Fyodor Dostoevsky, Collection novels Volume Three

In this book:
The Gambler
Poor Folk
Uncle's dream and
The Permanent Husband
The Idiot
The Grand Inquisitor

Translator:
Fred. Whishaw
C. J. Hogarth
H. P. Blavatsky
Eva Martin

Fyodor Dostoevsky (1821 – 1881), was a Russian novelist, short story writer, essayist, journalist and philosopher. Dostoyevsky's literary works explore human psychology in the context of the troubled political, social, and spiritual atmosphere of 19th-century Russia. He began writing in his 20s, and his first novel, Poor Folk, was published in 1846 when he was 25. His major works include Crime and Punishment (1866), The Idiot (1869), and The Brothers Karamazov (1880). His output consists of eleven novels, three novellas, seventeen short novels and numerous other works.

In this book:

The Gambler

I

At length I returned from two weeks leave of absence to find that my patrons had arrived three days ago in Roulettenberg. I received from them a welcome quite different to that which I had expected. The General eyed me coldly, greeted me in rather haughty fashion, and dismissed me to pay my respects to his sister. It was clear that from SOMEWHERE money had been acquired. I thought I could even detect a certain shamefacedness in the General's glance. Maria Philipovna, too, seemed distraught, and conversed with me with an air of detachment. Nevertheless, she took the money which I handed to her, counted it, and listened to what I had to tell. To luncheon there were expected that day a Monsieur Mezentsov, a French lady, and an Englishman; for, whenever money was in hand, a banquet in Muscovite style was always given. Polina Alexandrovna, on seeing me, inquired why I had been so long away. Then, without waiting for an answer, she departed. Evidently this was not mere accident, and I felt that I must throw some light upon matters. It was high time that I did so.

I was assigned a small room on the fourth floor of the hotel (for you must know that I belonged to the General's suite). So far as I could see, the party had already gained some notoriety in the place, which had come to look upon the General as a Russian nobleman of great wealth. Indeed, even before luncheon he charged me, among other things, to get two thousand-franc notes changed for him at the hotel counter, which put us in a position to be thought millionaires at all events for a week! Later, I was about to take Mischa and Nadia for a walk when a summons reached me from the staircase that I must attend the General. He began by deigning to inquire of me where I was going to take the children; and as he did so, I could see that he failed to look me in the eyes. He WANTED to do so, but each time was met by me with such a fixed, disrespectful stare that he desisted in confusion. In pompous language, however, which jumbled one sentence into another, and at length grew disconnected, he gave me to understand that I was to lead the children altogether away from the Casino, and out into the park. Finally his anger exploded, and he added sharply:

"I suppose you would like to take them to the Casino to play roulette? Well, excuse my speaking so plainly, but I know how addicted you are to gambling. Though I am not your mentor, nor wish to be, at least I have a right to require that you shall not actually compromise me."

"I have no money for gambling," I quietly replied.

"But you will soon be in receipt of some," retorted the General, reddening a little as he dived into his writing desk and applied himself to a memorandum book. From it he saw that he had 120 roubles of mine in his keeping.

"Let us calculate," he went on. "We must translate these roubles into thalers. Here—take 100 thalers, as a round sum. The rest will be safe in my hands."

In silence I took the money.

"You must not be offended at what I say," he continued. "You are too touchy about these things. What I have said I have said merely as a warning. To do so is no more than my right."

When returning home with the children before luncheon, I met a cavalcade of our party riding to view some ruins. Two splendid carriages, magnificently horsed, with Mlle. Blanche, Maria Philipovna, and Polina Alexandrovna in one of them, and the Frenchman, the Englishman, and the General in attendance on horseback! The passers-by stopped to stare at them, for the effect was splendid—the General could not have improved upon it. I calculated that, with the 4000 francs which I had brought with me, added to what my patrons seemed already to have acquired, the party must be in possession of at least 7000 or 8000 francs—though that would be none too much for Mlle. Blanche, who, with her mother and the Frenchman, was also lodging in our hotel. The latter gentleman was called by the lacqueys "Monsieur le Comte," and Mlle. Blanche's mother was dubbed "Madame la Comtesse." Perhaps in very truth they WERE "Comte et Comtesse."

I knew that "Monsieur le Comte" would take no notice of me when we met at dinner, as also that the General would not dream of introducing us, nor of recommending me to the "Comte." However, the latter had lived awhile in Russia, and knew that the person referred to as an "uchitel" is never looked upon as a bird of fine feather. Of course, strictly speaking, he knew me; but I was an uninvited guest at the luncheon—the General had forgotten to arrange otherwise, or I should have been dispatched to dine at the table d'hote. Nevertheless, I presented myself in such guise that the General looked at me with a touch of approval; and, though the good Maria Philipovna was for showing me my place, the fact of my having previously met the Englishman, Mr. Astley, saved me, and thenceforward I figured as one of the company.

This strange Englishman I had met first in Prussia, where we had happened to sit vis-a-vis in a railway train in which I was travelling to overtake our party; while, later, I had run across him in France, and again in Switzerland—twice within the space of two weeks! To think, therefore, that I should suddenly encounter him again here, in Roulettenberg! Never in my life had I known a more retiring man, for he was shy to the pitch of imbecility, yet well aware of the fact (for he was no fool). At the same time, he was a gentle, amiable sort of an individual, and, even on our first encounter in Prussia I had contrived to draw him out, and he had told me that he had just been to the North Cape, and was now anxious to visit the fair at Nizhni Novgorod. How he had come to make the General's acquaintance I do not know, but, apparently, he was much struck with Polina. Also, he was delighted that I should sit next him at table, for he appeared to look upon me as his bosom friend.

During the meal the Frenchman was in great feather: he was discursive and pompous to every one. In Moscow too, I remembered, he had blown a great many bubbles. Interminably he discoursed on finance and Russian politics, and though, at times, the General made feints to contradict him, he did so humbly, and as though wishing not wholly to lose sight of his own dignity.

For myself, I was in a curious frame of mind. Even before luncheon was half finished I had asked myself the old, eternal question: "WHY do I continue to dance attendance upon the General, instead of having left him and his family long ago?" Every now and then I would glance at Polina Alexandrovna, but she paid me no attention; until eventually I became so irritated that I decided to play the boor.

First of all I suddenly, and for no reason whatever, plunged loudly and gratuitously into the general conversation. Above everything I wanted to pick a quarrel with the Frenchman; and, with that end in view I turned to the General, and exclaimed in an overbearing sort of way—indeed, I think that I actually interrupted him—that that summer it had been almost impossible for a Russian to dine anywhere at tables d'hote. The General bent upon me a glance of astonishment.

"If one is a man of self-respect," I went on, "one risks abuse by so doing, and is forced to put up with insults of every kind. Both at Paris and on the Rhine, and even in Switzerland—there are so many Poles, with their sympathisers, the French, at these tables d'hote that one cannot get a word in edgeways if one happens only to be a Russian."

This I said in French. The General eyed me doubtfully, for he did not know whether to be angry or merely to feel surprised that I should so far forget myself.

"Of course, one always learns SOMETHING EVERYWHERE," said the Frenchman in a careless, contemptuous sort of tone.

"In Paris, too, I had a dispute with a Pole," I continued, "and then with a French officer who supported him. After that a section of the Frenchmen present took my part. They did so as soon as I told them the story of how once I threatened to spit into Monsignor's coffee."

"To spit into it?" the General inquired with grave disapproval in his tone, and a stare, of astonishment, while the Frenchman looked at me unbelievingly.

"Just so," I replied. "You must know that, on one occasion, when, for two days, I had felt certain that at any moment I might have to depart for Rome on business, I repaired to the Embassy of the Holy See in Paris, to have my passport visaed. There I encountered a sacristan of about fifty, and a man dry and cold of mien. After listening politely, but with great reserve, to my account of myself, this sacristan asked me to wait a little. I was in a great hurry to depart, but of course I sat down, pulled out a copy of L'Opinion Nationale, and fell to reading an extraordinary piece of invective against Russia which it happened to contain. As I was thus engaged I heard some one enter an adjoining room and ask for Monsignor; after which I saw the sacristan make a low bow to the visitor, and then another bow as the visitor took his leave. I ventured to remind the good man of my own business also; whereupon, with an expression of, if anything, increased dryness, he again asked me to wait. Soon a third visitor arrived who, like myself, had come on business (he was an Austrian of some sort); and as soon as ever he had stated his errand he was conducted upstairs! This made me very angry. I rose, approached the sacristan, and told him that, since Monsignor was receiving callers, his lordship might just as well finish off my affair as well. Upon this the sacristan shrunk back in astonishment. It simply passed his understanding that any insignificant Russian should dare to compare himself with other visitors of Monsignor's! In a tone of the utmost effrontery, as though he were delighted to have a chance of insulting me, he looked me up and down, and then said: "Do you suppose that Monsignor is going to put aside his coffee for YOU?" But I only cried the louder: "Let me tell you that I am going to SPIT into that coffee! Yes, and if you do not get me my passport visaed this very minute, I shall take it to Monsignor myself."

"What? While he is engaged with a Cardinal?" screeched the sacristan, again shrinking back in horror. Then, rushing to the door, he spread out his arms as though he would rather die than let me enter.

Thereupon I declared that I was a heretic and a barbarian—"Je suis heretique et barbare," I said, "and that these archbishops and cardinals and monsignors, and the rest of them, meant nothing at all to me. In a word, I showed him that I was not going to give way. He looked at me with an air of infinite resentment. Then he snatched up my passport, and departed with it upstairs. A minute later the passport had been visaed! Here it is now, if you care to see it,"—and I pulled out the document, and exhibited the Roman visa.

"But—" the General began.

"What really saved you was the fact that you proclaimed yourself a heretic and a barbarian," remarked the Frenchman with a smile. "Cela n'etait pas si bete."

"But is that how Russian subjects ought to be treated? Why, when they settle here they dare not utter even a word—they are ready even to deny the fact that they are Russians! At all events, at my hotel in Paris I received far more attention from the company after I had told them about the fracas with the sacristan. A fat Polish nobleman, who had been the most offensive of all who were present at the table d'hote, at once went upstairs, while some of the Frenchmen were simply disgusted when I told them that two years ago I had encountered a man at whom, in 1812, a French 'hero' fired for the mere fun of discharging his musket. That man was then a boy of ten and his family are still residing in Moscow."

"Impossible!" the Frenchman spluttered. "No French soldier would fire at a child!"

"Nevertheless the incident was as I say," I replied. "A very respected ex-captain told me the story, and I myself could see the scar left on his cheek."

The Frenchman then began chattering volubly, and the General supported him; but I recommended the former to read, for example, extracts from the memoirs of General Perovski, who, in 1812, was a prisoner in the hands of the French. Finally Maria Philipovna said something to interrupt the conversation. The General was furious with me for having started the altercation with the Frenchman. On the other hand, Mr. Astley seemed to take great pleasure in my brush with Monsieur, and, rising from the table, proposed that we should go and have a drink together. The same afternoon, at four o'clock, I went to have my customary talk with Polina Alexandrovna; and, the talk soon extended to a stroll. We entered the Park, and approached the Casino, where Polina seated herself upon a bench near the fountain, and sent Nadia away to a little distance to play with some other children. Mischa also I dispatched to play by the fountain, and in this fashion we—that is to say, Polina and myself—contrived to find ourselves alone.

Of course, we began by talking on business matters. Polina seemed furious when I handed her only 700 gulden, for she had thought to receive from Paris, as the proceeds of the pledging of her diamonds, at least 2000 gulden, or even more.

"Come what may, I MUST have money," she said. "And get it somehow I will—otherwise I shall be ruined."

I asked her what had happened during my absence.

"Nothing; except that two pieces of news have reached us from St. Petersburg. In the first place, my grandmother is very ill, and unlikely to last another couple of days. We had this from Timothy Petrovitch himself, and he is a reliable person. Every moment we are expecting to receive news of the end."

"All of you are on the tiptoe of expectation?" I queried.

"Of course—all of us, and every minute of the day. For a year-and-a-half now we have been looking for this."

"Looking for it?"

"Yes, looking for it. I am not her blood relation, you know—I am merely the General's step-daughter. Yet I am certain that the old lady has remembered me in her will."

"Yes, I believe that you WILL come in for a good deal," I said with some assurance.

"Yes, for she is fond of me. But how come you to think so?"

I answered this question with another one. "That Marquis of yours," I said, "—is HE also familiar with your family secrets?"

"And why are you yourself so interested in them?" was her retort as she eyed me with dry grimness.

"Never mind. If I am not mistaken, the General has succeeded in borrowing money of the Marquis."

"It may be so."

"Is it likely that the Marquis would have lent the money if he had not known something or other about your grandmother? Did you notice, too, that three times during luncheon, when speaking of her, he called her 'La Baboulenka'? [Dear little Grandmother]. What loving, friendly behaviour, to be sure!"

"Yes, that is true. As soon as ever he learnt that I was likely to inherit something from her he began to pay me his addresses. I thought you ought to know that."

"Then he has only just begun his courting? Why, I thought he had been doing so a long while!"

"You KNOW he has not," retorted Polina angrily. "But where on earth did you pick up this Englishman?" She said this after a pause.

"I KNEW you would ask about him!" Whereupon I told her of my previous encounters with Astley while travelling.

"He is very shy," I said, "and susceptible. Also, he is in love with you.—"

"Yes, he is in love with me," she replied.

"And he is ten times richer than the Frenchman. In fact, what does the Frenchman possess? To me it seems at least doubtful that he possesses anything at all."

"Oh, no, there is no doubt about it. He does possess some chateau or other. Last night the General told me that for certain. NOW are you satisfied?"

"Nevertheless, in your place I should marry the Englishman."

"And why?" asked Polina.

"Because, though the Frenchman is the handsomer of the two, he is also the baser; whereas the Englishman is not only a man of honour, but ten times the wealthier of the pair."

"Yes? But then the Frenchman is a marquis, and the cleverer of the two," remarked Polina imperturbably.

"Is that so?" I repeated.

"Yes; absolutely."

Polina was not at all pleased at my questions; I could see that she was doing her best to irritate me with the brusquerie of her answers. But I took no notice of this.

"It amuses me to see you grow angry," she continued. "However, inasmuch as I allow you to indulge in these questions and conjectures, you ought to pay me something for the privilege."

"I consider that I have a perfect right to put these questions to you," was my calm retort; "for the reason that I am ready to pay for them, and also care little what becomes of me."

Polina giggled.

"Last time you told me—when on the Shlangenberg—that at a word from me you would be ready to jump down a thousand feet into the abyss. Some day I may remind you of that saying, in order to see if you will be as good as your word. Yes, you may depend upon it that I shall do so. I hate you because I have allowed you to go to such lengths, and I also hate you and still more—because you are so necessary to me. For the time being I want you, so I must keep you."

Then she made a movement to rise. Her tone had sounded very angry. Indeed, of late her talks with me had invariably ended on a note of temper and irritation—yes, of real temper.

"May I ask you who is this Mlle. Blanche?" I inquired (since I did not wish Polina to depart without an explanation).

"You KNOW who she is—just Mlle. Blanche. Nothing further has transpired. Probably she will soon be Madame General—that is to say, if the rumours that Grandmamma is nearing her end should prove true. Mlle. Blanche, with her mother and her cousin, the Marquis, know very well that, as things now stand, we are ruined."

"And is the General at last in love?"

"That has nothing to do with it. Listen to me. Take these 700 florins, and go and play roulette with them. Win as much for me as you can, for I am badly in need of money."

So saying, she called Nadia back to her side, and entered the Casino, where she joined the rest of our party. For myself, I took, in musing astonishment, the first path to the left. Something had seemed to strike my brain when she told me to go and play roulette. Strangely enough, that something had also seemed to make me hesitate, and to set me analysing my feelings with regard to her. In fact, during the two weeks of my absence I had felt far more at my ease than I did now, on the day of my return; although, while travelling, I had moped like an imbecile, rushed about like a man in a fever, and actually beheld her in my dreams. Indeed, on one occasion (this happened in Switzerland, when I was asleep in the train) I had spoken aloud to her, and set all my fellow-travellers laughing. Again, therefore, I put to myself the question: "Do I, or do I not love her?" and again I could return myself no answer or, rather, for the hundredth time I told myself that I detested her. Yes, I detested her; there were moments (more especially at the close of our talks together) when I would gladly have given half my life to have strangled her! I swear that, had there, at such moments, been a sharp knife ready to my hand, I would have seized that knife with pleasure, and plunged it into her breast. Yet I also swear that if, on the Shlangenberg, she had REALLY said to me, "Leap into that abyss," I should have leapt into it, and with equal pleasure. Yes, this I knew well. One way or the other, the thing must soon be ended. She, too, knew it in some curious way; the thought that I was fully conscious of her inaccessibility, and of the impossibility of my ever realising my dreams, afforded her, I am certain, the keenest possible pleasure. Otherwise, is it likely that she, the cautious and clever woman that she was, would have indulged in this familiarity and openness with me? Hitherto (I concluded) she had looked upon me in the same light that the old Empress did upon her servant—the Empress who hesitated not to unrobe herself before her slave, since she did not account a slave a man. Yes, often Polina must have taken me for something less than a man!"

Still, she had charged me with a commission—to win what I could at roulette. Yet all the time I could not help wondering WHY it was so necessary for her to win something, and what new schemes could have sprung to birth in her ever-fertile brain. A host of new and unknown factors seemed to have arisen during the last two weeks. Well, it behoved me to divine them, and to probe them, and that as soon as possible. Yet not now: at the present moment I must repair to the roulette-table.

I confess I did not like it. Although I had made up my mind to play, I felt averse to doing so on behalf of some one else. In fact, it almost upset my balance, and I entered the gaming rooms with an angry feeling at my heart. At first glance the scene irritated me. Never at any time have I been able to bear the flunkeyishness which one meets in the Press of the world at large, but more especially in that of Russia, where, almost every evening, journalists write on two subjects in particular namely, on the splendour and luxury of the casinos to be found in the Rhenish towns, and on the heaps of gold which are daily to be seen lying on their tables. Those journalists are not paid for doing so: they write thus merely out of a spirit of disinterested complaisance. For there is nothing splendid about the establishments in question; and, not only are there no heaps of gold to be seen lying on their tables, but also there is very little money to be seen at all. Of course, during the season, some madman or another may make his appearance—generally an Englishman, or an Asiatic, or a Turk—and (as had happened during the summer of which I write) win or lose a great deal; but, as regards the rest of the crowd, it plays only for petty gulden, and seldom does much wealth figure on the board.

When, on the present occasion, I entered the gaming-rooms (for the first time in my life), it was several moments before I could even make up my mind to play. For one thing, the crowd oppressed me. Had I been playing for myself, I think I should have left at once, and never have embarked upon gambling at all, for I could feel my heart beginning to beat, and my heart was anything but cold-blooded. Also, I knew, I had long ago made up my mind, that never should I depart from Roulettenberg until some radical, some final, change had taken place in my fortunes. Thus, it must and would be. However ridiculous it may seem to you that I was expecting to win at roulette, I look upon the generally accepted opinion concerning the folly and the grossness of hoping to win at gambling as a thing even more absurd. For why is gambling a whit worse than any other method of acquiring money? How, for instance, is it worse than trade? True, out of a hundred persons, only one can win; yet what business is that of yours or of mine?

At all events, I confined myself at first simply to looking on, and decided to attempt nothing serious. Indeed, I felt that, if I began to do anything at all, I should do it in an absent-minded, haphazard sort of way—of that I felt certain. Also, it behoved me to learn the game itself; since, despite a thousand descriptions of roulette which I had read with ceaseless avidity, I knew nothing of its rules, and had never even seen it played.

In the first place, everything about it seemed to me so foul—so morally mean and foul. Yet I am not speaking of the hungry, restless folk who, by scores nay, even by hundreds—could be seen crowded around the gaming-tables. For in a desire to win quickly and to win much I can see nothing sordid; I have always applauded the opinion of a certain dead and gone, but cocksure, moralist who replied to the excuse that "one may always gamble moderately", by saying that to do so makes things worse, since, in that case, the profits too will always be moderate.

Insignificant profits and sumptuous profits do not stand on the same footing. No, it is all a matter of proportion. What may seem a small sum to a Rothschild may seem a large sum to me, and it is not the fault of stakes or of winnings that everywhere men can be found winning, can be found depriving their fellows of something, just as they do at roulette. As to the question whether stakes and winnings are, in themselves, immoral is another question altogether, and I wish to express no opinion upon it. Yet the very fact that I was full of a strong desire to win caused this gambling for gain, in spite of its attendant squalor, to contain, if you will, something intimate, something sympathetic, to my eyes: for it is always pleasant to see men dispensing with ceremony, and acting naturally, and in an unbuttoned mood....

Yet, why should I so deceive myself? I could see that the whole thing was a vain and unreasoning pursuit; and what, at the first glance, seemed to me the ugliest feature in this mob of roulette players was their respect for their occupation—the seriousness, and even the humility, with which they stood around the gaming tables. Moreover, I had always drawn sharp distinctions between a game which is de mauvais genre and a game which is permissible to a decent man. In fact, there are two sorts of gaming—namely, the game of the gentleman and the game of the plebs—the game for gain, and the game of the herd. Herein, as said, I draw sharp distinctions. Yet how essentially base are the distinctions! For instance, a gentleman may stake, say, five or ten louis d'or—seldom more, unless he is a very rich man, when he may stake, say, a thousand francs; but, he must do this simply for the love of the game itself—simply for sport, simply in order to observe the process of winning or of losing, and, above all things, as a man who remains quite uninterested in the possibility of his issuing a winner. If he wins, he will be at liberty, perhaps, to give vent to a laugh, or to pass a remark on the circumstance to a bystander, or to stake again, or to double his stake; but, even this he must do solely out of curiosity, and for the pleasure of watching the play of chances and of calculations, and not because of any vulgar desire to win. In a word, he must look upon the gaming-table, upon roulette, and upon trente et quarante, as mere relaxations which have been arranged solely for his amusement. Of the existence of the lures and gains upon which the bank is founded and maintained he must profess to have not an inkling. Best of all, he ought to imagine his fellow-gamblers and the rest of the mob which stands trembling over a coin to be equally rich and gentlemanly with himself, and playing solely for recreation and pleasure. This complete ignorance of the realities, this innocent view of mankind, is what, in my opinion, constitutes the truly aristocratic. For instance, I have seen even fond mothers so far indulge their guileless, elegant daughters—misses of fifteen or sixteen—as to give them a few gold coins and teach them how to play; and though the young ladies may have won or have lost, they have invariably laughed, and departed as though they were well pleased. In the same way, I saw our General once approach the table in a stolid, important manner. A lacquey darted to offer him a chair, but the General did not even notice him. Slowly he took out his money bags, and slowly extracted 300 francs in gold, which he staked on the black, and won. Yet he did not take up his winnings—he left them there on the table. Again the black turned up, and again he did not gather in what he had won; and when, in the third round, the RED turned up he lost, at a stroke, 1200 francs. Yet even then he rose with a smile, and thus preserved his reputation; yet I knew that his money bags must be chafing his heart, as well as that, had the stake been twice or thrice as much again, he would still have restrained himself from venting his disappointment.

On the other hand, I saw a Frenchman first win, and then lose, 30,000 francs cheerfully, and without a murmur. Yes; even if a gentleman should lose his whole substance, he must never give way to annoyance. Money must be so subservient to gentility as never to be worth a thought. Of course, the SUPREMELY aristocratic thing is to be entirely oblivious of the mire of rabble, with its setting; but sometimes a reverse course may be aristocratic to remark, to scan, and even to gape at, the mob (for preference, through a lorgnette), even as though one were taking the crowd and its squalor for a sort of raree show which had been organised specially for a gentleman's diversion. Though one may be squeezed by the crowd, one must look as though one were fully assured of being the observer—of having neither part nor lot with the observed. At the same time, to stare fixedly about one is unbecoming; for that, again, is ungentlemanly, seeing that no spectacle is worth an open stare—are no spectacles in the world which merit from a gentleman too pronounced an inspection.

However, to me personally the scene DID seem to be worth undisguised contemplation—more especially in view of the fact that I had come there not only to look at, but also to number myself sincerely and wholeheartedly with, the mob. As for my secret moral views, I had no room for them amongst my actual, practical opinions. Let that stand as written: I am writing only to relieve my conscience. Yet let me say also this: that from the first I have been consistent in having an intense aversion to any trial of my acts and thoughts by a moral standard. Another standard altogether has directed my life....

As a matter of fact, the mob was playing in exceedingly foul fashion. Indeed, I have an idea that sheer robbery was going on around that gaming-table. The croupiers who sat at the two ends of it had not only to watch the stakes, but also to calculate the game—an immense amount of work for two men! As for the crowd itself—well, it consisted mostly of Frenchmen. Yet I was not then taking notes merely in order to be able to give you a description of roulette, but in order to get my bearings as to my behaviour when I myself should begin to play. For example, I noticed that nothing was more common than for another's hand to stretch out and grab one's winnings whenever one had won. Then there would arise a dispute, and frequently an uproar; and it would be a case of "I beg of you to prove, and to produce witnesses to the fact, that the stake is yours."

At first the proceedings were pure Greek to me. I could only divine and distinguish that stakes were hazarded on numbers, on "odd" or "even," and on colours. Polina's money I decided to risk, that evening, only to the amount of 100 gulden. The thought that I was not going to play for myself quite unnerved me. It was an unpleasant sensation, and I tried hard to banish it. I had a feeling that, once I had begun to play for Polina, I should wreck my own fortunes. Also, I wonder if any one has EVER approached a gaming-table without falling an immediate prey to superstition? I began by pulling out fifty gulden, and staking them on "even." The wheel spun and stopped at 13. I had lost! With a feeling like a sick qualm, as though I would like to make my way out of the crowd and go home, I staked another fifty gulden—this time on the red. The red turned up. Next time I staked the 100 gulden just where they lay—and again the red turned up. Again I staked the whole sum, and again the red turned up. Clutching my 400 gulden, I placed 200 of them on twelve figures, to see what would come of it. The result was that the croupier paid me out three times my total stake! Thus from 100 gulden my store had grown to 800! Upon that such a curious, such an inexplicable, unwonted feeling overcame me that I decided to depart. Always the thought kept recurring to me that if I had been playing for myself alone I should never have had such luck. Once more I staked the whole 800 gulden on the "even." The wheel stopped at 4. I was paid out another 800 gulden, and, snatching up my pile of 1600, departed in search of Polina Alexandrovna.

I found the whole party walking in the park, and was able to get an interview with her only after supper. This time the Frenchman was absent from the meal, and the General seemed to be in a more expansive vein. Among other things, he thought it necessary to remind me that he would be sorry to see me playing at the gaming-tables. In his opinion, such conduct would greatly compromise him—especially if I were to lose much. "And even if you were to WIN much I should be compromised," he added in a meaning sort of way. "Of course I have no RIGHT to order your actions, but you yourself will agree that..." As usual, he did not finish his sentence. I answered drily that

I had very little money in my possession, and that, consequently, I was hardly in a position to indulge in any conspicuous play, even if I did gamble. At last, when ascending to my own room, I succeeded in handing Polina her winnings, and told her that, next time, I should not play for her.

"Why not?" she asked excitedly.

"Because I wish to play FOR MYSELF," I replied with a feigned glance of astonishment. "That is my sole reason."

"Then are you so certain that your roulette-playing will get us out of our difficulties?" she inquired with a quizzical smile.

I said very seriously, "Yes," and then added: "Possibly my certainty about winning may seem to you ridiculous; yet, pray leave me in peace."

Nonetheless she insisted that I ought to go halves with her in the day's winnings, and offered me 800 gulden on condition that henceforth, I gambled only on those terms; but I refused to do so, once and for all—stating, as my reason, that I found myself unable to play on behalf of any one else, "I am not unwilling so to do," I added, "but in all probability I should lose."

"Well, absurd though it be, I place great hopes on your playing of roulette," she remarked musingly; "wherefore, you ought to play as my partner and on equal shares; wherefore, of course, you will do as I wish."

Then she left me without listening to any further protests on my part.

III

On the morrow she said not a word to me about gambling. In fact, she purposely avoided me, although her old manner to me had not changed: the same serene coolness was hers on meeting me—a coolness that was mingled even with a spice of contempt and dislike. In short, she was at no pains to conceal her aversion to me. That I could see plainly. Also, she did not trouble to conceal from me the fact that I was necessary to her, and that she was keeping me for some end which she had in view. Consequently there became established between us relations which, to a large extent, were incomprehensible to me, considering her general pride and aloofness. For example, although she knew that I was madly in love with her, she allowed me to speak to her of my passion (though she could not well have showed her contempt for me more than by permitting me, unhindered and unrebuked, to mention to her my love).

"You see," her attitude expressed, "how little I regard your feelings, as well as how little I care for what you say to me, or for what you feel for me." Likewise, though she spoke as before concerning her affairs, it was never with complete frankness. In her contempt for me there were refinements. Although she knew well that I was aware of a certain circumstance in her life of something which might one day cause her trouble, she would speak to me about her affairs (whenever she had need of me for a given end) as though I were a slave or a passing acquaintance—yet tell them me only in so far as one would need to know them if one were going to be made temporary use of. Had I not known the whole chain of events, or had she not seen how much I was pained and disturbed by her teasing insistency, she would never have thought it worthwhile to soothe me with this frankness—even though, since she not infrequently used me to execute commissions that were not only troublesome, but risky, she ought, in my opinion, to have been frank in ANY case. But, forsooth, it was not worth her while to trouble about MY feelings—about the fact that I was uneasy, and, perhaps, thrice as put about by her cares and misfortunes as she was herself!

For three weeks I had known of her intention to take to roulette. She had even warned me that she would like me to play on her behalf, since it was unbecoming for her to play in person; and, from the tone of her words I had gathered that there was something on her mind besides a mere desire to win money. As if money could matter to HER! No, she had some end in view, and there were circumstances at which I could guess, but which I did not know for certain. True, the slavery and abasement in which she held me might have given me (such things often do so) the power to question her with abrupt directness (seeing that, inasmuch as I figured in her eyes as a mere slave and nonentity, she could not very well have taken offence at any rude curiosity); but the fact was that, though she let me question her, she never returned me a single answer, and at times did not so much as notice me. That is how matters stood.

Next day there was a good deal of talk about a telegram which, four days ago, had been sent to St. Petersburg, but to which there had come no answer. The General was visibly disturbed and moody, for the matter concerned his mother. The Frenchman, too, was excited, and after dinner the whole party talked long and seriously together—the Frenchman's tone being extraordinarily presumptuous and offhand to everybody. It almost reminded one of the proverb, "Invite a man to your table, and soon he will place his feet upon it." Even to Polina he was brusque almost to the point of rudeness. Yet still he seemed glad to join us in our walks in the Casino, or in our rides and drives about the town. I had long been aware of certain circumstances which bound the General to him; I had long been aware that in Russia they had hatched some scheme together although I did not know whether the plot had come to anything, or whether it was still only in the stage of being talked of. Likewise I was aware, in part, of a family secret—namely, that, last year, the Frenchman had bailed the General out of debt, and given him 30,000 roubles wherewith to pay his Treasury dues on retiring from the service. And now, of course, the General was in a vice—although the chief part in the affair was being played by Mlle. Blanche. Yes, of this last I had no doubt.

But WHO was this Mlle. Blanche? It was said of her that she was a Frenchwoman of good birth who, living with her mother, possessed a colossal fortune. It was also said that she was some relation to the Marquis, but only a distant one a cousin, or cousin-german, or something of the sort. Likewise I knew that, up to the time of my journey to Paris, she and the Frenchman had been more ceremonious towards our party—they had stood on a much more precise and delicate footing with them; but that now their acquaintanceship—their friendship, their intimacy—had taken on a much more off-hand and rough-and-ready air. Perhaps they thought that our means were too modest for them, and, therefore, unworthy of politeness or reticence. Also, for the last three days I had noticed certain looks which Astley had kept throwing at Mlle. Blanche and her mother; and it had occurred to me that he must have had some previous acquaintance with the pair. I had even surmised that the Frenchman too must have met Mr. Astley before. Astley was a man so shy, reserved, and taciturn in his manner that one might have looked for anything from him. At all events the Frenchman accorded him only the slightest of greetings, and scarcely even looked at him. Certainly he did not seem to be afraid of him; which was intelligible enough. But why did Mlle. Blanche also never look at the Englishman?—particularly since, a propos of something or another, the Marquis had declared the Englishman to be immensely and indubitably rich? Was not that a sufficient reason to make Mlle. Blanche look at the Englishman? Anyway the General seemed extremely uneasy; and, one could well understand what a telegram to announce the death of his mother would mean for him!

Although I thought it probable that Polina was avoiding me for a definite reason, I adopted a cold and indifferent air; for I felt pretty certain that it would not be long before she herself approached me. For two days, therefore, I devoted my attention to Mlle. Blanche. The poor General was in despair! To fall in love at fifty-five, and with such vehemence, is indeed a misfortune! And add to that his widowerhood, his children, his ruined property, his debts, and the woman with whom he had fallen in love! Though Mlle. Blanche was extremely good-looking, I may or may not be understood when I say that she had one of those faces which one is afraid of. At all events, I myself have always feared such women. Apparently about twenty-five years of age, she was tall and broad-shouldered, with shoulders that sloped; yet though her neck and bosom were ample in their proportions, her skin was dull yellow in colour, while her hair (which was extremely abundant—sufficient to make two coiffures) was as black as Indian ink. Add to that a pair of black eyes with yellowish whites, a proud glance, gleaming teeth, and lips which were perennially pomaded and redolent of musk. As for her dress, it was invariably rich, effective, and chic, yet in good taste. Lastly, her feet and hands were astonishing, and her voice a deep contralto. Sometimes, when she laughed, she displayed her teeth, but at ordinary times her air was taciturn and haughty—especially in the presence of Polina and Maria Philipovna. Yet she seemed to me almost destitute of education, and even of wits, though cunning and suspicious. This, apparently, was not because her life had been lacking in incident. Perhaps, if all were known, the Marquis was not her kinsman at all, nor her mother, her mother; but there was evidence that, in Berlin, where we had first come across the pair, they had possessed acquaintances of good standing. As for the Marquis himself, I doubt to this day if he was a Marquis—although about the fact that he had formerly belonged to high society (for instance, in Moscow and Germany) there could be no doubt whatever. What he had formerly been in France I had not a notion. All I knew was that he was said to possess a chateau. During the last two weeks I had looked for much to transpire, but am still ignorant whether at that time anything decisive ever passed between Mademoiselle and the General. Everything seemed to depend upon our means—upon whether the General would be able to flourish sufficient money in her face. If ever the news should arrive that the grandmother was not dead, Mlle. Blanche, I felt sure, would disappear in a twinkling. Indeed, it surprised and amused me to observe what a passion for intrigue I was developing. But how I loathed it all! With what pleasure would I have given everybody and everything the go-by! Only—I could not leave Polina. How, then, could I show contempt for those who surrounded her? Espionage is a base thing, but—what have I to do with that?

Mr. Astley, too, I found a curious person. I was only sure that he had fallen in love with Polina. A remarkable and diverting circumstance is the amount which may lie in the mien of a shy and painfully modest man who has been touched with the divine passion—especially when he would rather sink into the earth than betray himself by a single word or look. Though Mr. Astley frequently met us when we were out walking, he would merely take off his hat and pass us by, though I knew he was dying to join us. Even when invited to do so, he would refuse. Again, in places of amusement—in the Casino, at concerts, or near the fountain—he was never far from the spot where we were sitting. In fact, WHEREVER we were in the Park, in the forest, or on the Shlangenberg—one needed but to raise one's eyes and glance around to catch sight of at least a PORTION of Mr. Astley's frame sticking out—whether on an adjacent path or behind a bush. Yet never did he lose any chance of speaking to myself; and, one morning when we had met, and exchanged a couple of words, he burst out in his usual abrupt way, without saying "Good-morning."

"That Mlle. Blanche," he said. "Well, I have seen a good many women like her."

After that he was silent as he looked me meaningly in the face. What he meant I did not know, but to my glance of inquiry he returned only a dry nod, and a reiterated "It is so." Presently, however, he resumed:

"Does Mlle. Polina like flowers?"

"I really cannot say," was my reply.

"What? You cannot say?" he cried in great astonishment.

"No; I have never noticed whether she does so or not," I repeated with a smile.

"Hm! Then I have an idea in my mind," he concluded. Lastly, with a nod, he walked away with a pleased expression on his face. The conversation had been carried on in execrable French.

IV

Today has been a day of folly, stupidity, and ineptness. The time is now eleven o'clock in the evening, and I am sitting in my room and thinking. It all began, this morning, with my being forced to go and play roulette for Polina Alexandrovna. When she handed me over her store of six hundred gulden I exacted two conditions—namely, that I should not go halves with her in her winnings, if any (that is to say, I should not take anything for myself), and that she should explain to me, that same evening, why it was so necessary for her to win, and how much was the sum which she needed. For, I could not suppose that she was doing all this merely for the sake of money. Yet clearly she did need some money, and that as soon as possible, and for a special purpose. Well, she promised to explain matters, and I departed. There was a tremendous crowd in the gaming-rooms. What an arrogant, greedy crowd it was! I pressed forward towards the middle of the room until I had secured a seat at a croupier's elbow. Then I began to play in timid fashion, venturing only twenty or thirty gulden at a time. Meanwhile, I observed and took notes. It seemed to me that calculation was superfluous, and by no means possessed of the importance which certain other players attached to it, even though they sat with ruled papers in their hands, whereon they set down the coups, calculated the chances, reckoned, staked, and—lost exactly as we more simple mortals did who played without any reckoning at all.

However, I deduced from the scene one conclusion which seemed to me reliable—namely, that in the flow of fortuitous chances there is, if not a system, at all events a sort of order. This, of course, is a very strange thing. For instance, after a dozen middle figures there would always occur a dozen or so outer ones. Suppose the ball stopped twice at a dozen outer figures; it would then pass to a dozen of the first ones, and then, again, to a dozen of the middle ciphers, and fall upon them three or four times, and then revert to a dozen outers; whence, after another couple of rounds, the ball would again pass to the first figures, strike upon them once, and then return thrice to the middle series—continuing thus for an hour and a half, or two hours. One, three, two: one, three, two. It was all very curious. Again, for the whole of a day or a morning the red would alternate with the black, but almost without any order, and from moment to moment, so that scarcely two consecutive rounds would end upon either the one or the other. Yet, next day, or, perhaps, the next evening, the red alone would turn up, and attain a run of over two score, and continue so for quite a length of time—say, for a whole day. Of these circumstances the majority were pointed out to me by Mr. Astley, who stood by the gaming-table the whole morning, yet never once staked in person.

For myself, I lost all that I had on me, and with great speed. To begin with, I staked two hundred gulden on "even," and won. Then I staked the same amount again, and won: and so on some two or three times. At one moment I must have had in my hands—gathered there within a space of five minutes—about 4000 gulden. That, of course, was the proper moment for me to have departed, but there arose in me a strange sensation as of a challenge to Fate—as of a wish to deal her a blow on the cheek, and to put out my tongue at her. Accordingly I set down the largest stake allowed by the rules—namely, 4000 gulden—and lost. Fired by this mishap, I pulled out all the money left to me, staked it all on the same venture, and—again lost! Then I rose from the table, feeling as though I were stupefied. What had happened to me I did not know; but, before luncheon I told Polina of my losses—until which time I walked about the Park.

At luncheon I was as excited as I had been at the meal three days ago. Mlle. Blanche and the Frenchman were lunching with us, and it appeared that the former had been to the Casino that morning, and had seen my exploits there. So now she showed me more attention when talking to me; while, for his part, the Frenchman approached me, and asked outright if it had been my own money that I had lost. He appeared to be suspicious as to something being on foot between Polina and myself, but I merely fired up, and replied that the money had been all my own.

At this the General seemed extremely surprised, and asked me whence I had procured it; whereupon I replied that, though I had begun only with 100 gulden, six or seven rounds had increased my capital to 5000 or 6000 gulden, and that subsequently I had lost the whole in two rounds.

All this, of course, was plausible enough. During my recital I glanced at Polina, but nothing was to be discerned on her face. However, she had allowed me to fire up without correcting me, and from that I concluded that it was my cue to fire up, and to conceal the fact that I had been playing on her behalf. "At all events," I thought to myself, "she, in her turn, has promised to give me an explanation to-night, and to reveal to me something or another."

Although the General appeared to be taking stock of me, he said nothing. Yet I could see uneasiness and annoyance in his face. Perhaps his straitened circumstances made it hard for him to have to hear of piles of gold passing through the hands of an irresponsible fool like myself within the space of a quarter of an hour. Now, I have an idea that, last night, he and the Frenchman had a sharp encounter with one another. At all events they closeted themselves together, and then had a long and vehement discussion; after which the Frenchman departed in what appeared to be a passion, but returned, early this morning, to renew the combat. On hearing of my losses, however, he only remarked with a sharp, and even a malicious, air that "a man ought to go more carefully." Next, for some reason or another, he added that, "though a great many Russians go in for gambling, they are no good at the game."

"I think that roulette was devised specially for Russians," I retorted; and when the Frenchman smiled contemptuously at my reply I further remarked that I was sure I was right; also that, speaking of Russians in the capacity of gamblers, I had far more blame for them than praise—of that he could be quite sure.

"Upon what do you base your opinion?" he inquired.

"Upon the fact that to the virtues and merits of the civilised Westerner there has become historically added— though this is not his chief point—a capacity for acquiring capital; whereas, not only is the Russian incapable of acquiring capital, but also he exhausts it wantonly and of sheer folly. None the less we Russians often need money; wherefore, we are glad of, and greatly devoted to, a method of acquisition like roulette—whereby, in a couple of hours, one may grow rich without doing any work. This method, I repeat, has a great attraction for us, but since we play in wanton fashion, and without taking any trouble, we almost invariably lose."

"To a certain extent that is true," assented the Frenchman with a self-satisfied air.

"Oh no, it is not true," put in the General sternly. "And you," he added to me, "you ought to be ashamed of yourself for traducing your own country!"

"I beg pardon," I said. "Yet it would be difficult to say which is the worst of the two—Russian ineptitude or the German method of growing rich through honest toil."

"What an extraordinary idea," cried the General.

"And what a RUSSIAN idea!" added the Frenchman.

I smiled, for I was rather glad to have a quarrel with them.

"I would rather live a wandering life in tents," I cried, "than bow the knee to a German idol!"

"To WHAT idol?" exclaimed the General, now seriously angry.

"To the German method of heaping up riches. I have not been here very long, but I can tell you that what I have seen and verified makes my Tartar blood boil. Good Lord! I wish for no virtues of that kind. Yesterday I went for a walk of about ten versts; and, everywhere I found that things were even as we read of them in good German picture-books—that every house has its 'Fater,' who is horribly beneficent and extraordinarily honourable. So honourable is he that it is dreadful to have anything to do with him; and I cannot bear people of that sort. Each such 'Fater' has his family, and in the evenings they read improving books aloud. Over their roof-trees there murmur elms and chestnuts; the sun has sunk to his rest; a stork is roosting on the gable; and all is beautifully poetic and touching. Do not be angry, General. Let me tell you something that is even more touching than that. I can remember how, of an evening, my own father, now dead, used to sit under the lime trees in his little garden, and to read books aloud to myself and my mother. Yes, I know how things ought to be done. Yet every German family is bound to slavery and to submission to its 'Fater.' They work like oxen, and amass wealth like Jews. Suppose the 'Fater' has put by a certain number of gulden which he hands over to his eldest son, in order that the said son may acquire a trade or a small plot of land. Well, one result is to deprive the daughter of a dowry, and so leave her among the unwedded. For the same reason, the parents will have to sell the younger son into bondage or the ranks of the army, in order that he may earn more towards the family capital. Yes, such things ARE done, for I have been making inquiries on the subject. It is all done out of sheer rectitude—out of a rectitude which is magnified to the point of the younger son believing that he has been RIGHTLY sold, and that it is simply idyllic for the victim to rejoice when he is made over into pledge. What more have I to tell? Well, this—that matters bear just as hardly upon the eldest son. Perhaps he has his Gretchen to whom his heart is bound; but he cannot marry her, for the reason that he has not yet amassed sufficient gulden. So, the pair wait on in a mood of sincere and virtuous expectation, and smilingly deposit themselves in pawn the while. Gretchen's cheeks grow sunken, and she begins to wither; until at last, after some twenty years, their substance has multiplied, and sufficient gulden have been honourably and virtuously accumulated. Then the 'Fater' blesses his forty-year-old heir and the thirty-five-year-old Gretchen with the sunken bosom and the scarlet nose; after which he bursts, into tears, reads the pair a lesson on morality, and dies. In turn the eldest son becomes a virtuous 'Fater,' and the old story begins again. In fifty or sixty years' time the grandson of the original 'Fater' will have amassed a considerable sum; and that sum he will hand over to, his son, and the latter to HIS son, and so on for several generations; until at length there will issue a Baron Rothschild, or a 'Hoppe and Company,' or the devil knows what! Is it not a beautiful spectacle—the spectacle of a century or two of inherited labour, patience, intellect, rectitude, character, perseverance, and calculation, with a stork sitting on the roof above it all? What is more; they think there can never be anything better than this; wherefore, from their point of view they begin to judge the rest of the world, and to censure all who are at fault— that is to say, who are not exactly like themselves. Yes, there you have it in a nutshell. For my own part, I would rather grow fat after the Russian manner, or squander my whole substance at roulette. I have no wish to be 'Hoppe and Company' at the end of five generations. I want the money for MYSELF, for in no way do I look upon my personality as necessary to, or meet to be given over to, capital. I may be wrong, but there you have it. Those are MY views."

"How far you may be right in what you have said I do not know," remarked the General moodily; "but I DO know that you are becoming an insufferable farceur whenever you are given the least chance."

As usual, he left his sentence unfinished. Indeed, whenever he embarked upon anything that in the least exceeded the limits of daily small-talk, he left unfinished what he was saying. The Frenchman had listened to me contemptuously, with a slight protruding of his eyes; but, he could not have understood very much of my harangue. As for Polina, she had looked on with serene indifference. She seemed to have heard neither my voice nor any other during the progress of the meal.

V

Yes, she had been extraordinarily meditative. Yet, on leaving the table, she immediately ordered me to accompany her for a walk. We took the children with us, and set out for the fountain in the Park.

I was in such an irritated frame of mind that in rude and abrupt fashion I blurted out a question as to "why our Marquis de Griers had ceased to accompany her for strolls, or to speak to her for days together."

"Because he is a brute," she replied in rather a curious way. It was the first time that I had heard her speak so of De Griers: consequently, I was momentarily awed into silence by this expression of resentment.

"Have you noticed, too, that today he is by no means on good terms with the General?" I went on.

"Yes—and I suppose you want to know why," she replied with dry captiousness. "You are aware, are you not, that the General is mortgaged to the Marquis, with all his property? Consequently, if the General's mother does not die, the Frenchman will become the absolute possessor of everything which he now holds only in pledge."

"Then it is really the case that everything is mortgaged? I have heard rumours to that effect, but was unaware how far they might be true."

"Yes, they ARE true. What then?"

"Why, it will be a case of 'Farewell, Mlle. Blanche,'" I remarked; "for in such an event she would never become Madame General. Do you know, I believe the old man is so much in love with her that he will shoot himself if she should throw him over. At his age it is a dangerous thing to fall in love."

"Yes, something, I believe, WILL happen to him," assented Polina thoughtfully.

"And what a fine thing it all is!" I continued. "Could anything be more abominable than the way in which she has agreed to marry for money alone? Not one of the decencies has been observed; the whole affair has taken place without the least ceremony. And as for the grandmother, what could be more comical, yet more dastardly, than the sending of telegram after telegram to know if she is dead? What do you think of it, Polina Alexandrovna?"

"Yes, it is very horrible," she interrupted with a shudder. "Consequently, I am the more surprised that YOU should be so cheerful. What are YOU so pleased about? About the fact that you have gone and lost my money?"

"What? The money that you gave me to lose? I told you I should never win for other people—least of all for you. I obeyed you simply because you ordered me to; but you must not blame me for the result. I warned you that no good would ever come of it. You seem much depressed at having lost your money. Why do you need it so greatly?"

"Why do YOU ask me these questions?"

"Because you promised to explain matters to me. Listen. I am certain that, as soon as ever I 'begin to play for myself' (and I still have 120 gulden left), I shall win. You can then take of me what you require."

She made a contemptuous grimace.

"You must not be angry with me," I continued, "for making such a proposal. I am so conscious of being only a nonentity in your eyes that you need not mind accepting money from me. A gift from me could not possibly offend you. Moreover, it was I who lost your gulden."

She glanced at me, but, seeing that I was in an irritable, sarcastic mood, changed the subject.

"My affairs cannot possibly interest you," she said. "Still, if you DO wish to know, I am in debt. I borrowed some money, and must pay it back again. I have a curious, senseless idea that I am bound to win at the gaming-tables.

Why I think so I cannot tell, but I do think so, and with some assurance. Perhaps it is because of that assurance that I now find myself without any other resource."

"Or perhaps it is because it is so NECESSARY for you to win. It is like a drowning man catching at a straw. You yourself will agree that, unless he were drowning he would not mistake a straw for the trunk of a tree."

Polina looked surprised.

"What?" she said. "Do not you also hope something from it? Did you not tell me again and again, two weeks ago, that you were certain of winning at roulette if you played here? And did you not ask me not to consider you a fool for doing so? Were you joking? You cannot have been, for I remember that you spoke with a gravity which forbade the idea of your jesting."

"True," I replied gloomily. "I always felt certain that I should win. Indeed, what you say makes me ask myself— Why have my absurd, senseless losses of today raised a doubt in my mind? Yet I am still positive that, so soon as ever I begin to play for myself, I shall infallibly win."

"And why are you so certain?"

"To tell the truth, I do not know. I only know that I must win—that it is the one resource I have left. Yes, why do I feel so assured on the point?"

"Perhaps because one cannot help winning if one is fanatically certain of doing so."

"Yet I dare wager that you do not think me capable of serious feeling in the matter?"

"I do not care whether you are so or not," answered Polina with calm indifference. "Well, since you ask me, I DO doubt your ability to take anything seriously. You are capable of worrying, but not deeply. You are too ill-regulated and unsettled a person for that. But why do you want money? Not a single one of the reasons which you have given can be looked upon as serious."

"By the way," I interrupted, "you say you want to pay off a debt. It must be a large one. Is it to the Frenchman?"

"What do you mean by asking all these questions? You are very clever today. Surely you are not drunk?"

"You know that you and I stand on no ceremony, and that sometimes I put to you very plain questions. I repeat that I am your slave—and slaves cannot be shamed or offended."

"You talk like a child. It is always possible to comport oneself with dignity. If one has a quarrel it ought to elevate rather than to degrade one."

"A maxim straight from the copybook! Suppose I CANNOT comport myself with dignity. By that I mean that, though I am a man of self-respect, I am unable to carry off a situation properly. Do you know the reason? It is because we Russians are too richly and multifariously gifted to be able at once to find the proper mode of expression. It is all a question of mode. Most of us are so bounteously endowed with intellect as to require also a spice of genius to choose the right form of behaviour. And genius is lacking in us for the reason that so little genius at all exists. It belongs only to the French—though a few other Europeans have elaborated their forms so well as to be able to figure with extreme dignity, and yet be wholly undignified persons. That is why, with us, the mode is so all-important. The Frenchman may receive an insult—a real, a venomous insult: yet, he will not so much as frown. But a tweaking of the nose he cannot bear, for the reason that such an act is an infringement of the accepted, of the time-hallowed order of decorum. That is why our good ladies are so fond of Frenchmen—the Frenchman's manners, they say, are perfect! But in my opinion there is no such thing as a Frenchman's manners. The Frenchman is only a bird—the coq gaulois. At the same time, as I am not a woman, I do not properly understand the question. Cocks may be excellent birds. If I am wrong you must stop me. You ought to stop and correct me more often when I am speaking to you, for I am too apt to say everything that is in my head.

"You see, I have lost my manners. I agree that I have none, nor yet any dignity. I will tell you why. I set no store upon such things. Everything in me has undergone a cheek. You know the reason. I have not a single human thought in my head. For a long while I have been ignorant of what is going on in the world—here or in Russia. I have been to Dresden, yet am completely in the dark as to what Dresden is like. You know the cause of my obsession. I have no hope now, and am a mere cipher in your eyes; wherefore, I tell you outright that wherever I go I see only you—all the rest is a matter of indifference.

"Why or how I have come to love you I do not know. It may be that you are not altogether fair to look upon. Do you know, I am ignorant even as to what your face is like. In all probability, too, your heart is not comely, and it is possible that your mind is wholly ignoble."

"And because you do not believe in my nobility of soul you think to purchase me with money?" she said.

"WHEN have I thought to do so?" was my reply.

"You are losing the thread of the argument. If you do not wish to purchase me, at all events you wish to purchase my respect."

"Not at all. I have told you that I find it difficult to explain myself. You are hard upon me. Do not be angry at my chattering. You know why you ought not to be angry with me—that I am simply an imbecile. However, I do not mind if you ARE angry. Sitting in my room, I need but to think of you, to imagine to myself the rustle of your dress, and at once I fall almost to biting my hands. Why should you be angry with me? Because I call myself your slave? Revel, I pray you, in my slavery—revel in it. Do you know that sometimes I could kill you?—not because I do not love you, or am jealous of you, but, because I feel as though I could simply devour you... You are laughing!"

"No, I am not," she retorted. "But I order you, nevertheless, to be silent."

She stopped, well nigh breathless with anger. God knows, she may not have been a beautiful woman, yet I loved to see her come to a halt like this, and was therefore, the more fond of arousing her temper. Perhaps she divined this, and for that very reason gave way to rage. I said as much to her.

"What rubbish!" she cried with a shudder.

"I do not care," I continued. "Also, do you know that it is not safe for us to take walks together? Often I have a feeling that I should like to strike you, to disfigure you, to strangle you. Are you certain that it will never come to that? You are driving me to frenzy. Am I afraid of a scandal, or of your anger? Why should I fear your anger? I love without hope, and know that hereafter I shall love you a thousand times more. If ever I should kill you I should have to kill myself too. But I shall put off doing so as long as possible, for I wish to continue enjoying the unbearable pain which your coldness gives me. Do you know a very strange thing? It is that, with every day, my love for you increases—though that would seem to be almost an impossibility. Why should I not become a fatalist? Remember how, on the third day that we ascended the Shlangenberg, I was moved to whisper in your ear: 'Say but the word, and I will leap into the abyss.' Had you said it, I should have leapt. Do you not believe me?"

"What stupid rubbish!" she cried.

"I care not whether it be wise or stupid," I cried in return. "I only know that in your presence I must speak, speak, speak. Therefore, I am speaking. I lose all conceit when I am with you, and everything ceases to matter."

"Why should I have wanted you to leap from the Shlangenberg?" she said drily, and (I think) with wilful offensiveness. "THAT would have been of no use to me."

"Splendid!" I shouted. "I know well that you must have used the words 'of no use' in order to crush me. I can see through you. 'Of no use,' did you say? Why, to give pleasure is ALWAYS of use; and, as for barbarous, unlimited power—even if it be only over a fly—why, it is a kind of luxury. Man is a despot by nature, and loves to torture. You, in particular, love to do so."

I remember that at this moment she looked at me in a peculiar way. The fact is that my face must have been expressing all the maze of senseless, gross sensations which were seething within me. To this day I can remember, word for word, the conversation as I have written it down. My eyes were suffused with blood, and the foam had caked itself on my lips. Also, on my honour I swear that, had she bidden me cast myself from the summit of the Shlangenberg, I should have done it. Yes, had she bidden me in jest, or only in contempt and with a spit in my face, I should have cast myself down.

"Oh no! Why so? I believe you," she said, but in such a manner—in the manner of which, at times, she was a mistress—and with such a note of disdain and viperish arrogance in her tone, that God knows I could have killed her.

Yes, at that moment she stood in peril. I had not lied to her about that.

"Surely you are not a coward?" suddenly she asked me.

"I do not know," I replied. "Perhaps I am, but I do not know. I have long given up thinking about such things."

"If I said to you, 'Kill that man,' would you kill him?"

"Whom?"

"Whomsoever I wish?"

"The Frenchman?"

"Do not ask me questions; return me answers. I repeat, whomsoever I wish? I desire to see if you were speaking seriously just now."

She awaited my reply with such gravity and impatience that I found the situation unpleasant.

"Do YOU, rather, tell me," I said, "what is going on here? Why do you seem half-afraid of me? I can see for myself what is wrong. You are the step-daughter of a ruined and insensate man who is smitten with love for this devil of a Blanche. And there is this Frenchman, too, with his mysterious influence over you. Yet, you actually ask me such a question! If you do not tell me how things stand, I shall have to put in my oar and do something. Are you ashamed to be frank with me? Are you shy of me?"

"I am not going to talk to you on that subject. I have asked you a question, and am waiting for an answer."

"Well, then—I will kill whomsoever you wish," I said. "But are you REALLY going to bid me do such deeds?"

"Why should you think that I am going to let you off? I shall bid you do it, or else renounce me. Could you ever do the latter? No, you know that you couldn't. You would first kill whom I had bidden you, and then kill ME for having dared to send you away!"

Something seemed to strike upon my brain as I heard these words. Of course, at the time I took them half in jest and half as a challenge; yet, she had spoken them with great seriousness. I felt thunderstruck that she should so express herself, that she should assert such a right over me, that she should assume such authority and say outright: "Either you kill whom I bid you, or I will have nothing more to do with you." Indeed, in what she had said there was something so cynical and unveiled as to pass all bounds. For how could she ever regard me as the same after the killing was done? This was more than slavery and abasement; it was sufficient to bring a man back to his right senses. Yet, despite the outrageous improbability of our conversation, my heart shook within me.

Suddenly, she burst out laughing. We were seated on a bench near the spot where the children were playing—just opposite the point in the alley-way before the Casino where the carriages drew up in order to set down their occupants.

"Do you see that fat Baroness?" she cried. "It is the Baroness Burmergelm. She arrived three days ago. Just look at her husband—that tall, wizened Prussian there, with the stick in his hand. Do you remember how he stared at us the other day? Well, go to the Baroness, take off your hat to her, and say something in French."

"Why?"

"Because you have sworn that you would leap from the Shlangenberg for my sake, and that you would kill any one whom I might bid you kill. Well, instead of such murders and tragedies, I wish only for a good laugh. Go without answering me, and let me see the Baron give you a sound thrashing with his stick."

"Then you throw me out a challenge?—you think that I will not do it?"

"Yes, I do challenge you. Go, for such is my will."

"Then I WILL go, however mad be your fancy. Only, look here: shall you not be doing the General a great disservice, as well as, through him, a great disservice to yourself? It is not about myself I am worrying—it is about you and the General. Why, for a mere fancy, should I go and insult a woman?"

"Ah! Then I can see that you are only a trifler," she said contemptuously. "Your eyes are swimming with blood—but only because you have drunk a little too much at luncheon. Do I not know that what I have asked you to do is foolish and wrong, and that the General will be angry about it? But I want to have a good laugh, all the same. I want that, and nothing else. Why should you insult a woman, indeed? Well, you will be given a sound thrashing for so doing."

I turned away, and went silently to do her bidding. Of course the thing was folly, but I could not get out of it. I remember that, as I approached the Baroness, I felt as excited as a schoolboy. I was in a frenzy, as though I were drunk.

VI

Two days have passed since that day of lunacy. What a noise and a fuss and a chattering and an uproar there was! And what a welter of unseemliness and disorder and stupidity and bad manners! And I the cause of it all! Yet part of the scene was also ridiculous—at all events to myself it was so. I am not quite sure what was the matter with me—whether I was merely stupefied or whether I purposely broke loose and ran amok. At times my mind seems all confused; while at other times I seem almost to be back in my childhood, at the school desk, and to have done the deed simply out of mischief.

It all came of Polina—yes, of Polina. But for her, there might never have been a fracas. Or perhaps I did the deed in a fit of despair (though it may be foolish of me to think so)? What there is so attractive about her I cannot think. Yet there IS something attractive about her—something passing fair, it would seem. Others besides myself she has driven to distraction. She is tall and straight, and very slim. Her body looks as though it could be tied into a knot, or bent double, like a cord. The imprint of her foot is long and narrow. It is, a maddening imprint—yes, simply a maddening one! And her hair has a reddish tint about it, and her eyes are like cat's eyes—though able also to glance with proud, disdainful mien. On the evening of my first arrival, four months ago, I remember that she was sitting and holding an animated conversation with De Griers in the salon. And the way in which she looked at him was such that later, when I retired to my own room upstairs, I kept fancying that she had smitten him in the face—that she had smitten him right on the cheek, so peculiar had been her look as she stood confronting him. Ever since that evening I have loved her.

But to my tale.

I stepped from the path into the carriage-way, and took my stand in the middle of it. There I awaited the Baron and the Baroness. When they were but a few paces distant from me I took off my hat, and bowed.

I remember that the Baroness was clad in a voluminous silk dress, pale grey in colour, and adorned with flounces and a crinoline and train. Also, she was short and inordinately stout, while her gross, flabby chin completely concealed her neck. Her face was purple, and the little eyes in it had an impudent, malicious expression. Yet she walked as though she were conferring a favour upon everybody by so doing. As for the Baron, he was tall, wizened, bony-faced after the German fashion, spectacled, and, apparently, about forty-five years of age. Also, he had legs which seemed to begin almost at his chest—or, rather, at his chin! Yet, for all his air of peacock-like conceit, his clothes sagged a little, and his face wore a sheepish air which might have passed for profundity.

These details I noted within a space of a few seconds.

At first my bow and the fact that I had my hat in my hand barely caught their attention. The Baron only scowled a little, and the Baroness swept straight on.

"Madame la Baronne," said I, loudly and distinctly—embroidering each word, as it were—"j'ai l'honneur d'etre votre esclave."

Then I bowed again, put on my hat, and walked past the Baron with a rude smile on my face.

Polina had ordered me merely to take off my hat: the bow and the general effrontery were of my own invention. God knows what instigated me to perpetrate the outrage! In my frenzy I felt as though I were walking on air.

"Hein!" ejaculated—or, rather, growled—the Baron as he turned towards me in angry surprise.

I too turned round, and stood waiting in pseudo-courteous expectation. Yet still I wore on my face an impudent smile as I gazed at him. He seemed to hesitate, and his brows contracted to their utmost limits. Every moment his visage was growing darker. The Baroness also turned in my direction, and gazed at me in wrathful perplexity, while some of the passers-by also began to stare at us, and others of them halted outright.

"Hein!" the Baron vociferated again, with a redoubled growl and a note of growing wrath in his voice.

"Ja wohl!" I replied, still looking him in the eyes.

"Sind sie rasend?" he exclaimed, brandishing his stick, and, apparently, beginning to feel nervous. Perhaps it was my costume which intimidated him, for I was well and fashionably dressed, after the manner of a man who belongs to indisputably good society.

"Ja wo-o-ohl!" cried I again with all my might with a longdrawn rolling of the "ohl" sound after the fashion of the Berliners (who constantly use the phrase "Ja wohl!" in conversation, and more or less prolong the syllable "ohl" according as they desire to express different shades of meaning or of mood).

At this the Baron and the Baroness faced sharply about, and almost fled in their alarm. Some of the bystanders gave vent to excited exclamations, and others remained staring at me in astonishment. But I do not remember the details very well.

Wheeling quietly about, I returned in the direction of Polina Alexandrovna. But, when I had got within a hundred paces of her seat, I saw her rise and set out with the children towards the hotel.

At the portico I caught up to her.

"I have perpetrated the—the piece of idiocy," I said as I came level with her.

"Have you? Then you can take the consequences," she replied without so much as looking at me. Then she moved towards the staircase.

I spent the rest of the evening walking in the park. Thence I passed into the forest, and walked on until I found myself in a neighbouring principality. At a wayside restaurant I partook of an omelette and some wine, and was charged for the idyllic repast a thaler and a half.

Not until eleven o'clock did I return home—to find a summons awaiting me from the General.

Our party occupied two suites in the hotel; each of which contained two rooms. The first (the larger suite) comprised a salon and a smoking-room, with, adjoining the latter, the General's study. It was here that he was awaiting me as he stood posed in a majestic attitude beside his writing-table. Lolling on a divan close by was De Griers.

"My good sir," the General began, "may I ask you what this is that you have gone and done?"

"I should be glad," I replied, "if we could come straight to the point. Probably you are referring to my encounter of today with a German?"

"With a German? Why, the German was the Baron Burmergelm—a most important personage! I hear that you have been rude both to him and to the Baroness?"

"No, I have not."

"But I understand that you simply terrified them, my good sir?" shouted the General.

"Not in the least," I replied. "You must know that when I was in Berlin I frequently used to hear the Berliners repeat, and repellently prolong, a certain phrase—namely, 'Ja wohl!'; and, happening to meet this couple in the carriage-drive, I found, for some reason or another, that this phrase suddenly recurred to my memory, and exercised a rousing effect upon my spirits. Moreover, on the three previous occasions that I have met the Baroness she has walked towards me as though I were a worm which could easily be crushed with the foot. Not unnaturally, I too possess a measure of self-respect; wherefore, on THIS occasion I took off my hat, and said politely (yes, I assure you it was said politely): 'Madame, j'ai l'honneur d'etre votre esclave.' Then the Baron turned round, and said 'Hein!'; whereupon I felt moved to ejaculate in answer 'Ja wohl!' Twice I shouted it at him—the first time in an ordinary tone, and the second time with the greatest prolonging of the words of which I was capable. That is all."

I must confess that this puerile explanation gave me great pleasure. I felt a strong desire to overlay the incident with an even added measure of grossness; so, the further I proceeded, the more did the gusto of my proceeding increase.

"You are only making fun of me!" vociferated the General as, turning to the Frenchman, he declared that my bringing about of the incident had been gratuitous. De Griers smiled contemptuously, and shrugged his shoulders.

"Do not think THAT," I put in. "It was not so at all. I grant you that my behaviour was bad—I fully confess that it was so, and make no secret of the fact. I would even go so far as to grant you that my behaviour might well be called stupid and indecent tomfoolery; but, MORE than that it was not. Also, let me tell you that I am very sorry for my conduct. Yet there is one circumstance which, in my eyes, almost absolves me from regret in the matter. Of late—that is to say, for the last two or three weeks—I have been feeling not at all well. That is to say, I have been in a sick, nervous, irritable, fanciful condition, so that I have periodically lost control over myself. For instance, on more than one occasion I have tried to pick a quarrel even with Monsieur le Marquise here; and, under the circumstances, he had no choice but to answer me. In short, I have recently been showing signs of ill-health. Whether the Baroness Burmergelm will take this circumstance into consideration when I come to beg her pardon (for I do intend to make her amends) I do not know; but I doubt if she will, and the less so since, so far as I know, the circumstance is one which, of late, has begun to be abused in the legal world, in that advocates in criminal cases have taken to justifying their clients on the ground that, at the moment of the crime, they (the clients) were unconscious of what they were doing—that, in short, they were out of health. 'My client committed the murder—that is true; but he has no recollection of having committed it.' And doctors actually support these advocates by affirming that there really is such a malady—that there really can arise temporary delusions which make a man remember nothing of a given deed, or only a half or a quarter of it! But the Baron and Baroness are members of an older generation, as well as Prussian Junkers and landowners. To them such a process in the medico-judicial world will be unknown, and therefore, they are the more unlikely to accept any such explanation. What is YOUR opinion about it, General?"

"Enough, sir!" he thundered with barely restrained fury. "Enough, I say! Once and for all I must endeavour to rid myself of you and your impertinence. To justify yourself in the eyes of the Baron and Baroness will be impossible. Any intercourse with you, even though it be confined to a begging of their pardons, they would look upon as a degradation. I may tell you that, on learning that you formed part of, my household, the Baron approached me in the Casino, and demanded of me additional satisfaction. Do you understand, then, what it is that you have entailed upon me—upon ME, my good sir? You have entailed upon me the fact of my being forced to sue humbly to the Baron, and to give him my word of honour that this very day you shall cease to belong to my establishment!"

"Excuse me, General," I interrupted, "but did he make an express point of it that I should 'cease to belong to your establishment,' as you call it?"

"No; I, of my own initiative, thought that I ought to afford him that satisfaction; and, with it he was satisfied. So we must part, good sir. It is my duty to hand over to you forty gulden, three florins, as per the accompanying statement. Here is the money, and here the account, which you are at liberty to verify. Farewell. From henceforth we are strangers. From you I have never had anything but trouble and unpleasantness. I am about to call the landlord, and explain to him that from tomorrow onwards I shall no longer be responsible for your hotel expenses. Also I have the honour to remain your obedient servant."

I took the money and the account (which was indicted in pencil), and, bowing low to the General, said to him very gravely:

"The matter cannot end here. I regret very much that you should have been put to unpleasantness at the Baron's hands; but, the fault (pardon me) is your own. How came you to answer for me to the Baron? And what did you mean by saying that I formed part of your household? I am merely your family tutor—not a son of yours, nor yet your ward, nor a person of any kind for whose acts you need be responsible. I am a judicially competent person, a man of twenty-five years of age, a university graduate, a gentleman, and, until I met yourself, a complete stranger to you. Only my boundless respect for your merits restrains me from demanding satisfaction at your hands, as well as a further explanation as to the reasons which have led you to take it upon yourself to answer for my conduct."

So struck was he with my words that, spreading out his hands, he turned to the Frenchman, and interpreted to him that I had challenged himself (the General) to a duel. The Frenchman laughed aloud.

"Nor do I intend to let the Baron off," I continued calmly, but with not a little discomfiture at De Griers' merriment. "And since you, General, have today been so good as to listen to the Baron's complaints, and to enter into his concerns—since you have made yourself a participator in the affair—I have the honour to inform you that, tomorrow morning at the latest, I shall, in my own name, demand of the said Baron a formal explanation as to the reasons which have led him to disregard the fact that the matter lies between him and myself alone, and to put a slight upon me by referring it to another person, as though I were unworthy to answer for my own conduct."

Then there happened what I had foreseen. The General on hearing of this further intended outrage, showed the white feather.

"What?" he cried. "Do you intend to go on with this damned nonsense? Do you not realise the harm that it is doing me? I beg of you not to laugh at me, sir—not to laugh at me, for we have police authorities here who, out of respect for my rank, and for that of the Baron... In short, sir, I swear to you that I will have you arrested, and marched out of the place, to prevent any further brawling on your part. Do you understand what I say?" He was almost breathless with anger, as well as in a terrible fright.

"General," I replied with that calmness which he never could abide, "one cannot arrest a man for brawling until he has brawled. I have not so much as begun my explanations to the Baron, and you are altogether ignorant as to the form and time which my intended procedure is likely to assume. I wish but to disabuse the Baron of what is, to me, a shameful supposition—namely, that I am under the guardianship of a person who is qualified to exercise control over my free will. It is vain for you to disturb and alarm yourself."

"For God's sake, Alexis Ivanovitch, do put an end to this senseless scheme of yours!" he muttered, but with a sudden change from a truculent tone to one of entreaty as he caught me by the hand. "Do you know what is likely to come of it? Merely further unpleasantness. You will agree with me, I am sure, that at present I ought to move with especial care—yes, with very especial care. You cannot be fully aware of how I am situated. When we leave this place I shall be ready to receive you back into my household; but, for the time being I— Well, I cannot tell you all my reasons." With that he wound up in a despairing voice: "O Alexis Ivanovitch, Alexis Ivanovitch!"

I moved towards the door—begging him to be calm, and promising that everything should be done decently and in order; whereafter I departed.

Russians, when abroad, are over-apt to play the poltroon, to watch all their words, and to wonder what people are thinking of their conduct, or whether such and such a thing is 'comme il faut.' In short, they are over-apt to cosset themselves, and to lay claim to great importance. Always they prefer the form of behaviour which has once and for all become accepted and established. This they will follow slavishly whether in hotels, on promenades, at meetings, or when on a journey. But the General had avowed to me that, over and above such considerations as these, there were circumstances which compelled him to "move with especial care at present", and that the fact had actually made him poor-spirited and a coward—it had made him altogether change his tone towards me. This fact I took into my calculations, and duly noted it, for, of course, he MIGHT apply to the authorities tomorrow, and it behoved me to go carefully.

Yet it was not the General but Polina that I wanted to anger. She had treated me with such cruelty, and had got me into such a hole, that I felt a longing to force her to beseech me to stop. Of course, my tomfoolery might compromise her; yet certain other feelings and desires had begun to form themselves in my brain. If I was never to rank in her eyes as anything but a nonentity, it would not greatly matter if I figured as a draggle-tailed cockerel, and the Baron were to give me a good thrashing; but, the fact was that I desired to have the laugh of them all, and to come out myself unscathed. Let people see what they WOULD see. Let Polina, for once, have a good fright, and be forced to whistle me to heel again. But, however much she might whistle, she should see that I was at least no draggle-tailed cockerel!

I have just received a surprising piece of news. I have just met our chambermaid on the stairs, and been informed by her that Maria Philipovna departed today, by the night train, to stay with a cousin at Carlsbad. What can that mean? The maid declares that Madame packed her trunks early in the day. Yet how is it that no one else seems to have been aware of the circumstance? Or is it that I have been the only person to be unaware of it? Also, the maid has just told me that, three days ago, Maria Philipovna had some high words with the General. I understand, then! Probably the words were concerning Mlle. Blanche. Certainly something decisive is approaching.

VII

In the morning I sent for the maitre d'hotel, and explained to him that, in future, my bill was to be rendered to me personally. As a matter of fact, my expenses had never been so large as to alarm me, nor to lead me to quit the hotel; while, moreover, I still had 160 gulden left to me, and—in them—yes, in them, perhaps, riches awaited me. It was a curious fact, that, though I had not yet won anything at play, I nevertheless acted, thought, and felt as though I were sure, before long, to become wealthy—since I could not imagine myself otherwise.

Next, I bethought me, despite the earliness of the hour, of going to see Mr. Astley, who was staying at the Hotel de l'Angleterre (a hostelry at no great distance from our own). But suddenly De Griers entered my room. This had never before happened, for of late that gentleman and I had stood on the most strained and distant of terms—he attempting no concealment of his contempt for me (he even made an express, point of showing it), and I having no reason to desire his company. In short, I detested him. Consequently, his entry at the present moment the more astounded me. At once I divined that something out of the way was on the carpet.

He entered with marked affability, and began by complimenting me on my room. Then, perceiving that I had my hat in my hands, he inquired whither I was going so early; and, no sooner did he hear that I was bound for Mr. Astley's than he stopped, looked grave, and seemed plunged in thought.

He was a true Frenchman insofar as that, though he could be lively and engaging when it suited him, he became insufferably dull and wearisome as soon as ever the need for being lively and engaging had passed. Seldom is a Frenchman NATURALLY civil: he is civil only as though to order and of set purpose. Also, if he thinks it incumbent upon him to be fanciful, original, and out of the way, his fancy always assumes a foolish, unnatural vein, for the reason that it is compounded of trite, hackneyed forms. In short, the natural Frenchman is a conglomeration of commonplace, petty, everyday positiveness, so that he is the most tedious person in the world.—Indeed, I believe that none but greenhorns and excessively Russian people feel an attraction towards the French; for, to any man of sensibility, such a compendium of outworn forms—a compendium which is built up of drawing-room manners, expansiveness, and gaiety—becomes at once over-noticeable and unbearable.

"I have come to see you on business," De Griers began in a very off-hand, yet polite, tone; "nor will I seek to conceal from you the fact that I have come in the capacity of an emissary, of an intermediary, from the General. Having small knowledge of the Russian tongue, I lost most of what was said last night; but, the General has now explained matters, and I must confess that—"

"See here, Monsieur de Griers," I interrupted. "I understand that you have undertaken to act in this affair as an intermediary. Of course I am only 'un utchitel,' a tutor, and have never claimed to be an intimate of this household, nor to stand on at all familiar terms with it. Consequently, I do not know the whole of its circumstances. Yet pray explain to me this: have you yourself become one of its members, seeing that you are beginning to take such a part in everything, and are now present as an intermediary?"

The Frenchman seemed not over-pleased at my question. It was one which was too outspoken for his taste—and he had no mind to be frank with me.

"I am connected with the General," he said drily, "partly through business affairs, and partly through special circumstances. My principal has sent me merely to ask you to forego your intentions of last evening. What you contemplate is, I have no doubt, very clever; yet he has charged me to represent to you that you have not the slightest chance of succeeding in your end, since not only will the Baron refuse to receive you, but also he (the Baron) has at his disposal every possible means for obviating further unpleasantness from you. Surely you can see that yourself? What, then, would be the good of going on with it all? On the other hand, the General promises that at the first favourable opportunity he will receive you back into his household, and, in the meantime, will credit you with your salary—with 'vos appointements.' Surely that will suit you, will it not?"

Very quietly I replied that he (the Frenchman) was labouring under a delusion; that perhaps, after all, I should not be expelled from the Baron's presence, but, on the contrary, be listened to; finally, that I should be glad if Monsieur de Griers would confess that he was now visiting me merely in order to see how far I intended to go in the affair.

"Good heavens!" cried de Griers. "Seeing that the General takes such an interest in the matter, is there anything very unnatural in his desiring also to know your plans?"

Again I began my explanations, but the Frenchman only fidgeted and rolled his head about as he listened with an expression of manifest and unconcealed irony on his face. In short, he adopted a supercilious attitude. For my own part, I endeavoured to pretend that I took the affair very seriously. I declared that, since the Baron had gone and complained of me to the General, as though I were a mere servant of the General's, he had, in the first place, lost me my post, and, in the second place, treated me like a person to whom, as to one not qualified to answer for himself, it was not even worth while to speak. Naturally, I said, I felt insulted at this. Yet, comprehending as I did, differences of years, of social status, and so forth (here I could scarcely help smiling), I was not anxious to bring about further scenes by going personally to demand or to request satisfaction of the Baron. All that I felt was that I had a right to go in person and beg the Baron's and the Baroness's pardon—the more so since, of late, I had been feeling unwell and unstrung, and had been in a fanciful condition. And so forth, and so forth. Yet (I continued) the Baron's offensive behaviour to me of yesterday (that is to say, the fact of his referring the matter to the General) as well as his insistence that the General should deprive me of my post, had placed me in such a position that I could not well express my regret to him (the Baron) and to his good lady, for the reason that in all probability both he and the Baroness, with the world at large, would imagine that I was doing so merely because I hoped, by my action, to recover my post. Hence, I found myself forced to request the Baron to express to me HIS OWN regrets, as well as to express them in the most unqualified manner—to say, in fact, that he had never had any wish to insult me. After the Baron had done THAT, I should, for my part, at once feel free to express to him, whole-heartedly and without reserve, my own regrets. "In short," I declared in conclusion, "my one desire is that the Baron may make it possible for me to adopt the latter course."

"Oh fie! What refinements and subtleties!" exclaimed De Griers. "Besides, what have you to express regret for? Confess, Monsieur, Monsieur—pardon me, but I have forgotten your name—confess, I say, that all this is merely a plan to annoy the General? Or perhaps, you have some other and special end in view? Eh?"

"In return you must pardon ME, mon cher Marquis, and tell me what you have to do with it."

"The General—"

"But what of the General? Last night he said that, for some reason or another, it behoved him to 'move with especial care at present;' wherefore, he was feeling nervous. But I did not understand the reference."

"Yes, there DO exist special reasons for his doing so," assented De Griers in a conciliatory tone, yet with rising anger. "You are acquainted with Mlle. de Cominges, are you not?"

"Mlle. Blanche, you mean?"

"Yes, Mlle. Blanche de Cominges. Doubtless you know also that the General is in love with this young lady, and may even be about to marry her before he leaves here? Imagine, therefore, what any scene or scandal would entail upon him!"

"I cannot see that the marriage scheme need, be affected by scenes or scandals."

"Mais le Baron est si irascible—un caractere prussien, vous savez! Enfin il fera une querelle d'Allemand."

"I do not care," I replied, "seeing that I no longer belong to his household" (of set purpose I was trying to talk as senselessly as possible). "But is it quite settled that Mlle. is to marry the General? What are they waiting for? Why should they conceal such a matter—at all events from ourselves, the General's own party?"

"I cannot tell you. The marriage is not yet a settled affair, for they are awaiting news from Russia. The General has business transactions to arrange."

"Ah! Connected, doubtless, with madame his mother?"

De Griers shot at me a glance of hatred.

"To cut things short," he interrupted, "I have complete confidence in your native politeness, as well as in your tact and good sense. I feel sure that you will do what I suggest, even if it is only for the sake of this family which has received you as a kinsman into its bosom and has always loved and respected you."

"Be so good as to observe," I remarked, "that the same family has just EXPELLED me from its bosom. All that you are saying you are saying but for show; but, when people have just said to you, 'Of course we do not wish to turn you out, yet, for the sake of appearance's, you must PERMIT yourself to be turned out,' nothing can matter very much."

"Very well, then," he said, in a sterner and more arrogant tone. "Seeing that my solicitations have had no effect upon you, it is my duty to mention that other measures will be taken. There exist here police, you must remember, and this very day they shall send you packing. Que diable! To think of a blanc bec like yourself challenging a person like the Baron to a duel! Do you suppose that you will be ALLOWED to do such things? Just try doing them, and see if any one will be afraid of you! The reason why I have asked you to desist is that I can see that your conduct is causing the General annoyance. Do you believe that the Baron could not tell his lacquey simply to put you out of doors?"

"Nevertheless I should not GO out of doors," I retorted with absolute calm. "You are labouring under a delusion, Monsieur de Griers. The thing will be done in far better trim than you imagine. I was just about to start for Mr. Astley's, to ask him to be my intermediary—in other words, my second. He has a strong liking for me, and I do not think that he will refuse. He will go and see the Baron on MY behalf, and the Baron will certainly not decline to receive him. Although I am only a tutor—a kind of subaltern, Mr. Astley is known to all men as the nephew of a real English lord, the Lord Piebroch, as well as a lord in his own right. Yes, you may be pretty sure that the Baron will be civil to Mr. Astley, and listen to him. Or, should he decline to do so, Mr. Astley will take the refusal as a personal affront to himself (for you know how persistent the English are?) and thereupon introduce to the Baron a friend of his own (and he has many friends in a good position). That being so, picture to yourself the issue of the affair—an affair which will not quite end as you think it will."

This caused the Frenchman to bethink him of playing the coward. "Really things may be as this fellow says," he evidently thought. "Really he MIGHT be able to engineer another scene."

"Once more I beg of you to let the matter drop," he continued in a tone that was now entirely conciliatory. "One would think that it actually PLEASED you to have scenes! Indeed, it is a brawl rather than genuine satisfaction that you are seeking. I have said that the affair may prove to be diverting, and even clever, and that possibly you may attain something by it; yet none the less I tell you" (he said this only because he saw me rise and reach for my hat) "that I have come hither also to hand you these few words from a certain person. Read them, please, for I must take her back an answer."

So saying, he took from his pocket a small, compact, wafer-sealed note, and handed it to me. In Polina's handwriting I read:

"I hear that you are thinking of going on with this affair. You have lost your temper now, and are beginning to play the fool! Certain circumstances, however, I may explain to you later. Pray cease from your folly, and put a check upon yourself. For folly it all is. I have need of you, and, moreover, you have promised to obey me. Remember the Shlangenberg. I ask you to be obedient. If necessary, I shall even BID you be obedient.—Your own——POLINA.

"P.S.—If so be that you still bear a grudge against me for what happened last night, pray forgive me."

Everything, to my eyes, seemed to change as I read these words. My lips grew pale, and I began to tremble. Meanwhile, the cursed Frenchman was eyeing me discreetly and askance, as though he wished to avoid witnessing my confusion. It would have been better if he had laughed outright.

"Very well," I said, "you can tell Mlle. not to disturb herself. But," I added sharply, "I would also ask you why you have been so long in handing me this note? Instead of chattering about trifles, you ought to have delivered me the missive at once—if you have really come commissioned as you say."

"Well, pardon some natural haste on my part, for the situation is so strange. I wished first to gain some personal knowledge of your intentions; and, moreover, I did not know the contents of the note, and thought that it could be given you at any time."

"I understand," I replied. "So you were ordered to hand me the note only in the last resort, and if you could not otherwise appease me? Is it not so? Speak out, Monsieur de Griers."

"Perhaps," said he, assuming a look of great forbearance, but gazing at me in a meaning way.

I reached for my hat; whereupon he nodded, and went out. Yet on his lips I fancied that I could see a mocking smile. How could it have been otherwise?

"You and I are to have a reckoning later, Master Frenchman," I muttered as I descended the stairs. "Yes, we will measure our strength together." Yet my thoughts were all in confusion, for again something seemed to have struck me dizzy. Presently the air revived me a little, and, a couple of minutes later, my brain had sufficiently cleared to enable two ideas in particular to stand out in it. Firstly, I asked myself, which of the absurd, boyish, and extravagant threats which I had uttered at random last night had made everybody so alarmed? Secondly, what was the influence which this Frenchman appeared to exercise over Polina? He had but to give the word, and at once she did as he desired—at once she wrote me a note to beg of me to forbear! Of course, the relations between the pair had, from the first, been a riddle to me—they had been so ever since I had first made their acquaintance. But of late I had remarked in her a strong aversion for, even a contempt for—him, while, for his part, he had scarcely even looked at her, but had behaved towards her always in the most churlish fashion. Yes, I had noted that. Also, Polina herself had mentioned to me her dislike for him, and delivered herself of some remarkable confessions on the subject. Hence, he must have got her into his power somehow—somehow he must be holding her as in a vice.

VIII

All at once, on the Promenade, as it was called—that is to say, in the Chestnut Avenue—I came face to face with my Englishman.

"I was just coming to see you," he said; "and you appear to be out on a similar errand. So you have parted with your employers?"

"How do you know that?" I asked in astonishment. "Is EVERY ONE aware of the fact?"

"By no means. Not every one would consider such a fact to be of moment. Indeed, I have never heard any one speak of it."

"Then how come you to know it?"

"Because I have had occasion to do so. Whither are you bound? I like you, and was therefore coming to pay you a visit."

"What a splendid fellow you are, Mr. Astley!" I cried, though still wondering how he had come by his knowledge. "And since I have not yet had my coffee, and you have, in all probability, scarcely tasted yours, let us adjourn to the Casino Cafe, where we can sit and smoke and have a talk."

The cafe in question was only a hundred paces away; so, when coffee had been brought, we seated ourselves, and I lit a cigarette. Astley was no smoker, but, taking a seat by my side, he prepared himself to listen.

"I do not intend to go away," was my first remark. "I intend, on the contrary, to remain here."

"That I never doubted," he answered good-humouredly.

It is a curious fact that, on my way to see him, I had never even thought of telling him of my love for Polina. In fact, I had purposely meant to avoid any mention of the subject. Nor, during our stay in the place, had I ever made aught but the scantiest reference to it. You see, not only was Astley a man of great reserve, but also from the first I had perceived that Polina had made a great impression upon him, although he never spoke of her. But now, strangely enough, he had no sooner seated himself and bent his steely gaze upon me, than, for some reason or another, I felt moved to tell him everything—to speak to him of my love in all its phases. For an hour and a half did I discourse on the subject, and found it a pleasure to do so, even though this was the first occasion on which I had referred to the matter. Indeed, when, at certain moments, I perceived that my more ardent passages confused him, I purposely increased my ardour of narration. Yet one thing I regret: and that is that I made references to the Frenchman which were a little over-personal.

Mr. Astley sat without moving as he listened to me. Not a word nor a sound of any kind did he utter as he stared into my eyes. Suddenly, however, on my mentioning the Frenchman, he interrupted me, and inquired sternly whether I did right to speak of an extraneous matter (he had always been a strange man in his mode of propounding questions).

"No, I fear not," I replied.

"And concerning this Marquis and Mlle. Polina you know nothing beyond surmise?"

Again I was surprised that such a categorical question should come from such a reserved individual.

"No, I know nothing FOR CERTAIN about them" was my reply. "No—nothing."

"Then you have done very wrong to speak of them to me, or even to imagine things about them."

"Quite so, quite so," I interrupted in some astonishment. "I admit that. Yet that is not the question." Whereupon I related to him in detail the incident of two days ago. I spoke of Polina's outburst, of my encounter with the Baron, of my dismissal, of the General's extraordinary pusillanimity, and of the call which De Griers had that morning paid me. In conclusion, I showed Astley the note which I had lately received.

"What do you make of it?" I asked. "When I met you I was just coming to ask you your opinion. For myself, I could have killed this Frenchman, and am not sure that I shall not do so even yet."

"I feel the same about it," said Mr. Astley. "As for Mlle. Polina—well, you yourself know that, if necessity drives, one enters into relation with people whom one simply detests. Even between this couple there may be something which, though unknown to you, depends upon extraneous circumstances. For, my own part, I think that you may reassure yourself—or at all events partially. And as for Mlle. Polina's proceedings of two days ago, they were, of course, strange; not because she can have meant to get rid of you, or to earn for you a thrashing from the Baron's cudgel (which for some curious reason, he did not use, although he had it ready in his hands), but because such proceedings on the part of such—well, of such a refined lady as Mlle. Polina are, to say the least of it, unbecoming. But she cannot have guessed that you would carry out her absurd wish to the letter?"

"Do you know what?" suddenly I cried as I fixed Mr. Astley with my gaze. "I believe that you have already heard the story from some one—very possibly from Mlle. Polina herself?"

In return he gave me an astonished stare.

"Your eyes look very fiery," he said with a return of his former calm, "and in them I can read suspicion. Now, you have no right whatever to be suspicious. It is not a right which I can for a moment recognise, and I absolutely refuse to answer your questions."

"Enough! You need say no more," I cried with a strange emotion at my heart, yet not altogether understanding what had aroused that emotion in my breast. Indeed, when, where, and how could Polina have chosen Astley to be one of her confidants? Of late I had come rather to overlook him in this connection, even though Polina had always been a riddle to me—so much so that now, when I had just permitted myself to tell my friend of my infatuation in all its aspects, I had found myself struck, during the very telling, with the fact that in my relations with her I could specify nothing that was explicit, nothing that was positive. On the contrary, my relations had been purely fantastic, strange, and unreal; they had been unlike anything else that I could think of.

"Very well, very well," I replied with a warmth equal to Astley's own. "Then I stand confounded, and have no further opinions to offer. But you are a good fellow, and I am glad to know what you think about it all, even though I do not need your advice."

Then, after a pause, I resumed:

"For instance, what reason should you assign for the General taking fright in this way? Why should my stupid clowning have led the world to elevate it into a serious incident? Even De Griers has found it necessary to put in his oar (and he only interferes on the most important occasions), and to visit me, and to address to me the most earnest supplications. Yes, HE, De Griers, has actually been playing the suppliant to ME! And, mark you, although he came to me as early as nine o'clock, he had ready-prepared in his hand Mlle. Polina's note. When, I would ask, was that note written? Mlle. Polina must have been aroused from sleep for the express purpose of writing it. At all events the circumstance shows that she is an absolute slave to the Frenchman, since she actually begs my pardon in the note—actually begs my pardon! Yet what is her personal concern in the matter? Why is she interested in it at all? Why, too, is the whole party so afraid of this precious Baron? And what sort of a business do you call it for the General to be going to marry Mlle. Blanche de Cominges? He told me last night that, because of the circumstance, he must 'move with especial care at present.' What is your opinion of it all? Your look convinces me that you know more about it than I do."

Mr. Astley smiled and nodded.

"Yes, I think I DO know more about it than you do," he assented. "The affair centres around this Mlle. Blanche. Of that I feel certain."

"And what of Mlle. Blanche?" I cried impatiently (for in me there had dawned a sudden hope that this would enable me to discover something about Polina).

"Well, my belief is that at the present moment Mlle. Blanche has, in very truth, a special reason for wishing to avoid any trouble with the Baron and the Baroness. It might lead not only to some unpleasantness, but even to a scandal."

"Oh, oh!"

"Also I may tell you that Mlle. Blanche has been in Roulettenberg before, for she was staying here three seasons ago. I myself was in the place at the time, and in those days Mlle. Blanche was not known as Mlle. de Cominges, nor was her mother, the Widow de Cominges, even in existence. In any case no one ever mentioned the latter. De Griers, too, had not materialised, and I am convinced that not only do the parties stand in no relation to one another, but also they have not long enjoyed one another's acquaintance. Likewise, the Marquisate de Griers is of recent creation. Of that I have reason to be sure, owing to a certain circumstance. Even the name De Griers itself may be taken to be a new invention, seeing that I have a friend who once met the said 'Marquis' under a different name altogether."

"Yet he possesses a good circle of friends?"

"Possibly. Mlle. Blanche also may possess that. Yet it is not three years since she received from the local police, at the instance of the Baroness, an invitation to leave the town. And she left it."

"But why?"

"Well, I must tell you that she first appeared here in company with an Italian—a prince of some sort, a man who bore an historic name (Barberini or something of the kind). The fellow was simply a mass of rings and diamonds—real diamonds, too—and the couple used to drive out in a marvellous carriage. At first Mlle. Blanche played 'trente et quarante' with fair success, but, later, her luck took a marked change for the worse. I distinctly remember that in a single evening she lost an enormous sum. But worse was to ensue, for one fine morning her prince disappeared—horses, carriage, and all. Also, the hotel bill which he left unpaid was enormous. Upon this Mlle. Zelma (the name which she assumed after figuring as Madame Barberini) was in despair. She shrieked and howled all over the hotel, and even tore her clothes in her frenzy. In the hotel there was staying also a Polish count (you must know that ALL travelling Poles are counts!), and the spectacle of Mlle. Zelma tearing her clothes and, catlike, scratching her face with her beautiful, scented nails produced upon him a strong impression. So the pair had a talk together, and, by luncheon time, she was consoled. Indeed, that evening the couple entered the Casino arm-in-arm—Mlle. Zelma laughing loudly, according to her custom, and showing even more expansiveness in her manners than she had before shown. For instance, she thrust her way into the file of women roulette-players in the exact fashion of those ladies who, to clear a space for themselves at the tables, push their fellow-players roughly aside. Doubtless you have noticed them?"

"Yes, certainly."

"Well, they are not worth noticing. To the annoyance of the decent public they are allowed to remain here—at all events such of them as daily change 4000 franc notes at the tables (though, as soon as ever these women cease to do so, they receive an invitation to depart). However, Mlle. Zelma continued to change notes of this kind, but her play grew more and more unsuccessful, despite the fact that such ladies' luck is frequently good, for they have a surprising amount of cash at their disposal. Suddenly, the Count too disappeared, even as the Prince had done, and that same evening Mlle. Zelma was forced to appear in the Casino alone. On this occasion no one offered her a greeting. Two days later she had come to the end of her resources; whereupon, after staking and losing her last louis d'or she chanced to look around her, and saw standing by her side the Baron Burmergelm, who had been eyeing her with fixed disapproval. To his distaste, however, Mlle. paid no attention, but, turning to him with her well-known smile, requested him to stake, on her behalf, ten louis on the red. Later that evening a complaint from the Baroness led the authorities to request Mlle. not to re-enter the Casino. If you feel in any way surprised that I should know these petty and unedifying details, the reason is that I had them from a relative of mine who, later that evening, drove Mlle. Zelma in his carriage from Roulettenberg to Spa. Now, mark you, Mlle. wants to become Madame General, in order that, in future, she may be spared the receipt of such invitations from Casino authorities as she received three years ago. At present she is not playing; but that is only because, according to the signs, she is lending money to other players. Yes, that is a much more paying game. I even suspect that the unfortunate General is himself in her debt, as well as, perhaps, also De Griers. Or, it may be that the latter has entered into a partnership with her. Consequently you yourself will see that, until the marriage shall have been consummated, Mlle. would scarcely like to have the attention of the Baron and the Baroness drawn to herself. In short, to any one in her position, a scandal would be most detrimental. You form a member of the menage of these people; wherefore, any act of yours might cause such a scandal—and the more so since daily she appears in public arm in arm with the General or with Mlle. Polina. NOW do you understand?"

"No, I do not!" I shouted as I banged my fist down upon the table—banged it with such violence that a frightened waiter came running towards us. "Tell me, Mr. Astley, why, if you knew this history all along, and, consequently, always knew who this Mlle. Blanche is, you never warned either myself or the General, nor, most of all, Mlle. Polina" (who is accustomed to appear in the Casino—in public everywhere with Mlle. Blanche). "How could you do it?"

"It would have done no good to warn you," he replied quietly, "for the reason that you could have effected nothing. Against what was I to warn you? As likely as not, the General knows more about Mlle. Blanche even than I do; yet the unhappy man still walks about with her and Mlle. Polina. Only yesterday I saw this Frenchwoman riding, splendidly mounted, with De Griers, while the General was careering in their wake on a roan horse. He had said, that morning, that his legs were hurting him, yet his riding-seat was easy enough. As he passed I looked at him, and the thought occurred to me that he was a man lost for ever. However, it is no affair of mine, for I have only recently had the happiness to make Mlle. Polina's acquaintance. Also"—he added this as an afterthought—"I have already told you that I do not recognise your right to ask me certain questions, however sincere be my liking for you."

"Enough," I said, rising. "To me it is as clear as day that Mlle. Polina knows all about this Mlle. Blanche, but cannot bring herself to part with her Frenchman; wherefore, she consents also to be seen in public with Mlle. Blanche. You may be sure that nothing else would ever have induced her either to walk about with this Frenchwoman or to send me a note not to touch the Baron. Yes, it is THERE that the influence lies before which everything in the world must bow! Yet she herself it was who launched me at the Baron! The devil take it, but I was left no choice in the matter."

"You forget, in the first place, that this Mlle. de Cominges is the General's inamorata, and, in the second place, that Mlle. Polina, the General's step-daughter, has a younger brother and sister who, though they are the General's own children, are completely neglected by this madman, and robbed as well."

"Yes, yes; that is so. For me to go and desert the children now would mean their total abandonment; whereas, if I remain, I should be able to defend their interests, and, perhaps, to save a moiety of their property. Yes, yes; that is quite true. And yet, and yet—Oh, I can well understand why they are all so interested in the General's mother!"

"In whom?" asked Mr. Astley.

"In the old woman of Moscow who declines to die, yet concerning whom they are for ever expecting telegrams to notify the fact of her death."

"Ah, then of course their interests centre around her. It is a question of succession. Let that but be settled, and the General will marry, Mlle. Polina will be set free, and De Griers—"

"Yes, and De Griers?"

"Will be repaid his money, which is what he is now waiting for."

"What? You think that he is waiting for that?"

"I know of nothing else," asserted Mr. Astley doggedly.

"But, I do, I do!" I shouted in my fury. "He is waiting also for the old woman's will, for the reason that it awards Mlle. Polina a dowry. As soon as ever the money is received, she will throw herself upon the Frenchman's neck. All women are like that. Even the proudest of them become abject slaves where marriage is concerned. What Polina is good for is to fall head over ears in love. That is MY opinion. Look at her—especially when she is sitting alone, and plunged in thought. All this was pre-ordained and foretold, and is accursed. Polina could perpetrate any mad act. She—she—But who called me by name?" I broke off. "Who is shouting for me? I heard some one calling in Russian, 'Alexis Ivanovitch!' It was a woman's voice. Listen!"

At the moment, we were approaching my hotel. We had left the cafe long ago, without even noticing that we had done so.

"Yes, I DID hear a woman's voice calling, but whose I do not know. The someone was calling you in Russian. Ah! NOW I can see whence the cries come. They come from that lady there—the one who is sitting on the settee, the one who has just been escorted to the verandah by a crowd of lacqueys. Behind her see that pile of luggage! She must have arrived by train."

"But why should she be calling ME? Hear her calling again! See! She is beckoning to us!"

"Yes, so she is," assented Mr. Astley.

"Alexis Ivanovitch, Alexis Ivanovitch! Good heavens, what a stupid fellow!" came in a despairing wail from the verandah.

We had almost reached the portico, and I was just setting foot upon the space before it, when my hands fell to my sides in limp astonishment, and my feet glued themselves to the pavement!

IX

For on the topmost tier of the hotel verandah, after being carried up the steps in an armchair amid a bevy of footmen, maid-servants, and other menials of the hotel, headed by the landlord (that functionary had actually run out to meet a visitor who arrived with so much stir and din, attended by her own retinue, and accompanied by so great a pile of trunks and portmanteaux)—on the topmost tier of the verandah, I say, there was sitting—THE GRANDMOTHER! Yes, it was she—rich, and imposing, and seventy-five years of age—Antonida Vassilievna Tarassevitcha, landowner and grande dame of Moscow—the "La Baboulenka" who had caused so many telegrams to be sent off and received—who had been dying, yet not dying—who had, in her own person, descended upon us even as snow might fall from the clouds! Though unable to walk, she had arrived borne aloft in an armchair (her mode of conveyance for the last five years), as brisk, aggressive, self-satisfied, bolt-upright, loudly imperious, and generally abusive as ever. In fact, she looked exactly as she had on the only two occasions when I had seen her since my appointment to the General's household. Naturally enough, I stood petrified with astonishment. She had sighted me a hundred paces off! Even while she was being carried along in her chair she had recognised me, and called me by name and surname (which, as usual, after hearing once, she had remembered ever afterwards).

"And this is the woman whom they had thought to see in her grave after making her will!" I thought to myself. "Yet she will outlive us, and every one else in the hotel. Good Lord! what is going to become of us now? What on earth is to happen to the General? She will turn the place upside down!"

"My good sir," the old woman continued in a stentorian voice, "what are you standing THERE for, with your eyes almost falling out of your head? Cannot you come and say how-do-you-do? Are you too proud to shake hands? Or do you not recognise me? Here, Potapitch!" she cried to an old servant who, dressed in a frock coat and white waistcoat, had a bald, red head (he was the chamberlain who always accompanied her on her journeys). "Just think! Alexis Ivanovitch does not recognise me! They have buried me for good and all! Yes, and after sending hosts of telegrams to know if I were dead or not! Yes, yes, I have heard the whole story. I am very much alive, though, as you may see."

"Pardon me, Antonida Vassilievna," I replied good humouredly as I recovered my presence of mind. "I have no reason to wish you ill. I am merely rather astonished to see you. Why should I not be so, seeing how unexpected—"

"WHY should you be astonished? I just got into my chair, and came. Things are quiet enough in the train, for there is no one there to chatter. Have you been out for a walk?"

"Yes. I have just been to the Casino."

"Oh? Well, it is quite nice here," she went on as she looked about her. "The place seems comfortable, and all the trees are out. I like it very well. Are your people at home? Is the General, for instance, indoors?"

"Yes; and probably all of them."

"Do they observe the convenances, and keep up appearances? Such things always give one tone. I have heard that they are keeping a carriage, even as Russian gentlefolks ought to do. When abroad, our Russian people always cut a dash. Is Prascovia here too?"

"Yes. Polina Alexandrovna is here."

"And the Frenchwoman? However, I will go and look for them myself. Tell me the nearest way to their rooms. Do you like being here?"

"Yes, I thank you, Antonida Vassilievna."

"And you, Potapitch, you go and tell that fool of a landlord to reserve me a suitable suite of rooms. They must be handsomely decorated, and not too high up. Have my luggage taken up to them. But what are you tumbling over yourselves for? Why are you all tearing about? What scullions these fellows are!—Who is that with you?" she added to myself.

"A Mr. Astley," I replied.

"And who is Mr. Astley?"

"A fellow-traveller, and my very good friend, as well as an acquaintance of the General's."

"Oh, an Englishman? Then that is why he stared at me without even opening his lips. However, I like Englishmen. Now, take me upstairs, direct to their rooms. Where are they lodging?"

Madame was lifted up in her chair by the lacqueys, and I preceded her up the grand staircase. Our progress was exceedingly effective, for everyone whom we met stopped to stare at the cortege. It happened that the hotel had the reputation of being the best, the most expensive, and the most aristocratic in all the spa, and at every turn on the staircase or in the corridors we encountered fine ladies and important-looking Englishmen—more than one of whom hastened downstairs to inquire of the awestruck landlord who the newcomer was. To all such questions he returned the same answer—namely, that the old lady was an influential foreigner, a Russian, a Countess, and a grande dame, and that she had taken the suite which, during the previous week, had been tenanted by the Grande Duchesse de N.

Meanwhile the cause of the sensation—the Grandmother—was being borne aloft in her armchair. Every person whom she met she scanned with an inquisitive eye, after first of all interrogating me about him or her at the top of her voice. She was stout of figure, and, though she could not leave her chair, one felt, the moment that one first looked at her, that she was also tall of stature. Her back was as straight as a board, and never did she lean back in her seat. Also, her large grey head, with its keen, rugged features, remained always erect as she glanced about her in an imperious, challenging sort of way, with looks and gestures that clearly were unstudied. Though she had reached her seventy-sixth year, her face was still fresh, and her teeth had not decayed. Lastly, she was dressed in a black silk gown and white mobcap.

"She interests me tremendously," whispered Mr. Astley as, still smoking, he walked by my side. Meanwhile I was reflecting that probably the old lady knew all about the telegrams, and even about De Griers, though little or nothing about Mlle. Blanche. I said as much to Mr. Astley.

But what a frail creature is man! No sooner was my first surprise abated than I found myself rejoicing in the shock which we were about to administer to the General. So much did the thought inspire me that I marched ahead in the gayest of fashions.

Our party was lodging on the third floor. Without knocking at the door, or in any way announcing our presence, I threw open the portals, and the Grandmother was borne through them in triumph. As though of set purpose, the whole party chanced at that moment to be assembled in the General's study. The time was eleven o'clock, and it seemed that an outing of some sort (at which a portion of the party were to drive in carriages, and others to ride on horseback, accompanied by one or two extraneous acquaintances) was being planned. The General was present, and also Polina, the children, the latter's nurses, De Griers, Mlle. Blanche (attired in a riding-habit), her mother, the young Prince, and a learned German whom I beheld for the first time. Into the midst of this assembly the lacqueys conveyed Madame in her chair, and set her down within three paces of the General!

Good heavens! Never shall I forget the spectacle which ensued! Just before our entry, the General had been holding forth to the company, with De Griers in support of him. I may also mention that, for the last two or three days, Mlle. Blanche and De Griers had been making a great deal of the young Prince, under the very nose of the poor General. In short, the company, though decorous and conventional, was in a gay, familiar mood. But no sooner did the Grandmother appear than the General stopped dead in the middle of a word, and, with jaw dropping, stared hard at the old lady—his eyes almost starting out of his head, and his expression as spellbound as though he had just seen a basilisk. In return, the Grandmother stared at him silently and without moving—though with a look of mingled challenge, triumph, and ridicule in her eyes. For ten seconds did the pair remain thus eyeing one another, amid the profound silence of the company; and even De Griers sat petrified—an extraordinary look of uneasiness dawning on his face. As for Mlle. Blanche, she too stared wildly at the Grandmother, with eyebrows raised and her lips parted—while the Prince and the German savant contemplated the tableau in profound amazement. Only Polina looked anything but perplexed or surprised. Presently, however, she too turned as white as a sheet, and then reddened to her temples. Truly the Grandmother's arrival seemed to be a catastrophe for everybody! For my own part, I stood looking from the Grandmother to the company, and back again, while Mr. Astley, as usual, remained in the background, and gazed calmly and decorously at the scene.

"Well, here I am—and instead of a telegram, too!" the Grandmother at last ejaculated, to dissipate the silence. "What? You were not expecting me?"

"Antonida Vassilievna! O my dearest mother! But how on earth did you, did you—?" The mutterings of the unhappy General died away.

I verily believe that if the Grandmother had held her tongue a few seconds longer she would have had a stroke.

"How on earth did I WHAT?" she exclaimed. "Why, I just got into the train and came here. What else is the railway meant for? But you thought that I had turned up my toes and left my property to the lot of you. Oh, I know ALL about the telegrams which you have been dispatching. They must have cost you a pretty sum, I should think, for telegrams are not sent from abroad for nothing. Well, I picked up my heels, and came here. Who is this Frenchman? Monsieur de Griers, I suppose?"

"Oui, madame," assented De Griers. "Et, croyez, je suis si enchante! Votre sante—c'est un miracle vous voir ici. Une surprise charmante!"

"Just so. 'Charmante!' I happen to know you as a mountebank, and therefore trust you no more than THIS." She indicated her little finger. "And who is THAT?" she went on, turning towards Mlle. Blanche. Evidently the Frenchwoman looked so becoming in her riding-habit, with her whip in her hand, that she had made an impression upon the old lady. "Who is that woman there?"

"Mlle. de Cominges," I said. "And this is her mother, Madame de Cominges. They also are staying in the hotel."

"Is the daughter married?" asked the old lady, without the least semblance of ceremony.

"No," I replied as respectfully as possible, but under my breath.

"Is she good company?"

I failed to understand the question.

"I mean, is she or is she not a bore? Can she speak Russian? When this De Griers was in Moscow he soon learnt to make himself understood."

I explained to the old lady that Mlle. Blanche had never visited Russia.

"Bonjour, then," said Madame, with sudden brusquerie.

"Bonjour, madame," replied Mlle. Blanche with an elegant, ceremonious bow as, under cover of an unwonted modesty, she endeavoured to express, both in face and figure, her extreme surprise at such strange behaviour on the part of the Grandmother.

"How the woman sticks out her eyes at me! How she mows and minces!" was the Grandmother's comment. Then she turned suddenly to the General, and continued: "I have taken up my abode here, so am going to be your next-door neighbour. Are you glad to hear that, or are you not?"

"My dear mother, believe me when I say that I am sincerely delighted," returned the General, who had now, to a certain extent, recovered his senses; and inasmuch as, when occasion arose, he could speak with fluency, gravity, and a certain effect, he set himself to be expansive in his remarks, and went on: "We have been so dismayed and upset by the news of your indisposition! We had received such hopeless telegrams about you! Then suddenly—"

"Fibs, fibs!" interrupted the Grandmother.

"How on earth, too, did you come to decide upon the journey?" continued the General, with raised voice as he hurried to overlook the old lady's last remark. "Surely, at your age, and in your present state of health, the thing is so unexpected that our surprise is at least intelligible. However, I am glad to see you (as indeed, are we all"—he said this with a dignified, yet conciliatory, smile), "and will use my best endeavours to render your stay here as pleasant as possible."

"Enough! All this is empty chatter. You are talking the usual nonsense. I shall know quite well how to spend my time. How did I come to undertake the journey, you ask? Well, is there anything so very surprising about it? It was done quite simply. What is every one going into ecstasies about?—How do you do, Prascovia? What are YOU doing here?"

"And how are YOU, Grandmother?" replied Polina, as she approached the old lady. "Were you long on the journey?"

"The most sensible question that I have yet been asked! Well, you shall hear for yourself how it all happened. I lay and lay, and was doctored and doctored, until at last I drove the physicians from me, and called in an apothecary from Nicolai who had cured an old woman of a malady similar to my own—cured her merely with a little hayseed. Well, he did me a great deal of good, for on the third day I broke into a sweat, and was able to leave my bed. Then my German doctors held another consultation, put on their spectacles, and told me that if I would go abroad, and take a course of the waters, the indisposition would finally pass away. 'Why should it not?' I thought to myself. So I had got things ready, and on the following day, a Friday, set out for here. I occupied a special compartment in the train, and where ever I had to change I found at the station bearers who were ready to carry me for a few coppers. You have nice quarters here," she went on as she glanced around the room. "But where on earth did you get the money for them, my good sir? I thought that everything of yours had been mortgaged? This Frenchman alone must be your creditor for a good deal. Oh, I know all about it, all about it."

"I-I am surprised at you, my dearest mother," said the General in some confusion. "I-I am greatly surprised. But I do not need any extraneous control of my finances. Moreover, my expenses do not exceed my income, and we—"

"They do not exceed it? Fie! Why, you are robbing your children of their last kopeck—you, their guardian!"

"After this," said the General, completely taken aback, "—after what you have just said, I do not know whether—"

"You do not know what? By heavens, are you never going to drop that roulette of yours? Are you going to whistle all your property away?"

This made such an impression upon the General that he almost choked with fury.

"Roulette, indeed? I play roulette? Really, in view of my position—Recollect what you are saying, my dearest mother. You must still be unwell."

"Rubbish, rubbish!" she retorted. "The truth is that you CANNOT be got away from that roulette. You are simply telling lies. This very day I mean to go and see for myself what roulette is like. Prascovia, tell me what there is to be seen here; and do you, Alexis Ivanovitch, show me everything; and do you, Potapitch, make me a list of excursions. What IS there to be seen?" again she inquired of Polina.

"There is a ruined castle, and the Shlangenberg."

"The Shlangenberg? What is it? A forest?"

"No, a mountain on the summit of which there is a place fenced off. From it you can get a most beautiful view."

"Could a chair be carried up that mountain of yours?"

"Doubtless we could find bearers for the purpose," I interposed.

At this moment Theodosia, the nursemaid, approached the old lady with the General's children.

"No, I DON'T want to see them," said the Grandmother. "I hate kissing children, for their noses are always wet. How are you getting on, Theodosia?"

"I am very well, thank you, Madame," replied the nursemaid. "And how is your ladyship? We have been feeling so anxious about you!"

"Yes, I know, you simple soul—But who are those other guests?" the old lady continued, turning again to Polina. "For instance, who is that old rascal in the spectacles?"

"Prince Nilski, Grandmamma," whispered Polina.

"Oh, a Russian? Why, I had no idea that he could understand me! Surely he did not hear what I said? As for Mr. Astley, I have seen him already, and I see that he is here again. How do you do?" she added to the gentleman in question.

Mr. Astley bowed in silence.

"Have you NOTHING to say to me?" the old lady went on. "Say something, for goodness' sake! Translate to him, Polina."

Polina did so.

"I have only to say," replied Mr. Astley gravely, but also with alacrity, "that I am indeed glad to see you in such good health." This was interpreted to the Grandmother, and she seemed much gratified.

"How well English people know how to answer one!" she remarked. "That is why I like them so much better than French. Come here," she added to Mr. Astley. "I will try not to bore you too much. Polina, translate to him that I am staying in rooms on a lower floor. Yes, on a lower floor," she repeated to Astley, pointing downwards with her finger.

Astley looked pleased at receiving the invitation.

Next, the old lady scanned Polina, from head to foot with minute attention.

"I could almost have liked you, Prascovia," suddenly she remarked, "for you are a nice girl—the best of the lot. You have some character about you. I too have character. Turn round. Surely that is not false hair that you are wearing?"

"No, Grandmamma. It is my own."

"Well, well. I do not like the stupid fashions of today. You are very good looking. I should have fallen in love with you if I had been a man. Why do you not get married? It is time now that I was going. I want to walk, yet I always have to ride. Are you still in a bad temper?" she added to the General.

"No, indeed," rejoined the now mollified General.

"I quite understand that at your time of life—"

"Cette vieille est tombee en enfance," De Griers whispered to me.

"But I want to look round a little," the old lady added to the General. Will you lend me Alexis Ivanovitch for the purpose?

"As much as you like. But I myself—yes, and Polina and Monsieur de Griers too—we all of us hope to have the pleasure of escorting you."

"Mais, madame, cela sera un plaisir," De Griers commented with a bewitching smile.

"'Plaisir' indeed! Why, I look upon you as a perfect fool, monsieur." Then she remarked to the General: "I am not going to let you have any of my money. I must be off to my rooms now, to see what they are like. Afterwards we will look round a little. Lift me up."

Again the Grandmother was borne aloft and carried down the staircase amid a perfect bevy of followers—the General walking as though he had been hit over the head with a cudgel, and De Griers seeming to be plunged in thought. Endeavouring to be left behind, Mlle. Blanche next thought better of it, and followed the rest, with the Prince in her wake. Only the German savant and Madame de Cominges did not leave the General's apartments.

X

At spas—and, probably, all over Europe—hotel landlords and managers are guided in their allotment of rooms to visitors, not so much by the wishes and requirements of those visitors, as by their personal estimate of the same. It may also be said that these landlords and managers seldom make a mistake. To the Grandmother, however, our landlord, for some reason or another, allotted such a sumptuous suite that he fairly overreached himself; for he assigned her a suite consisting of four magnificently appointed rooms, with bathroom, servants' quarters, a separate room for her maid, and so on. In fact, during the previous week the suite had been occupied by no less a personage than a Grand Duchess: which circumstance was duly explained to the new occupant, as an excuse for raising the price of these apartments. The Grandmother had herself carried—or, rather, wheeled—through each room in turn, in order that she might subject the whole to a close and attentive scrutiny; while the landlord—an elderly, bald-headed man—walked respectfully by her side.

What every one took the Grandmother to be I do not know, but it appeared, at least, that she was accounted a person not only of great importance, but also, and still more, of great wealth; and without delay they entered her in the hotel register as "Madame la Generale, Princesse de Tarassevitcheva," although she had never been a princess in her life. Her retinue, her reserved compartment in the train, her pile of unnecessary trunks, portmanteaux, and strong-boxes, all helped to increase her prestige; while her wheeled chair, her sharp tone and voice, her eccentric questions (put with an air of the most overbearing and unbridled imperiousness), her whole figure—upright, rugged, and commanding as it was—completed the general awe in which she was held. As she inspected her new abode she ordered her chair to be stopped at intervals in order that, with finger extended towards some article of furniture, she might ply the respectfully smiling, yet secretly apprehensive, landlord with unexpected questions. She addressed them to him in French, although her pronunciation of the language was so bad that sometimes I had to translate them. For the most part, the landlord's answers were unsatisfactory, and failed to please her; nor were the questions themselves of a practical nature, but related, generally, to God knows what.

For instance, on one occasion she halted before a picture which, a poor copy of a well-known original, had a mythological subject.

"Of whom is this a portrait?" she inquired.

The landlord explained that it was probably that of a countess.

"But how know you that?" the old lady retorted.

"You live here, yet you cannot say for certain! And why is the picture there at all? And why do its eyes look so crooked?"

To all these questions the landlord could return no satisfactory reply, despite his floundering endeavours.

"The blockhead!" exclaimed the Grandmother in Russian.

Then she proceeded on her way—only to repeat the same story in front of a Saxon statuette which she had sighted from afar, and had commanded, for some reason or another, to be brought to her. Finally, she inquired of the landlord what was the value of the carpet in her bedroom, as well as where the said carpet had been manufactured; but, the landlord could do no more than promise to make inquiries.

"What donkeys these people are!" she commented. Next, she turned her attention to the bed.

"What a huge counterpane!" she exclaimed. "Turn it back, please." The lacqueys did so.

"Further yet, further yet," the old lady cried. "Turn it RIGHT back. Also, take off those pillows and bolsters, and lift up the feather bed."

The bed was opened for her inspection.

"Mercifully it contains no bugs," she remarked.

"Pull off the whole thing, and then put on my own pillows and sheets. The place is too luxurious for an old woman like myself. It is too large for any one person. Alexis Ivanovitch, come and see me whenever you are not teaching your pupils."

"After tomorrow I shall no longer be in the General's service," I replied, "but merely living in the hotel on my own account."

"Why so?"

"Because, the other day, there arrived from Berlin a German and his wife—persons of some importance; and, it chanced that, when taking a walk, I spoke to them in German without having properly compassed the Berlin accent."

"Indeed?"

"Yes: and this action on my part the Baron held to be an insult, and complained about it to the General, who yesterday dismissed me from his employ."

"But I suppose you must have threatened that precious Baron, or something of the kind? However, even if you did so, it was a matter of no moment."

"No, I did not. The Baron was the aggressor by raising his stick at me."

Upon that the Grandmother turned sharply to the General.

"What? You permitted yourself to treat your tutor thus, you nincompoop, and to dismiss him from his post? You are a blockhead—an utter blockhead! I can see that clearly."

"Do not alarm yourself, my dear mother," the General replied with a lofty air—an air in which there was also a tinge of familiarity. "I am quite capable of managing my own affairs. Moreover, Alexis Ivanovitch has not given you a true account of the matter."

"What did you do next?" The old lady inquired of me.

"I wanted to challenge the Baron to a duel," I replied as modestly as possible; "but the General protested against my doing so."

"And WHY did you so protest?" she inquired of the General. Then she turned to the landlord, and questioned him as to whether HE would not have fought a duel, if challenged. "For," she added, "I can see no difference between you and the Baron; nor can I bear that German visage of yours." Upon this the landlord bowed and departed, though he could not have understood the Grandmother's compliment.

"Pardon me, Madame," the General continued with a sneer, "but are duels really feasible?"

"Why not? All men are crowing cocks, and that is why they quarrel. YOU, though, I perceive, are a blockhead— a man who does not even know how to carry his breeding. Lift me up. Potapitch, see to it that you always have TWO bearers ready. Go and arrange for their hire. But we shall not require more than two, for I shall need only to be carried upstairs. On the level or in the street I can be WHEELED along. Go and tell them that, and pay them in advance, so that they may show me some respect. You too, Potapitch, are always to come with me, and YOU, Alexis Ivanovitch, are to point out to me this Baron as we go along, in order that I may get a squint at the precious 'Von.' And where is that roulette played?"

I explained to her that the game was carried on in the salons of the Casino; whereupon there ensued a string of questions as to whether there were many such salons, whether many people played in them, whether those people played a whole day at a time, and whether the game was managed according to fixed rules. At length, I thought it best to say that the most advisable course would be for her to go and see it for herself, since a mere description of it would be a difficult matter.

"Then take me straight there," she said, "and do you walk on in front of me, Alexis Ivanovitch."

"What, mother? Before you have so much as rested from your journey?" the General inquired with some solicitude. Also, for some reason which I could not divine, he seemed to be growing nervous; and, indeed, the whole party was evincing signs of confusion, and exchanging glances with one another. Probably they were thinking that it would be a ticklish—even an embarrassing—business to accompany the Grandmother to the Casino, where, very likely, she would perpetrate further eccentricities, and in public too! Yet on their own initiative they had offered to escort her!

"Why should I rest?" she retorted. "I am not tired, for I have been sitting still these past five days. Let us see what your medicinal springs and waters are like, and where they are situated. What, too, about that, that—what did you call it, Prascovia?—oh, about that mountain top?"

"Yes, we are going to see it, Grandmamma."

"Very well. Is there anything else for me to see here?"

"Yes! Quite a number of things," Polina forced herself to say.

"Martha, YOU must come with me as well," went on the old lady to her maid.

"No, no, mother!" ejaculated the General. "Really she cannot come. They would not admit even Potapitch to the Casino."

"Rubbish! Because she is my servant, is that a reason for turning her out? Why, she is only a human being like the rest of us; and as she has been travelling for a week she might like to look about her. With whom else could she go out but myself? She would never dare to show her nose in the street alone."

"But, mother—"

"Are you ashamed to be seen with me? Stop at home, then, and you will be asked no questions. A pretty General YOU are, to be sure! I am a general's widow myself. But, after all, why should I drag the whole party with me? I will go and see the sights with only Alexis Ivanovitch as my escort."

De Griers strongly insisted that EVERY ONE ought to accompany her. Indeed, he launched out into a perfect shower of charming phrases concerning the pleasure of acting as her cicerone, and so forth. Every one was touched with his words.

"Mais elle est tombee en enfance," he added aside to the General. "Seule, elle fera des betises." More than this I could not overhear, but he seemed to have got some plan in his mind, or even to be feeling a slight return of his hopes.

The distance to the Casino was about half a verst, and our route led us through the Chestnut Avenue until we reached the square directly fronting the building. The General, I could see, was a trifle reassured by the fact that, though our progress was distinctly eccentric in its nature, it was, at least, correct and orderly. As a matter of fact, the spectacle of a person who is unable to walk is not anything to excite surprise at a spa. Yet it was clear that the General had a great fear of the Casino itself: for why should a person who had lost the use of her limbs—more especially an old woman—be going to rooms which were set apart only for roulette? On either side of the wheeled chair walked Polina and Mlle. Blanche—the latter smiling, modestly jesting, and, in short, making herself so agreeable to the Grandmother that in the end the old lady relented towards her. On the other side of the chair Polina had to answer an endless flow of petty questions—such as "Who was it passed just now?" "Who is that coming along?" "Is the town a large one?" "Are the public gardens extensive?" "What sort of trees are those?" "What is the name of those hills?" "Do I see eagles flying yonder?" "What is that absurd-looking building?" and so forth. Meanwhile Astley whispered to me, as he walked by my side, that he looked for much to happen that morning. Behind the old lady's chair marched Potapitch and Martha—Potapitch in his frockcoat and white waistcoat, with a cloak over all, and the forty-year-old and rosy, but slightly grey-headed, Martha in a mobcap, cotton dress, and squeaking shoes. Frequently the old lady would twist herself round to converse with these servants. As for De Griers, he spoke as though he had made up his mind to do something (though it is also possible that he spoke in this manner merely in order to hearten the General, with whom he appeared to have held a conference). But, alas, the Grandmother had uttered the fatal words, "I am not going to give you any of my money;" and though De Griers might regard these words lightly, the General knew his mother better. Also, I noticed that De Griers and Mlle. Blanche were still exchanging looks; while of the Prince and the German savant I lost sight at the end of the Avenue, where they had turned back and left us.

Into the Casino we marched in triumph. At once, both in the person of the commissionaire and in the persons of the footmen, there sprang to life the same reverence as had arisen in the lacqueys of the hotel. Yet it was not without some curiosity that they eyed us.

Without loss of time, the Grandmother gave orders that she should be wheeled through every room in the establishment; of which apartments she praised a few, while to others she remained indifferent. Concerning everything, however, she asked questions. Finally we reached the gaming-salons, where a lacquey who was, acting as guard over the doors, flung them open as though he were a man possessed.

The Grandmother's entry into the roulette-salon produced a profound impression upon the public. Around the tables, and at the further end of the room where the trente-et-quarante table was set out, there may have been gathered from 150 to 200 gamblers, ranged in several rows. Those who had succeeded in pushing their way to the tables were standing with their feet firmly planted, in order to avoid having to give up their places until they should have finished their game (since merely to stand looking on—thus occupying a gambler's place for nothing—was not permitted). True, chairs were provided around the tables, but few players made use of them—more especially if there was a large attendance of the general public; since to stand allowed of a closer approach; and, therefore, of greater facilities for calculation and staking. Behind the foremost row were herded a second and a third row of people awaiting their turn; but sometimes their impatience led these people to stretch a hand through the first row, in order to deposit their stakes. Even third-row individuals would dart forward to stake; whence seldom did more than five or ten minutes pass without a scene over disputed money arising at one or another end of the table. On the other hand, the police of the Casino were an able body of men; and though to escape the crush was an impossibility, however much one might wish it, the eight croupiers apportioned to each table kept an eye upon the stakes, performed the necessary reckoning, and decided disputes as they arose.

In the last resort they always called in the Casino police, and the disputes would immediately come to an end. Policemen were stationed about the Casino in ordinary costume, and mingled with the spectators so as to make it impossible to recognise them. In particular they kept a lookout for pickpockets and swindlers, who simply swarmed in the roulette salons, and reaped a rich harvest. Indeed, in every direction money was being filched from pockets or purses—though, of course, if the attempt miscarried, a great uproar ensued. One had only to approach a roulette table, begin to play, and then openly grab some one else's winnings, for a din to be raised, and the thief to start vociferating that the stake was HIS; and, if the coup had been carried out with sufficient skill, and the witnesses wavered at all in their testimony, the thief would as likely as not succeed in getting away with the money, provided that the sum was not a large one—not large enough to have attracted the attention of the croupiers or some fellow-player. Moreover, if it were a stake of insignificant size, its true owner would sometimes decline to continue the dispute, rather than become involved in a scandal. Conversely, if the thief was detected, he was ignominiously expelled the building.

Upon all this the Grandmother gazed with open-eyed curiosity; and, on some thieves happening to be turned out of the place, she was delighted. Trente-et-quarante interested her but little; she preferred roulette, with its ever-revolving wheel. At length she expressed a wish to view the game closer; whereupon in some mysterious manner, the lacqueys and other officious agents (especially one or two ruined Poles of the kind who keep offering their services to successful gamblers and foreigners in general) at once found and cleared a space for the old lady among the crush, at the very centre of one of the tables, and next to the chief croupier; after which they wheeled her chair thither. Upon this a number of visitors who were not playing, but only looking on (particularly some Englishmen with their families), pressed closer forward towards the table, in order to watch the old lady from among the ranks of the gamblers. Many a lorgnette I saw turned in her direction, and the croupiers' hopes rose high that such an eccentric player was about to provide them with something out of the common. An old lady of seventy-five years who, though unable to walk, desired to play was not an everyday phenomenon. I too pressed forward towards the table, and ranged myself by the Grandmother's side; while Martha and Potapitch remained somewhere in the background among the crowd, and the General, Polina, and De Griers, with Mlle. Blanche, also remained hidden among the spectators.

At first the old lady did no more than watch the gamblers, and ply me, in a half-whisper, with sharp-broken questions as to who was so-and-so. Especially did her favour light upon a very young man who was plunging heavily, and had won (so it was whispered) as much as 40,000 francs, which were lying before him on the table in a heap of gold and bank-notes. His eyes kept flashing, and his hands shaking; yet all the while he staked without any sort of calculation—just what came to his hand, as he kept winning and winning, and raking and raking in his gains. Around him lacqueys fussed—placing chairs just behind where he was standing—and clearing the spectators from his vicinity, so that he should have more room, and not be crowded—the whole done, of course, in expectation of a generous largesse. From time to time other gamblers would hand him part of their winnings—being glad to let him stake for them as much as his hand could grasp; while beside him stood a Pole in a state of violent, but respectful, agitation, who, also in expectation of a generous largesse, kept whispering to him at intervals (probably telling him what to stake, and advising and directing his play). Yet never once did the player throw him a glance as he staked and staked, and raked in his winnings. Evidently, the player in question was dead to all besides.

For a few minutes the Grandmother watched him.

"Go and tell him," suddenly she exclaimed with a nudge at my elbow, "—go and tell him to stop, and to take his money with him, and go home. Presently he will be losing—yes, losing everything that he has now won." She seemed almost breathless with excitement.

"Where is Potapitch?" she continued. "Send Potapitch to speak to him. No, YOU must tell him, you must tell him,"—here she nudged me again—"for I have not the least notion where Potapitch is. Sortez, sortez," she shouted to the young man, until I leant over in her direction and whispered in her ear that no shouting was allowed, nor even loud speaking, since to do so disturbed the calculations of the players, and might lead to our being ejected.

"How provoking!" she retorted. "Then the young man is done for! I suppose he WISHES to be ruined. Yet I could not bear to see him have to return it all. What a fool the fellow is!" and the old lady turned sharply away.

On the left, among the players at the other half of the table, a young lady was playing, with, beside her, a dwarf. Who the dwarf may have been—whether a relative or a person whom she took with her to act as a foil—I do not know; but I had noticed her there on previous occasions, since, everyday, she entered the Casino at one o'clock precisely, and departed at two—thus playing for exactly one hour. Being well-known to the attendants, she always had a seat provided for her; and, taking some gold and a few thousand-franc notes out of her pocket—would begin quietly, coldly, and after much calculation, to stake, and mark down the figures in pencil on a paper, as though striving to work out a system according to which, at given moments, the odds might group themselves. Always she staked large coins, and either lost or won one, two, or three thousand francs a day, but not more; after which she would depart. The Grandmother took a long look at her.

"THAT woman is not losing," she said. "To whom does she belong? Do you know her? Who is she?"

"She is, I believe, a Frenchwoman," I replied.

"Ah! A bird of passage, evidently. Besides, I can see that she has her shoes polished. Now, explain to me the meaning of each round in the game, and the way in which one ought to stake."

Upon this I set myself to explain the meaning of all the combinations—of "rouge et noir," of "pair et impair," of "manque et passe," with, lastly, the different values in the system of numbers. The Grandmother listened attentively, took notes, put questions in various forms, and laid the whole thing to heart. Indeed, since an example of each system of stakes kept constantly occurring, a great deal of information could be assimilated with ease and celerity. The Grandmother was vastly pleased.

"But what is zero?" she inquired. "Just now I heard the flaxen-haired croupier call out 'zero!' And why does he keep raking in all the money that is on the table? To think that he should grab the whole pile for himself! What does zero mean?"

"Zero is what the bank takes for itself. If the wheel stops at that figure, everything lying on the table becomes the absolute property of the bank. Also, whenever the wheel has begun to turn, the bank ceases to pay out anything."

"Then I should receive nothing if I were staking?"

"No; unless by any chance you had PURPOSELY staked on zero; in which case you would receive thirty-five times the value of your stake."

"Why thirty-five times, when zero so often turns up? And if so, why do not more of these fools stake upon it?"

"Because the number of chances against its occurrence is thirty-six."

"Rubbish! Potapitch, Potapitch! Come here, and I will give you some money." The old lady took out of her pocket a tightly-clasped purse, and extracted from its depths a ten-gulden piece. "Go at once, and stake that upon zero."

"But, Madame, zero has only this moment turned up," I remonstrated; "wherefore, it may not do so again for ever so long. Wait a little, and you may then have a better chance."

"Rubbish! Stake, please."

"Pardon me, but zero might not turn up again until, say, tonight, even though you had staked thousands upon it. It often happens so."

"Rubbish, rubbish! Who fears the wolf should never enter the forest. What? We have lost? Then stake again."

A second ten-gulden piece did we lose, and then I put down a third. The Grandmother could scarcely remain seated in her chair, so intent was she upon the little ball as it leapt through the notches of the ever-revolving wheel. However, the third ten-gulden piece followed the first two. Upon this the Grandmother went perfectly crazy. She could no longer sit still, and actually struck the table with her fist when the croupier cried out, "Trente-six," instead of the desiderated zero.

"To listen to him!" fumed the old lady. "When will that accursed zero ever turn up? I cannot breathe until I see it. I believe that that infernal croupier is PURPOSELY keeping it from turning up. Alexis Ivanovitch, stake TWO golden pieces this time. The moment we cease to stake, that cursed zero will come turning up, and we shall get nothing."

"My good Madame—"

"Stake, stake! It is not YOUR money."

Accordingly I staked two ten-gulden pieces. The ball went hopping round the wheel until it began to settle through the notches. Meanwhile the Grandmother sat as though petrified, with my hand convulsively clutched in hers.

"Zero!" called the croupier.

"There! You see, you see!" cried the old lady, as she turned and faced me, wreathed in smiles. "I told you so! It was the Lord God himself who suggested to me to stake those two coins. Now, how much ought I to receive? Why do they not pay it out to me? Potapitch! Martha! Where are they? What has become of our party? Potapitch, Potapitch!"

"Presently, Madame," I whispered. "Potapitch is outside, and they would decline to admit him to these rooms. See! You are being paid out your money. Pray take it." The croupiers were making up a heavy packet of coins, sealed in blue paper, and containing fifty ten gulden pieces, together with an unsealed packet containing another twenty. I handed the whole to the old lady in a money-shovel.

"Faites le jeu, messieurs! Faites le jeu, messieurs! Rien ne va plus," proclaimed the croupier as once more he invited the company to stake, and prepared to turn the wheel.

"We shall be too late! He is going to spin again! Stake, stake!" The Grandmother was in a perfect fever. "Do not hang back! Be quick!" She seemed almost beside herself, and nudged me as hard as she could.

"Upon what shall I stake, Madame?"

"Upon zero, upon zero! Again upon zero! Stake as much as ever you can. How much have we got? Seventy ten-gulden pieces? We shall not miss them, so stake twenty pieces at a time."

"Think a moment, Madame. Sometimes zero does not turn up for two hundred rounds in succession. I assure you that you may lose all your capital."

"You are wrong—utterly wrong. Stake, I tell you! What a chattering tongue you have! I know perfectly well what I am doing." The old lady was shaking with excitement.

"But the rules do not allow of more than 120 gulden being staked upon zero at a time."

"How 'do not allow'? Surely you are wrong? Monsieur, monsieur—" here she nudged the croupier who was sitting on her left, and preparing to spin—"combien zero? Douze? Douze?"

I hastened to translate.

"Oui, Madame," was the croupier's polite reply. "No single stake must exceed four thousand florins. That is the regulation."

"Then there is nothing else for it. We must risk in gulden."

"Le jeu est fait!" the croupier called. The wheel revolved, and stopped at thirty. We had lost!

"Again, again, again! Stake again!" shouted the old lady. Without attempting to oppose her further, but merely shrugging my shoulders, I placed twelve more ten-gulden pieces upon the table. The wheel whirled around and around, with the Grandmother simply quaking as she watched its revolutions.

"Does she again think that zero is going to be the winning coup?" thought I, as I stared at her in astonishment. Yet an absolute assurance of winning was shining on her face; she looked perfectly convinced that zero was about to be called again. At length the ball dropped off into one of the notches.

"Zero!" cried the croupier.

"Ah!!!" screamed the old lady as she turned to me in a whirl of triumph.

I myself was at heart a gambler. At that moment I became acutely conscious both of that fact and of the fact that my hands and knees were shaking, and that the blood was beating in my brain. Of course this was a rare occasion— an occasion on which zero had turned up no less than three times within a dozen rounds; yet in such an event there was nothing so very surprising, seeing that, only three days ago, I myself had been a witness to zero turning up THREE TIMES IN SUCCESSION, so that one of the players who was recording the coups on paper was moved to remark that for several days past zero had never turned up at all!

With the Grandmother, as with any one who has won a very large sum, the management settled up with great attention and respect, since she was fortunate to have to receive no less than 4200 gulden. Of these gulden the odd 200 were paid her in gold, and the remainder in bank notes.

This time the old lady did not call for Potapitch; for that she was too preoccupied. Though not outwardly shaken by the event (indeed, she seemed perfectly calm), she was trembling inwardly from head to foot. At length, completely absorbed in the game, she burst out:

"Alexis Ivanovitch, did not the croupier just say that 4000 florins were the most that could be staked at any one time? Well, take these 4000, and stake them upon the red."

To oppose her was useless. Once more the wheel revolved.

"Rouge!" proclaimed the croupier.

Again 4000 florins—in all 8000!

"Give me them," commanded the Grandmother, "and stake the other 4000 upon the red again."

I did so.

"Rouge!" proclaimed the croupier.

"Twelve thousand!" cried the old lady. "Hand me the whole lot. Put the gold into this purse here, and count the bank notes. Enough! Let us go home. Wheel my chair away."

XI

THE chair, with the old lady beaming in it, was wheeled away towards the doors at the further end of the salon, while our party hastened to crowd around her, and to offer her their congratulations. In fact, eccentric as was her conduct, it was also overshadowed by her triumph; with the result that the General no longer feared to be publicly compromised by being seen with such a strange woman, but, smiling in a condescending, cheerfully familiar way, as though he were soothing a child, he offered his greetings to the old lady. At the same time, both he and the rest of the spectators were visibly impressed. Everywhere people kept pointing to the Grandmother, and talking about her. Many people even walked beside her chair, in order to view her the better while, at a little distance, Astley was carrying on a conversation on the subject with two English acquaintances of his. De Griers was simply overflowing with smiles and compliments, and a number of fine ladies were staring at the Grandmother as though she had been something curious.

"Quelle victoire!" exclaimed De Griers.

"Mais, Madame, c'etait du feu!" added Mlle. Blanche with an elusive smile.

"Yes, I have won twelve thousand florins," replied the old lady. "And then there is all this gold. With it the total ought to come to nearly thirteen thousand. How much is that in Russian money? Six thousand roubles, I think?"

However, I calculated that the sum would exceed seven thousand roubles—or, at the present rate of exchange, even eight thousand.

"Eight thousand roubles! What a splendid thing! And to think of you simpletons sitting there and doing nothing! Potapitch! Martha! See what I have won!"

"How DID you do it, Madame?" Martha exclaimed ecstatically. "Eight thousand roubles!"

"And I am going to give you fifty gulden apiece. There they are."

Potapitch and Martha rushed towards her to kiss her hand.

"And to each bearer also I will give a ten-gulden piece. Let them have it out of the gold, Alexis Ivanovitch. But why is this footman bowing to me, and that other man as well? Are they congratulating me? Well, let them have ten gulden apiece."

"Madame la princesse—Un pauvre expatrie—Malheur continuel—Les princes russes sont si genereux!" said a man who for some time past had been hanging around the old lady's chair—a personage who, dressed in a shabby frockcoat and coloured waistcoat, kept taking off his cap, and smiling pathetically.

"Give him ten gulden," said the Grandmother. "No, give him twenty. Now, enough of that, or I shall never get done with you all. Take a moment's rest, and then carry me away. Prascovia, I mean to buy a new dress for you tomorrow. Yes, and for you too, Mlle. Blanche. Please translate, Prascovia."

"Merci, Madame," replied Mlle. Blanche gratefully as she twisted her face into the mocking smile which usually she kept only for the benefit of De Griers and the General. The latter looked confused, and seemed greatly relieved when we reached the Avenue.

"How surprised Theodosia too will be!" went on the Grandmother (thinking of the General's nursemaid). "She, like yourselves, shall have the price of a new gown. Here, Alexis Ivanovitch! Give that beggar something" (a crooked-backed ragamuffin had approached to stare at us).

"But perhaps he is NOT a beggar—only a rascal," I replied.

"Never mind, never mind. Give him a gulden."

I approached the beggar in question, and handed him the coin. Looking at me in great astonishment, he silently accepted the gulden, while from his person there proceeded a strong smell of liquor.

"Have you never tried your luck, Alexis Ivanovitch?"

"No, Madame."

"Yet just now I could see that you were burning to do so?"

"I do mean to try my luck presently."

"Then stake everything upon zero. You have seen how it ought to be done? How much capital do you possess?"

"Two hundred gulden, Madame."

"Not very much. See here; I will lend you five hundred if you wish. Take this purse of mine." With that she added sharply to the General: "But YOU need not expect to receive any."

This seemed to upset him, but he said nothing, and De Griers contented himself by scowling.

"Que diable!" he whispered to the General. "C'est une terrible vieille."

"Look! Another beggar, another beggar!" exclaimed the grandmother. "Alexis Ivanovitch, go and give him a gulden."

As she spoke I saw approaching us a grey-headed old man with a wooden leg—a man who was dressed in a blue frockcoat and carrying a staff. He looked like an old soldier. As soon as I tendered him the coin he fell back a step or two, and eyed me threateningly.

"Was ist der Teufel!" he cried, and appended thereto a round dozen of oaths.

"The man is a perfect fool!" exclaimed the Grandmother, waving her hand. "Move on now, for I am simply famished. When we have lunched we will return to that place."

"What?" cried I. "You are going to play again?"

"What else do you suppose?" she retorted. "Are you going only to sit here, and grow sour, and let me look at you?"

"Madame," said De Griers confidentially, "les chances peuvent tourner. Une seule mauvaise chance, et vous perdrez tout—surtout avec votre jeu. C'etait terrible!"

"Oui; vous perdrez absolument," put in Mlle. Blanche.

"What has that got to do with YOU?" retorted the old lady. "It is not YOUR money that I am going to lose; it is my own. And where is that Mr. Astley of yours?" she added to myself.

"He stayed behind in the Casino."

"What a pity! He is such a nice sort of man!"

Arriving home, and meeting the landlord on the staircase, the Grandmother called him to her side, and boasted to him of her winnings—thereafter doing the same to Theodosia, and conferring upon her thirty gulden; after which she bid her serve luncheon. The meal over, Theodosia and Martha broke into a joint flood of ecstasy.

"I was watching you all the time, Madame," quavered Martha, "and I asked Potapitch what mistress was trying to do. And, my word! the heaps and heaps of money that were lying upon the table! Never in my life have I seen so much money. And there were gentlefolk around it, and other gentlefolk sitting down. So, I asked Potapitch where all these gentry had come from; for, thought I, maybe the Holy Mother of God will help our mistress among them. Yes, I prayed for you, Madame, and my heart died within me, so that I kept trembling and trembling. The Lord be with her, I thought to myself; and in answer to my prayer He has now sent you what He has done! Even yet I tremble—I tremble to think of it all."

"Alexis Ivanovitch," said the old lady, "after luncheon,—that is to say, about four o'clock—get ready to go out with me again. But in the meanwhile, good-bye. Do not forget to call a doctor, for I must take the waters. Now go and get rested a little."

I left the Grandmother's presence in a state of bewilderment.

Vainly I endeavoured to imagine what would become of our party, or what turn the affair would next take. I could perceive that none of the party had yet recovered their presence of mind—least of all the General. The factor of the Grandmother's appearance in place of the hourly expected telegram to announce her death (with, of course, resultant legacies) had so upset the whole scheme of intentions and projects that it was with a decided feeling of apprehension and growing paralysis that the conspirators viewed any future performances of the old lady at roulette. Yet this second factor was not quite so important as the first, since, though the Grandmother had twice declared that she did not intend to give the General any money, that declaration was not a complete ground for the abandonment of hope. Certainly De Griers, who, with the General, was up to the neck in the affair, had not wholly lost courage; and I felt sure that Mlle. Blanche also—Mlle. Blanche who was not only as deeply involved as the other two, but also expectant of becoming Madame General and an important legatee—would not lightly surrender the position, but would use her every resource of coquetry upon the old lady, in order to afford a contrast to the impetuous Polina, who was difficult to understand, and lacked the art of pleasing.

Yet now, when the Grandmother had just performed an astonishing feat at roulette; now, when the old lady's personality had been so clearly and typically revealed as that of a rugged, arrogant woman who was "tombee en enfance"; now, when everything appeared to be lost,—why, now the Grandmother was as merry as a child which plays with thistle-down. "Good Lord!" I thought with, may God forgive me, a most malicious smile, "every ten-gulden piece which the Grandmother staked must have raised a blister on the General's heart, and maddened De Griers, and driven Mlle. de Cominges almost to frenzy with the sight of this spoon dangling before her lips." Another factor is the circumstance that even when, overjoyed at winning, the Grandmother was distributing alms right and left, and taking every one to be a beggar, she again snapped out to the General that he was not going to be allowed any of her money—which meant that the old lady had quite made up her mind on the point, and was sure of it. Yes, danger loomed ahead.

All these thoughts passed through my mind during the few moments that, having left the old lady's rooms, I was ascending to my own room on the top storey. What most struck me was the fact that, though I had divined the chief, the stoutest, threads which united the various actors in the drama, I had, until now, been ignorant of the methods and secrets of the game. For Polina had never been completely open with me. Although, on occasions, it had happened that involuntarily, as it were, she had revealed to me something of her heart, I had noticed that in most cases—in fact, nearly always—she had either laughed away these revelations, or grown confused, or purposely imparted to them a false guise. Yes, she must have concealed a great deal from me. But, I had a presentiment that now the end of this strained and mysterious situation was approaching. Another stroke, and all would be finished and exposed. Of my own fortunes, interested though I was in the affair, I took no account. I was in the strange position of possessing but two hundred gulden, of being at a loose end, of lacking both a post, the means of subsistence, a shred of hope, and any plans for the future, yet of caring nothing for these things. Had not my mind been so full of Polina, I should have given myself up to the comical piquancy of the impending denouement, and laughed my fill at it. But the thought of Polina was torture to me. That her fate was settled I already had an inkling; yet that was not the thought which was giving me so much uneasiness. What I really wished for was to penetrate her secrets. I wanted her to come to me and say, "I love you," and, if she would not so come, or if to hope that she would ever do so was an unthinkable absurdity—why, then there was nothing else for me to want. Even now I do not know what I am wanting. I feel like a man who has lost his way. I yearn but to be in her presence, and within the circle of her light and splendour—to be there now, and forever, and for the whole of my life. More I do not know. How can I ever bring myself to leave her?

On reaching the third storey of the hotel I experienced a shock. I was just passing the General's suite when something caused me to look round. Out of a door about twenty paces away there was coming Polina! She hesitated for a moment on seeing me, and then beckoned me to her.

"Polina Alexandrovna!"

"Hush! Not so loud."

"Something startled me just now," I whispered, "and I looked round, and saw you. Some electrical influence seems to emanate from your form."

"Take this letter," she went on with a frown (probably she had not even heard my words, she was so preoccupied), "and hand it personally to Mr. Astley. Go as quickly as ever you can, please. No answer will be required. He himself—" She did not finish her sentence.

"To Mr. Astley?" I asked, in some astonishment.

But she had vanished again.

Aha! So the two were carrying on a correspondence! However, I set off to search for Astley—first at his hotel, and then at the Casino, where I went the round of the salons in vain. At length, vexed, and almost in despair, I was on my way home when I ran across him among a troop of English ladies and gentlemen who had been out for a ride. Beckoning to him to stop, I handed him the letter. We had barely time even to look at one another, but I suspected that it was of set purpose that he restarted his horse so quickly.

Was jealousy, then, gnawing at me? At all events, I felt exceedingly depressed, despite the fact that I had no desire to ascertain what the correspondence was about. To think that HE should be her confidant! "My friend, mine own familiar friend!" passed through my mind. Yet WAS there any love in the matter? "Of course not," reason whispered to me. But reason goes for little on such occasions. I felt that the matter must be cleared up, for it was becoming unpleasantly complex.

I had scarcely set foot in the hotel when the commissionaire and the landlord (the latter issuing from his room for the purpose) alike informed me that I was being searched for high and low—that three separate messages to ascertain my whereabouts had come down from the General. When I entered his study I was feeling anything but kindly disposed. I found there the General himself, De Griers, and Mlle. Blanche, but not Mlle.'s mother, who was a person whom her reputed daughter used only for show purposes, since in all matters of business the daughter fended for herself, and it is unlikely that the mother knew anything about them.

Some very heated discussion was in progress, and meanwhile the door of the study was open—an unprecedented circumstance. As I approached the portals I could hear loud voices raised, for mingled with the pert, venomous accents of De Griers were Mlle. Blanche's excited, impudently abusive tongue and the General's plaintive wail as, apparently, he sought to justify himself in something. But on my appearance every one stopped speaking, and tried to put a better face upon matters. De Griers smoothed his hair, and twisted his angry face into a smile—into the mean, studiedly polite French smile which I so detested; while the downcast, perplexed General assumed an air of dignity—though only in a mechanical way. On the other hand, Mlle. Blanche did not trouble to conceal the wrath that was sparkling in her countenance, but bent her gaze upon me with an air of impatient expectancy. I may remark that hitherto she had treated me with absolute superciliousness, and, so far from answering my salutations, had always ignored them.

"Alexis Ivanovitch," began the General in a tone of affectionate upbraiding, "may I say to you that I find it strange, exceedingly strange, that—In short, your conduct towards myself and my family— In a word, your—er—extremely—"

"Eh! Ce n'est pas ca," interrupted De Griers in a tone of impatience and contempt (evidently he was the ruling spirit of the conclave). "Mon cher monsieur, notre general se trompe. What he means to say is that he warns you—he begs of you most earnestly—not to ruin him. I use the expression because—"

"Why? Why?" I interjected.

"Because you have taken upon yourself to act as guide to this, to this—how shall I express it?—to this old lady, a cette pauvre terrible vieille. But she will only gamble away all that she has—gamble it away like thistledown. You yourself have seen her play. Once she has acquired the taste for gambling, she will never leave the roulette-table, but, of sheer perversity and temper, will stake her all, and lose it. In cases such as hers a gambler can never be torn away from the game; and then—and then—"

"And then," asseverated the General, "you will have ruined my whole family. I and my family are her heirs, for she has no nearer relatives than ourselves. I tell you frankly that my affairs are in great—very great disorder; how much they are so you yourself are partially aware. If she should lose a large sum, or, maybe, her whole fortune, what will become of us—of my children" (here the General exchanged a glance with De Griers) "or of me?" (here he looked at Mlle. Blanche, who turned her head contemptuously away). "Alexis Ivanovitch, I beg of you to save us."

"Tell me, General, how am I to do so? On what footing do I stand here?"

"Refuse to take her about. Simply leave her alone."

"But she would soon find some one else to take my place?"

"Ce n'est pas ca, ce n'est pas ca," again interrupted De Griers. "Que diable! Do not leave her alone so much as advise her, persuade her, draw her away. In any case do not let her gamble; find her some counter-attraction."

"And how am I to do that? If only you would undertake the task, Monsieur de Griers!" I said this last as innocently as possible, but at once saw a rapid glance of excited interrogation pass from Mlle. Blanche to De Griers, while in the face of the latter also there gleamed something which he could not repress.

"Well, at the present moment she would refuse to accept my services," said he with a gesture. "But if, later—"

Here he gave Mlle. Blanche another glance which was full of meaning; whereupon she advanced towards me with a bewitching smile, and seized and pressed my hands. Devil take it, but how that devilish visage of hers could change! At the present moment it was a visage full of supplication, and as gentle in its expression as that of a smiling, roguish infant. Stealthily, she drew me apart from the rest as though the more completely to separate me from them; and, though no harm came of her doing so—for it was merely a stupid manoeuvre, and no more—I found the situation very unpleasant.

The General hastened to lend her his support.

"Alexis Ivanovitch," he began, "pray pardon me for having said what I did just now—for having said more than I meant to do. I beg and beseech you, I kiss the hem of your garment, as our Russian saying has it, for you, and only you, can save us. I and Mlle. de Cominges, we all of us beg of you—But you understand, do you not? Surely you understand?" and with his eyes he indicated Mlle. Blanche. Truly he was cutting a pitiful figure!

At this moment three low, respectful knocks sounded at the door; which, on being opened, revealed a chambermaid, with Potapitch behind her—come from the Grandmother to request that I should attend her in her rooms. "She is in a bad humour," added Potapitch.

The time was half-past three.

"My mistress was unable to sleep," explained Potapitch; "so, after tossing about for a while, she suddenly rose, called for her chair, and sent me to look for you. She is now in the verandah."

"Quelle megere!" exclaimed De Griers.

True enough, I found Madame in the hotel verandah—much put about at my delay, for she had been unable to contain herself until four o'clock.

"Lift me up," she cried to the bearers, and once more we set out for the roulette-salons.

XII

The Grandmother was in an impatient, irritable frame of mind. Without doubt the roulette had turned her head, for she appeared to be indifferent to everything else, and, in general, seemed much distraught. For instance, she asked me no questions about objects en route, except that, when a sumptuous barouche passed us and raised a cloud of dust, she lifted her hand for a moment, and inquired, "What was that?" Yet even then she did not appear to hear my reply, although at times her abstraction was interrupted by sallies and fits of sharp, impatient fidgeting. Again, when I pointed out to her the Baron and Baroness Burmergelm walking to the Casino, she merely looked at them in an absent-minded sort of way, and said with complete indifference, "Ah!" Then, turning sharply to Potapitch and Martha, who were walking behind us, she rapped out:

"Why have YOU attached yourselves to the party? We are not going to take you with us every time. Go home at once." Then, when the servants had pulled hasty bows and departed, she added to me: "You are all the escort I need."

At the Casino the Grandmother seemed to be expected, for no time was lost in procuring her former place beside the croupier. It is my opinion that though croupiers seem such ordinary, humdrum officials—men who care nothing whether the bank wins or loses—they are, in reality, anything but indifferent to the bank's losing, and are given instructions to attract players, and to keep a watch over the bank's interests; as also, that for such services, these officials are awarded prizes and premiums. At all events, the croupiers of Roulettenberg seemed to look upon the Grandmother as their lawful prey—whereafter there befell what our party had foretold.

It happened thus:

As soon as ever we arrived the Grandmother ordered me to stake twelve ten-gulden pieces in succession upon zero. Once, twice, and thrice I did so, yet zero never turned up.

"Stake again," said the old lady with an impatient nudge of my elbow, and I obeyed.

"How many times have we lost?" she inquired—actually grinding her teeth in her excitement.

"We have lost 144 ten-gulden pieces," I replied. "I tell you, Madame, that zero may not turn up until nightfall."

"Never mind," she interrupted. "Keep on staking upon zero, and also stake a thousand gulden upon rouge. Here is a banknote with which to do so."

The red turned up, but zero missed again, and we only got our thousand gulden back.

"But you see, you see," whispered the old lady. "We have now recovered almost all that we staked. Try zero again. Let us do so another ten times, and then leave off."

By the fifth round, however, the Grandmother was weary of the scheme.

"To the devil with that zero!" she exclaimed. "Stake four thousand gulden upon the red."

"But, Madame, that will be so much to venture!" I remonstrated. "Suppose the red should not turn up?" The Grandmother almost struck me in her excitement. Her agitation was rapidly making her quarrelsome. Consequently, there was nothing for it but to stake the whole four thousand gulden as she had directed.

The wheel revolved while the Grandmother sat as bolt upright, and with as proud and quiet a mien, as though she had not the least doubt of winning.

"Zero!" cried the croupier.

At first the old lady failed to understand the situation; but, as soon as she saw the croupier raking in her four thousand gulden, together with everything else that happened to be lying on the table, and recognised that the zero which had been so long turning up, and on which we had lost nearly two hundred ten-gulden pieces, had at length, as though of set purpose, made a sudden reappearance—why, the poor old lady fell to cursing it, and to throwing herself about, and wailing and gesticulating at the company at large. Indeed, some people in our vicinity actually burst out laughing.

"To think that that accursed zero should have turned up NOW!" she sobbed. "The accursed, accursed thing! And, it is all YOUR fault," she added, rounding upon me in a frenzy. "It was you who persuaded me to cease staking upon it."

"But, Madame, I only explained the game to you. How am I to answer for every mischance which may occur in it?"

"You and your mischances!" she whispered threateningly. "Go! Away at once!"

"Farewell, then, Madame." And I turned to depart.

"No—stay," she put in hastily. "Where are you going to? Why should you leave me? You fool! No, no... stay here. It is I who was the fool. Tell me what I ought to do."

"I cannot take it upon myself to advise you, for you will only blame me if I do so. Play at your own discretion. Say exactly what you wish staked, and I will stake it."

"Very well. Stake another four thousand gulden upon the red. Take this banknote to do it with. I have still got twenty thousand roubles in actual cash."

"But," I whispered, "such a quantity of money—"

"Never mind. I cannot rest until I have won back my losses. Stake!"

I staked, and we lost.

"Stake again, stake again—eight thousand at a stroke!"

"I cannot, Madame. The largest stake allowed is four thousand gulden."

"Well, then; stake four thousand."

This time we won, and the Grandmother recovered herself a little.

"You see, you see!" she exclaimed as she nudged me. "Stake another four thousand."

I did so, and lost. Again, and yet again, we lost. "Madame, your twelve thousand gulden are now gone," at length I reported.

"I see they are," she replied with, as it were, the calmness of despair. "I see they are," she muttered again as she gazed straight in front of her, like a person lost in thought. "Ah well, I do not mean to rest until I have staked another four thousand."

"But you have no money with which to do it, Madame. In this satchel I can see only a few five percent bonds and some transfers—no actual cash."

"And in the purse?"

"A mere trifle."

"But there is a money-changer's office here, is there not? They told me I should be able to get any sort of paper security changed!"

"Quite so; to any amount you please. But you will lose on the transaction what would frighten even a Jew."

"Rubbish! I am DETERMINED to retrieve my losses. Take me away, and call those fools of bearers."

I wheeled the chair out of the throng, and, the bearers making their appearance, we left the Casino.

"Hurry, hurry!" commanded the Grandmother. "Show me the nearest way to the money-changer's. Is it far?"

"A couple of steps, Madame."

At the turning from the square into the Avenue we came face to face with the whole of our party—the General, De Griers, Mlle. Blanche, and her mother. Only Polina and Mr. Astley were absent.

"Well, well, well!" exclaimed the Grandmother. "But we have no time to stop. What do you want? I can't talk to you here."

I dropped behind a little, and immediately was pounced upon by De Griers.

"She has lost this morning's winnings," I whispered, "and also twelve thousand gulden of her original money. At the present moment we are going to get some bonds changed."

De Griers stamped his foot with vexation, and hastened to communicate the tidings to the General. Meanwhile we continued to wheel the old lady along.

"Stop her, stop her," whispered the General in consternation.

"You had better try and stop her yourself," I returned—also in a whisper.

"My good mother," he said as he approached her, "—my good mother, pray let, let—" (his voice was beginning to tremble and sink) "—let us hire a carriage, and go for a drive. Near here there is an enchanting view to be obtained. We-we-we were just coming to invite you to go and see it."

"Begone with you and your views!" said the Grandmother angrily as she waved him away.

"And there are trees there, and we could have tea under them," continued the General—now in utter despair.

"Nous boirons du lait, sur l'herbe fraiche," added De Griers with the snarl almost of a wild beast.

"Du lait, de l'herbe fraiche"—the idyll, the ideal of the Parisian bourgeois—his whole outlook upon "la nature et la verite"!

"Have done with you and your milk!" cried the old lady. "Go and stuff YOURSELF as much as you like, but my stomach simply recoils from the idea. What are you stopping for? I have nothing to say to you."

"Here we are, Madame," I announced. "Here is the moneychanger's office."

I entered to get the securities changed, while the Grandmother remained outside in the porch, and the rest waited at a little distance, in doubt as to their best course of action. At length the old lady turned such an angry stare upon them that they departed along the road towards the Casino.

The process of changing involved complicated calculations which soon necessitated my return to the Grandmother for instructions.

"The thieves!" she exclaimed as she clapped her hands together. "Never mind, though. Get the documents cashed—No; send the banker out to me," she added as an afterthought.

"Would one of the clerks do, Madame?"

"Yes, one of the clerks. The thieves!"

The clerk consented to come out when he perceived that he was being asked for by an old lady who was too infirm to walk; after which the Grandmother began to upbraid him at length, and with great vehemence, for his alleged usuriousness, and to bargain with him in a mixture of Russian, French, and German—I acting as interpreter. Meanwhile, the grave-faced official eyed us both, and silently nodded his head. At the Grandmother, in particular, he gazed with a curiosity which almost bordered upon rudeness. At length, too, he smiled.

"Pray recollect yourself!" cried the old lady. "And may my money choke you! Alexis Ivanovitch, tell him that we can easily repair to someone else."

"The clerk says that others will give you even less than he."

Of what the ultimate calculations consisted I do not exactly remember, but at all events they were alarming. Receiving twelve thousand florins in gold, I took also the statement of accounts, and carried it out to the Grandmother.

"Well, well," she said, "I am no accountant. Let us hurry away, hurry away." And she waved the paper aside.

"Neither upon that accursed zero, however, nor upon that equally accursed red do I mean to stake a cent," I muttered to myself as I entered the Casino.

This time I did all I could to persuade the old lady to stake as little as possible—saying that a turn would come in the chances when she would be at liberty to stake more. But she was so impatient that, though at first she agreed to do as I suggested, nothing could stop her when once she had begun. By way of prelude she won stakes of a hundred and two hundred gulden.

"There you are!" she said as she nudged me. "See what we have won! Surely it would be worth our while to stake four thousand instead of a hundred, for we might win another four thousand, and then—! Oh, it was YOUR fault before—all your fault!"

I felt greatly put out as I watched her play, but I decided to hold my tongue, and to give her no more advice.

Suddenly De Griers appeared on the scene. It seemed that all this while he and his companions had been standing beside us—though I noticed that Mlle. Blanche had withdrawn a little from the rest, and was engaged in flirting with the Prince. Clearly the General was greatly put out at this. Indeed, he was in a perfect agony of vexation. But Mlle. was careful never to look his way, though he did his best to attract her notice. Poor General! By turns his face blanched and reddened, and he was trembling to such an extent that he could scarcely follow the old lady's play. At length Mlle. and the Prince took their departure, and the General followed them.

"Madame, Madame," sounded the honeyed accents of De Griers as he leant over to whisper in the Grandmother's ear. "That stake will never win. No, no, it is impossible," he added in Russian with a writhe. "No, no!"

"But why not?" asked the Grandmother, turning round. "Show me what I ought to do."

Instantly De Griers burst into a babble of French as he advised, jumped about, declared that such and such chances ought to be waited for, and started to make calculations of figures. All this he addressed to me in my capacity as translator—tapping the table the while with his finger, and pointing hither and thither. At length he seized a pencil, and began to reckon sums on paper until he had exhausted the Grandmother's patience.

"Away with you!" she interrupted. "You talk sheer nonsense, for, though you keep on saying 'Madame, Madame,' you haven't the least notion what ought to be done. Away with you, I say!"

"Mais, Madame," cooed De Griers—and straightway started afresh with his fussy instructions.

"Stake just ONCE, as he advises," the Grandmother said to me, "and then we shall see what we shall see. Of course, his stake MIGHT win."

As a matter of fact, De Grier's one object was to distract the old lady from staking large sums; wherefore, he now suggested to her that she should stake upon certain numbers, singly and in groups. Consequently, in accordance with his instructions, I staked a ten-gulden piece upon several odd numbers in the first twenty, and five ten-gulden pieces upon certain groups of numbers-groups of from twelve to eighteen, and from eighteen to twenty-four. The total staked amounted to 160 gulden.

The wheel revolved. "Zero!" cried the croupier.

We had lost it all!

"The fool!" cried the old lady as she turned upon De Griers. "You infernal Frenchman, to think that you should advise! Away with you! Though you fuss and fuss, you don't even know what you're talking about."

Deeply offended, De Griers shrugged his shoulders, favoured the Grandmother with a look of contempt, and departed. For some time past he had been feeling ashamed of being seen in such company, and this had proved the last straw.

An hour later we had lost everything in hand.

"Home!" cried the Grandmother.

Not until we had turned into the Avenue did she utter a word; but from that point onwards, until we arrived at the hotel, she kept venting exclamations of "What a fool I am! What a silly old fool I am, to be sure!"

Arrived at the hotel, she called for tea, and then gave orders for her luggage to be packed.

"We are off again," she announced.

"But whither, Madame?" inquired Martha.

"What business is that of YOURS? Let the cricket stick to its hearth. [The Russian form of "Mind your own business."] Potapitch, have everything packed, for we are returning to Moscow at once. I have fooled away fifteen thousand roubles."

"Fifteen thousand roubles, good mistress? My God!" And Potapitch spat upon his hands—probably to show that he was ready to serve her in any way he could.

"Now then, you fool! At once you begin with your weeping and wailing! Be quiet, and pack. Also, run downstairs, and get my hotel bill."

"The next train leaves at 9:30, Madame," I interposed, with a view to checking her agitation.

"And what is the time now?"

"Half-past eight."

"How vexing! But, never mind. Alexis Ivanovitch, I have not a kopeck left; I have but these two bank notes. Please run to the office and get them changed. Otherwise I shall have nothing to travel with."

Departing on her errand, I returned half an hour later to find the whole party gathered in her rooms. It appeared that the news of her impending departure for Moscow had thrown the conspirators into consternation even greater than her losses had done. For, said they, even if her departure should save her fortune, what will become of the General later? And who is to repay De Griers? Clearly Mlle. Blanche would never consent to wait until the Grandmother was dead, but would at once elope with the Prince or someone else. So they had all gathered together—endeavouring to calm and dissuade the Grandmother. Only Polina was absent. For her part the Grandmother had nothing for the party but abuse.

"Away with you, you rascals!" she was shouting. "What have my affairs to do with you? Why, in particular, do you"—here she indicated De Griers—"come sneaking here with your goat's beard? And what do YOU"—here she turned to Mlle. Blanche "want of me? What are YOU finicking for?"

"Diantre!" muttered Mlle. under her breath, but her eyes were flashing. Then all at once she burst into a laugh and left the room—crying to the General as she did so: "Elle vivra cent ans!"

"So you have been counting upon my death, have you?" fumed the old lady. "Away with you! Clear them out of the room, Alexis Ivanovitch. What business is it of THEIRS? It is not THEIR money that I have been squandering, but my own."

The General shrugged his shoulders, bowed, and withdrew, with De Griers behind him.

"Call Prascovia," commanded the Grandmother, and in five minutes Martha reappeared with Polina, who had been sitting with the children in her own room (having purposely determined not to leave it that day). Her face looked grave and careworn.

"Prascovia," began the Grandmother, "is what I have just heard through a side wind true—namely, that this fool of a stepfather of yours is going to marry that silly whirligig of a Frenchwoman—that actress, or something worse? Tell me, is it true?"

"I do not know FOR CERTAIN, Grandmamma," replied Polina; "but from Mlle. Blanche's account (for she does not appear to think it necessary to conceal anything) I conclude that—"

"You need not say any more," interrupted the Grandmother energetically. "I understand the situation. I always thought we should get something like this from him, for I always looked upon him as a futile, frivolous fellow who gave himself unconscionable airs on the fact of his being a general (though he only became one because he retired as a colonel). Yes, I know all about the sending of the telegrams to inquire whether 'the old woman is likely to turn up her toes soon.' Ah, they were looking for the legacies! Without money that wretched woman (what is her name?—Oh, De Cominges) would never dream of accepting the General and his false teeth—no, not even for him to be her lacquey—since she herself, they say, possesses a pile of money, and lends it on interest, and makes a good thing out of it. However, it is not you, Prascovia, that I am blaming; it was not you who sent those telegrams. Nor, for that matter, do I wish to recall old scores. True, I know that you are a vixen by nature—that you are a wasp which will sting one if one touches it—yet, my heart is sore for you, for I loved your mother, Katerina. Now, will you leave everything here, and come away with me? Otherwise, I do not know what is to become of you, and it is not right that you should continue living with these people. Nay," she interposed, the moment that Polina attempted to speak, "I have not yet finished. I ask of you nothing in return. My house in Moscow is, as you know, large enough for a palace, and you could occupy a whole floor of it if you liked, and keep away from me for weeks together. Will you come with me or will you not?"

"First of all, let me ask of YOU," replied Polina, "whether you are intending to depart at once?"

"What? You suppose me to be jesting? I have said that I am going, and I AM going. Today I have squandered fifteen thousand roubles at that accursed roulette of yours, and though, five years ago, I promised the people of a certain suburb of Moscow to build them a stone church in place of a wooden one, I have been fooling away my money here! However, I am going back now to build my church."

"But what about the waters, Grandmamma? Surely you came here to take the waters?"

"You and your waters! Do not anger me, Prascovia. Surely you are trying to? Say, then: will you, or will you not, come with me?"

"Grandmamma," Polina replied with deep feeling, "I am very, very grateful to you for the shelter which you have so kindly offered me. Also, to a certain extent you have guessed my position aright, and I am beholden to you to such an extent that it may be that I will come and live with you, and that very soon; yet there are important reasons why—why I cannot make up my mind just yet. If you would let me have, say, a couple of weeks to decide in—?"

"You mean that you are NOT coming?"

"I mean only that I cannot come just yet. At all events, I could not well leave my little brother and sister here, since, since—if I were to leave them—they would be abandoned altogether. But if, Grandmamma, you would take the little ones AND myself, then, of course, I could come with you, and would do all I could to serve you" (this she said with great earnestness). "Only, without the little ones I CANNOT come."

"Do not make a fuss" (as a matter of fact Polina never at any time either fussed or wept). "The Great Foster—Father [Translated literally—The Great Poulterer] can find for all his chicks a place. You are not coming without the children? But see here, Prascovia. I wish you well, and nothing but well: yet I have divined the reason why you will not come. Yes, I know all, Prascovia. That Frenchman will never bring you good of any sort."

Polina coloured hotly, and even I started. "For," thought I to myself, "every one seems to know about that affair. Or perhaps I am the only one who does not know about it?"

"Now, now! Do not frown," continued the Grandmother. "But I do not intend to slur things over. You will take care that no harm befalls you, will you not? For you are a girl of sense, and I am sorry for you—I regard you in a different light to the rest of them. And now, please, leave me. Good-bye."

"But let me stay with you a little longer," said Polina.

"No," replied the other; "you need not. Do not bother me, for you and all of them have tired me out."

Yet when Polina tried to kiss the Grandmother's hand, the old lady withdrew it, and herself kissed the girl on the cheek. As she passed me, Polina gave me a momentary glance, and then as swiftly averted her eyes.

"And good-bye to you, also, Alexis Ivanovitch. The train starts in an hour's time, and I think that you must be weary of me. Take these five hundred gulden for yourself."

"I thank you humbly, Madame, but I am ashamed to—"

"Come, come!" cried the Grandmother so energetically, and with such an air of menace, that I did not dare refuse the money further.

"If, when in Moscow, you have no place where you can lay your head," she added, "come and see me, and I will give you a recommendation. Now, Potapitch, get things ready."

I ascended to my room, and lay down upon the bed. A whole hour I must have lain thus, with my head resting upon my hand. So the crisis had come! I needed time for its consideration. To-morrow I would have a talk with Polina. Ah! The Frenchman! So, it was true? But how could it be so? Polina and De Griers! What a combination!

No, it was too improbable. Suddenly I leapt up with the idea of seeking Astley and forcing him to speak. There could be no doubt that he knew more than I did. Astley? Well, he was another problem for me to solve.

Suddenly there came a knock at the door, and I opened it to find Potapitch awaiting me.

"Sir," he said, "my mistress is asking for you."

"Indeed? But she is just departing, is she not? The train leaves in ten minutes' time."

"She is uneasy, sir; she cannot rest. Come quickly, sir; do not delay."

I ran downstairs at once. The Grandmother was just being carried out of her rooms into the corridor. In her hands she held a roll of bank-notes.

"Alexis Ivanovitch," she cried, "walk on ahead, and we will set out again."

"But whither, Madame?"

"I cannot rest until I have retrieved my losses. March on ahead, and ask me no questions. Play continues until midnight, does it not?"

For a moment I stood stupefied—stood deep in thought; but it was not long before I had made up my mind.

"With your leave, Madame," I said, "I will not go with you."

"And why not? What do you mean? Is every one here a stupid good-for-nothing?"

"Pardon me, but I have nothing to reproach myself with. I merely will not go. I merely intend neither to witness nor to join in your play. I also beg to return you your five hundred gulden. Farewell."

Laying the money upon a little table which the Grandmother's chair happened to be passing, I bowed and withdrew.

"What folly!" the Grandmother shouted after me. "Very well, then. Do not come, and I will find my way alone. Potapitch, you must come with me. Lift up the chair, and carry me along."

I failed to find Mr. Astley, and returned home. It was now growing late—it was past midnight, but I subsequently learnt from Potapitch how the Grandmother's day had ended. She had lost all the money which, earlier in the day, I had got for her paper securities—a sum amounting to about ten thousand roubles. This she did under the direction of the Pole whom, that afternoon, she had dowered with two ten-gulden pieces. But before his arrival on the scene, she had commanded Potapitch to stake for her; until at length she had told him also to go about his business. Upon that the Pole had leapt into the breach. Not only did it happen that he knew the Russian language, but also he could speak a mixture of three different dialects, so that the pair were able to understand one another. Yet the old lady never ceased to abuse him, despite his deferential manner, and to compare him unfavourably with myself (so, at all events, Potapitch declared). "You," the old chamberlain said to me, "treated her as a gentleman should, but he—he robbed her right and left, as I could see with my own eyes. Twice she caught him at it, and rated him soundly. On one occasion she even pulled his hair, so that the bystanders burst out laughing. Yet she lost everything, sir—that is to say, she lost all that you had changed for her. Then we brought her home, and, after asking for some water and saying her prayers, she went to bed. So worn out was she that she fell asleep at once. May God send her dreams of angels! And this is all that foreign travel has done for us! Oh, my own Moscow! For what have we not at home there, in Moscow? Such a garden and flowers as you could never see here, and fresh air and apple-trees coming into blossom,—and a beautiful view to look upon. Ah, but what must she do but go travelling abroad? Alack, alack!"

XIII

Almost a month has passed since I last touched these notes—notes which I began under the influence of impressions at once poignant and disordered. The crisis which I then felt to be approaching has now arrived, but in a form a hundred times more extensive and unexpected than I had looked for. To me it all seems strange, uncouth, and tragic. Certain occurrences have befallen me which border upon the marvellous. At all events, that is how I view them. I view them so in one regard at least. I refer to the whirlpool of events in which, at the time, I was revolving. But the most curious feature of all is my relation to those events, for hitherto I had never clearly understood myself. Yet now the actual crisis has passed away like a dream. Even my passion for Polina is dead. Was it ever so strong and genuine as I thought? If so, what has become of it now? At times I fancy that I must be mad; that somewhere I am sitting in a madhouse; that these events have merely SEEMED to happen; that still they merely SEEM to be happening.

I have been arranging and re-perusing my notes (perhaps for the purpose of convincing myself that I am not in a madhouse). At present I am lonely and alone. Autumn is coming—already it is mellowing the leaves; and, as I sit brooding in this melancholy little town (and how melancholy the little towns of Germany can be!), I find myself taking no thought for the future, but living under the influence of passing moods, and of my recollections of the tempest which recently drew me into its vortex, and then cast me out again. At times I seem still to be caught within that vortex. At times, the tempest seems once more to be gathering, and, as it passes overhead, to be wrapping me in its folds, until I have lost my sense of order and reality, and continue whirling and whirling and whirling around.

Yet, it may be that I shall be able to stop myself from revolving if once I can succeed in rendering myself an exact account of what has happened within the month just past. Somehow I feel drawn towards the pen; on many and many an evening I have had nothing else in the world to do. But, curiously enough, of late I have taken to amusing myself with the works of M. Paul de Kock, which I read in German translations obtained from a wretched local library. These works I cannot abide, yet I read them, and find myself marvelling that I should be doing so. Somehow I seem to be afraid of any SERIOUS book—afraid of permitting any SERIOUS preoccupation to break the spell of the passing moment. So dear to me is the formless dream of which I have spoken, so dear to me are the impressions which it has left behind it, that I fear to touch the vision with anything new, lest it should dissolve in smoke. But is it so dear to me? Yes, it IS dear to me, and will ever be fresh in my recollections—even forty years hence....

So let me write of it, but only partially, and in a more abridged form than my full impressions might warrant.

First of all, let me conclude the history of the Grandmother. Next day she lost every gulden that she possessed. Things were bound to happen so, for persons of her type who have once entered upon that road descend it with ever-increasing rapidity, even as a sledge descends a toboggan-slide. All day until eight o'clock that evening did she play; and, though I personally did not witness her exploits, I learnt of them later through report.

All that day Potapitch remained in attendance upon her; but the Poles who directed her play she changed more than once. As a beginning she dismissed her Pole of the previous day—the Pole whose hair she had pulled—and took to herself another one; but the latter proved worse even than the former, and incurred dismissal in favour of the first Pole, who, during the time of his unemployment, had nevertheless hovered around the Grandmother's chair, and from time to time obtruded his head over her shoulder. At length the old lady became desperate, for the second Pole, when dismissed, imitated his predecessor by declining to go away; with the result that one Pole remained standing on the right of the victim, and the other on her left; from which vantage points the pair quarrelled, abused each other concerning the stakes and rounds, and exchanged the epithet "laidak" [Rascal] and other Polish terms of endearment. Finally, they effected a mutual reconciliation, and, tossing the money about anyhow, played simply at random. Once more quarrelling, each of them staked money on his own side of the Grandmother's chair (for instance, the one Pole staked upon the red, and the other one upon the black), until they had so confused and browbeaten the old lady that, nearly weeping, she was forced to appeal to the head croupier for protection, and to have the two Poles expelled. No time was lost in this being done, despite the rascals' cries and protestations that the old lady was in their debt, that she had cheated them, and that her general behaviour had been mean and dishonourable. The same evening the unfortunate Potapitch related the story to me with tears complaining that the two men had filled their pockets with money (he himself had seen them do it) which had been shamelessly pilfered from his mistress. For instance, one Pole demanded of the Grandmother fifty gulden for his trouble, and then staked the money by the side of her stake. She happened to win; whereupon he cried out that the winning stake was his, and hers the loser. As soon as the two Poles had been expelled, Potapitch left the room, and reported to the authorities that the men's pockets were full of gold; and, on the Grandmother also requesting the head croupier to look into the affair, the police made their appearance, and, despite the protests of the Poles (who, indeed, had been caught redhanded), their pockets were turned inside out, and the contents handed over to the Grandmother. In fact, in, view of the circumstance that she lost all day, the croupiers and other authorities of the Casino showed her every attention; and on her fame spreading through the town, visitors of every nationality—even the most knowing of them, the most distinguished—crowded to get a glimpse of "la vieille comtesse russe, tombee en enfance," who had lost "so many millions."

Yet with the money which the authorities restored to her from the pockets of the Poles the Grandmother effected very, very little, for there soon arrived to take his countrymen's place, a third Pole—a man who could speak Russian fluently, was dressed like a gentleman (albeit in lacqueyish fashion), and sported a huge moustache. Though polite enough to the old lady, he took a high hand with the bystanders. In short, he offered himself less as a servant than as an ENTERTAINER. After each round he would turn to the old lady, and swear terrible oaths to the effect that he was a "Polish gentleman of honour" who would scorn to take a kopeck of her money; and, though he repeated these oaths so often that at length she grew alarmed, he had her play in hand, and began to win on her behalf; wherefore, she felt that she could not well get rid of him. An hour later the two Poles who, earlier in the day, had been expelled from the Casino, made a reappearance behind the old lady's chair, and renewed their offers of service—even if it were only to be sent on messages; but from Potapitch I subsequently had it that between these rascals and the said "gentleman of honour" there passed a wink, as well as that the latter put something into their hands. Next, since the Grandmother had not yet lunched—she had scarcely for a moment left her chair—one of the two Poles ran to the restaurant of the Casino, and brought her thence a cup of soup, and afterwards some tea. In fact, BOTH the Poles hastened to perform this office. Finally, towards the close of the day, when it was clear that the Grandmother was about to play her last bank-note, there could be seen standing behind her chair no fewer than six natives of Poland—persons who, as yet, had been neither audible nor visible; and as soon as ever the old lady played the note in question, they took no further notice of her, but pushed their way past her chair to the table; seized the money, and staked it—shouting and disputing the while, and arguing with the "gentleman of honour" (who also had forgotten the Grandmother's existence), as though he were their equal. Even when the Grandmother had lost her all, and was returning (about eight o'clock) to the hotel, some three or four Poles could not bring themselves to leave her, but went on running beside her chair and volubly protesting that the Grandmother had cheated them, and that she ought to be made to surrender what was not her own. Thus the party arrived at the hotel; whence, presently, the gang of rascals was ejected neck and crop.

According to Potapitch's calculations, the Grandmother lost, that day, a total of ninety thousand roubles, in addition to the money which she had lost the day before. Every paper security which she had brought with her—five percent bonds, internal loan scrip, and what not—she had changed into cash. Also, I could not but marvel at the way in which, for seven or eight hours at a stretch, she sat in that chair of hers, almost never leaving the table. Again, Potapitch told me that there were three occasions on which she really began to win; but that, led on by false hopes, she was unable to tear herself away at the right moment. Every gambler knows how a person may sit a day and a night at cards without ever casting a glance to right or to left.

Meanwhile, that day some other very important events were passing in our hotel. As early as eleven o'clock—that is to say, before the Grandmother had quitted her rooms—the General and De Griers decided upon their last stroke. In other words, on learning that the old lady had changed her mind about departing, and was bent on setting out for the Casino again, the whole of our gang (Polina only excepted) proceeded en masse to her rooms, for the purpose of finally and frankly treating with her. But the General, quaking and greatly apprehensive as to his possible future, overdid things. After half an hour's prayers and entreaties, coupled with a full confession of his debts, and even of his passion for Mlle. Blanche (yes, he had quite lost his head), he suddenly adopted a tone of menace, and started to rage at the old lady—exclaiming that she was sullying the family honour, that she was making a public scandal of herself, and that she was smirching the fair name of Russia. The upshot was that the Grandmother turned him out of the room with her stick (it was a real stick, too!). Later in the morning he held several consultations with De Griers—the question which occupied him being: Is it in any way possible to make use of the police—to tell them that "this respected, but unfortunate, old lady has gone out of her mind, and is squandering her last kopeck," or something of the kind? In short, is it in any way possible to engineer a species of supervision over, or of restraint upon, the old lady? De Griers, however, shrugged his shoulders at this, and laughed in the General's face, while the old warrior went on chattering volubly, and running up and down his study. Finally De Griers waved his hand, and disappeared from view; and by evening it became known that he had left the hotel, after holding a very secret and important conference with Mlle. Blanche. As for the latter, from early morning she had taken decisive measures, by completely excluding the General from her presence, and bestowing upon him not a glance. Indeed, even when the General pursued her to the Casino, and met her walking arm in arm with the Prince, he (the General) received from her and her mother not the slightest recognition. Nor did the Prince himself bow. The rest of the day Mlle. spent in probing the Prince, and trying to make him declare himself; but in this she made a woeful mistake. The little incident occurred in the evening. Suddenly Mlle. Blanche realised that the Prince had not even a copper to his name, but, on the contrary, was minded to borrow of her money wherewith to play at roulette. In high displeasure she drove him from her presence, and shut herself up in her room.

The same morning I went to see—or, rather, to look for—Mr. Astley, but was unsuccessful in my quest. Neither in his rooms nor in the Casino nor in the Park was he to be found; nor did he, that day, lunch at his hotel as usual. However, at about five o'clock I caught sight of him walking from the railway station to the Hotel d'Angleterre. He seemed to be in a great hurry and much preoccupied, though in his face I could discern no actual traces of worry or perturbation. He held out to me a friendly hand, with his usual ejaculation of "Ah!" but did not check his stride. I turned and walked beside him, but found, somehow, that his answers forbade any putting of definite questions. Moreover, I felt reluctant to speak to him of Polina; nor, for his part, did he ask me any questions concerning her, although, on my telling him of the Grandmother's exploits, he listened attentively and gravely, and then shrugged his shoulders.

"She is gambling away everything that she has," I remarked.

"Indeed? She arrived at the Casino even before I had taken my departure by train, so I knew she had been playing. If I should have time I will go to the Casino to-night, and take a look at her. The thing interests me."

"Where have you been today?" I asked—surprised at myself for having, as yet, omitted to put to him that question.

"To Frankfort."

"On business?"

"On business."

What more was there to be asked after that? I accompanied him until, as we drew level with the Hotel des Quatre Saisons, he suddenly nodded to me and disappeared. For myself, I returned home, and came to the conclusion that, even had I met him at two o'clock in the afternoon, I should have learnt no more from him than I had done at five o'clock, for the reason that I had no definite question to ask. It was bound to have been so. For me to formulate the query which I really wished to put was a simple impossibility.

Polina spent the whole of that day either in walking about the park with the nurse and children or in sitting in her own room. For a long while past she had avoided the General and had scarcely had a word to say to him (scarcely a word, I mean, on any SERIOUS topic). Yes, that I had noticed. Still, even though I was aware of the position in which the General was placed, it had never occurred to me that he would have any reason to avoid HER, or to trouble her with family explanations. Indeed, when I was returning to the hotel after my conversation with Astley, and chanced to meet Polina and the children, I could see that her face was as calm as though the family disturbances had never touched her. To my salute she responded with a slight bow, and I retired to my room in a very bad humour.

Of course, since the affair with the Burmergelms I had exchanged not a word with Polina, nor had with her any kind of intercourse. Yet I had been at my wits' end, for, as time went on, there was arising in me an ever-seething dissatisfaction. Even if she did not love me she ought not to have trampled upon my feelings, nor to have accepted my confessions with such contempt, seeing that she must have been aware that I loved her (of her own accord she had allowed me to tell her as much). Of course the situation between us had arisen in a curious manner. About two months ago, I had noticed that she had a desire to make me her friend, her confidant—that she was making trial of me for the purpose; but, for some reason or another, the desired result had never come about, and we had fallen into the present strange relations, which had led me to address her as I had done. At the same time, if my love was distasteful to her, why had she not FORBIDDEN me to speak of it to her?

But she had not so forbidden me. On the contrary, there had been occasions when she had even INVITED me to speak. Of course, this might have been done out of sheer wantonness, for I well knew—I had remarked it only too often—that, after listening to what I had to say, and angering me almost beyond endurance, she loved suddenly to torture me with some fresh outburst of contempt and aloofness! Yet she must have known that I could not live without her. Three days had elapsed since the affair with the Baron, and I could bear the severance no longer. When, that afternoon, I met her near the Casino, my heart almost made me faint, it beat so violently. She too could not live without me, for had she not said that she had NEED of me? Or had that too been spoken in jest?

That she had a secret of some kind there could be no doubt. What she had said to the Grandmother had stabbed me to the heart. On a thousand occasions I had challenged her to be open with me, nor could she have been ignorant that I was ready to give my very life for her. Yet always she had kept me at a distance with that contemptuous air of hers; or else she had demanded of me, in lieu of the life which I offered to lay at her feet, such escapades as I had perpetrated with the Baron. Ah, was it not torture to me, all this? For could it be that her whole world was bound up with the Frenchman? What, too, about Mr. Astley? The affair was inexplicable throughout. My God, what distress it caused me!

Arrived home, I, in a fit of frenzy, indited the following:

"Polina Alexandrovna, I can see that there is approaching us an exposure which will involve you too. For the last time I ask of you—have you, or have you not, any need of my life? If you have, then make such dispositions as you wish, and I shall always be discoverable in my room if required. If you have need of my life, write or send for me."

I sealed the letter, and dispatched it by the hand of a corridor lacquey, with orders to hand it to the addressee in person. Though I expected no answer, scarcely three minutes had elapsed before the lacquey returned with "the compliments of a certain person."

Next, about seven o'clock, I was sent for by the General. I found him in his study, apparently preparing to go out again, for his hat and stick were lying on the sofa. When I entered he was standing in the middle of the room—his feet wide apart, and his head bent down. Also, he appeared to be talking to himself. But as soon as ever he saw me at the door he came towards me in such a curious manner that involuntarily I retreated a step, and was for leaving the room; whereupon he seized me by both hands, and, drawing me towards the sofa, and seating himself thereon, he forced me to sit down on a chair opposite him. Then, without letting go of my hands, he exclaimed with quivering lips and a sparkle of tears on his eyelashes:

"Oh, Alexis Ivanovitch! Save me, save me! Have some mercy upon me!"

For a long time I could not make out what he meant, although he kept talking and talking, and constantly repeating to himself, "Have mercy, mercy!" At length, however, I divined that he was expecting me to give him something in the nature of advice—or, rather, that, deserted by every one, and overwhelmed with grief and apprehension, he had bethought himself of my existence, and sent for me to relieve his feelings by talking and talking and talking.

In fact, he was in such a confused and despondent state of mind that, clasping his hands together, he actually went down upon his knees and begged me to go to Mlle. Blanche, and beseech and advise her to return to him, and to accept him in marriage.

"But, General," I exclaimed, "possibly Mlle. Blanche has scarcely even remarked my existence? What could I do with her?"

It was in vain that I protested, for he could understand nothing that was said to him, Next he started talking about the Grandmother, but always in a disconnected sort of fashion—his one thought being to send for the police.

"In Russia," said he, suddenly boiling over with indignation, "or in any well-ordered State where there exists a government, old women like my mother are placed under proper guardianship. Yes, my good sir," he went on, relapsing into a scolding tone as he leapt to his feet and started to pace the room, "do you not know this" (he seemed to be addressing some imaginary auditor in the corner) "—do you not know this, that in Russia old women like her are subjected to restraint, the devil take them?" Again he threw himself down upon the sofa.

A minute later, though sobbing and almost breathless, he managed to gasp out that Mlle. Blanche had refused to marry him, for the reason that the Grandmother had turned up in place of a telegram, and it was therefore clear that he had no inheritance to look for. Evidently, he supposed that I had hitherto been in entire ignorance of all this. Again, when I referred to De Griers, the General made a gesture of despair. "He has gone away," he said, "and everything which I possess is mortgaged to him. I stand stripped to my skin. Even of the money which you brought me from Paris, I know not if seven hundred francs be left. Of course that sum will do to go on with, but, as regards the future, I know nothing, I know nothing."

"Then how will you pay your hotel bill?" I cried in consternation. "And what shall you do afterwards?"

He looked at me vaguely, but it was clear that he had not understood—perhaps had not even heard—my questions. Then I tried to get him to speak of Polina and the children, but he only returned brief answers of "Yes, yes," and again started to maunder about the Prince, and the likelihood of the latter marrying Mlle. Blanche. "What on earth am I to do?" he concluded. "What on earth am I to do? Is this not ingratitude? Is it not sheer ingratitude?" And he burst into tears.

Nothing could be done with such a man. Yet to leave him alone was dangerous, for something might happen to him. I withdrew from his rooms for a little while, but warned the nursemaid to keep an eye upon him, as well as exchanged a word with the corridor lacquey (a very talkative fellow), who likewise promised to remain on the look-out.

Hardly had I left the General, when Potapitch approached me with a summons from the Grandmother. It was now eight o'clock, and she had returned from the Casino after finally losing all that she possessed. I found her sitting in her chair—much distressed and evidently fatigued. Presently Martha brought her up a cup of tea and forced her to drink it; yet, even then I could detect in the old lady's tone and manner a great change.

"Good evening, Alexis Ivanovitch," she said slowly, with her head drooping. "Pardon me for disturbing you again. Yes, you must pardon an old, old woman like myself, for I have left behind me all that I possess—nearly a hundred thousand roubles! You did quite right in declining to come with me this evening. Now I am without money—without a single groat. But I must not delay a moment; I must leave by the 9:30 train. I have sent for that English friend of yours, and am going to beg of him three thousand francs for a week. Please try and persuade him to think nothing of it, nor yet to refuse me, for I am still a rich woman who possesses three villages and a couple of mansions. Yes, the money shall be found, for I have not yet squandered EVERYTHING. I tell you this in order that he may have no doubts about—Ah, but here he is! Clearly he is a good fellow."

True enough, Astley had come hot-foot on receiving the Grandmother's appeal. Scarcely stopping even to reflect, and with scarcely a word, he counted out the three thousand francs under a note of hand which she duly signed. Then, his business done, he bowed, and lost no time in taking his departure.

"You too leave me, Alexis Ivanovitch," said the Grandmother. "All my bones are aching, and I still have an hour in which to rest. Do not be hard upon me, old fool that I am. Never again shall I blame young people for being frivolous. I should think it wrong even to blame that unhappy General of yours. Nevertheless, I do not mean to let him have any of my money (which is all that he desires), for the reason that I look upon him as a perfect blockhead, and consider myself, simpleton though I be, at least wiser than HE is. How surely does God visit old age, and punish it for its presumption! Well, good-bye. Martha, come and lift me up."

However, I had a mind to see the old lady off; and, moreover, I was in an expectant frame of mind—somehow I kept thinking that SOMETHING was going to happen; wherefore, I could not rest quietly in my room, but stepped out into the corridor, and then into the Chestnut Avenue for a few minutes' stroll. My letter to Polina had been clear and firm, and in the present crisis, I felt sure, would prove final. I had heard of De Griers' departure, and, however much Polina might reject me as a FRIEND, she might not reject me altogether as a SERVANT. She would need me to fetch and carry for her, and I was ready to do so. How could it have been otherwise?

Towards the hour of the train's departure I hastened to the station, and put the Grandmother into her compartment—she and her party occupying a reserved family saloon.

"Thanks for your disinterested assistance," she said at parting. "Oh, and please remind Prascovia of what I said to her last night. I expect soon to see her."

Then I returned home. As I was passing the door of the General's suite, I met the nursemaid, and inquired after her master. "There is nothing new to report, sir," she replied quietly. Nevertheless I decided to enter, and was just doing so when I halted thunderstruck on the threshold. For before me I beheld the General and Mlle. Blanche—laughing gaily at one another!—while beside them, on the sofa, there was seated her mother. Clearly the General was almost out of his mind with joy, for he was talking all sorts of nonsense, and bubbling over with a long-drawn, nervous laugh—a laugh which twisted his face into innumerable wrinkles, and caused his eyes almost to disappear.

Afterwards I learnt from Mlle. Blanche herself that, after dismissing the Prince and hearing of the General's tears, she bethought her of going to comfort the old man, and had just arrived for the purpose when I entered. Fortunately, the poor General did not know that his fate had been decided—that Mlle. had long ago packed her trunks in readiness for the first morning train to Paris!

Hesitating a moment on the threshold I changed my mind as to entering, and departed unnoticed. Ascending to my own room, and opening the door, I perceived in the semi-darkness a figure seated on a chair in the corner by the window. The figure did not rise when I entered, so I approached it swiftly, peered at it closely, and felt my heart almost stop beating. The figure was Polina!

XIV

The shock made me utter an exclamation.

"What is the matter? What is the matter?" she asked in a strange voice. She was looking pale, and her eyes were dim.

"What is the matter?" I re-echoed. "Why, the fact that you are HERE!"

"If I am here, I have come with all that I have to bring," she said. "Such has always been my way, as you shall presently see. Please light a candle."

I did so; whereupon she rose, approached the table, and laid upon it an open letter.

"Read it," she added.

"It is De Griers' handwriting!" I cried as I seized the document. My hands were so tremulous that the lines on the pages danced before my eyes. Although, at this distance of time, I have forgotten the exact phraseology of the missive, I append, if not the precise words, at all events the general sense.

"Mademoiselle," the document ran, "certain untoward circumstances compel me to depart in haste. Of course, you have of yourself remarked that hitherto I have always refrained from having any final explanation with you, for the reason that I could not well state the whole circumstances; and now to my difficulties the advent of the aged Grandmother, coupled with her subsequent proceedings, has put the final touch. Also, the involved state of my affairs forbids me to write with any finality concerning those hopes of ultimate bliss upon which, for a long while past, I have permitted myself to feed. I regret the past, but at the same time hope that in my conduct you have never been able to detect anything that was unworthy of a gentleman and a man of honour. Having lost, however, almost the whole of my money in debts incurred by your stepfather, I find myself driven to the necessity of saving the remainder; wherefore, I have instructed certain friends of mine in St. Petersburg to arrange for the sale of all the property which has been mortgaged to myself. At the same time, knowing that, in addition, your frivolous stepfather has squandered money which is exclusively yours, I have decided to absolve him from a certain moiety of the mortgages on his property, in order that you may be in a position to recover of him what you have lost, by suing him in legal fashion. I trust, therefore, that, as matters now stand, this action of mine may bring you some advantage. I trust also that this same action leaves me in the position of having fulfilled every obligation which is incumbent upon a man of honour and refinement. Rest assured that your memory will for ever remain graven in my heart."

"All this is clear enough," I commented. "Surely you did not expect aught else from him?" Somehow I was feeling annoyed.

"I expected nothing at all from him," she replied—quietly enough, to all outward seeming, yet with a note of irritation in her tone. "Long ago I made up my mind on the subject, for I could read his thoughts, and knew what he was thinking. He thought that possibly I should sue him—that one day I might become a nuisance." Here Polina halted for a moment, and stood biting her lips. "So of set purpose I redoubled my contemptuous treatment of him, and waited to see what he would do. If a telegram to say that we had become legatees had arrived from, St. Petersburg, I should have flung at him a quittance for my foolish stepfather's debts, and then dismissed him. For a long time I have hated him. Even in earlier days he was not a man; and now!—Oh, how gladly I could throw those fifty thousand roubles in his face, and spit in it, and then rub the spittle in!"

"But the document returning the fifty-thousand rouble mortgage—has the General got it? If so, possess yourself of it, and send it to De Griers."

"No, no; the General has not got it."

"Just as I expected! Well, what is the General going to do?" Then an idea suddenly occurred to me. "What about the Grandmother?" I asked.

Polina looked at me with impatience and bewilderment.

"What makes you speak of HER?" was her irritable inquiry. "I cannot go and live with her. Nor," she added hotly, "will I go down upon my knees to ANY ONE."

"Why should you?" I cried. "Yet to think that you should have loved De Griers! The villain, the villain! But I will kill him in a duel. Where is he now?"

"In Frankfort, where he will be staying for the next three days."

"Well, bid me do so, and I will go to him by the first train tomorrow," I exclaimed with enthusiasm.

She smiled.

"If you were to do that," she said, "he would merely tell you to be so good as first to return him the fifty thousand francs. What, then, would be the use of having a quarrel with him? You talk sheer nonsense."

I ground my teeth.

"The question," I went on, "is how to raise the fifty thousand francs. We cannot expect to find them lying about on the floor. Listen. What of Mr. Astley?" Even as I spoke a new and strange idea formed itself in my brain.

Her eyes flashed fire.

"What? YOU YOURSELF wish me to leave you for him?" she cried with a scornful look and a proud smile. Never before had she addressed me thus.

Then her head must have turned dizzy with emotion, for suddenly she seated herself upon the sofa, as though she were powerless any longer to stand.

A flash of lightning seemed to strike me as I stood there. I could scarcely believe my eyes or my ears. She DID love me, then! It WAS to me, and not to Mr. Astley, that she had turned! Although she, an unprotected girl, had come to me in my room—in an hotel room—and had probably compromised herself thereby, I had not understood!

Then a second mad idea flashed into my brain.

"Polina," I said, "give me but an hour. Wait here just one hour until I return. Yes, you MUST do so. Do you not see what I mean? Just stay here for that time."

And I rushed from the room without so much as answering her look of inquiry. She called something after me, but I did not return.

Sometimes it happens that the most insane thought, the most impossible conception, will become so fixed in one's head that at length one believes the thought or the conception to be reality. Moreover, if with the thought or the conception there is combined a strong, a passionate, desire, one will come to look upon the said thought or conception as something fated, inevitable, and foreordained—something bound to happen. Whether by this there is connoted something in the nature of a combination of presentiments, or a great effort of will, or a self-annulment of one's true expectations, and so on, I do not know; but, at all events that night saw happen to me (a night which I shall never forget) something in the nature of the miraculous. Although the occurrence can easily be explained by arithmetic, I still believe it to have been a miracle. Yet why did this conviction take such a hold upon me at the time, and remain with me ever since? Previously, I had thought of the idea, not as an occurrence which was ever likely to come about, but as something which NEVER could come about.

The time was a quarter past eleven o'clock when I entered the Casino in such a state of hope (though, at the same time, of agitation) as I had never before experienced. In the gaming-rooms there were still a large number of people, but not half as many as had been present in the morning.

At eleven o'clock there usually remained behind only the real, the desperate gamblers—persons for whom, at spas, there existed nothing beyond roulette, and who went thither for that alone. These gamesters took little note of what was going on around them, and were interested in none of the appurtenances of the season, but played from morning till night, and would have been ready to play through the night until dawn had that been possible. As it was, they used to disperse unwillingly when, at midnight, roulette came to an end. Likewise, as soon as ever roulette was drawing to a close and the head croupier had called "Les trois derniers coups," most of them were ready to stake on the last three rounds all that they had in their pockets—and, for the most part, lost it. For my own part I proceeded towards the table at which the Grandmother had lately sat; and, since the crowd around it was not very large, I soon obtained standing room among the ring of gamblers, while directly in front of me, on the green cloth, I saw marked the word "Passe."

"Passe" was a row of numbers from 19 to 36 inclusive; while a row of numbers from 1 to 18 inclusive was known as "Manque." But what had that to do with me? I had not noticed—I had not so much as heard the numbers upon which the previous coup had fallen, and so took no bearings when I began to play, as, in my place, any SYSTEMATIC gambler would have done. No, I merely extended my stock of twenty ten-gulden pieces, and threw them down upon the space "Passe" which happened to be confronting me.

"Vingt-deux!" called the croupier.

I had won! I staked upon the same again—both my original stake and my winnings.

"Trente-et-un!" called the croupier.

Again I had won, and was now in possession of eighty ten-gulden pieces. Next, I moved the whole eighty on to twelve middle numbers (a stake which, if successful, would bring me in a triple profit, but also involved a risk of two chances to one). The wheel revolved, and stopped at twenty-four. Upon this I was paid out notes and gold until I had by my side a total sum of two thousand gulden.

It was as in a fever that I moved the pile, en bloc, on to the red. Then suddenly I came to myself (though that was the only time during the evening's play when fear cast its cold spell over me, and showed itself in a trembling of the hands and knees). For with horror I had realised that I MUST win, and that upon that stake there depended all my life.

"Rouge!" called the croupier. I drew a long breath, and hot shivers went coursing over my body. I was paid out my winnings in bank-notes—amounting, of course, to a total of four thousand florins, eight hundred gulden (I could still calculate the amounts).

After that, I remember, I again staked two thousand florins upon twelve middle numbers, and lost. Again I staked the whole of my gold, with eight hundred gulden, in notes, and lost. Then madness seemed to come upon me, and seizing my last two thousand florins, I staked them upon twelve of the first numbers—wholly by chance, and at random, and without any sort of reckoning. Upon my doing so there followed a moment of suspense only comparable to that which Madame Blanchard must have experienced when, in Paris, she was descending earthwards from a balloon.

"Quatre!" called the croupier.

Once more, with the addition of my original stake, I was in possession of six thousand florins! Once more I looked around me like a conqueror—once more I feared nothing as I threw down four thousand of these florins upon the black. The croupiers glanced around them, and exchanged a few words; the bystanders murmured expectantly.

The black turned up. After that I do not exactly remember either my calculations or the order of my stakings. I only remember that, as in a dream, I won in one round sixteen thousand florins; that in the three following rounds, I lost twelve thousand; that I moved the remainder (four thousand) on to "Passe" (though quite unconscious of what I was doing—I was merely waiting, as it were, mechanically, and without reflection, for something) and won; and that, finally, four times in succession I lost. Yes, I can remember raking in money by thousands—but most frequently on the twelve, middle numbers, to which I constantly adhered, and which kept appearing in a sort of regular order—first, three or four times running, and then, after an interval of a couple of rounds, in another break of three or four appearances. Sometimes, this astonishing regularity manifested itself in patches; a thing to upset all the calculations of note—taking gamblers who play with a pencil and a memorandum book in their hands Fortune perpetrates some terrible jests at roulette!

Since my entry not more than half an hour could have elapsed. Suddenly a croupier informed me that I had, won thirty thousand florins, as well as that, since the latter was the limit for which, at any one time, the bank could make itself responsible, roulette at that table must close for the night. Accordingly, I caught up my pile of gold, stuffed it into my pocket, and, grasping my sheaf of bank-notes, moved to the table in an adjoining salon where a second game of roulette was in progress. The crowd followed me in a body, and cleared a place for me at the table; after which, I proceeded to stake as before—that is to say, at random and without calculating. What saved me from ruin I do not know.

Of course there were times when fragmentary reckonings DID come flashing into my brain. For instance, there were times when I attached myself for a while to certain figures and coups—though always leaving them, again before long, without knowing what I was doing.

In fact, I cannot have been in possession of all my faculties, for I can remember the croupiers correcting my play more than once, owing to my having made mistakes of the gravest order. My brows were damp with sweat, and my hands were shaking. Also, Poles came around me to proffer their services, but I heeded none of them. Nor did my luck fail me now. Suddenly, there arose around me a loud din of talking and laughter. "Bravo, bravo!" was the general shout, and some people even clapped their hands. I had raked in thirty thousand florins, and again the bank had had to close for the night!

"Go away now, go away now," a voice whispered to me on my right. The person who had spoken to me was a certain Jew of Frankfurt—a man who had been standing beside me the whole while, and occasionally helping me in my play.

"Yes, for God's sake go," whispered a second voice in my left ear. Glancing around, I perceived that the second voice had come from a modestly, plainly dressed lady of rather less than thirty—a woman whose face, though pale and sickly-looking, bore also very evident traces of former beauty. At the moment, I was stuffing the crumpled bank-notes into my pockets and collecting all the gold that was left on the table. Seizing up my last note for five hundred gulden, I contrived to insinuate it, unperceived, into the hand of the pale lady. An overpowering impulse had made me do so, and I remember how her thin little fingers pressed mine in token of her lively gratitude. The whole affair was the work of a moment.

Then, collecting my belongings, I crossed to where trente et quarante was being played—a game which could boast of a more aristocratic public, and was played with cards instead of with a wheel. At this diversion the bank made itself responsible for a hundred thousand thalers as the limit, but the highest stake allowable was, as in roulette, four thousand florins. Although I knew nothing of the game—and I scarcely knew the stakes, except those on black and red—I joined the ring of players, while the rest of the crowd massed itself around me. At this distance of time I cannot remember whether I ever gave a thought to Polina; I seemed only to be conscious of a vague pleasure in seizing and raking in the bank-notes which kept massing themselves in a pile before me.

But, as ever, fortune seemed to be at my back. As though of set purpose, there came to my aid a circumstance which not infrequently repeats itself in gaming. The circumstance is that not infrequently luck attaches itself to, say, the red, and does not leave it for a space of say, ten, or even fifteen, rounds in succession. Three days ago I had heard that, during the previous week there had been a run of twenty-two coups on the red—an occurrence never before known at roulette—so that men spoke of it with astonishment. Naturally enough, many deserted the red after a dozen rounds, and practically no one could now be found to stake upon it. Yet upon the black also—the antithesis of the red—no experienced gambler would stake anything, for the reason that every practised player knows the meaning of "capricious fortune." That is to say, after the sixteenth (or so) success of the red, one would think that the seventeenth coup would inevitably fall upon the black; wherefore, novices would be apt to back the latter in the seventeenth round, and even to double or treble their stakes upon it—only, in the end, to lose.

Yet some whim or other led me, on remarking that the red had come up consecutively for seven times, to attach myself to that colour. Probably this was mostly due to self-conceit, for I wanted to astonish the bystanders with the riskiness of my play. Also, I remember that—oh, strange sensation!—I suddenly, and without any challenge from my own presumption, became obsessed with a DESIRE to take risks. If the spirit has passed through a great many sensations, possibly it can no longer be sated with them, but grows more excited, and demands more sensations, and stronger and stronger ones, until at length it falls exhausted. Certainly, if the rules of the game had permitted even of my staking fifty thousand florins at a time, I should have staked them. All of a sudden I heard exclamations arising that the whole thing was a marvel, since the red was turning up for the fourteenth time!

"Monsieur a gagne cent mille florins," a voice exclaimed beside me.

I awoke to my senses. What? I had won a hundred thousand florins? If so, what more did I need to win? I grasped the banknotes, stuffed them into my pockets, raked in the gold without counting it, and started to leave the Casino. As I passed through the salons people smiled to see my bulging pockets and unsteady gait, for the weight which I was carrying must have amounted to half a pood! Several hands I saw stretched out in my direction, and as I passed I filled them with all the money that I could grasp in my own. At length two Jews stopped me near the exit.

"You are a bold young fellow," one said, "but mind you depart early tomorrow—as early as you can—for if you do not you will lose everything that you have won."

But I did not heed them. The Avenue was so dark that it was barely possible to distinguish one's hand before one's face, while the distance to the hotel was half a verst or so; but I feared neither pickpockets nor highwaymen. Indeed, never since my boyhood have I done that. Also, I cannot remember what I thought about on the way. I only felt a sort of fearful pleasure—the pleasure of success, of conquest, of power (how can I best express it?). Likewise, before me there flitted the image of Polina; and I kept remembering, and reminding myself, that it was to HER I was going, that it was in HER presence I should soon be standing, that it was SHE to whom I should soon be able to relate and show everything. Scarcely once did I recall what she had lately said to me, or the reason why I had left her, or all those varied sensations which I had been experiencing a bare hour and a half ago. No, those sensations seemed to be things of the past, to be things which had righted themselves and grown old, to be things concerning which we needed to trouble ourselves no longer, since, for us, life was about to begin anew. Yet I had just reached the end of the Avenue when there DID come upon me a fear of being robbed or murdered. With each step the fear increased until, in my terror, I almost started to run. Suddenly, as I issued from the Avenue, there burst upon me the lights of the hotel, sparkling with a myriad lamps! Yes, thanks be to God, I had reached home!

Running up to my room, I flung open the door of it. Polina was still on the sofa, with a lighted candle in front of her, and her hands clasped. As I entered she stared at me in astonishment (for, at the moment, I must have presented a strange spectacle). All I did, however, was to halt before her, and fling upon the table my burden of wealth.

XV

I remember, too, how, without moving from her place, or changing her attitude, she gazed into my face.

"I have won two hundred thousand francs!" cried I as I pulled out my last sheaf of bank-notes. The pile of paper currency occupied the whole table. I could not withdraw my eyes from it. Consequently, for a moment or two Polina escaped my mind. Then I set myself to arrange the pile in order, and to sort the notes, and to mass the gold in a separate heap. That done, I left everything where it lay, and proceeded to pace the room with rapid strides as I lost myself in thought. Then I darted to the table once more, and began to recount the money; until all of a sudden, as though I had remembered something, I rushed to the door, and closed and double-locked it. Finally I came to a meditative halt before my little trunk.

"Shall I put the money there until tomorrow?" I asked, turning sharply round to Polina as the recollection of her returned to me.

She was still in her old place—still making not a sound. Yet her eyes had followed every one of my movements. Somehow in her face there was a strange expression—an expression which I did not like. I think that I shall not be wrong if I say that it indicated sheer hatred.

Impulsively I approached her.

"Polina," I said, "here are twenty-five thousand florins—fifty thousand francs, or more. Take them, and tomorrow throw them in De Griers' face."

She returned no answer.

"Or, if you should prefer," I continued, "let me take them to him myself tomorrow—yes, early tomorrow morning. Shall I?"

Then all at once she burst out laughing, and laughed for a long while. With astonishment and a feeling of offence I gazed at her. Her laughter was too like the derisive merriment which she had so often indulged in of late—merriment which had broken forth always at the time of my most passionate explanations. At length she ceased, and frowned at me from under her eyebrows.

"I am NOT going to take your money," she said contemptuously.

"Why not?" I cried. "Why not, Polina?"

"Because I am not in the habit of receiving money for nothing."

"But I am offering it to you as a FRIEND in the same way I would offer you my very life."

Upon this she threw me a long, questioning glance, as though she were seeking to probe me to the depths.

"You are giving too much for me," she remarked with a smile. "The beloved of De Griers is not worth fifty thousand francs."

"Oh Polina, how can you speak so?" I exclaimed reproachfully. "Am I De Griers?"

"You?" she cried with her eyes suddenly flashing. "Why, I HATE you! Yes, yes, I HATE you! I love you no more than I do De Griers."

Then she buried her face in her hands, and relapsed into hysterics. I darted to her side. Somehow I had an intuition of something having happened to her which had nothing to do with myself. She was like a person temporarily insane.

"Buy me, would you, would you? Would you buy me for fifty thousand francs as De Griers did?" she gasped between her convulsive sobs.

I clasped her in my arms, kissed her hands and feet, and fell upon my knees before her.

Presently the hysterical fit passed away, and, laying her hands upon my shoulders, she gazed for a while into my face, as though trying to read it—something I said to her, but it was clear that she did not hear it. Her face looked so dark and despondent that I began to fear for her reason. At length she drew me towards herself—a trustful smile playing over her features; and then, as suddenly, she pushed me away again as she eyed me dimly.

Finally she threw herself upon me in an embrace.

"You love me?" she said. "DO you?—you who were willing even to quarrel with the Baron at my bidding?"

Then she laughed—laughed as though something dear, but laughable, had recurred to her memory. Yes, she laughed and wept at the same time. What was I to do? I was like a man in a fever. I remember that she began to say something to me—though WHAT I do not know, since she spoke with a feverish lisp, as though she were trying to tell me something very quickly. At intervals, too, she would break off into the smile which I was beginning to dread. "No, no!" she kept repeating. "YOU are my dear one; YOU are the man I trust." Again she laid her hands upon my shoulders, and again she gazed at me as she reiterated: "You love me, you love me? Will you ALWAYS love me?" I could not take my eyes off her. Never before had I seen her in this mood of humility and affection. True, the mood was the outcome of hysteria; but—! All of a sudden she noticed my ardent gaze, and smiled slightly. The next moment, for no apparent reason, she began to talk of Astley.

She continued talking and talking about him, but I could not make out all she said—more particularly when she was endeavouring to tell me of something or other which had happened recently. On the whole, she appeared to be laughing at Astley, for she kept repeating that he was waiting for her, and did I know whether, even at that moment, he was not standing beneath the window? "Yes, yes, he is there," she said. "Open the window, and see if he is not." She pushed me in that direction; yet, no sooner did I make a movement to obey her behest than she burst into laughter, and I remained beside her, and she embraced me.

"Shall we go away tomorrow?" presently she asked, as though some disturbing thought had recurred to her recollection. "How would it be if we were to try and overtake Grandmamma? I think we should do so at Berlin. And what think you she would have to say to us when we caught her up, and her eyes first lit upon us? What, too, about Mr. Astley? HE would not leap from the Shlangenberg for my sake! No! Of that I am very sure!"—and she laughed. "Do you know where he is going next year? He says he intends to go to the North Pole for scientific investigations, and has invited me to go with him! Ha, ha, ha! He also says that we Russians know nothing, can do nothing, without European help. But he is a good fellow all the same. For instance, he does not blame the General in the matter, but declares that Mlle. Blanche—that love—But no; I do not know, I do not know." She stopped suddenly, as though she had said her say, and was feeling bewildered. "What poor creatures these people are. How sorry I am for them, and for Grandmamma! But when are you going to kill De Griers? Surely you do not intend actually to murder him? You fool! Do you suppose that I should ALLOW you to fight De Griers? Nor shall you kill the Baron." Here she burst out laughing. "How absurd you looked when you were talking to the Burmergelms! I was watching you all the time—watching you from where I was sitting. And how unwilling you were to go when I sent you! Oh, how I laughed and laughed!"

Then she kissed and embraced me again; again she pressed her face to mine with tender passion. Yet I neither saw nor heard her, for my head was in a whirl....

It must have been about seven o'clock in the morning when I awoke. Daylight had come, and Polina was sitting by my side—a strange expression on her face, as though she had seen a vision and was unable to collect her thoughts. She too had just awoken, and was now staring at the money on the table. My head ached; it felt heavy. I attempted to take Polina's hand, but she pushed me from her, and leapt from the sofa. The dawn was full of mist, for rain had fallen, yet she moved to the window, opened it, and, leaning her elbows upon the window-sill, thrust out her head and shoulders to take the air. In this position did she remain for several minutes, without ever looking round at me, or listening to what I was saying. Into my head there came the uneasy thought: What is to happen now? How is it all to end? Suddenly Polina rose from the window, approached the table, and, looking at me with an expression of infinite aversion, said with lips which quivered with anger:

"Well? Are you going to hand me over my fifty thousand francs?"

"Polina, you say that AGAIN, AGAIN?" I exclaimed.

"You have changed your mind, then? Ha, ha, ha! You are sorry you ever promised them?"

On the table where, the previous night, I had counted the money there still was lying the packet of twenty five thousand florins. I handed it to her.

"The francs are mine, then, are they? They are mine?" she inquired viciously as she balanced the money in her hands.

"Yes; they have ALWAYS been yours," I said.

"Then TAKE your fifty thousand francs!" and she hurled them full in my face. The packet burst as she did so, and the floor became strewed with bank-notes. The instant that the deed was done she rushed from the room.

At that moment she cannot have been in her right mind; yet, what was the cause of her temporary aberration I cannot say. For a month past she had been unwell. Yet what had brought about this PRESENT condition of mind, above all things, this outburst? Had it come of wounded pride? Had it come of despair over her decision to come to me? Had it come of the fact that, presuming too much on my good fortune, I had seemed to be intending to desert her (even as De Griers had done) when once I had given her the fifty thousand francs? But, on my honour, I had never cherished any such intention. What was at fault, I think, was her own pride, which kept urging her not to trust me, but, rather, to insult me—even though she had not realised the fact. In her eyes I corresponded to De Griers, and therefore had been condemned for a fault not wholly my own. Her mood of late had been a sort of delirium, a sort of light-headedness—that I knew full well; yet, never had I sufficiently taken it into consideration. Perhaps she would not pardon me now? Ah, but this was THE PRESENT. What about the future? Her delirium and sickness were not likely to make her forget what she had done in bringing me De Griers' letter. No, she must have known what she was doing when she brought it.

Somehow I contrived to stuff the pile of notes and gold under the bed, to cover them over, and then to leave the room some ten minutes after Polina. I felt sure that she had returned to her own room; wherefore, I intended quietly to follow her, and to ask the nursemaid aid who opened the door how her mistress was. Judge, therefore, of my surprise when, meeting the domestic on the stairs, she informed me that Polina had not yet returned, and that she (the domestic) was at that moment on her way to my room in quest of her!

"Mlle. left me but ten minutes ago," I said. "What can have become of her?" The nursemaid looked at me reproachfully.

Already sundry rumours were flying about the hotel. Both in the office of the commissionaire and in that of the landlord it was whispered that, at seven o'clock that morning, the Fraulein had left the hotel, and set off, despite the rain, in the direction of the Hotel d'Angleterre. From words and hints let fall I could see that the fact of Polina having spent the night in my room was now public property. Also, sundry rumours were circulating concerning the General's family affairs. It was known that last night he had gone out of his mind, and paraded the hotel in tears; also, that the old lady who had arrived was his mother, and that she had come from Russia on purpose to forbid her son's marriage with Mlle. de Cominges, as well as to cut him out of her will if he should disobey her; also that, because he had disobeyed her, she had squandered all her money at roulette, in order to have nothing more to leave to him. "Oh, these Russians!" exclaimed the landlord, with an angry toss of the head, while the bystanders laughed and the clerk betook himself to his accounts. Also, every one had learnt about my winnings; Karl, the corridor lacquey, was the first to congratulate me. But with these folk I had nothing to do. My business was to set off at full speed to the Hotel d'Angleterre.

As yet it was early for Mr. Astley to receive visitors; but, as soon as he learnt that it was I who had arrived, he came out into the corridor to meet me, and stood looking at me in silence with his steel-grey eyes as he waited to hear what I had to say. I inquired after Polina.

"She is ill," he replied, still looking at me with his direct, unwavering glance.

"And she is in your rooms."

"Yes, she is in my rooms."

"Then you are minded to keep her there?"

"Yes, I am minded to keep her there."

"But, Mr. Astley, that will raise a scandal. It ought not to be allowed. Besides, she is very ill. Perhaps you had not remarked that?"

"Yes, I have. It was I who told you about it. Had she not been ill, she would not have gone and spent the night with you."

"Then you know all about it?"

"Yes; for last night she was to have accompanied me to the house of a relative of mine. Unfortunately, being ill, she made a mistake, and went to your rooms instead."

"Indeed? Then I wish you joy, Mr. Astley. Apropos, you have reminded me of something. Were you beneath my window last night? Every moment Mlle. Polina kept telling me to open the window and see if you were there; after which she always smiled."

"Indeed? No, I was not there; but I was waiting in the corridor, and walking about the hotel."

"She ought to see a doctor, you know, Mr. Astley."

"Yes, she ought. I have sent for one, and, if she dies, I shall hold you responsible."

This surprised me.

"Pardon me," I replied, "but what do you mean?"

"Never mind. Tell me if it is true that, last night, you won two hundred thousand thalers?"

"No; I won a hundred thousand florins."

"Good heavens! Then I suppose you will be off to Paris this morning?

"Why?"

"Because all Russians who have grown rich go to Paris," explained Astley, as though he had read the fact in a book.

"But what could I do in Paris in summer time?—I LOVE her, Mr. Astley! Surely you know that?"

"Indeed? I am sure that you do NOT. Moreover, if you were to stay here, you would lose everything that you possess, and have nothing left with which to pay your expenses in Paris. Well, good-bye now. I feel sure that today will see you gone from here."

"Good-bye. But I am NOT going to Paris. Likewise—pardon me—what is to become of this family? I mean that the affair of the General and Mlle. Polina will soon be all over the town."

"I daresay; yet, I hardly suppose that that will break the General's heart. Moreover, Mlle. Polina has a perfect right to live where she chooses. In short, we may say that, as a family, this family has ceased to exist."

I departed, and found myself smiling at the Englishman's strange assurance that I should soon be leaving for Paris. "I suppose he means to shoot me in a duel, should Polina die. Yes, that is what he intends to do." Now, although I was honestly sorry for Polina, it is a fact that, from the moment when, the previous night, I had approached the gaming-table, and begun to rake in the packets of bank-notes, my love for her had entered upon a new plane. Yes, I can say that now; although, at the time, I was barely conscious of it. Was I, then, at heart a gambler? Did I, after all, love Polina not so very much? No, no! As God is my witness, I loved her! Even when I was returning home from Mr. Astley's my suffering was genuine, and my self-reproach sincere. But presently I was to go through an exceedingly strange and ugly experience.

I was proceeding to the General's rooms when I heard a door near me open, and a voice call me by name. It was Mlle.'s mother, the Widow de Cominges who was inviting me, in her daughter's name, to enter.

I did so; whereupon, I heard a laugh and a little cry proceed from the bedroom (the pair occupied a suite of two apartments), where Mlle. Blanche was just arising.

"Ah, c'est lui! Viens, donc, bete! Is it true that you have won a mountain of gold and silver? J'aimerais mieux l'or."

"Yes," I replied with a smile.

"How much?"

"A hundred thousand florins."

"Bibi, comme tu es bete! Come in here, for I can't hear you where you are now. Nous ferons bombance, n'est-ce pas?"

Entering her room, I found her lolling under a pink satin coverlet, and revealing a pair of swarthy, wonderfully healthy shoulders—shoulders such as one sees in dreams—shoulders covered over with a white cambric nightgown which, trimmed with lace, stood out, in striking relief, against the darkness of her skin.

"Mon fils, as-tu du coeur?" she cried when she saw me, and then giggled. Her laugh had always been a very cheerful one, and at times it even sounded sincere.

"Tout autre—" I began, paraphrasing Corneille.

"See here," she prattled on. "Please search for my stockings, and help me to dress. Aussi, si tu n'es pas trop bete je te prends a Paris. I am just off, let me tell you."

"This moment?"

"In half an hour."

True enough, everything stood ready-packed—trunks, portmanteaux, and all. Coffee had long been served.

"Eh bien, tu verras Paris. Dis donc, qu'est-ce que c'est qu'un 'utchitel'? Tu etais bien bete quand tu etais 'utchitel.' Where are my stockings? Please help me to dress."

And she lifted up a really ravishing foot—small, swarthy, and not misshapen like the majority of feet which look dainty only in bottines. I laughed, and started to draw on to the foot a silk stocking, while Mlle. Blanche sat on the edge of the bed and chattered.

"Eh bien, que feras-tu si je te prends avec moi? First of all I must have fifty thousand francs, and you shall give them to me at Frankfurt. Then we will go on to Paris, where we will live together, et je te ferai voir des etoiles en plein jour. Yes, you shall see such women as your eyes have never lit upon."

"Stop a moment. If I were to give you those fifty thousand francs, what should I have left for myself?"

"Another hundred thousand francs, please to remember. Besides, I could live with you in your rooms for a month, or even for two; or even for longer. But it would not take us more than two months to get through fifty thousand francs; for, look you, je suis bonne enfante, et tu verras des etoiles, you may be sure."

"What? You mean to say that we should spend the whole in two months?"

"Certainly. Does that surprise you very much? Ah, vil esclave! Why, one month of that life would be better than all your previous existence. One month—et apres, le deluge! Mais tu ne peux comprendre. Va! Away, away! You are not worth it.—Ah, que fais-tu?"

For, while drawing on the other stocking, I had felt constrained to kiss her. Immediately she shrunk back, kicked me in the face with her toes, and turned me neck and prop out of the room.

"Eh bien, mon 'utchitel'," she called after me, "je t'attends, si tu veux. I start in a quarter of an hour's time."

I returned to my own room with my head in a whirl. It was not my fault that Polina had thrown a packet in my face, and preferred Mr. Astley to myself. A few bank-notes were still fluttering about the floor, and I picked them up. At that moment the door opened, and the landlord appeared—a person who, until now, had never bestowed upon me so much as a glance. He had come to know if I would prefer to move to a lower floor—to a suite which had just been tenanted by Count V.

For a moment I reflected.

"No!" I shouted. "My account, please, for in ten minutes I shall be gone."

"To Paris, to Paris!" I added to myself. "Every man of birth must make her acquaintance."

Within a quarter of an hour all three of us were seated in a family compartment—Mlle. Blanche, the Widow de Cominges, and myself. Mlle. kept laughing hysterically as she looked at me, and Madame re-echoed her; but I did not feel so cheerful. My life had broken in two, and yesterday had infected me with a habit of staking my all upon a card. Although it might be that I had failed to win my stake, that I had lost my senses, that I desired nothing better, I felt that the scene was to be changed only FOR A TIME. "Within a month from now," I kept thinking to myself, "I shall be back again in Roulettenberg; and THEN I mean to have it out with you, Mr. Astley!" Yes, as now I look back at things, I remember that I felt greatly depressed, despite the absurd gigglings of the egregious Blanche.

"What is the matter with you? How dull you are!" she cried at length as she interrupted her laughter to take me seriously to task.

"Come, come! We are going to spend your two hundred thousand francs for you, et tu seras heureux comme un petit roi. I myself will tie your tie for you, and introduce you to Hortense. And when we have spent your money you shall return here, and break the bank again. What did those two Jews tell you?—that the thing most needed is daring, and that you possess it? Consequently, this is not the first time that you will be hurrying to Paris with money in your pocket. Quant ... moi, je veux cinquante mille francs de rente, et alors."

"But what about the General?" I interrupted.

"The General? You know well enough that at about this hour every day he goes to buy me a bouquet. On this occasion, I took care to tell him that he must hunt for the choicest of flowers; and when he returns home, the poor fellow will find the bird flown. Possibly he may take wing in pursuit—ha, ha, ha! And if so, I shall not be sorry, for he could be useful to me in Paris, and Mr. Astley will pay his debts here."

In this manner did I depart for the Gay City.

XVI

Of Paris what am I to say? The whole proceeding was a delirium, a madness. I spent a little over three weeks there, and, during that time, saw my hundred thousand francs come to an end. I speak only of the ONE hundred thousand francs, for the other hundred thousand I gave to Mlle. Blanche in pure cash. That is to say, I handed her fifty thousand francs at Frankfurt, and, three days later (in Paris), advanced her another fifty thousand on note of hand. Nevertheless, a week had not elapsed ere she came to me for more money. "Et les cent mille francs qui nous restent," she added, "tu les mangeras avec moi, mon utchitel." Yes, she always called me her "utchitel." A person more economical, grasping, and mean than Mlle. Blanche one could not imagine. But this was only as regards HER OWN money. MY hundred thousand francs (as she explained to me later) she needed to set up her establishment in Paris, "so that once and for all I may be on a decent footing, and proof against any stones which may be thrown at me—at all events for a long time to come." Nevertheless, I saw nothing of those hundred thousand francs, for my own purse (which she inspected daily) never managed to amass in it more than a hundred francs at a time; and, generally the sum did not reach even that figure.

"What do you want with money?" she would say to me with air of absolute simplicity; and I never disputed the point. Nevertheless, though she fitted out her flat very badly with the money, the fact did not prevent her from saying when, later, she was showing me over the rooms of her new abode: "See what care and taste can do with the most wretched of means!" However, her "wretchedness" had cost fifty thousand francs, while with the remaining fifty thousand she purchased a carriage and horses.

Also, we gave a couple of balls—evening parties attended by Hortense and Lisette and Cleopatre, who were women remarkable both for the number of their liaisons and (though only in some cases) for their good looks. At these reunions I had to play the part of host—to meet and entertain fat mercantile parvenus who were impossible by reason of their rudeness and braggadocio, colonels of various kinds, hungry authors, and journalistic hacks—all of whom disported themselves in fashionable tailcoats and pale yellow gloves, and displayed such an aggregate of conceit and gasconade as would be unthinkable even in St. Petersburg—which is saying a great deal! They used to try to make fun of me, but I would console myself by drinking champagne and then lolling in a retiring-room. Nevertheless, I found it deadly work. "C'est un utchitel," Blanche would say of me, "qui a gagne deux cent mille francs, and but for me, would have had not a notion how to spend them. Presently he will have to return to his tutoring. Does any one know of a vacant post? You know, one must do something for him."

I had the more frequent recourse to champagne in that I constantly felt depressed and bored, owing to the fact that I was living in the most bourgeois commercial milieu imaginable—a milieu wherein every sou was counted and grudged. Indeed, two weeks had not elapsed before I perceived that Blanche had no real affection for me, even though she dressed me in elegant clothes, and herself tied my tie each day. In short, she utterly despised me. But that caused me no concern. Blase and inert, I spent my evenings generally at the Chateau des Fleurs, where I would get fuddled and then dance the cancan (which, in that establishment, was a very indecent performance) with eclat. At length, the time came when Blanche had drained my purse dry. She had conceived an idea that, during the term of our residence together, it would be well if I were always to walk behind her with a paper and pencil, in order to jot down exactly what she spent, what she had saved, what she was paying out, and what she was laying by. Well, of course I could not fail to be aware that this would entail a battle over every ten francs; so, although for every possible objection that I might make she had prepared a suitable answer, she soon saw that I made no objections, and therefore, had to start disputes herself. That is to say, she would burst out into tirades which were met only with silence as I lolled on a sofa and stared fixedly at the ceiling. This greatly surprised her. At first she imagined that it was due merely to the fact that I was a fool, "un utchitel"; wherefore she would break off her harangue in the belief that, being too stupid to understand, I was a hopeless case. Then she would leave the room, but return ten minutes later to resume the contest. This continued throughout her squandering of my money—a squandering altogether out of proportion to our means. An example is the way in which she changed her first pair of horses for a pair which cost sixteen thousand francs.

"Bibi," she said on the latter occasion as she approached me, "surely you are not angry?"

"No-o-o: I am merely tired," was my reply as I pushed her from me. This seemed to her so curious that straightway she seated herself by my side.

"You see," she went on, "I decided to spend so much upon these horses only because I can easily sell them again. They would go at any time for TWENTY thousand francs."

"Yes, yes. They are splendid horses, and you have got a splendid turn-out. I am quite content. Let me hear no more of the matter."

"Then you are not angry?"

"No. Why should I be? You are wise to provide yourself with what you need, for it will all come in handy in the future. Yes, I quite see the necessity of your establishing yourself on a good basis, for without it you will never earn your million. My hundred thousand francs I look upon merely as a beginning—as a mere drop in the bucket."

Blanche, who had by no means expected such declarations from me, but, rather, an uproar and protests, was rather taken aback.

"Well, well, what a man you are!" she exclaimed. "Mais tu as l'esprit pour comprendre. Sais-tu, mon garcon, although you are a tutor, you ought to have been born a prince. Are you not sorry that your money should be going so quickly?"

"No. The quicker it goes the better."

"Mais—sais-tu-mais dis donc, are you really rich? Mais sais-tu, you have too much contempt for money. Qu'est-ce que tu feras apres, dis donc?"

"Apres I shall go to Homburg, and win another hundred thousand francs."

"Oui, oui, c'est ca, c'est magnifique! Ah, I know you will win them, and bring them to me when you have done so. Dis donc—you will end by making me love you. Since you are what you are, I mean to love you all the time, and never to be unfaithful to you. You see, I have not loved you before parce que je croyais que tu n'es qu'un utchitel (quelque chose comme un lacquais, n'est-ce pas?) Yet all the time I have been true to you, parce que je suis bonne fille."

"You lie!" I interrupted. "Did I not see you, the other day, with Albert—with that black-jowled officer?"

"Oh, oh! Mais tu es—"

"Yes, you are lying right enough. But what makes you suppose that I should be angry? Rubbish! Il faut que jeunesse se passe. Even if that officer were here now, I should refrain from putting him out of the room if I thought you really cared for him. Only, mind you, do not give him any of my money. You hear?"

"You say, do you, that you would not be angry? Mais tu es un vrai philosophe, sais-tu? Oui, un vrai philosophe! Eh bien, je t'aimerai, je t'aimerai. Tu verras-tu seras content."

True enough, from that time onward she seemed to attach herself only to me, and in this manner we spent our last ten days together. The promised "etoiles" I did not see, but in other respects she, to a certain extent, kept her word. Moreover, she introduced me to Hortense, who was a remarkable woman in her way, and known among us as Therese Philosophe.

But I need not enlarge further, for to do so would require a story to itself, and entail a colouring which I am loth to impart to the present narrative. The point is that with all my faculties I desired the episode to come to an end as speedily as possible. Unfortunately, our hundred thousand francs lasted us, as I have said, for very nearly a month—which greatly surprised me. At all events, Blanche bought herself articles to the tune of eighty thousand francs, and the rest sufficed just to meet our expenses of living. Towards the close of the affair, Blanche grew almost frank with me (at least, she scarcely lied to me at all)—declaring, amongst other things, that none of the debts which she had been obliged to incur were going to fall upon my head. "I have purposely refrained from making you responsible for my bills or borrowings," she said, "for the reason that I am sorry for you. Any other woman in my place would have done so, and have let you go to prison. See, then, how much I love you, and how good-hearted I am! Think, too, what this accursed marriage with the General is going to cost me!"

True enough, the marriage took place. It did so at the close of our month together, and I am bound to suppose that it was upon the ceremony that the last remnants of my money were spent. With it the episode—that is to say, my sojourn with the Frenchwoman—came to an end, and I formally retired from the scene.

It happened thus: A week after we had taken up our abode in Paris there arrived thither the General. He came straight to see us, and thenceforward lived with us practically as our guest, though he had a flat of his own as well.

Blanche met him with merry badinage and laughter, and even threw her arms around him. In fact, she managed it so that he had to follow everywhere in her train—whether when promenading on the Boulevards, or when driving, or when going to the theatre, or when paying calls; and this use which she made of him quite satisfied the General. Still of imposing appearance and presence, as well as of fair height, he had a dyed moustache and whiskers (he had formerly been in the cuirassiers), and a handsome, though a somewhat wrinkled, face. Also, his manners were excellent, and he could carry a frockcoat well—the more so since, in Paris, he took to wearing his orders. To promenade the Boulevards with such a man was not only a thing possible, but also, so to speak, a thing advisable, and with this programme the good but foolish General had not a fault to find. The truth is that he had never counted upon this programme when he came to Paris to seek us out. On that occasion he had made his appearance nearly shaking with terror, for he had supposed that Blanche would at once raise an outcry, and have him put from the door; wherefore, he was the more enraptured at the turn that things had taken, and spent the month in a state of senseless ecstasy. Already I had learnt that, after our unexpected departure from Roulettenberg, he had had a sort of a fit—that he had fallen into a swoon, and spent a week in a species of garrulous delirium. Doctors had been summoned to him, but he had broken away from them, and suddenly taken a train to Paris. Of course Blanche's reception of him had acted as the best of all possible cures, but for long enough he carried the marks of his affliction, despite his present condition of rapture and delight. To think clearly, or even to engage in any serious conversation, had now become impossible for him; he could only ejaculate after each word "Hm!" and then nod his head in confirmation. Sometimes, also, he would laugh, but only in a nervous, hysterical sort of a fashion; while at other times he would sit for hours looking as black as night, with his heavy eyebrows knitted. Of much that went on he remained wholly oblivious, for he grew extremely absent-minded, and took to talking to himself. Only Blanche could awake him to any semblance of life. His fits of depression and moodiness in corners always meant either that he had not seen her for some while, or that she had gone out without taking him with her, or that she had omitted to caress him before departing. When in this condition, he would refuse to say what he wanted—nor had he the least idea that he was thus sulking and moping. Next, after remaining in this condition for an hour or two (this I remarked on two occasions when Blanche had gone out for the day—probably to see Albert), he would begin to look about him, and to grow uneasy, and to hurry about with an air as though he had suddenly remembered something, and must try and find it; after which, not perceiving the object of his search, nor succeeding in recalling what that object had been, he would as suddenly relapse into oblivion, and continue so until the reappearance of Blanche—merry, wanton, half-dressed, and laughing her strident laugh as she approached to pet him, and even to kiss him (though the latter reward he seldom received). Once, he was so overjoyed at her doing so that he burst into tears. Even I myself was surprised.

From the first moment of his arrival in Paris, Blanche set herself to plead with me on his behalf; and at such times she even rose to heights of eloquence—saying that it was for ME she had abandoned him, though she had almost become his betrothed and promised to become so; that it was for HER sake he had deserted his family; that, having been in his service, I ought to remember the fact, and to feel ashamed. To all this I would say nothing, however much she chattered on; until at length I would burst out laughing, and the incident would come to an end (at first, as I have said, she had thought me a fool, but since she had come to deem me a man of sense and sensibility). In short, I had the happiness of calling her better nature into play; for though, at first, I had not deemed her so, she was, in reality, a kind-hearted woman after her own fashion. "You are good and clever," she said to me towards the finish, "and my one regret is that you are also so wrong-headed. You will NEVER be a rich man!"

"Un vrai Russe—un Kalmuk" she usually called me.

Several times she sent me to give the General an airing in the streets, even as she might have done with a lacquey and her spaniel; but, I preferred to take him to the theatre, to the Bal Mabille, and to restaurants. For this purpose she usually allowed me some money, though the General had a little of his own, and enjoyed taking out his purse before strangers. Once I had to use actual force to prevent him from buying a phaeton at a price of seven hundred francs, after a vehicle had caught his fancy in the Palais Royal as seeming to be a desirable present for Blanche. What could SHE have done with a seven-hundred-franc phaeton?—and the General possessed in the world but a thousand francs! The origin even of those francs I could never determine, but imagined them to have emanated from Mr. Astley—the more so since the latter had paid the family's hotel bill. As for what view the General took of myself, I think that he never divined the footing on which I stood with Blanche. True, he had heard, in a dim sort of way, that I had won a good deal of money; but more probably he supposed me to be acting as secretary—or even as a kind of servant—to his inamorata. At all events, he continued to address me, in his old haughty style, as my superior. At times he even took it upon himself to scold me. One morning in particular, he started to sneer at me over our matutinal coffee. Though not a man prone to take offence, he suddenly, and for some reason of which to this day I am ignorant, fell out with me. Of course even he himself did not know the reason. To put things shortly, he began a speech which had neither beginning nor ending, and cried out, a batons rompus, that I was a boy whom he would soon put to rights—and so forth, and so forth. Yet no one could understand what he was saying, and at length Blanche exploded in a burst of laughter. Finally something appeased him, and he was taken out for his walk. More than once, however, I noticed that his depression was growing upon him; that he seemed to be feeling the want of somebody or something; that, despite Blanche's presence, he was missing some person in particular. Twice, on these occasions, did he plunge into a conversation with me, though he could not make himself intelligible, and only went on rambling about the service, his late wife, his home, and his property. Every now and then, also, some particular word would please him; whereupon he would repeat it a hundred times in the day—even though the word happened to express neither his thoughts nor his feelings. Again, I would try to get him to talk about his children, but always he cut me short in his old snappish way, and passed to another subject. "Yes, yes—my children," was all that I could extract from him. "Yes, you are right in what you have said about them." Only once did he disclose his real feelings. That was when we were taking him to the theatre, and suddenly he exclaimed: "My unfortunate children! Yes, sir, they are unfortunate children." Once, too, when I chanced to mention Polina, he grew quite bitter against her. "She is an ungrateful woman!" he exclaimed. "She is a bad and ungrateful woman! She has broken up a family. If there were laws here, I would have her impaled. Yes, I would." As for De Griers, the General would not have his name mentioned. "He has ruined me," he would say. "He has robbed me, and cut my throat. For two years he was a perfect nightmare to me. For months at a time he never left me in my dreams. Do not speak of him again."

It was now clear to me that Blanche and he were on the point of coming to terms; yet, true to my usual custom, I said nothing. At length, Blanche took the initiative in explaining matters. She did so a week before we parted.

"Il a du chance," she prattled, "for the Grandmother is now REALLY ill, and therefore, bound to die. Mr. Astley has just sent a telegram to say so, and you will agree with me that the General is likely to be her heir. Even if he should not be so, he will not come amiss, since, in the first place, he has his pension, and, in the second place, he will be content to live in a back room; whereas I shall be Madame General, and get into a good circle of society" (she was always thinking of this) "and become a Russian chatelaine. Yes, I shall have a mansion of my own, and peasants, and a million of money at my back."

"But, suppose he should prove jealous? He might demand all sorts of things, you know. Do you follow me?"

"Oh, dear no! How ridiculous that would be of him! Besides, I have taken measures to prevent it. You need not be alarmed. That is to say, I have induced him to sign notes of hand in Albert's name. Consequently, at any time I could get him punished. Isn't he ridiculous?"

"Very well, then. Marry him."

And, in truth, she did so—though the marriage was a family one only, and involved no pomp or ceremony. In fact, she invited to the nuptials none but Albert and a few other friends. Hortense, Cleopatre, and the rest she kept firmly at a distance. As for the bridegroom, he took a great interest in his new position. Blanche herself tied his tie, and Blanche herself pomaded him—with the result that, in his frockcoat and white waistcoat, he looked quite comme il faut.

"Il est, pourtant, TRES comme il faut," Blanche remarked when she issued from his room, as though the idea that he was "TRES comme il faut" had impressed even her. For myself, I had so little knowledge of the minor details of the affair, and took part in it so much as a supine spectator, that I have forgotten most of what passed on this occasion. I only remember that Blanche and the Widow figured at it, not as "de Cominges," but as "du Placet." Why they had hitherto been "de Cominges" I do not know—I only know that this entirely satisfied the General, that he liked the name "du Placet" even better than he had liked the name "de Cominges." On the morning of the wedding, he paced the salon in his gala attire and kept repeating to himself with an air of great gravity and importance: "Mlle. Blanche du Placet! Mlle. Blanche du Placet, du Placet!" He beamed with satisfaction as he did so. Both in the church and at the wedding breakfast he remained not only pleased and contented, but even proud. She too underwent a change, for now she assumed an air of added dignity.

"I must behave altogether differently," she confided to me with a serious air. "Yet, mark you, there is a tiresome circumstance of which I had never before thought—which is, how best to pronounce my new family name. Zagorianski, Zagozianski, Madame la Generale de Sago, Madame la Generale de Fourteen Consonants—oh these infernal Russian names! The LAST of them would be the best to use, don't you think?"

At length the time had come for us to part, and Blanche, the egregious Blanche, shed real tears as she took her leave of me. "Tu etais bon enfant" she said with a sob. "Je te croyais bete et tu en avais l'air, but it suited you." Then, having given me a final handshake, she exclaimed, "Attends!"; whereafter, running into her boudoir, she brought me thence two thousand-franc notes. I could scarcely believe my eyes! "They may come in handy for you," she explained, "for, though you are a very learned tutor, you are a very stupid man. More than two thousand francs, however, I am not going to give you, for the reason that, if I did so, you would gamble them all away. Now good-bye. Nous serons toujours bons amis, and if you win again, do not fail to come to me, et tu seras heureux."

I myself had still five hundred francs left, as well as a watch worth a thousand francs, a few diamond studs, and so on. Consequently, I could subsist for quite a length of time without particularly bestirring myself. Purposely I have taken up my abode where I am now partly to pull myself together, and partly to wait for Mr. Astley, who, I have learnt, will soon be here for a day or so on business. Yes, I know that, and then—and then I shall go to Homburg. But to Roulettenberg I shall not go until next year, for they say it is bad to try one's luck twice in succession at a table. Moreover, Homburg is where the best play is carried on.

XVII

It is a year and eight months since I last looked at these notes of mine. I do so now only because, being overwhelmed with depression, I wish to distract my mind by reading them through at random. I left them off at the point where I was just going to Homburg. My God, with what a light heart (comparatively speaking) did I write the concluding lines!—though it may be not so much with a light heart, as with a measure of self-confidence and unquenchable hope. At that time had I any doubts of myself? Yet behold me now. Scarcely a year and a half have passed, yet I am in a worse position than the meanest beggar. But what is a beggar? A fig for beggary! I have ruined myself—that is all. Nor is there anything with which I can compare myself; there is no moral which it would be of any use for you to read to me. At the present moment nothing could well be more incongruous than a moral. Oh, you self-satisfied persons who, in your unctuous pride, are forever ready to mouth your maxims—if only you knew how fully I myself comprehend the sordidness of my present state, you would not trouble to wag your tongues at me! What could you say to me that I do not already know? Well, wherein lies my difficulty? It lies in the fact that by a single turn of a roulette wheel everything for me, has become changed. Yet, had things befallen otherwise, these moralists would have been among the first (yes, I feel persuaded of it) to approach me with friendly jests and congratulations. Yes, they would never have turned from me as they are doing now! A fig for all of them! What am I? I am zero—nothing. What shall I be tomorrow? I may be risen from the dead, and have begun life anew. For still, I may discover the man in myself, if only my manhood has not become utterly shattered.

I went, I say, to Homburg, but afterwards went also to Roulettenberg, as well as to Spa and Baden; in which latter place, for a time, I acted as valet to a certain rascal of a Privy Councillor, by name Heintze, who until lately was also my master here. Yes, for five months I lived my life with lacqueys! That was just after I had come out of Roulettenberg prison, where I had lain for a small debt which I owed. Out of that prison I was bailed by—by whom? By Mr. Astley? By Polina? I do not know. At all events, the debt was paid to the tune of two hundred thalers, and I sallied forth a free man. But what was I to do with myself? In my dilemma I had recourse to this Heintze, who was a young scapegrace, and the sort of man who could speak and write three languages. At first I acted as his secretary, at a salary of thirty gulden a month, but afterwards I became his lacquey, for the reason that he could not afford to keep a secretary—only an unpaid servant. I had nothing else to turn to, so I remained with him, and allowed myself to become his flunkey. But by stinting myself in meat and drink I saved, during my five months of service, some seventy gulden; and one evening, when we were at Baden, I told him that I wished to resign my post, and then hastened to betake myself to roulette.

Oh, how my heart beat as I did so! No, it was not the money that I valued—what I wanted was to make all this mob of Heintzes, hotel proprietors, and fine ladies of Baden talk about me, recount my story, wonder at me, extol my doings, and worship my winnings. True, these were childish fancies and aspirations, but who knows but that I might meet Polina, and be able to tell her everything, and see her look of surprise at the fact that I had overcome so many adverse strokes of fortune. No, I had no desire for money for its own sake, for I was perfectly well aware that I should only squander it upon some new Blanche, and spend another three weeks in Paris after buying a pair of horses which had cost sixteen thousand francs. No, I never believed myself to be a hoarder; in fact, I knew only too well that I was a spendthrift. And already, with a sort of fear, a sort of sinking in my heart, I could hear the cries of the croupiers—"Trente et un, rouge, impair et passe," "Quarte, noir, pair et manque." How greedily I gazed upon the gaming-table, with its scattered louis d'or, ten-gulden pieces, and thalers; upon the streams of gold as they issued from the croupier's hands, and piled themselves up into heaps of gold scintillating as fire; upon the ell—long rolls of silver lying around the croupier. Even at a distance of two rooms I could hear the chink of that money—so much so that I nearly fell into convulsions.

Ah, the evening when I took those seventy gulden to the gaming table was a memorable one for me. I began by staking ten gulden upon passe. For passe I had always had a sort of predilection, yet I lost my stake upon it. This left me with sixty gulden in silver. After a moment's thought I selected zero—beginning by staking five gulden at a time. Twice I lost, but the third round suddenly brought up the desired coup. I could almost have died with joy as I received my one hundred and seventy-five gulden. Indeed, I have been less pleased when, in former times, I have won a hundred thousand gulden. Losing no time, I staked another hundred gulden upon the red, and won; two hundred upon the red, and won; four hundred upon the black, and won; eight hundred upon manque, and won. Thus, with the addition of the remainder of my original capital, I found myself possessed, within five minutes, of seventeen hundred gulden. Ah, at such moments one forgets both oneself and one's former failures! This I had gained by risking my very life. I had dared so to risk, and behold, again I was a member of mankind!

61

I went and hired a room, I shut myself up in it, and sat counting my money until three o'clock in the morning. To think that when I awoke on the morrow, I was no lacquey! I decided to leave at once for Homburg. There I should neither have to serve as a footman nor to lie in prison. Half an hour before starting, I went and ventured a couple of stakes—no more; with the result that, in all, I lost fifteen hundred florins. Nevertheless, I proceeded to Homburg, and have now been there for a month.

Of course, I am living in constant trepidation, playing for the smallest of stakes, and always looking out for something—calculating, standing whole days by the gaming-tables to watch the play—even seeing that play in my dreams—yet seeming, the while, to be in some way stiffening, to be growing caked, as it were, in mire. But I must conclude my notes, which I finish under the impression of a recent encounter with Mr. Astley. I had not seen him since we parted at Roulettenberg, and now we met quite by accident. At the time I was walking in the public gardens, and meditating upon the fact that not only had I still some fifty gulden in my possession, but also I had fully paid up my hotel bill three days ago. Consequently, I was in a position to try my luck again at roulette; and if I won anything I should be able to continue my play, whereas, if I lost what I now possessed, I should once more have to accept a lacquey's place, provided that, in the alternative, I failed to discover a Russian family which stood in need of a tutor. Plunged in these reflections, I started on my daily walk through the Park and forest towards a neighbouring principality. Sometimes, on such occasions, I spent four hours on the way, and would return to Homburg tired and hungry; but, on this particular occasion, I had scarcely left the gardens for the Park when I caught sight of Astley seated on a bench. As soon as he perceived me, he called me by name, and I went and sat down beside him; but, on noticing that he seemed a little stiff in his manner, I hastened to moderate the expression of joy which the sight of him had called forth.

"YOU here?" he said. "Well, I had an idea that I should meet you. Do not trouble to tell me anything, for I know all—yes, all. In fact, your whole life during the past twenty months lies within my knowledge."

"How closely you watch the doings of your old friends!" I replied. "That does you infinite credit. But stop a moment. You have reminded me of something. Was it you who bailed me out of Roulettenberg prison when I was lying there for a debt of two hundred gulden? SOMEONE did so."

"Oh dear no!—though I knew all the time that you were lying there."

"Perhaps you could tell me who DID bail me out?"

"No; I am afraid I could not."

"What a strange thing! For I know no Russians at all here, so it cannot have been a Russian who befriended me. In Russia we Orthodox folk DO go bail for one another, but in this case I thought it must have been done by some English stranger who was not conversant with the ways of the country."

Mr. Astley seemed to listen to me with a sort of surprise. Evidently he had expected to see me looking more crushed and broken than I was.

"Well," he said—not very pleasantly, "I am none the less glad to find that you retain your old independence of spirit, as well as your buoyancy."

"Which means that you are vexed at not having found me more abased and humiliated than I am?" I retorted with a smile.

Astley was not quick to understand this, but presently did so and laughed.

"Your remarks please me as they always did," he continued. "In those words I see the clever, triumphant, and, above all things, cynical friend of former days. Only Russians have the faculty of combining within themselves so many opposite qualities. Yes, most men love to see their best friend in abasement; for generally it is on such abasement that friendship is founded. All thinking persons know that ancient truth. Yet, on the present occasion, I assure you, I am sincerely glad to see that you are NOT cast down. Tell me, are you never going to give up gambling?"

"Damn the gambling! Yes, I should certainly have given it up, were it not that—"

"That you are losing? I thought so. You need not tell me any more. I know how things stand, for you have said that last in despair, and therefore, truthfully. Have you no other employment than gambling?"

"No; none whatever."

Astley gave me a searching glance. At that time it was ages since I had last looked at a paper or turned the pages of a book.

"You are growing blase," he said. "You have not only renounced life, with its interests and social ties, but the duties of a citizen and a man; you have not only renounced the friends whom I know you to have had, and every aim in life but that of winning money; but you have also renounced your memory. Though I can remember you in the strong, ardent period of your life, I feel persuaded that you have now forgotten every better feeling of that period—that your present dreams and aspirations of subsistence do not rise above pair, impair rouge, noir, the twelve middle numbers, and so forth."

"Enough, Mr. Astley!" I cried with some irritation—almost in anger. "Kindly do not recall to me any more recollections, for I can remember things for myself. Only for a time have I put them out of my head. Only until I shall have rehabilitated myself, am I keeping my memory dulled. When that hour shall come, you will see me arise from the dead."

"Then you will have to be here another ten years," he replied. "Should I then be alive, I will remind you—here, on this very bench—of what I have just said. In fact, I will bet you a wager that I shall do so."

"Say no more," I interrupted impatiently. "And to show you that I have not wholly forgotten the past, may I enquire where Mlle. Polina is? If it was not you who bailed me out of prison, it must have been she. Yet never have I heard a word concerning her."

"No, I do not think it was she. At the present moment she is in Switzerland, and you will do me a favour by ceasing to ask me these questions about her." Astley said this with a firm, and even an angry, air.

"Which means that she has dealt you a serious wound?" I burst out with an involuntary sneer.

"Mlle. Polina," he continued, "Is the best of all possible living beings; but, I repeat, that I shall thank you to cease questioning me about her. You never really knew her, and her name on your lips is an offence to my moral feeling."

"Indeed? On what subject, then, have I a better right to speak to you than on this? With it are bound up all your recollections and mine. However, do not be alarmed: I have no wish to probe too far into your private, your secret affairs. My interest in Mlle. Polina does not extend beyond her outward circumstances and surroundings. About them you could tell me in two words."

"Well, on condition that the matter shall end there, I will tell you that for a long time Mlle. Polina was ill, and still is so. My mother and sister entertained her for a while at their home in the north of England, and thereafter Mlle. Polina's grandmother (you remember the mad old woman?) died, and left Mlle. Polina a personal legacy of seven thousand pounds sterling. That was about six months ago, and now Mlle. is travelling with my sister's family—my sister having since married. Mlle.'s little brother and sister also benefited by the Grandmother's will, and are now being educated in London. As for the General, he died in Paris last month, of a stroke. Mlle. Blanche did well by him, for she succeeded in having transferred to herself all that he received from the Grandmother. That, I think, concludes all that I have to tell."

"And De Griers? Is he too travelling in Switzerland?"

"No; nor do I know where he is. Also I warn you once more that you had better avoid such hints and ignoble suppositions; otherwise you will assuredly have to reckon with me."

"What? In spite of our old friendship?"

"Yes, in spite of our old friendship."

"Then I beg your pardon a thousand times, Mr. Astley. I meant nothing offensive to Mlle. Polina, for I have nothing of which to accuse her. Moreover, the question of there being anything between this Frenchman and this Russian lady is not one which you and I need discuss, nor even attempt to understand."

"If," replied Astley, "you do not care to hear their names coupled together, may I ask you what you mean by the expressions 'this Frenchman,' 'this Russian lady,' and 'there being anything between them'? Why do you call them so particularly a 'Frenchman' and a 'Russian lady'?"

"Ah, I see you are interested, Mr. Astley. But it is a long, long story, and calls for a lengthy preface. At the same time, the question is an important one, however ridiculous it may seem at the first glance. A Frenchman, Mr. Astley, is merely a fine figure of a man. With this you, as a Britisher, may not agree. With it I also, as a Russian, may not agree—out of envy. Yet possibly our good ladies are of another opinion. For instance, one may look upon Racine as a broken-down, hobbledehoy, perfumed individual—one may even be unable to read him; and I too may think him the same, as well as, in some respects, a subject for ridicule. Yet about him, Mr. Astley, there is a certain charm, and, above all things, he is a great poet—though one might like to deny it. Yes, the Frenchman, the Parisian, as a national figure, was in process of developing into a figure of elegance before we Russians had even ceased to be bears. The Revolution bequeathed to the French nobility its heritage, and now every whippersnapper of a Parisian may possess manners, methods of expression, and even thoughts that are above reproach in form, while all the time he himself may share in that form neither in initiative nor in intellect nor in soul—his manners, and the rest, having come to him through inheritance. Yes, taken by himself, the Frenchman is frequently a fool of fools and a villain of villains. Per contra, there is no one in the world more worthy of confidence and respect than this young Russian lady. De Griers might so mask his face and play a part as easily to overcome her heart, for he has an imposing figure, Mr. Astley, and this young lady might easily take that figure for his real self—for the natural form of his heart and soul—instead of the mere cloak with which heredity has dowered him. And even though it may offend you, I feel bound to say that the majority also of English people are uncouth and unrefined, whereas we Russian folk can recognise beauty wherever we see it, and are always eager to cultivate the same. But to distinguish beauty of soul and personal originality there is needed far more independence and freedom than is possessed by our women, especially by our younger ladies. At all events, they need more EXPERIENCE. For instance, this Mlle. Polina—pardon me, but the name has passed my lips, and I cannot well recall it—is taking a very long time to make up her mind to prefer you to Monsieur de Griers. She may respect you, she may become your friend, she may open out her heart to you; yet over that heart there will be reigning that loathsome villain, that mean and petty usurer, De Griers. This will be due to obstinacy and self-love—to the fact that De Griers once appeared to her in the transfigured guise of a marquis, of a disenchanted and ruined liberal who was doing his best to help her family and the frivolous old General; and, although these transactions of his have since been exposed, you will find that the exposure has made no impression upon her mind. Only give her the De Griers of former days, and she will ask of you no more. The more she may detest the present De Griers, the more will she lament the De Griers of the past—even though the latter never existed but in her own imagination. You are a sugar refiner, Mr. Astley, are you not?"

"Yes, I belong to the well-known firm of Lovell and Co."

"Then see here. On the one hand, you are a sugar refiner, while, on the other hand, you are an Apollo Belvedere. But the two characters do not mix with one another. I, again, am not even a sugar refiner; I am a mere roulette gambler who has also served as a lacquey. Of this fact Mlle. Polina is probably well aware, since she appears to have an excellent force of police at her disposal."

"You are saying this because you are feeling bitter," said Astley with cold indifference. "Yet there is not the least originality in your words."

"I agree. But therein lies the horror of it all—that, how trepidation, playing ever mean and farcical my accusations may be, they are none the less TRUE. But I am only wasting words."

"Yes, you are, for you are only talking nonsense!" exclaimed my companion—his voice now trembling and his eyes flashing fire. "Are you aware," he continued, "that wretched, ignoble, petty, unfortunate man though you are, it was at HER request I came to Homburg, in order to see you, and to have a long, serious talk with you, and to report to her your feelings and thoughts and hopes—yes, and your recollections of her, too?"

"Indeed? Is that really so?" I cried—the tears beginning to well from my eyes. Never before had this happened.

"Yes, poor unfortunate," continued Astley. "She DID love you; and I may tell you this now for the reason that now you are utterly lost. Even if I were also to tell you that she still loves you, you would none the less have to remain where you are. Yes, you have ruined yourself beyond redemption. Once upon a time you had a certain amount of talent, and you were of a lively disposition, and your good looks were not to be despised. You might even have been useful to your country, which needs men like you. Yet you remained here, and your life is now over. I am not blaming you for this—in my view all Russians resemble you, or are inclined to do so. If it is not roulette, then it is something else. The exceptions are very rare. Nor are you the first to learn what a taskmaster is yours. For roulette is not exclusively a Russian game. Hitherto, you have honourably preferred to serve as a lacquey rather than to act as a thief; but what the future may have in store for you I tremble to think. Now good-bye. You are in want of money, I suppose? Then take these ten louis d'or. More I shall not give you, for you would only gamble it away. Take care of these coins, and farewell. Once more, TAKE CARE of them."

"No, Mr. Astley. After all that has been said I—"

"TAKE CARE of them!" repeated my friend. "I am certain you are still a gentleman, and therefore I give you the money as one gentleman may give money to another. Also, if I could be certain that you would leave both Homburg and the gaming-tables, and return to your own country, I would give you a thousand pounds down to start life afresh; but, I give you ten louis d'or instead of a thousand pounds for the reason that at the present time a thousand pounds and ten louis d'or will be all the same to you—you will lose the one as readily as you will the other. Take the money, therefore, and good-bye."

"Yes, I WILL take it if at the same time you will embrace me."

"With pleasure."

So we parted—on terms of sincere affection.

But he was wrong. If I was hard and undiscerning as regards Polina and De Griers, HE was hard and undiscerning as regards Russian people generally. Of myself I say nothing. Yet—yet words are only words. I need to ACT. Above all things I need to think of Switzerland. Tomorrow, tomorrow—Ah, but if only I could set things right tomorrow, and be born again, and rise again from the dead! But no—I cannot. Yet I must show her what I can do. Even if she should do no more than learn that I can still play the man, it would be worth it. Today it is too late, but TOMORROW...

Yet I have a presentiment that things can never be otherwise. I have got fifteen louis d'or in my possession, although I began with fifteen gulden. If I were to play carefully at the start—But no, no! Surely I am not such a fool as that? Yet WHY should I not rise from the dead? I should require at first but to go cautiously and patiently and the rest would follow. I should require but to put a check upon my nature for one hour, and my fortunes would be changed entirely. Yes, my nature is my weak point. I have only to remember what happened to me some months ago at Roulettenberg, before my final ruin. What a notable instance that was of my capacity for resolution! On the occasion in question I had lost everything—everything; yet, just as I was leaving the Casino, I heard another gulden give a rattle in my pocket! "Perhaps I shall need it for a meal," I thought to myself; but a hundred paces further on, I changed my mind, and returned. That gulden I staked upon manque—and there is something in the feeling that, though one is alone, and in a foreign land, and far from one's own home and friends, and ignorant of whence one's next meal is to come, one is nevertheless staking one's very last coin! Well, I won the stake, and in twenty minutes had left the Casino with a hundred and seventy gulden in my pocket! That is a fact, and it shows what a last remaining gulden can do.... But what if my heart had failed me, or I had shrunk from making up my mind? ...

No: tomorrow all shall be ended!

Poor Folk

April 8th

MY DEAREST BARBARA ALEXIEVNA,—How happy I was last night—how immeasurably, how impossibly happy! That was because for once in your life you had relented so far as to obey my wishes. At about eight o'clock I awoke from sleep (you know, my beloved one, that I always like to sleep for a short hour after my work is done)—I awoke, I say, and, lighting a candle, prepared my paper to write, and trimmed my pen. Then suddenly, for some reason or another, I raised my eyes—and felt my very heart leap within me! For you had understood what I wanted, you had understood what my heart was craving for. Yes, I perceived that a corner of the curtain in your window had been looped up and fastened to the cornice as I had suggested should be done; and it seemed to me that your dear face was glimmering at the window, and that you were looking at me from out of the darkness of your room, and that you were thinking of me. Yet how vexed I felt that I could not distinguish your sweet face clearly! For there was a time when you and I could see one another without any difficulty at all. Ah me, but old age is not always a blessing, my beloved one! At this very moment everything is standing awry to my eyes, for a man needs only to work late overnight in his writing of something or other for, in the morning, his eyes to be red, and the tears to be gushing from them in a way that makes him ashamed to be seen before strangers. However, I was able to picture to myself your beaming smile, my angel—your kind, bright smile; and in my heart there lurked just such a feeling as on the occasion when I first kissed you, my little Barbara. Do you remember that, my darling? Yet somehow you seemed to be threatening me with your tiny finger. Was it so, little wanton? You must write and tell me about it in your next letter.

But what think you of the plan of the curtain, Barbara? It is a charming one, is it not? No matter whether I be at work, or about to retire to rest, or just awaking from sleep, it enables me to know that you are thinking of me, and remembering me—that you are both well and happy. Then when you lower the curtain, it means that it is time that I, Makar Alexievitch, should go to bed; and when again you raise the curtain, it means that you are saying to me, "Good morning," and asking me how I am, and whether I have slept well. "As for myself," adds the curtain, "I am altogether in good health and spirits, glory be to God!" Yes, my heart's delight, you see how easy a plan it was to devise, and how much writing it will save us! It is a clever plan, is it not? And it was my own invention, too! Am I not cunning in such matters, Barbara Alexievna?

Well, next let me tell you, dearest, that last night I slept better and more soundly than I had ever hoped to do, and that I am the more delighted at the fact in that, as you know, I had just settled into a new lodging—a circumstance only too apt to keep one from sleeping! This morning, too, I arose (joyous and full of love) at cockcrow. How good seemed everything at that hour, my darling! When I opened my window I could see the sun shining, and hear the birds singing, and smell the air laden with scents of spring. In short, all nature was awaking to life again. Everything was in consonance with my mood; everything seemed fair and spring-like. Moreover, I had a fancy that I should fare well today. But my whole thoughts were bent upon you. "Surely," thought I, "we mortals who dwell in pain and sorrow might with reason envy the birds of heaven which know not either!" And my other thoughts were similar to these. In short, I gave myself up to fantastic comparisons. A little book which I have says the same kind of thing in a variety of ways. For instance, it says that one may have many, many fancies, my Barbara—that as soon as the spring comes on, one's thoughts become uniformly pleasant and sportive and witty, for the reason that, at that season, the mind inclines readily to tenderness, and the world takes on a more roseate hue. From that little book of mine I have culled the following passage, and written it down for you to see. In particular does the author express a longing similar to my own, where he writes:

"Why am I not a bird free to seek its quest?"

And he has written much else, God bless him!

But tell me, my love—where did you go for your walk this morning? Even before I had started for the office you had taken flight from your room, and passed through the courtyard—yes, looking as vernal-like as a bird in spring. What rapture it gave me to see you! Ah, little Barbara, little Barbara, you must never give way to grief, for tears are of no avail, nor sorrow. I know this well—I know it of my own experience. So do you rest quietly until you have regained your health a little. But how is our good Thedora? What a kind heart she has! You write that she is now living with you, and that you are satisfied with what she does. True, you say that she is inclined to grumble, but do not mind that, Barbara. God bless her, for she is an excellent soul!

But what sort of an abode have I lighted upon, Barbara Alexievna? What sort of a tenement, do you think, is this? Formerly, as you know, I used to live in absolute stillness—so much so that if a fly took wing it could plainly be heard buzzing. Here, however, all is turmoil and shouting and clatter. The PLAN of the tenement you know already. Imagine a long corridor, quite dark, and by no means clean. To the right a dead wall, and to the left a row of doors stretching as far as the line of rooms extends. These rooms are tenanted by different people—by one, by two, or by three lodgers as the case may be, but in this arrangement there is no sort of system, and the place is a perfect Noah's Ark. Most of the lodgers are respectable, educated, and even bookish people. In particular they include a tchinovnik (one of the literary staff in some government department), who is so well-read that he can expound Homer or any other author—in fact, ANYTHING, such a man of talent is he! Also, there are a couple of officers (for ever playing cards), a midshipman, and an English tutor. But, to amuse you, dearest, let me describe these people more categorically in my next letter, and tell you in detail about their lives. As for our landlady, she is a dirty little old woman who always walks about in a dressing-gown and slippers, and never ceases to shout at Theresa. I myself live in the kitchen—or, rather, in a small room which forms part of the kitchen. The latter is a very large, bright, clean, cheerful apartment with three windows in it, and a partition-wall which, running outwards from the front wall, makes a sort of little den, a sort of extra room, for myself. Everything in this den is comfortable and convenient, and I have, as I say, a window to myself. So much for a description of my dwelling-place. Do not think, dearest, that in all this there is any hidden intention. The fact that I live in the kitchen merely means that I live behind the partition wall in that apartment—that I live quite alone, and spend my time in a quiet fashion compounded of trifles. For furniture I have provided myself with a bed, a table, a chest of drawers, and two small chairs. Also, I have suspended an ikon. True, better rooms MAY exist in the world than this—much better rooms; yet COMFORT is the chief thing. In fact, I have made all my arrangements for comfort's sake alone; so do not for a moment imagine that I had any other end in view. And since your window happens to be just opposite to mine, and since the courtyard between us is narrow and I can see you as you pass,—why, the result is that this miserable wretch will be able to live at once more happily and with less outlay. The dearest room in this house costs, with board, thirty-five roubles—more than my purse could well afford; whereas MY room costs only twenty-four, though formerly I used to pay thirty, and so had to deny myself many things (I could drink tea but seldom, and never could indulge in tea and sugar as I do now). But, somehow, I do not like having to go without tea, for everyone else here is respectable, and the fact makes me ashamed. After all, one drinks tea largely to please one's fellow men, Barbara, and to give oneself tone and an air of gentility (though, of myself, I care little about such things, for I am not a man of the finicking sort). Yet think you that, when all things needful—boots and the rest—have been paid for, much will remain? Yet I ought not to grumble at my salary,—I am quite satisfied with it; it is sufficient. It has sufficed me now for some years, and, in addition, I receive certain gratuities.

Well good-bye, my darling. I have bought you two little pots of geraniums—quite cheap little pots, too—as a present. Perhaps you would also like some mignonette? Mignonette it shall be if only you will write to inform me of everything in detail. Also, do not misunderstand the fact that I have taken this room, my dearest. Convenience and nothing else, has made me do so. The snugness of the place has caught my fancy. Also, I shall be able to save money here, and to hoard it against the future. Already I have saved a little money as a beginning. Nor must you despise me because I am such an insignificant old fellow that a fly could break me with its wing. True, I am not a swashbuckler; but perhaps there may also abide in me the spirit which should pertain to every man who is at once resigned and sure of himself. Good-bye, then, again, my angel. I have now covered close upon a whole two sheets of notepaper, though I ought long ago to have been starting for the office. I kiss your hands, and remain ever your devoted slave, your faithful friend,

MAKAR DIEVUSHKIN.

P.S.—One thing I beg of you above all things—and that is, that you will answer this letter as FULLY as possible. With the letter I send you a packet of bonbons. Eat them for your health's sake, nor, for the love of God, feel any uneasiness about me. Once more, dearest one, good-bye.

April 8th

MY BELOVED MAKAR ALEXIEVITCH,—Do you know, must quarrel with you. Yes, good Makar Alexievitch, I really cannot accept your presents, for I know what they must have cost you—I know to what privations and self-denial they must have led. How many times have I not told you that I stand in need of NOTHING, of absolutely NOTHING, as well as that I shall never be in a position to recompense you for all the kindly acts with which you have loaded me? Why, for instance, have you sent me geraniums? A little sprig of balsam would not have mattered so much—but geraniums! Only have I to let fall an unguarded word—for example, about geraniums—and at once you buy me some! How much they must have cost you! Yet what a charm there is in them, with their flaming petals! Wherever did you get these beautiful plants? I have set them in my window as the most conspicuous place possible, while on the floor I have placed a bench for my other flowers to stand on (since you are good enough to enrich me with such presents). Unfortunately, Thedora, who, with her sweeping and polishing, makes a perfect sanctuary of my room, is not over-pleased at the arrangement. But why have you sent me also bonbons? Your letter tells me that something special is afoot with you, for I find in it so much about paradise and spring and sweet odours and the songs of birds. Surely, thought I to myself when I received it, this is as good as poetry! Indeed, verses are the only thing that your letter lacks, Makar Alexievitch.

And what tender feelings I can read in it—what roseate-coloured fancies! To the curtain, however, I had never given a thought. The fact is that when I moved the flower-pots, it LOOPED ITSELF up. There now!

Ah, Makar Alexievitch, you neither speak of nor give any account of what you have spent upon me. You hope thereby to deceive me, to make it seem as though the cost always falls upon you alone, and that there is nothing to conceal. Yet I KNOW that for my sake you deny yourself necessaries. For instance, what has made you go and take the room which you have done, where you will be worried and disturbed, and where you have neither elbow-space nor comfort—you who love solitude, and never like to have any one near you? To judge from your salary, I should think that you might well live in greater ease than that. Also, Thedora tells me that your circumstances used to be much more affluent than they are at present. Do you wish, then, to persuade me that your whole existence has been passed in loneliness and want and gloom, with never a cheering word to help you, nor a seat in a friend's chimney-corner? Ah, kind comrade, how my heart aches for you! But do not overtask your health, Makar Alexievitch. For instance, you say that your eyes are over-weak for you to go on writing in your office by candle-light. Then why do so? I am sure that your official superiors do not need to be convinced of your diligence!

Once more I implore you not to waste so much money upon me. I know how much you love me, but I also know that you are not rich.... This morning I too rose in good spirits. Thedora had long been at work; and it was time that I too should bestir myself. Indeed I was yearning to do so, so I went out for some silk, and then sat down to my labours. All the morning I felt light-hearted and cheerful. Yet now my thoughts are once more dark and sad—once more my heart is ready to sink.

Ah, what is going to become of me? What will be my fate? To have to be so uncertain as to the future, to have to be unable to foretell what is going to happen, distresses me deeply. Even to look back at the past is horrible, for it contains sorrow that breaks my very heart at the thought of it. Yes, a whole century in tears could I spend because of the wicked people who have wrecked my life!

But dusk is coming on, and I must set to work again. Much else should I have liked to write to you, but time is lacking, and I must hasten. Of course, to write this letter is a pleasure enough, and could never be wearisome; but why do you not come to see me in person? Why do you not, Makar Alexievitch? You live so close to me, and at least SOME of your time is your own. I pray you, come. I have just seen Theresa. She was looking so ill, and I felt so sorry for her, that I gave her twenty kopecks. I am almost falling asleep. Write to me in fullest detail, both concerning your mode of life, and concerning the people who live with you, and concerning how you fare with them. I should so like to know! Yes, you must write again. Tonight I have purposely looped the curtain up. Go to bed early, for, last night, I saw your candle burning until nearly midnight. Goodbye! I am now feeling sad and weary. Ah that I should have to spend such days as this one has been. Again good-bye.—Your friend,

BARBARA DOBROSELOVA.

April 8th

MY DEAREST BARBARA ALEXIEVNA,—To think that a day like this should have fallen to my miserable lot! Surely you are making fun of an old man?... However, it was my own fault—my own fault entirely. One ought not to grow old holding a lock of Cupid's hair in one's hand. Naturally one is misunderstood.... Yet man is sometimes a very strange being. By all the Saints, he will talk of doing things, yet leave them undone, and remain looking the kind of fool from whom may the Lord preserve us!... Nay, I am not angry, my beloved; I am only vexed to think that I should have written to you in such stupid, flowery phraseology. Today I went hopping and skipping to the office, for my heart was under your influence, and my soul was keeping holiday, as it were. Yes, everything seemed to be going well with me. Then I betook myself to my work. But with what result? I gazed around at the old familiar objects, at the old familiar grey and gloomy objects. They looked just the same as before. Yet WERE those the same inkstains, the same tables and chairs, that I had hitherto known? Yes, they WERE the same, exactly the same; so why should I have gone off riding on Pegasus' back? Whence had that mood arisen? It had arisen from the fact that a certain sun had beamed upon me, and turned the sky to blue. But why so? Why is it, sometimes, that sweet odours seem to be blowing through a courtyard where nothing of the sort can be? They must be born of my foolish fancy, for a man may stray so far into sentiment as to forget his immediate surroundings, and to give way to the superfluity of fond ardour with which his heart is charged. On the other hand, as I walked home from the office at nightfall my feet seemed to lag, and my head to be aching. Also, a cold wind seemed to be blowing down my back (enraptured with the spring, I had gone out clad only in a thin overcoat). Yet you have misunderstood my sentiments, dearest. They are altogether different to what you suppose. It is a purely paternal feeling that I have for you. I stand towards you in the position of a relative who is bound to watch over your lonely orphanhood. This I say in all sincerity, and with a single purpose, as any kinsman might do. For, after all, I AM a distant kinsman of yours—the seventh drop of water in the pudding, as the proverb has it—yet still a kinsman, and at the present time your nearest relative and protector, seeing that where you had the right to look for help and protection, you found only treachery and insult. As for poetry, I may say that I consider it unbecoming for a man of my years to devote his faculties to the making of verses. Poetry is rubbish. Even boys at school ought to be whipped for writing it.

Why do you write thus about "comfort" and "peace" and the rest? I am not a fastidious man, nor one who requires much. Never in my life have I been so comfortable as now. Why, then, should I complain in my old age? I have enough to eat, I am well dressed and booted. Also, I have my diversions. You see, I am not of noble blood. My father himself was not a gentleman; he and his family had to live even more plainly than I do. Nor am I a milksop. Nevertheless, to speak frankly, I do not like my present abode so much as I used to like my old one. Somehow the latter seemed more cosy, dearest. Of course, this room is a good one enough; in fact, in SOME respects it is the more cheerful and interesting of the two. I have nothing to say against it—no. Yet I miss the room that used to be so familiar to me. Old lodgers like myself soon grow as attached to our chattels as to a kinsman. My old room was such a snug little place! True, its walls resembled those of any other room—I am not speaking of that; the point is that the recollection of them seems to haunt my mind with sadness. Curious that recollections should be so mournful! Even what in that room used to vex me and inconvenience me now looms in a purified light, and figures in my imagination as a thing to be desired. We used to live there so quietly—I and an old landlady who is now dead. How my heart aches to remember her, for she was a good woman, and never overcharged for her rooms. Her whole time was spent in making patchwork quilts with knitting-needles that were an arshin [An ell.] long. Oftentimes we shared the same candle and board. Also she had a granddaughter, Masha—a girl who was then a mere baby, but must now be a girl of thirteen. This little piece of mischief, how she used to make us laugh the day long! We lived together, a happy family of three. Often of a long winter's evening we would first have tea at the big round table, and then betake ourselves to our work; the while that, to amuse the child and to keep her out of mischief, the old lady would set herself to tell stories. What stories they were!—though stories less suitable for a child than for a grown-up, educated person. My word! Why, I myself have sat listening to them, as I smoked my pipe, until I have forgotten about work altogether. And then, as the story grew grimmer, the little child, our little bag of mischief, would grow thoughtful in proportion, and clasp her rosy cheeks in her tiny hands, and, hiding her face, press closer to the old landlady. Ah, how I loved to see her at those moments! As one gazed at her one would fail to notice how the candle was flickering, or how the storm was swishing the snow about the courtyard. Yes, that was a goodly life, my Barbara, and we lived it for nearly twenty years.... How my tongue does carry me away! Maybe the subject does not interest you, and I myself find it a not over-easy subject to recall—especially at the present time.

Darkness is falling, and Theresa is busying herself with something or another. My head and my back are aching, and even my thoughts seem to be in pain, so strangely do they occur. Yes, my heart is sad today, Barbara.... What is it you have written to me?——"Why do you not come in PERSON to see me?" Dear one, what would people say? I should have but to cross the courtyard for people to begin noticing us, and asking themselves questions. Gossip and scandal would arise, and there would be read into the affair quite another meaning than the real one. No, little angel, it were better that I should see you tomorrow at Vespers. That will be the better plan, and less hurtful to us both. Nor must you chide me, beloved, because I have written you a letter like this (reading it through, I see it to be all odds and ends); for I am an old man now, dear Barbara, and an uneducated one. Little learning had I in my youth, and things refuse to fix themselves in my brain when I try to learn them anew. No, I am not skilled in letter-writing, Barbara, and, without being told so, or any one laughing at me for it, I know that, whenever I try to describe anything with more than ordinary distinctness, I fall into the mistake of talking sheer rubbish.... I saw you at your window today—yes, I saw you as you were drawing down the blind! Good-bye, goodbye, little Barbara, and may God keep you! Good-bye, my own Barbara Alexievna!—Your sincere friend,

MAKAR DIEVUSHKIN.

P.S.—Do not think that I could write to you in a satirical vein, for I am too old to show my teeth to no purpose, and people would laugh at me, and quote our Russian proverb: "Who diggeth a pit for another one, the same shall fall into it himself."

April 9th

MY DEAREST MAKAR ALEXIEVITCH,—Are not you, my friend and benefactor, just a little ashamed to repine and give way to such despondency? And surely you are not offended with me? Ah! Though often thoughtless in my speech, I never should have imagined that you would take my words as a jest at your expense. Rest assured that NEVER should I make sport of your years or of your character. Only my own levity is at fault; still more, the fact that I am so weary of life.

What will such a feeling not engender? To tell you the truth, I had supposed that YOU were jesting in your letter; wherefore, my heart was feeling heavy at the thought that you could feel so displeased with me. Kind comrade and helper, you will be doing me an injustice if for a single moment you ever suspect that I am lacking in feeling or in gratitude towards you. My heart, believe me, is able to appraise at its true worth all that you have done for me by protecting me from my enemies, and from hatred and persecution. Never shall I cease to pray to God for you; and, should my prayers ever reach Him and be received of Heaven, then assuredly fortune will smile upon you!

Today I am not well. By turns I shiver and flush with heat, and Thedora is greatly disturbed about me.... Do not scruple to come and see me, Makar Alexievitch. How can it concern other people what you do? You and I are well enough acquainted with each other, and one's own affairs are one's own affairs. Goodbye, Makar Alexievitch, for I have come to the end of all I had to say, and am feeling too unwell to write more. Again I beg of you not to be angry with me, but to rest assured of my constant respect and attachment.—Your humble, devoted servant,

BARBARA DOBROSELOVA.

April 12th

DEAREST MISTRESS BARBARA ALEXIEVNA,—I pray you, my beloved, to tell me what ails you. Every one of your letters fills me with alarm. On the other hand, in every letter I urge you to be more careful of yourself, and to wrap up yourself warmly, and to avoid going out in bad weather, and to be in all things prudent. Yet you go and disobey me! Ah, little angel, you are a perfect child! I know well that you are as weak as a blade of grass, and that, no matter what wind blows upon you, you are ready to fade. But you must be careful of yourself, dearest; you MUST look after yourself better; you MUST avoid all risks, lest you plunge your friends into desolation and despair.

Dearest, you also express a wish to learn the details of my daily life and surroundings. That wish I hasten to satisfy. Let me begin at the beginning, since, by doing so, I shall explain things more systematically. In the first place, on entering this house, one passes into a very bare hall, and thence along a passage to a mean staircase. The reception room, however, is bright, clean, and spacious, and is lined with redwood and metal-work. But the scullery you would not care to see; it is greasy, dirty, and odoriferous, while the stairs are in rags, and the walls so covered with filth that the hand sticks fast wherever it touches them. Also, on each landing there is a medley of boxes, chairs, and dilapidated wardrobes; while the windows have had most of their panes shattered, and everywhere stand washtubs filled with dirt, litter, eggshells, and fish-bladders. The smell is abominable. In short, the house is not a nice one.

As to the disposition of the rooms, I have described it to you already. True, they are convenient enough, yet every one of them has an ATMOSPHERE. I do not mean that they smell badly so much as that each of them seems to contain something which gives forth a rank, sickly-sweet odour. At first the impression is an unpleasant one, but a couple of minutes will suffice to dissipate it, for the reason that EVERYTHING here smells—people's clothes, hands, and everything else—and one grows accustomed to the rankness. Canaries, however, soon die in this house. A naval officer here has just bought his fifth. Birds cannot live long in such an air. Every morning, when fish or beef is being cooked, and washing and scrubbing are in progress, the house is filled with steam. Always, too, the kitchen is full of linen hanging out to dry; and since my room adjoins that apartment, the smell from the clothes causes me not a little annoyance. However, one can grow used to anything.

From earliest dawn the house is astir as its inmates rise, walk about, and stamp their feet. That is to say, everyone who has to go to work then gets out of bed. First of all, tea is partaken of. Most of the tea-urns belong to the landlady; and since there are not very many of them, we have to wait our turn. Anyone who fails to do so will find his teapot emptied and put away. On the first occasion, that was what happened to myself. Well, is there anything else to tell you? Already I have made the acquaintance of the company here. The naval officer took the initiative in calling upon me, and his frankness was such that he told me all about his father, his mother, his sister (who is married to a lawyer of Tula), and the town of Kronstadt. Also, he promised me his patronage, and asked me to come and take tea with him. I kept the appointment in a room where card-playing is continually in progress; and, after tea had been drunk, efforts were made to induce me to gamble. Whether or not my refusal seemed to the company ridiculous I cannot say, but at all events my companions played the whole evening, and were playing when I left. The dust and smoke in the room made my eyes ache. I declined, as I say, to play cards, and was, therefore, requested to discourse on philosophy, after which no one spoke to me at all—a result which I did not regret. In fact, I have no intention of going there again, since every one is for gambling, and for nothing but gambling. Even the literary tchinovnik gives such parties in his room—though, in his case, everything is done delicately and with a certain refinement, so that the thing has something of a retiring and innocent air.

In passing, I may tell you that our landlady is NOT a nice woman. In fact, she is a regular beldame. You have seen her once, so what do you think of her? She is as lanky as a plucked chicken in consumption, and, with Phaldoni (her servant), constitutes the entire staff of the establishment. Whether or not Phaldoni has any other name I do not know, but at least he answers to this one, and every one calls him by it. A red-haired, swine-jowled, snub-nosed, crooked lout, he is for ever wrangling with Theresa, until the pair nearly come to blows. In short, life is not overly pleasant in this place. Never at any time is the household wholly at rest, for always there are people sitting up to play cards. Sometimes, too, certain things are done of which it would be shameful for me to speak. In particular, hardened though I am, it astonishes me that men WITH FAMILIES should care to live in this Sodom. For example, there is a family of poor folk who have rented from the landlady a room which does not adjoin the other rooms, but is set apart in a corner by itself. Yet what quiet people they are! Not a sound is to be heard from them. The father—he is called Gorshkov—is a little grey-headed tchinovnik who, seven years ago, was dismissed from public service, and now walks about in a coat so dirty and ragged that it hurts one to see it. Indeed it is a worse coat even than mine! Also, he is so thin and frail (at times I meet him in the corridor) that his knees quake under him, his hands and head are tremulous with some disease (God only knows what!), and he so fears and distrusts everybody that he always walks alone. Reserved though I myself am, he is even worse. As for his family, it consists of a wife and three children. The eldest of the latter—a boy—is as frail as his father, while the mother—a woman who, formerly, must have been good looking, and still has a striking aspect in spite of her pallor—goes about in the sorriest of rags. Also I have heard that they are in debt to our landlady, as well as that she is not overly kind to them. Moreover, I have heard that Gorshkov lost his post through some unpleasantness or other—through a legal suit or process of which I could not exactly tell you the nature. Yes, they certainly are poor—Oh, my God, how poor! At the same time, never a sound comes from their room. It is as though not a soul were living in it. Never does one hear even the children—which is an unusual thing, seeing that children are ever ready to sport and play, and if they fail to do so it is a bad sign. One evening when I chanced to be passing the door of their room, and all was quiet in the house, I heard through the door a sob, and then a whisper, and then another sob, as though somebody within were weeping, and with such subdued bitterness that it tore my heart to hear the sound. In fact, the thought of these poor people never left me all night, and quite prevented me from sleeping.

Well, good-bye, my little Barbara, my little friend beyond price. I have described to you everything to the best of my ability. All today you have been in my thoughts; all today my heart has been yearning for you. I happen to know, dearest one, that you lack a warm cloak. To me too, these St. Petersburg springs, with their winds and their snow showers, spell death. Good heavens, how the breezes bite one! Do not be angry, beloved, that I should write like this. Style I have not. Would that I had! I write just what wanders into my brain, in the hope that I may cheer you up a little. Of course, had I had a good education, things might have been different; but, as things were, I could not have one. Never did I learn even to do simple sums!—Your faithful and unchangeable friend,

MAKAR DIEVUSHKIN.

April 25th

MY DEAREST MAKAR ALEXIEVITCH,—Today I met my cousin Sasha. To see her going to wrack and ruin shocked me terribly. Moreover, it has reached me, through a side wind, that she has been making inquiry for me, and dogging my footsteps, under the pretext that she wishes to pardon me, to forget the past, and to renew our acquaintance. Well, among other things she told me that, whereas you are not a kinsman of mine, that she is my nearest relative; that you have no right whatever to enter into family relations with us; and that it is wrong and shameful for me to be living upon your earnings and charity. Also, she said that I must have forgotten all that she did for me, though thereby she saved both myself and my mother from starvation, and gave us food and drink; that for two and a half years we caused her great loss; and, above all things, that she excused us what we owed her. Even my poor mother she did not spare. Would that she, my dead parent, could know how I am being treated! But God knows all about it.... Also, Anna declared that it was solely through my own fault that my fortunes declined after she had bettered them; that she is in no way responsible for what then happened; and that I have but myself to blame for having been either unable or unwilling to defend my honour. Great God! WHO, then, has been at fault? According to Anna, Hospodin [Mr.] Bwikov was only right when he declined to marry a woman who—But need I say it? It is cruel to hear such lies as hers. What is to become of me I do not know. I tremble and sob and weep. Indeed, even to write this letter has cost me two hours. At least it might have been thought that Anna would have confessed HER share in the past. Yet see what she says!... For the love of God do not be anxious about me, my friend, my only benefactor. Thedora is over apt to exaggerate matters. I am not REALLY ill. I have merely caught a little cold. I caught it last night while I was walking to Bolkovo, to hear Mass sung for my mother. Ah, mother, my poor mother! Could you but rise from the grave and learn what is being done to your daughter!

B. D.

May 20th

MY DEAREST LITTLE BARBARA,—I am sending you a few grapes, which are good for a convalescent person, and strongly recommended by doctors for the allayment of fever. Also, you were saying the other day that you would like some roses; wherefore, I now send you a bunch. Are you at all able to eat, my darling?—for that is the chief point which ought to be seen to. Let us thank God that the past and all its unhappiness are gone! Yes, let us give thanks to Heaven for that much! As for books, I cannot get hold of any, except for a book which, written in excellent style, is, I believe, to be had here. At all events, people keep praising it very much, and I have begged the loan of it for myself. Should you too like to read it? In this respect, indeed, I feel nervous, for the reason that it is so difficult to divine what your taste in books may be, despite my knowledge of your character. Probably you would like poetry—the poetry of sentiment and of love making? Well, I will send you a book of MY OWN poems. Already I have copied out part of the manuscript.

Everything with me is going well; so pray do not be anxious on my account, beloved. What Thedora told you about me was sheer rubbish. Tell her from me that she has not been speaking the truth. Yes, do not fail to give this mischief-maker my message. It is not the case that I have gone and sold a new uniform. Why should I do so, seeing that I have forty roubles of salary still to come to me? Do not be uneasy, my darling. Thedora is a vindictive woman—merely a vindictive woman. We shall yet see better days. Only do you get well, my angel—only do you get well, for the love of God, lest you grieve an old man. Also, who told you that I was looking thin? Slanders again—nothing but slanders! I am as healthy as could be, and have grown so fat that I am ashamed to be so sleek of paunch. Would that you were equally healthy!... Now goodbye, my angel. I kiss every one of your tiny fingers, and remain ever your constant friend,

MAKAR DIEVUSHKIN.

P.S.—But what is this, dearest one, that you have written to me? Why do you place me upon such a pedestal? Moreover, how could I come and visit you frequently? How, I repeat? Of course, I might avail myself of the cover of night; but, alas! the season of the year is what it is, and includes no night time to speak of. In fact, although, throughout your illness and delirium, I scarcely left your side for a moment, I cannot think how I contrived to do the many things that I did. Later, I ceased to visit you at all, for the reason that people were beginning to notice things, and to ask me questions. Yet, even so, a scandal has arisen. Theresa I trust thoroughly, for she is not a talkative woman; but consider how it will be when the truth comes out in its entirety! What THEN will folk not say and think? Nevertheless, be of good cheer, my beloved, and regain your health. When you have done so we will contrive to arrange a rendezvous out of doors.

June 1st

MY BELOVED MAKAR ALEXIEVITCH,—So eager am I to do something that will please and divert you in return for your care, for your ceaseless efforts on my behalf—in short, for your love for me—that I have decided to beguile a leisure hour for you by delving into my locker, and extracting thence the manuscript which I send you herewith. I began it during the happier period of my life, and have continued it at intervals since. So often have you asked me about my former existence—about my mother, about Pokrovski, about my sojourn with Anna Thedorovna, about my more recent misfortunes; so often have you expressed an earnest desire to read the manuscript in which (God knows why) I have recorded certain incidents of my life, that I feel no doubt but that the sending of it will give you sincere pleasure. Yet somehow I feel depressed when I read it, for I seem now to have grown twice as old as I was when I penned its concluding lines. Ah, Makar Alexievitch, how weary I am—how this insomnia tortures me! Convalescence is indeed a hard thing to bear!

B. D. ONE

UP to the age of fourteen, when my father died, my childhood was the happiest period of my life. It began very far away from here in the depths of the province of Tula, where my father filled the position of steward on the vast estates of the Prince P——. Our house was situated in one of the Prince's villages, and we lived a quiet, obscure, but happy, life. A gay little child was I—my one idea being ceaselessly to run about the fields and the woods and the garden. No one ever gave me a thought, for my father was always occupied with business affairs, and my mother with her housekeeping. Nor did any one ever give me any lessons—a circumstance for which I was not sorry. At earliest dawn I would hie me to a pond or a copse, or to a hay or a harvest field, where the sun could warm me, and I could roam wherever I liked, and scratch my hands with bushes, and tear my clothes in pieces. For this I used to get blamed afterwards, but I did not care.

Had it befallen me never to quit that village—had it befallen me to remain for ever in that spot—I should always have been happy; but fate ordained that I should leave my birthplace even before my girlhood had come to an end. In short, I was only twelve years old when we removed to St. Petersburg. Ah! how it hurts me to recall the mournful gatherings before our departure, and to recall how bitterly I wept when the time came for us to say farewell to all that I had held so dear! I remember throwing myself upon my father's neck, and beseeching him with tears to stay in the country a little longer; but he bid me be silent, and my mother, adding her tears to mine, explained that business matters compelled us to go. As a matter of fact, old Prince P—— had just died, and his heirs had dismissed my father from his post; whereupon, since he had a little money privately invested in St. Petersburg, he bethought him that his personal presence in the capital was necessary for the due management of his affairs. It was my mother who told me this. Consequently we settled here in St. Petersburg, and did not again move until my father died.

How difficult I found it to grow accustomed to my new life! At the time of our removal to St. Petersburg it was autumn—a season when, in the country, the weather is clear and keen and bright, all agricultural labour has come to an end, the great sheaves of corn are safely garnered in the byre, and the birds are flying hither and thither in clamorous flocks. Yes, at that season the country is joyous and fair, but here in St. Petersburg, at the time when we reached the city, we encountered nothing but rain, bitter autumn frosts, dull skies, ugliness, and crowds of strangers who looked hostile, discontented, and disposed to take offence. However, we managed to settle down—though I remember that in our new home there was much noise and confusion as we set the establishment in order. After this my father was seldom at home, and my mother had few spare moments; wherefore, I found myself forgotten.

The first morning after our arrival, when I awoke from sleep, how sad I felt! I could see that our windows looked out upon a drab space of wall, and that the street below was littered with filth. Passers-by were few, and as they walked they kept muffling themselves up against the cold.

Then there ensued days when dullness and depression reigned supreme. Scarcely a relative or an acquaintance did we possess in St. Petersburg, and even Anna Thedorovna and my father had come to loggerheads with one another, owing to the fact that he owed her money. In fact, our only visitors were business callers, and as a rule these came but to wrangle, to argue, and to raise a disturbance. Such visits would make my father look very discontented, and seem out of temper. For hours and hours he would pace the room with a frown on his face and a brooding silence on his lips. Even my mother did not dare address him at these times, while, for my own part, I used to sit reading quietly and humbly in a corner—not venturing to make a movement of any sort.

Three months after our arrival in St. Petersburg I was sent to a boarding-school. Here I found myself thrown among strange people; here everything was grim and uninviting, with teachers continually shouting at me, and my fellow-pupils for ever holding me up to derision, and myself constantly feeling awkward and uncouth. How strict, how exacting was the system! Appointed hours for everything, a common table, ever-insistent teachers! These things simply worried and tortured me. Never from the first could I sleep, but used to weep many a chill, weary night away. In the evenings everyone would have to repeat or to learn her lessons. As I crouched over a dialogue or a vocabulary, without daring even to stir, how my thoughts would turn to the chimney-corner at home, to my father, to my mother, to my old nurse, to the tales which the latter had been used to tell! How sad it all was! The memory of the merest trifle at home would please me, and I would think and think how nice things used to be at home. Once more I would be sitting in our little parlour at tea with my parents—in the familiar little parlour where everything was snug and warm! How ardently, how convulsively I would seem to be embracing my mother! Thus I would ponder, until at length tears of sorrow would softly gush forth and choke my bosom, and drive the lessons out of my head. For I never could master the tasks of the morrow; no matter how much my mistress and fellow-pupils might gird at me, no matter how much I might repeat my lessons over and over to myself, knowledge never came with the morning. Consequently, I used to be ordered the kneeling punishment, and given only one meal in the day. How dull and dispirited I used to feel! From the first my fellow-pupils used to tease and deride and mock me whenever I was saying my lessons. Also, they used to pinch me as we were on our way to dinner or tea, and to make groundless complaints of me to the head mistress. On the other hand, how heavenly it seemed when, on Saturday evening, my old nurse arrived to fetch me! How I would embrace the old woman in transports of joy! After dressing me, and wrapping me up, she would find that she could scarcely keep pace with me on the way home, so full was I of chatter and tales about one thing and another. Then, when I had arrived home merry and lighthearted, how fervently I would embrace my parents, as though I had not seen them for ten years. Such a fussing would there be—such a talking and a telling of tales! To everyone I would run with a greeting, and laugh, and giggle, and scamper about, and skip for very joy. True, my father and I used to have grave conversations about lessons and teachers and the French language and grammar; yet we were all very happy and contented together. Even now it thrills me to think of those moments. For my father's sake I tried hard to learn my lessons, for I could see that he was spending his last kopeck upon me, and himself subsisting God knows how. Every day he grew more morose and discontented and irritable; every day his character kept changing for the worse. He had suffered an influx of debts, nor were his business affairs prospering. As for my mother, she was afraid even to say a word, or to weep aloud, for fear of still further angering him. Gradually she sickened, grew thinner and thinner, and became taken with a painful cough. Whenever I reached home from school I would find every one low-spirited, and my mother shedding silent tears, and my father raging. Bickering and high words would arise, during which my father was wont to declare that, though he no longer derived the smallest pleasure or relaxation from life, and had spent his last coin upon my education, I had not yet mastered the French language. In short, everything began to go wrong, to turn to unhappiness; and for that circumstance, my father took vengeance upon myself and my mother. How he could treat my poor mother so I cannot understand. It used to rend my heart to see her, so hollow were her cheeks becoming, so sunken her eyes, so hectic her face. But it was chiefly around myself that the disputes raged. Though beginning only with some trifle, they would soon go on to God knows what. Frequently, even I myself did not know to what they related. Anything and everything would enter into them, for my father would say that I was an utter dunce at the French language; that the head mistress of my school was a stupid, common sort of women who cared nothing for morals; that he (my father) had not yet succeeded in obtaining another post; that Lamonde's "Grammar" was a wretched book—even a worse one than Zapolski's; that a great deal of money had been squandered upon me; that it was clear that I was wasting my time in repeating dialogues and vocabularies; that I alone was at fault, and that I must answer for everything. Yet this did not arise from any WANT OF LOVE for me on the part of my father, but rather from the fact that he was incapable of putting himself in my own and my mother's place. It came of a defect of character.

All these cares and worries and disappointments tortured my poor father until he became moody and distrustful. Next he began to neglect his health, with the result that, catching a chill, he died, after a short illness, so suddenly and unexpectedly that for a few days we were almost beside ourselves with the shock—my mother, in particular, lying for a while in such a state of torpor that I had fears for her reason. The instant my father was dead creditors seemed to spring up out of the ground, and to assail us en masse. Everything that we possessed had to be surrendered to them, including a little house which my father had bought six months after our arrival in St. Petersburg. How matters were finally settled I do not know, but we found ourselves roofless, shelterless, and without a copper. My mother was grievously ill, and of means of subsistence we had none. Before us there loomed only ruin, sheer ruin. At the time I was fourteen years old. Soon afterwards Anna Thedorovna came to see us, saying that she was a lady of property and our relative; and this my mother confirmed—though, true, she added that Anna was only a very DISTANT relative. Anna had never taken the least notice of us during my father's lifetime, yet now she entered our presence with tears in her eyes, and an assurance that she meant to better our fortunes. Having condoled with us on our loss and destitute position, she added that my father had been to blame for everything, in that he had lived beyond his means, and taken upon himself more than he was able to perform. Also, she expressed a wish to draw closer to us, and to forget old scores; and when my mother explained that, for her own part, she harboured no resentment against Anna, the latter burst into tears, and, hurrying my mother away to church, then and there ordered Mass to be said for the "dear departed," as she called my father. In this manner she effected a solemn reconciliation with my mother.

Next, after long negotiations and vacillations, coupled with much vivid description of our destitute position, our desolation, and our helplessness, Anna invited us to pay her (as she expressed it) a "return visit." For this my mother duly thanked her, and considered the invitation for a while; after which, seeing that there was nothing else to be done, she informed Anna Thedorovna that she was prepared, gratefully, to accept her offer. Ah, how I remember the morning when we removed to Vassilievski Island! [A quarter of St. Petersburg.] It was a clear, dry, frosty morning in autumn. My mother could not restrain her tears, and I too felt depressed. Nay, my very heart seemed to be breaking under a strange, undefined load of sorrow. How terrible it all seemed!...

II

AT first—that is to say, until my mother and myself grew used to our new abode—we found living at Anna Thedorovna's both strange and disagreeable. The house was her own, and contained five rooms, three of which she shared with my orphaned cousin, Sasha (whom she had brought up from babyhood); a fourth was occupied by my mother and myself; and the fifth was rented of Anna by a poor student named Pokrovski. Although Anna lived in good style—in far better style than might have been expected—her means and her avocation were conjectural. Never was she at rest; never was she not busy with some mysterious something or other. Also, she possessed a wide and varied circle of friends. The stream of callers was perpetual—although God only knows who they were, or what their business was. No sooner did my mother hear the door-bell ring than off she would carry me to our own apartment. This greatly displeased Anna, who used again and again to assure my mother that we were too proud for our station in life. In fact, she would sulk for hours about it. At the time I could not understand these reproaches, and it was not until long afterwards that I learned—or rather, I guessed—why eventually my mother declared that she could not go on living with Anna. Yes, Anna was a bad woman. Never did she let us alone. As to the exact motive why she had asked us to come and share her house with her I am still in the dark. At first she was not altogether unkind to us but, later, she revealed to us her real character—as soon, that is to say, as she saw that we were at her mercy, and had nowhere else to go. Yes, in early days she was quite kind to me—even offensively so, but afterwards, I had to suffer as much as my mother. Constantly did Anna reproach us; constantly did she remind us of her benefactions, and introduce us to her friends as poor relatives of hers whom, out of goodness of heart and for the love of Christ, she had received into her bosom. At table, also, she would watch every mouthful that we took; and, if our appetite failed, immediately she would begin as before, and reiterate that we were over-dainty, that we must not assume that riches would mean happiness, and that we had better go and live by ourselves. Moreover, she never ceased to inveigh against my father—saying that he had sought to be better than other people, and thereby had brought himself to a bad end; that he had left his wife and daughter destitute; and that, but for the fact that we had happened to meet with a kind and sympathetic Christian soul, God alone knew where we should have laid our heads, save in the street. What did that woman not say? To hear her was not so much galling as disgusting. From time to time my mother would burst into tears, her health grew worse from day to day, and her body was becoming sheer skin and bone. All the while, too, we had to work—to work from morning till night, for we had contrived to obtain some employment as occasional sempstresses. This, however, did not please Anna, who used to tell us that there was no room in her house for a modiste's establishment. Yet we had to get clothes to wear, to provide for unforeseen expenses, and to have a little money at our disposal in case we should some day wish to remove elsewhere. Unfortunately, the strain undermined my mother's health, and she became gradually weaker. Sickness, like a cankerworm, was gnawing at her life, and dragging her towards the tomb. Well could I see what she was enduring, what she was suffering. Yes, it all lay open to my eyes.

Day succeeded day, and each day was like the last one. We lived a life as quiet as though we had been in the country. Anna herself grew quieter in proportion as she came to realise the extent of her power over us. In nothing did we dare to thwart her. From her portion of the house our apartment was divided by a corridor, while next to us (as mentioned above) dwelt a certain Pokrovski, who was engaged in teaching Sasha the French and German languages, as well as history and geography—"all the sciences," as Anna used to say. In return for these services he received free board and lodging. As for Sasha, she was a clever, but rude and uncouth, girl of thirteen. On one occasion Anna remarked to my mother that it might be as well if I also were to take some lessons, seeing that my education had been neglected at school; and, my mother joyfully assenting, I joined Sasha for a year in studying under this Pokrovski.

The latter was a poor—a very poor—young man whose health would not permit of his undertaking the regular university course. Indeed, it was only for form's sake that we called him "The Student." He lived in such a quiet, humble, retiring fashion that never a sound reached us from his room. Also, his exterior was peculiar—he moved and walked awkwardly, and uttered his words in such a strange manner that at first I could never look at him without laughing. Sasha was for ever playing tricks upon him—more especially when he was giving us our lessons. But unfortunately, he was of a temperament as excitable as herself. Indeed, he was so irritable that the least trifle would send him into a frenzy, and set him shouting at us, and complaining of our conduct. Sometimes he would even rush away to his room before school hours were over, and sit there for days over his books, of which he had a store that was both rare and valuable. In addition, he acted as teacher at another establishment, and received payment for his services there; and, whenever he had received his fees for this extra work, he would hasten off and purchase more books.

In time I got to know and like him better, for in reality he was a good, worthy fellow—more so than any of the people with whom we otherwise came in contact. My mother in particular had a great respect for him, and, after herself, he was my best friend. But at first I was just an overgrown hoyden, and joined Sasha in playing the fool. For hours we would devise tricks to anger and distract him, for he looked extremely ridiculous when he was angry, and so diverted us the more (ashamed though I am now to admit it). But once, when we had driven him nearly to tears, I heard him say to himself under his breath, "What cruel children!" and instantly I repented—I began to feel sad and ashamed and sorry for him. I reddened to my ears, and begged him, almost with tears, not to mind us, nor to take offence at our stupid jests. Nevertheless, without finishing the lesson, he closed his book, and departed to his own room. All that day I felt torn with remorse. To think that we two children had forced him, the poor, the unhappy one, to remember his hard lot! And at night I could not sleep for grief and regret. Remorse is said to bring relief to the soul, but it is not so. How far my grief was internally connected with my conceit I do not know, but at least I did not wish him to think me a baby, seeing that I had now reached the age of fifteen years. Therefore, from that day onwards I began to torture my imagination with devising a thousand schemes which should compel Pokrovski to alter his opinion of me. At the same time, being yet shy and reserved by nature, I ended by finding that, in my present position, I could make up my mind to nothing but vague dreams (and such dreams I had). However, I ceased to join Sasha in playing the fool, while Pokrovski, for his part, ceased to lose his temper with us so much. Unfortunately this was not enough to satisfy my self-esteem.

At this point, I must say a few words about the strangest, the most interesting, the most pitiable human being that I have ever come across. I speak of him now—at this particular point in these memoirs—for the reason that hitherto I had paid him no attention whatever, and began to do so now only because everything connected with Pokrovski had suddenly become of absorbing interest in my eyes.

Sometimes there came to the house a ragged, poorly-dressed, grey-headed, awkward, amorphous—in short, a very strange-looking—little old man. At first glance it might have been thought that he was perpetually ashamed of something—that he had on his conscience something which always made him, as it were, bristle up and then shrink into himself. Such curious starts and grimaces did he indulge in that one was forced to conclude that he was scarcely in his right mind. On arriving, he would halt for a while by the window in the hall, as though afraid to enter; until, should any one happen to pass in or out of the door—whether Sasha or myself or one of the servants (to the latter he always resorted the most readily, as being the most nearly akin to his own class)—he would begin to gesticulate and to beckon to that person, and to make various signs. Then, should the person in question nod to him, or call him by name (the recognised token that no other visitor was present, and that he might enter freely), he would open the door gently, give a smile of satisfaction as he rubbed his hands together, and proceed on tiptoe to young Pokrovski's room. This old fellow was none other than Pokrovski's father.

Later I came to know his story in detail. Formerly a civil servant, he had possessed no additional means, and so had occupied a very low and insignificant position in the service. Then, after his first wife (mother of the younger Pokrovski) had died, the widower bethought him of marrying a second time, and took to himself a tradesman's daughter, who soon assumed the reins over everything, and brought the home to rack and ruin, so that the old man was worse off than before. But to the younger Pokrovski, fate proved kinder, for a landowner named Bwikov, who had formerly known the lad's father and been his benefactor, took the boy under his protection, and sent him to school. Another reason why this Bwikov took an interest in young Pokrovski was that he had known the lad's dead mother, who, while still a serving-maid, had been befriended by Anna Thedorovna, and subsequently married to the elder Pokrovski. At the wedding Bwikov, actuated by his friendship for Anna, conferred upon the young bride a dowry of five thousand roubles; but whither that money had since disappeared I cannot say. It was from Anna's lips that I heard the story, for the student Pokrovski was never prone to talk about his family affairs. His mother was said to have been very good-looking; wherefore, it is the more mysterious why she should have made so poor a match. She died when young—only four years after her espousal.

From school the young Pokrovski advanced to a gymnasium, [Secondary school.] and thence to the University, where Bwikov, who frequently visited the capital, continued to accord the youth his protection. Gradually, however, ill health put an end to the young man's university course; whereupon Bwikov introduced and personally recommended him to Anna Thedorovna, and he came to lodge with her on condition that he taught Sasha whatever might be required of him.

Grief at the harshness of his wife led the elder Pokrovski to plunge into dissipation, and to remain in an almost permanent condition of drunkenness. Constantly his wife beat him, or sent him to sit in the kitchen—with the result that in time, he became so inured to blows and neglect, that he ceased to complain. Still not greatly advanced in years, he had nevertheless endangered his reason through evil courses—his only sign of decent human feeling being his love for his son. The latter was said to resemble his dead mother as one pea may resemble another. What recollections, therefore, of the kind helpmeet of former days may not have moved the breast of the poor broken old man to this boundless affection for the boy? Of naught else could the father ever speak but of his son, and never did he fail to visit him twice a week. To come oftener he did not dare, for the reason that the younger Pokrovski did not like these visits of his father's. In fact, there can be no doubt that the youth's greatest fault was his lack of filial respect. Yet the father was certainly rather a difficult person to deal with, for, in the first place, he was extremely inquisitive, while, in the second place, his long-winded conversation and questions—questions of the most vapid and senseless order conceivable—always prevented the son from working. Likewise, the old man occasionally arrived there drunk. Gradually, however, the son was weaning his parent from his vicious ways and everlasting inquisitiveness, and teaching the old man to look upon him, his son, as an oracle, and never to speak without that son's permission.

On the subject of his Petinka, as he called him, the poor old man could never sufficiently rhapsodise and dilate. Yet when he arrived to see his son he almost invariably had on his face a downcast, timid expression that was probably due to uncertainty concerning the way in which he would be received. For a long time he would hesitate to enter, and if I happened to be there he would question me for twenty minutes or so as to whether his Petinka was in good health, as well as to the sort of mood he was in, whether he was engaged on matters of importance, what precisely he was doing (writing or meditating), and so on. Then, when I had sufficiently encouraged and reassured the old man, he would make up his mind to enter, and quietly and cautiously open the door. Next, he would protrude his head through the chink, and if he saw that his son was not angry, but threw him a nod, he would glide noiselessly into the room, take off his scarf, and hang up his hat (the latter perennially in a bad state of repair, full of holes, and with a smashed brim)—the whole being done without a word or a sound of any kind. Next, the old man would seat himself warily on a chair, and, never removing his eyes from his son, follow his every movement, as though seeking to gauge Petinka's state of mind. On the other hand, if the son was not in good spirits, the father would make a note of the fact, and at once get up, saying that he had "only called for a minute or two," that, "having been out for a long walk, and happening at the moment to be passing," he had "looked in for a moment's rest." Then silently and humbly the old man would resume his hat and scarf; softly he would open the door, and noiselessly depart with a forced smile on his face—the better to bear the disappointment which was seething in his breast, the better to help him not to show it to his son.

On the other hand, whenever the son received his father civilly the old man would be struck dumb with joy. Satisfaction would beam in his face, in his every gesture, in his every movement. And if the son deigned to engage in conversation with him, the old man always rose a little from his chair, and answered softly, sympathetically, with something like reverence, while strenuously endeavouring to make use of the most recherche (that is to say, the most ridiculous) expressions. But, alas! He had not the gift of words. Always he grew confused, and turned red in the face; never did he know what to do with his hands or with himself. Likewise, whenever he had returned an answer of any kind, he would go on repeating the same in a whisper, as though he were seeking to justify what he had just said. And if he happened to have returned a good answer, he would begin to preen himself, and to straighten his waistcoat, frockcoat and tie, and to assume an air of conscious dignity. Indeed, on these occasions he would feel so encouraged, he would carry his daring to such a pitch, that, rising softly from his chair, he would approach the bookshelves, take thence a book, and read over to himself some passage or another. All this he would do with an air of feigned indifference and sangfroid, as though he were free ALWAYS to use his son's books, and his son's kindness were no rarity at all. Yet on one occasion I saw the poor old fellow actually turn pale on being told by his son not to touch the books. Abashed and confused, he, in his awkward hurry, replaced the volume wrong side uppermost; whereupon, with a supreme effort to recover himself, he turned it round with a smile and a blush, as though he were at a loss how to view his own misdemeanour. Gradually, as already said, the younger Pokrovski weaned his father from his dissipated ways by giving him a small coin whenever, on three successive occasions, he (the father) arrived sober. Sometimes, also, the younger man would buy the older one shoes, or a tie, or a waistcoat; whereafter, the old man would be as proud of his acquisition as a peacock. Not infrequently, also, the old man would step in to visit ourselves, and bring Sasha and myself gingerbread birds or apples, while talking unceasingly of Petinka. Always he would beg of us to pay attention to our lessons, on the plea that Petinka was a good son, an exemplary son, a son who was in twofold measure a man of learning; after which he would wink at us so quizzingly with his left eye, and twist himself about in such amusing fashion, that we were forced to burst out laughing. My mother had a great liking for him, but he detested Anna Thedorovna—although in her presence he would be quieter than water and lowlier than the earth.

Soon after this I ceased to take lessons of Pokrovski. Even now he thought me a child, a raw schoolgirl, as much as he did Sasha; and this hurt me extremely, seeing that I had done so much to expiate my former behaviour. Of my efforts in this direction no notice had been taken, and the fact continued to anger me more and more. Scarcely ever did I address a word to my tutor between school hours, for I simply could not bring myself to do it. If I made the attempt I only grew red and confused, and rushed away to weep in a corner. How it would all have ended I do not know, had not a curious incident helped to bring about a rapprochement. One evening, when my mother was sitting in Anna Thedorovna's room, I crept on tiptoe to Pokrovski's apartment, in the belief that he was not at home. Some strange impulse moved me to do so. True, we had lived cheek by jowl with one another; yet never once had I caught a glimpse of his abode. Consequently my heart beat loudly—so loudly, indeed, that it seemed almost to be bursting from my breast. On entering the room I glanced around me with tense interest. The apartment was very poorly furnished, and bore few traces of orderliness. On table and chairs there lay heaps of books; everywhere were books and papers. Then a strange thought entered my head, as well as, with the thought, an unpleasant feeling of irritation. It seemed to me that my friendship, my heart's affection, meant little to him, for HE was well-educated, whereas I was stupid, and had learned nothing, and had read not a single book. So I stood looking wistfully at the long bookshelves where they groaned under their weight of volumes. I felt filled with grief, disappointment, and a sort of frenzy. I felt that I MUST read those books, and decided to do so—to read them one by one, and with all possible speed. Probably the idea was that, by learning whatsoever HE knew, I should render myself more worthy of his friendship. So, I made a rush towards the bookcase nearest me, and, without stopping further to consider matters, seized hold of the first dusty tome upon which my hands chanced to alight, and, reddening and growing pale by turns, and trembling with fear and excitement, clasped the stolen book to my breast with the intention of reading it by candle light while my mother lay asleep at night.

But how vexed I felt when, on returning to our own room, and hastily turning the pages, only an old, battered worm-eaten Latin work greeted my eyes! Without loss of time I retraced my steps. Just when I was about to replace the book I heard a noise in the corridor outside, and the sound of footsteps approaching. Fumblingly I hastened to complete what I was about, but the tiresome book had become so tightly wedged into its row that, on being pulled out, it caused its fellows to close up too compactly to leave any place for their comrade. To insert the book was beyond my strength; yet still I kept pushing and pushing at the row. At last the rusty nail which supported the shelf (the thing seemed to have been waiting on purpose for that moment!) broke off short; with the result that the shelf descended with a crash, and the books piled themselves in a heap on the floor! Then the door of the room opened, and Pokrovski entered!

I must here remark that he never could bear to have his possessions tampered with. Woe to the person, in particular, who touched his books! Judge, therefore, of my horror when books small and great, books of every possible shape and size and thickness, came tumbling from the shelf, and flew and sprang over the table, and under the chairs, and about the whole room. I would have turned and fled, but it was too late. "All is over!" thought I. "All is over! I am ruined, I am undone! Here have I been playing the fool like a ten-year-old child! What a stupid girl I am! The monstrous fool!"

Indeed, Pokrovski was very angry. "What? Have you not done enough?" he cried. "Are you not ashamed to be for ever indulging in such pranks? Are you NEVER going to grow sensible?" With that he darted forward to pick up the books, while I bent down to help him.

"You need not, you need not!" he went on. "You would have done far better not to have entered without an invitation."

Next, a little mollified by my humble demeanour, he resumed in his usual tutorial tone—the tone which he had adopted in his new-found role of preceptor:

"When are you going to grow steadier and more thoughtful? Consider yourself for a moment. You are no longer a child, a little girl, but a maiden of fifteen."

Then, with a desire (probably) to satisfy himself that I was no longer a being of tender years, he threw me a glance—but straightway reddened to his very ears. This I could not understand, but stood gazing at him in astonishment. Presently, he straightened himself a little, approached me with a sort of confused expression, and haltingly said something—probably it was an apology for not having before perceived that I was now a grown-up young person. But the next moment I understood. What I did I hardly know, save that, in my dismay and confusion, I blushed even more hotly than he had done and, covering my face with my hands, rushed from the room.

What to do with myself for shame I could not think. The one thought in my head was that he had surprised me in his room. For three whole days I found myself unable to raise my eyes to his, but blushed always to the point of weeping. The strangest and most confused of thoughts kept entering my brain. One of them—the most extravagant—was that I should dearly like to go to Pokrovski, and to explain to him the situation, and to make full confession, and to tell him everything without concealment, and to assure him that I had not acted foolishly as a minx, but honestly and of set purpose. In fact, I DID make up my mind to take this course, but lacked the necessary courage to do it. If I had done so, what a figure I should have cut! Even now I am ashamed to think of it.

A few days later, my mother suddenly fell dangerously ill. For two days past she had not left her bed, while during the third night of her illness she became seized with fever and delirium. I also had not closed my eyes during the previous night, but now waited upon my mother, sat by her bed, brought her drink at intervals, and gave her medicine at duly appointed hours. The next night I suffered terribly. Every now and then sleep would cause me to nod, and objects grow dim before my eyes. Also, my head was turning dizzy, and I could have fainted for very weariness. Yet always my mother's feeble moans recalled me to myself as I started, momentarily awoke, and then again felt drowsiness overcoming me. What torture it was! I do not know, I cannot clearly remember, but I think that, during a moment when wakefulness was thus contending with slumber, a strange dream, a horrible vision, visited my overwrought brain, and I awoke in terror. The room was nearly in darkness, for the candle was flickering, and throwing stray beams of light which suddenly illuminated the room, danced for a moment on the walls, and then disappeared. Somehow I felt afraid—a sort of horror had come upon me—my imagination had been over-excited by the evil dream which I had experienced, and a feeling of oppression was crushing my heart.... I leapt from the chair, and involuntarily uttered a cry—a cry wrung from me by the terrible, torturing sensation that was upon me. Presently the door opened, and Pokrovski entered.

I remember that I was in his arms when I recovered my senses. Carefully seating me on a bench, he handed me a glass of water, and then asked me a few questions—though how I answered them I do not know. "You yourself are ill," he said as he took my hand. "You yourself are VERY ill. You are feverish, and I can see that you are knocking yourself out through your neglect of your own health. Take a little rest. Lie down and go to sleep. Yes, lie down, lie down," he continued without giving me time to protest. Indeed, fatigue had so exhausted my strength that my eyes were closing from very weakness. So I lay down on the bench with the intention of sleeping for half an hour only; but, I slept till morning. Pokrovski then awoke me, saying that it was time for me to go and give my mother her medicine.

When the next evening, about eight o'clock, I had rested a little and was preparing to spend the night in a chair beside my mother (fixedly meaning not to go to sleep this time), Pokrovski suddenly knocked at the door. I opened it, and he informed me that, since, possibly, I might find the time wearisome, he had brought me a few books to read. I accepted the books, but do not, even now, know what books they were, nor whether I looked into them, despite the fact that I never closed my eyes the whole night long. The truth was that a strange feeling of excitement was preventing me from sleeping, and I could not rest long in any one spot, but had to keep rising from my chair, and walking about the room. Throughout my whole being there seemed to be diffused a kind of elation—of elation at Pokrovski's attentions, at the thought that he was anxious and uneasy about me. Until dawn I pondered and dreamed; and though I felt sure Pokrovski would not again visit us that night, I gave myself up to fancies concerning what he might do the following evening.

That evening, when everyone else in the house had retired to rest, Pokrovski opened his door, and opened a conversation from the threshold of his room. Although, at this distance of time, I cannot remember a word of what we said to one another, I remember that I blushed, grew confused, felt vexed with myself, and awaited with impatience the end of the conversation although I myself had been longing for the meeting to take place, and had spent the day in dreaming of it, and devising a string of suitable questions and replies. Yes, that evening saw the first strand in our friendship knitted; and each subsequent night of my mother's illness we spent several hours together. Little by little I overcame his reserve, but found that each of these conversations left me filled with a sense of vexation at myself. At the same time, I could see with secret joy and a sense of proud elation that I was leading him to forget his tiresome books. At last the conversation turned jestingly upon the upsetting of the shelf. The moment was a peculiar one, for it came upon me just when I was in the right mood for self-revelation and candour. In my ardour, my curious phase of exaltation, I found myself led to make a full confession of the fact that I had become wishful to learn, to KNOW, something, since I had felt hurt at being taken for a chit, a mere baby.... I repeat that that night I was in a very strange frame of mind. My heart was inclined to be tender, and there were tears standing in my eyes. Nothing did I conceal as I told him about my friendship for him, about my desire to love him, about my scheme for living in sympathy with him and comforting him, and making his life easier. In return he threw me a look of confusion mingled with astonishment, and said nothing. Then suddenly I began to feel terribly pained and disappointed, for I conceived that he had failed to understand me, or even that he might be laughing at me. Bursting into tears like a child, I sobbed, and could not stop myself, for I had fallen into a kind of fit; whereupon he seized my hand, kissed it, and clasped it to his breast—saying various things, meanwhile, to comfort me, for he was labouring under a strong emotion. Exactly what he said I do not remember—I merely wept and laughed by turns, and blushed, and found myself unable to speak a word for joy. Yet, for all my agitation, I noticed that about him there still lingered an air of constraint and uneasiness. Evidently, he was lost in wonder at my enthusiasm and raptures—at my curiously ardent, unexpected, consuming friendship. It may be that at first he was amazed, but that afterwards he accepted my devotion and words of invitation and expressions of interest with the same simple frankness as I had offered them, and responded to them with an interest, a friendliness, a devotion equal to my own, even as a friend or a brother would do. How happy, how warm was the feeling in my heart! Nothing had I concealed or repressed. No, I had bared all to his sight, and each day would see him draw nearer to me.

Truly I could not say what we did not talk about during those painful, yet rapturous, hours when, by the trembling light of a lamp, and almost at the very bedside of my poor sick mother, we kept midnight tryst. Whatsoever first came into our heads we spoke of—whatsoever came riven from our hearts, whatsoever seemed to call for utterance, found voice. And almost always we were happy. What a grievous, yet joyous, period it was—a period grievous and joyous at the same time! To this day it both hurts and delights me to recall it. Joyous or bitter though it was, its memories are yet painful. At least they seem so to me, though a certain sweetness assuaged the pain. So, whenever I am feeling heartsick and oppressed and jaded and sad those memories return to freshen and revive me, even as drops of evening dew return to freshen and revive, after a sultry day, the poor faded flower which has long been drooping in the noontide heat.

My mother grew better, but still I continued to spend the nights on a chair by her bedside. Often, too, Pokrovski would give me books. At first I read them merely so as to avoid going to sleep, but afterwards I examined them with more attention, and subsequently with actual avidity, for they opened up to me a new, an unexpected, an unknown, an unfamiliar world. New thoughts, added to new impressions, would come pouring into my heart in a rich flood; and the more emotion, the more pain and labour, it cost me to assimilate these new impressions, the dearer did they become to me, and the more gratefully did they stir my soul to its very depths. Crowding into my heart without giving it time even to breathe, they would cause my whole being to become lost in a wondrous chaos. Yet this spiritual ferment was not sufficiently strong wholly to undo me. For that I was too fanciful, and the fact saved me.

With the passing of my mother's illness the midnight meetings and long conversations between myself and Pokrovski came to an end. Only occasionally did we exchange a few words with one another—words, for the most part, that were of little purport or substance, yet words to which it delighted me to apportion their several meanings, their peculiar secret values. My life had now become full—I was happy; I was quietly, restfully happy. Thus did several weeks elapse....

One day the elder Pokrovski came to see us, and chattered in a brisk, cheerful, garrulous sort of way. He laughed, launched out into witticisms, and, finally, resolved the riddle of his transports by informing us that in a week's time it would be his Petinka's birthday, when, in honour of the occasion, he (the father) meant to don a new jacket (as well as new shoes which his wife was going to buy for him), and to come and pay a visit to his son. In short, the old man was perfectly happy, and gossiped about whatsoever first entered his head.

My lover's birthday! Thenceforward, I could not rest by night or day. Whatever might happen, it was my fixed intention to remind Pokrovski of our friendship by giving him a present. But what sort of present? Finally, I decided to give him books. I knew that he had long wanted to possess a complete set of Pushkin's works, in the latest edition; so, I decided to buy Pushkin. My private fund consisted of thirty roubles, earned by handiwork, and designed eventually to procure me a new dress, but at once I dispatched our cook, old Matrena, to ascertain the price of such an edition. Horrors! The price of the eleven volumes, added to extra outlay upon the binding, would amount to at least SIXTY roubles! Where was the money to come from? I thought and thought, yet could not decide. I did not like to resort to my mother. Of course she would help me, but in that case every one in the house would become aware of my gift, and the gift itself would assume the guise of a recompense—of payment for Pokrovski's labours on my behalf during the past year; whereas, I wished to present the gift ALONE, and without the knowledge of anyone. For the trouble that he had taken with me I wished to be his perpetual debtor—to make him no payment at all save my friendship. At length, I thought of a way out of the difficulty.

I knew that of the hucksters in the Gostinni Dvor one could sometimes buy a book—even one that had been little used and was almost entirely new—for a half of its price, provided that one haggled sufficiently over it; wherefore I determined to repair thither. It so happened that, next day, both Anna Thedorovna and ourselves were in want of sundry articles; and since my mother was unwell and Anna lazy, the execution of the commissions devolved upon me, and I set forth with Matrena.

Luckily, I soon chanced upon a set of Pushkin, handsomely bound, and set myself to bargain for it. At first more was demanded than would have been asked of me in a shop; but afterwards—though not without a great deal of trouble on my part, and several feints at departing—I induced the dealer to lower his price, and to limit his demands to ten roubles in silver. How I rejoiced that I had engaged in this bargaining! Poor Matrena could not imagine what had come to me, nor why I so desired to buy books. But, oh horror of horrors! As soon as ever the dealer caught sight of my capital of thirty roubles in notes, he refused to let the Pushkin go for less than the sum he had first named; and though, in answer to my prayers and protestations, he eventually yielded a little, he did so only to the tune of two-and-a-half roubles more than I possessed, while swearing that he was making the concession for my sake alone, since I was "a sweet young lady," and that he would have done so for no one else in the world. To think that only two-and-a-half roubles should still be wanting! I could have wept with vexation. Suddenly an unlooked-for circumstance occurred to help me in my distress.

Not far away, near another table that was heaped with books, I perceived the elder Pokrovski, and a crowd of four or five hucksters plaguing him nearly out of his senses. Each of these fellows was proffering the old man his own particular wares; and while there was nothing that they did not submit for his approval, there was nothing that he wished to buy. The poor old fellow had the air of a man who is receiving a thrashing. What to make of what he was being offered him he did not know. Approaching him, I inquired what he happened to be doing there; whereat the old man was delighted, since he liked me (it may be) no less than he did Petinka.

"I am buying some books, Barbara Alexievna," said he, "I am buying them for my Petinka. It will be his birthday soon, and since he likes books I thought I would get him some."

The old man always expressed himself in a very roundabout sort of fashion, and on the present occasion he was doubly, terribly confused. Of no matter what book he asked the price, it was sure to be one, two, or three roubles. The larger books he could not afford at all; he could only look at them wistfully, fumble their leaves with his finger, turn over the volumes in his hands, and then replace them. "No, no, that is too dear," he would mutter under his breath. "I must go and try somewhere else." Then again he would fall to examining copy-books, collections of poems, and almanacs of the cheaper order.

"Why should you buy things like those?" I asked him. "They are such rubbish!"

"No, no!" he replied. "See what nice books they are! Yes, they ARE nice books!" Yet these last words he uttered so lingeringly that I could see he was ready to weep with vexation at finding the better sorts of books so expensive. Already a little tear was trickling down his pale cheeks and red nose. I inquired whether he had much money on him; whereupon the poor old fellow pulled out his entire stock, wrapped in a piece of dirty newspaper, and consisting of a few small silver coins, with twenty kopecks in copper. At once I seized the lot, and, dragging him off to my huckster, said: "Look here. These eleven volumes of Pushkin are priced at thirty-two-and-a-half roubles, and I have only thirty roubles. Let us add to them these two-and-a-half roubles of yours, and buy the books together, and make them our joint gift." The old man was overjoyed, and pulled out his money en masse; whereupon the huckster loaded him with our common library. Stuffing it into his pockets, as well as filling both arms with it, he departed homewards with his prize, after giving me his word to bring me the books privately on the morrow.

Next day the old man came to see his son, and sat with him, as usual, for about an hour; after which he visited ourselves, wearing on his face the most comical, the most mysterious expression conceivable. Smiling broadly with satisfaction at the thought that he was the possessor of a secret, he informed me that he had stealthily brought the books to our rooms, and hidden them in a corner of the kitchen, under Matrena's care. Next, by a natural transition, the conversation passed to the coming fete-day; whereupon, the old man proceeded to hold forth extensively on the subject of gifts. The further he delved into his thesis, and the more he expounded it, the clearer could I see that on his mind there was something which he could not, dared not, divulge. So I waited and kept silent. The mysterious exaltation, the repressed satisfaction which I had hitherto discerned in his antics and grimaces and left-eyed winks gradually disappeared, and he began to grow momentarily more anxious and uneasy. At length he could contain himself no longer.

"Listen, Barbara Alexievna," he said timidly. "Listen to what I have got to say to you. When his birthday is come, do you take TEN of the books, and give them to him yourself—that is, FOR yourself, as being YOUR share of the gift. Then I will take the eleventh book, and give it to him MYSELF, as being my gift. If we do that, you will have a present for him and I shall have one—both of us alike."

"Why do you not want us to present our gifts together, Zachar Petrovitch?" I asked him.

"Oh, very well," he replied. "Very well, Barbara Alexievna. Only—only, I thought that—"

The old man broke off in confusion, while his face flushed with the exertion of thus expressing himself. For a moment or two he sat glued to his seat.

"You see," he went on, "I play the fool too much. I am forever playing the fool, and cannot help myself, though I know that it is wrong to do so. At home it is often cold, and sometimes there are other troubles as well, and it all makes me depressed. Well, whenever that happens, I indulge a little, and occasionally drink too much. Now, Petinka does not like that; he loses his temper about it, Barbara Alexievna, and scolds me, and reads me lectures. So I want by my gift to show him that I am mending my ways, and beginning to conduct myself better. For a long time past, I have been saving up to buy him a book—yes, for a long time past I have been saving up for it, since it is seldom that I have any money, unless Petinka happens to give me some. He knows that, and, consequently, as soon as ever he perceives the use to which I have put his money, he will understand that it is for his sake alone that I have acted."

My heart ached for the old man. Seeing him looking at me with such anxiety, I made up my mind without delay.

"I tell you what," I said. "Do you give him all the books."

"ALL?" he ejaculated. "ALL the books?"

"Yes, all of them."

"As my own gift?" "Yes, as your own gift."

"As my gift alone?"

"Yes, as your gift alone."

Surely I had spoken clearly enough, yet the old man seemed hardly to understand me.

"Well," said he after reflection, "that certainly would be splendid—certainly it would be most splendid. But what about yourself, Barbara Alexievna?"

"Oh, I shall give your son nothing."

"What?" he cried in dismay. "Are you going to give Petinka nothing—do you WISH to give him nothing?" So put about was the old fellow with what I had said, that he seemed almost ready to renounce his own proposal if only I would give his son something. What a kind heart he had! I hastened to assure him that I should certainly have a gift of some sort ready, since my one wish was to avoid spoiling his pleasure.

"Provided that your son is pleased," I added, "and that you are pleased, I shall be equally pleased, for in my secret heart I shall feel as though I had presented the gift."

This fully reassured the old man. He stopped with us another couple of hours, yet could not sit still for a moment, but kept jumping up from his seat, laughing, cracking jokes with Sasha, bestowing stealthy kisses upon myself, pinching my hands, and making silent grimaces at Anna Thedorovna. At length, she turned him out of the house. In short, his transports of joy exceeded anything that I had yet beheld.

On the festal day he arrived exactly at eleven o'clock, direct from Mass. He was dressed in a carefully mended frockcoat, a new waistcoat, and a pair of new shoes, while in his arms he carried our pile of books. Next we all sat down to coffee (the day being Sunday) in Anna Thedorovna's parlour. The old man led off the meal by saying that Pushkin was a magnificent poet. Thereafter, with a return to shamefacedness and confusion, he passed suddenly to the statement that a man ought to conduct himself properly; that, should he not do so, it might be taken as a sign that he was in some way overindulging himself; and that evil tendencies of this sort led to the man's ruin and degradation. Then the orator sketched for our benefit some terrible instances of such incontinence, and concluded by informing us that for some time past he had been mending his own ways, and conducting himself in exemplary fashion, for the reason that he had perceived the justice of his son's precepts, and had laid them to heart so well that he, the father, had really changed for the better: in proof whereof, he now begged to present to the said son some books for which he had long been setting aside his savings.

As I listened to the old man I could not help laughing and crying in a breath. Certainly he knew how to lie when the occasion required! The books were transferred to his son's room, and arranged upon a shelf, where Pokrovski at once guessed the truth about them. Then the old man was invited to dinner and we all spent a merry day together at cards and forfeits. Sasha was full of life, and I rivalled her, while Pokrovski paid me numerous attentions, and kept seeking an occasion to speak to me alone. But to allow this to happen I refused. Yes, taken all in all, it was the happiest day that I had known for four years.

But now only grievous, painful memories come to my recollection, for I must enter upon the story of my darker experiences. It may be that that is why my pen begins to move more slowly, and seems as though it were going altogether to refuse to write. The same reason may account for my having undertaken so lovingly and enthusiastically a recounting of even the smallest details of my younger, happier days. But alas! those days did not last long, and were succeeded by a period of black sorrow which will close only God knows when!

My misfortunes began with the illness and death of Pokrovski, who was taken worse two months after what I have last recorded in these memoirs. During those two months he worked hard to procure himself a livelihood since hitherto he had had no assured position. Like all consumptives, he never—not even up to his last moment—altogether abandoned the hope of being able to enjoy a long life. A post as tutor fell in his way, but he had never liked the profession; while for him to become a civil servant was out of the question, owing to his weak state of health. Moreover, in the latter capacity he would have had to have waited a long time for his first instalment of salary. Again, he always looked at the darker side of things, for his character was gradually being warped, and his health undermined by his illness, though he never noticed it. Then autumn came on, and daily he went out to business—that is to say, to apply for and to canvass for posts—clad only in a light jacket; with the result that, after repeated soakings with rain, he had to take to his bed, and never again left it. He died in mid-autumn at the close of the month of October.

Throughout his illness I scarcely ever left his room, but waited on him hand and foot. Often he could not sleep for several nights at a time. Often, too, he was unconscious, or else in a delirium; and at such times he would talk of all sorts of things—of his work, of his books, of his father, of myself. At such times I learned much which I had not hitherto known or divined about his affairs. During the early part of his illness everyone in the house looked askance at me, and Anna Thedorovna would nod her head in a meaning manner; but, I always looked them straight in the face, and gradually they ceased to take any notice of my concern for Pokrovski. At all events my mother ceased to trouble her head about it.

Sometimes Pokrovski would know who I was, but not often, for more usually he was unconscious. Sometimes, too, he would talk all night with some unknown person, in dim, mysterious language that caused his gasping voice to echo hoarsely through the narrow room as through a sepulchre; and at such times, I found the situation a strange one. During his last night he was especially lightheaded, for then he was in terrible agony, and kept rambling in his speech until my soul was torn with pity. Everyone in the house was alarmed, and Anna Thedorovna fell to praying that God might soon take him. When the doctor had been summoned, the verdict was that the patient would die with the morning.

That night the elder Pokrovski spent in the corridor, at the door of his son's room. Though given a mattress to lie upon, he spent his time in running in and out of the apartment. So broken with grief was he that he presented a dreadful spectacle, and appeared to have lost both perception and feeling. His head trembled with agony, and his body quivered from head to foot as at times he murmured to himself something which he appeared to be debating. Every moment I expected to see him go out of his mind. Just before dawn he succumbed to the stress of mental agony, and fell asleep on his mattress like a man who has been beaten; but by eight o'clock the son was at the point of death, and I ran to wake the father. The dying man was quite conscious, and bid us all farewell. Somehow I could not weep, though my heart seemed to be breaking.

The last moments were the most harassing and heartbreaking of all. For some time past Pokrovski had been asking for something with his failing tongue, but I had been unable to distinguish his words. Yet my heart had been bursting with grief. Then for an hour he had lain quieter, except that he had looked sadly in my direction, and striven to make some sign with his death-cold hands. At last he again essayed his piteous request in a hoarse, deep voice, but the words issued in so many inarticulate sounds, and once more I failed to divine his meaning. By turns I brought each member of the household to his bedside, and gave him something to drink, but he only shook his head sorrowfully. Finally, I understood what it was he wanted. He was asking me to draw aside the curtain from the window, and to open the casements. Probably he wished to take his last look at the daylight and the sun and all God's world. I pulled back the curtain, but the opening day was as dull and mournful—looking as though it had been the fast-flickering life of the poor invalid. Of sunshine there was none. Clouds overlaid the sky as with a shroud of mist, and everything looked sad, rainy, and threatening under a fine drizzle which was beating against the window-panes, and streaking their dull, dark surfaces with runlets of cold, dirty moisture. Only a scanty modicum of daylight entered to war with the trembling rays of the ikon lamp. The dying man threw me a wistful look, and nodded. The next moment he had passed away.

The funeral was arranged for by Anna Thedorovna. A plain coffin was bought, and a broken-down hearse hired; while, as security for this outlay, she seized the dead man's books and other articles. Nevertheless, the old man disputed the books with her, and, raising an uproar, carried off as many of them as he could—stuffing his pockets full, and even filling his hat. Indeed, he spent the next three days with them thus, and refused to let them leave his sight even when it was time for him to go to church. Throughout he acted like a man bereft of sense and memory. With quaint assiduity he busied himself about the bier—now straightening the candlestick on the dead man's breast, now snuffing and lighting the other candles. Clearly his thoughts were powerless to remain long fixed on any subject. Neither my mother nor Anna Thedorovna were present at the requiem, for the former was ill and the latter was at loggerheads with the old man. Only myself and the father were there. During the service a sort of panic, a sort of premonition of the future, came over me, and I could hardly hold myself upright. At length the coffin had received its burden and was screwed down; after which the bearers placed it upon a bier, and set out. I accompanied the cortege only to the end of the street. Here the driver broke into a trot, and the old man started to run behind the hearse—sobbing loudly, but with the motion of his running ever and anon causing the sobs to quaver and become broken off. Next he lost his hat, the poor old fellow, yet would not stop to pick it up, even though the rain was beating upon his head, and a wind was rising and the sleet kept stinging and lashing his face. It seemed as though he were impervious to the cruel elements as he ran from one side of the hearse to the other—the skirts of his old greatcoat flapping about him like a pair of wings. From every pocket of the garment protruded books, while in his hand he carried a specially large volume, which he hugged closely to his breast. The passers-by uncovered their heads and crossed themselves as the cortege passed, and some of them, having done so, remained staring in amazement at the poor old man. Every now and then a book would slip from one of his pockets and fall into the mud; whereupon somebody, stopping him, would direct his attention to his loss, and he would stop, pick up the book, and again set off in pursuit of the hearse. At the corner of the street he was joined by a ragged old woman; until at length the hearse turned a corner, and became hidden from my eyes. Then I went home, and threw myself, in a transport of grief, upon my mother's breast—clasping her in my arms, kissing her amid a storm of sobs and tears, and clinging to her form as though in my embraces I were holding my last friend on earth, that I might preserve her from death. Yet already death was standing over her....

June 11th

How I thank you for our walk to the Islands yesterday, Makar Alexievitch! How fresh and pleasant, how full of verdure, was everything! And I had not seen anything green for such a long time! During my illness I used to think that I should never get better, that I was certainly going to die. Judge, then, how I felt yesterday! True, I may have seemed to you a little sad, and you must not be angry with me for that. Happy and light-hearted though I was, there were moments, even at the height of my felicity, when, for some unknown reason, depression came sweeping over my soul. I kept weeping about trifles, yet could not say why I was grieved. The truth is that I am unwell—so much so, that I look at everything from the gloomy point of view. The pale, clear sky, the setting sun, the evening stillness—ah, somehow I felt disposed to grieve and feel hurt at these things; my heart seemed to be over-charged, and to be calling for tears to relieve it. But why should I write this to you? It is difficult for my heart to express itself; still more difficult for it to forego self-expression. Yet possibly you may understand me. Tears and laughter!... How good you are, Makar Alexievitch! Yesterday you looked into my eyes as though you could read in them all that I was feeling—as though you were rejoicing at my happiness. Whether it were a group of shrubs or an alleyway or a vista of water that we were passing, you would halt before me, and stand gazing at my face as though you were showing me possessions of your own. It told me how kind is your nature, and I love you for it. Today I am again unwell, for yesterday I wetted my feet, and took a chill. Thedora also is unwell; both of us are ailing. Do not forget me. Come and see me as often as you can.—Your own,
BARBARA ALEXIEVNA.

June 12th.

MY DEAREST BARBARA ALEXIEVNA—I had supposed that you meant to describe our doings of the other day in verse; yet from you there has arrived only a single sheet of writing. Nevertheless, I must say that, little though you have put into your letter, that little is not expressed with rare beauty and grace. Nature, your descriptions of rural scenes, your analysis of your own feelings—the whole is beautifully written. Alas, I have no such talent! Though I may fill a score of pages, nothing comes of it—I might as well never have put pen to paper. Yes, this I know from experience.

You say, my darling, that I am kind and good, that I could not harm my fellow-men, that I have power to comprehend the goodness of God (as expressed in nature's handiwork), and so on. It may all be so, my dearest one—it may all be exactly as you say. Indeed, I think that you are right. But if so, the reason is that when one reads such a letter as you have just sent me, one's heart involuntarily softens, and affords entrance to thoughts of a graver and weightier order. Listen, my darling; I have something to tell you, my beloved one.

I will begin from the time when I was seventeen years old and first entered the service—though I shall soon have completed my thirtieth year of official activity. I may say that at first I was much pleased with my new uniform;

and, as I grew older, I grew in mind, and fell to studying my fellow-men. Likewise I may say that I lived an upright life—so much so that at last I incurred persecution. This you may not believe, but it is true. To think that men so cruel should exist! For though, dearest one, I am dull and of no account, I have feelings like everyone else. Consequently, would you believe it, Barbara, when I tell you what these cruel fellows did to me? I feel ashamed to tell it you—and all because I was of a quiet, peaceful, good-natured disposition!

Things began with "this or that, Makar Alexievitch, is your fault." Then it went on to "I need hardly say that the fault is wholly Makar Alexievitch's." Finally it became "OF COURSE Makar Alexievitch is to blame." Do you see the sequence of things, my darling? Every mistake was attributed to me, until "Makar Alexievitch" became a byword in our department. Also, while making of me a proverb, these fellows could not give me a smile or a civil word. They found fault with my boots, with my uniform, with my hair, with my figure. None of these things were to their taste: everything had to be changed. And so it has been from that day to this. True, I have now grown used to it, for I can grow accustomed to anything (being, as you know, a man of peaceable disposition, like all men of small stature)—yet why should these things be? Whom have I harmed? Whom have I ever supplanted? Whom have I ever traduced to his superiors? No, the fault is that more than once I have asked for an increase of salary. But have I ever CABALLED for it? No, you would be wrong in thinking so, my dearest one. HOW could I ever have done so? You yourself have had many opportunities of seeing how incapable I am of deceit or chicanery.

Why then, should this have fallen to my lot?... However, since you think me worthy of respect, my darling, I do not care, for you are far and away the best person in the world.... What do you consider to be the greatest social virtue? In private conversation Evstafi Ivanovitch once told me that the greatest social virtue might be considered to be an ability to get money to spend. Also, my comrades used jestingly (yes, I know only jestingly) to propound the ethical maxim that a man ought never to let himself become a burden upon anyone. Well, I am a burden upon no one. It is my own crust of bread that I eat; and though that crust is but a poor one, and sometimes actually a maggoty one, it has at least been EARNED, and therefore, is being put to a right and lawful use. What therefore, ought I to do? I know that I can earn but little by my labours as a copyist; yet even of that little I am proud, for it has entailed WORK, and has wrung sweat from my brow. What harm is there in being a copyist? "He is only an amanuensis," people say of me. But what is there so disgraceful in that? My writing is at least legible, neat, and pleasant to look upon—and his Excellency is satisfied with it. Indeed, I transcribe many important documents. At the same time, I know that my writing lacks STYLE, which is why I have never risen in the service. Even to you, my dear one, I write simply and without tricks, but just as a thought may happen to enter my head. Yes, I know all this; but if everyone were to become a fine writer, who would there be left to act as copyists?... Whatsoever questions I may put to you in my letters, dearest, I pray you to answer them. I am sure that you need me, that I can be of use to you; and, since that is so, I must not allow myself to be distracted by any trifle. Even if I be likened to a rat, I do not care, provided that that particular rat be wanted by you, and be of use in the world, and be retained in its position, and receive its reward. But what a rat it is!

Enough of this, dearest one. I ought not to have spoken of it, but I lost my temper. Still, it is pleasant to speak the truth sometimes. Goodbye, my own, my darling, my sweet little comforter! I will come to you soon—yes, I will certainly come to you. Until I do so, do not fret yourself. With me I shall be bringing a book. Once more goodbye.—Your heartfelt well-wisher,

MAKAR DIEVUSHKIN.

June 20th.

MY DEAREST MAKAR ALEXIEVITCH—I am writing to you post-haste—I am hurrying my utmost to get my work finished in time. What do you suppose is the reason for this? It is because an opportunity has occurred for you to make a splendid purchase. Thedora tells me that a retired civil servant of her acquaintance has a uniform to sell—one cut to regulation pattern and in good repair, as well as likely to go very cheap. Now, DO not tell me that you have not got the money, for I know from your own lips that you HAVE. Use that money, I pray you, and do not hoard it. See what terrible garments you walk about in! They are shameful—they are patched all over! In fact, you have nothing new whatever. That this is so, I know for certain, and I care not WHAT you tell me about it. So listen to me for once, and buy this uniform. Do it for MY sake. Do it to show that you really love me.

You have sent me some linen as a gift. But listen to me, Makar Alexievitch. You are simply ruining yourself. Is it a jest that you should spend so much money, such a terrible amount of money, upon me? How you love to play the spendthrift! I tell you that I do not need it, that such expenditure is unnecessary. I know, I am CERTAIN, that you love me—therefore, it is useless to remind me of the fact with gifts. Nor do I like receiving them, since I know how much they must have cost you. No—put your money to a better use. I beg, I beseech of you, to do so. Also, you ask me to send you a continuation of my memoirs—to conclude them. But I know not how I contrived even to write as much of them as I did; and now I have not the strength to write further of my past, nor the desire to give it a single thought. Such recollections are terrible to me. Most difficult of all is it for me to speak of my poor mother, who left her destitute daughter a prey to villains. My heart runs blood whenever I think of it; it is so fresh in my memory that I cannot dismiss it from my thoughts, nor rest for its insistence, although a year has now elapsed since the events took place. But all this you know.

Also, I have told you what Anna Thedorovna is now intending. She accuses me of ingratitude, and denies the accusations made against herself with regard to Monsieur Bwikov. Also, she keeps sending for me, and telling me that I have taken to evil courses, but that if I will return to her, she will smooth over matters with Bwikov, and force him to confess his fault. Also, she says that he desires to give me a dowry. Away with them all! I am quite happy here with you and good Thedora, whose devotion to me reminds me of my old nurse, long since dead. Distant kinsman though you may be, I pray you always to defend my honour. Other people I do not wish to know, and would gladly forget if I could.... What are they wanting with me now? Thedora declares it all to be a trick, and says that in time they will leave me alone. God grant it be so!

B. D.

June 21st.

MY OWN, MY DARLING,—I wish to write to you, yet know not where to begin. Things are as strange as though we were actually living together. Also I would add that never in my life have I passed such happy days as I am spending at present. 'Tis as though God had blessed me with a home and a family of my own! Yes, you are my little daughter, beloved. But why mention the four sorry roubles that I sent you? You needed them; I know that from Thedora herself, and it will always be a particular pleasure to me to gratify you in anything. It will always be my one happiness in life. Pray, therefore, leave me that happiness, and do not seek to cross me in it. Things are not as you suppose. I have now reached the sunshine since, in the first place, I am living so close to you as almost to be with you (which is a great consolation to my mind), while, in the second place, a neighbour of mine named Rataziaev (the retired official who gives the literary parties) has today invited me to tea. This evening, therefore, there will be a gathering at which we shall discuss literature! Think of that my darling! Well, goodbye now. I have written this without any definite aim in my mind, but solely to assure you of my welfare. Through Theresa I have received your message that you need an embroidered cloak to wear, so I will go and purchase one. Yes, tomorrow I mean to purchase that embroidered cloak, and so give myself the pleasure of having satisfied one of your wants. I know where to go for such a garment. For the time being I remain your sincere friend,

MAKAR DIEVUSHKIN.

June 22nd.

MY DEAREST BARBARA ALEXIEVNA,—I have to tell you that a sad event has happened in this house—an event to excite one's utmost pity. This morning, about five o'clock, one of Gorshkov's children died of scarlatina, or something of the kind. I have been to pay the parents a visit of condolence, and found them living in the direst poverty and disorder. Nor is that surprising, seeing that the family lives in a single room, with only a screen to divide it for decency's sake. Already the coffin was standing in their midst—a plain but decent shell which had been bought ready-made. The child, they told me, had been a boy of nine, and full of promise. What a pitiful spectacle! Though not weeping, the mother, poor woman, looked broken with grief. After all, to have one burden the less on their shoulders may prove a relief, though there are still two children left—a babe at the breast and a little girl of six! How painful to see these suffering children, and to be unable to help them! The father, clad in an old, dirty frockcoat, was seated on a dilapidated chair. Down his cheeks there were coursing tears—though less through grief than owing to a long-standing affliction of the eyes. He was so thin, too! Always he reddens in the face when he is addressed, and becomes too confused to answer. A little girl, his daughter, was leaning against the coffin—her face looking so worn and thoughtful, poor mite! Do you know, I cannot bear to see a child look thoughtful. On the floor there lay a rag doll, but she was not playing with it as, motionless, she stood there with her finger to her lips. Even a bon-bon which the landlady had given her she was not eating. Is it not all sad, sad, Barbara?

MAKAR DIEVUSHKIN.

June 25th.

MY BELOVED MAKAR ALEXIEVITCH—I return you your book. In my opinion it is a worthless one, and I would rather not have it in my possession. Why do you save up your money to buy such trash? Except in jest, do such books really please you? However, you have now promised to send me something else to read. I will share the cost of it. Now, farewell until we meet again. I have nothing more to say.

B. D.

MY DEAR LITTLE BARBARA—To tell you the truth, I myself have not read the book of which you speak. That is to say, though I began to read it, I soon saw that it was nonsense, and written only to make people laugh. "However," thought I, "it is at least a CHEERFUL work, and so may please Barbara." That is why I sent it you.

Rataziaev has now promised to give me something really literary to read; so you shall soon have your book, my darling. He is a man who reflects; he is a clever fellow, as well as himself a writer—such a writer! His pen glides along with ease, and in such a style (even when he is writing the most ordinary, the most insignificant of articles) that I have often remarked upon the fact, both to Phaldoni and to Theresa. Often, too, I go to spend an evening with him. He reads aloud to us until five o'clock in the morning, and we listen to him. It is a revelation of things rather than a reading. It is charming, it is like a bouquet of flowers—there is a bouquet of flowers in every line of each page. Besides, he is such an approachable, courteous, kind-hearted fellow! What am I compared with him? Why, nothing, simply nothing! He is a man of reputation, whereas I—well, I do not exist at all. Yet he condescends to my level. At this very moment I am copying out a document for him. But you must not think that he finds any DIFFICULTY in condescending to me, who am only a copyist. No, you must not believe the base gossip that you may hear. I do copying work for him simply in order to please myself, as well as that he may notice me—a thing that always gives me pleasure. I appreciate the delicacy of his position. He is a good—a very good—man, and an unapproachable writer.

What a splendid thing is literature, Barbara—what a splendid thing! This I learnt before I had known Rataziaev even for three days. It strengthens and instructs the heart of man.... No matter what there be in the world, you will find it all written down in Rataziaev's works. And so well written down, too! Literature is a sort of picture—a sort of picture or mirror. It connotes at once passion, expression, fine criticism, good learning, and a document. Yes, I have learned this from Rataziaev himself. I can assure you, Barbara, that if only you could be sitting among us, and listening to the talk (while, with the rest of us, you smoked a pipe), and were to hear those present begin to argue and dispute concerning different matters, you would feel of as little account among them as I do; for I myself figure there only as a blockhead, and feel ashamed, since it takes me a whole evening to think of a single word to interpolate—and even then the word will not come! In a case like that a man regrets that, as the proverb has it, he should have reached man's estate but not man's understanding.... What do I do in my spare time? I sleep like a fool, though I would far rather be occupied with something else—say, with eating or writing, since the one is useful to oneself, and the other is beneficial to one's fellows. You should see how much money these fellows contrive to save! How much, for instance, does not Rataziaev lay by? A few days' writing, I am told, can earn him as much as three hundred roubles! Indeed, if a man be a writer of short stories or anything else that is interesting, he can sometimes pocket five hundred roubles, or a thousand, at a time! Think of it, Barbara! Rataziaev has by him a small manuscript of verses, and for it he is asking—what do you think? Seven thousand roubles! Why, one could buy a whole house for that sum! He has even refused five thousand for a manuscript, and on that occasion I reasoned with him, and advised him to accept the five thousand. But it was of no use. "For," said he, "they will soon offer me seven thousand," and kept to his point, for he is a man of some determination.

Suppose, now, that I were to give you an extract from "Passion in Italy" (as another work of his is called). Read this, dearest Barbara, and judge for yourself:

"Vladimir started, for in his veins the lust of passion had welled until it had reached boiling point.

"'Countess,' he cried, 'do you know how terrible is this adoration of mine, how infinite this madness? No! My fancies have not deceived me—I love you ecstatically, diabolically, as a madman might! All the blood that is in your husband's body could never quench the furious, surging rapture that is in my soul! No puny obstacle could thwart the all-destroying, infernal flame which is eating into my exhausted breast! Oh Zinaida, my Zinaida!'

"'Vladimir!' she whispered, almost beside herself, as she sank upon his bosom.

"'My Zinaida!' cried the enraptured Smileski once more.

"His breath was coming in sharp, broken pants. The lamp of love was burning brightly on the altar of passion, and searing the hearts of the two unfortunate sufferers.

"'Vladimir!' again she whispered in her intoxication, while her bosom heaved, her cheeks glowed, and her eyes flashed fire.

"Thus was a new and dread union consummated.

"Half an hour later the aged Count entered his wife's boudoir.

"'How now, my love?' said he. 'Surely it is for some welcome guest beyond the common that you have had the samovar [Tea-urn.] thus prepared?' And he smote her lightly on the cheek."

What think you of THAT, Barbara? True, it is a little too outspoken—there can be no doubt of that; yet how grand it is, how splendid! With your permission I will also quote you an extract from Rataziaev's story, Ermak and Zuleika:

"'You love me, Zuleika? Say again that you love me, you love me!'

"'I DO love you, Ermak,' whispered Zuleika.

"'Then by heaven and earth I thank you! By heaven and earth you have made me happy! You have given me all, all that my tortured soul has for immemorial years been seeking! 'Tis for this that you have led me hither, my guiding star—'tis for this that you have conducted me to the Girdle of Stone! To all the world will I now show my Zuleika, and no man, demon or monster of Hell, shall bid me nay! Oh, if men would but understand the mysterious passions of her tender heart, and see the poem which lurks in each of her little tears! Suffer me to dry those tears with my kisses! Suffer me to drink of those heavenly drops, Oh being who art not of this earth!'

"'Ermak,' said Zuleika, 'the world is cruel, and men are unjust. But LET them drive us from their midst—let them judge us, my beloved Ermak! What has a poor maiden who was reared amid the snows of Siberia to do with their cold, icy, self-sufficient world? Men cannot understand me, my darling, my sweetheart.'

"'Is that so? Then shall the sword of the Cossacks sing and whistle over their heads!' cried Ermak with a furious look in his eyes."

What must Ermak have felt when he learnt that his Zuleika had been murdered, Barbara?—that, taking advantages of the cover of night, the blind old Kouchoum had, in Ermak's absence, broken into the latter's tent, and stabbed his own daughter in mistake for the man who had robbed him of sceptre and crown?

"'Oh that I had a stone whereon to whet my sword!' cried Ermak in the madness of his wrath as he strove to sharpen his steel blade upon the enchanted rock. 'I would have his blood, his blood! I would tear him limb from limb, the villain!'"

Then Ermak, unable to survive the loss of his Zuleika, throws himself into the Irtisch, and the tale comes to an end.

Here, again, is another short extract—this time written in a more comical vein, to make people laugh:

"Do you know Ivan Prokofievitch Zheltopuzh? He is the man who took a piece out of Prokofi Ivanovitch's leg. Ivan's character is one of the rugged order, and therefore, one that is rather lacking in virtue. Yet he has a passionate relish for radishes and honey. Once he also possessed a friend named Pelagea Antonovna. Do you know Pelagea Antonovna? She is the woman who always puts on her petticoat wrong side outwards."

What humour, Barbara—what purest humour! We rocked with laughter when he read it aloud to us. Yes, that is the kind of man he is. Possibly the passage is a trifle over-frolicsome, but at least it is harmless, and contains no freethought or liberal ideas. In passing, I may say that Rataziaev is not only a supreme writer, but also a man of upright life—which is more than can be said for most writers.

What, do you think, is an idea that sometimes enters my head? In fact, what if I myself were to write something? How if suddenly a book were to make its appearance in the world bearing the title of "The Poetical Works of Makar Dievushkin"? What THEN, my angel? How should you view, should you receive, such an event? I may say of myself that never, after my book had appeared, should I have the hardihood to show my face on the Nevski Prospect; for would it not be too dreadful to hear every one saying, "Here comes the literateur and poet, Dievushkin—yes, it is Dievushkin himself." What, in such a case, should I do with my feet (for I may tell you that almost always my shoes are patched, or have just been resoled, and therefore look anything but becoming)? To think that the great writer Dievushkin should walk about in patched footgear! If a duchess or a countess should recognise me, what would she say, poor woman? Perhaps, though, she would not notice my shoes at all, since it may reasonably be supposed that countesses do not greatly occupy themselves with footgear, especially with the footgear of civil service officials (footgear may differ from footgear, it must be remembered). Besides, I should find that the countess had heard all about me, for my friends would have betrayed me to her—Rataziaev among the first of them, seeing that he often goes to visit Countess V., and practically lives at her house. She is said to be a woman of great intellect and wit. An artful dog, that Rataziaev!

But enough of this. I write this sort of thing both to amuse myself and to divert your thoughts. Goodbye now, my angel. This is a long epistle that I am sending you, but the reason is that today I feel in good spirits after dining at Rataziaev's. There I came across a novel which I hardly know how to describe to you. Do not think the worse of me on that account, even though I bring you another book instead (for I certainly mean to bring one). The novel in question was one of Paul de Kock's, and not a novel for you to read. No, no! Such a work is unfit for your eyes. In fact, it is said to have greatly offended the critics of St. Petersburg. Also, I am sending you a pound of bonbons— bought specially for yourself. Each time that you eat one, beloved, remember the sender. Only, do not bite the iced ones, but suck them gently, lest they make your teeth ache. Perhaps, too, you like comfits? Well, write and tell me if it is so. Goodbye, goodbye. Christ watch over you, my darling!—Always your faithful friend,

MAKAR DIEVUSHKIN.

MY DEAREST MAKAR ALEXIEVITCH—Thedora tells me that, should I wish, there are some people who will be glad to help me by obtaining me an excellent post as governess in a certain house. What think you, my friend? Shall I go or not? Of course, I should then cease to be a burden to you, and the post appears to be a comfortable one. On the other hand, the idea of entering a strange house appals me. The people in it are landed gentry, and they will begin to ask me questions, and to busy themselves about me. What answers shall I then return? You see, I am now so unused to society—so shy! I like to live in a corner to which I have long grown used. Yes, the place with which one is familiar is always the best. Even if for companion one has but sorrow, that place will still be the best.... God alone knows what duties the post will entail. Perhaps I shall merely be required to act as nursemaid; and in any case, I hear that the governess there has been changed three times in two years. For God's sake, Makar Alexievitch, advise me whether to go or not. Why do you never come near me now? Do let my eyes have an occasional sight of you. Mass on Sundays is almost the only time when we see one another. How retiring you have become! So also have I, even though, in a way, I am your kinswoman. You must have ceased to love me, Makar Alexievitch. I spend many a weary hour because of it. Sometimes, when dusk is falling, I find myself lonely—oh, so lonely! Thedora has gone out somewhere, and I sit here and think, and think, and think. I remember all the past, its joys and its sorrows. It passes before my eyes in detail, it glimmers at me as out of a mist; and as it does so, well-known faces appear, which seem actually to be present with me in this room! Most frequently of all, I see my mother. Ah, the dreams that come to me! I feel that my health is breaking, so weak am I. When this morning I arose, sickness took me until I vomited and vomited. Yes, I feel, I know, that death is approaching. Who will bury me when it has come? Who will visit my tomb? Who will sorrow for me? And now it is in a strange place, in the house of a stranger, that I may have to die! Yes, in a corner which I do not know!... My God, how sad a thing is life!... Why do you send me comfits to eat? Whence do you get the money to buy them? Ah, for God's sake keep the money, keep the money. Thedora has sold a carpet which I have made. She got fifty roubles for it, which is very good—I had expected less. Of the fifty roubles I shall give Thedora three, and with the remainder make myself a plain, warm dress. Also, I am going to make you a waistcoat—to make it myself, and out of good material.

Also, Thedora has brought me a book—"The Stories of Bielkin"—which I will forward you, if you would care to read it. Only, do not soil it, nor yet retain it, for it does not belong to me. It is by Pushkin. Two years ago I read these stories with my mother, and it would hurt me to read them again. If you yourself have any books, pray let me have them—so long as they have not been obtained from Rataziaev. Probably he will be giving you one of his own works when he has had one printed. How is it that his compositions please you so much, Makar Alexievitch? I think them SUCH rubbish!

—Now goodbye. How I have been chattering on! When feeling sad, I always like to talk of something, for it acts upon me like medicine—I begin to feel easier as soon as I have uttered what is preying upon my heart. Good bye, good-bye, my friend—Your own

B. D.

MY DEAREST BARBARA ALEXIEVNA—Away with melancholy! Really, beloved, you ought to be ashamed of yourself! How can you allow such thoughts to enter your head? Really and truly you are quite well; really and truly you are, my darling. Why, you are blooming—simply blooming. True, I see a certain touch of pallor in your face, but still you are blooming. A fig for dreams and visions! Yes, for shame, dearest! Drive away those fancies; try to despise them. Why do I sleep so well? Why am I never ailing? Look at ME, beloved. I live well, I sleep peacefully, I retain my health, I can ruffle it with my juniors. In fact, it is a pleasure to see me. Come, come, then, sweetheart! Let us have no more of this. I know that that little head of yours is capable of any fancy—that all too easily you take to dreaming and repining; but for my sake, cease to do so.

Are you to go to these people, you ask me? Never! No, no, again no! How could you think of doing such a thing as taking a journey? I will not allow it—I intend to combat your intention with all my might. I will sell my frockcoat, and walk the streets in my shirt sleeves, rather than let you be in want. But no, Barbara. I know you, I know you. This is merely a trick, merely a trick. And probably Thedora alone is to blame for it. She appears to be a foolish old woman, and to be able to persuade you to do anything. Do not believe her, my dearest. I am sure that you know what is what, as well as SHE does. Eh, sweetheart? She is a stupid, quarrelsome, rubbish-talking old woman who brought her late husband to the grave. Probably she has been plaguing you as much as she did him. No, no, dearest; you must not take this step. What should I do then? What would there be left for ME to do? Pray put the idea out of your head. What is it you lack here? I cannot feel sufficiently overjoyed to be near you, while, for your part, you love me well, and can live your life here as quietly as you wish. Read or sew, whichever you like—or read and do not sew. Only, do not desert me. Try, yourself, to imagine how things would seem after you had gone. Here am I sending you books, and later we will go for a walk. Come, come, then, my Barbara! Summon to your aid your reason, and cease to babble of trifles.

As soon as I can I will come and see you, and then you shall tell me the whole story. This will not do, sweetheart; this certainly will not do. Of course, I know that I am not an educated man, and have received but a sorry schooling, and have had no inclination for it, and think too much of Rataziaev, if you will; but he is my friend, and therefore, I must put in a word or two for him. Yes, he is a splendid writer. Again and again I assert that he writes magnificently. I do not agree with you about his works, and never shall. He writes too ornately, too laconically, with too great a wealth of imagery and imagination. Perhaps you have read him without insight, Barbara? Or perhaps you were out of spirits at the time, or angry with Thedora about something, or worried about some mischance? Ah, but you should read him sympathetically, and, best of all, at a time when you are feeling happy and contented and pleasantly disposed—for instance, when you have a bonbon or two in your mouth. Yes, that is the way to read Rataziaev. I do not dispute (indeed, who would do so?) that better writers than he exist—even far better; but they are good, and he is good too—they write well, and he writes well. It is chiefly for his own sake that he writes, and he is to be approved for so doing.

Now goodbye, dearest. More I cannot write, for I must hurry away to business. Be of good cheer, and the Lord God watch over you!—Your faithful friend,

MAKAR DIEVUSHKIN.

P.S—Thank you so much for the book, darling! I will read it through, this volume of Pushkin, and tonight come to you.

MY DEAR MAKAR ALEXIEVITCH—No, no, my friend, I must not go on living near you. I have been thinking the matter over, and come to the conclusion that I should be doing very wrong to refuse so good a post. I should at least have an assured crust of bread; I might at least set to work to earn my employers' favour, and even try to change my character if required to do so. Of course it is a sad and sorry thing to have to live among strangers, and to be forced to seek their patronage, and to conceal and constrain one's own personality—but God will help me. I must not remain forever a recluse, for similar chances have come my way before. I remember how, when a little girl at school, I used to go home on Sundays and spend the time in frisking and dancing about. Sometimes my mother would chide me for so doing, but I did not care, for my heart was too joyous, and my spirits too buoyant, for that. Yet as the evening of Sunday came on, a sadness as of death would overtake me, for at nine o'clock I had to return to school, where everything was cold and strange and severe—where the governesses, on Mondays, lost their tempers, and nipped my ears, and made me cry. On such occasions I would retire to a corner and weep alone; concealing my tears lest I should be called lazy. Yet it was not because I had to study that I used to weep, and in time I grew more used to things, and, after my schooldays were over, shed tears only when I was parting with friends....

It is not right for me to live in dependence upon you. The thought tortures me. I tell you this frankly, for the reason that frankness with you has become a habit. Cannot I see that daily, at earliest dawn, Thedora rises to do washing and scrubbing, and remains working at it until late at night, even though her poor old bones must be aching for want of rest? Cannot I also see that YOU are ruining yourself for me, and hoarding your last kopeck that you may spend it on my behalf? You ought not so to act, my friend, even though you write that you would rather sell your all than let me want for anything. I believe in you, my friend—I entirely believe in your good heart; but, you say that to me now (when, perhaps, you have received some unexpected sum or gratuity) and there is still the future to be thought of. You yourself know that I am always ailing—that I cannot work as you do, glad though I should be of any work if I could get it; so what else is there for me to do? To sit and repine as I watch you and Thedora? But how would that be of any use to you? AM I necessary to you, comrade of mine? HAVE I ever done you any good? Though I am bound to you with my whole soul, and love you dearly and strongly and wholeheartedly, a bitter fate has ordained that that love should be all that I have to give—that I should be unable, by creating for you subsistence, to repay you for all your kindness. Do not, therefore, detain me longer, but think the matter out, and give me your opinion on it. In expectation of which I remain your sweetheart,

B. D

July 1st.

Rubbish, rubbish, Barbara!—What you say is sheer rubbish. Stay here, rather, and put such thoughts out of your head. None of what you suppose is true. I can see for myself that it is not. Whatsoever you lack here, you have but to ask me for it. Here you love and are loved, and we might easily be happy and contented together. What could you want more? What have you to do with strangers? You cannot possibly know what strangers are like. I know it, though, and could have told you if you had asked me. There is a stranger whom I know, and whose bread I have eaten. He is a cruel man, Barbara—a man so bad that he would be unworthy of your little heart, and would soon tear it to pieces with his railings and reproaches and black looks. On the other hand, you are safe and well here—

you are as safe as though you were sheltered in a nest. Besides, you would, as it were, leave me with my head gone. For what should I have to do when you were gone? What could I, an old man, find to do? Are you not necessary to me? Are you not useful to me? Eh? Surely you do not think that you are not useful? You are of great use to me, Barbara, for you exercise a beneficial influence upon my life. Even at this moment, as I think of you, I feel cheered, for always I can write letters to you, and put into them what I am feeling, and receive from you detailed answers.... I have bought you a wardrobe, and also procured you a bonnet; so you see that you have only to give me a commission for it to be executed.... No—in what way are you not useful? What should I do if I were deserted in my old age? What would become of me? Perhaps you never thought of that, Barbara—perhaps you never said to yourself, "How could HE get on without me?" You see, I have grown so accustomed to you. What else would it end in, if you were to go away? Why, in my hiking to the Neva's bank and doing away with myself. Ah, Barbara, darling, I can see that you want me to be taken away to the Volkovo Cemetery in a broken-down old hearse, with some poor outcast of the streets to accompany my coffin as chief mourner, and the gravediggers to heap my body with clay, and depart and leave me there. How wrong of you, how wrong of you, my beloved! Yes, by heavens, how wrong of you! I am returning you your book, little friend; and, if you were to ask of me my opinion of it, I should say that never before in my life had I read a book so splendid. I keep wondering how I have hitherto contrived to remain such an owl. For what have I ever done? From what wilds did I spring into existence? I KNOW nothing—I know simply NOTHING. My ignorance is complete. Frankly, I am not an educated man, for until now I have read scarcely a single book—only "A Portrait of Man" (a clever enough work in its way), "The Boy Who Could Play Many Tunes Upon Bells", and "Ivik's Storks". That is all. But now I have also read "The Station Overseer" in your little volume; and it is wonderful to think that one may live and yet be ignorant of the fact that under one's very nose there may be a book in which one's whole life is described as in a picture. Never should I have guessed that, as soon as ever one begins to read such a book, it sets one on both to remember and to consider and to foretell events. Another reason why I liked this book so much is that, though, in the case of other works (however clever they be), one may read them, yet remember not a word of them (for I am a man naturally dull of comprehension, and unable to read works of any great importance),—although, as I say, one may read such works, one reads such a book as YOURS as easily as though it had been written by oneself, and had taken possession of one's heart, and turned it inside out for inspection, and were describing it in detail as a matter of perfect simplicity. Why, I might almost have written the book myself! Why not, indeed? I can feel just as the people in the book do, and find myself in positions precisely similar to those of, say, the character Samson Virin. In fact, how many good-hearted wretches like Virin are there not walking about amongst us? How easily, too, it is all described! I assure you, my darling, that I almost shed tears when I read that Virin so took to drink as to lose his memory, become morose, and spend whole days over his liquor; as also that he choked with grief and wept bitterly when, rubbing his eyes with his dirty hand, he bethought him of his wandering lamb, his daughter Dunasha! How natural, how natural! You should read the book for yourself. The thing is actually alive. Even I can see that; even I can realise that it is a picture cut from the very life around me. In it I see our own Theresa (to go no further) and the poor Tchinovnik—who is just such a man as this Samson Virin, except for his surname of Gorshkov. The book describes just what might happen to ourselves—to myself in particular. Even a count who lives in the Nevski Prospect or in Naberezhnaia Street might have a similar experience, though he might APPEAR to be different, owing to the fact that his life is cast on a higher plane. Yes, just the same things might happen to him—just the same things.... Here you are wishing to go away and leave us; yet, be careful lest it would not be I who had to pay the penalty of your doing so. For you might ruin both yourself and me. For the love of God, put away these thoughts from you, my darling, and do not torture me in vain. How could you, my poor little unfledged nestling, find yourself food, and defend yourself from misfortune, and ward off the wiles of evil men? Think better of it, Barbara, and pay no more heed to foolish advice and calumny, but read your book again, and read it with attention. It may do you much good.

I have spoken of Rataziaev's "The Station Overseer". However, the author has told me that the work is old-fashioned, since, nowadays, books are issued with illustrations and embellishments of different sorts (though I could not make out all that he said). Pushkin he adjudges a splendid poet, and one who has done honour to Holy Russia. Read your book again, Barbara, and follow my advice, and make an old man happy. The Lord God Himself will reward you. Yes, He will surely reward you.—Your faithful friend,

MAKAR DIEVUSHKIN.

MY DEAREST MAKAR ALEXIEVITCH,—Today Thedora came to me with fifteen roubles in silver. How glad was the poor woman when I gave her three of them! I am writing to you in great haste, for I am busy cutting out a waistcoat to send to you—buff, with a pattern of flowers. Also I am sending you a book of stories; some of which I have read myself, particularly one called "The Cloak." ... You invite me to go to the theatre with you. But will it not cost too much? Of course we might sit in the gallery. It is a long time (indeed I cannot remember when I last did so) since I visited a theatre! Yet I cannot help fearing that such an amusement is beyond our means. Thedora keeps nodding her head, and saying that you have taken to living above your income. I myself divine the same thing by the amount which you have spent upon me. Take care, dear friend, that misfortune does not come of it, for Thedora has also informed me of certain rumours concerning your inability to meet your landlady's bills. In fact, I am very anxious about you. Now, goodbye, for I must hasten away to see about another matter—about the changing of the ribands on my bonnet.

P.S.—Do you know, if we go to the theatre, I think that I shall wear my new hat and black mantilla. Will that not look nice?

July 7th.

MY DEAREST BARBARA ALEXIEVNA—SO much for yesterday! Yes, dearest, we have both been caught playing the fool, for I have become thoroughly bitten with the actress of whom I spoke. Last night I listened to her with all my ears, although, strangely enough, it was practically my first sight of her, seeing that only once before had I been to the theatre. In those days I lived cheek by jowl with a party of five young men—a most noisy crew— and one night I accompanied them, willy-nilly, to the theatre, though I held myself decently aloof from their doings, and only assisted them for company's sake. How those fellows talked to me of this actress! Every night when the theatre was open, the entire band of them (they always seemed to possess the requisite money) would betake themselves to that place of entertainment, where they ascended to the gallery, and clapped their hands, and repeatedly recalled the actress in question. In fact, they went simply mad over her. Even after we had returned home they would give me no rest, but would go on talking about her all night, and calling her their Glasha, and declaring themselves to be in love with "the canary-bird of their hearts." My defenseless self, too, they would plague about the woman, for I was as young as they. What a figure I must have cut with them on the fourth tier of the gallery! Yet, I never got a sight of more than just a corner of the curtain, but had to content myself with listening. She had a fine, resounding, mellow voice like a nightingale's, and we all of us used to clap our hands loudly, and to shout at the top of our lungs. In short, we came very near to being ejected. On the first occasion I went home walking as in a mist, with a single rouble left in my pocket, and an interval of ten clear days confronting me before next pay-day. Yet, what think you, dearest? The very next day, before going to work, I called at a French perfumer's, and spent my whole remaining capital on some eau-de-Cologne and scented soap! Why I did so I do not know. Nor did I dine at home that day, but kept walking and walking past her windows (she lived in a fourth-storey flat on the Nevski Prospect). At length I returned to my own lodging, but only to rest a short hour before again setting off to the Nevski Prospect and resuming my vigil before her windows. For a month and a half I kept this up—dangling in her train. Sometimes I would hire cabs, and discharge them in view of her abode; until at length I had entirely ruined myself, and got into debt. Then I fell out of love with her—I grew weary of the pursuit.... You see, therefore, to what depths an actress can reduce a decent man. In those days I was young. Yes, in those days I was VERY young.

M. D.

July 8th.

MY DEAREST BARBARA ALEXIEVNA,—The book which I received from you on the 6th of this month I now hasten to return, while at the same time hastening also to explain matters to you in this accompanying letter. What a misfortune, my beloved, that you should have brought me to such a pass! Our lots in life are apportioned by the Almighty according to our human deserts. To such a one He assigns a life in a general's epaulets or as a privy councillor—to such a one, I say, He assigns a life of command; whereas to another one, He allots only a life of unmurmuring toil and suffering. These things are calculated according to a man's CAPACITY. One man may be capable of one thing, and another of another, and their several capacities are ordered by the Lord God himself. I have now been thirty years in the public service, and have fulfilled my duties irreproachably, remained abstemious, and never been detected in any unbecoming behaviour. As a citizen, I may confess—I confess it freely—I have been guilty of certain shortcomings; yet those shortcomings have been combined with certain virtues. I am respected by my superiors, and even his Excellency has had no fault to find with me; and though I have never been shown any special marks of favour, I know that every one finds me at least satisfactory. Also, my writing is sufficiently legible and clear. Neither too rounded nor too fine, it is a running hand, yet always suitable. Of our staff only Ivan Prokofievitch writes a similar hand. Thus have I lived till the grey hairs of my old age; yet I can think of no serious fault committed. Of course, no one is free from MINOR faults. Everyone has some of them, and you among the rest, my beloved. But in grave or in audacious offences never have I been detected, nor in infringements of regulations, nor in breaches of the public peace. No, never! This you surely know, even as the author of your book must have known it. Yes, he also must have known it when he sat down to write. I had not expected this of you, my Barbara. I should never have expected it.

What? In future I am not to go on living peacefully in my little corner, poor though that corner be I am not to go on living, as the proverb has it, without muddying the water, or hurting any one, or forgetting the fear of the Lord God and of oneself? I am not to see, forsooth, that no man does me an injury, or breaks into my home—I am not to take care that all shall go well with me, or that I have clothes to wear, or that my shoes do not require mending, or that I be given work to do, or that I possess sufficient meat and drink? Is it nothing that, where the pavement is rotten, I have to walk on tiptoe to save my boots? If I write to you overmuch concerning myself, is it concerning ANOTHER man, rather, that I ought to write—concerning HIS wants, concerning HIS lack of tea to drink (and all the world needs tea)? Has it ever been my custom to pry into other men's mouths, to see what is being put into them? Have I ever been known to offend any one in that respect? No, no, beloved! Why should I desire to insult other folks when they are not molesting ME? Let me give you an example of what I mean. A man may go on slaving and slaving in the public service, and earn the respect of his superiors (for what it is worth), and then, for no visible reason at all, find himself made a fool of. Of course he may break out now and then (I am not now referring only to drunkenness), and (for example) buy himself a new pair of shoes, and take pleasure in seeing his feet looking well and smartly shod. Yes, I myself have known what it is to feel like that (I write this in good faith). Yet I am nonetheless astonished that Thedor Thedorovitch should neglect what is being said about him, and take no steps to defend himself. True, he is only a subordinate official, and sometimes loves to rate and scold; yet why should he not do so—why should he not indulge in a little vituperation when he feels like it? Suppose it to be NECESSARY, for FORM'S sake, to scold, and to set everyone right, and to shower around abuse (for, between ourselves, Barbara, our friend cannot get on WITHOUT abuse—so much so that every one humours him, and does things behind his back)? Well, since officials differ in rank, and every official demands that he shall be allowed to abuse his fellow officials in proportion to his rank, it follows that the TONE also of official abuse should become divided into ranks, and thus accord with the natural order of things. All the world is built upon the system that each one of us shall have to yield precedence to some other one, as well as to enjoy a certain power of abusing his fellows. Without such a provision the world could not get on at all, and simple chaos would ensue. Yet I am surprised that our Thedor should continue to overlook insults of the kind that he endures.

Why do I do my official work at all? Why is that necessary? Will my doing of it lead anyone who reads it to give me a greatcoat, or to buy me a new pair of shoes? No, Barbara. Men only read the documents, and then require me to write more. Sometimes a man will hide himself away, and not show his face abroad, for the mere reason that, though he has done nothing to be ashamed of, he dreads the gossip and slandering which are everywhere to be encountered. If his civic and family life have to do with literature, everything will be printed and read and laughed over and discussed; until at length, he hardly dare show his face in the street at all, seeing that he will have been described by report as recognisable through his gait alone! Then, when he has amended his ways, and grown gentler (even though he still continues to be loaded with official work), he will come to be accounted a virtuous, decent citizen who has deserved well of his comrades, rendered obedience to his superiors, wished noone any evil, preserved the fear of God in his heart, and died lamented. Yet would it not be better, instead of letting the poor fellow die, to give him a cloak while yet he is ALIVE—to give it to this same Thedor Thedorovitch (that is to say, to myself)? Yes, 'twere far better if, on hearing the tale of his subordinate's virtues, the chief of the department were to call the deserving man into his office, and then and there to promote him, and to grant him an increase of salary. Thus vice would be punished, virtue would prevail, and the staff of that department would live in peace together. Here we have an example from everyday, commonplace life. How, therefore, could you bring yourself to send me that book, my beloved? It is a badly conceived work, Barbara, and also unreal, for the reason that in creation such a Tchinovnik does not exist. No, again I protest against it, little Barbara; again I protest.—Your most humble, devoted servant,

M. D.

July 27th.

MY DEAREST MAKAR ALEXIEVITCH,—Your latest conduct and letters had frightened me, and left me thunderstruck and plunged in doubt, until what you have said about Thedor explained the situation. Why despair and go into such frenzies, Makar Alexievitch? Your explanations only partially satisfy me. Perhaps I did wrong to insist upon accepting a good situation when it was offered me, seeing that from my last experience in that way I derived a shock which was anything but a matter for jesting. You say also that your love for me has compelled you to hide yourself in retirement. Now, how much I am indebted to you I realised when you told me that you were spending for my benefit the sum which you are always reported to have laid by at your bankers; but, now that I have learned that you never possessed such a fund, but that, on hearing of my destitute plight, and being moved by it, you decided to spend upon me the whole of your salary—even to forestall it—and when I had fallen ill, actually to sell your clothes—when I learned all this I found myself placed in the harassing position of not knowing how to accept it all, nor what to think of it. Ah, Makar Alexievitch! You ought to have stopped at your first acts of charity—acts inspired by sympathy and the love of kinsfolk, rather than have continued to squander your means upon what was unnecessary. Yes, you have betrayed our friendship, Makar Alexievitch, in that you have not been open with me; and, now that I see that your last coin has been spent upon dresses and bon-bons and excursions and books and visits to the theatre for me, I weep bitter tears for my unpardonable improvidence in having accepted these things without giving so much as a thought to your welfare. Yes, all that you have done to give me pleasure has become converted into a source of grief, and left behind it only useless regret. Of late I have remarked that you were looking depressed; and though I felt fearful that something unfortunate was impending, what has happened would otherwise never have entered my head. To think that your better sense should so play you false, Makar Alexievitch! What will people think of you, and say of you? Who will want to know you? You whom, like everyone else, I have valued for your goodness of heart and modesty and good sense—YOU, I say, have now given way to an unpleasant vice of which you seem never before to have been guilty. What were my feelings when Thedora informed me that you had been discovered drunk in the street, and taken home by the police? Why, I felt petrified with astonishment—although, in view of the fact that you had failed me for four days, I had been expecting some such extraordinary occurrence. Also, have you thought what your superiors will say of you when they come to learn the true reason of your absence? You say that everyone is laughing at you, that every one has learnED of the bond which exists between us, and that your neighbours habitually refer to me with a sneer. Pay no attention to this, Makar Alexievitch; for the love of God, be comforted. Also, the incident between you and the officers has much alarmed me, although I had heard certain rumours concerning it. Pray explain to me what it means. You write, too, that you have been afraid to be open with me, for the reason that your confessions might lose you my friendship. Also, you say that you are in despair at the thought of being unable to help me in my illness, owing to the fact that you have sold everything which might have maintained me, and preserved me in sickness, as well as that you have borrowed as much as it is possible for you to borrow, and are daily experiencing unpleasantness with your landlady. Well, in failing to reveal all this to me you chose the worse course. Now, however, I know all. You have forced me to recognise that I have been the cause of your unhappy plight, as well as that my own conduct has brought upon myself a twofold measure of sorrow. The fact leaves me thunderstruck, Makar Alexievitch. Ah, friend, an infectious disease is indeed a misfortune, for now we poor and miserable folk must perforce keep apart from one another, lest the infection be increased. Yes, I have brought upon you calamities which never before in your humble, solitary life you had experienced. This tortures and exhausts me more than I can tell to think of.

Write to me quite frankly. Tell me how you came to embark upon such a course of conduct. Comfort, oh, comfort me if you can. It is not self-love that prompts me to speak of my own comforting, but my friendship and love for you, which will never fade from my heart. Goodbye. I await your answer with impatience. You have thought but poorly of me, Makar Alexievitch.—Your friend and lover,

BARBARA DOBROSELOVA.

July 28th.

MY PRICELESS BARBARA ALEXIEVNA,—What am I to say to you, now that all is over, and we are gradually returning to our old position? You say that you are anxious as to what will be thought of me. Let me tell you that the dearest thing in life to me is my self-respect; wherefore, in informing you of my misfortunes and misconduct, I would add that none of my superiors know of my doings, nor ever will know of them, and that therefore, I still enjoy a measure of respect in that quarter. Only one thing do I fear—I fear gossip. Garrulous though my landlady be, she said but little when, with the aid of your ten roubles, I today paid her part of her account; and as for the rest of my companions, they do not matter at all. So long as I have not borrowed money from them, I need pay them no attention. To conclude my explanations, let me tell you that I value your respect for me above everything in the world, and have found it my greatest comfort during this temporary distress of mine. Thank God, the first shock of things has abated, now that you have agreed not to look upon me as faithless and an egotist simply because I have deceived you. I wish to hold you to myself, for the reason that I cannot bear to part with you, and love you as my guardian angel.... I have now returned to work, and am applying myself diligently to my duties. Also, yesterday Evstafi Ivanovitch exchanged a word or two with me. Yet I will not conceal from you the fact that my debts are crushing me down, and that my wardrobe is in a sorry state. At the same time, these things do not REALLY matter and I would bid you not despair about them. Send me, however, another half-rouble if you can (though that half-rouble will stab me to the heart—stab me with the thought that it is not I who am helping you, but YOU who are helping ME). Thedora has done well to get those fifteen roubles for you. At the moment, fool of an old man that I am, I have no hope of acquiring any more money; but as soon as ever I do so, I will write to you and let you know all about it. What chiefly worries me is the fear of gossip. Goodbye, little angel.

I kiss your hands, and beseech you to regain your health. If this is not a detailed letter, the reason is that I must soon be starting for the office, in order that, by strict application to duty, I may make amends for the past. Further information concerning my doings (as well as concerning that affair with the officers) must be deferred until tonight.—Your affectionate and respectful friend,

MAKAR DIEVUSHKIN.

July 28th.

DEAREST LITTLE BARBARA,—It is YOU who have committed a fault—and one which must weigh heavily upon your conscience. Indeed, your last letter has amazed and confounded me,—so much so that, on once more looking into the recesses of my heart, I perceive that I was perfectly right in what I did. Of course I am not now referring to my debauch (no, indeed!), but to the fact that I love you, and to the fact that it is unwise of me to love you—very unwise. You know not how matters stand, my darling. You know not why I am BOUND to love you. Otherwise you would not say all that you do. Yet I am persuaded that it is your head rather than your heart that is speaking. I am certain that your heart thinks very differently.

What occurred that night between myself and those officers I scarcely know, I scarcely remember. You must bear in mind that for some time past I have been in terrible distress—that for a whole month I have been, so to speak, hanging by a single thread. Indeed, my position has been most pitiable. Though I hid myself from you, my landlady was forever shouting and railing at me. This would not have mattered a jot—the horrible old woman might have shouted as much as she pleased—had it not been that, in the first place, there was the disgrace of it, and, in the second place, she had somehow learned of our connection, and kept proclaiming it to the household until I felt perfectly deafened, and had to stop my ears. The point, however, is that other people did not stop their ears, but, on the contrary, pricked them. Indeed, I am at a loss what to do.

Really this wretched rabble has driven me to extremities. It all began with my hearing a strange rumour from Thedora—namely, that an unworthy suitor had been to visit you, and had insulted you with an improper proposal. That he had insulted you deeply I knew from my own feelings, for I felt insulted in an equal degree. Upon that, my angel, I went to pieces, and, losing all self-control, plunged headlong. Bursting into an unspeakable frenzy, I was at once going to call upon this villain of a seducer—though what to do next I knew not, seeing that I was fearful of giving you offence. Ah, what a night of sorrow it was, and what a time of gloom, rain, and sleet! Next, I was returning home, but found myself unable to stand upon my feet. Then Emelia Ilyitch happened to come by. He also is a tchinovnik—or rather, was a tchinovnik, since he was turned out of the service some time ago. What he was doing there at that moment I do not know; I only know that I went with him.... Surely it cannot give you pleasure to read of the misfortunes of your friend—of his sorrows, and of the temptations which he experienced?... On the evening of the third day Emelia urged me to go and see the officer of whom I have spoken, and whose address I had learned from our dvornik. More strictly speaking, I had noticed him when, on a previous occasion, he had come to play cards here, and I had followed him home. Of course I now see that I did wrong, but I felt beside myself when I heard them telling him stories about me. Exactly what happened next I cannot remember. I only remember that several other officers were present as well as he. Or it may be that I saw everything double—God alone knows. Also, I cannot exactly remember what I said. I only remember that in my fury I said a great deal. Then they turned me out of the room, and threw me down the staircase—pushed me down it, that is to say. How I got home you know. That is all. Of course, later I blamed myself, and my pride underwent a fall; but no extraneous person except yourself knows of the affair, and in any case it does not matter. Perhaps the affair is as you imagine it to have been, Barbara? One thing I know for certain, and that is that last year one of our lodgers, Aksenti Osipovitch, took a similar liberty with Peter Petrovitch, yet kept the fact secret, an absolute secret. He called him into his room (I happened to be looking through a crack in the partition-wall), and had an explanation with him in the way that a gentleman should—noone except myself being a witness of the scene; whereas, in my own case, I had no explanation at all. After the scene was over, nothing further transpired between Aksenti Osipovitch and Peter Petrovitch, for the reason that the latter was so desirous of getting on in life that he held his tongue. As a result, they bow and shake hands whenever they meet.... I will not dispute the fact that I have erred most grievously—that I should never dare to dispute, or that I have fallen greatly in my own estimation; but, I think I was fated from birth so to do—and one cannot escape fate, my beloved. Here, therefore, is a detailed explanation of my misfortunes and sorrows, written for you to read whenever you may find it convenient. I am far from well, beloved, and have lost all my gaiety of disposition, but I send you this letter as a token of my love, devotion, and respect, Oh dear lady of my affections.—Your humble servant,

MAKAR DIEVUSHKIN.

July 29th.

MY DEAREST MAKAR ALEXIEVITCH,—I have read your two letters, and they make my heart ache. See here, dear friend of mine. You pass over certain things in silence, and write about a PORTION only of your misfortunes. Can it be that the letters are the outcome of a mental disorder?... Come and see me, for God's sake. Come today, direct from the office, and dine with us as you have done before. As to how you are living now, or as to what settlement you have made with your landlady, I know not, for you write nothing concerning those two points, and seem purposely to have left them unmentioned. Au revoir, my friend. Come to me today without fail. You would do better ALWAYS to dine here. Thedora is an excellent cook. Goodbye—Your own,

BARBARA DOBROSELOVA.

August 1st.

MY DARLING BARBARA ALEXIEVNA,—Thank God that He has sent you a chance of repaying my good with good. I believe in so doing, as well as in the sweetness of your angelic heart. Therefore, I will not reproach you. Only I pray you, do not again blame me because in the decline of my life I have played the spendthrift. It was such a sin, was it not?—such a thing to do? And even if you would still have it that the sin was there, remember, little friend, what it costs me to hear such words fall from your lips. Do not be vexed with me for saying this, for my heart is fainting. Poor people are subject to fancies—this is a provision of nature. I myself have had reason to know this. The poor man is exacting. He cannot see God's world as it is, but eyes each passer-by askance, and looks around him uneasily in order that he may listen to every word that is being uttered. May not people be talking of him? How is it that he is so unsightly? What is he feeling at all? What sort of figure is he cutting on the one side or on the other? It is matter of common knowledge, my Barbara, that the poor man ranks lower than a rag, and will never earn the respect of any one. Yes, write about him as you like—let scribblers say what they choose about him—he will ever remain as he was. And why is this? It is because, from his very nature, the poor man has to wear his feelings on his sleeve, so that nothing about him is sacred, and as for his self-respect—! Well, Emelia told me the other day that once, when he had to collect subscriptions, official sanction was demanded for every single coin, since people thought that it would be no use paying their money to a poor man. Nowadays charity is strangely administered. Perhaps it has always been so. Either folk do not know how to administer it, or they are adept in the art—one of the two. Perhaps you did not know this, so I beg to tell it you. And how comes it that the poor man knows, is so conscious of it all? The answer is—by experience. He knows because any day he may see a gentleman enter a restaurant and ask himself, "What shall I have to eat today? I will have such and such a dish," while all the time the poor man will have nothing to eat that day but gruel. There are men, too—wretched busybodies—who walk about merely to see if they can find some wretched tchinovnik or broken-down official who has got toes projecting from his boots or his hair uncut! And when they have found such a one they make a report of the circumstance, and their rubbish gets entered on the file.... But what does it matter to you if my hair lacks the shears? If you will forgive me what may seem to you a piece of rudeness, I declare that the poor man is ashamed of such things with the sensitiveness of a young girl. YOU, for instance, would not care (pray pardon my bluntness) to unrobe yourself before the public eye; and in the same way, the poor man does not like to be pried at or questioned concerning his family relations, and so forth. A man of honour and self-respect such as I am finds it painful and grievous to have to consort with men who would deprive him of both.

Today I sat before my colleagues like a bear's cub or a plucked sparrow, so that I fairly burned with shame. Yes, it hurt me terribly, Barbara. Naturally one blushes when one can see one's naked toes projecting through one's boots, and one's buttons hanging by a single thread! As though on purpose, I seemed, on this occasion, to be peculiarly dishevelled. No wonder that my spirits fell. When I was talking on business matters to Stepan Karlovitch, he suddenly exclaimed, for no apparent reason, "Ah, poor old Makar Alexievitch!" and then left the rest unfinished. But I knew what he had in his mind, and blushed so hotly that even the bald patch on my head grew red. Of course the whole thing is nothing, but it worries me, and leads to anxious thoughts. What can these fellows know about me? God send that they know nothing! But I confess that I suspect, I strongly suspect, one of my colleagues. Let them only betray me! They would betray one's private life for a groat, for they hold nothing sacred.

I have an idea who is at the bottom of it all. It is Rataziaev. Probably he knows someone in our department to whom he has recounted the story with additions. Or perhaps he has spread it abroad in his own department, and thence, it has crept and crawled into ours. Everyone here knows it, down to the last detail, for I have seen them point at you with their fingers through the window. Oh yes, I have seen them do it. Yesterday, when I stepped across to dine with you, the whole crew were hanging out of the window to watch me, and the landlady exclaimed that the devil was in young people, and called you certain unbecoming names. But this is as nothing compared with Rataziaev's foul intention to place us in his books, and to describe us in a satire. He himself has declared that he is going to do so, and other people say the same. In fact, I know not what to think, nor what to decide. It is no use concealing the fact that you and I have sinned against the Lord God.... You were going to send me a book of some sort, to divert my mind—were you not, dearest? What book, though, could now divert me? Only such books as have never existed on earth. Novels are rubbish, and written for fools and for the idle. Believe me, dearest, I know it through long experience. Even should they vaunt Shakespeare to you, I tell you that Shakespeare is rubbish, and proper only for lampoons—Your own,

MAKAR DIEVUSHKIN.

August 2nd.

MY DEAREST MAKAR ALEXIEVITCH,—Do not disquiet yourself. God will grant that all shall turn out well. Thedora has obtained a quantity of work, both for me and herself, and we are setting about it with a will. Perhaps it will put us straight again. Thedora suspects my late misfortunes to be connected with Anna Thedorovna; but I do not care—I feel extraordinarily cheerful today. So you are thinking of borrowing more money? If so, may God preserve you, for you will assuredly be ruined when the time comes for repayment! You had far better come and live with us here for a little while. Yes, come and take up your abode here, and pay no attention whatever to what your landlady says. As for the rest of your enemies and ill-wishers, I am certain that it is with vain imaginings that you are vexing yourself.... In passing, let me tell you that your style differs greatly from letter to letter. Goodbye until we meet again. I await your coming with impatience—Your own,

B. D.

August 3rd.

MY ANGEL, BARBARA ALEXIEVNA,—I hasten to inform you, Oh light of my life, that my hopes are rising again. But, little daughter of mine—do you really mean it when you say that I am to indulge in no more borrowings? Why, I could not do without them. Things would go badly with us both if I did so. You are ailing. Consequently, I tell you roundly that I MUST borrow, and that I must continue to do so.

Also, I may tell you that my seat in the office is now next to that of a certain Emelia Ivanovitch. He is not the Emelia whom you know, but a man who, like myself, is a privy councillor, as well as represents, with myself, the senior and oldest official in our department. Likewise he is a good, disinterested soul, and one that is not over-talkative, though a true bear in appearance and demeanour. Industrious, and possessed of a handwriting purely English, his caligraphy is, it must be confessed, even worse than my own. Yes, he is a good soul. At the same time, we have never been intimate with one another. We have done no more than exchange greetings on meeting or parting, borrow one another's penknife if we needed one, and, in short, observe such bare civilities as convention demands. Well, today he said to me, "Makar Alexievitch, what makes you look so thoughtful?" and inasmuch as I could see that he wished me well, I told him all—or, rather, I did not tell him EVERYTHING, for that I do to no man (I have not the heart to do it); I told him just a few scattered details concerning my financial straits. "Then you ought to borrow," said he. "You ought to obtain a loan of Peter Petrovitch, who does a little in that way. I myself once borrowed some money of him, and he charged me fair and light interest." Well, Barbara, my heart leapt within me at these words. I kept thinking and thinking,—if only God would put it into the mind of Peter Petrovitch to be my benefactor by advancing me a loan! I calculated that with its aid I might both repay my landlady and assist yourself and get rid of my surroundings (where I can hardly sit down to table without the rascals making jokes about me). Sometimes his Excellency passes our desk in the office. He glances at me, and cannot but perceive how poorly I am dressed. Now, neatness and cleanliness are two of his strongest points. Even though he says nothing, I feel ready to die with shame when he approaches. Well, hardening my heart, and putting my diffidence into my ragged pocket, I approached Peter Petrovitch, and halted before him more dead than alive. Yet I was hopeful, and though, as it turned out, he was busily engaged in talking to Thedosei Ivanovitch, I walked up to him from behind, and plucked at his sleeve. He looked away from me, but I recited my speech about thirty roubles, et cetera, et cetera, of which, at first, he failed to catch the meaning. Even when I had explained matters to him more fully, he only burst out laughing, and said nothing. Again I addressed to him my request; whereupon, asking me what security I could give, he again buried himself in his papers, and went on writing without deigning me even a second glance. Dismay seized me. "Peter Petrovitch," I said, "I can offer you no security," but to this I added an explanation that some salary would, in time, be due to me, which I would make over to him, and account the loan my first debt. At that moment someone called him away, and I had to wait a little. On returning, he began to mend his pen as though he had not even noticed that I was there. But I was for myself this time. "Peter Petrovitch," I continued, "can you not do ANYTHING?" Still he maintained silence, and seemed not to have heard me. I waited and waited. At length I determined to make a final attempt, and plucked him by the sleeve. He muttered something, and, his pen mended, set about his writing. There was nothing for me to do but to depart. He and the rest of them are worthy fellows, dearest—that I do not doubt—but they are also proud, very proud. What have I to do with them? Yet I thought I would write and tell you all about it. Meanwhile Emelia Ivanovitch had been encouraging me with nods and smiles. He is a good soul, and has promised to recommend me to a friend of his who lives in

Viborskaia Street and lends money. Emelia declares that this friend will certainly lend me a little; so tomorrow, beloved, I am going to call upon the gentleman in question.... What do you think about it? It would be a pity not to obtain a loan. My landlady is on the point of turning me out of doors, and has refused to allow me any more board. Also, my boots are wearing through, and have lost every button—and I do not possess another pair! Could anyone in a government office display greater shabbiness? It is dreadful, my Barbara—it is simply dreadful!

MAKAR DIEVUSHKIN.

August 4th.

MY BELOVED MAKAR ALEXIEVITCH,—For God's sake borrow some money as soon as you can. I would not ask this help of you were it not for the situation in which I am placed. Thedora and myself cannot remain any longer in our present lodgings, for we have been subjected to great unpleasantness, and you cannot imagine my state of agitation and dismay. The reason is that this morning we received a visit from an elderly—almost an old—man whose breast was studded with orders. Greatly surprised, I asked him what he wanted (for at the moment Thedora had gone out shopping); whereupon he began to question me as to my mode of life and occupation, and then, without waiting for an answer, informed me that he was uncle to the officer of whom you have spoken; that he was very angry with his nephew for the way in which the latter had behaved, especially with regard to his slandering of me right and left; and that he, the uncle, was ready to protect me from the young spendthrift's insolence. Also, he advised me to have nothing to say to young fellows of that stamp, and added that he sympathised with me as though he were my own father, and would gladly help me in any way he could. At this I blushed in some confusion, but did not greatly hasten to thank him. Next, he took me forcibly by the hand, and, tapping my cheek, said that I was very good-looking, and that he greatly liked the dimples in my face (God only knows what he meant!). Finally he tried to kiss me, on the plea that he was an old man, the brute! At this moment Thedora returned; whereupon, in some confusion, he repeated that he felt a great respect for my modesty and virtue, and that he much wished to become acquainted with me; after which he took Thedora aside, and tried, on some pretext or another, to give her money (though of course she declined it). At last he took himself off—again reiterating his assurances, and saying that he intended to return with some earrings as a present; that he advised me to change my lodgings; and, that he could recommend me a splendid flat which he had in his mind's eye as likely to cost me nothing. Yes, he also declared that he greatly liked me for my purity and good sense; that I must beware of dissolute young men; and that he knew Anna Thedorovna, who had charged him to inform me that she would shortly be visiting me in person. Upon that, I understood all. What I did next I scarcely know, for I had never before found myself in such a position; but I believe that I broke all restraints, and made the old man feel thoroughly ashamed of himself—Thedora helping me in the task, and well-nigh turning him neck and crop out of the tenement. Neither of us doubt that this is Anna Thedorovna's work—for how otherwise could the old man have got to know about us?

Now, therefore, Makar Alexievitch, I turn to you for help. Do not, for God's sake, leave me in this plight. Borrow all the money that you can get, for I have not the wherewithal to leave these lodgings, yet cannot possibly remain in them any longer. At all events, this is Thedora's advice. She and I need at least twenty-five roubles, which I will repay you out of what I earn by my work, while Thedora shall get me additional work from day to day, so that, if there be heavy interest to pay on the loan, you shall not be troubled with the extra burden. Nay, I will make over to you all that I possess if only you will continue to help me. Truly, I grieve to have to trouble you when you yourself are so hardly situated, but my hopes rest upon you, and upon you alone. Goodbye, Makar Alexievitch. Think of me, and may God speed you on your errand!

B.D.

August 4th.

MY BELOVED BARBARA ALEXIEVNA,—These unlooked-for blows have shaken me terribly, and these strange calamities have quite broken my spirit. Not content with trying to bring you to a bed of sickness, these lickspittles and pestilent old men are trying to bring me to the same. And I assure you that they are succeeding—I assure you that they are. Yet I would rather die than not help you. If I cannot help you I SHALL die; but, to enable me to help you, you must flee like a bird out of the nest where these owls, these birds of prey, are seeking to peck you to death. How distressed I feel, my dearest! Yet how cruel you yourself are! Although you are enduring pain and insult, although you, little nestling, are in agony of spirit, you actually tell me that it grieves you to disturb me, and that you will work off your debt to me with the labour of your own hands! In other words, you, with your weak health, are proposing to kill yourself in order to relieve me to term of my financial embarrassments! Stop a moment, and think what you are saying. WHY should you sew, and work, and torture your poor head with anxiety, and spoil your beautiful eyes, and ruin your health? Why, indeed? Ah, little Barbara, little Barbara! Do you not see that I shall never be any good to you, never any good to you? At all events, I myself see it. Yet I WILL help you in your distress. I WILL overcome every difficulty, I WILL get extra work to do, I WILL copy out manuscripts for authors, I WILL go to the latter and force them to employ me, I WILL so apply myself to the work that they shall see that I am a good copyist (and good copyists, I know, are always in demand). Thus there will be no need for you to exhaust your strength, nor will I allow you to do so—I will not have you carry out your disastrous intention... Yes, little angel, I will certainly borrow some money. I would rather die than not do so. Merely tell me, my own darling, that I am not to shrink from heavy interest, and I will not shrink from it, I will not shrink from it—nay, I will shrink from nothing. I will ask for forty roubles, to begin with. That will not be much, will it, little Barbara? Yet will any one trust me even with that sum at the first asking? Do you think that I am capable of inspiring confidence at the first glance? Would the mere sight of my face lead any one to form of me a favourable opinion? Have I ever been able, remember you, to appear to anyone in a favourable light? What think you? Personally, I see difficulties in the way, and feel sick at heart at the mere prospect. However, of those forty roubles I mean to set aside twenty-five for yourself, two for my landlady, and the remainder for my own spending. Of course, I ought to give more than two to my landlady, but you must remember my necessities, and see for yourself that that is the most that can be assigned to her. We need say no more about it. For one rouble I shall buy me a new pair of shoes, for I scarcely know whether my old ones will take me to the office tomorrow morning. Also, a new neck-scarf is indispensable, seeing that the old one has now passed its first year; but, since you have promised to make of your old apron not only a scarf, but also a shirt-front, I need think no more of the article in question. So much for shoes and scarves. Next, for buttons. You yourself will agree that I cannot do without buttons; nor is there on my garments a single hem unfrayed. I tremble when I think that some day his Excellency may perceive my untidiness, and say—well, what will he NOT say? Yet I shall never hear what he says, for I shall have expired where I sit—expired of mere shame at the thought of having been thus exposed. Ah, dearest!... Well, my various necessities will have left me three roubles to go on with. Part of this sum I shall expend upon a half-pound of tobacco—for I cannot live without tobacco, and it is nine days since I last put a pipe into my mouth. To tell the truth, I shall buy the tobacco without acquainting you with the fact, although I ought not so to do. The pity of it all is that, while you are depriving yourself of everything, I keep solacing myself with various amenities—which is why I am telling you this, that the pangs of conscience may not torment me. Frankly, I confess that I am in desperate straits—in such straits as I have never yet known. My landlady flouts me, and I enjoy the respect of noone; my arrears and debts are terrible; and in the office, though never have I found the place exactly a paradise, noone has a single word to say to me. Yet I hide, I carefully hide, this from every one. I would hide my person in the same way, were it not that daily I have to attend the office where I have to be constantly on my guard against my fellows. Nevertheless, merely to be able to CONFESS this to you renews my spiritual strength. We must not think of these things, Barbara, lest the thought of them break our courage. I write them down merely to warn you NOT to think of them, nor to torture yourself with bitter imaginings. Yet, my God, what is to become of us? Stay where you are until I can come to you; after which I shall not return hither, but simply disappear. Now I have finished my letter, and must go and shave myself, inasmuch as, when that is done, one always feels more decent, as well as consorts more easily with decency. God speed me! One prayer to Him, and I must be off.

M. DIEVUSHKIN.

August 5th.

DEAREST MAKAR ALEXIEVITCH,—You must not despair. Away with melancholy! I am sending you thirty kopecks in silver, and regret that I cannot send you more. Buy yourself what you most need until tomorrow. I myself have almost nothing left, and what I am going to do I know not. Is it not dreadful, Makar Alexievitch? Yet do not be downcast—it is no good being that. Thedora declares that it would not be a bad thing if we were to remain in this tenement, since if we left it suspicions would arise, and our enemies might take it into their heads to look for us. On the other hand, I do not think it would be well for us to remain here. If I were feeling less sad I would tell you my reason.

What a strange man you are, Makar Alexievitch! You take things so much to heart that you never know what it is to be happy. I read your letters attentively, and can see from them that, though you worry and disturb yourself about me, you never give a thought to yourself. Yes, every letter tells me that you have a kind heart; but I tell YOU that that heart is overly kind. So I will give you a little friendly advice, Makar Alexievitch. I am full of gratitude towards you—I am indeed full for all that you have done for me, I am most sensible of your goodness; but, to think that I should be forced to see that, in spite of your own troubles (of which I have been the involuntary cause), you live for me alone—you live but for MY joys and MY sorrows and MY affection! If you take the affairs of another person so to heart, and suffer with her to such an extent, I do not wonder that you yourself are unhappy. Today, when you came to see me after office-work was done, I felt afraid even to raise my eyes to yours, for you looked so pale and desperate, and your face had so fallen in. Yes, you were dreading to have to tell me of your failure to borrow money—you were dreading to have to grieve and alarm me; but, when you saw that I came very near to smiling, the load was, I know, lifted from your heart. So do not be despondent, do not give way, but allow more rein to your better sense. I beg and implore this of you, for it will not be long before you see things take a turn for the better. You will but spoil your life if you constantly lament another person's sorrow. Goodbye, dear friend. I beseech you not to be over-anxious about me.

B. D.

August 5th.

MY DARLING LITTLE BARBARA,—This is well, this is well, my angel! So you are of opinion that the fact that I have failed to obtain any money does not matter? Then I too am reassured, I too am happy on your account. Also, I am delighted to think that you are not going to desert your old friend, but intend to remain in your present lodgings. Indeed, my heart was overcharged with joy when I read in your letter those kindly words about myself, as well as a not wholly unmerited recognition of my sentiments. I say this not out of pride, but because now I know how much you love me to be thus solicitous for my feelings. How good to think that I may speak to you of them! You bid me, darling, not be faint-hearted. Indeed, there is no need for me to be so. Think, for instance, of the pair of shoes which I shall be wearing to the office tomorrow! The fact is that over-brooding proves the undoing of a man—his complete undoing. What has saved me is the fact that it is not for myself that I am grieving, that I am suffering, but for YOU. Nor would it matter to me in the least that I should have to walk through the bitter cold without an overcoat or boots—I could bear it, I could well endure it, for I am a simple man in my requirements; but the point is—what would people say, what would every envious and hostile tongue exclaim, when I was seen without an overcoat? It is for OTHER folk that one wears an overcoat and boots. In any case, therefore, I should have needed boots to maintain my name and reputation; to both of which my ragged footgear would otherwise have spelled ruin. Yes, it is so, my beloved, and you may believe an old man who has had many years of experience, and knows both the world and mankind, rather than a set of scribblers and daubers.

But I have not yet told you in detail how things have gone with me today. During the morning I suffered as much agony of spirit as might have been experienced in a year. 'Twas like this: First of all, I went out to call upon the gentleman of whom I have spoken. I started very early, before going to the office. Rain and sleet were falling, and I hugged myself in my greatcoat as I walked along. "Lord," thought I, "pardon my offences, and send me fulfilment of all my desires;" and as I passed a church I crossed myself, repented of my sins, and reminded myself that I was unworthy to hold communication with the Lord God. Then I retired into myself, and tried to look at nothing; and so, walking without noticing the streets, I proceeded on my way. Everything had an empty air, and everyone whom I met looked careworn and preoccupied, and no wonder, for who would choose to walk abroad at such an early hour, and in such weather? Next a band of ragged workmen met me, and jostled me boorishly as they passed; upon which nervousness overtook me, and I felt uneasy, and tried hard not to think of the money that was my errand. Near the Voskresenski Bridge my feet began to ache with weariness, until I could hardly pull myself along; until presently I met with Ermolaev, a writer in our office, who, stepping aside, halted, and followed me with his eyes, as though to beg of me a glass of vodka. "Ah, friend," thought I, "go YOU to your vodka, but what have I to do with such stuff?" Then, sadly weary, I halted for a moment's rest, and thereafter dragged myself further on my way. Purposely I kept looking about me for something upon which to fasten my thoughts, with which to distract, to encourage myself; but there was nothing. Not a single idea could I connect with any given object, while, in addition, my appearance was so draggled that I felt utterly ashamed of it. At length I perceived from afar a gabled house that was built of yellow wood. This, I thought, must be the residence of the Monsieur Markov whom Emelia Ivanovitch had mentioned to me as ready to lend money on interest. Half unconscious of what I was doing, I asked a watchman if he could tell me to whom the house belonged; whereupon grudgingly, and as though he were vexed at something, the fellow muttered that it belonged to one Markov. Are ALL watchmen so unfeeling? Why did this one reply as he did? In any case I felt disagreeably impressed, for like always answers to like, and, no matter what position one is in, things invariably appear to correspond to it. Three times did I pass the house and walk the length of the street; until the further I walked, the worse became my state of mind. "No, never, never will he lend me anything!" I thought to myself, "He does not know me, and my affairs will seem to him ridiculous, and I shall cut a sorry figure. However, let fate decide for me. Only, let Heaven send that I do not afterwards repent me, and eat out my heart with remorse!" Softly I opened the wicket-gate. Horrors! A great ragged brute of a watch-dog came flying out at me, and foaming at the mouth, and nearly jumping out his skin! Curious is it to note what little, trivial incidents will nearly make a man crazy, and strike terror to his heart, and annihilate the firm purpose with which he has armed himself. At all events, I approached the house more dead than alive, and walked straight into another catastrophe. That is to say, not noticing the slipperiness of the threshold, I stumbled against an old woman who was filling milk-jugs from a pail, and sent the milk flying in every direction! The foolish old dame gave a start and a cry, and then demanded of me whither I had been coming, and what it was I wanted; after which she rated me soundly for my awkwardness. Always have I found something of the kind befall me when engaged on errands of this nature. It seems to be my destiny invariably to run into something. Upon that, the noise and the commotion brought out the mistress of the house—an old beldame of mean appearance. I addressed myself directly to her: "Does Monsieur Markov live here?" was my inquiry. "No," she replied, and then stood looking at me civilly enough. "But what want you with him?" she continued; upon which I told her about Emelia Ivanovitch and the rest of the business. As soon as I had finished, she called her daughter—a barefooted girl in her teens—and told her to summon her father from upstairs. Meanwhile, I was shown into a room which contained several portraits of generals on the walls and was furnished with a sofa, a large table, and a few pots of mignonette and balsam. "Shall I, or shall I not (come weal, come woe) take myself off?" was my thought as I waited there. Ah, how I longed to run away! "Yes," I continued, "I had better come again tomorrow, for the weather may then be better, and I shall not have upset the milk, and these generals will not be looking at me so fiercely." In fact, I had actually begun to move towards the door when Monsieur Markov entered—a grey-headed man with thievish eyes, and clad in a dirty dressing-gown fastened with a belt. Greetings over, I stumbled out something about Emelia Ivanovitch and forty roubles, and then came to a dead halt, for his eyes told me that my errand had been futile. "No." said he, "I have no money. Moreover, what security could you offer?" I admitted that I could offer none, but again added something about Emelia, as well as about my pressing needs. Markov heard me out, and then repeated that he had no money. "Ah," thought I, "I might have known this—I might have foreseen it!" And, to tell the truth, Barbara, I could have wished that the earth had opened under my feet, so chilled did I feel as he said what he did, so numbed did my legs grow as shivers began to run down my back. Thus I remained gazing at him while he returned my gaze with a look which said, "Well now, my friend? Why do you not go since you have no further business to do here?" Somehow I felt conscience-stricken. "How is it that you are in such need of money?" was what he appeared to be asking; whereupon, I opened my mouth (anything rather than stand there to no purpose at all!) but found that he was not even listening. "I have no money," again he said, "or I would lend you some with pleasure." Several times I repeated that I myself possessed a little, and that I would repay any loan from him punctually, most punctually, and that he might charge me what interest he liked, since I would meet it without fail. Yes, at that moment I remembered our misfortunes, our necessities, and I remembered your half-rouble. "No," said he, "I can lend you nothing without security," and clinched his assurance with an oath, the robber!

How I contrived to leave the house and, passing through Viborskaia Street, to reach the Voskresenski Bridge I do not know. I only remember that I felt terribly weary, cold, and starved, and that it was ten o'clock before I reached the office. Arriving, I tried to clean myself up a little, but Sniegirev, the porter, said that it was impossible for me to do so, and that I should only spoil the brush, which belonged to the Government. Thus, my darling, do such fellows rate me lower than the mat on which they wipe their boots! What is it that will most surely break me? It is not the want of money, but the LITTLE worries of life—these whisperings and nods and jeers. Any day his Excellency himself may round upon me. Ah, dearest, my golden days are gone. Today I have spent in reading your letters through; and the reading of them has made me sad. Goodbye, my own, and may the Lord watch over you!

M. DIEVUSHKIN.

P.S.—To conceal my sorrow I would have written this letter half jestingly; but, the faculty of jesting has not been given me. My one desire, however, is to afford you pleasure. Soon I will come and see you, dearest. Without fail I will come and see you.

August 11th.

O Barbara Alexievna, I am undone—we are both of us undone! Both of us are lost beyond recall! Everything is ruined—my reputation, my self-respect, all that I have in the world! And you as much as I. Never shall we retrieve what we have lost. I—I have brought you to this pass, for I have become an outcast, my darling. Everywhere I am laughed at and despised. Even my landlady has taken to abusing me. Today she overwhelmed me with shrill reproaches, and abased me to the level of a hearth-brush. And last night, when I was in Rataziaev's rooms, one of his friends began to read a scribbled note which I had written to you, and then inadvertently pulled out of my pocket. Oh beloved, what laughter there arose at the recital! How those scoundrels mocked and derided you and myself! I walked up to them and accused Rataziaev of breaking faith. I said that he had played the traitor. But he only replied that I had been the betrayer in the case, by indulging in various amours. "You have kept them very dark though, Mr. Lovelace!" said he—and now I am known everywhere by this name of "Lovelace." They know EVERYTHING about us, my darling, EVERYTHING—both about you and your affairs and about myself; and when today I was for sending Phaldoni to the bakeshop for something or other, he refused to go, saying that it was not his business. "But you MUST go," said I. "I will not," he replied. "You have not paid my mistress what you owe her, so I am not bound to run your errands." At such an insult from a raw peasant I lost my temper, and called him a fool; to which he retorted in a similar vein. Upon this I thought that he must be drunk, and told him so; whereupon he replied: "WHAT say you that I am? Suppose you yourself go and sober up, for I know that the other day you went to visit a woman, and that you got drunk with her on two grivenniks." To such a pass have things come! I feel ashamed to be seen alive. I am, as it were, a man proclaimed; I am in a worse plight even than a tramp who has lost his passport. How misfortunes are heaping themselves upon me! I am lost—I am lost for ever!

M. D.

August 13th.

MY BELOVED MAKAR ALEXIEVITCH,—It is true that misfortune is following upon misfortune. I myself scarcely know what to do. Yet, no matter how you may be fairing, you must not look for help from me, for only today I burned my left hand with the iron! At one and the same moment I dropped the iron, made a mistake in my work, and burned myself! So now I can no longer work. Also, these three days past, Thedora has been ailing. My anxiety is becoming positively torturous. Nevertheless, I send you thirty kopecks—almost the last coins that I have left to me, much as I should have liked to have helped you more when you are so much in need. I feel vexed to the point of weeping. Goodbye, dear friend of mine. You will bring me much comfort if only you will come and see me today.

B. D.

August 14th.

What is the matter with you, Makar Alexievitch? Surely you cannot fear the Lord God as you ought to do? You are not only driving me to distraction but also ruining yourself with this eternal solicitude for your reputation. You are a man of honour, nobility of character, and self-respect, as everyone knows; yet, at any moment, you are ready to die with shame! Surely you should have more consideration for your grey hairs. No, the fear of God has departed from you. Thedora has told you that it is out of my power to render you anymore help. See, therefore, to what a pass you have brought me! Probably you think it is nothing to me that you should behave so badly; probably you do not realise what you have made me suffer. I dare not set foot on the staircase here, for if I do so I am stared at, and pointed at, and spoken about in the most horrible manner. Yes, it is even said of me that I am "united to a drunkard." What a thing to hear! And whenever you are brought home drunk folk say, "They are carrying in that tchinovnik." THAT is not the proper way to make me help you. I swear that I MUST leave this place, and go and get work as a cook or a laundress. It is impossible for me to stay here. Long ago I wrote and asked you to come and see me, yet you have not come. Truly my tears and prayers must mean NOTHING to you, Makar Alexievitch! Whence, too, did you get the money for your debauchery? For the love of God be more careful of yourself, or you will be ruined. How shameful, how abominable of you! So the landlady would not admit you last night, and you spent the night on the doorstep? Oh, I know all about it. Yet if only you could have seen my agony when I heard the news!... Come and see me, Makar Alexievitch, and we will once more be happy together. Yes, we will read together, and talk of old times, and Thedora shall tell you of her pilgrimages in former days. For God's sake beloved, do not ruin both yourself and me. I live for you alone; it is for your sake alone that I am still here. Be your better self once more—the self which still can remain firm in the face of misfortune. Poverty is no crime; always remember that. After all, why should we despair? Our present difficulties will pass away, and God will right us. Only be brave. I send you two grivenniks for the purchase of some tobacco or anything else that you need; but, for the love of heaven, do not spend the money foolishly. Come you and see me soon; come without fail. Perhaps you may be ashamed to meet me, as you were before, but you NEED not feel like that—such shame would be misplaced. Only do bring with you sincere repentance and trust in God, who orders all things for the best.

B. D.

August 19th.

MY DEAREST BARBARA ALEXIEVNA,-Yes, I AM ashamed to meet you, my darling—I AM ashamed. At the same time, what is there in all this? Why should we not be cheerful again? Why should I mind the soles of my feet coming through my boots? The sole of one's foot is a mere bagatelle—it will never be anything but just a base, dirty sole. And shoes do not matter, either. The Greek sages used to walk about without them, so why should we coddle ourselves with such things? Yet why, also, should I be insulted and despised because of them? Tell Thedora that she is a rubbishy, tiresome, gabbling old woman, as well as an inexpressibly foolish one. As for my grey hairs, you are quite wrong about them, inasmuch as I am not such an old man as you think. Emelia sends you his greeting. You write that you are in great distress, and have been weeping. Well, I too am in great distress, and have been weeping. Nay, nay. I wish you the best of health and happiness, even as I am well and happy myself, so long as I may remain, my darling,—Your friend,

MAKAR DIEVUSHKIN.

August 21st.

MY DEAR AND KIND BARBARA ALEXIEVNA,—I feel that I am guilty, I feel that I have sinned against you. Yet also I feel, from what you say, that it is no use for me so to feel. Even before I had sinned I felt as I do now; but I gave way to despair, and the more so as recognised my fault. Darling, I am not cruel or hardhearted. To rend your little soul would be the act of a blood-thirsty tiger, whereas I have the heart of a sheep. You yourself know that I am not addicted to bloodthirstiness, and therefore that I cannot really be guilty of the fault in question, seeing that neither my mind nor my heart have participated in it.

Nor can I understand wherein the guilt lies. To me it is all a mystery. When you sent me those thirty kopecks, and thereafter those two grivenniks, my heart sank within me as I looked at the poor little money. To think that though you had burned your hand, and would soon be hungry, you could write to me that I was to buy tobacco! What was I to do? Remorselessly to rob you, an orphan, as any brigand might do? I felt greatly depressed, dearest. That is to say, persuaded that I should never do any good with my life, and that I was inferior even to the sole of my own boot, I took it into my head that it was absurd for me to aspire at all—rather, that I ought to account myself a disgrace and an abomination. Once a man has lost his self-respect, and has decided to abjure his better qualities and human dignity, he falls headlong, and cannot choose but do so. It is decreed of fate, and therefore I am not guilty in this respect.

That evening I went out merely to get a breath of fresh air, but one thing followed another—the weather was cold, all nature was looking mournful, and I had fallen in with Emelia. This man had spent everything that he possessed, and, at the time I met him, had not for two days tasted a crust of bread. He had tried to raise money by pawning, but what articles he had for the purpose had been refused by the pawnbrokers. It was more from sympathy for a fellow-man than from any liking for the individual that I yielded. That is how the fault arose, dearest.

He spoke of you, and I mingled my tears with his. Yes, he is a man of kind, kind heart—a man of deep feeling. I often feel as he did, dearest, and, in addition, I know how beholden to you I am. As soon as ever I got to know you I began both to realise myself and to love you; for until you came into my life I had been a lonely man—I had been, as it were, asleep rather than alive. In former days my rascally colleagues used to tell me that I was unfit even to be seen; in fact, they so disliked me that at length I began to dislike myself, for, being frequently told that I was stupid, I began to believe that I really was so. But the instant that YOU came into my life, you lightened the dark places in it, you lightened both my heart and my soul. Gradually, I gained rest of spirit, until I had come to see that I was no worse than other men, and that, though I had neither style nor brilliancy nor polish, I was still a MAN as regards my thoughts and feelings. But now, alas! pursued and scorned of fate, I have again allowed myself to abjure my own dignity. Oppressed of misfortune, I have lost my courage. Here is my confession to you, dearest. With tears I beseech you not to inquire further into the matter, for my heart is breaking, and life has grown indeed hard and bitter for me—Beloved, I offer you my respect, and remain ever your faithful friend,
MAKAR DIEVUSHKIN.

September 3rd.

The reason why I did not finish my last letter, Makar Alexievitch, was that I found it so difficult to write. There are moments when I am glad to be alone—to grieve and repine without any one to share my sorrow: and those moments are beginning to come upon me with ever-increasing frequency. Always in my reminiscences I find something which is inexplicable, yet strongly attractive—so much so that for hours together I remain insensible to my surroundings, oblivious of reality. Indeed, in my present life there is not a single impression that I encounter—pleasant or the reverse—which does not recall to my mind something of a similar nature in the past. More particularly is this the case with regard to my childhood, my golden childhood. Yet such moments always leave me depressed. They render me weak, and exhaust my powers of fancy; with the result that my health, already not good, grows steadily worse.

However, this morning it is a fine, fresh, cloudless day, such as we seldom get in autumn. The air has revived me and I greet it with joy. Yet to think that already the fall of the year has come! How I used to love the country in autumn! Then but a child, I was yet a sensitive being who loved autumn evenings better than autumn mornings. I remember how beside our house, at the foot of a hill, there lay a large pond, and how the pond—I can see it even now!—shone with a broad, level surface that was as clear as crystal. On still evenings this pond would be at rest, and not a rustle would disturb the trees which grew on its banks and overhung the motionless expanse of water. How fresh it used to seem, yet how cold! The dew would be falling upon the turf, lights would be beginning to shine forth from the huts on the pond's margin, and the cattle would be wending their way home. Then quietly I would slip out of the house to look at my beloved pond, and forget myself in contemplation. Here and there a fisherman's bundle of brushwood would be burning at the water's edge, and sending its light far and wide over the surface. Above, the sky would be of a cold blue colour, save for a fringe of flame-coloured streaks on the horizon that kept turning ever paler and paler; and when the moon had come out there would be wafted through the limpid air the sounds of a frightened bird fluttering, of a bulrush rubbing against its fellows in the gentle breeze, and of a fish rising with a splash. Over the dark water there would gather a thin, transparent mist; and though, in the distance, night would be looming, and seemingly enveloping the entire horizon, everything closer at hand would be standing out as though shaped with a chisel—banks, boats, little islands, and all. Beside the margin a derelict barrel would be turning over and over in the water; a switch of laburnum, with yellowing leaves, would go meandering through the reeds; and a belated gull would flutter up, dive again into the cold depths, rise once more, and disappear into the mist. How I would watch and listen to these things! How strangely good they all would seem! But I was a mere infant in those days—a mere child.

Yes, truly I loved autumn-tide—the late autumn when the crops are garnered, and field work is ended, and the evening gatherings in the huts have begun, and everyone is awaiting winter. Then does everything become more mysterious, the sky frowns with clouds, yellow leaves strew the paths at the edge of the naked forest, and the forest itself turns black and blue—more especially at eventide when damp fog is spreading and the trees glimmer in the depths like giants, like formless, weird phantoms. Perhaps one may be out late, and had got separated from one's companions. Oh horrors! Suddenly one starts and trembles as one seems to see a strange-looking being peering from out of the darkness of a hollow tree, while all the while the wind is moaning and rattling and howling through the forest—moaning with a hungry sound as it strips the leaves from the bare boughs, and whirls them into the air. High over the tree-tops, in a widespread, trailing, noisy crew, there fly, with resounding cries, flocks of birds which seem to darken and overlay the very heavens. Then a strange feeling comes over one, until one seems to hear the voice of some one whispering: "Run, run, little child! Do not be out late, for this place will soon have become dreadful! Run, little child! Run!" And at the words terror will possess one's soul, and one will rush and rush until one's breath is spent—until, panting, one has reached home.

At home, however, all will look bright and bustling as we children are set to shell peas or poppies, and the damp twigs crackle in the stove, and our mother comes to look fondly at our work, and our old nurse, Iliana, tells us stories of bygone days, or terrible legends concerning wizards and dead men. At the recital we little ones will press closer to one another, yet smile as we do so; when suddenly, everyone becomes silent. Surely somebody has knocked at the door?... But nay, nay; it is only the sound of Frolovna's spinning-wheel. What shouts of laughter arise! Later one will be unable to sleep for fear of the strange dreams which come to visit one; or, if one falls asleep, one will soon wake again, and, afraid to stir, lie quaking under the coverlet until dawn. And in the morning, one will arise as fresh as a lark and look at the window, and see the fields overlaid with hoarfrost, and fine icicles hanging from the naked branches, and the pond covered over with ice as thin as paper, and a white steam rising from the surface, and birds flying overhead with cheerful cries. Next, as the sun rises, he throws his glittering beams everywhere, and melts the thin, glassy ice until the whole scene has come to look bright and clear and exhilarating; and as the fire begins to crackle again in the stove, we sit down to the tea-urn, while, chilled with the night cold, our black dog, Polkan, will look in at us through the window, and wag his tail with a cheerful air. Presently, a peasant will pass the window in his cart bound for the forest to cut firewood, and the whole party will feel merry and contented together. Abundant grain lies stored in the byres, and great stacks of wheat are glowing comfortably in the morning sunlight. Everyone is quiet and happy, for God has blessed us with a bounteous harvest, and we know that there will be abundance of food for the wintertide. Yes, the peasant may rest assured that his family will not want for aught. Song and dance will arise at night from the village girls, and on festival days everyone will repair to God's house to thank Him with grateful tears for what He has done.... Ah, a golden time was my time of childhood!...

Carried away by these memories, I could weep like a child. Everything, everything comes back so clearly to my recollection! The past stands out so vividly before me! Yet in the present everything looks dim and dark! How will it all end?—how? Do you know, I have a feeling, a sort of sure premonition, that I am going to die this coming autumn; for I feel terribly, oh so terribly ill! Often do I think of death, yet feel that I should not like to die here and be laid to rest in the soil of St. Petersburg. Once more I have had to take to my bed, as I did last spring, for I have never really recovered. Indeed I feel so depressed! Thedora has gone out for the day, and I am alone. For a long while past I have been afraid to be left by myself, for I keep fancying that there is someone else in the room, and that that someone is speaking to me. Especially do I fancy this when I have gone off into a reverie, and then suddenly awoken from it, and am feeling bewildered. That is why I have made this letter such a long one; for, when

I am writing, the mood passes away. Goodbye. I have neither time nor paper left for more, and must close. Of the money which I saved to buy a new dress and hat, there remains but a single rouble; but, I am glad that you have been able to pay your landlady two roubles, for they will keep her tongue quiet for a time. And you must repair your wardrobe.

Goodbye once more. I am so tired! Nor can I think why I am growing so weak—why it is that even the smallest task now wearies me? Even if work should come my way, how am I to do it? That is what worries me above all things.

B. D.

September 5th.

MY BELOVED BARBARA,—Today I have undergone a variety of experiences. In the first place, my head has been aching, and towards evening I went out to get a breath of fresh air along the Fontanka Canal. The weather was dull and damp, and even by six o'clock, darkness had begun to set in. True, rain was not actually falling, but only a mist like rain, while the sky was streaked with masses of trailing cloud. Crowds of people were hurrying along Naberezhnaia Street, with faces that looked strange and dejected. There were drunken peasants; snub-nosed old harridans in slippers; bareheaded artisans; cab drivers; every species of beggar; boys; a locksmith's apprentice in a striped smock, with lean, emaciated features which seemed to have been washed in rancid oil; an ex-soldier who was offering penknives and copper rings for sale; and so on, and so on. It was the hour when one would expect to meet no other folk than these. And what a quantity of boats there were on the canal. It made one wonder how they could all find room there. On every bridge were old women selling damp gingerbread or withered apples, and every woman looked as damp and dirty as her wares. In short, the Fontanka is a saddening spot for a walk, for there is wet granite under one's feet, and tall, dingy buildings on either side of one, and wet mist below and wet mist above. Yes, all was dark and gloomy there this evening.

By the time I had returned to Gorokhovaia Street darkness had fallen and the lamps had been lit. However, I did not linger long in that particular spot, for Gorokhovaia Street is too noisy a place. But what sumptuous shops and stores it contains! Everything sparkles and glitters, and the windows are full of nothing but bright colours and materials and hats of different shapes. One might think that they were decked merely for display; but no,—people buy these things, and give them to their wives! Yes, it IS a sumptuous place. Hordes of German hucksters are there, as well as quite respectable traders. And the quantities of carriages which pass along the street! One marvels that the pavement can support so many splendid vehicles, with windows like crystal, linings made of silk and velvet, and lacqueys dressed in epaulets and wearing swords! Into some of them I glanced, and saw that they contained ladies of various ages. Perhaps they were princesses and countesses! Probably at that hour such folk would be hastening to balls and other gatherings. In fact, it was interesting to be able to look so closely at a princess or a great lady. They were all very fine. At all events, I had never before seen such persons as I beheld in those carriages....

Then I thought of you. Ah, my own, my darling, it is often that I think of you and feel my heart sink. How is it that YOU are so unfortunate, Barbara? How is it that YOU are so much worse off than other people? In my eyes you are kind-hearted, beautiful, and clever—why, then, has such an evil fate fallen to your lot? How comes it that you are left desolate—you, so good a human being! While to others happiness comes without an invitation at all? Yes, I know—I know it well—that I ought not to say it, for to do so savours of free-thought; but why should that raven, Fate, croak out upon the fortunes of one person while she is yet in her mother's womb, while another person it permits to go forth in happiness from the home which has reared her? To even an idiot of an Ivanushka such happiness is sometimes granted. "You, you fool Ivanushka," says Fate, "shall succeed to your grandfather's money-bags, and eat, drink, and be merry; whereas YOU (such and such another one) shall do no more than lick the dish, since that is all that you are good for." Yes, I know that it is wrong to hold such opinions, but involuntarily the sin of so doing grows upon one's soul. Nevertheless, it is you, my darling, who ought to be riding in one of those carriages. Generals would have come seeking your favour, and, instead of being clad in a humble cotton dress, you would have been walking in silken and golden attire. Then you would not have been thin and wan as now, but fresh and plump and rosy-cheeked as a figure on a sugar-cake. Then should I too have been happy—happy if only I could look at your lighted windows from the street, and watch your shadow—happy if only I could think that you were well and happy, my sweet little bird! Yet how are things in reality? Not only have evil folk brought you to ruin, but there comes also an old rascal of a libertine to insult you! Just because he struts about in a frockcoat, and can ogle you through a gold-mounted lorgnette, the brute thinks that everything will fall into his hands—that you are bound to listen to his insulting condescension! Out upon him! But why is this? It is because you are an orphan, it is because you are unprotected, it is because you have no powerful friend to afford you the decent support which is your due. WHAT do such facts matter to a man or to men to whom the insulting of an orphan is an offence allowed? Such fellows are not men at all, but mere vermin, no matter what they think themselves to be. Of that I am certain. Why, an organ-grinder whom I met in Gorokhovaia Street would inspire more respect than they do, for at least he walks about all day, and suffers hunger—at least he looks for a stray, superfluous groat to earn him subsistence, and is, therefore, a true gentleman, in that he supports himself. To beg alms he would be ashamed; and, moreover, he works for the benefit of mankind just as does a factory machine. "So far as in me lies," says he, "I will give you pleasure." True, he is a pauper, and nothing but a pauper; but, at least he is an HONOURABLE pauper. Though tired and hungry, he still goes on working—working in his own peculiar fashion, yet still doing honest labour. Yes, many a decent fellow whose labour may be disproportionate to its utility pulls the forelock to no one, and begs his bread of no one. I myself resemble that organ-grinder. That is to say, though not exactly he, I resemble him in this respect, that I work according to my capabilities, and so far as in me lies. More could be asked of no one; nor ought I to be adjudged to do more.

Apropos of the organ-grinder, I may tell you, dearest, that today I experienced a double misfortune. As I was looking at the grinder, certain thoughts entered my head and I stood wrapped in a reverie. Some cabmen also had halted at the spot, as well as a young girl, with a yet smaller girl who was dressed in rags and tatters. These people had halted there to listen to the organ-grinder, who was playing in front of some one's windows. Next, I caught sight of a little urchin of about ten—a boy who would have been good-looking but for the fact that his face was pinched and sickly. Almost barefooted, and clad only in a shirt, he was standing agape to listen to the music—a pitiful childish figure. Nearer to the grinder a few more urchins were dancing, but in the case of this lad his hands and feet looked numbed, and he kept biting the end of his sleeve and shivering. Also, I noticed that in his hands he had a paper of some sort. Presently a gentleman came by, and tossed the grinder a small coin, which fell straight into a box adorned with a representation of a Frenchman and some ladies. The instant he heard the rattle of the coin, the boy started, looked timidly round, and evidently made up his mind that I had thrown the money; whereupon, he ran to me with his little hands all shaking, and said in a tremulous voice as he proffered me his paper: "Pl-please sign this." I turned over the paper, and saw that there was written on it what is usual under such circumstances. "Kind friends I am a sick mother with three hungry children. Pray help me. Though soon I shall be dead, yet, if you will not forget my little ones in this world, neither will I forget you in the world that is to come." The thing seemed clear enough; it was a matter of life and death. Yet what was I to give the lad? Well, I gave him nothing. But my heart ached for him. I am certain that, shivering with cold though he was, and perhaps hungry, the poor lad was not lying. No, no, he was not lying.

The shameful point is that so many mothers take no care of their children, but send them out, half-clad, into the cold. Perhaps this lad's mother also was a feckless old woman, and devoid of character? Or perhaps she had no one to work for her, but was forced to sit with her legs crossed—a veritable invalid? Or perhaps she was just an old rogue who was in the habit of sending out pinched and hungry boys to deceive the public? What would such a boy learn from begging letters? His heart would soon be rendered callous, for, as he ran about begging, people would pass him by and give him nothing. Yes, their hearts would be as stone, and their replies rough and harsh. "Away with you!" they would say. "You are seeking but to trick us." He would hear that from every one, and his heart would grow hard, and he would shiver in vain with the cold, like some poor little fledgling that has fallen out of the nest. His hands and feet would be freezing, and his breath coming with difficulty; until, look you, he would begin to cough, and disease, like an unclean parasite, would worm its way into his breast until death itself had overtaken him—overtaken him in some foetid corner whence there was no chance of escape. Yes, that is what his life would become.

There are many such cases. Ah, Barbara, it is hard to hear "For Christ's sake!" and yet pass the suppliant by and give nothing, or say merely: "May the Lord give unto you!" Of course, SOME supplications mean nothing (for supplications differ greatly in character). Occasionally supplications are long, drawn-out and drawling, stereotyped and mechanical—they are purely begging supplications. Requests of this kind it is less hard to refuse, for they are purely professional and of long standing. "The beggar is overdoing it," one thinks to oneself. "He knows the trick too well." But there are other supplications which voice a strange, hoarse, unaccustomed note, like that today when I took the poor boy's paper. He had been standing by the kerbstone without speaking to anybody—save that at last to myself he said, "For the love of Christ give me a groat!" in a voice so hoarse and broken that I started, and felt a queer sensation in my heart, although I did not give him a groat. Indeed, I had not a groat on me. Rich folk dislike hearing poor people complain of their poverty. "They disturb us," they say, "and are impertinent as well. Why should poverty be so impertinent? Why should its hungry moans prevent us from sleeping?"

To tell you the truth, my darling, I have written the foregoing not merely to relieve my feelings, but, also, still more, to give you an example of the excellent style in which I can write. You yourself will recognise that my style was formed long ago, but of late such fits of despondency have seized upon me that my style has begun to correspond to my feelings; and though I know that such correspondence gains one little, it at least renders one a certain justice. For not unfrequently it happens that, for some reason or another, one feels abased, and inclined to value oneself at nothing, and to account oneself lower than a dishclout; but this merely arises from the fact that at the time one is feeling harassed and depressed, like the poor boy who today asked of me alms. Let me tell you an allegory, dearest, and do you hearken to it. Often, as I hasten to the office in the morning, I look around me at the city—I watch it awaking, getting out of bed, lighting its fires, cooking its breakfast, and becoming vocal; and at the sight, I begin to feel smaller, as though some one had dealt me a rap on my inquisitive nose. Yes, at such times I slink along with a sense of utter humiliation in my heart. For one would have but to see what is passing within those great, black, grimy houses of the capital, and to penetrate within their walls, for one at once to realise what good reason there is for self-depredation and heart-searching. Of course, you will note that I am speaking figuratively rather than literally.

Let us look at what is passing within those houses. In some dingy corner, perhaps, in some damp kennel which is supposed to be a room, an artisan has just awakened from sleep. All night he has dreamt—IF such an insignificant fellow is capable of dreaming?—about the shoes which last night he mechanically cut out. He is a master-shoemaker, you see, and therefore able to think of nothing but his one subject of interest. Nearby are some squalling children and a hungry wife. Nor is he the only man that has to greet the day in this fashion. Indeed, the incident would be nothing—it would not be worth writing about, save for another circumstance. In that same house ANOTHER person—a person of great wealth-may also have been dreaming of shoes; but, of shoes of a very different pattern and fashion (in a manner of speaking, if you understand my metaphor, we are all of us shoemakers). This, again, would be nothing, were it not that the rich person has no one to whisper in his ear: "Why dost thou think of such things? Why dost thou think of thyself alone, and live only for thyself—thou who art not a shoemaker? THY children are not ailing. THY wife is not hungry. Look around thee. Can'st thou not find a subject more fitting for thy thoughts than thy shoes?" That is what I want to say to you in allegorical language, Barbara. Maybe it savours a little of free-thought, dearest; but, such ideas WILL keep arising in my mind and finding utterance in impetuous speech. Why, therefore, should one not value oneself at a groat as one listens in fear and trembling to the roar and turmoil of the city? Maybe you think that I am exaggerating things—that this is a mere whim of mine, or that I am quoting from a book? No, no, Barbara. You may rest assured that it is not so. Exaggeration I abhor, with whims I have nothing to do, and of quotation I am guiltless.

I arrived home today in a melancholy mood. Sitting down to the table, I had warmed myself some tea, and was about to drink a second glass of it, when there entered Gorshkov, the poor lodger. Already, this morning, I had noticed that he was hovering around the other lodgers, and also seeming to want to speak to myself. In passing I may say that his circumstances are infinitely worse than my own; for, only think of it, he has a wife and children! Indeed, if I were he, I do not know what I should do. Well, he entered my room, and bowed to me with the pus standing, as usual, in drops on his eyelashes, his feet shuffling about, and his tongue unable, at first, to articulate a word. I motioned him to a chair (it was a dilapidated enough one, but I had no other), and asked him to have a glass of tea. To this he demurred—for quite a long time he demurred, but at length he accepted the offer. Next, he was for drinking the tea without sugar, and renewed his excuses, but upon the sugar I insisted. After long resistance and many refusals, he DID consent to take some, but only the smallest possible lump; after which, he assured me that his tea was perfectly sweet. To what depths of humility can poverty reduce a man! "Well, what is it, my good sir?" I inquired of him; whereupon he replied: "It is this, Makar Alexievitch. You have once before been my benefactor. Pray again show me the charity of God, and assist my unfortunate family. My wife and children have nothing to eat. To think that a father should have to say this!" I was about to speak again when he interrupted me. "You see," he continued, "I am afraid of the other lodgers here. That is to say, I am not so much afraid of, as ashamed to address them, for they are a proud, conceited lot of men. Nor would I have troubled even you, my friend and former benefactor, were it not that I know that you yourself have experienced misfortune and are in debt; wherefore, I have ventured to come and make this request of you, in that I know you not only to be kind-hearted, but also to be in need, and for that reason the more likely to sympathise with me in my distress." To this he added an apology for his awkwardness and presumption. I replied that, glad though I should have been to serve him, I had nothing, absolutely nothing, at my disposal. "Ah, Makar Alexievitch," he went on, "surely it is not much that I am asking of you? My-my wife and children are starving. C-could you not afford me just a grivennik?" At that my heart contracted, "How these people put me to shame!" thought I. But I had only twenty kopecks left, and upon them I had been counting for meeting my most pressing requirements. "No, good sir, I cannot," said I. "Well, what you will," he persisted. "Perhaps ten kopecks?" Well I got out my cash-box, and gave him the twenty. It was a good deed. To think that such poverty should exist! Then I had some further talk with him. "How is it," I asked him, "that, though you are in such straits, you have hired a room at five roubles?" He replied that though, when he engaged the room six months ago, he paid three months' rent in advance, his affairs had subsequently turned out badly, and never righted themselves since. You see, Barbara, he was sued at law by a merchant who had defrauded the Treasury in the matter of a contract. When the fraud was discovered the merchant was prosecuted, but the transactions in which he had engaged involved Gorshkov, although the latter had been guilty only of negligence, want of prudence, and culpable indifference to the Treasury's interests. True, the affair had taken place some years ago, but various obstacles had since combined to thwart Gorshkov. "Of the disgrace put upon me," said he to me, "I am innocent. True, I to a certain extent disobeyed orders, but never did I commit theft or embezzlement." Nevertheless the affair lost him his character. He was dismissed the service, and though not adjudged capitally guilty, has been unable since to recover from the merchant a large sum of money which is his by right, as spared to him (Gorshkov) by the legal tribunal. True, the tribunal in question did not altogether believe in Gorshkov, but I do so. The matter is of a nature so complex and crooked that probably a hundred years would be insufficient to unravel it; and, though it has now to a certain extent been cleared up, the merchant still holds the key to the situation. Personally I side with Gorshkov, and am very sorry for him. Though lacking a post of any kind, he still refuses to despair, though his resources are completely exhausted. Yes, it is a tangled affair, and meanwhile he must live, for, unfortunately, another child which has been born to him has entailed upon the family fresh expenses. Also, another of his children recently fell ill and died—which meant yet further expense. Lastly, not only is his wife in bad health, but he himself is suffering from a complaint of long standing. In short, he has had a very great deal to undergo. Yet he declares that daily he expects a favourable issue to his affair—that he has no doubt of it whatever. I am terribly sorry for him, and said what I could to give him comfort, for he is a man who has been much bullied and misled. He had come to me for protection from his troubles, so I did my best to soothe him. Now, goodbye, my darling. May Christ watch over you and preserve your health. Dearest one, even to think of you is like medicine to my ailing soul. Though I suffer for you, I at least suffer gladly.—Your true friend,

MAKAR DIEVUSHKIN.

September 9th.

MY DEAREST BARBARA ALEXIEVNA,—I am beside myself as I take up my pen, for a most terrible thing has happened. My head is whirling round. Ah, beloved, how am I to tell you about it all? I had never foreseen what has happened. But no—I cannot say that I had NEVER foreseen it, for my mind DID get an inkling of what was coming, through my seeing something very similar to it in a dream.

I will tell you the whole story—simply, and as God may put it into my heart. Today I went to the office as usual, and, upon arrival, sat down to write. You must know that I had been engaged on the same sort of work yesterday, and that, while executing it, I had been approached by Timothei Ivanovitch with an urgent request for a particular document. "Makar Alexievitch," he had said, "pray copy this out for me. Copy it as quickly and as carefully as you can, for it will require to be signed today." Also let me tell you, dearest, that yesterday I had not been feeling myself, nor able to look at anything. I had been troubled with grave depression—my breast had felt chilled, and my head clouded. All the while I had been thinking of you, my darling. Well, I set to work upon the copying, and executed it cleanly and well, except for the fact that, whether the devil confused my mind, or a mysterious fate so ordained, or the occurrence was simply bound to happen, I left out a whole line of the document, and thus made nonsense of it! The work had been given me too late for signature last night, so it went before his Excellency this morning. I reached the office at my usual hour, and sat down beside Emelia Ivanovitch. Here I may remark that for a long time past I have been feeling twice as shy and diffident as I used to do; I have been finding it impossible to look people in the face. Let only a chair creak, and I become more dead than alive. Today, therefore, I crept humbly to my seat and sat down in such a crouching posture that Efim Akimovitch (the most touchy man in the world) said to me sotto voce: "What on earth makes you sit like that, Makar Alexievitch?" Then he pulled such a grimace that everyone near us rocked with laughter at my expense. I stopped my ears, frowned, and sat without moving, for I found this the best method of putting a stop to such merriment. All at once I heard a bustle and a commotion and the sound of someone running towards us. Did my ears deceive me? It was I who was being summoned in peremptory tones! My heart started to tremble within me, though I could not say why. I only know that never in my life before had it trembled as it did then. Still I clung to my chair—and at that moment was hardly myself at all. The voices were coming nearer and nearer, until they were shouting in my ear: "Dievushkin! Dievushkin! Where is Dievushkin?" Then at length I raised my eyes, and saw before me Evstafi Ivanovitch. He said to me: "Makar Alexievitch, go at once to his Excellency. You have made a mistake in a document." That was all, but it was enough, was it not? I felt dead and cold as ice—I felt absolutely deprived of the power of sensation; but, I rose from my seat and went whither I had been bidden. Through one room, through two rooms, through three rooms I passed, until I was conducted into his Excellency's cabinet itself. Of my thoughts at that moment I can give no exact account. I merely saw his Excellency standing before me, with a knot of people around him. I have an idea that I did not salute him—that I forgot to do so. Indeed, so panic-stricken was I, that my teeth were chattering and my knees knocking together. In the first place, I was greatly ashamed of my appearance (a glance into a mirror on the right had frightened me with the reflection of myself that it presented), and, in the second place, I had always been accustomed to comport myself as though no such person as I existed. Probably his Excellency had never before known that I was even alive. Of course, he might have heard, in passing, that there was a man named Dievushkin in his department; but never for a moment had he had any intercourse with me.

He began angrily: "What is this you have done, sir? Why are you not more careful? The document was wanted in a hurry, and you have gone and spoiled it. What do you think of it?"—the last being addressed to Evstafi Ivanovitch. More I did not hear, except for some flying exclamations of "What negligence and carelessness! How awkward this is!" and so on. I opened my mouth to say something or other; I tried to beg pardon, but could not. To attempt to leave the room, I had not the hardihood. Then there happened something the recollection of which causes the pen to tremble in my hand with shame. A button of mine—the devil take it!—a button of mine that was hanging by a single thread suddenly broke off, and hopped and skipped and rattled and rolled until it had reached the feet of his Excellency himself—this amid a profound general silence! THAT was what came of my intended self-justification and plea for mercy! THAT was the only answer that I had to return to my chief!

The sequel I shudder to relate. At once his Excellency's attention became drawn to my figure and costume. I remembered what I had seen in the mirror, and hastened to pursue the button. Obstinacy of a sort seized upon me, and I did my best to arrest the thing, but it slipped away, and kept turning over and over, so that I could not grasp it, and made a sad spectacle of myself with my awkwardness. Then there came over me a feeling that my last remaining strength was about to leave me, and that all, all was lost—reputation, manhood, everything! In both ears I seemed to hear the voices of Theresa and Phaldoni. At length, however, I grasped the button, and, raising and straightening myself, stood humbly with clasped hands—looking a veritable fool! But no. First of all I tried to attach the button to the ragged threads, and smiled each time that it broke away from them, and smiled again. In the beginning his Excellency had turned away, but now he threw me another glance, and I heard him say to Evstafi Ivanovitch: "What on earth is the matter with the fellow? Look at the figure he cuts! Who to God is he?" Ah, beloved, only to hear that, "Who to God is he?" Truly I had made myself a marked man! In reply to his Excellency Evstafi murmured: "He is no one of any note, though his character is good. Besides, his salary is sufficient as the scale goes." "Very well, then; but help him out of his difficulties somehow," said his Excellency. "Give him a trifle of salary in advance." "It is all forestalled," was the reply. "He drew it some time ago. But his record is good. There is nothing against him." At this I felt as though I were in Hell fire. I could actually have died! "Well, well," said his Excellency, "let him copy out the document a second time. Dievushkin, come here. You are to make another copy of this paper, and to make it as quickly as possible." With that he turned to some other officials present, issued to them a few orders, and the company dispersed. No sooner had they done so than his Excellency hurriedly pulled out a pocket-book, took thence a note for a hundred roubles, and, with the words, "Take this. It is as much as I can afford. Treat it as you like," placed the money in my hand! At this, dearest, I started and trembled, for I was moved to my very soul. What next I did I hardly know, except that I know that I seized his Excellency by the hand. But he only grew very red, and then—no, I am not departing by a hair's-breadth from the truth—it is true—that he took this unworthy hand in his, and shook it! Yes, he took this hand of mine in his, and shook it, as though I had been his equal, as though I had been a general like himself! "Go now," he said. "This is all that I can do for you. Make no further mistakes, and I will overlook your fault."

What I think about it is this: I beg of you and of Thedora, and had I any children I should beg of them also, to pray ever to God for his Excellency. I should say to my children: "For your father you need not pray; but for his Excellency, I bid you pray until your lives shall end." Yes, dear one—I tell you this in all solemnity, so hearken well unto my words—that though, during these cruel days of our adversity, I have nearly died of distress of soul at the sight of you and your poverty, as well as at the sight of myself and my abasement and helplessness, I yet care less for the hundred roubles which his Excellency has given me than for the fact that he was good enough to take the hand of a wretched drunkard in his own and press it. By that act he restored me to myself. By that act he revived my courage, he made life forever sweet to me.... Yes, sure am I that, sinner though I be before the Almighty, my prayers for the happiness and prosperity of his Excellency will yet ascend to the Heavenly Throne!...

But, my darling, for the moment I am terribly agitated and distraught. My heart is beating as though it would burst my breast, and all my body seems weak.... I send you forty-five roubles in notes. Another twenty I shall give to my landlady, and the remaining thirty-five I shall keep—twenty for new clothes and fifteen for actual living expenses. But these experiences of the morning have shaken me to the core, and I must rest awhile. It is quiet, very quiet, here. My breath is coming in jerks—deep down in my breast I can hear it sobbing and trembling.... I will come and see you soon, but at the moment my head is aching with these various sensations. God sees all things, my darling, my priceless treasure!—Your steadfast friend,

MAKAR DIEVUSHKIN.

September 10th.

MY BELOVED MAKAR ALEXIEVITCH,—I am unspeakably rejoiced at your good fortune, and fully appreciate the kindness of your superior. Now, take a rest from your cares. Only do not AGAIN spend money to no advantage. Live as quietly and as frugally as possible, and from today begin always to set aside something, lest misfortune again overtake you. Do not, for God's sake, worry yourself—Thedora and I will get on somehow. Why have you sent me so much money? I really do not need it—what I had already would have been quite sufficient. True, I shall soon be needing further funds if I am to leave these lodgings, but Thedora is hoping before long to receive repayment of an old debt. Of course, at least TWENTY roubles will have to be set aside for indispensable requirements, but the remainder shall be returned to you. Pray take care of it, Makar Alexievitch. Now, goodbye. May your life continue peacefully, and may you preserve your health and spirits. I would have written to you at greater length had I not felt so terribly weary. Yesterday I never left my bed. I am glad that you have promised to come and see me. Yes, you MUST pay me a visit.

B. D.

September 11th.

MY DARLING BARBARA ALEXIEVNA,—I implore you not to leave me now that I am once more happy and contented. Disregard what Thedora says, and I will do anything in the world for you. I will behave myself better, even if only out of respect for his Excellency, and guard my every action. Once more we will exchange cheerful letters with one another, and make mutual confidence of our thoughts and joys and sorrows (if so be that we shall know any more sorrows?). Yes, we will live twice as happily and comfortably as of old. Also, we will exchange books.... Angel of my heart, a great change has taken place in my fortunes—a change very much for the better. My landlady has become more accommodating; Theresa has recovered her senses; even Phaldoni springs to do my bidding. Likewise, I have made my peace with Rataziaev. He came to see me of his own accord, the moment that he heard the glad tidings. There can be no doubt that he is a good fellow, that there is no truth in the slanders that one hears of him. For one thing, I have discovered that he never had any intention of putting me and yourself into a book. This he told me himself, and then read to me his latest work. As for his calling me "Lovelace," he had intended no rudeness or indecency thereby. The term is merely one of foreign derivation, meaning a clever fellow, or, in more literary and elegant language, a gentleman with whom one must reckon. That is all; it was a mere harmless jest, my beloved. Only ignorance made me lose my temper, and I have expressed to him my regret.... How beautiful is the weather today, my little Barbara! True, there was a slight frost in the early morning, as though scattered through a sieve, but it was nothing, and the breeze soon freshened the air. I went out to buy some shoes, and obtained a splendid pair. Then, after a stroll along the Nevski Prospect, I read "The Daily Bee". This reminds me that I have forgotten to tell you the most important thing of all. It happened like this:

This morning I had a talk with Emelia Ivanovitch and Aksenti Michaelovitch concerning his Excellency. Apparently, I am not the only person to whom he has acted kindly and been charitable, for he is known to the whole world for his goodness of heart. In many quarters his praises are to be heard; in many quarters he has called forth tears of gratitude. Among other things, he undertook the care of an orphaned girl, and married her to an official, the son of a poor widow, and found this man place in a certain chancellory, and in other ways benefited him. Well, dearest, I considered it to be my duty to add my mite by publishing abroad the story of his Excellency's gracious treatment of myself. Accordingly, I related the whole occurrence to my interlocutors, and concealed not a single detail. In fact, I put my pride into my pocket—though why should I feel ashamed of having been elated by such an occurrence? "Let it only be noised afield," said I to myself, and it will resound greatly to his Excellency's credit.—So I expressed myself enthusiastically on the subject and never faltered. On the contrary, I felt proud to have such a story to tell. I referred to every one concerned (except to yourself, of course, dearest)—to my landlady, to Phaldoni, to Rataziaev, to Markov. I even mentioned the matter of my shoes! Some of those standing by laughed—in fact every one present did so, but probably it was my own figure or the incident of my shoes—more particularly the latter—that excited merriment, for I am sure it was not meant ill-naturedly. My hearers may have been young men, or well off; certainly they cannot have been laughing with evil intent at what I had said. Anything against his Excellency CANNOT have been in their thoughts. Eh, Barbara?

Even now I cannot wholly collect my faculties, so upset am I by recent events.... Have you any fuel to go on with, Barbara? You must not expose yourself to cold. Also, you have depressed my spirits with your fears for the future. Daily I pray to God on your behalf. Ah, HOW I pray to Him!... Likewise, have you any woollen stockings to wear, and warm clothes generally? Mind you, if there is anything you need, you must not hurt an old man's feelings by failing to apply to him for what you require. The bad times are gone now, and the future is looking bright and fair.

But what bad times they were, Barbara, even though they be gone, and can no longer matter! As the years pass on we shall gradually recover ourselves. How clearly I remember my youth! In those days I never had a kopeck to spare. Yet, cold and hungry though I was, I was always light-hearted. In the morning I would walk the Nevski Prospect, and meet nice-looking people, and be happy all day. Yes, it was a glorious, a glorious time! It was good to be alive, especially in St. Petersburg. Yet it is but yesterday that I was beseeching God with tears to pardon me my sins during the late sorrowful period—to pardon me my murmurings and evil thoughts and gambling and drunkenness. And you I remembered in my prayers, for you alone have encouraged and comforted me, you alone have given me advice and instruction. I shall never forget that, dearest. Today I gave each one of your letters a kiss.... Goodbye, beloved. I have been told that there is going to be a sale of clothing somewhere in this neighbourhood. Once more goodbye, goodbye, my angel—Yours in heart and soul,

MAKAR DIEVUSHKIN.

September 15th.

MY DEAREST MAKAR ALEXIEVITCH,—I am in terrible distress. I feel sure that something is about to happen. The matter, my beloved friend, is that Monsieur Bwikov is again in St. Petersburg, for Thedora has met him. He was driving along in a drozhki, but, on meeting Thedora, he ordered the coachman to stop, sprang out, and inquired of her where she was living; but this she would not tell him. Next, he said with a smile that he knew quite well who was living with her (evidently Anna Thedorovna had told him); whereupon Thedora could hold out no longer, but then and there, in the street, railed at and abused him—telling him that he was an immoral man, and the cause of all my misfortunes. To this he replied that a person who did not possess a groat must surely be rather badly off; to which Thedora retorted that I could always either live by the labour of my hands or marry—that it was not so much a question of my losing posts as of my losing my happiness, the ruin of which had led almost to my death. In reply he observed that, though I was still quite young, I seemed to have lost my wits, and that my "virtue appeared to be under a cloud" (I quote his exact words). Both I and Thedora had thought that he does not know where I live; but, last night, just as I had left the house to make a few purchases in the Gostinni Dvor, he appeared at our rooms (evidently he had not wanted to find me at home), and put many questions to Thedora concerning our way of living. Then, after inspecting my work, he wound up with: "Who is this tchinovnik friend of yours?" At the moment you happened to be passing through the courtyard, so Thedora pointed you out, and the man peered at you, and laughed. Thedora next asked him to depart—telling him that I was still ill from grief, and that it would give me great pain to see him there; to which, after a pause, he replied that he had come because he had had nothing better to do. Also, he was for giving Thedora twenty-five roubles, but, of course, she declined them. What does it all mean? Why has he paid this visit? I cannot understand his getting to know about me. I am lost in conjecture. Thedora, however, says that Aksinia, her sister-in-law (who sometimes comes to see her), is acquainted with a laundress named Nastasia, and that this woman has a cousin in the position of watchman to a department of which a certain friend of Anna Thedorovna's nephew forms one of the staff. Can it be, therefore, that an intrigue has been hatched through THIS channel? But Thedora may be entirely mistaken. We hardly know what to think. What if he should come again? The very thought terrifies me. When Thedora told me of this last night such terror seized upon me that I almost swooned away. What can the man be wanting? At all events, I refuse to know such people. What have they to do with my wretched self? Ah, how I am haunted with anxiety, for every moment I keep thinking that Bwikov is at hand! WHAT will become of me? WHAT MORE has fate in store for me? For Christ's sake come and see me, Makar Alexievitch! For Christ's sake come and see me soon.

September 18th.

MY BELOVED BARBARA ALEXIEVNA,—Today there took place in this house a most lamentable, a most mysterious, a most unlooked-for occurrence. First of all, let me tell you that poor Gorshkov has been entirely absolved of guilt. The decision has been long in coming, but this morning he went to hear the final resolution read. It was entirely in his favour. Any culpability which had been imputed to him for negligence and irregularity was removed by the resolution. Likewise, he was authorised to recover of the merchant a large sum of money. Thus, he stands entirely justified, and has had his character cleansed from all stain. In short, he could not have wished for a more complete vindication. When he arrived home at three o'clock he was looking as white as a sheet, and his lips were quivering. Yet there was a smile on his face as he embraced his wife and children. In a body the rest of us ran to congratulate him, and he was greatly moved by the act. Bowing to us, he pressed our hands in turn. As he did so I thought, somehow, that he seemed to have grown taller and straighter, and that the pus-drops seemed to have disappeared from his eyelashes. Yet how agitated he was, poor fellow! He could not rest quietly for two minutes together, but kept picking up and then dropping whatsoever came to his hand, and bowing and smiling without intermission, and sitting down and getting up, and again sitting down, and chattering God only knows what about his honour and his good name and his little ones. How he did talk—yes, and weep too! Indeed, few of ourselves could refrain from tears; although Rataziaev remarked (probably to encourage Gorshkov) that honour mattered nothing when one had nothing to eat, and that money was the chief thing in the world, and that for it alone ought God to be thanked. Then he slapped Gorshkov on the shoulder, but I thought that Gorshkov somehow seemed hurt at this. He did not express any open displeasure, but threw Rataziaev a curious look, and removed his hand from his shoulder. ONCE upon a time he would not have acted thus; but characters differ. For example, I myself should have hesitated, at such a season of rejoicing, to seem proud, even though excessive deference and civility at such a moment might have been construed as a lapse both of moral courage and of mental vigour. However, this is none of my business. All that Gorshkov said was: "Yes, money IS a good thing, glory be to God!" In fact, the whole time that we remained in his room he kept repeating to himself: "Glory be to God, glory be to God!" His wife ordered a richer and more delicate meal than usual, and the landlady herself cooked it, for at heart she is not a bad woman. But until the meal was served Gorshkov could not remain still. He kept entering everyone's room in turn (whether invited thither or not), and, seating himself smilingly upon a chair, would sometimes say something, and sometimes not utter a word, but get up and go out again. In the naval officer's room he even took a pack of playing-cards into his hand, and was thereupon invited to make a fourth in a game; but after losing a few times, as well as making several blunders in his play, he abandoned the pursuit. "No," said he, "that is the sort of man that I am—that is all that I am good for," and departed. Next, encountering myself in the corridor, he took my hands in his, and gazed into my face with a rather curious air. Then he pressed my hands again, and moved away still smiling, smiling, but in an odd, weary sort of manner, much as a corpse might smile. Meanwhile his wife was weeping for joy, and everything in their room was decked in holiday guise. Presently dinner was served, and after they had dined Gorshkov said to his wife: "See now, dearest, I am going to rest a little while;" and with that went to bed. Presently he called his little daughter to his side, and, laying his hand upon the child's head, lay a long while looking at her. Then he turned to his wife again, and asked her: "What of Petinka? Where is our Petinka?" whereupon his wife crossed herself, and replied: "Why, our Petinka is dead!" "Yes, yes, I know—of course," said her husband. "Petinka is now in the Kingdom of Heaven." This showed his wife that her husband was not quite in his right senses—that the recent occurrence had upset him; so she said: "My dearest, you must sleep awhile." "I will do so," he replied, "—at once—I am rather—" And he turned over, and lay silent for a time. Then again he turned round and tried to say something, but his wife could not hear what it was. "What do you say?" she inquired, but he made no reply. Then again she waited a few moments until she thought to herself, "He has gone to sleep," and departed to spend an hour with the landlady. At the end of that hour she returned—only to find that her husband had not yet awoken, but was still lying motionless. "He is sleeping very soundly," she reflected as she sat down and began to work at something or other. Since then she has told us that when half an hour or so had elapsed she fell into a reverie. What she was thinking of she cannot remember, save that she had forgotten altogether about her husband. Then she awoke with a curious sort of sensation at her heart. The first thing that struck her was the deathlike stillness of the room. Glancing at the bed, she perceived her husband to be lying in the same position as before. Thereupon she approached him, turned the coverlet back, and saw that he was stiff and cold—that he had died suddenly, as though smitten with a stroke. But of what precisely he died God only knows. The affair has so terribly impressed me that even now I cannot fully collect my thoughts. It would scarcely be believed that a human being could die so simply—and he such a poor, needy wretch, this Gorshkov! What a fate, what a fate, to be sure! His wife is plunged in tears and panic-stricken, while his little daughter has run away somewhere to hide herself. In their room, however, all is bustle and confusion, for the doctors are about to make an autopsy on the corpse. But I cannot tell you things for certain; I only know that I am most grieved, most grieved. How sad to think that one never knows what even a day, what even an hour, may bring forth! One seems to die to so little purpose!—Your own

MAKAR DIEVUSHKIN.

September 19th.

MY BELOVED BARBARA ALEXIEVNA,—I hasten to let you know that Rataziaev has found me some work to do for a certain writer—the latter having submitted to him a large manuscript. Glory be to God, for this means a large amount of work to do. Yet, though the copy is wanted in haste, the original is so carelessly written that I hardly know how to set about my task. Indeed, certain parts of the manuscript are almost undecipherable. I have agreed to do the work for forty kopecks a sheet. You see therefore (and this is my true reason for writing to you), that we shall soon be receiving money from an extraneous source. Goodbye now, as I must begin upon my labours.—Your sincere friend,

MAKAR DIEVUSHKIN.

September 23rd.

MY DEAREST MAKAR ALEXIEVITCH,—I have not written to you these three days past for the reason that I have been so worried and alarmed.

Three days ago Bwikov came again to see me. At the time I was alone, for Thedora had gone out somewhere. As soon as I opened the door the sight of him so terrified me that I stood rooted to the spot, and could feel myself turning pale. Entering with his usual loud laugh, he took a chair, and sat down. For a long while I could not collect my thoughts; I just sat where I was, and went on with my work. Soon his smile faded, for my appearance seemed somehow to have struck him. You see, of late I have grown thin, and my eyes and cheeks have fallen in, and my face has become as white as a sheet; so that anyone who knew me a year ago would scarcely recognise me now. After a prolonged inspection, Bwikov seemed to recover his spirits, for he said something to which I duly replied. Then again he laughed. Thus he sat for a whole hour—talking to me the while, and asking me questions about one thing and another. At length, just before he rose to depart, he took me by the hand, and said (to quote his exact words): "Between ourselves, Barbara Alexievna, that kinswoman of yours and my good friend and acquaintance—I refer to Anna Thedorovna—is a very bad woman," (he also added a grosser term of opprobrium). "First of all she led your cousin astray, and then she ruined yourself. I also have behaved like a villain, but such is the way of the world." Again he laughed. Next, having remarked that, though not a master of eloquence, he had always considered that obligations of gentility obliged him to have with me a clear and outspoken explanation, he went on to say that he sought my hand in marriage; that he looked upon it as a duty to restore to me my honour; that he could offer me riches; that, after marriage, he would take me to his country seat in the Steppes, where we would hunt hares; that he intended never to visit St. Petersburg again, since everything there was horrible, and he had to entertain a worthless nephew whom he had sworn to disinherit in favour of a legal heir; and, finally, that it was to obtain such a legal heir that he was seeking my hand in marriage. Lastly, he remarked that I seemed to be living in very poor circumstances (which was not surprising, said he, in view of the kennel that I inhabited); that I should die if I remained a month longer in that den; that all lodgings in St. Petersburg were detestable; and that he would be glad to know if I was in want of anything.

So thunderstruck was I with the proposal that I could only burst into tears. These tears he interpreted as a sign of gratitude, for he told me that he had always felt assured of my good sense, cleverness, and sensibility, but that hitherto he had hesitated to take this step until he should have learned precisely how I was getting on. Next he asked me some questions about YOU; saying that he had heard of you as a man of good principle, and that since he was unwilling to remain your debtor, would a sum of five hundred roubles repay you for all you had done for me? To this I replied that your services to myself had been such as could never be requited with money; whereupon, he exclaimed that I was talking rubbish and nonsense; that evidently I was still young enough to read poetry; that romances of this kind were the undoing of young girls, that books only corrupted morality, and that, for his part, he could not abide them. "You ought to live as long as I have done," he added, "and THEN you will see what men can be."

With that he requested me to give his proposal my favourable consideration—saying that he would not like me to take such an important step unguardedly, since want of thought and impetuosity often spelt ruin to youthful inexperience, but that he hoped to receive an answer in the affirmative. "Otherwise," said he, "I shall have no choice but to marry a certain merchant's daughter in Moscow, in order that I may keep my vow to deprive my nephew of the inheritance."—Then he pressed five hundred roubles into my hand—to buy myself some bonbons, as he phrased it—and wound up by saying that in the country I should grow as fat as a doughnut or a cheese rolled in butter; that at the present moment he was extremely busy; and that, deeply engaged in business though he had been all day, he had snatched the present opportunity of paying me a visit. At length he departed.

For a long time I sat plunged in reflection. Great though my distress of mind was, I soon arrived at a decision.... My friend, I am going to marry this man; I have no choice but to accept his proposal. If anyone could save me from this squalor, and restore to me my good name, and avert from me future poverty and want and misfortune, he is the man to do it. What else have I to look for from the future? What more am I to ask of fate? Thedora declares that one need NEVER lose one's happiness; but what, I ask HER, can be called happiness under such circumstances as mine? At all events I see no other road open, dear friend. I see nothing else to be done. I have worked until I have ruined my health. I cannot go on working forever. Shall I go out into the world? Nay; I am worn to a shadow with grief, and become good for nothing. Sickly by nature, I should merely be a burden upon other folks. Of course this marriage will not bring me paradise, but what else does there remain, my friend—what else does there remain? What other choice is left?

I had not asked your advice earlier for the reason that I wanted to think the matter over alone. However, the decision which you have just read is unalterable, and I am about to announce it to Bwikov himself, who in any case has pressed me for a speedy reply, owing to the fact (so he says) that his business will not wait nor allow him to remain here longer, and that therefore, no trifle must be allowed to stand in its way. God alone knows whether I shall be happy, but my fate is in His holy, His inscrutable hand, and I have so decided. Bwikov is said to be kind-hearted. He will at least respect me, and perhaps I shall be able to return that respect. What more could be looked for from such a marriage?

I have now told you all, Makar Alexievitch, and feel sure that you will understand my despondency. Do not, however, try to divert me from my intention, for all your efforts will be in vain. Think for a moment; weigh in your heart for a moment all that has led me to take this step. At first my anguish was extreme, but now I am quieter. What awaits me I know not. What must be must be, and as God may send....

Bwikov has just arrived, so I am leaving this letter unfinished. Otherwise I had much else to say to you. Bwikov is even now at the door!...

September 23rd.

MY BELOVED BARBARA ALEXIEVNA,—I hasten to reply to you—I hasten to express to you my extreme astonishment.... In passing, I may mention that yesterday we buried poor Gorshkov....

Yes, Bwikov has acted nobly, and you have no choice but to accept him. All things are in God's hands. This is so, and must always be so; and the purposes of the Divine Creator are at once good and inscrutable, as also is Fate, which is one with Him....

Thedora will share your happiness—for, of course, you will be happy, and free from want, darling, dearest, sweetest of angels! But why should the matter be so hurried? Oh, of course—Monsieur Bwikov's business affairs. Only a man who has no affairs to see to can afford to disregard such things. I got a glimpse of Monsieur Bwikov as he was leaving your door. He is a fine-looking man—a very fine-looking man; though that is not the point that I should most have noticed had I been quite myself at the time....

In the future shall we be able to write letters to one another? I keep wondering and wondering what has led you to say all that you have said. To think that just when twenty pages of my copying are completed THIS has happened!... I suppose you will be able to make many purchases now—to buy shoes and dresses and all sorts of things? Do you remember the shops in Gorokhovaia Street of which I used to speak?...

But no. You ought not to go out at present—you simply ought not to, and shall not. Presently, you will he able to buy many, many things, and to, keep a carriage. Also, at present the weather is bad. Rain is descending in pailfuls, and it is such a soaking kind of rain that—that you might catch cold from it, my darling, and the chill might go to your heart. Why should your fear of this man lead you to take such risks when all the time I am here to do your bidding? So Thedora declares great happiness to be awaiting you, does she? She is a gossiping old woman, and evidently desires to ruin you.

Shall you be at the all-night Mass this evening, dearest? I should like to come and see you there. Yes, Bwikov spoke but the truth when he said that you are a woman of virtue, wit, and good feeling. Yet I think he would do far better to marry the merchant's daughter. What think YOU about it? Yes, 'twould be far better for him. As soon as it grows dark tonight I mean to come and sit with you for an hour. Tonight twilight will close in early, so I shall soon be with you. Yes, come what may, I mean to see you for an hour. At present, I suppose, you are expecting Bwikov, but I will come as soon as he has gone. So stay at home until I have arrived, dearest.

MAKAR DIEVUSHKIN.

September 27th.

DEAR MAKAR ALEXIEVITCH,—Bwikov has just informed me that I must have at least three dozen linen blouses; so I must go at once and look for sempstresses to make two out of the three dozen, since time presses. Indeed, Monsieur Bwikov is quite angry about the fuss which these fripperies are entailing, seeing that there remain but five days before the wedding, and we are to depart on the following day. He keeps rushing about and declaring that no time ought to be wasted on trifles. I am terribly worried, and scarcely able to stand on my feet. There is so much to do, and, perhaps, so much that were better left undone! Moreover, I have no blond or other lace; so THERE is another item to be purchased, since Bwikov declares that he cannot have his bride look like a cook, but, on the contrary, she must "put the noses of the great ladies out of joint." That is his expression. I wish, therefore, that you would go to Madame Chiffon's, in Gorokhovaia Street, and ask her, in the first place, to send me some sempstresses, and, in the second place, to give herself the trouble of coming in person, as I am too ill to go out. Our new flat is very cold, and still in great disorder. Also, Bwikov has an aunt who is at her last gasp through old age, and may die before our departure. He himself, however, declares this to be nothing, and says that she will soon recover. He is not yet living with me, and I have to go running hither and thither to find him. Only Thedora is acting as my servant, together with Bwikov's valet, who oversees everything, but has been absent for the past three days.

Each morning Bwikov goes to business, and loses his temper. Yesterday he even had some trouble with the police because of his thrashing the steward of these buildings... I have no one to send with this letter so I am going to post it... Ah! I had almost forgotten the most important point—which is that I should like you to go and tell Madame Chiffon that I wish the blond lace to be changed in conformity with yesterday's patterns, if she will be good enough to bring with her a new assortment. Also say that I have altered my mind about the satin, which I wish to be tamboured with crochet-work; also, that tambour is to be used with monograms on the various garments. Do you hear? Tambour, not smooth work. Do not forget that it is to be tambour. Another thing I had almost forgotten,

113

which is that the lappets of the fur cloak must be raised, and the collar bound with lace. Please tell her these things, Makar Alexievitch.—Your friend,

B. D.

P.S.—I am so ashamed to trouble you with my commissions! This is the third morning that you will have spent in running about for my sake. But what else am I to do? The whole place is in disorder, and I myself am ill. Do not be vexed with me, Makar Alexievitch. I am feeling so depressed! What is going to become of me, dear friend, dear, kind, old Makar Alexievitch? I dread to look forward into the future. Somehow I feel apprehensive; I am living, as it were, in a mist. Yet, for God's sake, forget none of my commissions. I am so afraid lest you should make a mistake! Remember that everything is to be tambour work, not smooth.

September 27th.

MY BELOVED BARBARA ALEXIEVNA,—I have carefully fulfilled your commissions. Madame Chiffon informs me that she herself had thought of using tambour work as being more suitable (though I did not quite take in all she said). Also, she has informed me that, since you have given certain directions in writing, she has followed them (though again I do not clearly remember all that she said—I only remember that she said a very great deal, for she is a most tiresome old woman). These observations she will soon be repeating to you in person. For myself, I feel absolutely exhausted, and have not been to the office today...

Do not despair about the future, dearest. To save you trouble I would visit every shop in St. Petersburg. You write that you dare not look forward into the future. But by tonight, at seven o'clock, you will have learned all, for Madame Chiffon will have arrived in person to see you. Hope on, and everything will order itself for the best. Of course, I am referring only to these accursed gewgaws, to these frills and fripperies! Ah me, ah me, how glad I shall be to see you, my angel! Yes, how glad I shall be! Twice already today I have passed the gates of your abode. Unfortunately, this Bwikov is a man of such choler that—Well, things are as they are.

MAKAR DIEVUSHKIN.

September 28th.

MY DEAREST MAKAR ALEXIEVITCH,—For God's sake go to the jeweller's, and tell him that, after all, he need not make the pearl and emerald earrings. Monsieur Bwikov says that they will cost him too much, that they will burn a veritable hole in his pocket. In fact, he has lost his temper again, and declares that he is being robbed. Yesterday he added that, had he but known, but foreseen, these expenses, he would never have married. Also, he says that, as things are, he intends only to have a plain wedding, and then to depart. "You must not look for any dancing or festivity or entertainment of guests, for our gala times are still in the air." Such were his words. God knows I do not want such things, but none the less Bwikov has forbidden them. I made him no answer on the subject, for he is a man all too easily irritated. What, what is going to become of me?

B. D.

September 28th.

MY BELOVED BARBARA ALEXIEVNA,—All is well as regards the jeweller. Unfortunately, I have also to say that I myself have fallen ill, and cannot rise from bed. Just when so many things need to be done, I have gone and caught a chill, the devil take it! Also I have to tell you that, to complete my misfortunes, his Excellency has been pleased to become stricter. Today he railed at and scolded Emelia Ivanovitch until the poor fellow was quite put about. That is the sum of my news.

No—there is something else concerning which I should like to write to you, but am afraid to obtrude upon your notice. I am a simple, dull fellow who writes down whatsoever first comes into his head—Your friend,

MAKAR DIEVUSHKIN.

September 29th.

MY OWN BARBARA ALEXIEVNA,—Today, dearest, I saw Thedora, who informed me that you are to be married tomorrow, and on the following day to go away—for which purpose Bwikov has ordered a post-chaise....

Well, of the incident of his Excellency, I have already told you. Also I have verified the bill from the shop in Gorokhovaia Street. It is correct, but very long. Why is Monsieur Bwikov so out of humour with you? Nay, but you must be of good cheer, my darling. I am so, and shall always be so, so long as you are happy. I should have come to the church tomorrow, but, alas, shall be prevented from doing so by the pain in my loins. Also, I would have written an account of the ceremony, but that there will be no one to report to me the details....

Yes, you have been a very good friend to Thedora, dearest. You have acted kindly, very kindly, towards her. For every such deed God will bless you. Good deeds never go unrewarded, nor does virtue ever fail to win the crown of divine justice, be it early or be it late. Much else should I have liked to write to you. Every hour, every minute I could occupy in writing. Indeed I could write to you forever! Only your book, "The Stories of Bielkin", is left to me. Do not deprive me of it, I pray you, but suffer me to keep it. It is not so much because I wish to read the book for its own sake, as because winter is coming on, when the evenings will be long and dreary, and one will want to read at least SOMETHING.

Do you know, I am going to move from my present quarters into your old ones, which I intend to rent from Thedora; for I could never part with that good old woman. Moreover, she is such a splendid worker. Yesterday I inspected your empty room in detail, and inspected your embroidery-frame, with the work still hanging on it. It had been left untouched in its corner. Next, I inspected the work itself, of which there still remained a few remnants, and saw that you had used one of my letters for a spool upon which to wind your thread. Also, on the table I found a scrap of paper which had written on it, "My dearest Makar Alexievitch I hasten to—" that was all. Evidently, someone had interrupted you at an interesting point. Lastly, behind a screen there was your little bed.... Oh darling of darlings!!!... Well, goodbye now, goodbye now, but for God's sake send me something in answer to this letter!

MAKAR DIEVUSHKIN.

September 30th.

MY BELOVED MAKAR ALEXIEVITCH,—All is over! The die is cast! What my lot may have in store I know not, but I am submissive to the will of God. Tomorrow, then, we depart. For the last time, I take my leave of you, my friend beyond price, my benefactor, my dear one! Do not grieve for me, but try to live happily. Think of me sometimes, and may the blessing of Almighty God light upon you! For myself, I shall often have you in remembrance, and recall you in my prayers. Thus our time together has come to an end. Little comfort in my new life shall I derive from memories of the past. The more, therefore, shall I cherish the recollection of you, and the dearer will you ever be to my heart. Here, you have been my only friend; here, you alone have loved me. Yes, I have seen all, I have known all—I have throughout known how well you love me. A single smile of mine, a single stroke from my pen, has been able to make you happy.... But now you must forget me.... How lonely you will be! Why should you stay here at all, kind, inestimable, but solitary, friend of mine?

To your care I entrust the book, the embroidery frame, and the letter upon which I had begun. When you look upon the few words which the letter contains you will be able mentally to read in thought all that you would have liked further to hear or receive from me—all that I would so gladly have written, but can never now write. Think sometimes of your poor little Barbara who loved you so well. All your letters I have left behind me in the top drawer of Thedora's chest of drawers... You write that you are ill, but Monsieur Bwikov will not let me leave the house today; so that I can only write to you. Also, I will write again before long. That is a promise. Yet God only knows when I shall be able to do so....

Now we must bid one another forever farewell, my friend, my beloved, my own! Yes, it must be forever! Ah, how at this moment I could embrace you! Goodbye, dear friend—goodbye, goodbye! May you ever rest well and happy! To the end I shall keep you in my prayers. How my heart is aching under its load of sorrow!... Monsieur Bwikov is just calling for me....—Your ever loving

B.

P.S.—My heart is full! It is full to bursting of tears! Sorrow has me in its grip, and is tearing me to pieces. Goodbye. My God, what grief! Do not, do not forget your poor Barbara!

BELOVED BARBARA—MY JEWEL, MY PRICELESS ONE,—You are now almost en route, you are now just about to depart! Would that they had torn my heart out of my breast rather than have taken you away from me! How could you allow it? You weep, yet you go! And only this moment I have received from you a letter stained with your tears! It must be that you are departing unwillingly; it must be that you are being abducted against your will; it must be that you are sorry for me; it must be that—that you LOVE me!...

Yet how will it fare with you now? Your heart will soon have become chilled and sick and depressed. Grief will soon have sucked away its life; grief will soon have rent it in twain! Yes, you will die where you be, and be laid to rest in the cold, moist earth where there is no one to bewail you. Monsieur Bwikov will only be hunting hares!...

Ah, my darling, my darling! WHY did you come to this decision? How could you bring yourself to take such a step? What have you done, have you done, have you done? Soon they will be carrying you away to the tomb; soon your beauty will have become defiled, my angel. Ah, dearest one, you are as weak as a feather. And where have I been all this time? What have I been thinking of? I have treated you merely as a forward child whose head was aching. Fool that I was, I neither saw nor understood. I have behaved as though, right or wrong, the matter was in no way my concern. Yes, I have been running about after fripperies!... Ah, but I WILL leave my bed. Tomorrow I WILL rise sound and well, and be once more myself....

Dearest, I could throw myself under the wheels of a passing vehicle rather than that you should go like this. By what right is it being done?... I will go with you; I will run behind your carriage if you will not take me—yes, I will run, and run so long as the power is in me, and until my breath shall have failed. Do you know whither you are going? Perhaps you will not know, and will have to ask me? Before you there lie the Steppes, my darling—only the Steppes, the naked Steppes, the Steppes that are as bare as the palm of my hand. THERE there live only heartless old women and rude peasants and drunkards. THERE the trees have already shed their leaves. THERE there abide but rain and cold. Why should you go thither? True, Monsieur Bwikov will have his diversions in that country—he will be able to hunt the hare; but what of yourself? Do you wish to become a mere estate lady? Nay; look at yourself, my seraph of heaven. Are you in any way fitted for such a role? How could you play it? To whom should I write letters? To whom should I send these missives? Whom should I call "my darling"? To whom should I apply that name of endearment? Where, too, could I find you?

When you are gone, Barbara, I shall die—for certain I shall die, for my heart cannot bear this misery. I love you as I love the light of God; I love you as my own daughter; to you I have devoted my love in its entirety; only for you have I lived at all; only because you were near me have I worked and copied manuscripts and committed my views to paper under the guise of friendly letters.

Perhaps you did not know all this, but it has been so. How, then, my beloved, could you bring yourself to leave me? Nay, you MUST not go—it is impossible, it is sheerly, it is utterly, impossible. The rain will fall upon you, and you are weak, and will catch cold. The floods will stop your carriage. No sooner will it have passed the city barriers than it will break down, purposely break down. Here, in St. Petersburg, they are bad builders of carriages. Yes, I know well these carriage-builders. They are jerry-builders who can fashion a toy, but nothing that is durable. Yes, I swear they can make nothing that is durable.... All that I can do is to go upon my knees before Monsieur Bwikov, and to tell him all, to tell him all. Do you also tell him all, dearest, and reason with him. Tell him that you MUST remain here, and must not go. Ah, why did he not marry that merchant's daughter in Moscow? Let him go and marry her now. She would suit him far better and for reasons which I well know. Then I could keep you. For what is he to you, this Monsieur Bwikov? Why has he suddenly become so dear to your heart? Is it because he can buy you gewgaws? What are THEY? What use are THEY? They are so much rubbish. One should consider human life rather than mere finery.

Nevertheless, as soon as I have received my next instalment of salary I mean to buy you a new cloak. I mean to buy it at a shop with which I am acquainted. Only, you must wait until my next installment is due, my angel of a Barbara. Ah, God, my God! To think that you are going away into the Steppes with Monsieur Bwikov—that you are going away never to return!... Nay, nay, but you SHALL write to me. You SHALL write me a letter as soon as you have started, even if it be your last letter of all, my dearest. Yet will it be your last letter? How has it come about so suddenly, so irrevocably, that this letter should be your last? Nay, nay; I will write, and you shall write—yes, NOW, when at length I am beginning to improve my style. Style? I do not know what I am writing. I never do know what I am writing. I could not possibly know, for I never read over what I have written, nor correct its orthography. At the present moment, I am writing merely for the sake of writing, and to put as much as possible into this last letter of mine....

Ah, dearest, my pet, my own darling!...

Uncle's dream and
The Permanent Husband

CHAPTER I.

Maria Alexandrovna Moskaleva was the principal lady of Mordasoff—there was no doubt whatever on that point! She always bore herself as though *she* did not care a fig for anyone, but as though no one else could do without *her*. True, there were uncommonly few who loved her—in fact I may say that very many detested her; still, everyone was afraid of her, and that was what she liked!

Now, why did Maria Alexandrovna, who dearly loves scandal, and cannot sleep at night unless she has heard something new and piquant the day before,—why, or how did she know how to bear herself so that it would never strike anyone, looking at her, to suppose that the dignified lady was the most inveterate scandal-monger in the world—or at all events in Mordasoff? On the contrary, anyone would have said at once, that scandals and such-like pettiness must vanish in her presence; and that scandal-mongers, caught red-handed by Maria Alexandrovna, would blush and tremble, like schoolboys at the entrance of the master; and that the talk would immediately be diverted into channels of the loftiest and most sublime subjects so soon as she entered the room. Maria Alexandrovna knew many deadly and scandalous secrets of certain other Mordasoff inhabitants, which, if she liked to reveal them at any convenient opportunity, would produce results little less terrible than the earthquake of Lisbon. Still, she was very quiet about the secrets she knew, and never let them out except in cases of absolute need, and then only to her nearest and dearest friends. She liked to hint that she knew certain things, and frighten people out of their wits; preferring to keep them in a state of perpetual terror, rather than crush them altogether.

This was real talent—the talent of tactics.

We all considered Maria Alexandrovna as our type and model of irreproachable *comme-il-faut*! She had no rival in this respect in Mordasoff! She could kill and annihilate and pulverize any rival with a single word. We have seen her do it; and all the while she would look as though she had not even observed that she had let the fatal word fall.

Everyone knows that this trait is a speciality of the highest circles.

Her circle of friends was large. Many visitors to Mordasoff left the town again in an ecstasy over her reception of them, and carried on a correspondence with her afterwards! Somebody even addressed some poetry to her, which she showed about the place with great pride. The novelist who came to the town used to read his novel to her of an evening, and ended by dedicating it to her; which produced a very agreeable effect. A certain German professor, who came from Carlsbad to inquire into the question of a little worm with horns which abounds in our part of the world, and who wrote and published four large quarto volumes about this same little insect, was so delighted and ravished with her amiability and kindness that to this very day he carries on a most improving correspondence upon moral subjects from far Carlsbad!

Some people have compared Maria Alexandrovna, in certain respects, with Napoleon. Of course it may have been her enemies who did so, in order to bring Maria Alexandrovna to scorn; but all I can say is, How is it that Napoleon, when he rose to his highest, that *too* high estate of his, became giddy and fell? Historians of the old school have ascribed this to the fact that he was not only not of royal blood, but was not even a gentleman! and therefore when he rose too high, he thought of his proper place, the ground, became giddy and fell! But why did not Maria Alexandrovna's head whirl? And how was it that she could always keep her place as the first lady of Mordasoff?

People have often said this sort of thing of Maria Alexandrovna; for instance: "Oh—yes, but how would she act under such and such difficult circumstances?" Yet, when the circumstances arose, Maria Alexandrovna invariably rose also to the emergency! For instance, when her husband—Afanassy Matveyevitch—was obliged to throw up his appointment, out of pure incapacity and feebleness of intellect, just before the government inspector came down to look into matters, all Mordasoff danced with delight to think that she would be down on her knees to this inspector, begging and beseeching and weeping and praying—in fact, that she would drop her wings and fall; but, bless you, nothing of the sort happened! Maria Alexandrovna quite understood that her husband was beyond praying for: he must retire. So she only rearranged her affairs a little, in such a manner that she lost not a scrap of her influence in the place, and her house still remained the acknowledged head of all Mordasoff Society!

The procurer's wife, Anna Nicolaevna Antipova, the sworn foe of Maria Alexandrovna, though a friend so far as could be judged outside, had already blown the trumpet of victory over her rival! But when Society found that Maria Alexandrovna was extremely difficult to put down, they were obliged to conclude that the latter had struck her roots far deeper than they had thought for.

As I have mentioned Afanassy Matveyevitch, Maria Alexandrovna's husband, I may as well add a few words about him in this place.

Firstly, then, he was a most presentable man, so far as exterior goes, and a very high-principled person besides; but in critical moments he used to lose his head and stand looking like a sheep which has come across a new gate. He looked very majestic and dignified in his dress-coat and white tie at dinner parties, and so on; but his dignity only lasted until he opened his mouth to speak; for then—well, you'd better have shut your ears, ladies and gentlemen, when he began to talk—that's all! Everyone agreed that he was quite unworthy to be Maria Alexandrovna's husband. He only sat in his place by virtue of his wife's genius. In my humble opinion he ought long ago to have been derogated to the office of frightening sparrows in the kitchen garden. There, and only there, would he have been in his proper sphere, and doing some good to his fellow countrymen.

Therefore, I think Maria Alexandrovna did a very wise thing when she sent him away to her village, about a couple of miles from town, where she possessed a property of some hundred and twenty souls—which, to tell the truth, was all she had to keep up the respectability and grandeur of her noble house upon!

Everybody knew that Afanassy was only kept because he had earned a salary and perquisites; so that when he ceased to earn the said salary and perquisites, it surprised no-one to learn that he was sent away—"returned empty" to the village, as useless and fit for nothing! In fact, everyone praised his wife for her soundness of judgment and decision of character!

Afanassy lived in clover at the village. I called on him there once and spent a very pleasant hour. He tied on his white ties, cleaned his boots himself (not because he had no-one to do it for him, but for the sake of art, for he loved to have them *shine*), went to the bath as often as he could, had tea four times a day, and was as contented as possible.

Do you remember, a year and a half ago, the dreadful stories that were afoot about Zenaida, Maria Alexandrovna's and Afanassy's daughter? Zenaida was undoubtedly a fine, handsome, well-educated girl; but she was now twenty-three years old, and not married yet. Among the reasons put forth for Zenaida being still a maid, one of the strongest was those dark rumours about a strange attachment, a year and a half ago, with the schoolmaster of the place—rumours not hushed up even to this day. Yes, to this very day they tell of a love-letter, written by Zina, as she was called, and handed all about Mordasoff. But kindly tell me, who ever saw this letter? If it went from hand to hand what became of it? Everyone seems to have heard of it, but no one ever saw it! At all events, *I* have never met anyone who actually saw the letter with his own eyes. If you drop a hint to Maria Alexandrovna about it, she simply does not understand you.

Well, supposing that there *was* something, and that Zina did write such a letter; what dexterity and skill of Maria Alexandrovna, to have so ably nipped the bud of the scandal! I feel sure that Zina *did* write the letter; but Maria Alexandrovna has managed so well that there is not a trace, not a shred of evidence of the existence of it. Goodness knows how she must have worked and planned to save the reputation of this only daughter of hers; but she managed it somehow.

As for Zina not having married, there's nothing surprising in that. Why, what sort of a husband could be found for her in Mordasoff? Zina ought to marry a reigning prince, if anyone! Did you ever see such a beauty among beauties as Zina? I think not. Of course, she was very proud—too proud.

There was Mosgliakoff—some people said she was likely to end by marrying *him*; but I never thought so. Why, what was there in Mosgliakoff? True, he was young and good looking, and possessed an estate of a hundred and fifty souls, and was a Petersburg swell; but, in the first place, I don't think there was much inside his head. He was such a funny, new-idea sort of man. Besides, what is an estate of a hundred and fifty souls, according to present notions? Oh, no; that's a marriage that never could come off.

There, kind reader, all you have just read was written by me some five months ago, for my own amusement. I admit, I am rather partial to Maria Alexandrovna; and I wished to write some sort of laudatory account of that charming woman, and to mould it into the form of one of those playful "letters to a friend," purporting to have been written in the old golden days (which will never return—thank Heaven!) to one of the periodicals of the time, "The Northern Bee," or some such paper. But since I have no "friend," and since I am, besides, naturally of a timid disposition, and especially so as to my literary efforts, the essay remained on my writing-table, as a memorial of my early literary attempts and in memory of the peaceful occupation of a moment or two of leisure.

Well, five months have gone by, and lo! great things have happened at Mordasoff!

Prince K—— drove into the town at an early hour one fine morning, and put up at Maria Alexandrovna's house! The prince only stayed three days, but his visit proved pregnant with the most fatal consequences. I will say more—the prince brought about what was, in a certain sense, a revolution in the town, an account of which revolution will, of course, comprise some of the most important events that have ever happened in Mordasoff; and I have determined at last, after many heart-sinkings and flutterings, and much doubt, to arrange the story into the orthodox literary form of a novel, and present it to the indulgent Public! My tale will include a narrative of the Rise and Greatness and Triumphant Fall of Maria Alexandrovna, and of all her House in Mordasoff, a theme both worthy of, and attractive to any writer!

Of course I must first explain why there should have been anything extraordinary in the fact that Prince K—— came to Mordasoff, and put up at Maria Alexandrovna's mansion. And in order to do this, I must first be allowed to say a few words about this same Prince K——. This I shall now do. A short biography of the nobleman is absolutely necessary to the further working out of my story. So, reader, you must excuse me.

CHAPTER II.

I will begin, then, by stating that Prince K—— was not so very, very old, although, to look at him, you would think he *must* fall to pieces every moment, so decayed, or rather, worn-out was he. At Mordasoff all sorts of strange things were told of him. Some declared that the old prince's wits had forsaken him. All agreed that it was passing strange that the owner of a magnificent property of four thousand souls, a man of rank, and one who could have, if he liked, a great influence, and play a great part in his country's affairs; that such a man should live all alone upon his estate, and make an absolute hermit of himself, as did Prince K——. Many who had known him a few years before insisted upon it that he was very far from loving solitude then, and was as unlike a hermit as anyone could possibly be.

However, here is all I have been able to learn authentically as to his antecedents, etc.:—

Some time or other, in his younger days—which must have been a mighty long while ago,—the prince made a most brilliant entry into life. He knocked about and enjoyed himself, and sang romantic songs, and wrote epigrams, and led a fast life generally, very often abroad, and was full of gifts and intellectual capacity.

Of course he very soon ran through his means, and when old age approached, he suddenly found himself almost penniless. Somebody recommended him to betake himself to his country seat, which was about to be sold by public auction. So off he went with that intention; but called in at Mordasoff, and stopped there six months. He liked this provincial life, and while in our town he spent every farthing he had left in the world, continuing his reckless life as of old, galivanting about, and forming intimacies with half the ladies of Mordasoff.

He was a kind-hearted, good sort of a man, but, of course, not without certain princely failings, which, however, were accounted here to be nothing but evidences of the highest breeding, and for this reason caused a good effect instead of aversion. The ladies, especially, were in a state of perpetual ecstasy over their dear guest. They cherished the fondest and tenderest recollections of him. There were also strange traditions and rumours about the prince. It was said that he spent more than half the day at his toilet table; and that he was, in fact, made up of all sorts of little bits. No one could say when or how he had managed to fall to pieces so completely.

He wore a wig, whiskers, moustache, and even an "espagnole," all false to a hair, and of a lovely raven black; besides which he painted and rouged every day. It was even said that he managed to do away with his wrinkles by means of *hidden springs*—hidden somehow in his wig. It was said, further, that he wore stays, in consequence of the want of a rib which he had lost in Italy, through being caused to fly, involuntarily, out of a window during a certain love affair. He limped with his left foot, and it was whispered that the said foot was a cork one—a very scientific member, made for him in place of the real one which came to grief during another love affair, in Paris this time. But what will not people say? At all events, I know for a fact that his right eye was a glass one; beautifully made, I confess, but still—glass. His teeth were false too.

For whole days at a time he used to wash himself in all sorts of patent waters and scents and pomades.

However, no one could deny that even then he was beginning to indulge in senile drivel and chatter. It appeared his career was about over; he had seen his best days, everyone knew that he had not a copeck left in the world!

Then, suddenly and unexpectedly, an old relative of his—who had always lived in Paris, but from whom he never had had the slightest hope of inheritance—died, after having buried her legal heir exactly a month before! The prince, to his utter astonishment, turned out to be the next heir, and a beautiful property of four thousand serfs, just forty miles from Mordasoff, became his—absolutely and unquestionably!

He immediately started off to Petersburg, to see to his affairs. Before he departed, however, the ladies of our town gave him a magnificent subscription banquet. They tell how bewitching and delightful the prince was at this last dinner; how he punned and joked and told the most *unusual* stories; and how he promised to come to Donchanovo (his new property) very soon, and gave his word that on his arrival he would give endless balls and garden parties and picnics and fireworks and entertainments of all kinds, for his friends here.

For a whole year after his departure, the ladies of the place talked of nothing but these promised festivities; and awaited the arrival of the "dear old man" with the utmost impatience. At last the prince arrived; but to the disappointment and astonishment of everyone, he did not even call in at Mordasoff on the way; and on his arrival at Donchanovo he shut himself up there, as I have expressed it before, like a very hermit.

All sorts of fantastic rumours were bruited about, and from this time the prince's life and history became most secret, mysterious, and incomprehensible.

In the first place, it was declared that the prince had not been very successful in St. Petersburg; that many of his relations—future heirs and heirs presumptive, and so on, had wished to put the Prince under some kind of restraint, on the plea of "feebleness of intellect;" probably fearing that he would run through this property as he had done with the last! And more, some of them went so far as to suggest that he should be popped into a lunatic asylum; and he was only saved by the interference of one of the nearest of kin, who pointed out that the poor old prince was more than half dead already, and that the rest of him must inevitably soon die too; and that then the property would come down to them safely enough without the need of the lunatic asylum. I repeat, what will not people say? Especially at our place, Mordasoff! All this, it was said, had frightened the prince dreadfully; so that his nature seemed to change entirely, and he came down to live a hermit life at Donchanovo.

Some of our Mordasoff folk went over to welcome him on his arrival; but they were either not received at all or received in the strangest fashion. The prince did not recognise his old friends: many people explained that he did not *wish* to recognise them. Among other visitors to Donchanovo was the Governor.

On the return of the latter from his visit, he declared that the prince was undoubtedly a little "off his head." The Governor always made a face if anyone reminded him of this visit of his to Donchanovo. The ladies were dreadfully offended.

At last an important fact was revealed: namely, that there was with the prince, and apparently in authority over him, some unknown person of the name of Stepanida Matveyevna, who had come down with him from St. Petersburg; an elderly fat woman in a calico dress, who went about with the house-keys in her hand; and that the prince obeyed this woman like a little child, and did not dare take a step without her leave; that she washed him and dressed him and soothed and petted him just like a nurse with a baby; and lastly, that she kept all visitors away from him, even relations—who, little by little, had begun to pervade the place rather too frequently, for the purpose of seeing that all was right.

It was said that this person managed not only the prince, but his estate too: she turned off bailiffs and clerks, she encashed the rents, she looked after things in general—and did it well, too; so that the peasants blessed their fate under her rule.

As for the prince, it was rumoured that he spent his days now almost entirely at his toilet-table, trying on wigs and dress-coats, and that the rest of his time was spent playing cards and games with Stepanida Matveyevna, and riding on a quiet old English mare. On such occasions his nurse always accompanied him in a covered droshky, because the prince liked to ride out of bravado, but was most unsafe in his saddle.

He had been seen on foot too, in a long great coat and a straw hat with a wide brim; a pink silk lady's tie round his neck, and a basket on his arm for mushrooms and flowers and berries, and so on, which he collected. The nurse accompanied him, and a few yards behind walked a manservant, while a carriage was in attendance on the high road at the side. When any peasant happened to meet him, and with low bow, and hat in hand, said, "Good morning, your highness—our beloved Sun, and Father of us all," or some such Russian greeting, he would stick his eye-glass in his eye, nod his head and say, with great urbanity, and in French, "Bon jour, mon ami, bon jour!"

Lots of other rumours there were—in fact, our folks could not forget that the prince lived so near them.

What, then, must have been the general amazement when one fine day it was trumpeted abroad that the prince—their curious old hermit-prince, had arrived at Mordasoff, and put up at Maria Alexandrovna's house!

Agitation and bewilderment were the order of the day; everybody waited for explanations, and asked one another what could be the meaning of this mystery? Some proposed to go and see for themselves; all agreed that it was *most* extraordinary. The ladies wrote notes to each other, came and whispered to one another, and sent their maids and husbands to find out more.

What was particularly strange was, why had the prince put up at Maria Alexandrovna's, and not somewhere else? This fact annoyed everyone; but, most of all, Mrs. Antipova, who happened to be a distant relative of the prince.

However, in order to clear up all these mysteries and find an answer to all these questions, we must ourselves go and see Maria Alexandrovna. Will you follow me in, kind reader? It is only ten in the morning, certainly, as you point out; but I daresay she will receive such intimate friends, all the same. Oh, yes; she'll see us all right.

CHAPTER III.

It is ten o'clock in the morning, and we are at Maria Alexandrovna's, and in that room which the mistress calls her "salon" on great occasions; she has a boudoir besides.

In this salon the walls are prettily papered, and the floor is nicely painted; the furniture is mostly red; there is a fireplace, and on the mantelpiece a bronze clock with some figure—a Cupid—upon it, in dreadfully bad taste. There are large looking-glasses between the windows. Against the back wall there stands a magnificent grand piano—Zina's—for Zina is a musician. On a table in the middle of the room hisses a silver tea-urn, with a very pretty tea-set alongside of it.

There is a lady pouring out tea, a distant relative of the family, and living with Maria Alexandrovna in that capacity, one Nastasia Petrovna Ziablova. She is a widow of over thirty, a brunette with a fresh-looking face and lively black eyes, not at all bad looking.

She is of a very animated disposition, laughs a great deal, is fond of scandal, of course; and can manage her own little affairs very nicely. She has two children somewhere, being educated. She would much like to marry again. Her last husband was a military man.

Maria Alexandrovna herself is sitting at the fire in a very benign frame of mind; she is dressed in a pale-green dress, which becomes her very well; she is unspeakably delighted at the arrival of the Prince, who, at this moment, is sitting upstairs, at his toilet table. She is so happy, that she does not even attempt to conceal her joy. A young man is standing before her and relating something in an animated way; one can see in his eyes that he wishes to curry favour with his listener.

This young fellow is about twenty-five years old, and his manners are decidedly good, though he has a silly way of going into raptures, and has, besides, a good deal too much of the "funny man" about him. He is well dressed and his hair is light; he is not a bad-looking fellow. But we have already heard of this gentleman: he is Mr. Mosgliakoff. Maria Alexandrovna considers him rather a stupid sort of a man, but receives him very well. He is an aspirant for the hand of her daughter Zina, whom, according to his own account, he loves to distraction. In his conversation, he refers to Zina every other minute, and does his best to bring a smile to her lips by his witty remarks; but the girl is evidently very cool and indifferent with him. At this moment she is standing away at the side near the piano, turning over the leaves of some book.

This girl is one of those women who create a sensation amounting almost to amazement when they appear in society. She is lovely to an almost impossible extent, a brunette with splendid black eyes, a grand figure and divine bust. Her shoulders and arms are like an antique statue; her gait that of an empress. She is a little pale to-day; but her lips, with the gleam of her pearly teeth between them, are things to dream of, if you once get a sight of them. Her expression is severe and serious.

Mr. Mosgliakoff is evidently afraid of her intent gaze; at all events, he seems to cower before her when she looks at him. She is very simply dressed, in a white muslin frock—the white suits her admirably. But then,*everything* suits her! On her finger is a hair ring: it does not look as though the hair was her mother's, from the colour. Mosgliakoff has never dared to ask her whose hair it is. This morning she seems to be in a peculiarly depressed humour; she appears to be very much preoccupied and silent: but her mother is quite ready to talk enough for both; albeit she glances continually at Zina, as though anxious for her, but timidly, too, as if afraid of her.

"I am *so* pleased, Pavel Alexandrovitch," she chirps to Mosgliakoff; "*so* happy, that I feel inclined to cry the news out of the window to every passer-by. Not to speak of the delightful surprise—to both Zina and myself—of seeing you a whole fortnight sooner than we expected you—that, of course, 'goes without saying'; but I am so, *so* pleased that you should have brought this dear prince with you. You don't know how I love that fascinating old man. No, no! You would never believe it. You young people don't understand this sort of rapture; you never would believe me, assure you as much as ever I pleased.

"Don't you remember, Zina, how much he was to me at that time—six years ago? Why, I was his guide, his sister, his mother! There was something delightfully ingenuous and ennobling in our intimacy—one might say*pastoral*; I don't know what to call it—it was delightful. That is why the poor dear prince thinks of *my* house, and only mine, with gratitude, now. Do you know, Pavel Alexandrovitch, perhaps you have *saved* him by thus bringing him to me? I have thought of him with quaking of heart all these six years—you'd hardly believe it,— and *dreamed* of him, too. They say that wretch of a woman has bewitched and ruined him; but you've got him out of the net at last. We must make the best of our opportunity now, and save him outright. Do tell me again, how did you manage it? Describe your meeting and all in detail; I only heard the chief point of the story just now, and I do so like details. So, he's still at his toilet table now, is he?—"

"Yes. It was all just as I told you, Maria Alexandrovna!" begins Mosgliakoff readily—delighted to repeat his story ten times over, if required—"I had driven all night, and not slept a wink. You can imagine what a hurry I was in to arrive here," he adds, turning to Zina; "in a word, I swore at the driver, yelled for fresh horses, kicked up a row at every post station: my adventures would fill a volume. Well, exactly at six o'clock in the morning I arrived at the last station, Igishova. 'Horses, horses!' I shouted, 'let's have fresh horses quick; I'm not going to get out.' I frightened the post-station man's wife out of her wits; she had a small baby in her arms, and I have an idea that its mother's fright will affect said baby's supply of the needful. Well, the sunrise was splendid—fine frosty morning— lovely! but I hadn't time to look at anything. I got my horses—I had to deprive some other traveller of his pair; he was a professor, and we nearly fought a duel about it.

"They told me some prince had driven off a quarter of an hour ago. He had slept here, and was driving his own horses; but I didn't attend to anything. Well, just seven miles from town, at a turn of the road, I saw that some surprising event had happened. A huge travelling carriage was lying on its side; the coachman and two flunkeys stood outside it, apparently dazed, while from inside the carriage came heart-rending lamentations and cries. I thought I'd pass by and let them all be—; it was no affair of mine: but humanity insisted, and would not take a denial. (I think it is Heine says that humanity shoves its nose in everywhere!) So I stopped; and my driver and myself, with the other fellows, lifted the carriage on to its legs again, or perhaps I should say wheels, as it had no legs.

"I thought to myself, 'This is that very prince they mentioned!' So, I looked in. Good Heavens! it was our prince! Here was a meeting, if you like! I yelled at him, 'Prince—uncle!' Of course he hardly knew me at the first glance, but he very soon recognised me. At least, I don't believe he knows who I am really, even *now*; I think he takes me for someone else, not a relation. I saw him last seven years ago, as a boy; I remember *him*, because he struck me so; but how was he to remember *me*? At all events, I told him my name, and he embraced me ecstatically; and all the while he himself was crying and trembling with fright. He really was *crying*, I'll take my oath he was! I saw it with my own eyes.

"Well, we talked a bit, and at last I persuaded him to get into my trap with me, and call in at Mordasoff, if only for one day, to rest and compose his feelings. He told me that Stepanida Matveyevna had had a letter from Moscow, saying that her father, or daughter, or both, with all her family, were dying; and that she had wavered for a long time, and at last determined to go away for ten days. The prince sat out one day, and then another, and then a third, measuring wigs, and powdering and pomading himself; then he grew sick of it, and determined to go and see an old friend, a priest called Misael, who lived at the Svetozersk Hermitage. Some of the household, being afraid of the great Stepanida's wrath, opposed the prince's proposed journey; but the latter insisted, and started last night after dinner. He slept at Igishova, and went off this morning again, at sunrise. Just at the turn going down to the Reverend Mr. Misael's, the carriage went over, and the prince was very nearly shot down the ravine."

"Then I step in and save the prince, and persuade him to come and pay a visit to our mutual friend, Maria Alexandrovna (of whom the prince told me that she is the most delightful and charming woman he has ever known). And so here we are, and the prince is now upstairs attending to his wigs and so on, with the help of his valet, whom he took along with him, and whom he always would and will take with him wherever he goes; because he would sooner die than appear before ladies without certain little secret touches which require the valet's hand. There you are, that's the whole story."

"Why, what a humourist he is, isn't he, Zina?" said the lady of the house. "How beautifully you told the story! Now, listen, Paul: one question; explain to me clearly how you are related to the prince; you call him uncle!"

"I really don't know, Maria Alexandrovna; seventh, cousin I think, or something of that sort. My aunt knows all about it; it was she who made me go down to see him at Donchanova, when I got kicked out by Stepanida! I simply call him 'uncle,' and he answers me; that's about all our relationship."

"Well, I repeat, it was Providence that made you bring him straight to my house as you did. I tremble to think of what might have happened to the poor dear prince if somebody else, and not I, had got hold of him! Why, they'd have torn him to pieces among them, and picked his bones! They'd have pounced on him as on a new-found mine; they might easily have robbed him; they are capable of it. You have no idea, Paul, of the depth of meanness and greediness to which the people of this place have fallen!"

"But, my dear good Maria Alexandrovna—as if he would ever *think* of bringing him anywhere but to yourself,"said the widow, pouring out a cup of tea; "you don't suppose he would have taken the prince to Mrs. Antipova's, surely, do you?"

"Dear me, how very long he is coming out," said Maria Alexandrovna, impatiently rising from her chair; "it really is quite strange!"

"Strange! what, of uncle? Oh dear, no! he'll probably be another five hours or so putting himself together; besides, since he has no memory whatever, he has very likely quite forgotten that he has come to your house! Why, he's a most extraordinary man, Maria Alexandrovna."

"Oh don't, don't! Don't talk like that!"

"Why not, Maria Alexandrovna? He is a lump of composition, not a man at all! Remember, you haven't seen him for six years, and I saw him half an hour ago. He is half a corpse; he's only the memory of a man; they've forgotten to bury him! Why, his eye is made of glass, and his leg of cork, and he goes on wires; he even talks on wires!"

Maria Alexandrovna's face took a serious expression. "What nonsense you talk," she said; "and aren't you ashamed of yourself, you, a young man and a relation too—to talk like that of a most honourable old nobleman! not to mention his incomparable personal goodness and kindness" (her voice here trembled with emotion). "He is a relic, a chip, so to speak, of our old aristocracy. I know, my dear young friend, that all this flightiness on your part, proceeds from those 'new ideas' of which you are so fond of talking; but, goodness me, I've seen a good deal more of life than you have: I'm a mother; and though I see the greatness and nobleness, if you like, of these 'new ideas,' yet I can understand the practical side of things too! Now, this gentleman is an old man, and that is quite enough to render him ridiculous in your eyes. You, who talk of emancipating your serfs, and 'doing something for posterity,' indeed! I tell you what it is, it's your Shakespeare! You stuff yourself full of Shakespeare, who has long ago outlived his time, my dear Paul; and who, if he lived now, with all his wisdom, would never make head or tail of our way of life!"

"If there be any chivalry left in our modern society, it is only in the highest circles of the aristocracy. A prince is a prince either in a hovel or in a palace! *You* are more or less a representative of the highest circles; your extraction is aristocratic. I, too, am not altogether a stranger to the upper ten, and it's a bad fledgling that fouls its own nest! However, my dear Paul, you'll forget your Shakespeare yet, and you'll understand all this much better than I can explain it. I foresee it! Besides, I'm sure you are only joking; you did not mean what you said. Stay here, dear Paul, will you? I'm just going upstairs to make inquiries after the prince, he may want something." And Maria Alexandrovna left the room hurriedly.

"Maria Alexandrovna seems highly delighted that Mrs. Antipova, who thinks so much of herself, did not get hold of the prince!" remarked the widow; "Mrs. Antipova must be gnashing her teeth with annoyance just now! She's a relation, too, as I've been pointing out to Maria Alexandrovna."

Observing that no one answered her, and casting her eyes on Zina and Mosgliakoff, the widow suddenly recollected herself, and discreetly left the room, as though to fetch something. However, she rewarded herself for her discretion, by putting her ear to the keyhole, as soon as she had closed the door after her.

Pavel Alexandrovitch immediately turned to Zina. He was in a state of great agitation; his voice shook.

"Zenaida Afanassievna, are you angry with me?" he began, in a timid, beseechful tone.

"With you? Why?" asked Zina, blushing a little, and raising her magnificent eyes to his face.

"For coming earlier. I couldn't help it; I couldn't wait another fortnight; I dreamed of you every night; so I flew off to learn my fate. But you are frowning, you are angry;—oh; am I really not to hear anything definite, even now?"

Zina distinctly and decidedly frowned.

"I supposed you would speak of this," she said, with her eyes drooped again, but with a firm and severe voice, in which some annoyance was perceptible; "and as the expectation of it was very tedious, the sooner you had your say, the better! You insist upon an answer again, do you? Very well, I say *wait*, just as I said it before. I now repeat, as I did then, that I have not as yet decided, and cannot therefore promise to be your wife. You cannot force a girl to such a decision, Pavel Alexandrovitch! However, to relieve your mind, I will add, that I do not as yet refuse you absolutely; and pray observe that I give you thus much hope of a favourable reply, merely out of forced deference to your impatience and agitation; and that if I think fit afterwards to reject you altogether, you are not to blame me for having given you false hopes. So now you know."

"Oh, but—but—what's the use of that? What hope am I to get out of that, Zina?" cried Mosgliakoff in piteous tones.

"Recollect what I have said, and draw whatever you please from the words; that's your business. I shall add nothing. I do not refuse you; I merely say—wait! And I repeat, I reserve the free right of rejecting you afterwards if I choose so to do. Just one more word: if you come here before the fixed time relying on outside protection, or even on my mother's influence to help you gain your end, let me tell you, you make a great mistake; if you worry me now, I shall refuse you outright. I hope we understand each other now, and that I shall hear no more of this, until the period I named to you for my decision." All this was said quietly and drily, and without a pause, as if learnt by rote. Paul felt foolish; but just at this moment Maria Alexandrovna entered the room, and the widow after her.

"I think he's just coming, Zina! Nastasia Petrovna, make some new tea quick, please!" The good lady was considerably agitated.

"Mrs. Antipova has sent her maid over to inquire about the prince already. How angry she must be feeling just now," remarked the widow, as she commenced to pass over the tea-urn.

"And what's that to me!" replied Maria Alexandrovna, over her shoulder. "Just as though *I* care what she thinks! *I* shall not send a maid to her kitchen to inquire, I assure you! And I am surprised, downright *surprised*, that, not only you, but all the town, too, should suppose that that wretched woman is my enemy! I appeal to you, Paul—you know us both. Why should I be her enemy, now? Is it a question of precedence? Pooh! I don't care about precedence! She may be first, if she likes, and I shall be readiest of all to go and congratulate her on the fact. Besides, it's all nonsense! Why, I take her part; I *must* take her part. People malign her; *why* do you all fall upon her so? Because she's young, and likes to be smart; is that it? Dear me, I think finery is a good bit better than some other failings—like Natalia Dimitrievna's, for instance, who has a taste for things that cannot be mentioned in polite society. Or is it that Mrs. Antipova goes out too much, and never stays at home? My goodness! why, the woman has never had any education; naturally she doesn't care to sit down to read, or anything of that sort. True, she coquets and makes eyes at everybody who looks at her. But why do people tell her that she's pretty? especially as she only has a pale face, and nothing else to boast of.

"She is amusing at a dance, I admit; but why do people tell her that she dances the polka so well? She wears hideous hats and things; but it's not her fault that nature gave her no gift of good taste. She talks scandal; but that's the custom of the place—who doesn't here? That fellow, Sushikoff, with his whiskers, goes to see her pretty often while her husband plays cards, but that *may* be merely a trumped-up tale; at all events I always say so, and take her part in every way! But, good heavens! here's the prince at last! 'Tis he, 'tis he! I recognise him! I should know him out of a thousand! At last I see you! At last, my Prince!" cried Maria Alexandrovna,—and she rushed to greet the prince as he entered the room.

CHAPTER IV.

At first sight you would not take this prince for an old man at all, and it is only when you come near and take a good look at him, that you see he is merely a dead man working on wires. All the resources of science are brought to bear upon this mummy, in order to give it the appearance of life and youth. A marvellous wig, glorious whiskers, moustache and napoleon—all of the most raven black—cover half his face. He is painted and powdered with very great skill, so much so that one can hardly detect any wrinkles. What has become of them, goodness only knows.

He is dressed in the pink of fashion, just as though he had walked straight out of a tailor's fashion-page. His coat, his gloves, tie, his waistcoat, his linen, are all in perfect taste, and in the very last mode. The prince limps slightly, but so slightly that one would suppose he did it on purpose because *that* was in fashion too. In his eye he wears a glass—in the eye which is itself glass already.

He was soaked with scent. His speech and manner of pronouncing certain syllables was full of affectation; and this was, perhaps, all that he retained of the mannerisms and tricks of his younger days. For if the prince had not quite lost his wits as yet, he had certainly parted with nearly every vestige of his memory, which—alas!—is a thing which no amount of perfumeries and wigs and rouge and tight-lacing will renovate. He continually forgets words in the midst of conversation, and loses his way, which makes it a matter of some difficulty to carry on a conversation with him. However, Maria Alexandrovna has confidence in her inborn dexterity, and at sight of the prince she flies into a condition of unspeakable rapture.

"Oh! but you've not changed, you've not changed a *bit*!" she cries, seizing her guest by both hands, and popping him into a comfortable arm-chair. "Sit down, dear Prince, do sit down! Six years, prince, six whole long years since we saw each other, and not a letter, not a little tiny scrap of a note all the while. *Oh*, how naughty you have been, prince! And *how* angry I have been with you, my dear friend! But, tea! tea! Good Heavens, Nastasia Petrovna, tea for the prince, quick!"

"Th—thanks, thanks; I'm very s—orry!" stammered the old man (I forgot to mention that he stammered a little, but he did even this as though it were the fashion to do it). "Very s—sorry; fancy, I—I wanted to co—come last year, but they t—told me there was cho—cho—cholera here."

"There was foot and mouth disease here, uncle," put in Mosgliakoff, by way of distinguishing himself. Maria Alexandrovna gave him a severe look.

"Ye—yes, foot and mouth disease, or something of that s—sort," said the prince; "so I st—stayed at home. Well, and how's your h—husband, my dear Anna Nic—Nicolaevna? Still at his proc—procuror's work?"

"No, prince!" said Maria Alexandrovna, a little disconcerted. "My husband is not a procurer."

"I'll bet anything that uncle has mixed you up with Anna Nicolaevna Antipova," said Mosgliakoff, but stopped suddenly on observing the look on Maria Alexandrovna's face.

"Ye—yes, of course, Anna Nicolaevna. A—An. What the deuce! I'm always f—forgetting; Antipova, Antipova, of course," continued the prince.

"No, prince, you have made a great mistake," remarked Maria Alexandrovna, with a bitter smile. "I am not Anna Nicolaevna at all, and I confess I should never have believed that you would not recognise me. You have astonished me, prince. I am your old friend, Maria Alexandrovna Moskaloff. Don't you remember Maria Alexandrovna?"

"M—Maria Alexandrovna! think of that; and I thought she was w—what's her name. Y—yes, Anna Vasilievna! *C'est délicieux.* W—why I thought you were going to take me to this A—Anna Matveyevna. Dear me! *C'est ch—charmant!* It often happens so w—with me. I get taken to the wrong house; but I'm v—very pleased, v—very pleased! So you're not Nastasia Va—silievna? How interesting."

"I'm Maria Alexandrovna, prince; *Maria Alexandrovna*! Oh! how naughty you are, Prince, to forget your best, best friend!"

"Ye—es! ye—yes! best friend; best friend, for—forgive me!" stammered the old man, staring at Zina.

"That's my daughter Zina. You are not acquainted yet, prince. She wasn't here when you were last in the town, in the year —— you know."

"Oh, th—this is your d—daughter!" muttered the old man, staring hungrily at Zina through his glasses. "Dear me, dear me. *Ch—charmante, ch—armante!* But what a lo—ovely girl," he added, evidently impressed.

"Tea! prince," remarked Maria Alexandrovna, directing his attention to the page standing before him with the tray. The prince took a cup, and examined the boy, who had a nice fresh face of his own.

"Ah! this is your l—little boy? Wh—what a charming little b—boy! and does he be—behave nicely?"

"But, prince," interrupted Maria Alexandrovna, impatiently, "what is this dreadful occurrence I hear of? I confess I was nearly beside myself with terror when I heard of it. Were you not hurt at all? *Do* take care. One cannot make light of this sort of thing."

"Upset, upset; the c—coachman upset me!" cried the prince, with unwonted vivacity. "I thought it was the end of the world, and I was fri—frightened out of my wits. I didn't expect it; I didn't, indeed! and my co—oachman is to blame for it all. I trust you, my friend, to lo—ok into the matter well. I feel sure he was making an attempt on my life!"

"All right, all right, uncle," said Paul; "I'll see about it. But look here—forgive him, just this once, uncle; just this once, won't you?"

"N—not I! Not for anything! I'm sure he wants my life, he and Lavrenty too. It's—it's the 'new ideas;' it's Com—Communism, in the fullest sense of the word. I daren't meet them anywhere."

"You are right, you are quite right, prince," cried Maria Alexandrovna. "You don't know how I suffer myself from these wretched people. I've just been obliged to change two of my servants; and you've no idea how*stupid* they are, prince."

"Ye—yes! quite so!" said the prince, delighted—as all old men are whose senile chatter is listened to with servility. "But I like a fl—flunky to look stupid; it gives them presence. There's my Terenty, now. You remember Terenty, my friend? Well, the f—first time I ever looked at him I said, 'You shall be my ha—hall porter.' He's stupid, phen—phen—omenally stupid, he looks like a she—sheep; but his dig—dignity and majesty are wonderful. When I look at him he seems to be composing some l—learned dis—sertation. He's just like the German philosopher, Kant, or like some fa—fat old turkey, and that's just what one wants in a serving-man."

Maria Alexandrovna laughed, and clapped her hands in the highest state of ecstasy; Paul supported her with all his might; Nastasia Petrovna laughed too; and even Zina smiled.

"But, prince, how clever, how witty, how *humorous* you are!" cried Maria Alexandrovna. "What a wonderful gilt of remarking the smallest refinements of character. And for a man like you to eschew all society, and shut yourself up for five years! With such talents! Why, prince, you could *write*, you could be an author. You could emulate Von Vezin, Gribojedoff, Gogol!"

"Ye—yes! ye—yes!" said the delighted prince. "I can reproduce things I see, very well. And, do you know, I used to be a very wi—witty fellow indeed, some time ago. I even wrote a play once. There were some very smart couplets, I remember; but it was never acted."

"Oh! how nice it would be to read it over, especially just *now*, eh, Zina? for we are thinking of getting up a play, you must know, prince, for the benefit of the 'martyrs of the Fatherland,' the wounded soldiers. There, now, how handy your play would come in!"

"Certainly, certainly. I—I would even write you another. I think I've quite forgotten the old one. I remember there were two or three such epigrams that (here the prince kissed his own hand to convey an idea of the exquisite wit of his lines) I recollect when I was abroad I made a real furore. I remember Lord Byron well; we were great friends; you should have seen him dance the mazurka one day during the Vienna Congress."

"Lord Byron, uncle?—Surely not!"

"Ye—yes, Lord Byron. Perhaps it was not Lord Byron, though, perhaps it was someone else; no, it wasn't Lord Byron, it was some Pole; I remember now. A won—der-ful fellow that Pole was! He said he was a C—Count, and he turned out to be a c—cook—shop man! But he danced the mazurka won—der—fully, and broke his leg at last. I recollect I wrote some lines at the time:—

"Our little Pole
Danced like blazes."

—How did it go on, now? Wait a minute! No, I can't remember."

"I'll tell you, uncle. It must have been like this," said Paul, becoming more and more inspired:—
"But he tripped in a hole,
Which stopped his crazes."

"Ye—yes, that was it, I think, or something very like it. I don't know, though—perhaps it wasn't. Anyhow, the lines were very sm—art. I forget a good deal of what I have seen and done. I'm so b—busy now!"

"But do let me hear how you have employed your time in your solitude, dear prince," said Maria Alexandrovna. "I must confess that I have thought of you so often, and often, that I am burning with impatience to hear more about you and your doings."

"Employed my time? Oh, very busy; very busy, ge—generally. One rests, you see, part of the day; and then I imagine a good many things."

"I should think you have a very strong imagination, haven't you, uncle?" remarked Paul.

"Exceptionally so, my dear fellow. I sometimes imagine things which amaze even myself! When I was at Kadueff,—by-the-by, you were vice-governor of Kadueff, weren't you?"

"I, uncle! Why, what are you thinking of?"

"No? Just fancy, my dear fellow! and I've been thinking all this time how f—funny that the vice-governor of Kadueff should be here with quite a different face: he had a fine intelligent, dig—dignified face, you know. A wo—wonderful fellow! Always writing verses, too; he was rather like the Ki—King of Diamonds from the side view, but—"

"No, prince," interrupted Maria Alexandrovna. "I assure you, you'll ruin yourself with the life you are leading! To make a hermit of oneself for five years, and see no one, and hear no one: you're a lost man, dear prince! Ask any one of those who love you, they'll all tell you the same; you're a lost man!"

"No," cried the prince, "really?"

"Yes, I assure you of it! I am speaking to you as a sister—as a friend! I am telling you this because you are very dear to me, and because the memory of the past is sacred to me. No, no! You must change your way of living; otherwise you will fall ill, and break up, and die!"

"Gracious heavens! Surely I shan't d—die so soon?" cried the old man. "You—you are right about being ill; I am ill now and then. I'll tell you all the sy—symptoms! I'll de—detail them to you. Firstly I—"

"Uncle, don't you think you had better tell us all about it another day?" Paul interrupted hurriedly. "I think we had better be starting just now, don't you?"

"Yes—yes, perhaps, perhaps. But remind me to tell you another time; it's a most interesting case, I assure you!"

"But listen, my dear prince!" Maria Alexandrovna resumed, "why don't you try being doctored abroad?"

"Ab—road? Yes, yes—I shall certainly go abroad. I remember when I was abroad, about '20; it was delightfully g—gay and jolly. I very nearly married a vi—viscountess, a French woman. I was fearfully in love, but som—somebody else married her, not I. It was a very s—strange thing. I had only gone away for a coup—couple of hours, and this Ger—German baron fellow came and carried her off! He went into a ma—madhouse afterwards!"

"Yes, dear prince, you must look after your health. There are such good doctors abroad; and—besides, the mere change of life, what will not that alone do for you! You *must* desert your dear Donchanovo, if only for a time!"

"C—certainly, certainly! I've long meant to do it. I'm going to try hy—hydropathy!"

"Hydropathy?"

"Yes. I've tried it once before: I was abroad, you know, and they persuaded me to try drinking the wa—waters. There wasn't anything the matter with me, but I agreed, just out of deli—delicacy for their feelings; and I did seem to feel easier, somehow. So I drank, and drank, and dra—ank up a whole waterfall; and I assure you if I hadn't fallen ill just then I should have been quite well, th—thanks to the water! But, I confess, you've frightened me so about these ma—maladies and things, I feel quite put out. I'll come back d—directly!"

"Why, prince, where are you off to?" asked Maria Alexandrovna in surprise.

"Directly, directly. I'm just going to note down an i—idea!"

"What sort of idea?" cried Paul, bursting with laughter.

Maria Alexandrovna lost all patience.

"I cannot understand what you find to laugh at!" she cried, as the old man disappeared; "to laugh at an honourable old man, and turn every word of his into ridicule—presuming on his angelic good nature. I assure you I *blushed* for you, Paul Alexandrovitch! Why, what do you see in him to laugh at? I never saw anything funny about him!"

"Well, I laugh because he does not recognise people, and talks such nonsense!"

"That's simply the result of his sad life, of his dreadful five years' captivity, under the guardianship of that she-devil! You should *pity*, not laugh at him! He did not even know *me*; you saw it yourself. I tell you it's a crying shame; he must be saved, at all costs! I recommend him to go abroad so that he may get out of the clutches of that—beast of a woman!"

"Do you know what—we must find him a wife!" cried Paul.

"Oh, Mr. Mosgliakoff, you are too bad; you really are too bad!"

"No, no, Maria Alexandrovna; I assure you, this time I'm speaking in all seriousness. Why *not* marry him off? Isn't it rather a brilliant idea? What harm can marriage do him? On the contrary, he is in that position that such a step alone can save him! In the first place, he will get rid of that fox of a woman; and, secondly, he may find some girl, or better still some widow—kind, good, wise and gentle, and poor, who will look after him as his own daughter would, and who will be sensible of the honour he does her in making her his wife! And what could be better for the old fellow than to have such a person about him, rather than the—woman he has now? Of course she must be nice-looking, for uncle appreciates good looks; didn't you observe how he stared at Miss Zina?"

"But how will you find him such a bride?" asked Nastasia Petrovna, who had listened intently to Paul's suggestion.

"What a question! Why, you yourself, if you pleased! and why not, pray? In the first place, you are good-looking, you are a widow, you are generous, you are poor (at least I don't think you are very rich). Then you are a very reasonable woman: you'll learn to love him, and take good care of him; you'll send that other woman to the deuce, and take your husband abroad, where you will feed him on pudding and lollipops till the moment of his quitting this wicked world, which will be in about a year, or in a couple of months perhaps. After that, you emerge a princess, a rich widow, and, as a prize for your goodness to the old gentleman, you'll marry a fine young marquis, or a governor-general, or somebody of the sort! There—that's a pretty enough prospect, isn't it?"

"Tfu! Goodness me! I should fall in love with him at once, out of pure gratitude, if he only proposed to me!" said the widow, with her black eyes all ablaze; "but, of course, it's all nonsense!"

"Nonsense, is it? Shall I make it sound sense, then, for you? Ask me prettily, and if I don't make you his betrothed by this evening, you may cut my little finger off! Why, there's nothing in the world easier than to talk uncle into anything you please! He'll only say, 'Ye—yes, ye—yes,' just as you heard him now! We'll marry him so that he doesn't know anything about it, if you like? We'll deceive him and marry him, if you please! Any way you like, it can be done! Why, it's for his own good; it's out of pity for himself! Don't you think, seriously, Nastasia Petrovna, that you had better put on some smart clothes in any case?"

Paul's enthusiasm amounted by now to something like madness, while the widow's mouth watered at his idea, in spite of her better judgment.

"I know, I know I look horridly untidy!" she said. "I go about anyhow, nowadays! There's nothing to dress for. Do I really look like a regular cook?"

All this time Maria Alexandrovna sat still, with a strange expression on her face. I shall not be far wrong if I say that she listened to Paul's wild suggestion with a look of terror, almost: she was confused and startled; at last she recollected herself, and spoke.

"All this is very nice, of course; but at the same time it is utter nonsense, and perfectly out of the question!" she observed cuttingly.

"Why, why, my good Maria Alexandrovna? Why is it such nonsense, or why out of the question?"

"For many reasons; and, principally because you are, as the prince is also, a guest in my house; and I cannot permit anyone to forget their respect towards my establishment! I shall consider your words as a joke, Paul Alexandrovitch, and nothing more! Here comes the prince—thank goodness!"

"Here I am!" cried the old man as he entered. "It's a wo—wonderful thing how many good ideas of all s—sorts I'm having to-day! and another day I may spend the whole of it without a single one! As—tonishing? not one all day!"

"Probably the result of your accident, to-day, uncle! Your nerves got shaken up, you see, and ——"

"Ye—yes, I think so, I think so too; and I look on the accident as pro—fitable, on the whole; and therefore I'm going to excuse the coachman. I don't think it was an at—tempt on my life, after all, do you? Besides, he was punished a little while a—go, when his beard was sh—shaved off!"

"Beard shaved off? Why, uncle, his beard is as big as a German state!"

"Ye—yes, a German state, you are very happy in your ex—pressions, my boy! but it's a fa—false one. Fancy what happened: I sent for a price-current for false hair and beards, and found advertisements for splendid ser—vants' and coachmen's beards, very cheap—extraordinarily so! I sent for one, and it certainly was a be—auty. But when we wanted to clap it on the coachman, we found he had one of his own t—twice as big; so I thought, shall I cut off his, or let him wear it, and send this one b—back? and I decided to shave his off, and let him wear the f—false one!"

"On the theory that art is higher than nature, I suppose uncle?"

"Yes, yes! Just so—and I assure you, when we cut off his beard he suffered as much as though we were depriving him of all he held most dear! But we must be go—going, my boy!"

"But I hope, dear prince, that you will only call upon the governor!" cried Maria Alexandrovna, in great agitation. "You are *mine* now, Prince; you belong to *my* family for the whole of this day! Of course I will say nothing about the society of this place. Perhaps you are thinking of paying Anna Nicolaevna a visit? I will not say a word to dissuade you; but at the same time I am quite convinced that—time will show! Remember one thing, dear Prince, that I am your sister, your nurse, your guardian for to-day at least, and oh!—I tremble for you. You don't know these people, Prince, as I do! You don't know them fully: but time will teach you all you do not know."

"Trust me, Maria Alexandrovna!" said Paul, "it shall all be exactly as I have promised you!"

"Oh—but you're such a weathercock! I can never trust *you*! I shall wait for you at dinner time, Prince; we dine early. How sorry I am that my husband happens to be in the country on such an occasion! How happy he would have been to see you! He esteems you so highly, Prince; he is so sincerely attached to you!"

"Your husband? dear me! So you have a h—husband, too!" observed the old man.

"Oh, prince, prince! how forgetful you are! Why, you have *quite*, quite forgotten the past! My husband, Afanassy Matveyevitch, surely you must remember him? He is in the country: but you have seen him thousands of times before! Don't you remember—Afanassy Matveyevitch!"

"Afanassy Matveyevitch. Dear me!—and in the co—country! how very charming! So you have a husband! dear me, I remember a vaudeville very like that, something about—

"The husband's here,
And his wife at Tvere."

Charming, charming—such a good rhyme too; and it's a most ri—diculous story! Charming, charming; the wife's away, you know, at Jaroslaf or Tv—— or somewhere, and the husband is——is——Dear me! I'm afraid I've forgotten what we were talking about! Yes, yes—we must be going, my boy! *Au revoir, madame; adieu, ma charmante demoiselle*" he added, turning to Zina, and putting the ends of her fingers to his lips.

"Come back to dinner,—to dinner, prince! don't forget to come back here quick!" cried Maria Alexandrovna after them as they went out; "be back to dinner!"

CHAPTER V.

"Nastasia Petrovna, I think you had better go and see what is doing in the kitchen!" observed Maria Alexandrovna, as she returned from seeing the prince off. "I'm sure that rascal Nikitka will spoil the dinner! Probably he's drunk already!" The widow obeyed.

As the latter left the room, she glanced suspiciously at Maria Alexandrovna, and observed that the latter was in a high state of agitation. Therefore, instead of going to look after Nikitka, she went through the "Salon," along the passage to her own room, and through that to a dark box-room, where the old clothes of the establishment and such things were stored. There she approached the locked door on tiptoe; and stifling her breath, she bent to the keyhole, through which she peeped, and settled herself to listen intently. This door, which was always kept shut, was one of the three doors communicating with the room where Maria Alexandrovna and Zina were now left alone. Maria Alexandrovna always considered Nastasia an untrustworthy sort of woman, although extremely silly into the bargain. Of course she had suspected the widow—more than once—of eavesdropping; but it so happened that at the moment Madame Moskaleva was too agitated and excited to think of the usual precautions.

She was sitting in her arm-chair and gazing at Zina. Zina felt that her mother was looking at her, and was conscious of an unpleasant sensation at her heart.

"Zina!"

Zina slowly turned her head towards the speaker, and lifted her splendid dark eyes to hers.

"Zina, I wish to speak to you on a most important matter!"

Zina adopted an attentive air, and sat still with folded hands, waiting for light. In her face there was an expression of annoyance as well as irony, which she did her best to hide.

"I wish to ask you first, Zina, what you thought of *that* Mosgliakoff, to-day?"

"You have known my opinion of him for a long time!" replied Zina, surlily.

"Yes, yes, of course! but I think he is getting just a little *too* troublesome, with his continual bothering you—"

"Oh, but he says he is in love with me, in which case his importunity is pardonable!"

"Strange! You used not to be so ready to find his offences pardonable; you used to fly out at him if ever I mentioned his name!"

"Strange, too, that you always defended him, and were so very anxious that I should marry him!—and now you are the first to attack him!"

"Yes; I don't deny, Zina, that I did wish, then, to see you married to Mosgliakoff! It was painful to me to witness your continual grief, your sufferings, which I can well realize—whatever you may think to the contrary!—and which deprived me of my rest at night! I determined at last that there was but one great change of life that would ever save you from the sorrows of the past, and that change was matrimony! We are not rich; we cannot afford to go abroad. All the asses in the place prick their long ears, and wonder that you should be unmarried at twenty-three years old; and they must needs invent all sorts of stories to account for the fact! As if I would marry you to one of our wretched little town councillors, or to Ivan Ivanovitch, the family lawyer! There are no husbands for *you* in this place, Zina! Of course Paul Mosgliakoff is a silly sort of a fellow, but he is better than these people here: he is fairly born, at least, and he has 150 serfs and landed property, all of which is better than living by bribes and corruption, and goodness knows what jobbery besides, as these do! and that is why I allowed my eyes to rest on him. But I give you my solemn word, I never had any real sympathy for him! and if Providence has sent you someone better now, oh, my dear girl, how fortunate that you have not given your word to Mosgliakoff! You didn't tell him anything for certain to-day, did you, Zina?"

"What is the use of beating about the bush, when the whole thing lies in a couple of words?" said Zina, with some show of annoyance.

"Beating about the bush, Zina? Is that the way to speak to your mother? But what am I? You have long ceased to trust to your poor mother! You have long looked upon me as your enemy, and not as your mother at all!"

"Oh, come mother! you and I are beyond quarrelling about an expression! Surely we understand one another by now? It is about time we did, anyhow!"

"But you offend me, my child! you will not believe that I am ready to devote *all, all* I can give, in order to establish your destiny on a safe and happy footing!"

Zina looked angrily and sarcastically at her mother.

"Would not you like to marry me to this old prince, now, in order to establish my destiny on a safe and happy footing?"

"I have not said a word about it; but, as you mention the fact, I will say that if you *were* to marry the prince it would be a very happy thing for you, and—"

"Oh! Well, I consider the idea utter nonsense!" cried the girl passionately. "Nonsense, humbug! and what's more, I think you have a good deal too much poetical inspiration, mamma; you are a woman poet in the fullest sense of the term, and they call you by that name here! You are always full of projects; and the impracticability and absurdity of your ideas does not in the least discourage you. I felt, when the prince was sitting here, that you had that notion in your head. When Mosgliakoff was talking nonsense there about marrying the old man to somebody I read all your thoughts in your face. I am ready to bet any money that you are thinking of it now, and that you have come to me now about this very question! However, as your perpetual projects on my behalf are beginning to weary me to death, I must beg you not to say one word about it, not *one word*, mamma; do you hear me? *not one word*; and I beg you will remember what I say!" She was panting with rage.

"You are a child, Zina; a poor sorrow-worn, sick child!" said Maria Alexandrovna in tearful accents. "You speak to your poor mother disrespectfully; you wound me deeply, my dear; there is not another mother in the world who would have borne what I have to bear from you every day! But you are suffering, you are sick, you are sorrowful, and I am your mother, and, first of all, I am a Christian woman! I must bear it all, and forgive it. But one word, Zina: if I had really thought of the union you suggest, why would you consider it so impracticable and absurd? In my opinion, Mosgliakoff has never said a wiser thing than he did to-day, when he declared that marriage was what alone could save the prince,—not, of course, marriage with that slovenly slut, Nastasia; there he certainly *did* make a fool of himself!"

"Now look here, mamma; do you ask me this out of pure curiosity, or with design? Tell me the truth."

"All I ask is, why does it appear to you to be so absurd?"

"Good heavens, mother, you'll drive me wild! What a fate!" cried Zina, stamping her foot with impatience. "I'll tell you why, if you can't see for yourself. Not to mention all the other evident absurdities of the plan, to take advantage of the weakened wits of a poor old man, and deceive him and marry him—an old cripple, in order to get hold of his money,—and then every day and every hour to wish for his death, is, in my opinion, not only nonsense, but so mean, *so* mean, mamma, that I—I can't congratulate you on your brilliant idea; that's all I can say!"

There was silence for one minute.

"Zina, do you remember all that happened two years ago?" asked Maria Alexandrovna of a sudden.

Zina trembled.

"Mamma!" she said, severely, "you promised me solemnly never to mention that again."

"And I ask you now, as solemnly, my dear child, to allow me to break that promise, just once! I have never broken it before. Zina! the time has come for a full and clear understanding between us! These two years of silence have been terrible. We cannot go on like this. I am ready to pray you, on my knees, to let me speak. Listen, Zina, your own mother who bore you beseeches you, on her knees! And I promise you faithfully, Zina, and solemnly, on the word of an unhappy but adoring mother, that never, under any circumstances, not even to save my life, will I ever mention the subject again. This shall be the last time, but it is absolutely necessary!"

Maria Alexandrovna counted upon the effect of her words, and with reason:

"Speak, then!" said Zina, growing whiter every moment.

"Thank you, Zina!——Two years ago there came to the house, to teach your little brother Mitya, since dead, a tutor——"

"Why do you begin so solemnly, mamma? Why all this eloquence, all these quite unnecessary details, which are painful to me, and only too well known to both of us?" cried Zina with a sort of irritated disgust.

"Because, my dear child, I, your mother, felt in some degree bound to justify myself before you; and also because I wish to present this whole question to you from an entirely new point of view, and not from that mistaken position which you are accustomed to take up with regard to it; and because, lastly, I think you will thus better understand the conclusion at which I shall arrive upon the whole question. Do not think, dear child, that I wish to trifle with your heart! No, Zina, you will find in me a real mother; and perhaps, with tears streaming from your eyes, you will ask and beseech at my feet—at the feet of the '*mean woman*,' as you have just called me,—yes, and pray for that reconciliation which you have rejected so long! That's why I wish to recall all, Zina, *all* that has happened, from the very beginning; and without this I shall not speak at all!"

"Speak, then!" repeated Zina, cursing the necessity for her mother's eloquence from the very bottom of her heart.

"I continue then, Zina!——This tutor, a master of the parish school, almost a boy, makes upon you what is, to me, a totally inexplicable impression. I built too much upon my confidence in your good sense, or your noble pride, and principally upon the fact of his insignificance—(I must speak out!)—to allow myself to harbour the slightest suspicion of you! And then you suddenly come to me, one fine day, and state that you intend to marry the man! Zina, it was putting a knife to my heart! I gave a shriek and lost consciousness.

"But of course you remember all this. Of course I thought it my duty to use all my power over you, which power you called tyranny. Think for yourself—a boy, the son of a deacon, receiving a salary of twelve roubles a month—a writer of weak verses which are printed, out of pity, in the 'library of short readings.' A man, a boy, who could talk of nothing but that accursed Shakespeare,—this boy to be the husband of Zenaida Moskaloff! Forgive me, Zina, but the very thought of it all makes me *wild*!

"I rejected him, of course. But no power would stop *you*; your father only blinked his eyes, as usual, and could not even understand what I was telling him about. You continue your relations with this boy, even giving him rendezvous, and, worst of all, you allow yourself to correspond with him!

"Rumours now begin to flit about town: I am assailed with hints; they blow their trumpets of joy and triumph; and suddenly all my fears and anticipations are verified! You and he quarrel over something or other; he shows himself to be a boy (I can't call him a man!), who is utterly unworthy of you, and threatens to show your letters all over the town! On hearing this threat, you, beside yourself with irritation, boxed his ears. Yes, Zina, I am aware of even that fact! I know all, all! But to continue—the wretched boy shows one of your letters the very same day to that ne'er-do-well Zanshin, and within an hour Natalie Dimitrievna holds it in her hands—my deadly enemy! The same evening the miserable fellow attempts to put an end to himself, in remorse. In a word, there is a fearful scandal stirred up. That slut, Nastasia, comes panting to me with the dreadful news; she tells me that Natalie Dimitrievna has had your letter for a whole hour. In a couple of hours the whole town will learn of your foolishness! I bore it all. I did not fall down in a swoon; but oh, the blows, the blows you dealt to my heart, Zina!

That shameless scum of the earth, Nastasia, says she will get the letter back for two hundred roubles! I myself run over, in thin shoes, too, through the snow to the Jew Baumstein, and pledge my diamond clasps—a keepsake of my dear mother's! In a couple of hours the letter is in my hands! Nastasia had stolen it; she had broken open a desk, and your honour was safe!

"But what a dreadful day you had sentenced me to live! I noticed some grey hairs among my raven locks for the first time, next morning! Zina, you have judged this boy's action yourself now! You can admit now, and perhaps smile a bitter smile over the admission, that it was beyond the limits of good sense to wish to entrust your fate to this youth.

"But since that fatal time you are wretched, my child, you are miserable! You cannot forget him, or rather not him—for he was never worthy of you,—but you cannot forget the phantom of your past joy! This wretched young fellow is now on the point of death—consumption, they say; and you, angel of goodness that you are! you do not wish to marry while he is alive, because you fear to harass him in his last days; because to this day he is miserable with jealousy, though I am convinced that he never loved you in the best and highest sense of the word! I know well that, hearing of Mosgliakoff's proposal to you, he has been in a flutter of jealousy, and has spied upon you and your actions ever since; and you—you have been merciful to him, my child. And oh! God knows how I have watered my pillow with tears for you!"

"Oh, mother, do drop all this sort of thing!" cried Zina, with inexpressible agony in her tone. "Surely we needn't hear all about your pillow!" she added, sharply. "Can't we get on without all this declamation and pirouetting?"

"You do not believe me, Zina! Oh! do not look so unfriendly at me, my child! My eyes have not been dry these two years. I have hidden my tears from you; but I am changed, Zina mine, much changed and in many ways! I have long known of your feelings, Zina, but I admit I have only lately realized the depth of your mental anguish. Can you blame me, my child, if I looked upon this attachment of yours as romanticism—called into being by that accursed Shakespeare, who shoves his nose in everywhere where he isn't wanted?

"What mother would blame me for my fears of that kind, for my measures, for the severity of my judgment? But now, understanding as I do, and realizing your two years' sufferings, I can estimate the depth of your real feelings. Believe me, I understand you far better than you understand yourself! I am convinced that you love not him—not this unnatural boy,—but your lost happiness, your broken hopes, your cracked idol!

"I have loved too—perhaps more deeply than yourself; I, too, have suffered, I, too, have lost my exalted ideals and seen them levelled with the earth; and therefore who can blame me now—and, above all, can *you* blame me now,—if I consider a marriage with the prince to be the one saving, the one *essential* move left to you in your present position"?

Zina listened to this long declamation with surprise. She knew well that her mother never adopted this tone without good reason. However this last and unexpected conclusion fairly amazed her.

"You don't mean to say you seriously entertain the idea of marrying me to this prince?" she cried bewildered, and gazing at her mother almost with alarm; "that this is no mere idea, no project, no flighty inspiration, but your deliberate intention? I *have* guessed right, then? And pray, *how* is this marriage going to save me? and *why* is it essential to me in my present position? And—and what has all this to do with what you have been talking about?——I cannot understand you, mother,—not a bit!"

"And *I* can't understand, angel mine, how you *cannot* see the connection of it all!" cried Maria Alexandrovna, in her turn. "In the first place, you would pass into new society, into a new world. You would leave for ever this loathsome little town, so full of sad memories for you; where you meet neither friends nor kindness; where they have bullied and maligned you; where all these—these *magpies* hate you because you are good looking! You could go abroad this very spring, to Italy, Switzerland, Spain!—to Spain, Zina, where the Alhambra is, and where the Guadalquiver flows—no wretched little stream like this of ours!"

"But, one moment, mother; you talk as though I were married already, or at least as if the prince had made me an offer!"

"Oh, no—oh dear, no! don't bother yourself about that, my angel! I know what I'm talking about! Let me proceed. I've said my 'firstly;' now, then, for my 'secondly!' I understand, dear child, with what loathing you would give your hand to that Mosgliakoff!——"

"I know, without your telling me so, that I shall never be *his* wife!" cried Zina, angrily, and with flashing eyes.

"If only you knew, my angel, how I understand and enter into your loathing for him! It is dreadful to vow before the altar that you will love a man whom you *cannot* love—how dreadful to belong to one whom you cannot esteem! And he insists on your *love*—he only marries you for love. I can see it by the way he looks at you! Why deceive ourselves? I have suffered from the same thing for twenty-five years; your father ruined me—he, so to speak, sucked up my youth! You have seen my tears many a time!——"

"Father's away in the country, don't touch *him*, please!" said Zina.

"I know you always take his part! Oh, Zina, my very heart trembled within me when I thought to arrange your marriage with Mosgliakoff for financial reasons! I trembled for the consequences. But with the prince it is different, you need not deceive him; you cannot be expected to give him your *love*, not your *love*—oh, no! and he is not in a state to ask it of you!"

"Good heavens, what nonsense! I do assure you you are in error from the very first step—from the first and most important step! Understand, that I do not care to make a martyr of myself for some unknown reason! Know, also, that I shall not marry anyone at all; I shall remain a maid. You have bitten my head off for the last two years because I would not marry. Well, you must accept the fact, and make the best of it; that's all I can say, and so it shall be!"

"But Zina, darling—my Zina, don't be so cross before you have heard me out! What a hot-headed little person you are, to be sure! Let me show you the matter from my point of view, and you'll agree with me—you really will! The prince will live a year—two at most; and surely it is better to be a young widow than a decayed old maid! Not to mention the fact that you will be a princess—free, rich, independent! I dare say you look with contempt upon all these calculations—founded upon his death; but I am a mother, and what mother will blame me for my foresight?

"And if you, my angel of kindness, are unwilling to marry, even now, out of tenderness for that wretched boy's feelings, oh, think, think how, by marrying this prince, you will rejoice his heart and soothe and comfort his soul! For if he has a single particle of commonsense, he must understand that jealousy of this old man were *too*absurd—*too* ridiculous! He will understand that you marry him—for money, for convenience; that stern necessity compels you to it!

"And lastly, he will understand that—that,—well I simply wish to say, that, upon the prince's death, you will be at liberty to marry whomsoever you please."

"That's a truly simple arrangement! All I have to do is to marry this prince, rob him of his money, and then count upon his death in order to marry my lover! You are a clever arithmetician, mamma; you do your sums and get your totals nicely. You wish to seduce me by offering me this! Oh, I understand you, mamma—I understand you well! You cannot resist the expression of your noble sentiments and exalted ideas, even in the manufacture of a nasty business. Why can't you say simply and straightforwardly, 'Zina, this is a dirty affair, but it will pay us, so please agree with me?' at all events, that would be candid and frank on your part."

"But, my dear child, why, *why* look at it from this point of view? Why look at it under the light of suspicion as*deceit*, and low cunning, and covetousness? You consider my calculations as meanness, as deceit; but, by all that is good and true, where is the meanness? Show me the deceit. Look at yourself in the glass: you are so beautiful, that a kingdom would be a fair price for you! And suddenly you, you, the possessor of this divine beauty, sacrifice yourself, in order to soothe the last years of an old man's life! You would be like a beautiful star, shedding your light over the evening of his days. You would be like the fresh green ivy, twining in and about his old age; not the stinging nettle that this wretched woman at his place is, fastening herself upon him, and thirstily sucking his blood! Surely his money, his rank are not worthy of being put in the scales beside *you*? Where is the meanness of it; where is the deceit of all this? You don't know what you are saying, Zina."

"I suppose they *are* worthy of being weighed against me, if I am to marry a cripple for them! No, mother, however you look at it, it is deceit, and you can't get out of *that*!"

"On the contrary, my dear child, I can look at it from a high, almost from an exalted—nay, Christian—point of view. You, yourself, told me once, in a fit of temporary insanity of some sort, that you wished to be a sister of charity. You had suffered; you said your heart could love no more. If, then, you cannot love, turn your thoughts to the higher aspect of the case. This poor old man has also suffered—he is unhappy. I have known him, and felt the deepest sympathy towards him—akin to love,—for many a year. Be his friend, his daughter, be his plaything, even, if you like; but warm his old heart, and you are doing a good work—a virtuous, kind, noble work of love.

"He may be funny to look at; don't think of that. He's but half a man—pity him! You are a Christian girl—do whatever is right by him; and this will be medicine for your own heart-wounds; employment, action, all this will heal you too, and where is the deceit here? But you do not believe me. Perhaps you think that I am deceiving myself when I thus talk of duty and of action. You think that I, a woman of the world, have no right to good feeling and the promptings of duty and virtue. Very well, do not trust me, if you like: insult me, do what you please to your poor mother; but you will have to admit that her words carry the stamp of good sense,—they are saving words! Imagine that someone else is talking to you, not I. Shut your eyes, and fancy that some invisible being is speaking. What is worrying you is the idea that all this is for money—a sort of sale or purchase. Very well, then *refuse* the money, if it is so loathsome to your eyes. Leave just as much as is absolutely necessary for yourself, and give the rest to the poor. Help *him*, if you like, the poor fellow who lies there a-dying!"

"He would never accept my help!" muttered Zina, as though to herself.

"He would not, but his mother would!" said Maria Alexandrovna. "She would take it, and keep her secret. You sold your ear-rings, a present from your aunt, half a year or so ago, and helped her; *I* know all about it! I know, too, that the woman washes linen in order to support her unfortunate son!"

"He will soon be where he requires no more help!"

"I know, I understand your hints." Maria Alexandrovna sighed a real sigh. "They say he is in a consumption, and must die.

"But *who* says so?

"I asked the doctor the other day, because, having a tender heart, Zina, I felt interested in the poor fellow. The doctor said that he was convinced the malady was *not* consumption; that it was dangerous, no doubt, but still*not* consumption, only some severe affection of the lungs. Ask him yourself! He certainly told me that under different conditions—change of climate and of his style of living,—the sick man might well recover. He said—and I have read it too, somewhere, that off Spain there is a wonderful island, called Malaga—I think it was Malaga; anyhow, the name was like some wine, where, not only ordinary sufferers from chest maladies, but even consumptive patients, recover entirely, solely by virtue of the climate, and that sick people go there on purpose to be cured.

"Oh, but Spain—the Alhambra alone—and the lemons, and the riding on mules. All this is enough in itself to impress a poetical nature. You think he would not accept your help, your money—for such a journey? Very well—deceit is permissible where it may save a man's life.

"Give him hope, too! Promise him your love; promise to marry him when you are a widow! Anything in the world can be said with care and tact! Your own mother would not counsel you to an ignoble deed, Zina. You will do as I say, to save this boy's life; and with this object, everything is permissible! You will revive his hope; he will himself begin to think of his health, and listen to what the doctor says to him. He will do his best to resuscitate his dead happiness; and if he gets well again, even if you never marry him, you will have saved him—raised him from the dead!

"I can look at him with some sympathy. I admit I can, now! Perhaps sorrow has changed him for the better; and I say frankly, if he should be worthy of you when you become a widow, marry him, by all means! You will be rich then, and independent. You can not only cure him, but, having done so, you can give him position in the world—a career! Your marriage to him will then be possible and pardonable, not, as now, an absolute impossibility!

"For what would become of both of you were you to be capable of such madness *now*? Universal contempt, beggary; smacking little boys, which is part of his duty; the reading of Shakespeare; perpetual, hopeless life in Mordasoff; and lastly his certain death, which will undoubtedly take place before long unless he is taken away from here!

"While, if you resuscitate him—if you raise him from the dead, as it were, you raise him to a good, useful, and virtuous life! He may then enter public life—make himself rank, and a name! At the least, even if he must die, he will die happy, at peace with himself, in your arms—for he will be by then assured of your love and forgiveness of the past, and lying beneath the scent of myrtles and lemons, beneath the tropical sky of the South. Oh, Zina, all this is within your grasp, and all—all is *gain*. Yes, and all to be had by merely marrying this prince."

Maria Alexandrovna broke off, and for several minutes there was silence; not a word was said on either side: Zina was in a state of indescribable agitation. I say indescribable because I will not attempt to describe Zina's feelings: I cannot guess at them; but I *think* that Maria Alexandrovna had found the road to her heart.

Not knowing how her words had sped with her daughter, Maria Alexandrovna now began to work her busy brain to imagine and prepare herself for every possible humour that Zina might prove to be in; but at last she concluded that she had happened upon the right track after all. Her rude hand had touched the sorest place in Zina's heart, but her crude and absurd sentimental twaddle had not blinded her daughter. "However, that doesn't matter"—thought the mother. "All I care to do is to make her *think*; I wish my ideas to stick!" So she reflected, and she gained her end; the effect was made—the arrow reached the mark. Zina had listened hungrily as her mother spoke; her cheeks were burning, her breast heaved.

"Listen, mother," she said at last, with decision; though the sudden pallor of her face showed clearly what the decision had cost her. "Listen mother——" But at this moment a sudden noise in the entrance hall, and a shrill female voice, asking for Maria Alexandrovna, interrupted Zina, while her mother jumped up from her chair.

"Oh! the devil fly away with this magpie of a woman!" cried the latter furiously. "Why, I nearly drove her out by force only a fortnight ago!" she added, almost in despair. "I can't, I can't receive her now. Zina, this question is too important to be put off: she must have news for me or she never would have dared to come. I won't receive the old —— Oh! *how* glad I am to see you, dear Sophia Petrovna. What lucky chance brought *you* to see me? What a *charming* surprise!" said Maria Alexandrovna, advancing to receive her guest.

Zina escaped out of the room.

Mrs. Colonel Tarpuchin, or Sophia Petrovna, was only morally like a magpie; she was more akin to the sparrow tribe, viewed physically. She was a little bit of a woman of fifty summers or so, with lively eyes, and yellow patches all over her face. On her little wizened body and spare limbs she wore a black silk dress, which was perpetually on the rustle: for this little woman could never sit still for an instant.

This was the most inveterate and bitterest scandal-monger in the town. She took her stand on the fact that she was a Colonel's wife, though she often fought with her husband, the Colonel, and scratched his face handsomely on such occasions.

Add to this, that it was her custom to drink four glasses of "vodki" at lunch, or earlier, and four more in the evening; and that she hated Mrs. Antipova to madness.

"I've just come in for a minute, *mon ange*," she panted; "it's no use sitting down—no time! I wanted to let you know what's going on, simply that the whole town has gone mad over this prince. Our 'beauties,' you know what I mean! are all after him, fishing for him, pulling him about, giving him champagne—you would not believe it! *would* you now? How on earth you could ever have let him out of the house, I can't understand! Are you aware that he's at Natalia Dimitrievna's at this moment?"

"At *Natalia Dimitrievna's*?" cried Maria Alexandrovna jumping up. "Why, he was only going to see the Governor, and then call in for one moment at the Antipova's!"

"Oh, yes, just for one moment—of course! Well, catch him if you can, there! That's all I can say. He found the Governor 'out,' and went on to Mrs. Antipova's, where he has promised to dine. There Natalia caught him—she is never away from Mrs. Antipova nowadays,—and persuaded him to come away with her to lunch. So there's your prince! catch him if you can!"

"But how—Mosgliakoff's with him—he promised—"

"Mosgliakoff, indeed,—why, he's gone too! and they'll be playing at cards and clearing him out before he knows where he is! And the things Natalia is saying, too—out loud if you please! She's telling the prince to his face that you, *you* have got hold of him with certain views—*vous comprenez?*"

"She calmly tells him this to his face! Of course he doesn't understand a word of it, and simply sits there like a soaked cat, and says 'Ye—yes!' And would you believe it, she has trotted out her Sonia—a girl of fifteen, in a dress down to her knees—my word on it? Then she has sent for that little orphan—Masha; she's in a short dress too,—why, I swear it doesn't reach her knees. I looked at it carefully through my pince-nez! She's stuck red caps with some sort of feathers in them on their heads, and set them to dance some silly dance to the piano accompaniment for the prince's benefit! You know his little weakness as to our sex,—well, you can imagine him staring at them through his glass and saying, '*Charmant!*—What figures!' Tfu! They've turned the place into a music hall! Call that a dance! I was at school at Madame Jarne's, I know, and there were plenty of princesses and countesses there with me, too; and I know I danced before senators and councillors, and earned their applause, too: but as for this dance—it's a low can-can, and nothing more! I simply *burned* with shame,—I couldn't stand it, and came out."

"How! have you been at Natalia Dimitrievna's? Why, you——!"

"What!—she offended me last week? is that what you you mean? Oh, but, my dear, I *had* to go and have a peep at the prince—else, when should I have seen him? As if I would have gone *near* her but for this wretched old prince. Imagine—chocolate handed round and *me left out*. I'll let her have it for that, some day! Well, good-bye, *mon ange*: I must hurry off to Akulina, and let her know all about it. You may say good-bye to the prince; he won't come near you again now! He has no memory left, you know, and Mrs. Antipova will simply carry him off bodily to her house. He'll think it's all right——They're all afraid of you, you know; they think that you want to get hold of him—you understand! Zina, you know!"

"*Quelle horreur!*"

"Oh, yes, I know! I tell you—the whole town is talking about it! Mrs. Antipova is going to make him stay to dinner—and then she'll just keep him! She's doing it to spite *you*, my angel. I had a look in at her back premises. *Such* arrangements, my dear. Knives clattering, people running about for champagne. I tell you what you must do—go and grab him as he comes out from Natalia Dimitrievna's to Antipova's to dinner. He promised *you* first, he's *your* guest. Tfu! don't you be laughed at by this brace of chattering magpies—good for nothing baggage, both of them. 'Procuror's lady,' indeed! Why, I'm a Colonel's wife. Tfu!—*Mais adieu, mon ange*. I have my own sledge at the door, or I'd go with you."

Having got rid of this walking newspaper, Maria Alexandrovna waited a moment, to free herself of a little of her super-abundant agitation. Mrs. Colonel's advice was good and practical. There was no use losing time,—none to lose, in fact. But the greatest difficulty of all was as yet unsettled.

Maria Alexandrovna flew to Zina's room.

Zina was walking up and down, pale, with hands folded and head bent on her bosom: there were tears in her eyes, but Resolve was there too, and sparkled in the glance which she threw on her mother as the latter entered the room. She hastily dried her tears, and a sarcastic smile played on her lips once more.

"Mamma," she began, anticipating her mother's speech "you have already wasted much of your eloquence over me—too much! But you have not blinded me; I am not a child. To do the work of a sister of mercy, without the slightest call thereto,—to justify one's meanness—meanness proceeding in reality from the purest egotism, by attributing to it noble ends,—all this is a sort of Jesuitism which cannot deceive *me*. Listen! I repeat, all *this could not deceive me*, and I wish you to understand that!"

"But, dearest child!" began her mother, in some alarm.

"Be quiet, mamma; have patience, and hear me out. In spite of the full consciousness that all this is pure Jesuitism, and in spite of my full knowledge of the absolutely ignoble character of such an act, I accept your proposition in full,—you hear me—*in full*; and inform you hereby, that I am ready to marry the prince. More! I am ready to help you to the best of my power in your endeavours to lure the prince into making me an offer. Why do I do this? You need not know that; enough that I have consented. I have consented to the whole thing—to bringing him his boots, to serving him; I will dance for him, that my meanness may be in some sort atoned. I shall do all I possibly can so that he shall never regret that he married me! But in return for my consent I insist upon knowing *how* you intend to bring the matter about? Since you have spoken so warmly on the subject—I know you!—I am convinced you must have some definite plan of operation in your head. Be frank for once in your life; your candour is the essential condition upon which alone I give my consent. I shall not decide until you have told me what I require!"

Maria Alexandrovna was so surprised by the unexpected conclusion at which Zina arrived, that she stood before the latter some little while, dumb with amazement, and staring at her with all her eyes. Prepared to have to combat the stubborn romanticism of her daughter—whose obstinate nobility of character she always feared,—she had suddenly heard this same daughter consent to all that her mother had required of her.

Consequently, the matter had taken a very different complexion. Her eyes sparkled with delight:

"Zina, Zina!" she cried; "you are my life, my——"

She could say no more, but fell to embracing and kissing her daughter.

"Oh, mother, I don't *want* all this kissing!" cried Zina, with impatience and disgust. "I don't need all this rapture on your part; all I want is a plain answer to my question!"

"But, Zina, I love you; I adore you, darling, and you repel me like this! I am working for your happiness, child!"

Tears sparkled in her eyes. Maria Alexandrovna really loved her daughter, in her own way, and just now she actually felt deeply, for once in her life—thanks to her agitation, and the success of her eloquence.

Zina, in spite of her present distorted view of things in general, knew that her mother loved her; but this love only annoyed her; she would much rather—it would have been easier for her—if it had been hate!

"Well, well; don't be angry, mamma—I'm so excited just now!" she said, to soothe her mother's feelings.

"I'm not angry, I'm not angry, darling! I know you are much agitated!" cried Maria Alexandrovna. "You say, my child, that you wish me to be candid: very well, I will; I will be *quite* frank, I assure you. But you might have trusted me! Firstly, then, I must tell you that I have no actually organized plan yet—no *detailed* plan, that is. You must understand, with that clever little head of yours, you must see, Zina, that I *cannot* have such a plan, all cut out. I even anticipate some difficulties. Why, that magpie of a woman has just been telling me all sorts of things. We ought to be quick, by the bye; you see, I am quite open with you! But I swear to you that the end shall be attained!" she added, ecstatically. "My convictions are not the result of a poetical nature, as you told me just now; they are founded on facts. I rely on the weakness of the prince's intellect—which is a canvas upon which one can stitch any pattern one pleases!

"The only fear is, we may be interfered with! But a fool of a woman like that is not going to get the better of*me*!" she added, stamping her foot, and with flashing eyes. "That's my part of the business, though; and to manage it thoroughly I must begin as soon as possible—in fact, the whole thing, or the most important part of it, must be arranged this very day!"

"Very well, mamma; but now listen to one more piece of candour. Do you know why I am so interested in your plan of operations, and do not trust it? because I am not sure of myself! I have told you already that I consent to this——meanness; but I must warn you that if I find the details of your plan of operations *too* dirty, too mean and repulsive, I shall not be able to stand it, and shall assuredly throw you over. I know that this is a new pettiness, to consent to a wicked thing and then fear the dirt in which it floats! But what's to be done? So it will be, and I warn you!"

"But Zina, dear child, where is the wickedness in this?" asked Maria Alexandrovna timidly. "It is simply a matter of a marriage for profit; everybody does it! Look at it in this light, and you will see there is nothing particular in it; it is good 'form' enough!"

"Oh, mamma, don't try to play the fox over me! Don't you see that I have consented to everything—to*everything*? What else do you require of me? Don't be alarmed if I call things by their proper names! For all you know it may be my only comfort!" And a bitter smile played over her lips.

"Very well, very well, dear! we may disagree as to ideas and yet be very fond of one another. But if you are afraid of the working of my plan, and dread that you will see any baseness or meanness about it, leave it all to me, dear, and I guarantee you that not a particle of dirt shall soil you! Your hands shall be clean! As if I would be the one to compromise you! Trust me entirely, and all shall go grandly and with dignity; all shall be done worthily; there shall be no scandal—even if there be a whisper afterwards, we shall all be out of the way, far off! We shall not stay here, of course! Let them *howl* if they like, *we* won't care. Besides, they are not worth bothering about, and I wonder at your being so frightened of these people, Zina. Don't be angry with me! how can you be so frightened, with your proud nature?"

"I'm not frightened; you don't understand me a bit!" said Zina, in a tone of annoyance.

"Very well, darling; don't be angry. I only talk like this because these people about here are always stirring up mud, if they can; while you—this is the first time in your life you have done a mean action.—*Mean* action! What an old fool I am! On the contrary, this is a most generous, *noble* act! I'll prove this to you once more, Zina. Firstly, then, it all depends upon the point of view you take up——"

"Oh! bother your proofs, mother. I've surely had enough of them by now," cried Zina angrily, and stamped her foot on the floor.

"Well, darling, I won't; it was stupid of me—I won't!"

There was another moment's silence. Maria Alexandrovna looked into her daughter's eyes as a little dog looks into the eyes of its mistress.

"I don't understand how you are going to set about it," said Zina at last, in a tone of disgust. "I feel sure you will only plunge yourself into a pool of shame! I'm not thinking of these people about here. I despise their opinions; but it would be very ignominious for *you*."

"Oh! if that's all, my dear child, don't bother your head about it: please, *please* don't! Let us be agreed about it, and then you need not fear for me. Dear me! if you but knew, though, what things I have done, and kept my skin whole! I tell you this is *nothing* in comparison with *real* difficulties which I have arranged successfully. Only let me try. But, first of all we must get the prince *alone*, and that as soon as possible. That's the first move: all the rest will depend upon the way we manage this. However, I can foresee the result. They'll all rise against us; but I'll manage *them* all right! I'm a little nervous about Mosgliakoff. He——"

"Mosgliakoff!" said Zina, contemptuously.

"Yes, but don't you be afraid, Zina! I'll give you my word I'll work him so that he shall help us himself. You don't know me yet, my Zina. My child, when I heard about this old prince having arrived this morning, the idea, as it were, shone out all at once in my brain! Who would have thought of his really coming to us like this! It is a chance such as you might wait for a thousand years in vain. Zina, my angel! there's no shame in what you are doing. What *is* wrong is to marry a man whom you loathe. Your marriage with the prince will be no *real*marriage; it is simply a domestic contract. It is he, the old fool, who gains by it. It is *he* who is made unspeakably, immeasurably happy. Oh! Zina, how lovely you look to-day. If I were a man I would give you half a kingdom if you but raised your finger for it! *Asses* they all are! Who wouldn't kiss a hand like this?" and Maria Alexandrovna kissed her daughter's hand warmly. "Why, this is my own flesh and blood, Zina. What's to be done afterwards? You won't part with me, will you? You won't drive your old mother away when you are happy yourself? No, darling, for though we have quarrelled often enough, you have not such another friend as I am, Zina! You——"

"Mamma, if you've made up your mind to it all, perhaps it is time you set about making some move in the matter. We are losing time," said Zina, impatiently.

"Yes, it is, it is indeed time; and here am I gabbling on while they are all doing their best to seduce the prince away from us. I must be off at once. I shall find them, and bring the prince back by force, if need be. Good-bye, Zina, darling child. Don't be afraid, and don't look sad, dear; please don't! It will be all well, nay, *gloriously*well! Good-bye, good-bye!"

Maria Alexandrovna made the sign of the Cross over Zina, and dashed out of the room. She stopped one moment at her looking-glass to see that all was right, and then, in another minute, was seated in her carriage and careering through the Mordasoff streets. Maria Alexandrovna lived in good style, and her carriage was always in waiting at that hour in case of need.

"No, no, my dears! it's not for *you* to outwit me," she thought, as she drove along. "Zina agrees; so half the work is done. Oh, Zina, Zina! so your imagination is susceptible to pretty little visions, is it? and I *did* treat her to a pretty little picture. She was really touched at last; and how lovely the child looked to-day! If I had her beauty I should turn half Europe topsy-turvy. But wait a bit, it's all right. Shakespeare will fly away to another world when you're a princess, my dear, and know a few people. What does she know? Mordasoff and the tutor! And what a princess she will make. I *love* to see her pride and pluck. She looks at you like any queen. And not to know her own good! However, she soon will. Wait a bit; let this old fool die, and then the boy, and I'll marry her to a reigning prince yet! The only thing I'm afraid of is—haven't I trusted her too much? Didn't I allow my feelings to run away with me too far? I am anxious about her. I am anxious, anxious!"

Thus Maria Alexandrovna reflected as she drove along. She was a busy woman, was Maria Alexandrovna.

Zina, left alone, continued her solitary walk up and down the room with folded hands and thoughtful brow. She had a good deal to think of! Over and over again she repeated, "It's time—it's time—oh, it's time!" What did this ejaculation mean? Once or twice tears glistened on her long silken eyelashes, and she did not attempt to wipe them away.

Her mother worried herself in vain, as far as Zina was concerned; for her daughter had quite made up her mind:—she was ready, come what might!

"Wait a bit!" said the widow to herself, as she picked her way out of her hiding-place, after having observed and listened to the interview between Zina and her mother. "And I was thinking of a wedding dress for myself; I positively thought the prince would really come my way! So much for *my* wedding dress—what a fool I was! Oho! Maria Alexandrovna—I'm a baggage, am I—and a beggar;—and I took a bribe of two hundred roubles from you, did I? And I didn't spend it on expenses connected with your precious daughter's letter, did I? and break open a desk for your sake with my own hands! Yes, madam; I'll teach you what sort of a baggage Nastasia Petrovna is; both of you shall know her a little better yet! Wait a bit!"

CHAPTER VII.

Maria Alexandrovna's genius had conceived a great and daring project.

To marry her daughter to a rich man, a prince, and a cripple; to marry her secretly, to take advantage of the senile feebleness of her guest, to marry her daughter to this old man *burglariously*, as her enemies would call it,—was not only a daring, it was a downright audacious, project.

Of course, in case of success, it would be a profitable undertaking enough; but in the event of *non*-success, what an ignominious position for the authors of such a failure.

Maria Alexandrovna knew all this, but she did not despair. She had been through deeper mire than this, as she had rightly informed Zina.

Undoubtedly all this looked rather too like a robbery on the high road to be altogether pleasant; but Maria Alexandrovna did not dwell much on this thought. She had one very simple but very pointed notion on the subject: namely, this—"*once married they can't be unmarried again.*"

It was a simple, but very pleasant reflection, and the very thought of it gave Maria Alexandrovna a tingling sensation in all her limbs. She was in a great state of agitation, and sat in her carriage as if on pins and needles. She was anxious to begin the fray: her grand plan of operations was drawn up; but there were thousands of small details to be settled, and these must depend upon circumstances. She was not agitated by fear of failure—oh dear, no! all she minded was delay! she feared the delay and obstructions that might be put in her way by the Mordasoff ladies, whose pretty ways she knew so well! She was well aware that probably at this moment the whole town knew all about her present intentions, though she had not revealed them to a living soul. She had found out by painful experience that nothing, not the most secret event, could happen in her house in the morning but it was known at the farthest end of the town by the evening.

Of course, no anticipation, no presentiment, deterred or deceived Maria Alexandrovna: she might feel such sensations at times, but she despised them. Now, this is what had happened in the town this morning, and of which our heroine was as yet only partly informed. About mid-day, that is, just three hours after the prince's arrival at Mordasoff, extraordinary rumours began to circulate about the town.

Whence came they? Who spread them? None could say; but they spread like wild-fire. Everyone suddenly began to assure his neighbour that Maria Alexandrovna had engaged her daughter to the prince; that Mosgliakoff had notice to quit, and that all was settled and signed, and the penniless, twenty-three-year-old Zina was to be the princess.

Whence came this rumour? Could it be that Maria Alexandrovna was so thoroughly known that her friends could anticipate her thoughts and actions under any given circumstances?

The fact is, every inhabitant of a provincial town lives under a glass case; there is no possibility of his keeping anything whatever secret from his honourable co-dwellers in the place. They know *everything*; they know it, too, better than he does himself. Every provincial person should be a psychologist by nature; and that is why I have been surprised, often and often, to observe when I am among provincials that there is not a great number of psychologists—as one would expect,—but an infinite number of dreadful asses. However, this a digression.

The rumour thus spread, then, was a thunder-like and startling shock to the Mordasoff system. Such a marriage—a marriage with this prince—appeared to all to be a thing so very desirable, so brilliant, that the strange side of the affair had not seemed to strike anyone as yet!

One more circumstance must be noticed. Zina was even more detested in the place than her mother; why, I don't know. Perhaps her beauty was the prime cause. Perhaps, too, it was that Maria Alexandrovna was, as it were, one of themselves, a fruit of their own soil: if she was to go away she might even be missed; she kept the place alive more or less—it might be dull without her! But with Zina it was quite a different matter: she lived more in the clouds than in the town of Mordasoff. She was no company for these good people; she could not pair with them. Perhaps she bore herself towards them, unconsciously though, too haughtily.

And now this same Zina, this haughty girl, about whom there were certain scandalous stories afloat, this same Zina was to become a millionaire, a princess, and a woman of rank and eminence!

In a couple of years she might marry again, some duke, perhaps, or a general, maybe a Governor; their own Governor was a widower, and very fond of the ladies! Then she would be the first lady of their province! Why, the very thought of such a thing would be intolerable: in fact, this rumour of Zina's marriage with the prince aroused more irritation in Mordasoff than any other piece of gossip within the memory of man!

People told each other that it was a sin and a shame, that the prince was crazy, that the old man was being deceived, caught, robbed—anything you like; that the prince must be saved from the bloodthirsty talons he had floundered into; that the thing was simply robbery, immorality. And why were any others worse than Zina? Why should not somebody else marry the prince?

Maria Alexandrovna only guessed at all this at present—but that was quite enough. She knew that the whole town would rise up and use all and every means to defeat her ends. Why, they had tried to "confiscate" the prince already; she would have to retrieve him by force, and if she should succeed in luring or forcing him back now, she could not keep him tied to her apron-strings for ever. Again, what was to prevent this whole troop of Mordasoff gossips from coming *en masse* to her salon, under such a plausible plea, too, that she would not be able to turn them out. She knew well that if kicked out of the door these good people would get in at the window—a thing which had actually happened before now at Mordasoff.

In a word, there was not an hour, not a moment to be lost; and meanwhile things were not even begun. A brilliant idea now struck Maria Alexandrovna. We shall hear what this idea was in its proper place, meanwhile I will only state that my heroine dashed through the streets of Mordasoff, looking like a threatening storm-cloud as she swept along full of the stern and implacable resolve that the prince should come back if she had to drag him, and fight for him; and that all Mordasoff might fall in ruins but she should have her way!

Her first move was successful—it could not have been more so.

She chanced to meet the prince in the street, and carried him off to dinner with her.

If my reader wishes to know *how* this feat was accomplished with such a circle of enemies about and around her, and how she managed to make such a fool of Mrs. Antipova, then I must be allowed to point out that such a question is an insult to Maria Alexandrovna. As if *she* were not capable of outwitting any Antipova that ever breathed!

She simply "arrested" the prince at her rival's very door, as he alighted there with Mosgliakoff, in spite of the latter's terror of a scandal, and in spite of everything else; and she popped the old man into the carriage beside her. Of course the prince made very little resistance, and as usual, forgot all about the episode in a couple of minutes, and was as happy as possible.

At dinner he was hilarious to a degree; he made jokes and fun, and told stories which had no ends, or which he tacked on to ends belonging to other stories, without remarking the fact.

He had had three glasses of champagne at lunch at Natalie Dimitrievna's. He now took more wine, and his old head whirled with it. Maria Alexandrovna plied him well. The dinner was very good: the mistress of the house kept the company alive with most bewitching airs and manners,—at least so it should have been, but all excepting herself and the prince were terribly dull on this occasion. Zina sat silent and grave. Mosgliakoff was clearly off his feed: he was very thoughtful; and as this was unusual Maria Alexandrovna was considerably anxious about him.

The widow looked cross and cunning; she continually made mysterious signs to Mosgliakoff on the sly; but the latter took no notice of them.

If the mistress herself had not been so amiable and bewitching, the dinner party might have been mistaken for a lunch at a funeral!

Meanwhile Maria Alexandrovna's condition of mind was in reality excited and agitated to a terrible degree. Zina alone terrified her by her tragic look and tearful eyes. And there was another difficulty—for that accursed Mosgliakoff would probably sit about and get in the way of business! One could not well set about it with him in the room!

So, Maria Alexandrovna rose from the table in some agitation.

But what was her amazement, her joyful surprise, when Mosgliakoff came up to her after dinner, of his own accord, and suddenly and most unexpectedly informed her that he must—to his infinite regret—leave the house on important business for a short while.

"Why, where are you going to?" she asked, with great show of regret.

"Well, you see," began Mosgliakoff, rather disconcerted and uncomfortable, "I have to—*may* I come to you for advice?"

"What is it—what is it?"

"Why, you see, my godfather Borodueff—you know the man; I met him in the street to-day, and he is dreadfully angry with me, says I am grown so *proud*, that though I have been in Mordasoff three times I have never shown my nose inside his doors. He asked me to come in for a cup of tea at five—it's four now. He has no children, you know,—and he is worth a million of roubles—*more*, they say; and if I marry Zina—you see,—and he's seventy years old now!"

"Why, my good boy, of course, of course!—what are you thinking of? You must not neglect that sort of thing—go at once, of course! I *thought* you looked preoccupied at dinner. You ought to have gone this morning and shewn him that you cared for him, and so on. Oh, you boys, you boys!" cried Maria Alexandrovna with difficulty concealing her joy.

"Thanks, thanks, Maria Alexandrovna! you've made a man of me again! I declare I quite feared telling you—for I know you didn't think much of the connection.—He is a common sort of old fellow, I know! So good-bye—my respects to Zina, and apologies—I must be off, of course I shall be back soon!"

"Good-bye—take my blessing with you; say something polite to the old man for me; I have long changed my opinion of him; I have grown to like the real old Russian style of the man. *Au revoir, mon ami, au revoir!*"

"Well, it *is* a mercy that the devil has carried him off, out of the way!" she reflected, flushing with joy as Paul took his departure out of the room. But Paul had only just reached the hall and was putting on his fur coat when to him appeared—goodness knows whence—the widow, Nastasia Petrovna. She had been waiting for him.

"Where are you going to?" she asked, holding him by the arm.

"To my godfather Borodueff's—a rich old fellow; I want him to leave me money. Excuse me—I'm in rather a hurry!"

Mosgliakoff was in a capital humour!

"Oh! then say good-bye to your betrothed!" remarked the widow, cuttingly.

"And why 'good-bye'?"

"Why; you think she's yours already, do you? and they are going to marry her to the prince! I heard them say so myself!"

"To the prince? Oh, come now, Nastasia Petrovna!"

"Oh, it's not a case of 'come now' at all! Would you like to see and hear it for yourself? Put down your coat, and come along here,—this way!"

"Excuse me, Nastasia Petrovna, but I don't understand what you are driving at!"

"Oh! you'll understand fast enough if you just bend down here and listen! The comedy is probably just beginning!"

"What comedy?"

"Hush! don't talk so loud! The comedy of humbugging *you*. This morning, when you went away with the prince, Maria Alexandrovna spent a whole hour talking Zina over into marrying the old man! She told her that nothing was easier than to lure the prince into marrying her; and all sorts of other things that were enough to make one sick! Zina agreed. You should have heard the pretty way in which *you* were spoken of! They think you simply a fool! Zina said plump out that she would never marry you! Listen now, listen!"

"Why—why—it would be most godless cunning," Paul stammered, looking sheepishly into Nastasia's eyes.

"Well, just you listen—you'll hear that, and more besides!"

"But how am I to listen?"

"Here, bend down here. Do you see that keyhole!"

"Oh! but, Nastasia Petrovna, I can't eavesdrop, you know!"

"Oh, nonsense, nonsense! Put your pride in your pocket! You've come, and you must listen now!"

"Well, at all events——"

"Oh! if you can't bear to be an eavesdropper, let it alone, and be made a fool of! One goes out of one's way solely out of pity for you, and you must needs make difficulties! What is it to me? I'm not doing this for myself! *I* shall leave the house before night, in any case!"

Paul, steeling his heart, bent to the keyhole.

His pulses were raging and throbbing. He did not realise what was going on, or what he was doing, or where he was.

CHAPTER VIII.

"So you were very gay, prince, at Natalia Dimitrievna's?" asked Maria Alexandrovna, surveying the battlefield before her; she was anxious to begin the conversation as innocently as possible; but her heart beat loud with hope and agitation.

After dinner the Prince had been carried off to the salon, where he was first received in the morning. Maria Alexandrovna prided herself on this room, and always used it on state occasions.

The old man, after his six glasses of champagne, was not very steady on his legs; but he talked away all the more, for the same reason.

Surveying the field of battle before the fray, Maria Alexandrovna had observed with satisfaction that the voluptuous old man had already begun to regard Zina with great tenderness, and her maternal heart beat high with joy.

"Oh! ch—charming—very gay indeed!" replied the prince, "and, do you know, Nat—alia Dimitrievna is a wo—wonderful woman, a ch—charming woman!"

Howsoever busy with her own high thoughts and exalted ideas, Maria Alexandrovna's heart waxed wrathful to hear such a loud blast of praise on her rival's account.

"Oh! Prince," she began, with flashing eyes, "if Natalia Dimitrievna is a charming woman in your eyes, then I really don't know *what* to think! After such a statement, dear Prince, you must not claim to know society here—no, no!"

"Really! You sur—pr—prise me!"

"I assure you—I assure you, *mon cher* Prince! Listen Zina, I must just tell the prince that absurd story about what Natalia Dimitrievna did when she was here last week. Dearest prince, I am not a scandal-monger, but I must, I really *must* tell you this, if only to make you laugh, and to show you a living picture, as it were, of what people are like in this place! Well, last week this Natalia Dimitrievna came to call upon me. Coffee was brought in, and I had to leave the room for a moment—I forget why—at all events, I went out. Now, I happened to have remarked how much sugar there was in the silver sugar basin; it was quite full. Well, I came back in a few minutes—looked at the sugar basin, and!——three lumps—three little wretched lumps at the very bottom of the basin, prince!—and she was all alone in the room, mind! Now that woman has a large house of her own, and lots of money! Of course this is merely a funny story—but you can judge from this what sort of people one has to deal with here!"

"N—no! you don't mean it!" said the prince, in real astonishment. "What a gr—eedy woman! Do you mean to say she ate it all up?"

"There, prince, and that's your 'charming woman!' What do you think of *that* nice little bit of lady-like conduct? I think I should have died of shame if I had ever allowed myself to do such a dirty thing as that!"

"Ye—yes, ye—yes! but, do you know, she is a real '*belle femme*' all the same!"

"What! Natalia Dimitrievna? My dear prince; why, she is a mere tub of a woman! Oh! prince, prince! what have you said? I expected far better taste of *you*, prince!"

"Ye—yes, tub—tub, of course! but she's a n—nice figure, a nice figure! And the girl who danced—oh! a nice figure too, a very nice figure of a wo—woman!"

"What, Sonia? Why she's a mere child, prince? She's only thirteen years old."

"Ye—yes, ye—yes, of course; but her figure de—velops very fast—charming, charming! And the other da—ancing girl, she's de—veloping too—nicely: she's dirty rather—she might have washed her hands, but very at—tractive, charming!" and the prince raised his glass again and hungrily inspected Zina. "*Mais quelle charmante personne!*—what a lovely girl!" he muttered, melting with satisfaction.

"Zina, play us something, or—better still, sing us a song! How she sings, prince! she's an artiste—a real artiste; oh if you only knew, dear prince," continued Maria Alexandrovna, in a half whisper, as Zina rose to go to the piano with her stately but quiet gait and queenly composure, which evidently told upon the old man; "if you only knew what a daughter that is to me! how she can love; how tender, how affectionate she is to me! what taste she has, what a heart!"

"Ye—yes! ye—yes! taste. And do you know, I have only known one woman in all my life who could compare with her in love—liness. It was the late C—ountess Nainsky: she died thirty years ago, a w—onderful woman, and her beauty was quite sur—passing. She married her co—ook at last."

"Her cook, prince?"

"Ye—yes, her cook, a Frenchman, abroad. She bought him a count's title a—broad; he was a good-looking fellow enough, with little moustaches——"

"And how did they get on?"

"Oh, very well indeed; however, they p—arted very soon; they quarrelled about some sa—sauce. He robbed her—and bo—olted."

"Mamma, what shall I play?" asked Zina.

"Better sing us something, Zina. *How* she sings, prince! Do you like music?"

"Oh, ye—yes! charming, charming. I love music pass—sionately. I knew Beethoven, abroad."

"Knew Beethoven!" cried Maria Alexandrovna, ecstatically. "Imagine, Zina, the prince knew Beethoven! Oh, prince, did you really, *really* know the great Beethoven?"

"Ye—yes, we were great friends, Beet—hoven and I; he was always taking snuff—such a funny fellow!"

"What, Beethoven?"

"Yes, Beethoven; or it may have been some other German fellow—I don't know; there are a great many Germans there. I forget."

"Well, what shall I sing, mamma?" asked Zina again.

"Oh Zina darling, do sing us that lovely ballad all about knights, you know, and the girl who lived in a castle and loved a troubadour. Don't you know! Oh, prince, how I do *love* all those knightly stories and songs, and the castles! Oh! the castles, and life in the middle ages, and the troubadours, and heralds and all. Shall I accompany you, Zina? Sit down near here, prince. Oh! those castles, those castles!"

"Ye—yes, ye—yes, castles; I love ca—astles too!" observed the prince, staring at Zina all the while with the whole of his one eye, as if he would like to eat her up at once. "But, good heavens," he cried, "that song! I know that s—song. I heard that song years—years ago! Oh! how that song reminds me of so—omething. Oh, oh."

I will not attempt to describe the ecstatic state of the prince while Zina sang.

She warbled an old French ballad which had once been all the fashion. Zina sang it beautifully; her lovely face, her glorious eyes, her fine sweet contralto voice, all this went to the prince's heart at once; and her dark thick hair, her heaving bosom, her proud, beautiful, stately figure as she sat at the piano, and played and sang, quite finished him. He never took his eyes off her, he panted with excitement. His old heart, partially revivified with champagne, with the music, and with awakening recollections (and who is there who has no beloved memories of the past?), his old heart beat faster and faster. It was long since it had last beat in this way. He was ready to fall on his knees at her feet, when Zina stopped singing, and he was almost in tears with various emotions.

"Oh, my charming, charming child," he cried, putting his lips to her fingers, "you have ra—vished me quite—quite! I remember all now. Oh charming, charming child!——"

The poor prince could not finish his sentence.

Maria Alexandrovna felt that the moment had arrived for her to make a move.

"Why, *why* do you bury yourself alive as you do, prince?" she began, solemnly. "So much taste, so much vital energy, so many rich gifts of the mind and soul—and to hide yourself in solitude all your days; to flee from mankind, from your friends. Oh, it is unpardonable! Prince, bethink yourself. Look up at life again with open eyes. Call up your dear memories of the past; think of your golden youth—your golden, careless, happy days of youth! Wake them, wake them from the dead, Prince! and wake yourself, too; and recommence life among men and women and society! Go abroad—to Italy, to Spain, oh, to Spain, Prince! You must have a guide, a heart that will love and respect, and sympathize with you! You have friends; summon them about you! Give the word, and they will rally round you in crowds! I myself will be the first to throw up everything, and answer to your cry! I remembered our old friendship, my Prince; and I will sacrifice husband, home, all, and follow you. Yes, and were I but young and lovely, like my daughter here, I would be your fellow, your friend, your *wife*, if you said but the word!"

"And I am convinced that you were a most charming creature in your day, too!" said the prince, blowing his nose violently. His eyes were full of tears.

141

"We live again in our children," said Maria Alexandrovna, with great feeling. "I, too, have my guardian angel, and that is this child, my daughter, Prince, the partner of my heart and of all my thoughts! She has refused seven offers because she is unwilling to leave me! So that she will go too, when you accompany me abroad."

"In that case, I shall certainly go abroad," cried the prince with animation. "As—suredly I shall go! And if only I could ve—venture to hope—oh! you be—witching child, charming, be—witching child!" And the prince recommenced to kiss Zina's fingers. The poor old man was evidently meditating going down on his knees before her.

"But, Prince," began Maria Alexandrovna again, feeling that the opportunity had arrived for another display of eloquence. "But, Prince, you say, 'If only I could flatter myself into indulging any hope!' Why, what a strange man you are, Prince. Surely you do not suppose that you are unworthy the flattering attention of *any* woman! It is not only youth that constitutes true beauty. Remember that you are, so to speak, a chip of the tree of aristocracy. You are a representative of all the most knightly, most refined taste and culture and manners. Did not Maria fall in love with the old man Mazeppa? I remember reading that Lauzun, that fascinating marquis of the court of Louis (I forget which), when he was an old, bent and bowed man, won the heart of one of the youngest and most beautiful women about the court.

"And who told you you are an old man? Who taught you that nonsense? Do men like you ever grow old? You, with your wealth of taste and wit, and animation and vital energy and brilliant manners! Just you make your appearance at some watering-place abroad with a young wife on your arm—some lovely young girl like my Zina, for instance—of course I merely mention her as an example, nothing more,—and you will see at once what a colossal effect you will produce: you, a scion of our aristocracy; she a beauty among beauties! You will lead her triumphantly on your arm; she, perhaps, will sing in some brilliant assemblage; you will delight the company with your wit. Why, all the people of the place will crowd to see you! All Europe will ring with your renown, for every newspaper and feuilleton at the Waters will be full of you. And yet you say, 'If I could but *venture* to *hope*,' indeed!"

"The feuilletons! yes—ye—yes, and the newspapers," said the prince, growing more and more feeble with love, but not understanding half of Maria Alexandrovna's tall talk. "But, my child, if you're not tired, do repeat that song which you have just sung so cha—armingly once more."

"Oh! but, Prince, she has other lovely songs, still prettier ones; don't you remember *L'Hirondelle*? You must have heard it, haven't you?"

"Ye—yes, I remember it; at least I've for—gotten it. No, no! the one you have just sung. I don't want the Hir—ondelle! I want that other song," whined the prince, just like any child.

Zina sang again.

This time the prince could not contain himself; he fell on his knees at her feet, he cried, he sobbed:

"Oh, my beautiful *chatelaine*!" he cried in his shaky old voice—shaky with old age and emotion combined. "Oh, my charming, charming *chatelaine*! oh, my dear child! You have re—minded me of so much that is long, long passed! I always thought then that things must be fairer in the future than in the present. I used to sing duets with the vis—countess in this very ballad! And now, oh! I don't know what to do, I don't know *what* to do!"

The prince panted and choked as he spoke; his tongue seemed to find it difficult to move; some of his words were almost unintelligible. It was clear that he was in the last stage of emotional excitement. Maria Alexandrovna immediately poured oil on the fire.

"Why, Prince, I do believe you are falling in love with my Zina," she cried, feeling that the moment was a solemn one.

The prince's reply surpassed her fondest expectations.

"I am madly in love with her!" cried the old man, all animated, of a sudden. He was still on his knees, and he trembled with excitement as he spoke. "I am ready to give my life for her! And if only I could hope, if only I might have a little hope—I,—but, lift me up; I feel so weak. I—if only she would give me the hope that I might offer her my heart, I—she should sing ballads to me every day; and I could look at her, and look and gaze and gaze at her.——Oh, my God! my God!"

"Prince, Prince! you are offering her your hand. You want to take her from me, my Zina! my darling, my *ange*, my own dear child, Zina! No, Zina, no, I can't let you go! They must tear you from me, Zina. They must tear you first from your mother's arms!"

Maria Alexandrovna sprang to her daughter, and caught her up in a close embrace, conscious, withal, of serious physical resistance on Zina's part. The fond mother was a little overdoing it.

Zina felt this with all her soul, and she looked on at the whole comedy with inexpressible loathing.

However, she held her tongue, and that was all the fond mother required of her.

"She has refused nine men because she will not leave me!" said Maria. "But this time, I fear—my heart tells me that we are doomed to part! I noticed just now how she looked at you, Prince. You have impressed her with your aristocratic manner, with your refinement. Oh! Prince, you are going to separate us—I feel it, I feel it!"

"I ad—ore her!" murmured the poor old man, still trembling like an autumnal leaf.

"And you'll consent to leave your mother!" cried Maria Alexandrovna, throwing herself upon her daughter once more. Zina made haste to bring this, to her, painful scene to an end. She stretched her pretty hand silently to the prince, and even forced herself to smile. The prince reverently took the little hand into his own, and covered it with kisses.

"I am only this mo—ment beginning to live," he muttered, in a voice that seemed choking with rapture and ecstasy.

"Zina," began Maria Alexandrovna, solemnly, "look well at this man! This is the most honest and upright and noble man of all the men I know. He is a knight of the middle ages! But she knows it, Prince, she knows it too well; to my grief I say it. Oh! why did you come here? I am surrendering my treasure to you—my angel! Oh! take care of her, Prince. Her mother entreats you to watch over her. And what mother could blame my grief!"

"Enough, mamma! that's enough," said Zina, quietly.

"Protect her from all hurt and insult, Prince! Can I rely upon your sword to flash in the face of the vile scandal-monger who dares to offend my Zina?"

"Enough, mother, I tell you! am I——?"

"Ye—yes, ye—yes, it shall flash all right," said the prince. "But I want to be married now, at once. I—I'm only just learning what it is to live. I want to send off to Donchanovo at once. I want to send for some di—iamonds I have there. I want to lay them at her feet.——I——"

"What noble ardour! what ecstasy of love! what noble, generous feelings you have, Prince!" cried Maria Alexandrovna. "And you could bury yourself—*bury* yourself, far from the world and society! I shall remind you of this a thousand times! I go mad when I think of that *hellish* woman."

"What could I do? I was fri—ghtened!" stammered the prince in a whining voice: "they wanted to put me in a lu—unatic asylum! I was dreadfully alarmed!"

"In a lunatic asylum? Ah, the scoundrels! oh, the inhuman wretches! Ah, the low cunning of them! Yes, Prince; I had heard of it. But the lunacy was in these people, not in *you*. Why, *why* was it—what for?"

"I don't know myself, what it was for," replied the poor old man, feebly sinking into his chair; "I was at a ball, don't you know, and told some an—ecdote or other and they didn't like it; and so they got up a scandal and a ro—ow."

"Surely that was not all, Prince?"

"No;—the—I was playing cards with Prince Paul De—mentieff, and I was cleared out: you see, I had two kings and three quee—ns, three kings and two qu—eens; or I should say—one king—and some queens—I know I had——."

"And it was for this? Oh, the hellish inhumanity of some people! You are weeping, Prince; but be of good cheer—it is all over now! Now I shall be at hand, dearest Prince,—I shall not leave Zina; and we shall see which of them will dare to say a word to you, *then*! And do you know, my Prince, your marriage will expose them! it will shame them! They will see that you are a man—that a lovely girl like our Zina would never have married a madman! You shall raise your head proudly now, and look them straight in the face!"

"Ye—yes; I shall look them straight in the f—ace!" murmured the prince, slowly shutting his eyes.

Maria Alexandrovna saw that her work was done: the prince was tired out with love and emotion. She was only wasting her eloquence!

"Prince, you are disturbed and tired, I see you are!" she said; "you must rest, you must take a good rest after so much agitation," she added, bending over him maternally.

"Ye—yes, ye—yes; I should like to lie down a little," said the old man.

"Of course, of course! you must lie down! those agitating scenes——stop, I will escort you myself, and arrange your couch with my own hands! Why are you looking so hard at that portrait, Prince? That is my mother's picture; she was an angel—not a woman! Oh, why is she not among us at this joyful moment!"

"Ye—yes; charming—charming! Do you know, I had a mother too,—a princess, and imagine! a re—markably, a re—markably fat woman she was; but that is not what I was going to say,——I—I feel a little weak, and——Au revoir, my charming child—to-morrow—to-day—I will—I—I—Au revoir, au revoir!" Here the poor old fellow tried to kiss his hand, but slipped, and nearly fell over the threshold of the door.

"Take care, dear Prince—take care! lean on my arm!" cried Maria Alexandrovna.

"Charming, ch—arming!" he muttered, as he left the room. "I am only now le—learning to live!"

Zina was left alone.

A terrible oppression weighed down her heart. She felt a sensation of loathing which nearly suffocated her. She despised herself—her cheeks burned. With folded hands, and teeth biting hard into her lips, she stood in one spot, motionless. The tears of shame streamed from her eyes,——and at this moment the door opened, and Paul Mosgliakoff entered the room!

CHAPTER IX.

He had heard all—*all*.

He did not actually enter the room, but stood at the door, pale with excitement and fury. Zina looked at him in amazement.

"So that's the sort of person you are!" he cried panting. "At last I have found you out, have I?"

"Found me out?" repeated Zina, looking at him as though he were a madman. Suddenly her eyes flashed with rage. "How dare you address me like that?" she cried, advancing towards him.

"I have heard all!" said Mosgliakoff solemnly, but involuntarily taking a step backwards.

"You heard? I see—you have been eavesdropping!" cried Zina, looking at him with disdain.

"Yes, I have been eavesdropping! Yes—I consented to do a mean action, and my reward is that I have found out that you, too, are——I don't know how to express to you what I think you!" he replied, looking more and more timid under Zina's eyes.

"And supposing that you *have* heard all: what right have you to blame me? What right have you to speak to me so insolently, in any case?"

"*I!—I?* what right have *I?* and *you* can ask me this? You are going to marry this prince, and I have no right to say a word! Why, you gave me your promise—is that nothing?"

"When?"

"How, when?"

"Did not I tell you that morning, when you came to me with your sentimental nonsense—did I not tell you that I could give you no decided answer?"

"But you did not reject me; you did not send me away. I see—you kept me hanging in reserve, in case of need! You lured me into your net! I see, I see it all!"

An expression of pain flitted over Zina's careworn face, as though someone had suddenly stabbed her to the heart; but she mastered her feelings.

"If I didn't turn you out of the house," she began deliberately and very clearly, though her voice had a scarcely perceptible tremor in it, "I refrained from such a course purely out of pity. You begged me yourself to postpone, to give you time, not to say you 'No,' to study you better, and 'then,' you said, 'then, when you know what a fine fellow I am, perhaps you will not refuse me!' These were your own words, or very like them, at the very beginning of your courtship!—you cannot deny them! And now you dare to tell me that I 'lured you into my net,' just as though you did not notice my expression of loathing when you made your appearance this morning! You came a fortnight sooner than I expected you, and I did not hide my disgust; on the contrary, I made it evident—you must have noticed it—I know you did; because you asked me whether I was angry because you had come sooner than you promised! Let me tell you that people who do not, and do not *care* to, hide their loathing for a man can hardly be accused of luring that man into their net! You dare to tell me that I was keeping you in reserve! Very well; my answer to that is, that I judged of you like this: 'Though he may not be endowed with much intellect, still he may turn out to be a good enough fellow; and if so, it might be possible to marry him.' However, being persuaded, now, that you are a fool, and a *mischievous* fool into the bargain,—having found out this fact, to my great joy,—it only remains for me now to wish you every happiness and a pleasant journey. Good-bye!"

With these words Zina turned her back on him, and deliberately made for the door.

Mosgliakoff, seeing that all was lost, boiled over with fury.

"Oh! so I'm a fool!" he yelled; "I'm a fool, am I? Very well, good-bye! But before I go, the whole town shall know of this! They shall all hear how you and your mother made the old man drunk, and then swindled him! I shall let the whole world know it! You shall see what Mosgliakoff can do!"

Zina trembled and stopped, as though to answer; but on reflection, she contented herself by shrugging her shoulders; glanced contemptuously at Mosgliakoff, and left the room, banging the door after her.

At this moment Maria Alexandrovna made her appearance. She heard Mosgliakoff's exclamation, and, divining at once what had happened, trembled with terror. Mosgliakoff still in the house, and near the prince! Mosgliakoff about to spread the news all over the town! At this moment, when secrecy, if only for a short time, was essential! But Maria Alexandrovna was quick at calculations: she thought, with an eagle flight of the mind, over all the circumstances of the case, and her plan for the pacification of Mosgliakoff was ready in an instant!

"What is it, *mon ami*?" she said, entering the room, and holding out her hand to him with friendly warmth.

"How—'*mon ami*?'" cried the enraged Mosgliakoff. "*Mon ami*, indeed! the moment after you have abused and reviled me like a pickpocket! No, no! Not quite so green, my good lady! I'm not to be so easily imposed upon again!"

"I am sorry, extremely sorry, to see you in such a *strange* condition of mind, Paul Alexandrovitch! What expressions you use! You do not take the trouble to choose your words before ladies—oh, fie!"

"Before ladies? Ho ho! You—you are—you are anything you like—but not a lady!" yelled Mosgliakoff.

I don't quite know what he meant, but it was something very terrible, you may be sure!

Maria Alexandrovna looked benignly in his face:

"Sit down!" she said, sorrowfully, showing him a chair, the same that the old prince had reclined in a quarter of an hour before.

"But listen, *will* you listen, Maria Alexandrovna? You look at me just as though you were not the least to blame; in fact, as though *I* were the guilty party! Really, Maria Alexandrovna, this is a little *too* much of a good thing! No human being can stand that sort of thing, Maria Alexandrovna! You must be aware of that fact!"

"My dear friend," replied Maria Alexandrovna—"you will allow me to continue to call you by that name, for you have no better friend than I am!—my friend, you are suffering—you are amazed and bewildered; your heart is sore, and therefore the tone of your remarks to me is perhaps not surprising. But I have made up my mind to open my heart to you, especially as I am, perhaps, in some degree to blame before you. Sit down; let us talk it over!"

Maria Alexandrovna's voice was tender to a sickly extent. Her face showed the pain she was suffering. The amazed Mosgliakoff sat down beside her in the arm-chair.

"You hid somewhere, and listened, I suppose?" she began, looking reproachfully into his face.

"Yes I did, of course I did; and a good thing too! What a fool I should have looked if I hadn't! At all events now I know what you have been plotting against me!" replied the injured man, rudely; encouraging and supporting himself by his own fury.

"And you—and you—with your principles, and with your bringing up, could condescend to such an action—Oh, oh!"

Mosgliakoff jumped up.

"Maria Alexandrovna, this is a little too much!" he cried. "Consider what *you* condescend to do, with *your* principles, and *then* judge of other people."

"One more question," she continued, without replying to his outburst: "who recommended you to be an eavesdropper; who told you anything; who is the spy here? That's what I wish to know!"

"Oh, excuse me; that I shall *not* tell you!"

"Very well; I know already. I said, Paul, that I was in some degree to blame before you. But if you look into the matter you will find that if I am to blame it is solely in consequence of my anxiety to do you a good turn!"

"*What?* a good turn—*me?* No, no, madam! I assure you I am not to be caught again! I'm not quite such a fool!"

He moved so violently in his arm-chair that it shook again.

"Now, do be cool, if you can, my good friend. Listen to me attentively, and you will find that what I say is only the bare truth. In the first place I was anxious to inform you of all that has just taken place, in which case you would have learned everything, down to the smallest detail, without being obliged to descend to eavesdropping! If I did not tell you all before, it was simply because the whole matter was in an embryo condition in my mind. It was then quite possible that what *has* happened would never happen. You see, I am quite open with you.

"In the second place, do not blame my daughter. She loves you to distraction; and it was only by the exercise of my utmost influence that I persuaded her to drop you, and accept the prince's offer."

"I have just had the pleasure of receiving convincing proof of her 'love to distraction!'" remarked Mosgliakoff, ironically and bitterly.

"Very well. But how did you speak to *her*? As a lover should speak? Again, ought *any* man of respectable position and tone to speak like that? You insulted and wounded her!"

"Never mind about my 'tone' now! All I can say is that this morning, when I went away with the prince, in spite of both of you having been as sweet as honey to me before, you reviled me behind my back like a pickpocket! *I* know all about it, you see!"

"Yes, from the same dirty source, I suppose?" said Maria Alexandrovna, smiling disdainfully. "Yes, Paul, I *did* revile you: I pitched into you considerably, and I admit it frankly. But it was simply that I was *bound* to blacken you before her. Why? Because, as I have said, I required her to consent to leave you, and this consent was so difficult to tear from her! Short-sighted man that you are! If she had not loved you, why should I have required

145

so to blacken your character? Why should I have been obliged to take this extreme step? Oh! you don't know all! I was forced to use my fullest maternal authority in order to erase you from her heart; and with all my influence and skill I only succeeded in erasing your dear image superficially and partially! If you saw and heard all just now, it cannot have escaped you that Zina did not once, by either word or gesture, encourage or confirm my words to the prince? Throughout the whole scene she said not one word. She sang, but like an automaton! Her whole soul was in anguish, and at last, out of pity for her, I took the prince away. I am sure, she cried, when I left her alone! When you entered the room you must have observed tears in her eyes?"

Mosgliakoff certainly did recall the fact that when he rushed into the room Zina was crying.

"But you—*you*—why were *you* so against me, Maria Alexandrovna?" he cried. "Why did you revile me and malign me, as you admit you did?"

"Ah, now that's quite a different question. Now, if you had only asked me reasonably at the beginning, you should have had your answer long ago! Yes, you are right. It was I, and I alone, who did it all. Do not think of Zina in the matter. Now, *why* did I do it? I reply, in the first place, for Zina's sake. The prince is rich, influential, has great connections, and in marrying him Zina will make a brilliant match. Very well; then if the prince dies—as perhaps he will die soon, for we are all mortal,—Zina is still young, a widow, a princess, and probably very rich. Then she can marry whom she pleases; she may make another brilliant match if she likes. But of course she will marry the man she loves, and loved before, the man whose heart she wounded by accepting the prince. Remorse alone would be enough to make her marry the man whom she had loved and so deeply injured!"

"Hem!" said Paul, gazing at his boots thoughtfully.

"In the second place," continued Maria, "and I will put this shortly, because, though you read a great deal of your beloved Shakespeare, and extract his finest thoughts and ideals, yet you are very young, and cannot, perhaps, apply what you read. You may not understand my feelings in this matter: listen, however. *I* am giving my Zina to this prince partly for the prince's own sake, because I wish to save him by this marriage. We are old friends; he is the dearest and best of men, he is a knightly, chivalrous gentleman, and he lives helpless and miserable in the claws of that devil of a woman at Donchanovo! Heaven knows that I persuaded Zina into this marriage by putting it to her that she would be performing a great and noble action. I represented her as being the stay and the comfort and the darling and the idol of a poor old man, who probably would not live another year at the most! I showed her that thus his last days should be made happy with love and light and friendship, instead of wretched with fear and the society of a detestable woman. Oh! do not blame Zina. She is guiltless. I am not—I admit it; for if there have been calculations it is I who have made them! But I calculated for her, Paul; for her, not myself! I have outlived my time; I have thought but for my child, and what mother could blame me for this?" Tears sparkled in the fond mother's eyes. Mosgliakoff listened in amazement to all this eloquence, winking his eyes in bewilderment.

"Yes, yes, of course! You talk well, Maria Alexandrovna, but you forget—you gave me your word, you encouraged me, you gave me my hopes; and where am I now? I have to stand aside and look a fool!"

"But, my dear Paul, you don't surely suppose that I have not thought of you too! Don't you see the huge, immeasurable gain to yourself in all this? A gain so vast that I was bound in your interest to act as I did!"

"Gain for me! How so?" asked Paul, in the most abject state of confusion and bewilderment.

"Gracious Heavens! do you mean to say you are really so simple and so short-sighted as to be unable to see *that*?" cried Maria Alexandrovna, raising her eyes to the ceiling in a pious manner. "Oh! youth, youth! That's what comes of steeping one's soul in Shakespeare! You ask me, my dear friend Paul, where is the gain to you in all this. Allow me to make a little digression. Zina loves you—that is an undoubted fact. But I have observed that at the same time, and in spite of her evident love, she is not quite sure of your good feeling and devotion to her; and for this reason she is sometimes cold and self-restrained in your presence. Have you never observed this yourself, Paul?"

"Certainly; I did this very day; but go on, what do you deduce from that fact?"

"There, you see! you have observed it yourself; then of course I am right. She is not quite sure of the *lasting* quality of your feeling for her! I am a mother, and I may be permitted to read the heart of my child. Now, then, supposing that instead of rushing into the room and reproaching, vilifying, even *swearing* at and insulting this sweet, pure, beautiful, proud being, instead of hurling contempt and vituperation at her head—supposing that instead of all this you had received the bad news with composure, with tears of grief, maybe; perhaps even with despair—but at the same time with noble composure of soul——"

"H'm!"

"No, no—don't interrupt me! I wish to show you the picture as it is. Very well, supposing, then, that you had come to her and said, 'Zina, I love you better than my life, but family considerations must separate us; I understand these considerations—they are devised for your greater happiness, and I dare not oppose them. Zina, I forgive you; be happy, if you can!'—think what effect such noble words would have wrought upon her heart!"

"Yes—yes, that's all very true, I quite understand that much! but if I *had* said all this, I should have had to go all the same, without satisfaction!"

"No, no, no! don't interrupt me! I wish to show you the *whole* picture in all its detail, in order to impress you fully and satisfactorily. Very well, then, imagine now that you meet her in society some time afterwards: you meet perhaps at a ball—in the brilliant light of a ball-room, under the soothing strains of music, and in the midst of worldly women and of all that is gay and beautiful. You alone are sad—thoughtful—pale,—you lean against some pillar (where you are visible, however!) and watch her. She is dancing. You hear the strains of Strauss, and the wit and merriment around you, but you are sad and wretched.

"What, think you, will Zina make of it? With what sort of eyes will she gaze on you as you stand there? 'And I could doubt this man!' she will think, 'this man who sacrificed all, all, for my sake—even to the mortal wounding of his heart!' Of course the old love will awake in her bosom and will swell with irresistible power!"

Maria Alexandrovna stopped to take breath. Paul moved violently from side to side of his chair.

"Zina now goes abroad for the benefit of the prince's health—to Italy—to Spain," she continued, "where the myrtle and the lemon tree grow, where the sky is so blue, the beautiful Guadalquiver flows! to the land of love, where none can live without loving; where roses and kisses—so to speak—breathe in the very air around. You follow her—you sacrifice your business, friends, everything, and follow her. And so your love grows and increases with irresistible might. Of course that love is irreproachable—innocent—you will languish for one another—you will meet frequently; of course others will malign and vilify you both, and call your love by baser names—but your love is innocent, as I have purposely said; I am her mother—it is not for me to teach you evil, but good. At all events the prince is not in the condition to keep a very sharp look-out upon you; but if he did, as if there would be the slightest ground for base suspicion? Well, the prince dies at last, and then, who will marry Zina, if not yourself? You are so distant a relative of the prince's that there could be no obstacle to the match; you marry her—she is young still, and rich. You are a grandee in an instant! you, too, are rich now! I will take care that the prince's will is made as it should be; and lastly, Zina, now convinced of your loyalty and faithfulness, will look on you hereafter as her hero, as her paragon of virtue and self-sacrifice! Oh! you must be blind,—*blind*, not to observe and calculate your own profit when it lies but a couple of strides from you, grinning at you, as it were, and saying, 'Here, I am yours, take me! Oh, Paul, Paul!'"

"Maria Alexandrovna!" cried Mosgliakoff, in great agitation and excitement, "I see it all! I have been rude, and a fool, and a scoundrel too!" He jumped up from his chair and tore his hair.

"Yes, and unbusinesslike, that's the chief thing—unbusinesslike, and blindly so!" added Maria Alexandrovna.

"I'm an ass! Maria Alexandrovna," he cried in despair. "All is lost now, and I loved her to madness!"

"Maybe all is not lost yet!" said this successful orator softly, and as though thinking out some idea.

"Oh! if only it could be so! help me—teach me. Oh! save me, save me!"

Mosgliakoff burst into tears.

"My dear boy," said Maria Alexandrovna, sympathetically, and holding out her hand, "you acted impulsively, from the depth and heat of your passion—in fact, out of your great love for her; you were in despair, you had forgotten yourself; she must understand all that!"

"Oh! I love her madly! I am ready to sacrifice everything for her!" cried Mosgliakoff.

"Listen! I will justify you before her."

"Oh, Maria Alexandrovna!"

"Yes, I will. I take it upon myself! You come with me, and you shall tell her exactly what I said!"

"Oh, how kind, how good you are! Can't we go at once, Maria Alexandrovna?"

"Goodness gracious, no! What a very green hand you are, Paul! She's far too proud! she would take it as a new rudeness and impertinence! To-morrow I shall arrange it all comfortably for you: but now, couldn't you get out of the way somewhere for a while, to that godfather of yours, for instance? You could come back in the evening, if you pleased; but my advice would be to stay away!"

"Yes, yes! I'll go—of course! Good heavens, you've made a man of me again!—Well, but look here—one more question:—What if the prince does *not* die so soon?"

"Oh, my dear boy, how delightfully naïve you are! On the contrary, we must pray for his good health! We must wish with all our hearts for long life to this dear, good, and chivalrous old man! I shall be the first to pray day and night for the happiness of my beloved daughter! But alas! I fear the prince's case is hopeless; you see, they must visit the capital now, to bring Zina out into society.—I dreadfully fear that all this may prove fatal to him; however, we'll pray, Paul, we can't do more, and the rest is in the hands of a kind Providence. You see what I mean? Very well—good-bye, my dear boy, bless you! Be a man, and wait patiently—be a man, that's the chief thing! I never doubted your generosity of character; but be brave—good-bye!" She pressed his hand warmly, and Mosgliakoff walked out of the room on tip-toes.

"There goes *one* fool, got rid of satisfactorily!" observed Maria Alexandrovna to herself,—"but there are more behind——!"

At this moment the door opened, and Zina entered the room. She was paler than usual, and her eyes were all ablaze.

"Mamma!" she said, "be quick about this business, or I shall not be able to hold out. It is all so dirty and mean that I feel I must run out of the house if it goes on. Don't drive me to desperation! I warn you—don't weary me out—don't weary me out!"

"Zina—what is it, my darling? You—you've been listening?" cried Maria Alexandrovna, gazing intently and anxiously at her daughter.

"Yes, I have; but you need not try to make me ashamed of myself as you succeeded in doing with that fool. Now listen: I solemnly swear that if you worry and annoy me by making me play various mean and odious parts in this comedy of yours,—I swear to you that I will throw up the whole business and put an end to it in a moment. It is quite enough that I have consented to be a party in the main and essence of the base transactions; but—but—I did not know myself, I am poisoned and suffocated with the stench of it!"—So saying, she left the room and banged the door after her.

Maria Alexandrovna looked fixedly after her for a moment, and reflected.

"I must make haste," she cried, rousing herself; "*she* is the greatest danger and difficulty of all! If these detestable people do not let us alone, instead of acting the town-criers all over the place (as I fear they are doing already!)—all will be lost! She won't stand the worry of it—she'll drop the business altogether!—At all hazards, I must get the prince to the country house, and that quickly, too! I shall be off there at once, first, and bring my fool of a husband up: he shall be made useful for once in his life! Meanwhile the prince shall have his sleep out, and when he wakes up I shall be back and ready to cart him away bodily!"

She rang the bell.

"Are the horses ready?" she inquired of the man.

"Yes, madam, long ago!" said the latter.

She had ordered the carriage the moment after she had taken the prince upstairs.

Maria Alexandrovna dressed hurriedly, and then looked in at Zina's room for a moment, before starting, in order to tell her the outlines of her plan of operations, and at the same time to give Zina a few necessary instructions. But her daughter could not listen to her. She was lying on her bed with face hidden in the pillows, crying, and was tearing her beautiful hair with her long white hands: occasionally she trembled violently for a moment, as though a blast of cold had passed through all her veins. Her mother began to speak to her, but Zina did not even raise her head!

Having stood over her daughter in a state of bewilderment for some little while, Maria Alexandrovna left the room; and to make up for lost time bade the coachman drive like fury, as she stepped into the carriage.

"I don't quite like Zina having listened!" she thought as she rattled away. "I gave Mosgliakoff very much the same argument as to herself: she is proud, and may easily have taken offence! H'm! Well, the great thing is to be in time with all the arrangements,—before people know what I am up to! Good heavens, fancy, if my fool of a husband were to be out!!"

And at the very thought of such a thing, Maria Alexandrovna's rage so overcame her that it was clear her poor husband would fare badly for his sins if he proved to be not at home! She twisted and turned in her place with impatience,—the horses almost galloped with the carriage at their heels.

CHAPTER X.

On they flew.

I have said already that this very day, on her first drive after the prince, Maria Alexandrovna had been inspired with a great idea! and I promised to reveal this idea in its proper place. But I am sure the reader has guessed it already!—It was, to "confiscate" the prince in her turn, and carry him off to the village where, at this moment, her husband Afanassy Matveyevitch vegetated alone.

I must admit that our heroine was growing more and more anxious as the day went on; but this is often the case with heroes of all kinds, just before they attain their great ends! Some such instinct whispered to her that it was not safe to remain in Mordasoff another hour, if it could be avoided;—but once in the country house, the whole town might go mad and stand on its head, for all she cared!

Of course she must not lose time, even there! All sorts of things might happen—even the police might interfere. (Reader, I shall never believe, for my part, that my heroine really had the slightest fear of the vulgar police force; but as it has been rumoured in Mordasoff that at this moment such a thought *did* pass through her brain, why, I must record the fact.)

In a word she saw clearly that Zina's marriage with the prince must be brought about at once, without delay! It was easily done: the priest at the village should perform the ceremony; why not the day after to-morrow? or indeed, in case of need, to-morrow? Marriages had often been brought about in less time than this—in two hours, she had heard! It would be easy enough to persuade the prince that haste and simplicity would be in far better taste than all the usual pomps and vanities of common everyday weddings. In fact, she relied upon her skill in putting the matter to the old man as a fitting dramatic issue to a romantic story of love, and thus to touch the most sensitive string of his chivalrous heart.

In case of absolute need there was always the possibility of making him drunk, or rather of *keeping* him perpetually drunk. And then, come what might, Zina would be a princess! And if this marriage were fated to produce scandal among the prince's relations and friends in St. Petersburg and Moscow, Maria Alexandrovna comforted herself with the reflection that marriages in high life nearly always *were* productive of scandal; and that such a result might fairly be looked upon as "good form," and as peculiar to aristocratic circles.

Besides, she felt sure that Zina need only show herself in society, with her mamma to support her, and every one of all those countesses and princes should very soon either acknowledge her of their own accord, or yield to the head-washing that Maria Alexandrovna felt herself so competent to give to any or all of them, individually or collectively.

It was in consequence of these reflections that Maria Alexandrovna was now hastening with all speed towards her village, in order to bring back Afanassy Matveyevitch, whose presence she considered absolutely necessary at this crisis. It was desirable that her husband should appear and invite the prince down to the country: she relied upon the appearance of the father of the family, in dress-coat and white tie, hastening up to town on the first rumours of the prince's arrival there, to produce a very favourable impression upon the old man's self-respect: it would flatter him; and after such a courteous action, followed by a polite and warmly-couched invitation to the country, the prince would hardly refuse to go.

At last the carriage stopped at the door of a long low wooden house, surrounded by old lime trees. This was the country house, Maria Alexandrovna's village residence.

Lights were burning inside.

"Where's my old fool?" cried Maria Alexandrovna bursting like a hurricane into the sitting-room.

"Whats this towel lying here for?—Oh!—he's been wiping his head, has he. What, the baths again! and tea—of course tea!—always tea! Well, what are you winking your eyes at me for, you old fool?—Here, why is his hair not cropped? Grisha, Grisha!—here; why didn't you cut your master's hair, as I told you?"

Maria Alexandrovna, on entering the room, had intended to greet her husband more kindly than this; but seeing that he had just been to the baths and that he was drinking tea with great satisfaction, as usual, she could not restrain her irritable feelings.

She felt the contrast between her own activity and intellectual energy, and the stolid indifference and sheep-like contentedness of her husband, and it went to her heart!

Meanwhile the "old fool," or to put it more politely, he who had been addressed by that title, sat at the tea-urn, and stared with open mouth, in abject alarm, opening and shutting his lips as he gazed at the wife of his bosom, who had almost petrified him by her sudden appearance.

At the door stood the sleepy, fat Grisha, looking on at the scene, and blinking both eyes at periodical intervals.

"I couldn't cut his hair as you wished, because he wouldn't let me!" he growled at last. " 'You'd better let me do it!'—I said, 'or the mistress'll be down one of these days, and then we shall both catch it!' "

"No," he says, "I want it like this now, and you shall cut it on Sunday. I like it long!"

"What!—So you wish to curl it without my leave, do you! What an idea—as if you could wear curls with your sheep-face underneath! Good gracious, what a mess you've made of the place; and what's the smell—what have you been doing, idiot, eh!" cried Maria Alexandrovna, waxing more and more angry, and turning furiously upon the wretched and perfectly innocent Afanassy!

"Mam—mammy!" muttered the poor frightened master of the house, gazing with frightened eyes at the mistress, and blinking with all his might—"mammy!"

"How many times have I dinned into your stupid head that I am *not* your 'mammy.' How can I be your mammy, you idiotic pigmy? How dare you call a noble lady by such a name; a lady whose proper place is in the highest circles, not beside an ass like yourself!"

"Yes—yes,—but—but, you *are* my legal wife, you know, after all;—so I—it was husbandly affection you know———" murmured poor Afanassy, raising both hands to his head as he spoke, to defend his hair from the tugs he evidently expected.

"Oh, idiot that you are! did anyone ever hear such a ridiculous answer as that—legal wife, indeed! Who ever heard the expression '*legal* wife,' in good society—nasty low expression! And how dare you remind me that I am your wife, when I use all my power and do all I possibly can at every moment to forget the fact, eh? What are you covering your head with your hands for? Look at his hair—now: wet, as wet as reeds! it will take three hours to dry that head! How on earth am I to take him like this? How can he show his face among respectable people? What am I to do?"

And Maria Alexandrovna bit her finger-nails with rage as she walked furiously up and down the room.

It was no very great matter, of course; and one that was easily set right; but Maria Alexandrovna required a vent for her feelings and felt the need of emptying out her accumulated wrath upon the head of the wretched Afanassy Matveyevitch; for tyranny is a habit recallable at need.

Besides, everyone knows how great a contrast there is between the sweetness and refinement shown by many ladies of a certain class on the stage, as it were, of society life, and the revelations of character behind the scenes at home; and I was anxious to bring out this contrast for my reader's benefit.

Afanassy watched the movements of his terrible spouse in fear and trembling; perspiration formed upon his brow as he gazed.

"Grisha!" she cried at last, "dress your master this instant! Dress-coat, black trousers, white waistcoat and tie, quick! Where's his hairbrush—quick, quick!"

"Mam—my! Why, I've just been to the bath. I shall catch cold if I go up to town just now!"

"You won't catch cold!"

"But—mammy, my hair's quite wet!"

"We'll dry it in a minute. Here, Grisha, take this brush and brush away till he's dry,—harder—harder—much harder! There, that's better!"

Grisha worked like a man. For the greater convenience of his herculean task he seized his master's shoulder with one hand as he rubbed violently with the other. Poor Afanassy grunted and groaned and almost wept.

"Now, then, lift him up a bit. Where's the pomatum? Bend your head, duffer!—bend lower, you abject dummy!" And Maria Alexandrovna herself undertook to pomade her husband's hair, ploughing her hands through it without the slightest pity. Afanassy heartily wished that his shock growth had been cut. He winced, and groaned and moaned, but did not cry out under the painful operation.

"You suck my life-blood out of me—bend lower, you idiot!" remarked the fond wife—"bend lower still, I tell you!"

"How have I sucked your life blood?" asked the victim, bending his head as low as circumstances permitted.

"Fool!—allegorically, of course—can't you understand? Now, then, comb it yourself. Here, Grisha, dress him, quick!"

Our heroine threw herself into an arm-chair, and critically watched the ceremony of adorning her husband. Meanwhile the latter had a little opportunity to get his breath once more and compose his feelings generally; so that when matters arrived at the point where the tie is tied, he had even developed so much audacity as to express opinions of his own as to how the bow should be manufactured.

At last, having put his dress-coat on, the lord of the manor was his brave self again, and gazed at his highly ornate person in the glass with great satisfaction and complacency.

"Where are you going to take me to?" he now asked, smiling at his reflected self.

Maria Alexandrovna could not believe her ears.

"What—*what*? How *dare* you ask me where I am taking you to, sir!"

"But—mammy—I must know, you know———"

"Hold your tongue! You let me hear you call me mammy again, especially where we are going to now! you sha'n't have any tea for a month!"

The frightened consort held his peace.

"Look at that, now! You haven't got a single 'order' to put on—sloven!" she continued, looking at his black coat with contempt.

"The Government awards orders, mammy; and I am not a sloven, but a town councillor!" said Afanassy, with a sudden excess of noble wrath.

"What, what—*what*! So you've learned to argue now, have you—you mongrel, you? However, I haven't time to waste over you now, or I'd———but I sha'n't forget it. Here, Grisha, give him his fur coat and his hat—quick; and look here, Grisha, when I'm gone, get these three rooms ready, and the green room, and the corner bedroom.

Quick—find your broom; take the coverings off the looking-glasses and clocks, and see that all is ready and tidy within an hour. Put on a dress coat, and see that the other men have gloves: don't lose time. Quick, now!"

She entered the carriage, followed by Afanassy. The latter sat bewildered and lost.

Meanwhile Maria Alexandrovna reflected as to how best she could drum into her husband's thick skull certain essential instructions with regard to the present situation of affairs. But Afanassy anticipated her.

"I had a very original dream to-day, Maria Alexandrovna," he observed quite unexpectedly, in the middle of a long silence.

"Tfu! idiot. I thought you were going to say something of terrific interest, from the look of you. Dream, indeed! How dare you mention your miserable dreams to me! Original, too! Listen here: if you dare so much as remind me of the word 'dream,' or say anything else, either, where we are going to-day, I—I don't know *what* I won't do to you! Now, look here: Prince K. has arrived at my house. Do you remember Prince K.?"

"Oh, yes, mammy, I remember; and why has he done us this honour?"

"Be quiet; that's not your business. Now, you are to invite him, with all the amiability you can, to come down to our house in the country, at once! That is what I am taking you up for. And if you dare so much as breathe another word of any kind, either to-day or to-morrow, or next day, without leave from me, you shall herd geese for a whole year. You're not to say a single word, mind! and that's all you have to think of. Do you understand, now?"

"Well, but if I'm asked anything?"

"Hold your tongue all the same!"

"Oh, but I can't do that—I can't do——"

"Very well, then; you can say 'H'm,' or something of that sort, to give them the idea that you are very wise indeed, and like to think well before answering."

"H'm."

"Understand me, now. I am taking you up because you are to make it appear that you have just heard of the prince's visit, and have hastened up to town in a transport of joy to express your unbounded respect and gratitude to him, and to invite him at once to your country house! Do you understand me?"

"H'm."

"I don't want you to say 'H'm' *now*, you fool! You must answer *me* when I speak!"

"All right—all right, mammy. All shall be as you wish; but why am I to ask the prince down?"

"What—what! arguing again. What business is it of yours *why* you are to invite him? How dare you ask questions!"

"Why it's all the same thing, mammy. How am I to invite him if I must not say a word?"

"Oh, I shall do all the talking. All you have to do is to bow. Do you hear? *Bow*; and hold your hat in your hand and look polite. Do you understand, or not?"

"I understand, mam—Maria-Alexandrovna."

"The prince is very witty, indeed; so mind, if he says anything either to yourself or anyone else, you are to laugh cordially and merrily. Do you hear me?"

"H'm."

"Don't say 'H'm' to *me*, I tell you. You are to answer me plainly and simply. Do you hear me, or not?"

"Yes, yes; I hear you, of course. That's all right. I only say 'H'm,' for practice; I want to get into the way of saying it. But look here, mammy, it's all very well; you say I'm not to speak, and if he speaks to me I'm to look at him and laugh—but what if he asks me a question?"

"Oh—you dense log of a man! I tell you again, you are to be quiet. *I'll* answer for you. You have simply got to look polite, and smile!"

"But he'll think I am dumb!" said Afanassy.

"Well, and what if he does. Let him! You'll conceal the fact that you are a fool, anyhow!"

"H'm, and if *other* people ask me questions?"

"No one will; there'll be no one to ask you. But if there *should* be anyone else in the room, and they ask you questions, all you have to do is to smile sarcastically. Do you know what a sarcastic smile is?"

"What, a witty sort of smile, is it, mammy?"

"I'll let you know about it! *Witty*, indeed! Why, who would think of expecting anything witty from a fool like you. No, sir, a jesting smile—*jesting* and *contemptuous*!"

"H'm."

"Good heavens. I'm afraid for this idiot," thought Maria Alexandrovna to herself. "I really think it would have been almost better to leave him behind, after all." So thinking, nervous and anxious, Maria Alexandrovna drove on. She looked out of the window, and she fidgeted, and she bustled the coachman up. The horses were almost flying through the air; but to her they appeared to be crawling. Afanassy sat silent and thoughtful in the corner of the carriage, practising his lessons. At last the carriage arrived at the town house.

Hardly, however, had Maria Alexandrovna mounted the outer steps when she became aware of a fine pair of horses trotting up—drawing a smart sledge with a hood to it. In fact, the very "turn-out" in which Anna Nicolaevna Antipova was generally to be seen.

Two ladies sat in the sledge. One of these was, of course, Mrs. Antipova herself; the other was Natalia Dimitrievna, of late the great friend and ally of the former lady.

Maria Alexandrovna's heart sank.

But she had no time to say a word, before another smart vehicle drove up, in which there reclined yet another guest. Exclamations of joy and delight were now heard.

"Maria Alexandrovna! and Afanassy Matveyevitch! Just arrived, too! Where from? How extremely delightful! And here we are, you see, just driven up at the right moment. We are going to spend the evening with you. What a delightful surprise."

The guests alighted and fluttered up the steps like so many swallows.

Maria Alexandrovna could neither believe her eyes nor her ears.

"Curse you all!" she said to herself. "This looks like a plot—it must be seen to; but it takes more than a flight of magpies like *you* to get to windward of *me*. Wait a little!!"

CHAPTER XI.

Mosgliakoff went out from Maria Alexandrovna's house to all appearances quite pacified. She had fired his ardour completely. His imagination was kindled.

He did not go to his godfather's, for he felt the need of solitude. A terrific rush of heroic and romantic thoughts surged over him, and gave him no rest.

He pictured to himself the solemn explanation he should have with Zina, then the generous throbs of his all-forgiving heart; his pallor and despair at the future ball in St. Petersburg; then Spain, the Guadalquiver, and love, and the old dying prince joining their hands with his last blessing. Then came thoughts of his beautiful wife, devoted to himself, and never ceasing to wonder at and admire her husband's heroism and exalted refinement of taste and conduct. Then, among other things, the attention which he should attract among the ladies of the highest circles, into which he would of course enter, thanks to his marriage with Zina—widow of the Prince K.: then the inevitable appointments, first as a vice-governor, with the delightful accompaniment of salary: in a word, all, *all* that Maria Alexandrovna's eloquence had pictured to his imagination, now marched in triumphant procession through his brain, soothing and attracting and flattering his self-love.

And yet—(I really cannot explain this phenomenon, however!)—and yet, no sooner did the first flush of this delightful sunrise of future delights pass off and fade away, than the annoying thought struck him: this is all very well, but it is in the future: and now, to-day, I shall look a dreadful fool. As he reflected thus, he looked up and found that he had wandered a long way, to some of the dirty back slums of the town. A wet snow was falling; now and again he met another belated pedestrian like himself. The outer circumstances began to anger Mosgliakoff, which was a bad sign; for when things are going well with us we are always inclined to see everything in a rose-coloured light.

Paul could not help remembering that up to now he had been in the habit of cutting a dash at Mordasoff. He had enjoyed being treated at all the houses he went to in the town, as Zina's accepted lover, and to be congratulated, as he often was, upon the honour of that distinction. He was proud of being her future husband; and here he was now with notice to quit. He would be laughed at. He couldn't tell everybody about the future scene in the ball-room at St. Petersburg, and the Guadalquiver, and all that! And then a thought came out into prominence, which had been uncomfortably fidgeting about in his brain for some time: "Was it all true? *Would* it really come about as Maria Alexandrovna had predicted?"

Here it struck him that Maria Alexandrovna was an amazingly cunning woman; that, however worthy she might be of universal esteem, still she was a known scandal-monger, and lied from morning to night! that, again, she probably had some good reason for wishing him out of the place to-night. He next bethought him of Zina, and of her parting look at him, which was very far from being expressive of passionate love; he remembered also, that, less than an hour ago she had called him a fool.

As he thought of the last fact Paul stopped in his tracks, as though shot; blushed, and almost cried for very shame! At this very moment he was unfortunate enough to lose his footing on the slippery pavement, and to go head-first into a snow-heap. As he stood shaking himself dry, a whole troop of dogs, which had long trotted barking at his heels, flew at him. One of them, a wretched little half-starved beast, went so far as to fix her teeth into his fur coat and hang therefrom. Swearing and striking out, Paul cleared his way out of the yelping pack at last, in a fury, and with rent clothes; and making his way as fast as he could to the corner of the street, discovered that he hadn't the slightest idea where he was. He walked up lanes, and down streets, and round corners, and lost himself more and more hopelessly; also his temper. "The devil take all these confounded exalted ideas!" he growled, half aloud; "and the archfiend take every one of you, you and your Guadalquivers and humbug!"

Mosgliakoff was not in a pretty humour at this moment.

At last, tired and horribly angry, after two hours of walking, he reached the door of Maria Alexandrovna's house.

Observing a host of carriages standing outside, he paused to consider.

"Surely she has not a party to-night!" he thought, "and if she has, *why* has she a party?"

He inquired of the servants, and found out that Maria Alexandrovna had been out of town, and had fetched up Afanassy Matveyevitch, gorgeous in his dress-suit and white tie. He learned, further, that the prince was awake, but had not as yet made his appearance in the "salon."

On receiving this information, Paul Mosgliakoff said not a word, but quietly made his way upstairs to his uncle's room.

He was in that frame of mind in which a man determines to commit some desperate act, out of revenge, aware at the time, and wide awake to the fact that he is about to do the deed, but forgetting entirely that he may very likely regret it all his life afterwards!

Entering the prince's room, he found that worthy seated before the glass, with a perfectly bare head, but with whiskers and napoleon stuck on. His wig was in the hands of his old and grey valet, his favourite Ivan Pochomitch, and the latter was gravely and thoughtfully combing it out.

As for the prince, he was indeed a pitiable object! He was not half awake yet, for one thing; he sat as though he were still dazed with sleep; he kept opening and shutting his mouth, and stared at Mosgliakoff as though he did not know him!

"Well, how are you, uncle?" asked Mosgliakoff.

"What, it's you, is it!" said the prince. "Ye—yes; I've been as—leep a little while! Oh, heavens!" he cried suddenly, with great animation, "why, I've got no wi—ig on!"

"Oh, never mind that, uncle; I'll help you on with it, if you like!"

"Dear me; now you've found out my se—ecret! I told him to shut the door. Now, my friend, you must give me your word in—stantly, that you'll never breathe a hint of this to anyone—I mean about my hair being ar—tificial!"

"Oh, uncle! As if I could be guilty of such meanness?" cried Paul, who was anxious to please the prince, for reasons of his own.

"Ye—yes, ye—yes. Well, as I see you are a good fe—ellow, I—I'll just as—tonish you a little: I'll tell you all my secrets! How do you like my mous—tache, my dear boy?"

"Wonderful, uncle, wonderful! It astonishes me that you should have been able to keep it so long!"

"Sp—are your wonder, my friend, it's ar—tificial!"

"No!! That's difficult to believe! Well, and your whiskers, uncle! admit—you black them, now *don't* you?"

"Black them? Not—only I don't black them, but they, too, are ar—tificial!" said the Prince, regarding Mosgliakoff with a look of triumph.

"*What!* Artificial? No, no, uncle! I can't believe *that*! You're laughing at me!"

"*Parole d'honneur, mon ami!*" cried the delighted old man; "and fancy, all—everybody is taken in by them just as you were! Even Stepanida Matveyevna cannot believe they are not real, sometimes, although she often sticks them on herself! But, I am sure, my dear friend, you will keep my se—cret. Give me your word!"

"I do give you my word, uncle! But surely you do not suppose I would be so mean as to divulge it?"

"Oh, my boy! I had such a fall to-day, without you. The coachman upset me out of the carriage again!"

"How? When?"

"Why, we were driving to the mo—nastery, when?——"

"I know, uncle: that was early this morning!"

"No, no! A couple of hours ago, not more! I was driving along with him, and he suddenly took and up—set me!"

"Why, my dear uncle, you were asleep," began Paul, in amazement!

"Ye—yes, ye—yes. I did have a sleep; and then I drove away, at least I—at least I—dear me, how strange it all seems!"

"I assure you, uncle, you have been dreaming! You saw all this in a dream! You have been sleeping quietly here since just after dinner!"

"No!" And the prince reflected. "Ye—yes. Perhaps I did see it all in a dream! However, I can remember all I saw quite well. First, I saw a large bull with horns; and then I saw a pro—curor, and I think he had huge horns too. Then there was Napoleon Buonaparte. Did you ever hear, my boy, that people say I am so like Napoleon Buonaparte? But my profile is very like some old pope. What do you think about it, my bo—oy?"

"I think you are much more like Napoleon Buonaparte, uncle!"

"Why, ye—yes, of course—full face; so I am, my boy, so I am! I dreamt of him on his is—land, and do you know he was such a merry, talk—ative fellow, he quite am—used me!"

"Who, uncle—Napoleon?" asked Mosgliakoff, looking thoughtfully at the old man. A strange idea was beginning to occupy his brain—an idea which he could not quite put into shape as yet.

"Ye—yes, ye—yes, Nap—oleon. We talked about philosophical subjects. And do you know, my boy, I became quite sorry that the English had been so hard upon him. Of course, though, if one didn't chain him up, he would be flying at people's throats again! Still I'm sorry for him. Now I should have managed him quite differently. I should have put him on an uninhabited island."

"Why uninhabited, uncle?" asked Mosgliakoff, absently.

"Well, well, an inhabited one, then; but the in—habitants must be good sort of people. And I should arrange all sorts of amusements for him, at the State's charge: theatres, balle's, and so on. And, of course, he should walk about, under proper su—pervision. Then he should have tarts (he liked tarts, you know), as many tarts as ever he pleased. I should treat him like a fa—ather; and he would end by being sorry for his sins, see if he wouldn't!"

Mosgliakoff listened absently to all this senile gabble, and bit his nails with impatience. He was anxious to turn the conversation on to the subject of marriage. He did not know quite clearly why he wished to do so, but his heart was boiling over with anger.

Suddenly the old man made an exclamation of surprise.

"Why, my dear boy, I declare I've forgotten to tell you about it. Fancy, I made an offer of marriage to-day!"

"An offer of marriage, uncle?" cried Paul, brightening up.

"Why, ye—yes! an offer. Pachomief, are you going? All right! Away with you! Ye—yes, *c'est une charmante personne*. But I confess, I took the step rather rash—ly. I only begin to see that now. Dear me! dear, dear me!"

"Excuse me, uncle; but *when* did you make this offer?"

"Well, I admit I don't know exactly *when* I made it! Perhaps I dre—dreamed it; I don't know. Dear me, how very strange it all seems!"

Mosgliakoff trembled with joy: his new idea blazed forth in full developed glory.

"And *whom* did you propose to?" he asked impatiently.

"The daughter of the house, my boy; that beau—tiful girl. I—I forget what they call her. Bu—but, my dear boy, you see I—I can't possibly marry. What am I to do?"

"Oh! of course, you are done for if you marry, that's clear. But let me ask you one more question, uncle. Are you perfectly certain that you actually made her an offer of marriage?"

"Ye—yes, I'm sure of it; I—I——."

"And what if you dreamed the whole thing, just as you did that you were upset out of the carriage a second time?"

"Dear me! dear me! I—I really think I may have dreamed it; it's very awkward. I don't know how to show myself there, now. H—how could I find out, dear boy, for certain? Couldn't I get to know by some outside way whether I really did make her an offer of ma—arriage or not? Why, just you think of my dreadful po—sition!"

"Do you know, uncle, I don't think we need trouble ourselves to find out at all."

"Why, wh—what then?"

"I am convinced that you were dreaming."

"I—I think so myself, too, my dear fellow; es—pecially as I often have that sort of dream."

"You see, uncle, you had a drop of wine for lunch, and then another drop or two for dinner, don't you know; and so you may easily have——"

"Ye—yes, quite so, quite so; it may easily have been that."

"Besides, my dear uncle, however excited you may have been, you would never have taken such a senseless step in your waking moments. So far as I know you, uncle, you are a man of the highest and most deliberate judgment, and I am positive that——"

"Ye—yes, ye—yes."

"Why, only imagine—if your relations were to get to hear of such a thing. My goodness, uncle! they were cruel enough to you before. What do you suppose they would do *now*, eh?"

"Goodness gracious!" cried the frightened old prince. "Good—ness gracious! Wh—why, what would they do, do you think?"

"Do? Why, of course, they would all screech out that you had acted under the influence of insanity: in fact, that you were mad; that you had been swindled, and that you must be put under proper restraint. In fact, they'd pop you into some lunatic asylum."

Mosgliakoff was well aware of the best method of frightening the poor old man out of his wits.

"Gracious heavens!" cried the latter, trembling like a leaflet with horror. "Gra—cious heavens! would they really do that?"

"Undoubtedly; and, knowing this, uncle, think for yourself. Could you possibly have done such a thing with your eyes open? As if you don't understand what's good for you just as well as your neighbours. I solemnly affirm that you saw all this in a dream!"

"Of course, of course; un—doubtedly in a dream, un—doubtedly so! What a clever fellow you are, my dear boy; you saw it at once. I am deeply grate—ful to you for putting me right. I was really quite under the im—pression I had actually done it."

"And how glad I am that I met you, uncle, before you went in there! Just fancy, what a mess you might have made of it! You might have gone in thinking you were engaged to the girl, and behaved in the capacity of accepted lover. Think how fearfully dangerous——."

"Ye—yes, of course; most dangerous!"

"Why, remember, this girl is twenty-three years old. Nobody will marry her, and suddenly *you*, a rich and eminent man of rank and title, appear on the scene as her accepted swain. They would lay hold of the idea at once, and act up to it, and swear that you really were her future husband, and would marry you off, too. I daresay they would even count upon your speedy death, and make their calculations accordingly."

"No!"

"Then again, uncle; a man of your dignity——"

"Ye—yes, quite so, dig—nity!"

"And wisdom,—and amiability——"

"Quite so; wis—dom—wisdom!"

"And then—a prince into the bargain! Good gracious, uncle, as if a man like yourself would make such a match as *that*, if you really did mean marrying! What would your relations say?"

"Why, my dear boy, they'd simply ea—eat me up,—I—I know their cunning and malice of old! My dear fellow—you won't believe it—but I assure you I was afraid they were going to put me into a lun—atic asylum! a common ma—ad-house! Goodness me, think of that! Whatever should I have done with myself all day in a ma—ad-house?"

"Of course, of course! Well, I won't leave your side, then, uncle, when you go downstairs. There are guests there too!"

"Guests? dear me! I—I——"

"Don't be afraid, uncle; I shall be by you!"

"I—I'm *so* much obliged to you, my dear boy; you have simply sa—ved me, you have indeed! But, do you know what,—I think I'd better go away altogether!"

"To-morrow, uncle! to-morrow morning at seven! and this evening you must be sure to say, in the presence of everybody, that you are starting away at seven next morning: you must say good-bye to-night!"

"Un—doubtedly, undoubtedly—I shall go;—but what if they talk to me as though I were engaged to the young wo—oman?"

"Don't you fear, uncle! I shall be there! And mind, whatever they say or hint to you, you must declare that you dreamed the whole thing—as indeed you did, of course?"

"Ye—yes, quite so, un—doubtedly so! But, do you know my dear boy, it was a most be—witching dream, for all that! She is a wond—erfully lovely girl, my boy,—such a figure—bewitching—be—witching!"

"Well, *au revoir*, uncle! I'm going down, now, and you——"

"How! How! you are not going to leave me alone?" cried the old man, greatly alarmed.

"No, no—oh no, uncle; but we must enter the room separately. First, I will go in, and then you come down; that will be better!"

"Very well, very well. Besides, I just want to note down one little i—dea——"

"Capital, uncle! jot it down, and then come at once; don't wait any longer; and to-morrow morning——"

"And to-morrow morning away we go to the Her—mitage, straight to the Her—mitage! Charming—charm—ing! but, do you know, my boy,—she's a fas—cinating girl—she is indeed! be—witching! Such a bust! and, really, if I were to marry, I—I—really——"

"No, no, uncle! Heaven forbid!"

"Yes—yes—quite so—Heaven for—bid!—well, *au revoir*, my friend—I'll come directly; by the bye—I meant to ask you, have you read Kazanoff's Memoirs?"

"Yes, uncle. Why?"

"Yes, yes, quite so—I forget what I wanted to say——"

"You'll remember afterwards, uncle! *au revoir!*"

"*Au revoir*, my boy, *au revoir*—but, I say, it was a bewitching dream, a most be—witching dream!"

CHAPTER XII.

"Here we all are, all of us, come to spend the evening; Proskovia Ilinishna is coming too, and Luisa Karlovna and all!" cried Mrs. Antipova as she entered the salon, and looked hungrily round. She was a neat, pretty little woman! she was well-dressed, and knew it.

She looked greedily around, as I say, because she had an idea that the prince and Zina were hidden together somewhere about the room.

"Yes, and Katerina Petrovna, and Felisata Michaelovna are coming as well," added Natalia Dimitrievna, a huge woman—whose figure had pleased the prince so much, and who looked more like a grenadier than anything else. This monster had been hand and glove with little Mrs. Antipova for the last three weeks; they were now quite inseparable. Natalia looked as though she could pick her little friend up and swallow her, bones and all, without thinking.

"I need not say with what *rapture* I welcome you both to my house, and for a whole evening, too!" piped Maria Alexandrovna, a little recovered from her first shock of amazement; "but do tell me, what miracle is it that has brought you all to-day, when I had quite despaired of ever seeing anyone of you in my house again?"

"Oh, oh! my *dear* Maria Alexandrovna!" said Natalia, very affectedly, but sweetly. The attributes of sweetness and affectation were a curious contrast to her personal appearance.

"You see, dearest Maria Alexandrovna," chirped Mrs. Antipova, "we really must get on with the private theatricals question! It was only this very day that Peter Michaelovitch was saying how *bad* it was of us to have made no progress towards rehearsing, and so on; and that it was quite time we brought all our silly squabbles to an end! Well, four of us got together to-day, and then it struck us 'Let's all go to Maria Alexandrovna's, and settle the matter once for all!' So Natalia Dimitrievna let all the rest know that we were to meet here! We'll soon settle it—I don't think we should allow it to be said that we do nothing but 'squabble' over the preliminaries and get no farther, do *you*, dear Maria Alexandrovna?" She added, playfully, and kissing our heroine affectionately, "Goodness me, Zenaida, I declare you grow prettier every day!" And she betook herself to embracing Zina with equal affection.

"She has nothing else to do, but sit and grow more and more beautiful!" said Natalia with great sweetness, rubbing her huge hands together.

"Oh, the devil take them all! they know I care nothing about private theatricals—cursed magpies!" reflected Maria Alexandrovna, beside herself with rage.

"Especially, dear, as that delightful prince is with you just now. You know there is a private theatre in his house at Donchanof, and we have discovered that somewhere or other there, there are a lot of old theatrical properties and decorations and scenery. The prince was at my house to-day, but I was so surprised to see him that it all went clean out of my head and I forgot to ask him. Now we'll broach the subject before him. You must support me and we'll persuade him to send us all the old rubbish that can be found. We want to get the prince to come and see the play, too! He is sure to subscribe, isn't he—as it is for the poor? Perhaps he would even take a part; he is such a dear, kind, willing old man. If only he did, it would make the fortune of our play!"

"Of course he will take a part! why, he can be made to play *any* part!" remarked Natalia significantly.

Mrs. Antipova had not exaggerated. Guests poured in every moment! Maria Alexandrovna hardly had time to receive one lot and make the usual exclamations of surprise and delight exacted by the laws of etiquette before another arrival would be announced.

I will not undertake to describe all these good people. I will only remark that every one of them, on arrival, looked about her cunningly; and that every face wore an expression of expectation and impatience.

Some of them came with the distinct intention of witnessing some scene of a delightfully scandalous nature, and were prepared to be very angry indeed if it should turn out that they were obliged to leave the house without the gratification of their hopes.

All behaved in the most amiable and affectionate manner towards their hostess; but Maria Alexandrovna firmly braced her nerves for battle.

Many apparently natural and innocent questions were asked about the prince; but in each one might be detected some hint or insinuation.

Tea came in, and people moved about and changed places: one group surrounded the piano; Zina was requested to play and sing, but answered drily that she was not quite well—and the paleness of her face bore out this assertion. Inquiries were made for Mosgliakoff; and these inquiries were addressed to Zina.

Maria Alexandrovna proved that she had the eyes and ears of ten ordinary mortals. She saw and heard all that was going on in every corner of the room; she heard and answered every question asked, and answered readily and cleverly. She was dreadfully anxious about Zina, however, and wondered why she did not leave the room, as she usually did on such occasions.

Poor Afanassy came in for his share of notice, too. It was the custom of these amiable people of Mordasoff to do their best to set Maria Alexandrovna and her husband "by the ears;" but to-day there were hopes of extracting valuable news and secrets out of the candid simplicity of the latter.

Maria Alexandrovna watched the state of siege into which the wretched Afanassy was thrown, with great anxiety; he was answering "H'm!" to all questions put to him, as instructed; but with so wretched an expression and so extremely artificial a mien that Maria Alexandrovna could barely restrain her wrath.

"Maria Alexandrovna! your husband won't have a word to say to me!" remarked a sharp-faced little lady with a devil-may-care manner, as though she cared nothing for anybody, and was not to be abashed under any circumstances. "Do ask him to be a *little* more courteous towards ladies!"

"I really don't know myself what can have happened to him to-day!" said Maria Alexandrovna, interrupting her conversation with Mrs. Antipova and Natalia, and laughing merrily; "he is so *dreadfully* uncommunicative! He has scarcely said a word even to *me*, all day! Why don't you answer Felisata Michaelovna, Afanassy? What did you ask him?"

"But, but—why, mammy, you told me yourself"—began the bewildered and lost Afanassy. At this moment he was standing at the fireside with one hand placed inside his waistcoat, in an artistic position which he had chosen deliberately, on mature reflection,—and he was sipping his tea. The questions of the ladies had so confused him that he was blushing like a girl.

When he began the justification of himself recorded above, he suddenly met so dreadful a look in the eyes of his infuriated spouse that he nearly lost all consciousness, for terror!

Uncertain what to do, but anxious to recover himself and win back her favour once more, he said nothing, but took a gulp of tea to restore his scattered senses.

Unfortunately the tea was too hot; which fact, together with the hugeness of the gulp he took—quite upset him. He burned his throat, choked, sent the cup flying, and burst into such a fit of coughing that he was obliged to leave the room for a time, awakening universal astonishment by his conduct.

In a word, Maria Alexandrovna saw clearly enough that her guests knew all about it, and had assembled with malicious intent! The situation was dangerous! They were quite capable of confusing and overwhelming the feeble-minded old prince before her very eyes! They might even carry him off bodily—after stirring up a quarrel between the old man and herself! *Anything* might happen.

But fate had prepared her one more surprise. The door opened and in came Mosgliakoff—who, as she thought, was far enough away at his godfather's, and would not come near her to-night! She shuddered as though something had hurt her.

Mosgliakoff stood a moment at the door, looking around at the company. He was a little bewildered, and could not conceal his agitation, which showed itself very clearly in his expression.

"Why, it's Paul Alexandrovitch! and you told us he had gone to his godfather's, Maria Alexandrovna. We were told you had hidden yourself away from us, Paul Alexandrovitch!" cried Natalia.

"Hidden myself?" said Paul, with a crooked sort of a smile. "What a strange expression! Excuse me, Natalia Dimitrievna, but I never hide from anyone; I have no cause to do so, that I know of! Nor do I ever hide anyone else!" he added, looking significantly at Maria Alexandrovna.

Maria Alexandrovna trembled in her shoes.

"Surely this fool of a man is not up to anything disagreeable!" she thought. "No, no! that would be worse than anything!" She looked curiously and anxiously into his eyes.

"Is it true, Paul Alexandrovitch, that you have just been politely dismissed?—the Government service, I mean, of course!" remarked the daring Felisata Michaelovna, looking impertinently into his eyes.

"Dismissed! How dismissed? I'm simply changing my department, that's all! I am to be placed at Petersburg!" Mosgliakoff answered, drily.

"Oh! well, I congratulate you!" continued the bold young woman. "We were alarmed to hear that you were trying for a—a place down here at Mordasoff. The berths here are wretched, Paul Alexandrovitch—no good at all, I assure you!"

"I don't know—there's a place as teacher at the school, vacant, I believe," remarked Natalia.

This was such a crude and palpable insinuation that even Mrs. Antipova was ashamed of her friend, and kicked her, under the table.

"You don't suppose Paul Alexandrovitch would accept the place vacated by a wretched little schoolmaster!"said Felisata Michaelovna.

But Paul did not answer. He turned at this moment, and encountered Afanassy Matveyevitch, just returning into the room. The latter offered him his hand. Mosgliakoff, like a fool, looked beyond poor Afanassy, and did not take his outstretched hand: annoyed to the limits of endurance, he stepped up to Zina, and muttered, gazing angrily into her eyes:

"This is all thanks to you! Wait a bit; you shall see this very day whether I am a fool or not!"

"Why put off the revelation? It is clear enough already!" said Zina, aloud, staring contemptuously at her former lover.

Mosgliakoff hurriedly left her. He did not half like the loud tone she spoke in.

"Have you been to your godfather's?" asked Maria Alexandrovna at last, determined to sound matters in this direction.

"No, I've just been with uncle."

"With your uncle! What! have you just come from the prince now?"

"Oh—oh! and we were told the prince was asleep!" added Natalia Dimitrievna, looking daggers at Maria Alexandrovna.

"Do not be disturbed about the prince, Natalia Dimitrievna," replied Paul, "he is awake now, and quite restored to his senses. He was persuaded to drink a good deal too much wine, first at your house, and then here; so that he quite lost his head, which never was too strong. However, I have had a talk with him, and he now seems to have entirely recovered his judgment, thank God! He is coming down directly to take his leave, Maria Alexandrovna, and to thank you for all your kind hospitality; and to-morrow morning early we are off to the Hermitage. Thence I shall myself see him safe home to Donchanovo, in order that he may be far from the temptation to further excesses like that of to-day. There I shall give him over into the hands of Stepanida Matveyevna, who must be back at home by this time, and who will assuredly never allow him another opportunity of going on his travels, I'll answer for that!"

So saying, Mosgliakoff stared angrily at Maria Alexandrovna. The latter sat still, apparently dumb with amazement. I regret to say—it gives me great pain to record it—that, perhaps for the first time in her life, my heroine was decidedly alarmed.

"So the prince is off to-morrow morning! Dear me; why is that?" inquired Natalia Dimitrievna, very sweetly, of Maria Alexandrovna.

"Yes. How is that?" asked Mrs. Antipova, in astonishment.

"Yes; dear me! how comes that, I wonder!" said two or three voices. "How can that be? When we were told— dear me! How very strange!"

But the mistress of the house could not find words to reply in.

However, at this moment the general attention was distracted by a most unwonted and eccentric episode. In the next room was heard a strange noise—sharp exclamations and hurrying feet, which was followed by the sudden appearance of Sophia Petrovna, the fidgety guest who had called upon Maria Alexandrovna in the morning.

Sophia Petrovna was a very eccentric woman indeed—so much so that even the good people of Mordasoff could not support her, and had lately voted her out of society. I must observe that every evening, punctually at seven, this lady was in the habit of having, what she called, "a snack," and that after this snack, which she declared was for the benefit of her liver, her condition was well *emancipated*, to use no stronger term. She was in this very condition, as described, now, as she appeared flinging herself into Maria Alexandrovna's salon.

"Oho! so this is how you treat me, Maria Alexandrovna!" she shouted at the top of her voice. "Oh! don't be afraid, I shall not inflict myself upon you for more than a minute! I won't sit down. I just came in to see if what they said was true! Ah! so you go in for balls and receptions and parties, and Sophia Petrovna is to sit at home alone, and knit stockings, is she? You ask the whole town in, and leave me out, do you? Yes, and I was *mon ange*, and 'dear,' and all the rest of it when I came in to warn you of Natalia Dimitrievna having got hold of the prince! And now this very Natalia Dimitrievna, whom you swore at like a pickpocket, and who was just about as polite when she spoke of you, is here among your guests? Oh, don't mind *me*, Natalia Dimitrievna, *I* don't want your *chocolat à la santé* at a penny the ounce, six cups to the ounce! thanks, I can do better at home; t'fu, a good deal better."

"Evidently!" observed Natalia Dimitrievna.

"But—goodness gracious, Sophia Petrovna!" cried the hostess, flushing with annoyance; "what is it all about? Do show a little common sense!"

"Oh, don't bother about me, Maria Alexandrovna, thank you! I know all about it—oh, dear me, yes!—*I* know all about it!" cried Sophia Petrovna, in her shrill squeaky voice, from among the crowd of guests who now surrounded her, and who seemed to derive immense satisfaction from this unexpected scene. "Oh, yes, I know all about it, I assure you! Your friend Nastasia came over and told me all! You got hold of the old prince, made him drunk and persuaded him to make an offer of marriage to your daughter Zina—whom nobody else will marry; and I daresay you suppose you are going to be a very great lady, indeed—a sort of duchess in lace and jewellery. Tfu! Don't flatter yourself; you may not be aware that I, too, am a colonel's lady! and if you don't care to ask me to your betrothal parties, you needn't: I scorn and despise you and your parties too! I've seen honester women than you, you know! I have dined at Countess Zalichvatsky's; a chief commissioner proposed for my hand! A lot *I* care for your invitations. Tfu!"

"Look here, Sophia Petrovna," said Maria Alexandrovna, beside herself with rage; "I assure you that people do not indulge in this sort of sally at respectable houses; especially in *the condition you are now in*! And let me tell you that if you do not immediately relieve me of your presence and eloquence, I shall be obliged to take the matter into my own hands!"

"Oh, I know—you'll get your people to turn me out! Don't trouble yourself—I know the way out! Good-bye,—marry your daughter to whom you please, for all I care. And as for *you*, Natalia Dimitrievna, I will thank you not to laugh at me! I may not have been asked here, but at all events *I* did not dance a can-can for the prince's benefit. What may *you* be laughing at, Mrs. Antipova? I suppose you haven't heard that your *great friend* Lushiloff has broken his leg?—he has just been taken home. Tfu! Good-bye, Maria Alexandrovna—good luck to you! Tfu!"

Sophia Petrovna now disappeared. All the guests laughed; Maria Alexandrovna was in a state of indescribable fury.

"I think the good lady must have been drinking!" said Natalia Dimitrievna, sweetly.

"But what audacity!"

"*Quelle abominable femme!*"

"What a raving lunatic!"

"But really, what excessively improper things she says!"

"Yes, but what *could* she have meant by a 'betrothal party?' What sort of a betrothal party is this?" asked Felisata Michaelovna innocently.

"It is too bad—too bad!" Maria Alexandrovna burst out at last. "It is just such abominable women as this that sow nonsensical rumours about! it is not the fact that there *are* such women about, Felisata Michaelovna, that is so surprising; the astonishing part of the matter is that ladies can be found who support and encourage them, and believe their abominable tales, and——"

"The prince, the prince!" cried all the guests at once.

"Oh, oh, here he is—the dear, dear prince!"

"Well, thank goodness, we shall hear all the particulars now!" murmured Felisata Michaelovna to her neighbour.

CHAPTER XIII.

The prince entered and smiled benignly around.

All the agitation which his conversation with Mosgliakoff, a quarter of an hour since, had aroused in his chicken-heart vanished at the sight of the ladies.

Those gentle creatures received him with chirps and exclamations of joy. Ladies always petted our old friend the prince, and were—as a rule—wonderfully familiar with him. He had a way of amusing them with his own individuality which was astonishing! Only this morning Felisata Michaelovna had announced that she would sit on his knee with the greatest pleasure, if he liked; "because he was such a dear old pet of an old man!"

Maria Alexandrovna fastened her eyes on him, to read—if she could—if it were but the slightest indication of his state of mind, and to get a possible idea for a way out of this horribly critical position. But there was nothing to be made of *his* face; it was just as before—just as ever it was!

"Ah—h! here's the prince at last!" cried several voices. "Oh, Prince, how we have waited and waited for you!"

"With impatience, Prince, with impatience!" another chorus took up the strain.

"Dear me, how very flat—tering!" said the old man, settling himself near the tea-table.

The ladies immediately surrounded him. There only remained Natalia Dimitrievna and Mrs. Antipova with the hostess. Afanassy stood and smiled with great courtesy.

Mosgliakoff also smiled as he gazed defiantly at Zina, who, without taking the slightest notice of him, took a chair near her father, and sat down at the fireside.

"Prince, do tell us—is it true that you are about to leave us so soon?" asked Felisata Michaelovna.

"Yes, yes, *mesdames*; I am going abroad almost im—mediately!"

"Abroad, Prince, abroad? Why, what can have caused you to take such a step as that?" cried several ladies at once.

"Yes—yes, abroad," said the prince; "and do you know it is principally for the sake of the new i—deas——"

"How, new ideas? what new ideas—what does he mean?" the astonished ladies asked of one another.

"Ye—yes. Quite so—new ideas!" repeated the prince with an air of deep conviction, "everybody goes abroad now for new ideas, and I'm going too, to see if I can pick any up."

Up to this moment Maria Alexandrovna had listened to the conversation observantly; but it now struck her that the prince had entirely forgotten her existence—which would not do!

"Allow me, Prince, to introduce my husband, Afanassy Matveyevitch. He hastened up from our country seat so soon as ever he heard of your arrival in our house."

Afanassy, under the impression that he was being praised, smiled amiably and beamed all over.

"Very happy, very happy—Afanassy Mat—veyevitch!" said the prince. "Wait a moment: your name reminds me of something, Afanassy Mat—veyevitch; ye—yes, you are the man down at the village! Charming, charm—ing! Very glad, I'm sure. Do you remember, my boy," (to Paul) "the nice little rhyme we fitted out to him? What was it?"

"Oh, I know, prince," said Felisata Michaelovna—

" 'When the husband's away
The wife will play!'

"Wasn't that it? We had it last year at the theatre."

"Yes, yes, quite so, ye—yes, 'the wife will play!' That's it: charming, charming. So you are that ve—ry man? Dear me, I'm *very* glad, I'm sure," said the prince, stretching out his hand, but not rising from his chair. "Dear me, and how is your health, my dear sir?"

"H'm!"

"Oh, he's quite well, thank you, prince, *quite* well," answered Maria Alexandrovna quickly.

"Ye—yes, I see he is—he looks it! And are you still at the vill—age? Dear me, very pleased, I'm sure; why, how red he looks, and he's always laugh—ing."

Afanassy smiled and bowed, and even "scraped," as the prince spoke, but at the last observation he suddenly, and without warning or apparent reason, burst into loud fits of laughter.

The ladies were delighted. Zina flushed up, and with flashing eyes darted a look at her mother, who, in her turn, was boiling over with rage.

It was time to change the conversation.

"Did you have a nice nap, prince?" she inquired in honied accents; but at the same time giving Afanassy to understand, with very un-honied looks that he might go—well, anywhere!

"Oh, I slept won—derfully, wonderfully? And do you know, I had such a most fascinating, be—witching dream!"

"A dream? how delightful! I do so love to hear people tell their dreams," cried Felisata.

"Oh, a fas—cinating dream," stammered the old man again, "quite be—witching, but all the more a dead secret for that very reas—on."

"Oh, Prince, you don't mean to say you can't tell us?" said Mrs. Antipova. "I suppose it's an *extraordinary* dream, isn't it?"

"A dead secret!" repeated the prince, purposely whetting the curiosity of the ladies, and enjoying the fun.

"Then it *must* be interesting, oh, *dreadfully* interesting," cried other ladies.

"I don't mind taking a bet that the prince dreamed that he was kneeling at some lovely woman's feet and making a declaration of love," said Felisata Michaelovna. "Confess, now, prince, that it was so? confess, dear prince, confess."

"Yes, Prince, confess!" the chorus took up the cry. The old man listened solemnly until the last voice was hushed. The ladies' guesswork flattered his vanity wonderfully; he was as pleased as he could be. "Though I did say that my dream was a dead se—cret," he replied at last, "still I am obliged to confess, dear lady, that to my great as—tonishment you have almost exactly guessed it."

"I've guessed it, I've guessed it," cried Felisata, in a rapture of joy. "Well, prince, say what you like, but it's your *plain* duty to tell us the name of your beauty; come now, *isn't* it?"

"Of course, of course, prince."

"Is she in this town?"

"Dear prince, *do* tell us."

"*Darling* prince, do, *do* tell us; you positively *must*," was heard on all sides.

"*Mesdames, mes—dames*; if you must know, I will go so far as to say that it is the most charming, and be—witching, and vir—tuous lady I know," said the prince, unctuously.

"The most bewitching? and belonging to this place? Who *can* it be?" cried the ladies, interchanging looks and signs.

"Why, of course, the young lady who is considered the reigning beauty here," remarked Natalia Dimitrievna, rubbing her hands and looking hard at Zina with those cat's-eyes of hers. All joined her in staring at Zina.

"But, prince, if you dream those sort of things, why should not you marry somebody *bona fide*?" asked Felisata, looking around her with a significant expression.

"We would marry you off beautifully, prince!" said somebody else.

"Oh, dear prince, *do* marry!" chirped another.

"Marry, marry, *do* marry!" was now the cry on all sides.

"Ye—yes. Why should I not ma—arry!" said the old man, confused and bewildered with all the cries and exclamations around him.

"Uncle!" cried Mosgliakoff.

"Ye—yes, my boy, quite so; I un—derstand what you mean. I may as well tell you, ladies, that I am not in a position to marry again; and having passed one most delightful evening with our fascinating hostess, I must start away to-morrow to the Hermitage, and then I shall go straight off abroad, and study the question of the enlightenment of Europe."

Zina shuddered, and looked over at her mother with an expression of unspeakable anguish.

But Maria Alexandrovna had now made up her mind how to act; all this while she had played a mere waiting game, observing closely and carefully all that was said or done, although she could see only too clearly that her plans were undermined, and that her foes had come about her in numbers which were too great to be altogether pleasant.

At last, however, she comprehended the situation, she thought, completely. She had gauged how the matter stood in all its branches, and she determined to slay the hundred-headed hydra at one fell blow!

With great majesty, then, she rose from her seat, and approached the tea-table, stalking across the room with firm and dignified tread, as she looked around upon her pigmy foes. The fire of inspiration blazed in her eyes. She resolved to smite once, and annihilate this vile nest of poisonous scandal-adders: to destroy the miserable Mosgliakoff, as though he were a blackbeetle, and with one triumphant blow to reassert all her influence over this miserable old idiot-prince!

Some audacity was requisite for such a performance, of course; but Maria Alexandrovna had not even to put her hand in her pocket for a supply of that particular commodity.

"*Mesdames*," she began, solemnly, and with much dignity (Maria Alexandrovna was always a great admirer of solemnity); "*mesdames*, I have been a listener to your conversation—to your witty remarks and merry jokes—long enough, and I consider that my turn has come, at last, to put in a word in contribution.

"You are aware we have all met here accidentally (to my great joy, I must add—to my very great joy); but, though I should be the first to refuse to divulge a family secret before the strictest rules of ordinary propriety rendered such a revelation necessary, yet, as my dear guest here appears to me to have given us to understand, by covert hints and insinuations, that he is not averse to the matter becoming common property (he will forgive me if I have mistaken his intentions!)—I cannot help feeling that the prince is not only not averse, but actually desires me to make known our great family secret. Am I right, Prince?"

"Ye—yes, quite so, quite so! Very glad, ve—ry glad, I'm sure!" said the prince, who had not the remotest idea what the good lady was talking about!

Maria Alexandrovna, for greater effect, now paused to take breath, and looked solemnly and proudly around upon the assembled guests, all of whom were now listening with greedy but slightly disturbed curiosity to what their hostess was about to reveal to them.

Mosgliakoff shuddered; Zina flushed up, and arose from her seat; Afanassy, seeing that something important was about to happen, blew his nose violently, in order to be ready for any emergency.

"Yes, ladies; I am ready—nay, gratified—to entrust my family secret to your keeping!——This evening, the prince, overcome by the beauty and virtues of my daughter, has done her the honour of proposing to me for her hand. Prince," she concluded, in trembling tearful accents, "dear Prince; you must not, you cannot blame me for my candour! It is only my overwhelming joy that could have torn this dear secret prematurely from my heart: and what mother is there who will blame me in such a case as this?"

Words fail me to describe the effect produced by this most unexpected sally on the part of Maria Alexandrovna. All present appeared to be struck dumb with amazement. These perfidious guests, who had thought to frighten

Maria Alexandrovna by showing her that they knew her secret; who thought to annihilate her by the premature revelation of that secret; who thought to overwhelm her, for the present, with their hints and insinuations; these guests were themselves struck down and pulverized by this fearless candour on her part! Such audacious frankness argued the consciousness of strength.

"So that the prince actually, and of his own free-will is really going to marry Zina? So they did not drink and bully and swindle him into it? So he is not to be married burglariously and forcibly? So Maria Alexandrovna is not afraid of anybody? Then we can't knock this marriage on the head—since the prince is not being married compulsorily!"

Such were the questions and exclamations the visitors now put to themselves and each other.

But very soon the whispers which the hostess's words had awakened all over the room, suddenly changed to chirps and exclamations of joy.

Natalia Dimitrievna was the first to come forward and embrace Maria Alexandrovna; then came Mrs. Antipova; next Felisata Michaelovna. All present were shortly on their feet and moving about, changing places. Many of the ladies were pale with rage. Some began to congratulate Zina, who was confused enough without; some attached themselves to the wretched Afanassy Matveyevitch. Maria Alexandrovna stretched her arms theatrically, and embraced her daughter—almost by force.

The prince alone gazed upon the company with a sort of confused wonder; but he smiled on as before. He seemed to be pleased with the scene. At sight of the mother and daughter embracing, he took out his handkerchief, and wiped his eye, in the corner of which there really was a tear.

Of course the company fell upon him with their congratulations before very long.

"I congratulate you, Prince! I congratulate you!" came from all sides at once.

"So you *are* going to be married, Prince?"

"So you *really are* going to marry?"

"Dear Prince! You really are to be married, then?"

"Ye—yes, ye—yes; quite so, quite so!" replied the old fellow, delighted beyond measure with all the rapture and atmosphere of congratulation around him; "and I confess what I like best of all, is the ve—ery kind in—terest you all take in me! I shall never forget it, never for—get it! Charming! charming! You have brought the tears to my eyes!"

"Kiss me, prince!" cried Felisata Michaelovna, in stentorian tones.

"And I con—fess further," continued the Prince, as well as the constant physical interruptions from all sides allowed him; "I confess I am beyond measure as—tonished that Maria Alexandrovna, our revered hostess, should have had the extraordinary penet—ration to guess my dream! She might have dreamed it herself, instead of me. Ex—traordinary perspicacity! Won—derful, wonderful!"

"Oh, prince; your dream again!"

"Oh, come, prince! admit—confess!" cried one and all.

"Yes, prince, it is no use concealing it now; it is time we divulged this secret of ours!" said Maria Alexandrovna, severely and decidedly. "I quite entered into your refined, allegorical manner; the delightful delicacy with which you gave me to understand, by means of subtle insinuations, that you wished the fact of your engagement to be made known. Yes, ladies, it is all true! This very evening the prince knelt at my daughter's feet, and actually, and by no means in a dream, made a solemn proposal of marriage to her!"

"Yes—yes, quite so! just exactly like that; and under the very cir—cumstances she describes: just like re—ality," said the old man. "My dear young lady," he continued, bowing with his greatest courtesy to Zina, who had by no means recovered from her amazement as yet; "my dear young lady, I swear to you, I should never have dared thus to bring your name into pro—minence, if others had not done so before me! It was a most be—witching dream! a be—witching dream! and I am doubly happy that I have been per—mitted to describe it. Charming—charming!"

"Dear me! how very curious it is: he insists on sticking to his idea about a dream!" whispered Mrs. Antipova to the now slightly paling Maria Alexandrovna. Alas! that great woman had felt her heart beating more quickly than she liked without this last little reminder!

"What does it mean?" whispered the ladies among themselves.

"Excuse me, prince," began Maria Alexandrovna, with a miserable attempt at a smile, "but I confess you astonish me a great deal! What is this strange idea of yours about a dream? I confess I had thought you were joking up to this moment; but—if it be a joke on your part, it is exceedingly out of place! I should like—I am*anxious* to ascribe your conduct to absence of mind, but——"

"Yes; it may really be a case of absence of mind!" put in Natalia Dimitrievna in a whisper.

"Yes—yes—of course, quite so; it may easily be absence of mind!" confirmed the prince, who clearly did not in the least comprehend what they were trying to get out of him; "and with regard to this subject, let me tell you a little an—ecdote. I was asked to a funeral at Petersburg, and I went and made a little mis—take about it and thought it was a birthday par—ty! So I brought a lovely bouquet of cam—ellias! When I came in and saw the master of the house lying in state on a table, I didn't know where to lo—ok, or what to do with my ca—mellias, I assure you!"

"Yes; but, Prince, this is not the moment for stories!" observed Maria Alexandrovna, with great annoyance."Of course, my daughter has no need to beat up a husband; but at the same time, I must repeat that you yourself here, just by the piano, made her an offer of marriage. *I* did not ask you to do it! I may say I was amazed to hear it! However, since the episode of your proposal, I may say that I have thought of nothing else; and I have only waited for your appearance to talk the matter over with you. But now—well, I am a mother, and this is my daughter. You speak of a dream. I supposed, naturally, that you were anxious to make your engagement known by the medium of an allegory. Well, I am perfectly well aware that someone may have thought fit to confuse your mind on this matter; in fact, I may say that I have my suspicions as to the individual responsible for such a——however, kindly explain yourself, Prince; explain yourself quickly and satisfactorily. You cannot be permitted to jest in this fashion in a respectable house."

"Ye—yes—quite so, quite so; one should not jest in respectable houses," remarked the prince, still bewildered, but beginning gradually to grow a little disconcerted.

"But that is no answer to my question, Prince. I ask you to reply categorically. I insist upon your confirming—confirming here and at once—the fact that this very evening you made a proposal of marriage to my daughter!"

"Quite so—quite so; I am ready to confirm that! But I have told the com—pany all about it, and Felisata Michaelovna ac—tually guessed my dream!"

"*Not dream!* it was *not* a dream!" shouted Maria Alexandrovna furiously. "It was not a dream, Prince, but you were wide awake. Do you hear? Awake—you were *awake*!"

"Awake?" cried the prince, rising from his chair in astonishment. "Well, there you are, my friend; it has come about just as you said," he added, turning to Mosgliakoff. "But I assure you, most es—teemed Maria Alexandrovna, that you are under a del—usion. I am quite convinced that I saw the whole scene in a dream!"

"Goodness gracious!" cried Maria Alexandrovna.

"Do not disturb yourself, dear Maria Alexandrovna," said Natalia Dimitrievna, "probably the prince has forgotten; he will recollect himself by and by."

"I am astonished at you, Natalia Dimitrievna!" said the now furious hostess. "As if people forget this sort of thing! Excuse me, Prince, but are you laughing at us, or what are you doing? Are you trying to act one of Dumas' heroes, or Lauzun or Ferlacourt, or somebody? But, if you will excuse me saying so, you are a good deal too old for that sort of thing, and I assure you, your amiable little play-acting will not do here! My daughter is not a French viscountess! I tell you, this very evening and in this very spot here, my daughter sang a ballad to you, and you, amazed at the beauty of her singing, went down on your knees and made her a proposal of marriage. I am not talking in my sleep, am I? Surely I am wide awake? Speak, Prince, am I asleep, or not?"

"Ye—yes, of course, of course—quite so. I don't know," said the bewildered old man. "I mean, I don't think I am drea—ming now; but, a little while ago I *was* asleep, you see; and while asleep I had this dream, that I——"

"Goodness me, Prince, I tell you you were *not* dreaming. *Not dreaming*, do you hear? *Not* dreaming! What on earth do you mean? Are you raving, Prince, or what?"

"Ye—yes; deuce only knows. I don't know! It seems to me I'm getting be—wildered," said the prince, looking around him in a state of considerable mental perturbation.

"But, my dear Prince, how can you possibly have *dreamed* this, when I can tell you all the minutest details of your proposal and of the circumstances attending it? You have not told any of us of these details. How could I possibly have known what you dreamed?"

"But, perhaps the prince *did* tell someone of his dream, in detail," remarked Natalia Dimitrievna.

"Ye—yes, quite so—quite so! Perhaps I did tell someone all about my dream, in detail," said the now completely lost and bewildered prince.

"Here's a nice comedy!" whispered Felisata Michaelovna to her neighbour.

"My goodness me! this is too much for *anybody's* patience!" cried Maria Alexandrovna, beside herself with helpless rage. "Do you hear me, Prince? She sang you a ballad—*sang you a ballad*! Surely you didn't dream that too?"

"Certainly—cer—tainly, quite so. It really did seem to me that she sang me a ballad," murmured the prince; and a ray of recollection seemed to flash across his face. "My friend," he continued, addressing Mosgliakoff, "I believe I forgot to tell you, there was a ballad sung—a ballad all about castles and knights; and some trou—badour or other came in. Of course, of course, I remember it all quite well. I recoll—ect I did turn over the ballad. It puzzles me much, for now it seems as though I had really heard the ballad, and not dreamt it all."

"I confess, uncle," said Mosgliakoff, as calmly as he could, though his voice shook with agitation, "I confess I do not see any difficulty in bringing your actual experience and your dream into strict conformity; it is consistent enough. You probably *did* hear the ballad. Miss Zenaida sings beautifully; probably you all adjourned into this room and Zenaida Afanassievna sang you the song. Of course, I was not there myself, but in all probability this ballad reminded you of old times; very likely it reminded you of that very vicomtesse with whom you used once to sing, and of whom you were speaking to-day; well, and then, when you went up for your nap and lay down, thinking of the delightful impressions made upon you by the ballad and all, you dreamed that you were in love and made an offer of marriage to the lady who had inspired you with that feeling."

Maria Alexandrovna was struck dumb by this display of barefaced audacity.

"Why, ye—yes, my boy, yes, of course; that's exactly how it really wa—as!" cried the prince, in an ecstasy of delight. "Of course it was the de—lightful impressions that caused me to dream it. I certainly re—member the song; and then I went away and dreamed about my pro—posal, and that I really wished to marry! The viscountess was there too. How beautifully you have unravelled the diffi—culty, my dear boy. Well, now I am quite convinced that it was all a dream. Maria Alex—androvna! I assure you, you are under a delu—usion: it was a dream. I should not think of trifling with your feelings otherwise."

"Oh, indeed! Now I perceive very clearly whom we have to thank for making this dirty mess of our affairs!"cried Maria Alexandrovna, beside herself with rage, and turning to Mosgliakoff: "You are the man, sir—the*dishonest* person. It is you who stirred up this mud! It is you that puzzled an unhappy old idiot into this eccentric behaviour, because you yourself were rejected! But we shall be quits, my friend, for this offence! You shall pay, you shall pay! Wait a bit, my dishonest friend; wait a bit!"

"Maria Alexandrovna!" cried Mosgliakoff, blushing in his turn until he looked as red as a boiled lobster, "your words are so, so——to such an extent—I really don't know how to express my opinion of you. No lady would ever permit herself to—to—. At all events I am but protecting my relative. You must allow that to *allure* an old man like this is, is——."

"Quite so, quite so; *allure*," began the prince, trying to hide himself behind Mosgliakoff.

"Afanassy Matveyevitch!" cried Maria Alexandrovna, in unnatural tones; "do you hear, sir, how these people are shaming and insulting me? Have you *quite* exempted yourself from all the responsibilities of a man? Or are you actually a—a wooden block, instead of the father of a family? What do you stand blinking there for? eh! Any other husband would have wiped out such an insult to his family with the blood of the offender long ago."

"Wife!" began Afanassy, solemnly, delighted, and proud to find that a need for him had sprung up for once in his life. "Wife, are you quite certain, now, that *you* did not dream all this? You might so easily have fallen asleep and dreamed it, and then muddled it all up with what really happened, you know, and so——"

But Afanassy Matveyevitch was never destined to complete his ingenious, but unlucky guess.

Up to this moment the guests had all restrained themselves, and had managed, cleverly enough, to keep up an appearance of solid and judicial interest in the proceedings. But at the first sound, almost, of Afanassy's voice, a burst of uncontrollable laughter rose like a tempest from all parts of the room.

Maria Alexandrovna, forgetting all the laws of propriety in her fury, tried to rush at her unlucky consort; but she was held back by force, or, doubtless, she would have scratched out that gentleman's eyes.

Natalia Dimitrievna took advantage of the occasion to add a little, if only a little, drop more of poison to the bitter cup.

"But, dear Maria Alexandrovna," she said, in the sweetest honied tones, "perhaps it may be that it really *was*so, as your husband suggests, and that you are actually under a strange delusion?"

"How! What was a delusion?" cried Maria Alexandrovna, not quite catching the remark.

"Why, my dear Maria, I was saying, *mightn't* it have been so, dear, after all? These sort of things *do* happen sometimes, you know!"

"*What* sort of things do happen, eh? What are you trying to do with me? What am I to make of you?"

"Why, perhaps, dear, you really *did* dream it all!"

"What? *dream* it! *I* dreamed it? And you dare suggest such a thing to me—straight to my face?"

"Oh, why not? Perhaps it really was the case," observed Felisata Michaelovna.

"Ye—yes, quite so, very likely it act—ually *was* the case," muttered the old prince.

"He, too—gracious Heaven!" cried poor Maria Alexandrovna, wringing her hands.

"Dear me, how you do worry yourself, Maria Alexandrovna. You should remember that dreams are sent us by a good Providence. If Providence so wills it, there is no more to be said. Providence gives the word, and we can neither weep nor be angry at its dictum."

"Quite so, quite so. We can't be a—angry about it," observed the prince.

"Look here; do you take me for a lunatic, or not?" said Maria Alexandrovna. She spoke with difficulty, so dreadfully was she panting with fury. It was more than flesh and blood could stand. She hurriedly grasped a chair, and fell fainting into it. There was a scene of great excitement.

"She has fainted in obedience to the laws of propriety!" observed Natalia Dimitrievna to Mrs. Antipova. But at this moment—at this moment when the general bewilderment and confusion had reached its height, and when the scene was strained to the last possible point of excitement, another actor suddenly stepped to the front; one who had been silent hitherto, but who immediately threw quite a different complexion on the scene.

<h2 style="text-align:center">CHAPTER XIV.</h2>

Zenaida, or Zina Afanassievna, was an individual of an extremely romantic turn of mind.

I don't know whether it really was that she had read too much of "that fool Shakespeare," with her "little tutor fellow," as Maria Alexandrovna insisted; but, at all events she was very romantic. However, never, in all her experience of Mordasoff life, had Zina before made such an ultra-romantic, or perhaps I might call it *heroic*, display as on the occasion of the sally which I am now about to describe.

Pale, and with resolution in her eyes, yet almost trembling with agitation, and wonderfully beautiful in her anger and scorn, she stepped to the front.

Gazing around at all, defiantly, she approached her mother in the midst of the sudden silence which had fallen on all present. Her mother roused herself from her swoon at the first indication of a projected movement on Zina's part, and she now opened her eyes.

"Mamma!" cried Zina, "why should we deceive anyone? Why befoul ourselves with more lies? Everything is so foul already that surely it is not worth while to bemean ourselves any further by attempting to gloss over the filth!"

"Zina, Zina! what are you thinking of? *Do* recollect yourself!" cried Maria Alexandrovna, frightened out of her wits, and jumping briskly up from her chair.

"I told you, mamma—I told you before, that I should not be able to last out the length of this shameful and ignominious business!" continued Zina. "Surely we need no further bemean and befoul ourselves! I will take it all on myself, mamma. I am the basest of all, for lending myself, of my own free will, to this abominable intrigue! You are my mother; you love me, I know, and you wished to arrange matters for my happiness, as you thought best, and according to your lights. *Your* conduct, therefore, is pardonable; but mine! oh, no! never, never!"

"Zina, Zina! surely you are not going to tell the whole story? Oh! woe, woe! I felt that the knife would pierce my heart!"

"Yes, mamma, I shall tell all; I am disgraced, you—we all of us are disgraced——"

"Zina, you are exaggerating! you are beside yourself; and you don't know what you are saying. And why say anything about it? The ignominy and disgrace is not on our side, dear child; I will show in a moment that it is not on our side!"

"No, mamma, no!" cried Zina, with a quiver of rage in her voice, "I do not wish to remain silent any longer before these—persons, whose opinion I despise, and who have come here for the purpose of laughing at us. I do not wish to stand insult from any one of them; none of them have any right to throw dirt at me; every single one of them would be ready at any moment to do things thirty times as bad as anything either I or you have done or would do! Dare they, *can* they constitute themselves our judges?"

"Listen to that!"

"There's a pretty little speech for you!"

"Why, that's *us* she's abusing"!

"A nice sort of creature she is herself!"

These and other such-like exclamations greeted the conclusion of Zina's speech.

"Oh, she simply doesn't know what she's talking about!" observed Natalia Dimitrievna.

We will make a digression, and remark that Natalia Dimitrievna was quite right there!

For if Zina did not consider these women competent to judge herself, why should she trouble herself to make those exposures and admissions which she proposed to reveal in their presence? Zina was in much too great a hurry. (She always was,—so the best heads in Mordasoff had agreed!) All might have been set right; all might have been satisfactorily arranged! Maria Alexandrovna was a great deal to blame this night, too! She had been too much "in a hurry," like her daughter,—and too arrogant! She should have simply raised the laugh at the old prince's expense, and turned him out of the house! But Zina, in despite of all common sense (as indicated above), and of the sage opinions of all Mordasoff, addressed herself to the prince:

"Prince," she said to the old man, who actually rose from his arm-chair to show his respect for the speaker, so much was he struck by her at this moment!—"Prince forgive us; we have deceived you; we entrapped you——"

"*Will* you be quiet, you wretched girl?" cried Maria Alexandrovna, wild with rage.

"My dear young lady—my dear child, my darling child!" murmured the admiring prince.

But the proud haughty character of Zina had led her on to cross the barrier of all propriety;—she even forgot her own mother who lay fainting at her feet—a victim to the self-exposure her daughter indulged in.

"Yes, prince, we both cheated you. Mamma was in fault in that she determined that I must marry you; and I in that I consented thereto. We filled you with wine; I sang to you and postured and posed for your admiration. We tricked you, a weak defenceless old man, we *tricked* you (as Mr. Mosgliakoff would express it!) for the sake of your wealth, and your rank. All this was shockingly mean, and I freely admit the fact. But I swear to you, Prince, that I consented to all this baseness from motives which were *not* base. I wished,—but what a wretch I am! it is doubly mean to justify one's conduct in such a case as this! But I will tell you, Prince, that if I had accepted anything from you, I should have made it up to you for it, by being your plaything, your servant, your—your ballet dancer, your slave—anything you wished. I had sworn to this, and I should have kept my oath."

A severe spasm at the throat stopped her for a moment; while all the guests sat and listened like so many blocks of wood, their eyes and mouths wide open.

This unexpected, and to them perfectly unintelligible sally on Zina's part had utterly confounded them. The old prince alone was touched to tears, though he did not understand half that Zina said.

"But I will marry you, my beau—t—iful child, I *will* marry you, if you like"—he murmured, "and est—eem it a great honour, too! But I as—sure you it was all a dream,—what does it mat—ter what I dream? Why should you take it so to heart? I don't seem to under—stand it all; please explain, my dear friend, what it all means!" he added, to Paul.

"As for you, Pavel Alexandrovitch," Zina recommenced, also turning to Mosgliakoff, "you whom I had made up my mind, at one time, to look upon as my future husband; you who have now so cruelly revenged yourself upon me; must you needs have allied yourself to these people here, whose object at all times is to humiliate and shame me? And you said that you loved me! However, it is not for me to preach moralities to you, for I am worse than all! I wronged you, distinctly, in holding out false hopes and half promises. I never loved you, and if I had agreed to be your wife, it would have been solely with the view of getting away from here, out of this accursed town, and free of all this meanness and baseness. However, I swear to you that had I married you, I should have been a good and faithful wife! You have taken a cruel vengeance upon me, and if that flatters your pride, then——"

"Zina!" cried Mosgliakoff.

"If you still hate me——"

"Zina!!"

"If you ever did love me——"

"Zenaida Afanassievna!"

"Zina, Zina—my child!" cried Maria Alexandrovna.

"I am a blackguard, Zina—a blackguard, and nothing else!" cried Mosgliakoff; while all the assembled ladies gave way to violent agitation. Cries of amazement and of wrath broke upon the silence; but Mosgliakoff himself stood speechless and miserable, without a thought and without a word to plead for him!

"I am an ass, Zina," he cried at last, in an outburst of wild despair,—"an ass! oh far, far worse than an ass. But I will prove to you, Zina, that even an ass can behave like a generous human being! Uncle, I cheated you! I, I—it was I who cheated you: you were *not* asleep,—you were wide awake when you made this lady an offer of marriage! And I—scoundrel that I was—out of revenge because I was rejected by her myself, persuaded you that you had dreamed it all!"

"Dear me, what wonderful and interesting revelations we are being treated to now!" whispered Natalia to Mrs. Antipova.

"My dear friend," replied the prince, "com—pose yourself, do! I assure you—you quite start—led me with that sudden ex—clamation of yours! Besides, you are labouring under a delusion;—I will marr—y the lady, of course, if ne—cessary. But you told me, yourself, it was all a dre—eam!"

"Oh, how am I to tell you? Do show me, somebody, how to explain to him! Uncle, uncle! this is an important matter—a most important family affair! Think of that, uncle—just try to realise that——"

"Wait a bit, my boy—wait a bit: let me think! First there was my coachman, Theophile——"

"Oh, never mind Theophile now, for goodness sake!"

"Of course we need not waste time over The—ophile. Well—then came Na—poleon; and then we seemed to be sitting at tea, and some la—dy came and ate up all our su—gar!"

"But, uncle!" cried Mosgliakoff, at his wits' end, "it was Maria Alexandrovna herself told us that anecdote about Natalia Dimitrievna! I was here myself and heard it!—I was a blackguard, and listened at the keyhole!"

"How, Maria Alexandrovna!" cried Natalia, "you've told the prince too, have you, that I stole sugar out of your basin? So I come to you to steal your sugar, do I, eh! do I?"

166

"Get away from me!" cried Maria Alexandrovna, with the abandonment of utter despair.

"Oh, dear no! I shall do nothing of the sort, Maria Alexandrovna! I steal your sugar, do I? I tell you you shall not talk of me like that, madam—you dare not! I have long suspected you of spreading this sort of rubbish abroad about me! Sophia Petrovna came and told me all about it. So I stole your sugar, did I, eh?"

"But, my dear la—dies!" said the prince, "it was only part of a dream! What do my dreams matter?——"

"Great tub of a woman!" muttered Maria Alexandrovna through her teeth.

"What! what! I'm a tub, too, am I?" shrieked Natalia Dimitrievna. "And what are you yourself, pray? Oh, I have long known that you call me a tub, madam. Never mind!—at all events my husband is a man, madam, and not a fool, like yours!"

"Ye—yes—quite so! I remember there *was* something about a tub, too!" murmured the old man, with a vague recollection of his late conversation with Maria Alexandrovna.

"What—*you*, too? *you* join in abusing a respectable woman of noble extraction, do you? How dare you call me names, prince—you wretched old one-legged misery! I'm a tub am I, you one-legged old abomination?"

"Wha—at, madam, I one-legged?"

"Yes—one-legged and toothless, sir; that's what you are!"

"Yes, and one-eyed too!" shouted Maria Alexandrovna.

"And what's more, you wear stays instead of having your own ribs!" added Natalia Dimitrievna.

"His face is all on wire springs!"

"He hasn't a hair of his own to swear by!"

"Even the old fool's moustache is stuck on!" put in Maria Alexandrovna.

"Well, Ma—arie Alexandrovna, give me the credit of having a nose of my ve—ry own, at all events!" said the prince, overwhelmed with confusion under these unexpected disclosures. "My friend, it must have been you betrayed me! *you* must have told them that my hair is stuck on?"

"Uncle, what an idea, I——!"

"My dear boy, I can't stay here any lon—ger, take me away somewhere—*quelle société*! Where have you brought me to, eh?—Gracious Hea—eaven, what dreadful soc—iety!"

"Idiot! scoundrel!" shrieked Maria Alexandrovna.

"Goodness!" said the unfortunate old prince. "I can't quite remember just now what I came here for at all—I suppose I shall reme—mber directly. Take me away, quick, my boy, or I shall be torn to pieces here! Besides, I have an i—dea that I want to make a note of——"

"Come along, uncle—it isn't very late; I'll take you over to an hotel at once, and I'll move over my own things too."

"Ye—yes, of course, a ho—tel! Good-bye, my charming child; you alone, you—are the only vir—tuous one of them all; you are a no—oble child. Good-bye, my charming girl! Come along, my friend;—oh, good gra—cious, what people!"

I will not attempt to describe the end of this disagreeable scene, after the prince's departure.

The guests separated in a hurricane of scolding and abuse and mutual vituperation, and Maria Alexandrovna was at last left alone amid the ruins and relics of her departed glory.

Alas, alas! Power, glory, weight—all had disappeared in this one unfortunate evening. Maria Alexandrovna quite realised that there was no chance of her ever again mounting to the height from which she had now fallen. Her long preeminence and despotism over society in general had collapsed.

What remained to her? Philosophy? She was wild with the madness of despair all night! Zina was dishonoured—scandals would circulate, never-ceasing scandals; and—oh! it was dreadful!

As a faithful historian, I must record that poor Afanassy was the scapegoat this night; he "caught it" so terribly that he eventually disappeared; he had hidden himself in the garret, and was there starved to death almost, with cold, all night.

The morning came at last; but it brought nothing good with it! Misfortunes never come singly.

CHAPTER XV.

If fate makes up its mind to visit anyone with misfortune, there is no end to its malice! This fact has often been remarked by thinkers; and, as if the ignominy of last night were not enough, the same malicious destiny had prepared for this family more, yea, and worse—evils to come!

By ten o'clock in the morning a strange and almost incredible rumour was in full swing all over the town: it was received by society, of course, with full measure of spiteful joy, just as we all love to receive delightfully scandalous stories of anyone about us.

"To lose one's sense of shame to such an extent!" people said one to another.

"To humiliate oneself so, and to neglect the first rules of propriety! To loose the bands of decency altogether like this, really!" etc., etc.

But here is what had happened.

Early in the morning, something after six o'clock, a poor piteous-looking old woman came hurriedly to the door of Maria Alexandrovna's house, and begged the maid to wake Miss Zina up as quickly, as possible,—*only* Miss Zina, and very quietly, so that her mother should not hear of it, if possible.

Zina, pale and miserable, ran out to the old woman immediately.

The latter fell at Zina's feet and kissed them and begged her with tears to come with her at once to see poor Vaísia, her son, who had been so bad, *so* bad all night that she did not think he could live another day.

The old woman told Zina that Vaísia had sent to beg her to come and bid him farewell in this his death hour: he conjured her to come by all the blessed angels, and by all their past—otherwise he must die in despair.

Zina at once decided to go, in spite of the fact that, by so doing, she would be justifying all the scandal and slanders disseminated about her in former days, as to the intercepted letter, her visits to him, and so on. Without a word to her mother, then, she donned her cloak and started off with the old woman, passing through the whole length of the town, into one of the poorest slums of Mordasof—and stopped at a little low wretched house, with small miserable windows, and snow piled round the basement for warmth.

In this house, in a tiny room, more than half of which was occupied by an enormous stove, on a wretched bed, and covered with a miserably thin quilt, lay a young man, pale and haggard: his eyes were ablaze with the fire of fever, his hands were dry and thin, and he was breathing with difficulty and very hoarsely. He looked as though he might have been handsome once, but disease had put its finger on his features and made them dreadful to look upon and sad withal, as are so many dying consumptive patients' faces.

His old mother who had fed herself for a year past with the conviction that her son would recover, now saw at last that Vaísia was not to live. She stood over him, bowed down with her grief—tearless, and looked and looked, and could not look enough; and felt, but could not realize, that this dear son of hers must in a few days be buried in the miserable Mordasof churchyard, far down beneath the snow and frozen earth!

But Vaísia was not looking at her at this moment! His poor suffering face was at rest now, and happy; for he saw before him the dear image which he had thought of, dreamed of, and loved through all the long sad nights of his illness, for the last year and a half! He realised that she forgave him, and had come, like an angel of God, to tell him of her forgiveness, here, on his deathbed.

She pressed his hands, wept over him, stood and smiled over him, looked at him once more with those wonderful eyes of hers, and all the past, the undying ever-present past rose up before the mind's eye of the dying man. The spark of life flashed up again in his soul, as though to show, now that it was about to die out for ever on this earth, how hard, how hard it was to see so sweet a light fade away.

"Zina, Zina!" he said, "my Zina, do not weep; don't grieve, Zina, don't remind me that I must die! Let me gaze at you, so—so,—and feel that our two souls have come together once more—that you have forgiven me! Let me kiss your dear hands again, as I used, and so let me die without noticing the approach of death.

"How thin you have grown, Zina! and how sweetly you are looking at me now, my Zina! Do you remember how you used to laugh, in bygone days? Oh, Zina, my angel, I shall not ask you to forgive me,—I will not remember anything about—that, you know what! for if you *do* forgive me, I can never forgive myself!

"All the long, long nights, Zina, I have lain here and thought, and thought; and I have long since decided that I had better die, Zina; for I am not fit to live!"

Zina wept, and silently pressed his hands, as though she would stop him talking so.

"Why do you cry so?" continued the sick man. "Is it because I am dying? but all the past is long since dead and buried, Zina, my angel! You are wiser than I am, you know I am a bad, wicked man; surely you cannot love me still? Do you know what it has cost me to realise that I am a bad man? I, who have always prided myself before the world—and what on? Purity of heart, generosity of aim! Yes, Zina, so I did, while we read Shakespeare; and in theory I was pure and generous. Yet, how did I prove these qualities in practice?"

"Oh, don't! don't!" sobbed Zina, "you are not fair to yourself: don't talk like this, please don't!"

"Don't stop me, Zina! You forgave me, my angel; I know you forgave me long ago, but you must have judged me, and you know what sort of man I really am; and that is what tortures me so! I am unworthy of your love, Zina! And you were good and true, not only in theory, but in practice too! You told your mother you would marry me, and no one else, and you would have kept your word! Do you know, Zina, I never realized before what you would sacrifice in marrying me! I could not even see that you might die of hunger if you did so! All I thought of was that

168

you would be the bride of a great poet (in the future), and I could not understand your reasons for wishing to delay our union! So I reproached you and bullied you, and despised you and suspected you, and at last I committed the crime of showing your letter! I was not even a scoundrel at that moment! I was simply a worm-man. Ah! how you must have despised me! No, it is well that I am dying; it is well that you did not marry me! I should not have understood your sacrifice, and I should have worried you, and perhaps, in time, have learned to hate you, and ... but now it is good, it is best so! my bitter tears can at least cleanse my heart before I die. Ah! Zina! Zina! love me, love me as you did before for a little, little while! just for the last hour of my life. I know I am not worthy of it, but—oh, my angel, my Zina!"

Throughout this speech Zina, sobbing herself, had several times tried to stop the speaker; but he would not listen. He felt that he must unburden his soul by speaking out, and continued to talk—though with difficulty, panting, and with choking and husky utterance.

"Oh, if only you had never seen me and never loved me," said Zina, "you would have lived on now! Ah, *why* did we ever meet?"

"No, no, darling, don't blame yourself because I am dying! think of all my self-love, my romanticism! I am to blame for all, myself! Did they ever tell you my story in full? Do you remember, three years ago, there was a criminal here sentenced to death? This man heard that a criminal was never executed whilst ill! so he got hold of some wine, mixed tobacco in it, and drank it. The effect was to make him so dreadfully sick, with blood-spitting, that his lungs became affected; he was taken to a hospital, and a few weeks after he died of virulent consumption! Well, on that day, you know, after the letter, it struck me that I would do the same; and why do you think I chose consumption? Because I was afraid of any more sudden death? Perhaps. But, oh, Zina! believe me, a romantic nonsense played a great part in it; at all events, I had an idea that it would be striking and grand for me to be lying here, dying of consumption, and you standing and wringing your hands for woe that *love* should have brought me to this! You should come, I thought, and beg my pardon on your knees, and I should forgive you and die in your arms!"

"Oh, don't! don't!" said Zina, "don't talk of it now, dear! you are not really like that. Think of our happy days together, think of something else—not that, not that!"

"Oh, but it's so bitter to me, darling; and that's why I must speak of it. I havn't seen you for a year and a half, you know, and all that time I have been alone; and I don't think there was one single minute of all that time when I have not thought of you, my angel, Zina! And, oh! how I longed to do something to earn a better opinion from you! Up to these very last days I have never believed that I should really die; it has not killed me all at once, you know. I have long walked about with my lungs affected. For instance, I have longed to become a great poet suddenly, to publish a poem such as has never appeared before on this earth; I intended to pour my whole soul and being into it, so that wherever I was, or wherever *you* were, I should always be with you and remind you of myself in my poems! And my greatest longing of all was that you should think it all over and say to yourself at last some day, 'No, he is not such a wretch as I thought, after all!' It was stupid of me, Zina, stupid—stupid—wasn't it, darling?"

"No, no, Vaísia—no!" cried Zina. She fell on his breast and kissed his poor hot, dry hands.

"And, oh! how jealous I have been of you all this time, Zina! I think I should have died if I had heard of your wedding. I kept a watch over you, you know; I had a spy—there!" (he nodded towards his mother). "She used to go over and bring me news. You never loved Mosgliakoff—now *did* you, Zina? Oh, my darling, my darling, will you remember me when I am dead? Oh, I know you will; but years go by, Zina, and hearts grow cold, and yours will cool too, and you'll forget me, Zina!"

"No, no, never! I shall never marry. You are my first love, and my only—only—undying love!"

"But all things die, Zina, even our memories, and our good and noble feelings die also, and in their place comes reason. No, no, Zina, be happy, and live long. Love another if you can, you cannot love a poor dead man for ever! But think of me now and then, if only seldom; don't think of my faults: forgive them! For oh, Zina, there was good in that sweet love of ours as well as evil. Oh, golden, golden days never to be recalled! Listen, darling, I have always loved the sunset hour—remember me at that time, will you? Oh no, no! why must I die? oh *how* I should love to live on now. Think of that time—oh, just think of it! it was all spring then, the sun shone so bright, the flowers were so sweet, ah me! and look, now—look!"

And the poor thin finger pointed to the frozen window-pane. Then he seized Zina's hand and pressed it tight over his eyes, and sighed bitterly—bitterly! His sobs nearly burst his poor suffering breast.... And so he continued suffering and talking all the long day. Zina comforted and soothed him as she best could, but she too was full of deadly grief and pain. She told him—she promised him—never to forget; that she would never love again as she loved him; and he believed her and wept, and smiled again, and kissed her hands. And so the day passed.

Meanwhile, Maria Alexandrovna had sent some ten times for Zina, begging her not to ruin her reputation irretrievably. At last, at dusk, she determined to go herself; she was out of her wits with terror and grief.

Having called Zina out into the next room, she proceeded to beg and pray her, on her knees, "to spare this last dagger at her heart!"

Zina had come out from the sick-room ill: her head was on fire,—she heard, but could not comprehend, what her mother said; and Marie Alexandrovna was obliged to leave the house again in despair, for Zina had determined to sit up all night with Vaísia.

She never left his bedside, but the poor fellow grew worse and worse. Another day came, but there was no hope that the sick man would see its close. His old mother walked about as though she had lost all control of her actions; grief had turned her head for the time; she gave her son medicines, but he would none of them! His death agony dragged on and on! He could not speak now, and only hoarse inarticulate sounds proceeded from his throat. To the very last instant he stared and stared at Zina, and never took his eyes off her; and when their light failed them he still groped with uncertain fingers for her hand, to press and fondle it in his own!

Meanwhile the short winter day was waning! And when at even the last sunbeam gilded the frozen window-pane of the little room, the soul of the sufferer fled in pursuit of it out of the emaciated body that had kept it prisoner.

The old mother, seeing that there was nothing left her now but the lifeless body of her beloved Vaísia, wrung her hands, and with a loud cry flung herself on his dead breast.

"This is your doing, you viper, you cursed snake," she yelled to Zina, in her despair; "it was you ruined and killed him, you wicked, wretched girl." But Zina heard nothing. She stood over the dead body like one bereft of her senses.

At last she bent over him, made the sign of the Cross, kissed him, and mechanically left the room. Her eyes were ablaze, her head whirled. Two nights without sleep, combined with her turbulent feelings, were almost too much for her reason; she had a sort of confused consciousness that all her past had just been torn out of her heart, and that a new life was beginning for her, dark and threatening.

But she had not gone ten paces when Mosgliakoff suddenly seemed to start up from the earth at her feet.

He must have been waiting for her here.

"Zenaida Afanassievna," he began, peering all around him in what looked like timid haste; it was still pretty light. "Zenaida Afanassievna, of course I am an ass, or, if you please, perhaps not quite an ass, for I really think I am acting rather generously this time. Excuse my blundering, but I am rather confused, from a variety of causes."

Zina glanced at him almost unconsciously, and silently went on her way. There was not much room for two on the narrow pavement, and as Zina did not make way for Paul, the latter was obliged to walk on the road at the side, which he did, never taking his eyes off her face.

"Zenaida Afanassievna," he continued, "I have thought it all over, and if you are agreeable I am willing to renew my proposal of marriage. I am even ready to forget all that has happened; all the ignominy of the last two days, and to forgive it—but on one condition: that while we are still here our engagement is to remain a strict secret. You will depart from this place as soon as ever you can, and I shall quietly follow you. We will be married secretly, somewhere, so that nobody shall know anything about it; and then we'll be off to St. Petersburg by express post— don't take more than a small bag—eh? What say you, Zenaida Afanassievna; tell me quick, please, I can't stay here. We might be seen together, you know."

Zina did not answer a word; she only looked at Mosgliakoff; but it was such a look that he understood all instantly, bowed, and disappeared down the next lane.

"Dear me," he said to himself, "what's the meaning of this? The day before yesterday she became so jolly humble, and blamed herself all round. I've come on the wrong day, evidently!"

Meanwhile event followed event in Mordasof.

A very tragical circumstance occurred.

The old prince, who moved over to the hotel with Mosgliakoff, fell very ill that same night, dangerously ill. All Mordasof knew of it in the morning; the doctor never left his side. That evening a consultation of all the local medical talent was held over the old man (the invitations to which were issued in Latin); but in spite of the Latin and all they could do for him, the poor prince was quite off his head; he raved and asked his doctor to sing him some ballad or other; raved about wigs, and occasionally cried out as though frightened.

The Mordasof doctors decided that the hospitality of the town had given the prince inflammation of the stomach, which had somehow "gone to the head."

There might be some subordinate moral causes to account for the attack; but at all events he ought to have died long ago; and so he would certainly die now.

In this last conclusion they were not far wrong; for the poor old prince breathed his last three days after, at the hotel.

This event impressed the Mordasof folk considerably. No one had expected such a tragical turn of affairs. They went in troops to the hotel to view the poor old body, and there they wagged their heads wisely and ended by passing severe judgment upon "the murderers of the unfortunate Prince,"—meaning thereby, of course, Maria

Alexandrovna and her daughter. They predicted that this matter would go further. Mosgliakoff was in a dreadful state of perturbation: he did not know what to do with the body. Should he take it back to Donchanof! or what? Perhaps he would be held responsible for the old man's death, as he had brought him here? He did not like the look of things. The Mordasof people were less than useless for advice, they were all far too frightened to hazard a word.

But suddenly the scene changed.

One fine evening a visitor arrived—no less a person than the eminent Prince Shepetiloff, a young man of thirty-five, with colonel's epaulettes, a relative of the dead man. His arrival created a great stir among all classes at Mordasof.

It appeared that this gentleman had lately left St. Petersburg, and had called in at Donchanof. Finding no one there, he had followed the prince to Mordasof, where the news and circumstances of the old man's death fell upon him like a thunder-clap!

Even the governor felt a little guilty while detailing the story of the prince's death: all Mordasof felt and looked guilty.

This visitor took the matter entirely into his own hands, and Mosgliakoff made himself scarce before the presence of the prince's real nephew, and disappeared, no one knew whither.

The body was taken to the monastery, and all the Mordasof ladies flocked thither to the funeral. It was rumoured that Maria Alexandrovna was to be present, and that she was to go on her knees before the coffin, and loudly pray for pardon; and that all this was in conformity with the laws of the country.

Of course this was all nonsense, and Maria Alexandrovna never went near the place!

I forgot to state that the latter had carried off Zina to the country house, not deeming it possible to continue to live in the town. There she sat, and trembled over all the second-hand news she could get hold of as to events occurring at Mordasof.

The funeral procession passed within half a mile of her country house; so that Maria Alexandrovna could get a good view of the long train of carriages looking black against the white snow roads; but she could not bear the sight, and left the window.

Before the week was out, she and her daughter moved to Moscow, taking Afanassy Matveyevitch with them; and, within a month, the country house and town house were both for sale.

And so Mordasof lost its most eminent inhabitant for ever!

Afanassy Matveyevitch was said to be for sale with the country house.

A year—two years went by, and Mordasof had quite forgotten Maria Alexandrovna, or nearly so! Alas! so wags the world! It was said that she had bought another estate, and had moved over to some other provincial capital; where, of course, she had everybody under her thumb; that Zina was not yet married; and that Afanassy Matveyevitch—but why repeat all this nonsense? None of it was true; it was but rumour!——

It is three years since I wrote the last words of the above chronicles of Mordasof, and whoever would have believed that I should have to unfold my MS., and add another piece of news to my narrative?

Well, to business!—

Let's begin with Paul Mosgliakoff.—After leaving Mordasof, he went straight to St. Petersburg, where he very soon obtained the clerkship he had applied for. He then promptly forgot all about Mordasof, and the events enacted there. He enjoyed life, went into society, fell in love, made another offer of marriage, and had to swallow another snub; became disgusted with Petersburg life, and joined an expedition to one of the remote quarters of our vast empire.

This expedition passed through its perils of land and water, and arrived in due course at the capital of the remote province which was its destination.

There the members were well received by the governor, and a ball was arranged for their entertainment.

Mosgliakoff was delighted. He donned his best Petersburg uniform, and proceeded to the large ball-room with the full intention of producing a great and startling effect. His first duty was to make his bow to the governor-general's lady, of whom it was rumoured that she was young, and very lovely.

He advanced then, with some little "swagger," but was suddenly rooted to the spot with amazement. Before him stood Zina, beautifully dressed, proud and haughty, and sparkling with diamonds! She did not recognize him; her eyes rested a moment on his face, and then passed on to glance at some other person.

Paul immediately departed to a safe and quiet corner, and there button-holed a young civilian whom he questioned, and from whom he learned certain most interesting facts. He learned that the governor-general had married a very rich and very lovely lady in Moscow, two years since; that his wife was certainly very beautiful, but, at the same time, excessively proud and haughty, and danced with none but generals. That the governor's lady had a mother, a lady of rank and fashion, who had followed them from Moscow; that this lady was very clever and wise, but that even she was quite under the thumb of her daughter; as for the general (the governor), he doted on his wife.

Mosgliakoff inquired after our old friend Afanassy; but in their "remote province" nothing was known of that gentleman.

Feeling a little more at home presently, Paul began to walk about the room, and shortly espied Maria Alexandrovna herself. She was wonderfully dressed, and was surrounded by a bevy of ladies who evidently dwelt in the glory of her patronage: she appeared to be exceedingly amiable to them—wonderfully so!

Paul plucked up courage and introduced himself. Maria Alexandrovna seemed to give a shudder at first sight of him, but in an instant she was herself again. She was kind enough to recognise Paul, and to ask him all sorts of questions as to his Petersburg experiences, and so on. She never said a word about Mordasof, however. She behaved as though no such place existed.

After a minute or so, and having dropped a question as to some Petersburg prince whom Paul had never so much as heard of, she turned to speak to another young gentleman standing by, and in a second or two was entirely oblivious of Mosgliakoff. With a sarcastic smile our friend passed on into the large hall. Feeling offended—though he knew not why—he decided not to dance. So he leant his back against one of the pillars, and for a couple of hours did nothing but follow Zina about with his eyes. But alas! all the grace of his figure and attitude, and all the fascinations of his general appearance were lost upon her, she never looked at him.

At last, with legs stiff from standing, tired, hungry, and feeling miserable generally, he went home. Here he tossed about half the night thinking of the past, and next morning, having the chance of joining a branch party of his expedition, he accepted the opportunity with delight, and left the town at once.

The bells tinkled, the horses trotted gaily along, kicking up snowballs as they went. Paul Mosgliakoff fell to thinking, then he fell to snoring, and so he continued until the third station from the start; there he awoke fresh and jolly, and with the new scenery came newer, and healthier, and pleasanter thoughts.

THE END OF "UNCLE'S DREAM."

THE PERMANENT HUSBAND.
CHAPTER I.

Summer had come, and Velchaninoff, contrary to his expectations, was still in St. Petersburg. His trip to the south of Russia had fallen through, and there seemed no end to the business which had detained him.

This business—which was a lawsuit as to certain property—had taken a very disagreeable aspect. Three months ago the thing had appeared to be by no means complicated—in fact, there had seemed to be scarcely any question as to the rights and wrongs of the matter, but all seemed to change suddenly.

"Everything else seems to have changed for the worse, too!" said Velchaninoff to himself, over and over again.

He was employing a clever lawyer—an eminent man, and an expensive one, too; but in his impatience and suspicion he began to interfere in the matter himself. He read and wrote papers—all of which the lawyer put into his waste-paper basket—*holus bolus*; called in continually at the courts and offices, made inquiries, and confused and worried everybody concerned in the matter; so at least the lawyer declared, and begged him for mercy's sake to go away to the country somewhere.

But he could not make up his mind to do so. He stayed in town and enjoyed the dust, and the hot nights, and the closeness of the air of St. Petersburg, things which are enough to destroy anyone's nerves. His lodgings were somewhere near the Great Theatre; he had lately taken them, and did not like them. Nothing went well with him; his hypochondria increased with each day, and he had long been a victim to that disorder.

Velchaninoff was a man who had seen a great deal of the world; he was not quite young, thirty-eight years old—perhaps thirty-nine, or so; and all this "old age," as he called it, had "fallen upon him quite unawares." However, as he himself well understood, he had aged more in the *quality* than in the number of the years of his life; and if his infirmities were really creeping upon him, they must have come from within and not from outside causes. He looked young enough still. He was a tall, stout man, with light-brown thick hair, without a suspicion of white about it, and a light beard that reached half way down his chest. At first sight you might have supposed him to be of a lax, careless disposition or character, but on studying him more closely you would have found that, on the contrary, the man was decidedly a stickler for the proprieties of this world, and withal brought up in the ways and graces of the very best society. His manners were very good—free but graceful—in spite of this lately-acquired habit of grumbling and reviling things in general. He was still full of the most perfect, aristocratic self-confidence: probably he did not himself suspect to how great an extent this was so, though he was a most decidedly intelligent, I may say clever, even talented man. His open, healthy-looking face was distinguished by an almost feminine refinement, which quality gained him much attention from the fair sex. He had large blue eyes—eyes which ten years ago had known well how to persuade and attract; such clear, merry, careless eyes they had been, that they invariably brought over to his side any person he wished to gain. Now, when he was nearly forty years old, their ancient, kind, frank expression had died out of them, and a certain cynicism—a cunning—an irony very often, and yet another variety of expression, of late—an expression of melancholy or pain, undefined but keen, had taken the place of the earlier attractive qualities of his eyes. This expression of melancholy especially showed itself when he was alone; and it was a strange fact that the gay, careless, happy fellow of a couple of years ago, the man who could tell a funny story so inimitably, should now love nothing so well as to be all alone. He intended to throw up most of his friends—a quite unnecessary step, in spite of his present financial difficulties. Probably his vanity was to blame for this intention: he could not bear to see his old friends in his present position; with his vain suspicious character it would be most unpalatable to him.

But his vanity began to change its nature in solitude. It did not grow less, on the contrary; but it seemed to develop into a special type of vanity which was unlike its old self. This new vanity suffered from entirely different causes, "*higher* causes, if I may so express it," he said, "and if there really be higher and lower motives in this world."

He defined these "higher things" as matters which he could not laugh at, or turn to ridicule when happening in his own individual experience. Of course it would be quite another thing with the same subjects in society; by *himself* he could not ridicule then; but put him among other people, and he would be the first to tear himself from all of those secret resolutions of his conscience made in solitude, and laugh them to scorn.

Very often, on rising from his bed in the morning, he would feel ashamed of the thoughts and feelings which had animated him during the long sleepless night—and his nights of late had been sleepless. He seemed suspicious of everything and everybody, great and small, and grew mistrustful of himself.

One fact stood out clearly, and that was that during those sleepless nights his thoughts and opinions took huge leaps and bounds, sometimes changing entirely from the thoughts and opinions of the daytime. This fact struck him very forcibly; and he took occasion to consult an eminent medical friend. He spoke in fun, but the doctor informed him that the fact of feelings and opinions changing during meditations at night, and during sleeplessness, was one long recognised by science; and that that was especially the case with persons of strong thinking power, and of acute feelings. He stated further that very often the beliefs of a whole life are uprooted under the melancholy influence of night and inability to sleep, and that often the most fateful resolutions are made under the same influence; that sometimes this impressionability to the mystic influence of the dark hours amounted to a malady, in which case measures must be taken, the radical manner of living should be changed, diet considered, a journey undertaken if possible, etc., etc.

Velchaninoff listened no further, but he was sure that in his own case there was decided malady.

Very soon his morning meditations began to partake of the nature of those of the night, but they were more bitter. Certain events of his life now began to recur to his memory more and more vividly; they would strike him suddenly, and without apparent reason: things which had been forgotten for ten or fifteen years—some so long ago that he thought it miraculous that he should have been able to recall them at all. But that was not all—for, after all, what man who has seen any life has not hundreds of such recollections of the past? The principal point was that all this past came back to him now with an absolutely new light thrown upon it, and he seemed to look at it from an entirely new and unexpected point of view. Why did some of his acts appear to him now to be nothing better than crimes? It was not merely in the judgment of his intellect that these things appeared so to him now—had it been only his poor sick mind, he would not have trusted it; but his whole being seemed to condemn him; he would curse and even weep over these recollections of the past! If anyone had told him a couple of years since that he would *weep* over anything, he would have laughed the idea to scorn.

At first he recalled the unpleasant experiences of his life: certain failures in society, humiliations; he remembered how some designing person had so successfully blackened his character that he was requested to cease his visits to a certain house; how once, and not so very long ago, he had been publicly insulted, and had not challenged the offender; how once an epigram had been fastened to his name by some witty person, in the midst of a party of pretty women and he had not found a reply; he remembered several unpaid debts, and how he had most stupidly run through two very respectable fortunes.

Then he began to recall facts belonging to a "higher" order. He remembered that he had once insulted a poor old grey-headed clerk, and that the latter had covered his face with his hands and cried, which Velchaninoff had thought a great joke at the time, but now looked upon in quite another light. Then he thought how he had once, merely for fun, set a scandal going about the beautiful little wife of a certain schoolmaster, and how the husband had got to hear the rumour. He (Velchaninoff) had left the town shortly after and did not know how the matter had ended; but now he fell to wondering and picturing to himself the possible consequences of his action; and goodness knows where this theme would not have taken him to if he had not suddenly recalled another picture: that of a poor girl, whom he had been ashamed of and never thought of loving, but whom he had betrayed and forsaken, her and her child, when he left St. Petersburg. He had afterwards searched for this girl and her baby for a whole year, but never found them.

Of this sort of recollections there were, alas! but too many; and each one seemed to bring along with it a train of others. His vanity began to suffer, little by little, under these memories. I have said that his vanity had developed into a new type of vanity. There were moments (few albeit) in which he was not even ashamed of having no carriage of his own, now; or of being seen by one of his former friends in shabby clothes; or when, if seen and looked at by such a person contemptuously, he was high-minded enough to suppress even a frown. Of course such moments of self-oblivion were rare; but, as I said before, his vanity began little by little to change away from its former quarters and to centre upon one question which was perpetually ranging itself before his intellect. "There is some power or other," he would muse, sarcastically, "somewhere, which is extremely interested in my morals, and sends me these damnable recollections and tears of remorse! Let them come, by all means; but they have not the slightest effect on me! for I haven't a scrap of independence about me, in spite of my wretched forty years, I know that for certain. Why, if it were to happen so that I should gain anything by spreading another scandal about that schoolmaster's wife, (for instance, that she had accepted presents from me, or something of that sort), I should certainly spread it without a thought."

But though no other opportunity ever did occur of maligning the schoolmistress, yet the very thought alone that *if* such an opportunity were to occur he would inevitably seize it was almost fatal to him at times. He was not tortured with memory at every moment of his life; he had intervals of time to breathe and rest in. But the longer he stayed, the more unpleasant did he find his life in St. Petersburg. July came in. At certain moments he felt inclined to throw up his lawsuit and all, and go down to the Crimea; but after an hour or so he would despise his own idea, and laugh at himself for entertaining it.

"These thoughts won't be driven away by a mere journey down south," he said to himself, "when they have once begun to annoy me; besides, if I am easy in my conscience now, I surely need not try to run away from any such worrying recollections of past days!" "Why should I go after all?" he resumed, in a strain of melancholy philosophizing; "this place is a very heaven for a hypochondriac like myself, what with the dust and the heat, and the discomfort of this house, what with the nonsensical swagger and pretence of all these wretched little 'civil servants' in the departments I frequent! Everyone is delightfully candid—and candour is undoubtedly worthy of all respect! I *won't* go away—I'll stay and die here rather than go!"

CHAPTER II.

It was the third of July. The heat and closeness of the air had become quite unbearable. The day had been a busy one for Velchaninoff—he had been walking and driving about without rest, and had still in prospect a visit in the evening to a certain state councillor who lived somewhere on the Chornaya Riéchka (black stream), and whom he was anxious to drop in upon unexpectedly.

At six o'clock our hero issued from his house once more, and trudged off to dine at a restaurant on the Nefsky, near the police-bridge—a second-rate sort of place, but French. Here he took his usual corner, and ordered his usual dinner, and waited.

He always had a rouble[1] dinner, and paid for his wine extra, which moderation he looked upon as a discreet sacrifice to the temporary financial embarrassment under which he was suffering.

He regularly went through the ceremony of wondering how he could bring himself to eat "such nastiness," and yet as regularly he demolished every morsel, and with excellent show of appetite too, just as though he had eaten nothing for three days.

"This appetite can't be healthy!" he murmured to himself sometimes, observing his own voracity. However, on this particular occasion, he sat down to his dinner in a miserably bad humour: he threw his hat angrily away somewhere, tipped his chair back,—and reflected.

He was in the sort of humour that if his next neighbour—dining at the little table near him—were to rattle his plate, or if the boy serving him were to make any little blunder, or, in fact, if any little petty annoyance were to put him out of a sudden, he was quite capable of shouting at the offender, and, in fact, of kicking up a serious row on the smallest pretext.

Soup was served to him. He took up his spoon, and was about to commence operations, when he suddenly threw it down again, and started from his seat. An unexpected thought had struck him, and in an instant he had realized why he had been plunged in gloom and mental perturbation during the last few days. Goodness knows why he thus suddenly became inspired, as it were, with the truth; but so it was. He jumped from his chair, and in an instant it all stood out before him as plain as his five fingers! "It's all that hat!" he muttered to himself; "it's all simply and solely that damnable round hat, with the crape band round it; that's the reason and cause of all my worries these last days!"

He began to think; and the more he thought, the more dejected he became, and the more astonishing appeared the "remarkable circumstance of the hat."

"But, hang it all, there *is* no circumstance!" he growled to himself. "What circumstance do I mean? There's been nothing in the nature of an event or occurrence!"

The fact of the matter was this: Nearly a fortnight since, he had met for the first time, somewhere about the corner of the Podiacheskaya, a gentleman with crape round his hat. There was nothing particular about the man— he was just like all others; but as he passed Velchaninoff he had stared at him so fixedly that it was impossible to avoid noticing him, and more than noticing—observing him attentively.

The man's face seemed to be familiar to Velchaninoff. He had evidently seen him somewhere and at some time or other.

"But one sees thousands of people during one's life," thought Velchaninoff; "one can't remember every face!" So he had gone on his way, and before he was twenty yards further, to all appearances he had forgotten all about the meeting, in spite of the strength of the first impression made upon him.

And yet he had *not* forgotten; for the impression remained all day, and a very original impression it was, too,—a kind of objectless feeling of anger against he knew not what. He remembered his exact feelings at this moment, a fortnight after the occurrence: how he had been puzzled by the angry nature of his sentiments at the time, and puzzled to such an extent that he had never for a moment connected his ill-humour with the meeting of the morning, though he had felt as cross as possible all day. But the gentleman with the crape band had not lost much time about reminding Velchaninoff of his existence, for the very next day he met the latter again, on the Nefsky Prospect and again he had stared in a peculiarly fixed way at him.

Velchaninoff flared up and spat on the ground in irritation—Russian like, but a moment after he was wondering at his own wrath. "There are faces, undoubtedly," he reflected, "which fill one with disgust at first sight; but I certainly *have* met that fellow somewhere or other.

"Yes, I *have* met him before!" he muttered again, half an hour later.

And again, as on the last occasion, he was in a vile humour all that evening, and even went so far as to have a bad dream in the night; and yet it never entered his head to imagine that the cause of his bad temper on both occasions had been the accidental meeting with the gentleman in mourning, although on the second evening he had remembered and thought of the chance encounter two or three times.

He had even flared up angrily to think that "such a dirty-looking cad" should presume to linger in his memory so long; he would have felt it humiliating to himself to imagine for a moment that such a wretched creature could possibly be in any way connected with the agitated condition of his feelings.

Two days later the pair had met once more at the landing place of one of the small Neva ferry steamers.

On the third occasion Velchaninoff was ready to swear that the man recognised him, and had pressed through the crowd towards him; had even dared to stretch out his hand and call him by name. As to this last fact he was not quite certain, however. "At all events, who the deuce *is* he?" thought Velchaninoff, "and why can't the idiot come up and speak to me if he really does recognise me; and if he so much wishes to do so?" With these thoughts Velchaninoff had taken a droshky and started off for the Smolney Monastery, where his lawyer lived.

Half an hour later he was engaged in his usual quarrel with that gentleman.

But that same evening he was in a worse humour than ever, and his night was spent in fantastic dreams and imaginings, which were anything but pleasant. "I suppose it's bile!" he concluded, as he paid his matutinal visit to the looking-glass.

This was the third meeting.

Then, for five days there was not a sign of the man; and yet, much to his distaste, Velchaninoff could not, for the life of him, avoid thinking of the man with the crape band.

He caught himself musing over the fellow. "What have I to do with him?" he thought. "What can his business in St. Petersburg be?—he looks busy: and whom is he in mourning for? He clearly recognises me, but I don't know in the least who he is! And why do such people as he is put crape on their hats? it doesn't seem 'the thing' for them, somehow! I believe I shall recognise this fellow if I ever get a good close look at him!"

And there came over him that sensation we all know so well—the same feeling that one has when one can't for the life of one think of the required word; every other word comes up; associations with the right word come up; occasions when one has used the word come up; one wanders round and round the immediate vicinity of the word wanted, but the actual word itself will not appear, though you may break your head to get at it!

"Let's see, now: it was—yes—some while since. It was—where on earth was it? There was a—oh! devil take whatever there was or wasn't there! What does it matter to me?" he broke off angrily of a sudden. "I'm not going to lower myself by thinking of a little cad like that!"

He felt very angry; but when, in the evening, he remembered that he had been so upset, and recollected the cause of his anger, he felt the disagreeable sensation of having been caught by someone doing something wrong.

This fact puzzled and annoyed him.

"There must be some reason for my getting so angry at the mere recollection of that man's face," he thought, but he didn't finish thinking it out.

But the next evening he was still more indignant; and this time, he really thought, with good cause. "Such audacity is unparalleled!" he said to himself.

The fact of the matter is, there had been a fourth meeting with the man of the crape hat band. The latter had apparently arisen from the earth and confronted him. But let me explain what had happened.

It so chanced that Velchaninoff had just met, accidentally, that very state-councillor mentioned a few pages back, whom he had been so anxious to see, and on whom he had intended to pounce unexpectedly at his country house. This gentleman evidently avoided Velchaninoff, but at the same time was most necessary to the latter in his lawsuit. Consequently, when Velchaninoff met him, the one was delighted, while the other was very much the reverse. Velchaninoff had immediately button-holed him, and walked down the street with him, talking; doing his very utmost to keep the sly old fox to the subject on which it was so necessary that he should be pumped. And it was just at this most important moment, when Velchaninoff's intellect was all on the *qui vive* to catch up the slightest hints of what he wished to get at, while the foxy old councillor (aware of the fact) was doing his best to reveal nothing, that the former, taking his eyes from his companion's face for one instant, beheld the gentleman of the crape hatband walking along the other side of the road, and looking at him—nay, *watching* him, evidently—and apparently smiling!

"Devil take him!" said Velchaninoff, bursting out into fury at once, while the "old fox" instantly disappeared, "and I should have succeeded in another minute. Curse that dirty little hound! he's simply spying me. I'll—I'll hire somebody to—I'll take my oath he laughed at me! D—n him, I'll thrash him. I wish I had a stick with me. I'll—I'll buy one! I won't leave this matter so. Who the deuce is he? I *will* know! Who is he?"

At last, three days after this fourth encounter, we find Velchaninoff sitting down to dinner at his restaurant, as recorded a page or two back, in a state of mind bordering upon the furious. He could not conceal the state of his feelings from himself, in spite of all his pride. He was obliged to confess at last, that all his anxiety, his irritation, his state of agitation generally, must undoubtedly be connected with, and absolutely attributed to, the appearance of the wretched-looking creature with the crape hatband, in spite of his insignificance.

"I may be a hypochondriac," he reflected, "and I may be inclined to make an elephant out of a gnat; but how does it help me? What use is it to me if I persuade myself to believe that *perhaps* all this is fancy? Why, if every dirty little wretch like that is to have the power of upsetting a man like myself, why—it's—it's simply unbearable!"

Undoubtedly, at this last (fifth) encounter of to-day, the elephant had proved himself a very small gnat indeed. The "crape man" had appeared suddenly, as usual, and had passed by Velchaninoff, but without looking up at him this time; indeed, he had gone by with downcast eyes, and had even seemed anxious to pass unobserved. Velchaninoff had turned rapidly round and shouted as loud as ever he could at him.

"Hey!" he cried. "You! Crape hatband! You want to escape notice this time, do you? Who are you?"

Both the question and the whole idea of calling after the man were absurdly foolish, and Velchaninoff knew it the moment he had said the words. The man had turned round, stopped for an instant, lost his head, smiled—half made up his mind to say something,—had waited half a minute in painful indecision, then twisted suddenly round again, and "bolted" without a word. Velchaninoff gazed after him in amazement. "What if it be *I* that haunt *him*, and not he me, after all?" he thought. However, Velchaninoff ate up his dinner, and then drove off to pounce upon the town councillor at the latter's house, if he could.

The councillor was not in; and he was informed that he would scarcely be at home before three or four in the morning, because he had gone to a "name's-day party."

Velchaninoff felt that this was too bad! In his rage he determined to follow and hunt the fellow up at the party: he actually took a droshky, and started off with that wild idea; but luckily he thought better of it on the way, got out of the vehicle and walked away towards the "Great Theatre," near which he lived. He felt that he must have motion; also he *must* absolutely sleep well this coming night: in order to sleep he must be tired; so he walked all the way home—a fairly long walk, and arrived there about half-past ten, as tired as he could wish.

His lodging, which he had taken last March, and had abused ever since, apologising to himself for living "in such a hole," and at the same time excusing himself for the fact by the reflection that it was only for a while, and that he had dropped quite accidentally into St. Petersburg—thanks to that cursed lawsuit!—his lodging, I say, was by no means so bad as he made it out to be!

The entrance certainly was a little dark, and dirty-looking, being just under the arch of the gateway. But he had two fine large light rooms on the second floor, separated by the entrance hall: one of these rooms overlooked the yard and the other the street. Leading out of the former of these was a smaller room, meant to be used as a bedroom; but Velchaninoff had filled it with a disordered array of books and papers, and preferred to sleep in one of the large rooms, the one overlooking the street, to wit.

His bed was made for him, every day, upon the large divan. The rooms were full of good furniture, and some valuable ornaments and pictures were scattered about, but the whole place was in dreadful disorder; the fact being that at this time Velchaninoff was without a regular servant. His one domestic had gone away to stay with her friends in the country; he thought of taking a man, but decided that it was not worth while for a short time; besides he hated flunkeys, and ended by making arrangements with his dvornik's sister Martha, who was to come up every morning and "do out" his rooms, he leaving the key with her as he went out each day. Martha did absolutely nothing towards tidying the place and robbed him besides, but he didn't care, he liked to be alone in the house. But solitude is all very well within certain limits, and Velchaninoff found that his nerves could not stand all this sort of thing at certain bilious moments; and it so fell out that he began to loathe his room more and more every time he entered it.

However, on this particular evening he hardly gave himself time to undress; he threw himself on his bed, and determined that nothing should make him think of *anything*, and that he would fall asleep at once.

And, strangely enough, his head had hardly touched the pillow before he actually was asleep; and this was the first time for a month past that such a thing had occurred.

He awoke at about two, considerably agitated; he had dreamed certain very strange dreams, reminding him of the incoherent wanderings of fever.

The subject seemed to be some crime which he had committed and concealed, but of which he was accused by a continuous flow of people who swarmed into his rooms for the purpose. The crowd which had already collected within was enormous, and yet they continued to pour in in such numbers that the door was never shut for an instant.

But his whole interest seemed to centre in one strange looking individual,—a man who seemed to have once been very closely and intimately connected with him, but who had died long ago and now reappeared for some reason or other.

The most tormenting part of the matter was that Velchaninoff could not recollect who this man was,—he could not remember his name,—though he recollected the fact that he had once dearly loved him. All the rest of the people swarming into the room seemed to be waiting for the final word of this man,—either the condemnation or the justification of Velchaninoff was to be pronounced by him,—and everyone was impatiently waiting to hear him speak.

But he sat motionless at the table, and would not open his lips to say a word of any sort.

The uproar continued, the general annoyance increased, and, suddenly, Velchaninoff himself strode up to the man in a fury, and smote him because he would not speak. Velchaninoff felt the strangest satisfaction in having thus smitten him; his heart seemed to freeze in horror for what he had done, and in acute suffering for the crime involved in his action,—but in that very sensation of freezing at the heart lay the sense of satisfaction which he felt.

Exasperated more and more, he struck the man a second and a third time; and then—in a sort of intoxication of fury and terror, which amounted to actual insanity, and yet bore within it a germ of delightful satisfaction, he ceased to count his blows, and rained them in without ceasing.

He felt he must destroy, annihilate, demolish all this.

Suddenly something strange happened; everyone present had given a dreadful cry and turned expectantly towards the door, while at the same moment there came three terrific peals of the hall-bell, so violent that it appeared someone was anxious to pull the bell-handle out.

Velchaninoff awoke, started up in a second, and made for the door; he was persuaded that the ring at the bell had been no dream or illusion, but that someone had actually rung, and was at that moment standing at the front door.

"It would be *too* unnatural if such a clear and unmistakable ring should turn out to be nothing but an item of a dream!" he thought. But, to his surprise, it proved that such was nevertheless the actual state of the case! He opened the door and went out on to the landing; he looked downstairs and about him, but there was not a soul to be seen. The bell hung motionless. Surprised, but pleased, he returned into his room. He lit a candle, and suddenly remembered that he had left the door closed, but not locked and chained. He had often returned home before this evening and forgotten to lock the door behind him, without attaching any special significance to the fact; his maid had often respectfully protested against such neglect while with him. He now returned to the entrance hall to make the door fast; before doing so he opened it, however, and had one more look about the stairs. He then shut the door and fastened the chain and hook, but did not take the trouble to turn the key in the lock.

Some clock struck half-past two at this moment, so that he had had three hours' sleep—more or less.

His dream had agitated him to such an extent that he felt unwilling to lie down again at once; he decided to walk up and down the room two or three times first, just long enough to smoke a cigar. Having half-dressed himself, he went to the window, drew the heavy curtains aside and pulled up one of the blinds, it was almost full daylight. These light summer nights of St. Petersburg always had a bad effect upon his nerves, and of late they had added to the causes of his sleeplessness, so that a few weeks since he had invested in these thick curtains, which completely shut out the light when drawn close.

Having thus let in the sunshine, quite oblivious of the lighted candle on the table, he commenced to walk up and down the room. Still feeling the burden of his dream upon him, its impression was even now at work upon his mind, he still felt a painfully guilty sensation about him, caused by the fact that he had allowed himself to raise his hand against "that man" and strike him. "But, my dear sir!" he argued with himself, "it was not a man at all! the whole thing was a dream! what's the use of worrying yourself for nothing?"

Velchaninoff now became obstinately convinced that he was a sick man, and that to his sickly state of body was to be attributed all his perturbation of mind. He was an invalid.

It had always been a weak point with Velchaninoff that he hated to think of himself as growing old or infirm; and yet in his moments of anger he loved to exaggerate one or the other in order to worry himself.

"It's old age," he now muttered to himself, as he paced up and down the room. "I'm becoming an old fogey—that's the fact of the matter! I'm losing my memory—see ghosts, and have dreams, and hear bells ring—curse it all! I know these dreams of old, they always herald fever with me. I dare swear that the whole business of this man with the crape hatband has been a dream too! I was perfectly right yesterday, he isn't haunting me the least bit in the world; it is I that am haunting *him*! I've invented a pretty little ghost-story about him and then climb under the table in terror at my own creation! Why do I call him a little cad, too? he may be a most respectable individual for all I know! His face is a disagreeable one, certainly, though there is nothing hideous about it! He dresses just like anyone else. I don't know—there's something about his look—There I go again! What the devil have I got to do with his look? what a fool I am—just as though I could not live without the dirty little wretch—curse him!"

Among other thoughts connected with this haunting crape-man was one which puzzled Velchaninoff immensely; he felt convinced that at some time or other he had known the man, and known him very intimately; and that now the latter, when meeting him, always laughed at him because he was aware of some great secret of his former life, or because he was amused to see Velchaninoff's present humiliating condition of poverty.

Mechanically our hero approached the window in order to get a breath of fresh air—when he was suddenly seized with a violent fit of shuddering;—a feeling came over him that something unusual and unheard-of was happening before his very eyes.

He had not had time to open the window when something he saw caused him to slip behind the corner of the curtain, and hide himself.

The man in the crape hatband was standing on the opposite side of the street.

He was standing with his face turned directly towards Velchaninoff's window, but evidently unaware of the latter's presence there, and was carefully examining the house, and apparently considering some question connected with it.

He seemed to come to a decision after a moment's thought, and raised his finger to his forehead; then he looked quietly about him, and ran swiftly across the road on tiptoe. He reached the gate, and entered it; this gate was often left open on summer nights until two or three in the morning.

"He's coming to me," muttered Velchaninoff, and with equal caution he left the window, and ran to the front door; arrived in the hall, he stood in breathless expectation before the door, and placed his trembling hand carefully upon the hook which he had fastened a few minutes since, and stood listening for the tread of the expected footfall on the stairs. His heart was beating so loud that he was afraid he might miss the sound of the cautious steps approaching.

He could understand nothing of what was happening, but it seemed clear that his dream was about to be realised.

Velchaninoff was naturally brave. He loved risk for its own sake, and very often ran into useless dangers, with no one by to see, to please himself. But this was different, somehow; he was not himself, and yet he was as brave as ever, but with something added. He made out every movement of the stranger from behind his own door.

"Ah!—there he comes!—he's on the steps now!—here he comes!—he's up now!—now he's looking down stairs and all about, and crouching down! Aha! there's his hand on the door-handle—he's trying it!—he thought he would find it unlocked!—then he must know that I *do* leave it unlocked sometimes!—He's trying it again!—I suppose he thinks the hook may slip!—he doesn't care to go away without doing anything!"

So ran Velchaninoff's thoughts, and so indeed followed the man's actions. There was no doubt about it, someone was certainly standing outside and trying the door-handle, carefully and cautiously pulling at the door itself, and, in fact, endeavouring to effect an entrance; equally sure was it that the person so doing must have his own object in trying to sneak into another man's house at dead of night. But Velchaninoff's plan of action was laid, and he awaited the proper moment; he was anxious to seize a good opportunity—slip the hook and chain—open the door wide, suddenly, and stand face to face with this bugbear, and then ask him what the deuce he wanted there.

No sooner devised than executed.

Awaiting the proper moment, Velchaninoff suddenly slipped the hook, pushed the door wide, and almost tumbled over the man with the crape hatband!

CHAPTER III.

The crape-man stood rooted to the spot dumb with astonishment.

Both men stood opposite one another on the landing, and both stared in each other's eyes, silent and motionless.

So passed a few moments, and suddenly, like a flash of lightning, Velchaninoff became aware of the identity of his guest.

At the same moment the latter seemed to guess that Velchaninoff had recognised him. Velchaninoff could see it in his eyes. In one instant the visitor's whole face was all ablaze with its very sweetest of smiles.

"Surely I have the pleasure of speaking to Aleksey Ivanovitch?" he asked, in the most dulcet of voices, comically inappropriate to the circumstances of the case.

"Surely you are Pavel Pavlovitch Trusotsky?" asked Velchaninoff, in return, after a pause, and with an expression of much perplexity.

"I had the pleasure of your acquaintance ten years ago at T——, and, if I may remind you of the fact, we were almost intimate friends."

"Quite so—oh yes! but it is now three o'clock in the morning, and you have been trying my lock for the last ten minutes."

"Three o'clock!" cried the visitor, looking at his watch with an air of melancholy surprise.

"Why, so it is! dear me—three o'clock! forgive me, Aleksey Ivanovitch! I ought to have found it out before thinking of paying you a visit. I will do myself the honour of calling to explain another day, and now I—."

"Oh no;—no, no! If you are to explain at all let's have it at once; this moment!" interrupted Velchaninoff warmly. "Kindly step in here, into the room! You must have meant to come in, you know; you didn't come here at night, like this, simply for the pleasure of trying my lock?"

He felt excited, and at the same time was conscious of a sort of timidity; he could not collect his thoughts. He was ashamed of himself for it. There was no danger, no mystery about the business, nothing but the silly figure of Pavel Pavlovitch.

And yet he could not feel satisfied that there was nothing particular in it; he felt afraid of something to come, he knew not what or when.

However, he made the man enter, seated him in a chair, and himself sat down on the side of his bed, a yard or so off, and rested his elbows on his knees while he quietly waited for the other to begin. He felt irritated; he stared at his visitor and let his thoughts run. Strangely enough, the other never opened his mouth; he seemed to be entirely oblivious of the fact that it was his duty to speak. Nay, he was even looking enquiringly at Velchaninoff as though quite expecting that the latter would speak to *him*!

Perhaps he felt a little uncomfortable at first, somewhat as a mouse must feel when he finds himself unexpectedly in the trap.

Velchaninoff very soon lost his patience.

"Well?" he cried, "you are not a fantasy or a dream or anything of that kind, are you? You aren't a corpse, are you? Come, my friend, this is not a game or play. I want your explanation, please!"

The visitor fidgeted about a little, smiled, and began to speak cautiously.

"So far as I can see," he said, "the time of night of my visit is what surprises you, and that I should have come as I did; in fact, when I remember the past, and our intimacy, and all that, I am astonished myself; but the fact is, I did not mean to come in at all, and if I did so it was purely an accident."

"An accident! Why, I saw you creeping across the road on tip-toes!"

"You saw me? Indeed! Come, then you know as much or more about the matter than I do; but I see I am annoying you. This is how it was: I've been in town three weeks or so on business. I am Pavel Pavlovitch Trusotsky, you recognized me yourself, my business in town is to effect an exchange of departments. I am trying for a situation in another place—one with a large increase of salary; but all this is beside the point; the fact of the matter is, I believe I have been delaying my business on purpose. I believe if everything were settled at this moment I should still be dawdling in this St. Petersburg of yours in my present condition of mind. I go wandering about as though I had lost all interest in things, and were rather glad of the fact, in my present condition of mind."

"What condition of mind?" asked Velchaninoff, frowning.

The visitor raised his eyes to Velchaninoff's, lifted his hat from the ground beside him, and with great dignity pointed out the black crape band.

"There, sir, in *that* condition of mind!" he observed.

Velchaninoff stared stupidly at the crape, and thence at the man's face. Suddenly his face flushed up in a hot blush for a moment, and he was violently agitated.

"Not Natalia Vasilievna, surely?"

"Yes, Natalia Vasilievna! Last March! Consumption, sir, and almost suddenly—all over in two or three months— and here am I left as you see me!"

So saying, Pavel Pavlovitch, with much show of feeling, bent his bald head down and kept it bent for some ten seconds, while he held out his two hands, in one of which was the hat with the band, in explanatory emotion.

This gesture, and the man's whole air, seemed to brighten Velchaninoff up; he smiled sarcastically for one instant, not more at present, for the news of this lady's death (he had known her so long ago, and had forgotten her many a year since) had made a quite unexpected impression upon his mind.

"Is it possible!" he muttered, using the first words that came to his lips, "and pray why did you not come here and tell me at once?"

"Thanks for your kind interest, I see and value it, in spite of——"

"In spite of what?"

"In spite of so many years of separation you at once sympathised with my sorrow—and in fact with myself, and so fully too—that I feel naturally grateful. That's all I had to tell you, sir! Don't suppose I doubt my friends, you know; why, even here, in this place, I could put my finger on several very sincere friends indeed (for instance, Stepan Michailovitch Bagantoff); but remember, my dear Aleksey Ivanovitch—nine years have passed since we were acquaintances—or friends, if you'll allow me to say so—and meanwhile you have never been to see us, never written."

The guest sang all this out as though he were reading it from music, but kept his eyes fixed on the ground the while, although, of course, he saw what was going on above his eyelashes exceedingly well all the same.

Velchaninoff had found his head by this time.

With a strange sort of fascinated attention, which strengthened itself every moment, he continued to gaze at and listen to Pavel Pavlovitch, and of a sudden, when the latter stopped speaking, a flood of curious ideas swept unexpectedly through his brain.

"But look here," he cried, "how is it that I never recognized you all this while?—we've met five times, at least, in the streets!"

"Quite so—I am perfectly aware of the circumstance. You chanced to meet me two or three times, and——"

"No, no! *you* met *me*, you know—not I you!" Velchaninoff suddenly burst into a roar of laughter, and rose from his seat. Pavel Pavlovitch paused a moment, looked keenly at Velchaninoff, and then continued:

"As to your not recognizing me, in the first place you might easily have forgotten me by now; and besides, I have had small-pox since last we met, and I daresay my face is a good deal marked."

"Smallpox? why, how did you manage that?—he has had it, though, by Jove!" cried Velchaninoff. "What a funny fellow you are—however, go on, don't stop."

Velchaninoff's spirits were rising higher and higher; he was beginning to feel wonderfully light-hearted. That feeling of agitation which had lately so disturbed him had given place to quite a different sentiment. He now began to stride up and down the room, very quickly.

"I was going to say," resumed Pavel Pavlovitch, "that though I have met you several times, and though I quite intended to come and look you up, when I was arranging my visit to Petersburg, still, I was in that condition of mind, you know, and my wits have so suffered since last March, that——"

"Wits since last March,—yes, go on: wait a minute—do you smoke?"

"Oh—you know, Natalia Vasilievna, never—"

"Quite so; but since March—eh?"

"Well—I might, a cigarette or so."

"Here you are, then! Light up and go on,—go on! you interest me wonderfully."

Velchaninoff lit a cigar and sat down on his bed again. Pavel Pavlovitch paused a moment.

"But what a state of agitation you seem to be in yourself!" said he, "are you quite well?"

"Oh, curse my health!" cried Velchaninoff,—"you go on!"

The visitor observed his host's agitation with satisfaction; he went on with his share of the talking with more confidence.

"What am I to go on about?" he asked. "Imagine me, Alexey Ivanovitch—a broken man,—not simply broken, but gone at the root, as it were; a man forced to change his whole manner of living, after twenty years of married life, wandering about the dusty roads without an object,—mind lost—almost oblivious of his own self,—and yet, as it were, taking some sort of intoxicated delight in his loneliness! Isn't it natural that if I should, at such a moment of self-forgetfulness come across a friend—even a *dear* friend, I might prefer to avoid him for that moment? and isn't it equally natural that at another moment I should long to see and speak with some one who has been an eye-witness of, or a partaker, so to speak, in my never-to-be-recalled past? and to rush—not only in the day, but at night, if it so happens,—to rush to the embrace of such a man?—yes, even if one has to wake him up at three in the morning to do it! I was wrong in my time, not in my estimate of my friend, though, for at this moment I feel the full rapture of success; my rash action has been successful: I have found sympathy! As for the time of night, I confess I thought it was not twelve yet! You see, one sups of grief, and it intoxicates one,—at least, not grief, exactly, it's more the condition of mind—the new state of things that affects me."

"Dear me, how oddly you express yourself!" said Velchaninoff, rising from his seat once more, and becoming quite serious again.

"Oddly, do I? Perhaps."

"Look here: are you joking?"

"Joking!" cried Pavel Pavlovitch, in shocked surprise; "*joking*—at the very moment when I am telling you of——"

"Oh—be quiet about that! for goodness sake."

Velchaninoff started off on his journey up and down the room again.

So matters stood for five minutes or so: the visitor seemed inclined to rise from his chair, but Velchaninoff bade him sit still, and Pavel Pavlovitch obediently flopped into his seat again.

"How changed you are!" said the host at last, stopping in front of the other chair, as though suddenly struck with the idea; "fearfully changed!"

"Wonderful! you're quite another man!"

"That's hardly surprising! *nine* years, sir!"

"No, no, no! years have nothing to do with it! it's not in appearance you are so changed: it's something else!"

"Well, sir, the nine years might account for anything."

"Perhaps it's only since March, eh?"

"Ha-ha! you are playful, sir," said Pavel Pavlovitch, laughing slyly. "But, if I may ask it, wherein am I so changed?"

"Oh—why, you used to be such a staid, sober, correct Pavel Pavlovitch; such a wise Pavel Pavlovitch; and now you're a good-for-nothing sort of Pavel Pavlovitch."

Velchaninoff was in that state of irritation when the steadiest, gravest people will sometimes say rather more than they mean.

"Good-for-nothing, am I? and *wise* no longer, I suppose, eh?" chuckled Pavel Pavlovitch, with disagreeable satisfaction.

"Wise, indeed! My dear sir, I'm afraid you are not sober," replied Velchaninoff; and added to himself, "I am pretty fairly insolent myself, but I can't compare with this little cad! And what on earth is the fellow driving at?"

"Oh, my dear, good, my best of Alexey Ivanovitches," said the visitor suddenly, most excitedly, and twisting about on his chair, "and why *should* I be sober? We are not moving in the brilliant walks of society—you and I—

just now. We are but two dear old friends come together in the full sincerity of perfect love, to recall and talk over that sweet mutual tie of which the dear departed formed so treasured a link in our friendship."

So saying, the sensitive gentleman became so carried away by his feelings that he bent his head down once more, to hide his emotion, and buried his face in his hat.

Velchaninoff looked on with an uncomfortable feeling of disgust.

"I can't help thinking the man is simply silly," he thought; "and yet—no, no—his face is so red he must be drunk. But drunk or not drunk, what does the little wretch want with me? That's the puzzle."

"Do you remember—oh, *don't* you remember—our delightful little evenings—dancing sometimes, or sometimes literary—at Simeon Simeonovitch's?" continued the visitor, gradually removing his hat from before his face, and apparently growing more and more enthusiastic over the memories of the past, "and our little readings—you and she and myself—and our first meeting, when you came in to ask for information about something connected with your business in the town, and commenced shouting angrily at me; don't you remember—when suddenly in came Natalia Vasilievna, and within ten minutes you were our dear friend, and so remained for exactly a year? Just like Turgenieff's story 'The Provincialka!' "

Velchaninoff had continued his walk up and down the room during this *tirade*, with his eyes on the ground, listening impatiently and with disgust—but listening *hard*, all the same.

"It never struck me to think of 'The Provincialka' in connection with the matter," he interrupted. "And look here, why do you talk in that sneaking, whining sort of voice? You never used to do that. Your whole manner is unlike yourself."

"Quite so, quite so. I used to be more silent, I know. I used to love to listen while others talked. You remember how well the dear departed talked—the wit and grace of her conversation. As to The Provincialka, I remember she and I used often to compare your friendship for us to certain episodes in that piece, and especially to the doings of one Stupendief. It really was remarkably like that character and his doings."

"What Stupendief do you mean, confound it all?" cried Velchaninoff, stamping his foot with rage. The name seemed to have evoked certain most irritating thoughts in his mind.

"Why, Stupendief, don't you know, the 'husband' in 'Provincialka,' " whined Pavel Pavlovitch, in the very sweetest of tones; "but that belongs to another set of fond memories—after you departed, in fact, when Mr. Bagantoff had honoured us with his friendship, just as you had done before him, only that his lasted five whole years."

"Bagantoff? What Bagantoff? Do you mean that same Bagantoff who was serving down in your town? Why, he also——"

"Yes, yes! quite so. He also, he also!" cried the enthusiastic Pavel Pavlovitch, seizing upon Velchaninoff's accidental slip. "Of course! So that there you are—there's the whole company. Bagantoff played the 'count,' the dear departed was the 'Provincialka,' and I was the 'husband,' only that the part was taken away from me, for incapacity, I suppose!"

"Yes; fancy *you* a Stupendief. You're a—you're first a Pavel Pavlovitch Trusotsky!" said Velchaninoff, contemptuously, and very unceremoniously. "But look here! Bagantoff is in town; I know he is, for I have seen him. Why don't you go to see *him* as well as myself?"

"My dear sir, I've been there every day for the last three weeks. He won't receive me; he's ill, and can't receive! And, do you know, I have found out that he really is very ill! Fancy my feelings—a five-year's friend! Oh, my dear Alexey Ivanovitch! you don't know what my feelings are in my present condition of mind. I assure you, at one moment I long for the earth to open and swallow me up, and the next I feel that I *must* find one of those old friends, eyewitnesses of the past, as it were, if only to weep on his bosom, only to weep, sir—give you my word."

"Well, that's about enough for to-night; don't you think so?" said Velchaninoff, cuttingly.

"Oh, too—too much!" cried the other, rising. "It must be four o'clock; and here am I agitating your feelings in the most selfish way."

"Now, look here; I shall call upon you myself, and I hope that you will then——but, tell me honestly, are you drunk to-night?"

"Drunk! not the least in the world!"

"Did you drink nothing before you came here, or earlier?"

"Do you know, my dear Alexey Ivanovitch, you are quite in a high fever!"

"Good-night. I shall call to-morrow."

"And I have noticed it all the evening, really quite delirious!" continued Pavel Pavlovitch, licking his lips, as it were, with satisfaction as he pursued this theme. "I am really quite ashamed that I should have allowed myself to be so awkward as to agitate you. Well, well; I'm going! Now you must lie down at once and go to sleep."

"You haven't told me where you live," shouted Velchaninoff after him as he left the room.

"Oh, didn't I? Pokrofsky Hotel."

Pavel Pavlovitch was out on the stairs now.

"Stop!" cried Velchaninoff, once more. "You are not 'running away,' are you?"

"How do you mean, 'running away?'" asked Pavel Pavlovitch, turning round at the third step, and grinning back at him, with his eyes staring very wide open.

Instead of replying, Velchaninoff banged the door fiercely, locked and bolted it, and went fuming back into his room. Arrived there, he spat on the ground, as though to get rid of the taste of something loathsome.

He then stood motionless for at least five minutes, in the centre of the room; after which he threw himself upon his bed, and fell asleep in an instant.

The forgotten candle burned itself out in its socket.

CHAPTER IV.

Velchaninoff slept soundly until half-past nine, at which hour he started up, sat down on the side of his bed, and began to think.

His thoughts quickly fixed themselves upon the death of "that woman."

The agitating impression wrought upon his mind by yesterday's news as to her death had left a painful feeling of mental perturbation.

This morning the whole of the events of nine years back stood out before his mind's eye with extraordinary distinctness.

He had loved this woman, Natalia Vasilievna—Trusotsky's wife,—he had loved her, and had acted the part of her lover during the time which he had spent in their provincial town (while engaged in business connected with a legacy); he had lived there a whole year, though his business did not require by any means so long a visit; in fact, the tie above mentioned had detained him in the place.

He had been so completely under the influence of this passion, that Natalia Vasilievna had held him in a species of slavery. He would have obeyed the slightest whim or the wildest caprice of the woman, at that time. He had never, before or since, experienced anything approaching to the infatuation she had caused.

When the time came for departing, Velchaninoff had been in a state of such absolute despair, though the parting was to have been but a short one, that he had begged Natalia Vasilievna to leave all and fly across the frontier with him; and it was only by laughing him out of the idea (though she had at first encouraged it herself, probably for a joke), and by unmercifully chaffing him, that the lady eventually persuaded Velchaninoff to depart alone.

However, he had not been a couple of months in St. Petersburg before he found himself asking himself that question which he had never to this day been able to answer satisfactorily, namely, "*Did* he love this woman at all, or was it nothing but the infatuation of the moment?" He did not ask this question because he was conscious of any new passion taking root in his heart; on the contrary, during those first two months in town he had been in that condition of mind that he had not so much as looked at a woman, though he had met hundreds, and had returned to his old society ways at once. And yet he knew perfectly well that if he were to return to T—— he would instantly fall into the meshes of his passion for Natalia Vasilievna once more, in spite of the question which he could not answer as to the reality of his love for her.

Five years later he was as convinced of this fact as ever, although the very thought of it was detestable to him, and although he did not remember the name of Natalia Vasilievna but with loathing.

He was ashamed of that episode at T——. He could not understand how he (Velchaninoff) could ever have allowed himself to become the victim of such a stupid passion. He blushed whenever he thought of the shameful business—blushed, and even wept for shame.

He managed to forget his remorse after a few more years—he felt sure that he had "lived it down;" and yet now, after nine years, here was the whole thing resuscitated by the news of Natalia's death.

At all events, however, now, as he sat on his bed with agitating thoughts swarming through his brain, he could not but feel that the fact of her being dead was a consolation, amidst all the painful reflections which the mention of her name had called up.

"Surely I am a little sorry for her?" he asked himself.

Well, he certainly did not feel that sensation of hatred for her now; he could think of her and judge her now without passion of any kind, and therefore more justly.

He had long since been of opinion that in all probability there had been nothing more in Natalia Vasilievna than is to be found in every lady of good provincial society, and that he himself had created the whole "fantasy" of his worship and her worshipfulness; but though he had formed this opinion, he always doubted its correctness, and he still felt that doubt now. Facts existed to contradict the theory. For instance, this Bagantoff had lived for several years at T——, and had been no less a victim to passion for this woman, and had been as helpless as Velchaninoff himself under her witchery. Bagantoff, though a young idiot (as Velchaninoff expressed it), was nevertheless a scion of the very highest society in St. Petersburg. His career was in St. Petersburg, and it was significant that such a man should have wasted five important years of his life at T—— simply out of love for this woman. It was said that he had only returned to Petersburg even then because the lady had had enough of him; so that, all things considered, there must have been something which rendered Natalia Vasilievna preeminently attractive among women.

Yet the woman was not rich; she was not even pretty (if not absolutely *plain*!) Velchaninoff had known her when she was twenty-eight years old. Her face was capable of taking a pleasing expression, but her eyes were not good—they were too hard. She was a thin, bony woman to look at. Her mind was intelligent, but narrow and one-sided. She had tact and taste, especially as to dress. Her character was firm and overbearing. She was never wrong (in her own opinion) or unjust. The unfaithfulness towards her husband never caused her the slightest remorse; she hated corruption, and yet she was herself corrupt; and she believed in herself absolutely. Nothing could ever have persuaded her that she herself was actually depraved; Velchaninoff believed that she really did not know that her own corruption was corrupt. He considered her to be "one of those women who only exist to be unfaithful wives." Such women never remain unmarried,—it is the law of their nature to marry,—their husband is their first lover, and he is always to blame for anything that may happen afterwards; the unfaithful wife herself being invariably *absolutely* in the right, and of course perfectly innocent.

So thought Velchaninoff; and he was convinced that such a type of woman actually existed; but he was no less convinced that there also existed a corresponding type of men, born to be the husbands of such women. In his opinion the mission of such men was to be, so to speak, "permanent husbands,"—that is, to be husbands all their lives, and nothing else.

Velchaninoff had not the smallest doubt as to the existence of these two types, and Pavel Pavlovitch Trusotsky was, in his opinion, an excellent representative of the male type. Of course, the Pavel Pavlovitch of last night was by no means the same Pavel Pavlovitch as he had known at T——. He had found an extraordinary change in the man; and yet, on reflection, he was bound to admit that the change was but natural, for that he could only have remained what he was so long as his wife lived; and that now he was but a part of a whole, allowed to wander at will—that is, an imperfect being, a surprising, an incomprehensible sort of a *thing*, without proper balance.

As for the Pavel Pavlovitch of T——, this is what Velchaninoff remembered of him:

Pavel Pavlovitch had been a husband, of course,—a formality,—and that was all. If, for instance, he was a clerk of department besides, he was so merely in his capacity of, and as a part of his responsibility as—a husband. He worked for his wife, and for her social position. He had been thirty-five years old at that time, and was possessed of some considerable property. He had not shown any special talent, nor, on the other hand, any marked incapacity in his professional employment; his position had been decidedly a good one.

Natalia Vasilievna had been respected and looked up to by all; not that she valued their respect in the least,—she considered it merely as her due. She was a good hostess, and had schooled Pavel Pavlovitch into polite manners, so that he was able to receive and entertain the very best society passably well.

He might be a clever man, for all Velchaninoff knew, but as Natalia Vasilievna did not like her husband to talk much, there was little opportunity of judging. He may have had many good qualities, as well as bad; but the good ones were, so to speak, kept put away in their cases, and the bad ones were stifled and not allowed to appear. Velchaninoff remembered, for instance, that Pavel Pavlovitch had once or twice shown a disposition to laugh at those about him, but this unworthy proclivity had been very promptly subdued. He had been fond of telling stories, but this was not allowed either; or, if permitted at all, the anecdote was to be of the shortest and most uninteresting description.

Pavel Pavlovitch had a circle of private friends outside the house, with whom he was fain, at times, to taste the flowing bowl; but this vicious tendency was radically stamped out as soon as possible.

And yet, with all this, Natalia Vasilievna appeared, to the uninitiated, to be the most obedient of wives, and doubtless considered herself so. Pavel Pavlovitch may have been desperately in love with her,—no one could say as to this.

Velchaninoff had frequently asked himself during his life at T——, whether Pavel Pavlovitch ever suspected his wife of having formed the tie with himself, of which mention has been made. Velchaninoff had several times questioned Natalia Vasilievna on this point, seriously enough; but had invariably been told, with some show of annoyance, that her husband neither did know, nor ever could know; and that "all there might be to know was not his business!"

Another trait in her character was that she never laughed at Pavel Pavlovitch, and never found him funny in any sense; and that she would have been down on any person who dared to be rude to him, at once!

Pavel Pavlovitch's reference to the pleasant little readings enjoyed by the trio nine years ago was accurate; they used to read Dickens' novels together. Velchaninoff or Trusotsky reading aloud, while Natalia Vasilievna worked. The life at T—— had ended suddenly, and so far as Velchaninoff was concerned, in a way which drove him almost to the verge of madness. The fact is, he was simply turned out—although it was all managed in such a way that he never observed that he was being thrown over like an old worn-out shoe.

A young artillery officer had appeared in the town a month or so before Velchaninoff's departure and had made acquaintance with the Trusotsky's. The trio became a quartet. Before long Velchaninoff was informed that for many reasons a separation was absolutely necessary; Natalia Vasilievna adduced a hundred excellent reasons why this had become unavoidable—and especially one which quite settled the matter. After his stormy attempt to persuade Natalia Vasilievna to fly with him to Paris—or anywhere,—Velchaninoff had ended by going to St. Petersburg alone—for two or three months at the *very most*, as he said,—otherwise he would refuse to go at all, in spite of every reason and argument Natalia might adduce.

Exactly two months later Velchaninoff had received a letter from Natalia Vasilievna, begging him to come no more to T——, because that she already loved another. As to the principal reason which she had brought forward in favour of his immediate departure, she now informed him that she had made a mistake. Velchaninoff remembered the young artilleryman, and understood,—and so the matter had ended, once and for all. A year or two after this Bagantoff appeared at T——, and an intimacy between Natalia Vasilievna and the former had sprung up which lasted for five years. This long period of constancy, Velchaninoff attributed to advancing age on the part of Natalia. He sat on the side of his bed for nearly an hour and thought. At last he roused himself, rang for Mavra and his coffee, drank it off quickly—dressed—and punctually at eleven was on his way to the Pokrofsky Hotel: he felt rather ashamed of his behaviour to Pavel Pavlovitch last night. Velchaninoff put down all that phantasmagoria of the trying of the lock and so on to Pavel Pavlovitch's drunken condition and to other reasons,—but he did not know why he was now on his way to make fresh relations with the husband of that woman, since their acquaintanceship and intercourse had come to so natural and simple a termination; yet something seemed to draw him thither—some strong current of impulse,—and he went.

CHAPTER V.

Pavel Pavlovitch was not thinking of "running away," and goodness knows why Velchaninoff should have asked him such a question last night—he did not know himself why he had said it!

He was directed to the Petrofsky Hotel, and found the building at once. At the hotel he was told that Pavel Pavlovitch had now engaged a furnished lodging in the back part of the same house.

Mounting the dirty and narrow stairs indicated, as far as the third storey, he suddenly became aware of someone crying. It sounded like the weeping of a child of some seven or eight years of age; it was a bitter, but a more or less suppressed sort of crying, and with it came the sound of a grown man's voice, apparently trying to quiet the child—anxious that its sobbing and crying should not be heard,—and yet only succeeding in making it cry the louder.

The man's voice did not seem in any way sympathetic with the child's grief; and the latter appeared to be begging for forgiveness.

Making his way into a narrow dark passage with two doors on each side of it, Velchaninoff met a stout-looking, elderly woman, in very careless morning attire, and inquired for Pavel Pavlovitch.

She tapped the door with her fingers in response to his inquiry—the same door, apparently, whence issued the noises just mentioned. Her fat face seemed to flush with indignation as she did so.

"He appears to be amusing himself in there!" she said, and proceeded downstairs.

Velchaninoff was about to knock, but thought better of it and opened the door without ceremony.

In the very middle of a room furnished with plain, but abundant furniture, stood Pavel Pavlovitch in his shirt-sleeves, very red in the face, trying to persuade a little girl to do something or other, and using cries and gestures, and what looked to Velchaninoff very like kicks, in order to effect his purpose. The child appeared to be some seven or eight years of age, and was poorly dressed in a short black stuff frock. She seemed to be in a most hysterical condition, crying and stretching out her arms to Pavel Pavlovitch, as though begging and entreating him to allow her to do whatever it might be she desired.

On Velchaninoff's appearance the scene changed in an instant. No sooner did her eyes fall on the visitor than the child made for the door of the next room, with a cry of alarm; while Pavel Pavlovitch—thrown out for one little instant—immediately relaxed into smiles of great sweetness—exactly as he had done last night, when Velchaninoff suddenly opened his front door and caught him standing outside.

"Alexey Ivanovitch!" he cried in real surprise; "who ever would have thought it! Sit down—sit down—take the sofa—or this chair,—sit down, my dear sir! I'll just put on——" and he rushed for his coat and threw it on, leaving his waistcoat behind.

"Don't stand on ceremony with me," said Velchaninoff sitting down; "stay as you are!"

"No, sir, no! excuse me—I insist upon standing on ceremony. There, now! I'm a little more respectable! Dear me, now, who ever would have thought of seeing *you* here!—not I, for one!"

Pavel Pavlovitch sat down on the edge of a chair, which he turned so as to face Velchaninoff.

"And pray *why* shouldn't you have expected me? I told you last night that I was coming this morning!"

"I thought you wouldn't come, sir—I did indeed; in fact, when I thought over yesterday's visit, I despaired of ever seeing you again: I did indeed, sir!"

Velchaninoff glanced round the room meanwhile. The place was very untidy; the bed was unmade; the clothes thrown about the floor; on the table were two coffee tumblers with the dregs of coffee still in them, and a bottle of champagne half finished, and with a tumbler standing alongside it. He glanced at the next room, but all was quiet there; the little girl had hidden herself, and was as still as a mouse.

"You don't mean to say you drink that stuff at this time of day?" he asked, indicating the champagne bottle.

"It's only a remnant," explained Pavel Pavlovitch, a little confused.

"My word! You *are* a changed man!"

"Bad habits, sir; and all of a sudden. All dating from that time, sir. Give you my word, I couldn't resist it. But I'm all right now—I'm not drunk—I shan't talk twaddle as I did last night; don't be afraid sir, it's all right! From that very day, sir; give you my word it is! And if anyone had told me half a year ago that I should become like this,—if they had shown me my face in a glass then as I should be *now*, I should have given them the lie, sir; I should indeed!"

"Hem! Then you *were* drunk last night?"

"Yes—I was!" admitted Pavel Pavlovitch, a little guiltily—"not exactly *drunk*, a little *beyond* drunk!—I tell you this by way of explanation, because I'm always worse *after* being drunk! If I'm only a little drunk, still the violence and unreasonableness of intoxication come out afterwards, and stay out too; and then I feel my grief the more keenly. I daresay my grief is responsible for my drinking. I am capable of making an awful fool of myself and offending people when I'm drunk. I daresay I seemed strange enough to you last night?"

"Don't you remember what you said and did?"

"Assuredly I do—I remember everything!"

"Listen to me, Pavel Pavlovitch: I have thought it over and have come to very much the same conclusion as you did yourself," began Velchaninoff gently; "besides—I believe I was a little too irritable towards you last night—too impatient,—I admit it gladly; the fact is—I am not very well sometimes, and your sudden arrival, you know, in the middle of the night——"

"In the middle of the night: you are quite right—it was!" said Pavel Pavlovitch, wagging his head assentingly; "how in the world could I have brought myself to do such a thing? I shouldn't have come in, though, if you hadn't opened the door. I should have gone as I came. I called on you about a week ago, and did not find you at home, and I daresay I should never have called again; for I am rather proud—Alexey Ivanovitch—in spite of my present state. Whenever I have met you in the streets I have always said to myself, 'What if he doesn't know me and rejects me—nine years is no joke!' and I did not dare try you for fear of being snubbed. Yesterday, thanks to that sort of thing, you know," (he pointed to the bottle), "I didn't know what time it was, and—it's lucky you are the kind of man you are, Alexey Ivanovitch, or I should despair of preserving your acquaintance, after yesterday! You remember old times, Alexey Ivanovitch!"

Velchaninoff listened keenly to all this. The man seemed to be talking seriously enough, and even with some dignity; and yet he had not believed a single word that Pavel Pavlovitch had uttered from the very first moment that he entered the room.

"Tell me, Pavel Pavlovitch," said Velchaninoff at last, "—I see you are not quite alone here,—whose little girl is that I saw when I came in?"

Pavel Pavlovitch looked surprised and raised his eyebrow; but he gazed back at Velchaninoff with candour and apparent amiability:

"Whose little girl? Why that's our Liza!" he said, smiling affably.

"What Liza?" asked Velchaninoff,—and something seemed to cause him to shudder inwardly.

The sensation was dreadfully sudden. Just now, on entering the room and seeing Liza, he had felt surprised more or less,—but had not been conscious of the slightest feeling of presentiment,—indeed he had had no special thought about the matter, at the moment.

"Why—*our* Liza!—our daughter Liza!" repeated Pavel Pavlovitch, smiling.

"Your daughter? Do you mean to say that you and Natalia Vasilievna had children?" asked Velchaninoff timidly, and in a very low tone of voice indeed!

"Of course—but—what a fool I am—how in the world should *you* know! Providence sent us the gift after you had gone!"

Pavel Pavlovitch jumped off his chair in apparently pleasurable excitement.

"I heard nothing of it!" said Velchaninoff, looking very pale.

"How should you? how should you?" repeated Pavel Pavlovitch with ineffable sweetness. "We had quite lost hope of any children—as you may remember,—when suddenly Heaven sent us this little one. And, oh! my feelings—Heaven alone knows what I felt! Just a year after you went, I think—no, wait a bit—not a year by a long way!—Let's see, you left us in October, or November, didn't you?"

"I left T—— on the twelfth of September, I remember well."

"Hum! September was it? Dear me! Well, then, let's see—September, October, November, December, January, February, March, April—to the 8th of May—that was Liza's birthday—eight months all but a bit; and if you could only have seen the dear departed, how rejoiced——"

"Show her to me—call her in!" the words seemed to tear themselves from Velchaninoff, whether he liked it or no.

"Certainly—this moment!" cried Pavel Pavlovitch, forgetting that he had not finished his previous sentence, or ignoring the fact; and he hastily left the room, and entered the small chamber adjoining.

Three or four minutes passed by, while Velchaninoff heard the rapid interchange of whispers going on, and an occasional rather louder sound of Liza's voice, apparently entreating her father to leave her alone—so Velchaninoff concluded.

At last the two came out.

"There you are—she's dreadfully shy and proud," said Pavel Pavlovitch; "just like her mother."

Liza entered the room without tears, but with eyes downcast, her father leading her by the hand. She was a tall, slight, and very pretty little girl. She raised her large blue eyes to the visitor's face with curiosity; but only glanced surlily at him, and dropped them again. There was that in her expression that one always sees in children when they look on some new guest for the first time—retiring to a corner, and looking out at him thence seriously and mistrustingly; only that there was a something in her manner beyond the usual childish mistrust—so, at least thought Velchaninoff.

Her father brought her straight up to the visitor.

"There—this gentleman knew mother very well. He was our friend; you mustn't be shy,—give him your hand!"

The child bowed slightly, and timidly stretched out her hand.

"Natalia Vasilievna never would teach her to curtsey; she liked her to bow, English fashion, and give her hand," explained Pavel Pavlovitch, gazing intently at Velchaninoff.

Velchaninoff knew perfectly well that the other was keenly examining him at this moment, but he made no attempt to conceal his agitation: he sat motionless on his chair and held the child's hand in his, gazing into her face the while.

But Liza was apparently much preoccupied, and did not take her eyes off her father's face; she listened timidly to every word he said.

Velchaninoff recognised her large blue eyes at once; but what specially struck him was the refined pallor of her face, and the colour of her hair; these traits were altogether too significant, in his eyes! Her features, on the other hand, and the set of her lips, reminded him keenly of Natalia Vasilievna. Meanwhile Pavel Pavlovitch was in the middle of some apparently most interesting tale—one of great sentiment seemingly,—but Velchaninoff did not hear a word of it until the last few words struck upon his ear:

"... So that you can't imagine what our joy was when Providence sent us this gift, Alexey Ivanovitch! She was everything to me, for I felt that if it should be the will of Heaven to deprive me of my other joy, I should still have Liza left to me; that's what I felt, sir, I did indeed!"

"And Natalia Vasilievna?" asked Velchaninoff.

"Oh, Natalia Vasilievna—" began Pavel Pavlovitch, smiling with one side of his mouth; "she never used to like to say much—as you know yourself; but she told me on her deathbed—deathbed! you know, sir—to the very day of her death she used to get so angry and say that they were trying to cure her with a lot of nasty medicines when she had nothing the matter but a simple little feverish attack; and that when Koch arrived (you remember our old doctor Koch?) he would make her all right in a fortnight. Why, five hours before she died she was talking of fixing that day three weeks for a visit to her Aunt, Liza's godmother, at her country place!" Velchaninoff here started from his seat, but still held the child's hand. He could not help thinking that there was something reproachful in the girl's persistent stare in her father's face.

"Is she ill?" he asked hurriedly, and his voice had a strange tone in it.

"No! I don't think so" said Pavel Pavlovitch; "but, you see our way of living here, and all that: she's a strange child and very nervous, besides! After her mother's death she was quite ill and hysterical for a fortnight. Just before you came in she was crying like anything; and do you know what about, sir? Do you hear me, Liza?—You listen!—Simply because I was going out, and wished to leave her behind, and because she said I didn't love her so well as I used to in her mother's time. That's what she pitches into me for! Fancy a child like this getting hold of such an idea!—a child who ought to be playing at dolls, instead of developing ideas of that sort! The thing is, she has no one to play with here."

"Then—then—are you two quite alone here?"

"Quite! a servant comes in once a day, that's all!"

"And when you go out, do you leave her quite alone?"

"Of course! What else am I to do? Yesterday I locked her in that room, and that's what all the tears were about this morning. What could I do? the day before yesterday she went down into the yard all by herself, and a boy took a shot at her head with a stone! Not only that, but she must needs go and cling on to everybody she met, and ask where I had gone to! That's not so very pleasant, you see! But I oughtn't to complain when I say I am going out for an hour and then stay out till four in the morning, as I did last night! The landlady came and let her out: she had the door broken open! Nice for my feelings, eh! It's all the result of the eclipse that came over my life; nothing but that, sir!"

"Papa!" said the child, timidly and anxiously.

"Now, then! none of that again! What did I tell you yesterday?"

"I won't; I won't!" cried the child hurriedly, clasping her hands before her entreatingly.

"Come! things can't be allowed to go on in this way!" said Velchaninoff impatiently, and with authority. "In the first place, you are a man of property; how can you possibly live in a hole like this, and in such disorder?"

"This place! Oh, but we shall probably have left this place within a week; and I've spent a lot of money here, as it is, though I may be 'a man of property;' and——"

"Very well, that'll do," interrupted Velchaninoff with growing impatience, "now, I'll make you a proposition: you have just said that you intend to stay another week—perhaps two. I have a house here—or rather I know a family where I am as much at home as at my own fireside, and have been so for twenty years. The family I mean is the Pogoryeltseffs—Alexander Pavlovitch Pogoryeltseff is a state councillor (he may be of use to you in your business!) They are now living in the country—they have a beautiful country villa; Claudia Petrovna, the lady of the house, is like a sister—like a mother to me; they have eight children. Let me take Liza down to them without loss of time! they'll receive her with joy, and they'll treat her like their own little daughter—they will, indeed!"

Velchaninoff was in a great hurry, and much excited, and he did not conceal his feelings.

"I'm afraid it's impossible!" said Pavel Pavlovitch with a grimace, looking straight into his visitor's eyes, very cunningly, as it seemed to Velchaninoff.

"Why! why, impossible?"

"Oh, why! to let the child go—so suddenly, you know, of course with such a sincere well-wisher as yourself—it's not that!—but a strange house—and such swells, too!—I don't know whether they would receive her!"

"But I tell you I'm like a son of the house!" cried Velchaninoff, almost angrily. "Claudia Petrovna will be delighted to take her, at one word from me! She'd receive her as though she were my own daughter. Deuce take it, sir, you know you are only humbugging me,—what's the use of talking about it?"

He stamped his foot.

"No—no! I mean to say—don't it look a little strange? Oughtn't I to call once or twice first?—such a smart house as you say theirs is—don't you see——"

"I tell you it's the simplest house in the world; it isn't 'smart' in the least bit," cried Velchaninoff; "they have a lot of children: it will make another girl of her!—I'll introduce you there myself, to-morrow, if you like. Of course you'll have to go and thank them, and all that. You shall go down every day with me, if you please."

"Oh, but——"

"Nonsense! You know it's nonsense! Now look here: you come to me this evening—I'll put you up for the night—and we'll start off early to-morrow and be down there by twelve."

"Benefactor!—and I may spend the night at your house?" cried Pavel Pavlovitch, instantly consenting to the plan with the greatest cordiality,—"you are really *too* good! And where's their country house?"

"At the Liesnoy."

"But look here, how about her dress? Such a house, you know,—a father's heart shrinks——"

"Nonsense!—she's in mourning—what else could she wear but a black dress like this? it's exactly the thing; you couldn't imagine anything more so!—you might let her have some clean linen with her, and give her a cleaner neck-handkerchief."

"Directly, directly. We'll get her linen together in a couple of minutes—it's just home from the wash!"

"Send for a carriage—can you? Tell them to let us have it at once, so as not to waste time."

But now an unexpected obstacle arose: Liza absolutely rejected the plan; she had listened to it with terror, and if Velchaninoff had, in his excited argument with Pavel Pavlovitch, had time to glance at the child's face, he would have observed her expression of absolute despair at this moment.

"I won't go!" she said, quietly but firmly.

"There—look at that! Just like her mamma!"

"I'm *not* like mamma, I'm *not* like mamma!" cried Liza, wringing her little hands in despair. "Oh, papa—papa!"she added, "if you desert me—" she suddenly threw herself upon the alarmed Velchaninoff—"If you take me away—" she cried—"I'll——"

But Liza had no time to finish her sentence, for Pavel Pavlovitch suddenly seized her by the arm and collar and hustled her into the next room with unconcealed rage. For several minutes Velchaninoff listened to the whispering going on there,—whisperings and seemingly subdued crying on the part of Liza. He was about to follow the pair, when suddenly out came Pavel Pavlovitch, and stated—with a disagreeable grin—that Liza would come directly.

Velchaninoff tried not to look at him and kept his eyes fixed on the other side of the room.

The elderly woman whom Velchaninoff had met on the stairs also made her appearance, and packed Liza's things into a neat little carpet bag.

"Is it you that are going to take the little lady away, sir?" she asked; "if so, you are doing a good deed! She's a nice quiet child, and you are saving her from goodness knows what, here!"

"Oh! come—Maria Sisevna,"—began Pavel Pavlovitch.

"Well? What? Isn't it true! Arn't you ashamed to let a girl of her intelligence see the things that you allow to go on here? The carriage has arrived for you, sir,—*you* ordered one for the Liesnoy, didn't you?"

"Yes."

"Well, good luck to you!"

Liza came out, looking very pale and with downcast eyes; she took her bag, but never glanced in Velchaninoff's direction. She restrained herself and did not throw herself upon her father, as she had done before—not even to say good-bye. She evidently did not wish to look at him.

Her father kissed her and patted her head in correct form; her lip curled during the operation, the chin trembled a little, but she did not raise her eyes to her father's.

Pavel Pavlovitch looked pale, and his hands shook; Velchaninoff saw that plainly enough, although he did his best not to see the man at all. He (Velchaninoff) had but one thought, and that was how to get away at once!

Downstairs was old Maria Sisevna, waiting to say good-bye; and more kissing was done. Liza had just climbed into the carriage when suddenly she caught sight of her father's face; she gave a loud cry and wrung her hands,—in another minute she would have been out of the carriage and away, but luckily the vehicle went on and she was too late!

CHAPTER VI.

"Are you feeling faint?" asked Velchaninoff of his companion, frightened out of his wits: "I'll tell him to stop and get you some water, shall I?"

She looked at him angrily and reproachfully.

"Where are you taking me to?" she asked coldly and abruptly.

"To a very beautiful house, Liza. There are plenty of children,—they'll all love you there, they are so kind! Don't be angry with me, Liza; I wish you well, you know!"

In truth, Velchaninoff would have looked strange at this moment to any acquaintance, if such had happened to see him!

"How—how—how—oh! *how* wicked you are!" said Liza, fighting with suppressed tears, and flashing her fine angry eyes at him.

"But Liza—I——"

"You are bad—bad—and wicked!" cried Liza. She wrung her hands.

Velchaninoff was beside himself.

"Oh, Liza, Liza! if only you knew what despair you are causing me!" he said.

"Is it true that he is coming down to-morrow?" asked the child haughtily—"is it true or not?"

"Quite true—I shall bring him down myself,—I shall take him and bring him!"

"He will deceive you somehow!" cried the child, drooping her eyes.

"Doesn't he love you, then, Liza?"

"No."

"Has he ill-treated you,—has he?"

Liza looked gloomily at her questioner, and said nothing. She then turned away from him and sat still and depressed.

Velchaninoff commenced to talk: he tried to win her,—he spoke warmly—excitedly—feverishly.

Liza listened incredulously and with a hostile air,—but still she listened. Her attention delighted him beyond measure;—he went so far as to explain to her what it meant when a man took to drink. He said that he loved her and would himself look after her father.

At last Liza raised her eyes and gazed fixedly at him.

Then Velchaninoff began to speak of her mother and of how well he had known her; and he saw that his tales attracted her. Little by little she began to reply to his questions, but very cautiously and in an obstinately monosyllabic way.

She would answer nothing to his chief inquiries; as to her former relations with her father, for instance, she maintained an obstinate silence.

While speaking to her, Velchaninoff held the child's hand in his own, as before; and she did not try to take it away.

Liza said enough to make it apparent that she had loved her father more than her mother at first, because that her father had loved the child better than her mother did; but that when her mother had died and was lying dead, Liza wept over her and kissed her, and ever since then she had loved her mother more than all—all there was in the whole world—and that every night she thought of her and loved her.

But Liza was very proud, and suddenly recollecting herself and finding that she was saying a great deal more than she had meant to reveal, she paused, and relapsed into obstinate silence once more, and gazed at Velchaninoff with something like hatred in her eyes, considering that he had beguiled her into the revelations just made.

By the end of the journey, however, her hysterical condition was nearly over, but she was very silent and sat looking morosely about her, obstinately silent and gloomy, like a little wild animal.

The fact that she was being taken to a strange house where she had never been before did not seem so far to weigh upon her; Velchaninoff saw clearly enough that other things distressed her, and principally that she was ashamed—ashamed that her father should have let her go so easily—thrown her away, as it were—into Velchaninoff's arms.

"She's ill," thought the latter, "and perhaps very ill; she has been bullied and ill-treated. Oh! that drunken, blackguardly wretch of a fellow!" He hurried on the coachman. Velchaninoff trusted greatly to the fresh air, to the garden, to the children, to the new life, now; as to the future, he was in no sort of doubt at all, his hopes were clear and defined. One thing he was quite sure of, and that was that he had never before felt what now swelled within his soul, and that the sensation would last for ever and ever.

"I have an object at last! this is Life!" he said to himself enthusiastically.

Many thoughts welled into his brain just now, but he would have none of them; he did not care to think of details at this moment, for without details the future was all so clear and so beautiful, and so safe and indestructible!

The basis of his plan was simple enough; it was simply this, in the language of his own thoughts:

"I shall so work upon that drunken little blackguard that he will leave Liza with the Pogoryeltseffs, and go away alone—at first, 'for a time,' of course!—and so Liza shall remain behind for me! what more do I want? The plan will suit him, too!—else why does he bully her like this?"

The carriage arrived at last.

It was certainly a very beautiful place. They were met first of all by a troop of noisy children, who overflowed on to the front-door steps. Velchaninoff had not been down for some time, and the delight of the little ones to see him was excessive—they were very fond of him.

The elder ones shouted, before he had left the carriage, by way of chaff:

"How's the lawsuit getting on, eh?" and the smaller gang took up the joke, and all clamoured the same question: it was a pet joke in this establishment to chaff Velchaninoff about his lawsuit. But when Liza climbed down the carriage steps, she was instantly surrounded and stared at with true juvenile curiosity. Then Claudia Petrovna and her husband came out, and both of them good-humouredly bantered Velchaninoff about his lawsuit.

Claudia Petrovna was a lady of some thirty-seven summers, stout and well-favoured, and with a sweet fresh-looking face. Her husband was a man of fifty-five, a clever and long-headed man of the world, but above all, a good and kind-hearted friend to anyone requiring kindness.

The Pogoryeltseffs' house was in the full sense of the word a "home" to Velchaninoff, as the latter had stated. There was rather more here, however; for, twenty years since Claudia had very nearly married young Velchaninoff almost a boy at that time, and a student at the university.

This had been his first experience of love—and very hot and fiery and funny—and sweet it was! The end of it was, however, that Claudia married Mr Pogoryeltseff. Five years later she and Velchaninoff had met again, and a quiet candid friendship had sprung up between them. Since then there had always been a warmth, a speciality about their friendship, a radiance which overspread it and glorified their relations one to the other. There was nothing here that Velchaninoff could remember with shame—all was pure and sweet; and this was perhaps the reason why the friendship was specially dear to Velchaninoff; he had not experienced many such platonic intimacies.

In this house Velchaninoff was simple and happy, confessed his sins, played with the children and lectured them, and never bothered his head about outside matters; he had promised the Pogoryeltseffs that he would live a few more years alone in the world, and then move over to their household for good and all; and he looked forward to that good time coming with all seriousness.

Velchaninoff now gave all the information about Liza which he thought fit, though his simple request would have been amply sufficient here.

Claudia Petrovna kissed the little "orphan," and promised to do all she possibly could for her; and the children carried Liza off to play in the garden. Half an hour passed in conversation, and then Velchaninoff rose to depart: he was in such a hurry, that his friends could not help remarking upon the fact. He had not been near them for three weeks, they said, and now he only stayed half an hour! Velchaninoff laughed and promised to come down to-morrow. Someone observed that Velchaninoff's state of agitation was remarkable, even for *him*! Whereupon the latter jumped up, seized Claudia Petrovna's hand, and, under pretence of having forgotten to tell her something most important about Liza, he led her into another room.

"Do you remember," he began, "what I told you, and only you,—even your husband does not know of it—about my year of life down at T——?"

"Oh yes! only too well! You have often spoken of it."

"No—I did not 'speak about it,' I *confessed*, and only to yourself; but I never told you the lady's name. It was Trusotsky, the wife of this Trusotsky; it is she who has died, and this little Liza is her child—*my* child!"

"Is this certain? Are you quite sure there is no mistake?" asked Claudia Petrovna, with some agitation.

"Quite, quite certain!" said Velchaninoff enthusiastically. He then gave a short, hasty, and excited narrative of all that had occurred. Claudia had heard it all before, excepting the lady's name.

The fact is, Velchaninoff had always been so afraid that one of his friends might some fine day meet Madame Trusotsky at T——, and wonder how in the world he could have loved such a woman as that, that he had never revealed her name to a single soul; not even to Claudia Petrovna, his great friend.

"And does the 'father' know nothing of it?" asked Claudia, having heard the tale out.

"N—no; he knows—you see, that's just what is bothering me now. I haven't sifted the matter as yet," resumed Velchaninoff hotly. "He must know—he *does* know. I remarked that fact both yesterday and to-day. But I wish to discover *how much* he knows. That's why I am hurrying back now; he is coming to-night. He knows all about Bagantoff; but how about myself? You know how such wives can deceive their husbands! If an angel from Heaven were to come down and convict a woman, her husband will still trust her, and give the angel the lie. "Oh! don't nod your head at me, don't judge me! I have long since judged and convicted myself. You see, this morning I felt so sure that he knew all, that I compromised myself before him. Fancy, I was really ashamed of having been rude to him last night. He only called in to see me out of the pure unconquerably malicious desire to show me that he knew all the offence, and knew who was the offender! I behaved like a fool; I gave myself into his hands too easily; I was too heated; he came at such a feverish moment for me. I tell you, he has been bullying Liza, simply to 'let off bile,'—you understand. He needs a safety-valve for his offended feelings, and vents them upon *anyone*, even a little child!

"It is exasperation, and quite natural. We must treat him in a Christian spirit, my friend; and do you know, I wish to change my way of treating him, entirely; I wish to be particularly kind to him. That will be a good action on my part, for I am to blame before him, I know I am; there's no disguising the fact! Besides, once at T——, it so happened that I required four thousand roubles at a moment's notice. Well, the fellow gave me the money, without a receipt, at once, and with every manifestation of delight to be able to serve me! And I took the money from his hands,—I did, indeed! I took it as though he were a friend. Think of that!"

"Very well; only be careful!" said Claudia Petrovna. "You are so enthusiastic that I am really alarmed for you! Of course Liza shall now be no less than my own daughter to me; but there is so much to know and to settle yet!

Above all, be very careful and observant! You are not nearly careful enough when you are happy! You are much too exalted an individual to be cautious, when you are happy!" she added with a smile.

The whole family went out to see Velchaninoff off. The children brought Liza along with them; they had been playing in the garden. They seemed to look at her now with even more perplexity then at first! The girl became dreadfully shy when Velchaninoff kissed her before all, and promised to come down next day and bring her father with him. To the last moment she did not say a single word, and never looked at him at all; but just before he was about to start she seized his hand and drew him away to one side, looking imploringly in his face: she evidently had something to say to him. Velchaninoff immediately took her into an adjoining room.

"What is it, Liza?" he asked, kindly and encouragingly; but she drew him farther away,—into the very farthest corner of the room, anxious to get well out of sight and hearing of the rest.

"What is it, Liza? What is it?" But she was still silent, and could not make up her mind to speak; she stared with her motionless, large blue eyes, into his face, and in every lineament of her little face was betrayed the wildest terror and anxiety. "He'll—hang himself!" she whispered at last, as though she were talking in her sleep. "Who will hang himself?" asked Velchaninoff, in alarm. "He will—*he*! He tried to hang himself to a hook last night!" said the child, panting with haste and excitement;"I saw it myself! To-day he tried it again,—he wishes to hang himself; he told me so!—he told me so! He wanted to, long ago; he has always wanted to do it! I saw it myself—in the night!" "Impossible!" muttered Velchaninoff, incredulously. Liza suddenly threw herself into his arms, kissed his hands, and cried. She could hardly breathe for sobbing; she was begging and imploring Velchaninoff, but he could not understand what she was trying to say. Velchaninoff never afterwards forgot the terrible look of this distressed child; he thought of it waking and thought of it sleeping—how she had come to him in her despair as to her last hope, and hysterically begged and prayed him to help her! "And to think of her being so deeply attached to him!" he reflected jealously, as he drove, impatient and feverish, towards town. "She said herself that she loved her mother better;—perhaps she hates him, and doesn't love him at all! And what's all that nonsense about 'hanging himself!' What did she mean by that? As if he would hang himself, the fool! I must sift the matter—the whole matter. I must settle this business once and for ever—and quickly!"

CHAPTER VII.

He was in a great hurry to "know all." In order to lose no time about finding out what he felt he must know at once, he told the coachman to drive him straight to Trusotsky's rooms. On the way he changed his mind; "let him come to me, himself," he thought, "and meanwhile I can attend to my cursed law business."

But to-day he really felt that he was too absent to attend to anything at all; and at five o'clock he set out with the intention of dining. And at this moment, for the first time, an amusing idea struck him. What if he really only hindered his law business by meddling as he did, and hunting his wretched lawyer about the place, when the latter plainly avoided meeting him? Velchaninoff laughed merrily over this idea. "And yet," he thought; "if this notion had struck me in the evening instead of now, how angry I should have been!" He laughed again, more merrily than before. But in spite of his merriness he grew more and more thoughtful and impatient, and could settle to nothing, nor could he think out what he most wanted to reflect upon.

"I *must* have that fellow here!" he said at length; "I must read the mystery of *him* first of all, and then I can settle what to do next. There's a duel in this business!"

Returning home at seven o'clock he did not find Pavel Pavlovitch there, which fact first surprised him, then angered him, then depressed him, and at last, frightened him.

"God knows, God knows how it will all end!" he cried; first trying to settle himself on a sofa, and then marching up and down the room, and all the while looking at his watch every other minute.

At length—at about nine o'clock—Pavel Pavlovitch appeared.

"If this man was cunning enough to mean it he could not have managed better in order to put me into a state of nervousness!" thought Velchaninoff, though his heart bounded for joy to see his guest arrive.

To Velchaninoff's cordial inquiry as to why he was so late, Pavel Pavlovitch smiled disagreeably—took a seat with easy familiarity, carelessly threw his crapebound hat on a chair,—and made himself perfectly at home. Velchaninoff observed and took stock of the careless manner adopted by his visitor; it was not like yesterday. Velchaninoff then quietly, and in a few words, gave Pavel Pavlovitch an account of what he had done with Liza, of how kindly she had been received, of how good it would be for the child down there; then he led the conversation to the topic of the Pogoryeltseffs, leaving Liza out of the talking altogether, and spoke of how kind the whole family were, of how long he had known them, and so on.

Pavel Pavlovitch listened absently, occasionally looking ironically at his host from under his eyelashes.

"What an enthusiast you are!" he muttered at last, smiling very unpleasantly.

"Hum, you seem in a bad humour to-day!" remarked Velchaninoff with annoyance.

"And why shouldn't I be as wicked as my neighbours?" cried Pavel Pavlovitch suddenly! He said this so abruptly that he gave one the idea that he had pounced out of a corner where he had been lurking, on purpose to make a dash at the first opportunity.

"Oh dear me! do as you like, pray!" laughed Velchaninoff; "I only thought something had put you out, perhaps!"

"So it has," cried Pavel Pavlovitch, as though proud of the fact.

"Well, what was it?"

Pavel Pavlovitch waited a moment or two before he replied.

"Why it's that Stepan Michailovitch Bagantoff of ours—up to his tricks again; he's a shining light among the highest circles of society—he is!"

"Wouldn't he receive you again—or what?"

"N—no! not quite that, this time; on the contrary I was allowed to go in for the first time on record, and I had the honour of musing over his features, too!—but he happened to be a corpse, that's all!"

"What! Bagantoff dead?" cried Velchaninoff, in the greatest astonishment; though there was no particular reason why he *should* be surprised.

"Yes—my unalterable—six-years-standing friend is dead!—died yesterday at about mid-day, and I knew nothing of it! Perhaps he died just when I called there—who knows? To-morrow is the funeral! he's in his coffin at this moment! Died of nervous fever; and they let me in to see him—they did indeed!—to contemplate his features! I told them I was a great friend—and therefore they allowed me in! A pretty trick he has played me—this dear friend of six years' standing! why—perhaps I came to St. Petersburg *specially for him*!"

"Well—it's hardly worth your while to be angry with him about it, is it—he didn't die on purpose!" said Velchaninoff laughing.

"Oh, but I'm speaking out of pure sympathy—he was a *dear* friend to me! oh a *very* dear friend!"

Pavel Pavlovitch gave a smile of detestable irony and cunning.

"Do you know what, Alexey Ivanovitch," he resumed, "I think you ought to treat me to something,—I have often treated you; I used to be your host every blessed day, sir, at T——, for a whole year! Send for a bottle of wine, do—my throat is so dry!"

"With pleasure—why didn't you say so before! what would you like?"

"Don't say 'you!' say 'we'! we'll drink together of course!" said Pavel Pavlovitch defiantly, but at the same time looking into Velchaninoff's eyes with some concern.

"Shall it be champagne?"

"Of course! it isn't time for vodki yet!"

Velchaninoff rose slowly—rang the bell and gave Mavra the necessary orders.

"We'll drink to this happy meeting of friends after nine years' parting!" said Pavel Pavlovitch, with a very inappropriate and unnecessary giggle. "Why, you are the only real, true friend left to me now! Bagantoff is no more! it quite reminds one of the great poet:

"Great Patroclus is no more,
Mean Thersites liveth yet!"

—and so on,—don't you know!"

At the name "Thersites" Pavel Pavlovitch touched his own breast.

"I wish you would speak plainly, you pig of a fellow!" said Velchaninoff to himself, "I hate hints!" His own anger was on the rise, and he had long been struggling with his self-restraint.

"Look here,—tell me this, since you consider Bagantoff to have been guilty before you (as I see you do) surely you must be glad that your betrayer is dead? What are you so angry about?"

"Glad! Why should I be glad?"

"I judge by what I should imagine your feelings to be."

"Ha-ha! well, this time you are a little bit in error as to my feelings, for once! A certain sage has said 'my good enemy is dead, but I have a still better one alive! ha-ha!"

"Well but you saw him alive for five years at a stretch,—I should have thought that was enough to contemplate his features in!" said Velchaninoff angrily and contemptuously.

"Yes, but how was I to know then, sir?" snapped Pavel Pavlovitch—jumping out of an ambush once more, as it were,—delighted to be asked a question which he had long awaited; "why, what do you take me for, Alexey

Ivanovitch?" at this moment there was in the speaker's face a new expression altogether, transfiguring entirely the hitherto merely disagreeably malicious look upon it.

"Do you mean to say you knew nothing of it?" said Velchaninoff in astonishment.

"How! Didn't know? As if I could have known it and——Oh, you race of Jupiters! you reckon a man to be no better than a dog, and judge of him by your own sentiments. Look here, sir,—there, look at that." So saying, he brought his fist madly down upon the table with a resounding bang, and immediately afterwards looked frightened at his own act.

Velchaninoff's face beamed.

"Listen, Pavel Pavlovitch," he said; "it is entirely the same thing to me whether you knew or did not know all about it. If you did not know, so much the more honourable is it for you; but—I can't understand why you should have selected me for your confidant."

"I wasn't talking of you; don't be angry, it wasn't about you," muttered Pavel Pavlovitch, with his eyes fixed on the ground.

At this moment, Mavra entered with the champagne.

"Here it is!" cried Pavel Pavlovitch, immensely delighted at the appearance of the wine. "Now then, tumblers my good girl, tumblers quick! Capital! Thank you, we don't require you any more, my good Mavra. What! you've drawn the cork? Excellent creature. Well, ta-ta! off with you."

Mavra's advent with the bottle so encouraged him that he again looked at Velchaninoff with some defiance.

"Now confess," he giggled suddenly, "confess that you are very curious indeed to hear about all this, and that it is by no means 'entirely the same to you,' as you declared! Confess that you would be miserable if I were to get up and go away this very minute without telling you anything more."

"Not the least in the world, I assure you!"

Pavel Pavlovitch smiled; and his smile said, as plainly as words could, "That's a lie!"

"Well, let's to business," he said, and poured out two glasses of champagne.

"Here's a toast," he continued, raising his goblet, "to the health in Paradise of our dear departed friend Bagantoff."

He raised his glass and drank.

"I won't drink such a toast as that!" said Velchaninoff; and put his glass down on the table.

"Why not? It's a very pretty toast."

"Look here, were you drunk when you came here?"

"A little; why?"

"Oh—nothing particular. Only it appeared to me that yesterday, and especially this morning, you were sincerely sorry for the loss of Natalia Vasilievna."

"And who says I am not sorry now?" cried Pavel Pavlovitch, as if somebody had pulled a string and made him snap the words out, like a doll.

"No, I don't mean that; but you must admit you may be in error about Bagantoff; and that's a serious matter!"

Pavel Pavlovitch grinned and gave a wink.

"Hey! Wouldn't you just like to know how I found out about Bagantoff, eh?"

Velchaninoff blushed.

"I repeat, it's all the same to me," he said; and added to himself, "Hadn't I better pitch him and the bottle out of the window together." He was blushing more and more now.

Pavel Pavlovitch poured himself out another glass.

"I'll tell you directly how I found out all about Mr. Bagantoff, and your burning wish shall be satisfied. For you are a fiery sort of man, you know, Alexey Ivanovitch, oh, dreadfully so! Ha-ha-ha. Just give me a cigarette first, will you, for ever since March——"

"Here's a cigarette for you."

"Ever since March I have been a depraved man, sir, and this is how it all came about. Listen. Consumption, as you know, my dear friend" (Pavel Pavlovitch was growing more and more familiar!), "is an interesting malady. One sees a man dying of consumption without a suspicion that to-morrow is to be his last day. Well, I told you how Natalia Vasilievna, up to five hours before her death, talked about going to visit her aunt, who lived thirty miles or so away, and starting in a fortnight. You know how some ladies—and gentlemen, too, I daresay—have the bad habit of keeping a lot of old rubbish by them, in the way of love-letters and so on. It would be much safer to stick them all into the fire, wouldn't it? But no, they must keep every little scrap of paper in drawers and desks, and endorse it and classify it, and tie it up in bundles, for each year and month and class! I don't know whether they find this consoling to their feelings afterwards, or what. Well, since she was arranging a visit to her aunt just five hours before her death, Natalia Vasilievna naturally did not expect to die so soon; in fact, she was expecting old Doctor Koch down till the last; and so, when Natalia Vasilievna *did* die, she left behind her a beautiful little black desk all

194

inlaid with mother-of-pearl, and bound with silver, in her bureau; oh, a lovely little box, an heirloom left her by her grandmother, with a lock and key all complete. Well, sir, in this box everything—I mean *everything*, you know, for every day and hour for the last twenty years—was disclosed; and since Mr. Bagantoff had a decided taste for literature (indeed, he had published a passionate novel once, I am told, in a newspaper!)—consequently there were about a hundred examples of his genius in the desk, ranging over a period of five years. Some of these talented effusions were covered with pencilled remarks by Natalia Vasilievna herself! Pleasant, that, for a fond husband's feelings, sir, eh?"

Velchaninoff quickly cast his thoughts back over the past, and remembered that he had never written a single letter or a single note to Natalia Vasilievna.

He had written a couple of letters from St. Petersburg, but, according to a previous arrangement, he had addressed them to both Mr. and Mrs. Trusotsky together. He had not answered Natalia Vasilievna's last letter—which had contained his dismissal—at all.

Having ended his speech, Pavel Pavlovitch relapsed into silence, and sat smiling repulsively for a whole minute or so.

"Why don't you answer my question, my friend?" he asked, at length, evidently disturbed by Velchaninoff's silence.

"What question?"

"As to the pleasure I must have felt as a fond husband, upon opening the desk."

"Your feelings are no business of mine!" said the other bitterly, rising and commencing to stride up and down the room.

"I wouldn't mind betting that you are thinking at this very moment: 'What a pig of a fellow he is to parade his shame like this!' Ha-ha! dear me, what a squeamish gentleman you are to be sure!"

"Not at all. I was thinking nothing of the sort; on the contrary, I consider that you are—besides being more or less intoxicated—so put out by the death of the man who has injured you that you are not yourself. There's nothing surprising in it at all! I quite understand why you wish Bagantoff were still alive, and am ready to respect your annoyance, but——"

"And pray *why* do you suppose that I wish Bagantoff were alive?"

"Oh, that's your affair!"

"I'll take my oath you are thinking of a duel!"

"Devil take it, sir!" cried Velchaninoff, obliged to hold himself tighter than ever. "I was thinking that you, like every respectable person in similar circumstances, would act openly and candidly and straightforwardly, and not humiliate yourself with comical antics and silly grimaces, and ridiculous complaints and detestable innuendoes, which only heap greater shame upon you. I say I was thinking you would act like a respectable person."

"Ha-ha-ha!—but perhaps I am *not* a respectable person!"

"Oh, well, that's your own affair again and yet, if so, what in the devil's name could you want with Bagantoff alive?"

"Oh, my dear sir, I should have liked just to have a nice peep at a dear old friend, that's all. We should have got hold of a bottle of wine, and drunk it together!"

"He wouldn't have drunk with *you*!"

"Why not? *Noblesse oblige?* Why, *you* are drinking with me. Wherein is he better than you?"

"I have not drunk with you."

"Wherefore this sudden pride, sir?"

Velchaninoff suddenly burst into a fit of nervous, irritable laughter.

"Why, deuce take it all!" he cried, "you are quite a different type to what I believed. I thought you were nothing but a 'permanent husband,' but I find you are a sort of bird of prey."

"What! 'permanent husband?' What is a 'permanent husband?' " asked Pavel Pavlovitch, pricking up his ears.

"Oh—just one type of husbands—that's all, it's too long to explain. Come, you'd better get out now; it's quite time you went. I'm sick of you!"

"And bird of prey, sir; what did that mean?"

"I said you were a bird of prey for a joke."

"Yes; but—bird of prey—tell me what you mean, Alexey Ivanovitch, for goodness sake!"

"Come, come, that's quite enough!" shouted Velchaninoff, suddenly flaring up and speaking at the top of his voice. "It's time you went; get out of this, will you?"

"No, sir, it's *not* enough!" cried Pavel Pavlovitch, jumping up, too. "Even if you *are* sick of me, sir, it's not enough; for you must first drink and clink glasses with me. I won't go before you do! No, no; oh dear no! drink first; it's *not* enough yet."

"Pavel Pavlovitch, will you go to the devil or will you not?"

"With pleasure, sir. I'll go to the devil with pleasure; but first we must drink. You say you don't wish to drink*with me*; but *I wish you* to drink with me—actually *with me*."

Pavel Pavlovitch was grimacing and giggling no longer. He seemed to be suddenly transfigured again, and was as different from the Pavel Pavlovitch of but a few moments since as he could possibly be, both in appearance and in the tone of his voice; so much so that Velchaninoff was absolutely confounded.

"Come, Alexey Ivanovitch, let's drink!—don't refuse me!" continued Pavel Pavlovitch, seizing the other tightly by the hand and gazing into his face with an extraordinary expression.

It was clear there was more in this matter than the mere question of drinking a glass of wine.

"Well," muttered Velchaninoff, "but that's nothing but dregs!"

"No, there's just a couple of glasses left—it's quite clear. Now then, clink glasses and drink. There, I'll take your glass and you take mine." They touched glasses and drank.

"Oh, Alexey Ivanovitch! now that we've drunk together—oh!" Pavel Pavlovitch suddenly raised his hand to his forehead and sat still for a few moments.

Velchaninoff trembled with excitement. He thought Pavel Pavlovitch was about to disclose *all*; but Pavel Pavlovitch said nothing whatever. He only looked at him, and quietly smiled his detestable cunning smile in the other's face.

"What do you want with me, you drunken wretch?" cried Velchaninoff, furious, and stamping his foot upon the floor; "you are making a fool of me!"

"Don't shout so—don't shout! Why make such a noise?" cried Pavel Pavlovitch. "I'm not making a fool of you! Do you know what you are to me now?" and he suddenly seized Velchaninoff's hand, and kissed it before Velchaninoff could recollect himself.

"There, that's what you are to me *now*; and now I'll go to the devil."

"Wait a bit—stop!" cried Velchaninoff, recollecting himself; "there's something I wished to say to you."

Pavel Pavlovitch turned back from the door.

"You see," began Velchaninoff, blushing and keeping his eye well away from the other, "you ought to go with me to the Pogoryeltseffs to-morrow—just to thank them, you know, and make their acquaintance."

"Of course, of course; quite so!" said Pavel Pavlovitch readily, and making a gesture of the hand to imply that he knew his duty, and there was no need to remind him of it.

"Besides Liza expects you anxiously—I promised her."

"Liza?" Pavel Pavlovitch turned quickly once more upon him. "Liza? Do you know, sir, what this Liza has been to me—has been and is?" he cried passionately and almost beside himself; "but—no!—afterwards—that shall be afterwards! Meanwhile it's not enough for me, Alexey Ivanovitch, that we have drunk together; there's another satisfaction I must have, sir!" He placed his hat on a chair, and, panting with excitement, gazed at his companion with much the same expression as before.

"Kiss me, Alexey Ivanovitch!"

"Are you drunk?" cried the other, drawing back.

"Yes, I am—but kiss me all the same, Alexey Ivanovitch—oh, do! I kissed your hand just now, you know."

Alexey Ivanovitch was silent for a few moments, as though stunned by the blow of a cudgel. Then he quickly bent down to Pavel Pavlovitch (who was about the height of his shoulder), and kissed his lips, from which proceeded a disagreeably powerful odour of wine. He performed the action as though not quite certain of what he was doing.

"Well! *now, now!*" cried Pavel Pavlovitch, with drunken enthusiasm, and with his eyes flashing fiercely; "*now*—look here—I'll tell you what! I thought at that time: 'Surely not *he*, too! If *this* man,' I thought, 'if *this* man is guilty too—then whom am I ever to trust again!' "

Pavel Pavlovitch suddenly burst into tears.

"So now you must understand *how* dear a friend you are to me henceforth." With these words he took his hat and rushed out of the room.

Velchaninoff stood for several minutes in one spot, just as he had done after Pavel Pavlovitch's first visit.

"It's merely a drunken sally—nothing more!" he muttered. "Absolutely nothing further!" he repeated, when he was undressed and settled down in his bed.

CHAPTER VIII.

Next morning, while waiting for Pavel Pavlovitch, who had promised to be in good time in order to drive down to the Pogoryeltseffs with him, Velchaninoff walked up and down the room, sipped his coffee, and every other minute reflected upon one and the same idea; namely, that he felt like a man who had awaked from sleep with the deep impression of having received a box on the ear the last thing at night.

"Hm!" he thought, anxiously, "he understands the state of the case only too well; he'll take it out of me by means of Liza!" The dear image of the poor little girl danced before his eyes. His heart beat quicker when he reflected that to-day—in a couple of hours—he would see *his own* Liza once more. "Yes—there's no question about it," he said to himself; "my whole end and aim in life is *there* now! What do I care about all these 'memories' and boxes on the ear; and what have I lived for up to now?—for sorrow and discomfort—that's all! but *now*, now—it's all different!"

But in spite of his ecstatic feelings he grew more and more thoughtful.

"He is worrying me for Liza, that's plain; and he bullies Liza—he is going to take it out of me that way—for *all*! Hm! at all events I cannot possibly allow such sallies as his of last night," and Velchaninoff blushed hotly "and here's half-past eleven and he hasn't come yet." He waited long—till half-past twelve, and his anguish of impatience grew more and more keen. Pavel Pavlovitch did not appear. At length the idea began to take shape that Pavel Pavlovitch naturally would not come again for the sole purpose of another scene like that of last night. The thought filled Velchaninoff with despair. "The brute knows I am depending upon him—and what on earth am I to do now about Liza? How can I make my appearance without him?"

At last he could bear it no longer and set off to the Pokrofsky at one o'clock to look for Pavel Pavlovitch.

At the lodging, Velchaninoff was informed that Pavel Pavlovitch had not been at home all night, and had only called in at nine o'clock, stayed a quarter of an hour, and had gone out again.

Velchaninoff stood at the door listening to the servants' report, mechanically tried the handle, recollected himself, and asked to see Maria Sisevna.

The latter obeyed his summons at once.

She was a kind-hearted old creature, of generous feelings, as Velchaninoff described her afterwards to Claudia Petrovna. Having first enquired as to his journey yesterday with Liza, Maria launched into anecdotes of Pavel Pavlovitch. She declared that she would long ago have turned her lodger out neck and crop, but for the child. Pavel Pavlovitch had been turned out of the hotel for generally disreputable behaviour. "Oh, he does dreadful things!" she continued. "Fancy his telling the poor child, in anger, that she wasn't his daughter, but——"

"Oh no, no! impossible!" cried Velchaninoff in alarm.

"I heard it myself! She's only a small child, of course, but that sort of thing doesn't do before an intelligent child like her! She cried dreadfully—she was quite upset. We had a catastrophe in the house a short while since. Some commissionnaire or somebody took a room in the evening, and hung himself before morning. He had bolted with money, they say. Well, crowds of people came in to stare at him. Pavel Pavlovitch wasn't at home, but the child had escaped and was wandering about; and she must needs go with the rest to see the sight. I saw her looking at the suicide with an extraordinary expression, and carried her off at once, of course; and fancy, I hardly managed to get home with her—trembling all over she was—when off she goes in a dead faint, and it was all I could do to bring her round at all. I don't know whether she's epileptic or what—and ever since that she has been ill. When her father heard, he came and pinched her all over—he doesn't beat her; he always pinches her like that,—then he went out and got drunk somewhere, and came back and frightened her. 'I'm going to hang myself too,' he says, 'because of you. I shall hang myself on that blind string there,' he says, and he makes a loop in the string before her very eyes. The poor little thing went quite out of her mind with terror, and cried and clasped him round with her little arms. 'I'll be good—I'll be good!' she shrieks. It was a pitiful sight—it was, indeed!"

Velchaninoff, though prepared for strange revelations concerning Pavel Pavlovitch and his ways, was quite dumbfounded by these tales; he could scarcely believe his ears.

Maria Sisevna told him many more such little anecdotes. Among others, there was one occasion, when, if she (Maria) had not been by, Liza would have thrown herself out of the window.

Pavel Pavlovitch had come staggering out of the room muttering, "I shall smash her head in with a stick! I shall murder her like a dog!" and he had gone away, repeating this over and over again to himself.

Velchaninoff hired a carriage and set off towards the Pogoryeltseffs. Before he had left the town behind him, the carriage was delayed by a block at a cross road, just by a small bridge, over which was passing, at the moment, a long funeral procession. There were carriages waiting to move on on both sides of the bridge, and a considerable crowd of foot passengers besides.

The funeral was evidently of some person of considerable importance, for the train of private and hired vehicles was a very long one; and at the window of one of these carriages in the procession Velchaninoff suddenly beheld the face of Pavel Pavlovitch.

Velchaninoff would not have believed his eyes, but that Pavel Pavlovitch nodded his head and smiled to him. He seemed to be delighted to have recognised Velchaninoff; he even began to kiss his hand out of the window.

Velchaninoff jumped out of his own vehicle, and in spite of policemen, crowd, and everything else, elbowed his way to Pavel Pavlovitch's carriage window. He found the latter sitting alone.

"What are you doing?" he cried. "Why didn't you come to my house? Why are you here?"

"I'm paying a debt; don't shout so! I'm repaying a debt," said Pavel Pavlovitch, giggling and winking. "I'm escorting the mortal remains of my dear friend Stepan Michailovitch Bagantoff!"

"What absurdity, you drunken, insane creature," cried Velchaninoff louder than ever, and beside himself with outraged feeling. "Get out and come with me. Quick! get out instantly!"

"I can't. It's a debt——"

"I'll pull you out, then!" shouted Velchaninoff.

"Then I'll scream, sir, I'll scream!" giggled Pavel Pavlovitch, as merrily as ever, just as though the whole thing was a joke. However, he retreated into the further corner of the carriage, all the same.

"Look out, sir, look out! You'll be knocked down!" cried a policeman.

Sure enough, an outside carriage was making its way on to the bridge from the side, stopping the procession, and causing a commotion. Velchaninoff was obliged to spring aside, and the press of carriages and people immediately separated him from Pavel Pavlovitch. He shrugged his shoulders and returned to his own vehicle.

"It's all the same. I couldn't take such a fellow with me, anyhow," he reflected, still all of a tremble with excitement and the rage of disgust. When he repeated Maria Sisevna's story, and his meeting at the funeral, to Claudia Petrovna afterwards, the latter became buried in deep thought.

"I am anxious for you," she said at last. "You must break off all relations with that man, and as soon as possible."

"Oh, he's nothing but a drunken fool!" cried Velchaninoff passionately; "as if I am to be afraid of *him*! And how can I break off relations with him? Remember Liza!"

Meanwhile Liza was lying ill; fever had set in last night, and an eminent doctor was momentarily expected from town! He had been sent for early this morning.

These news quite upset Velchaninoff. Claudia Petrovna took him in to see the patient.

"I observed her very carefully yesterday," she said, stopping at the door of Liza's room before entering it. "She is a proud and morose child. She is ashamed of being with us, and of having been thrown over by her father. In my opinion that is the whole secret of her illness."

"How 'thrown over'? Why do you suppose that he has thrown her over?"

"The simple fact that he allowed her to come here to a strange house, and with a man who was also a stranger, or nearly so; or, at all events, with whom his relations were such that——"

"Oh, but I took her myself, almost by force."

Liza was not surprised to see Velchaninoff alone. She only smiled bitterly, and turned her hot face to the wall. She made no reply to his passionate promises to bring her father down to-morrow without fail, or to his timid attempts at consolation.

As soon as Velchaninoff left the sick child's presence, he burst into tears.

The doctor did not arrive until evening. On seeing the patient he frightened everybody by his very first remark, observing that it was a pity he had not been sent for before.

When informed that the child had only been taken ill last night, he could not believe it at first.

"Well, it all depends upon how this night is passed," he decided at last.

Having made all necessary arrangements, he took his departure, promising to come as early as possible next morning.

Velchaninoff was anxious to stay the night, but Claudia Petrovna begged him to try once more "to bring down that brute of a man."

"Try once more!" cried Velchaninoff, passionately; "why, I'll tie him hand and foot and bring him along myself!"

The idea that he would tie Pavel Pavlovitch up and carry him down in his arms overpowered Velchaninoff, and filled him with impatience to execute his frantic desire.

"I don't feel the slightest bit guilty before him any more," he said to Claudia Petrovna, at parting, "and I withdraw all my servile, abject words of yesterday—all I said to you," he added, wrathfully.

Liza lay with closed eyes, apparently asleep; she seemed to be better. When Velchaninoff bent cautiously over her in order to kiss—if it were but the edge of her bed linen—she suddenly opened her eyes, just as though she had been waiting for him, and whispered, "Take me away!"

It was but a quiet, sad petition—without a trace of yesterday's irritation; but at the same time there was that in her voice which betrayed that she made the request in the full knowledge that it could not be assented to.

No sooner did Velchaninoff, in despair, begin to assure her as tenderly as he could that what she desired was impossible, than she silently closed her eyes and said not another word, just as though she neither saw nor heard him.

Arrived in town Velchaninoff told his man to drive him to the Pokrofsky. It was ten o'clock at night.

Pavel Pavlovitch was not at his lodgings. Velchaninoff waited for him half an hour, walking up and down the passage in a state of feverish impatience. Maria Sisevna assured him at last that Pavel Pavlovitch would not come in until the small hours.

"Well, then, I'll return here before daylight," he said, beside himself with desperation, and he went home to his own rooms.

What was his amazement, when, on arriving at the gate of his house, he learned from Mavra that "yesterday's visitor" had been waiting for him ever since before ten o'clock.

"He's had some tea," she added, "and sent me for wine again—the same wine as yesterday. He gave me the money to buy it with."

CHAPTER IX.

Pavel Pavlovitch had made himself very comfortable. He was sitting in the same chair as he had occupied yesterday, smoking a cigar, and had just poured the fourth and last tumbler of champagne out of the bottle.

The teapot and a half-emptied tumbler of tea stood on the table beside him; his red face beamed with benevolence. He had taken off his coat, and sat in his shirt sleeves.

"Forgive me, dearest of friends," he cried, catching sight of Velchaninoff, and hastening to put on his coat, "I took it off to make myself thoroughly comfortable."

Velchaninoff approached him menacingly.

"You are not quite tipsy yet, are you? Can you understand what is said to you?"

Paul Pavlovitch became a little confused.

"No, not quite. I've been thinking of the dear deceased a bit, but I'm not quite drunk yet."

"Can you understand what I say?"

"My dear sir, I came here on purpose to understand you."

"Very well, then I shall begin at once by telling you that you are an ass, sir!" cried Velchaninoff, at the top of his voice.

"Why, if you begin that way where will you end, I wonder!" said Pavel Pavlovitch, clearly alarmed more than a little.

Velchaninoff did not listen, but roared again,

"Your daughter is dying—she is very ill! Have you thrown her over altogether, or not?"

"Oh, surely she isn't dying yet?"

"I tell you she's ill; very, very ill—dangerously ill."

"What, fits? or——"

"Don't talk nonsense. I tell you she is very dangerously ill. You ought to go down, if only for that reason."

"What, to thank your friends, eh? to return thanks for their hospitality? Of course, quite so; I well understand, Alexey Ivanovitch—dearest of friends!" He suddenly seized Velchaninoff by both hands, and added with intoxicated sentiment, almost melted to tears, "Alexey Ivanovitch, don't shout at me—don't shout at me, please! If you do, I may throw myself into the Neva—I don't know!—and we have such important things to talk over. There's lots of time to go to the Pogoryeltseffs another day."

Velchaninoff did his best to restrain his wrath. "You are drunk, and therefore I don't understand what you are driving at," he said sternly. "I'm ready to come to an explanation with you at any moment you like—delighted!— the the sooner the better. But first let me tell you that I am going to take my own measures to secure you. You will sleep here to-night, and to-morrow I shall take you with me to see Liza. I shall not let you go again. I shall bind you, if necessary, and carry you down myself. How do you like this sofa to sleep on?" he added, panting, and indicating a wide, soft divan opposite his own sofa, against the other wall.

"Oh—anything will do for me!"

"Very well, you shall have this sofa. Here, take these things—here are sheets, blankets, pillow" (Velchaninoff pulled all these things out of a cupboard, and tossed them impatiently to Pavel Pavlovitch, who humbly stood and received them); "now then, make your bed,—come, bustle up!"

Pavel Pavlovitch laden with bed clothes had been standing in the middle of the room with a stupid drunken leer on his face, irresolute; but at Velchaninoff's second bidding he hurriedly began the task of making his bed, moving the table away from in front of it, and smoothing a sheet over the seat of the divan. Velchaninoff approached to help him. He was more or less gratified with his guest's alarm and submission.

"Now, drink up that wine and lie down!" was his next command. He felt that he *must* order this man about, he could not help himself. "I suppose you took upon yourself to order this wine, did you?"

"I did—I did, sir! I sent for the wine, Alexey Ivanovitch, because I knew *you* would not send out again!"

"Well, it's a good thing that you knew that; but I desire that you should know still more. I give you notice that I have taken my own measures for the future, I'm not going to put up with any more of your antics."

"Oh, I quite understand, Alexey Ivanovitch, that that sort of thing could only happen once!" said Pavel Pavlovitch, giggling feebly.

At this reply Velchaninoff, who had been marching up and down the room stopped solemnly before Pavel Pavlovitch.

"Pavel Pavlovitch," he said, "speak plainly! You are a clever fellow—I admit the fact freely,—but I assure you you are going on a false track now. Speak plainly, and act like an honest man, and I give you my word of honour that I will answer all you wish to know."

Pavel Pavlovitch grinned his disagreeable grin (which always drove Velchaninoff wild) once more.

"Wait!" cried the latter. "No humbug now, please; I see through you. I repeat that I give you my word of honour to reply candidly to anything you may like to ask, and to give you every sort of satisfaction—reasonable or even unreasonable—that you please. *Oh!* how I wish I could make you understand me!"

"Since you are so very kind," began Pavel Pavlovitch, cautiously bending towards him, "I may tell you that I am very much interested as to what you said yesterday about 'bird of prey'?"

Velchaninoff spat on the ground in utter despair and disgust, and recommenced his walk up and down the room, quicker than ever.

"No, no, Alexey Ivanovitch, don't spurn my question; you don't know how interested I am in it. I assure you I came here on purpose to ask you about it. I know I'm speaking indistinctly, but you'll forgive me that. I've read the expression before. Tell me now, was Bagantoff a 'bird of prey,' or—the other thing? How is one to distinguish one from the other?"

Velchaninoff went on walking up and down, and answered nothing for some minutes.

"The bird of prey, sir," he began suddenly, stopping in front of Pavel Pavlovitch, and speaking vehemently, "is the man who would poison Bagantoff while drinking champagne with him under the cloak of goodfellowship, as you did with me yesterday, instead of escorting his wretched body to the burial ground as you did—the deuce only knows why, and with what dirty, mean, underhand, petty motives, which only recoil upon yourself and make you viler than you already are. Yes, sir, recoil upon yourself!"

"Quite so, quite so, I oughtn't to have gone," assented Pavel Pavlovitch, "but aren't you a little——"

"The bird of prey is not a man who goes and learns his grievance off by heart, like a lesson, and whines it about the place, grimacing and posing, and hanging it round other people's necks, and who spends all his time in such pettifogging. Is it true you wanted to hang yourself? Come, is it true, or not?"

"I—I don't know—I may have when I was drunk—I don't remember. You see, Alexey Ivanovitch, it wouldn't be quite nice for me to go poisoning people. I'm too high up in the service, and I have money, too, you know—and I may wish to marry again, who knows."

"Yes; you'd be sent to Siberia, which would be awkward."

"Quite so; though they say the penal servitude is not so bad as it was. But you remind me of an anecdote, Alexey Ivanovitch. I thought of it in the carriage, and meant to tell you afterwards. Well! you may remember Liftsoff at T——. He came while you were there. His younger brother—who is rather a swell, too—was serving at L—— under the governor, and one fine day he happened to quarrel with Colonel Golubenko in the presence of ladies, and of one lady especially. Liftsoff considered himself insulted, but concealed his grievance; and, meanwhile, Golubenko proposed to a certain lady and was accepted. Would you believe it, Liftsoff made great friends with Golubenko, and even volunteered to be best man at his wedding. But when the ceremony was all over, and Liftsoff approached the bridegroom to wish him joy and kiss him, as usual, he took the opportunity of sticking a knife into Golubenko. Fancy! his own best man stuck him! Well, what does the assassin do but run about the room crying. 'Oh! what have I done? Oh! what have I done?' says he, and throws himself on everyone's neck by turns, ladies and all! Ha-ha-ha! He starved to death in Siberia, sir! One is a little sorry for Golubenko; but he recovered, after all."

"I don't understand why you told me that story," said Velchaninoff, frowning heavily.

"Why, because he stuck the other fellow with a knife," giggled Pavel Pavlovitch, "which proves that he was no type, but an ass of a fellow, who could so forget the ordinary manners of society as to hang around ladies' necks, and in the presence of the governor, too—and yet he stuck the other fellow. Ha-ha-ha! He did what he intended to do, that's all, sir!"

"Go to the devil, will you—you and your miserable humbug—you miserable humbug yourself," yelled Velchaninoff, wild with rage and fury, and panting so that he could hardly get his words out. "You think you are going to alarm *me*, do you, you frightener of children—you mean beast—you low scoundrel you?—scoundrel—scoundrel—scoundrel!" He had quite forgotten himself in his rage.

Pavel Pavlovitch shuddered all over; his drunkenness seemed to vanish in an instant; his lips trembled and shook.

"Are you calling *me* a scoundrel, Alexey Ivanovitch—*you*—*me*?"

But Velchaninoff was himself again now.

"I'll apologise if you like," he said, and relapsed into gloomy silence. After a moment he added, "But only on condition that you yourself agree to speak out fully, and at once."

"In your place I should apologise unconditionally, Alexey Ivanovitch."

"Very well; so be it then." Velchaninoff was silent again for a while. "I apologise," he resumed; "but admit yourself, Pavel Pavlovitch, that I need not feel myself in any way bound to you after this. I mean with regard to *anything*—not only this particular matter."

"All right! Why, what is there to settle between us?" laughed Pavel Pavlovitch, without looking up.

"In that case, so much the better—so much the better. Come, drink up your wine and get into bed, for I shall not let you go now, anyhow."

"Oh, my wine—never mind my wine!" muttered Pavel Pavlovitch; but he went to the table all the same, and took up his tumbler of champagne which had long been poured out. Either he had been drinking copiously before, or there was some other unknown cause at work, but his hand shook so as he drank the wine that a quantity of it was spilled over his waistcoat and the floor. However, he drank it all, to the last drop, as though he could not leave the tumbler without emptying it. He then placed the empty glass on the table, approached his bed, sat down on it, and began to undress.

"I think perhaps I had better *not* sleep here," he said suddenly, with one boot off, and half undressed.

"Well, I *don't* think so," said Velchaninoff, who was walking up and down, without looking at him.

Pavel Pavlovitch finished undressing and lay down. A quarter of an hour later Velchaninoff also got into bed, and put the candle out.

He soon began to doze uncomfortably. Some new trouble seemed to have suddenly come over him and worried him, and at the same time he felt a sensation of shame that he could allow himself to be worried by the new trouble. Velchaninoff was just falling definitely asleep, however, when a rustling sound awoke him. He immediately glanced at Pavel Pavlovitch's bed. The room was quite dark, the blinds being down and curtains drawn; but it seemed to him that Pavel Pavlovitch was not lying in his bed; he seemed to be sitting on the side of it.

"What's the matter?" cried Velchaninoff.

"A ghost, sir," said Pavel Pavlovitch, in a low tone, after a few moments of silence.

"What? What sort of a ghost?"

"Th—there—in that room—just at the door, I seemed to see a ghost!"

"Whose ghost?" asked Velchaninoff, pausing a minute before putting the question.

"Natalia Vasilievna's!"

Velchaninoff jumped out of bed and walked to the door, whence he could see into the room opposite, across the passage. There were no curtains in that room, so that it was much lighter than his own.

"There's nothing there at all. You are drunk; lie down again!" he said, and himself set the example, rolling his blanket around him.

Pavel Pavlovitch said nothing, but lay down as he was told.

"Did you ever see any ghosts before?" asked Velchaninoff suddenly, ten minutes later.

"I think I saw one once," said Pavel Pavlovitch in the same low voice; after which there was silence once more. Velchaninoff was not sure whether he had been asleep or not, but an hour or so had passed, when suddenly he was wide awake again. Was it a rustle that awoke him? He could not tell; but one thing was evident—in the midst of the profound darkness of the room something white stood before him; not quite close to him, but about the middle of the room. He sat up in bed, and stared for a full minute.

"Is that you, Pavel Pavlovitch?" he asked. His voice sounded very weak.

There was no reply; but there was not the slightest doubt of the fact that someone was standing there.

"Is that you, Pavel Pavlovitch?" cried Velchaninoff again, louder this time; in fact, so loud that if the former had been asleep in bed he must have started up and answered.

But there was no reply again. It seemed to Velchaninoff that the white figure had approached nearer to him.

Then something strange happened; something seemed to "let go" within Velchaninoff's system, and he commenced to shout at the top of his voice, just as he had done once before this evening, in the wildest and maddest way possible, panting so that he could hardly articulate his words: "If you—drunken ass that you are—dare to think that you could frighten *me*, I'll turn my face to the wall, and not look round once the whole night, to show you how little I am afraid of you—a fool like you—if you stand there from now till morning! I despise you!" So saying, Velchaninoff twisted round with his face to the wall, rolled his blanket round him, and lay motionless, as though turned to stone. A deathlike stillness supervened.

Did the ghost stand where it was, or had it moved? He could not tell; but his heart beat, and beat, and beat—At least five minutes went by, and then, not a couple of paces from his bed, there came the feeble voice of Pavel Pavlovitch:

"I got up, Alexey Ivanovitch, to look for a little water. I couldn't find any, and was just going to look about nearer your bed——"

"Then why didn't you answer when I called?" cried Velchaninoff angrily, after a minute's pause.

"I was frightened; you shouted so, you alarmed me!"

"You'll find a caraffe and glass over there, on the little table. Light a candle."

"Oh, I'll find it without. You'll forgive me, Alexey Ivanovitch, for frightening you so; I felt thirsty so suddenly."

But Velchaninoff said nothing. He continued to lie with his face to the wall, and so he lay all night, without turning round once. Was he anxious to keep his word and show his contempt for Pavel Pavlovitch? He did not know himself why he did it; his nervous agitation and perturbation were such that he could not sleep for a long while, he felt quite delirious. At last he fell asleep, and awoke at past nine o'clock next morning. He started up just as though someone had struck him, and sat down on the side of his bed. But Pavel Pavlovitch was not to be seen. His empty, rumpled bed was there, but its occupant had flown before daybreak.

"I thought so!" cried Velchaninoff, bringing the palm of his right hand smartly to his forehead.

CHAPTER X.

The doctor's anxiety was justified; Liza grew worse, so much so that it was clear she was far more seriously ill than Velchaninoff and Claudia Petrovna had thought the day before.

When the former arrived in the morning, Liza was still conscious, though burning with fever. He assured his friend Claudia, afterwards, that the child had smiled at him and held out her little hot hand. Whether she actually did so, or whether he so much longed for her to do so that he imagined it done, is uncertain.

By the evening, however, Liza was quite unconscious, and so she remained during the whole of her illness. Ten days after her removal to the country she died.

This was a sad period for Velchaninoff; the Pogoryeltseffs were quite anxious on his account. He was with them for the greater part of the time, and during the last few days of the little one's illness, he used to sit all alone for hours together in some corner, apparently thinking of nothing. Claudia Petrovna would attempt to distract him but he hardly answered her, and conversation was clearly painful to him. Claudia was quite surprised that "all this" should affect him so deeply.

The children were the best consolation and distraction for him; with them he could even laugh and play at intervals. Every hour, at least, he would rise from his chair and creep on tip-toes to the sick-room to look at the little invalid. Sometimes he imagined that she knew him; he had no hope for her recovery—none of the family had any hope; but he never left the precincts of the child's chamber, sitting principally in the next room.

Twice, however, he had evinced great activity of a sudden; he had jumped up and started off for town, where he had called upon all the most eminent doctors of the place, and arranged consultations between them. The last consultation was on the day before Liza's death.

Claudia Petrovna had spoken seriously to him a day or two since, as to the absolute necessity of hunting up Pavel Pavlovitch Trusotsky, because in case of anything happening to Liza, she could not be buried without certain documents from him.

Velchaninoff promised to write to him, and did write a couple of lines, which he took to the Pokrofsky. Pavel Pavlovitch was not at home, as usual, but he left the letter to the care of Maria Sisevna.

At last Liza died—on a lovely summer evening, just as the sun was setting; and only then did Velchaninoff rouse himself.

When the little one was laid out, all covered with flowers, and dressed in a fair white frock belonging to one of Claudia Petrovna's children, Velchaninoff came up to the lady of the house, and told her with flashing eyes that he would now go and fetch the murderer. Regardless of all advice to put off his search until to-morrow he started for town immediately.

He knew where to find Pavel Pavlovitch. He had not been in town exclusively to find the doctors those two days. Occasionally, while watching the dying child, he had been struck with the idea that if he could only find and bring down Pavel Pavlovitch she might hear his voice and be called back, as it were, from the darkness of delirium; at such moments he had been seized with desperation, and twice he had started up and driven wildly off to town in order to find Pavel Pavlovitch.

The latter's room was the same as before, but it was useless to look for him there, for, according to Maria Sisevna's report, he was now two or three days absent from home at a stretch, and was generally to be found with some friends in the Voznecensky.

Arrived in town about ten o'clock, Velchaninoff went straight to these latter people, and securing the services of a member of the family to assist in finding Pavel Pavlovitch, set out on his quest. He did not know what he should do with Pavel Pavlovitch when found, whether he should kill him then and there, or simply inform him of the death of the child, and of the necessity for his assistance in arranging for her funeral. After a long and fruitless search Velchaninoff found Pavel Pavlovitch quite accidentally; he was quarrelling with some person in the street—tipsy as usual, and seemed to be getting the worst of the controversy, which appeared to be about a money claim.

On catching sight of Velchaninoff, Pavel Pavlovitch stretched out his arms to him and begged for help; while his opponent—observing Velchaninoff's athletic figure—made off. Pavel Pavlovitch shook his fist after him triumphantly, and hooted at him with cries of victory; but this amusement was brought to a sudden conclusion by Velchaninoff, who, impelled by some mysterious motive—which he could not analyse, took him by the shoulders, and began to shake him violently, so violently that his teeth chattered.

Pavel Pavlovitch ceased to shout after his opponent, and gazed with a stupid tipsy expression of alarm at his new antagonist. Velchaninoff, having shaken him till he was tired, and not knowing what to do next with him, set him down violently on the pavement, backwards.

"Liza is dead!" he said.

Pavel Pavlovitch sat on the pavement and stared, he was too far gone to take in the news. At last he seemed to realize.

"Dead!" he whispered, in a strange inexplicable tone. Velchaninoff was not sure whether his face was simply twitching, or whether he was trying to grin in his usual disagreeable way; but the next moment the drunkard raised his shaking hand to cross himself. He then struggled to his feet and staggered off, appearing totally oblivious of the fact that such a person as Velchaninoff existed.

However, the latter very soon pursued and caught him, seizing him once more by the shoulder.

"Do you understand, you drunken sot, that without you the funeral arrangements cannot be made?" he shouted, panting with rage.

Pavel Pavlovitch turned his head.

"The artillery—lieutenant—don't you remember him?" he muttered, thickly.

"*What?*" cried Velchaninoff, with a shudder.

"He's her father—find him! he'll bury her!"

"You liar! You said that out of pure malice. I thought you'd invent something of the sort!"

Quite beside himself with passion Velchaninoff brought down his powerful fist with all his strength on Pavel Pavlovitch's head; another moment and he might have followed up the blow and slain the man as he stood. His victim never winced, but he turned upon Velchaninoff a face of such insane terrible passion, that his whole visage looked distorted.

"Do you understand Russian?" he asked more firmly, as though his fury had chased away the effects of drunkenness. "Very well, then, you are a——!" (here followed a specimen of the very vilest language which the Russian tongue could furnish); "and now you can go back to her!" So saying he tore himself from Velchaninoff's grasp, nearly knocking himself over with the effort, and staggered away. Velchaninoff did not follow him.

Next day, however, a most respectable-looking middle-aged man arrived at the Pogoryeltseft's house, in civil uniform, and handed to Claudia Petrovna a packet addressed to her "from Pavel Pavlovitch Trusotsky."

In this packet was a sum of three hundred roubles, together with all certificates necessary for Liza's funeral. Pavel Pavlovitch had written a short note couched in very polite and correct phraseology, and thanking Claudia Petrovna sincerely "for her great kindness to the orphan—kindness for which heaven alone could recompense her." He added rather confusedly that severe illness prevented his personal presence at the funeral of his "tenderly loved and unfortunate daughter," but that he "felt he could repose all confidence (as to the ceremony being fittingly performed) in the angelic goodness of Claudia Petrovna." The three hundred roubles, he explained, were to go

203

towards the funeral and other expenses. If there should be any of the money left after defraying all charges, Claudia Petrovna was requested to spend the same in prayers for the repose of the soul of the deceased.

Nothing further was to be discovered by questioning the messenger; and it was soon evident that the latter knew nothing, excepting that he had only consented to act as bearer of the packet, in response to the urgent appeal of Pavel Pavlovitch.

Pogoryeltseff was a little offended by the offer of money for expenses, and would have sent it back, but Claudia Petrovna suggested that a receipt should be taken from the cemetery authorities for the cost of the funeral (since one could not well refuse to allow a man to bury his own child), together with a document undertaking that the rest of the three hundred roubles should be spent in prayer for the soul of Liza.

Velchaninoff afterwards posted an envelope containing these two papers to Trusotsky's lodging.

After the funeral Velchaninoff disappeared from the country altogether. He wandered about town for a whole fortnight, knocking up against people as he went blindly through the streets. Now and then he spent a whole day lying in his bed, oblivious of the most ordinary needs and occupations; the Pogoryeltseffs often invited him to their house, and he invariably promised to come, and as invariably forgot all about it. Claudia Petrovna went as far as to call for him herself, but she did not find him at home. The same thing happened with his lawyer, who had some good news to tell him. The difference with his opponent had been settled advantageously for Velchaninoff, the former having accepted a small bonification and renounced his claim to the property in dispute. All that was wanting was the formal acquiescence of Velchaninoff himself.

Finding him at home at last, after many endeavours, the lawyer was excessively surprised to discover that Velchaninoff was as callous and cool as to the result of his (the lawyer's) labours, as he had before been ardent and excitable.

The hottest days of July had now arrived, but Velchaninoff was oblivious of everything. His grief swelled and ached at his heart like some internal boil; his greatest sorrow was that Liza had not had time to know him, and died without ever guessing how fondly he loved her. The sweet new beacon of his life, which had glimmered for a short while within his heart, was extinguished once more, and lost in eternal gloom.

The whole object of his existence, as he now told himself at every moment, should have been that Liza might feel his love about her and around her, each day, each hour, each moment of her life.

"There can be no higher aim or object than this in life," he thought, in gloomy ecstasy. "If there be other aims in life, none can be holier or better than this of mine. All my old unworthy life should have been purified and atoned for by my love for Liza; in place of myself—my sinful, worn-out, useless life—I should have bequeathed to the world a sweet, pure, beautiful being, in whose innocence all my guilt should have been absorbed, and lost, and forgiven, and in her I should have forgiven myself."

Such thoughts would flit through Velchaninoff's head as he mused sorrowfully over the memory of the dead child. He thought over all he had seen of her; he recalled her little face all burning with fever, then lying at rest in her coffin, covered with lovely flowers. He remembered that once he had noticed that one of her fingers was quite black from some bruise or pinch—goodness knows what had made it so, but it was the sight of that little finger which had filled him with longing to go straight away and *murder* Pavel Pavlovitch.

"Do you know what Liza is to me?" Pavel had said, he recollected, one day; and now he understood the exclamation. It was no pretence of love, no posturing and nonsense—it was real love! How, then, could the wretch have been so cruel to a child whom he so dearly loved? He could not bear to think of it, the question was painful, and quite unanswerable.

One day he wandered down—he knew not exactly how—to the cemetery where Liza was buried, and hunted up her grave. This was the first time he had been there since the funeral; he had never dared to go there before, fearing that the visit would be too painful. But strangely enough, when he found the little mound and had bent down and kissed it, he felt happier and lighter at heart than before.

It was a lovely evening, the sun was setting, the tall grass waved about the tombs, and a bee hummed somewhere near him. The flowers and crosses placed on the tomb by Claudia Petrovna were still there. A ray of hope blazed up in his heart for the first time for many a long day. "How light-hearted I feel," he thought, as he felt the spell of the quiet of God's Acre, and the hush of the beautiful still evening. A flow of some indefinable faith in something poured into his heart.

"This is Liza's gift," he thought; "this is Liza herself talking to me!"

It was quite dark when he left the cemetery and turned his steps homewards.

Not far from the gate of the burial ground there stood a small inn or public-house, and through the open windows he could see the people inside sitting at tables. It instantly struck Velchaninoff that one of the guests, sitting nearest to the window, was Pavel Pavlovitch, and that the latter had seen him and was observing him curiously.

He went on further, but before very long he heard footsteps pursuing him. It was, of course, Pavel Pavlovitch. Probably the unusually serene and peaceful expression of Velchaninoff's face as he went by had attracted and encouraged him.

He soon caught Velchaninoff up, and smiled timidly at him, but not with the old drunken grin. He did not appear to be in the smallest degree drunk.

"Good evening," said Pavel Pavlovitch.

"How d'ye do?" replied Velchaninoff.

CHAPTER XI.

By replying thus to Pavel Pavlovitch's greeting Velchaninoff surprised himself. It seemed strange indeed to him that he should now meet this man without any feeling of anger, and that there should be something quite novel in his feelings towards Pavel Pavlovitch—a sort of call to new relations with him.

"What a lovely evening!" said Pavel Pavlovitch, looking observantly into the other's eyes.

"So you haven't gone away yet!" murmured Velchaninoff, not in a tone of inquiry, but as though musing upon the fact as he continued to walk on.

"I've been a good deal delayed; but I've obtained my petition, my new post, with rise of salary. I'm off the day after to-morrow for certain."

"What? You've obtained the new situation?"

"And why not?" said Pavel Pavlovitch, with a crooked smile.

"Oh, I meant nothing particular by my remark!" said Velchaninoff frowning, and glancing sidelong at his companion. To his surprise Pavel Pavlovitch, both in dress and appearance, even down to the hat with the crape band, was incomparably neater and tidier-looking than he was wont to be a fortnight since.

"Why was he sitting in the public-house then?" thought Velchaninoff. This fact puzzled him much.

"I wished to let you know of my other great joy, Alexey Ivanovitch!" resumed Pavel.

"Joy?"

"I'm going to marry."

"What?"

"Yes, sir! after sorrow, joy! It is ever thus in life. Oh! Alexey Ivanovitch, I should so much like if—but you look as though you were in a great hurry."

"Yes, I am in a hurry, and I am ill besides." He felt as though he would give anything to get rid of the man; the feeling of readiness to develop new and better relations with him had vanished in a moment.

"I should so much like——"

Pavel Pavlovitch did not finish his sentence; Velchaninoff kept silence and waited.

"In that case, perhaps another time—if we should happen to meet."

"Yes, yes, another time," said Velchaninoff quickly, continuing to move along, and never looking at his companion.

Nothing was said for another minute or two. Pavel Pavlovitch continued to trot alongside.

"In that case, *au revoir*," he blurted, at last. "*Au revoir!* I hope——"

Velchaninoff did not think it necessary to hear him complete his sentence; he left Pavel, and returned home much agitated. The meeting with "that fellow" had been too much for his present state of mind. As he lay down upon his bed the thought came over him once more: "Why was that fellow there, close to the cemetery?" He determined to go down to the Pogoryeltseffs' next morning; not that he felt inclined to go—any sympathy was intolerably painful to him,—but they had been so kind and so anxious about him, that he must really make up his mind to go. But next day, while finishing his breakfast, he felt terribly disinclined for the visit; he felt, as it were, shy of meeting them for the first time after his grief. "Shall I go or not?" he was saying to himself, as he sat at his table. When suddenly, to his extreme amazement, in walked Pavel Pavlovitch.

In spite of yesterday's *rencontre*, Velchaninoff could not have believed that this man would ever enter his rooms again; and when he now saw him appear, he gazed at him in such absolute astonishment, that he simply did not know what to say. But Pavel Pavlovitch took the management of the matter into his own hands; he said "good morning," and sat down in the very same chair which he had occupied on his last visit, three weeks since.

This circumstance reminded Velchaninoff too painfully of that visit, and he glared at his visitor with disgust and some agitation.

"You are surprised, I see!" said Pavel Pavlovitch, reading the other's expression.

He seemed to be both freer, more at his ease, and yet more timid than yesterday. His outward appearance was very curious to behold; for Pavel Pavlovitch was not only *neatly* dressed, he was "got up" in the pink of fashion. He had on a neat summer overcoat, with a pair of light trousers and a white waistcoat; his gloves, his gold eye-glasses (quite a new acquisition), and his linen were quite above all criticism; he wafted an odour of sweet scent when he moved. He looked funny, but his appearance awakened strange thoughts besides.

"Of course I have surprised you, Alexey Ivanovitch," he said, twisting himself about; "I see it. But in my opinion there should be a something exalted, something higher—untouched and unattainable by petty discords, or the ordinary conditions of life, between man and man. Don't you agree with me, sir?"

"Pavel Pavlovitch, say what you have to say as quickly as you can, and without further ceremony," said Velchaninoff, frowning angrily.

"In a couple of words, sir," said Pavel, hurriedly, "I am going to be married, and I am now off to see my bride—at once. She lives in the country; and what I desire is, the profound honour of introducing *you* to the family, sir; in fact, I have come here to petition you, sir" (Pavel Pavlovitch bent his head deferentially)—"to beg you to go down with me."

"Go down with you? Where to?" cried the other, his eyes starting out of his head.

"To their house in the country, sir. Forgive me, my dear sir, if I am too agitated, and confuse my words; but I am so dreadfully afraid of hearing you refuse me."

He looked at Velchaninoff plaintively.

"You wish me to accompany you to see your bride?" said Velchaninoff, staring keenly at Pavel Pavlovitch; he could not believe either his eyes or his ears.

"Yes—yes, sir!" murmured Pavel, who had suddenly become timid to a painful degree. "Don't be angry, Alexey Ivanovitch, it is not my audacity that prompts me to ask you this; I do it with all humility, and conscious of the unusual nature of my petition. I—I thought perhaps you would not refuse my humble request."

"In the first place, the thing is absolutely out of the question," said Velchaninoff, turning away in considerable mental perturbation.

"It is only my immeasurable longing that prompts me to ask you. I confess I have a reason for desiring it, which reason I propose to reveal to you afterwards; just now I——"

"The thing is quite impossible, however you may look at it. You must admit yourself that it is so!" cried Velchaninoff. Both men had risen from their chairs in the excitement of the conversation.

"Not at all—not at all; it is quite possible, sir. In the first place, I merely propose to introduce you as my friend; and in the second place, you know the family already, the Zachlebnikoff's—State Councillor Zachlebnikoff!"

"What? how so?" cried Velchaninoff. This was the very man whom he had so often tried to find at home, and whom he never succeeded in hunting down—the very lawyer who had acted for his adversary in the late legal proceedings.

"Why, certainly—certainly!" cried Pavel Pavlovitch, apparently taking heart at Velchaninoff's extreme display of amazement. "The very same man whom I saw you talking to in the street one day; when I watched you from the other side of the road, I was waiting my turn to speak to him then. We served in the same department twelve years since. I had no thought of all this that day I saw you with him; the whole idea is quite new and sudden—only a week old."

"But—excuse me; why, surely this is a most respectable family, isn't it?" asked Velchaninoff, naïvely.

"Well, and what if it is respectable?" said Pavel, with a twist.

"Oh, no—of course, I meant nothing; but, so far as I could judge from what I saw, there——"

"They remember—they remember your coming down," cried Pavel delightedly. "I told them all sorts of flattering things about you."

"But, look here, how are you to marry within three months of your late wife's death?"

"Oh! the wedding needn't be at once. The wedding can come off in nine or ten months, so that I shall have been in mourning exactly a year. Believe me, my dear sir, it's all most charming—first place, Fedosie Petrovitch has known me since I was a child; he knew my late wife; he knows how much income I have; he knows all about my little private capital, and all about my new increase of salary. So that you see the whole thing is a mere matter of weights and scales."

"Is she a daughter of his, then?"

"I'll tell you all about it," said Pavel, licking his lips with pleasure. "May I smoke a cigarette? Now, you see, men like Fedosie Petrovitch Zachlebnikoff are much valued in the State; but, excepting for a few perquisites allowed them, the pay is wretched; they live well enough, but they cannot possibly lay by money. Now, imagine, this man has eight daughters and only one little boy: if he were to die there would be nothing but a wretched little pension to keep the lot of them. Just imagine now—*boots* alone for such a family, eh? Well, out of these eight girls five are marriageable, the eldest is twenty-four already (a splendid girl, she is, you shall see her for yourself). The sixth is a girl of fifteen, still at school. Well, all those five elder girls have to be trotted about and shown off, and what does all that sort of thing cost the poor father, sir? They must be married. Then suddenly I appear on the scene—the first probable bridegroom in the family, and they all know that I have money. Well, there you are, sir—the thing's done."

Pavel Pavlovitch was intoxicated with enthusiasm.

"Are you engaged to the eldest?"

"N—no;—not the eldest. I am wooing the sixth girl, the one at school."

"What?" cried Velchaninoff, laughing in spite of himself. "Why, you say yourself she's only fifteen years old."

"Fifteen *now*, sir; but she'll be sixteen in nine months—sixteen and three months—so why not? It wouldn't be quite nice to make the engagement public just yet, though; so there's to be nothing formal at present, it's only a private arrangement between the parents and myself so far. Believe me, my dear sir, the whole thing is apple-pie, regular and charming."

"Then it isn't quite settled yet?"

"Oh, *quite* settled—quite settled. Believe me, it's all as right and tight as——"

"Does *she* know?"

"Well, you see, just for form's sake, it is not actually talked about—to her I mean,—but she *knows* well enough. Oh! now you *will* make me happy this once, Alexey Ivanovitch, won't you?" he concluded, with extreme timidity of voice and manner.

"But why should *I* go with you? However," added Velchaninoff impatiently, "as I am not going in any case, I don't see why I should hear any reasons you may adduce for my accompanying you."

"Alexey Ivanovitch!——"

"Oh, come! you don't suppose I am going to sit down in a carriage with you alongside, and drive down there! Come, just think for yourself!"

The feeling of disgust and displeasure which Pavel Pavlovitch had awakened in him before, had now started into life again after the momentary distraction of the man's foolery about his bride. He felt that in another minute or two he might kick the fellow out before he realized what he was doing. He felt angry with himself for some reason or other.

"Sit down, Alexey Ivanovitch, sit down! You shall not repent it!" said Pavel Pavlovitch in a wheedling voice. "No, no, no!" he added, deprecating the impatient gesture which Velchaninoff made at this moment. "Alexey Ivanovitch, I entreat you to pause before you decide definitely. I see you have quite misunderstood me. I quite realize that I am not for you, nor you for me! I am not quite so absurd as to be unaware of that fact. The service I ask of you now shall not compromise you in any way for the future. I am going away the day after to-morrow, for certain; let this one day be an exceptional one for me, sir. I came to you founding my hopes upon the generosity and nobility of your heart, Alexey Ivanovitch—upon those special tender feelings which may, perhaps, have been aroused in you by late events. Am I explaining myself clearly, sir; or do you still misunderstand me?"

The agitation of Pavel Pavlovitch was increasing with every moment.

Velchaninoff gazed curiously at him.

"You ask a service of me," he said thoughtfully, "and insist strongly upon my performance of it. This is very suspicious, in my opinion; I must know more."

"The whole service I ask is merely that you will come with me; and I promise, when we return that I will lay bare my heart to you as though we were at a confessional. Trust me this once, Alexey Ivanovitch!"

But Velchaninoff still held out, and the more obstinately because he was conscious of a certain worrying feeling which he had had ever since Pavel Pavlovitch began to talk about his bride. Whether this feeling was simple curiosity, or something quite inexplicable, he knew not. Whatever it was it urged him to agree, and go. And the more the instinct urged him, the more he resisted it.

He sat and thought for a long time, his head resting on his hand, while Pavel Pavlovitch buzzed about him and continued to repeat his arguments.

"Very well," he said at last, "very well, I'll go." He was agitated almost to trembling pitch. Pavel was radiant.

"Then, Alexey Ivanovitch, change your clothes—dress up, will you? Dress up in your own style—you know so well how to do it."

Pavel Pavlovitch danced about Velchaninoff as he dressed. His state of mind was exuberantly blissful.

"What in the world does the fellow mean by it all?" thought Velchaninoff.

"I'm going to ask you one more favour yet, Alexey Ivanovitch," cried the other. "You've consented to come; you must be my guide, sir, too."

"For instance, how?"

"Well, for instance, here's an important question—the crape. Which ought I to do—tear it off, or leave it on?"

"Just as you like."

"No, I want your opinion. What should you do yourself, if you were wearing crape, under the circumstances? My own idea was, that if I left it on, I should be giving a proof of the fidelity of my affections. A very flattering recommendation, eh, sir?"

"Oh, take it off, of course."

"Do you really think it's a matter of 'of course'?" Pavel Pavlovitch reflected. "No," he continued, "do you know, I think I'd rather leave it on."

"Well, do as you like! He doesn't trust me, at all events, which is one good thing," thought Velchaninoff.

They left the house at last. Pavel looked over his companion's smart costume with intense satisfaction. Velchaninoff was greatly surprised at Pavel's conduct, but not less so at his own. At the gate there stood a very superior open carriage.

"H'm! so you had a carriage in waiting, had you? Then you were quite convinced that I would consent to come down with you, I suppose?"

"I took the carriage for my own use, but I was nearly sure you would come," said Pavel Pavlovitch, who wore the air of a man whose cup of happiness is full to the brim.

"Don't you think you are a little too sanguine in trusting so much to my benevolence?" asked Velchaninoff, as they took their seats and started. He smiled as he spoke, but his heart was full of annoyance.

"Well, Alexey Ivanovitch, it is not for *you* to call me a fool for that," replied Pavel, firmly and impressively.

"H'm! and Liza?" thought Velchaninoff, but he chased the idea away, he felt as though it were sacrilege to think of her here; and immediately another thought came in, namely, how small, how petty a creature he must be himself to harbour such a thought—such a mean, paltry sentiment in connection with Liza's sacred name. So angry was he, that he felt as though he must stop the carriage and get out, even though it cost him a struggle with Pavel Pavlovitch to do so.

But at this moment Pavel spoke, and the old feeling of desire to go with him re-entered his soul. "Alexey Ivanovitch," Pavel said, "are you a judge of articles of value?"

"What sort of articles?"

"Diamonds."

"Yes."

"I wish to take down a present with me. What do you think? Ought I to give her one, or not?"

"Quite unnecessary, I should think."

"But I wish to do it, badly. The only thing is, what shall I give?—a whole set, brooch, ear-rings, bracelet, and all, or only one article?"

"How much do you wish to spend?"

"Oh, four or five hundred roubles."

"Bosh!"

"What, too much?"

"Buy one bracelet for about a hundred."

This advice depressed Pavel Pavlovitch; he grew wondrous melancholy. He was terribly anxious to spend a lot of money, and buy the whole set. He insisted upon the necessity of doing so.

A shop was reached and entered, and Pavel bought a bracelet after all, and that not the one he chose himself, but the one which his companion fixed upon. Pavel wished to buy both. When the shopman, who originally asked one hundred and seventy five, let the bracelet go for a hundred and fifty roubles, Pavel Pavlovitch was anything but pleased. He was most anxious to spend a lot of money on the young lady, and would have gladly paid two hundred roubles for the same goods, on the slightest encouragement.

"It doesn't matter, my being in a hurry to give her presents, does it?" he began excitedly, when they were back in the carriage, and rolling along once more. "They are not 'swells' at all; they live most simply. Innocence loves presents," he continued, smiling cunningly. "You laughed just now, Alexey Ivanovitch, when I said that the girl was only fifteen; but, you know, what specially struck me about her was, that she still goes to school, with a sweet little bag in her hand, containing copy books and pencils. Ha-ha-ha! It was the little satchel that'fetched' me. I do love innocence, Alexey Ivanovitch. I don't care half so much for good looks as for innocence. Fancy, she and her friend were sitting in the corner there, the other day, and roared with laughter because the cat jumped from a cupboard on to the sofa, and fell down all of a heap. Why, it smells of fresh apples, that does, sir. Shall I take off the crape, eh?"

"Do as you like!"

"Well, I'll take it off!" He took his hat, tore the crape off, and threw the latter into the road.

Velchaninoff remarked that as he put his hat on his bald head once more, he wore an expression of the simplest and frankest hope and delight.

208

"Is he *really* that sort of man?" thought Velchaninoff with annoyance. "He surely *can't* be trundling me down here without some underhand motive—impossible! He *can't* be trusting entirely to my generosity?" This last idea seemed to fill him with indignation. "What *is* this clown of a fellow?" he continued to reflect. "Is he a fool, an idiot, or simply a 'permanent husband'? I can't make head or tail of it all!"

CHAPTER XII.

The Zachlebnikoffs were certainly, as Velchaninoff had expressed it, a most respectable family. Zachlebnikoff himself was a most eminently dignified and "solid" gentleman to look at. What Pavel Pavlovitch had said as to their resources was, however, quite true; they lived well, but if paterfamilias were to die, it would be very awkward for the rest.

Old Zachlebnikoff received Velchaninoff most cordially. He was no longer the legal opponent; he appeared now in a far more agreeable guise.

"I congratulate you," he said at once, "upon the issue. I did my best to arrange it so, and your lawyer was a capital fellow to deal with. You have your sixty thousand without trouble or worry, you see; and if we hadn't squared it we might have fought on for two or three years."

Velchaninoff was introduced to the lady of the house as well—an elderly, simple-looking, worn woman. Then the girls began to troop in, one by one and occasionally two together. But, somehow, there seemed to be even more than Velchaninoff had been led to expect; ten or a dozen were collected already—he could not count them exactly. It turned out that some were friends from the neighbouring houses.

The Zachlebnikoffs' country house was a large wooden structure of no particular style of architecture, but handsome enough, and was possessed of a fine large garden. There were, however, two or three other houses built round the latter, so that the garden was common property for all, which fact resulted in great intimacy between the Zachlebnikoff girls and the young ladies of the neighbouring houses.

Velchaninoff discovered, almost from the first moment, that his arrival—in the capacity of Pavel Pavlovitch's friend, desiring an introduction to the family—was expected, and looked forward to as a solemn and important occasion.

Being an expert in such matters he very soon observed that there was even more than this in his reception. Judging from the extra politeness of the parents, and by the exceeding smartness of the young ladies, he could not help suspecting that Pavel Pavlovitch had been improving the occasion, and that he had—not, of course, in so many words—given to understand that Velchaninoff was a single man—dull and disconsolate, and had represented him as likely enough at any moment to change his manner of living and set up an establishment, especially as he had just come in for a considerable inheritance. He thought that Katerina Fedosievna, the eldest girl—twenty-four years of age, and a splendid girl according to Pavel's description—seemed rather "got up to kill," from the look of her. She was eminent, even among her well-dressed sisters, for special elegance of costume, and for a certain originality about the make-up of her abundant hair.

The rest of the girls all looked as though they were well aware that Velchaninoff was making acquaintance with the family "for Katie," and had come down "to have a look at her." Their looks and words all strengthened the impression that they were acting with this supposition in view, as the day went on.

Katerina Fedosievna was a fine tall girl, rather plump, and with an extremely pleasing face. She seemed to be of a quiet, if not actually sleepy, disposition.

"Strange, that such a fine girl should be unmarried," thought Velchaninoff, as he watched her with much satisfaction.

All the sisters were nice-looking, and there were several pretty faces among the friends assembled. Velchaninoff was much diverted by the presence of all these young ladies.

Nadejda Fedosievna, the school-girl and bride elect of Pavel Pavlovitch, had not as yet condescended to appear. Velchaninoff awaited her coming with a degree of impatience which surprised and amused him. At last she came, and came with effect, too, accompanied by a lively girl, her friend—Maria Nikitishna—who was considerably older than herself and a very old friend of the family, having been governess in a neighbouring house for some years. She was quite one of the family, and boasted of about twenty-three years of age. She was much esteemed by all the girls, and evidently acted at present as guide, philosopher, and friend to Nadia (Nadejda). Velchaninoff saw at the first glance that all the girls were against Pavel Pavlovitch, friends and all; and when Nadia came in, it did not take him long to discover that she absolutely *hated* him. He observed, further, that Pavel Pavlovitch either did not, or *would not*, notice this fact.

Nadia was the prettiest of all the girls—a little *brunette*, with an impudent audacious expression; she might have been a Nihilist from the independence of her look. The sly little creature had a pair of flashing eyes and a most charming smile, though as often as not her smile was more full of mischief and wickedness than of amiability; her lips and teeth were wonders; she was slender but well put together, and the expression of her face was thoughtful though at the same time childish.

"Fifteen years old" was imprinted in every feature of her face and every motion of her body. It appeared afterwards that Pavel Pavlovitch had actually seen the girl for the first time with a little satchel in her hand, coming back from school. She had ceased to carry the satchel since that day.

The present brought down by Pavel Pavlovitch proved a failure, and was the cause of a very painful impression.

Pavel Pavlovitch no sooner saw his bride elect enter the room than he approached her with a broad grin on his face. He gave his present with the preface that he "offered it in recognition of the agreeable sensation experienced by him at his last visit upon the occasion of Nadejda Fedosievna singing a certain song to the pianoforte," and there he stopped in confusion and stood before her lost and miserable, shoving the jeweller's box into her hand. Nadia, however, would not take the present, and drew her hands away.

She approached her mother imperiously (the latter looked much put out), and said aloud: "I won't take it, mother." Nadia was blushing with shame and anger.

"Take it and say 'thank you' to Pavel Pavlovitch for it," said her father quietly but firmly. He was very far from pleased.

"Quite unnecessary, quite unnecessary!" he muttered to Pavel Pavlovitch.

Nadia, seeing there was nothing else to be done, took the case and curtsied—just as children do, giving a little bob down and then a bob up again, as if she had been on springs.

One of the sisters came across to look at the present whereupon Nadia handed it over to her unopened, thereby showing that she did not care so much as to look at it herself.

The bracelet was taken out and handed around from one to the other of the company; but all examined it silently, and some even ironically, only the mother of the family muttered that the bracelet was "very pretty."

Pavel Pavlovitch would have been delighted to see the earth open and swallow him up.

Velchaninoff helped the wretched man out of the mess. He suddenly began to talk loudly and eloquently about the first thing that struck him, and before five minutes had passed he had won the attention of everyone in the room. He was a wonderfully clever society talker. He had the knack of putting on an air of absolute sincerity, and of impressing his hearers with the belief that he considered them equally sincere; he was able to act the simple, careless, and happy young fellow to perfection. He was a master of the art of interlarding his talk with occasional flashes of real wit, apparently spontaneous but actually pre-arranged, and very likely *stale*, in so far that he had himself made the joke before.

But to-day he was particularly successful; he felt that he must talk on and talk well, and he knew that before many moments were past he should succeed in monopolizing all eyes and all ears—that no joke should be laughed at but his own, and no voice heard but his.

And sure enough the spell of his presence seemed to produce a wonderful effect; in a while the talking and laughter became general, with Velchaninoff as the centre and motor of all. Mrs. Zachlebnikoff's kind face lighted up with real pleasure, and Katie's pretty eyes were alight with absolute fascination, while her whole visage glowed with delight.

Only Nadia frowned at him, and watched him keenly from beneath her dark lashes. It was clear that she was prejudiced against him. This last fact only roused Velchaninoff to greater exertions. The mischievous Maria Nikitishna, however, as Nadia's ally, succeeded in playing off a successful piece of chaff against Velchaninoff; she pretended that Pavel Pavlovitch had represented Velchaninoff as the friend of his childhood, thereby making the latter out to be some seven or eight years older than he really was. Velchaninoff liked the look of Maria, notwithstanding.

Pavel Pavlovitch was the picture of perplexity. He quite understood the success which his "friend" was achieving, and at first he felt glad and proud of that success, laughing at the jokes and taking a share of the conversation; but for some reason or other he gradually relapsed into thoughtfulness, and thence into melancholy—which fact was sufficiently plain from the expression of his lugubrious and careworn physiognomy.

"Well, my dear fellow, you are the sort of guest one need not exert oneself to entertain," said old Zachlebnikoff at last, rising and making for his private study, where he had business of importance awaiting his attention; "and I was led to believe that you were the most morose of hypochondriacs. Dear me! what mistakes one does make about other people, to be sure!"

There was a grand piano in the room, and Velchaninoff suddenly turned to Nadia and remarked:

"You sing, don't you?"

"Who told you I did?" said Nadia curtly.

"Pavel Pavlovitch."

"It isn't true; I only sing for a joke—I have no voice."

"Oh, but I have no voice either, and yet I sing!"

"Well, you sing to us first, and then I'll sing," said Nadia, with sparkling eyes; "not now though—after dinner. I hate music," she added, "I'm so sick of the piano. We have singing and strumming going on all day here;—and Katie is the only one of us all worth hearing!"

Velchaninoff immediately attacked Katie, and besieged her with petitions to play. This attention from him to her eldest daughter so pleased mamma that she flushed up with satisfaction.

Katie went to the piano, blushing like a school-girl, and evidently much ashamed of herself for blushing; she played some little piece of Haydn's correctly enough but without much expression.

When she had finished Velchaninoff praised the music warmly—Haydn's music generally, and this little piece in particular. He looked at Katie too, with admiration, and his expression seemed to say. "By Jove, you're a fine girl!" So eloquent was his look that everyone in the room was able to read it, and especially Katie herself.

"What a pretty garden you have!" said Velchaninoff after a short pause, looking through the glass doors of the balcony. "Let's all go out; may we?"

"Oh, yes! do let's go out!" cried several voices together. He seemed to have hit upon the very thing most desired by all.

So they all adjourned into the garden, and walked about there until dinner-time; and Velchaninoff had the opportunity of making closer acquaintance with some of the girls of the establishment. Two or three young fellows "dropped in" from the neighbouring houses—a student, a school-boy, and another young fellow of about twenty in a pair of huge spectacles. Each of these young fellows immediately attached himself to the particular young lady of his choice.

The young man in spectacles no sooner arrived than he went aside with Nadia and Maria Nikitishna, and entered into an animated whispering conversation with them, with much frowning and impatience of manner.

This gentleman seemed to consider it his mission to treat Pavel Pavlovitch with the most ineffable contempt.

Some of the girls proposed a game. One of them suggested "Proverbs," but it was voted dull; another suggested acting, but the objection was made that they never knew how to finish off.

"It may be more successful with you," said Nadia to Velchaninoff confidentially. "You know we all thought you were Pavel Pavlovitch's friend, but it appears that he was only boasting. I am *very* glad you have come—for a certain reason!" she added, looking knowingly into Velchaninoff's face, and then retreating back again to Maria's wing, blushing.

"We'll play 'Proverbs' in the evening," said another, "and we'll all chaff Pavel Pavlovitch; *you* must help us too!"

"We *are* so glad you're come—it's so dull here as a rule," said a third, a funny-looking red-haired girl, whose face was comically hot, with running apparently. Goodness knows where she had dropped from; Velchaninoff had not observed her arrive.

Pavel Pavlovitch's agitation increased every moment. Meanwhile Velchaninoff took the opportunity of making great friends with Nadia. She had ceased to frown at him as before, and had now developed the wildest of spirits, dancing and jumping about, singing and whistling, and occasionally even catching hold of his hand in her innocent friendliness.

She was very happy indeed, apparently; but she took no more notice of Pavel Pavlovitch than if he had not been there at all.

Pavel Pavlovitch was very jealous of all this, and once or twice when Nadia and Velchaninoff talked apart, he joined them and rudely interrupted their conversation by interposing his anxious face between them.

Katia could not help being fully aware by this time that their charming guest had not come in for her sake, as had been believed by the family; indeed, it was clear that Nadia interested him so much that she excluded everyone else, to a considerable extent, from his attention. However, in spite of this, her good-natured face retained its amiability of expression all the same. She seemed to be happy enough witnessing the happiness of the rest and listening to the merry talk; she could not take a large share in the conversation herself, poor girl!

"What a fine girl your sister, Katerina Fedosievna is," remarked Velchaninoff to Nadia.

"Katia? I should think so! there is no better girl in the world. She's our family angel! I'm in love with her myself!" replied Nadia enthusiastically.

At last, dinner was announced, and a very good dinner it was, several courses being added for the benefit of the guests: a bottle of tokay made its appearance, and champagne was handed round in honour of the occasion. The good humour of the company was general, old Zachlebnikoff was in high spirits, having partaken of an extra glass of wine this evening. So infectious was the hilarity that even Pavel Pavlovitch took heart of grace and made a pun.

From the end of the table where he sat beside the lady of the house, there suddenly came a loud laugh from the delighted girls who had been fortunate enough to hear the virgin attempt.

"Papa, papa, Pavel Pavlovitch has made a joke!" cried several at once: "he says that there is quite a 'galaxy of gals' here!"

"Oho! he's made a pun too, has he?" cried the old fellow. "Well, what is it, let's have it!" He turned to Pavel Pavlovitch with beaming face, prepared to roar over the latter's joke.

"Why, I tell you, he says there's quite a 'galaxy of gals.' "

"Well, go on, where's the joke?" repeated papa, still dense to the merits of the pun, but beaming more and more with benevolent desire to see it.

"Oh, papa, how stupid you are not to see it. Why 'gals' and 'galaxy,' don't you see?—he says there's quite a galaxy of gals!"

"Oh! oh!" guffawed the old gentleman, "Ha-ha! Well, we'll hope he'll make a better one next time, that's all."

"Pavel Pavlovitch can't acquire all the perfections at once," said Maria Nikitishna. "Oh, my goodness! he's swallowed a bone—look!" she added, jumping up from her chair.

The alarm was general, and Maria's delight was great.

Poor Pavel Pavlovitch had only choked over a glass of wine, which he seized and drank to hide his confusion; but Maria declared that it was a fishbone—that she had seen it herself, and that people had been known to die of swallowing a bone just like that.

"Clap him on the back!" cried somebody.

It appeared that there were numerous kind friends ready to perform this friendly office, and poor Pavel protested in vain that it was nothing but a common choke. The belabouring went on until the coughing fit was over, and it became evident that mischievous Maria was at the bottom of it all.

After dinner old Mr. Zachlebnikoff retired for his post-prandial nap, bidding the young people enjoy themselves in the garden as best they might.

"You enjoy yourself, too!" he added to Pavel Pavlovitch, tapping the latter's shoulder affably as he went by.

When the party were all collected in the garden once more, Pavel suddenly approached Velchaninoff: "One moment," he whispered, pulling the latter by the coat-sleeve.

The two men went aside into a lonely by-path.

"None of that here, please; I won't allow it here!" said Pavel Pavlovitch in a choking whisper.

"None of what? Who?" asked Velchaninoff, staring with all his eyes.

Pavel Pavlovitch said nothing more, but gazed furiously at his companion, his lips trembling in a desperate attempt at a pretended smile. At this moment the voices of several of the girls broke in upon them, calling them to some game. Velchaninoff shrugged his shoulders and re-joined the party. Pavel followed him.

"I'm sure Pavel Pavlovitch was borrowing a handkerchief from you, wasn't he? He forgot his handkerchief last time too. Pavel Pavlovitch has forgotten his handkerchief again, and he has a cold as usual!" cried Maria.

"Oh, Pavel Pavlovitch, why didn't you say so?" cried Mrs. Zachlebnikoff, making towards the house; "you shall have one at once."

In vain poor Pavel protested that he had two of those necessary articles, and was *not* suffering from a cold. Mrs. Zachlebnikoff was glad of the excuse for retiring to the house, and heard nothing. A few moments afterwards a maid pursued Pavel with a handkerchief, to the confusion of the latter gentleman.

A game of "proverbs" was now proposed. All sat down, and the young man with spectacles was made to retire to a considerable distance and wait there with his nose close up against the wall and his back turned until the proverb should have been chosen and the words arranged. Velchaninoff was the next in turn to be the questioner.

Then the cry arose for Pavel Pavlovitch, and the latter, who had more or less recovered his good humour by this time, proceeded to the spot indicated; and, resolved to do his duty like a man, took his stand with his nose to the wall, ready to stay there motionless until called. The red-haired young lady was detailed to watch him, in case of fraud on his part.

No sooner, however, had the wretched Pavel taken up his position at the wall, than the whole party took to their heels and ran away as fast as their legs could carry them.

"Run quick!" whispered the girls to Velchaninoff, in despair, for he had not started with them.

"Why, what's happened? What's the matter?" asked the latter, keeping up as best he could.

"Don't make a noise! we want to get away and let him go on standing there—that's all."

Katia, it appeared, did not like this practical joke. When the last stragglers of the party arrived at the end of the garden, among them Velchaninoff, the latter found Katia angrily scolding the rest of the girls.

"Very well," she was saying, "I won't tell mother this time; but I shall go away myself: it's too bad! What will the poor fellow's feelings be, standing all alone there, and finding us fled!"

And off she went. The rest, however, were entirely unsympathizing, and enjoyed the joke thoroughly. Velchaninoff was entreated to appear entirely unconscious when Pavel Pavlovitch should appear again, just as though nothing whatever had happened. It was a full quarter of an hour before Pavel put in an appearance, two thirds, at least, of that time he must have stood at the wall. When he reached the party he found everyone busy over a game of *Goriélki*, laughing and shouting and making themselves thoroughly happy.

Wild with rage, Pavel Pavlovitch again made straight for Velchaninoff, and tugged him by the coat-sleeve.

"One moment, sir!"

"Oh, my goodness! he's always coming in with his 'one moments'!" said someone.

"A handkerchief wanted again probably!" shouted someone else after the pair as they retired.

"Come now, this time it was you! You were the originator of this insult!" muttered Pavel, his teeth chattering with fury.

Velchaninoff interrupted him, and strongly recommended Pavel to bestir himself to be merrier.

"You are chaffed because you get angry," he said; "if you try to be jolly instead of sulky you'll be let alone!"

To his surprise these words impressed Pavel deeply; he was quiet at once, and returned to the party with a guilty air, and immediately began to take part in the games engaged in once more. He was not further bullied at present, and within half an hour his good humour seemed quite re-established.

To Velchaninoff's astonishment, however, he never seemed to presume to speak to Nadia, although he kept as close to her, on all occasions, as he possibly could. He seemed to take his position as quite natural, and was not put out by her contemptuous air towards him.

Pavel Pavlovitch was teased once more, however, before the evening ended.

A game of "Hide-and-seek" was commenced, and Pavel had hidden in a small room in the house. Being observed entering there by someone, he was locked in, and left there raging for an hour. Meanwhile, Velchaninoff learned the "special reason" for Nadia's joy at his arrival. Maria conducted him to a lonely alley, where Nadia was awaiting him alone.

"I have quite convinced myself," began the latter, when they were left alone, "that you are not nearly so great a friend of Pavel Pavlovitch as he gave us to understand. I have also convinced myself that you alone can perform a certain great service for me. Here is his horrid bracelet" (she drew the case out of her pocket)—"I wish to ask you to be so kind as to return it to him; I cannot do so myself, because I am quite determined never to speak to him again all my life. You can tell him so from me, and better add that he is not to worry me with any more of his nasty presents. I'll let him know something else I have to say through other channels. Will you do this for me?"

"Oh, for goodness sake, spare me!" cried Velchaninoff, almost wringing his hands.

"How spare you?" cried poor Nadia. Her artificial tone put on for the occasion had collapsed at once before this check, and she was nearly crying. Velchaninoff burst out laughing.

"I don't mean—I should be delighted, you know—but the thing is, I have my own accounts to settle with him!"

"I knew you weren't his friend, and that he was lying. I shall never marry him—never! You may rely on that! I don't understand how he could dare—at all events, you really *must* give him back this horrid bracelet. What am I to do if you don't? I *must* have it given back to him this very day. He'll catch it if he interferes with father about me!"

At this moment the spectacled young gentleman issued from the shrubs at their elbow.

"You are bound to return the bracelet!" he burst out furiously, upon Velchaninoff, "if only out of respect to the rights of woman——"

He did not finish the sentence, for Nadia pulled him away from beside Velchaninoff with all her strength.

"How stupid you are," she cried; "go away. How dare you listen? I told you to stand a long way off!" She stamped her foot with rage, and for some while after the young fellow had slunk away she continued to walk along with flashing eyes, furious with indignation. "You wouldn't believe how stupid he is!" she cried at last. "You laugh, but think of my feelings!"

"That's not *he*, is it?" laughed Velchaninoff.

"Of course not. How could you imagine such a thing! It's only his friend, and how he can choose such friends I can't understand! They say he is a 'future motive-power,' but I don't see it. Alexey Ivanovitch, for the last time—I have no one else to ask—will you give the bracelet back or not?"

"Very well, I will. Give it to me!"

"Oh, you dear, good Alexey Ivanovitch, thanks!" she cried, enthusiastic with delight. "I'll sing all the evening for that! I sing beautifully, you know! I was telling you a wicked story before dinner. Oh, I *wish* you would come down here again; I'd tell you *all*, then, and lots of other things besides—for you are a dear, kind, good fellow, like—like Katia!"

And sure enough when they reached home she sat down and sang a couple of songs in a voice which, though entirely untrained, was of great natural sweetness and considerable strength.

When the party returned from the garden they had found Pavel Pavlovitch drinking tea with the old folks on the balcony. He had probably been talking on serious topics, as he was to take his departure the day after to-morrow for nine months. He never so much as glanced at Velchaninoff and the rest when they entered; but he evidently had not complained to the authorities, and all was quiet as yet. But, when Nadia began to sing, he came in. Nadia did not answer a single one of his questions, but he did not seem offended by this, and took his stand behind her chair. Once there, his whole appearance gave it to be understood that that was his own place by right, and that he allowed none to dispute it.

"It's Alexey Ivanovitch's turn to sing now!" cried the girls, when Nadia's song was finished, and all crowded round to hear Velchaninoff, who sat down to accompany himself. He chose a song of Glinke's, too much neglected nowadays; it ran:—

"When from your merry lips

Tenderness flows," &c.

Velchaninoff seemed to address the words to Nadia exclusively, but the whole party stood around him. His voice had long since gone the way of all flesh, but it was clear that he must have had a good one once, and it so happened that Velchaninoff had heard this particular song many years ago, from Glinkes' own lips, when a student at the university, and remembered the great effect that it had made upon him when he first heard it. The song was full of the most intense passion of expression, and Velchaninoff sang it well, with his eyes fixed upon Nadia.

Amid the applause that followed the completion of the performance, Pavel Pavlovitch came forward, seized Nadia's hand and drew her away from the proximity of Velchaninoff; he then returned to the latter at the piano, and, with every evidence of frantic rage, whispered to him, his lips all of a tremble,

"One moment with you!"

Velchaninoff, seeing that the man was capable of worse things in his then frame of mind, took Pavel's hand and led him out through the balcony into the garden—quite dark now.

"Do you understand, sir, that you must come away at once—*this very minute*?" said Pavel Pavlovitch.

"No, sir, I do not!"

"Do you remember," continued Pavel in his frenzied whisper, "do you remember that you begged me to tell you *all, everything*—down to the smallest details? Well, the time has come for telling you all—come!"

Velchaninoff considered a moment, glanced once more at Pavel Pavlovitch, and consented to go.

"Oh! stay and have another cup of tea!" said Mrs. Zachlebnikoff, when this decision was announced.

"Pavel Pavlovitch, why are you taking Alexey Ivanovitch away?" cried the girls, with angry looks. As for Nadia, she looked so cross with Pavel, that the latter felt absolutely uncomfortable; but he did not give in.

"Oh, but I am very much obliged to Pavel Pavlovitch," said Velchaninoff, "for reminding me of some most important business which I must attend to this very evening, and which I might have forgotten," laughed Velchaninoff, as he shook hands with his host and made his bow to the ladies, especially to Katia, as the family thought.

"You must come again soon!" said the host; "we have been so glad to see you; it was so good of you to come!"

"Yes, *so* glad!" said the lady of the house.

"Do come again soon!" cried the girls, as Pavel Pavlovitch and Velchaninoff took their seats in the carriage;"Alexey Ivanovitch, *do* come back soon!" And with these voices in their ears they drove away.

CHAPTER XIII.

In spite of Velchaninoff's apparently happy day, the feeling of annoyance and suffering at his heart had hardly actually left him for a single moment. Before he sang the song he had not known what to do with himself, or suppressed anger and melancholy—perhaps that was the reason why he had sung with so much feeling and passion.

"To think that I could so have lowered myself as to forget everything!" he thought—and then despised himself for thinking it; "it is more humiliating still to cry over what is done," he continued. "Far better to fly into a passion with someone instead."

"Fool!" he muttered—looking askance at Pavel Pavlovitch, who sat beside him as still as a mouse. Pavel Pavlovitch preserved a most obstinate silence—probably concentrating and ranging his energies. He occasionally took his hat off, impatiently, and wiped the perspiration from his forehead.

Once—and once only—Pavel spoke, to the coachman, he asked whether there was going to be a thunder-storm.

"Wheugh!" said the man, "I should think so! It's been a steamy day—just the day for it!"

By the time town was reached—half-past ten—the whole sky was overcast.

"I am coming to your house," said Pavel to Velchaninoff, when almost at the door.

"Quite so; but I warn you, I feel very unwell to-night!"

"All right—I won't stay too long."

When the two men passed under the gateway, Pavel Pavlovitch disappeared into the 'dvornik's' room for a minute, to speak to Mavra.

"What did you go in there for?" asked Velchaninoff severely as they mounted the stairs and reached his own door.

"Oh—nothing—nothing at all,—just to tell them about the coachman.——"

"Very well. Mind, I shall not allow you to drink!"

Pavel Pavlovitch did not answer.

Velchaninoff lit a candle, while Pavel threw himself into a chair;—then the former came and stood menacingly before him.

"I may have told you I should have *my* last word to say to-night, as well as you!" he said with suppressed anger in his voice and manner: "Here it is. I consider conscientiously that things are square between you and me, now; and therefore there is no more to be said, understand me, about *anything*. Since this is so, had you not better go, and let me close the door after you?"

"Let's cry 'quits' first, Alexey Ivanovitch," said Pavel Pavlovitch, gazing into Velchaninoff's eyes with great sweetness.

"Quits?" cried the latter, in amazement; "you strange man, what are we to cry quits about? Are you harping upon your promise of a 'last word'?"

"Yes."

"Oh, well, we have nothing more to cry quits for. We have been quits long since," said Velchaninoff.

"Dear me, do you really think so?" cried Pavel Pavlovitch, in a shrill, sharp voice, pressing his two hands tightly together, finger to finger, as he held them up before his breast.

Velchaninoff said nothing. He rose from his seat and began to walk up and down the room. The word "Liza" resounded through and through his soul like the voice of a bell.

"Well, what is there that you still consider unsettled between us?" he asked at last, looking angrily at Pavel, who had never ceased to follow him with his eyes—always holding his hands before his breast, finger tip to finger tip.

"Don't go down there any more," said Pavel, almost in a whisper, and rising from his seat with every indication of humble entreaty.

"*What!* is *that* all?" cried Velchaninoff, bursting into an angry laugh; "good heavens, man, you have done nothing but surprise me all day." He had begun in a tone of exasperation, but he now abruptly changed both voice and expression, and continued with an air of deep feeling. "Listen," he said, "listen to me. I don't think I have ever felt so deeply humiliated as I am feeling now, in consequence of the events of to-day. In the first place, that I should have condescended to go down with you at all, and in the second place, all that happened there. It has been such a day of pettifogging—pitiful pettifogging. I have profaned and lowered myself by taking a share in it all, and forgetting——Well, it's done now. But look here—you fell upon me to-day, unawares—upon a sick man. Oh, you needn't excuse yourself; at all events I shall certainly *not* go there again. I have not the slightest interest in so doing," he concluded, with an air of decision.

"No, really!" cried Pavel Pavlovitch, making no secret of his delight and exultation.

Velchaninoff glanced contemptuously at him, and recommenced his march up and down the room.

"You have determined to be happy under any circumstances, I suppose?" he observed, after a pause. He could not resist making the remark disdainfully.

"Yes, I have," said Pavel, quietly.

"It's no business of mine that he's a fool and a knave, out of pure idiocy!" thought Velchaninoff. "I can't help hating him, though I feel that he is not even worth hating."

"I'm a permanent husband," said Pavel Pavlovitch, with the most exquisitely servile irony, at his own expense. "I remember you using that expression, Alexey Ivanovitch, long ago, when you were with us at T——. I remember many of your original phrases of that time, and when you spoke of 'permanent husbands,' the other day, I recollected the expression."

At this point Mavra entered the room with a bottle of champagne and two glasses.

"Forgive me, Alexey Ivanovitch," said Pavel, "you know I can't get on without it. Don't consider it an audacity on my part—think of it as a mere bit of by-play unworthy your notice."

"Well," consented Velchaninoff, with a look of disgust, "but I must remind you that I don't feel well, and that—"

"One little moment—I'll go at once, I really will—I *must* just drink *one* glass, my throat is so——"

He seized the bottle eagerly, and poured himself out a glass, drank it greedily at a gulp, and sat down. He looked at Velchaninoff almost tenderly.

"What a nasty looking beast!" muttered the latter to himself.

"It's all her friends that make her like that," said Pavel, suddenly, with animation.

"What? Oh, you refer to the lady. I——"

"And, besides, she is so very young still, you see," resumed Pavel. "I shall be her slave—she shall see a little society, and a bit of the world. She will change, sir, entirely."

"I mustn't forget to give him back the bracelet, by-the-bye," thought Velchaninoff, frowning, as he felt for the case in his coat pocket.

"You said just now that I am determined to be happy, Alexey Ivanovitch," continued Pavel, confidentially, and with almost touching earnestness. "I *must* marry, else what will become of me? You see for yourself" (he pointed to the bottle), "and that's only a hundredth part of what I demean myself to nowadays. I cannot get on without marrying again, sir; I *must* have a new faith. If I can but believe in some one again, sir, I shall rise—I shall be saved."

"Why are you telling *me* all this?" exclaimed Velchaninoff, very nearly laughing in his face; it seemed so absurdly inconsistent.

"Look here," he continued, roaring the words out, "let me know now, once for all, why did you drag me down there? what good was I to do you there?"

"I—I wished to try——," began Pavel, with some confusion.

"Try what?"

"The effect, sir. You see, Alexey Ivanovitch, I have only been visiting there a week" (he grew more and more confused), "and yesterday, when I met you, I thought to myself that I had never seen her yet in society; that is, in the society of other *men* besides myself—a stupid idea, I know it is—I was very anxious to try—you know my wretchedly jealous nature." He suddenly raised his head and blushed violently.

"He *can't* be telling me the truth!" thought Velchaninoff; he was struck dumb with surprise.

"Well, go on!" he muttered at last.

"Well, I see it was all her pretty childish nature, sir—that and her friends together. You must forgive my stupid conduct towards yourself to-day, Alexey Ivanovitch. I will never do it again—never again, sir, I assure you!"

"I shall never be there to give you the opportunity," replied Velchaninoff with a laugh.

"That's partly why I say it," said Pavel.

"Oh, come! I'm not the only man in the world you know!" said the other irritably.

"I am sorry to hear you say that, Alexey Ivanovitch. My esteem for Nadejda is such that I——"

"Oh, forgive me, forgive me! I meant nothing, I assure you! Only it surprises me that you should have expected so much of me—that you trusted me so completely."

"I trusted you entirely, sir, solely on account of—all that has passed."

"So that you still consider me the most honourable of men?" Velchaninoff paused, the naïve nature of his sudden question surprised even himself.

"I always did think you that, sir!" said Pavel, hanging his head.

"Of course, quite so—I didn't mean quite that—I wanted to say, in spite of all prejudices you may have formed, you——"

"Yes, in spite of all prejudices!"

"And when you first came to Petersburg?" asked Velchaninoff, who himself felt the monstrosity of his own inquisitive questions, but could not resist putting them.

"I considered you the most honourable of men when I first came to Petersburg, sir; no less. I always respected you, Alexey Ivanovitch!"

Pavel Pavlovitch raised his eyes and looked at his companion without the smallest trace of confusion.

Velchaninoff suddenly felt cowed and afraid. He was anxious that nothing should result—nothing disagreeable—from this conversation, since he himself was responsible for having initiated it.

"I loved you, Alexey Ivanovitch; all that year at T—— I loved you—you did not observe it," continued Pavel Pavlovitch, his voice trembling with emotion, to the great discomfiture of his companion. "You did not observe my affection, because I was too lowly a being to deserve any sort of notice; but it was unnecessary that you should observe my love. Well, sir, and all these nine years I have thought of you, for I have never known such a year of life as that year was." (Pavel's eyes seemed to have a special glare in them at this point.) "I remembered many of your sayings and expressions, sir, and I thought of you always as a man imbued with the loftiest sentiments, and gifted with knowledge and intellect, sir—of the highest order—a man of grand ideas. 'Great ideas do not proceed so frequently from greatness of intellect, as from elevation of taste and feeling.' You yourself said that, sir, once. I dare say you have forgotten the fact, but you did say it. Therefore I always thought of you, sir, as a man of taste and feeling; consequently I concluded—consequently I trusted you, in spite of everything."

Pavel Pavlovitch's chin suddenly began to tremble. Velchaninoff was frightened out of his wits. This unexpected tone must be put an end to at all hazards.

"Enough, Pavel Pavlovitch!" he said softly, blushing violently and with some show of irritation. "And why—why (Velchaninoff suddenly began to shout passionately)—why do you come hanging round the neck of a sick man, a worried man—a man who is almost out of his wits with fever and annoyance of all sorts, and drag him into this abyss of lies and mirage and vision and shame—and unnatural, disproportionate, distorted nonsense! Yes, sir, that's the most shameful part of the whole business—the disproportionate nonsense of what you say! You know it's all humbug; both of us are mean wretches—both of us; and if you like I'll prove to you at once that not only you don't love me, but that you loathe and hate me with all your heart, and that you are a liar, whether you know it or not! You took me down to see your bride, not—not a bit in the world to try how she would behave in the society of other men—absurd idea!—You simply saw me, yesterday, and your vile impulse led you to carry me off there in order that you might show me the girl, and say, as it were. There, look at that! She's to be mine! Try your hand *there* if you can! It was nothing but your challenge to me! You may not have known it, but this was so, as I say; and you felt the impulse which I have described. Such a challenge could not be made without hatred; consequently you hate me."

Velchaninoff almost *rushed* up and down the room as he shouted the above words; and with every syllable the humiliating consciousness that he was allowing himself to descend to the level of Pavel Pavlovitch afflicted him and tormented him more and more!

"I was only anxious to be at peace with you, Alexey Ivanovitch!" said Pavel sadly, his chin and lips working again.

Velchaninoff flew into a violent rage, as if he had been insulted in the most unexampled manner.

"I tell you once more, sir," he cried, "that you have attached yourself to a sick and irritated man, in order that you may surprise him into saying something unseemly in his madness! We are, I tell you, man, we are men of different worlds. Understand me! between us two there is a grave," he hissed in his fury, and stopped.

"And how do you know,—sir," cried Pavel Pavlovitch, his face suddenly becoming all twisted, and deadly white to look at, as he strode up to Velchaninoff, "how do you know what that grave means to me, sir, here!"(He beat his breast with terrible earnestness, droll though he looked.) "Yes, sir, we both stand on the brink of the grave, but on my side there is more, sir, than on yours—yes, more, more, more!" he hissed, beating his breast without pause—"more than on yours—the grave means more to me than to you!"

But at this moment a loud ring at the bell brought both men to their senses. Someone was ringing so loud that the bell-wire was in danger of snapping.

"People don't ring like that for me, observed Velchaninoff angrily."

"No more they do for me, sir! I assure you they don't!" said Pavel Pavlovitch anxiously. He had become the quiet timid Pavel again in a moment. Velchaninoff frowned and went to open the door.

"Mr. Velchaninoff, if I am not mistaken?" said a strange voice, apparently belonging to some young and very self-satisfied person, at the door.

"What is it?"

"I have been informed that Mr. Trusotsky is at this moment in your rooms. I must see him at once."

Velchaninoff felt inclined to send this self-satisfied looking young gentleman flying downstairs again; but he reflected—refrained, stood aside and let him in.

"Here is Mr. Trusotsky. Come in."

CHAPTER XIV.

A young fellow of some nineteen summers entered the room; he might have been even younger, to judge by his handsome but self-satisfied and very juvenile face.

He was not badly dressed, at all events his clothes fitted him well; in stature he was a little above the middle height; he had thick black hair, and dark, bold eyes—and these were the striking features of his face. Unfortunately his nose was a little too broad and tip-tilted, otherwise he would have been a really remarkably good-looking young fellow.—He came in with some pretension.

"I believe I have the opportunity of speaking to Mr. Trusotsky?" he observed deliberately, and bringing out the word opportunity with much apparent satisfaction, as though he wished to accentuate the fact that he could not possibly be supposed to feel either honour or pleasure in meeting Mr. Trusotsky. Velchaninoff thought he knew what all this meant; Pavel Pavlovitch seemed to have an inkling of the state of affairs, too. His expression was one of anxiety, but he did not show the white feather.

"Not having the honour of your acquaintance," he said with dignity, "I do not understand what sort of business you can have with me."

"Kindly listen to me first, and you can then let me know your ideas on the subject," observed the young gentleman, pulling out his tortoiseshell glasses, and focusing the champagne bottle with them. Having deliberately inspected that object, he put up his glasses again, and fixing his attention once more upon Pavel Pavlovitch, remarked:

"Alexander Loboff."

"What about Alexander Loboff?"

"That's my name. You've not heard of me?"

"No."

"H'm! Well, I don't know when you should have, now I think of it; but I've come on important business concerning yourself. I suppose I can sit down? I'm tired."

"Oh, pray sit down," said Velchaninoff, but not before the young man had taken a chair. In spite of the pain at his heart Velchaninoff could not help being interested in this impudent youngling.

There seemed to be something in his good-looking, fresh young face that reminded him of Nadia.

"You can sit down too," observed Loboff, indicating an empty seat to Pavel Pavlovitch, with a careless nod of his head.

"Thank you; I shall stand."

"Very well, but you'll soon get tired. You need not go away, I think, Mr. Velchaninoff."

"I have nowhere to go to, my good sir, I am at home."

"As you like; I confess I should prefer your being present while I have an explanation with this gentleman. Nadejda Fedosievna has given you a flattering enough character, sir, to me."

"Nonsense; how could she have had time to do so?"

"Immediately after you left. Now, Mr. Trusotsky, this is what I wish to observe," he continued to Pavel, the latter still standing in front of him; "we, that is Nadejda Fedosievna and myself, have long loved one another, and have plighted our troth. You have suddenly come between us as an obstruction; I have come to tell you that you had better clear out of the way at once. Are you prepared to adopt my suggestion?"

Pavel Pavlovitch took a step backward in amazement; his face paled visibly, but in a moment a spiteful smile curled his lip.

"Not in the slightest degree prepared, sir," he said, laconically.

"Dear me," said the young fellow, settling himself comfortably in his chair, and throwing one leg over the other.

"Indeed, I do not know whom I am speaking to," added Pavel Pavlovitch, "so that it can't hardly be worth your while to continue."

So saying he sat down at last.

"I *said* you'd get tired," remarked the youth. "I informed you just now," he added, "that my name is Alexander Loboff, and that Nadejda and I have plighted our troth; consequently you cannot truthfully say, as you did say just now, that you don't know who I am, nor can you honestly assert that you do not see what we can have to talk about. Not to speak of myself—there is Nadejda Fedosievna to be considered—the lady to whom you have so impudently attached yourself: that alone is matter sufficient for explanation between us."

All this the young fellow rattled off carelessly enough, as if the thing were so self-evident that it hardly needed mentioning. While talking, he raised his eye-glass once more, and inspected some object for an instant, putting the glass back in his pocket immediately afterwards.

"Excuse me, young man," began Pavel Pavlovitch: but the words "young man" were fatal.

"At any other moment," observed the youth, "I should of course forbid your calling me 'young man' at once; but you must admit that in this case my youth is my principal advantage over yourself, and that even this very day you would have given anything—nay, at the moment when you presented your bracelet—to be just a little bit younger."

"Cheeky young brat!" muttered Velchaninoff.

"In any case," began Pavel Pavlovitch, with dignity, "I do not consider your reasons as set forth—most questionable and improper reasons at the best—sufficient to justify the continuance of this conversation. I see your 'business' is mere childishness and nonsense: to-morrow I shall have the pleasure of an explanation with Mr. Zachlebnikoff, my respected friend. Meanwhile, sir, perhaps you will make it convenient to—depart."

"That's the sort of man he is," cried the youth, hotly, turning to Velchaninoff: "he is not content with being as good as kicked out of the place, and having faces made at him, but he must go down again to-morrow to carry tales about us to Mr. Zachlebnikoff. Do you not prove by this, you obstinate man, that you wish to carry off the young lady by force? that you desire to *buy* her of people who preserve—thanks to the relics of barbarism still triumphant among us—a species of power over her? Surely she showed you sufficiently clearly that she*despises* you? You have had your wretched tasteless present of to-day—that bracelet thing—returned to you; what more do you want?"

"Excuse me, no bracelet has been, or can be returned to me," said Pavel Pavlovitch, with a shudder of anxiety, however.

"How so? hasn't Mr. Velchaninoff given it to you?"

"Oh, the deuce take you, sir," thought Velchaninoff. "Nadejda Fedosievna certainly did give me this case for you, Pavel Pavlovitch," he said; "I did not wish to take it, but she was anxious that I should: here it is, I'm very sorry."

He took out the case and laid it down on the table before the enraged Pavel Pavlovitch.

"How is it you have not handed it to him before?" asked the young man severely.

"I had no time, as you may conclude," said Velchaninoff with a frown.

"H'm! Strange circumstance!"

"*What*, sir?"

"Well, you must admit it *is* strange! However, I am quite prepared to believe that there has been some mistake."

Velchaninoff would have given worlds to get up and drub the impertinent young rascal and drag him out of the house by the ear; but he could not contain himself, and burst out laughing. The boy immediately followed suit and laughed too.

But for Pavel Pavlovitch it was no laughing matter.

If Velchaninoff had seen the ferocious look which the former cast at him at the moment when he and Loboff laughed, he would have realized that Pavel Pavlovitch was in the act of passing a fatal limit of forbearance. He did not see the look; but it struck him that it was only fair to stand up for Pavel now.

"Listen, Mr. Loboff," he said, in friendly tones, "not to enter into the consideration of other matters, I may point out that Mr. Trusotsky brings with him, in his wooing of Miss Zachlebnikoff, a name and circumstances fully well-known to that esteemed family; in the second place, he brings a fairly respectable position in the world; and thirdly, he brings wealth. Therefore he may well be surprised to find himself confronted by such a rival as yourself—a gentleman of great wealth, doubtless, but at the same time so very young, that he could not possibly look upon you as a serious rival; therefore, again, he is quite right in begging you to bring the conversation to an end."

"What do you mean by 'so very young'? I was nineteen a month since; by the law I might have been married long ago. That's a sufficient answer to your argument."

"But what father would consent to allowing his daughter to marry you *now*—even though you may be a Rothschild to come, or a benefactor to humanity in the future. A man of nineteen years old is not capable of answering for himself and yet you are ready to take on your own responsibility another being—in other words, a being who is as much a child as you are yourself. Why, it is hardly even honourable on your part, is it? I have presumed to address you thus, because you yourself referred the matter to me as a sort of arbiter between yourself and Pavel Pavlovitch."

"Yes, by-the-bye, 'Pavel Pavlovitch,' I forgot he was called that," remarked the youth. "I wonder why I thought of him all along as 'Vassili Petrovitch.' Look here, sir (addressing Velchaninoff), you have not surprised me in the least. I knew you were all tarred with one brush. It is strange that you should have been described to me as a man of some originality. However, to business. All that you have said is, of course, utter nonsense; not only is there nothing 'dishonourable' about my intentions, as you permitted yourself to suggest, but the fact of the matter is entirely the reverse, as I hope to prove to you by-and-bye. In the first place, we have promised each other marriage, besides which I have given her my word that if she ever repents of her promise she shall have her full liberty to throw me over. I have given her surety to that effect before witnesses."

"I bet anything your friend—what's his name?—Predposiloff invented that idea," cried Velchaninoff.

"He-he-he!" giggled Pavel Pavlovitch contemptuously.

"What is that person giggling about? You are right, sir, it was Predposiloff's idea. But I don't think you and I quite understand one another, do we? and I had such a good report of you. How old are you? Are you fifty yet?"

"Stick to business, if you please."

"Forgive the liberty. I did not mean anything offensive. Well, to proceed. I am no millionaire, and I am no great benefactor to humanity (to reply to your arguments), but I shall manage to keep myself and my wife. Of course I have nothing now; I was brought up, in fact, in their house from my childhood."

"How so?"

"Oh, because I am a distant relative of this Mr. Zachlebnikoff's wife. When my people died, he took me in and sent me to school. The old fellow is really quite a kind-hearted man, if you only knew it."

219

"I do know it!"

"Yes, he's an old fogey rather, but a kind-hearted old fellow; but I left him four months ago and began to keep myself. I first joined a railway office at ten roubles a month, and am now in a notary's place at twenty-five. I made him a formal proposal for her a fortnight since. He first laughed like mad, and afterwards fell into a violent rage, and Nadia was locked up. She bore it heroically. He had been furious with me before for throwing up a post in his department which he procured for me. You see he is a good and kind old fellow at home, but get him in his office and—oh, my word!—he's a sort of *Jupiter Tonans*! I told him straight out that I didn't like his ways; but the great row was—thanks to the second chief at the office; he said I insulted him, but I only told him he was an ignorant beggar. So I threw them all up, and went in for the notary business. Listen to that! What a clap! We shall have a thunder-storm directly! What a good thing I arrived before the rain! I came here on foot, you know, all the way, nearly at a run, too!"

"How in the world did you find an opportunity of speaking to Miss Nadia then? especially since you are not allowed to meet."

"Oh, one can always get over the railing; then there's that red-haired girl, she helps, and Maria Nikitishna—oh, but she's a snake, that girl! What's the matter? Are you afraid of the thunder-storm?"

"No, I'm ill—seriously ill!"

Velchaninoff had risen from his seat with a fearful sudden pain in his chest, and was trying to walk up and down the room.

"Oh, really! then I'm disturbing you. I shall go at once," said the youth, jumping up.

"No, you don't disturb me!" said Velchaninoff ceremoniously.

"How not; of course I do, if you've got the stomach ache! Well now, Vassili—what's your name—Pavel Pavlovitch, let's conclude this matter. I will formulate my question for once into words which will adapt themselves to your understanding: Are you prepared to renounce your claim to the hand of Nadejda Fedosievna before her parents, and in my presence, with all due formality?"

"No, sir; not in the slightest degree prepared," said Pavel Pavlovitch witheringly; "and allow me to say once more that all this is childish and absurd, and that you had better clear out!"

"Take care," said the youth, holding up a warning forefinger; "better give it up now, for I warn you that otherwise you will spend a lot of money down there, and take a lot of trouble; and when you come back in nine months you will be turned out of the house by Nadejda Fedosievna herself; and if you don't go *then*, it will be the worse for you. Excuse me for saying so, but at present you are like the dog in the manger. Think over it, and be sensible for once in your life."

"Spare me the moral, if you please," began Pavel Pavlovitch furiously; "and as for your low threats I shall take my measures to-morrow—*serious* measures."

"Low threats? pooh! You are low yourself to take them as such. Very well, I'll wait till to-morrow then; but if you—there's the thunder again!—*au revoir*—very glad to have met you, sir." He nodded to Velchaninoff and made off hurriedly, evidently anxious to reach home before the rain.

CHAPTER XV.

"You see, you see!" cried Pavel to Velchaninoff, the instant that the young fellow's back was turned.

"Yes; you are not going to succeed there," said Velchaninoff. He would not have been so abrupt and careless of Pavel's feelings if it had not been for the dreadful pain in his chest.

Pavel Pavlovitch shuddered as though from a sudden scald. "Well, sir, and you—you were loth to give me back the bracelet, eh?"

"I hadn't time."

"Oh! you were sorry—you pitied me, as true friend pities friend!"

"Oh, well, I pitied you, then!" Velchaninoff was growing angrier every moment. However, he informed Pavel Pavlovitch shortly as to how he had received the bracelet, and how Nadia had almost forced it upon him.

"You must understand," he added, "that otherwise I should never have agreed to accept the commission; there are quite enough disagreeables already."

"You liked the job, and accepted it with pleasure," giggled Pavel Pavlovitch.

"That is foolish on your part; but I suppose you must be forgiven. You must have seen from that boy's behaviour that I play no part in this matter. Others are the principal actors, not I!"

"At all events the job had attractions for you." Pavel Pavlovitch sat down and poured out a glass of wine.

"You think I shall knuckle under to that young gentleman? Pooh! I shall drive him out to-morrow, sir, like dust. I'll smoke this little gentleman out of his nursery, sir; you see if I don't." He drank his wine off at a gulp, and poured out some more. He seemed to grow freer as the moments went by; he talked glibly now.

"Ha-ha! Sachinka and Nadienka![2] darling little children. Ha-ha-ha!" He was beside himself with fury.

At this moment, a terrific crash of thunder startled the silence, and was followed by flashes of lightning and sheets of heavy rain. Pavel Pavlovitch rose and shut the window.

"The fellow asked you if you were afraid of the thunder; do you remember? Ha-ha-ha! Velchaninoff afraid of thunder! And all that about 'fifty years old' wasn't bad, eh? Ha-ha-ha!" Pavel Pavlovitch was in a spiteful mood.

"You seem to have settled yourself here," said Velchaninoff, who could hardly speak for agony. "Do as you like, I must lie down."

"Come, you wouldn't turn a *dog* out to-night!" replied Pavel, glad of a grievance.

"Of course, sit down; drink your wine—do anything you like," murmured Velchaninoff, as he laid himself flat on his divan, and groaned with pain.

"Am I to spend the night? Aren't you afraid?"

"What of?" asked Velchaninoff, raising his head slightly.

"Oh, nothing. Only last time you seemed to be a little alarmed, that's all."

"You are a fool!" said the other angrily, as he turned his face to the wall.

"Very well, sir; all right," said Pavel.

Velchaninoff fell asleep within a minute or so of lying down. The unnatural strain of the day, and his sickly state of health together, had suddenly undermined his strength, and he was as weak as a child. But physical pain would have its own, and soon conquered weakness and sleep; in an hour he was wide awake again, and rose from the divan in anguish. Pavel Pavlovitch was asleep on the other sofa. He was dressed, and in his boots; his hat lay on the floor, and his eye-glass hung by its cord almost to the ground. Velchaninoff did not wake his guest. The room was full of tobacco smoke, and the bottle was empty; he looked savagely at the sleeping drunkard.

Having twisted himself painfully off his bed, Velchaninoff began to walk about, groaning and thinking of his agony; he could lie no longer.

He was alarmed for this pain in his chest, and not without reason. He was subject to these attacks, and had been so for many years; but they came seldom, luckily—once a year or two years. On such occasions, his agony was so dreadful for some ten hours or so that he invariably believed that he must be actually dying.

This night, his anguish was terrible; it was too late to send for the doctor, but it was far from morning yet. He staggered up and down the room, and before long his groans became loud and frequent.

The noise awoke Pavel Pavlovitch. He sat up on his divan, and for some time gazed in terror and perplexity upon Velchaninoff, as the latter walked moaning up and down. At last he gathered his senses, and enquired anxiously what was the matter.

Velchaninoff muttered something unintelligible.

"It's your kidneys—I'm sure it is," cried Pavel, very wide awake of a sudden. "I remember Peter Kuzmich used to have the same sort of attacks. The kidneys—why, one can die of it. Let me go and fetch Mavra."

"No, no; I don't want anything," muttered Velchaninoff, waving him off irritably.

But Pavel Pavlovitch—goodness knows why—was beside himself with anxiety; he was as much exercised as though the matter at issue were the saving of his own son's life. He insisted on immediate compresses, and told Velchaninoff he must drink two or three cups of very hot weak tea—boiling hot. He ran for Mavra, lighted the fire in the kitchen, put the kettle on, put the sick man back to bed, covered him up, and within twenty minutes had the first hot application all ready, as well as the tea.

"Hot plates, sir, hot plates," he cried, as he clapped the first, wrapped in a napkin, on to Velchaninoff's chest. "I have nothing else handy; but I give you my word it's as good as anything else. Drink this tea quick, never mind if you scald your tongue—life is dearer. You can die of this sort of thing, you know." He sent sleepy Mavra out of her wits with flurry; the plates were changed every couple of minutes. At the third application, and after having taken two cups of scalding tea, Velchaninoff suddenly felt decidedly better.

"Capital! thank God! if we can once get the better of the pain it's a good sign!" cried Pavel, delightedly, and away he ran for another plate and some more tea.

"If only we can beat the pain down!" he kept muttering to himself every minute.

In half an hour the agony was passed, but the sick man was so completely knocked up that, in spite of Pavel's repeated entreaties to be allowed to apply "just one more plate," he could bear no more. His eyes were drooping from weakness.

"Sleep—sleep," he muttered faintly.

"Very well," consented Pavel, "go to sleep."

"Are you spending the night here? What time is it?"

"Nearly two."

"You must sleep here."

"Yes, yes—all right. I will."

A moment after the sick man called to Pavel again.

"You—you—" muttered the former faintly, as Pavel ran up and bent over him, "you are better than I am. I understand all—all—thank you!"

"Go to sleep!" whispered Pavel Pavlovitch, as he crept back to his divan on tip-toes.

Velchaninoff, dozing off, heard Pavel quietly make his bed, undress and lie down, all very softly, and then put the light out.

Undoubtedly Velchaninoff fell asleep very quietly when the light was once out; he remembered that much afterwards. Yet all the while he was asleep, and until he awoke, he dreamed that he could not go to sleep in spite of his weakness. At length he dreamed that he was delirious, and that he could not for the life of him chase away the visions which crowded in upon him, although he was conscious the whole while they *were* but visions and not reality. The apparition was familiar to him. He thought that his front door was open, and that his room gradually filled with people pouring in. At the table in the middle of the room, sat one man exactly as had been the case a month before, during one of his dreams. As on the previous occasion, this man leant on his elbow at the table and would not speak; he was in a round hat with a crape band.

"How?" thought the dreamer. "Was it really Pavel Pavlovitch last time as well?" However, when he looked at the man's face, he was convinced that it was quite another person.

"Why has he a crape band, then?" thought Velchaninoff in perplexity.

The noise and chattering of all these people was dreadful; they seemed even more exasperated with Velchaninoff than on the former occasion. They were all threatening him with something or other, shaking their fists at him, and shouting something which he could not understand.

"It's all a vision," he dreamed, "I know quite well that I am up and about, because I could not lie still for anguish!"

Yet the cries and noise at times seemed so real that he was now and again half-convinced of their reality.

"Surely this *can't* be delirium!" he thought. "What on earth do all these people want of me—my God!"

Yet if it were not a vision, surely all these cries would have roused Pavel Pavlovitch? There he was, fast asleep in his divan!

Then something suddenly occurred as in the old dream. Another crowd of people surged in, crushing those who were already collected inside. These new arrivals carried something large and heavy; he could judge of the weight by their footsteps labouring upstairs.

Those in the room cried, "They're bringing it! they're bringing it!"

Every eye flashed as it turned and glared at Velchaninoff; every hand threatened him and then pointed to the stairs.

Undoubtedly it was reality, not delirium. Velchaninoff thought that he stood up and raised himself on tip-toes, in order to see over the heads of the crowd. He wanted to know what was being carried in.

His heart beat wildly, wildly, wildly; and suddenly, as in his former dream, there came one—two—three loud rings at the bell.

And again, the sound of the bell was so distinct and clear that he felt it *could* not be a dream. He gave a cry, and awoke; but he did not rush to the door as on the former occasion.

What sudden idea was it that guided his movements? Had he any idea at all, or was it impulse that prompted him what to do? He sprang up in bed, with arms outstretched, as though to ward off an attack, straight towards the divan where Pavel Pavlovitch was sleeping.

His hands encountered other hands outstretched in his direction; consequently some one must have been standing over him.

The curtains were drawn, but it was not absolutely dark, because a faint light came from the next room, which had no curtains.

Suddenly something cut the palm of his left hand, some of his fingers causing him sharp pain. He instantly realized that he had seized a knife or a razor, and he closed his hand upon it with the rapidity of thought.

At that moment something fell to the ground with a hard metallic sound.

Velchaninoff was probably three times as strong as Pavel Pavlovitch, but the struggle lasted for a long while—at least three minutes.

The former, however, forced his adversary to the earth, and bent his arms back behind his head; then he paused, for he was most anxious to tie the hands. Holding the assassin's wrist with his wounded left hand, he felt for the blind cord with his right. For a long while he could not find it; at last he grasped it, and tore it down.

He was amazed afterwards at the unnatural strength which he must have displayed during all this.

During the whole of the struggle neither man spoke a word; only their heavy breathing was audible, and the inarticulate sounds emitted by both as they fought.

At length, having secured his opponent's hands, Velchaninoff left him on the ground, rose, drew the curtains, and pulled up the blind.

The deserted street was light now. He opened the window, and stood breathing in the fresh air for a few moments. It was a little past four o'clock. He shut the window once more, fetched a towel and bound up his cut hand as tightly as he could to stop the flow of blood.

At his feet he caught sight of the opened razor lying on the carpet; he picked it up, wiped it, and put it by in its own case, which he now saw he had left upon the little cupboard beside the divan which Pavel Pavlovitch occupied. He locked the cupboard.

Having completed all these arrangements, he approached Pavel Pavlovitch and looked at him. Meanwhile the latter had managed to raise himself from the floor and reach a chair; he was now sitting in it—undressed to his shirt, which was stained with marks of blood both back and front—Velchaninoff's blood, not his own.

Of course this was Pavel Pavlovitch; but it would have been only natural for any one who had known him before, and saw him at this moment, to doubt his identity. He sat upright in his chair—very stiffly, owing to the uncomfortable position of his tightly bound hands behind his back; his face looked yellow and crooked, and he shuddered every other moment. He gazed intently, but with an expression of dazed perplexity, at Velchaninoff.

Suddenly he smiled gravely, and nodding towards a carafe of water on the table, muttered, "A little drop!" Velchaninoff poured some into a glass, and held it for him to drink.

Pavel gulped a couple of mouthfuls greedily—then suddenly raised his head and gazed intently at Velchaninoff standing over him; he said nothing, however, but finished the water. He then sighed deeply.

Velchaninoff took his pillows and some of his clothing, and went into the next room, locking Pavel Pavlovitch behind him.

His pain had quite disappeared, but he felt very weak after the strain of his late exertion. Goodness knows whence came his strength for the trial; he tried to think, but he could not collect his ideas, the shock had been too great.

His eyes would droop now and again, sometimes for ten minutes at a time; then he would shudder, wake up, remember all that had passed and raise the blood-stained rag bound about his hand to prove the reality of his thoughts; then he would relapse into eager, feverish thought. One thing was quite certain, Pavel Pavlovitch had intended to cut his throat, though, perhaps, a quarter of an hour before the fatal moment he had not known that he would make the attempt. Perhaps he had seen the razor case last evening, and thought nothing of it, only remembering the fact that it was there. The razors were usually locked up, and only yesterday Velchaninoff had taken one out in order to make himself neat for his visit to the country, and had omitted to lock it up again.

"If he had premeditated murdering me, he would certainly have provided himself with a knife or a pistol long ago; he could not have relied on my razors, which he never saw until yesterday," concluded Velchaninoff.

At last the clock struck six. Velchaninoff arose, dressed himself, and went into Pavel Pavlovitch's room. As he opened the door he wondered why he had ever locked it, and why he had not allowed Pavel to go away at once.

To his surprise the prisoner was dressed, he had doubtless found means to get his hands loose. He was sitting in an arm-chair, but rose when Velchaninoff entered. His hat was in his hand.

His anxious look seemed to say as plain as words:—

"Don't talk to me! It's no use talking—don't talk to me!"

"Go!" said Velchaninoff. "Take your jewel-case!" he added.

Pavel Pavlovitch turned back and seized his bracelet-case, stuffing it into his pocket, and went out.

Velchaninoff stood in the hall, waiting to shut the front door after him.

Their looks met for the last time. Pavel Pavlovitch stopped, and the two men gazed into each others eyes for five seconds or so, as though in indecision. At length Velchaninoff faintly waved him away with his hand.

"Go!" he said, only half aloud, as he closed the door and turned the key.

CHAPTER XVI.

A feeling of immense happiness took possession of Velchaninoff; something was finished, and done with, and settled. Some huge anxiety was at an end, so it seemed to him. This anxiety had lasted five weeks.

He raised his hand and looked at the blood-stained rag bound about it.

"Oh, yes!" he thought, "it is, indeed, all over now."

And all this morning—the first time for many a day, he did not even once think of Liza; just as if the blood from those cut fingers had wiped out that grief as well, and made him "quits" with it.

He quite realized how terrible was the danger which he had passed through.

"For those people," he thought, "who do not know a minute or two before-hand that they are going to murder you, when they once get the knife into their hands, and feel the first touch of warm blood—Good Heaven! they not only cut your throat, they hack your head off afterwards—right off!"

Velchaninoff could not sit at home, he *must* go out and let something happen to him, and he walked about in hopes of something turning up; he longed to *talk*, and it struck him that he might fairly go to the doctor and talk to him, and have his hand properly bound up.

The doctor inquired how he hurt his hand, which made Velchaninoff laugh like mad; he was on the point of telling all, but refrained. Several times during the day he was on the point of telling others the whole story. Once it was to a perfect stranger in a restaurant, with whom he had begun to converse on his own initiative. Before this day he had hated the very idea of speaking to strangers in the public restaurants.

He went into a shop and ordered some new clothes, not with the idea of visiting the Pogoryeltseffs however—the thought of any such visit was distasteful to him; besides he could not leave town, he felt that he must stay and see what was going to happen.

Velchaninoff dined and enjoyed his dinner, talking affably to his neighbour and to the waiter as well. When evening fell he went home, his head was whirling a little, and he felt slightly delirious; the first sight of his rooms gave him quite a start. He walked round them and reflected. He visited the kitchen, which he had hardly ever done before in his life, and thought, "This is where they heated the plates last night." He locked the doors carefully, and lit his candles earlier than usual. As he shut the door he remembered that he had asked Mavra, as he passed the dvornik's lodging, whether Pavel Pavlovitch had been. Just as if the latter could possibly have been near the place!

Having then carefully locked himself in, he opened the little cupboard where his razors were kept, and took out "the" razor. There was still some of the blood on the bone handle. He put the razor back again, and locked the cupboard.

He was sleepy; he felt that he must go to sleep as speedily as possible, otherwise he would be useless "for to-morrow," and to-morrow seemed to him for some reason or other to be about to be a fateful day for him.

But all those thoughts which had crowded in upon him all day, and had never left him for a moment, were still in full swing within his brain; he thought, and thought, and thought, and could not fall asleep.

If Pavel Pavlovitch arrived at murdering point accidentally, had he ever seriously thought of murder even for a single evil instant before? Velchaninoff decided the question strangely enough: Pavel Pavlovitch *had* the desire to murder him, but did not himself know of the existence of this desire.

"It seems an absurd conclusion; but so it is!" thought Velchaninoff.

Pavel Pavlovitch did not come to Petersburg to look out for a new appointment, nor did he come for the sake of finding Bagantoff, in spite of his rage when the latter died. No! he despised Bagantoff thoroughly. Pavel Pavlovitch had come to St. Petersburg for *him*, and had brought Liza with him, for him alone, Velchaninoff.

"Did *I* expect to have my throat cut?" Velchaninoff decided that he *had* expected it, from the moment when he saw Pavel Pavlovitch in the carriage following in Bagantoff's funeral procession. "That is I expected something—of course, not exactly to have my throat cut! And surely—surely, it was not all *bonâ fide* yesterday," he reflected, raising his head from the pillow in the excitement of the idea. "*Surely* it cannot have been all in good faith that that fellow assured me of his love for me, beating his breast, and with his under lip trembling, as he spoke!

"Yes, it was absolutely *bonâ fide*!" he decided. "This quasimodo of T—— was quite good enough and generous enough to fall in love with his wife's lover—his wife in whom he never observed 'anything' during the twenty years of their married life.

"He respected and loved me for nine years, and remembered both me and my sayings. My goodness, to think of that! and I knew nothing whatever of all this! Oh, no! he was not lying yesterday! But did he love me *while* he declared his love for me, and said that we must be 'quits!' Yes, he did, he loved me spitefully—and spiteful love is sometimes the strongest of all.

"I daresay I made a colossal impression upon him down at T——, for it is just upon such Schiller-like men that one is liable to make a colossal impression. He exaggerated my value a thousand fold; perhaps it was my 'philosophical retirement' that struck him! It would be curious to discover precisely what it was that made so great an impression upon him. Who knows, it may have been that I wore a good pair of gloves, and knew how to put them on. These quasimodo fellows love æstheticism to distraction! Give them a start in the direction of admiration for yourself, and they will do all the rest, and give you a thousand times more than your due of every virtue that exists; will fight to the death for you with pleasure, if you ask it of them. How high he must have held my aptitude for illusionizing others; perhaps that has struck him as much as anything else! for he remarked: 'If *this* man deceived me, whom am I ever to trust again!'

"After such a cry as that a man may well turn wild beast.

"And he came here to 'embrace and weep over me,' as he expressed it. H'm! that means he came to cut my throat, and *thought* that he came to embrace and weep over me. He brought Liza with him, too.

"What if I *had* wept with him and embraced him? Perhaps he really would have fully and entirely forgiven me—for he was yearning to forgive me, I could see that! And all this turned to drunkenness and bestiality at the first check. Yes, Pavel Pavlovitch, the most deformed of all deformities is the abortion with noble feelings. And this man was foolish enough to take me down to see his 'bride.' My goodness! his bride! Only such a lunatic of a fellow could ever have developed so wild an idea as a 'new existence' to be inaugurated by an alliance between himself and Nadia. But you are not to blame, Pavel Pavlovitch, you are a deformity, and all your ideas and actions and aspirations must of necessity be deformed. But deformity though he be, why in the world was *my* sanction, *my* blessing, as it were, necessary to his union with Miss Zachlebnikoff? Perhaps he sincerely hoped that there, with so much sweet innocence and charm around us, we should fall into each other's arms in some leafy spot, and weep out our differences on each other's shoulders?

"Was *murder* in his thoughts when I caught him standing between our beds that first time, in the darkness? No. I think not. And yet the first idea of it may have entered his soul as he stood there—And if I had not left the razors out, probably nothing would have happened. Surely that is so; for he avoided me for weeks—he was *sorry* for me, and avoided me. He chose Bagantoff to expend his wrath upon, first, not me! He jumped out of bed and fussed over the hot plates, to divert his mind from murder perhaps—from the knife to charity! Perhaps he tried to save both himself and me by his hot plates!"

So mused Velchaninoff, his poor overwrought brain working on and on, and jumping from conclusion to conclusion with the endless activity of fever, until he fell asleep. Next morning he awoke with no less tired brain and body, but with a new terror, an unexpected and novel feeling of dread hanging over him.

This dread consisted in the fact that he felt that he, Velchaninoff, must go and see Pavel Pavlovitch that very day; he knew not why he must go, but he felt drawn to go, as though by some unseen force. The idea was too loathsome to look into, so he left it to take care of itself as an unalterable fact. The madness of it, however, was modified, and the whole aspect of the thought became more reasonable, after a while, when it took shape and resolved itself into a conviction in Velchaninoff's mind that Pavel Pavlovitch had returned home, locked himself up, and hung himself to the bedpost, as Maria Sisevna had described of the wretched suicide witnessed by poor Liza.

"Why should the fool hang himself?" he repeated over and over again; yet the thought *would* return that he was bound to hang himself, as Liza had said that he threatened to do. Velchaninoff could not help adding that if he were in Pavel Pavlovitch's place he would probably do the same.

So the end of it was that instead of going out to his dinner, he set off for Pavel Pavlovitch's lodging, "just to ask Maria Sisevna after him." But before he had reached the street he paused and his face flushed up with shame. "Surely I am not going there to embrace and weep over him! Surely I am not going to add this one last pitiful folly to the long list of my late shameful actions!"

However, his good providence saved him from this "pitiful folly," for he had hardly passed through the large gateway into the street, when Alexander Loboff suddenly collided with him. The young fellow was dashing along in a state of great excitement.

"I was just coming to you. Our friend Pavel Pavlovitch—a nice sort of fellow he is——"

"Has he hung himself?" gasped Velchaninoff.

"Hung himself? Who? Why?" asked Loboff, with his eyes starting out of his head.

"Oh! go on, I meant nothing!"

"Tfu! What a funny line your thoughts seem to take. He hasn't hung himself a bit—why in the world should he?—on the contrary, he's gone away. I've just seen him off! My goodness, how that fellow can drink! We had three bottles of wine. Predposiloff was there too—but how the fellow drinks! Good heavens! he was singing in the carriage when the train went off! He thought of you, and kissed his hand to you, and sent his love. He's a scamp, that fellow, eh?"

Young Loboff had apparently had quite his share of the three bottles, his face was flushed and his utterance thick. Velchaninoff roared with laughter.

"So you ended up by weeping over each others shoulders, did you? Ha-ha-ha! Oh, you poetical, Schiller-ish, funny fellows, you!"

"Don't scold us. You must know he went down *there* yesterday and to-day, and he has withdrawn. He 'sneaked' like anything about Nadia and me. They've shut her up. There was such a row, but we wouldn't give way—and, my word, how the fellow drinks! He was always talking about you; but, of course, he is no companion for you. You are, more or less, a respectable sort of man, and must have belonged to society at some time of your life, though you seem to have retired into private life just now. Is it poverty, or what? I couldn't make head or tail of Pavel Pavlovitch's story."

"Oh! Then it was he who gave you those interesting details about me?"

"Yes; don't be cross about it. It's better to be a citizen than 'a swell' any-day! The thing is one does not know whom to respect in Russia nowadays! Don't you think it a diseased feature of the times, in Russia, that one doesn't know whom to respect?"

"Quite so, quite so. Well, go on about Pavel Pavlovitch——"

"Well, he sat down in the railway carriage and began singing, then he cried a bit. It was really disgusting to see the fellow. I hate fools! Then he began to throw money to beggars 'for the repose of Liza's soul,' he said. Is that his wife?"

"Daughter."

"What's the matter with your hand?"

"I cut it."

"H'm! Never mind, cheer up! It'll be all right soon! I am glad that fellow has gone, you know,—confound him! But I bet anything he'll marry as soon as he arrives at his place."

"Well, what of that? You are going to marry, too!"

"I! That's quite a different affair! What a funny man you are! Why, if *you* are fifty, he must be sixty! Well, ta-ta! Glad I met you—can't come in—don't ask me—no time!"

He started off at a run, but turned a minute after and came back.

"What a fool I am!" he cried, "I forgot all about it—he sent you a letter. Here it is. How was it you didn't see him off? Ta-ta!"

Velchaninoff returned home and opened the letter, which was sealed and addressed to himself.

There was not a syllable inside in Pavel Pavlovitch's own hand writing; but he drew out another letter, and knew the writing at once. It was an old, faded, yellow-looking sheet of paper, and the ink was faint and discoloured; the letter was addressed to Velchaninoff, and written ten years before—a couple of months after his departure from T——. He had never received a copy of this one, but another letter, which he well remembered, had evidently been written and sent instead of it; he could tell that by the substance of the faded document in his hand. In this present letter Natalia Vasilievna bade farewell to him for ever (as she had done in the other communication), and informed him that she expected her confinement in a few months. She added, for his consolation, that she would find an opportunity of purveying his child to him in good time, and pointed out that their friendship was now cemented for ever. She begged him to love her no longer, because she could no longer return his love, but authorized him to pay a visit to T—— after a year's absence, in order to see the child. Goodness only knows why she had not sent this letter, but had changed it for another!

Velchaninoff was deadly pale when he read this document; but he imagined Pavel Pavlovitch finding it in the family box of black wood with mother-of-pearl ornamentation and silver mounting, and reading it for the first time!

"I should think he, too, grew as pale as a corpse," he reflected, catching sight of his own face in the looking-glass. "Perhaps he read it and then closed his eyes and hoped and prayed that when he opened them again the dreadful letter would be nothing but a sheet of white paper once more! Perhaps the poor fellow tried this desperate expedient two or three times before he accepted the truth!"

CHAPTER XVII.
THE PERMANENT HUSBAND.

Two years have elapsed since the events recorded in the foregoing chapters, and we find our friend Velchaninoff, one lovely summer day, seated in a railway carriage on his way to Odessa; he was making the journey for the purpose of seeing a great friend, and of being introduced to a lady whose acquaintance he had long wished to make.

Without entering into any details, we may remark that Velchaninoff was entirely changed during these last two years. He was no longer the miserable, fanciful hypochondriac of those dark days. He had returned to society and to his friends, who gladly forgave him his temporary relapse into seclusion. Even those whom he had ceased to bow to, when met, were now among the first to extend the hand of friendship once more, and asked no questions—just as though he had been abroad on private business, which was no affair of theirs.

His success in the legal matters of which we have heard, and the fact of having his sixty thousand roubles safe at his bankers—enough to keep him all his life—was the elixir which brought him back to health and spirits. His premature wrinkles departed, his eyes grew brighter, and his complexion better; he became more active and vigorous—in fact, as he sat thinking in a comfortable first-class carriage, he looked a very different man from the Velchaninoff of two years ago.

The next station to be reached was that at which passengers were expected to dine, forty minutes being allowed for this purpose.

It so happened that Velchaninoff, while seated at the dinner table, was able to do a service to a lady who was also dining there. This lady was young and nice looking, though rather too flashily dressed, and was accompanied by a young officer who unfortunately was scarcely in a befitting condition for ladies' society, having refreshed himself at the bar to an unnecessary extent. This young man succeeded in quarrelling with another person equally unfit for ladies' society, and a brawl ensued, which threatened to land both parties upon the table in close proximity to the lady. Velchaninoff interfered, and removed the brawlers to a safe distance, to the great and almost boundless gratitude of the alarmed lady, who hailed him as her "guardian angel." Velchaninoff was interested in the young woman, who looked like a respectable provincial lady—of provincial manners and taste, as her dress and gestures showed.

A conversation was opened, and the lady immediately commenced to lament that her husband was "never by when he was wanted," and that he had now gone and hidden himself somewhere just because he happened to be required.

"Poor fellow, he'll catch it for this," thought Velchaninoff. "If you will tell me your husband's name," he added aloud, "I will find him, with pleasure."

"Pavel Pavlovitch," hiccupped the young officer.

"Your husband's name is Pavel Pavlovitch, is it?" inquired Velchaninoff with curiosity, and at the same moment a familiar bald head was interposed between the lady and himself.

"Here you are *at last*," cried the wife, hysterically.

It was indeed Pavel Pavlovitch.

He gazed in amazement and dread at Velchaninoff, falling back before him just as though he saw a ghost. So great was his consternation, that for some time it was clear that he did not understand a single word of what his wife was telling him—which was that Velchaninoff had acted as her guardian angel, and that he (Pavel) ought to be ashamed of himself for never being at hand when he was wanted.

At last Pavel Pavlovitch shuddered, and woke up to consciousness.

Velchaninoff suddenly burst out laughing. "Why, we are old friends"—he cried, "friends from childhood!" He clapped his hand familiarly and encouragingly on Pavel's shoulder. Pavel smiled wanly. "Hasn't he ever spoken to you of Velchaninoff?"

"No, never," said the wife, a little confused.

"Then introduce me to your wife, you faithless friend!"

"This—this is Mr. Velchaninoff!" muttered Pavel Pavlovitch, looking the picture of confusion.

All went swimmingly after this. Pavel Pavlovitch was despatched to cater for the party, while his lady informed Velchaninoff that they were on their way from O——, where Pavel Pavlovitch served, to their country place—a lovely house, she said, some twenty-five miles away. There they hoped to receive a party of friends, and if Mr. Velchaninoff would be so very kind as to take pity on their rustic home, and honour it with a visit, she should do her best to show her gratitude to the guardian angel who, etc., etc. Velchaninoff replied that he would be delighted; and that he was an idle man, and always free—adding a compliment or two which caused the fair lady to blush with delight, and to tell Pavel Pavlovitch, who now returned from his quest, that Alexey Ivanovitch had been so kind as to promise to pay them a visit next week, and stay a whole month.

Pavel Pavlovitch, to the amazed wrath of his wife, smiled a sickly smile, and said nothing.

After dinner the party bade farewell to Velchaninoff, and returned to their carriage, while the latter walked up and down the platform smoking his cigar; he knew that Pavel Pavlovitch would return to talk to him.

So it turned out. Pavel came up with an expression of the most anxious and harassed misery. Velchaninoff smiled, took his arm, led him to a seat, and sat down beside him. He did not say anything, for he was anxious that Pavel should make the first move.

"So you are coming to us?" murmured the latter at last, plunging *in medias res*.

"I knew you'd begin like that! you haven't changed an atom!" cried Velchaninoff, roaring with laughter, and slapping him confidentially on the back. "Surely, you don't really suppose that I ever had the smallest intention of visiting you—and staying a month too!"

Pavel Pavlovitch gave a start.

"Then you're *not* coming?" he cried, without an attempt to hide his joy.

"No, no! of course not!" replied Velchaninoff, laughing. He did not know why, but all this was exquisitely droll to him; and the further it went the funnier it seemed.

"Really—are you really serious?" cried Pavel, jumping up.

"Yes; I tell you, I won't come—not for the world!"

"But what will my wife say now? She thinks you intend to come!"

"Oh, tell her I've broken my leg—or anything you like!"

"She won't believe!" said Pavel, looking anxious.

"Ha-ha-ha! You catch it at home, I see! Tell me, who is that young officer?"

"Oh, a distant relative of mine—an unfortunate young fellow——"

"Pavel Pavlovitch!" cried a voice from the carriage, "the second bell has rung!"

Pavel was about to move off—Velchaninoff stopped him.

"Shall I go and tell your wife how you tried to cut my throat?" he said.

"What are you thinking of—God forbid!" cried Pavel, in a terrible fright.

"Well, go along, then!" said the other, loosing his hold of Pavel's shoulder.

"Then—then—you won't come, will you?" said Pavel once more, timidly and despairingly, and clasping his hands in entreaty.

"No—I won't—I swear!—run away—you'll be late!" He put out his hand mechanically, then recollected himself, and shuddered. Pavel did not take the proffered hand, he withdrew his own.

The third bell rang.

An instantaneous but total change seemed to have come over both. Something snapped within Velchaninoff's heart—so it seemed to him, and he who had been roaring with laughter a moment before, seized Pavel Pavlovitch angrily by the shoulder.

"If I—*I* offer you my hand, sir" (he showed the scar on the palm of his left hand)—"if *I* can offer you my hand, sir, I should think *you* might accept it!" he hissed with white and trembling lips.

Pavel Pavlovitch grew deadly white also, his lips quivered and a convulsion seemed to run through his features:

"And—Liza?" he whispered quickly. Suddenly his whole face worked, and tears started to his eyes.

Velchaninoff stood like a log before him.

"Pavel Pavlovitch! Pavel Pavlovitch!" shrieked the voice from the carriage, in despairing accents, as though some one were being murdered.

Pavel roused himself and started to run. At that moment the engine whistled, and the train moved off. Pavel Pavlovitch just managed to cling on, and so climb into his carriage, as it moved out of the station.

Velchaninoff waited for another train, and then continued his journey to Odessa.

The Grand Inquisitor

[Dedicated by the Translator to those sceptics who clamour so loudly, both in print and private letters—"Show us the wonder-working 'Brothers,' let them come out publicly—and we will believe in them!"]

[The following is an extract from M. Dostoevsky's celebrated novel, The Brothers Karamazof, the last publication from the pen of the great Russian novelist, who died a few months ago, just as the concluding chapters appeared in print. Dostoevsky is beginning to be recognized as one of the ablest and profoundest among Russian writers. His characters are invariably typical portraits drawn from various classes of Russian society, strikingly life-like and realistic to the highest degree. The following extract is a cutting satire on modern theology generally and the Roman Catholic religion in particular. The idea is that Christ revisits earth, coming to Spain at the period of the Inquisition, and is at once arrested as a heretic by the Grand Inquisitor. One of the three brothers of the story, Ivan, a rank materialist and an atheist of the new school, is supposed to throw this conception into the form of a poem, which he describes to Alyosha—the youngest of the brothers, a young Christian mystic brought up by a "saint" in a monastery—as follows: (—Ed. Theosophist, Nov., 1881)]

"Quite impossible, as you see, to start without an introduction," laughed Ivan. "Well, then, I mean to place the event described in the poem in the sixteenth century, an age—as you must have been told at school—when it was the great fashion among poets to make the denizens and powers of higher worlds descend on earth and mix freely with mortals... In France all the notaries' clerks, and the monks in the cloisters as well, used to give grand performances, dramatic plays in which long scenes were enacted by the Madonna, the angels, the saints, Christ, and even by God Himself. In those days, everything was very artless and primitive. An instance of it may be found in Victor Hugo's drama, Notre Dame de Paris, where, at the Municipal Hall, a play called Le Bon Jugement de la Tres-sainte et Gracièuse Vierge Marie, is enacted in honour of Louis XI, in which the Virgin appears personally to pronounce her 'good judgment.' In Moscow, during the prepetrean period, performances of nearly the same character, chosen especially from the Old Testament, were also in great favour. Apart from such plays, the world was overflooded with mystical writings, 'verses'—the heroes of which were always selected from the ranks of angels, saints and other heavenly citizens answering to the devotional purposes of the age. The recluses of our monasteries, like the Roman Catholic monks, passed their time in translating, copying, and even producing original compositions upon such subjects, and that, remember, during the Tarter period!... In this connection, I am reminded of a poem compiled in a convent—a translation from the Greek, of course—called, 'The Travels of the Mother of God among the Damned,' with fitting illustrations and a boldness of conception inferior nowise to that of Dante. The 'Mother of God' visits hell, in company with the archangel Michael as her cicerone to guide her through the legions of the 'damned.' She sees them all, and is witness to their multifarious tortures. Among the many other exceedingly remarkably varieties of torments—every category of sinners having its own—there is one especially worthy of notice, namely a class of the 'damned' sentenced to gradually sink in a burning lake of brimstone and fire. Those whose sins cause them to sink so low that they no longer can rise to the surface are for ever forgotten by God, i.e., they fade out from the omniscient memory, says the poem—an expression, by the way, of an extraordinary profundity of thought, when closely analysed. The Virgin is terribly shocked, and falling down upon her knees in tears before the throne of God, begs that all she has seen in hell—all, all without exception, should have their sentences remitted to them. Her dialogue with God is colossally interesting. She supplicates, she will not leave Him. And when God, pointing to the pierced hands and feet of her Son, cries, 'How can I forgive His executioners?' She then commands that all the saints, martyrs, angels and archangels, should prostrate themselves with her before the Immutable and Changeless One and implore Him to change His wrath into mercy and—forgive them all. The poem closes upon her obtaining from God a compromise, a kind of yearly respite of tortures between Good Friday and Trinity, a chorus of the 'damned' singing loud praises to God from their 'bottomless pit,' thanking and telling Him:

> Thou art right, O Lord, very right,
> Thou hast condemned us justly.

"My poem is of the same character.

"In it, it is Christ who appears on the scene. True, He says nothing, but only appears and passes out of sight. Fifteen centuries have elapsed since He left the world with the distinct promise to return 'with power and great glory'; fifteen long centuries since His prophet cried, 'Prepare ye the way of the Lord!' since He Himself had foretold, while yet on earth, 'Of that day and hour knoweth no man, no, not the angels of heaven but my Father only.' But Christendom expects Him still. ...

"It waits for Him with the same old faith and the same emotion; aye, with a far greater faith, for fifteen centuries have rolled away since the last sign from heaven was sent to man,

> And blind faith remained alone
> To lull the trusting heart,
> As heav'n would send a sign no more.

"True, again, we have all heard of miracles being wrought ever since the 'age of miracles' passed away to return no more. We had, and still have, our saints credited with performing the most miraculous cures; and, if we can believe their biographers, there have been those among them who have been personally visited by the Queen of Heaven. But Satan sleepeth not, and the first germs of doubt, and ever-increasing unbelief in such wonders, already had begun to sprout in Christendom as early as the sixteenth century. It was just at that time that a new and terrible heresy first made its appearance in the north of Germany.* [*Luther's reform] A great star 'shining as it were a lamp... fell upon the fountains waters'... and 'they were made bitter.' This 'heresy' blasphemously denied 'miracles.' But those who had remained faithful believed all the more ardently, the tears of mankind ascended to Him as heretofore, and the Christian world was expecting Him as confidently as ever; they loved Him and hoped in Him, thirsted and hungered to suffer and die for Him just as many of them had done before.... So many centuries had weak, trusting humanity implored Him, crying with ardent faith and fervour: 'How long, O Lord, holy and true, dost Thou not come!' So many long centuries hath it vainly appealed to Him, that at last, in His inexhaustible compassion, He consenteth to answer the prayer.... He decideth that once more, if it were but for one short hour, the people—His long-suffering, tortured, fatally sinful, his loving and child-like, trusting people—shall behold Him again. The scene of action is placed by me in Spain, at Seville, during that terrible period of the Inquisition, when, for the greater glory of God, stakes were flaming all over the country.

> Burning wicked heretics,
> In grand auto-da-fes.

"This particular visit has, of course, nothing to do with the promised Advent, when, according to the programme, 'after the tribulation of those days,' He will appear 'coming in the clouds of heaven.' For, that 'coming of the Son of Man,' as we are informed, will take place as suddenly 'as the lightning cometh out of the east and shineth even unto the west.' No; this once, He desired to come unknown, and appear among His children, just when the bones of the heretics, sentenced to be burnt alive, had commenced crackling at the flaming stakes. Owing to His limitless mercy, He mixes once more with mortals and in the same form in which He was wont to appear fifteen centuries ago. He descends, just at the very moment when before king, courtiers, knights, cardinals, and the fairest dames of court, before the whole population of Seville, upwards of a hundred wicked heretics are being roasted, in a magnificent auto-da-fe ad majorem Dei gloriam, by the order of the powerful Cardinal Grand Inquisitor.

"He comes silently and unannounced; yet all—how strange—yea, all recognize Him, at once! The population rushes towards Him as if propelled by some irresistible force; it surrounds, throngs, and presses around, it follows Him.... Silently, and with a smile of boundless compassion upon His lips, He crosses the dense crowd, and moves softly on. The Sun of Love burns in His heart, and warm rays of Light, Wisdom and Power beam forth from His eyes, and pour down their waves upon the swarming multitudes of the rabble assembled around, making their hearts vibrate with returning love. He extends His hands over their heads, blesses them, and from mere contact with Him, aye, even with His garments, a healing power goes forth. An old man, blind from his birth, cries, 'Lord, heal me, that I may see Thee!' and the scales falling off the closed eyes, the blind man beholds Him... The crowd weeps for joy, and kisses the ground upon which He treads. Children strew flowers along His path and sing to Him, 'Hosanna!' It is He, it is Himself, they say to each other, it must be He, it can be none other but He! He pauses at the portal of the old cathedral, just as a wee white coffin is carried in, with tears and great lamentations. The lid is off, and in the coffin lies the body of a fair-child, seven years old, the only child of an eminent citizen of the city. The little corpse lies buried in flowers. 'He will raise the child to life!' confidently shouts the crowd to the weeping mother. The officiating priest who had come to meet the funeral procession, looks perplexed, and frowns. A loud cry is suddenly heard, and the bereaved mother prostrates herself at His feet. 'If it be Thou, then bring back my child to life!' she cries beseechingly. The procession halts, and the little coffin is gently lowered at his feet. Divine compassion beams forth from His eyes, and as He looks at the child, His lips are heard to whisper once more, 'Talitha Cumi'—and 'straightway the damsel arose.' The child rises in her coffin. Her little hands still hold the nosegay of white roses which after death was placed in them, and, looking round with large astonished eyes she smiles sweetly .... The crowd is violently excited. A terrible commotion rages among them, the populace shouts and loudly weeps, when suddenly, before the cathedral door, appears the Cardinal Grand Inquisitor himself.... He is tall, gaunt-looking old man of nearly four-score years and ten, with a stern, withered face, and deeply sunken eyes, from the cavity of which glitter two fiery sparks. He has laid aside his gorgeous cardinal's robes in which he had appeared before the people at the auto da-fe of the enemies of the Romish Church, and is now clad in his old, rough, monkish cassock. His sullen assistants and slaves of the 'holy guard' are following at a distance. He pauses before the crowd and observes. He has seen all. He has witnessed the placing of the little coffin at His feet, the calling back to life. And now, his dark, grim face has grown still darker; his bushy grey eyebrows nearly meet, and his sunken eye flashes with sinister light. Slowly raising his finger, he commands his minions to arrest Him....

"Such is his power over the well-disciplined, submissive and now trembling people, that the thick crowds immediately give way, and scattering before the guard, amid dead silence and without one breath of protest, allow them to lay their sacrilegious hands upon the stranger and lead Him away.... That same populace, like one man, now bows its head to the ground before the old Inquisitor, who blesses it and slowly moves onward. The guards conduct their prisoner to the ancient building of the Holy Tribunal; pushing Him into a narrow, gloomy, vaulted prison-cell, they lock Him in and retire....

"The day wanes, and night—a dark, hot breathless Spanish night—creeps on and settles upon the city of Seville. The air smells of laurels and orange blossoms. In the Cimmerian darkness of the old Tribunal Hall the iron door of the cell is suddenly thrown open, and the Grand Inquisitor, holding a dark lantern, slowly stalks into the dungeon. He is alone, and, as the heavy door closes behind him, he pauses at the threshold, and, for a minute or two, silently and gloomily scrutinizes the Face before him. At last approaching with measured steps, he sets his lantern down upon the table and addresses Him in these words:

"'It is Thou! ... Thou!' ... Receiving no reply, he rapidly continues: 'Nay, answer not; be silent! ... And what couldst Thou say? ... I know but too well Thy answer.... Besides, Thou hast no right to add one syllable to that which was already uttered by Thee before.... Why shouldst Thou now return, to impede us in our work? For Thou hast come but for that only, and Thou knowest it well. But art Thou as well aware of what awaits Thee in the morning? I do not know, nor do I care to know who thou mayest be: be it Thou or only thine image, to-morrow I will condemn and burn Thee on the stake, as the most wicked of all the heretics; and that same people, who to-day were kissing Thy feet, to-morrow at one bend of my finger, will rush to add fuel to Thy funeral pile... Wert Thou aware of this?' he adds, speaking as if in solemn thought, and never for one instant taking his piercing glance off the meek Face before him."....

"I can hardly realize the situation described—what is all this, Ivan?" suddenly interrupted Alyosha, who had remained silently listening to his brother. "Is this an extravagant fancy, or some mistake of the old man, an impossible quid pro quo?"

"Let it be the latter, if you like," laughed Ivan, "since modern realism has so perverted your taste that you feel unable to realize anything from the world of fancy.... Let it be a quid pro quo, if you so choose it. Again, the Inquisitor is ninety years old, and he might have easily gone mad with his one idee fixe of power; or, it might have as well been a delirious vision, called forth by dying fancy, overheated by the auto-da-fe of the hundred heretics in that forenoon.... But what matters for the poem, whether it was a quid pro quo or an uncontrollable fancy? The question is, that the old man has to open his heart; that he must give out his thought at last; and that the hour has come when he does speak it out, and says loudly that which for ninety years he has kept secret within his own breast."

"And his prisoner, does He never reply? Does He keep silent, looking at him, without saying a word?"

"Of course; and it could not well be otherwise," again retorted Ivan. "The Grand Inquisitor begins from his very first words by telling Him that He has no right to add one syllable to that which He had said before. To make the situation clear at once, the above preliminary monologue is intended to convey to the reader the very fundamental idea which underlies Roman Catholicism—as well as I can convey it, his words mean, in short: 'Everything was given over by Thee to the Pope, and everything now rests with him alone; Thou hast no business to return and thus hinder us in our work.' In this sense the Jesuits not only talk but write likewise.

"'Hast thou the right to divulge to us a single one of the mysteries of that world whence Thou comest?' enquires of Him my old Inquisitor, and forthwith answers for Him. 'Nay, Thou has no such right. For, that would be adding to that which was already said by Thee before; hence depriving people of that freedom for which Thou hast so stoutly stood up while yet on earth.... Anything new that Thou would now proclaim would have to be regarded as an attempt to interfere with that freedom of choice, as it would come as a new and a miraculous revelation superseding the old revelation of fifteen hundred years ago, when Thou didst so repeatedly tell the people: "The truth shall make you free." Behold then, Thy "free" people now!' adds the old man with sombre irony. 'Yea!... it has cost us dearly.' he continues, sternly looking at his victim. 'But we have at last accomplished our task, and—in Thy name.... For fifteen long centuries we had to toil and suffer owing to that "freedom": but now we have prevailed and our work is done, and well and strongly it is done. ....Believest not Thou it is so very strong? ... And why should Thou look at me so meekly as if I were not worthy even of Thy indignation?... Know then, that now, and

231

only now, Thy people feel fully sure and satisfied of their freedom; and that only since they have themselves and of their own free will delivered that freedom unto our hands by placing it submissively at our feet. But then, that is what we have done. Is it that which Thou has striven for? Is this the kind of "freedom" Thou has promised them?'"

"Now again, I do not understand," interrupted Alyosha. "Does the old man mock and laugh?"

"Not in the least. He seriously regards it as a great service done by himself, his brother monks and Jesuits, to humanity, to have conquered and subjected unto their authority that freedom, and boasts that it was done but for the good of the world. 'For only now,' he says (speaking of the Inquisition) 'has it become possible to us, for the first time, to give a serious thought to human happiness. Man is born a rebel, and can rebels be ever happy?... Thou has been fairly warned of it, but evidently to no use, since Thou hast rejected the only means which could make mankind happy; fortunately at Thy departure Thou hast delivered the task to us.... Thou has promised, ratifying the pledge by Thy own words, in words giving us the right to bind and unbind... and surely, Thou couldst not think of depriving us of it now!'"

"But what can he mean by the words, 'Thou has been fairly warned'?" asked Alexis.

"These words give the key to what the old man has to say for his justification... But listen—

"'The terrible and wise spirit, the spirit of self annihilation and non-being,' goes on the Inquisitor, 'the great spirit of negation conversed with Thee in the wilderness, and we are told that he "tempted" Thee... Was it so? And if it were so, then it is impossible to utter anything more truthful than what is contained in his three offers, which Thou didst reject, and which are usually called "temptations." Yea; if ever there was on earth a genuine striking wonder produced, it was on that day of Thy three temptations, and it is precisely in these three short sentences that the marvelous miracle is contained. If it were possible that they should vanish and disappear for ever, without leaving any trace, from the record and from the memory of man, and that it should become necessary again to devise, invent, and make them reappear in Thy history once more, thinkest Thou that all the world's sages, all the legislators, initiates, philosophers and thinkers, if called upon to frame three questions which should, like these, besides answering the magnitude of the event, express in three short sentences the whole future history of this our world and of mankind—dost Thou believe, I ask Thee, that all their combined efforts could ever create anything equal in power and depth of thought to the three propositions offered Thee by the powerful and all-wise spirit in the wilderness? Judging of them by their marvelous aptness alone, one can at once perceive that they emanated not from a finite, terrestrial intellect, but indeed, from the Eternal and the Absolute. In these three offers we find, blended into one and foretold to us, the complete subsequent history of man; we are shown three images, so to say, uniting in them all the future axiomatic, insoluble problems and contradictions of human nature, the world over. In those days, the wondrous wisdom contained in them was not made so apparent as it is now, for futurity remained still veiled; but now, when fifteen centuries have elapsed, we see that everything in these three questions is so marvelously foreseen and foretold, that to add to, or to take away from, the prophecy one jot, would be absolutely impossible!

"'Decide then thyself.' sternly proceeded the Inquisitor, 'which of ye twain was right: Thou who didst reject, or he who offered? Remember the subtle meaning of question the first, which runs thus: Wouldst Thou go into the world empty-handed? Would Thou venture thither with Thy vague and undefined promise of freedom, which men, dull and unruly as they are by nature, are unable so much as to understand, which they avoid and fear?—for never was there anything more unbearable to the human race than personal freedom! Dost Thou see these stones in the desolate and glaring wilderness? Command that these stones be made bread—and mankind will run after Thee, obedient and grateful like a herd of cattle. But even then it will be ever diffident and trembling, lest Thou should take away Thy hand, and they lose thereby their bread! Thou didst refuse to accept the offer for fear of depriving men of their free choice; for where is there freedom of choice where men are bribed with bread? Man shall not live by bread alone—was Thine answer. Thou knewest not, it seems, that it was precisely in the name of that earthly bread that the terrestrial spirit would one day rise against, struggle with, and finally conquer Thee, followed by the hungry multitudes shouting: "Who is like unto that Beast, who maketh fire come down from heaven upon the earth!" Knowest Thou not that, but a few centuries hence, and the whole of mankind will have proclaimed in its wisdom and through its mouthpiece, Science, that there is no more crime, hence no more sin on earth, but only hungry people? "Feed us first and then command us to be virtuous!" will be the words written upon the banner lifted against Thee—a banner which shall destroy Thy Church to its very foundations, and in the place of Thy Temple shall raise once more the terrible Tower of Babel; and though its building be left unfinished, as was that of the first one, yet the fact will remain recorded that Thou couldst, but wouldst not, prevent the attempt to build that new tower by accepting the offer, and thus saving mankind a millennium of useless suffering on earth. And it is to us that the people will return again. They will search for us catacombs, as we shall once more be persecuted and martyred—and they will begin crying unto us: "Feed us, for they who promised us the fire from heaven have deceived us!" It is then that we will finish building their tower for them. For they alone who feed them shall finish it, and we shall feed them in Thy name, and lying to them that it is in that name. Oh, never, never, will they learn to feed themselves without our help! No science will ever give them bread so long as they remain free, so long as they refuse to lay that freedom at our feet, and say: "Enslave, but feed us!" That day must come when men will understand that freedom and daily bread enough to satisfy all are unthinkable and can never be had together, as men will never be able to fairly divide the two among themselves. And they will also learn that they can never be free, for they are weak, vicious, miserable nonentities born wicked and rebellious. Thou has promised to them the bread of life, the bread of heaven; but I ask Thee again, can that bread ever equal in the sight of the weak and the vicious, the ever ungrateful human race, their daily bread on earth? And even supposing that thousands and tens of thousands follow Thee in the name of, and for the sake of, Thy heavenly bread, what will become of the millions and hundreds of millions of human beings to weak to scorn the earthly for the sake of Thy heavenly bread? Or is it but those tens of thousands chosen among the great and the mighty, that are so dear to Thee, while the remaining millions, innumerable as the grains of sand in the seas, the weak and the loving, have to be used as material for the former? No, no! In our sight and for our purpose the weak and the lowly are the more dear to us. True, they are vicious and rebellious, but we will force them into obedience, and it is they who will admire us the most. They will regard us as gods, and feel grateful to those who have consented to lead the masses and bear their burden of freedom by ruling over them—so terrible will that freedom at last appear to men! Then we will tell them that it is in obedience to Thy will and in Thy name that we rule over them. We will deceive them once more and lie to them once again—for never, never more will we allow Thee to come among us. In this deception we will find our suffering, for we must needs lie eternally, and never cease to lie!

"Such is the secret meaning of "temptation" the first, and that is what Thou didst reject in the wilderness for the sake of that freedom which Thou didst prize above all. Meanwhile Thy tempter's offer contained another great world-mystery. By accepting the "bread," Thou wouldst have satisfied and answered a universal craving, a ceaseless longing alive in the heart of every individual human being, lurking in the breast of collective mankind, that most perplexing problem—"whom or what shall we worship?" There exists no greater or more painful anxiety for a man who has freed himself from all religious bias, than how he shall soonest find a new object or idea to worship. But man seeks to bow before that only which is recognized by the greater majority, if not by all his fellow-men, as having a right to be worshipped; whose rights are so unquestionable that men agree unanimously to bow down to it. For the chief concern of these miserable creatures is not to find and worship the idol of their own choice, but to discover that which all others will believe in, and consent to bow down to in a mass. It is that instinctive need of having a worship in common that is the chief suffering of every man, the chief concern of mankind from the beginning of times. It is for that universality of religious worship that people destroyed each other by sword. Creating gods unto themselves, they forwith began appealing to each other: "Abandon your deities, come and bow down to ours, or death to ye and your idols!" And so will they do till the end of this world; they will do so even then, when all the gods themselves have disappeared, for then men will prostrate themselves before and worship some idea. Thou didst know, Thou couldst not be ignorant of, that mysterious fundamental principle in human nature, and still thou hast rejected the only absolute banner offered Thee, to which all the nations would remain true, and before which all would have bowed—the banner of earthly bread, rejected in the name of freedom and of "bread in the kingdom of God"! Behold, then, what Thou hast done furthermore for that "freedom's" sake! I repeat to Thee, man has no greater anxiety in life than to find some one to whom he can make over that gift of freedom with which the unfortunate creature is born. But he alone will prove capable of silencing and quieting their consciences, that shall succeed in possessing himself of the freedom of men. With "daily bread" an irresistible power was offered Thee: show a man "bread" and he will follow Thee, for what can he resist less than the attraction of bread? But if, at the same time, another succeed in possessing himself of his conscience—oh! then even Thy bread will be forgotten, and man will follow him who seduced his conscience. So far Thou wert right. For the mystery of human being does not solely rest in the desire to live, but in the problem—for what should one live at all? Without a clear perception of his reasons for living, man will never consent to live, and will rather destroy himself than tarry on earth, though he be surrounded with bread. This is the truth. But what has happened? Instead of getting hold of man's freedom, Thou has enlarged it still more! Hast Thou again forgotten that to man rest and even death are preferable to a free choice between the knowledge of Good and Evil? Nothing seems more seductive in his eyes than freedom of conscience, and nothing proves more painful. And behold! instead of laying a firm foundation whereon to rest once for all man's conscience, Thou hast chosen to stir up in him all that is abnormal, mysterious, and indefinite, all that is beyond human strength, and has acted as if Thou never hadst any love for him, and yet Thou wert He who came to "lay down His life for His friends!" Thou hast burdened man's soul with anxieties hitherto unknown to him. Thirsting for human love freely given, seeking to enable man, seduced and charmed by Thee, to follow Thy path of his own free-will, instead of the old and wise law which held him in subjection, Thou hast given him the right henceforth to choose and freely decide what is good and bad for him, guided but by Thine image in his heart. But hast Thou never dreamt of the probability, nay, of the certainty, of that same man one day rejected finally, and controverting even Thine image and Thy truth, once he would find himself laden with such a terrible burden as freedom of choice? That a time would surely come when men would exclaim that Truth and Light cannot be in Thee, for no one could have left them in a greater perplexity and mental suffering than Thou has done, lading them with so many cares and insoluble problems. Thus, it is Thyself who hast laid the foundation for the destruction of Thine own kingdom and no one but Thou is to be blamed for it.

"'Meantime, every chance of success was offered Thee. There are three Powers, three unique Forces upon earth, capable of conquering for ever by charming the conscience of these weak rebels—men—for their own good; and these Forces are: Miracle, Mystery and Authority. Thou hast rejected all the three, and thus wert the first to set them an example. When the terrible and all-wise spirit placed Thee on a pinnacle of the temple and said unto Thee, "If Thou be the son of God, cast Thyself down, for it is written, He shall give His angels charge concerning Thee: and in their hands they shall bear Thee up, lest at any time Thou dash Thy foot against a stone!"—for thus Thy faith in Thy father should have been made evident, Thou didst refuse to accept his suggestion and didst not follow it. Oh, undoubtedly, Thou didst act in this with all the magnificent pride of a god, but then men—that weak and rebel race—are they also gods, to understand Thy refusal? Of course, Thou didst well know that by taking one single step forward, by making the slightest motion to throw Thyself down, Thou wouldst have tempted "the Lord Thy God," lost suddenly all faith in Him, and dashed Thyself to atoms against that same earth which Thou camest to save, and thus wouldst have allowed the wise spirit which tempted Thee to triumph and rejoice. But, then, how many such as Thee are to be found on this globe, I ask Thee? Couldst Thou ever for a moment imagine that men would have the same strength to resist such a temptation? Is human nature calculated to reject miracle, and trust, during the most terrible moments in life, when the most momentous, painful and perplexing problems struggle within man's soul, to the free decisions of his heart for the true solution? Oh, Thou knewest well that that action of Thine would remain recorded in books for ages to come, reaching to the confines of the globe, and Thy hope was, that following Thy example, man would remain true to his God, without needing any miracle to keep his faith alive! But Thou knewest not, it seems, that no sooner would man reject miracle than he would reject God likewise, for he seeketh less God than "a sign" from Him. And thus, as it is beyond the power of man to remain without miracles, so, rather than live without, he will create for himself new wonders of his own making; and he will bow to and worship the soothsayer's miracles, the old witch's sorcery, were he a rebel, a heretic, and an atheist a hundred times over. Thy refusal to come down from the cross when people, mocking and wagging their heads were saying to Thee—"Save Thyself if Thou be the son of God, and we will believe in Thee," was due to the same determination—not to enslave man through miracle, but to obtain faith in Thee freely and apart from any miraculous influence. Thou thirstest for free and uninfluenced love, and refuses the passionate adoration of the slave before a Potency which would have subjected his will once for ever. Thou judgest of men too highly here, again, for though rebels they be, they are born slaves and nothing more. Behold, and judge of them once more, now that fifteen centuries have elapsed since that moment. Look at them, whom Thou didst try to elevate unto Thee! I swear man is weaker and lower than Thou hast ever imagined him to be! Can he ever do that which Thou art said to have accomplished? By valuing him so highly Thou hast acted as if there were no love for him in Thine heart, for Thou hast demanded of him more than he could ever give—Thou, who lovest him more than Thyself! Hadst Thou esteemed him less, less wouldst Thou have demanded of him, and that would have been more like love, for his burden would have been made thereby lighter. Man is weak and cowardly. What matters it, if he now riots and rebels throughout the world against our will and power, and prides himself upon that rebellion? It is but the petty pride and vanity of a school-boy. It is the rioting of little children, getting up a mutiny in the class-room and driving their schoolmaster out of it. But it will not last long, and when the day of their triumph is over, they will have to pay dearly for it. They will destroy the temples and raze them to the ground, flooding the earth with blood. But the foolish children will have to learn some day that, rebels though they be and riotous from nature, they are too weak to maintain the spirit of mutiny for any length of time. Suffused with idiotic tears, they will confess that He who created them rebellious undoubtedly did so but to mock them. They will pronounce these words in despair, and such blasphemous utterances will but add to their misery—for human nature cannot endure blasphemy, and takes her own revenge in the end.

"'And thus, after all Thou has suffered for mankind and its freedom, the present fate of men may be summed up in three words: Unrest, Confusion, Misery! Thy great prophet John records in his vision, that he saw, during the first resurrection of the chosen servants of God—"the number of them which were sealed" in their foreheads, "twelve thousand" of every tribe. But were they, indeed, as many? Then they must have been gods, not men. They had shared Thy Cross for long years, suffered scores of years' hunger and thirst in dreary wildernesses and deserts, feeding upon locusts and roots—and of these children of free love for Thee, and self-sacrifice in Thy name, Thou mayest well feel proud. But remember that these are but a few thousands—of gods, not men; and how about all others? And why should the weakest be held guilty for not being able to endure what the strongest have endured? Why should a soul incapable of containing such terrible gifts be punished for its weakness? Didst Thou really come to, and for, the "elect" alone? If so, then the mystery will remain for ever mysterious to our finite minds. And if a mystery, then were we right to proclaim it as one, and preach it, teaching them that neither their freely given love to Thee nor freedom of conscience were essential, but only that incomprehensible mystery which they must blindly obey even against the dictates of their conscience. Thus did we. We corrected and improved Thy teaching and based it upon "Miracle, Mystery, and Authority." And men rejoiced at finding themselves led once more like a herd of cattle, and at finding their hearts at last delivered of the terrible burden laid upon them by Thee, which caused them so much suffering. Tell me, were we right in doing as we did. Did not we show our great love for humanity, by realizing in such a humble spirit its helplessness, by so mercifully lightening its great burden, and by permitting and remitting for its weak nature every sin, provided it be committed with our authorization? For what, then, hast Thou come again to trouble us in our work? And why lookest Thou at me so penetratingly with Thy meek eyes, and in such a silence? Rather shouldst Thou feel wroth, for I need not Thy love, I reject it, and love Thee not, myself. Why should I conceal the truth from Thee? I know but too well with whom I am now talking! What I had to say was known to Thee before, I read it in Thine eye. How should I conceal from Thee our secret? If perchance Thou wouldst hear it from my own lips, then listen: We are not with Thee, but with him, and that is our secret! For centuries have we abandoned Thee to follow him, yes—eight centuries. Eight hundred years now since we accepted from him the gift rejected by Thee with indignation; that last gift which he offered Thee from the high mountain when, showing all the kingdoms of the world and the glory of them, he saith unto Thee: "All these things will I give Thee, if Thou will fall down and worship me!" We took Rome from him and the glaive of Caesar, and declared ourselves alone the kings of this earth, its sole kings, though our work is not yet fully accomplished. But who is to blame for it? Our work is but in its incipient stage, but it is nevertheless started. We may have long to wait until its culmination, and mankind have to suffer much, but we shall reach the goal some day, and become sole Caesars, and then will be the time to think of universal happiness for men.

"'Thou couldst accept the glaive of Caesar Thyself; why didst Thou reject the offer? By accepting from the powerful spirit his third offer Thou would have realized every aspiration man seeketh for himself on earth; man would have found a constant object for worship; one to deliver his conscience up to, and one that should unite all together into one common and harmonious ant-hill; for an innate necessity for universal union constitutes the third and final affliction of mankind. Humanity as a whole has ever aspired to unite itself universally. Many were, the great nations with great histories, but the greater they were, the more unhappy they felt, as they felt the stronger necessity of a universal union among men. Great conquerors, like Timoor and Tchengis-Khan, passed like a cyclone upon the face of the earth in their efforts to conquer the universe, but even they, albeit unconsciously, expressed the same aspiration towards universal and common union. In accepting the kingdom of the world and Caesar's purple, one would found a universal kingdom and secure to mankind eternal peace. And who can rule mankind better than those who have possessed themselves of man's conscience, and hold in their hand man's daily bread? Having accepted Caesar's glaive and purple, we had, of course, but to deny Thee, to henceforth follow him alone. Oh, centuries of intellectual riot and rebellious free thought are yet before us, and their science will end by anthropophagy, for having begun to build their Babylonian tower without our help they will have to end by anthropophagy. But it is precisely at that time that the Beast will crawl up to us in full submission, and lick the soles of our feet, and sprinkle them with tears of blood and we shall sit upon the scarlet-colored Beast, and lifting up high the golden cup "full of abomination and filthiness," shall show written upon it the word "Mystery"! But it is only then that men will see the beginning of a kingdom of peace and happiness. Thou art proud of Thine own elect, but Thou has none other but these elect, and we—we will give rest to all. But that is not the end. Many are those among thine elect and the laborers of Thy vineyard, who, tired of waiting for Thy coming, already have carried and will yet carry, the great fervor of their hearts and their spiritual strength into another field, and will end by lifting up against Thee Thine own banner of freedom. But it is Thyself Thou hast to thank. Under our rule and sway all will be happy, and will neither rebel nor destroy each other as they did while under Thy free banner. Oh, we will take good care to prove to them that they will become absolutely free only when they have abjured their freedom in our favor and submit to us absolutely. Thinkest Thou we shall be right or still lying? They will convince themselves of our rightness, for they will see what a depth of degrading slavery and strife that liberty of Thine has led them into. Liberty, Freedom of Thought and Conscience, and Science will lead them into such impassable chasms, place them face to face before such wonders and insoluble mysteries, that some of them—more rebellious and ferocious than the rest—will destroy themselves; others—rebellious but weak—will destroy each other; while the remainder, weak, helpless and miserable, will crawl back to our feet and cry: "'Yes; right were ye, oh Fathers of Jesus; ye alone are in possession of His mystery, and we return to you, praying that ye save us from ourselves!" Receiving their bread from us, they will clearly see that we take the bread from them, the bread made by their own hands, but to give it back to them in equal shares and that without any miracle; and having ascertained that, though we have not changed stones into bread, yet bread they have, while every other bread turned verily in their own hands into stones, they will be only to glad to have it so. Until that day, they will never be happy. And who is it that helped the most to blind them, tell me? Who separated the flock and scattered it over ways unknown if it be not Thee? But we

235

will gather the sheep once more and subject them to our will for ever. We will prove to them their own weakness and make them humble again, whilst with Thee they have learnt but pride, for Thou hast made more of them than they ever were worth. We will give them that quiet, humble happiness, which alone benefits such weak, foolish creatures as they are, and having once had proved to them their weakness, they will become timid and obedient, and gather around us as chickens around their hen. They will wonder at and feel a superstitious admiration for us, and feel proud to be led by men so powerful and wise that a handful of them can subject a flock a thousand millions strong. Gradually men will begin to fear us. They will nervously dread our slightest anger, their intellects will weaken, their eyes become as easily accessible to tears as those of children and women; but we will teach them an easy transition from grief and tears to laughter, childish joy and mirthful song. Yes; we will make them work like slaves, but during their recreation hours they shall have an innocent child-like life, full of play and merry laughter. We will even permit them sin, for, weak and helpless, they will feel the more love for us for permitting them to indulge in it. We will tell them that every kind of sin will be remitted to them, so long as it is done with our permission; that we take all these sins upon ourselves, for we so love the world, that we are even willing to sacrifice our souls for its satisfaction. And, appearing before them in the light of their scapegoats and redeemers, we shall be adored the more for it. They will have no secrets from us. It will rest with us to permit them to live with their wives and concubines, or to forbid them, to have children or remain childless, either way depending on the degree of their obedience to us; and they will submit most joyfully to us the most agonizing secrets of their souls— all, all will they lay down at our feet, and we will authorize and remit them all in Thy name, and they will believe us and accept our mediation with rapture, as it will deliver them from their greatest anxiety and torture—that of having to decide freely for themselves. And all will be happy, all except the one or two hundred thousands of their rulers. For it is but we, we the keepers of the great Mystery who will be miserable. There will be thousands of millions of happy infants, and one hundred thousand martyrs who have taken upon themselves the curse of knowledge of good and evil. Peaceable will be their end, and peacefully will they die, in Thy name, to find behind the portals of the grave—but death. But we will keep the secret inviolate, and deceive them for their own good with the mirage of life eternal in Thy kingdom. For, were there really anything like life beyond the grave, surely it would never fall to the lot of such as they! People tell us and prophesy of Thy coming and triumphing once more on earth; of Thy appearing with the army of Thy elect, with Thy proud and mighty ones; but we will answer Thee that they have saved but themselves while we have saved all. We are also threatened with the great disgrace which awaits the whore, "Babylon the great, the mother of harlots"—who sits upon the Beast, holding in her hands the Mystery, the word written upon her forehead; and we are told that the weak ones, the lambs shall rebel against her and shall make her desolate and naked. But then will I arise, and point out to Thee the thousands of millions of happy infants free from any sin. And we who have taken their sins upon us, for their own good, shall stand before Thee and say: "Judge us if Thou canst and darest!" Know then that I fear Thee not. Know that I too have lived in the dreary wilderness, where I fed upon locusts and roots, that I too have blessed freedom with which thou hast blessed men, and that I too have once prepared to join the ranks of Thy elect, the proud and the mighty. But I awoke from my delusion and refused since then to serve insanity. I returned to join the legion of those who corrected Thy mistakes. I left the proud and returned to the really humble, and for their own happiness. What I now tell thee will come to pass, and our kingdom shall be built, I tell Thee not later than to-morrow Thou shalt see that obedient flock which at one simple motion of my hand will rush to add burning coals to Thy stake, on which I will burn Thee for having dared to come and trouble us in our work. For, if there ever was one who deserved more than any of the others our inquisitorial fires—it is Thee! To-morrow I will burn Thee. Dixi'."

Ivan paused. He had entered into the situation and had spoken with great animation, but now he suddenly burst out laughing.

"But all that is absurd!" suddenly exclaimed Alyosha, who had hitherto listened perplexed and agitated but in profound silence. "Your poem is a glorification of Christ, not an accusation, as you, perhaps, meant to be. And who will believe you when you speak of 'freedom'? Is it thus that we Christians must understand it? It is Rome (not all Rome, for that would be unjust), but the worst of the Roman Catholics, the Inquisitors and Jesuits, that you have been exposing! Your Inquisitor is an impossible character. What are these sins they are taking upon themselves? Who are those keepers of mystery who took upon themselves a curse for the good of mankind? Who ever met them? We all know the Jesuits, and no one has a good word to say in their favor; but when were they as you depict them? Never, never! The Jesuits are merely a Romish army making ready for their future temporal kingdom, with a mitred emperor—a Roman high priest at their head. That is their ideal and object, without any mystery or elevated suffering. The most prosaic thirsting for power, for the sake of the mean and earthly pleasures of life, a desire to enslave their fellow-men, something like our late system of serfs, with themselves at the head as landed proprietors—that is all that they can be accused of. They may not believe in God, that is also possible, but your suffering Inquisitor is simply—a fancy!"

"Hold, hold!" interrupted Ivan, smiling. "Do not be so excited. A fancy, you say; be it so! Of course, it is a fancy. But stop. Do you really imagine that all this Catholic movement during the last centuries is naught but a desire for power for the mere purpose of 'mean pleasures'? Is this what your Father Paissiy taught you?"

"No, no, quite the reverse, for Father Paissiy once told me something very similar to what you yourself say, though, of course, not that—something quite different," suddenly added Alexis, blushing.

"A precious piece of information, notwithstanding your 'not that.' I ask you, why should the Inquisitors and the Jesuits of your imagination live but for the attainment of 'mean material pleasures?' Why should there not be found among them one single genuine martyr suffering under a great and holy idea and loving humanity with all his heart? Now let us suppose that among all these Jesuits thirsting and hungering but after 'mean material pleasures' there may be one, just one like my old Inquisitor, who had himself fed upon roots in the wilderness, suffered the tortures of damnation while trying to conquer flesh, in order to become free and perfect, but who had never ceased to love humanity, and who one day prophetically beheld the truth; who saw as plain as he could see that the bulk of humanity could never be happy under the old system, that it was not for them that the great Idealist had come and died and dreamt of His Universal Harmony. Having realized that truth, he returned into the world and joined—intelligent and practical people. Is this so impossible?"

"Joined whom? What intelligent and practical people?" exclaimed Alyosha quite excited. "Why should they be more intelligent than other men, and what secrets and mysteries can they have? They have neither. Atheism and infidelity is all the secret they have. Your Inquisitor does not believe in God, and that is all the Mystery there is in it!"

"It may be so. You have guessed rightly there. And it is so, and that is his whole secret; but is this not the acutest sufferings for such a man as he, who killed all his young life in asceticism in the desert, and yet could not cure himself of his love towards his fellowmen? Toward the end of his life he becomes convinced that it is only by following the advice of the great and terrible spirit that the fate of these millions of weak rebels, these 'half-finished samples of humanity created in mockery' can be made tolerable. And once convinced of it, he sees as clearly that to achieve that object, one must follow blindly the guidance of the wise spirit, the fearful spirit of death and destruction, hence accept a system of lies and deception and lead humanity consciously this time toward death and destruction, and moreover, be deceiving them all the while in order to prevent them from realizing where they are being led, and so force the miserable blind men to feel happy, at least while here on earth. And note this: a wholesale deception in the name of Him, in whose ideal the old man had so passionately, so fervently, believed during nearly his whole life! Is this no suffering? And were such a solitary exception found amidst, and at the head of, that army 'that thirsts for power but for the sake of the mean pleasures of life,' think you one such man would not suffice to bring on a tragedy? Moreover, one single man like my Inquisitor as a principal leader, would prove sufficient to discover the real guiding idea of the Romish system with all its armies of Jesuits, the greatest and chiefest conviction that the solitary type described in my poem has at no time ever disappeared from among the chief leaders of that movement. Who knows but that terrible old man, loving humanity so stubbornly and in such an original way, exists even in our days in the shape of a whole host of such solitary exceptions, whose existence is not due to mere chance, but to a well-defined association born of mutual consent, to a secret league, organized several centuries back, in order to guard the Mystery from the indiscreet eyes of the miserable and weak people, and only in view of their own happiness? And so it is; it cannot be otherwise. I suspect that even Masons have some such Mystery underlying the basis of their organization, and that it is just the reason why the Roman Catholic clergy hate them so, dreading to find in them rivals, competition, the dismemberment of the unity of the idea, for the realization of which one flock and one Shepherd are needed. However, in defending my idea, I look like an author whose production is unable to stand criticism. Enough of this."

"You are, perhaps, a Mason yourself!" exclaimed Alyosha. "You do not believe in God," he added, with a note of profound sadness in his voice. But suddenly remarking that his brother was looking at him with mockery, "How do you mean then to bring your poem to a close?" he unexpectedly enquired, casting his eyes downward, "or does it break off here?"

"My intention is to end it with the following scene: Having disburdened his heart, the Inquisitor waits for some time to hear his prisoner speak in His turn. His silence weighs upon him. He has seen that his captive has been attentively listening to him all the time, with His eyes fixed penetratingly and softly on the face of his jailer, and evidently bent upon not replying to him. The old man longs to hear His voice, to hear Him reply; better words of bitterness and scorn than His silence. Suddenly He rises; slowly and silently approaching the Inquisitor, He bends towards him and softly kisses the bloodless, four-score and-ten-year-old lips. That is all the answer. The Grand Inquisitor shudders. There is a convulsive twitch at the corner of his mouth. He goes to the door, opens it, and addressing Him, 'Go,' he says, 'go, and return no more... do not come again... never, never!' and—lets Him out into the dark night. The prisoner vanishes."

"And the old man?"

237

"The kiss burns his heart, but the old man remains firm in his own ideas and unbelief."

"And you, together with him? You too!" despairingly exclaimed Alyosha, while Ivan burst into a still louder fit of laughter.

The Idiot

Towards the end of November, during a thaw, at nine o'clock one morning, a train on the Warsaw and Petersburg railway was approaching the latter city at full speed. The morning was so damp and misty that it was only with great difficulty that the day succeeded in breaking; and it was impossible to distinguish anything more than a few yards away from the carriage windows.

Some of the passengers by this particular train were returning from abroad; but the third-class carriages were the best filled, chiefly with insignificant persons of various occupations and degrees, picked up at the different stations nearer town. All of them seemed weary, and most of them had sleepy eyes and a shivering expression, while their complexions generally appeared to have taken on the colour of the fog outside.

When day dawned, two passengers in one of the third-class carriages found themselves opposite each other. Both were young fellows, both were rather poorly dressed, both had remarkable faces, and both were evidently anxious to start a conversation. If they had but known why, at this particular moment, they were both remarkable persons, they would undoubtedly have wondered at the strange chance which had set them down opposite to one another in a third-class carriage of the Warsaw Railway Company.

One of them was a young fellow of about twenty-seven, not tall, with black curling hair, and small, grey, fiery eyes. His nose was broad and flat, and he had high cheek bones; his thin lips were constantly compressed into an impudent, ironical—it might almost be called a malicious—smile; but his forehead was high and well formed, and atoned for a good deal of the ugliness of the lower part of his face. A special feature of this physiognomy was its death-like pallor, which gave to the whole man an indescribably emaciated appearance in spite of his hard look, and at the same time a sort of passionate and suffering expression which did not harmonize with his impudent, sarcastic smile and keen, self-satisfied bearing. He wore a large fur—or rather astrachan—overcoat, which had kept him warm all night, while his neighbour had been obliged to bear the full severity of a Russian November night entirely unprepared. His wide sleeveless mantle with a large cape to it—the sort of cloak one sees upon travellers during the winter months in Switzerland or North Italy—was by no means adapted to the long cold journey through Russia, from Eydkuhnen to St. Petersburg.

The wearer of this cloak was a young fellow, also of about twenty-six or twenty-seven years of age, slightly above the middle height, very fair, with a thin, pointed and very light coloured beard; his eyes were large and blue, and had an intent look about them, yet that heavy expression which some people affirm to be a peculiarity as well as evidence, of an epileptic subject. His face was decidedly a pleasant one for all that; refined, but quite colourless, except for the circumstance that at this moment it was blue with cold. He held a bundle made up of an old faded silk handkerchief that apparently contained all his travelling wardrobe, and wore thick shoes and gaiters, his whole appearance being very un-Russian.

His black-haired neighbour inspected these peculiarities, having nothing better to do, and at length remarked, with that rude enjoyment of the discomforts of others which the common classes so often show:

"Cold?"

"Very," said his neighbour, readily, "and this is a thaw, too. Fancy if it had been a hard frost! I never thought it would be so cold in the old country. I've grown quite out of the way of it."

"What, been abroad, I suppose?"

"Yes, straight from Switzerland."

"Wheugh! my goodness!" The black-haired young fellow whistled, and then laughed.

The conversation proceeded. The readiness of the fair-haired young man in the cloak to answer all his opposite neighbour's questions was surprising. He seemed to have no suspicion of any impertinence or inappropriateness in the fact of such questions being put to him. Replying to them, he made known to the inquirer that he certainly had been long absent from Russia, more than four years; that he had been sent abroad for his health; that he had suffered from some strange nervous malady—a kind of epilepsy, with convulsive spasms. His interlocutor burst out laughing several times at his answers; and more than ever, when to the question, "whether he had been cured?" the patient replied:

"No, they did not cure me."

"Hey! that's it! You stumped up your money for nothing, and we believe in those fellows, here!" remarked the black-haired individual, sarcastically.

"Gospel truth, sir, Gospel truth!" exclaimed another passenger, a shabbily dressed man of about forty, who looked like a clerk, and possessed a red nose and a very blotchy face. "Gospel truth! All they do is to get hold of our good Russian money free, gratis, and for nothing."

"Oh, but you're quite wrong in my particular instance," said the Swiss patient, quietly. "Of course I can't argue the matter, because I know only my own case; but my doctor gave me money—and he had very little—to pay my journey back, besides having kept me at his own expense, while there, for nearly two years."

"Why? Was there no one else to pay for you?" asked the black-haired one.

"No—Mr. Pavlicheff, who had been supporting me there, died a couple of years ago. I wrote to Mrs. General Epanchin at the time (she is a distant relative of mine), but she did not answer my letter. And so eventually I came back."

"And where have you come to?"

"That is—where am I going to stay? I—I really don't quite know yet, I—"

Both the listeners laughed again.

"I suppose your whole set-up is in that bundle, then?" asked the first.

"I bet anything it is!" exclaimed the red-nosed passenger, with extreme satisfaction, "and that he has precious little in the luggage van!—though of course poverty is no crime—we must remember that!"

It appeared that it was indeed as they had surmised. The young fellow hastened to admit the fact with wonderful readiness.

"Your bundle has some importance, however," continued the clerk, when they had laughed their fill (it was observable that the subject of their mirth joined in the laughter when he saw them laughing); "for though I dare say it is not stuffed full of friedrichs d'or and louis d'or—judge from your costume and gaiters—still—if you can add to your possessions such a valuable property as a relation like Mrs. General Epanchin, then your bundle becomes a significant object at once. That is, of course, if you really are a relative of Mrs. Epanchin's, and have not made a little error through—well, absence of mind, which is very common to human beings; or, say—through a too luxuriant fancy?"

"Oh, you are right again," said the fair-haired traveller, "for I really am *almost* wrong when I say she and I are related. She is hardly a relation at all; so little, in fact, that I was not in the least surprised to have no answer to my letter. I expected as much."

"H'm! you spent your postage for nothing, then. H'm! you are candid, however—and that is commendable. H'm! Mrs. Epanchin—oh yes! a most eminent person. I know her. As for Mr. Pavlicheff, who supported you in Switzerland, I know him too—at least, if it was Nicolai Andreevitch of that name? A fine fellow he was—and had a property of four thousand souls in his day."

"Yes, Nicolai Andreevitch—that was his name," and the young fellow looked earnestly and with curiosity at the all-knowing gentleman with the red nose.

This sort of character is met with pretty frequently in a certain class. They are people who know everyone—that is, they know where a man is employed, what his salary is, whom he knows, whom he married, what money his wife had, who are his cousins, and second cousins, etc., etc. These men generally have about a hundred pounds a year to live on, and they spend their whole time and talents in the amassing of this style of knowledge, which they reduce—or raise—to the standard of a science.

During the latter part of the conversation the black-haired young man had become very impatient. He stared out of the window, and fidgeted, and evidently longed for the end of the journey. He was very absent; he would appear to listen—and heard nothing; and he would laugh of a sudden, evidently with no idea of what he was laughing about.

"Excuse me," said the red-nosed man to the young fellow with the bundle, rather suddenly; "whom have I the honour to be talking to?"

"Prince Lef Nicolaievitch Muishkin," replied the latter, with perfect readiness.

"Prince Muishkin? Lef Nicolaievitch? H'm! I don't know, I'm sure! I may say I have never heard of such a person," said the clerk, thoughtfully. "At least, the name, I admit, is historical. Karamsin must mention the family name, of course, in his history—but as an individual—one never hears of any Prince Muishkin nowadays."

"Of course not," replied the prince; "there are none, except myself. I believe I am the last and only one. As to my forefathers, they have always been a poor lot; my own father was a sublieutenant in the army. I don't know how Mrs. Epanchin comes into the Muishkin family, but she is descended from the Princess Muishkin, and she, too, is the last of her line."

"And did you learn science and all that, with your professor over there?" asked the black-haired passenger.

"Oh yes—I did learn a little, but—"

"I've never learned anything whatever," said the other.

"Oh, but I learned very little, you know!" added the prince, as though excusing himself. "They could not teach me very much on account of my illness."

"Do you know the Rogojins?" asked his questioner, abruptly.

"No, I don't—not at all! I hardly know anyone in Russia. Why, is that your name?"

"Yes, I am Rogojin, Parfen Rogojin."

"Parfen Rogojin? dear me—then don't you belong to those very Rogojins, perhaps—" began the clerk, with a very perceptible increase of civility in his tone.

"Yes—those very ones," interrupted Rogojin, impatiently, and with scant courtesy. I may remark that he had not once taken any notice of the blotchy-faced passenger, and had hitherto addressed all his remarks direct to the prince.

"Dear me—is it possible?" observed the clerk, while his face assumed an expression of great deference and servility—if not of absolute alarm: "what, a son of that very Semen Rogojin—hereditary honourable citizen—who died a month or so ago and left two million and a half of roubles?"

"And how do *you* know that he left two million and a half of roubles?" asked Rogojin, disdainfully, and not deigning so much as to look at the other. "However, it's true enough that my father died a month ago, and that here am I returning from Pskoff, a month after, with hardly a boot to my foot. They've treated me like a dog! I've been ill of fever at Pskoff the whole time, and not a line, nor farthing of money, have I received from my mother or my confounded brother!"

"And now you'll have a million roubles, at least—goodness gracious me!" exclaimed the clerk, rubbing his hands.

"Five weeks since, I was just like yourself," continued Rogojin, addressing the prince, "with nothing but a bundle and the clothes I wore. I ran away from my father and came to Pskoff to my aunt's house, where I caved in at once with fever, and he went and died while I was away. All honour to my respected father's memory—but he uncommonly nearly killed me, all the same. Give you my word, prince, if I hadn't cut and run then, when I did, he'd have murdered me like a dog."

"I suppose you angered him somehow?" asked the prince, looking at the millionaire with considerable curiosity. But though there may have been something remarkable in the fact that this man was heir to millions of roubles there was something about him which surprised and interested the prince more than that. Rogojin, too, seemed to have taken up the conversation with unusual alacrity it appeared that he was still in a considerable state of excitement, if not absolutely feverish, and was in real need of someone to talk to for the mere sake of talking, as safety-valve to his agitation.

As for his red-nosed neighbour, the latter—since the information as to the identity of Rogojin—hung over him, seemed to be living on the honey of his words and in the breath of his nostrils, catching at every syllable as though it were a pearl of great price.

"Oh, yes; I angered him—I certainly did anger him," replied Rogojin. "But what puts me out so is my brother. Of course my mother couldn't do anything—she's too old—and whatever brother Senka says is law for her! But why couldn't he let me know? He sent a telegram, they say. What's the good of a telegram? It frightened my aunt so that she sent it back to the office unopened, and there it's been ever since! It's only thanks to Konief that I heard at all; he wrote me all about it. He says my brother cut off the gold tassels from my father's coffin, at night 'because they're worth a lot of money!' says he. Why, I can get him sent off to Siberia for that alone, if I like; it's sacrilege. Here, you—scarecrow!" he added, addressing the clerk at his side, "is it sacrilege or not, by law?"

"Sacrilege, certainly—certainly sacrilege," said the latter.

"And it's Siberia for sacrilege, isn't it?"

"Undoubtedly so; Siberia, of course!"

"They will think that I'm still ill," continued Rogojin to the prince, "but I sloped off quietly, seedy as I was, took the train and came away. Aha, brother Senka, you'll have to open your gates and let me in, my boy! I know he told tales about me to my father—I know that well enough but I certainly did rile my father about Nastasia Philipovna that's very sure, and that was my own doing."

"Nastasia Philipovna?" said the clerk, as though trying to think out something.

"Come, you know nothing about *her*," said Rogojin, impatiently.

"And supposing I do know something?" observed the other, triumphantly.

"Bosh! there are plenty of Nastasia Philipovnas. And what an impertinent beast you are!" he added angrily. "I thought some creature like you would hang on to me as soon as I got hold of my money."

"Oh, but I do know, as it happens," said the clerk in an aggravating manner. "Lebedeff knows all about her. You are pleased to reproach me, your excellency, but what if I prove that I am right after all? Nastasia Phillpovna's family name is Barashkoff—I know, you see—and she is a very well known lady, indeed, and comes of a good family, too. She is connected with one Totski, Afanasy Ivanovitch, a man of considerable property, a director of companies, and so on, and a great friend of General Epanchin, who is interested in the same matters as he is."

"My eyes!" said Rogojin, really surprised at last. "The devil take the fellow, how does he know that?"

"Why, he knows everything—Lebedeff knows everything! I was a month or two with Lihachof after his father died, your excellency, and while he was knocking about—he's in the debtor's prison now—I was with him, and he couldn't do a thing without Lebedeff; and I got to know Nastasia Philipovna and several people at that time."

"Nastasia Philipovna? Why, you don't mean to say that she and Lihachof—" cried Rogojin, turning quite pale.

"No, no, no, no, no! Nothing of the sort, I assure you!" said Lebedeff, hastily. "Oh dear no, not for the world! Totski's the only man with any chance there. Oh, no! He takes her to his box at the opera at the French theatre of an evening, and the officers and people all look at her and say, 'By Jove, there's the famous Nastasia Philipovna!' but no one ever gets any further than that, for there is nothing more to say."

"Yes, it's quite true," said Rogojin, frowning gloomily; "so Zaleshoff told me. I was walking about the Nefsky one fine day, prince, in my father's old coat, when she suddenly came out of a shop and stepped into her carriage. I swear I was all of a blaze at once. Then I met Zaleshoff—looking like a hair-dresser's assistant, got up as fine as I don't know who, while I looked like a tinker. 'Don't flatter yourself, my boy,' said he; 'she's not for such as you; she's a princess, she is, and her name is Nastasia Philipovna Barashkoff, and she lives with Totski, who wishes to get rid of her because he's growing rather old—fifty-five or so—and wants to marry a certain beauty, the loveliest woman in all Petersburg.' And then he told me that I could see Nastasia Philipovna at the opera-house that evening, if I liked, and described which was her box. Well, I'd like to see my father allowing any of us to go to the theatre; he'd sooner have killed us, any day. However, I went for an hour or so and saw Nastasia Philipovna, and I never slept a wink all night after. Next morning my father happened to give me two government loan bonds to sell, worth nearly five thousand roubles each. 'Sell them,' said he, 'and then take seven thousand five hundred roubles to the office, give them to the cashier, and bring me back the rest of the ten thousand, without looking in anywhere on the way; look sharp, I shall be waiting for you.' Well, I sold the bonds, but I didn't take the seven thousand roubles to the office; I went straight to the English shop and chose a pair of earrings, with a diamond the size of a nut in each. They cost four hundred roubles more than I had, so I gave my name, and they trusted me. With the earrings I went at once to Zaleshoff's. 'Come on!' I said, 'come on to Nastasia Philipovna's,' and off we went without more ado. I tell you I hadn't a notion of what was about me or before me or below my feet all the way; I saw nothing whatever. We went straight into her drawing-room, and then she came out to us.

"I didn't say right out who I was, but Zaleshoff said: 'From Parfen Rogojin, in memory of his first meeting with you yesterday; be so kind as to accept these!'

"She opened the parcel, looked at the earrings, and laughed.

"'Thank your friend Mr. Rogojin for his kind attention,' says she, and bowed and went off. Why didn't I die there on the spot? The worst of it all was, though, that the beast Zaleshoff got all the credit of it! I was short and abominably dressed, and stood and stared in her face and never said a word, because I was shy, like an ass! And there was he all in the fashion, pomaded and dressed out, with a smart tie on, bowing and scraping; and I bet anything she took him for me all the while!

"'Look here now,' I said, when we came out, 'none of your interference here after this-do you understand?' He laughed: 'And how are you going to settle up with your father?' says he. I thought I might as well jump into the Neva at once without going home first; but it struck me that I wouldn't, after all, and I went home feeling like one of the damned."

"My goodness!" shivered the clerk. "And his father," he added, for the prince's instruction, "and his father would have given a man a ticket to the other world for ten roubles any day—not to speak of ten thousand!"

The prince observed Rogojin with great curiosity; he seemed paler than ever at this moment.

"What do you know about it?" cried the latter. "Well, my father learned the whole story at once, and Zaleshoff blabbed it all over the town besides. So he took me upstairs and locked me up, and swore at me for an hour. 'This is only a foretaste,' says he; 'wait a bit till night comes, and I'll come back and talk to you again.'

"Well, what do you think? The old fellow went straight off to Nastasia Philipovna, touched the floor with his forehead, and began blubbering and beseeching her on his knees to give him back the diamonds. So after awhile she brought the box and flew out at him. 'There,' she says, 'take your earrings, you wretched old miser; although they are ten times dearer than their value to me now that I know what it must have cost Parfen to get them! Give Parfen my compliments,' she says, 'and thank him very much!' Well, I meanwhile had borrowed twenty-five roubles from a friend, and off I went to Pskoff to my aunt's. The old woman there lectured me so that I left the house and went on a drinking tour round the public-houses of the place. I was in a high fever when I got to Pskoff, and by nightfall I was lying delirious in the streets somewhere or other!"

"Oho! we'll make Nastasia Philipovna sing another song now!" giggled Lebedeff, rubbing his hands with glee. "Hey, my boy, we'll get her some proper earrings now! We'll get her such earrings that—"

"Look here," cried Rogojin, seizing him fiercely by the arm, "look here, if you so much as name Nastasia Philipovna again, I'll tan your hide as sure as you sit there!"

"Aha! do—by all means! if you tan my hide you won't turn me away from your society. You'll bind me to you, with your lash, for ever. Ha, ha! here we are at the station, though."

Sure enough, the train was just steaming in as he spoke.

Though Rogojin had declared that he left Pskoff secretly, a large collection of friends had assembled to greet him, and did so with profuse waving of hats and shouting.

"Why, there's Zaleshoff here, too!" he muttered, gazing at the scene with a sort of triumphant but unpleasant smile. Then he suddenly turned to the prince: "Prince, I don't know why I have taken a fancy to you; perhaps because I met you just when I did. But no, it can't be that, for I met this fellow" (nodding at Lebedeff) "too, and I have not taken a fancy to him by any means. Come to see me, prince; we'll take off those gaiters of yours and dress you up in a smart fur coat, the best we can buy. You shall have a dress coat, best quality, white waistcoat, anything you like, and your pocket shall be full of money. Come, and you shall go with me to Nastasia Philipovna's. Now then will you come or no?"

"Accept, accept, Prince Lef Nicolaievitch" said Lebedef solemnly; "don't let it slip! Accept, quick!"

Prince Muishkin rose and stretched out his hand courteously, while he replied with some cordiality:

"I will come with the greatest pleasure, and thank you very much for taking a fancy to me. I dare say I may even come today if I have time, for I tell you frankly that I like you very much too. I liked you especially when you told us about the diamond earrings; but I liked you before that as well, though you have such a dark-clouded sort of face. Thanks very much for the offer of clothes and a fur coat; I certainly shall require both clothes and coat very soon. As for money, I have hardly a copeck about me at this moment."

"You shall have lots of money; by the evening I shall have plenty; so come along!"

"That's true enough, he'll have lots before evening!" put in Lebedeff.

"But, look here, are you a great hand with the ladies? Let's know that first?" asked Rogojin.

"Oh no, oh no!" said the prince; "I couldn't, you know—my illness—I hardly ever saw a soul."

"H'm! well—here, you fellow-you can come along with me now if you like!" cried Rogojin to Lebedeff, and so they all left the carriage.

Lebedeff had his desire. He went off with the noisy group of Rogojin's friends towards the Voznesensky, while the prince's route lay towards the Litaynaya. It was damp and wet. The prince asked his way of passers-by, and finding that he was a couple of miles or so from his destination, he determined to take a droshky.

II.

General Epanchin lived in his own house near the Litaynaya. Besides this large residence—five-sixths of which was let in flats and lodgings-the general was owner of another enormous house in the Sadovaya bringing in even more rent than the first. Besides these houses he had a delightful little estate just out of town, and some sort of factory in another part of the city. General Epanchin, as everyone knew, had a good deal to do with certain government monopolies; he was also a voice, and an important one, in many rich public companies of various descriptions; in fact, he enjoyed the reputation of being a well-to-do man of busy habits, many ties, and affluent means. He had made himself indispensable in several quarters, amongst others in his department of the government; and yet it was a known fact that Fedor Ivanovitch Epanchin was a man of no education whatever, and had absolutely risen from the ranks.

This last fact could, of course, reflect nothing but credit upon the general; and yet, though unquestionably a sagacious man, he had his own little weaknesses-very excusable ones,—one of which was a dislike to any allusion to the above circumstance. He was undoubtedly clever. For instance, he made a point of never asserting himself when he would gain more by keeping in the background; and in consequence many exalted personages valued him principally for his humility and simplicity, and because "he knew his place." And yet if these good people could only have had a peep into the mind of this excellent fellow who "knew his place" so well! The fact is that, in spite of his knowledge of the world and his really remarkable abilities, he always liked to appear to be carrying out other people's ideas rather than his own. And also, his luck seldom failed him, even at cards, for which he had a passion that he did not attempt to conceal. He played for high stakes, and moved, altogether, in very varied society.

As to age, General Epanchin was in the very prime of life; that is, about fifty-five years of age,—the flowering time of existence, when real enjoyment of life begins. His healthy appearance, good colour, sound, though discoloured teeth, sturdy figure, preoccupied air during business hours, and jolly good humour during his game at cards in the evening, all bore witness to his success in life, and combined to make existence a bed of roses to his excellency. The general was lord of a flourishing family, consisting of his wife and three grown-up daughters. He had married young, while still a lieutenant, his wife being a girl of about his own age, who possessed neither beauty nor education, and who brought him no more than fifty souls of landed property, which little estate served, however, as a nest-egg for far more important accumulations. The general never regretted his early marriage, or regarded it as a foolish youthful escapade; and he so respected and feared his wife that he was very near loving her. Mrs. Epanchin came of the princely stock of Muishkin, which if not a brilliant, was, at all events, a decidedly ancient family; and she was extremely proud of her descent.

With a few exceptions, the worthy couple had lived through their long union very happily. While still young the wife had been able to make important friends among the aristocracy, partly by virtue of her family descent, and partly by her own exertions; while, in after life, thanks to their wealth and to the position of her husband in the service, she took her place among the higher circles as by right.

During these last few years all three of the general's daughters—Alexandra, Adelaida, and Aglaya—had grown up and matured. Of course they were only Epanchins, but their mother's family was noble; they might expect considerable fortunes; their father had hopes of attaining to very high rank indeed in his country's service-all of which was satisfactory. All three of the girls were decidedly pretty, even the eldest, Alexandra, who was just twenty-five years old. The middle daughter was now twenty-three, while the youngest, Aglaya, was twenty. This youngest girl was absolutely a beauty, and had begun of late to attract considerable attention in society. But this was not all, for every one of the three was clever, well educated, and accomplished.

It was a matter of general knowledge that the three girls were very fond of one another, and supported each other in every way; it was even said that the two elder ones had made certain sacrifices for the sake of the idol of the household, Aglaya. In society they not only disliked asserting themselves, but were actually retiring. Certainly no one could blame them for being too arrogant or haughty, and yet everybody was well aware that they were proud and quite understood their own value. The eldest was musical, while the second was a clever artist, which fact she had concealed until lately. In a word, the world spoke well of the girls; but they were not without their enemies, and occasionally people talked with horror of the number of books they had read.

They were in no hurry to marry. They liked good society, but were not too keen about it. All this was the more remarkable, because everyone was well aware of the hopes and aims of their parents.

It was about eleven o'clock in the forenoon when the prince rang the bell at General Epanchin's door. The general lived on the first floor or flat of the house, as modest a lodging as his position permitted. A liveried servant opened the door, and the prince was obliged to enter into long explanations with this gentleman, who, from the first glance, looked at him and his bundle with grave suspicion. At last, however, on the repeated positive assurance that he really was Prince Muishkin, and must absolutely see the general on business, the bewildered domestic showed him into a little ante-chamber leading to a waiting-room that adjoined the general's study, there handing him over to another servant, whose duty it was to be in this ante-chamber all the morning, and announce visitors to the general. This second individual wore a dress coat, and was some forty years of age; he was the general's special study servant, and well aware of his own importance.

"Wait in the next room, please; and leave your bundle here," said the door-keeper, as he sat down comfortably in his own easy-chair in the ante-chamber. He looked at the prince in severe surprise as the latter settled himself in another chair alongside, with his bundle on his knees.

"If you don't mind, I would rather sit here with you," said the prince; "I should prefer it to sitting in there."

"Oh, but you can't stay here. You are a visitor—a guest, so to speak. Is it the general himself you wish to see?"

The man evidently could not take in the idea of such a shabby-looking visitor, and had decided to ask once more.

"Yes—I have business—" began the prince.

"I do not ask you what your business may be, all I have to do is to announce you; and unless the secretary comes in here I cannot do that."

The man's suspicions seemed to increase more and more. The prince was too unlike the usual run of daily visitors; and although the general certainly did receive, on business, all sorts and conditions of men, yet in spite of this fact the servant felt great doubts on the subject of this particular visitor. The presence of the secretary as an intermediary was, he judged, essential in this case.

"Surely you—are from abroad?" he inquired at last, in a confused sort of way. He had begun his sentence intending to say, "Surely you are not Prince Muishkin, are you?"

"Yes, straight from the train! Did not you intend to say, 'Surely you are not Prince Muishkin?' just now, but refrained out of politeness?"

"H'm!" grunted the astonished servant.

"I assure you I am not deceiving you; you shall not have to answer for me. As to my being dressed like this, and carrying a bundle, there's nothing surprising in that—the fact is, my circumstances are not particularly rosy at this moment."

"H'm!—no, I'm not afraid of that, you see; I have to announce you, that's all. The secretary will be out directly-that is, unless you—yes, that's the rub—unless you—come, you must allow me to ask you—you've not come to beg, have you?"

"Oh dear no, you can be perfectly easy on that score. I have quite another matter on hand."

"You must excuse my asking, you know. Your appearance led me to think—but just wait for the secretary; the general is busy now, but the secretary is sure to come out."

"Oh—well, look here, if I have some time to wait, would you mind telling me, is there any place about where I could have a smoke? I have my pipe and tobacco with me."

"*Smoke?*" said the man, in shocked but disdainful surprise, blinking his eyes at the prince as though he could not believe his senses. "No, sir, you cannot smoke here, and I wonder you are not ashamed of the very suggestion. Ha, ha! a cool idea that, I declare!"

"Oh, I didn't mean in this room! I know I can't smoke here, of course. I'd adjourn to some other room, wherever you like to show me to. You see, I'm used to smoking a good deal, and now I haven't had a puff for three hours; however, just as you like."

"Now how on earth am I to announce a man like that?" muttered the servant. "In the first place, you've no right in here at all; you ought to be in the waiting-room, because you're a sort of visitor—a guest, in fact—and I shall catch it for this. Look here, do you intend to take up you abode with us?" he added, glancing once more at the prince's bundle, which evidently gave him no peace.

"No, I don't think so. I don't think I should stay even if they were to invite me. I've simply come to make their acquaintance, and nothing more."

"Make their acquaintance?" asked the man, in amazement, and with redoubled suspicion. "Then why did you say you had business with the general?"

"Oh well, very little business. There is one little matter—some advice I am going to ask him for; but my principal object is simply to introduce myself, because I am Prince Muishkin, and Madame Epanchin is the last of her branch of the house, and besides herself and me there are no other Muishkins left."

"What—you're a relation then, are you?" asked the servant, so bewildered that he began to feel quite alarmed.

"Well, hardly so. If you stretch a point, we are relations, of course, but so distant that one cannot really take cognizance of it. I once wrote to your mistress from abroad, but she did not reply. However, I have thought it right to make acquaintance with her on my arrival. I am telling you all this in order to ease your mind, for I see you are still far from comfortable on my account. All you have to do is to announce me as Prince Muishkin, and the object of my visit will be plain enough. If I am received—very good; if not, well, very good again. But they are sure to receive me, I should think; Madame Epanchin will naturally be curious to see the only remaining representative of her family. She values her Muishkin descent very highly, if I am rightly informed."

The prince's conversation was artless and confiding to a degree, and the servant could not help feeling that as from visitor to common serving-man this state of things was highly improper. His conclusion was that one of two things must be the explanation—either that this was a begging impostor, or that the prince, if prince he were, was simply a fool, without the slightest ambition; for a sensible prince with any ambition would certainly not wait about in ante-rooms with servants, and talk of his own private affairs like this. In either case, how was he to announce this singular visitor?

"I really think I must request you to step into the next room!" he said, with all the insistence he could muster.

"Why? If I had been sitting there now, I should not have had the opportunity of making these personal explanations. I see you are still uneasy about me and keep eyeing my cloak and bundle. Don't you think you might go in yourself now, without waiting for the secretary to come out?"

"No, no! I can't announce a visitor like yourself without the secretary. Besides the general said he was not to be disturbed—he is with the Colonel C—. Gavrila Ardalionovitch goes in without announcing."

"Who may that be? a clerk?"

"What? Gavrila Ardalionovitch? Oh no; he belongs to one of the companies. Look here, at all events put your bundle down, here."

"Yes, I will if I may; and—can I take off my cloak"

"Of course; you can't go in *there* with it on, anyhow."

The prince rose and took off his mantle, revealing a neat enough morning costume—a little worn, but well made. He wore a steel watch chain and from this chain there hung a silver Geneva watch. Fool the prince might be, still, the general's servant felt that it was not correct for him to continue to converse thus with a visitor, in spite of the fact that the prince pleased him somehow.

"And what time of day does the lady receive?" the latter asked, reseating himself in his old place.

"Oh, that's not in *my* province! I believe she receives at any time; it depends upon the visitors. The dressmaker goes in at eleven. Gavrila Ardalionovitch is allowed much earlier than other people, too; he is even admitted to early lunch now and then."

"It is much warmer in the rooms here than it is abroad at this season," observed the prince; "but it is much warmer there out of doors. As for the houses—a Russian can't live in them in the winter until he gets accustomed to them."

"Don't they heat them at all?"

"Well, they do heat them a little; but the houses and stoves are so different to ours."

"H'm! were you long away?"

"Four years! and I was in the same place nearly all the time,—in one village."

"You must have forgotten Russia, hadn't you?"

"Yes, indeed I had—a good deal; and, would you believe it, I often wonder at myself for not having forgotten how to speak Russian? Even now, as I talk to you, I keep saying to myself 'how well I am speaking it.' Perhaps that is partly why I am so talkative this morning. I assure you, ever since yesterday evening I have had the strongest desire to go on and on talking Russian."

"H'm! yes; did you live in Petersburg in former years?"

This good flunkey, in spite of his conscientious scruples, really could not resist continuing such a very genteel and agreeable conversation.

"In Petersburg? Oh no! hardly at all, and now they say so much is changed in the place that even those who did know it well are obliged to relearn what they knew. They talk a good deal about the new law courts, and changes there, don't they?"

"H'm! yes, that's true enough. Well now, how is the law over there, do they administer it more justly than here?"

"Oh, I don't know about that! I've heard much that is good about our legal administration, too. There is no capital punishment here for one thing."

"Is there over there?"

"Yes—I saw an execution in France—at Lyons. Schneider took me over with him to see it."

"What, did they hang the fellow?"

"No, they cut off people's heads in France."

"What did the fellow do?—yell?"

"Oh no—it's the work of an instant. They put a man inside a frame and a sort of broad knife falls by machinery—they call the thing a guillotine—it falls with fearful force and weight—the head springs off so quickly that you can't wink your eye in between. But all the preparations are so dreadful. When they announce the sentence, you know, and prepare the criminal and tie his hands, and cart him off to the scaffold—that's the fearful part of the business. The people all crowd round—even women—though they don't at all approve of women looking on."

"No, it's not a thing for women."

"Of course not—of course not!—bah! The criminal was a fine intelligent fearless man; Le Gros was his name; and I may tell you—believe it or not, as you like—that when that man stepped upon the scaffold he *cried*, he did indeed,—he was as white as a bit of paper. Isn't it a dreadful idea that he should have cried—cried! Whoever heard of a grown man crying from fear—not a child, but a man who never had cried before—a grown man of forty-five years. Imagine what must have been going on in that man's mind at such a moment; what dreadful convulsions his whole spirit must have endured; it is an outrage on the soul that's what it is. Because it is said 'thou shalt not kill,' is he to be killed because he murdered some one else? No, it is not right, it's an impossible theory. I assure you, I saw the sight a month ago and it's dancing before my eyes to this moment. I dream of it, often."

The prince had grown animated as he spoke, and a tinge of colour suffused his pale face, though his way of talking was as quiet as ever. The servant followed his words with sympathetic interest. Clearly he was not at all anxious to bring the conversation to an end. Who knows? Perhaps he too was a man of imagination and with some capacity for thought.

"Well, at all events it is a good thing that there's no pain when the poor fellow's head flies off," he remarked.

"Do you know, though," cried the prince warmly, "you made that remark now, and everyone says the same thing, and the machine is designed with the purpose of avoiding pain, this guillotine I mean; but a thought came into my head then: what if it be a bad plan after all? You may laugh at my idea, perhaps—but I could not help its occurring to me all the same. Now with the rack and tortures and so on—you suffer terrible pain of course; but then your torture is bodily pain only (although no doubt you have plenty of that) until you die. But *here* I should imagine the most terrible part of the whole punishment is, not the bodily pain at all—but the certain knowledge that in an hour,—then in ten minutes, then in half a minute, then now—this very *instant*—your soul must quit your body and that you will no longer be a man—and that this is certain, *certain!* That's the point—the certainty of it. Just that instant when you place your head on the block and hear the iron grate over your head—then—that quarter of a second is the most awful of all.

"This is not my own fantastical opinion—many people have thought the same; but I feel it so deeply that I'll tell you what I think. I believe that to execute a man for murder is to punish him immeasurably more dreadfully than is equivalent to his crime. A murder by sentence is far more dreadful than a murder committed by a criminal. The man who is attacked by robbers at night, in a dark wood, or anywhere, undoubtedly hopes and hopes that he may yet escape until the very moment of his death. There are plenty of instances of a man running away, or imploring for mercy—at all events hoping on in some degree—even after his throat was cut. But in the case of an execution, that last hope—having which it is so immeasurably less dreadful to die,—is taken away from the wretch and *certainty* substituted in its place! There is his sentence, and with it that terrible certainty that he cannot possibly escape death—which, I consider, must be the most dreadful anguish in the world. You may place a soldier before a cannon's mouth in battle, and fire upon him—and he will still hope. But read to that same soldier his death-sentence, and he will either go mad or burst into tears. Who dares to say that any man can suffer this without going mad? No, no! it is an abuse, a shame, it is unnecessary—why should such a thing exist? Doubtless there may be men who have been sentenced, who have suffered this mental anguish for a while and then have been reprieved; perhaps such men may have been able to relate their feelings afterwards. Our Lord Christ spoke of this anguish and dread. No! no! no! No man should be treated so, no man, no man!"

The servant, though of course he could not have expressed all this as the prince did, still clearly entered into it and was greatly conciliated, as was evident from the increased amiability of his expression. "If you are really very anxious for a smoke," he remarked, "I think it might possibly be managed, if you are very quick about it. You see they might come out and inquire for you, and you wouldn't be on the spot. You see that door there? Go in there and you'll find a little room on the right; you can smoke there, only open the window, because I ought not to allow it really, and—." But there was no time, after all.

A young fellow entered the ante-room at this moment, with a bundle of papers in his hand. The footman hastened to help him take off his overcoat. The new arrival glanced at the prince out of the corners of his eyes.

"This gentleman declares, Gavrila Ardalionovitch," began the man, confidentially and almost familiarly, "that he is Prince Muishkin and a relative of Madame Epanchin's. He has just arrived from abroad, with nothing but a bundle by way of luggage—."

The prince did not hear the rest, because at this point the servant continued his communication in a whisper.

Gavrila Ardalionovitch listened attentively, and gazed at the prince with great curiosity. At last he motioned the man aside and stepped hurriedly towards the prince.

"Are you Prince Muishkin?" he asked, with the greatest courtesy and amiability.

He was a remarkably handsome young fellow of some twenty-eight summers, fair and of middle height; he wore a small beard, and his face was most intelligent. Yet his smile, in spite of its sweetness, was a little thin, if I may so call it, and showed his teeth too evenly; his gaze though decidedly good-humoured and ingenuous, was a trifle too inquisitive and intent to be altogether agreeable.

"Probably when he is alone he looks quite different, and hardly smiles at all!" thought the prince.

He explained about himself in a few words, very much the same as he had told the footman and Rogojin beforehand.

Gavrila Ardalionovitch meanwhile seemed to be trying to recall something.

"Was it not you, then, who sent a letter a year or less ago—from Switzerland, I think it was—to Elizabetha Prokofievna (Mrs. Epanchin)?"

"It was."

"Oh, then, of course they will remember who you are. You wish to see the general? I'll tell him at once—he will be free in a minute; but you—you had better wait in the ante-chamber,—hadn't you? Why is he here?" he added, severely, to the man.

"I tell you, sir, he wished it himself!"

At this moment the study door opened, and a military man, with a portfolio under his arm, came out talking loudly, and after bidding good-bye to someone inside, took his departure.

"You there, Gania?" cried a voice from the study, "come in here, will you?"

Gavrila Ardalionovitch nodded to the prince and entered the room hastily.

A couple of minutes later the door opened again and the affable voice of Gania cried:

"Come in please, prince!"

III.

General Ivan Fedorovitch Epanchin was standing in the middle of the room, and gazed with great curiosity at the prince as he entered. He even advanced a couple of steps to meet him.

The prince came forward and introduced himself.

"Quite so," replied the general, "and what can I do for you?"

"Oh, I have no special business; my principal object was to make your acquaintance. I should not like to disturb you. I do not know your times and arrangements here, you see, but I have only just arrived. I came straight from the station. I am come direct from Switzerland."

The general very nearly smiled, but thought better of it and kept his smile back. Then he reflected, blinked his eyes, stared at his guest once more from head to foot; then abruptly motioned him to a chair, sat down himself, and waited with some impatience for the prince to speak.

Gania stood at his table in the far corner of the room, turning over papers.

"I have not much time for making acquaintances, as a rule," said the general, "but as, of course, you have your object in coming, I—"

"I felt sure you would think I had some object in view when I resolved to pay you this visit," the prince interrupted; "but I give you my word, beyond the pleasure of making your acquaintance I had no personal object whatever."

"The pleasure is, of course, mutual; but life is not all pleasure, as you are aware. There is such a thing as business, and I really do not see what possible reason there can be, or what we have in common to—"

"Oh, there is no reason, of course, and I suppose there is nothing in common between us, or very little; for if I am Prince Muishkin, and your wife happens to be a member of my house, that can hardly be called a 'reason.' I quite understand that. And yet that was my whole motive for coming. You see I have not been in Russia for four years, and knew very little about anything when I left. I had been very ill for a long time, and I feel now the need of a few good friends. In fact, I have a certain question upon which I much need advice, and do not know whom to go to for it. I thought of your family when I was passing through Berlin. 'They are almost relations,' I said to myself,' so I'll begin with them; perhaps we may get on with each other, I with them and they with me, if they are kind people;' and I have heard that you are very kind people!"

"Oh, thank you, thank you, I'm sure," replied the general, considerably taken aback. "May I ask where you have taken up your quarters?"

"Nowhere, as yet."

"What, straight from the station to my house? And how about your luggage?"

"I only had a small bundle, containing linen, with me, nothing more. I can carry it in my hand, easily. There will be plenty of time to take a room in some hotel by the evening."

"Oh, then you *do* intend to take a room?"

"Of course."

"To judge from your words, you came straight to my house with the intention of staying there."

"That could only have been on your invitation. I confess, however, that I should not have stayed here even if you had invited me, not for any particular reason, but because it is—well, contrary to my practice and nature, somehow."

"Oh, indeed! Then it is perhaps as well that I neither *did* invite you, nor *do* invite you now. Excuse me, prince, but we had better make this matter clear, once for all. We have just agreed that with regard to our relationship there is not much to be said, though, of course, it would have been very delightful to us to feel that such relationship did actually exist; therefore, perhaps—"

"Therefore, perhaps I had better get up and go away?" said the prince, laughing merrily as he rose from his place; just as merrily as though the circumstances were by no means strained or difficult. "And I give you my word, general, that though I know nothing whatever of manners and customs of society, and how people live and all that, yet I felt quite sure that this visit of mine would end exactly as it has ended now. Oh, well, I suppose it's all right; especially as my letter was not answered. Well, good-bye, and forgive me for having disturbed you!"

The prince's expression was so good-natured at this moment, and so entirely free from even a suspicion of unpleasant feeling was the smile with which he looked at the general as he spoke, that the latter suddenly paused, and appeared to gaze at his guest from quite a new point of view, all in an instant.

"Do you know, prince," he said, in quite a different tone, "I do not know you at all, yet, and after all, Elizabetha Prokofievna would very likely be pleased to have a peep at a man of her own name. Wait a little, if you don't mind, and if you have time to spare?"

"Oh, I assure you I've lots of time, my time is entirely my own!" And the prince immediately replaced his soft, round hat on the table. "I confess, I thought Elizabetha Prokofievna would very likely remember that I had written her a letter. Just now your servant—outside there—was dreadfully suspicious that I had come to beg of you. I noticed that! Probably he has very strict instructions on that score; but I assure you I did not come to beg. I came to make some friends. But I am rather bothered at having disturbed you; that's all I care about.—"

"Look here, prince," said the general, with a cordial smile, "if you really are the sort of man you appear to be, it may be a source of great pleasure to us to make your better acquaintance; but, you see, I am a very busy man, and have to be perpetually sitting here and signing papers, or off to see his excellency, or to my department, or somewhere; so that though I should be glad to see more of people, nice people—you see, I—however, I am sure you are so well brought up that you will see at once, and—but how old are you, prince?"

"Twenty-six."

"No? I thought you very much younger."

"Yes, they say I have a 'young' face. As to disturbing you I shall soon learn to avoid doing that, for I hate disturbing people. Besides, you and I are so differently constituted, I should think, that there must be very little in common between us. Not that I will ever believe there is *nothing* in common between any two people, as some declare is the case. I am sure people make a great mistake in sorting each other into groups, by appearances; but I am boring you, I see, you—"

"Just two words: have you any means at all? Or perhaps you may be intending to undertake some sort of employment? Excuse my questioning you, but—"

"Oh, my dear sir, I esteem and understand your kindness in putting the question. No; at present I have no means whatever, and no employment either, but I hope to find some. I was living on other people abroad. Schneider, the professor who treated me and taught me, too, in Switzerland, gave me just enough money for my journey, so that now I have but a few copecks left. There certainly is one question upon which I am anxious to have advice, but—"

"Tell me, how do you intend to live now, and what are your plans?" interrupted the general.

"I wish to work, somehow or other."

"Oh yes, but then, you see, you are a philosopher. Have you any talents, or ability in any direction—that is, any that would bring in money and bread? Excuse me again—"

"Oh, don't apologize. No, I don't think I have either talents or special abilities of any kind; on the contrary. I have always been an invalid and unable to learn much. As for bread, I should think—"

The general interrupted once more with questions; while the prince again replied with the narrative we have heard before. It appeared that the general had known Pavlicheff; but why the latter had taken an interest in the prince, that young gentleman could not explain; probably by virtue of the old friendship with his father, he thought.

The prince had been left an orphan when quite a little child, and Pavlicheff had entrusted him to an old lady, a relative of his own, living in the country, the child needing the fresh air and exercise of country life. He was educated, first by a governess, and afterwards by a tutor, but could not remember much about this time of his life. His fits were so frequent then, that they made almost an idiot of him (the prince used the expression "idiot" himself). Pavlicheff had met Professor Schneider in Berlin, and the latter had persuaded him to send the boy to Switzerland, to Schneider's establishment there, for the cure of his epilepsy, and, five years before this time, the prince was sent off. But Pavlicheff had died two or three years since, and Schneider had himself supported the young fellow, from that day to this, at his own expense. Although he had not quite cured him, he had greatly improved his condition; and now, at last, at the prince's own desire, and because of a certain matter which came to the ears of the latter, Schneider had despatched the young man to Russia.

The general was much astonished.

"Then you have no one, absolutely *no* one in Russia?" he asked.

"No one, at present; but I hope to make friends; and then I have a letter from—"

"At all events," put in the general, not listening to the news about the letter, "at all events, you must have learned*something*, and your malady would not prevent your undertaking some easy work, in one of the departments, for instance?"

"Oh dear no, oh no! As for a situation, I should much like to find one for I am anxious to discover what I really am fit for. I have learned a good deal in the last four years, and, besides, I read a great many Russian books."

"Russian books, indeed? Then, of course, you can read and write quite correctly?"

"Oh dear, yes!"

"Capital! And your handwriting?"

"Ah, there I am *really* talented! I may say I am a real caligraphist. Let me write you something, just to show you," said the prince, with some excitement.

"With pleasure! In fact, it is very necessary. I like your readiness, prince; in fact, I must say—I—I—like you very well, altogether," said the general.

"What delightful writing materials you have here, such a lot of pencils and things, and what beautiful paper! It's a charming room altogether. I know that picture, it's a Swiss view. I'm sure the artist painted it from nature, and that I have seen the very place—"

"Quite likely, though I bought it here. Gania, give the prince some paper. Here are pens and paper; now then, take this table. What's this?" the general continued to Gania, who had that moment taken a large photograph out of his portfolio, and shown it to his senior. "Halloa! Nastasia Philipovna! Did she send it you herself? Herself?" he inquired, with much curiosity and great animation.

"She gave it me just now, when I called in to congratulate her. I asked her for it long ago. I don't know whether she meant it for a hint that I had come empty-handed, without a present for her birthday, or what," added Gania, with an unpleasant smile.

"Oh, nonsense, nonsense," said the general, with decision. "What extraordinary ideas you have, Gania! As if she would hint; that's not her way at all. Besides, what could *you* give her, without having thousands at your disposal? You might have given her your portrait, however. Has she ever asked you for it?"

"No, not yet. Very likely she never will. I suppose you haven't forgotten about tonight, have you, Ivan Fedorovitch? You were one of those specially invited, you know."

"Oh no, I remember all right, and I shall go, of course. I should think so! She's twenty-five years old today! And, you know, Gania, you must be ready for great things; she has promised both myself and Afanasy Ivanovitch that she will give a decided answer tonight, yes or no. So be prepared!"

Gania suddenly became so ill at ease that his face grew paler than ever.

"Are you sure she said that?" he asked, and his voice seemed to quiver as he spoke.

"Yes, she promised. We both worried her so that she gave in; but she wished us to tell you nothing about it until the day."

The general watched Gania's confusion intently, and clearly did not like it.

"Remember, Ivan Fedorovitch," said Gania, in great agitation, "that I was to be free too, until her decision; and that even then I was to have my 'yes or no' free."

"Why, don't you, aren't you—" began the general, in alarm.

"Oh, don't misunderstand—"

"But, my dear fellow, what are you doing, what do you mean?"

"Oh, I'm not rejecting her. I may have expressed myself badly, but I didn't mean that."

"Reject her! I should think not!" said the general with annoyance, and apparently not in the least anxious to conceal it. "Why, my dear fellow, it's not a question of your rejecting her, it is whether you are prepared to receive her consent joyfully, and with proper satisfaction. How are things going on at home?"

"At home? Oh, I can do as I like there, of course; only my father will make a fool of himself, as usual. He is rapidly becoming a general nuisance. I don't ever talk to him now, but I hold him in check, safe enough. I swear if it had not been for my mother, I should have shown him the way out, long ago. My mother is always crying, of course, and my sister sulks. I had to tell them at last that I intended to be master of my own destiny, and that I expect to be obeyed at home. At least, I gave my sister to understand as much, and my mother was present."

"Well, I must say, I cannot understand it!" said the general, shrugging his shoulders and dropping his hands. "You remember your mother, Nina Alexandrovna, that day she came and sat here and groaned—and when I asked her what was the matter, she says, 'Oh, it's such a *dishonour* to us!' dishonour! Stuff and nonsense! I should like to know who can reproach Nastasia Philipovna, or who can say a word of any kind against her. Did she mean because Nastasia had been living with Totski? What nonsense it is! You would not let her come near your daughters, says Nina Alexandrovna. What next, I wonder? I don't see how she can fail to—to understand—"

"Her own position?" prompted Gania. "She does understand. Don't be annoyed with her. I have warned her not to meddle in other people's affairs. However, although there's comparative peace at home at present, the storm will break if anything is finally settled tonight."

The prince heard the whole of the foregoing conversation, as he sat at the table, writing. He finished at last, and brought the result of his labour to the general's desk.

"So this is Nastasia Philipovna," he said, looking attentively and curiously at the portrait. "How wonderfully beautiful!" he immediately added, with warmth. The picture was certainly that of an unusually lovely woman. She was photographed in a black silk dress of simple design, her hair was evidently dark and plainly arranged, her eyes were deep and thoughtful, the expression of her face passionate, but proud. She was rather thin, perhaps, and a little pale. Both Gania and the general gazed at the prince in amazement.

"How do you know it's Nastasia Philipovna?" asked the general; "you surely don't know her already, do you?"

"Yes, I do! I have only been one day in Russia, but I have heard of the great beauty!" And the prince proceeded to narrate his meeting with Rogojin in the train and the whole of the latter's story.

"There's news!" said the general in some excitement, after listening to the story with engrossed attention.

"Oh, of course it's nothing but humbug!" cried Gania, a little disturbed, however. "It's all humbug; the young merchant was pleased to indulge in a little innocent recreation! I have heard something of Rogojin!"

"Yes, so have I!" replied the general. "Nastasia Philipovna told us all about the earrings that very day. But now it is quite a different matter. You see the fellow really has a million of roubles, and he is passionately in love. The whole story smells of passion, and we all know what this class of gentry is capable of when infatuated. I am much afraid of some disagreeable scandal, I am indeed!"

"You are afraid of the million, I suppose," said Gania, grinning and showing his teeth.

"And you are *not*, I presume, eh?"

"How did he strike you, prince?" asked Gania, suddenly. "Did he seem to be a serious sort of a man, or just a common rowdy fellow? What was your own opinion about the matter?"

While Gania put this question, a new idea suddenly flashed into his brain, and blazed out, impatiently, in his eyes. The general, who was really agitated and disturbed, looked at the prince too, but did not seem to expect much from his reply.

"I really don't quite know how to tell you," replied the prince, "but it certainly did seem to me that the man was full of passion, and not, perhaps, quite healthy passion. He seemed to be still far from well. Very likely he will be in bed again in a day or two, especially if he lives fast."

"No! do you think so?" said the general, catching at the idea.

"Yes, I do think so!"

"Yes, but the sort of scandal I referred to may happen at any moment. It may be this very evening," remarked Gania to the general, with a smile.

"Of course; quite so. In that case it all depends upon what is going on in her brain at this moment."

"You know the kind of person she is at times."

"How? What kind of person is she?" cried the general, arrived at the limits of his patience. "Look here, Gania, don't you go annoying her tonight. What you are to do is to be as agreeable towards her as ever you can. Well, what are you smiling at? You must understand, Gania, that I have no interest whatever in speaking like this. Whichever way the question is settled, it will be to my advantage. Nothing will move Totski from his resolution, so I run no risk. If there is anything I desire, you must know that it is your benefit only. Can't you trust me? You are a sensible fellow, and I have been counting on you; for, in this matter, that, that—"

"Yes, that's the chief thing," said Gania, helping the general out of his difficulties again, and curling his lips in an envenomed smile, which he did not attempt to conceal. He gazed with his fevered eyes straight into those of the general, as though he were anxious that the latter might read his thoughts.

The general grew purple with anger.

"Yes, of course it is the chief thing!" he cried, looking sharply at Gania. "What a very curious man you are, Gania! You actually seem to be *glad* to hear of this millionaire fellow's arrival—just as though you wished for an excuse to get out of the whole thing. This is an affair in which you ought to act honestly with both sides, and give due warning, to avoid compromising others. But, even now, there is still time. Do you understand me? I wish to know whether you desire this arrangement or whether you do not? If not, say so,—and—and welcome! No one is trying to force you into the snare, Gavrila Ardalionovitch, if you see a snare in the matter, at least."

"I do desire it," murmured Gania, softly but firmly, lowering his eyes; and he relapsed into gloomy silence.

The general was satisfied. He had excited himself, and was evidently now regretting that he had gone so far. He turned to the prince, and suddenly the disagreeable thought of the latter's presence struck him, and the certainty that he must have heard every word of the conversation. But he felt at ease in another moment; it only needed one glance at the prince to see that in that quarter there was nothing to fear.

"Oh!" cried the general, catching sight of the prince's specimen of caligraphy, which the latter had now handed him for inspection. "Why, this is simply beautiful; look at that, Gania, there's real talent there!"

On a sheet of thick writing-paper the prince had written in medieval characters the legend:

"The gentle Abbot Pafnute signed this."

"There," explained the prince, with great delight and animation, "there, that's the abbot's real signature—from a manuscript of the fourteenth century. All these old abbots and bishops used to write most beautifully, with such taste and so much care and diligence. Have you no copy of Pogodin, general? If you had one I could show you another type. Stop a bit—here you have the large round writing common in France during the eighteenth century. Some of the letters are shaped quite differently from those now in use. It was the writing current then, and employed by public writers generally. I copied this from one of them, and you can see how good it is. Look at the well-rounded a and d. I have tried to translate the French character into the Russian letters—a difficult thing to do, but I think I have succeeded fairly. Here is a fine sentence, written in a good, original hand—'Zeal triumphs over all.' That is the script of the Russian War Office. That is how official documents addressed to important personages should be written. The letters are round, the type black, and the style somewhat remarkable. A stylist would not allow these ornaments, or attempts at flourishes—just look at these unfinished tails!—but it has distinction and really depicts the soul of the writer. He would like to give play to his imagination, and follow the inspiration of his genius, but a soldier is only at ease in the guard-room, and the pen stops half-way, a slave to discipline. How delightful! The first time I met an example of this handwriting, I was positively astonished, and where do you think I chanced to find it? In Switzerland, of all places! Now that is an ordinary English hand. It can hardly be improved, it is so refined and exquisite—almost perfection. This is an example of another kind, a mixture of styles. The copy was given me by a French commercial traveller. It is founded on the English, but the downstrokes are a little blacker, and more marked. Notice that the oval has some slight modification—it is more rounded. This writing allows for flourishes; now a flourish is a dangerous thing! Its use requires such taste, but, if successful, what a distinction it gives to the whole! It results in an incomparable type—one to fall in love with!"

"Dear me! How you have gone into all the refinements and details of the question! Why, my dear fellow, you are not a caligraphist, you are an artist! Eh, Gania?"

"Wonderful!" said Gania. "And he knows it too," he added, with a sarcastic smile.

"You may smile,—but there's a career in this," said the general. "You don't know what a great personage I shall show this to, prince. Why, you can command a situation at thirty-five roubles per month to start with. However, it's half-past twelve," he concluded, looking at his watch; "so to business, prince, for I must be setting to work and shall not see you again today. Sit down a minute. I have told you that I cannot receive you myself very often, but I should like to be of some assistance to you, some small assistance, of a kind that would give you satisfaction. I shall find you a place in one of the State departments, an easy place—but you will require to be accurate. Now, as to your plans—in the house, or rather in the family of Gania here—my young friend, whom I hope you will know better—his mother and sister have prepared two or three rooms for lodgers, and let them to highly recommended young fellows, with board and attendance. I am sure Nina Alexandrovna will take you in on my recommendation. There you will be comfortable and well taken care of; for I do not think, prince, that you are the sort of man to be left to the mercy of Fate in a town like Petersburg. Nina Alexandrovna, Gania's mother, and Varvara Alexandrovna, are ladies for whom I have the highest possible esteem and respect. Nina Alexandrovna is the wife of General Ardalion Alexandrovitch, my old brother in arms, with whom, I regret to say, on account of certain circumstances, I am no longer acquainted. I give you all this information, prince, in order to make it clear to you that I am personally recommending you to this family, and that in so doing, I am more or less taking upon myself to answer for you. The terms are most reasonable, and I trust that your salary will very shortly prove amply sufficient for your expenditure. Of course pocket-money is a necessity, if only a little; do not be angry, prince, if I strongly recommend you to avoid carrying money in your pocket. But as your purse is quite empty at the present moment, you must allow me to press these twenty-five roubles upon your acceptance, as something to begin with. Of course we will settle this little matter another time, and if you are the upright, honest man you look, I anticipate very little trouble between us on that score. Taking so much interest in you as you may perceive I do, I am not without my object, and you shall know it in good time. You see, I am perfectly candid with you. I hope, Gania, you have nothing to say against the prince's taking up his abode in your house?"

"Oh, on the contrary! my mother will be very glad," said Gania, courteously and kindly.

"I think only one of your rooms is engaged as yet, is it not? That fellow Ferd-Ferd—"

"Ferdishenko."

"Yes—I don't like that Ferdishenko. I can't understand why Nastasia Philipovna encourages him so. Is he really her cousin, as he says?"

"Oh dear no, it's all a joke. No more cousin than I am."

"Well, what do you think of the arrangement, prince?"

"Thank you, general; you have behaved very kindly to me; all the more so since I did not ask you to help me. I don't say that out of pride. I certainly did not know where to lay my head tonight. Rogojin asked me to come to his house, of course, but—"

"Rogojin? No, no, my good fellow. I should strongly recommend you, paternally,—or, if you prefer it, as a friend,—to forget all about Rogojin, and, in fact, to stick to the family into which you are about to enter."

"Thank you," began the prince; "and since you are so very kind there is just one matter which I—"

"You must really excuse me," interrupted the general, "but I positively haven't another moment now. I shall just tell Elizabetha Prokofievna about you, and if she wishes to receive you at once—as I shall advise her—I strongly recommend you to ingratiate yourself with her at the first opportunity, for my wife may be of the greatest service to you in many ways. If she cannot receive you now, you must be content to wait till another time. Meanwhile you, Gania, just look over these accounts, will you? We mustn't forget to finish off that matter—"

The general left the room, and the prince never succeeded in broaching the business which he had on hand, though he had endeavoured to do so four times.

Gania lit a cigarette and offered one to the prince. The latter accepted the offer, but did not talk, being unwilling to disturb Gania's work. He commenced to examine the study and its contents. But Gania hardly so much as glanced at the papers lying before him; he was absent and thoughtful, and his smile and general appearance struck the prince still more disagreeably now that the two were left alone together.

Suddenly Gania approached our hero who was at the moment standing over Nastasia Philipovna's portrait, gazing at it.

"Do you admire that sort of woman, prince?" he asked, looking intently at him. He seemed to have some special object in the question.

"It's a wonderful face," said the prince, "and I feel sure that her destiny is not by any means an ordinary, uneventful one. Her face is smiling enough, but she must have suffered terribly—hasn't she? Her eyes show it— those two bones there, the little points under her eyes, just where the cheek begins. It's a proud face too, terribly proud! And I—I can't say whether she is good and kind, or not. Oh, if she be but good! That would make all well!"

"And would you marry a woman like that, now?" continued Gania, never taking his excited eyes off the prince's face.

"I cannot marry at all," said the latter. "I am an invalid."

"Would Rogojin marry her, do you think?"

"Why not? Certainly he would, I should think. He would marry her tomorrow!—marry her tomorrow and murder her in a week!"

Hardly had the prince uttered the last word when Gania gave such a fearful shudder that the prince almost cried out.

"What's the matter?" said he, seizing Gania's hand.

"Your highness! His excellency begs your presence in her excellency's apartments!" announced the footman, appearing at the door.

The prince immediately followed the man out of the room.

IV.

All three of the Miss Epanchins were fine, healthy girls, well-grown, with good shoulders and busts, and strong—almost masculine—hands; and, of course, with all the above attributes, they enjoyed capital appetites, of which they were not in the least ashamed.

Elizabetha Prokofievna sometimes informed the girls that they were a little too candid in this matter, but in spite of their outward deference to their mother these three young women, in solemn conclave, had long agreed to modify the unquestioning obedience which they had been in the habit of according to her; and Mrs. General Epanchin had judged it better to say nothing about it, though, of course, she was well aware of the fact.

It is true that her nature sometimes rebelled against these dictates of reason, and that she grew yearly more capricious and impatient; but having a respectful and well-disciplined husband under her thumb at all times, she found it possible, as a rule, to empty any little accumulations of spleen upon his head, and therefore the harmony of the family was kept duly balanced, and things went as smoothly as family matters can.

Mrs. Epanchin had a fair appetite herself, and generally took her share of the capital mid-day lunch which was always served for the girls, and which was nearly as good as a dinner. The young ladies used to have a cup of coffee each before this meal, at ten o'clock, while still in bed. This was a favourite and unalterable arrangement with them. At half-past twelve, the table was laid in the small dining-room, and occasionally the general himself appeared at the family gathering, if he had time.

Besides tea and coffee, cheese, honey, butter, pan-cakes of various kinds (the lady of the house loved these best), cutlets, and so on, there was generally strong beef soup, and other substantial delicacies.

On the particular morning on which our story has opened, the family had assembled in the dining-room, and were waiting the general's appearance, the latter having promised to come this day. If he had been one moment late, he would have been sent for at once; but he turned up punctually.

As he came forward to wish his wife good-morning and kiss her hands, as his custom was, he observed something in her look which boded ill. He thought he knew the reason, and had expected it, but still, he was not altogether comfortable. His daughters advanced to kiss him, too, and though they did not look exactly angry, there was something strange in their expression as well.

The general was, owing to certain circumstances, a little inclined to be too suspicious at home, and needlessly nervous; but, as an experienced father and husband, he judged it better to take measures at once to protect himself from any dangers there might be in the air.

However, I hope I shall not interfere with the proper sequence of my narrative too much, if I diverge for a moment at this point, in order to explain the mutual relations between General Epanchin's family and others acting a part in this history, at the time when we take up the thread of their destiny. I have already stated that the general, though he was a man of lowly origin, and of poor education, was, for all that, an experienced and talented husband and father. Among other things, he considered it undesirable to hurry his daughters to the matrimonial altar and to worry them too much with assurances of his paternal wishes for their happiness, as is the custom among parents of many grown-up daughters. He even succeeded in ranging his wife on his side on this question, though he found the feat very difficult to accomplish, because unnatural; but the general's arguments were conclusive, and founded upon obvious facts. The general considered that the girls' taste and good sense should be allowed to develop and mature deliberately, and that the parents' duty should merely be to keep watch, in order that no strange or undesirable choice be made; but that the selection once effected, both father and mother were bound from that moment to enter heart and soul into the cause, and to see that the matter progressed without hindrance until the altar should be happily reached.

Besides this, it was clear that the Epanchins' position gained each year, with geometrical accuracy, both as to financial solidity and social weight; and, therefore, the longer the girls waited, the better was their chance of making a brilliant match.

But again, amidst the incontrovertible facts just recorded, one more, equally significant, rose up to confront the family; and this was, that the eldest daughter, Alexandra, had imperceptibly arrived at her twenty-fifth birthday.

253

Almost at the same moment, Afanasy Ivanovitch Totski, a man of immense wealth, high connections, and good standing, announced his intention of marrying. Afanasy Ivanovitch was a gentleman of fifty-five years of age, artistically gifted, and of most refined tastes. He wished to marry well, and, moreover, he was a keen admirer and judge of beauty.

Now, since Totski had, of late, been upon terms of great cordiality with Epanchin, which excellent relations were intensified by the fact that they were, so to speak, partners in several financial enterprises, it so happened that the former now put in a friendly request to the general for counsel with regard to the important step he meditated. Might he suggest, for instance, such a thing as a marriage between himself and one of the general's daughters?

Evidently the quiet, pleasant current of the family life of the Epanchins was about to undergo a change.

The undoubted beauty of the family, *par excellence*, was the youngest, Aglaya, as aforesaid. But Totski himself, though an egotist of the extremest type, realized that he had no chance there; Aglaya was clearly not for such as he.

Perhaps the sisterly love and friendship of the three girls had more or less exaggerated Aglaya's chances of happiness. In their opinion, the latter's destiny was not merely to be very happy; she was to live in a heaven on earth. Aglaya's husband was to be a compendium of all the virtues, and of all success, not to speak of fabulous wealth. The two elder sisters had agreed that all was to be sacrificed by them, if need be, for Aglaya's sake; her dowry was to be colossal and unprecedented.

The general and his wife were aware of this agreement, and, therefore, when Totski suggested himself for one of the sisters, the parents made no doubt that one of the two elder girls would probably accept the offer, since Totski would certainly make no difficulty as to dowry. The general valued the proposal very highly. He knew life, and realized what such an offer was worth.

The answer of the sisters to the communication was, if not conclusive, at least consoling and hopeful. It made known that the eldest, Alexandra, would very likely be disposed to listen to a proposal.

Alexandra was a good-natured girl, though she had a will of her own. She was intelligent and kind-hearted, and, if she were to marry Totski, she would make him a good wife. She did not care for a brilliant marriage; she was eminently a woman calculated to soothe and sweeten the life of any man; decidedly pretty, if not absolutely handsome. What better could Totski wish?

So the matter crept slowly forward. The general and Totski had agreed to avoid any hasty and irrevocable step. Alexandra's parents had not even begun to talk to their daughters freely upon the subject, when suddenly, as it were, a dissonant chord was struck amid the harmony of the proceedings. Mrs. Epanchin began to show signs of discontent, and that was a serious matter. A certain circumstance had crept in, a disagreeable and troublesome factor, which threatened to overturn the whole business.

This circumstance had come into existence eighteen years before. Close to an estate of Totski's, in one of the central provinces of Russia, there lived, at that time, a poor gentleman whose estate was of the wretchedest description. This gentleman was noted in the district for his persistent ill-fortune; his name was Barashkoff, and, as regards family and descent, he was vastly superior to Totski, but his estate was mortgaged to the last acre. One day, when he had ridden over to the town to see a creditor, the chief peasant of his village followed him shortly after, with the news that his house had been burnt down, and that his wife had perished with it, but his children were safe.

Even Barashkoff, inured to the storms of evil fortune as he was, could not stand this last stroke. He went mad and died shortly after in the town hospital. His estate was sold for the creditors; and the little girls—two of them, of seven and eight years of age respectively,—were adopted by Totski, who undertook their maintenance and education in the kindness of his heart. They were brought up together with the children of his German bailiff. Very soon, however, there was only one of them left—Nastasia Philipovna—for the other little one died of whooping-cough. Totski, who was living abroad at this time, very soon forgot all about the child; but five years after, returning to Russia, it struck him that he would like to look over his estate and see how matters were going there, and, arrived at his bailiff's house, he was not long in discovering that among the children of the latter there now dwelt a most lovely little girl of twelve, sweet and intelligent, and bright, and promising to develop beauty of most unusual quality-as to which last Totski was an undoubted authority.

He only stayed at his country seat a few days on this occasion, but he had time to make his arrangements. Great changes took place in the child's education; a good governess was engaged, a Swiss lady of experience and culture. For four years this lady resided in the house with little Nastia, and then the education was considered complete. The governess took her departure, and another lady came down to fetch Nastia, by Totski's instructions. The child was now transported to another of Totski's estates in a distant part of the country. Here she found a delightful little house, just built, and prepared for her reception with great care and taste; and here she took up her abode together with the lady who had accompanied her from her old home. In the house there were two experienced maids, musical instruments of all sorts, a charming "young lady's library," pictures, paint-boxes, a lap-dog, and everything to make life agreeable. Within a fortnight Totski himself arrived, and from that time he appeared to have taken a great fancy to this part of the world and came down each summer, staying two and three months at a time. So passed four years peacefully and happily, in charming surroundings.

At the end of that time, and about four months after Totski's last visit (he had stayed but a fortnight on this occasion), a report reached Nastasia Philipovna that he was about to be married in St. Petersburg, to a rich, eminent, and lovely woman. The report was only partially true, the marriage project being only in an embryo condition; but a great change now came over Nastasia Philipovna. She suddenly displayed unusual decision of character; and without wasting time in thought, she left her country home and came up to St. Petersburg, straight to Totski's house, all alone.

The latter, amazed at her conduct, began to express his displeasure; but he very soon became aware that he must change his voice, style, and everything else, with this young lady; the good old times were gone. An entirely new and different woman sat before him, between whom and the girl he had left in the country last July there seemed nothing in common.

In the first place, this new woman understood a good deal more than was usual for young people of her age; so much indeed, that Totski could not help wondering where she had picked up her knowledge. Surely not from her "young lady's library"? It even embraced legal matters, and the "world" in general, to a considerable extent.

Her character was absolutely changed. No more of the girlish alternations of timidity and petulance, the adorable naivete, the reveries, the tears, the playfulness... It was an entirely new and hitherto unknown being who now sat and laughed at him, and informed him to his face that she had never had the faintest feeling for him of any kind, except loathing and contempt—contempt which had followed closely upon her sensations of surprise and bewilderment after her first acquaintance with him.

This new woman gave him further to understand that though it was absolutely the same to her whom he married, yet she had decided to prevent this marriage—for no particular reason, but that she *chose* to do so, and because she wished to amuse herself at his expense for that it was "quite her turn to laugh a little now!"

Such were her words—very likely she did not give her real reason for this eccentric conduct; but, at all events, that was all the explanation she deigned to offer.

Meanwhile, Totski thought the matter over as well as his scattered ideas would permit. His meditations lasted a fortnight, however, and at the end of that time his resolution was taken. The fact was, Totski was at that time a man of fifty years of age; his position was solid and respectable; his place in society had long been firmly fixed upon safe foundations; he loved himself, his personal comforts, and his position better than all the world, as every respectable gentleman should!

At the same time his grasp of things in general soon showed Totski that he now had to deal with a being who was outside the pale of the ordinary rules of traditional behaviour, and who would not only threaten mischief but would undoubtedly carry it out, and stop for no one.

There was evidently, he concluded, something at work here; some storm of the mind, some paroxysm of romantic anger, goodness knows against whom or what, some insatiable contempt—in a word, something altogether absurd and impossible, but at the same time most dangerous to be met with by any respectable person with a position in society to keep up.

For a man of Totski's wealth and standing, it would, of course, have been the simplest possible matter to take steps which would rid him at once from all annoyance; while it was obviously impossible for Nastasia Philipovna to harm him in any way, either legally or by stirring up a scandal, for, in case of the latter danger, he could so easily remove her to a sphere of safety. However, these arguments would only hold good in case of Nastasia acting as others might in such an emergency. She was much more likely to overstep the bounds of reasonable conduct by some extraordinary eccentricity.

Here the sound judgment of Totski stood him in good stead. He realized that Nastasia Philipovna must be well aware that she could do nothing by legal means to injure him, and that her flashing eyes betrayed some entirely different intention.

Nastasia Philipovna was quite capable of ruining herself, and even of perpetrating something which would send her to Siberia, for the mere pleasure of injuring a man for whom she had developed so inhuman a sense of loathing and contempt. He had sufficient insight to understand that she valued nothing in the world—herself least of all— and he made no attempt to conceal the fact that he was a coward in some respects. For instance, if he had been told that he would be stabbed at the altar, or publicly insulted, he would undoubtedly have been frightened; but not so much at the idea of being murdered, or wounded, or insulted, as at the thought that if such things were to happen he would be made to look ridiculous in the eyes of society.

He knew well that Nastasia thoroughly understood him and where to wound him and how, and therefore, as the marriage was still only in embryo, Totski decided to conciliate her by giving it up. His decision was strengthened by the fact that Nastasia Philipovna had curiously altered of late. It would be difficult to conceive how different she was physically, at the present time, to the girl of a few years ago. She was pretty then... but now!... Totski laughed angrily when he thought how short-sighted he had been. In days gone by he remembered how he had looked at her beautiful eyes, how even then he had marvelled at their dark mysterious depths, and at their wondering gaze which seemed to seek an answer to some unknown riddle. Her complexion also had altered. She was now exceedingly pale, but, curiously, this change only made her more beautiful. Like most men of the world, Totski had rather despised such a cheaply-bought conquest, but of late years he had begun to think differently about it. It had struck him as long ago as last spring that he ought to be finding a good match for Nastasia; for instance, some respectable and reasonable young fellow serving in a government office in another part of the country. How maliciously Nastasia laughed at the idea of such a thing, now!

However, it appeared to Totski that he might make use of her in another way; and he determined to establish her in St. Petersburg, surrounding her with all the comforts and luxuries that his wealth could command. In this way he might gain glory in certain circles.

Five years of this Petersburg life went by, and, of course, during that time a great deal happened. Totski's position was very uncomfortable; having "funked" once, he could not totally regain his ease. He was afraid, he did not know why, but he was simply *afraid* of Nastasia Philipovna. For the first two years or so he had suspected that she wished to marry him herself, and that only her vanity prevented her telling him so. He thought that she wanted him to approach her with a humble proposal from his own side. But to his great, and not entirely pleasurable amazement, he discovered that this was by no means the case, and that were he to offer himself he would be refused. He could not understand such a state of things, and was obliged to conclude that it was pride, the pride of an injured and imaginative woman, which had gone to such lengths that it preferred to sit and nurse its contempt and hatred in solitude rather than mount to heights of hitherto unattainable splendour. To make matters worse, she was quite impervious to mercenary considerations, and could not be bribed in any way.

Finally, Totski took cunning means to try to break his chains and be free. He tried to tempt her in various ways to lose her heart; he invited princes, hussars, secretaries of embassies, poets, novelists, even Socialists, to see her; but not one of them all made the faintest impression upon Nastasia. It was as though she had a pebble in place of a heart, as though her feelings and affections were dried up and withered for ever.

She lived almost entirely alone; she read, she studied, she loved music. Her principal acquaintances were poor women of various grades, a couple of actresses, and the family of a poor schoolteacher. Among these people she was much beloved.

She received four or five friends sometimes, of an evening. Totski often came. Lately, too, General Epanchin had been enabled with great difficulty to introduce himself into her circle. Gania made her acquaintance also, and others were Ferdishenko, an ill-bred, and would-be witty, young clerk, and Ptitsin, a money-lender of modest and polished manners, who had risen from poverty. In fact, Nastasia Philipovna's beauty became a thing known to all the town; but not a single man could boast of anything more than his own admiration for her; and this reputation of hers, and her wit and culture and grace, all confirmed Totski in the plan he had now prepared.

And it was at this moment that General Epanchin began to play so large and important a part in the story.

When Totski had approached the general with his request for friendly counsel as to a marriage with one of his daughters, he had made a full and candid confession. He had said that he intended to stop at no means to obtain his freedom; even if Nastasia were to promise to leave him entirely alone in future, he would not (he said) believe and trust her; words were not enough for him; he must have solid guarantees of some sort. So he and the general determined to try what an attempt to appeal to her heart would effect. Having arrived at Nastasia's house one day, with Epanchin, Totski immediately began to speak of the intolerable torment of his position. He admitted that he was to blame for all, but candidly confessed that he could not bring himself to feel any remorse for his original guilt towards herself, because he was a man of sensual passions which were inborn and ineradicable, and that he had no power over himself in this respect; but that he wished, seriously, to marry at last, and that the whole fate of the most desirable social union which he contemplated, was in her hands; in a word, he confided his all to her generosity of heart.

General Epanchin took up his part and spoke in the character of father of a family; he spoke sensibly, and without wasting words over any attempt at sentimentality, he merely recorded his full admission of her right to be the arbiter of Totski's destiny at this moment. He then pointed out that the fate of his daughter, and very likely of both his other daughters, now hung upon her reply.

To Nastasia's question as to what they wished her to do, Totski confessed that he had been so frightened by her, five years ago, that he could never now be entirely comfortable until she herself married. He immediately added that such a suggestion from him would, of course, be absurd, unless accompanied by remarks of a more pointed nature. He very well knew, he said, that a certain young gentleman of good family, namely, Gavrila Ardalionovitch Ivolgin, with whom she was acquainted, and whom she received at her house, had long loved her passionately, and would give his life for some response from her. The young fellow had confessed this love of his to him (Totski) and had also admitted it in the hearing of his benefactor, General Epanchin. Lastly, he could not help being of opinion that Nastasia must be aware of Gania's love for her, and if he (Totski) mistook not, she had looked with some favour upon it, being often lonely, and rather tired of her present life. Having remarked how difficult it was for him, of all people, to speak to her of these matters, Totski concluded by saying that he trusted Nastasia Philipovna would not look with contempt upon him if he now expressed his sincere desire to guarantee her future by a gift of seventy-five thousand roubles. He added that the sum would have been left her all the same in his will, and that therefore she must not consider the gift as in any way an indemnification to her for anything, but that there was no reason, after all, why a man should not be allowed to entertain a natural desire to lighten his conscience, etc., etc.; in fact, all that would naturally be said under the circumstances. Totski was very eloquent all through, and, in conclusion, just touched on the fact that not a soul in the world, not even General Epanchin, had ever heard a word about the above seventy-five thousand roubles, and that this was the first time he had ever given expression to his intentions in respect to them.

Nastasia Philipovna's reply to this long rigmarole astonished both the friends considerably.

Not only was there no trace of her former irony, of her old hatred and enmity, and of that dreadful laughter, the very recollection of which sent a cold chill down Totski's back to this very day; but she seemed charmed and really glad to have the opportunity of talking seriously with him for once in a way. She confessed that she had long wished to have a frank and free conversation and to ask for friendly advice, but that pride had hitherto prevented her; now, however, that the ice was broken, nothing could be more welcome to her than this opportunity.

First, with a sad smile, and then with a twinkle of merriment in her eyes, she admitted that such a storm as that of five years ago was now quite out of the question. She said that she had long since changed her views of things, and recognized that facts must be taken into consideration in spite of the feelings of the heart. What was done was done and ended, and she could not understand why Totski should still feel alarmed.

She next turned to General Epanchin and observed, most courteously, that she had long since known of his daughters, and that she had heard none but good report; that she had learned to think of them with deep and sincere respect. The idea alone that she could in any way serve them, would be to her both a pride and a source of real happiness.

It was true that she was lonely in her present life; Totski had judged her thoughts aright. She longed to rise, if not to love, at least to family life and new hopes and objects, but as to Gavrila Ardalionovitch, she could not as yet say much. She thought it must be the case that he loved her; she felt that she too might learn to love him, if she could be sure of the firmness of his attachment to herself; but he was very young, and it was a difficult question to decide. What she specially liked about him was that he worked, and supported his family by his toil.

She had heard that he was proud and ambitious; she had heard much that was interesting of his mother and sister, she had heard of them from Mr. Ptitsin, and would much like to make their acquaintance, but—another question!— would they like to receive her into their house? At all events, though she did not reject the idea of this marriage, she desired not to be hurried. As for the seventy-five thousand roubles, Mr. Totski need not have found any difficulty or awkwardness about the matter; she quite understood the value of money, and would, of course, accept the gift. She thanked him for his delicacy, however, but saw no reason why Gavrila Ardalionovitch should not know about it.

She would not marry the latter, she said, until she felt persuaded that neither on his part nor on the part of his family did there exist any sort of concealed suspicions as to herself. She did not intend to ask forgiveness for anything in the past, which fact she desired to be known. She did not consider herself to blame for anything that had happened in former years, and she thought that Gavrila Ardalionovitch should be informed as to the relations which had existed between herself and Totski during the last five years. If she accepted this money it was not to be considered as indemnification for her misfortune as a young girl, which had not been in any degree her own fault, but merely as compensation for her ruined life.

She became so excited and agitated during all these explanations and confessions that General Epanchin was highly gratified, and considered the matter satisfactorily arranged once for all. But the once bitten Totski was twice shy, and looked for hidden snakes among the flowers. However, the special point to which the two friends particularly trusted to bring about their object (namely, Gania's attractiveness for Nastasia Philipovna), stood out more and more prominently; the pourparlers had commenced, and gradually even Totski began to believe in the possibility of success.

Before long Nastasia and Gania had talked the matter over. Very little was said—her modesty seemed to suffer under the infliction of discussing such a question. But she recognized his love, on the understanding that she bound herself to nothing whatever, and that she reserved the right to say "no" up to the very hour of the marriage ceremony. Gania was to have the same right of refusal at the last moment.

It soon became clear to Gania, after scenes of wrath and quarrellings at the domestic hearth, that his family were seriously opposed to the match, and that Nastasia was aware of this fact was equally evident. She said nothing about it, though he daily expected her to do so.

There were several rumours afloat, before long, which upset Totski's equanimity a good deal, but we will not now stop to describe them; merely mentioning an instance or two. One was that Nastasia had entered into close and secret relations with the Epanchin girls—a most unlikely rumour; another was that Nastasia had long satisfied herself of the fact that Gania was merely marrying her for money, and that his nature was gloomy and greedy, impatient and selfish, to an extraordinary degree; and that although he had been keen enough in his desire to achieve a conquest before, yet since the two friends had agreed to exploit his passion for their own purposes, it was clear enough that he had begun to consider the whole thing a nuisance and a nightmare.

In his heart passion and hate seemed to hold divided sway, and although he had at last given his consent to marry the woman (as he said), under the stress of circumstances, yet he promised himself that he would "take it out of her," after marriage.

Nastasia seemed to Totski to have divined all this, and to be preparing something on her own account, which frightened him to such an extent that he did not dare communicate his views even to the general. But at times he would pluck up his courage and be full of hope and good spirits again, acting, in fact, as weak men do act in such circumstances.

However, both the friends felt that the thing looked rosy indeed when one day Nastasia informed them that she would give her final answer on the evening of her birthday, which anniversary was due in a very short time.

A strange rumour began to circulate, meanwhile; no less than that the respectable and highly respected General Epanchin was himself so fascinated by Nastasia Philipovna that his feeling for her amounted almost to passion. What he thought to gain by Gania's marriage to the girl it was difficult to imagine. Possibly he counted on Gania's complaisance; for Totski had long suspected that there existed some secret understanding between the general and his secretary. At all events the fact was known that he had prepared a magnificent present of pearls for Nastasia's birthday, and that he was looking forward to the occasion when he should present his gift with the greatest excitement and impatience. The day before her birthday he was in a fever of agitation.

Mrs. Epanchin, long accustomed to her husband's infidelities, had heard of the pearls, and the rumour excited her liveliest curiosity and interest. The general remarked her suspicions, and felt that a grand explanation must shortly take place—which fact alarmed him much.

This is the reason why he was so unwilling to take lunch (on the morning upon which we took up this narrative) with the rest of his family. Before the prince's arrival he had made up his mind to plead business, and "cut" the meal; which simply meant running away.

He was particularly anxious that this one day should be passed—especially the evening—without unpleasantness between himself and his family; and just at the right moment the prince turned up—"as though Heaven had sent him on purpose," said the general to himself, as he left the study to seek out the wife of his bosom.

V.

Mrs. General Epanchin was a proud woman by nature. What must her feelings have been when she heard that Prince Muishkin, the last of his and her line, had arrived in beggar's guise, a wretched idiot, a recipient of charity—all of which details the general gave out for greater effect! He was anxious to steal her interest at the first swoop, so as to distract her thoughts from other matters nearer home.

Mrs. Epanchin was in the habit of holding herself very straight, and staring before her, without speaking, in moments of excitement.

She was a fine woman of the same age as her husband, with a slightly hooked nose, a high, narrow forehead, thick hair turning a little grey, and a sallow complexion. Her eyes were grey and wore a very curious expression at times. She believed them to be most effective—a belief that nothing could alter.

"What, receive him! Now, at once?" asked Mrs. Epanchin, gazing vaguely at her husband as he stood fidgeting before her.

"Oh, dear me, I assure you there is no need to stand on ceremony with him," the general explained hastily. "He is quite a child, not to say a pathetic-looking creature. He has fits of some sort, and has just arrived from Switzerland, straight from the station, dressed like a German and without a farthing in his pocket. I gave him twenty-five roubles to go on with, and am going to find him some easy place in one of the government offices. I should like you to ply him well with the victuals, my dears, for I should think he must be very hungry."

"You astonish me," said the lady, gazing as before. "Fits, and hungry too! What sort of fits?"

"Oh, they don't come on frequently, besides, he's a regular child, though he seems to be fairly educated. I should like you, if possible, my dears," the general added, making slowly for the door, "to put him through his paces a bit, and see what he is good for. I think you should be kind to him; it is a good deed, you know—however, just as you like, of course—but he is a sort of relation, remember, and I thought it might interest you to see the young fellow, seeing that this is so."

"Oh, of course, mamma, if we needn't stand on ceremony with him, we must give the poor fellow something to eat after his journey; especially as he has not the least idea where to go to," said Alexandra, the eldest of the girls.

"Besides, he's quite a child; we can entertain him with a little hide-and-seek, in case of need," said Adelaida.

"Hide-and-seek? What do you mean?" inquired Mrs. Epanchin.

"Oh, do stop pretending, mamma," cried Aglaya, in vexation. "Send him up, father; mother allows."

The general rang the bell and gave orders that the prince should be shown in.

"Only on condition that he has a napkin under his chin at lunch, then," said Mrs. Epanchin, "and let Fedor, or Mavra, stand behind him while he eats. Is he quiet when he has these fits? He doesn't show violence, does he?"

"On the contrary, he seems to be very well brought up. His manners are excellent—but here he is himself. Here you are, prince—let me introduce you, the last of the Muishkins, a relative of your own, my dear, or at least of the same name. Receive him kindly, please. They'll bring in lunch directly, prince; you must stop and have some, but you must excuse me. I'm in a hurry, I must be off—"

"We all know where *you* must be off to!" said Mrs. Epanchin, in a meaning voice.

"Yes, yes—I must hurry away, I'm late! Look here, dears, let him write you something in your albums; you've no idea what a wonderful caligraphist he is, wonderful talent! He has just written out 'Abbot Pafnute signed this' for me. Well, *au revoir!*"

"Stop a minute; where are you off to? Who is this abbot?" cried Mrs. Epanchin to her retreating husband in a tone of excited annoyance.

"Yes, my dear, it was an old abbot of that name-I must be off to see the count, he's waiting for me, I'm late— Good-bye! *Au revoir*, prince!"—and the general bolted at full speed.

"Oh, yes—I know what count you're going to see!" remarked his wife in a cutting manner, as she turned her angry eyes on the prince. "Now then, what's all this about?—What abbot—Who's Pafnute?" she added, brusquely.

"Mamma!" said Alexandra, shocked at her rudeness.

Aglaya stamped her foot.

"Nonsense! Let me alone!" said the angry mother. "Now then, prince, sit down here, no, nearer, come nearer the light! I want to have a good look at you. So, now then, who is this abbot?"

"Abbot Pafnute," said our friend, seriously and with deference.

"Pafnute, yes. And who was he?"

Mrs. Epanchin put these questions hastily and brusquely, and when the prince answered she nodded her head sagely at each word he said.

"The Abbot Pafnute lived in the fourteenth century," began the prince; "he was in charge of one of the monasteries on the Volga, about where our present Kostroma government lies. He went to Oreol and helped in the great matters then going on in the religious world; he signed an edict there, and I have seen a print of his signature; it struck me, so I copied it. When the general asked me, in his study, to write something for him, to show my handwriting, I wrote 'The Abbot Pafnute signed this,' in the exact handwriting of the abbot. The general liked it very much, and that's why he recalled it just now."

"Aglaya, make a note of 'Pafnute,' or we shall forget him. H'm! and where is this signature?"

"I think it was left on the general's table."

"Let it be sent for at once!"

"Oh, I'll write you a new one in half a minute," said the prince, "if you like!"

"Of course, mamma!" said Alexandra. "But let's have lunch now, we are all hungry!"

"Yes; come along, prince," said the mother, "are you very hungry?"

"Yes; I must say that I am pretty hungry, thanks very much."

"H'm! I like to see that you know your manners; and you are by no means such a person as the general thought fit to describe you. Come along; you sit here, opposite to me," she continued, "I wish to be able to see your face. Alexandra, Adelaida, look after the prince! He doesn't seem so very ill, does he? I don't think he requires a napkin under his chin, after all; are you accustomed to having one on, prince?"

"Formerly, when I was seven years old or so. I believe I wore one; but now I usually hold my napkin on my knee when I eat."

"Of course, of course! And about your fits?"

"Fits?" asked the prince, slightly surprised. "I very seldom have fits nowadays. I don't know how it may be here, though; they say the climate may be bad for me."

"He talks very well, you know!" said Mrs. Epanchin, who still continued to nod at each word the prince spoke. "I really did not expect it at all; in fact, I suppose it was all stuff and nonsense on the general's part, as usual. Eat away, prince, and tell me where you were born, and where you were brought up. I wish to know all about you, you interest me very much!"

The prince expressed his thanks once more, and eating heartily the while, recommenced the narrative of his life in Switzerland, all of which we have heard before. Mrs. Epanchin became more and more pleased with her guest; the girls, too, listened with considerable attention. In talking over the question of relationship it turned out that the prince was very well up in the matter and knew his pedigree off by heart. It was found that scarcely any connection existed between himself and Mrs. Epanchin, but the talk, and the opportunity of conversing about her family tree, gratified the latter exceedingly, and she rose from the table in great good humour.

"Let's all go to my boudoir," she said, "and they shall bring some coffee in there. That's the room where we all assemble and busy ourselves as we like best," she explained. "Alexandra, my eldest, here, plays the piano, or reads or sews; Adelaida paints landscapes and portraits (but never finishes any); and Aglaya sits and does nothing. I don't work too much, either. Here we are, now; sit down, prince, near the fire and talk to us. I want to hear you relate something. I wish to make sure of you first and then tell my old friend, Princess Bielokonski, about you. I wish you to know all the good people and to interest them. Now then, begin!"

"Mamma, it's rather a strange order, that!" said Adelaida, who was fussing among her paints and paint-brushes at the easel. Aglaya and Alexandra had settled themselves with folded hands on a sofa, evidently meaning to be listeners. The prince felt that the general attention was concentrated upon himself.

"I should refuse to say a word if I were ordered to tell a story like that!" observed Aglaya.

"Why? what's there strange about it? He has a tongue. Why shouldn't he tell us something? I want to judge whether he is a good story-teller; anything you like, prince-how you liked Switzerland, what was your first impression, anything. You'll see, he'll begin directly and tell us all about it beautifully."

"The impression was forcible—" the prince began.

"There, you see, girls," said the impatient lady, "he *has* begun, you see."

"Well, then, *let* him talk, mamma," said Alexandra. "This prince is a great humbug and by no means an idiot," she whispered to Aglaya.

"Oh, I saw that at once," replied the latter. "I don't think it at all nice of him to play a part. What does he wish to gain by it, I wonder?"

"My first impression was a very strong one," repeated the prince. "When they took me away from Russia, I remember I passed through many German towns and looked out of the windows, but did not trouble so much as to ask questions about them. This was after a long series of fits. I always used to fall into a sort of torpid condition after such a series, and lost my memory almost entirely; and though I was not altogether without reason at such times, yet I had no logical power of thought. This would continue for three or four days, and then I would recover myself again. I remember my melancholy was intolerable; I felt inclined to cry; I sat and wondered and wondered uncomfortably; the consciousness that everything was strange weighed terribly upon me; I could understand that it was all foreign and strange. I recollect I awoke from this state for the first time at Basle, one evening; the bray of a donkey aroused me, a donkey in the town market. I saw the donkey and was extremely pleased with it, and from that moment my head seemed to clear."

"A donkey? How strange! Yet it is not strange. Anyone of us might fall in love with a donkey! It happened in mythological times," said Madame Epanchin, looking wrathfully at her daughters, who had begun to laugh. "Go on, prince."

"Since that evening I have been specially fond of donkeys. I began to ask questions about them, for I had never seen one before; and I at once came to the conclusion that this must be one of the most useful of animals—strong, willing, patient, cheap; and, thanks to this donkey, I began to like the whole country I was travelling through; and my melancholy passed away."

"All this is very strange and interesting," said Mrs. Epanchin. "Now let's leave the donkey and go on to other matters. What are you laughing at, Aglaya? and you too, Adelaida? The prince told us his experiences very cleverly; he saw the donkey himself, and what have you ever seen? *You* have never been abroad."

"I have seen a donkey though, mamma!" said Aglaya.

"And I've heard one!" said Adelaida. All three of the girls laughed out loud, and the prince laughed with them.

"Well, it's too bad of you," said mamma. "You must forgive them, prince; they are good girls. I am very fond of them, though I often have to be scolding them; they are all as silly and mad as march hares."

"Oh, why shouldn't they laugh?" said the prince. "I shouldn't have let the chance go by in their place, I know. But I stick up for the donkey, all the same; he's a patient, good-natured fellow."

"Are you a patient man, prince? I ask out of curiosity," said Mrs. Epanchin.

All laughed again.

"Oh, that wretched donkey again, I see!" cried the lady. "I assure you, prince, I was not guilty of the least—"

"Insinuation? Oh! I assure you, I take your word for it." And the prince continued laughing merrily.

"I must say it's very nice of you to laugh. I see you really are a kind-hearted fellow," said Mrs. Epanchin.

"I'm not always kind, though."

"I am kind myself, and *always* kind too, if you please!" she retorted, unexpectedly; "and that is my chief fault, for one ought not to be always kind. I am often angry with these girls and their father; but the worst of it is, I am always kindest when I am cross. I was very angry just before you came, and Aglaya there read me a lesson—

thanks, Aglaya, dear—come and kiss me—there—that's enough" she added, as Aglaya came forward and kissed her lips and then her hand. "Now then, go on, prince. Perhaps you can think of something more exciting than about the donkey, eh?"

"I must say, again, *I* can't understand how you can expect anyone to tell you stories straight away, so," said Adelaida. "I know I never could!"

"Yes, but the prince can, because he is clever—cleverer than you are by ten or twenty times, if you like. There, that's so, prince; and seriously, let's drop the donkey now—what else did you see abroad, besides the donkey?"

"Yes, but the prince told us about the donkey very cleverly, all the same," said Alexandra. "I have always been most interested to hear how people go mad and get well again, and that sort of thing. Especially when it happens suddenly."

"Quite so, quite so!" cried Mrs. Epanchin, delighted. "I see you *can* be sensible now and then, Alexandra. You were speaking of Switzerland, prince?"

"Yes. We came to Lucerne, and I was taken out in a boat. I felt how lovely it was, but the loveliness weighed upon me somehow or other, and made me feel melancholy."

"Why?" asked Alexandra.

"I don't know; I always feel like that when I look at the beauties of nature for the first time; but then, I was ill at that time, of course!"

"Oh, but I should like to see it!" said Adelaida; "and I don't know *when* we shall ever go abroad. I've been two years looking out for a good subject for a picture. I've done all I know. 'The North and South I know by heart,' as our poet observes. Do help me to a subject, prince."

"Oh, but I know nothing about painting. It seems to me one only has to look, and paint what one sees."

"But I don't know *how* to see!"

"Nonsense, what rubbish you talk!" the mother struck in. "Not know how to see! Open your eyes and look! If you can't see here, you won't see abroad either. Tell us what you saw yourself, prince!"

"Yes, that's better," said Adelaida; "the prince *learned to see* abroad."

"Oh, I hardly know! You see, I only went to restore my health. I don't know whether I learned to see, exactly. I was very happy, however, nearly all the time."

"Happy! you can be happy?" cried Aglaya. "Then how can you say you did not learn to see? I should think you could teach*us* to see!"

"Oh! *do* teach us," laughed Adelaida.

"Oh! I can't do that," said the prince, laughing too. "I lived almost all the while in one little Swiss village; what can I teach you? At first I was only just not absolutely dull; then my health began to improve—then every day became dearer and more precious to me, and the longer I stayed, the dearer became the time to me; so much so that I could not help observing it; but why this was so, it would be difficult to say."

"So that you didn't care to go away anywhere else?"

"Well, at first I did; I was restless; I didn't know however I should manage to support life—you know there are such moments, especially in solitude. There was a waterfall near us, such a lovely thin streak of water, like a thread but white and moving. It fell from a great height, but it looked quite low, and it was half a mile away, though it did not seem fifty paces. I loved to listen to it at night, but it was then that I became so restless. Sometimes I went and climbed the mountain and stood there in the midst of the tall pines, all alone in the terrible silence, with our little village in the distance, and the sky so blue, and the sun so bright, and an old ruined castle on the mountain-side, far away. I used to watch the line where earth and sky met, and longed to go and seek there the key of all mysteries, thinking that I might find there a new life, perhaps some great city where life should be grander and richer—and then it struck me that life may be grand enough even in a prison."

"I read that last most praiseworthy thought in my manual, when I was twelve years old," said Aglaya.

"All this is pure philosophy," said Adelaida. "You are a philosopher, prince, and have come here to instruct us in your views."

"Perhaps you are right," said the prince, smiling. "I think I am a philosopher, perhaps, and who knows, perhaps I do wish to teach my views of things to those I meet with?"

"Your philosophy is rather like that of an old woman we know, who is rich and yet does nothing but try how little she can spend. She talks of nothing but money all day. Your great philosophical idea of a grand life in a prison and your four happy years in that Swiss village are like this, rather," said Aglaya.

"As to life in a prison, of course there may be two opinions," said the prince. "I once heard the story of a man who lived twelve years in a prison—I heard it from the man himself. He was one of the persons under treatment with my professor; he had fits, and attacks of melancholy, then he would weep, and once he tried to commit suicide. *His* life in prison was sad enough; his only acquaintances were spiders and a tree that grew outside his grating-but I think I had better tell you of another man I met last year. There was a very strange feature in this case, strange because of its extremely rare occurrence. This man had once been brought to the scaffold in company with several others, and had had the sentence of death by shooting passed upon him for some political crime. Twenty minutes later he had been reprieved and some other punishment substituted; but the interval between the two sentences, twenty minutes, or at least a quarter of an hour, had been passed in the certainty that within a few minutes he must die. I was very anxious to hear him speak of his impressions during that dreadful time, and I several times inquired of him as to what he thought and felt. He remembered everything with the most accurate and extraordinary distinctness, and declared that he would never forget a single iota of the experience.

"About twenty paces from the scaffold, where he had stood to hear the sentence, were three posts, fixed in the ground, to which to fasten the criminals (of whom there were several). The first three criminals were taken to the posts, dressed in long white tunics, with white caps drawn over their faces, so that they could not see the rifles pointed at them. Then a group of soldiers took their stand opposite to each post. My friend was the eighth on the list, and therefore he would have been among the third lot to go up. A priest went about among them with a cross: and there was about five minutes of time left for him to live.

"He said that those five minutes seemed to him to be a most interminable period, an enormous wealth of time; he seemed to be living, in these minutes, so many lives that there was no need as yet to think of that last moment, so that he made several arrangements, dividing up the time into portions—one for saying farewell to his companions, two minutes for that; then a couple more for thinking over his own life and career and all about himself; and another minute for a last look around. He remembered having divided his time like this quite well. While saying good-bye to his friends he recollected asking one of them some very usual everyday question, and being much interested in the answer. Then having bade farewell, he embarked upon those two minutes which he had allotted to looking into himself; he knew beforehand what he was going to think about. He wished to put it to himself as quickly and clearly as possible, that here was he, a living, thinking man, and that in three minutes he would be nobody; or if somebody or something, then what and where? He thought he would decide this question once for all in these last three minutes. A little way off there stood a church, and its gilded spire glittered in the sun. He remembered staring stubbornly at this spire, and at the rays of light sparkling from it. He could not tear his eyes from these rays of light; he got the idea that these rays were his new nature, and that in three minutes he would become one of them, amalgamated somehow with them.

"The repugnance to what must ensue almost immediately, and the uncertainty, were dreadful, he said; but worst of all was the idea, 'What should I do if I were not to die now? What if I were to return to life again? What an eternity of days, and all mine! How I should grudge and count up every minute of it, so as to waste not a single instant!' He said that this thought weighed so upon him and became such a terrible burden upon his brain that he could not bear it, and wished they would shoot him quickly and have done with it."

The prince paused and all waited, expecting him to go on again and finish the story.

"Is that all?" asked Aglaya.

"All? Yes," said the prince, emerging from a momentary reverie.

"And why did you tell us this?"

"Oh, I happened to recall it, that's all! It fitted into the conversation—"

"You probably wish to deduce, prince," said Alexandra, "that moments of time cannot be reckoned by money value, and that sometimes five minutes are worth priceless treasures. All this is very praiseworthy; but may I ask about this friend of yours, who told you the terrible experience of his life? He was reprieved, you say; in other words, they did restore to him that 'eternity of days.' What did he do with these riches of time? Did he keep careful account of his minutes?"

"Oh no, he didn't! I asked him myself. He said that he had not lived a bit as he had intended, and had wasted many, and many a minute."

"Very well, then there's an experiment, and the thing is proved; one cannot live and count each moment; say what you like, but one *cannot*."

"That is true," said the prince, "I have thought so myself. And yet, why shouldn't one do it?"

"You think, then, that you could live more wisely than other people?" said Aglaya.

"I have had that idea."

"And you have it still?"

"Yes—I have it still," the prince replied.

He had contemplated Aglaya until now, with a pleasant though rather timid smile, but as the last words fell from his lips he began to laugh, and looked at her merrily.

"You are not very modest!" said she.

"But how brave you are!" said he. "You are laughing, and I—that man's tale impressed me so much, that I dreamt of it afterwards; yes, I dreamt of those five minutes..."

He looked at his listeners again with that same serious, searching expression.

"You are not angry with me?" he asked suddenly, and with a kind of nervous hurry, although he looked them straight in the face.

"Why should we be angry?" they cried.

"Only because I seem to be giving you a lecture, all the time!"

At this they laughed heartily.

"Please don't be angry with me," continued the prince. "I know very well that I have seen less of life than other people, and have less knowledge of it. I must appear to speak strangely sometimes..."

He said the last words nervously.

"You say you have been happy, and that proves you have lived, not less, but more than other people. Why make all these excuses?" interrupted Aglaya in a mocking tone of voice. "Besides, you need not mind about lecturing us; you have nothing to boast of. With your quietism, one could live happily for a hundred years at least. One might show you the execution of a felon, or show you one's little finger. You could draw a moral from either, and be quite satisfied. That sort of existence is easy enough."

"I can't understand why you always fly into a temper," said Mrs. Epanchin, who had been listening to the conversation and examining the faces of the speakers in turn. "I do not understand what you mean. What has your little finger to do with it? The prince talks well, though he is not amusing. He began all right, but now he seems sad."

"Never mind, mamma! Prince, I wish you had seen an execution," said Aglaya. "I should like to ask you a question about that, if you had."

"I have seen an execution," said the prince.

"You have!" cried Aglaya. "I might have guessed it. That's a fitting crown to the rest of the story. If you have seen an execution, how can you say you lived happily all the while?"

"But is there capital punishment where you were?" asked Adelaida.

"I saw it at Lyons. Schneider took us there, and as soon as we arrived we came in for that."

"Well, and did you like it very much? Was it very edifying and instructive?" asked Aglaya.

"No, I didn't like it at all, and was ill after seeing it; but I confess I stared as though my eyes were fixed to the sight. I could not tear them away."

"I, too, should have been unable to tear my eyes away," said Aglaya.

"They do not at all approve of women going to see an execution there. The women who do go are condemned for it afterwards in the newspapers."

"That is, by contending that it is not a sight for women they admit that it is a sight for men. I congratulate them on the deduction. I suppose you quite agree with them, prince?"

"Tell us about the execution," put in Adelaida.

"I would much rather not, just now," said the prince, a little disturbed and frowning slightly.

"You don't seem to want to tell us," said Aglaya, with a mocking air.

"No,—the thing is, I was telling all about the execution a little while ago, and—"

"Whom did you tell about it?"

"The man-servant, while I was waiting to see the general."

"Our man-servant?" exclaimed several voices at once.

"Yes, the one who waits in the entrance hall, a greyish, red-faced man—"

"The prince is clearly a democrat," remarked Aglaya.

"Well, if you could tell Aleksey about it, surely you can tell us too."

"I do so want to hear about it," repeated Adelaida.

"Just now, I confess," began the prince, with more animation, "when you asked me for a subject for a picture, I confess I had serious thoughts of giving you one. I thought of asking you to draw the face of a criminal, one minute before the fall of the guillotine, while the wretched man is still standing on the scaffold, preparatory to placing his neck on the block."

"What, his face? only his face?" asked Adelaida. "That would be a strange subject indeed. And what sort of a picture would that make?"

"Oh, why not?" the prince insisted, with some warmth. "When I was in Basle I saw a picture very much in that style—I should like to tell you about it; I will some time or other; it struck me very forcibly."

"Oh, you shall tell us about the Basle picture another time; now we must have all about the execution," said Adelaida. "Tell us about that face as; it appeared to your imagination-how should it be drawn?—just the face alone, do you mean?"

"It was just a minute before the execution," began the prince, readily, carried away by the recollection and evidently forgetting everything else in a moment; "just at the instant when he stepped off the ladder on to the scaffold. He happened to look in my direction: I saw his eyes and understood all, at once—but how am I to describe it? I do so wish you or somebody else could draw it, you, if possible. I thought at the time what a picture it would make. You must imagine all that went before, of course, all—all. He had lived in the prison for some time and had not expected that the execution would take place for at least a week yet—he had counted on all the formalities and so on taking time; but it so happened that his papers had been got ready quickly. At five o'clock in the morning he was asleep—it was October, and at five in the morning it was cold and dark. The governor of the prison comes in on tip-toe and touches the sleeping man's shoulder gently. He starts up. 'What is it?' he says. 'The execution is fixed for ten o'clock.' He was only just awake, and would not believe at first, but began to argue that his papers would not be out for a week, and so on. When he was wide awake and realized the truth, he became very silent and argued no more—so they say; but after a bit he said: 'It comes very hard on one so suddenly' and then he was silent again and said nothing.

"The three or four hours went by, of course, in necessary preparations—the priest, breakfast, (coffee, meat, and some wine they gave him; doesn't it seem ridiculous?) And yet I believe these people give them a good breakfast out of pure kindness of heart, and believe that they are doing a good action. Then he is dressed, and then begins the procession through the town to the scaffold. I think he, too, must feel that he has an age to live still while they cart him along. Probably he thought, on the way, 'Oh, I have a long, long time yet. Three streets of life yet! When we've passed this street there'll be that other one; and then that one where the baker's shop is on the right; and when shall we get there? It's ages, ages!' Around him are crowds shouting, yelling—ten thousand faces, twenty thousand eyes. All this has to be endured, and especially the thought: 'Here are ten thousand men, and not one of them is going to be executed, and yet I am to die.' Well, all that is preparatory.

"At the scaffold there is a ladder, and just there he burst into tears—and this was a strong man, and a terribly wicked one, they say! There was a priest with him the whole time, talking; even in the cart as they drove along, he talked and talked. Probably the other heard nothing; he would begin to listen now and then, and at the third word or so he had forgotten all about it.

"At last he began to mount the steps; his legs were tied, so that he had to take very small steps. The priest, who seemed to be a wise man, had stopped talking now, and only held the cross for the wretched fellow to kiss. At the foot of the ladder he had been pale enough; but when he set foot on the scaffold at the top, his face suddenly became the colour of paper, positively like white notepaper. His legs must have become suddenly feeble and helpless, and he felt a choking in his throat—you know the sudden feeling one has in moments of terrible fear, when one does not lose one's wits, but is absolutely powerless to move? If some dreadful thing were suddenly to happen; if a house were just about to fall on one;—don't you know how one would long to sit down and shut one's eyes and wait, and wait? Well, when this terrible feeling came over him, the priest quickly pressed the cross to his lips, without a word—a little silver cross it was—and he kept on pressing it to the man's lips every second. And whenever the cross touched his lips, the eyes would open for a moment, and the legs moved once, and he kissed the cross greedily, hurriedly—just as though he were anxious to catch hold of something in case of its being useful to him afterwards, though he could hardly have had any connected religious thoughts at the time. And so up to the very block.

"How strange that criminals seldom swoon at such a moment! On the contrary, the brain is especially active, and works incessantly—probably hard, hard, hard—like an engine at full pressure. I imagine that various thoughts must beat loud and fast through his head—all unfinished ones, and strange, funny thoughts, very likely!—like this, for instance: 'That man is looking at me, and he has a wart on his forehead! and the executioner has burst one of his buttons, and the lowest one is all rusty!' And meanwhile he notices and remembers everything. There is one point that cannot be forgotten, round which everything else dances and turns about; and because of this point he cannot faint, and this lasts until the very final quarter of a second, when the wretched neck is on the block and the victim listens and waits and *knows*—that's the point, he *knows* that he is just *now* about to die, and listens for the rasp of the iron over his head. If I lay there, I should certainly listen for that grating sound, and hear it, too! There would probably be but the tenth part of an instant left to hear it in, but one would certainly hear it. And imagine, some people declare that when the head flies off it is *conscious* of having flown off! Just imagine what a thing to realize! Fancy if consciousness were to last for even five seconds!

"Draw the scaffold so that only the top step of the ladder comes in clearly. The criminal must be just stepping on to it, his face as white as note-paper. The priest is holding the cross to his blue lips, and the criminal kisses it, and knows and sees and understands everything. The cross and the head—there's your picture; the priest and the executioner, with his two assistants, and a few heads and eyes below. Those might come in as subordinate accessories—a sort of mist. There's a picture for you." The prince paused, and looked around.

"Certainly that isn't much like quietism," murmured Alexandra, half to herself.

"Now tell us about your love affairs," said Adelaida, after a moment's pause.

The prince gazed at her in amazement.

"You know," Adelaida continued, "you owe us a description of the Basle picture; but first I wish to hear how you fell in love. Don't deny the fact, for you did, of course. Besides, you stop philosophizing when you are telling about anything."

"Why are you ashamed of your stories the moment after you have told them?" asked Aglaya, suddenly.

"How silly you are!" said Mrs. Epanchin, looking indignantly towards the last speaker.

"Yes, that wasn't a clever remark," said Alexandra.

"Don't listen to her, prince," said Mrs. Epanchin; "she says that sort of thing out of mischief. Don't think anything of their nonsense, it means nothing. They love to chaff, but they like you. I can see it in their faces—I know their faces."

"I know their faces, too," said the prince, with a peculiar stress on the words.

"How so?" asked Adelaida, with curiosity.

"What do *you* know about our faces?" exclaimed the other two, in chorus.

But the prince was silent and serious. All awaited his reply.

"I'll tell you afterwards," he said quietly.

"Ah, you want to arouse our curiosity!" said Aglaya. "And how terribly solemn you are about it!"

"Very well," interrupted Adelaida, "then if you can read faces so well, you *must* have been in love. Come now; I've guessed—let's have the secret!"

"I have not been in love," said the prince, as quietly and seriously as before. "I have been happy in another way."

"How, how?"

"Well, I'll tell you," said the prince, apparently in a deep reverie.

VI.

"Here you all are," began the prince, "settling yourselves down to listen to me with so much curiosity, that if I do not satisfy you you will probably be angry with me. No, no! I'm only joking!" he added, hastily, with a smile.

"Well, then—they were all children there, and I was always among children and only with children. They were the children of the village in which I lived, and they went to the school there—all of them. I did not teach them, oh no; there was a master for that, one Jules Thibaut. I may have taught them some things, but I was among them just as an outsider, and I passed all four years of my life there among them. I wished for nothing better; I used to tell them everything and hid nothing from them. Their fathers and relations were very angry with me, because the children could do nothing without me at last, and used to throng after me at all times. The schoolmaster was my greatest enemy in the end! I had many enemies, and all because of the children. Even Schneider reproached me. What were they afraid of? One can tell a child everything, anything. I have often been struck by the fact that parents know their children so little. They should not conceal so much from them. How well even little children understand that their parents conceal things from them, because they consider them too young to understand! Children are capable of giving advice in the most important matters. How can one deceive these dear little birds, when they look at one so sweetly and confidingly? I call them birds because there is nothing in the world better than birds!

"However, most of the people were angry with me about one and the same thing; but Thibaut simply was jealous of me. At first he had wagged his head and wondered how it was that the children understood what I told them so well, and could not learn from him; and he laughed like anything when I replied that neither he nor I could teach them very much, but that *they* might teach us a good deal.

"How he could hate me and tell scandalous stories about me, living among children as he did, is what I cannot understand. Children soothe and heal the wounded heart. I remember there was one poor fellow at our professor's who was being treated for madness, and you have no idea what those children did for him, eventually. I don't think he was mad, but only terribly unhappy. But I'll tell you all about him another day. Now I must get on with this story.

"The children did not love me at first; I was such a sickly, awkward kind of a fellow then—and I know I am ugly. Besides, I was a foreigner. The children used to laugh at me, at first; and they even went so far as to throw stones at me, when they saw me kiss Marie. I only kissed her once in my life—no, no, don't laugh!" The prince hastened to suppress the smiles of his audience at this point. "It was not a matter of *love* at all! If only you knew what a miserable creature she was, you would have pitied her, just as I did. She belonged to our village. Her mother was an old, old woman, and they used to sell string and thread, and soap and tobacco, out of the window of their little house, and lived on the pittance they gained by this trade. The old woman was ill and very old, and could hardly move. Marie was her daughter, a girl of twenty, weak and thin and consumptive; but still she did heavy work at the houses around, day by day. Well, one fine day a commercial traveller betrayed her and carried her off; and a week later he deserted her. She came home dirty, draggled, and shoeless; she had walked for a whole week without shoes; she had slept in the fields, and caught a terrible cold; her feet were swollen and sore, and her hands torn and scratched all over. She never had been pretty even before; but her eyes were quiet, innocent, kind eyes.

"She was very quiet always—and I remember once, when she had suddenly begun singing at her work, everyone said, 'Marie tried to sing today!' and she got so chaffed that she was silent for ever after. She had been treated kindly in the place before; but when she came back now—ill and shunned and miserable—not one of them all had the slightest sympathy for her. Cruel people! Oh, what hazy understandings they have on such matters! Her mother was the first to show the way. She received her wrathfully, unkindly, and with contempt. 'You have disgraced me,' she said. She was the first to cast her into ignominy; but when they all heard that Marie had returned to the village, they ran out to see her and crowded into the little cottage—old men, children, women, girls—such a hurrying, stamping, greedy crowd. Marie was lying on the floor at the old woman's feet, hungry, torn, draggled, crying, miserable.

"When everyone crowded into the room she hid her face in her dishevelled hair and lay cowering on the floor. Everyone looked at her as though she were a piece of dirt off the road. The old men scolded and condemned, and the young ones laughed at her. The women condemned her too, and looked at her contemptuously, just as though she were some loathsome insect.

"Her mother allowed all this to go on, and nodded her head and encouraged them. The old woman was very ill at that time, and knew she was dying (she really did die a couple of months later), and though she felt the end approaching she never thought of forgiving her daughter, to the very day of her death. She would not even speak to her. She made her sleep on straw in a shed, and hardly gave her food enough to support life.

"Marie was very gentle to her mother, and nursed her, and did everything for her; but the old woman accepted all her services without a word and never showed her the slightest kindness. Marie bore all this; and I could see when I got to know her that she thought it quite right and fitting, considering herself the lowest and meanest of creatures.

"When the old woman took to her bed finally, the other old women in the village sat with her by turns, as the custom is there; and then Marie was quite driven out of the house. They gave her no food at all, and she could not get any work in the village; none would employ her. The men seemed to consider her no longer a woman, they said such dreadful things to her. Sometimes on Sundays, if they were drunk enough, they used to throw her a penny or two, into the mud, and Marie would silently pick up the money. She had began to spit blood at that time.

"At last her rags became so tattered and torn that she was ashamed of appearing in the village any longer. The children used to pelt her with mud; so she begged to be taken on as assistant cowherd, but the cowherd would not have her. Then she took to helping him without leave; and he saw how valuable her assistance was to him, and did not drive her away again; on the contrary, he occasionally gave her the remnants of his dinner, bread and cheese. He considered that he was being very kind. When the mother died, the village parson was not ashamed to hold Marie up to public derision and shame. Marie was standing at the coffin's head, in all her rags, crying.

"A crowd of people had collected to see how she would cry. The parson, a young fellow ambitious of becoming a great preacher, began his sermon and pointed to Marie. 'There,' he said, 'there is the cause of the death of this venerable woman'—(which was a lie, because she had been ill for at least two years)—'there she stands before you, and dares not lift her eyes from the ground, because she knows that the finger of God is upon her. Look at her tatters and rags—the badge of those who lose their virtue. Who is she? her daughter!' and so on to the end.

"And just fancy, this infamy pleased them, all of them, nearly. Only the children had altered—for then they were all on my side and had learned to love Marie.

"This is how it was: I had wished to do something for Marie; I longed to give her some money, but I never had a farthing while I was there. But I had a little diamond pin, and this I sold to a travelling pedlar; he gave me eight francs for it—it was worth at least forty.

"I long sought to meet Marie alone; and at last I did meet her, on the hillside beyond the village. I gave her the eight francs and asked her to take care of the money because I could get no more; and then I kissed her and said that she was not to suppose I kissed her with any evil motives or because I was in love with her, for that I did so solely out of pity for her, and because from the first I had not accounted her as guilty so much as unfortunate. I longed to console and encourage her somehow, and to assure her that she was not the low, base thing which she and others strove to make out; but I don't think she understood me. She stood before me, dreadfully ashamed of herself, and with downcast eyes; and when I had finished she kissed my hand. I would have kissed hers, but she drew it away. Just at this moment the whole troop of children saw us. (I found out afterwards that they had long kept a watch upon me.) They all began whistling and clapping their hands, and laughing at us. Marie ran away at once; and when I tried to talk to them, they threw stones at me. All the village heard of it the same day, and Marie's position became worse than ever. The children would not let her pass now in the streets, but annoyed her and threw dirt at her more than before. They used to run after her—she racing away with her poor feeble lungs panting and gasping, and they pelting her and shouting abuse at her.

"Once I had to interfere by force; and after that I took to speaking to them every day and whenever I could. Occasionally they stopped and listened; but they teased Marie all the same.

"I told them how unhappy Marie was, and after a while they stopped their abuse of her, and let her go by silently. Little by little we got into the way of conversing together, the children and I. I concealed nothing from them, I told them all. They listened very attentively and soon began to be sorry for Marie. At last some of them took to saying 'Good-morning' to her, kindly, when they met her. It is the custom there to salute anyone you meet with 'Good-morning' whether acquainted or not. I can imagine how astonished Marie was at these first greetings from the children.

"Once two little girls got hold of some food and took it to her, and came back and told me. They said she had burst into tears, and that they loved her very much now. Very soon after that they all became fond of Marie, and at the same time they began to develop the greatest affection for myself. They often came to me and begged me to tell them stories. I think I must have told stories well, for they did so love to hear them. At last I took to reading up interesting things on purpose to pass them on to the little ones, and this went on for all the rest of my time there, three years. Later, when everyone—even Schneider—was angry with me for hiding nothing from the children, I pointed out how foolish it was, for they always knew things, only they learnt them in a way that soiled their minds but not so from me. One has only to remember one's own childhood to admit the truth of this. But nobody was convinced... It was two weeks before her mother died that I had kissed Marie; and when the clergyman preached that sermon the children were all on my side.

"When I told them what a shame it was of the parson to talk as he had done, and explained my reason, they were so angry that some of them went and broke his windows with stones. Of course I stopped them, for that was not right, but all the village heard of it, and how I caught it for spoiling the children! Everyone discovered now that the little ones had taken to being fond of Marie, and their parents were terribly alarmed; but Marie was so happy. The children were forbidden to meet her; but they used to run out of the village to the herd and take her food and things; and sometimes just ran off there and kissed her, and said, '*Je vous aime, Marie!*' and then trotted back again. They imagined that I was in love with Marie, and this was the only point on which I did not undeceive them, for they got such enjoyment out of it. And what delicacy and tenderness they showed!

"In the evening I used to walk to the waterfall. There was a spot there which was quite closed in and hidden from view by large trees; and to this spot the children used to come to me. They could not bear that their dear Leon should love a poor girl without shoes to her feet and dressed all in rags and tatters. So, would you believe it, they actually clubbed together, somehow, and bought her shoes and stockings, and some linen, and even a dress! I can't understand how they managed it, but they did it, all together. When I asked them about it they only laughed and shouted, and the little girls clapped their hands and kissed me. I sometimes went to see Marie secretly, too. She had become very ill, and could hardly walk. She still went with the herd, but could not help the herdsman any longer. She used to sit on a stone near, and wait there almost motionless all day, till the herd went home. Her consumption was so advanced, and she was so weak, that she used to sit with closed eyes, breathing heavily. Her face was as thin as a skeleton's, and sweat used to stand on her white brow in large drops. I always found her sitting just like that. I used to come up quietly to look at her; but Marie would hear me, open her eyes, and tremble violently as she kissed my hands. I did not take my hand away because it made her happy to have it, and so she would sit and cry quietly. Sometimes she tried to speak; but it was very difficult to understand her. She was almost like a madwoman, with excitement and ecstasy, whenever I came. Occasionally the children came with me; when they did so, they would stand some way off and keep guard over us, so as to tell me if anybody came near. This was a great pleasure to them.

"When we left her, Marie used to relapse at once into her old condition, and sit with closed eyes and motionless limbs. One day she could not go out at all, and remained at home all alone in the empty hut; but the children very soon became aware of the fact, and nearly all of them visited her that day as she lay alone and helpless in her miserable bed.

"For two days the children looked after her, and then, when the village people got to know that Marie was really dying, some of the old women came and took it in turns to sit by her and look after her a bit. I think they began to be a little sorry for her in the village at last; at all events they did not interfere with the children any more, on her account.

"Marie lay in a state of uncomfortable delirium the whole while; she coughed dreadfully. The old women would not let the children stay in the room; but they all collected outside the window each morning, if only for a moment, and shouted '*Bon jour, notre bonne Marie!*' and Marie no sooner caught sight of, or heard them, and she became quite animated at once, and, in spite of the old women, would try to sit up and nod her head and smile at them, and thank them. The little ones used to bring her nice things and sweets to eat, but she could hardly touch anything. Thanks to them, I assure you, the girl died almost perfectly happy. She almost forgot her misery, and seemed to accept their love as a sort of symbol of pardon for her offence, though she never ceased to consider herself a dreadful sinner. They used to flutter at her window just like little birds, calling out: '*Nous t'aimons, Marie!*'

"She died very soon; I had thought she would live much longer. The day before her death I went to see her for the last time, just before sunset. I think she recognized me, for she pressed my hand.

"Next morning they came and told me that Marie was dead. The children could not be restrained now; they went and covered her coffin with flowers, and put a wreath of lovely blossoms on her head. The pastor did not throw any more shameful words at the poor dead woman; but there were very few people at the funeral. However, when it came to carrying the coffin, all the children rushed up, to carry it themselves. Of course they could not do it alone, but they insisted on helping, and walked alongside and behind, crying.

"They have planted roses all round her grave, and every year they look alter the flowers and make Marie's resting-place as beautiful as they can. I was in ill odour after all this with the parents of the children, and especially with the parson and schoolmaster. Schneider was obliged to promise that I should not meet them and talk to them; but we conversed from a distance by signs, and they used to write me sweet little notes. Afterwards I came closer than ever to those little souls, but even then it was very dear to me, to have them so fond of me.

"Schneider said that I did the children great harm by my pernicious 'system'; what nonsense that was! And what did he mean by my system? He said afterwards that he believed I was a child myself—just before I came away. 'You have the form and face of an adult' he said, 'but as regards soul, and character, and perhaps even intelligence, you are a child in the completest sense of the word, and always will be, if you live to be sixty.' I laughed very much, for of course that is nonsense. But it is a fact that I do not care to be among grown-up people and much prefer the society of children. However kind people may be to me, I never feel quite at home with them, and am always glad to get back to my little companions. Now my companions have always been children, not because I was a child myself once, but because young things attract me. On one of the first days of my stay in Switzerland, I was strolling about alone and miserable, when I came upon the children rushing noisily out of school, with their slates and bags, and books, their games, their laughter and shouts—and my soul went out to them. I stopped and laughed happily as I watched their little feet moving so quickly. Girls and boys, laughing and crying; for as they went home many of them found time to fight and make peace, to weep and play. I forgot my troubles in looking at them. And then, all those three years, I tried to understand why men should be for ever tormenting themselves. I lived the life of a child there, and thought I should never leave the little village; indeed, I was far from thinking that I should ever return to Russia. But at last I recognized the fact that Schneider could not keep me any longer. And then something so important happened, that Schneider himself urged me to depart. I am going to see now if can get good advice about it. Perhaps my lot in life will be changed; but that is not the principal thing. The principal thing is the entire change that has already come over me. I left many things behind me—too many. They have gone. On the journey I said to myself, 'I am going into the world of men. I don't know much, perhaps, but a new life has begun for me.' I made up my mind to be honest, and steadfast in accomplishing my task. Perhaps I shall meet with troubles and many disappointments, but I have made up my mind to be polite and sincere to everyone; more cannot be asked of me. People may consider me a child if they like. I am often called an idiot, and at one time I certainly was so ill that I was nearly as bad as an idiot; but I am not an idiot now. How can I possibly be so when I know myself that I am considered one?

"When I received a letter from those dear little souls, while passing through Berlin, I only then realized how much I loved them. It was very, very painful, getting that first little letter. How melancholy they had been when they saw me off! For a month before, they had been talking of my departure and sorrowing over it; and at the waterfall, of an evening, when we parted for the night, they would hug me so tight and kiss me so warmly, far more so than before. And every now and then they would turn up one by one when I was alone, just to give me a kiss and a hug, to show their love for me. The whole flock went with me to the station, which was about a mile from the village, and every now and then one of them would stop to throw his arms round me, and all the little girls had tears in their voices, though they tried hard not to cry. As the train steamed out of the station, I saw them all standing on the platform waving to me and crying 'Hurrah!' till they were lost in the distance.

"I assure you, when I came in here just now and saw your kind faces (I can read faces well) my heart felt light for the first time since that moment of parting. I think I must be one of those who are born to be in luck, for one does not often meet with people whom one feels he can love from the first sight of their faces; and yet, no sooner do I step out of the railway carriage than I happen upon you!

"I know it is more or less a shamefaced thing to speak of one's feelings before others; and yet here am I talking like this to you, and am not a bit ashamed or shy. I am an unsociable sort of fellow and shall very likely not come to see you again for some time; but don't think the worse of me for that. It is not that I do not value your society; and you must never suppose that I have taken offence at anything.

"You asked me about your faces, and what I could read in them; I will tell you with the greatest pleasure. You, Adelaida Ivanovna, have a very happy face; it is the most sympathetic of the three. Not to speak of your natural beauty, one can look at your face and say to one's self, 'She has the face of a kind sister.' You are simple and merry, but you can see into another's heart very quickly. That's what I read in your face.

"You too, Alexandra Ivanovna, have a very lovely face; but I think you may have some secret sorrow. Your heart is undoubtedly a kind, good one, but you are not merry. There is a certain suspicion of 'shadow' in your face, like in that of Holbein's Madonna in Dresden. So much for your face. Have I guessed right?

"As for your face, Lizabetha Prokofievna, I not only think, but am perfectly *sure*, that you are an absolute child—in all, in all, mind, both good and bad—and in spite of your years. Don't be angry with me for saying so; you know what my feelings for children are. And do not suppose that I am so candid out of pure simplicity of soul. Oh dear no, it is by no means the case! Perhaps I have my own very profound object in view."

VII.

When the prince ceased speaking all were gazing merrily at him—even Aglaya; but Lizabetha Prokofievna looked the jolliest of all.

"Well!" she cried, "we *have* 'put him through his paces,' with a vengeance! My dears, you imagined, I believe, that you were about to patronize this young gentleman, like some poor *protégé* picked up somewhere, and taken under your magnificent protection. What fools we were, and what a specially big fool is your father! Well done, prince! I assure you the general actually asked me to put you through your paces, and examine you. As to what you said about my face, you are absolutely correct in your judgment. I am a child, and know it. I knew it long before you said so; you have expressed my own thoughts. I think your nature and mine must be extremely alike, and I am very glad of it. We are like two drops of water, only you are a man and I a woman, and I've not been to Switzerland, and that is all the difference between us."

"Don't be in a hurry, mother; the prince says that he has some motive behind his simplicity," cried Aglaya.

"Yes, yes, so he does," laughed the others.

"Oh, don't you begin bantering him," said mamma. "He is probably a good deal cleverer than all three of you girls put together. We shall see. Only you haven't told us anything about Aglaya yet, prince; and Aglaya and I are both waiting to hear."

"I cannot say anything at present. I'll tell you afterwards."

"Why? Her face is clear enough, isn't it?"

"Oh yes, of course. You are very beautiful, Aglaya Ivanovna, so beautiful that one is afraid to look at you."

"Is that all? What about her character?" persisted Mrs. Epanchin.

"It is difficult to judge when such beauty is concerned. I have not prepared my judgment. Beauty is a riddle."

"That means that you have set Aglaya a riddle!" said Adelaida. "Guess it, Aglaya! But she's pretty, prince, isn't she?"

"Most wonderfully so," said the latter, warmly, gazing at Aglaya with admiration. "Almost as lovely as Nastasia Philipovna, but quite a different type."

All present exchanged looks of surprise.

"As lovely as *who?*" said Mrs. Epanchin. "As *Nastasia Philipovna?* Where have you seen Nastasia Philipovna? What Nastasia Philipovna?"

"Gavrila Ardalionovitch showed the general her portrait just now."

"How so? Did he bring the portrait for my husband?"

"Only to show it. Nastasia Philipovna gave it to Gavrila Ardalionovitch today, and the latter brought it here to show to the general."

"I must see it!" cried Mrs. Epanchin. "Where is the portrait? If she gave it to him, he must have it; and he is still in the study. He never leaves before four o'clock on Wednesdays. Send for Gavrila Ardalionovitch at once. No, I don't long to see him so much. Look here, dear prince, *be* so kind, will you? Just step to the study and fetch this portrait! Say we want to look at it. Please do this for me, will you?"

"He is a nice fellow, but a little too simple," said Adelaida, as the prince left the room.

"He is, indeed," said Alexandra; "almost laughably so at times."

Neither one nor the other seemed to give expression to her full thoughts.

"He got out of it very neatly about our faces, though," said Aglaya. "He flattered us all round, even mamma."

"Nonsense!" cried the latter. "He did not flatter me. It was I who found his appreciation flattering. I think you are a great deal more foolish than he is. He is simple, of course, but also very knowing. Just like myself."

"How stupid of me to speak of the portrait," thought the prince as he entered the study, with a feeling of guilt at his heart, "and yet, perhaps I was right after all." He had an idea, unformed as yet, but a strange idea.

Gavrila Ardalionovitch was still sitting in the study, buried in a mass of papers. He looked as though he did not take his salary from the public company, whose servant he was, for a sinecure.

He grew very wroth and confused when the prince asked for the portrait, and explained how it came about that he had spoken of it.

"Oh, curse it all," he said; "what on earth must you go blabbing for? You know nothing about the thing, and yet—idiot!" he added, muttering the last word to himself in irrepressible rage.

"I am very sorry; I was not thinking at the time. I merely said that Aglaya was almost as beautiful as Nastasia Philipovna."

Gania asked for further details; and the prince once more repeated the conversation. Gania looked at him with ironical contempt the while.

"Nastasia Philipovna," he began, and there paused; he was clearly much agitated and annoyed. The prince reminded him of the portrait.

"Listen, prince," said Gania, as though an idea had just struck him, "I wish to ask you a great favour, and yet I really don't know—"

He paused again, he was trying to make up his mind to something, and was turning the matter over. The prince waited quietly. Once more Gania fixed him with intent and questioning eyes.

"Prince," he began again, "they are rather angry with me, in there, owing to a circumstance which I need not explain, so that I do not care to go in at present without an invitation. I particularly wish to speak to Aglaya, but I have written a few words in case I shall not have the chance of seeing her" (here the prince observed a small note in his hand), "and I do not know how to get my communication to her. Don't you think you could undertake to give it to her at once, but only to her, mind, and so that no one else should see you give it? It isn't much of a secret, but still—Well, will you do it?"

"I don't quite like it," replied the prince.

"Oh, but it is absolutely necessary for me," Gania entreated. "Believe me, if it were not so, I would not ask you; how else am I to get it to her? It is most important, dreadfully important!"

Gania was evidently much alarmed at the idea that the prince would not consent to take his note, and he looked at him now with an expression of absolute entreaty.

"Well, I will take it then."

"But mind, nobody is to see!" cried the delighted Gania "And of course I may rely on your word of honour, eh?"

"I won't show it to anyone," said the prince.

"The letter is not sealed—" continued Gania, and paused in confusion.

"Oh, I won't read it," said the prince, quite simply.

He took up the portrait, and went out of the room.

Gania, left alone, clutched his head with his hands.

"One word from her," he said, "one word from her, and I may yet be free."

He could not settle himself to his papers again, for agitation and excitement, but began walking up and down the room from corner to corner.

The prince walked along, musing. He did not like his commission, and disliked the idea of Gania sending a note to Aglaya at all; but when he was two rooms distant from the drawing-room, where they all were, he stopped as though recalling something; went to the window, nearer the light, and began to examine the portrait in his hand.

He longed to solve the mystery of something in the face Nastasia Philipovna, something which had struck him as he looked at the portrait for the first time; the impression had not left him. It was partly the fact of her marvellous beauty that struck him, and partly something else. There was a suggestion of immense pride and disdain in the face almost of hatred, and at the same time something confiding and very full of simplicity. The contrast aroused a deep sympathy in his heart as he looked at the lovely face. The blinding loveliness of it was almost intolerable, this pale thin face with its flaming eyes; it was a strange beauty.

The prince gazed at it for a minute or two, then glanced around him, and hurriedly raised the portrait to his lips. When, a minute after, he reached the drawing-room door, his face was quite composed. But just as he reached the door he met Aglaya coming out alone.

"Gavrila Ardalionovitch begged me to give you this," he said, handing her the note.

Aglaya stopped, took the letter, and gazed strangely into the prince's eyes. There was no confusion in her face; a little surprise, perhaps, but that was all. By her look she seemed merely to challenge the prince to an explanation as to how he and Gania happened to be connected in this matter. But her expression was perfectly cool and quiet, and even condescending.

So they stood for a moment or two, confronting one another. At length a faint smile passed over her face, and she passed by him without a word.

Mrs. Epanchin examined the portrait of Nastasia Philipovna for some little while, holding it critically at arm's length.

"Yes, she is pretty," she said at last, "even very pretty. I have seen her twice, but only at a distance. So you admire this kind of beauty, do you?" she asked the prince, suddenly.

"Yes, I do—this kind."

"Do you mean especially this kind?"

"Yes, especially this kind."

"Why?"

"There is much suffering in this face," murmured the prince, more as though talking to himself than answering the question.

"I think you are wandering a little, prince," Mrs. Epanchin decided, after a lengthened survey of his face; and she tossed the portrait on to the table, haughtily.

Alexandra took it, and Adelaida came up, and both the girls examined the photograph. Just then Aglaya entered the room.

"What a power!" cried Adelaida suddenly, as she earnestly examined the portrait over her sister's shoulder.

"Whom? What power?" asked her mother, crossly.

"Such beauty is real power," said Adelaida. "With such beauty as that one might overthrow the world." She returned to her easel thoughtfully.

Aglaya merely glanced at the portrait—frowned, and put out her underlip; then went and sat down on the sofa with folded hands. Mrs. Epanchin rang the bell.

"Ask Gavrila Ardalionovitch to step this way," said she to the man who answered.

"Mamma!" cried Alexandra, significantly.

"I shall just say two words to him, that's all," said her mother, silencing all objection by her manner; she was evidently seriously put out. "You see, prince, it is all secrets with us, just now—all secrets. It seems to be the etiquette of the house, for some reason or other. Stupid nonsense, and in a matter which ought to be approached with all candour and open-heartedness. There is a marriage being talked of, and I don't like this marriage—"

"Mamma, what are you saying?" said Alexandra again, hurriedly.

"Well, what, my dear girl? As if you can possibly like it yourself? The heart is the great thing, and the rest is all rubbish—though one must have sense as well. Perhaps sense is really the great thing. Don't smile like that, Aglaya. I don't contradict myself. A fool with a heart and no brains is just as unhappy as a fool with brains and no heart. I am one and you are the other, and therefore both of us suffer, both of us are unhappy."

"Why are you so unhappy, mother?" asked Adelaida, who alone of all the company seemed to have preserved her good temper and spirits up to now.

"In the first place, because of my carefully brought-up daughters," said Mrs. Epanchin, cuttingly; "and as that is the best reason I can give you we need not bother about any other at present. Enough of words, now! We shall see how both of you (I don't count Aglaya) will manage your business, and whether you, most revered Alexandra Ivanovna, will be happy with your fine mate."

"Ah!" she added, as Gania suddenly entered the room, "here's another marrying subject. How do you do?" she continued, in response to Gania's bow; but she did not invite him to sit down. "You are going to be married?"

"Married? how—what marriage?" murmured Gania, overwhelmed with confusion.

"Are you about to take a wife? I ask,—if you prefer that expression."

"No, no I—I—no!" said Gania, bringing out his lie with a tell-tale blush of shame. He glanced keenly at Aglaya, who was sitting some way off, and dropped his eyes immediately.

Aglaya gazed coldly, intently, and composedly at him, without taking her eyes off his face, and watched his confusion.

"No? You say no, do you?" continued the pitiless Mrs. General. "Very well, I shall remember that you told me this Wednesday morning, in answer to my question, that you are not going to be married. What day is it, Wednesday, isn't it?"

"Yes, I think so!" said Adelaida.

"You never know the day of the week; what's the day of the month?"

"Twenty-seventh!" said Gania.

"Twenty-seventh; very well. Good-bye now; you have a good deal to do, I'm sure, and I must dress and go out. Take your portrait. Give my respects to your unfortunate mother, Nina Alexandrovna. *Au revoir*, dear prince, come in and see us often, do; and I shall tell old Princess Bielokonski about you. I shall go and see her on purpose. And listen, my dear boy, I feel sure that God has sent you to Petersburg from Switzerland on purpose for me. Maybe you will have other things to do, besides, but you are sent chiefly for my sake, I feel sure of it. God sent you to me! *Au revoir!* Alexandra, come with me, my dear."

Mrs. Epanchin left the room.

Gania—confused, annoyed, furious—took up his portrait, and turned to the prince with a nasty smile on his face.

"Prince," he said, "I am just going home. If you have not changed your mind as to living with us, perhaps you would like to come with me. You don't know the address, I believe?"

"Wait a minute, prince," said Aglaya, suddenly rising from her seat, "do write something in my album first, will you? Father says you are a most talented caligraphist; I'll bring you my book in a minute." She left the room.

"Well, *au revoir*, prince," said Adelaida, "I must be going too." She pressed the prince's hand warmly, and gave him a friendly smile as she left the room. She did not so much as look at Gania.

"This is your doing, prince," said Gania, turning on the latter so soon as the others were all out of the room. "This is your doing, sir! *You* have been telling them that I am going to be married!" He said this in a hurried whisper, his eyes flashing with rage and his face ablaze. "You shameless tattler!"

"I assure you, you are under a delusion," said the prince, calmly and politely. "I did not even know that you were to be married."

"You heard me talking about it, the general and me. You heard me say that everything was to be settled today at Nastasia Philipovna's, and you went and blurted it out here. You lie if you deny it. Who else could have told them? Devil take it, sir, who could have told them except yourself? Didn't the old woman as good as hint as much to me?"

"If she hinted to you who told her you must know best, of course; but I never said a word about it."

"Did you give my note? Is there an answer?" interrupted Gania, impatiently.

But at this moment Aglaya came back, and the prince had no time to reply.

"There, prince," said she, "there's my album. Now choose a page and write me something, will you? There's a pen, a new one; do you mind a steel one? I have heard that you caligraphists don't like steel pens."

Conversing with the prince, Aglaya did not even seem to notice that Gania was in the room. But while the prince was getting his pen ready, finding a page, and making his preparations to write, Gania came up to the fireplace where Aglaya was standing, to the right of the prince, and in trembling, broken accents said, almost in her ear:

"One word, just one word from you, and I'm saved."

The prince turned sharply round and looked at both of them. Gania's face was full of real despair; he seemed to have said the words almost unconsciously and on the impulse of the moment.

Aglaya gazed at him for some seconds with precisely the same composure and calm astonishment as she had shown a little while before, when the prince handed her the note, and it appeared that this calm surprise and seemingly absolute incomprehension of what was said to her, were more terribly overwhelming to Gania than even the most plainly expressed disdain would have been.

"What shall I write?" asked the prince.

"I'll dictate to you," said Aglaya, coming up to the table. "Now then, are you ready? Write, 'I never condescend to bargain!' Now put your name and the date. Let me see it."

The prince handed her the album.

"Capital! How beautifully you have written it! Thanks so much. *Au revoir*, prince. Wait a minute,"; she added, "I want to give you something for a keepsake. Come with me this way, will you?"

The prince followed her. Arrived at the dining-room, she stopped.

"Read this," she said, handing him Gania's note.

The prince took it from her hand, but gazed at her in bewilderment.

"Oh! I *know* you haven't read it, and that you could never be that man's accomplice. Read it, I wish you to read it."

The letter had evidently been written in a hurry:

"My fate is to be decided today" (it ran), *"you know how. This day I must give my word irrevocably. I have no right to ask your help, and I dare not allow myself to indulge in any hopes; but once you said just one word, and that word lighted up the night of my life, and became the beacon of my days. Say one more such word, and save me from utter ruin. Only tell me, 'break off the whole thing!' and I will do so this very day. Oh! what can it cost you to say just this one word? In doing so you will but be giving me a sign of your sympathy for me, and of your pity; only this, only this; nothing more, nothing. I dare not indulge in any hope, because I am unworthy of it. But if you say but this word, I will take up my cross again with joy, and return once more to my battle with poverty. I shall meet the storm and be glad of it; I shall rise up with renewed strength.*

"Send me back then this one word of sympathy, only sympathy, I swear to you; and oh! do not be angry with the audacity of despair, with the drowning man who has dared to make this last effort to save himself from perishing beneath the waters.

"G.L."

"This man assures me," said Aglaya, scornfully, when the prince had finished reading the letter, "that the words 'break off everything' do not commit me to anything whatever; and himself gives me a written guarantee to that effect, in this letter. Observe how ingenuously he underlines certain words, and how crudely he glosses over his hidden thoughts. He must know that if he 'broke off everything,' *first*, by himself, and without telling me a word about it or having the slightest hope on my account, that in that case I should perhaps be able to change my opinion of him, and even accept his—friendship. He must know that, but his soul is such a wretched thing. He knows it and cannot make up his mind; he knows it and yet asks for guarantees. He cannot bring himself to *trust*, he wants me to give him hopes of myself before he lets go of his hundred thousand roubles. As to the 'former word' which he declares 'lighted up the night of his life,' he is simply an impudent liar; I merely pitied him once. But he is audacious and shameless. He immediately began to hope, at that very moment. I saw it. He has tried to catch me ever since; he is still fishing for me. Well, enough of this. Take the letter and give it back to him, as soon as you have left our house; not before, of course."

"And what shall I tell him by way of answer?"

"Nothing—of course! That's the best answer. Is it the case that you are going to live in his house?"

"Yes, your father kindly recommended me to him."

"Then look out for him, I warn you! He won't forgive you easily, for taking back the letter."

Aglaya pressed the prince's hand and left the room. Her face was serious and frowning; she did not even smile as she nodded good-bye to him at the door.

"I'll just get my parcel and we'll go," said the prince to Gania, as he re-entered the drawing-room. Gania stamped his foot with impatience. His face looked dark and gloomy with rage.

At last they left the house behind them, the prince carrying his bundle.

"The answer—quick—the answer!" said Gania, the instant they were outside. "What did she say? Did you give the letter?" The prince silently held out the note. Gania was struck motionless with amazement.

"How, what? my letter?" he cried. "He never delivered it! I might have guessed it, oh! curse him! Of course she did not understand what I meant, naturally! Why—why—*why* didn't you give her the note, you—"

"Excuse me; I was able to deliver it almost immediately after receiving your commission, and I gave it, too, just as you asked me to. It has come into my hands now because Aglaya Ivanovna has just returned it to me."

"How? When?"

"As soon as I finished writing in her album for her, and when she asked me to come out of the room with her (you heard?), we went into the dining-room, and she gave me your letter to read, and then told me to return it."

"To *read?*" cried Gania, almost at the top of his voice; "to *read*, and you read it?"

And again he stood like a log in the middle of the pavement; so amazed that his mouth remained open after the last word had left it.

"Yes, I have just read it."

"And she gave it you to read herself—*herself?*"

"Yes, herself; and you may believe me when I tell you that I would not have read it for anything without her permission."

Gania was silent for a minute or two, as though thinking out some problem. Suddenly he cried:

"It's impossible, she cannot have given it to you to read! You are lying. You read it yourself!"

"I am telling you the truth," said the prince in his former composed tone of voice; "and believe me, I am extremely sorry that the circumstance should have made such an unpleasant impression upon you!"

"But, you wretched man, at least she must have said something? There must be *some* answer from her!"

"Yes, of course, she did say something!"

"Out with it then, damn it! Out with it at once!" and Gania stamped his foot twice on the pavement.

"As soon as I had finished reading it, she told me that you were fishing for her; that you wished to compromise her so far as to receive some hopes from her, trusting to which hopes you might break with the prospect of receiving a hundred thousand roubles. She said that if you had done this without bargaining with her, if you had broken with the money prospects without trying to force a guarantee out of her first, she might have been your friend. That's all, I think. Oh no, when I asked her what I was to say, as I took the letter, she replied that 'no answer is the best answer.' I think that was it. Forgive me if I do not use her exact expressions. I tell you the sense as I understood it myself."

Ungovernable rage and madness took entire possession of Gania, and his fury burst out without the least attempt at restraint.

"Oh! that's it, is it!" he yelled. "She throws my letters out of the window, does she! Oh! and she does not condescend to bargain, while I *do*, eh? We shall see, we shall see! I shall pay her out for this."

He twisted himself about with rage, and grew paler and paler; he shook his fist. So the pair walked along a few steps. Gania did not stand on ceremony with the prince; he behaved just as though he were alone in his room. He clearly counted the latter as a nonentity. But suddenly he seemed to have an idea, and recollected himself.

"But how was it?" he asked, "how was it that you (idiot that you are)," he added to himself, "were so very confidential a couple of hours after your first meeting with these people? How was that, eh?"

Up to this moment jealousy had not been one of his torments; now it suddenly gnawed at his heart.

"That is a thing I cannot undertake to explain," replied the prince. Gania looked at him with angry contempt.

"Oh! I suppose the present she wished to make to you, when she took you into the dining-room, was her confidence, eh?"

"I suppose that was it; I cannot explain it otherwise?"

"But why, *why?* Devil take it, what did you do in there? Why did they fancy you? Look here, can't you remember exactly what you said to them, from the very beginning? Can't you remember?"

"Oh, we talked of a great many things. When first I went in we began to speak of Switzerland."

"Oh, the devil take Switzerland!"

"Then about executions."

"Executions?"

"Yes—at least about one. Then I told the whole three years' story of my life, and the history of a poor peasant girl—"

"Oh, damn the peasant girl! go on, go on!" said Gania, impatiently.

"Then how Schneider told me about my childish nature, and—"

"Oh, *curse* Schneider and his dirty opinions! Go on."

"Then I began to talk about faces, at least about the *expressions* of faces, and said that Aglaya Ivanovna was nearly as lovely as Nastasia Philipovna. It was then I blurted out about the portrait—"

"But you didn't repeat what you heard in the study? You didn't repeat that—eh?"

"No, I tell you I did *not.*"

"Then how did they—look here! Did Aglaya show my letter to the old lady?"

"Oh, there I can give you my fullest assurance that she did *not.* I was there all the while—she had no time to do it!"

"But perhaps you may not have observed it, oh, you damned idiot, you!" he shouted, quite beside himself with fury. "You can't even describe what went on."

Gania having once descended to abuse, and receiving no check, very soon knew no bounds or limit to his licence, as is often the way in such cases. His rage so blinded him that he had not even been able to detect that this "idiot," whom he was abusing to such an extent, was very far from being slow of comprehension, and had a way of taking in an impression, and afterwards giving it out again, which was very un-idiotic indeed. But something a little unforeseen now occurred.

"I think I ought to tell you, Gavrila Ardalionovitch," said the prince, suddenly, "that though I once was so ill that I really was little better than an idiot, yet now I am almost recovered, and that, therefore, it is not altogether pleasant to be called an idiot to my face. Of course your anger is excusable, considering the treatment you have just experienced; but I must remind you that you have twice abused me rather rudely. I do not like this sort of thing, and especially so at the first time of meeting a man, and, therefore, as we happen to be at this moment standing at a crossroad, don't you think we had better part, you to the left, homewards, and I to the right, here? I have twenty-five roubles, and I shall easily find a lodging."

Gania was much confused, and blushed for shame "Do forgive me, prince!" he cried, suddenly changing his abusive tone for one of great courtesy. "For Heaven's sake, forgive me! You see what a miserable plight I am in, but you hardly know anything of the facts of the case as yet. If you did, I am sure you would forgive me, at least partially. Of course it was inexcusable of me, I know, but—"

"Oh, dear me, I really do not require such profuse apologies," replied the prince, hastily. "I quite understand how unpleasant your position is, and that is what made you abuse me. So come along to your house, after all. I shall be delighted—"

"I am not going to let him go like this," thought Gania, glancing angrily at the prince as they walked along. "The fellow has sucked everything out of me, and now he takes off his mask—there's something more than appears, here we shall see. It shall all be as clear as water by tonight, everything!"

But by this time they had reached Gania's house.

VIII.

The flat occupied by Gania and his family was on the third floor of the house. It was reached by a clean light staircase, and consisted of seven rooms, a nice enough lodging, and one would have thought a little too good for a clerk on two thousand roubles a year. But it was designed to accommodate a few lodgers on board terms, and had been taken a few months since, much to the disgust of Gania, at the urgent request of his mother and his sister, Varvara Ardalionovna, who longed to do something to increase the family income a little, and fixed their hopes upon letting lodgings. Gania frowned upon the idea. He thought it *infra dig,* and did not quite like appearing in society afterwards—that society in which he had been accustomed to pose up to now as a young man of rather brilliant prospects. All these concessions and rebuffs of fortune, of late, had wounded his spirit severely, and his temper had become extremely irritable, his wrath being generally quite out of proportion to the cause. But if he had made up his mind to put up with this sort of life for a while, it was only on the plain understanding with his inner self that he would very soon change it all, and have things as he chose again. Yet the very means by which he hoped to make this change threatened to involve him in even greater difficulties than he had had before.

The flat was divided by a passage which led straight out of the entrance-hall. Along one side of this corridor lay the three rooms which were designed for the accommodation of the "highly recommended" lodgers. Besides these three rooms there was another small one at the end of the passage, close to the kitchen, which was allotted to General Ivolgin, the nominal master of the house, who slept on a wide sofa, and was obliged to pass into and out of his room through the kitchen, and up or down the back stairs. Colia, Gania's young brother, a school-boy of thirteen, shared this room with his father. He, too, had to sleep on an old sofa, a narrow, uncomfortable thing with a torn rug over it; his chief duty being to look after his father, who needed to be watched more and more every day.

The prince was given the middle room of the three, the first being occupied by one Ferdishenko, while the third was empty.

But Gania first conducted the prince to the family apartments. These consisted of a "salon," which became the dining-room when required; a drawing-room, which was only a drawing-room in the morning, and became Gania's study in the evening, and his bedroom at night; and lastly Nina Alexandrovna's and Varvara's bedroom, a small, close chamber which they shared together.

In a word, the whole place was confined, and a "tight fit" for the party. Gania used to grind his teeth with rage over the state of affairs; though he was anxious to be dutiful and polite to his mother. However, it was very soon apparent to anyone coming into the house, that Gania was the tyrant of the family.

Nina Alexandrovna and her daughter were both seated in the drawing-room, engaged in knitting, and talking to a visitor, Ivan Petrovitch Ptitsin.

The lady of the house appeared to be a woman of about fifty years of age, thin-faced, and with black lines under the eyes. She looked ill and rather sad; but her face was a pleasant one for all that; and from the first word that fell from her lips, any stranger would at once conclude that she was of a serious and particularly sincere nature. In spite of her sorrowful expression, she gave the idea of possessing considerable firmness and decision.

Her dress was modest and simple to a degree, dark and elderly in style; but both her face and appearance gave evidence that she had seen better days.

Varvara was a girl of some twenty-three summers, of middle height, thin, but possessing a face which, without being actually beautiful, had the rare quality of charm, and might fascinate even to the extent of passionate regard.

She was very like her mother: she even dressed like her, which proved that she had no taste for smart clothes. The expression of her grey eyes was merry and gentle, when it was not, as lately, too full of thought and anxiety. The same decision and firmness was to be observed in her face as in her mother's, but her strength seemed to be more vigorous than that of Nina Alexandrovna. She was subject to outbursts of temper, of which even her brother was a little afraid.

The present visitor, Ptitsin, was also afraid of her. This was a young fellow of something under thirty, dressed plainly, but neatly. His manners were good, but rather ponderously so. His dark beard bore evidence to the fact that he was not in any government employ. He could speak well, but preferred silence. On the whole he made a decidedly agreeable impression. He was clearly attracted by Varvara, and made no secret of his feelings. She trusted him in a friendly way, but had not shown him any decided encouragement as yet, which fact did not quell his ardour in the least.

Nina Alexandrovna was very fond of him, and had grown quite confidential with him of late. Ptitsin, as was well known, was engaged in the business of lending out money on good security, and at a good rate of interest. He was a great friend of Gania's.

After a formal introduction by Gania (who greeted his mother very shortly, took no notice of his sister, and immediately marched Ptitsin out of the room), Nina Alexandrovna addressed a few kind words to the prince and forthwith requested Colia, who had just appeared at the door, to show him to the "middle room."

Colia was a nice-looking boy. His expression was simple and confiding, and his manners were very polite and engaging.

"Where's your luggage?" he asked, as he led the prince away to his room.

"I had a bundle; it's in the entrance hall."

"I'll bring it you directly. We only have a cook and one maid, so I have to help as much as I can. Varia looks after things, generally, and loses her temper over it. Gania says you have only just arrived from Switzerland?"

"Yes."

"Is it jolly there?"

"Very."

"Mountains?"

"Yes."

"I'll go and get your bundle."

Here Varvara joined them.

"The maid shall bring your bed-linen directly. Have you a portmanteau?"

"No; a bundle—your brother has just gone to the hall for it."

"There's nothing there except this," said Colia, returning at this moment. "Where did you put it?"

"Oh! but that's all I have," said the prince, taking it.

"Ah! I thought perhaps Ferdishenko had taken it."

"Don't talk nonsense," said Varia, severely. She seemed put out, and was only just polite with the prince.

"Oho!" laughed the boy, "you can be nicer than that to *me*, you know—I'm not Ptitsin!"

"You ought to be whipped, Colia, you silly boy. If you want anything" (to the prince) "please apply to the servant. We dine at half-past four. You can take your dinner with us, or have it in your room, just as you please. Come along, Colia, don't disturb the prince."

At the door they met Gania coming in.

"Is father in?" he asked. Colia whispered something in his ear and went out.

"Just a couple of words, prince, if you'll excuse me. Don't blab over *there* about what you may see here, or in this house as to all that about Aglaya and me, you know. Things are not altogether pleasant in this establishment—devil take it all! You'll see. At all events keep your tongue to yourself for *today*."

"I assure you I 'blabbed' a great deal less than you seem to suppose," said the prince, with some annoyance. Clearly the relations between Gania and himself were by no means improving.

"Oh I well; I caught it quite hot enough today, thanks to you. However, I forgive you."

"I think you might fairly remember that I was not in any way bound, I had no reason to be silent about that portrait. You never asked me not to mention it."

"Pfu! what a wretched room this is—dark, and the window looking into the yard. Your coming to our house is, in no respect, opportune. However, it's not *my* affair. I don't keep the lodgings."

Ptitsin here looked in and beckoned to Gania, who hastily left the room, in spite of the fact that he had evidently wished to say something more and had only made the remark about the room to gain time. The prince had hardly had time to wash and tidy himself a little when the door opened once more, and another figure appeared.

This was a gentleman of about thirty, tall, broad-shouldered, and red-haired; his face was red, too, and he possessed a pair of thick lips, a wide nose, small eyes, rather bloodshot, and with an ironical expression in them; as though he were perpetually winking at someone. His whole appearance gave one the idea of impudence; his dress was shabby.

He opened the door just enough to let his head in. His head remained so placed for a few seconds while he quietly scrutinized the room; the door then opened enough to admit his body; but still he did not enter. He stood on the threshold and examined the prince carefully. At last he gave the door a final shove, entered, approached the prince, took his hand and seated himself and the owner of the room on two chairs side by side.

"Ferdishenko," he said, gazing intently and inquiringly into the prince's eyes.

"Very well, what next?" said the latter, almost laughing in his face.

"A lodger here," continued the other, staring as before.

"Do you wish to make acquaintance?" asked the prince.

"Ah!" said the visitor, passing his fingers through his hair and sighing. He then looked over to the other side of the room and around it. "Got any money?" he asked, suddenly.

"Not much."

"How much?"

"Twenty-five roubles."

"Let's see it."

The prince took his banknote out and showed it to Ferdishenko. The latter unfolded it and looked at it; then he turned it round and examined the other side; then he held it up to the light.

"How strange that it should have browned so," he said, reflectively. "These twenty-five rouble notes brown in a most extraordinary way, while other notes often grow paler. Take it."

The prince took his note. Ferdishenko rose.

"I came here to warn you," he said. "In the first place, don't lend me any money, for I shall certainly ask you to."

"Very well."

"Shall you pay here?"

"Yes, I intend to."

"Oh! I *don't* intend to. Thanks. I live here, next door to you; you noticed a room, did you? Don't come to me very often; I shall see you here quite often enough. Have you seen the general?"

"No."

"Nor heard him?"

"No; of course not."

"Well, you'll both hear and see him soon; he even tries to borrow money from me. *Avis au lecteur.* Good-bye; do you think a man can possibly live with a name like Ferdishenko?"

"Why not?"

"Good-bye."

And so he departed. The prince found out afterwards that this gentleman made it his business to amaze people with his originality and wit, but that it did not as a rule "come off." He even produced a bad impression on some people, which grieved him sorely; but he did not change his ways for all that.

As he went out of the prince's room, he collided with yet another visitor coming in. Ferdishenko took the opportunity of making several warning gestures to the prince from behind the new arrival's back, and left the room in conscious pride.

This next arrival was a tall red-faced man of about fifty-five, with greyish hair and whiskers, and large eyes which stood out of their sockets. His appearance would have been distinguished had it not been that he gave the idea of being rather dirty. He was dressed in an old coat, and he smelled of vodka when he came near. His walk was effective, and he clearly did his best to appear dignified, and to impress people by his manner.

This gentleman now approached the prince slowly, and with a most courteous smile; silently took his hand and held it in his own, as he examined the prince's features as though searching for familiar traits therein.

"'Tis he, 'tis he!" he said at last, quietly, but with much solemnity. "As though he were alive once more. I heard the familiar name-the dear familiar name—and, oh! how it reminded me of the irrevocable past—Prince Muishkin, I believe?"

"Exactly so."

"General Ivolgin—retired and unfortunate. May I ask your Christian and generic names?"

"Lef Nicolaievitch."

"So, so—the son of my old, I may say my childhood's friend, Nicolai Petrovitch."

"My father's name was Nicolai Lvovitch."

"Lvovitch," repeated the general without the slightest haste, and with perfect confidence, just as though he had not committed himself the least in the world, but merely made a little slip of the tongue. He sat down, and taking the prince's hand, drew him to a seat next to himself.

"I carried you in my arms as a baby," he observed.

"Really?" asked the prince. "Why, it's twenty years since my father died."

"Yes, yes—twenty years and three months. We were educated together; I went straight into the army, and he—"

"My father went into the army, too. He was a sub-lieutenant in the Vasiliefsky regiment."

"No, sir—in the Bielomirsky; he changed into the latter shortly before his death. I was at his bedside when he died, and gave him my blessing for eternity. Your mother—" The general paused, as though overcome with emotion.

"She died a few months later, from a cold," said the prince.

"Oh, not cold—believe an old man—not from a cold, but from grief for her prince. Oh—your mother, your mother! heigh-ho! Youth—youth! Your father and I—old friends as we were—nearly murdered each other for her sake."

The prince began to be a little incredulous.

"I was passionately in love with her when she was engaged—engaged to my friend. The prince noticed the fact and was furious. He came and woke me at seven o'clock one morning. I rise and dress in amazement; silence on both sides. I understand it all. He takes a couple of pistols out of his pocket—across a handkerchief—without witnesses. Why invite witnesses when both of us would be walking in eternity in a couple of minutes? The pistols are loaded; we stretch the handkerchief and stand opposite one another. We aim the pistols at each other's hearts. Suddenly tears start to our eyes, our hands shake; we weep, we embrace—the battle is one of self-sacrifice now! The prince shouts, 'She is yours;' I cry, 'She is yours—' in a word, in a word—You've come to live with us, hey?"

"Yes—yes—for a while, I think," stammered the prince.

"Prince, mother begs you to come to her," said Colia, appearing at the door.

The prince rose to go, but the general once more laid his hand in a friendly manner on his shoulder, and dragged him down on to the sofa.

"As the true friend of your father, I wish to say a few words to you," he began. "I have suffered—there was a catastrophe. I suffered without a trial; I had no trial. Nina Alexandrovna my wife, is an excellent woman, so is my daughter Varvara. We have to let lodgings because we are poor—a dreadful, unheard-of come-down for us—for me, who should have been a governor-general; but we are very glad to have *you*, at all events. Meanwhile there is a tragedy in the house."

The prince looked inquiringly at the other.

"Yes, a marriage is being arranged—a marriage between a questionable woman and a young fellow who might be a flunkey. They wish to bring this woman into the house where my wife and daughter reside, but while I live and breathe she shall never enter my doors. I shall lie at the threshold, and she shall trample me underfoot if she does. I hardly talk to Gania now, and avoid him as much as I can. I warn you of this beforehand, but you cannot fail to observe it. But you are the son of my old friend, and I hope—"

"Prince, be so kind as to come to me for a moment in the drawing-room," said Nina Alexandrovna herself, appearing at the door.

"Imagine, my dear," cried the general, "it turns out that I have nursed the prince on my knee in the old days." His wife looked searchingly at him, and glanced at the prince, but said nothing. The prince rose and followed her; but hardly had they reached the drawing-room, and Nina Alexandrovna had begun to talk hurriedly, when in came the general. She immediately relapsed into silence. The master of the house may have observed this, but at all events he did not take any notice of it; he was in high good humour.

"A son of my old friend, dear," he cried; "surely you must remember Prince Nicolai Lvovitch? You saw him at—at Tver."

"I don't remember any Nicolai Lvovitch. Was that your father?" she inquired of the prince.

"Yes, but he died at Elizabethgrad, not at Tver," said the prince, rather timidly. "So Pavlicheff told me."

"No, Tver," insisted the general; "he removed just before his death. You were very small and cannot remember; and Pavlicheff, though an excellent fellow, may have made a mistake."

"You knew Pavlicheff then?"

"Oh, yes—a wonderful fellow; but I was present myself. I gave him my blessing."

"My father was just about to be tried when he died," said the prince, "although I never knew of what he was accused. He died in hospital."

"Oh! it was the Kolpakoff business, and of course he would have been acquitted."

"Yes? Do you know that for a fact?" asked the prince, whose curiosity was aroused by the general's words.

"I should think so indeed!" cried the latter. "The court-martial came to no decision. It was a mysterious, an impossible business, one might say! Captain Larionoff, commander of the company, had died; his command was handed over to the prince for the moment. Very well. This soldier, Kolpakoff, stole some leather from one of his comrades, intending to sell it, and spent the money on drink. Well! The prince—you understand that what follows took place in the presence of the sergeant-major, and a corporal—the prince rated Kolpakoff soundly, and threatened to have him flogged. Well, Kolpakoff went back to the barracks, lay down on a camp bedstead, and in a quarter of an hour was dead: you quite understand? It was, as I said, a strange, almost impossible, affair. In due course Kolpakoff was buried; the prince wrote his report, the deceased's name was removed from the roll. All as it should be, is it not? But exactly three months later at the inspection of the brigade, the man Kolpakoff was found in the third company of the second battalion of infantry, Novozemlianski division, just as if nothing had happened!"

"What?" said the prince, much astonished.

"It did not occur—it's a mistake!" said Nina Alexandrovna quickly, looking, at the prince rather anxiously. "*Mon mari se trompe*," she added, speaking in French.

"My dear, '*se trompe*' is easily said. Do you remember any case at all like it? Everybody was at their wits' end. I should be the first to say '*qu'on se trompe*,' but unfortunately I was an eye-witness, and was also on the commission of inquiry. Everything proved that it was really he, the very same soldier Kolpakoff who had been given the usual military funeral to the sound of the drum. It is of course a most curious case—nearly an impossible one. I recognize that... but—"

"Father, your dinner is ready," said Varvara at this point, putting her head in at the door.

"Very glad, I'm particularly hungry. Yes, yes, a strange coincidence—almost a psychological—"

"Your soup'll be cold; do come."

"Coming, coming," said the general. "Son of my old friend—" he was heard muttering as he went down the passage.

"You will have to excuse very much in my husband, if you stay with us," said Nina Alexandrovna; "but he will not disturb you often. He dines alone. Everyone has his little peculiarities, you know, and some people perhaps have more than those who are most pointed at and laughed at. One thing I must beg of you—if my husband applies to you for payment for board and lodging, tell him that you have already paid me. Of course anything paid by you to the general would be as fully settled as if paid to me, so far as you are concerned; but I wish it to be so, if you please, for convenience' sake. What is it, Varia?"

Varia had quietly entered the room, and was holding out the portrait of Nastasia Philipovna to her mother.

Nina Alexandrovna started, and examined the photograph intently, gazing at it long and sadly. At last she looked up inquiringly at Varia.

"It's a present from herself to him," said Varia; "the question is to be finally decided this evening."

"This evening!" repeated her mother in a tone of despair, but softly, as though to herself. "Then it's all settled, of course, and there's no hope left to us. She has anticipated her answer by the present of her portrait. Did he show it you himself?" she added, in some surprise.

"You know we have hardly spoken to each other for a whole month. Ptitsin told me all about it; and the photo was lying under the table, and I picked it up."

"Prince," asked Nina Alexandrovna, "I wanted to inquire whether you have known my son long? I think he said that you had only arrived today from somewhere."

The prince gave a short narrative of what we have heard before, leaving out the greater part. The two ladies listened intently.

"I did not ask about Gania out of curiosity," said the elder, at last. "I wish to know how much you know about him, because he said just now that we need not stand on ceremony with you. What, exactly, does that mean?"

At this moment Gania and Ptitsin entered the room together, and Nina Alexandrovna immediately became silent again. The prince remained seated next to her, but Varia moved to the other end of the room; the portrait of Nastasia Philipovna remained lying as before on the work-table. Gania observed it there, and with a frown of annoyance snatched it up and threw it across to his writing-table, which stood at the other end of the room.

"Is it today, Gania?" asked Nina Alexandrovna, at last.

"Is what today?" cried the former. Then suddenly recollecting himself, he turned sharply on the prince. "Oh," he growled, "I see, you are here, that explains it! Is it a disease, or what, that you can't hold your tongue? Look here, understand once for all, prince—"

"I am to blame in this, Gania—no one else," said Ptitsin.

Gania glanced inquiringly at the speaker.

"It's better so, you know, Gania—especially as, from one point of view, the matter may be considered as settled," said Ptitsin; and sitting down a little way from the table he began to study a paper covered with pencil writing.

Gania stood and frowned, he expected a family scene. He never thought of apologizing to the prince, however.

"If it's all settled, Gania, then of course Mr. Ptitsin is right," said Nina Alexandrovna. "Don't frown. You need not worry yourself, Gania; I shall ask you no questions. You need not tell me anything you don't like. I assure you I have quite submitted to your will." She said all this, knitting away the while as though perfectly calm and composed.

Gania was surprised, but cautiously kept silence and looked at his mother, hoping that she would express herself more clearly. Nina Alexandrovna observed his cautiousness and added, with a bitter smile:

"You are still suspicious, I see, and do not believe me; but you may be quite at your ease. There shall be no more tears, nor questions—not from my side, at all events. All I wish is that you may be happy, you know that. I have submitted to my fate; but my heart will always be with you, whether we remain united, or whether we part. Of course I only answer for myself—you can hardly expect your sister—"

"My sister again," cried Gania, looking at her with contempt and almost hate. "Look here, mother, I have already given you my word that I shall always respect you fully and absolutely, and so shall everyone else in this house, be it who it may, who shall cross this threshold."

Gania was so much relieved that he gazed at his mother almost affectionately.

"I was not at all afraid for myself, Gania, as you know well. It was not for my own sake that I have been so anxious and worried all this time! They say it is all to be settled to-day. What is to be settled?"

"She has promised to tell me tonight at her own house whether she consents or not," replied Gania.

"We have been silent on this subject for three weeks," said his mother, "and it was better so; and now I will only ask you one question. How can she give her consent and make you a present of her portrait when you do not love her? How can such a—such a—"

"Practised hand—eh?"

"I was not going to express myself so. But how could you so blind her?"

Nina Alexandrovna's question betrayed intense annoyance. Gania waited a moment and then said, without taking the trouble to conceal the irony of his tone:

"There you are, mother, you are always like that. You begin by promising that there are to be no reproaches or insinuations or questions, and here you are beginning them at once. We had better drop the subject—we had, really. I shall never leave you, mother; any other man would cut and run from such a sister as this. See how she is looking at me at this moment! Besides, how do you know that I am blinding Nastasia Philipovna? As for Varia, I don't care—she can do just as she pleases. There, that's quite enough!"

Gania's irritation increased with every word he uttered, as he walked up and down the room. These conversations always touched the family sores before long.

"I have said already that the moment she comes in I go out, and I shall keep my word," remarked Varia.

"Out of obstinacy" shouted Gania. "You haven't married, either, thanks to your obstinacy. Oh, you needn't frown at me, Varvara! You can go at once for all I care; I am sick enough of your company. What, you are going to leave us are you, too?" he cried, turning to the prince, who was rising from his chair.

Gania's voice was full of the most uncontrolled and uncontrollable irritation.

The prince turned at the door to say something, but perceiving in Gania's expression that there was but that one drop wanting to make the cup overflow, he changed his mind and left the room without a word. A few minutes later he was aware from the noisy voices in the drawing room, that the conversation had become more quarrelsome than ever after his departure.

He crossed the salon and the entrance-hall, so as to pass down the corridor into his own room. As he came near the front door he heard someone outside vainly endeavouring to ring the bell, which was evidently broken, and only shook a little, without emitting any sound.

The prince took down the chain and opened the door. He started back in amazement—for there stood Nastasia Philipovna. He knew her at once from her photograph. Her eyes blazed with anger as she looked at him. She quickly pushed by him into the hall, shouldering him out of her way, and said, furiously, as she threw off her fur cloak:

"If you are too lazy to mend your bell, you should at least wait in the hall to let people in when they rattle the bell handle. There, now, you've dropped my fur cloak—dummy!"

Sure enough the cloak was lying on the ground. Nastasia had thrown it off her towards the prince, expecting him to catch it, but the prince had missed it.

"Now then—announce me, quick!"

The prince wanted to say something, but was so confused and astonished that he could not. However, he moved off towards the drawing-room with the cloak over his arm.

"Now then, where are you taking my cloak to? Ha, ha, ha! Are you mad?"

The prince turned and came back, more confused than ever. When she burst out laughing, he smiled, but his tongue could not form a word as yet. At first, when he had opened the door and saw her standing before him, he had become as pale as death; but now the red blood had rushed back to his cheeks in a torrent.

"Why, what an idiot it is!" cried Nastasia, stamping her foot with irritation. "Go on, do! Whom are you going to announce?"

"Nastasia Philipovna," murmured the prince.

"And how do you know that?" she asked him, sharply.

"I have never seen you before!"

"Go on, announce me—what's that noise?"

"They are quarrelling," said the prince, and entered the drawing-room, just as matters in there had almost reached a crisis. Nina Alexandrovna had forgotten that she had "submitted to everything!" She was defending Varia. Ptitsin was taking her part, too. Not that Varia was afraid of standing up for herself. She was by no means that sort of a girl; but her brother was becoming ruder and more intolerable every moment. Her usual practice in such cases as the present was to say nothing, but stare at him, without taking her eyes off his face for an instant. This manoeuvre, as she well knew, could drive Gania distracted.

Just at this moment the door opened and the prince entered, announcing:

"Nastasia Philipovna!"

IX.

Silence immediately fell on the room; all looked at the prince as though they neither understood, nor hoped to understand. Gania was motionless with horror.

Nastasia's arrival was a most unexpected and overwhelming event to all parties. In the first place, she had never been before. Up to now she had been so haughty that she had never even asked Gania to introduce her to his parents. Of late she had not so much as mentioned them. Gania was partly glad of this; but still he had put it to her debit in the account to be settled after marriage.

He would have borne anything from her rather than this visit. But one thing seemed to him quite clear-her visit now, and the present of her portrait on this particular day, pointed out plainly enough which way she intended to make her decision!

The incredulous amazement with which all regarded the prince did not last long, for Nastasia herself appeared at the door and passed in, pushing by the prince again.

"At last I've stormed the citadel! Why do you tie up your bell?" she said, merrily, as she pressed Gania's hand, the latter having rushed up to her as soon as she made her appearance. "What are you looking so upset about? Introduce me, please!"

The bewildered Gania introduced her first to Varia, and both women, before shaking hands, exchanged looks of strange import. Nastasia, however, smiled amiably; but Varia did not try to look amiable, and kept her gloomy expression. She did not even vouchsafe the usual courteous smile of etiquette. Gania darted a terrible glance of wrath at her for this, but Nina Alexandrovna mended matters a little when Gania introduced her at last. Hardly, however, had the old lady begun about her "highly gratified feelings," and so on, when Nastasia left her, and flounced into a chair by Gania's side in the corner by the window, and cried: "Where's your study? and where are the—the lodgers? You do take in lodgers, don't you?"

Gania looked dreadfully put out, and tried to say something in reply, but Nastasia interrupted him:

"Why, where are you going to squeeze lodgers in here? Don't you use a study? Does this sort of thing pay?" she added, turning to Nina Alexandrovna.

"Well, it is troublesome, rather," said the latter; "but I suppose it will 'pay' pretty well. We have only just begun, however—"

Again Nastasia Philipovna did not hear the sentence out. She glanced at Gania, and cried, laughing, "What a face! My goodness, what a face you have on at this moment!"

Indeed, Gania did not look in the least like himself. His bewilderment and his alarmed perplexity passed off, however, and his lips now twitched with rage as he continued to stare evilly at his laughing guest, while his countenance became absolutely livid.

There was another witness, who, though standing at the door motionless and bewildered himself, still managed to remark Gania's death-like pallor, and the dreadful change that had come over his face. This witness was the prince, who now advanced in alarm and muttered to Gania:

"Drink some water, and don't look like that!"

It was clear that he came out with these words quite spontaneously, on the spur of the moment. But his speech was productive of much—for it appeared that all Gania's rage now overflowed upon the prince. He seized him by the shoulder and gazed with an intensity of loathing and revenge at him, but said nothing—as though his feelings were too strong to permit of words.

General agitation prevailed. Nina Alexandrovna gave a little cry of anxiety; Ptitsin took a step forward in alarm; Colia and Ferdishenko stood stock still at the door in amazement;—only Varia remained coolly watching the scene from under her eyelashes. She did not sit down, but stood by her mother with folded hands. However, Gania recollected himself almost immediately. He let go of the prince and burst out laughing.

"Why, are you a doctor, prince, or what?" he asked, as naturally as possible. "I declare you quite frightened me! Nastasia Philipovna, let me introduce this interesting character to you—though I have only known him myself since the morning."

Nastasia gazed at the prince in bewilderment. "Prince? He a Prince? Why, I took him for the footman, just now, and sent him in to announce me! Ha, ha, ha, isn't that good!"

"Not bad that, not bad at all!" put in Ferdishenko, "*se non è vero*—"

"I rather think I pitched into you, too, didn't I? Forgive me—do! Who is he, did you say? What prince? Muishkin?" she added, addressing Gania.

"He is a lodger of ours," explained the latter.

"An idiot!"—the prince distinctly heard the word half whispered from behind him. This was Ferdishenko's voluntary information for Nastasia's benefit.

"Tell me, why didn't you put me right when I made such a dreadful mistake just now?" continued the latter, examining the prince from head to foot without the slightest ceremony. She awaited the answer as though convinced that it would be so foolish that she must inevitably fail to restrain her laughter over it.

"I was astonished, seeing you so suddenly—" murmured the prince.

"How did you know who I was? Where had you seen me before? And why were you so struck dumb at the sight of me? What was there so overwhelming about me?"

"Oho! ho, ho, ho!" cried Ferdishenko. "*Now* then, prince! My word, what things I would say if I had such a chance as that! My goodness, prince—go on!"

"So should I, in your place, I've no doubt!" laughed the prince to Ferdishenko; then continued, addressing Nastasia: "Your portrait struck me very forcibly this morning; then I was talking about you to the Epanchins; and then, in the train, before I reached Petersburg, Parfen Rogojin told me a good deal about you; and at the very moment that I opened the door to you I happened to be thinking of you, when—there you stood before me!"

"And how did you recognize me?"

"From the portrait!"

"What else?"

"I seemed to imagine you exactly as you are—I seemed to have seen you somewhere."

"Where—where?"

"I seem to have seen your eyes somewhere; but it cannot be! I have not seen you—I never was here before. I may have dreamed of you, I don't know."

The prince said all this with manifest effort—in broken sentences, and with many drawings of breath. He was evidently much agitated. Nastasia Philipovna looked at him inquisitively, but did not laugh.

"Bravo, prince!" cried Ferdishenko, delighted.

At this moment a loud voice from behind the group which hedged in the prince and Nastasia Philipovna, divided the crowd, as it were, and before them stood the head of the family, General Ivolgin. He was dressed in evening clothes; his moustache was dyed.

This apparition was too much for Gania. Vain and ambitious almost to morbidness, he had had much to put up with in the last two months, and was seeking feverishly for some means of enabling himself to lead a more presentable kind of existence. At home, he now adopted an attitude of absolute cynicism, but he could not keep this up before Nastasia Philipovna, although he had sworn to make her pay after marriage for all he suffered now. He was experiencing a last humiliation, the bitterest of all, at this moment—the humiliation of blushing for his own kindred in his own house. A question flashed through his mind as to whether the game was really worth the candle.

For that had happened at this moment, which for two months had been his nightmare; which had filled his soul with dread and shame—the meeting between his father and Nastasia Philipovna. He had often tried to imagine such an event, but had found the picture too mortifying and exasperating, and had quietly dropped it. Very likely he anticipated far worse things than was at all necessary; it is often so with vain persons. He had long since determined, therefore, to get his father out of the way, anywhere, before his marriage, in order to avoid such a meeting; but when Nastasia entered the room just now, he had been so overwhelmed with astonishment, that he had not thought of his father, and had made no arrangements to keep him out of the way. And now it was too late—there he was, and got up, too, in a dress coat and white tie, and Nastasia in the very humour to heap ridicule on him and his family circle; of this last fact, he felt quite persuaded. What else had she come for? There were his mother and his sister sitting before her, and she seemed to have forgotten their very existence already; and if she behaved like that, he thought, she must have some object in view.

Ferdishenko led the general up to Nastasia Philipovna.

"Ardalion Alexandrovitch Ivolgin," said the smiling general, with a low bow of great dignity, "an old soldier, unfortunate, and the father of this family; but happy in the hope of including in that family so exquisite—"

He did not finish his sentence, for at this moment Ferdishenko pushed a chair up from behind, and the general, not very firm on his legs, at this post-prandial hour, flopped into it backwards. It was always a difficult thing to put this warrior to confusion, and his sudden descent left him as composed as before. He had sat down just opposite to Nastasia, whose fingers he now took, and raised to his lips with great elegance, and much courtesy. The general had once belonged to a very select circle of society, but he had been turned out of it two or three years since on account of certain weaknesses, in which he now indulged with all the less restraint; but his good manners remained with him to this day, in spite of all.

Nastasia Philipovna seemed delighted at the appearance of this latest arrival, of whom she had of course heard a good deal by report.

"I have heard that my son—" began Ardalion Alexandrovitch.

"Your son, indeed! A nice papa you are! *You* might have come to see me anyhow, without compromising anyone. Do you hide yourself, or does your son hide you?"

"The children of the nineteenth century, and their parents—" began the general, again.

"Nastasia Philipovna, will you excuse the general for a moment? Someone is inquiring for him," said Nina Alexandrovna in a loud voice, interrupting the conversation.

"Excuse him? Oh no, I have wished to see him too long for that. Why, what business can he have? He has retired, hasn't he? You won't leave me, general, will you?"

"I give you my word that he shall come and see you—but he—he needs rest just now."

"General, they say you require rest," said Nastasia Philipovna, with the melancholy face of a child whose toy is taken away.

Ardalion Alexandrovitch immediately did his best to make his foolish position a great deal worse.

"My dear, my dear!" he said, solemnly and reproachfully, looking at his wife, with one hand on his heart.

"Won't you leave the room, mamma?" asked Varia, aloud.

"No, Varia, I shall sit it out to the end."

Nastasia must have overheard both question and reply, but her vivacity was not in the least damped. On the contrary, it seemed to increase. She immediately overwhelmed the general once more with questions, and within five minutes that gentleman was as happy as a king, and holding forth at the top of his voice, amid the laughter of almost all who heard him.

Colia jogged the prince's arm.

"Can't *you* get him out of the room, somehow? *Do*, please," and tears of annoyance stood in the boy's eyes. "Curse that Gania!" he muttered, between his teeth.

"Oh yes, I knew General Epanchin well," General Ivolgin was saying at this moment; "he and Prince Nicolai Ivanovitch Muishkin—whose son I have this day embraced after an absence of twenty years—and I, were three inseparables. Alas one is in the grave, torn to pieces by calumnies and bullets; another is now before you, still battling with calumnies and bullets—"

"Bullets?" cried Nastasia.

"Yes, here in my chest. I received them at the siege of Kars, and I feel them in bad weather now. And as to the third of our trio, Epanchin, of course after that little affair with the poodle in the railway carriage, it was all *up* between us."

"Poodle? What was that? And in a railway carriage? Dear me," said Nastasia, thoughtfully, as though trying to recall something to mind.

"Oh, just a silly, little occurrence, really not worth telling, about Princess Bielokonski's governess, Miss Smith, and—oh, it is really not worth telling!"

"No, no, we must have it!" cried Nastasia merrily.

"Yes, of course," said Ferdishenko. "C'est du nouveau."

"Ardalion," said Nina Alexandrovitch, entreatingly.

"Papa, you are wanted!" cried Colia.

"Well, it is a silly little story, in a few words," began the delighted general. "A couple of years ago, soon after the new railway was opened, I had to go somewhere or other on business. Well, I took a first-class ticket, sat down, and began to smoke, or rather *continued* to smoke, for I had lighted up before. I was alone in the carriage. Smoking is not allowed, but is not prohibited either; it is half allowed—so to speak, winked at. I had the window open."

"Suddenly, just before the whistle, in came two ladies with a little poodle, and sat down opposite to me; not bad-looking women; one was in light blue, the other in black silk. The poodle, a beauty with a silver collar, lay on light blue's knee. They looked haughtily about, and talked English together. I took no notice, just went on smoking. I observed that the ladies were getting angry—over my cigar, doubtless. One looked at me through her tortoise-shell eyeglass.

"I took no notice, because they never said a word. If they didn't like the cigar, why couldn't they say so? Not a word, not a hint! Suddenly, and without the very slightest suspicion of warning, 'light blue' seizes my cigar from between my fingers, and, wheugh! out of the window with it! Well, on flew the train, and I sat bewildered, and the young woman, tall and fair, and rather red in the face, too red, glared at me with flashing eyes.

"I didn't say a word, but with extreme courtesy, I may say with most refined courtesy, I reached my finger and thumb over towards the poodle, took it up delicately by the nape of the neck, and chucked it out of the window, after the cigar. The train went flying on, and the poodle's yells were lost in the distance."

"Oh, you naughty man!" cried Nastasia, laughing and clapping her hands like a child.

"Bravo!" said Ferdishenko. Ptitsin laughed too, though he had been very sorry to see the general appear. Even Colia laughed and said, "Bravo!"

"And I was right, truly right," cried the general, with warmth and solemnity, "for if cigars are forbidden in railway carriages, poodles are much more so."

"Well, and what did the lady do?" asked Nastasia, impatiently.

"She—ah, that's where all the mischief of it lies!" replied Ivolgin, frowning. "Without a word, as it were, of warning, she slapped me on the cheek! An extraordinary woman!"

"And you?"

The general dropped his eyes, and elevated his brows; shrugged his shoulders, tightened his lips, spread his hands, and remained silent. At last he blurted out:

"I lost my head!"

"Did you hit her?"

"No, oh no!—there was a great flare-up, but I didn't hit her! I had to struggle a little, purely to defend myself; but the very devil was in the business. It turned out that 'light blue' was an Englishwoman, governess or something, at Princess Bielokonski's, and the other woman was one of the old-maid princesses Bielokonski. Well, everybody knows what great friends the princess and Mrs. Epanchin are, so there was a pretty kettle of fish. All the Bielokonskis went into mourning for the poodle. Six princesses in tears, and the Englishwoman shrieking!

"Of course I wrote an apology, and called, but they would not receive either me or my apology, and the Epanchins cut me, too!"

"But wait," said Nastasia. "How is it that, five or six days since, I read exactly the same story in the paper, as happening between a Frenchman and an English girl? The cigar was snatched away exactly as you describe, and the poodle was chucked out of the window after it. The slapping came off, too, as in your case; and the girl's dress was light blue!"

The general blushed dreadfully; Colia blushed too; and Ptitsin turned hastily away. Ferdishenko was the only one who laughed as gaily as before. As to Gania, I need not say that he was miserable; he stood dumb and wretched and took no notice of anybody.

"I assure you," said the general, "that exactly the same thing happened to myself!"

"I remembered there was some quarrel between father and Miss Smith, the Bielokonski's governess," said Colia.

"How very curious, point for point the same anecdote, and happening at different ends of Europe! Even the light blue dress the same," continued the pitiless Nastasia. "I must really send you the paper."

"You must observe," insisted the general, "that my experience was two years earlier."

"Ah! that's it, no doubt!"

Nastasia Philipovna laughed hysterically.

"Father, will you hear a word from me outside!" said Gania, his voice shaking with agitation, as he seized his father by the shoulder. His eyes shone with a blaze of hatred.

At this moment there was a terrific bang at the front door, almost enough to break it down. Some most unusual visitor must have arrived. Colia ran to open.

X.

The entrance-hall suddenly became full of noise and people. To judge from the sounds which penetrated to the drawing-room, a number of people had already come in, and the stampede continued. Several voices were talking and shouting at once; others were talking and shouting on the stairs outside; it was evidently a most extraordinary visit that was about to take place.

Everyone exchanged startled glances. Gania rushed out towards the dining-room, but a number of men had already made their way in, and met him.

"Ah! here he is, the Judas!" cried a voice which the prince recognized at once. "How d'ye do, Gania, you old blackguard?"

"Yes, that's the man!" said another voice.

There was no room for doubt in the prince's mind: one of the voices was Rogojin's, and the other Lebedeff's.

Gania stood at the door like a block and looked on in silence, putting no obstacle in the way of their entrance, and ten or a dozen men marched in behind Parfen Rogojin. They were a decidedly mixed-looking collection, and some of them came in in their furs and caps. None of them were quite drunk, but all appeared to be considerably excited.

They seemed to need each other's support, morally, before they dared come in; not one of them would have entered alone but with the rest each one was brave enough. Even Rogojin entered rather cautiously at the head of his troop; but he was evidently preoccupied. He appeared to be gloomy and morose, and had clearly come with some end in view. All the rest were merely chorus, brought in to support the chief character. Besides Lebedeff there was the dandy Zalesheff, who came in without his coat and hat, two or three others followed his example; the rest were more uncouth. They included a couple of young merchants, a man in a great-coat, a medical student, a little Pole, a small fat man who laughed continuously, and an enormously tall stout one who apparently put great faith in the strength of his fists. A couple of "ladies" of some sort put their heads in at the front door, but did not dare come any farther. Colia promptly banged the door in their faces and locked it.

"Hallo, Gania, you blackguard! You didn't expect Rogojin, eh?" said the latter, entering the drawing-room, and stopping before Gania.

But at this moment he saw, seated before him, Nastasia Philipovna. He had not dreamed of meeting her here, evidently, for her appearance produced a marvellous effect upon him. He grew pale, and his lips became actually blue.

"I suppose it is true, then!" he muttered to himself, and his face took on an expression of despair. "So that's the end of it! Now you, sir, will you answer me or not?" he went on suddenly, gazing at Gania with ineffable malice. "Now then, you—"

He panted, and could hardly speak for agitation. He advanced into the room mechanically; but perceiving Nina Alexandrovna and Varia he became more or less embarrassed, in spite of his excitement. His followers entered after him, and all paused a moment at sight of the ladies. Of course their modesty was not fated to be long-lived, but for a moment they were abashed. Once let them begin to shout, however, and nothing on earth should disconcert them.

"What, you here too, prince?" said Rogojin, absently, but a little surprised all the same "Still in your gaiters, eh?" He sighed, and forgot the prince next moment, and his wild eyes wandered over to Nastasia again, as though attracted in that direction by some magnetic force.

Nastasia looked at the new arrivals with great curiosity. Gania recollected himself at last.

"Excuse me, sirs," he said, loudly, "but what does all this mean?" He glared at the advancing crowd generally, but addressed his remarks especially to their captain, Rogojin. "You are not in a stable, gentlemen, though you may think it—my mother and sister are present."

"Yes, I see your mother and sister," muttered Rogojin, through his teeth; and Lebedeff seemed to feel himself called upon to second the statement.

"At all events, I must request you to step into the salon," said Gania, his rage rising quite out of proportion to his words, "and then I shall inquire—"

"What, he doesn't know me!" said Rogojin, showing his teeth disagreeably. "He doesn't recognize Rogojin!" He did not move an inch, however.

"I have met you somewhere, I believe, but—"

"Met me somewhere, pfu! Why, it's only three months since I lost two hundred roubles of my father's money to you, at cards. The old fellow died before he found out. Ptitsin knows all about it. Why, I've only to pull out a three-rouble note and show it to you, and you'd crawl on your hands and knees to the other end of the town for it; that's the sort of man you are. Why, I've come now, at this moment, to buy you up! Oh, you needn't think that because I wear these boots I have no money. I have lots of money, my beauty,—enough to buy up you and all yours together. So I shall, if I like to! I'll buy you up! I will!" he yelled, apparently growing more and more intoxicated and excited. "Oh, Nastasia Philipovna! don't turn me out! Say one word, do! Are you going to marry this man, or not?"

Rogojin asked his question like a lost soul appealing to some divinity, with the reckless daring of one appointed to die, who has nothing to lose.

He awaited the reply in deadly anxiety.

Nastasia Philipovna gazed at him with a haughty, ironical expression of face; but when she glanced at Nina Alexandrovna and Varia, and from them to Gania, she changed her tone, all of a sudden.

"Certainly not; what are you thinking of? What could have induced you to ask such a question?" she replied, quietly and seriously, and even, apparently, with some astonishment.

"No? No?" shouted Rogojin, almost out of his mind with joy. "You are not going to, after all? And they told me—oh, Nastasia Philipovna—they said you had promised to marry him, *him!* As if you *could* do it!—him—pooh! I don't mind saying it to everyone—I'd buy him off for a hundred roubles, any day pfu! Give him a thousand, or three if he likes, poor devil, and he'd cut and run the day before his wedding, and leave his bride to me! Wouldn't you, Gania, you blackguard? You'd take three thousand, wouldn't you? Here's the money! Look, I've come on purpose to pay you off and get your receipt, formally. I said I'd buy you up, and so I will."

"Get out of this, you drunken beast!" cried Gania, who was red and white by turns.

Rogojin's troop, who were only waiting for an excuse, set up a howl at this. Lebedeff stepped forward and whispered something in Parfen's ear.

"You're right, clerk," said the latter, "you're right, tipsy spirit—you're right!—Nastasia Philipovna," he added, looking at her like some lunatic, harmless generally, but suddenly wound up to a pitch of audacity, "here are eighteen thousand roubles, and—and you shall have more—." Here he threw a packet of bank-notes tied up in white paper, on the table before her, not daring to say all he wished to say.

"No—no—no!" muttered Lebedeff, clutching at his arm. He was clearly aghast at the largeness of the sum, and thought a far smaller amount should have been tried first.

"No, you fool—you don't know whom you are dealing with—and it appears I am a fool, too!" said Parfen, trembling beneath the flashing glance of Nastasia. "Oh, curse it all! What a fool I was to listen to you!" he added, with profound melancholy.

Nastasia Philipovna, observing his woe-begone expression, suddenly burst out laughing.

"Eighteen thousand roubles, for me? Why, you declare yourself a fool at once," she said, with impudent familiarity, as she rose from the sofa and prepared to go. Gania watched the whole scene with a sinking of the heart.

"Forty thousand, then—forty thousand roubles instead of eighteen! Ptitsin and another have promised to find me forty thousand roubles by seven o'clock tonight. Forty thousand roubles—paid down on the nail!"

The scene was growing more and more disgraceful; but Nastasia Philipovna continued to laugh and did not go away. Nina Alexandrovna and Varia had both risen from their places and were waiting, in silent horror, to see what would happen. Varia's eyes were all ablaze with anger; but the scene had a different effect on Nina Alexandrovna. She paled and trembled, and looked more and more like fainting every moment.

"Very well then, a *hundred* thousand! a hundred thousand! paid this very day. Ptitsin! find it for me. A good share shall stick to your fingers—come!"

"You are mad!" said Ptitsin, coming up quickly and seizing him by the hand. "You're drunk—the police will be sent for if you don't look out. Think where you are."

"Yes, he's boasting like a drunkard," added Nastasia, as though with the sole intention of goading him.

"I do *not* boast! You shall have a hundred thousand, this very day. Ptitsin, get the money, you gay usurer! Take what you like for it, but get it by the evening! I'll show that I'm in earnest!" cried Rogojin, working himself up into a frenzy of excitement.

"Come, come; what's all this?" cried General Ivolgin, suddenly and angrily, coming close up to Rogojin. The unexpectedness of this sally on the part of the hitherto silent old man caused some laughter among the intruders.

"Halloa! what's this now?" laughed Rogojin. "You come along with me, old fellow! You shall have as much to drink as you like."

"Oh, it's too horrible!" cried poor Colia, sobbing with shame and annoyance.

"Surely there must be someone among all of you here who will turn this shameless creature out of the room?" cried Varia, suddenly. She was shaking and trembling with rage.

"That's me, I suppose. I'm the shameless creature!" cried Nastasia Philipovna, with amused indifference. "Dear me, and I came—like a fool, as I am—to invite them over to my house for the evening! Look how your sister treats me, Gavrila Ardalionovitch."

For some moments Gania stood as if stunned or struck by lightning, after his sister's speech. But seeing that Nastasia Philipovna was really about to leave the room this time, he sprang at Varia and seized her by the arm like a madman.

"What have you done?" he hissed, glaring at her as though he would like to annihilate her on the spot. He was quite beside himself, and could hardly articulate his words for rage.

"What have I done? Where are you dragging me to?"

"Do you wish me to beg pardon of this creature because she has come here to insult our mother and disgrace the whole household, you low, base wretch?" cried Varia, looking back at her brother with proud defiance.

A few moments passed as they stood there face to face, Gania still holding her wrist tightly. Varia struggled once—twice—to get free; then could restrain herself no longer, and spat in his face.

"There's a girl for you!" cried Nastasia Philipovna. "Mr. Ptitsin, I congratulate you on your choice."

Gania lost his head. Forgetful of everything he aimed a blow at Varia, which would inevitably have laid her low, but suddenly another hand caught his. Between him and Varia stood the prince.

"Enough—enough!" said the latter, with insistence, but all of a tremble with excitement.

"Are you going to cross my path for ever, damn you!" cried Gania; and, loosening his hold on Varia, he slapped the prince's face with all his force.

Exclamations of horror arose on all sides. The prince grew pale as death; he gazed into Gania's eyes with a strange, wild, reproachful look; his lips trembled and vainly endeavoured to form some words; then his mouth twisted into an incongruous smile.

"Very well—never mind about me; but I shall not allow you to strike her!" he said, at last, quietly. Then, suddenly, he could bear it no longer, and covering his face with his hands, turned to the wall, and murmured in broken accents:

"Oh! how ashamed you will be of this afterwards!"

Gania certainly did look dreadfully abashed. Colia rushed up to comfort the prince, and after him crowded Varia, Rogojin and all, even the general.

"It's nothing, it's nothing!" said the prince, and again he wore the smile which was so inconsistent with the circumstances.

"Yes, he will be ashamed!" cried Rogojin. "You will be properly ashamed of yourself for having injured such a—such a sheep" (he could not find a better word). "Prince, my dear fellow, leave this and come away with me. I'll show you how Rogojin shows his affection for his friends."

Nastasia Philipovna was also much impressed, both with Gania's action and with the prince's reply.

Her usually thoughtful, pale face, which all this while had been so little in harmony with the jests and laughter which she had seemed to put on for the occasion, was now evidently agitated by new feelings, though she tried to conceal the fact and to look as though she were as ready as ever for jesting and irony.

"I really think I must have seen him somewhere!" she murmured seriously enough.

"Oh, aren't you ashamed of yourself—aren't you ashamed? Are you really the sort of woman you are trying to represent yourself to be? Is it possible?" The prince was now addressing Nastasia, in a tone of reproach, which evidently came from his very heart.

Nastasia Philipovna looked surprised, and smiled, but evidently concealed something beneath her smile and with some confusion and a glance at Gania she left the room.

However, she had not reached the outer hall when she turned round, walked quickly up to Nina Alexandrovna, seized her hand and lifted it to her lips.

"He guessed quite right. I am not that sort of woman," she whispered hurriedly, flushing red all over. Then she turned again and left the room so quickly that no one could imagine what she had come back for. All they saw was that she said something to Nina Alexandrovna in a hurried whisper, and seemed to kiss her hand. Varia, however, both saw and heard all, and watched Nastasia out of the room with an expression of wonder.

Gania recollected himself in time to rush after her in order to show her out, but she had gone. He followed her to the stairs.

"Don't come with me," she cried, "*Au revoir*, till the evening—do you hear? *Au revoir!*"

He returned thoughtful and confused; the riddle lay heavier than ever on his soul. He was troubled about the prince, too, and so bewildered that he did not even observe Rogojin's rowdy band crowd past him and step on his toes, at the door as they went out. They were all talking at once. Rogojin went ahead of the others, talking to Ptitsin, and apparently insisting vehemently upon something very important.

"You've lost the game, Gania" he cried, as he passed the latter.

Gania gazed after him uneasily, but said nothing.

XI.

The prince now left the room and shut himself up in his own chamber. Colia followed him almost at once, anxious to do what he could to console him. The poor boy seemed to be already so attached to him that he could hardly leave him.

"You were quite right to go away!" he said. "The row will rage there worse than ever now; and it's like this every day with us—and all through that Nastasia Philipovna."

"You have so many sources of trouble here, Colia," said the prince.

"Yes, indeed, and it is all our own fault. But I have a great friend who is much worse off even than we are. Would you like to know him?"

"Yes, very much. Is he one of your school-fellows?"

"Well, not exactly. I will tell you all about him some day.... What do you think of Nastasia Philipovna? She is beautiful, isn't she? I had never seen her before, though I had a great wish to do so. She fascinated me. I could forgive Gania if he were to marry her for love, but for money! Oh dear! that is horrible!"

"Yes, your brother does not attract me much."

"I am not surprised at that. After what you... But I do hate that way of looking at things! Because some fool, or a rogue pretending to be a fool, strikes a man, that man is to be dishonoured for his whole life, unless he wipes out the disgrace with blood, or makes his assailant beg forgiveness on his knees! I think that so very absurd and tyrannical. Lermontoff's Bal Masque is based on that idea—a stupid and unnatural one, in my opinion; but he was hardly more than a child when he wrote it."

"I like your sister very much."

"Did you see how she spat in Gania's face! Varia is afraid of no one. But you did not follow her example, and yet I am sure it was not through cowardice. Here she comes! Speak of a wolf and you see his tail! I felt sure that she would come. She is very generous, though of course she has her faults."

Varia pounced upon her brother.

"This is not the place for you," said she. "Go to father. Is he plaguing you, prince?"

"Not in the least; on the contrary, he interests me."

"Scolding as usual, Varia! It is the worst thing about her. After all, I believe father may have started off with Rogojin. No doubt he is sorry now. Perhaps I had better go and see what he is doing," added Colia, running off.

"Thank God, I have got mother away, and put her to bed without another scene! Gania is worried—and ashamed—not without reason! What a spectacle! I have come to thank you once more, prince, and to ask you if you knew Nastasia Philipovna before?"

"No, I have never known her."

"Then what did you mean, when you said straight out to her that she was not really 'like that'? You guessed right, I fancy. It is quite possible she was not herself at the moment, though I cannot fathom her meaning. Evidently she meant to hurt and insult us. I have heard curious tales about her before now, but if she came to invite us to her house, why did she behave so to my mother? Ptitsin knows her very well; he says he could not understand her today. With Rogojin, too! No one with a spark of self-respect could have talked like that in the house of her... Mother is extremely vexed on your account, too...

"That is nothing!" said the prince, waving his hand.

"But how meek she was when you spoke to her!"

"Meek! What do you mean?"

"You told her it was a shame for her to behave so, and her manner changed at once; she was like another person. You have some influence over her, prince," added Varia, smiling a little.

The door opened at this point, and in came Gania most unexpectedly.

He was not in the least disconcerted to see Varia there, but he stood a moment at the door, and then approached the prince quietly.

"Prince," he said, with feeling, "I was a blackguard. Forgive me!" His face gave evidence of suffering. The prince was considerably amazed, and did not reply at once. "Oh, come, forgive me, forgive me!" Gania insisted, rather impatiently. "If you like, I'll kiss your hand. There!"

The prince was touched; he took Gania's hands, and embraced him heartily, while each kissed the other.

"I never, never thought you were like that," said Muishkin, drawing a deep breath. "I thought you—you weren't capable of—"

"Of what? Apologizing, eh? And where on earth did I get the idea that you were an idiot? You always observe what other people pass by unnoticed; one could talk sense to you, but—"

"Here is another to whom you should apologize," said the prince, pointing to Varia.

"No, no! they are all enemies! I've tried them often enough, believe me," and Gania turned his back on Varia with these words.

"But if I beg you to make it up?" said Varia.

"And you'll go to Nastasia Philipovna's this evening—"

"If you insist: but, judge for yourself, can I go, ought I to go?"

"But she is not that sort of woman, I tell you!" said Gania, angrily. "She was only acting."

"I know that—I know that; but what a part to play! And think what she must take *you* for, Gania! I know she kissed mother's hand, and all that, but she laughed at you, all the same. All this is not good enough for seventy-five thousand roubles, my dear boy. You are capable of honourable feelings still, and that's why I am talking to you so. Oh! *do* take care what you are doing! Don't you know yourself that it will end badly, Gania?"

So saying, and in a state of violent agitation, Varia left the room.

"There, they are all like that," said Gania, laughing, "just as if I do not know all about it much better than they do."

He sat down with these words, evidently intending to prolong his visit.

"If you know it so well," said the prince a little timidly, "why do you choose all this worry for the sake of the seventy-five thousand, which, you confess, does not cover it?"

"I didn't mean that," said Gania; "but while we are upon the subject, let me hear your opinion. Is all this worry worth seventy-five thousand or not?

"Certainly not."

"Of course! And it would be a disgrace to marry so, eh?"

"A great disgrace."

"Oh, well, then you may know that I shall certainly do it, now. I shall certainly marry her. I was not quite sure of myself before, but now I am. Don't say a word: I know what you want to tell me—"

"No. I was only going to say that what surprises me most of all is your extraordinary confidence."

"How so? What in?"

"That Nastasia Philipovna will accept you, and that the question is as good as settled; and secondly, that even if she did, you would be able to pocket the money. Of course, I know very little about it, but that's my view. When a man marries for money it often happens that the wife keeps the money in her own hands."

"Of course, you don't know all; but, I assure you, you needn't be afraid, it won't be like that in our case. There are circumstances," said Gania, rather excitedly. "And as to her answer to me, there's no doubt about that. Why should you suppose she will refuse me?"

"Oh, I only judge by what I see. Varvara Ardalionovna said just now—"

"Oh she—they don't know anything about it! Nastasia was only chaffing Rogojin. I was alarmed at first, but I have thought better of it now; she was simply laughing at him. She looks on me as a fool because I show that I meant her money, and doesn't realize that there are other men who would deceive her in far worse fashion. I'm not going to pretend anything, and you'll see she'll marry me, all right. If she likes to live quietly, so she shall; but if she gives me any of her nonsense, I shall leave her at once, but I shall keep the money. I'm not going to look a fool; that's the first thing, not to look a fool."

"But Nastasia Philipovna seems to me to be such a *sensible* woman, and, as such, why should she run blindly into this business? That's what puzzles me so," said the prince.

"You don't know all, you see; I tell you there are things—and besides, I'm sure that she is persuaded that I love her to distraction, and I give you my word I have a strong suspicion that she loves me, too—in her own way, of course. She thinks she will be able to make a sort of slave of me all my life; but I shall prepare a little surprise for her. I don't know whether I ought to be confidential with you, prince; but, I assure you, you are the only decent fellow I have come across. I have not spoken so sincerely as I am doing at this moment for years. There are uncommonly few honest people about, prince; there isn't one honester than Ptitsin, he's the best of the lot. Are you laughing? You don't know, perhaps, that blackguards like honest people, and being one myself I like you. *Why* am I a blackguard? Tell me honestly, now. They all call me a blackguard because of her, and I have got into the way of thinking myself one. That's what is so bad about the business."

"*I* for one shall never think you a blackguard again," said the prince. "I confess I had a poor opinion of you at first, but I have been so joyfully surprised about you just now; it's a good lesson for me. I shall never judge again without a thorough trial. I see now that you are not only not a blackguard, but are not even quite spoiled. I see that you are quite an ordinary man, not original in the least degree, but rather weak."

Gania laughed sarcastically, but said nothing. The prince, seeing that he did not quite like the last remark, blushed, and was silent too.

"Has my father asked you for money?" asked Gania, suddenly.

"No."

"Don't give it to him if he does. Fancy, he was a decent, respectable man once! He was received in the best society; he was not always the liar he is now. Of course, wine is at the bottom of it all; but he is a good deal worse than an innocent liar now. Do you know that he keeps a mistress? I can't understand how mother is so long-suffering. Did he tell you the story of the siege of Kars? Or perhaps the one about his grey horse that talked? He loves to enlarge on these absurd histories." And Gania burst into a fit of laughter. Suddenly he turned to the prince and asked: "Why are you looking at me like that?"

"I am surprised to see you laugh in that way, like a child. You came to make friends with me again just now, and you said, 'I will kiss your hand, if you like,' just as a child would have said it. And then, all at once you are talking of this mad project—of these seventy-five thousand roubles! It all seems so absurd and impossible."

"Well, what conclusion have you reached?"

"That you are rushing madly into the undertaking, and that you would do well to think it over again. It is more than possible that Varvara Ardalionovna is right."

"Ah! now you begin to moralize!" I know that I am only a child, very well," replied Gania impatiently. "That is proved by my having this conversation with you. It is not for money only, prince, that I am rushing into this affair," he continued, hardly master of his words, so closely had his vanity been touched. "If I reckoned on that I should certainly be deceived, for I am still too weak in mind and character. I am obeying a passion, an impulse perhaps, because I have but one aim, one that overmasters all else. You imagine that once I am in possession of these seventy-five thousand roubles, I shall rush to buy a carriage... No, I shall go on wearing the old overcoat I have worn for three years, and I shall give up my club. I shall follow the example of men who have made their fortunes. When Ptitsin was seventeen he slept in the street, he sold pen-knives, and began with a copeck; now he has sixty thousand roubles, but to get them, what has he not done? Well, I shall be spared such a hard beginning, and shall start with a little capital. In fifteen years people will say, 'Look, that's Ivolgin, the king of the Jews!' You say that I have no originality. Now mark this, prince—there is nothing so offensive to a man of our time and race than to be told that he is wanting in originality, that he is weak in character, has no particular talent, and is, in short, an ordinary person. You have not even done me the honour of looking upon me as a rogue. Do you know, I could have knocked you down for that just now! You wounded me more cruelly than Epanchin, who thinks me capable of selling him my wife! Observe, it was a perfectly gratuitous idea on his part, seeing there has never been any discussion of it between us! This has exasperated me, and I am determined to make a fortune! I will do it! Once I am rich, I shall be a genius, an extremely original man. One of the vilest and most hateful things connected with money is that it can buy even talent; and will do so as long as the world lasts. You will say that this is childish—or romantic. Well, that will be all the better for me, but the thing shall be done. I will carry it through. He laughs most, who laughs last. Why does Epanchin insult me? Simply because, socially, I am a nobody. However, enough for the present. Colia has put his nose in to tell us dinner is ready, twice. I'm dining out. I shall come and talk to you now and then; you shall be comfortable enough with us. They are sure to make you one of the family. I think you and I will either be great friends or enemies. Look here now, supposing I had kissed your hand just now, as I offered to do in all sincerity, should I have hated you for it afterwards?"

"Certainly, but not always. You would not have been able to keep it up, and would have ended by forgiving me," said the prince, after a pause for reflection, and with a pleasant smile.

"Oho, how careful one has to be with you, prince! Haven't you put a drop of poison in that remark now, eh? By the way—ha, ha, ha!—I forgot to ask, was I right in believing that you were a good deal struck yourself with Nastasia Philipovna."

"Ye-yes."

"Are you in love with her?"

"N-no."

"And yet you flush up as red as a rosebud! Come—it's all right. I'm not going to laugh at you. Do you know she is a very virtuous woman? Believe it or not, as you like. You think she and Totski—not a bit of it, not a bit of it! Not for ever so long!*Au revoir!*"

289

Gania left the room in great good humour. The prince stayed behind, and meditated alone for a few minutes. At length, Colia popped his head in once more.

"I don't want any dinner, thanks, Colia. I had too good a lunch at General Epanchin's."

Colia came into the room and gave the prince a note; it was from the general and was carefully sealed up. It was clear from Colia's face how painful it was to him to deliver the missive. The prince read it, rose, and took his hat.

"It's only a couple of yards," said Colia, blushing.

"He's sitting there over his bottle—and how they can give him credit, I cannot understand. Don't tell mother I brought you the note, prince; I have sworn not to do it a thousand times, but I'm always so sorry for him. Don't stand on ceremony, give him some trifle, and let that end it."

"Come along, Colia, I want to see your father. I have an idea," said the prince.

XII.

Colia took the prince to a public-house in the Litaynaya, not far off. In one of the side rooms there sat at a table— looking like one of the regular guests of the establishment—Ardalion Alexandrovitch, with a bottle before him, and a newspaper on his knee. He was waiting for the prince, and no sooner did the latter appear than he began a long harangue about something or other; but so far gone was he that the prince could hardly understand a word.

"I have not got a ten-rouble note," said the prince; "but here is a twenty-five. Change it and give me back the fifteen, or I shall be left without a farthing myself."

"Oh, of course, of course; and you quite understand that I—"

"Yes; and I have another request to make, general. Have you ever been at Nastasia Philipovna's?"

"I? I? Do you mean me? Often, my friend, often! I only pretended I had not in order to avoid a painful subject. You saw today, you were a witness, that I did all that a kind, an indulgent father could do. Now a father of altogether another type shall step into the scene. You shall see; the old soldier shall lay bare this intrigue, or a shameless woman will force her way into a respectable and noble family."

"Yes, quite so. I wished to ask you whether you could show me the way to Nastasia Philipovna's tonight. I must go; I have business with her; I was not invited but I was introduced. Anyhow I am ready to trespass the laws of propriety if only I can get in somehow or other."

"My dear young friend, you have hit on my very idea. It was not for this rubbish I asked you to come over here" (he pocketed the money, however, at this point), "it was to invite your alliance in the campaign against Nastasia Philipovna tonight. How well it sounds, 'General Ivolgin and Prince Muishkin.' That'll fetch her, I think, eh? Capital! We'll go at nine; there's time yet."

"Where does she live?"

"Oh, a long way off, near the Great Theatre, just in the square there—It won't be a large party."

The general sat on and on. He had ordered a fresh bottle when the prince arrived; this took him an hour to drink, and then he had another, and another, during the consumption of which he told pretty nearly the whole story of his life. The prince was in despair. He felt that though he had but applied to this miserable old drunkard because he saw no other way of getting to Nastasia Philipovna's, yet he had been very wrong to put the slightest confidence in such a man.

At last he rose and declared that he would wait no longer. The general rose too, drank the last drops that he could squeeze out of the bottle, and staggered into the street.

Muishkin began to despair. He could not imagine how he had been so foolish as to trust this man. He only wanted one thing, and that was to get to Nastasia Philipovna's, even at the cost of a certain amount of impropriety. But now the scandal threatened to be more than he had bargained for. By this time Ardalion Alexandrovitch was quite intoxicated, and he kept his companion listening while he discoursed eloquently and pathetically on subjects of all kinds, interspersed with torrents of recrimination against the members of his family. He insisted that all his troubles were caused by their bad conduct, and time alone would put an end to them.

At last they reached the Litaynaya. The thaw increased steadily, a warm, unhealthy wind blew through the streets, vehicles splashed through the mud, and the iron shoes of horses and mules rang on the paving stones. Crowds of melancholy people plodded wearily along the footpaths, with here and there a drunken man among them.

"Do you see those brightly-lighted windows?" said the general. "Many of my old comrades-in-arms live about here, and I, who served longer, and suffered more than any of them, am walking on foot to the house of a woman of rather questionable reputation! A man, look you, who has thirteen bullets on his breast!... You don't believe it? Well, I can assure you it was entirely on my account that Pirogoff telegraphed to Paris, and left Sebastopol at the greatest risk during the siege. Nelaton, the Tuileries surgeon, demanded a safe conduct, in the name of science, into the besieged city in order to attend my wounds. The government knows all about it. 'That's the Ivolgin with thirteen bullets in him!' That's how they speak of me.... Do you see that house, prince? One of my old friends lives on the first floor, with his large family. In this and five other houses, three overlooking Nevsky, two in the Morskaya, are all that remain of my personal friends. Nina Alexandrovna gave them up long ago, but I keep in touch with them still... I may say I find refreshment in this little coterie, in thus meeting my old acquaintances and subordinates, who worship me still, in spite of all. General Sokolovitch (by the way, I have not called on him lately, or seen Anna Fedorovna)... You know, my dear prince, when a person does not receive company himself, he gives up going to other people's houses involuntarily. And yet... well... you look as if you didn't believe me.... Well now, why should I not present the son of my old friend and companion to this delightful family—General Ivolgin and Prince Muishkin? You will see a lovely girl—what am I saying—a lovely girl? No, indeed, two, three! Ornaments of this city and of society: beauty, education, culture—the woman question—poetry—everything! Added to which is the fact that each one will have a dot of at least eighty thousand roubles. No bad thing, eh?... In a word I absolutely must introduce you to them: it is a duty, an obligation. General Ivolgin and Prince Muishkin. Tableau!"

"At once? Now? You must have forgotten..." began the prince.

"No, I have forgotten nothing. Come! This is the house—up this magnificent staircase. I am surprised not to see the porter, but .... it is a holiday... and the man has gone off... Drunken fool! Why have they not got rid of him? Sokolovitch owes all the happiness he has had in the service and in his private life to me, and me alone, but... here we are."

The prince followed quietly, making no further objection for fear of irritating the old man. At the same time he fervently hoped that General Sokolovitch and his family would fade away like a mirage in the desert, so that the visitors could escape, by merely returning downstairs. But to his horror he saw that General Ivolgin was quite familiar with the house, and really seemed to have friends there. At every step he named some topographical or biographical detail that left nothing to be desired on the score of accuracy. When they arrived at last, on the first floor, and the general turned to ring the bell to the right, the prince decided to run away, but a curious incident stopped him momentarily.

"You have made a mistake, general," said he. "The name on the door is Koulakoff, and you were going to see General Sokolovitch."

"Koulakoff... Koulakoff means nothing. This is Sokolovitch's flat, and I am ringing at his door.... What do I care for Koulakoff?... Here comes someone to open."

In fact, the door opened directly, and the footman informed the visitors that the family were all away.

"What a pity! What a pity! It's just my luck!" repeated Ardalion Alexandrovitch over and over again, in regretful tones. "When your master and mistress return, my man, tell them that General Ivolgin and Prince Muishkin desired to present themselves, and that they were extremely sorry, excessively grieved..."

Just then another person belonging to the household was seen at the back of the hall. It was a woman of some forty years, dressed in sombre colours, probably a housekeeper or a governess. Hearing the names she came forward with a look of suspicion on her face.

"Marie Alexandrovna is not at home," said she, staring hard at the general. "She has gone to her mother's, with Alexandra Michailovna."

"Alexandra Michailovna out, too! How disappointing! Would you believe it, I am always so unfortunate! May I most respectfully ask you to present my compliments to Alexandra Michailovna, and remind her... tell her, that with my whole heart I wish for her what she wished for herself on Thursday evening, while she was listening to Chopin's Ballade. She will remember. I wish it with all sincerity. General Ivolgin and Prince Muishkin!"

The woman's face changed; she lost her suspicious expression.

"I will not fail to deliver your message," she replied, and bowed them out.

As they went downstairs the general regretted repeatedly that he had failed to introduce the prince to his friends.

"You know I am a bit of a poet," said he. "Have you noticed it? The poetic soul, you know." Then he added suddenly—"But after all... after all I believe we made a mistake this time! I remember that the Sokolovitch's live in another house, and what is more, they are just now in Moscow. Yes, I certainly was at fault. However, it is of no consequence."

"Just tell me," said the prince in reply, "may I count still on your assistance? Or shall I go on alone to see Nastasia Philipovna?"

"Count on my assistance? Go alone? How can you ask me that question, when it is a matter on which the fate of my family so largely depends? You don't know Ivolgin, my friend. To trust Ivolgin is to trust a rock; that's how the first squadron I commanded spoke of me. 'Depend upon Ivolgin,' said they all, 'he is as steady as a rock.' But, excuse me, I must just call at a house on our way, a house where I have found consolation and help in all my trials for years."

"You are going home?"

"No... I wish... to visit Madame Terentieff, the widow of Captain Terentieff, my old subordinate and friend. She helps me to keep up my courage, and to bear the trials of my domestic life, and as I have an extra burden on my mind today..."

"It seems to me," interrupted the prince, "that I was foolish to trouble you just now. However, at present you... Good-bye!"

"Indeed, you must not go away like that, young man, you must not!" cried the general. "My friend here is a widow, the mother of a family; her words come straight from her heart, and find an echo in mine. A visit to her is merely an affair of a few minutes; I am quite at home in her house. I will have a wash, and dress, and then we can drive to the Grand Theatre. Make up your mind to spend the evening with me.... We are just there—that's the house... Why, Colia! you here! Well, is Marfa Borisovna at home or have you only just come?"

"Oh no! I have been here a long while," replied Colia, who was at the front door when the general met him. "I am keeping Hippolyte company. He is worse, and has been in bed all day. I came down to buy some cards. Marfa Borisovna expects you. But what a state you are in, father!" added the boy, noticing his father's unsteady gait. "Well, let us go in."

On meeting Colia the prince determined to accompany the general, though he made up his mind to stay as short a time as possible. He wanted Colia, but firmly resolved to leave the general behind. He could not forgive himself for being so simple as to imagine that Ivolgin would be of any use. The three climbed up the long staircase until they reached the fourth floor where Madame Terentieff lived.

"You intend to introduce the prince?" asked Colia, as they went up.

"Yes, my boy. I wish to present him: General Ivolgin and Prince Muishkin! But what's the matter?... what?... How is Marfa Borisovna?"

"You know, father, you would have done much better not to come at all! She is ready to eat you up! You have not shown yourself since the day before yesterday and she is expecting the money. Why did you promise her any? You are always the same! Well, now you will have to get out of it as best you can."

They stopped before a somewhat low doorway on the fourth floor. Ardalion Alexandrovitch, evidently much out of countenance, pushed Muishkin in front.

"I will wait here," he stammered. "I should like to surprise her. ...."

Colia entered first, and as the door stood open, the mistress of the house peeped out. The surprise of the general's imagination fell very flat, for she at once began to address him in terms of reproach.

Marfa Borisovna was about forty years of age. She wore a dressing-jacket, her feet were in slippers, her face painted, and her hair was in dozens of small plaits. No sooner did she catch sight of Ardalion Alexandrovitch than she screamed:

"There he is, that wicked, mean wretch! I knew it was he! My heart misgave me!"

The old man tried to put a good face on the affair.

"Come, let us go in—it's all right," he whispered in the prince's ear.

But it was more serious than he wished to think. As soon as the visitors had crossed the low dark hall, and entered the narrow reception-room, furnished with half a dozen cane chairs, and two small card-tables, Madame Terentieff, in the shrill tones habitual to her, continued her stream of invectives.

"Are you not ashamed? Are you not ashamed? You barbarian! You tyrant! You have robbed me of all I possessed—you have sucked my bones to the marrow. How long shall I be your victim? Shameless, dishonourable man!"

"Marfa Borisovna! Marfa Borisovna! Here is... the Prince Muishkin! General Ivolgin and Prince Muishkin," stammered the disconcerted old man.

"Would you believe," said the mistress of the house, suddenly addressing the prince, "would you believe that that man has not even spared my orphan children? He has stolen everything I possessed, sold everything, pawned everything; he has left me nothing—nothing! What am I to do with your IOU's, you cunning, unscrupulous rogue? Answer, devourer! answer, heart of stone! How shall I feed my orphans? with what shall I nourish them? And now he has come, he is drunk! He can scarcely stand. How, oh how, have I offended the Almighty, that He should bring this curse upon me! Answer, you worthless villain, answer!"

But this was too much for the general.

"Here are twenty-five roubles, Marfa Borisovna... it is all that I can give... and I owe even these to the prince's generosity—my noble friend. I have been cruelly deceived. Such is... life... Now... Excuse me, I am very weak," he continued, standing in the centre of the room, and bowing to all sides. "I am faint; excuse me! Lenotchka... a cushion... my dear!"

Lenotchka, a little girl of eight, ran to fetch the cushion at once, and placed it on the rickety old sofa. The general meant to have said much more, but as soon as he had stretched himself out, he turned his face to the wall, and slept the sleep of the just.

With a grave and ceremonious air, Marfa Borisovna motioned the prince to a chair at one of the card-tables. She seated herself opposite, leaned her right cheek on her hand, and sat in silence, her eyes fixed on Muishkin, now and again sighing deeply. The three children, two little girls and a boy, Lenotchka being the eldest, came and leant on the table and also stared steadily at him. Presently Colia appeared from the adjoining room.

"I am very glad indeed to have met you here, Colia," said the prince. "Can you do something for me? I must see Nastasia Philipovna, and I asked Ardalion Alexandrovitch just now to take me to her house, but he has gone to sleep, as you see. Will you show me the way, for I do not know the street? I have the address, though; it is close to the Grand Theatre."

"Nastasia Philipovna? She does not live there, and to tell you the truth my father has never been to her house! It is strange that you should have depended on him! She lives near Wladimir Street, at the Five Corners, and it is quite close by. Will you go directly? It is just half-past nine. I will show you the way with pleasure."

Colia and the prince went off together. Alas! the latter had no money to pay for a cab, so they were obliged to walk.

"I should have liked to have taken you to see Hippolyte," said Colia. "He is the eldest son of the lady you met just now, and was in the next room. He is ill, and has been in bed all day. But he is rather strange, and extremely sensitive, and I thought he might be upset considering the circumstances in which you came... Somehow it touches me less, as it concerns my father, while it is *his* mother. That, of course, makes a great difference. What is a terrible disgrace to a woman, does not disgrace a man, at least not in the same way. Perhaps public opinion is wrong in condemning one sex, and excusing the other. Hippolyte is an extremely clever boy, but so prejudiced. He is really a slave to his opinions."

"Do you say he is consumptive?"

"Yes. It really would be happier for him to die young. If I were in his place I should certainly long for death. He is unhappy about his brother and sisters, the children you saw. If it were possible, if we only had a little money, we should leave our respective families, and live together in a little apartment of our own. It is our dream. But, do you know, when I was talking over your affair with him, he was angry, and said that anyone who did not call out a man who had given him a blow was a coward. He is very irritable to-day, and I left off arguing the matter with him. So Nastasia Philipovna has invited you to go and see her?"

"To tell the truth, she has not."

"Then how do you come to be going there?" cried Colia, so much astonished that he stopped short in the middle of the pavement. "And... and are you going to her 'At Home' in that costume?"

"I don't know, really, whether I shall be allowed in at all. If she will receive me, so much the better. If not, the matter is ended. As to my clothes—what can I do?"

"Are you going there for some particular reason, or only as a way of getting into her society, and that of her friends?"

"No, I have really an object in going... That is, I am going on business it is difficult to explain, but..."

"Well, whether you go on business or not is your affair, I do not want to know. The only important thing, in my eyes, is that you should not be going there simply for the pleasure of spending your evening in such company—cocottes, generals, usurers! If that were the case I should despise and laugh at you. There are terribly few honest people here, and hardly any whom one can respect, although people put on airs—Varia especially! Have you noticed, prince, how many adventurers there are nowadays? Especially here, in our dear Russia. How it has happened I never can understand. There used to be a certain amount of solidity in all things, but now what happens? Everything is exposed to the public gaze, veils are thrown back, every wound is probed by careless fingers. We are for ever present at an orgy of scandalous revelations. Parents blush when they remember their old-fashioned morality. At Moscow lately a father was heard urging his son to stop at nothing—at nothing, mind you!—to get money! The press seized upon the story, of course, and now it is public property. Look at my father, the general! See what he is, and yet, I assure you, he is an honest man! Only... he drinks too much, and his morals are not all we could desire. Yes, that's true! I pity him, to tell the truth, but I dare not say so, because everybody would laugh at me—but I do pity him! And who are the really clever men, after all? Money-grubbers, every one of them, from the first to the last. Hippolyte finds excuses for money-lending, and says it is a necessity. He talks about the economic movement, and the ebb and flow of capital; the devil knows what he means. It makes me angry to hear him talk so, but he is soured by his troubles. Just imagine-the general keeps his mother-but she lends him money! She lends it for a week or ten days at very high interest! Isn't it disgusting? And then, you would hardly believe it, but my mother—Nina Alexandrovna—helps Hippolyte in all sorts of ways, sends him money and clothes. She even goes as far as helping the children, through Hippolyte, because their mother cares nothing about them, and Varia does the same."

"Well, just now you said there were no honest nor good people about, that there were only money-grubbers—and here they are quite close at hand, these honest and good people, your mother and Varia! I think there is a good deal of moral strength in helping people in such circumstances."

"Varia does it from pride, and likes showing off, and giving herself airs. As to my mother, I really do admire her—yes, and honour her. Hippolyte, hardened as he is, feels it. He laughed at first, and thought it vulgar of her—but now, he is sometimes quite touched and overcome by her kindness. H'm! You call that being strong and good? I will remember that! Gania knows nothing about it. He would say that it was encouraging vice."

"Ah, Gania knows nothing about it? It seems there are many things that Gania does not know," exclaimed the prince, as he considered Colia's last words.

"Do you know, I like you very much indeed, prince? I shall never forget about this afternoon."

"I like you too, Colia."

"Listen to me! You are going to live here, are you not?" said Colia. "I mean to get something to do directly, and earn money. Then shall we three live together? You, and I, and Hippolyte? We will hire a flat, and let the general come and visit us. What do you say?"

"It would be very pleasant," returned the prince. "But we must see. I am really rather worried just now. What! are we there already? Is that the house? What a long flight of steps! And there's a porter! Well, Colia I don't know what will come of it all."

The prince seemed quite distracted for the moment.

"You must tell me all about it tomorrow! Don't be afraid. I wish you success; we agree so entirely I that can do so, although I do not understand why you are here. Good-bye!" cried Colia excitedly. "Now I will rush back and tell Hippolyte all about our plans and proposals! But as to your getting in—don't be in the least afraid. You will see her. She is so original about everything. It's the first floor. The porter will show you."

XIII.

The prince was very nervous as he reached the outer door; but he did his best to encourage himself with the reflection that the worst thing that could happen to him would be that he would not be received, or, perhaps, received, then laughed at for coming.

But there was another question, which terrified him considerably, and that was: what was he going to do when he *did* get in? And to this question he could fashion no satisfactory reply.

If only he could find an opportunity of coming close up to Nastasia Philipovna and saying to her: "Don't ruin yourself by marrying this man. He does not love you, he only loves your money. He told me so himself, and so did Aglaya Ivanovna, and I have come on purpose to warn you"—but even that did not seem quite a legitimate or practicable thing to do. Then, again, there was another delicate question, to which he could not find an answer; dared not, in fact, think of it; but at the very idea of which he trembled and blushed. However, in spite of all his fears and heart-quakings he went in, and asked for Nastasia Philipovna.

Nastasia occupied a medium-sized, but distinctly tasteful, flat, beautifully furnished and arranged. At one period of these five years of Petersburg life, Totski had certainly not spared his expenditure upon her. He had calculated upon her eventual love, and tried to tempt her with a lavish outlay upon comforts and luxuries, knowing too well how easily the heart accustoms itself to comforts, and how difficult it is to tear one's self away from luxuries which have become habitual and, little by little, indispensable.

Nastasia did not reject all this, she even loved her comforts and luxuries, but, strangely enough, never became, in the least degree, dependent upon them, and always gave the impression that she could do just as well without them. In fact, she went so far as to inform Totski on several occasions that such was the case, which the latter gentleman considered a very unpleasant communication indeed.

But, of late, Totski had observed many strange and original features and characteristics in Nastasia, which he had neither known nor reckoned upon in former times, and some of these fascinated him, even now, in spite of the fact that all his old calculations with regard to her were long ago cast to the winds.

A maid opened the door for the prince (Nastasia's servants were all females) and, to his surprise, received his request to announce him to her mistress without any astonishment. Neither his dirty boots, nor his wide-brimmed hat, nor his sleeveless cloak, nor his evident confusion of manner, produced the least impression upon her. She helped him off with his cloak, and begged him to wait a moment in the ante-room while she announced him.

The company assembled at Nastasia Philipovna's consisted of none but her most intimate friends, and formed a very small party in comparison with her usual gatherings on this anniversary.

In the first place there were present Totski, and General Epanchin. They were both highly amiable, but both appeared to be labouring under a half-hidden feeling of anxiety as to the result of Nastasia's deliberations with regard to Gania, which result was to be made public this evening.

Then, of course, there was Gania who was by no means so amiable as his elders, but stood apart, gloomy, and miserable, and silent. He had determined not to bring Varia with him; but Nastasia had not even asked after her, though no sooner had he arrived than she had reminded him of the episode between himself and the prince. The general, who had heard nothing of it before, began to listen with some interest, while Gania, drily, but with perfect candour, went through the whole history, including the fact of his apology to the prince. He finished by declaring that the prince was a most extraordinary man, and goodness knows why he had been considered an idiot hitherto, for he was very far from being one.

Nastasia listened to all this with great interest; but the conversation soon turned to Rogojin and his visit, and this theme proved of the greatest attraction to both Totski and the general.

Ptitsin was able to afford some particulars as to Rogojin's conduct since the afternoon. He declared that he had been busy finding money for the latter ever since, and up to nine o'clock, Rogojin having declared that he must absolutely have a hundred thousand roubles by the evening. He added that Rogojin was drunk, of course; but that he thought the money would be forthcoming, for the excited and intoxicated rapture of the fellow impelled him to give any interest or premium that was asked of him, and there were several others engaged in beating up the money, also.

All this news was received by the company with somewhat gloomy interest. Nastasia was silent, and would not say what she thought about it. Gania was equally uncommunicative. The general seemed the most anxious of all, and decidedly uneasy. The present of pearls which he had prepared with so much joy in the morning had been accepted but coldly, and Nastasia had smiled rather disagreeably as she took it from him. Ferdishenko was the only person present in good spirits.

Totski himself, who had the reputation of being a capital talker, and was usually the life and soul of these entertainments, was as silent as any on this occasion, and sat in a state of, for him, most uncommon perturbation.

The rest of the guests (an old tutor or schoolmaster, goodness knows why invited; a young man, very timid, and shy and silent; a rather loud woman of about forty, apparently an actress; and a very pretty, well-dressed German lady who hardly said a word all the evening) not only had no gift for enlivening the proceedings, but hardly knew what to say for themselves when addressed. Under these circumstances the arrival of the prince came almost as a godsend.

The announcement of his name gave rise to some surprise and to some smiles, especially when it became evident, from Nastasia's astonished look, that she had not thought of inviting him. But her astonishment once over, Nastasia showed such satisfaction that all prepared to greet the prince with cordial smiles of welcome.

"Of course," remarked General Epanchin, "he does this out of pure innocence. It's a little dangerous, perhaps, to encourage this sort of freedom; but it is rather a good thing that he has arrived just at this moment. He may enliven us a little with his originalities."

"Especially as he asked himself," said Ferdishenko.

"What's that got to do with it?" asked the general, who loathed Ferdishenko.

"Why, he must pay toll for his entrance," explained the latter.

"H'm! Prince Muishkin is not Ferdishenko," said the general, impatiently. This worthy gentleman could never quite reconcile himself to the idea of meeting Ferdishenko in society, and on an equal footing.

"Oh general, spare Ferdishenko!" replied the other, smiling. "I have special privileges."

"What do you mean by special privileges?"

"Once before I had the honour of stating them to the company. I will repeat the explanation to-day for your excellency's benefit. You see, excellency, all the world is witty and clever except myself. I am neither. As a kind of compensation I am allowed to tell the truth, for it is a well-known fact that only stupid people tell 'the truth.' Added to this, I am a spiteful man, just because I am not clever. If I am offended or injured I bear it quite patiently until the man injuring me meets with some misfortune. Then I remember, and take my revenge. I return the injury sevenfold, as Ivan Petrovitch Ptitsin says. (Of course he never does so himself.) Excellency, no doubt you recollect Kryloff's fable, 'The Lion and the Ass'? Well now, that's you and I. That fable was written precisely for us."

"You seem to be talking nonsense again, Ferdishenko," growled the general.

"What is the matter, excellency? I know how to keep my place. When I said just now that we, you and I, were the lion and the ass of Kryloff's fable, of course it is understood that I take the role of the ass. Your excellency is the lion of which the fable remarks:

'A mighty lion, terror of the woods,
 Was shorn of his great prowess by old age.'

And I, your excellency, am the ass."

"I am of your opinion on that last point," said Ivan Fedorovitch, with ill-concealed irritation.

All this was no doubt extremely coarse, and moreover it was premeditated, but after all Ferdishenko had persuaded everyone to accept him as a buffoon.

"If I am admitted and tolerated here," he had said one day, "it is simply because I talk in this way. How can anyone possibly receive such a man as I am? I quite understand. Now, could I, a Ferdishenko, be allowed to sit shoulder to shoulder with a clever man like Afanasy Ivanovitch? There is one explanation, only one. I am given the position because it is so entirely inconceivable!"

But these vulgarities seemed to please Nastasia Philipovna, although too often they were both rude and offensive. Those who wished to go to her house were forced to put up with Ferdishenko. Possibly the latter was not mistaken in imagining that he was received simply in order to annoy Totski, who disliked him extremely. Gania also was often made the butt of the jester's sarcasms, who used this method of keeping in Nastasia Philipovna's good graces.

"The prince will begin by singing us a fashionable ditty," remarked Ferdishenko, and looked at the mistress of the house, to see what she would say.

"I don't think so, Ferdishenko; please be quiet," answered Nastasia Philipovna dryly.

"A-ah! if he is to be under special patronage, I withdraw my claws."

But Nastasia Philipovna had now risen and advanced to meet the prince.

"I was so sorry to have forgotten to ask you to come, when I saw you," she said, "and I am delighted to be able to thank you personally now, and to express my pleasure at your resolution."

So saying she gazed into his eyes, longing to see whether she could make any guess as to the explanation of his motive in coming to her house. The prince would very likely have made some reply to her kind words, but he was so dazzled by her appearance that he could not speak.

Nastasia noticed this with satisfaction. She was in full dress this evening; and her appearance was certainly calculated to impress all beholders. She took his hand and led him towards her other guests. But just before they reached the drawing-room door, the prince stopped her, and hurriedly and in great agitation whispered to her:

"You are altogether perfection; even your pallor and thinness are perfect; one could not wish you otherwise. I did so wish to come and see you. I—forgive me, please—"

"Don't apologize," said Nastasia, laughing; "you spoil the whole originality of the thing. I think what they say about you must be true, that you are so original.—So you think me perfection, do you?"

"Yes."

"H'm! Well, you may be a good reader of riddles but you are wrong *there*, at all events. I'll remind you of this, tonight."

Nastasia introduced the prince to her guests, to most of whom he was already known.

Totski immediately made some amiable remark. All seemed to brighten up at once, and the conversation became general. Nastasia made the prince sit down next to herself.

"Dear me, there's nothing so very curious about the prince dropping in, after all," remarked Ferdishenko.

"It's quite a clear case," said the hitherto silent Gania. "I have watched the prince almost all day, ever since the moment when he first saw Nastasia Philipovna's portrait, at General Epanchin's. I remember thinking at the time what I am now pretty sure of; and what, I may say in passing, the prince confessed to myself."

Gania said all this perfectly seriously, and without the slightest appearance of joking; indeed, he seemed strangely gloomy.

"I did not confess anything to you," said the prince, blushing. "I only answered your question."

"Bravo! That's frank, at any rate!" shouted Ferdishenko, and there was general laughter.

"Oh prince, prince! I never should have thought it of you;" said General Epanchin. "And I imagined you a philosopher! Oh, you silent fellows!"

"Judging from the fact that the prince blushed at this innocent joke, like a young girl, I should think that he must, as an honourable man, harbour the noblest intentions," said the old toothless schoolmaster, most unexpectedly; he had not so much as opened his mouth before. This remark provoked general mirth, and the old fellow himself laughed loudest of the lot, but ended with a stupendous fit of coughing.

Nastasia Philipovna, who loved originality and drollery of all kinds, was apparently very fond of this old man, and rang the bell for more tea to stop his coughing. It was now half-past ten o'clock.

"Gentlemen, wouldn't you like a little champagne now?" she asked. "I have it all ready; it will cheer us up—do now—no ceremony!"

This invitation to drink, couched, as it was, in such informal terms, came very strangely from Nastasia Philipovna. Her usual entertainments were not quite like this; there was more style about them. However, the wine was not refused; each guest took a glass excepting Gania, who drank nothing.

It was extremely difficult to account for Nastasia's strange condition of mind, which became more evident each moment, and which none could avoid noticing.

She took her glass, and vowed she would empty it three times that evening. She was hysterical, and laughed aloud every other minute with no apparent reason—the next moment relapsing into gloom and thoughtfulness.

Some of her guests suspected that she must be ill; but concluded at last that she was expecting something, for she continued to look at her watch impatiently and unceasingly; she was most absent and strange.

"You seem to be a little feverish tonight," said the actress.

"Yes; I feel quite ill. I have been obliged to put on this shawl—I feel so cold," replied Nastasia. She certainly had grown very pale, and every now and then she tried to suppress a trembling in her limbs.

"Had we not better allow our hostess to retire?" asked Totski of the general.

"Not at all, gentlemen, not at all! Your presence is absolutely necessary to me tonight," said Nastasia, significantly.

As most of those present were aware that this evening a certain very important decision was to be taken, these words of Nastasia Philipovna's appeared to be fraught with much hidden interest. The general and Totski exchanged looks; Gania fidgeted convulsively in his chair.

"Let's play at some game!" suggested the actress.

"I know a new and most delightful game, added Ferdishenko.

"What is it?" asked the actress.

"Well, when we tried it we were a party of people, like this, for instance; and somebody proposed that each of us, without leaving his place at the table, should relate something about himself. It had to be something that he really and honestly considered the very worst action he had ever committed in his life. But he was to be honest—that was the chief point! He wasn't to be allowed to lie."

"What an extraordinary idea!" said the general.

"That's the beauty of it, general!"

"It's a funny notion," said Totski, "and yet quite natural—it's only a new way of boasting."

"Perhaps that is just what was so fascinating about it."

"Why, it would be a game to cry over—not to laugh at!" said the actress.

"Did it succeed?" asked Nastasia Philipovna. "Come, let's try it, let's try it; we really are not quite so jolly as we might be—let's try it! We may like it; it's original, at all events!"

"Yes," said Ferdishenko; "it's a good idea—come along—the men begin. Of course no one need tell a story if he prefers to be disobliging. We must draw lots! Throw your slips of paper, gentlemen, into this hat, and the prince shall draw for turns. It's a very simple game; all you have to do is to tell the story of the worst action of your life. It's as simple as anything. I'll prompt anyone who forgets the rules!"

No one liked the idea much. Some smiled, some frowned some objected, but faintly, not wishing to oppose Nastasia's wishes; for this new idea seemed to be rather well received by her. She was still in an excited, hysterical state, laughing convulsively at nothing and everything. Her eyes were blazing, and her cheeks showed two bright red spots against the white. The melancholy appearance of some of her guests seemed to add to her sarcastic humour, and perhaps the very cynicism and cruelty of the game proposed by Ferdishenko pleased her. At all events she was attracted by the idea, and gradually her guests came round to her side; the thing was original, at least, and might turn out to be amusing. "And supposing it's something that one—one can't speak about before ladies?" asked the timid and silent young man.

"Why, then of course, you won't say anything about it. As if there are not plenty of sins to your score without the need of those!" said Ferdishenko.

"But I really don't know which of my actions is the worst," said the lively actress.

"Ladies are exempted if they like."

"And how are you to know that one isn't lying? And if one lies the whole point of the game is lost," said Gania.

"Oh, but think how delightful to hear how one's friends lie! Besides you needn't be afraid, Gania; everybody knows what your worst action is without the need of any lying on your part. Only think, gentlemen,"—and Ferdishenko here grew quite enthusiastic, "only think with what eyes we shall observe one another tomorrow, after our tales have been told!"

"But surely this is a joke, Nastasia Philipovna?" asked Totski. "You don't really mean us to play this game."

"Whoever is afraid of wolves had better not go into the wood," said Nastasia, smiling.

"But, pardon me, Mr. Ferdishenko, is it possible to make a game out of this kind of thing?" persisted Totski, growing more and more uneasy. "I assure you it can't be a success."

"And why not? Why, the last time I simply told straight off about how I stole three roubles."

"Perhaps so; but it is hardly possible that you told it so that it seemed like truth, or so that you were believed. And, as Gavrila Ardalionovitch has said, the least suggestion of a falsehood takes all point out of the game. It seems to me that sincerity, on the other hand, is only possible if combined with a kind of bad taste that would be utterly out of place here."

"How subtle you are, Afanasy Ivanovitch! You astonish me," cried Ferdishenko. "You will remark, gentleman, that in saying that I could not recount the story of my theft so as to be believed, Afanasy Ivanovitch has very ingeniously implied that I am not capable of thieving—(it would have been bad taste to say so openly); and all the time he is probably firmly convinced, in his own mind, that I am very well capable of it! But now, gentlemen, to business! Put in your slips, ladies and gentlemen—is yours in, Mr. Totski? So—then we are all ready; now prince, draw, please." The prince silently put his hand into the hat, and drew the names. Ferdishenko was first, then Ptitsin, then the general, Totski next, his own fifth, then Gania, and so on; the ladies did not draw.

"Oh, dear! oh, dear!" cried Ferdishenko. "I did so hope the prince would come out first, and then the general. Well, gentlemen, I suppose I must set a good example! What vexes me much is that I am such an insignificant creature that it matters nothing to anybody whether I have done bad actions or not! Besides, which am I to choose? It's an *embarras de richesse*. Shall I tell how I became a thief on one occasion only, to convince Afanasy Ivanovitch that it is possible to steal without being a thief?"

"Do go on, Ferdishenko, and don't make unnecessary preface, or you'll never finish," said Nastasia Philipovna. All observed how irritable and cross she had become since her last burst of laughter; but none the less obstinately did she stick to her absurd whim about this new game. Totski sat looking miserable enough. The general lingered over his champagne, and seemed to be thinking of some story for the time when his turn should come.

<h2 style="text-align:center">XIV.</h2>

"I have no wit, Nastasia Philipovna," began Ferdishenko, "and therefore I talk too much, perhaps. Were I as witty, now, as Mr. Totski or the general, I should probably have sat silent all the evening, as they have. Now, prince, what do you think?—are there not far more thieves than honest men in this world? Don't you think we may say there does not exist a single person so honest that he has never stolen anything whatever in his life?"

"What a silly idea," said the actress. "Of course it is not the case. I have never stolen anything, for one."

"H'm! very well, Daria Alexeyevna; you have not stolen anything—agreed. But how about the prince, now—look how he is blushing!"

"I think you are partially right, but you exaggerate," said the prince, who had certainly blushed up, of a sudden, for some reason or other.

"Ferdishenko—either tell us your story, or be quiet, and mind your own business. You exhaust all patience," cuttingly and irritably remarked Nastasia Philipovna.

"Immediately, immediately! As for my story, gentlemen, it is too stupid and absurd to tell you.

"I assure you I am not a thief, and yet I have stolen; I cannot explain why. It was at Semeon Ivanovitch Ishenka's country house, one Sunday. He had a dinner party. After dinner the men stayed at the table over their wine. It struck me to ask the daughter of the house to play something on the piano; so I passed through the corner room to join the ladies. In that room, on Maria Ivanovna's writing-table, I observed a three-rouble note. She must have taken it out for some purpose, and left it lying there. There was no one about. I took up the note and put it in my pocket; why, I can't say. I don't know what possessed me to do it, but it was done, and I went quickly back to the dining-room and reseated myself at the dinner-table. I sat and waited there in a great state of excitement. I talked hard, and told lots of stories, and laughed like mad; then I joined the ladies.

"In half an hour or so the loss was discovered, and the servants were being put under examination. Daria, the housemaid was suspected. I exhibited the greatest interest and sympathy, and I remember that poor Daria quite lost her head, and that I began assuring her, before everyone, that I would guarantee her forgiveness on the part of her mistress, if she would confess her guilt. They all stared at the girl, and I remember a wonderful attraction in the reflection that here was I sermonizing away, with the money in my own pocket all the while. I went and spent the three roubles that very evening at a restaurant. I went in and asked for a bottle of Lafite, and drank it up; I wanted to be rid of the money.

"I did not feel much remorse either then or afterwards; but I would not repeat the performance—believe it or not as you please. There—that's all."

"Only, of course that's not nearly your worst action," said the actress, with evident dislike in her face.

"That was a psychological phenomenon, not an action," remarked Totski.

"And what about the maid?" asked Nastasia Philipovna, with undisguised contempt.

"Oh, she was turned out next day, of course. It's a very strict household, there!"

"And you allowed it?"

"I should think so, rather! I was not going to return and confess next day," laughed Ferdishenko, who seemed a little surprised at the disagreeable impression which his story had made on all parties.

"How mean you were!" said Nastasia.

"Bah! you wish to hear a man tell of his worst actions, and you expect the story to come out goody-goody! One's worst actions always are mean. We shall see what the general has to say for himself now. All is not gold that glitters, you know; and because a man keeps his carriage he need not be specially virtuous, I assure you, all sorts of people keep carriages. And by what means?"

In a word, Ferdishenko was very angry and rapidly forgetting himself; his whole face was drawn with passion. Strange as it may appear, he had expected much better success for his story. These little errors of taste on Ferdishenko's part occurred very frequently. Nastasia trembled with rage, and looked fixedly at him, whereupon he relapsed into alarmed silence. He realized that he had gone a little too far.

"Had we not better end this game?" asked Totski.

"It's my turn, but I plead exemption," said Ptitsin.

"You don't care to oblige us?" asked Nastasia.

"I cannot, I assure you. I confess I do not understand how anyone can play this game."

"Then, general, it's your turn," continued Nastasia Philipovna, "and if you refuse, the whole game will fall through, which will disappoint me very much, for I was looking forward to relating a certain 'page of my own life.' I am only waiting for you and Afanasy Ivanovitch to have your turns, for I require the support of your example," she added, smiling.

"Oh, if you put it in that way," cried the general, excitedly, "I'm ready to tell the whole story of my life, but I must confess that I prepared a little story in anticipation of my turn."

Nastasia smiled amiably at him; but evidently her depression and irritability were increasing with every moment. Totski was dreadfully alarmed to hear her promise a revelation out of her own life.

"I, like everyone else," began the general, "have committed certain not altogether graceful actions, so to speak, during the course of my life. But the strangest thing of all in my case is, that I should consider the little anecdote which I am now about to give you as a confession of the worst of my 'bad actions.' It is thirty-five years since it all happened, and yet I cannot to this very day recall the circumstances without, as it were, a sudden pang at the heart.

"It was a silly affair—I was an ensign at the time. You know ensigns—their blood is boiling water, their circumstances generally penurious. Well, I had a servant Nikifor who used to do everything for me in my quarters, economized and managed for me, and even laid hands on anything he could find (belonging to other people), in order to augment our household goods; but a faithful, honest fellow all the same.

"I was strict, but just by nature. At that time we were stationed in a small town. I was quartered at an old widow's house, a lieutenant's widow of eighty years of age. She lived in a wretched little wooden house, and had not even a servant, so poor was she.

"Her relations had all died off—her husband was dead and buried forty years since; and a niece, who had lived with her and bullied her up to three years ago, was dead too; so that she was quite alone.

"Well, I was precious dull with her, especially as she was so childish that there was nothing to be got out of her. Eventually, she stole a fowl of mine; the business is a mystery to this day; but it could have been no one but herself. I requested to be quartered somewhere else, and was shifted to the other end of the town, to the house of a merchant with a large family, and a long beard, as I remember him. Nikifor and I were delighted to go; but the old lady was not pleased at our departure.

"Well, a day or two afterwards, when I returned from drill, Nikifor says to me: 'We oughtn't to have left our tureen with the old lady, I've nothing to serve the soup in.'

"I asked how it came about that the tureen had been left. Nikifor explained that the old lady refused to give it up, because, she said, we had broken her bowl, and she must have our tureen in place of it; she had declared that I had so arranged the matter with herself.

"This baseness on her part of course aroused my young blood to fever heat; I jumped up, and away I flew.

"I arrived at the old woman's house beside myself. She was sitting in a corner all alone, leaning her face on her hand. I fell on her like a clap of thunder. 'You old wretch!' I yelled and all that sort of thing, in real Russian style. Well, when I began cursing at her, a strange thing happened. I looked at her, and she stared back with her eyes starting out of her head, but she did not say a word. She seemed to sway about as she sat, and looked and looked at me in the strangest way. Well, I soon stopped swearing and looked closer at her, asked her questions, but not a word could I get out of her. The flies were buzzing about the room and only this sound broke the silence; the sun was setting outside; I didn't know what to make of it, so I went away.

"Before I reached home I was met and summoned to the major's, so that it was some while before I actually got there. When I came in, Nikifor met me. 'Have you heard, sir, that our old lady is dead?' '*dead*, when?' 'Oh, an hour and a half ago.' That meant nothing more nor less than that she was dying at the moment when I pounced on her and began abusing her.

"This produced a great effect upon me. I used to dream of the poor old woman at nights. I really am not superstitious, but two days after, I went to her funeral, and as time went on I thought more and more about her. I said to myself, 'This woman, this human being, lived to a great age. She had children, a husband and family, friends and relations; her household was busy and cheerful; she was surrounded by smiling faces; and then suddenly they are gone, and she is left alone like a solitary fly... like a fly, cursed with the burden of her age. At last, God calls her to Himself. At sunset, on a lovely summer's evening, my little old woman passes away—a thought, you will notice, which offers much food for reflection—and behold! instead of tears and prayers to start her on her last journey, she has insults and jeers from a young ensign, who stands before her with his hands in his pockets, making a terrible row about a soup tureen!' Of course I was to blame, and even now that I have time to look back at it calmly, I pity the poor old thing no less. I repeat that I wonder at myself, for after all I was not really responsible. Why did she take it into her head to die at that moment? But the more I thought of it, the more I felt the weight of it upon my mind; and I never got quite rid of the impression until I put a couple of old women into an almshouse and kept them there at my own expense. There, that's all. I repeat I dare say I have committed many a grievous sin in my day; but I cannot help always looking back upon this as the worst action I have ever perpetrated."

"H'm! and instead of a bad action, your excellency has detailed one of your noblest deeds," said Ferdishenko. "Ferdishenko is 'done.'"

"Dear me, general," said Nastasia Philipovna, absently, "I really never imagined you had such a good heart."

The general laughed with great satisfaction, and applied himself once more to the champagne.

It was now Totski's turn, and his story was awaited with great curiosity—while all eyes turned on Nastasia Philipovna, as though anticipating that his revelation must be connected somehow with her. Nastasia, during the whole of his story, pulled at the lace trimming of her sleeve, and never once glanced at the speaker. Totski was a handsome man, rather stout, with a very polite and dignified manner. He was always well dressed, and his linen was exquisite. He had plump white hands, and wore a magnificent diamond ring on one finger.

"What simplifies the duty before me considerably, in my opinion," he began, "is that I am bound to recall and relate the very worst action of my life. In such circumstances there can, of course, be no doubt. One's conscience very soon informs one what is the proper narrative to tell. I admit, that among the many silly and thoughtless actions of my life, the memory of one comes prominently forward and reminds me that it lay long like a stone on my heart. Some twenty years since, I paid a visit to Platon Ordintzeff at his country-house. He had just been elected marshal of the nobility, and had come there with his young wife for the winter holidays. Anfisa Alexeyevna's birthday came off just then, too, and there were two balls arranged. At that time Dumas-fils' beautiful work, *La Dame aux Camélias*—a novel which I consider imperishable—had just come into fashion. In the provinces all the ladies were in raptures over it, those who had read it, at least. Camellias were all the fashion. Everyone inquired for them, everybody wanted them; and a grand lot of camellias are to be got in a country town—as you all know—and two balls to provide for!

"Poor Peter Volhofskoi was desperately in love with Anfisa Alexeyevna. I don't know whether there was anything—I mean I don't know whether he could possibly have indulged in any hope. The poor fellow was beside himself to get her a bouquet of camellias. Countess Sotski and Sophia Bespalova, as everyone knew, were coming with white camellia bouquets. Anfisa wished for red ones, for effect. Well, her husband Platon was driven desperate to find some. And the day before the ball, Anfisa's rival snapped up the only red camellias to be had in the place, from under Platon's nose, and Platon—wretched man—was done for. Now if Peter had only been able to step in at this moment with a red bouquet, his little hopes might have made gigantic strides. A woman's gratitude under such circumstances would have been boundless—but it was practically an impossibility.

"The night before the ball I met Peter, looking radiant. 'What is it?' I ask. 'I've found them, Eureka!' 'No! where, where?' 'At Ekshaisk (a little town fifteen miles off) there's a rich old merchant, who keeps a lot of canaries, has no children, and he and his wife are devoted to flowers. He's got some camellias.' 'And what if he won't let you have them?' 'I'll go on my knees and implore till I get them. I won't go away.' 'When shall you start?' 'Tomorrow morning at five o'clock.' 'Go on,' I said, 'and good luck to you.'

"I was glad for the poor fellow, and went home. But an idea got hold of me somehow. I don't know how. It was nearly two in the morning. I rang the bell and ordered the coachman to be waked up and sent to me. He came. I gave him a tip of fifteen roubles, and told him to get the carriage ready at once. In half an hour it was at the door. I got in and off we went.

"By five I drew up at the Ekshaisky inn. I waited there till dawn, and soon after six I was off, and at the old merchant Trepalaf's.

"'Camellias!' I said, 'father, save me, save me, let me have some camellias!' He was a tall, grey old man—a terrible-looking old gentleman. 'Not a bit of it,' he says. 'I won't.' Down I went on my knees. 'Don't say so, don't—think what you're doing!' I cried; 'it's a matter of life and death!' 'If that's the case, take them,' says he. So up I get, and cut such a bouquet of red camellias! He had a whole greenhouse full of them—lovely ones. The old fellow sighs. I pull out a hundred roubles. 'No, no!' says he, 'don't insult me that way.' 'Oh, if that's the case, give it to the village hospital,' I say. 'Ah,' he says, 'that's quite a different matter; that's good of you and generous. I'll pay it in there for you with pleasure.' I liked that old fellow, Russian to the core, *de la vraie souche*. I went home in raptures, but took another road in order to avoid Peter. Immediately on arriving I sent up the bouquet for Anfisa to see when she awoke.

"You may imagine her ecstasy, her gratitude. The wretched Platon, who had almost died since yesterday of the reproaches showered upon him, wept on my shoulder. Of course poor Peter had no chance after this.

"I thought he would cut my throat at first, and went about armed ready to meet him. But he took it differently; he fainted, and had brain fever and convulsions. A month after, when he had hardly recovered, he went off to the Crimea, and there he was shot.

"I assure you this business left me no peace for many a long year. Why did I do it? I was not in love with her myself; I'm afraid it was simply mischief—pure 'cussedness' on my part.

"If I hadn't seized that bouquet from under his nose he might have been alive now, and a happy man. He might have been successful in life, and never have gone to fight the Turks."

Totski ended his tale with the same dignity that had characterized its commencement.

Nastasia Philipovna's eyes were flashing in a most unmistakable way, now; and her lips were all a-quiver by the time Totski finished his story.

All present watched both of them with curiosity.

"You were right, Totski," said Nastasia, "it is a dull game and a stupid one. I'll just tell my story, as I promised, and then we'll play cards."

"Yes, but let's have the story first!" cried the general.

"Prince," said Nastasia Philipovna, unexpectedly turning to Muishkin, "here are my old friends, Totski and General Epanchin, who wish to marry me off. Tell me what you think. Shall I marry or not? As you decide, so shall it be."

Totski grew white as a sheet. The general was struck dumb. All present started and listened intently. Gania sat rooted to his chair.

"Marry whom?" asked the prince, faintly.

"Gavrila Ardalionovitch Ivolgin," said Nastasia, firmly and evenly.

There were a few seconds of dead silence.

The prince tried to speak, but could not form his words; a great weight seemed to lie upon his breast and suffocate him.

"N-no! don't marry him!" he whispered at last, drawing his breath with an effort.

"So be it, then. Gavrila Ardalionovitch," she spoke solemnly and forcibly, "you hear the prince's decision? Take it as my decision; and let that be the end of the matter for good and all."

"Nastasia Philipovna!" cried Totski, in a quaking voice.

"Nastasia Philipovna!" said the general, in persuasive but agitated tones.

Everyone in the room fidgeted in their places, and waited to see what was coming next.

"Well, gentlemen!" she continued, gazing around in apparent astonishment; "what do you all look so alarmed about? Why are you so upset?"

"But—recollect, Nastasia Philipovna." stammered Totski, "you gave a promise, quite a free one, and—and you might have spared us this. I am confused and bewildered, I know; but, in a word, at such a moment, and before company, and all so-so-irregular, finishing off a game with a serious matter like this, a matter of honour, and of heart, and—"

"I don't follow you, Afanasy Ivanovitch; you are losing your head. In the first place, what do you mean by 'before company'? Isn't the company good enough for you? And what's all that about 'a game'? I wished to tell my little story, and I told it! Don't you like it? You heard what I said to the prince? 'As you decide, so it shall be!' If he had said 'yes,' I should have given my consent! But he said 'no,' so I refused. Here was my whole life hanging on his one word! Surely I was serious enough?"

"The prince! What on earth has the prince got to do with it? Who the deuce is the prince?" cried the general, who could conceal his wrath no longer.

"The prince has this to do with it—that I see in him for the first time in all my life, a man endowed with real truthfulness of spirit, and I trust him. He trusted me at first sight, and I trust him!"

"It only remains for me, then, to thank Nastasia Philipovna for the great delicacy with which she has treated me," said Gania, as pale as death, and with quivering lips. "That is my plain duty, of course; but the prince—what has he to do in the matter?"

"I see what you are driving at," said Nastasia Philipovna. "You imply that the prince is after the seventy-five thousand roubles—I quite understand you. Mr. Totski, I forgot to say, 'Take your seventy-five thousand roubles'—I don't want them. I let you go free for nothing—take your freedom! You must need it. Nine years and three months' captivity is enough for anybody. Tomorrow I shall start afresh—today I am a free agent for the first time in my life.

"General, you must take your pearls back, too—give them to your wife—here they are! Tomorrow I shall leave this flat altogether, and then there'll be no more of these pleasant little social gatherings, ladies and gentlemen."

So saying, she scornfully rose from her seat as though to depart.

"Nastasia Philipovna! Nastasia Philipovna!"

The words burst involuntarily from every mouth. All present started up in bewildered excitement; all surrounded her; all had listened uneasily to her wild, disconnected sentences. All felt that something had happened, something had gone very far wrong indeed, but no one could make head or tail of the matter.

At this moment there was a furious ring at the bell, and a great knock at the door—exactly similar to the one which had startled the company at Gania's house in the afternoon.

"Ah, ah! here's the climax at last, at half-past twelve!" cried Nastasia Philipovna. "Sit down, gentlemen, I beg you. Something is about to happen."

So saying, she reseated herself; a strange smile played on her lips. She sat quite still, but watched the door in a fever of impatience.

"Rogojin and his hundred thousand roubles, no doubt of it," muttered Ptitsin to himself.

XV.

Katia, the maid-servant, made her appearance, terribly frightened.

"Goodness knows what it means, ma'am," she said. "There is a whole collection of men come—all tipsy—and want to see you. They say that 'it's Rogojin, and she knows all about it.'"

"It's all right, Katia, let them all in at once."

"Surely not *all*, ma'am? They seem so disorderly—it's dreadful to see them."

"Yes *all*, Katia, all—every one of them. Let them in, or they'll come in whether you like or no. Listen! what a noise they are making! Perhaps you are offended, gentlemen, that I should receive such guests in your presence? I am very sorry, and ask your forgiveness, but it cannot be helped—and I should be very grateful if you could all stay and witness this climax. However, just as you please, of course."

The guests exchanged glances; they were annoyed and bewildered by the episode; but it was clear enough that all this had been pre-arranged and expected by Nastasia Philipovna, and that there was no use in trying to stop her now—for she was little short of insane.

Besides, they were naturally inquisitive to see what was to happen. There was nobody who would be likely to feel much alarm. There were but two ladies present; one of whom was the lively actress, who was not easily frightened, and the other the silent German beauty who, it turned out, did not understand a word of Russian, and seemed to be as stupid as she was lovely.

Her acquaintances invited her to their "At Homes" because she was so decorative. She was exhibited to their guests like a valuable picture, or vase, or statue, or firescreen. As for the men, Ptitsin was one of Rogojin's friends; Ferdishenko was as much at home as a fish in the sea, Gania, not yet recovered from his amazement, appeared to be chained to a pillory. The old professor did not in the least understand what was happening; but when he noticed how extremely agitated the mistress of the house, and her friends, seemed, he nearly wept, and trembled with fright: but he would rather have died than leave Nastasia Philipovna at such a crisis, for he loved her as if she were his own granddaughter. Afanasy Ivanovitch greatly disliked having anything to do with the affair, but he was too much interested to leave, in spite of the mad turn things had taken; and a few words that had dropped from the lips of Nastasia puzzled him so much, that he felt he could not go without an explanation. He resolved therefore, to see it out, and to adopt the attitude of silent spectator, as most suited to his dignity. General Epanchin alone determined to depart. He was annoyed at the manner in which his gift had been returned, as though he had condescended, under the influence of passion, to place himself on a level with Ptitsin and Ferdishenko, his self-respect and sense of duty now returned together with a consciousness of what was due to his social rank and official importance. In short, he plainly showed his conviction that a man in his position could have nothing to do with Rogojin and his companions. But Nastasia interrupted him at his first words.

"Ah, general!" she cried, "I was forgetting! If I had only foreseen this unpleasantness! I won't insist on keeping you against your will, although I should have liked you to be beside me now. In any case, I am most grateful to you for your visit, and flattering attention... but if you are afraid..."

"Excuse me, Nastasia Philipovna," interrupted the general, with chivalric generosity. "To whom are you speaking? I have remained until now simply because of my devotion to you, and as for danger, I am only afraid that the carpets may be ruined, and the furniture smashed!... You should shut the door on the lot, in my opinion. But I confess that I am extremely curious to see how it ends."

"Rogojin!" announced Ferdishenko.

"What do you think about it?" said the general in a low voice to Totski. "Is she mad? I mean mad in the medical sense of the word .... eh?"

"I've always said she was predisposed to it," whispered Afanasy Ivanovitch slyly. "Perhaps it is a fever!"

Since their visit to Gania's home, Rogojin's followers had been increased by two new recruits—a dissolute old man, the hero of some ancient scandal, and a retired sub-lieutenant. A laughable story was told of the former. He possessed, it was said, a set of false teeth, and one day when he wanted money for a drinking orgy, he pawned them, and was never able to reclaim them! The officer appeared to be a rival of the gentleman who was so proud of his fists. He was known to none of Rogojin's followers, but as they passed by the Nevsky, where he stood begging, he had joined their ranks. His claim for the charity he desired seemed based on the fact that in the days of his prosperity he had given away as much as fifteen roubles at a time. The rivals seemed more than a little jealous of one another. The athlete appeared injured at the admission of the "beggar" into the company. By nature taciturn, he now merely growled occasionally like a bear, and glared contemptuously upon the "beggar," who, being somewhat of a man of the world, and a diplomatist, tried to insinuate himself into the bear's good graces. He was a much smaller man than the athlete, and doubtless was conscious that he must tread warily. Gently and without argument he alluded to the advantages of the English style in boxing, and showed himself a firm believer in Western institutions. The athlete's lips curled disdainfully, and without honouring his adversary with a formal denial, he exhibited, as if by accident, that peculiarly Russian object—an enormous fist, clenched, muscular, and covered with red hairs! The sight of this pre-eminently national attribute was enough to convince anybody, without words, that it was a serious matter for those who should happen to come into contact with it.

None of the band were very drunk, for the leader had kept his intended visit to Nastasia in view all day, and had done his best to prevent his followers from drinking too much. He was sober himself, but the excitement of this chaotic day—the strangest day of his life—had affected him so that he was in a dazed, wild condition, which almost resembled drunkenness.

He had kept but one idea before him all day, and for that he had worked in an agony of anxiety and a fever of suspense. His lieutenants had worked so hard from five o'clock until eleven, that they actually had collected a hundred thousand roubles for him, but at such terrific expense, that the rate of interest was only mentioned among them in whispers and with bated breath.

As before, Rogojin walked in advance of his troop, who followed him with mingled self-assertion and timidity. They were specially frightened of Nastasia Philipovna herself, for some reason.

Many of them expected to be thrown downstairs at once, without further ceremony, the elegant and irresistible Zaleshoff among them. But the party led by the athlete, without openly showing their hostile intentions, silently nursed contempt and even hatred for Nastasia Philipovna, and marched into her house as they would have marched into an enemy's fortress. Arrived there, the luxury of the rooms seemed to inspire them with a kind of respect, not unmixed with alarm. So many things were entirely new to their experience—the choice furniture, the pictures, the great statue of Venus. They followed their chief into the salon, however, with a kind of impudent curiosity. There, the sight of General Epanchin among the guests, caused many of them to beat a hasty retreat into the adjoining room, the "boxer" and "beggar" being among the first to go. A few only, of whom Lebedeff made one, stood their ground; he had contrived to walk side by side with Rogojin, for he quite understood the importance of a man who had a fortune of a million odd roubles, and who at this moment carried a hundred thousand in his hand. It may be added that the whole company, not excepting Lebedeff, had the vaguest idea of the extent of their powers, and of how far they could safely go. At some moments Lebedeff was sure that right was on their side; at others he tried uneasily to remember various cheering and reassuring articles of the Civil Code.

Rogojin, when he stepped into the room, and his eyes fell upon Nastasia, stopped short, grew white as a sheet, and stood staring; it was clear that his heart was beating painfully. So he stood, gazing intently, but timidly, for a few seconds. Suddenly, as though bereft of his senses, he moved forward, staggering helplessly, towards the table. On his way he collided against Ptitsin's chair, and put his dirty foot on the lace skirt of the silent lady's dress; but he neither apologized for this, nor even noticed it.

On reaching the table, he placed upon it a strange-looking object, which he had carried with him into the drawing-room. This was a paper packet, some six or seven inches thick, and eight or nine in length, wrapped in an old newspaper, and tied round three or four times with string.

Having placed this before her, he stood with drooped arms and head, as though awaiting his sentence.

His costume was the same as it had been in the morning, except for a new silk handkerchief round his neck, bright green and red, fastened with a huge diamond pin, and an enormous diamond ring on his dirty forefinger.

Lebedeff stood two or three paces behind his chief; and the rest of the band waited about near the door.

The two maid-servants were both peeping in, frightened and amazed at this unusual and disorderly scene.

"What is that?" asked Nastasia Philipovna, gazing intently at Rogojin, and indicating the paper packet.

"A hundred thousand," replied the latter, almost in a whisper.

"Oh! so he kept his word—there's a man for you! Well, sit down, please—take that chair. I shall have something to say to you presently. Who are all these with you? The same party? Let them come in and sit down. There's room on that sofa, there are some chairs and there's another sofa! Well, why don't they sit down?"

Sure enough, some of the brave fellows entirely lost their heads at this point, and retreated into the next room. Others, however, took the hint and sat down, as far as they could from the table, however; feeling braver in proportion to their distance from Nastasia.

Rogojin took the chair offered him, but he did not sit long; he soon stood up again, and did not reseat himself. Little by little he began to look around him and discern the other guests. Seeing Gania, he smiled venomously and muttered to himself, "Look at that!"

He gazed at Totski and the general with no apparent confusion, and with very little curiosity. But when he observed that the prince was seated beside Nastasia Philipovna, he could not take his eyes off him for a long while, and was clearly amazed. He could not account for the prince's presence there. It was not in the least surprising that

Rogojin should be, at this time, in a more or less delirious condition; for not to speak of the excitements of the day, he had spent the night before in the train, and had not slept more than a wink for forty-eight hours.

"This, gentlemen, is a hundred thousand roubles," said Nastasia Philipovna, addressing the company in general, "here, in this dirty parcel. This afternoon Rogojin yelled, like a madman, that he would bring me a hundred thousand in the evening, and I have been waiting for him all the while. He was bargaining for me, you know; first he offered me eighteen thousand; then he rose to forty, and then to a hundred thousand. And he has kept his word, see! My goodness, how white he is! All this happened this afternoon, at Gania's. I had gone to pay his mother a visit—my future family, you know! And his sister said to my very face, surely somebody will turn this shameless creature out. After which she spat in her brother Gania's face—a girl of character, that!"

"Nastasia Philipovna!" began the general, reproachfully. He was beginning to put his own interpretation on the affair.

"Well, what, general? Not quite good form, eh? Oh, nonsense! Here have I been sitting in my box at the French theatre for the last five years like a statue of inaccessible virtue, and kept out of the way of all admirers, like a silly little idiot! Now, there's this man, who comes and pays down his hundred thousand on the table, before you all, in spite of my five years of innocence and proud virtue, and I dare be sworn he has his sledge outside waiting to carry me off. He values me at a hundred thousand! I see you are still angry with me, Gania! Why, surely you never really wished to take *me* into your family? *me*, Rogojin's mistress! What did the prince say just now?"

"I never said you were Rogojin's mistress—you are *not!*" said the prince, in trembling accents.

"Nastasia Philipovna, dear soul!" cried the actress, impatiently, "do be calm, dear! If it annoys you so—all this—do go away and rest! Of course you would never go with this wretched fellow, in spite of his hundred thousand roubles! Take his money and kick him out of the house; that's the way to treat him and the likes of him! Upon my word, if it were my business, I'd soon clear them all out!"

The actress was a kind-hearted woman, and highly impressionable. She was very angry now.

"Don't be cross, Daria Alexeyevna!" laughed Nastasia. "I was not angry when I spoke; I wasn't reproaching Gania. I don't know how it was that I ever could have indulged the whim of entering an honest family like his. I saw his mother—and kissed her hand, too. I came and stirred up all that fuss, Gania, this afternoon, on purpose to see how much you could swallow—you surprised me, my friend—you did, indeed. Surely you could not marry a woman who accepts pearls like those you knew the general was going to give me, on the very eve of her marriage? And Rogojin! Why, in your own house and before your own brother and sister, he bargained with me! Yet you could come here and expect to be betrothed to me before you left the house! You almost brought your sister, too. Surely what Rogojin said about you is not really true: that you would crawl all the way to the other end of the town, on hands and knees, for three roubles?"

"Yes, he would!" said Rogojin, quietly, but with an air of absolute conviction.

"H'm! and he receives a good salary, I'm told. Well, what should you get but disgrace and misery if you took a wife you hated into your family (for I know very well that you do hate me)? No, no! I believe now that a man like you would murder anyone for money—sharpen a razor and come up behind his best friend and cut his throat like a sheep—I've read of such people. Everyone seems money-mad nowadays. No, no! I may be shameless, but you are far worse. I don't say a word about that other—"

"Nastasia Philipovna, is this really you? You, once so refined and delicate of speech. Oh, what a tongue! What dreadful things you are saying," cried the general, wringing his hands in real grief.

"I am intoxicated, general. I am having a day out, you know—it's my birthday! I have long looked forward to this happy occasion. Daria Alexeyevna, you see that nosegay-man, that Monsieur aux Camelias, sitting there laughing at us?"

"I am not laughing, Nastasia Philipovna; I am only listening with all my attention," said Totski, with dignity.

"Well, why have I worried him, for five years, and never let him go free? Is he worth it? He is only just what he ought to be—nothing particular. He thinks I am to blame, too. He gave me my education, kept me like a countess. Money—my word! What a lot of money he spent over me! And he tried to find me an honest husband first, and then this Gania, here. And what do you think? All these five years I did not live with him, and yet I took his money, and considered I was quite justified.

"You say, take the hundred thousand and kick that man out. It is true, it is an abominable business, as you say. I might have married long ago, not Gania—Oh, no!—but that would have been abominable too.

"Would you believe it, I had some thoughts of marrying Totski, four years ago! I meant mischief, I confess—but I could have had him, I give you my word; he asked me himself. But I thought, no! it's not worthwhile to take such advantage of him. No! I had better go on to the streets, or accept Rogojin, or become a washerwoman or something—for I have nothing of my own, you know. I shall go away and leave everything behind, to the last rag—he shall have it all back. And who would take me without anything? Ask Gania, there, whether he would. Why, even Ferdishenko wouldn't have me!"

"No, Ferdishenko would not; he is a candid fellow, Nastasia Philipovna," said that worthy. "But the prince would. You sit here making complaints, but just look at the prince. I've been observing him for a long while."

Nastasia Philipovna looked keenly round at the prince.

"Is that true?" she asked.

"Quite true," whispered the prince.

"You'll take me as I am, with nothing?"

"I will, Nastasia Philipovna."

"Here's a pretty business!" cried the general. "However, it might have been expected of him."

The prince continued to regard Nastasia with a sorrowful, but intent and piercing, gaze.

"Here's another alternative for me," said Nastasia, turning once more to the actress; "and he does it out of pure kindness of heart. I know him. I've found a benefactor. Perhaps, though, what they say about him may be true—that he's an—we know what. And what shall you live on, if you are really so madly in love with Rogojin's mistress, that you are ready to marry her—eh?"

"I take you as a good, honest woman, Nastasia Philipovna—not as Rogojin's mistress."

"Who? I?—good and honest?"

"Yes, you."

"Oh, you get those ideas out of novels, you know. Times are changed now, dear prince; the world sees things as they really are. That's all nonsense. Besides, how can you marry? You need a nurse, not a wife."

The prince rose and began to speak in a trembling, timid tone, but with the air of a man absolutely sure of the truth of his words.

"I know nothing, Nastasia Philipovna. I have seen nothing. You are right so far; but I consider that you would be honouring me, and not I you. I am a nobody. You have suffered, you have passed through hell and emerged pure, and that is very much. Why do you shame yourself by desiring to go with Rogojin? You are delirious. You have returned to Mr. Totski his seventy-five thousand roubles, and declared that you will leave this house and all that is in it, which is a line of conduct that not one person here would imitate. Nastasia Philipovna, I love you! I would die for you. I shall never let any man say one word against you, Nastasia Philipovna! and if we are poor, I can work for both."

As the prince spoke these last words a titter was heard from Ferdishenko; Lebedeff laughed too. The general grunted with irritation; Ptitsin and Totski barely restrained their smiles. The rest all sat listening, open-mouthed with wonder.

"But perhaps we shall not be poor; we may be very rich, Nastasia Philipovna," continued the prince, in the same timid, quivering tones. "I don't know for certain, and I'm sorry to say I haven't had an opportunity of finding out all day; but I received a letter from Moscow, while I was in Switzerland, from a Mr. Salaskin, and he acquaints me with the fact that I am entitled to a very large inheritance. This letter—"

The prince pulled a letter out of his pocket.

"Is he raving?" said the general. "Are we really in a mad-house?"

There was silence for a moment. Then Ptitsin spoke.

"I think you said, prince, that your letter was from Salaskin? Salaskin is a very eminent man, indeed, in his own world; he is a wonderfully clever solicitor, and if he really tells you this, I think you may be pretty sure that he is right. It so happens, luckily, that I know his handwriting, for I have lately had business with him. If you would allow me to see it, I should perhaps be able to tell you."

The prince held out the letter silently, but with a shaking hand.

"What, what?" said the general, much agitated.

"What's all this? Is he really heir to anything?"

All present concentrated their attention upon Ptitsin, reading the prince's letter. The general curiosity had received a new fillip. Ferdishenko could not sit still. Rogojin fixed his eyes first on the prince, and then on Ptitsin, and then back again; he was extremely agitated. Lebedeff could not stand it. He crept up and read over Ptitsin's shoulder, with the air of a naughty boy who expects a box on the ear every moment for his indiscretion.

XVI.

"It's good business," said Ptitsin, at last, folding the letter and handing it back to the prince. "You will receive, without the slightest trouble, by the last will and testament of your aunt, a very large sum of money indeed."

"Impossible!" cried the general, starting up as if he had been shot.

Ptitsin explained, for the benefit of the company, that the prince's aunt had died five months since. He had never known her, but she was his mother's own sister, the daughter of a Moscow merchant, one Paparchin, who had died a bankrupt. But the elder brother of this same Paparchin, had been an eminent and very rich merchant. A year since it had so happened that his only two sons had both died within the same month. This sad event had so affected the old man that he, too, had died very shortly after. He was a widower, and had no relations left, excepting the prince's aunt, a poor woman living on charity, who was herself at the point of death from dropsy; but who had time, before she died, to set Salaskin to work to find her nephew, and to make her will bequeathing her newly-acquired fortune to him.

It appeared that neither the prince, nor the doctor with whom he lived in Switzerland, had thought of waiting for further communications; but the prince had started straight away with Salaskin's letter in his pocket.

"One thing I may tell you, for certain," concluded Ptitsin, addressing the prince, "that there is no question about the authenticity of this matter. Anything that Salaskin writes you as regards your unquestionable right to this inheritance, you may look upon as so much money in your pocket. I congratulate you, prince; you may receive a million and a half of roubles, perhaps more; I don't know. All I *do* know is that Paparchin was a very rich merchant indeed."

"Hurrah!" cried Lebedeff, in a drunken voice. "Hurrah for the last of the Muishkins!"

"My goodness me! and I gave him twenty-five roubles this morning as though he were a beggar," blurted out the general, half senseless with amazement. "Well, I congratulate you, I congratulate you!" And the general rose from his seat and solemnly embraced the prince. All came forward with congratulations; even those of Rogojin's party who had retreated into the next room, now crept softly back to look on. For the moment even Nastasia Philipovna was forgotten.

But gradually the consciousness crept back into the minds of each one present that the prince had just made her an offer of marriage. The situation had, therefore, become three times as fantastic as before.

Totski sat and shrugged his shoulders, bewildered. He was the only guest left sitting at this time; the others had thronged round the table in disorder, and were all talking at once.

It was generally agreed, afterwards, in recalling that evening, that from this moment Nastasia Philipovna seemed entirely to lose her senses. She continued to sit still in her place, looking around at her guests with a strange, bewildered expression, as though she were trying to collect her thoughts, and could not. Then she suddenly turned to the prince, and glared at him with frowning brows; but this only lasted one moment. Perhaps it suddenly struck her that all this was a jest, but his face seemed to reassure her. She reflected, and smiled again, vaguely.

"So I am really a princess," she whispered to herself, ironically, and glancing accidentally at Daria Alexeyevna's face, she burst out laughing.

"Ha, ha, ha!" she cried, "this is an unexpected climax, after all. I didn't expect this. What are you all standing up for, gentlemen? Sit down; congratulate me and the prince! Ferdishenko, just step out and order some more champagne, will you? Katia, Pasha," she added suddenly, seeing the servants at the door, "come here! I'm going to be married, did you hear? To the prince. He has a million and a half of roubles; he is Prince Muishkin, and has asked me to marry him. Here, prince, come and sit by me; and here comes the wine. Now then, ladies and gentlemen, where are your congratulations?"

"Hurrah!" cried a number of voices. A rush was made for the wine by Rogojin's followers, though, even among them, there seemed some sort of realization that the situation had changed. Rogojin stood and looked on, with an incredulous smile, screwing up one side of his mouth.

"Prince, my dear fellow, do remember what you are about," said the general, approaching Muishkin, and pulling him by the coat sleeve.

Nastasia Philipovna overheard the remark, and burst out laughing.

"No, no, general!" she cried. "You had better look out! I am the princess now, you know. The prince won't let you insult me. Afanasy Ivanovitch, why don't you congratulate me? I shall be able to sit at table with your new wife, now. Aha! you see what I gain by marrying a prince! A million and a half, and a prince, and an idiot into the bargain, they say. What better could I wish for? Life is only just about to commence for me in earnest. Rogojin, you are a little too late. Away with your paper parcel! I'm going to marry the prince; I'm richer than you are now."

But Rogojin understood how things were tending, at last. An inexpressibly painful expression came over his face. He wrung his hands; a groan made its way up from the depths of his soul.

"Surrender her, for God's sake!" he said to the prince.

All around burst out laughing.

"What? Surrender her to *you?*" cried Daria Alexeyevna. "To a fellow who comes and bargains for a wife like a moujik! The prince wishes to marry her, and you—"

"So do I, so do I! This moment, if I could! I'd give every farthing I have to do it."

"You drunken moujik," said Daria Alexeyevna, once more. "You ought to be kicked out of the place."

The laughter became louder than ever.

"Do you hear, prince?" said Nastasia Philipovna. "Do you hear how this moujik of a fellow goes on bargaining for your bride?"

"He is drunk," said the prince, quietly, "and he loves you very much."

"Won't you be ashamed, afterwards, to reflect that your wife very nearly ran away with Rogojin?"

"Oh, you were raving, you were in a fever; you are still half delirious."

"And won't you be ashamed when they tell you, afterwards, that your wife lived at Totski's expense so many years?"

"No; I shall not be ashamed of that. You did not so live by your own will."

"And you'll never reproach me with it?"

"Never."

"Take care, don't commit yourself for a whole lifetime."

"Nastasia Philipovna." said the prince, quietly, and with deep emotion, "I said before that I shall esteem your consent to be my wife as a great honour to myself, and shall consider that it is you who will honour me, not I you, by our marriage. You laughed at these words, and others around us laughed as well; I heard them. Very likely I expressed myself funnily, and I may have looked funny, but, for all that, I believe I understand where honour lies, and what I said was but the literal truth. You were about to ruin yourself just now, irrevocably; you would never have forgiven yourself for so doing afterwards; and yet, you are absolutely blameless. It is impossible that your life should be altogether ruined at your age. What matter that Rogojin came bargaining here, and that Gavrila Ardalionovitch would have deceived you if he could? Why do you continually remind us of these facts? I assure you once more that very few could find it in them to act as you have acted this day. As for your wish to go with Rogojin, that was simply the idea of a delirious and suffering brain. You are still quite feverish; you ought to be in bed, not here. You know quite well that if you had gone with Rogojin, you would have become a washer-woman next day, rather than stay with him. You are proud, Nastasia Philipovna, and perhaps you have really suffered so much that you imagine yourself to be a desperately guilty woman. You require a great deal of petting and looking after, Nastasia Philipovna, and I will do this. I saw your portrait this morning, and it seemed quite a familiar face to me; it seemed to me that the portrait-face was calling to me for help. I—I shall respect you all my life, Nastasia Philipovna," concluded the prince, as though suddenly recollecting himself, and blushing to think of the sort of company before whom he had said all this.

Ptitsin bowed his head and looked at the ground, overcome by a mixture of feelings. Totski muttered to himself: "He may be an idiot, but he knows that flattery is the best road to success here."

The prince observed Gania's eyes flashing at him, as though they would gladly annihilate him then and there.

"That's a kind-hearted man, if you like," said Daria Alexeyevna, whose wrath was quickly evaporating.

"A refined man, but—lost," murmured the general.

Totski took his hat and rose to go. He and the general exchanged glances, making a private arrangement, thereby, to leave the house together.

"Thank you, prince; no one has ever spoken to me like that before," began Nastasia Philipovna. "Men have always bargained for me, before this; and not a single respectable man has ever proposed to marry me. Do you hear, Afanasy Ivanovitch? What do *you* think of what the prince has just been saying? It was almost immodest, wasn't it? You, Rogojin, wait a moment, don't go yet! I see you don't intend to move however. Perhaps I may go with you yet. Where did you mean to take me to?"

"To Ekaterinhof," replied Lebedeff. Rogojin simply stood staring, with trembling lips, not daring to believe his ears. He was stunned, as though from a blow on the head.

"What are you thinking of, my dear Nastasia?" said Daria Alexeyevna in alarm. "What are you saying?" "You are not going mad, are you?"

Nastasia Philipovna burst out laughing and jumped up from the sofa.

"You thought I should accept this good child's invitation to ruin him, did you?" she cried. "That's Totski's way, not mine. He's fond of children. Come along, Rogojin, get your money ready! We won't talk about marrying just at this moment, but let's see the money at all events. Come! I may not marry you, either. I don't know. I suppose you thought you'd keep the money, if I did! Ha, ha, ha! nonsense! I have no sense of shame left. I tell you I have been Totski's concubine. Prince, you must marry Aglaya Ivanovna, not Nastasia Philipovna, or this fellow Ferdishenko will always be pointing the finger of scorn at you. You aren't afraid, I know; but I should always be afraid that I had ruined you, and that you would reproach me for it. As for what you say about my doing you honour by marrying you-well, Totski can tell you all about that. You had your eye on Aglaya, Gania, you know you had; and you might have married her if you had not come bargaining. You are all like this. You should choose, once for all, between disreputable women, and respectable ones, or you are sure to get mixed. Look at the general, how he's staring at me!"

"This is too horrible," said the general, starting to his feet. All were standing up now. Nastasia was absolutely beside herself.

"I am very proud, in spite of what I am," she continued. "You called me 'perfection' just now, prince. A nice sort of perfection to throw up a prince and a million and a half of roubles in order to be able to boast of the fact afterwards! What sort of a wife should I make for you, after all I have said? Afanasy Ivanovitch, do you observe I have really and truly thrown away a million of roubles? And you thought that I should consider your wretched seventy-five thousand, with Gania thrown in for a husband, a paradise of bliss! Take your seventy-five thousand back, sir; you did not reach the hundred thousand. Rogojin cut a better dash than you did. I'll console Gania myself; I have an idea about that. But now I must be off! I've been in prison for ten years. I'm free at last! Well, Rogojin, what are you waiting for? Let's get ready and go."

"Come along!" shouted Rogojin, beside himself with joy. "Hey! all of you fellows! Wine! Round with it! Fill the glasses!"

"Get away!" he shouted frantically, observing that Daria Alexeyevna was approaching to protest against Nastasia's conduct. "Get away, she's mine, everything's mine! She's a queen, get away!"

He was panting with ecstasy. He walked round and round Nastasia Philipovna and told everybody to "keep their distance."

All the Rogojin company were now collected in the drawing-room; some were drinking, some laughed and talked: all were in the highest and wildest spirits. Ferdishenko was doing his best to unite himself to them; the general and Totski again made an attempt to go. Gania, too stood hat in hand ready to go; but seemed to be unable to tear his eyes away from the scene before him.

"Get out, keep your distance!" shouted Rogojin.

"What are you shouting about there!" cried Nastasia "I'm not yours yet. I may kick you out for all you know I haven't taken your money yet; there it all is on the table. Here, give me over that packet! Is there a hundred thousand roubles in that one packet? Pfu! what abominable stuff it looks! Oh! nonsense, Daria Alexeyevna; you surely did not expect me to ruin*him?*" (indicating the prince). "Fancy him nursing me! Why, he needs a nurse himself! The general, there, will be his nurse now, you'll see. Here, prince, look here! Your bride is accepting money. What a disreputable woman she must be! And you wished to marry her! What are you crying about? Is it a bitter dose? Never mind, you shall laugh yet. Trust to time." (In spite of these words there were two large tears rolling down Nastasia's own cheeks.) "It's far better to think twice of it now than afterwards. Oh! you mustn't cry like that! There's Katia crying, too. What is it, Katia, dear? I shall leave you and Pasha a lot of things, I've laid them out for you already; but good-bye, now. I made an honest girl like you serve a low woman like myself. It's better so, prince, it is indeed. You'd begin to despise me afterwards—we should never be happy. Oh! you needn't swear, prince, I shan't believe you, you know. How foolish it would be, too! No, no; we'd better say good-bye and part friends. I am a bit of a dreamer myself, and I used to dream of you once. Very often during those five years down at his estate I used to dream and think, and I always imagined just such a good, honest, foolish fellow as you, one who should come and say to me: 'You are an innocent woman, Nastasia Philipovna, and I adore you.' I dreamt of you often. I used to think so much down there that I nearly went mad; and then this fellow here would come down. He would stay a couple of months out of the twelve, and disgrace and insult and deprave me, and then go; so that I longed to drown myself in the pond a thousand times over; but I did not dare do it. I hadn't the heart, and now— well, are you ready, Rogojin?"

"Ready—keep your distance, all of you!"

"We're all ready," said several of his friends. "The troikas [Sledges drawn by three horses abreast.] are at the door, bells and all."

Nastasia Philipovna seized the packet of bank-notes.

"Gania, I have an idea. I wish to recompense you—why should you lose all? Rogojin, would he crawl for three roubles as far as the Vassiliostrof?"

"Oh, wouldn't he just!"

"Well, look here, Gania. I wish to look into your heart once more, for the last time. You've worried me for the last three months—now it's my turn. Do you see this packet? It contains a hundred thousand roubles. Now, I'm going to throw it into the fire, here—before all these witnesses. As soon as the fire catches hold of it, you put your hands into the fire and pick it out—without gloves, you know. You must have bare hands, and you must turn your sleeves up. Pull it out, I say, and it's all yours. You may burn your fingers a little, of course; but then it's a hundred thousand roubles, remember—it won't take you long to lay hold of it and snatch it out. I shall so much admire you if you put your hands into the fire for my money. All here present may be witnesses that the whole packet of money is yours if you get it out. If you don't get it out, it shall burn. I will let no one else come; away—get away, all of you—it's my money! Rogojin has bought me with it. Is it my money, Rogojin?"

"Yes, my queen; it's your own money, my joy."

"Get away then, all of you. I shall do as I like with my own—don't meddle! Ferdishenko, make up the fire, quick!"

"Nastasia Philipovna, I can't; my hands won't obey me," said Ferdishenko, astounded and helpless with bewilderment.

"Nonsense," cried Nastasia Philipovna, seizing the poker and raking a couple of logs together. No sooner did a tongue of flame burst out than she threw the packet of notes upon it.

Everyone gasped; some even crossed themselves.

"She's mad—she's mad!" was the cry.

"Oughtn't-oughtn't we to secure her?" asked the general of Ptitsin, in a whisper; "or shall we send for the authorities? Why, she's mad, isn't she—isn't she, eh?"

"N-no, I hardly think she is actually mad," whispered Ptitsin, who was as white as his handkerchief, and trembling like a leaf. He could not take his eyes off the smouldering packet.

"She's mad surely, isn't she?" the general appealed to Totski.

"I told you she wasn't an ordinary woman," replied the latter, who was as pale as anyone.

"Oh, but, positively, you know—a hundred thousand roubles!"

"Goodness gracious! good heavens!" came from all quarters of the room.

All now crowded round the fire and thronged to see what was going on; everyone lamented and gave vent to exclamations of horror and woe. Some jumped up on chairs in order to get a better view. Daria Alexeyevna ran into the next room and whispered excitedly to Katia and Pasha. The beautiful German disappeared altogether.

"My lady! my sovereign!" lamented Lebedeff, falling on his knees before Nastasia Philipovna, and stretching out his hands towards the fire; "it's a hundred thousand roubles, it is indeed, I packed it up myself, I saw the money! My queen, let me get into the fire after it—say the word-I'll put my whole grey head into the fire for it! I have a poor lame wife and thirteen children. My father died of starvation last week. Nastasia Philipovna, Nastasia Philipovna!" The wretched little man wept, and groaned, and crawled towards the fire.

"Away, out of the way!" cried Nastasia. "Make room, all of you! Gania, what are you standing there for? Don't stand on ceremony. Put in your hand! There's your whole happiness smouldering away, look! Quick!"

But Gania had borne too much that day, and especially this evening, and he was not prepared for this last, quite unexpected trial.

The crowd parted on each side of him and he was left face to face with Nastasia Philipovna, three paces from her. She stood by the fire and waited, with her intent gaze fixed upon him.

Gania stood before her, in his evening clothes, holding his white gloves and hat in his hand, speechless and motionless, with arms folded and eyes fixed on the fire.

A silly, meaningless smile played on his white, death-like lips. He could not take his eyes off the smouldering packet; but it appeared that something new had come to birth in his soul—as though he were vowing to himself that he would bear this trial. He did not move from his place. In a few seconds it became evident to all that he did not intend to rescue the money.

"Hey! look at it, it'll burn in another minute or two!" cried Nastasia Philipovna. "You'll hang yourself afterwards, you know, if it does! I'm not joking."

The fire, choked between a couple of smouldering pieces of wood, had died down for the first few moments after the packet was thrown upon it. But a little tongue of fire now began to lick the paper from below, and soon, gathering courage, mounted the sides of the parcel, and crept around it. In another moment, the whole of it burst into flames, and the exclamations of woe and horror were redoubled.

"Nastasia Philipovna!" lamented Lebedeff again, straining towards the fireplace; but Rogojin dragged him away, and pushed him to the rear once more.

The whole of Rogojin's being was concentrated in one rapturous gaze of ecstasy. He could not take his eyes off Nastasia. He stood drinking her in, as it were. He was in the seventh heaven of delight.

"Oh, what a queen she is!" he ejaculated, every other minute, throwing out the remark for anyone who liked to catch it. "That's the sort of woman for me! Which of you would think of doing a thing like that, you blackguards, eh?" he yelled. He was hopelessly and wildly beside himself with ecstasy.

The prince watched the whole scene, silent and dejected.

"I'll pull it out with my teeth for one thousand," said Ferdishenko.

"So would I," said another, from behind, "with pleasure. Devil take the thing!" he added, in a tempest of despair, "it will all be burnt up in a minute—It's burning, it's burning!"

"It's burning, it's burning!" cried all, thronging nearer and nearer to the fire in their excitement.

"Gania, don't be a fool! I tell you for the last time."

"Get on, quick!" shrieked Ferdishenko, rushing wildly up to Gania, and trying to drag him to the fire by the sleeve of his coat. "Get it, you dummy, it's burning away fast! Oh—*damn* the thing!"

Gania hurled Ferdishenko from him; then he turned sharp round and made for the door. But he had not gone a couple of steps when he tottered and fell to the ground.

"He's fainted!" the cry went round.

"And the money's burning still," Lebedeff lamented.

"Burning for nothing," shouted others.

"Katia-Pasha! Bring him some water!" cried Nastasia Philipovna. Then she took the tongs and fished out the packet.

Nearly the whole of the outer covering was burned away, but it was soon evident that the contents were hardly touched. The packet had been wrapped in a threefold covering of newspaper, and the notes were safe. All breathed more freely.

"Some dirty little thousand or so may be touched," said Lebedeff, immensely relieved, "but there's very little harm done, after all."

"It's all his—the whole packet is for him, do you hear—all of you?" cried Nastasia Philipovna, placing the packet by the side of Gania. "He restrained himself, and didn't go after it; so his self-respect is greater than his thirst for money. All right—he'll come to directly—he must have the packet or he'll cut his throat afterwards. There! He's coming to himself. General, Totski, all of you, did you hear me? The money is all Gania's. I give it to him, fully conscious of my action, as recompense for—well, for anything he thinks best. Tell him so. Let it lie here beside him. Off we go, Rogojin! Goodbye, prince. I have seen a man for the first time in my life. Goodbye, Afanasy Ivanovitch—and thanks!"

The Rogojin gang followed their leader and Nastasia Philipovna to the entrance-hall, laughing and shouting and whistling.

In the hall the servants were waiting, and handed her her fur cloak. Martha, the cook, ran in from the kitchen. Nastasia kissed them all round.

"Are you really throwing us all over, little mother? Where, where are you going to? And on your birthday, too!" cried the four girls, crying over her and kissing her hands.

"I am going out into the world, Katia; perhaps I shall be a laundress. I don't know. No more of Afanasy Ivanovitch, anyhow. Give him my respects. Don't think badly of me, girls."

The prince hurried down to the front gate where the party were settling into the troikas, all the bells tinkling a merry accompaniment the while. The general caught him up on the stairs:

"Prince, prince!" he cried, seizing hold of his arm, "recollect yourself! Drop her, prince! You see what sort of a woman she is. I am speaking to you like a father."

The prince glanced at him, but said nothing. He shook himself free, and rushed on downstairs.

The general was just in time to see the prince take the first sledge he could get, and, giving the order to Ekaterinhof, start off in pursuit of the troikas. Then the general's fine grey horse dragged that worthy home, with some new thoughts, and some new hopes and calculations developing in his brain, and with the pearls in his pocket, for he had not forgotten to bring them along with him, being a man of business. Amid his new thoughts and ideas there came, once or twice, the image of Nastasia Philipovna. The general sighed.

"I'm sorry, really sorry," he muttered. "She's a ruined woman. Mad! mad! However, the prince is not for Nastasia Philipovna now,—perhaps it's as well."

Two more of Nastasia's guests, who walked a short distance together, indulged in high moral sentiments of a similar nature.

"Do you know, Totski, this is all very like what they say goes on among the Japanese?" said Ptitsin. "The offended party there, they say, marches off to his insulter and says to him, 'You insulted me, so I have come to rip myself open before your eyes;' and with these words he does actually rip his stomach open before his enemy, and considers, doubtless, that he is having all possible and necessary satisfaction and revenge. There are strange characters in the world, sir!"

"H'm! and you think there was something of this sort here, do you? Dear me—a very remarkable comparison, you know! But you must have observed, my dear Ptitsin, that I did all I possibly could. I could do no more than I did. And you must admit that there are some rare qualities in this woman. I felt I could not speak in that Bedlam, or I should have been tempted to cry out, when she reproached me, that she herself was my best justification. Such a woman could make anyone forget all reason—everything! Even that moujik, Rogojin, you saw, brought her a hundred thousand roubles! Of course, all that happened tonight was ephemeral, fantastic, unseemly—yet it lacked neither colour nor originality. My God! What might not have been made of such a character combined with such beauty! Yet in spite of all efforts—in spite of all education, even—all those gifts are wasted! She is an uncut diamond.... I have often said so."

And Afanasy Ivanovitch heaved a deep sigh.

PART II

I.

Two days after the strange conclusion to Nastasia Philipovna's birthday party, with the record of which we concluded the first part of this story, Prince Muishkin hurriedly left St. Petersburg for Moscow, in order to see after some business connected with the receipt of his unexpected fortune.

It was said that there were other reasons for his hurried departure; but as to this, and as to his movements in Moscow, and as to his prolonged absence from St. Petersburg, we are able to give very little information.

The prince was away for six months, and even those who were most interested in his destiny were able to pick up very little news about him all that while. True, certain rumours did reach his friends, but these were both strange and rare, and each one contradicted the last.

Of course the Epanchin family was much interested in his movements, though he had not had time to bid them farewell before his departure. The general, however, had had an opportunity of seeing him once or twice since the eventful evening, and had spoken very seriously with him; but though he had seen the prince, as I say, he told his family nothing about the circumstance. In fact, for a month or so after his departure it was considered not the thing to mention the prince's name in the Epanchin household. Only Mrs. Epanchin, at the commencement of this period, had announced that she had been "cruelly mistaken in the prince!" and a day or two after, she had added, evidently alluding to him, but not mentioning his name, that it was an unalterable characteristic of hers to be mistaken in people. Then once more, ten days later, after some passage of arms with one of her daughters, she had remarked sententiously. "We have had enough of mistakes. I shall be more careful in future!" However, it was impossible to avoid remarking that there was some sense of oppression in the household—something unspoken, but felt; something strained. All the members of the family wore frowning looks. The general was unusually busy; his family hardly ever saw him.

As to the girls, nothing was said openly, at all events; and probably very little in private. They were proud damsels, and were not always perfectly confidential even among themselves. But they understood each other thoroughly at the first word on all occasions; very often at the first glance, so that there was no need of much talking as a rule.

One fact, at least, would have been perfectly plain to an outsider, had any such person been on the spot; and that was, that the prince had made a very considerable impression upon the family, in spite of the fact that he had but once been inside the house, and then only for a short time. Of course, if analyzed, this impression might have proved to be nothing more than a feeling of curiosity; but be it what it might, there it undoubtedly was.

Little by little, the rumours spread about town became lost in a maze of uncertainty. It was said that some foolish young prince, name unknown, had suddenly come into possession of a gigantic fortune, and had married a French ballet dancer. This was contradicted, and the rumour circulated that it was a young merchant who had come into the enormous fortune and married the great ballet dancer, and that at the wedding the drunken young fool had burned seventy thousand roubles at a candle out of pure bravado.

However, all these rumours soon died down, to which circumstance certain facts largely contributed. For instance, the whole of the Rogojin troop had departed, with him at their head, for Moscow. This was exactly a week after a dreadful orgy at the Ekaterinhof gardens, where Nastasia Philipovna had been present. It became known that after this orgy Nastasia Philipovna had entirely disappeared, and that she had since been traced to Moscow; so that the exodus of the Rogojin band was found consistent with this report.

There were rumours current as to Gania, too; but circumstances soon contradicted these. He had fallen seriously ill, and his illness precluded his appearance in society, and even at business, for over a month. As soon as he had recovered, however, he threw up his situation in the public company under General Epanchin's direction, for some unknown reason, and the post was given to another. He never went near the Epanchins' house at all, and was exceedingly irritable and depressed.

Varvara Ardalionovna married Ptitsin this winter, and it was said that the fact of Gania's retirement from business was the ultimate cause of the marriage, since Gania was now not only unable to support his family, but even required help himself.

We may mention that Gania was no longer mentioned in the Epanchin household any more than the prince was; but that a certain circumstance in connection with the fatal evening at Nastasia's house became known to the general, and, in fact, to all the family the very next day. This fact was that Gania had come home that night, but had refused to go to bed. He had awaited the prince's return from Ekaterinhof with feverish impatience.

On the latter's arrival, at six in the morning, Gania had gone to him in his room, bringing with him the singed packet of money, which he had insisted that the prince should return to Nastasia Philipovna without delay. It was said that when Gania entered the prince's room, he came with anything but friendly feelings, and in a condition of despair and misery; but that after a short conversation, he had stayed on for a couple of hours with him, sobbing continuously and bitterly the whole time. They had parted upon terms of cordial friendship.

The Epanchins heard about this, as well as about the episode at Nastasia Philipovna's. It was strange, perhaps, that the facts should become so quickly, and fairly accurately, known. As far as Gania was concerned, it might have been supposed that the news had come through Varvara Ardalionovna, who had suddenly become a frequent visitor of the Epanchin girls, greatly to their mother's surprise. But though Varvara had seen fit, for some reason, to make friends with them, it was not likely that she would have talked to them about her brother. She had plenty of pride, in spite of the fact that in thus acting she was seeking intimacy with people who had practically shown her brother the door. She and the Epanchin girls had been acquainted in childhood, although of late they had met but rarely. Even now Varvara hardly ever appeared in the drawing-room, but would slip in by a back way. Lizabetha Prokofievna, who disliked Varvara, although she had a great respect for her mother, was much annoyed by this sudden intimacy, and put it down to the general "contrariness" of her daughters, who were "always on the lookout for some new way of opposing her." Nevertheless, Varvara continued her visits.

A month after Muishkin's departure, Mrs. Epanchin received a letter from her old friend Princess Bielokonski (who had lately left for Moscow), which letter put her into the greatest good humour. She did not divulge its contents either to her daughters or the general, but her conduct towards the former became affectionate in the extreme. She even made some sort of confession to them, but they were unable to understand what it was about. She actually relaxed towards the general a little—he had been long disgraced—and though she managed to quarrel with them all the next day, yet she soon came round, and from her general behaviour it was to be concluded that she had had good news of some sort, which she would like, but could not make up her mind, to disclose.

However, a week later she received another letter from the same source, and at last resolved to speak.

She solemnly announced that she had heard from old Princess Bielokonski, who had given her most comforting news about "that queer young prince." Her friend had hunted him up, and found that all was going well with him. He had since called in person upon her, making an extremely favourable impression, for the princess had received him each day since, and had introduced him into several good houses.

The girls could see that their mother concealed a great deal from them, and left out large pieces of the letter in reading it to them.

However, the ice was broken, and it suddenly became possible to mention the prince's name again. And again it became evident how very strong was the impression the young man had made in the household by his one visit there. Mrs. Epanchin was surprised at the effect which the news from Moscow had upon the girls, and they were no less surprised that after solemnly remarking that her most striking characteristic was "being mistaken in people" she should have troubled to obtain for the prince the favour and protection of so powerful an old lady as the Princess Bielokonski. As soon as the ice was thus broken, the general lost no time in showing that he, too, took the greatest interest in the subject. He admitted that he was interested, but said that it was merely in the business side of the question. It appeared that, in the interests of the prince, he had made arrangements in Moscow for a careful watch to be kept upon the prince's business affairs, and especially upon Salaskin. All that had been said as to the prince being an undoubted heir to a fortune turned out to be perfectly true; but the fortune proved to be much smaller than was at first reported. The estate was considerably encumbered with debts; creditors turned up on all sides, and the prince, in spite of all advice and entreaty, insisted upon managing all matters of claim himself—which, of course, meant satisfying everybody all round, although half the claims were absolutely fraudulent.

Mrs. Epanchin confirmed all this. She said the princess had written to much the same effect, and added that there was no curing a fool. But it was plain, from her expression of face, how strongly she approved of this particular young fool's doings. In conclusion, the general observed that his wife took as great an interest in the prince as though he were her own son; and that she had commenced to be especially affectionate towards Aglaya was a self-evident fact.

All this caused the general to look grave and important. But, alas! this agreeable state of affairs very soon changed once more.

A couple of weeks went by, and suddenly the general and his wife were once more gloomy and silent, and the ice was as firm as ever. The fact was, the general, who had heard first, how Nastasia Philipovna had fled to Moscow and had been discovered there by Rogojin; that she had then disappeared once more, and been found again by Rogojin, and how after that she had almost promised to marry him, now received news that she had once more disappeared, almost on the very day fixed for her wedding, flying somewhere into the interior of Russia this time, and that Prince Muishkin had left all his affairs in the hands of Salaskin and disappeared also—but whether he was with Nastasia, or had only set off in search of her, was unknown.

Lizabetha Prokofievna received confirmatory news from the princess—and alas, two months after the prince's first departure from St. Petersburg, darkness and mystery once more enveloped his whereabouts and actions, and in the Epanchin family the ice of silence once more formed over the subject. Varia, however, informed the girls of what had happened, she having received the news from Ptitsin, who generally knew more than most people.

To make an end, we may say that there were many changes in the Epanchin household in the spring, so that it was not difficult to forget the prince, who sent no news of himself.

The Epanchin family had at last made up their minds to spend the summer abroad, all except the general, who could not waste time in "travelling for enjoyment," of course. This arrangement was brought about by the persistence of the girls, who insisted that they were never allowed to go abroad because their parents were too anxious to marry them off. Perhaps their parents had at last come to the conclusion that husbands might be found abroad, and that a summer's travel might bear fruit. The marriage between Alexandra and Totski had been broken off. Since the prince's departure from St. Petersburg no more had been said about it; the subject had been dropped without ceremony, much to the joy of Mrs. General, who, announced that she was "ready to cross herself with both hands" in gratitude for the escape. The general, however, regretted Totski for a long while. "Such a fortune!" he sighed, "and such a good, easy-going fellow!"

After a time it became known that Totski had married a French marquise, and was to be carried off by her to Paris, and then to Brittany.

"Oh, well," thought the general, "he's lost to us for good, now."

So the Epanchins prepared to depart for the summer.

But now another circumstance occurred, which changed all the plans once more, and again the intended journey was put off, much to the delight of the general and his spouse.

A certain Prince S—— arrived in St. Petersburg from Moscow, an eminent and honourable young man. He was one of those active persons who always find some good work with which to employ themselves. Without forcing himself upon the public notice, modest and unobtrusive, this young prince was concerned with much that happened in the world in general.

He had served, at first, in one of the civil departments, had then attended to matters connected with the local government of provincial towns, and had of late been a corresponding member of several important scientific societies. He was a man of excellent family and solid means, about thirty-five years of age.

Prince S—— made the acquaintance of the general's family, and Adelaida, the second girl, made a great impression upon him. Towards the spring he proposed to her, and she accepted him. The general and his wife were delighted. The journey abroad was put off, and the wedding was fixed for a day not very distant.

The trip abroad might have been enjoyed later on by Mrs. Epanchin and her two remaining daughters, but for another circumstance.

It so happened that Prince S—— introduced a distant relation of his own into the Epanchin family—one Evgenie Pavlovitch, a young officer of about twenty-eight years of age, whose conquests among the ladies in Moscow had been proverbial. This young gentleman no sooner set eyes on Aglaya than he became a frequent visitor at the house. He was witty, well-educated, and extremely wealthy, as the general very soon discovered. His past reputation was the only thing against him.

Nothing was said; there were not even any hints dropped; but still, it seemed better to the parents to say nothing more about going abroad this season, at all events. Aglaya herself perhaps was of a different opinion.

All this happened just before the second appearance of our hero upon the scene.

By this time, to judge from appearances, poor Prince Muishkin had been quite forgotten in St. Petersburg. If he had appeared suddenly among his acquaintances, he would have been received as one from the skies; but we must just glance at one more fact before we conclude this preface.

Colia Ivolgin, for some time after the prince's departure, continued his old life. That is, he went to school, looked after his father, helped Varia in the house, and ran her errands, and went frequently to see his friend, Hippolyte.

The lodgers had disappeared very quickly—Ferdishenko soon after the events at Nastasia Philipovna's, while the prince went to Moscow, as we know. Gania and his mother went to live with Varia and Ptitsin immediately after the latter's wedding, while the general was housed in a debtor's prison by reason of certain IOU's given to the captain's widow under the impression that they would never be formally used against him. This unkind action much surprised poor Ardalion Alexandrovitch, the victim, as he called himself, of an "unbounded trust in the nobility of the human heart."

When he signed those notes of hand he never dreamt that they would be a source of future trouble. The event showed that he was mistaken. "Trust in anyone after this! Have the least confidence in man or woman!" he cried in bitter tones, as he sat with his new friends in prison, and recounted to them his favourite stories of the siege of Kars, and the resuscitated soldier. On the whole, he accommodated himself very well to his new position. Ptitsin and Varia declared that he was in the right place, and Gania was of the same opinion. The only person who deplored his fate was poor Nina Alexandrovna, who wept bitter tears over him, to the great surprise of her household, and, though always in feeble health, made a point of going to see him as often as possible.

Since the general's "mishap," as Colia called it, and the marriage of his sister, the boy had quietly possessed himself of far more freedom. His relations saw little of him, for he rarely slept at home. He made many new friends; and was moreover, a frequent visitor at the debtor's prison, to which he invariably accompanied his mother. Varia, who used to be always correcting him, never spoke to him now on the subject of his frequent absences, and the whole household was surprised to see Gania, in spite of his depression, on quite friendly terms with his brother. This was something new, for Gania had been wont to look upon Colia as a kind of errand-boy, treating him with contempt, threatening to "pull his ears," and in general driving him almost wild with irritation. It seemed now that Gania really needed his brother, and the latter, for his part, felt as if he could forgive Gania much since he had returned the hundred thousand roubles offered to him by Nastasia Philipovna. Three months after the departure of the prince, the Ivolgin family discovered that Colia had made acquaintance with the Epanchins, and was on very friendly terms with the daughters. Varia heard of it first, though Colia had not asked her to introduce him. Little by little the family grew quite fond of him. Madame Epanchin at first looked on him with disdain, and received him coldly, but in a short time he grew to please her, because, as she said, he "was candid and no flatterer"——a very true description. From the first he put himself on an equality with his new friends, and though he sometimes read newspapers and books to the mistress of the house, it was simply because he liked to be useful.

One day, however, he and Lizabetha Prokofievna quarrelled seriously about the "woman question," in the course of a lively discussion on that burning subject. He told her that she was a tyrant, and that he would never set foot in her house again. It may seem incredible, but a day or two after, Madame Epanchin sent a servant with a note begging him to return, and Colia, without standing on his dignity, did so at once.

Aglaya was the only one of the family whose good graces he could not gain, and who always spoke to him haughtily, but it so happened that the boy one day succeeded in giving the proud maiden a surprise.

It was about Easter, when, taking advantage of a momentary tête-à-tête Colia handed Aglaya a letter, remarking that he "had orders to deliver it to her privately." She stared at him in amazement, but he did not wait to hear what she had to say, and went out. Aglaya broke the seal, and read as follows:

"Once you did me the honour of giving me your confidence. Perhaps you have quite forgotten me now! How is it that I am writing to you? I do not know; but I am conscious of an irresistible desire to remind you of my existence, especially you. How many times I have needed all three of you; but only you have dwelt always in my mind's eye. I need you—I need you very much. I will not write about myself. I have nothing to tell you. But I long for you to be happy. Are you happy? That is all I wished to say to you—Your brother,

"Pr. L. Muishkin."

On reading this short and disconnected note, Aglaya suddenly blushed all over, and became very thoughtful.

It would be difficult to describe her thoughts at that moment. One of them was, "Shall I show it to anyone?" But she was ashamed to show it. So she ended by hiding it in her table drawer, with a very strange, ironical smile upon her lips.

Next day, she took it out, and put it into a large book, as she usually did with papers which she wanted to be able to find easily. She laughed when, about a week later, she happened to notice the name of the book, and saw that it was Don Quixote, but it would be difficult to say exactly why.

I cannot say, either, whether she showed the letter to her sisters.

But when she had read it herself once more, it suddenly struck her that surely that conceited boy, Colia, had not been the one chosen correspondent of the prince all this while. She determined to ask him, and did so with an exaggerated show of carelessness. He informed her haughtily that though he had given the prince his permanent address when the latter left town, and had offered his services, the prince had never before given him any commission to perform, nor had he written until the following lines arrived, with Aglaya's letter. Aglaya took the note, and read it.

"Dear Colia,—Please be so kind as to give the enclosed sealed letter to Aglaya Ivanovna. Keep well—Ever your loving,

"Pr. L. Muishkin."

"It seems absurd to trust a little pepper-box like you," said Aglaya, as she returned the note, and walked past the "pepper-box" with an expression of great contempt.

This was more than Colia could bear. He had actually borrowed Gania's new green tie for the occasion, without saying why he wanted it, in order to impress her. He was very deeply mortified.

II.

It was the beginning of June, and for a whole week the weather in St. Petersburg had been magnificent. The Epanchins had a luxurious country-house at Pavlofsk, [One of the fashionable summer resorts near St. Petersburg.] and to this spot Mrs. Epanchin determined to proceed without further delay. In a couple of days all was ready, and the family had left town. A day or two after this removal to Pavlofsk, Prince Muishkin arrived in St. Petersburg by the morning train from Moscow. No one met him; but, as he stepped out of the carriage, he suddenly became aware of two strangely glowing eyes fixed upon him from among the crowd that met the train. On endeavouring to re-

314

discover the eyes, and see to whom they belonged, he could find nothing to guide him. It must have been a hallucination. But the disagreeable impression remained, and without this, the prince was sad and thoughtful already, and seemed to be much preoccupied.

His cab took him to a small and bad hotel near the Litaynaya. Here he engaged a couple of rooms, dark and badly furnished. He washed and changed, and hurriedly left the hotel again, as though anxious to waste no time. Anyone who now saw him for the first time since he left Petersburg would judge that he had improved vastly so far as his exterior was concerned. His clothes certainly were very different; they were more fashionable, perhaps even too much so, and anyone inclined to mockery might have found something to smile at in his appearance. But what is there that people will not smile at?

The prince took a cab and drove to a street near the Nativity, where he soon discovered the house he was seeking. It was a small wooden villa, and he was struck by its attractive and clean appearance; it stood in a pleasant little garden, full of flowers. The windows looking on the street were open, and the sound of a voice, reading aloud or making a speech, came through them. It rose at times to a shout, and was interrupted occasionally by bursts of laughter.

Prince Muishkin entered the court-yard, and ascended the steps. A cook with her sleeves turned up to the elbows opened the door. The visitor asked if Mr. Lebedeff were at home.

"He is in there," said she, pointing to the salon.

The room had a blue wall-paper, and was well, almost pretentiously, furnished, with its round table, its divan, and its bronze clock under a glass shade. There was a narrow pier-glass against the wall, and a chandelier adorned with lustres hung by a bronze chain from the ceiling.

When the prince entered, Lebedeff was standing in the middle of the room, his back to the door. He was in his shirt-sleeves, on account of the extreme heat, and he seemed to have just reached the peroration of his speech, and was impressively beating his breast.

His audience consisted of a youth of about fifteen years of age with a clever face, who had a book in his hand, though he was not reading; a young lady of twenty, in deep mourning, stood near him with an infant in her arms; another girl of thirteen, also in black, was laughing loudly, her mouth wide open; and on the sofa lay a handsome young man, with black hair and eyes, and a suspicion of beard and whiskers. He frequently interrupted the speaker and argued with him, to the great delight of the others.

"Lukian Timofeyovitch! Lukian Timofeyovitch! Here's someone to see you! Look here!... a gentleman to speak to you!... Well, it's not my fault!" and the cook turned and went away red with anger.

Lebedeff started, and at sight of the prince stood like a statue for a moment. Then he moved up to him with an ingratiating smile, but stopped short again.

"Prince! ex-ex-excellency!" he stammered. Then suddenly he ran towards the girl with the infant, a movement so unexpected by her that she staggered and fell back, but next moment he was threatening the other child, who was standing, still laughing, in the doorway. She screamed, and ran towards the kitchen. Lebedeff stamped his foot angrily; then, seeing the prince regarding him with amazement, he murmured apologetically—"Pardon to show respect!... he-he!"

"You are quite wrong..." began the prince.

"At once... at once... in one moment!"

He rushed like a whirlwind from the room, and Muishkin looked inquiringly at the others.

They were all laughing, and the guest joined in the chorus.

"He has gone to get his coat," said the boy.

"How annoying!" exclaimed the prince. "I thought... Tell me, is he..."

"You think he is drunk?" cried the young man on the sofa. "Not in the least. He's only had three or four small glasses, perhaps five; but what is that? The usual thing!"

As the prince opened his mouth to answer, he was interrupted by the girl, whose sweet face wore an expression of absolute frankness.

"He never drinks much in the morning; if you have come to talk business with him, do it now. It is the best time. He sometimes comes back drunk in the evening; but just now he passes the greater part of the evening in tears, and reads passages of Holy Scripture aloud, because our mother died five weeks ago."

"No doubt he ran off because he did not know what to say to you," said the youth on the divan. "I bet he is trying to cheat you, and is thinking how best to do it."

Just then Lebedeff returned, having put on his coat.

"Five weeks!" said he, wiping his eyes. "Only five weeks! Poor orphans!"

"But why wear a coat in holes," asked the girl, "when your new one is hanging behind the door? Did you not see it?"

"Hold your tongue, dragon-fly!" he scolded. "What a plague you are!" He stamped his foot irritably, but she only laughed, and answered:

"Are you trying to frighten me? I am not Tania, you know, and I don't intend to run away. Look, you are waking Lubotchka, and she will have convulsions again. Why do you shout like that?"

"Well, well! I won't again," said the master of the house his anxiety getting the better of his temper. He went up to his daughter, and looked at the child in her arms, anxiously making the sign of the cross over her three times. "God bless her! God bless her!" he cried with emotion. "This little creature is my daughter Luboff," addressing the prince. "My wife, Helena, died—at her birth; and this is my big daughter Vera, in mourning, as you see; and this, this, oh, this pointing to the young man on the divan...

"Well, go on! never mind me!" mocked the other. "Don't be afraid!"

"Excellency! Have you read that account of the murder of the Zemarin family, in the newspaper?" cried Lebedeff, all of a sudden.

"Yes," said Muishkin, with some surprise.

"Well, that is the murderer! It is he—in fact—"

"What do you mean?" asked the visitor.

"I am speaking allegorically, of course; but he will be the murderer of a Zemarin family in the future. He is getting ready. ..."

They all laughed, and the thought crossed the prince's mind that perhaps Lebedeff was really trifling in this way because he foresaw inconvenient questions, and wanted to gain time.

"He is a traitor! a conspirator!" shouted Lebedeff, who seemed to have lost all control over himself. "A monster! a slanderer! Ought I to treat him as a nephew, the son of my sister Anisia?"

"Oh! do be quiet! You must be drunk! He has taken it into his head to play the lawyer, prince, and he practices speechifying, and is always repeating his eloquent pleadings to his children. And who do you think was his last client? An old woman who had been robbed of five hundred roubles, her all, by some rogue of a usurer, besought him to take up her case, instead of which he defended the usurer himself, a Jew named Zeidler, because this Jew promised to give him fifty roubles...."

"It was to be fifty if I won the case, only five if I lost," interrupted Lebedeff, speaking in a low tone, a great contrast to his earlier manner.

"Well! naturally he came to grief: the law is not administered as it used to be, and he only got laughed at for his pains. But he was much pleased with himself in spite of that. 'Most learned judge!' said he, 'picture this unhappy man, crippled by age and infirmities, who gains his living by honourable toil—picture him, I repeat, robbed of his all, of his last mouthful; remember, I entreat you, the words of that learned legislator, "Let mercy and justice alike rule the courts of law."' Now, would you believe it, excellency, every morning he recites this speech to us from beginning to end, exactly as he spoke it before the magistrate. To-day we have heard it for the fifth time. He was just starting again when you arrived, so much does he admire it. He is now preparing to undertake another case. I think, by the way, that you are Prince Muishkin? Colia tells me you are the cleverest man he has ever known...."

"The cleverest in the world," interrupted his uncle hastily.

"I do not pay much attention to that opinion," continued the young man calmly. "Colia is very fond of you, but he," pointing to Lebedeff, "is flattering you. I can assure you I have no intention of flattering you, or anyone else, but at least you have some common-sense. Well, will you judge between us? Shall we ask the prince to act as arbitrator?" he went on, addressing his uncle.

"I am so glad you chanced to come here, prince."

"I agree," said Lebedeff, firmly, looking round involuntarily at his daughter, who had come nearer, and was listening attentively to the conversation.

"What is it all about?" asked the prince, frowning. His head ached, and he felt sure that Lebedeff was trying to cheat him in some way, and only talking to put off the explanation that he had come for.

"I will tell you all the story. I am his nephew; he did speak the truth there, although he is generally telling lies. I am at the University, and have not yet finished my course. I mean to do so, and I shall, for I have a determined character. I must, however, find something to do for the present, and therefore I have got employment on the railway at twenty-four roubles a month. I admit that my uncle has helped me once or twice before. Well, I had twenty roubles in my pocket, and I gambled them away. Can you believe that I should be so low, so base, as to lose money in that way?"

"And the man who won it is a rogue, a rogue whom you ought not to have paid!" cried Lebedeff.

"Yes, he is a rogue, but I was obliged to pay him," said the young man. "As to his being a rogue, he is assuredly that, and I am not saying it because he beat you. He is an ex-lieutenant, prince, dismissed from the service, a teacher of boxing, and one of Rogojin's followers. They are all lounging about the pavements now that Rogojin has turned them off. Of course, the worst of it is that, knowing he was a rascal, and a card-sharper, I none the less played palki with him, and risked my last rouble. To tell the truth, I thought to myself, 'If I lose, I will go to my uncle, and I am sure he will not refuse to help me.' Now that was base-cowardly and base!"

"That is so," observed Lebedeff quietly; "cowardly and base."

"Well, wait a bit, before you begin to triumph," said the nephew viciously; for the words seemed to irritate him. "He is delighted! I came to him here and told him everything: I acted honourably, for I did not excuse myself. I spoke most severely of my conduct, as everyone here can witness. But I must smarten myself up before I take up my new post, for I am really like a tramp. Just look at my boots! I cannot possibly appear like this, and if I am not at the bureau at the time appointed, the job will be given to someone else; and I shall have to try for another. Now I only beg for fifteen roubles, and I give my word that I will never ask him for anything again. I am also ready to promise to repay my debt in three months' time, and I will keep my word, even if I have to live on bread and water. My salary will amount to seventy-five roubles in three months. The sum I now ask, added to what I have borrowed already, will make a total of about thirty-five roubles, so you see I shall have enough to pay him and confound him! if he wants interest, he shall have that, too! Haven't I always paid back the money he lent me before? Why should he be so mean now? He grudges my having paid that lieutenant; there can be no other reason! That's the kind he is—a dog in the manger!"

"And he won't go away!" cried Lebedeff. "He has installed himself here, and here he remains!"

"I have told you already, that I will not go away until I have got what I ask. Why are you smiling, prince? You look as if you disapproved of me."

"I am not smiling, but I really think you are in the wrong, somewhat," replied Muishkin, reluctantly.

"Don't shuffle! Say plainly that you think that I am quite wrong, without any 'somewhat'! Why 'somewhat'?"

"I will say you are quite wrong, if you wish."

"If I wish! That's good, I must say! Do you think I am deceived as to the flagrant impropriety of my conduct? I am quite aware that his money is his own, and that my action—As much like an attempt at extortion. But you-you don't know what life is! If people don't learn by experience, they never understand. They must be taught. My intentions are perfectly honest; on my conscience he will lose nothing, and I will pay back the money with interest. Added to which he has had the moral satisfaction of seeing me disgraced. What does he want more? and what is he good for if he never helps anyone? Look what he does himself! just ask him about his dealings with others, how he deceives people! How did he manage to buy this house? You may cut off my head if he has not let you in for something—and if he is not trying to cheat you again. You are smiling. You don't believe me?"

"It seems to me that all this has nothing to do with your affairs," remarked the prince.

"I have lain here now for three days," cried the young man without noticing, "and I have seen a lot! Fancy! he suspects his daughter, that angel, that orphan, my cousin—he suspects her, and every evening he searches her room, to see if she has a lover hidden in it! He comes here too on tiptoe, creeping softly—oh, so softly—and looks under the sofa—my bed, you know. He is mad with suspicion, and sees a thief in every corner. He runs about all night long; he was up at least seven times last night, to satisfy himself that the windows and doors were barred, and to peep into the oven. That man who appears in court for scoundrels, rushes in here in the night and prays, lying prostrate, banging his head on the ground by the half-hour—and for whom do you think he prays? Who are the sinners figuring in his drunken petitions? I have heard him with my own ears praying for the repose of the soul of the Countess du Barry! Colia heard it too. He is as mad as a March hare!"

"You hear how he slanders me, prince," said Lebedeff, almost beside himself with rage. "I may be a drunkard, an evil-doer, a thief, but at least I can say one thing for myself. He does not know—how should he, mocker that he is?—that when he came into the world it was I who washed him, and dressed him in his swathing-bands, for my sister Anisia had lost her husband, and was in great poverty. I was very little better off than she, but I sat up night after night with her, and nursed both mother and child; I used to go downstairs and steal wood for them from the house-porter. How often did I sing him to sleep when I was half dead with hunger! In short, I was more than a father to him, and now—now he jeers at me! Even if I did cross myself, and pray for the repose of the soul of the Comtesse du Barry, what does it matter? Three days ago, for the first time in my life, I read her biography in an historical dictionary. Do you know who she was? You there!" addressing his nephew. "Speak! do you know?"

"Of course no one knows anything about her but you," muttered the young man in a would-be jeering tone.

"She was a Countess who rose from shame to reign like a Queen. An Empress wrote to her, with her own hand, as '*Ma chère cousine*.' At a *lever-du-roi* one morning (do you know what a *lever-du-roi* was?)—a Cardinal, a Papal legate, offered to put on her stockings; a high and holy person like that looked on it as an honour! Did you know this? I see by your expression that you did not! Well, how did she die? Answer!"

"Oh! do stop—you are too absurd!"

"This is how she died. After all this honour and glory, after having been almost a Queen, she was guillotined by that butcher, Samson. She was quite innocent, but it had to be done, for the satisfaction of the fishwives of Paris. She was so terrified, that she did not understand what was happening. But when Samson seized her head, and pushed her under the knife with his foot, she cried out: 'Wait a moment! wait a moment, monsieur!' Well, because of that moment of bitter suffering, perhaps the Saviour will pardon her other faults, for one cannot imagine a greater agony. As I read the story my heart bled for her. And what does it matter to you, little worm, if I implored the Divine mercy for her, great sinner as she was, as I said my evening prayer? I might have done it because I doubted if anyone had ever crossed himself for her sake before. It may be that in the other world she will rejoice to think that a sinner like herself has cried to heaven for the salvation of her soul. Why are you laughing? You believe nothing, atheist! And your story was not even correct! If you had listened to what I was saying, you would have heard that I did not only pray for the Comtesse du Barry. I said, 'Oh Lord! give rest to the soul of that great sinner, the Comtesse du Barry, and to all unhappy ones like her.' You see that is quite a different thing, for how many sinners there are, how many women, who have passed through the trials of this life, are now suffering and groaning in purgatory! I prayed for you, too, in spite of your insolence and impudence, also for your fellows, as it seems that you claim to know how I pray..."

"Oh! that's enough in all conscience! Pray for whom you choose, and the devil take them and you! We have a scholar here; you did not know that, prince?" he continued, with a sneer. "He reads all sorts of books and memoirs now."

"At any rate, your uncle has a kind heart," remarked the prince, who really had to force himself to speak to the nephew, so much did he dislike him.

"Oh, now you are going to praise him! He will be set up! He puts his hand on his heart, and he is delighted! I never said he was a man without heart, but he is a rascal—that's the pity of it. And then, he is addicted to drink, and his mind is unhinged, like that of most people who have taken more than is good for them for years. He loves his children—oh, I know that well enough! He respected my aunt, his late wife... and he even has a sort of affection for me. He has remembered me in his will."

"I shall leave you nothing!" exclaimed his uncle angrily.

"Listen to me, Lebedeff," said the prince in a decided voice, turning his back on the young man. "I know by experience that when you choose, you can be business-like.. I. I have very little time to spare, and if you... By the way—excuse me—what is your Christian name? I have forgotten it."

"Ti-Ti-Timofey."

"And?"

"Lukianovitch."

Everyone in the room began to laugh.

"He is telling lies!" cried the nephew. "Even now he cannot speak the truth. He is not called Timofey Lukianovitch, prince, but Lukian Timofeyovitch. Now do tell us why you must needs lie about it? Lukian or Timofey, it is all the same to you, and what difference can it make to the prince? He tells lies without the least necessity, simply by force of habit, I assure you."

"Is that true?" said the prince impatiently.

"My name really is Lukian Timofeyovitch," acknowledged Lebedeff, lowering his eyes, and putting his hand on his heart.

"Well, for God's sake, what made you say the other?"

"To humble myself," murmured Lebedeff.

"What on earth do you mean? Oh I if only I knew where Colia was at this moment!" cried the prince, standing up, as if to go.

"I can tell you all about Colia," said the young man

"Oh! no, no!" said Lebedeff, hurriedly.

"Colia spent the night here, and this morning went after his father, whom you let out of prison by paying his debts—Heaven only knows why! Yesterday the general promised to come and lodge here, but he did not appear. Most probably he slept at the hotel close by. No doubt Colia is there, unless he has gone to Pavlofsk to see the Epanchins. He had a little money, and was intending to go there yesterday. He must be either at the hotel or at Pavlofsk."

"At Pavlofsk! He is at Pavlofsk, undoubtedly!" interrupted Lebedeff.... "But come—let us go into the garden—we will have coffee there...." And Lebedeff seized the prince's arm, and led him from the room. They went across the yard, and found themselves in a delightful little garden with the trees already in their summer dress of green, thanks to the unusually fine weather. Lebedeff invited his guest to sit down on a green seat before a table of the same colour fixed in the earth, and took a seat facing him. In a few minutes the coffee appeared, and the prince did not refuse it. The host kept his eyes fixed on Muishkin, with an expression of passionate servility.

"I knew nothing about your home before," said the prince absently, as if he were thinking of something else.

"Poor orphans," began Lebedeff, his face assuming a mournful air, but he stopped short, for the other looked at him inattentively, as if he had already forgotten his own remark. They waited a few minutes in silence, while Lebedeff sat with his eyes fixed mournfully on the young man's face.

"Well!" said the latter, at last rousing himself. "Ah! yes! You know why I came, Lebedeff. Your letter brought me. Speak! Tell me all about it."

The clerk, rather confused, tried to say something, hesitated, began to speak, and again stopped. The prince looked at him gravely.

"I think I understand, Lukian Timofeyovitch: you were not sure that I should come. You did not think I should start at the first word from you, and you merely wrote to relieve your conscience. However, you see now that I have come, and I have had enough of trickery. Give up serving, or trying to serve, two masters. Rogojin has been here these three weeks. Have you managed to sell her to him as you did before? Tell me the truth."

"He discovered everything, the monster... himself......"

"Don't abuse him; though I dare say you have something to complain of...."

"He beat me, he thrashed me unmercifully!" replied Lebedeff vehemently. "He set a dog on me in Moscow, a bloodhound, a terrible beast that chased me all down the street."

"You seem to take me for a child, Lebedeff. Tell me, is it a fact that she left him while they were in Moscow?"

"Yes, it is a fact, and this time, let me tell you, on the very eve of their marriage! It was a question of minutes when she slipped off to Petersburg. She came to me directly she arrived—'Save me, Lukian! find me some refuge, and say nothing to the prince!' She is afraid of you, even more than she is of him, and in that she shows her wisdom!" And Lebedeff slily put his finger to his brow as he said the last words.

"And now it is you who have brought them together again?"

"Excellency, how could I, how could I prevent it?"

"That will do. I can find out for myself. Only tell me, where is she now? At his house? With him?"

"Oh no! Certainly not! 'I am free,' she says; you know how she insists on that point. 'I am entirely free.' She repeats it over and over again. She is living in Petersburgskaia, with my sister-in-law, as I told you in my letter."

"She is there at this moment?"

"Yes, unless she has gone to Pavlofsk: the fine weather may have tempted her, perhaps, into the country, with Daria Alexeyevna. 'I am quite free,' she says. Only yesterday she boasted of her freedom to Nicolai Ardalionovitch—a bad sign," added Lebedeff, smiling.

"Colia goes to see her often, does he not?"

"He is a strange boy, thoughtless, and inclined to be indiscreet."

"Is it long since you saw her?"

"I go to see her every day, every day."

"Then you were there yesterday?"

"N-no: I have not been these three last days."

"It is a pity you have taken too much wine, Lebedeff I want to ask you something... but..."

"All right! all right! I am not drunk," replied the clerk, preparing to listen.

"Tell me, how was she when you left her?"

"She is a woman who is seeking..."

"Seeking?"

"She seems always to be searching about, as if she had lost something. The mere idea of her coming marriage disgusts her; she looks on it as an insult. She cares as much for *him* as for a piece of orange-peel—not more. Yet I am much mistaken if she does not look on him with fear and trembling. She forbids his name to be mentioned before her, and they only meet when unavoidable. He understands, well enough! But it must be gone through. She is restless, mocking, deceitful, violent...."

"Deceitful and violent?"

"Yes, violent. I can give you a proof of it. A few days ago she tried to pull my hair because I said something that annoyed her. I tried to soothe her by reading the Apocalypse aloud."

"What?" exclaimed the prince, thinking he had not heard aright.

"By reading the Apocalypse. The lady has a restless imagination, he-he! She has a liking for conversation on serious subjects, of any kind; in fact they please her so much, that it flatters her to discuss them. Now for fifteen years at least I have studied the Apocalypse, and she agrees with me in thinking that the present is the epoch represented by the third horse, the black one whose rider holds a measure in his hand. It seems to me that everything is ruled by measure in our century; all men are clamouring for their rights; 'a measure of wheat for a penny, and three measures of barley for a penny.' But, added to this, men desire freedom of mind and body, a pure heart, a healthy life, and all God's good gifts. Now by pleading their rights alone, they will never attain all this, so the white horse, with his rider Death, comes next, and is followed by Hell. We talked about this matter when we met, and it impressed her very much."

"Do you believe all this?" asked Muishkin, looking curiously at his companion.

"I both believe it and explain it. I am but a poor creature, a beggar, an atom in the scale of humanity. Who has the least respect for Lebedeff? He is a target for all the world, the butt of any fool who chooses to kick him. But in interpreting revelation I am the equal of anyone, great as he may be! Such is the power of the mind and the spirit. I have made a lordly personage tremble, as he sat in his armchair... only by talking to him of things concerning the spirit. Two years ago, on Easter Eve, His Excellency Nil Alexeyovitch, whose subordinate I was then, wished to hear what I had to say, and sent a message by Peter Zakkaritch to ask me to go to his private room. 'They tell me you expound the prophecies relating to Antichrist,' said he, when we were alone. 'Is that so?' 'Yes,' I answered unhesitatingly, and I began to give some comments on the Apostle's allegorical vision. At first he smiled, but when we reached the numerical computations and correspondences, he trembled, and turned pale. Then he begged me to close the book, and sent me away, promising to put my name on the reward list. That took place as I said on the eve of Easter, and eight days later his soul returned to God."

"What?"

"It is the truth. One evening after dinner he stumbled as he stepped out of his carriage. He fell, and struck his head on the curb, and died immediately. He was seventy-three years of age, and had a red face, and white hair; he deluged himself with scent, and was always smiling like a child. Peter Zakkaritch recalled my interview with him, and said, '*you foretold his death.*'"

The prince rose from his seat, and Lebedeff, surprised to see his guest preparing to go so soon, remarked: "You are not interested?" in a respectful tone.

"I am not very well, and my head aches. Doubtless the effect of the journey," replied the prince, frowning.

"You should go into the country," said Lebedeff timidly.

The prince seemed to be considering the suggestion.

"You see, I am going into the country myself in three days, with my children and belongings. The little one is delicate; she needs change of air; and during our absence this house will be done up. I am going to Pavlofsk."

"You are going to Pavlofsk too?" asked the prince sharply. "Everybody seems to be going there. Have you a house in that neighbourhood?"

"I don't know of many people going to Pavlofsk, and as for the house, Ivan Ptitsin has let me one of his villas rather cheaply. It is a pleasant place, lying on a hill surrounded by trees, and one can live there for a mere song. There is good music to be heard, so no wonder it is popular. I shall stay in the lodge. As to the villa itself..."

"Have you let it?"

"N-no—not exactly."

"Let it to me," said the prince.

Now this was precisely what Lebedeff had made up his mind to do in the last three minutes. Not that he had any difficulty in finding a tenant; in fact the house was occupied at present by a chance visitor, who had told Lebedeff that he would perhaps take it for the summer months. The clerk knew very well that this "*perhaps*" meant "*certainly*," but as he thought he could make more out of a tenant like the prince, he felt justified in speaking vaguely about the present inhabitant's intentions. "This is quite a coincidence," thought he, and when the subject of price was mentioned, he made a gesture with his hand, as if to waive away a question of so little importance.

"Oh well, as you like!" said Muishkin. "I will think it over. You shall lose nothing!"

They were walking slowly across the garden.

"But if you... I could..." stammered Lebedeff, "if... if you please, prince, tell you something on the subject which would interest you, I am sure." He spoke in wheedling tones, and wriggled as he walked along.

Muishkin stopped short.

"Daria Alexeyevna also has a villa at Pavlofsk."

"Well?"

"A certain person is very friendly with her, and intends to visit her pretty often."

"Well?"

"Aglaya Ivanovna..."

"Oh stop, Lebedeff!" interposed Muishkin, feeling as if he had been touched on an open wound. "That... that has nothing to do with me. I should like to know when you are going to start. The sooner the better as far as I am concerned, for I am at an hotel."

They had left the garden now, and were crossing the yard on their way to the gate.

"Well, leave your hotel at once and come here; then we can all go together to Pavlofsk the day after tomorrow."

"I will think about it," said the prince dreamily, and went off.

The clerk stood looking after his guest, struck by his sudden absent-mindedness. He had not even remembered to say goodbye, and Lebedeff was the more surprised at the omission, as he knew by experience how courteous the prince usually was.

III.

It was now close on twelve o'clock.

The prince knew that if he called at the Epanchins' now he would only find the general, and that the latter might probably carry him straight off to Pavlofsk with him; whereas there was one visit he was most anxious to make without delay.

So at the risk of missing General Epanchin altogether, and thus postponing his visit to Pavlofsk for a day, at least, the prince decided to go and look for the house he desired to find.

The visit he was about to pay was, in some respects, a risky one. He was in two minds about it, but knowing that the house was in the Gorohovaya, not far from the Sadovaya, he determined to go in that direction, and to try to make up his mind on the way.

Arrived at the point where the Gorohovaya crosses the Sadovaya, he was surprised to find how excessively agitated he was. He had no idea that his heart could beat so painfully.

One house in the Gorohovaya began to attract his attention long before he reached it, and the prince remembered afterwards that he had said to himself: "That is the house, I'm sure of it." He came up to it quite curious to discover whether he had guessed right, and felt that he would be disagreeably impressed to find that he had actually done so. The house was a large gloomy-looking structure, without the slightest claim to architectural beauty, in colour a dirty green. There are a few of these old houses, built towards the end of the last century, still standing in that part of St. Petersburg, and showing little change from their original form and colour. They are solidly built, and are remarkable for the thickness of their walls, and for the fewness of their windows, many of which are covered by gratings. On the ground-floor there is usually a money-changer's shop, and the owner lives over it. Without as well as within, the houses seem inhospitable and mysterious—an impression which is difficult to explain, unless it has something to do with the actual architectural style. These houses are almost exclusively inhabited by the merchant class.

Arrived at the gate, the prince looked up at the legend over it, which ran:

"House of Rogojin, hereditary and honourable citizen."

He hesitated no longer; but opened the glazed door at the bottom of the outer stairs and made his way up to the second storey. The place was dark and gloomy-looking; the walls of the stone staircase were painted a dull red. Rogojin and his mother and brother occupied the whole of the second floor. The servant who opened the door to Muishkin led him, without taking his name, through several rooms and up and down many steps until they arrived at a door, where he knocked.

Parfen Rogojin opened the door himself.

On seeing the prince he became deadly white, and apparently fixed to the ground, so that he was more like a marble statue than a human being. The prince had expected some surprise, but Rogojin evidently considered his visit an impossible and miraculous event. He stared with an expression almost of terror, and his lips twisted into a bewildered smile.

"Parfen! perhaps my visit is ill-timed. I—I can go away again if you like," said Muishkin at last, rather embarrassed.

"No, no; it's all right, come in," said Parfen, recollecting himself.

They were evidently on quite familiar terms. In Moscow they had had many occasions of meeting; indeed, some few of those meetings were but too vividly impressed upon their memories. They had not met now, however, for three months.

The deathlike pallor, and a sort of slight convulsion about the lips, had not left Rogojin's face. Though he welcomed his guest, he was still obviously much disturbed. As he invited the prince to sit down near the table, the latter happened to turn towards him, and was startled by the strange expression on his face. A painful recollection flashed into his mind. He stood for a time, looking straight at Rogojin, whose eyes seemed to blaze like fire. At last Rogojin smiled, though he still looked agitated and shaken.

"What are you staring at me like that for?" he muttered. "Sit down."

The prince took a chair.

"Parfen," he said, "tell me honestly, did you know that I was coming to Petersburg or no?"

"Oh, I supposed you were coming," the other replied, smiling sarcastically, "and I was right in my supposition, you see; but how was I to know that you would come *today?*"

A certain strangeness and impatience in his manner impressed the prince very forcibly.

"And if you had known that I was coming today, why be so irritated about it?" he asked, in quiet surprise.

"Why did you ask me?"

"Because when I jumped out of the train this morning, two eyes glared at me just as yours did a moment since."

"Ha! and whose eyes may they have been?" said Rogojin, suspiciously. It seemed to the prince that he was trembling.

"I don't know; I thought it was a hallucination. I often have hallucinations nowadays. I feel just as I did five years ago when my fits were about to come on."

"Well, perhaps it was a hallucination, I don't know," said Parfen.

He tried to give the prince an affectionate smile, and it seemed to the latter as though in this smile of his something had broken, and that he could not mend it, try as he would.

"Shall you go abroad again then?" he asked, and suddenly added, "Do you remember how we came up in the train from Pskoff together? You and your cloak and leggings, eh?"

And Rogojin burst out laughing, this time with unconcealed malice, as though he were glad that he had been able to find an opportunity for giving vent to it.

"Have you quite taken up your quarters here?" asked the prince

"Yes, I'm at home. Where else should I go to?"

"We haven't met for some time. Meanwhile I have heard things about you which I should not have believed to be possible."

"What of that? People will say anything," said Rogojin drily.

"At all events, you've disbanded your troop—and you are living in your own house instead of being fast and loose about the place; that's all very good. Is this house all yours, or joint property?"

"It is my mother's. You get to her apartments by that passage."

"Where's your brother?"

"In the other wing."

"Is he married?"

"Widower. Why do you want to know all this?"

The prince looked at him, but said nothing. He had suddenly relapsed into musing, and had probably not heard the question at all. Rogojin did not insist upon an answer, and there was silence for a few moments.

"I guessed which was your house from a hundred yards off," said the prince at last.

"Why so?"

"I don't quite know. Your house has the aspect of yourself and all your family; it bears the stamp of the Rogojin life; but ask me why I think so, and I can tell you nothing. It is nonsense, of course. I am nervous about this kind of thing troubling me so much. I had never before imagined what sort of a house you would live in, and yet no sooner did I set eyes on this one than I said to myself that it must be yours."

"Really!" said Rogojin vaguely, not taking in what the prince meant by his rather obscure remarks.

The room they were now sitting in was a large one, lofty but dark, well furnished, principally with writing-tables and desks covered with papers and books. A wide sofa covered with red morocco evidently served Rogojin for a bed. On the table beside which the prince had been invited to seat himself lay some books; one containing a marker where the reader had left off, was a volume of Solovieff's History. Some oil-paintings in worn gilded frames hung on the walls, but it was impossible to make out what subjects they represented, so blackened were they by smoke and age. One, a life-sized portrait, attracted the prince's attention. It showed a man of about fifty, wearing a long riding-coat of German cut. He had two medals on his breast; his beard was white, short and thin; his face yellow and wrinkled, with a sly, suspicious expression in the eyes.

"That is your father, is it not?" asked the prince.

"Yes, it is," replied Rogojin with an unpleasant smile, as if he had expected his guest to ask the question, and then to make some disagreeable remark.

"Was he one of the Old Believers?"

"No, he went to church, but to tell the truth he really preferred the old religion. This was his study and is now mine. Why did you ask if he were an Old Believer?"

"Are you going to be married here?"

"Ye-yes!" replied Rogojin, starting at the unexpected question.

"Soon?"

"You know yourself it does not depend on me."

"Parfen, I am not your enemy, and I do not intend to oppose your intentions in any way. I repeat this to you now just as I said it to you once before on a very similar occasion. When you were arranging for your projected marriage in Moscow, I did not interfere with you—you know I did not. That first time she fled to me from you, from the very altar almost, and begged me to 'save her from you.' Afterwards she ran away from me again, and you found her and arranged your marriage with her once more; and now, I hear, she has run away from you and come to Petersburg. Is it true? Lebedeff wrote me to this effect, and that's why I came here. That you had once more

322

arranged matters with Nastasia Philipovna I only learned last night in the train from a friend of yours, Zaleshoff—if you wish to know.

"I confess I came here with an object. I wished to persuade Nastasia to go abroad for her health; she requires it. Both mind and body need a change badly. I did not intend to take her abroad myself. I was going to arrange for her to go without me. Now I tell you honestly, Parfen, if it is true that all is made up between you, I will not so much as set eyes upon her, and I will never even come to see you again.

"You know quite well that I am telling the truth, because I have always been frank with you. I have never concealed my own opinion from you. I have always told you that I consider a marriage between you and her would be ruin to her. You would also be ruined, and perhaps even more hopelessly. If this marriage were to be broken off again, I admit I should be greatly pleased; but at the same time I have not the slightest intention of trying to part you. You may be quite easy in your mind, and you need not suspect me. You know yourself whether I was ever really your rival or not, even when she ran away and came to me.

"There, you are laughing at me—I know why you laugh. It is perfectly true that we lived apart from one another all the time, in different towns. I told you before that I did not love her with love, but with pity! You said then that you understood me; did you really understand me or not? What hatred there is in your eyes at this moment! I came to relieve your mind, because you are dear to me also. I love you very much, Parfen; and now I shall go away and never come back again. Goodbye."

The prince rose.

"Stay a little," said Parfen, not leaving his chair and resting his head on his right hand. "I haven't seen you for a long time."

The prince sat down again. Both were silent for a few moments.

"When you are not with me I hate you, Lef Nicolaievitch. I have loathed you every day of these three months since I last saw you. By heaven I have!" said Rogojin. "I could have poisoned you at any minute. Now, you have been with me but a quarter of an hour, and all my malice seems to have melted away, and you are as dear to me as ever. Stay here a little longer."

"When I am with you you trust me; but as soon as my back is turned you suspect me," said the prince, smiling, and trying to hide his emotion.

"I trust your voice, when I hear you speak. I quite understand that you and I cannot be put on a level, of course."

"Why did you add that?—There! Now you are cross again," said the prince, wondering.

"We were not asked, you see. We were made different, with different tastes and feelings, without being consulted. You say you love her with pity. I have no pity for her. She hates me—that's the plain truth of the matter. I dream of her every night, and always that she is laughing at me with another man. And so she does laugh at me. She thinks no more of marrying me than if she were changing her shoe. Would you believe it, I haven't seen her for five days, and I daren't go near her. She asks me what I come for, as if she were not content with having disgraced me—"

"Disgraced you! How?"

"Just as though you didn't know! Why, she ran away from me, and went to you. You admitted it yourself, just now."

"But surely you do not believe that she..."

"That she did not disgrace me at Moscow with that officer. Zemtuznikoff? I know for certain she did, after having fixed our marriage-day herself!"

"Impossible!" cried the prince.

"I know it for a fact," replied Rogojin, with conviction.

"It is not like her, you say? My friend, that's absurd. Perhaps such an act would horrify her, if she were with you, but it is quite different where I am concerned. She looks on me as vermin. Her affair with Keller was simply to make a laughing-stock of me. You don't know what a fool she made of me in Moscow; and the money I spent over her! The money! the money!"

"And you can marry her now, Parfen! What will come of it all?" said the prince, with dread in his voice.

Rogojin gazed back gloomily, and with a terrible expression in his eyes, but said nothing.

"I haven't been to see her for five days," he repeated, after a slight pause. "I'm afraid of being turned out. She says she's still her own mistress, and may turn me off altogether, and go abroad. She told me this herself," he said, with a peculiar glance at Muishkin. "I think she often does it merely to frighten me. She is always laughing at me, for some reason or other; but at other times she's angry, and won't say a word, and that's what I'm afraid of. I took her a shawl one day, the like of which she might never have seen, although she did live in luxury and she gave it away to her maid, Katia. Sometimes when I can keep away no longer, I steal past the house on the sly, and once I watched at the gate till dawn—I thought something was going on—and she saw me from the window. She asked me what I should do if I found she had deceived me. I said, 'You know well enough.'"

"What did she know?" cried the prince.

"How was I to tell?" replied Rogojin, with an angry laugh. "I did my best to catch her tripping in Moscow, but did not succeed. However, I caught hold of her one day, and said: 'You are engaged to be married into a respectable family, and do you know what sort of a woman you are? *That's* the sort of woman you are,' I said."

"You told her that?"

"Yes."

"Well, go on."

"She said, 'I wouldn't even have you for a footman now, much less for a husband.' 'I shan't leave the house,' I said, 'so it doesn't matter.' 'Then I shall call somebody and have you kicked out,' she cried. So then I rushed at her, and beat her till she was bruised all over."

"Impossible!" cried the prince, aghast.

"I tell you it's true," said Rogojin quietly, but with eyes ablaze with passion.

"Then for a day and a half I neither slept, nor ate, nor drank, and would not leave her. I knelt at her feet: 'I shall die here,' I said, 'if you don't forgive me; and if you have me turned out, I shall drown myself; because, what should I be without you now?' She was like a madwoman all that day; now she would cry; now she would threaten me with a knife; now she would abuse me. She called in Zaleshoff and Keller, and showed me to them, shamed me in their presence. 'Let's all go to the theatre,' she says, 'and leave him here if he won't go—it's not my business. They'll give you some tea, Parfen Semeonovitch, while I am away, for you must be hungry.' She came back from the theatre alone. 'Those cowards wouldn't come,' she said. 'They are afraid of you, and tried to frighten me, too. "He won't go away as he came," they said, "he'll cut your throat—see if he doesn't." Now, I shall go to my bedroom, and I shall not even lock my door, just to show you how much I am afraid of you. You must be shown that once for all. Did you have tea?' 'No,' I said, 'and I don't intend to.' 'Ha, ha! you are playing off your pride against your stomach! That sort of heroism doesn't sit well on you,' she said.

"With that she did as she had said she would; she went to bed, and did not lock her door. In the morning she came out. 'Are you quite mad?' she said, sharply. 'Why, you'll die of hunger like this.' 'Forgive me,' I said. 'No, I won't, and I won't marry you. I've said it. Surely you haven't sat in this chair all night without sleeping?' 'I didn't sleep,' I said. 'H'm! how sensible of you. And are you going to have no breakfast or dinner today?' 'I told you I wouldn't. Forgive me!' 'You've no idea how unbecoming this sort of thing is to you,' she said, 'it's like putting a saddle on a cow's back. Do you think you are frightening me? My word, what a dreadful thing that you should sit here and eat no food! How terribly frightened I am!' She wasn't angry long, and didn't seem to remember my offence at all. I was surprised, for she is a vindictive, resentful woman—but then I thought that perhaps she despised me too much to feel any resentment against me. And that's the truth.

"She came up to me and said, 'Do you know who the Pope of Rome is?' 'I've heard of him,' I said. 'I suppose you've read the Universal History, Parfen Semeonovitch, haven't you?' she asked. 'I've learned nothing at all,' I said. 'Then I'll lend it to you to read. You must know there was a Roman Pope once, and he was very angry with a certain Emperor; so the Emperor came and neither ate nor drank, but knelt before the Pope's palace till he should be forgiven. And what sort of vows do you think that Emperor was making during all those days on his knees? Stop, I'll read it to you!' Then she read me a lot of verses, where it said that the Emperor spent all the time vowing vengeance against the Pope. 'You don't mean to say you don't approve of the poem, Parfen Semeonovitch,' she says. 'All you have read out is perfectly true,' say I. 'Aha!' says she, 'you admit it's true, do you? And you are making vows to yourself that if I marry you, you will remind me of all this, and take it out of me.' 'I don't know,' I say, 'perhaps I was thinking like that, and perhaps I was not. I'm not thinking of anything just now.' 'What are your thoughts, then?' 'I'm thinking that when you rise from your chair and go past me, I watch you, and follow you with my eyes; if your dress does but rustle, my heart sinks; if you leave the room, I remember every little word and action, and what your voice sounded like, and what you said. I thought of nothing all last night, but sat here listening to your sleeping breath, and heard you move a little, twice.' 'And as for your attack upon me,' she says, 'I suppose you never once thought of *that?*' 'Perhaps I did think of it, and perhaps not,' I say. And what if I don't either forgive you or marry, you' 'I tell you I shall go and drown myself.' 'H'm!' she said, and then relapsed into silence. Then she got angry, and went out. 'I suppose you'd murder me before you drowned yourself, though!' she cried as she left the room.

"An hour later, she came to me again, looking melancholy. 'I will marry you, Parfen Semeonovitch,' she says, not because I'm frightened of you, but because it's all the same to me how I ruin myself. And how can I do it better? Sit down; they'll bring you some dinner directly. And if I do marry you, I'll be a faithful wife to you—you need not doubt that.' Then she thought a bit, and said, 'At all events, you are not a flunkey; at first, I thought you were no better than a flunkey.' And she arranged the wedding and fixed the day straight away on the spot.

"Then, in another week, she had run away again, and came here to Lebedeff's; and when I found her here, she said to me, 'I'm not going to renounce you altogether, but I wish to put off the wedding a bit longer yet—just as long as I like—for I am still my own mistress; so you may wait, if you like.' That's how the matter stands between us now. What do you think of all this, Lef Nicolaievitch?"

"'What do you think of it yourself?" replied the prince, looking sadly at Rogojin.

"As if I can think anything about it! I—" He was about to say more, but stopped in despair.

The prince rose again, as if he would leave.

"At all events, I shall not interfere with you!" he murmured, as though making answer to some secret thought of his own.

"I'll tell you what!" cried Rogojin, and his eyes flashed fire. "I can't understand your yielding her to me like this; I don't understand it. Have you given up loving her altogether? At first you suffered badly—I know it—I saw it. Besides, why did you come post-haste after us? Out of pity, eh? He, he, he!" His mouth curved in a mocking smile.

"Do you think I am deceiving you?" asked the prince.

"No! I trust you—but I can't understand. It seems to me that your pity is greater than my love." A hungry longing to speak his mind out seemed to flash in the man's eyes, combined with an intense anger.

"Your love is mingled with hatred, and therefore, when your love passes, there will be the greater misery," said the prince. "I tell you this, Parfen—"

"What! that I'll cut her throat, you mean?"

The prince shuddered.

"You'll hate her afterwards for all your present love, and for all the torment you are suffering on her account now. What seems to me the most extraordinary thing is, that she can again consent to marry you, after all that has passed between you. When I heard the news yesterday, I could hardly bring myself to believe it. Why, she has run twice from you, from the very altar rails, as it were. She must have some presentiment of evil. What can she want with you now? Your money? Nonsense! Besides, I should think you must have made a fairly large hole in your fortune already. Surely it is not because she is so very anxious to find a husband? She could find many a one besides yourself. Anyone would be better than you, because you will murder her, and I feel sure she must know that but too well by now. Is it because you love her so passionately? Indeed, that may be it. I have heard that there are women who want just that kind of love... but still..." The prince paused, reflectively.

"What are you grinning at my father's portrait again for?" asked Rogojin, suddenly. He was carefully observing every change in the expression of the prince's face.

"I smiled because the idea came into my head that if it were not for this unhappy passion of yours you might have, and would have, become just such a man as your father, and that very quickly, too. You'd have settled down in this house of yours with some silent and obedient wife. You would have spoken rarely, trusted no one, heeded no one, and thought of nothing but making money."

"Laugh away! She said exactly the same, almost word for word, when she saw my father's portrait. It's remarkable how entirely you and she are at one now-a-days."

"What, has she been here?" asked the prince with curiosity.

"Yes! She looked long at the portrait and asked all about my father. 'You'd be just such another,' she said at last, and laughed. 'You have such strong passions, Parfen,' she said, 'that they'd have taken you to Siberia in no time if you had not, luckily, intelligence as well. For you have a good deal of intelligence.' (She said this—believe it or not. The first time I ever heard anything of that sort from her.) 'You'd soon have thrown up all this rowdyism that you indulge in now, and you'd have settled down to quiet, steady money-making, because you have little education; and here you'd have stayed just like your father before you. And you'd have loved your money so that you'd amass not two million, like him, but ten million; and you'd have died of hunger on your money bags to finish up with, for you carry everything to extremes.' There, that's exactly word for word as she said it to me. She never talked to me like that before. She always talks nonsense and laughs when she's with me. We went all over this old house together. 'I shall change all this,' I said, 'or else I'll buy a new house for the wedding.' 'No, no!' she said, 'don't touch anything; leave it all as it is; I shall live with your mother when I marry you.'

"I took her to see my mother, and she was as respectful and kind as though she were her own daughter. Mother has been almost demented ever since father died—she's an old woman. She sits and bows from her chair to everyone she sees. If you left her alone and didn't feed her for three days, I don't believe she would notice it. Well, I took her hand, and I said, 'Give your blessing to this lady, mother, she's going to be my wife.' So Nastasia kissed mother's hand with great feeling. 'She must have suffered terribly, hasn't she?' she said. She saw this book here lying before me. 'What! have you begun to read Russian history?' she asked. She told me once in Moscow, you know, that I had better get Solovieff's Russian History and read it, because I knew nothing. 'That's good,' she said, 'you go on like that, reading books. I'll make you a list myself of the books you ought to read first—shall I?' She had never once spoken to me like this before; it was the first time I felt I could breathe before her like a living creature."

"I'm very, very glad to hear of this, Parfen," said the prince, with real feeling. "Who knows? Maybe God will yet bring you near to one another."

"Never, never!" cried Rogojin, excitedly.

"Look here, Parfen; if you love her so much, surely you must be anxious to earn her respect? And if you do so wish, surely you may hope to? I said just now that I considered it extraordinary that she could still be ready to marry you. Well, though I cannot yet understand it, I feel sure she must have some good reason, or she wouldn't do it. She is sure of your love; but besides that, she must attribute *something* else to you—some good qualities, otherwise the thing would not be. What you have just said confirms my words. You say yourself that she found it possible to speak to you quite differently from her usual manner. You are suspicious, you know, and jealous, therefore when anything annoying happens to you, you exaggerate its significance. Of course, of course, she does not think so ill of you as you say. Why, if she did, she would simply be walking to death by drowning or by the knife, with her eyes wide open, when she married you. It is impossible! As if anybody would go to their death deliberately!"

Rogojin listened to the prince's excited words with a bitter smile. His conviction was, apparently, unalterable.

"How dreadfully you look at me, Parfen!" said the prince, with a feeling of dread.

"Water or the knife?" said the latter, at last. "Ha, ha—that's exactly why she is going to marry me, because she knows for certain that the knife awaits her. Prince, can it be that you don't even yet see what's at the root of it all?"

"I don't understand you."

"Perhaps he really doesn't understand me! They do say that you are a—you know what! She loves another—there, you can understand that much! Just as I love her, exactly so she loves another man. And that other man is—do you know who? It's you. There—you didn't know that, eh?"

"I?"

"You, you! She has loved you ever since that day, her birthday! Only she thinks she cannot marry you, because it would be the ruin of you. 'Everybody knows what sort of a woman I am,' she says. She told me all this herself, to my very face! She's afraid of disgracing and ruining you, she says, but it doesn't matter about me. She can marry me all right! Notice how much consideration she shows for me!"

"But why did she run away to me, and then again from me to—"

"From you to me? Ha, ha! that's nothing! Why, she always acts as though she were in a delirium now-a-days! Either she says, 'Come on, I'll marry you! Let's have the wedding quickly!' and fixes the day, and seems in a hurry for it, and when it begins to come near she feels frightened; or else some other idea gets into her head—goodness knows! you've seen her—you know how she goes on—laughing and crying and raving! There's nothing extraordinary about her having run away from you! She ran away because she found out how dearly she loved you. She could not bear to be near you. You said just now that I had found her at Moscow, when she ran away from you. I didn't do anything of the sort; she came to me herself, straight from you. 'Name the day—I'm ready!' she said. 'Let's have some champagne, and go and hear the gipsies sing!' I tell you she'd have thrown herself into the water long ago if it were not for me! She doesn't do it because I am, perhaps, even more dreadful to her than the water! She's marrying me out of spite; if she marries me, I tell you, it will be for spite!"

"But how do you, how can you—" began the prince, gazing with dread and horror at Rogojin.

"Why don't you finish your sentence? Shall I tell you what you were thinking to yourself just then? You were thinking, 'How can she marry him after this? How can it possibly be permitted?' Oh, I know what you were thinking about!"

"I didn't come here for that purpose, Parfen. That was not in my mind—"

"That may be! Perhaps you didn't *come* with the idea, but the idea is certainly there *now!* Ha, ha! well, that's enough! What are you upset about? Didn't you really know it all before? You astonish me!"

"All this is mere jealousy—it is some malady of yours, Parfen! You exaggerate everything," said the prince, excessively agitated. "What are you doing?"

"Let go of it!" said Parfen, seizing from the prince's hand a knife which the latter had at that moment taken up from the table, where it lay beside the history. Parfen replaced it where it had been.

"I seemed to know it—I felt it, when I was coming back to Petersburg," continued the prince, "I did not want to come, I wished to forget all this, to uproot it from my memory altogether! Well, good-bye—what is the matter?"

He had absently taken up the knife a second time, and again Rogojin snatched it from his hand, and threw it down on the table. It was a plain looking knife, with a bone handle, a blade about eight inches long, and broad in proportion, it did not clasp.

Seeing that the prince was considerably struck by the fact that he had twice seized this knife out of his hand, Rogojin caught it up with some irritation, put it inside the book, and threw the latter across to another table.

"Do you cut your pages with it, or what?" asked Muishkin, still rather absently, as though unable to throw off a deep preoccupation into which the conversation had thrown him.

"Yes."

"It's a garden knife, isn't it?"

"Yes. Can't one cut pages with a garden knife?"

"It's quite new."

"Well, what of that? Can't I buy a new knife if I like?" shouted Rogojin furiously, his irritation growing with every word.

The prince shuddered, and gazed fixedly at Parfen. Suddenly he burst out laughing.

"Why, what an idea!" he said. "I didn't mean to ask you any of these questions; I was thinking of something quite different! But my head is heavy, and I seem so absent-minded nowadays! Well, good-bye—I can't remember what I wanted to say—good-bye!"

"Not that way," said Rogojin.

"There, I've forgotten that too!"

"This way—come along—I'll show you."

IV.

They passed through the same rooms which the prince had traversed on his arrival. In the largest there were pictures on the walls, portraits and landscapes of little interest. Over the door, however, there was one of strange and rather striking shape; it was six or seven feet in length, and not more than a foot in height. It represented the Saviour just taken from the cross.

The prince glanced at it, but took no further notice. He moved on hastily, as though anxious to get out of the house. But Rogojin suddenly stopped underneath the picture.

"My father picked up all these pictures very cheap at auctions, and so on," he said; "they are all rubbish, except the one over the door, and that is valuable. A man offered five hundred roubles for it last week."

"Yes—that's a copy of a Holbein," said the prince, looking at it again, "and a good copy, too, so far as I am able to judge. I saw the picture abroad, and could not forget it—what's the matter?"

Rogojin had dropped the subject of the picture and walked on. Of course his strange frame of mind was sufficient to account for his conduct; but, still, it seemed queer to the prince that he should so abruptly drop a conversation commenced by himself. Rogojin did not take any notice of his question.

"Lef Nicolaievitch," said Rogojin, after a pause, during which the two walked along a little further, "I have long wished to ask you, do you believe in God?"

"How strangely you speak, and how odd you look!" said the other, involuntarily.

"I like looking at that picture," muttered Rogojin, not noticing, apparently, that the prince had not answered his question.

"That picture! That picture!" cried Muishkin, struck by a sudden idea. "Why, a man's faith might be ruined by looking at that picture!"

"So it is!" said Rogojin, unexpectedly. They had now reached the front door.

The prince stopped.

"How?" he said. "What do you mean? I was half joking, and you took me up quite seriously! Why do you ask me whether I believe in God?"

"Oh, no particular reason. I meant to ask you before—many people are unbelievers nowadays, especially Russians, I have been told. You ought to know—you've lived abroad."

Rogojin laughed bitterly as he said these words, and opening the door, held it for the prince to pass out. Muishkin looked surprised, but went out. The other followed him as far as the landing of the outer stairs, and shut the door behind him. They both now stood facing one another, as though oblivious of where they were, or what they had to do next.

"Well, good-bye!" said the prince, holding out his hand.

"Good-bye," said Rogojin, pressing it hard, but quite mechanically.

The prince made one step forward, and then turned round.

"As to faith," he said, smiling, and evidently unwilling to leave Rogojin in this state—"as to faith, I had four curious conversations in two days, a week or so ago. One morning I met a man in the train, and made acquaintance with him at once. I had often heard of him as a very learned man, but an atheist; and I was very glad of the opportunity of conversing with so eminent and clever a person. He doesn't believe in God, and he talked a good deal about it, but all the while it appeared to me that he was speaking *outside the subject*. And it has always struck me, both in speaking to such men and in reading their books, that they do not seem really to be touching on that at all, though on the surface they may appear to do so. I told him this, but I dare say I did not clearly express what I meant, for he could not understand me.

"That same evening I stopped at a small provincial hotel, and it so happened that a dreadful murder had been committed there the night before, and everybody was talking about it. Two peasants—elderly men and old friends—had had tea together there the night before, and were to occupy the same bedroom. They were not drunk but one of them had noticed for the first time that his friend possessed a silver watch which he was wearing on a chain. He was by no means a thief, and was, as peasants go, a rich man; but this watch so fascinated him that he could not restrain himself. He took a knife, and when his friend turned his back, he came up softly behind, raised his eyes to heaven, crossed himself, and saying earnestly—'God forgive me, for Christ's sake!' he cut his friend's throat like a sheep, and took the watch."

Rogojin roared with laughter. He laughed as though he were in a sort of fit. It was strange to see him laughing so after the sombre mood he had been in just before.

"Oh, I like that! That beats anything!" he cried convulsively, panting for breath. "One is an absolute unbeliever; the other is such a thorough—going believer that he murders his friend to the tune of a prayer! Oh, prince, prince, that's too good for anything! You can't have invented it. It's the best thing I've heard!"

"Next morning I went out for a stroll through the town," continued the prince, so soon as Rogojin was a little quieter, though his laughter still burst out at intervals, "and soon observed a drunken-looking soldier staggering about the pavement. He came up to me and said, 'Buy my silver cross, sir! You shall have it for fourpence—it's real silver.' I looked, and there he held a cross, just taken off his own neck, evidently, a large tin one, made after the Byzantine pattern. I fished out fourpence, and put his cross on my own neck, and I could see by his face that he was as pleased as he could be at the thought that he had succeeded in cheating a foolish gentleman, and away he went to drink the value of his cross. At that time everything that I saw made a tremendous impression upon me. I had understood nothing about Russia before, and had only vague and fantastic memories of it. So I thought, 'I will wait awhile before I condemn this Judas. Only God knows what may be hidden in the hearts of drunkards.'

"Well, I went homewards, and near the hotel I came across a poor woman, carrying a child—a baby of some six weeks old. The mother was quite a girl herself. The baby was smiling up at her, for the first time in its life, just at that moment; and while I watched the woman she suddenly crossed herself, oh, so devoutly! 'What is it, my good woman I asked her. (I was never but asking questions then!) Exactly as is a mother's joy when her baby smiles for the first time into her eyes, so is God's joy when one of His children turns and prays to Him for the first time, with all his heart!' This is what that poor woman said to me, almost word for word; and such a deep, refined, truly religious thought it was—a thought in which the whole essence of Christianity was expressed in one flash—that is, the recognition of God as our Father, and of God's joy in men as His own children, which is the chief idea of Christ. She was a simple country-woman—a mother, it's true—and perhaps, who knows, she may have been the wife of the drunken soldier!

"Listen, Parfen; you put a question to me just now. This is my reply. The essence of religious feeling has nothing to do with reason, or atheism, or crime, or acts of any kind—it has nothing to do with these things—and never had. There is something besides all this, something which the arguments of the atheists can never touch. But the principal thing, and the conclusion of my argument, is that this is most clearly seen in the heart of a Russian. This is a conviction which I have gained while I have been in this Russia of ours. Yes, Parfen! there is work to be done; there is work to be done in this Russian world! Remember what talks we used to have in Moscow! And I never wished to come here at all; and I never thought to meet you like this, Parfen! Well, well—good-bye—good-bye! God be with you!"

He turned and went downstairs.

"Lef Nicolaievitch!" cried Parfen, before he had reached the next landing. "Have you got that cross you bought from the soldier with you?"

"Yes, I have," and the prince stopped again.

"Show it me, will you?"

A new fancy! The prince reflected, and then mounted the stairs once more. He pulled out the cross without taking it off his neck.

"Give it to me," said Parfen.

"Why? do you—"

The prince would rather have kept this particular cross.

"I'll wear it; and you shall have mine. I'll take it off at once."

"You wish to exchange crosses? Very well, Parfen, if that's the case, I'm glad enough—that makes us brothers, you know."

The prince took off his tin cross, Parfen his gold one, and the exchange was made.

Parfen was silent. With sad surprise the prince observed that the look of distrust, the bitter, ironical smile, had still not altogether left his newly-adopted brother's face. At moments, at all events, it showed itself but too plainly,

At last Rogojin took the prince's hand, and stood so for some moments, as though he could not make up his mind. Then he drew him along, murmuring almost inaudibly,

"Come!"

They stopped on the landing, and rang the bell at a door opposite to Parfen's own lodging.

An old woman opened to them and bowed low to Parfen, who asked her some questions hurriedly, but did not wait to hear her answer. He led the prince on through several dark, cold-looking rooms, spotlessly clean, with white covers over all the furniture.

Without the ceremony of knocking, Parfen entered a small apartment, furnished like a drawing-room, but with a polished mahogany partition dividing one half of it from what was probably a bedroom. In one corner of this room sat an old woman in an arm-chair, close to the stove. She did not look very old, and her face was a pleasant, round one; but she was white-haired and, as one could detect at the first glance, quite in her second childhood. She wore a black woollen dress, with a black handkerchief round her neck and shoulders, and a white cap with black ribbons. Her feet were raised on a footstool. Beside her sat another old woman, also dressed in mourning, and silently knitting a stocking; this was evidently a companion. They both looked as though they never broke the silence. The first old woman, so soon as she saw Rogojin and the prince, smiled and bowed courteously several times, in token of her gratification at their visit.

"Mother," said Rogojin, kissing her hand, "here is my great friend, Prince Muishkin; we have exchanged crosses; he was like a real brother to me at Moscow at one time, and did a great deal for me. Bless him, mother, as you would bless your own son. Wait a moment, let me arrange your hands for you."

But the old lady, before Parfen had time to touch her, raised her right hand, and, with three fingers held up, devoutly made the sign of the cross three times over the prince. She then nodded her head kindly at him once more.

"There, come along, Lef Nicolaievitch; that's all I brought you here for," said Rogojin.

When they reached the stairs again he added:

"She understood nothing of what I said to her, and did not know what I wanted her to do, and yet she blessed you; that shows she wished to do so herself. Well, goodbye; it's time you went, and I must go too."

He opened his own door.

"Well, let me at least embrace you and say goodbye, you strange fellow!" cried the prince, looking with gentle reproach at Rogojin, and advancing towards him. But the latter had hardly raised his arms when he dropped them again. He could not make up his mind to it; he turned away from the prince in order to avoid looking at him. He could not embrace him.

"Don't be afraid," he muttered, indistinctly, "though I have taken your cross, I shall not murder you for your watch." So saying, he laughed suddenly, and strangely. Then in a moment his face became transfigured; he grew deadly white, his lips trembled, his eyes burned like fire. He stretched out his arms and held the prince tightly to him, and said in a strangled voice:

"Well, take her! It's Fate! She's yours. I surrender her.... Remember Rogojin!" And pushing the prince from him, without looking back at him, he hurriedly entered his own flat, and banged the door.

V.

It was late now, nearly half-past two, and the prince did not find General Epanchin at home. He left a card, and determined to look up Colia, who had a room at a small hotel near. Colia was not in, but he was informed that he might be back shortly, and had left word that if he were not in by half-past three it was to be understood that he had gone to Pavlofsk to General Epanchin's, and would dine there. The prince decided to wait till half-past three, and ordered some dinner. At half-past three there was no sign of Colia. The prince waited until four o'clock, and then strolled off mechanically wherever his feet should carry him.

In early summer there are often magnificent days in St. Petersburg—bright, hot and still. This happened to be such a day.

For some time the prince wandered about without aim or object. He did not know the town well. He stopped to look about him on bridges, at street corners. He entered a confectioner's shop to rest, once. He was in a state of nervous excitement and perturbation; he noticed nothing and no one; and he felt a craving for solitude, to be alone with his thoughts and his emotions, and to give himself up to them passively. He loathed the idea of trying to answer the questions that would rise up in his heart and mind. "I am not to blame for all this," he thought to himself, half unconsciously.

Towards six o'clock he found himself at the station of the Tsarsko-Selski railway.

He was tired of solitude now; a new rush of feeling took hold of him, and a flood of light chased away the gloom, for a moment, from his soul. He took a ticket to Pavlofsk, and determined to get there as fast as he could, but something stopped him; a reality, and not a fantasy, as he was inclined to think it. He was about to take his place in a carriage, when he suddenly threw away his ticket and came out again, disturbed and thoughtful. A few moments later, in the street, he recalled something that had bothered him all the afternoon. He caught himself engaged in a strange occupation which he now recollected he had taken up at odd moments for the last few hours—it was looking about all around him for something, he did not know what. He had forgotten it for a while, half an hour or so, and now, suddenly, the uneasy search had recommenced.

But he had hardly become conscious of this curious phenomenon, when another recollection suddenly swam through his brain, interesting him for the moment, exceedingly. He remembered that the last time he had been engaged in looking around him for the unknown something, he was standing before a cutler's shop, in the window of which were exposed certain goods for sale. He was extremely anxious now to discover whether this shop and these goods really existed, or whether the whole thing had been a hallucination.

He felt in a very curious condition today, a condition similar to that which had preceded his fits in bygone years.

He remembered that at such times he had been particularly absentminded, and could not discriminate between objects and persons unless he concentrated special attention upon them.

He remembered seeing something in the window marked at sixty copecks. Therefore, if the shop existed and if this object were really in the window, it would prove that he had been able to concentrate his attention on this article at a moment when, as a general rule, his absence of mind would have been too great to admit of any such concentration; in fact, very shortly after he had left the railway station in such a state of agitation.

So he walked back looking about him for the shop, and his heart beat with intolerable impatience. Ah! here was the very shop, and there was the article marked "60 cop." Of course, it's sixty copecks, he thought, and certainly worth no more. This idea amused him and he laughed.

But it was a hysterical laugh; he was feeling terribly oppressed. He remembered clearly that just here, standing before this window, he had suddenly turned round, just as earlier in the day he had turned and found the dreadful eyes of Rogojin fixed upon him. Convinced, therefore, that in this respect at all events he had been under no delusion, he left the shop and went on.

This must be thought out; it was clear that there had been no hallucination at the station then, either; something had actually happened to him, on both occasions; there was no doubt of it. But again a loathing for all mental exertion overmastered him; he would not think it out now, he would put it off and think of something else. He remembered that during his epileptic fits, or rather immediately preceding them, he had always experienced a moment or two when his whole heart, and mind, and body seemed to wake up to vigour and light; when he became filled with joy and hope, and all his anxieties seemed to be swept away for ever; these moments were but presentiments, as it were, of the one final second (it was never more than a second) in which the fit came upon him. That second, of course, was inexpressible. When his attack was over, and the prince reflected on his symptoms, he used to say to himself: "These moments, short as they are, when I feel such extreme consciousness of myself, and consequently more of life than at other times, are due only to the disease—to the sudden rupture of normal conditions. Therefore they are not really a higher kind of life, but a lower." This reasoning, however, seemed to end in a paradox, and lead to the further consideration:—"What matter though it be only disease, an abnormal tension of the brain, if when I recall and analyze the moment, it seems to have been one of harmony and beauty in the highest degree—an instant of deepest sensation, overflowing with unbounded joy and rapture, ecstatic devotion, and completest life?" Vague though this sounds, it was perfectly comprehensible to Muishkin, though he knew that it was but a feeble expression of his sensations.

That there was, indeed, beauty and harmony in those abnormal moments, that they really contained the highest synthesis of life, he could not doubt, nor even admit the possibility of doubt. He felt that they were not analogous to the fantastic and unreal dreams due to intoxication by hashish, opium or wine. Of that he could judge, when the attack was over. These instants were characterized—to define it in a word—by an intense quickening of the sense of personality. Since, in the last conscious moment preceding the attack, he could say to himself, with full understanding of his words: "I would give my whole life for this one instant," then doubtless to him it really was worth a lifetime. For the rest, he thought the dialectical part of his argument of little worth; he saw only too clearly that the result of these ecstatic moments was stupefaction, mental darkness, idiocy. No argument was possible on that point. His conclusion, his estimate of the "moment," doubtless contained some error, yet the reality of the sensation troubled him. What's more unanswerable than a fact? And this fact had occurred. The prince had confessed unreservedly to himself that the feeling of intense beatitude in that crowded moment made the moment worth a lifetime. "I feel then," he said one day to Rogojin in Moscow, "I feel then as if I understood those amazing words—'There shall be no more time.'" And he added with a smile: "No doubt the epileptic Mahomet refers to that same moment when he says that he visited all the dwellings of Allah, in less time than was needed to empty his pitcher of water." Yes, he had often met Rogojin in Moscow, and many were the subjects they discussed. "He told me I had been a brother to him," thought the prince. "He said so today, for the first time."

He was sitting in the Summer Garden on a seat under a tree, and his mind dwelt on the matter. It was about seven o'clock, and the place was empty. The stifling atmosphere foretold a storm, and the prince felt a certain charm in the contemplative mood which possessed him. He found pleasure, too, in gazing at the exterior objects around him. All the time he was trying to forget some thing, to escape from some idea that haunted him; but melancholy thoughts came back, though he would so willingly have escaped from them. He remembered suddenly how he had been talking to the waiter, while he dined, about a recently committed murder which the whole town was discussing, and as he thought of it something strange came over him. He was seized all at once by a violent desire, almost a temptation, against which he strove in vain.

He jumped up and walked off as fast as he could towards the "Petersburg Side." [One of the quarters of St. Petersburg.] He had asked someone, a little while before, to show him which was the Petersburg Side, on the banks of the Neva. He had not gone there, however; and he knew very well that it was of no use to go now, for he would certainly not find Lebedeff's relation at home. He had the address, but she must certainly have gone to Pavlofsk, or Colia would have let him know. If he were to go now, it would merely be out of curiosity, but a sudden, new idea had come into his head.

However, it was something to move on and know where he was going. A minute later he was still moving on, but without knowing anything. He could no longer think out his new idea. He tried to take an interest in all he saw; in the sky, in the Neva. He spoke to some children he met. He felt his epileptic condition becoming more and more developed. The evening was very close; thunder was heard some way off.

The prince was haunted all that day by the face of Lebedeff's nephew whom he had seen for the first time that morning, just as one is haunted at times by some persistent musical refrain. By a curious association of ideas, the young man always appeared as the murderer of whom Lebedeff had spoken when introducing him to Muishkin. Yes, he had read something about the murder, and that quite recently. Since he came to Russia, he had heard many stories of this kind, and was interested in them. His conversation with the waiter, an hour ago, chanced to be on the subject of this murder of the Zemarins, and the latter had agreed with him about it. He thought of the waiter again, and decided that he was no fool, but a steady, intelligent man: though, said he to himself, "God knows what he may really be; in a country with which one is unfamiliar it is difficult to understand the people one meets." He was beginning to have a passionate faith in the Russian soul, however, and what discoveries he had made in the last six months, what unexpected discoveries! But every soul is a mystery, and depths of mystery lie in the soul of a Russian. He had been intimate with Rogojin, for example, and a brotherly friendship had sprung up between them—yet did he really know him? What chaos and ugliness fills the world at times! What a self-satisfied rascal is that nephew of Lebedeff's! "But what am I thinking," continued the prince to himself. "Can he really have committed that crime? Did he kill those six persons? I seem to be confusing things... how strange it all is.... My head goes round... And Lebedeff's daughter—how sympathetic and charming her face was as she held the child in her arms! What an innocent look and child-like laugh she had! It is curious that I had forgotten her until now. I expect Lebedeff adores her—and I really believe, when I think of it, that as sure as two and two make four, he is fond of that nephew, too!"

Well, why should he judge them so hastily! Could he really say what they were, after one short visit? Even Lebedeff seemed an enigma today. Did he expect to find him so? He had never seen him like that before. Lebedeff and the Comtesse du Barry! Good Heavens! If Rogojin should really kill someone, it would not, at any rate, be such a senseless, chaotic affair. A knife made to a special pattern, and six people killed in a kind of delirium. But Rogojin also had a knife made to a special pattern. Can it be that Rogojin wishes to murder anyone? The prince began to tremble violently. "It is a crime on my part to imagine anything so base, with such cynical frankness." His face reddened with shame at the thought; and then there came across him as in a flash the memory of the incidents at the Pavlofsk station, and at the other station in the morning; and the question asked him by Rogojin about *the eyes* and Rogojin's cross, that he was even now wearing; and the benediction of Rogojin's mother; and his embrace on the darkened staircase—that last supreme renunciation—and now, to find himself full of this new "idea," staring into shop-windows, and looking round for things—how base he was!

Despair overmastered his soul; he would not go on, he would go back to his hotel; he even turned and went the other way; but a moment after he changed his mind again and went on in the old direction.

Why, here he was on the Petersburg Side already, quite close to the house! Where was his "idea"? He was marching along without it now. Yes, his malady was coming back, it was clear enough; all this gloom and heaviness, all these "ideas," were nothing more nor less than a fit coming on; perhaps he would have a fit this very day.

But just now all the gloom and darkness had fled, his heart felt full of joy and hope, there was no such thing as doubt. And yes, he hadn't seen her for so long; he really must see her. He wished he could meet Rogojin; he would take his hand, and they would go to her together. His heart was pure, he was no rival of Parfen's. Tomorrow, he would go and tell him that he had seen her. Why, he had only come for the sole purpose of seeing her, all the way from Moscow! Perhaps she might be here still, who knows? She might not have gone away to Pavlofsk yet.

Yes, all this must be put straight and above-board, there must be no more passionate renouncements, such as Rogojin's. It must all be clear as day. Cannot Rogojin's soul bear the light? He said he did not love her with sympathy and pity; true, he added that "your pity is greater than my love," but he was not quite fair on himself there. Kin! Rogojin reading a book—wasn't that sympathy beginning? Did it not show that he comprehended his relations with her? And his story of waiting day and night for her forgiveness? That didn't look quite like passion alone.

And as to her face, could it inspire nothing but passion? Could her face inspire passion at all now? Oh, it inspired suffering, grief, overwhelming grief of the soul! A poignant, agonizing memory swept over the prince's heart.

Yes, agonizing. He remembered how he had suffered that first day when he thought he observed in her the symptoms of madness. He had almost fallen into despair. How could he have lost his hold upon her when she ran away from him to Rogojin? He ought to have run after her himself, rather than wait for news as he had done. Can Rogojin have failed to observe, up to now, that she is mad? Rogojin attributes her strangeness to other causes, to passion! What insane jealousy! What was it he had hinted at in that suggestion of his? The prince suddenly blushed, and shuddered to his very heart.

But why recall all this? There was insanity on both sides. For him, the prince, to love this woman with passion, was unthinkable. It would be cruel and inhuman. Yes. Rogojin is not fair to himself; he has a large heart; he has aptitude for sympathy. When he learns the truth, and finds what a pitiable being is this injured, broken, half-insane creature, he will forgive her all the torment she has caused him. He will become her slave, her brother, her friend. Compassion will teach even Rogojin, it will show him how to reason. Compassion is the chief law of human existence. Oh, how guilty he felt towards Rogojin! And, for a few warm, hasty words spoken in Moscow, Parfen had called him "brother," while he—but no, this was delirium! It would all come right! That gloomy Parfen had implied that his faith was waning; he must suffer dreadfully. He said he liked to look at that picture; it was not that he liked it, but he felt the need of looking at it. Rogojin was not merely a passionate soul; he was a fighter. He was fighting for the restoration of his dying faith. He must have something to hold on to and believe, and someone to believe in. What a strange picture that of Holbein's is! Why, this is the street, and here's the house, No. 16.

The prince rang the bell, and asked for Nastasia Philipovna. The lady of the house came out, and stated that Nastasia had gone to stay with Daria Alexeyevna at Pavlofsk, and might be there some days.

Madame Filisoff was a little woman of forty, with a cunning face, and crafty, piercing eyes. When, with an air of mystery, she asked her visitor's name, he refused at first to answer, but in a moment he changed his mind, and left strict instructions that it should be given to Nastasia Philipovna. The urgency of his request seemed to impress Madame Filisoff, and she put on a knowing expression, as if to say, "You need not be afraid, I quite understand." The prince's name evidently was a great surprise to her. He stood and looked absently at her for a moment, then turned, and took the road back to his hotel. But he went away not as he came. A great change had suddenly come over him. He went blindly forward; his knees shook under him; he was tormented by "ideas"; his lips were blue, and trembled with a feeble, meaningless smile. His demon was upon him once more.

What had happened to him? Why was his brow clammy with drops of moisture, his knees shaking beneath him, and his soul oppressed with a cold gloom? Was it because he had just seen these dreadful eyes again? Why, he had left the Summer Garden on purpose to see them; that had been his "idea." He had wished to assure himself that he would see them once more at that house. Then why was he so overwhelmed now, having seen them as he expected? just as though he had not expected to see them! Yes, they were the very same eyes; and no doubt about it. The same that he had seen in the crowd that morning at the station, the same that he had surprised in Rogojin's rooms some hours later, when the latter had replied to his inquiry with a sneering laugh, "Well, whose eyes were they?" Then for the third time they had appeared just as he was getting into the train on his way to see Aglaya. He had had a strong impulse to rush up to Rogojin, and repeat his words of the morning "Whose eyes are they?" Instead he had fled from the station, and knew nothing more, until he found himself gazing into the window of a cutler's shop, and wondering if a knife with a staghorn handle would cost more than sixty copecks. And as the prince sat dreaming in the Summer Garden under a lime-tree, a wicked demon had come and whispered in his car: "Rogojin has been spying upon you and watching you all the morning in a frenzy of desperation. When he finds you have not gone to Pavlofsk—a terrible discovery for him—he will surely go at once to that house in Petersburg Side, and watch for you there, although only this morning you gave your word of honour not to see *her*, and swore that you had not come to Petersburg for that purpose." And thereupon the prince had hastened off to that house, and what was there in the fact that he had met Rogojin there? He had only seen a wretched, suffering creature, whose state of mind was gloomy and miserable, but most comprehensible. In the morning Rogojin had seemed to be trying to keep out of the way; but at the station this afternoon he had stood out, he had concealed himself, indeed, less than the prince himself; at the house, now, he had stood fifty yards off on the other side of the road, with folded hands, watching, plainly in view and apparently desirous of being seen. He had stood there like an accuser, like a judge, not like a—a what?

And why had not the prince approached him and spoken to him, instead of turning away and pretending he had seen nothing, although their eyes met? (Yes, their eyes had met, and they had looked at each other.) Why, he had himself wished to take Rogojin by the hand and go in together, he had himself determined to go to him on the morrow and tell him that he had seen her, he had repudiated the demon as he walked to the house, and his heart had been full of joy.

Was there something in the whole aspect of the man, today, sufficient to justify the prince's terror, and the awful suspicions of his demon? Something seen, but indescribable, which filled him with dreadful presentiments? Yes, he was convinced of it—convinced of what? (Oh, how mean and hideous of him to feel this conviction, this presentiment! How he blamed himself for it!) "Speak if you dare, and tell me, what is the presentiment?" he repeated to himself, over and over again. "Put it into words, speak out clearly and distinctly. Oh, miserable coward that I am!" The prince flushed with shame for his own baseness. "How shall I ever look this man in the face again? My God, what a day! And what a nightmare, what a nightmare!"

There was a moment, during this long, wretched walk back from the Petersburg Side, when the prince felt an irresistible desire to go straight to Rogojin's, wait for him, embrace him with tears of shame and contrition, and tell him of his distrust, and finish with it—once for all.

But here he was back at his hotel.

How often during the day he had thought of this hotel with loathing—its corridor, its rooms, its stairs. How he had dreaded coming back to it, for some reason.

"What a regular old woman I am today," he had said to himself each time, with annoyance. "I believe in every foolish presentiment that comes into my head."

He stopped for a moment at the door; a great flush of shame came over him. "I am a coward, a wretched coward," he said, and moved forward again; but once more he paused.

Among all the incidents of the day, one recurred to his mind to the exclusion of the rest; although now that his self-control was regained, and he was no longer under the influence of a nightmare, he was able to think of it calmly. It concerned the knife on Rogojin's table. "Why should not Rogojin have as many knives on his table as he chooses?" thought the prince, wondering at his suspicions, as he had done when he found himself looking into the cutler's window. "What could it have to do with me?" he said to himself again, and stopped as if rooted to the ground by a kind of paralysis of limb such as attacks people under the stress of some humiliating recollection.

The doorway was dark and gloomy at any time; but just at this moment it was rendered doubly so by the fact that the thunder-storm had just broken, and the rain was coming down in torrents.

And in the semi-darkness the prince distinguished a man standing close to the stairs, apparently waiting.

There was nothing particularly significant in the fact that a man was standing back in the doorway, waiting to come out or go upstairs; but the prince felt an irresistible conviction that he knew this man, and that it was Rogojin. The man moved on up the stairs; a moment later the prince passed up them, too. His heart froze within him. "In a minute or two I shall know all," he thought.

The staircase led to the first and second corridors of the hotel, along which lay the guests' bedrooms. As is often the case in Petersburg houses, it was narrow and very dark, and turned around a massive stone column.

On the first landing, which was as small as the necessary turn of the stairs allowed, there was a niche in the column, about half a yard wide, and in this niche the prince felt convinced that a man stood concealed. He thought he could distinguish a figure standing there. He would pass by quickly and not look. He took a step forward, but could bear the uncertainty no longer and turned his head.

The eyes—the same two eyes—met his! The man concealed in the niche had also taken a step forward. For one second they stood face to face.

Suddenly the prince caught the man by the shoulder and twisted him round towards the light, so that he might see his face more clearly.

Rogojin's eyes flashed, and a smile of insanity distorted his countenance. His right hand was raised, and something glittered in it. The prince did not think of trying to stop it. All he could remember afterwards was that he seemed to have called out:

"Parfen! I won't believe it."

Next moment something appeared to burst open before him: a wonderful inner light illuminated his soul. This lasted perhaps half a second, yet he distinctly remembered hearing the beginning of the wail, the strange, dreadful wail, which burst from his lips of its own accord, and which no effort of will on his part could suppress.

Next moment he was absolutely unconscious; black darkness blotted out everything.

He had fallen in an epileptic fit.

As is well known, these fits occur instantaneously. The face, especially the eyes, become terribly disfigured, convulsions seize the limbs, a terrible cry breaks from the sufferer, a wail from which everything human seems to be blotted out, so that it is impossible to believe that the man who has just fallen is the same who emitted the dreadful cry. It seems more as though some other being, inside the stricken one, had cried. Many people have borne witness to this impression; and many cannot behold an epileptic fit without a feeling of mysterious terror and dread.

Such a feeling, we must suppose, overtook Rogojin at this moment, and saved the prince's life. Not knowing that it was a fit, and seeing his victim disappear head foremost into the darkness, hearing his head strike the stone steps below with a crash, Rogojin rushed downstairs, skirting the body, and flung himself headlong out of the hotel, like a raving madman.

The prince's body slipped convulsively down the steps till it rested at the bottom. Very soon, in five minutes or so, he was discovered, and a crowd collected around him.

A pool of blood on the steps near his head gave rise to grave fears. Was it a case of accident, or had there been a crime? It was, however, soon recognized as a case of epilepsy, and identification and proper measures for restoration followed one another, owing to a fortunate circumstance. Colia Ivolgin had come back to his hotel about seven o'clock, owing to a sudden impulse which made him refuse to dine at the Epanchins', and, finding a note from the prince awaiting him, had sped away to the latter's address. Arrived there, he ordered a cup of tea and sat sipping it in the coffee-room. While there he heard excited whispers of someone just found at the bottom of the stairs in a fit; upon which he had hurried to the spot, with a presentiment of evil, and at once recognized the prince.

The sufferer was immediately taken to his room, and though he partially regained consciousness, he lay long in a semi-dazed condition.

The doctor stated that there was no danger to be apprehended from the wound on the head, and as soon as the prince could understand what was going on around him, Colia hired a carriage and took him away to Lebedeff's. There he was received with much cordiality, and the departure to the country was hastened on his account. Three days later they were all at Pavlofsk.

VI.

Lebedeff's country-house was not large, but it was pretty and convenient, especially the part which was let to the prince.

A row of orange and lemon trees and jasmines, planted in green tubs, stood on the fairly wide terrace. According to Lebedeff, these trees gave the house a most delightful aspect. Some were there when he bought it, and he was so charmed with the effect that he promptly added to their number. When the tubs containing these plants arrived at the villa and were set in their places, Lebedeff kept running into the street to enjoy the view of the house, and every time he did so the rent to be demanded from the future tenant went up with a bound.

This country villa pleased the prince very much in his state of physical and mental exhaustion. On the day that they left for Pavlofsk, that is the day after his attack, he appeared almost well, though in reality he felt very far from it. The faces of those around him for the last three days had made a pleasant impression. He was pleased to see, not only Colia, who had become his inseparable companion, but Lebedeff himself and all the family, except the nephew, who had left the house. He was also glad to receive a visit from General Ivolgin, before leaving St. Petersburg.

It was getting late when the party arrived at Pavlofsk, but several people called to see the prince, and assembled in the verandah. Gania was the first to arrive. He had grown so pale and thin that the prince could hardly recognize him. Then came Varia and Ptitsin, who were rusticating in the neighbourhood. As to General Ivolgin, he scarcely budged from Lebedeff's house, and seemed to have moved to Pavlofsk with him. Lebedeff did his best to keep Ardalion Alexandrovitch by him, and to prevent him from invading the prince's quarters. He chatted with him confidentially, so that they might have been taken for old friends. During those three days the prince had noticed that they frequently held long conversations; he often heard their voices raised in argument on deep and learned subjects, which evidently pleased Lebedeff. He seemed as if he could not do without the general. But it was not only Ardalion Alexandrovitch whom Lebedeff kept out of the prince's way. Since they had come to the villa, he treated his own family the same. Upon the pretext that his tenant needed quiet, he kept him almost in isolation, and Muishkin protested in vain against this excess of zeal. Lebedeff stamped his feet at his daughters and drove them away if they attempted to join the prince on the terrace; not even Vera was excepted.

"They will lose all respect if they are allowed to be so free and easy; besides it is not proper for them," he declared at last, in answer to a direct question from the prince.

"Why on earth not?" asked the latter. "Really, you know, you are making yourself a nuisance, by keeping guard over me like this. I get bored all by myself; I have told you so over and over again, and you get on my nerves more than ever by waving your hands and creeping in and out in the mysterious way you do."

It was a fact that Lebedeff, though he was so anxious to keep everyone else from disturbing the patient, was continually in and out of the prince's room himself. He invariably began by opening the door a crack and peering in to see if the prince was there, or if he had escaped; then he would creep softly up to the arm-chair, sometimes making Muishkin jump by his sudden appearance. He always asked if the patient wanted anything, and when the latter replied that he only wanted to be left in peace, he would turn away obediently and make for the door on tip-toe, with deprecatory gestures to imply that he had only just looked in, that he would not speak a word, and would go away and not intrude again; which did not prevent him from reappearing in ten minutes or a quarter of an hour.

Colia had free access to the prince, at which Lebedeff was quite disgusted and indignant. He would listen at the door for half an hour at a time while the two were talking. Colia found this out, and naturally told the prince of his discovery.

"Do you think yourself my master, that you try to keep me under lock and key like this?" said the prince to Lebedeff. "In the country, at least, I intend to be free, and you may make up your mind that I mean to see whom I like, and go where I please."

"Why, of course," replied the clerk, gesticulating with his hands.

The prince looked him sternly up and down.

"Well, Lukian Timofeyovitch, have you brought the little cupboard that you had at the head of your bed with you here?"

"No, I left it where it was."

"Impossible!"

"It cannot be moved; you would have to pull the wall down, it is so firmly fixed."

"Perhaps you have one like it here?"

"I have one that is even better, much better; that is really why I bought this house."

"Ah! What visitor did you turn away from my door, about an hour ago?"

"The-the general. I would not let him in; there is no need for him to visit you, prince... I have the deepest esteem for him, he is a—a great man. You don't believe it? Well, you will see, and yet, most excellent prince, you had much better not receive him."

"May I ask why? and also why you walk about on tiptoe and always seem as if you were going to whisper a secret in my ear whenever you come near me?"

"I am vile, vile; I know it!" cried Lebedeff, beating his breast with a contrite air. "But will not the general be too hospitable for you?"

"Too hospitable?"

"Yes. First, he proposes to come and live in my house. Well and good; but he sticks at nothing; he immediately makes himself one of the family. We have talked over our respective relations several times, and discovered that we are connected by marriage. It seems also that you are a sort of nephew on his mother's side; he was explaining it to me again only yesterday. If you are his nephew, it follows that I must also be a relation of yours, most excellent prince. Never mind about that, it is only a foible; but just now he assured me that all his life, from the day he was made an ensign to the 11th of last June, he has entertained at least two hundred guests at his table every day. Finally, he went so far as to say that they never rose from the table; they dined, supped, and had tea, for fifteen hours at a stretch. This went on for thirty years without a break; there was barely time to change the table-cloth; directly one person left, another took his place. On feast-days he entertained as many as three hundred guests, and they numbered seven hundred on the thousandth anniversary of the foundation of the Russian Empire. It amounts to a passion with him; it makes one uneasy to hear of it. It is terrible to have to entertain people who do things on such a scale. That is why I wonder whether such a man is not too hospitable for you and me."

"But you seem to be on the best of terms with him?"

"Quite fraternal—I look upon it as a joke. Let us be brothers-in-law, it is all the same to me,—rather an honour than not. But in spite of the two hundred guests and the thousandth anniversary of the Russian Empire, I can see that he is a very remarkable man. I am quite sincere. You said just now that I always looked as if I was going to tell you a secret; you are right. I have a secret to tell you: a certain person has just let me know that she is very anxious for a secret interview with you."

"Why should it be secret? Not at all; I will call on her myself tomorrow."

"No, oh no!" cried Lebedeff, waving his arms; "if she is afraid, it is not for the reason you think. By the way, do you know that the monster comes every day to inquire after your health?"

"You call him a monster so often that it makes me suspicious."

"You must have no suspicions, none whatever," said Lebedeff quickly. "I only want you to know that the person in question is not afraid of him, but of something quite, quite different."

"What on earth is she afraid of, then? Tell me plainly, without any more beating about the bush," said the prince, exasperated by the other's mysterious grimaces.

"Ah that is the secret," said Lebedeff, with a smile.

"Whose secret?"

"Yours. You forbade me yourself to mention it before you, most excellent prince," murmured Lebedeff. Then, satisfied that he had worked up Muishkin's curiosity to the highest pitch, he added abruptly: "She is afraid of Aglaya Ivanovna."

The prince frowned for a moment in silence, and then said suddenly:

"Really, Lebedeff, I must leave your house. Where are Gavrila Ardalionovitch and the Ptitsins? Are they here? Have you chased them away, too?"

"They are coming, they are coming; and the general as well. I will open all the doors; I will call all my daughters, all of them, this very minute," said Lebedeff in a low voice, thoroughly frightened, and waving his hands as he ran from door to door.

At that moment Colia appeared on the terrace; he announced that Lizabetha Prokofievna and her three daughters were close behind him.

Moved by this news, Lebedeff hurried up to the prince.

"Shall I call the Ptitsins, and Gavrila Ardalionovitch? Shall I let the general in?" he asked.

"Why not? Let in anyone who wants to see me. I assure you, Lebedeff, you have misunderstood my position from the very first; you have been wrong all along. I have not the slightest reason to hide myself from anyone," replied the prince gaily.

Seeing him laugh, Lebedeff thought fit to laugh also, and though much agitated his satisfaction was quite visible.

Colia was right; the Epanchin ladies were only a few steps behind him. As they approached the terrace other visitors appeared from Lebedeff's side of the house-the Ptitsins, Gania, and Ardalion Alexandrovitch.

The Epanchins had only just heard of the prince's illness and of his presence in Pavlofsk, from Colia; and up to this time had been in a state of considerable bewilderment about him. The general brought the prince's card down from town, and Mrs. Epanchin had felt convinced that he himself would follow his card at once; she was much excited.

In vain the girls assured her that a man who had not written for six months would not be in such a dreadful hurry, and that probably he had enough to do in town without needing to bustle down to Pavlofsk to see them. Their mother was quite angry at the very idea of such a thing, and announced her absolute conviction that he would turn up the next day at latest.

So next day the prince was expected all the morning, and at dinner, tea, and supper; and when he did not appear in the evening, Mrs. Epanchin quarrelled with everyone in the house, finding plenty of pretexts without so much as mentioning the prince's name.

On the third day there was no talk of him at all, until Aglaya remarked at dinner: "Mamma is cross because the prince hasn't turned up," to which the general replied that it was not his fault.

Mrs. Epanchin misunderstood the observation, and rising from her place she left the room in majestic wrath. In the evening, however, Colia came with the story of the prince's adventures, so far as he knew them. Mrs. Epanchin was triumphant; although Colia had to listen to a long lecture. "He idles about here the whole day long, one can't get rid of him; and then when he is wanted he does not come. He might have sent a line if he did not wish to inconvenience himself."

At the words "one can't get rid of him," Colia was very angry, and nearly flew into a rage; but he resolved to be quiet for the time and show his resentment later. If the words had been less offensive he might have forgiven them, so pleased was he to see Lizabetha Prokofievna worried and anxious about the prince's illness.

She would have insisted on sending to Petersburg at once, for a certain great medical celebrity; but her daughters dissuaded her, though they were not willing to stay behind when she at once prepared to go and visit the invalid. Aglaya, however, suggested that it was a little unceremonious to go *en masse* to see him.

"Very well then, stay at home," said Mrs. Epanchin, "and a good thing too, for Evgenie Pavlovitch is coming down and there will be no one at home to receive him."

Of course, after this, Aglaya went with the rest. In fact, she had never had the slightest intention of doing otherwise.

Prince S., who was in the house, was requested to escort the ladies. He had been much interested when he first heard of the prince from the Epanchins. It appeared that they had known one another before, and had spent some time together in a little provincial town three months ago. Prince S. had greatly taken to him, and was delighted with the opportunity of meeting him again.

The general had not come down from town as yet, nor had Evgenie Pavlovitch arrived.

It was not more than two or three hundred yards from the Epanchins' house to Lebedeff's. The first disagreeable impression experienced by Mrs. Epanchin was to find the prince surrounded by a whole assembly of other guests—not to mention the fact that some of those present were particularly detestable in her eyes. The next annoying circumstance was when an apparently strong and healthy young fellow, well dressed, and smiling, came forward to meet her on the terrace, instead of the half-dying unfortunate whom she had expected to see.

She was astonished and vexed, and her disappointment pleased Colia immensely. Of course he could have undeceived her before she started, but the mischievous boy had been careful not to do that, foreseeing the probably laughable disgust that she would experience when she found her dear friend, the prince, in good health. Colia was indelicate enough to voice the delight he felt at his success in managing to annoy Lizabetha Prokofievna, with whom, in spite of their really amicable relations, he was constantly sparring.

"Just wait a while, my boy!" said she; "don't be too certain of your triumph." And she sat down heavily, in the arm-chair pushed forward by the prince.

Lebedeff, Ptitsin, and General Ivolgin hastened to find chairs for the young ladies. Varia greeted them joyfully, and they exchanged confidences in ecstatic whispers.

"I must admit, prince, I was a little put out to see you up and about like this—I expected to find you in bed; but I give you my word, I was only annoyed for an instant, before I collected my thoughts properly. I am always wiser on second thoughts, and I dare say you are the same. I assure you I am as glad to see you well as though you were my own son,—yes, and more; and if you don't believe me the more shame to you, and it's not my fault. But that spiteful boy delights in playing all sorts of tricks. You are his patron, it seems. Well, I warn you that one fine morning I shall deprive myself of the pleasure of his further acquaintance."

"What have I done wrong now?" cried Colia. "What was the good of telling you that the prince was nearly well again? You would not have believed me; it was so much more interesting to picture him on his death-bed."

"How long do you remain here, prince?" asked Madame Epanchin.

"All the summer, and perhaps longer."

"You are alone, aren't you,—not married?"

"No, I'm not married!" replied the prince, smiling at the ingenuousness of this little feeler.

"Oh, you needn't laugh! These things do happen, you know! Now then—why didn't you come to us? We have a wing quite empty. But just as you like, of course. Do you lease it from *him?*—this fellow, I mean," she added, nodding towards Lebedeff. "And why does he always wriggle so?"

At that moment Vera, carrying the baby in her arms as usual, came out of the house, on to the terrace. Lebedeff kept fidgeting among the chairs, and did not seem to know what to do with himself, though he had no intention of going away. He no sooner caught sight of his daughter, than he rushed in her direction, waving his arms to keep her away; he even forgot himself so far as to stamp his foot.

"Is he mad?" asked Madame Epanchin suddenly.

"No, he..."

"Perhaps he is drunk? Your company is rather peculiar," she added, with a glance at the other guests....

"But what a pretty girl! Who is she?"

"That is Lebedeff's daughter—Vera Lukianovna."

"Indeed? She looks very sweet. I should like to make her acquaintance."

The words were hardly out of her mouth, when Lebedeff dragged Vera forward, in order to present her.

"Orphans, poor orphans!" he began in a pathetic voice.

"The child she carries is an orphan, too. She is Vera's sister, my daughter Luboff. The day this babe was born, six weeks ago, my wife died, by the will of God Almighty.... Yes... Vera takes her mother's place, though she is but her sister... nothing more... nothing more..."

"And you! You are nothing more than a fool, if you'll excuse me! Well! well! you know that yourself, I expect," said the lady indignantly.

Lebedeff bowed low. "It is the truth," he replied, with extreme respect.

"Oh, Mr. Lebedeff, I am told you lecture on the Apocalypse. Is it true?" asked Aglaya.

"Yes, that is so... for the last fifteen years."

"I have heard of you, and I think read of you in the newspapers."

"No, that was another commentator, whom the papers named. He is dead, however, and I have taken his place," said the other, much delighted.

"We are neighbours, so will you be so kind as to come over one day and explain the Apocalypse to me?" said Aglaya. "I do not understand it in the least."

"Allow me to warn you," interposed General Ivolgin, "that he is the greatest charlatan on earth." He had taken the chair next to the girl, and was impatient to begin talking. "No doubt there are pleasures and amusements peculiar to the country," he continued, "and to listen to a pretended student holding forth on the book of the Revelations may be as good as any other. It may even be original. But... you seem to be looking at me with some surprise—may I introduce myself—General Ivolgin—I carried you in my arms as a baby—"

"Delighted, I'm sure," said Aglaya; "I am acquainted with Varvara Ardalionovna and Nina Alexandrovna." She was trying hard to restrain herself from laughing.

Mrs. Epanchin flushed up; some accumulation of spleen in her suddenly needed an outlet. She could not bear this General Ivolgin whom she had once known, long ago—in society.

"You are deviating from the truth, sir, as usual!" she remarked, boiling over with indignation; "you never carried her in your life!"

"You have forgotten, mother," said Aglaya, suddenly. "He really did carry me about,—in Tver, you know. I was six years old, I remember. He made me a bow and arrow, and I shot a pigeon. Don't you remember shooting a pigeon, you and I, one day?"

"Yes, and he made me a cardboard helmet, and a little wooden sword—I remember!" said Adelaida.

"Yes, I remember too!" said Alexandra. "You quarrelled about the wounded pigeon, and Adelaida was put in the corner, and stood there with her helmet and sword and all."

The poor general had merely made the remark about having carried Aglaya in his arms because he always did so begin a conversation with young people. But it happened that this time he had really hit upon the truth, though he had himself entirely forgotten the fact. But when Adelaida and Aglaya recalled the episode of the pigeon, his mind became filled with memories, and it is impossible to describe how this poor old man, usually half drunk, was moved by the recollection.

"I remember—I remember it all!" he cried. "I was captain then. You were such a lovely little thing—Nina Alexandrovna!—Gania, listen! I was received then by General Epanchin."

"Yes, and look what you have come to now!" interrupted Mrs. Epanchin. "However, I see you have not quite drunk your better feelings away. But you've broken your wife's heart, sir—and instead of looking after your children, you have spent your time in public-houses and debtors' prisons! Go away, my friend, stand in some corner and weep, and bemoan your fallen dignity, and perhaps God will forgive you yet! Go, go! I'm serious! There's nothing so favourable for repentance as to think of the past with feelings of remorse!"

There was no need to repeat that she was serious. The general, like all drunkards, was extremely emotional and easily touched by recollections of his better days. He rose and walked quietly to the door, so meekly that Mrs. Epanchin was instantly sorry for him.

"Ardalion Alexandrovitch," she cried after him, "wait a moment, we are all sinners! When you feel that your conscience reproaches you a little less, come over to me and we'll have a talk about the past! I dare say I am fifty times more of a sinner than you are! And now go, go, good-bye, you had better not stay here!" she added, in alarm, as he turned as though to come back.

"Don't go after him just now, Colia, or he'll be vexed, and the benefit of this moment will be lost!" said the prince, as the boy was hurrying out of the room.

"Quite true! Much better to go in half an hour or so said Mrs. Epanchin.

"That's what comes of telling the truth for once in one's life!" said Lebedeff. "It reduced him to tears."

"Come, come! the less *you* say about it the better—to judge from all I have heard about you!" replied Mrs. Epanchin.

The prince took the first opportunity of informing the Epanchin ladies that he had intended to pay them a visit that day, if they had not themselves come this afternoon, and Lizabetha Prokofievna replied that she hoped he would still do so.

By this time some of the visitors had disappeared.

Ptitsin had tactfully retreated to Lebedeff's wing; and Gania soon followed him.

The latter had behaved modestly, but with dignity, on this occasion of his first meeting with the Epanchins since the rupture. Twice Mrs. Epanchin had deliberately examined him from head to foot; but he had stood fire without flinching. He was certainly much changed, as anyone could see who had not met him for some time; and this fact seemed to afford Aglaya a good deal of satisfaction.

"That was Gavrila Ardalionovitch, who just went out, wasn't it?" she asked suddenly, interrupting somebody else's conversation to make the remark.

"Yes, it was," said the prince.

"I hardly knew him; he is much changed, and for the better!"

"I am very glad," said the prince.

"He has been very ill," added Varia.

"How has he changed for the better?" asked Mrs. Epanchin. "I don't see any change for the better! What's better in him? Where did you get *that* idea from? *what*'S better?"

"There's nothing better than the 'poor knight'!" said Colia, who was standing near the last speaker's chair.

"I quite agree with you there!" said Prince S., laughing.

"So do I," said Adelaida, solemnly.

"*What* poor knight?" asked Mrs. Epanchin, looking round at the face of each of the speakers in turn. Seeing, however, that Aglaya was blushing, she added, angrily:

"What nonsense you are all talking! What do you mean by poor knight?"

"It's not the first time this urchin, your favourite, has shown his impudence by twisting other people's words," said Aglaya, haughtily.

Every time that Aglaya showed temper (and this was very often), there was so much childish pouting, such "school-girlishness," as it were, in her apparent wrath, that it was impossible to avoid smiling at her, to her own unutterable indignation. On these occasions she would say, "How can they, how *dare* they laugh at me?"

This time everyone laughed at her, her sisters, Prince S., Prince Muishkin (though he himself had flushed for some reason), and Colia. Aglaya was dreadfully indignant, and looked twice as pretty in her wrath.

"He's always twisting round what one says," she cried.

"I am only repeating your own exclamation!" said Colia. "A month ago you were turning over the pages of your Don Quixote, and suddenly called out 'there is nothing better than the poor knight.' I don't know whom you were referring to, of course, whether to Don Quixote, or Evgenie Pavlovitch, or someone else, but you certainly said these words, and afterwards there was a long conversation..."

"You are inclined to go a little too far, my good boy, with your guesses," said Mrs. Epanchin, with some show of annoyance.

"But it's not I alone," cried Colia. "They all talked about it, and they do still. Why, just now Prince S. and Adelaida Ivanovna declared that they upheld 'the poor knight'; so evidently there does exist a 'poor knight'; and if it were not for Adelaida Ivanovna, we should have known long ago who the 'poor knight' was."

"Why, how am I to blame?" asked Adelaida, smiling.

"You wouldn't draw his portrait for us, that's why you are to blame! Aglaya Ivanovna asked you to draw his portrait, and gave you the whole subject of the picture. She invented it herself; and you wouldn't."

"What was I to draw? According to the lines she quoted:

"'From his face he never lifted
  That eternal mask of steel.'"

"What sort of a face was I to draw? I couldn't draw a mask."

"I don't know what you are driving at; what mask do you mean?" said Mrs. Epanchin, irritably. She began to see pretty clearly though what it meant, and whom they referred to by the generally accepted title of "poor knight." But what specially annoyed her was that the prince was looking so uncomfortable, and blushing like a ten-year-old child.

"Well, have you finished your silly joke?" she added, "and am I to be told what this 'poor knight' means, or is it a solemn secret which cannot be approached lightly?"

But they all laughed on.

"It's simply that there is a Russian poem," began Prince S., evidently anxious to change the conversation, "a strange thing, without beginning or end, and all about a 'poor knight.' A month or so ago, we were all talking and laughing, and looking up a subject for one of Adelaida's pictures—you know it is the principal business of this family to find subjects for Adelaida's pictures. Well, we happened upon this 'poor knight.' I don't remember who thought of it first—"

"Oh! Aglaya Ivanovna did," said Colia.

"Very likely—I don't recollect," continued Prince S.

"Some of us laughed at the subject; some liked it; but she declared that, in order to make a picture of the gentleman, she must first see his face. We then began to think over all our friends' faces to see if any of them would do, and none suited us, and so the matter stood; that's all. I don't know why Nicolai Ardalionovitch has brought up the joke now. What was appropriate and funny then, has quite lost all interest by this time."

"Probably there's some new silliness about it," said Mrs. Epanchin, sarcastically.

"There is no silliness about it at all—only the profoundest respect," said Aglaya, very seriously. She had quite recovered her temper; in fact, from certain signs, it was fair to conclude that she was delighted to see this joke going so far; and a careful observer might have remarked that her satisfaction dated from the moment when the fact of the prince's confusion became apparent to all.

"'Profoundest respect!' What nonsense! First, insane giggling, and then, all of a sudden, a display of 'profoundest respect.' Why respect? Tell me at once, why have you suddenly developed this 'profound respect,' eh?"

"Because," replied Aglaya gravely, "in the poem the knight is described as a man capable of living up to an ideal all his life. That sort of thing is not to be found every day among the men of our times. In the poem it is not stated exactly what the ideal was, but it was evidently some vision, some revelation of pure Beauty, and the knight wore round his neck, instead of a scarf, a rosary. A device—A. N. B.—the meaning of which is not explained, was inscribed on his shield—"

"No, A. N. D.," corrected Colia.

"I say A. N. B., and so it shall be!" cried Aglaya, irritably. "Anyway, the 'poor knight' did not care what his lady was, or what she did. He had chosen his ideal, and he was bound to serve her, and break lances for her, and acknowledge her as the ideal of pure Beauty, whatever she might say or do afterwards. If she had taken to stealing, he would have championed her just the same. I think the poet desired to embody in this one picture the whole spirit of medieval chivalry and the platonic love of a pure and high-souled knight. Of course it's all an ideal, and in the 'poor knight' that spirit reached the utmost limit of asceticism. He is a Don Quixote, only serious and not comical. I used not to understand him, and laughed at him, but now I love the 'poor knight,' and respect his actions."

So ended Aglaya; and, to look at her, it was difficult, indeed, to judge whether she was joking or in earnest.

"Pooh! he was a fool, and his actions were the actions of a fool," said Mrs. Epanchin; "and as for you, young woman, you ought to know better. At all events, you are not to talk like that again. What poem is it? Recite it! I want to hear this poem! I have hated poetry all my life. Prince, you must excuse this nonsense. We neither of us like this sort of thing! Be patient!"

They certainly were put out, both of them.

The prince tried to say something, but he was too confused, and could not get his words out. Aglaya, who had taken such liberties in her little speech, was the only person present, perhaps, who was not in the least embarrassed. She seemed, in fact, quite pleased.

She now rose solemnly from her seat, walked to the centre of the terrace, and stood in front of the prince's chair. All looked on with some surprise, and Prince S. and her sisters with feelings of decided alarm, to see what new frolic she was up to; it had gone quite far enough already, they thought. But Aglaya evidently thoroughly enjoyed the affectation and ceremony with which she was introducing her recitation of the poem.

Mrs. Epanchin was just wondering whether she would not forbid the performance after all, when, at the very moment that Aglaya commenced her declamation, two new guests, both talking loudly, entered from the street. The new arrivals were General Epanchin and a young man.

Their entrance caused some slight commotion.

VII.

The young fellow accompanying the general was about twenty-eight, tall, and well built, with a handsome and clever face, and bright black eyes, full of fun and intelligence.

Aglaya did not so much as glance at the new arrivals, but went on with her recitation, gazing at the prince the while in an affected manner, and at him alone. It was clear to him that she was doing all this with some special object.

But the new guests at least somewhat eased his strained and uncomfortable position. Seeing them approaching, he rose from his chair, and nodding amicably to the general, signed to him not to interrupt the recitation. He then got behind his chair, and stood there with his left hand resting on the back of it. Thanks to this change of position, he was able to listen to the ballad with far less embarrassment than before. Mrs. Epanchin had also twice motioned to the new arrivals to be quiet, and stay where they were.

The prince was much interested in the young man who had just entered. He easily concluded that this was Evgenie Pavlovitch Radomski, of whom he had already heard mention several times. He was puzzled, however, by the young man's plain clothes, for he had always heard of Evgenie Pavlovitch as a military man. An ironical smile played on Evgenie's lips all the while the recitation was proceeding, which showed that he, too, was probably in the secret of the 'poor knight' joke. But it had become quite a different matter with Aglaya. All the affectation of manner which she had displayed at the beginning disappeared as the ballad proceeded. She spoke the lines in so serious and exalted a manner, and with so much taste, that she even seemed to justify the exaggerated solemnity with which she had stepped forward. It was impossible to discern in her now anything but a deep feeling for the spirit of the poem which she had undertaken to interpret.

Her eyes were aglow with inspiration, and a slight tremor of rapture passed over her lovely features once or twice. She continued to recite:

"Once there came a vision glorious,
Mystic, dreadful, wondrous fair;
Burned itself into his spirit,
And abode for ever there!

"Never more—from that sweet moment—
Gazéd he on womankind;
He was dumb to love and wooing
And to all their graces blind.

"Full of love for that sweet vision,
Brave and pure he took the field;
With his blood he stained the letters
N. P. B. upon his shield.

"'Lumen caeli, sancta Rosa!'
Shouting on the foe he fell,
And like thunder rang his war-cry
O'er the cowering infidel.

"Then within his distant castle,
Home returned, he dreamed his days—
Silent, sad,—and when death took him
He was mad, the legend says."

When recalling all this afterwards the prince could not for the life of him understand how to reconcile the beautiful, sincere, pure nature of the girl with the irony of this jest. That it was a jest there was no doubt whatever; he knew that well enough, and had good reason, too, for his conviction; for during her recitation of the ballad Aglaya had deliberately changed the letters A. N. B. into N. P. B. He was quite sure she had not done this by accident, and that his ears had not deceived him. At all events her performance—which was a joke, of course, if rather a crude one,—was premeditated. They had evidently talked (and laughed) over the 'poor knight' for more than a month.

Yet Aglaya had brought out these letters N. P. B. not only without the slightest appearance of irony, or even any particular accentuation, but with so even and unbroken an appearance of seriousness that assuredly anyone might have supposed that these initials were the original ones written in the ballad. The thing made an uncomfortable impression upon the prince. Of course Mrs. Epanchin saw nothing either in the change of initials or in the insinuation embodied therein. General Epanchin only knew that there was a recitation of verses going on, and took no further interest in the matter. Of the rest of the audience, many had understood the allusion and wondered both at the daring of the lady and at the motive underlying it, but tried to show no sign of their feelings. But Evgenie Pavlovitch (as the prince was ready to wager) both comprehended and tried his best to show that he comprehended; his smile was too mocking to leave any doubt on that point.

"How beautiful that is!" cried Mrs. Epanchin, with sincere admiration. "Whose is it?"

"Pushkin's, mama, of course! Don't disgrace us all by showing your ignorance," said Adelaida.

"As soon as we reach home give it to me to read."

"I don't think we have a copy of Pushkin in the house."

"There are a couple of torn volumes somewhere; they have been lying about from time immemorial," added Alexandra.

"Send Feodor or Alexey up by the very first train to buy a copy, then.—Aglaya, come here—kiss me, dear, you recited beautifully! but," she added in a whisper, "if you were sincere I am sorry for you. If it was a joke, I do not approve of the feelings which prompted you to do it, and in any case you would have done far better not to recite it at all. Do you understand?—Now come along, young woman; we've sat here too long. I'll speak to you about this another time."

Meanwhile the prince took the opportunity of greeting General Epanchin, and the general introduced Evgenie Pavlovitch to him.

"I caught him up on the way to your house," explained the general. "He had heard that we were all here."

"Yes, and I heard that you were here, too," added Evgenie Pavlovitch; "and since I had long promised myself the pleasure of seeking not only your acquaintance but your friendship, I did not wish to waste time, but came straight on. I am sorry to hear that you are unwell."

"Oh, but I'm quite well now, thank you, and very glad to make your acquaintance. Prince S. has often spoken to me about you," said Muishkin, and for an instant the two men looked intently into one another's eyes.

The prince remarked that Evgenie Pavlovitch's plain clothes had evidently made a great impression upon the company present, so much so that all other interests seemed to be effaced before this surprising fact.

His change of dress was evidently a matter of some importance. Adelaida and Alexandra poured out a stream of questions; Prince S., a relative of the young man, appeared annoyed; and Ivan Fedorovitch quite excited. Aglaya alone was not interested. She merely looked closely at Evgenie for a minute, curious perhaps as to whether civil or military clothes became him best, then turned away and paid no more attention to him or his costume. Lizabetha Prokofievna asked no questions, but it was clear that she was uneasy, and the prince fancied that Evgenie was not in her good graces.

"He has astonished me," said Ivan Fedorovitch. "I nearly fell down with surprise. I could hardly believe my eyes when I met him in Petersburg just now. Why this haste? That's what I want to know. He has always said himself that there is no need to break windows."

Evgenie Pavlovitch remarked here that he had spoken of his intention of leaving the service long ago. He had, however, always made more or less of a joke about it, so no one had taken him seriously. For that matter he joked about everything, and his friends never knew what to believe, especially if he did not wish them to understand him.

"I have only retired for a time," said he, laughing. "For a few months; at most for a year."

"But there is no necessity for you to retire at all," complained the general, "as far as I know."

"I want to go and look after my country estates. You advised me to do that yourself," was the reply. "And then I wish to go abroad."

After a few more expostulations, the conversation drifted into other channels, but the prince, who had been an attentive listener, thought all this excitement about so small a matter very curious. "There must be more in it than appears," he said to himself.

"I see the 'poor knight' has come on the scene again," said Evgenie Pavlovitch, stepping to Aglaya's side.

To the amazement of the prince, who overheard the remark, Aglaya looked haughtily and inquiringly at the questioner, as though she would give him to know, once for all, that there could be no talk between them about the 'poor knight,' and that she did not understand his question.

"But not now! It is too late to send to town for a Pushkin now. It is much too late, I say!" Colia was exclaiming in a loud voice. "I have told you so at least a hundred times."

"Yes, it is really much too late to send to town now," said Evgenie Pavlovitch, who had escaped from Aglaya as rapidly as possible. "I am sure the shops are shut in Petersburg; it is past eight o'clock," he added, looking at his watch.

"We have done without him so far," interrupted Adelaida in her turn. "Surely we can wait until to-morrow."

"Besides," said Colia, "it is quite unusual, almost improper, for people in our position to take any interest in literature. Ask Evgenie Pavlovitch if I am not right. It is much more fashionable to drive a waggonette with red wheels."

"You got that from some magazine, Colia," remarked Adelaida.

"He gets most of his conversation in that way," laughed Evgenie Pavlovitch. "He borrows whole phrases from the reviews. I have long had the pleasure of knowing both Nicholai Ardalionovitch and his conversational methods, but this time he was not repeating something he had read; he was alluding, no doubt, to my yellow waggonette, which has, or had, red wheels. But I have exchanged it, so you are rather behind the times, Colia."

The prince had been listening attentively to Radomski's words, and thought his manner very pleasant. When Colia chaffed him about his waggonette he had replied with perfect equality and in a friendly fashion. This pleased Muishkin.

At this moment Vera came up to Lizabetha Prokofievna, carrying several large and beautifully bound books, apparently quite new.

"What is it?" demanded the lady.

"This is Pushkin," replied the girl. "Papa told me to offer it to you."

"What? Impossible!" exclaimed Mrs. Epanchin.

"Not as a present, not as a present! I should not have taken the liberty," said Lebedeff, appearing suddenly from behind his daughter. "It is our own Pushkin, our family copy, Annenkoff's edition; it could not be bought now. I beg to suggest, with great respect, that your excellency should buy it, and thus quench the noble literary thirst which is consuming you at this moment," he concluded grandiloquently.

"Oh! if you will sell it, very good—and thank you. You shall not be a loser! But for goodness' sake, don't twist about like that, sir! I have heard of you; they tell me you are a very learned person. We must have a talk one of these days. You will bring me the books yourself?"

"With the greatest respect... and... and veneration," replied Lebedeff, making extraordinary grimaces.

"Well, bring them, with or without respect, provided always you do not drop them on the way; but on the condition," went on the lady, looking full at him, "that you do not cross my threshold. I do not intend to receive you today. You may send your daughter Vera at once, if you like. I am much pleased with her."

"Why don't you tell him about them?" said Vera impatiently to her father. "They will come in, whether you announce them or not, and they are beginning to make a row. Lef Nicolaievitch,"—she addressed herself to the prince—"four men are here asking for you. They have waited some time, and are beginning to make a fuss, and papa will not bring them in."

"Who are these people?" said the prince.

"They say that they have come on business, and they are the kind of men, who, if you do not see them here, will follow you about the street. It would be better to receive them, and then you will get rid of them. Gavrila Ardalionovitch and Ptitsin are both there, trying to make them hear reason."

"Pavlicheff's son! It is not worth while!" cried Lebedeff. "There is no necessity to see them, and it would be most unpleasant for your excellency. They do not deserve..."

"What? Pavlicheff's son!" cried the prince, much perturbed. "I know... I know—but I entrusted this matter to Gavrila Ardalionovitch. He told me..."

At that moment Gania, accompanied by Ptitsin, came out to the terrace. From an adjoining room came a noise of angry voices, and General Ivolgin, in loud tones, seemed to be trying to shout them down. Colia rushed off at once to investigate the cause of the uproar.

"This is most interesting!" observed Evgenie Pavlovitch.

"I expect he knows all about it!" thought the prince.

"What, the son of Pavlicheff? And who may this son of Pavlicheff be?" asked General Epanchin with surprise; and looking curiously around him, he discovered that he alone had no clue to the mystery. Expectation and suspense were on every face, with the exception of that of the prince, who stood gravely wondering how an affair so entirely personal could have awakened such lively and widespread interest in so short a time.

Aglaya went up to him with a peculiarly serious look

"It will be well," she said, "if you put an end to this affair yourself *at once*: but you must allow us to be your witnesses. They want to throw mud at you, prince, and you must be triumphantly vindicated. I give you joy beforehand!"

"And I also wish for justice to be done, once for all," cried Madame Epanchin, "about this impudent claim. Deal with them promptly, prince, and don't spare them! I am sick of hearing about the affair, and many a quarrel I have had in your cause. But I confess I am anxious to see what happens, so do make them come out here, and we will remain. You have heard people talking about it, no doubt?" she added, turning to Prince S.

"Of course," said he. "I have heard it spoken about at your house, and I am anxious to see these young men!"

"They are Nihilists, are they not?"

"No, they are not Nihilists," explained Lebedeff, who seemed much excited. "This is another lot—a special group. According to my nephew they are more advanced even than the Nihilists. You are quite wrong, excellency, if you think that your presence will intimidate them; nothing intimidates them. Educated men, learned men even, are to be found among Nihilists; these go further, in that they are men of action. The movement is, properly speaking, a derivative from Nihilism—though they are only known indirectly, and by hearsay, for they never advertise their doings in the papers. They go straight to the point. For them, it is not a question of showing that Pushkin is stupid, or that Russia must be torn in pieces. No; but if they have a great desire for anything, they believe they have a right to get it even at the cost of the lives, say, of eight persons. They are checked by no obstacles. In fact, prince, I should not advise you..."

But Muishkin had risen, and was on his way to open the door for his visitors.

"You are slandering them, Lebedeff," said he, smiling.

"You are always thinking about your nephew's conduct. Don't believe him, Lizabetha Prokofievna. I can assure you Gorsky and Daniloff are exceptions—and that these are only... mistaken. However, I do not care about receiving them here, in public. Excuse me, Lizabetha Prokofievna. They are coming, and you can see them, and then I will take them away. Please come in, gentlemen!"

Another thought tormented him: He wondered was this an arranged business—arranged to happen when he had guests in his house, and in anticipation of his humiliation rather than of his triumph? But he reproached himself bitterly for such a thought, and felt as if he should die of shame if it were discovered. When his new visitors appeared, he was quite ready to believe himself infinitely less to be respected than any of them.

Four persons entered, led by General Ivolgin, in a state of great excitement, and talking eloquently.

"He is for me, undoubtedly!" thought the prince, with a smile. Colia also had joined the party, and was talking with animation to Hippolyte, who listened with a jeering smile on his lips.

The prince begged the visitors to sit down. They were all so young that it made the proceedings seem even more extraordinary. Ivan Fedorovitch, who really understood nothing of what was going on, felt indignant at the sight of these youths, and would have interfered in some way had it not been for the extreme interest shown by his wife in the affair. He therefore remained, partly through curiosity, partly through good-nature, hoping that his presence might be of some use. But the bow with which General Ivolgin greeted him irritated him anew; he frowned, and decided to be absolutely silent.

As to the rest, one was a man of thirty, the retired officer, now a boxer, who had been with Rogojin, and in his happier days had given fifteen roubles at a time to beggars. Evidently he had joined the others as a comrade to give them moral, and if necessary material, support. The man who had been spoken of as "Pavlicheff's son," although he gave the name of Antip Burdovsky, was about twenty-two years of age, fair, thin and rather tall. He was remarkable for the poverty, not to say uncleanliness, of his personal appearance: the sleeves of his overcoat were greasy; his dirty waistcoat, buttoned up to his neck, showed not a trace of linen; a filthy black silk scarf, twisted till it resembled a cord, was round his neck, and his hands were unwashed. He looked round with an air of insolent effrontery. His face, covered with pimples, was neither thoughtful nor even contemptuous; it wore an expression of complacent satisfaction in demanding his rights and in being an aggrieved party. His voice trembled, and he spoke so fast, and with such stammerings, that he might have been taken for a foreigner, though the purest Russian blood ran in his veins. Lebedeff's nephew, whom the reader has seen already, accompanied him, and also the youth named Hippolyte Terentieff. The latter was only seventeen or eighteen. He had an intelligent face, though it was usually irritated and fretful in expression. His skeleton-like figure, his ghastly complexion, the brightness of his eyes, and the red spots of colour on his cheeks, betrayed the victim of consumption to the most casual glance. He coughed persistently, and panted for breath; it looked as though he had but a few weeks more to live. He was nearly dead with fatigue, and fell, rather than sat, into a chair. The rest bowed as they came in; and being more or less abashed, put on an air of extreme self-assurance. In short, their attitude was not that which one would have expected in men who professed to despise all trivialities, all foolish mundane conventions, and indeed everything, except their own personal interests.

"Antip Burdovsky," stuttered the son of Pavlicheff.

"Vladimir Doktorenko," said Lebedeff's nephew briskly, and with a certain pride, as if he boasted of his name.

"Keller," murmured the retired officer.

"Hippolyte Terentieff," cried the last-named, in a shrill voice.

They sat now in a row facing the prince, and frowned, and played with their caps. All appeared ready to speak, and yet all were silent; the defiant expression on their faces seemed to say, "No, sir, you don't take us in!" It could be felt that the first word spoken by anyone present would bring a torrent of speech from the whole deputation.

VIII.

"I *did* not expect you, gentlemen," began the prince. "I have been ill until to-day. A month ago," he continued, addressing himself to Antip Burdovsky, "I put your business into Gavrila Ardalionovitch Ivolgin's hands, as I told you then. I do not in the least object to having a personal interview... but you will agree with me that this is hardly the time... I propose that we go into another room, if you will not keep me long... As you see, I have friends here, and believe me..."

"Friends as many as you please, but allow me," interrupted the harsh voice of Lebedeff's nephew—"allow me to tell you that you might have treated us rather more politely, and not have kept us waiting at least two hours...

"No doubt... and I... is that acting like a prince? And you... you may be a general! But I... I am not your valet! And I... I..." stammered Antip Burdovsky.

He was extremely excited; his lips trembled, and the resentment of an embittered soul was in his voice. But he spoke so indistinctly that hardly a dozen words could be gathered.

"It was a princely action!" sneered Hippolyte.

"If anyone had treated me so," grumbled the boxer.

"I mean to say that if I had been in Burdovsky's place...I..."

"Gentlemen, I did not know you were there; I have only just been informed, I assure you," repeated Muishkin.

"We are not afraid of your friends, prince," remarked Lebedeff's nephew, "for we are within our rights."

The shrill tones of Hippolyte interrupted him. "What right have you... by what right do you demand us to submit this matter, about Burdovsky... to the judgment of your friends? We know only too well what the judgment of your friends will be!..."

This beginning gave promise of a stormy discussion. The prince was much discouraged, but at last he managed to make himself heard amid the vociferations of his excited visitors.

"If you," he said, addressing Burdovsky—"if you prefer not to speak here, I offer again to go into another room with you... and as to your waiting to see me, I repeat that I only this instant heard..."

"Well, you have no right, you have no right, no right at all!... Your friends indeed!"... gabbled Burdovsky, defiantly examining the faces round him, and becoming more and more excited. "You have no right!..." As he ended thus abruptly, he leant forward, staring at the prince with his short-sighted, bloodshot eyes. The latter was so astonished, that he did not reply, but looked steadily at him in return.

"Lef Nicolaievitch!" interposed Madame Epanchin, suddenly, "read this at once, this very moment! It is about this business."

She held out a weekly comic paper, pointing to an article on one of its pages. Just as the visitors were coming in, Lebedeff, wishing to ingratiate himself with the great lady, had pulled this paper from his pocket, and presented it to her, indicating a few columns marked in pencil. Lizabetha Prokofievna had had time to read some of it, and was greatly upset.

"Would it not be better to peruse it alone..." later asked the prince, nervously.

"No, no, read it—read it at once directly, and aloud, aloud!" cried she, calling Colia to her and giving him the journal.—"Read it aloud, so that everyone may hear it!"

An impetuous woman, Lizabetha Prokofievna sometimes weighed her anchors and put out to sea quite regardless of the possible storms she might encounter. Ivan Fedorovitch felt a sudden pang of alarm, but the others were merely curious, and somewhat surprised. Colia unfolded the paper, and began to read, in his clear, high-pitched voice, the following article:

"Proletarians and scions of nobility! An episode of the brigandage of today and every day! Progress! Reform! Justice!"

"Strange things are going on in our so-called Holy Russia in this age of reform and great enterprises; this age of patriotism in which hundreds of millions are yearly sent abroad; in which industry is encouraged, and the hands of Labour paralyzed, etc.; there is no end to this, gentlemen, so let us come to the point. A strange thing has happened to a scion of our defunct aristocracy. (De profundis!) The grandfathers of these scions ruined themselves at the gaming-tables; their fathers were forced to serve as officers or subalterns; some have died just as they were about to be tried for innocent thoughtlessness in the handling of public funds. Their children are sometimes congenital idiots, like the hero of our story; sometimes they are found in the dock at the Assizes, where they are generally acquitted by the jury for edifying motives; sometimes they distinguish themselves by one of those burning scandals that amaze the public and add another blot to the stained record of our age. Six months ago—that is, last winter—this particular scion returned to Russia, wearing gaiters like a foreigner, and shivering with cold in an old scantily-lined cloak. He had come from Switzerland, where he had just undergone a successful course of treatment for idiocy (sic!). Certainly Fortune favoured him, for, apart from the interesting malady of which he was cured in Switzerland (can there be a cure for idiocy?) his story proves the truth of the Russian proverb that 'happiness is the right of certain classes!' Judge for yourselves. Our subject was an infant in arms when he lost his father, an officer who died just as he was about to be court-martialled for gambling away the funds of his company, and perhaps also for flogging a subordinate to excess (remember the good old days, gentlemen). The orphan was brought up by the charity of a very rich Russian landowner. In the good old days, this man, whom we will call P——, owned four thousand souls as serfs (souls as serfs!—can you understand such an expression, gentlemen? I cannot; it must be looked up in a dictionary before one can understand it; these things of a bygone day are already unintelligible to us). He appears to have been one of those Russian parasites who lead an idle existence abroad, spending the summer at some spa, and the winter in Paris, to the greater profit of the organizers of public balls. It may safely be said that the manager of the Chateau des Fleurs (lucky man!) pocketed at least a third of the money paid by Russian peasants to their lords in the days of serfdom. However this may be, the gay P—— brought up the orphan like a prince, provided him with tutors and governesses (pretty, of course!) whom he chose himself in Paris. But the little aristocrat, the last of his noble race, was an idiot. The governesses, recruited at the Chateau des Fleurs, laboured in vain; at twenty years of age their pupil could not speak in any language, not even Russian. But ignorance of the latter was still excusable. At last P—— was seized with a strange notion; he imagined that in Switzerland they could change an idiot into a mail of sense. After all, the idea was quite logical; a parasite and landowner naturally supposed that intelligence was a marketable commodity like everything else, and that in Switzerland especially it could be bought for money. The case was entrusted to a celebrated Swiss professor, and cost thousands of roubles; the treatment lasted five years. Needless to say, the idiot did not become intelligent, but it is alleged that he grew into something more or less resembling a man. At this stage P—— died suddenly, and, as usual, he had made no will and left his affairs in disorder. A crowd of eager claimants arose, who cared nothing about any last scion of a noble race undergoing treatment in Switzerland, at the expense of the deceased, as a congenital idiot. Idiot though he was, the noble scion tried to cheat his professor, and they say he succeeded in getting him to continue the treatment gratis for two years, by concealing the death of his benefactor. But the professor himself was a charlatan. Getting anxious at last when no money was forthcoming, and alarmed above all by his patient's appetite, he presented him with a pair of old gaiters and a shabby cloak and packed him off to Russia, third class. It would seem that Fortune had turned her back upon our hero. Not at all; Fortune, who lets whole populations die of hunger, showered all her gifts at once upon the little aristocrat, like Kryloff's Cloud which passes over an arid plain and empties itself into the sea. He had scarcely arrived in St. Petersburg, when a relation of his mother's (who was of bourgeois origin, of course), died at Moscow. He was a merchant, an Old Believer, and he had no children. He left a fortune of several millions in good current coin, and everything came to our noble scion, our gaitered baron, formerly treated for idiocy in a Swiss lunatic asylum. Instantly the scene changed, crowds of friends gathered round our baron, who meanwhile had lost his head over a celebrated demi-mondaine; he even discovered some relations; moreover a number of young girls of high birth burned to be united to him in lawful matrimony. Could anyone possibly imagine a better match? Aristocrat, millionaire, and idiot, he has every advantage! One might hunt in vain for his equal, even with the lantern of Diogenes; his like is not to be had even by getting it made to order!"

"Oh, I don't know what this means" cried Ivan Fedorovitch, transported with indignation.

"Leave off, Colia," begged the prince. Exclamations arose on all sides.

"Let him go on reading at all costs!" ordered Lizabetha Prokofievna, evidently preserving her composure by a desperate effort. "Prince, if the reading is stopped, you and I will quarrel."

Colia had no choice but to obey. With crimson cheeks he read on unsteadily:

"But while our young millionaire dwelt as it were in the Empyrean, something new occurred. One fine morning a man called upon him, calm and severe of aspect, distinguished, but plainly dressed. Politely, but in dignified terms, as befitted his errand, he briefly explained the motive for his visit. He was a lawyer of enlightened views; his client was a young man who had consulted him in confidence. This young man was no other than the son of P——, though he bears another name. In his youth P——, the sensualist, had seduced a young girl, poor but respectable. She was a serf, but had received a European education. Finding that a child was expected, he hastened her marriage with a man of noble character who had loved her for a long time. He helped the young couple for a time, but he was soon obliged to give up, for the high-minded husband refused to accept anything from him. Soon the careless nobleman forgot all about his former mistress and the child she had borne him; then, as we know, he died intestate. P——'s son, born after his mother's marriage, found a true father in the generous man whose name he bore. But when he also died, the orphan was left to provide for himself, his mother now being an invalid who had lost the use of her limbs. Leaving her in a distant province, he came to the capital in search of pupils. By dint of daily toil he earned enough to enable him to follow the college courses, and at last to enter the university. But what can one earn by teaching the children of Russian merchants at ten copecks a lesson, especially with an invalid mother to keep? Even her death did not much diminish the hardships of the young man's struggle for existence. Now this is the question: how, in the name of justice, should our scion have argued the case? Our readers will think, no doubt, that he would say to himself: 'P—— showered benefits upon me all my life; he spent tens of thousands of roubles to educate me, to provide me with governesses, and to keep me under treatment in Switzerland. Now I am a millionaire, and P——'s son, a noble young man who is not responsible for the faults of his careless and forgetful father, is wearing himself out giving ill-paid lessons. According to justice, all that was done for me ought to have been done for him. The enormous sums spent upon me were not really mine; they came to me by an error of blind Fortune, when they ought to have gone to P——'s son. They should have gone to benefit him, not me, in whom P—— interested himself by a mere caprice, instead of doing his duty as a father. If I wished to behave nobly, justly, and with delicacy, I ought to bestow half my fortune upon the son of my benefactor; but as economy is my favourite virtue, and I know this is not a case in which the law can intervene, I will not give up half my millions. But it would be too openly vile, too flagrantly infamous, if I did not at least restore to P——'s son the tens of thousands of roubles spent in curing my idiocy. This is simply a case of conscience and of strict justice. Whatever would have become of me if P—— had not looked after my education, and had taken care of his own son instead of me?'

"No, gentlemen, our scions of the nobility do not reason thus. The lawyer, who had taken up the matter purely out of friendship to the young man, and almost against his will, invoked every consideration of justice, delicacy, honour, and even plain figures; in vain, the ex-patient of the Swiss lunatic asylum was inflexible. All this might pass, but the sequel is absolutely unpardonable, and not to be excused by any interesting malady. This millionaire, having but just discarded the old gaiters of his professor, could not even understand that the noble young man slaving away at his lessons was not asking for charitable help, but for his rightful due, though the debt was not a legal one; that, correctly speaking, he was not asking for anything, but it was merely his friends who had thought fit to bestir themselves on his behalf. With the cool insolence of a bloated capitalist, secure in his millions, he majestically drew a banknote for fifty roubles from his pocket-book and sent it to the noble young man as a humiliating piece of charity. You can hardly believe it, gentlemen! You are scandalized and disgusted; you cry out in indignation! But that is what he did! Needless to say, the money was returned, or rather flung back in his face. The case is not within the province of the law, it must be referred to the tribunal of public opinion; this is what we now do, guaranteeing the truth of all the details which we have related."

When Colia had finished reading, he handed the paper to the prince, and retired silently to a corner of the room, hiding his face in his hands. He was overcome by a feeling of inexpressible shame; his boyish sensitiveness was wounded beyond endurance. It seemed to him that something extraordinary, some sudden catastrophe had occurred, and that he was almost the cause of it, because he had read the article aloud.

Yet all the others were similarly affected. The girls were uncomfortable and ashamed. Lizabetha Prokofievna restrained her violent anger by a great effort; perhaps she bitterly regretted her interference in the matter; for the present she kept silence. The prince felt as very shy people often do in such a case; he was so ashamed of the conduct of other people, so humiliated for his guests, that he dared not look them in the face. Ptitsin, Varia, Gania, and Lebedeff himself, all looked rather confused. Stranger still, Hippolyte and the "son of Pavlicheff" also seemed slightly surprised, and Lebedeff's nephew was obviously far from pleased. The boxer alone was perfectly calm; he twisted his moustaches with affected dignity, and if his eyes were cast down it was certainly not in confusion, but rather in noble modesty, as if he did not wish to be insolent in his triumph. It was evident that he was delighted with the article.

"The devil knows what it means," growled Ivan Fedorovitch, under his breath; "it must have taken the united wits of fifty footmen to write it."

"May I ask your reason for such an insulting supposition, sir?" said Hippolyte, trembling with rage.

"You will admit yourself, general, that for an honourable man, if the author is an honourable man, that is an—an insult," growled the boxer suddenly, with convulsive jerkings of his shoulders.

"In the first place, it is not for you to address me as 'sir,' and, in the second place, I refuse to give you any explanation," said Ivan Fedorovitch vehemently; and he rose without another word, and went and stood on the first step of the flight that led from the verandah to the street, turning his back on the company. He was indignant with Lizabetha Prokofievna, who did not think of moving even now.

"Gentlemen, gentlemen, let me speak at last," cried the prince, anxious and agitated. "Please let us understand one another. I say nothing about the article, gentlemen, except that every word is false; I say this because you know it as well as I do. It is shameful. I should be surprised if any one of you could have written it."

"I did not know of its existence till this moment," declared Hippolyte. "I do not approve of it."

"I knew it had been written, but I would not have advised its publication," said Lebedeff's nephew, "because it is premature."

"I knew it, but I have a right. I... I..." stammered the "son of Pavlicheff."

"What! Did you write all that yourself? Is it possible?" asked the prince, regarding Burdovsky with curiosity.

"One might dispute your right to ask such questions," observed Lebedeff's nephew.

"I was only surprised that Mr. Burdovsky should have—however, this is what I have to say. Since you had already given the matter publicity, why did you object just now, when I began to speak of it to my friends?"

"At last!" murmured Lizabetha Prokofievna indignantly.

Lebedeff could restrain himself no longer; he made his way through the row of chairs.

"Prince," he cried, "you are forgetting that if you consented to receive and hear them, it was only because of your kind heart which has no equal, for they had not the least right to demand it, especially as you had placed the matter in the hands of Gavrila Ardalionovitch, which was also extremely kind of you. You are also forgetting, most excellent prince, that you are with friends, a select company; you cannot sacrifice them to these gentlemen, and it is only for you to have them turned out this instant. As the master of the house I shall have great pleasure ...."

"Quite right!" agreed General Ivolgin in a loud voice.

"That will do, Lebedeff, that will do—" began the prince, when an indignant outcry drowned his words.

"Excuse me, prince, excuse me, but now that will not do," shouted Lebedeff's nephew, his voice dominating all the others. "The matter must be clearly stated, for it is obviously not properly understood. They are calling in some legal chicanery, and upon that ground they are threatening to turn us out of the house! Really, prince, do you think we are such fools as not to be aware that this matter does not come within the law, and that legally we cannot claim a rouble from you? But we are also aware that if actual law is not on our side, human law is for us, natural law, the law of common-sense and conscience, which is no less binding upon every noble and honest man—that is, every man of sane judgment—because it is not to be found in miserable legal codes. If we come here without fear of being turned out (as was threatened just now) because of the imperative tone of our demand, and the unseemliness of such a visit at this late hour (though it was not late when we arrived, we were kept waiting in your anteroom), if, I say, we came in without fear, it is just because we expected to find you a man of sense; I mean, a man of honour and conscience. It is quite true that we did not present ourselves humbly, like your flatterers and parasites, but holding up our heads as befits independent men. We present no petition, but a proud and free demand (note it well, we do not beseech, we demand!). We ask you fairly and squarely in a dignified manner. Do you believe that in this affair of Burdovsky you have right on your side? Do you admit that Pavlicheff overwhelmed you with benefits, and perhaps saved your life? If you admit it (which we take for granted), do you intend, now that you are a millionaire, and do you not think it in conformity with justice, to indemnify Burdovsky? Yes or no? If it is yes, or, in other words, if you possess what you call honour and conscience, and we more justly call common-sense, then accede to our demand, and the matter is at an end. Give us satisfaction, without entreaties or thanks from us; do not expect thanks from us, for what you do will be done not for our sake, but for the sake of justice. If you refuse to satisfy us, that is, if your answer is no, we will go away at once, and there will be an end of the matter. But we will tell you to your face before the present company that you are a man of vulgar and undeveloped mind; we will openly deny you the right to speak in future of your honour and conscience, for you have not paid the fair price of such a right. I have no more to say—I have put the question before you. Now turn us out if you dare. You can do it; force is on your side. But remember that we do not beseech, we demand! We do not beseech, we demand!"

With these last excited words, Lebedeff's nephew was silent.

"We demand, we demand, we demand, we do not beseech," spluttered Burdovsky, red as a lobster.

The speech of Lebedeff's nephew caused a certain stir among the company; murmurs arose, though with the exception of Lebedeff, who was still very much excited, everyone was careful not to interfere in the matter.

347

Strangely enough, Lebedeff, although on the prince's side, seemed quite proud of his nephew's eloquence. Gratified vanity was visible in the glances he cast upon the assembled company.

"In my opinion, Mr. Doktorenko," said the prince, in rather a low voice, "you are quite right in at least half of what you say. I would go further and say that you are altogether right, and that I quite agree with you, if there were not something lacking in your speech. I cannot undertake to say precisely what it is, but you have certainly omitted something, and you cannot be quite just while there is something lacking. But let us put that aside and return to the point. Tell me what induced you to publish this article. Every word of it is a calumny, and I think, gentlemen, that you have been guilty of a mean action."

"Allow me—"

"Sir—"

"What? What? What?" cried all the visitors at once, in violent agitation.

"As to the article," said Hippolyte in his croaking voice, "I have told you already that we none of us approve of it! There is the writer," he added, pointing to the boxer, who sat beside him. "I quite admit that he has written it in his old regimental manner, with an equal disregard for style and decency. I know he is a cross between a fool and an adventurer; I make no bones about telling him so to his face every day. But after all he is half justified; publicity is the lawful right of every man; consequently, Burdovsky is not excepted. Let him answer for his own blunders. As to the objection which I made just now in the name of all, to the presence of your friends, I think I ought to explain, gentlemen, that I only did so to assert our rights, though we really wished to have witnesses; we had agreed unanimously upon the point before we came in. We do not care who your witnesses may be, or whether they are your friends or not. As they cannot fail to recognize Burdovsky's right (seeing that it is mathematically demonstrable), it is just as well that the witnesses should be your friends. The truth will only be more plainly evident."

"It is quite true; we had agreed upon that point," said Lebedeff's nephew, in confirmation.

"If that is the case, why did you begin by making such a fuss about it?" asked the astonished prince.

The boxer was dying to get in a few words; owing, no doubt, to the presence of the ladies, he was becoming quite jovial.

"As to the article, prince," he said, "I admit that I wrote it, in spite of the severe criticism of my poor friend, in whom I always overlook many things because of his unfortunate state of health. But I wrote and published it in the form of a letter, in the paper of a friend. I showed it to no one but Burdovsky, and I did not read it all through, even to him. He immediately gave me permission to publish it, but you will admit that I might have done so without his consent. Publicity is a noble, beneficent, and universal right. I hope, prince, that you are too progressive to deny this?"

"I deny nothing, but you must confess that your article—"

"Is a bit thick, you mean? Well, in a way that is in the public interest; you will admit that yourself, and after all one cannot overlook a blatant fact. So much the worse for the guilty parties, but the public welfare must come before everything. As to certain inaccuracies and figures of speech, so to speak, you will also admit that the motive, aim, and intention, are the chief thing. It is a question, above all, of making a wholesome example; the individual case can be examined afterwards; and as to the style—well, the thing was meant to be humorous, so to speak, and, after all, everybody writes like that; you must admit it yourself! Ha, ha!"

"But, gentlemen, I assure you that you are quite astray," exclaimed the prince. "You have published this article upon the supposition that I would never consent to satisfy Mr. Burdovsky. Acting on that conviction, you have tried to intimidate me by this publication and to be revenged for my supposed refusal. But what did you know of my intentions? It may be that I have resolved to satisfy Mr. Burdovsky's claim. I now declare openly, in the presence of these witnesses, that I will do so."

"The noble and intelligent word of an intelligent and most noble man, at last!" exclaimed the boxer.

"Good God!" exclaimed Lizabetha Prokofievna involuntarily.

"This is intolerable," growled the general.

"Allow me, gentlemen, allow me," urged the prince.

"I will explain matters to you. Five weeks ago I received a visit from Tchebaroff, your agent, Mr. Burdovsky. You have given a very flattering description of him in your article, Mr. Keller," he continued, turning to the boxer with a smile, "but he did not please me at all. I saw at once that Tchebaroff was the moving spirit in the matter, and, to speak frankly, I thought he might have induced you, Mr. Burdovsky, to make this claim, by taking advantage of your simplicity."

"You have no right.... I am not simple," stammered Burdovsky, much agitated.

"You have no sort of right to suppose such things," said Lebedeff's nephew in a tone of authority.

"It is most offensive!" shrieked Hippolyte; "it is an insulting suggestion, false, and most ill-timed."

"I beg your pardon, gentlemen; please excuse me," said the prince. "I thought absolute frankness on both sides would be best, but have it your own way. I told Tchebaroff that, as I was not in Petersburg, I would commission a friend to look into the matter without delay, and that I would let you know, Mr. Burdovsky. Gentlemen, I have no hesitation in telling you that it was the fact of Tchebaroff's intervention that made me suspect a fraud. Oh! do not take offence at my words, gentlemen, for Heaven's sake do not be so touchy!" cried the prince, seeing that Burdovsky was getting excited again, and that the rest were preparing to protest. "If I say I suspected a fraud, there is nothing personal in that. I had never seen any of you then; I did not even know your names; I only judged by Tchebaroff; I am speaking quite generally—if you only knew how I have been 'done' since I came into my fortune!"

"You are shockingly naive, prince," said Lebedeff's nephew in mocking tones.

"Besides, though you are a prince and a millionaire, and even though you may really be simple and good-hearted, you can hardly be outside the general law," Hippolyte declared loudly.

"Perhaps not; it is very possible," the prince agreed hastily, "though I do not know what general law you allude to. I will go on—only please do not take offence without good cause. I assure you I do not mean to offend you in the least. Really, it is impossible to speak three words sincerely without your flying into a rage! At first I was amazed when Tchebaroff told me that Pavlicheff had a son, and that he was in such a miserable position. Pavlicheff was my benefactor, and my father's friend. Oh, Mr. Keller, why does your article impute things to my father without the slightest foundation? He never squandered the funds of his company nor ill-treated his subordinates, I am absolutely certain of it; I cannot imagine how you could bring yourself to write such a calumny! But your assertions concerning Pavlicheff are absolutely intolerable! You do not scruple to make a libertine of that noble man; you call him a sensualist as coolly as if you were speaking the truth, and yet it would not be possible to find a chaster man. He was even a scholar of note, and in correspondence with several celebrated scientists, and spent large sums in the interests of science. As to his kind heart and his good actions, you were right indeed when you said that I was almost an idiot at that time, and could hardly understand anything—(I could speak and understand Russian, though),—but now I can appreciate what I remember—"

"Excuse me," interrupted Hippolyte, "is not this rather sentimental? You said you wished to come to the point; please remember that it is after nine o'clock."

"Very well, gentlemen—very well," replied the prince. "At first I received the news with mistrust, then I said to myself that I might be mistaken, and that Pavlicheff might possibly have had a son. But I was absolutely amazed at the readiness with which the son had revealed the secret of his birth at the expense of his mother's honour. For Tchebaroff had already menaced me with publicity in our interview...."

"What nonsense!" Lebedeff's nephew interrupted violently.

"You have no right—you have no right!" cried Burdovsky.

"The son is not responsible for the misdeeds of his father; and the mother is not to blame," added Hippolyte, with warmth.

"That seems to me all the more reason for sparing her," said the prince timidly.

"Prince, you are not only simple, but your simplicity is almost past the limit," said Lebedeff's nephew, with a sarcastic smile.

"But what right had you?" said Hippolyte in a very strange tone.

"None—none whatever," agreed the prince hastily. "I admit you are right there, but it was involuntary, and I immediately said to myself that my personal feelings had nothing to do with it,—that if I thought it right to satisfy the demands of Mr. Burdovsky, out of respect for the memory of Pavlicheff, I ought to do so in any case, whether I esteemed Mr. Burdovsky or not. I only mentioned this, gentlemen, because it seemed so unnatural to me for a son to betray his mother's secret in such a way. In short, that is what convinced me that Tchebaroff must be a rogue, and that he had induced Mr. Burdovsky to attempt this fraud."

"But this is intolerable!" cried the visitors, some of them starting to their feet.

"Gentlemen, I supposed from this that poor Mr. Burdovsky must be a simple-minded man, quite defenceless, and an easy tool in the hands of rogues. That is why I thought it my duty to try and help him as 'Pavlicheff's son'; in the first place by rescuing him from the influence of Tchebaroff, and secondly by making myself his friend. I have resolved to give him ten thousand roubles; that is about the sum which I calculate that Pavlicheff must have spent on me."

"What, only ten thousand!" cried Hippolyte.

"Well, prince, your arithmetic is not up to much, or else you are mighty clever at it, though you affect the air of a simpleton," said Lebedeff's nephew.

"I will not accept ten thousand roubles," said Burdovsky.

"Accept, Antip," whispered the boxer eagerly, leaning past the back of Hippolyte's chair to give his friend this piece of advice. "Take it for the present; we can see about more later on."

"Look here, Mr. Muishkin," shouted Hippolyte, "please understand that we are not fools, nor idiots, as your guests seem to imagine; these ladies who look upon us with such scorn, and especially this fine gentleman" (pointing to Evgenie Pavlovitch) "whom I have not the honour of knowing, though I think I have heard some talk about him—"

"Really, really, gentlemen," cried the prince in great agitation, "you are misunderstanding me again. In the first place, Mr. Keller, you have greatly overestimated my fortune in your article. I am far from being a millionaire. I have barely a tenth of what you suppose. Secondly, my treatment in Switzerland was very far from costing tens of thousands of roubles. Schneider received six hundred roubles a year, and he was only paid for the first three years. As to the pretty governesses whom Pavlicheff is supposed to have brought from Paris, they only exist in Mr. Keller's imagination; it is another calumny. According to my calculations, the sum spent on me was very considerably under ten thousand roubles, but I decided on that sum, and you must admit that in paying a debt I could not offer Mr. Burdovsky more, however kindly disposed I might be towards him; delicacy forbids it; I should seem to be offering him charity instead of rightful payment. I don't know how you cannot see that, gentlemen! Besides, I had no intention of leaving the matter there. I meant to intervene amicably later on and help to improve poor Mr. Burdovsky's position. It is clear that he has been deceived, or he would never have agreed to anything so vile as the scandalous revelations about his mother in Mr. Keller's article. But, gentlemen, why are you getting angry again? Are we never to come to an understanding? Well, the event has proved me right! I have just seen with my own eyes the proof that my conjecture was correct!" he added, with increasing eagerness.

He meant to calm his hearers, and did not perceive that his words had only increased their irritation.

"What do you mean? What are you convinced of?" they demanded angrily.

"In the first place, I have had the opportunity of getting a correct idea of Mr. Burdovsky. I see what he is for myself. He is an innocent man, deceived by everyone! A defenceless victim, who deserves indulgence! Secondly, Gavrila Ardalionovitch, in whose hands I had placed the matter, had his first interview with me barely an hour ago. I had not heard from him for some time, as I was away, and have been ill for three days since my return to St. Petersburg. He tells me that he has exposed the designs of Tchebaroff and has proof that justifies my opinion of him. I know, gentlemen, that many people think me an idiot. Counting upon my reputation as a man whose purse-strings are easily loosened, Tchebaroff thought it would be a simple matter to fleece me, especially by trading on my gratitude to Pavlicheff. But the main point is—listen, gentlemen, let me finish!—the main point is that Mr. Burdovsky is not Pavlicheff's son at all. Gavrila Ardalionovitch has just told me of his discovery, and assures me that he has positive proofs. Well, what do you think of that? It is scarcely credible, even after all the tricks that have been played upon me. Please note that we have positive proofs! I can hardly believe it myself, I assure you; I do not yet believe it; I am still doubtful, because Gavrila Ardalionovitch has not had time to go into details; but there can be no further doubt that Tchebaroff is a rogue! He has deceived poor Mr. Burdovsky, and all of you, gentlemen, who have come forward so nobly to support your friend—(he evidently needs support, I quite see that!). He has abused your credulity and involved you all in an attempted fraud, for when all is said and done this claim is nothing else!"

"What! a fraud? What, he is not Pavlicheff's son? Impossible!"

These exclamations but feebly expressed the profound bewilderment into which the prince's words had plunged Burdovsky's companions.

"Certainly it is a fraud! Since Mr. Burdovsky is not Pavlicheff's son, his claim is neither more nor less than attempted fraud (supposing, of course, that he had known the truth), but the fact is that he has been deceived. I insist on this point in order to justify him; I repeat that his simple-mindedness makes him worthy of pity, and that he cannot stand alone; otherwise he would have behaved like a scoundrel in this matter. But I feel certain that he does not understand it! I was just the same myself before I went to Switzerland; I stammered incoherently; one tries to express oneself and cannot. I understand that. I am all the better able to pity Mr. Burdovsky, because I know from experience what it is to be like that, and so I have a right to speak. Well, though there is no such person as 'Pavlicheff's son,' and it is all nothing but a humbug, yet I will keep to my decision, and I am prepared to give up ten thousand roubles in memory of Pavlicheff. Before Mr. Burdovsky made this claim, I proposed to found a school with this money, in memory of my benefactor, but I shall honour his memory quite as well by giving the ten thousand roubles to Mr. Burdovsky, because, though he was not Pavlicheff's son, he was treated almost as though he were. That is what gave a rogue the opportunity of deceiving him; he really did think himself Pavlicheff's son. Listen, gentlemen; this matter must be settled; keep calm; do not get angry; and sit down! Gavrila Ardalionovitch will explain everything to you at once, and I confess that I am very anxious to hear all the details myself. He says that he has even been to Pskoff to see your mother, Mr. Burdovsky; she is not dead, as the article which was just read to us makes out. Sit down, gentlemen, sit down!"

The prince sat down, and at length prevailed upon Burdovsky's company to do likewise. During the last ten or twenty minutes, exasperated by continual interruptions, he had raised his voice, and spoken with great vehemence.

Now, no doubt, he bitterly regretted several words and expressions which had escaped him in his excitement. If he had not been driven beyond the limits of endurance, he would not have ventured to express certain conjectures so openly. He had no sooner sat down than his heart was torn by sharp remorse. Besides insulting Burdovsky with the supposition, made in the presence of witnesses, that he was suffering from the complaint for which he had himself been treated in Switzerland, he reproached himself with the grossest indelicacy in having offered him the ten thousand roubles before everyone. "I ought to have waited till to-morrow and offered him the money when we were alone," thought Muishkin. "Now it is too late, the mischief is done! Yes, I am an idiot, an absolute idiot!" he said to himself, overcome with shame and regret.

Till then Gavrila Ardalionovitch had sat apart in silence. When the prince called upon him, he came and stood by his side, and in a calm, clear voice began to render an account of the mission confided to him. All conversation ceased instantly. Everyone, especially the Burdovsky party, listened with the utmost curiosity.

IX.

"You will not deny, I am sure," said Gavrila Ardalionovitch, turning to Burdovsky, who sat looking at him with wide-open eyes, perplexed and astonished. You will not deny, seriously, that you were born just two years after your mother's legal marriage to Mr. Burdovsky, your father. Nothing would be easier than to prove the date of your birth from well-known facts; we can only look on Mr. Keller's version as a work of imagination, and one, moreover, extremely offensive both to you and your mother. Of course he distorted the truth in order to strengthen your claim, and to serve your interests. Mr. Keller said that he previously consulted you about his article in the paper, but did not read it to you as a whole. Certainly he could not have read that passage. ....

"As a matter of fact, I did not read it," interrupted the boxer, "but its contents had been given me on unimpeachable authority, and I..."

"Excuse me, Mr. Keller," interposed Gavrila Ardalionovitch. "Allow me to speak. I assure you your article shall be mentioned in its proper place, and you can then explain everything, but for the moment I would rather not anticipate. Quite accidentally, with the help of my sister, Varvara Ardalionovna Ptitsin, I obtained from one of her intimate friends, Madame Zoubkoff, a letter written to her twenty-five years ago, by Nicolai Andreevitch Pavlicheff, then abroad. After getting into communication with this lady, I went by her advice to Timofei Fedorovitch Viazovkin, a retired colonel, and one of Pavlicheff's oldest friends. He gave me two more letters written by the latter when he was still in foreign parts. These three documents, their dates, and the facts mentioned in them, prove in the most undeniable manner, that eighteen months before your birth, Nicolai Andreevitch went abroad, where he remained for three consecutive years. Your mother, as you are well aware, has never been out of Russia.... It is too late to read the letters now; I am content to state the fact. But if you desire it, come to me tomorrow morning, bring witnesses and writing experts with you, and I will prove the absolute truth of my story. From that moment the question will be decided."

These words caused a sensation among the listeners, and there was a general movement of relief. Burdovsky got up abruptly.

"If that is true," said he, "I have been deceived, grossly deceived, but not by Tchebaroff: and for a long time past, a long time. I do not wish for experts, not I, nor to go to see you. I believe you. I give it up.... But I refuse the ten thousand roubles. Good-bye."

"Wait five minutes more, Mr. Burdovsky," said Gavrila Ardalionovitch pleasantly. "I have more to say. Some rather curious and important facts have come to light, and it is absolutely necessary, in my opinion, that you should hear them. You will not regret, I fancy, to have the whole matter thoroughly cleared up."

Burdovsky silently resumed his seat, and bent his head as though in profound thought. His friend, Lebedeff's nephew, who had risen to accompany him, also sat down again. He seemed much disappointed, though as self-confident as ever. Hippolyte looked dejected and sulky, as well as surprised. He had just been attacked by a violent fit of coughing, so that his handkerchief was stained with blood. The boxer looked thoroughly frightened.

"Oh, Antip!" cried he in a miserable voice, "I did say to you the other day—the day before yesterday—that perhaps you were not really Pavlicheff's son!"

There were sounds of half-smothered laughter at this.

"Now, that is a valuable piece of information, Mr. Keller," replied Gania. "However that may be, I have private information which convinces me that Mr. Burdovsky, though doubtless aware of the date of his birth, knew nothing at all about Pavlicheff's sojourn abroad. Indeed, he passed the greater part of his life out of Russia, returning at intervals for short visits. The journey in question is in itself too unimportant for his friends to recollect it after more than twenty years; and of course Mr. Burdovsky could have known nothing about it, for he was not born. As the event has proved, it was not impossible to find evidence of his absence, though I must confess that chance has helped me in a quest which might very well have come to nothing. It was really almost impossible for Burdovsky or Tchebaroff to discover these facts, even if it had entered their heads to try. Naturally they never dreamt..."

Here the voice of Hippolyte suddenly intervened.

"Allow me, Mr. Ivolgin," he said irritably. "What is the good of all this rigmarole? Pardon me. All is now clear, and we acknowledge the truth of your main point. Why go into these tedious details? You wish perhaps to boast of the cleverness of your investigation, to cry up your talents as detective? Or perhaps your intention is to excuse Burdovsky, by roving that he took up the matter in ignorance? Well, I consider that extremely impudent on your part! You ought to know that Burdovsky has no need of being excused or justified by you or anyone else! It is an insult! The affair is quite painful enough for him without that. Will nothing make you understand?"

"Enough! enough! Mr. Terentieff," interrupted Gania.

"Don't excite yourself; you seem very ill, and I am sorry for that. I am almost done, but there are a few facts to which I must briefly refer, as I am convinced that they ought to be clearly explained once for all...." A movement of impatience was noticed in his audience as he resumed: "I merely wish to state, for the information of all concerned, that the reason for Mr. Pavlicheff's interest in your mother, Mr. Burdovsky, was simply that she was the sister of a serf-girl with whom he was deeply in love in his youth, and whom most certainly he would have married but for her sudden death. I have proofs that this circumstance is almost, if not quite, forgotten. I may add that when your mother was about ten years old, Pavlicheff took her under his care, gave her a good education, and later, a considerable dowry. His relations were alarmed, and feared he might go so far as to marry her, but she gave her hand to a young land-surveyor named Burdovsky when she reached the age of twenty. I can even say definitely that it was a marriage of affection. After his wedding your father gave up his occupation as land-surveyor, and with his wife's dowry of fifteen thousand roubles went in for commercial speculations. As he had had no experience, he was cheated on all sides, and took to drink in order to forget his troubles. He shortened his life by his excesses, and eight years after his marriage he died. Your mother says herself that she was left in the direst poverty, and would have died of starvation had it not been for Pavlicheff, who generously allowed her a yearly pension of six hundred roubles. Many people recall his extreme fondness for you as a little boy. Your mother confirms this, and agrees with others in thinking that he loved you the more because you were a sickly child, stammering in your speech, and almost deformed—for it is known that all his life Nicolai Andreevitch had a partiality for unfortunates of every kind, especially children. In my opinion this is most important. I may add that I discovered yet another fact, the last on which I employed my detective powers. Seeing how fond Pavlicheff was of you,—it was thanks to him you went to school, and also had the advantage of special teachers—his relations and servants grew to believe that you were his son, and that your father had been betrayed by his wife. I may point out that this idea was only accredited generally during the last years of Pavlicheff's life, when his next-of-kin were trembling about the succession, when the earlier story was quite forgotten, and when all opportunity for discovering the truth had seemingly passed away. No doubt you, Mr. Burdovsky, heard this conjecture, and did not hesitate to accept it as true. I have had the honour of making your mother's acquaintance, and I find that she knows all about these reports. What she does not know is that you, her son, should have listened to them so complaisantly. I found your respected mother at Pskoff, ill and in deep poverty, as she has been ever since the death of your benefactor. She told me with tears of gratitude how you had supported her; she expects much of you, and believes fervently in your future success..."

"Oh, this is unbearable!" said Lebedeff's nephew impatiently. "What is the good of all this romancing?"

"It is revolting and unseemly!" cried Hippolyte, jumping up in a fury.

Burdovsky alone sat silent and motionless.

"What is the good of it?" repeated Gavrila Ardalionovitch, with pretended surprise. "Well, firstly, because now perhaps Mr. Burdovsky is quite convinced that Mr. Pavlicheff's love for him came simply from generosity of soul, and not from paternal duty. It was most necessary to impress this fact upon his mind, considering that he approved of the article written by Mr. Keller. I speak thus because I look on you, Mr. Burdovsky, as an honourable man. Secondly, it appears that there was no intention of cheating in this case, even on the part of Tchebaroff. I wish to say this quite plainly, because the prince hinted a while ago that I too thought it an attempt at robbery and extortion. On the contrary, everyone has been quite sincere in the matter, and although Tchebaroff may be somewhat of a rogue, in this business he has acted simply as any sharp lawyer would do under the circumstances. He looked at it as a case that might bring him in a lot of money, and he did not calculate badly; because on the one hand he speculated on the generosity of the prince, and his gratitude to the late Mr. Pavlicheff, and on the other to his chivalrous ideas as to the obligations of honour and conscience. As to Mr. Burdovsky, allowing for his principles, we may acknowledge that he engaged in the business with very little personal aim in view. At the instigation of Tchebaroff and his other friends, he decided to make the attempt in the service of truth, progress, and humanity. In short, the conclusion may be drawn that, in spite of all appearances, Mr. Burdovsky is a man of irreproachable character, and thus the prince can all the more readily offer him his friendship, and the assistance of which he spoke just now..."

"Hush! hush! Gavrila Ardalionovitch!" cried Muishkin in dismay, but it was too late.

"I said, and I have repeated it over and over again," shouted Burdovsky furiously, "that I did not want the money. I will not take it... why...I will not... I am going away!"

He was rushing hurriedly from the terrace, when Lebedeff's nephew seized his arms, and said something to him in a low voice. Burdovsky turned quickly, and drawing an addressed but unsealed envelope from his pocket, he threw it down on a little table beside the prince.

"There's the money!... How dare you?... The money!"

"Those are the two hundred and fifty roubles you dared to send him as a charity, by the hands of Tchebaroff," explained Doktorenko.

"The article in the newspaper put it at fifty!" cried Colia.

"I beg your pardon," said the prince, going up to Burdovsky. "I have done you a great wrong, but I did not send you that money as a charity, believe me. And now I am again to blame. I offended you just now." (The prince was much distressed; he seemed worn out with fatigue, and spoke almost incoherently.) "I spoke of swindling... but I did not apply that to you. I was deceived .... I said you were... afflicted... like me... But you are not like me... you give lessons... you support your mother. I said you had dishonoured your mother, but you love her. She says so herself... I did not know... Gavrila Ardalionovitch did not tell me that... Forgive me! I dared to offer you ten thousand roubles, but I was wrong. I ought to have done it differently, and now... there is no way of doing it, for you despise me..."

"I declare, this is a lunatic asylum!" cried Lizabetha Prokofievna.

"Of course it is a lunatic asylum!" repeated Aglaya sharply, but her words were overpowered by other voices. Everybody was talking loudly, making remarks and comments; some discussed the affair gravely, others laughed. Ivan Fedorovitch Epanchin was extremely indignant. He stood waiting for his wife with an air of offended dignity. Lebedeff's nephew took up the word again.

"Well, prince, to do you justice, you certainly know how to make the most of your—let us call it infirmity, for the sake of politeness; you have set about offering your money and friendship in such a way that no self-respecting man could possibly accept them. This is an excess of ingenuousness or of malice—you ought to know better than anyone which word best fits the case."

"Allow me, gentlemen," said Gavrila Ardalionovitch, who had just examined the contents of the envelope, "there are only a hundred roubles here, not two hundred and fifty. I point this out, prince, to prevent misunderstanding."

"Never mind, never mind," said the prince, signing to him to keep quiet.

"But we do mind," said Lebedeff's nephew vehemently. "Prince, your 'never mind' is an insult to us. We have nothing to hide; our actions can bear daylight. It is true that there are only a hundred roubles instead of two hundred and fifty, but it is all the same."

"Why, no, it is hardly the same," remarked Gavrila Ardalionovitch, with an air of ingenuous surprise.

"Don't interrupt, we are not such fools as you think, Mr. Lawyer," cried Lebedeff's nephew angrily. "Of course there is a difference between a hundred roubles and two hundred and fifty, but in this case the principle is the main point, and that a hundred and fifty roubles are missing is only a side issue. The point to be emphasized is that Burdovsky will not accept your highness's charity; he flings it back in your face, and it scarcely matters if there are a hundred roubles or two hundred and fifty. Burdovsky has refused ten thousand roubles; you heard him. He would not have returned even a hundred roubles if he was dishonest! The hundred and fifty roubles were paid to Tchebaroff for his travelling expenses. You may jeer at our stupidity and at our inexperience in business matters; you have done all you could already to make us look ridiculous; but do not dare to call us dishonest. The four of us will club together every day to repay the hundred and fifty roubles to the prince, if we have to pay it in instalments of a rouble at a time, but we will repay it, with interest. Burdovsky is poor, he has no millions. After his journey to see the prince Tchebaroff sent in his bill. We counted on winning... Who would not have done the same in such a case?"

"Who indeed?" exclaimed Prince S.

"I shall certainly go mad, if I stay here!" cried Lizabetha Prokofievna.

"It reminds me," said Evgenie Pavlovitch, laughing, "of the famous plea of a certain lawyer who lately defended a man for murdering six people in order to rob them. He excused his client on the score of poverty. 'It is quite natural,' he said in conclusion, 'considering the state of misery he was in, that he should have thought of murdering these six people; which of you, gentlemen, would not have done the same in his place?'"

"Enough," cried Lizabetha Prokofievna abruptly, trembling with anger, "we have had enough of this balderdash!"

In a state of terrible excitement she threw back her head, with flaming eyes, casting looks of contempt and defiance upon the whole company, in which she could no longer distinguish friend from foe. She had restrained herself so long that she felt forced to vent her rage on somebody. Those who knew Lizabetha Prokofievna saw at once how it was with her. "She flies into these rages sometimes," said Ivan Fedorovitch to Prince S. the next day, "but she is not often so violent as she was yesterday; it does not happen more than once in three years."

"Be quiet, Ivan Fedorovitch! Leave me alone!" cried Mrs. Epanchin. "Why do you offer me your arm now? You had not sense enough to take me away before. You are my husband, you are a father, it was your duty to drag me away by force, if in my folly I refused to obey you and go quietly. You might at least have thought of your daughters. We can find our way out now without your help. Here is shame enough for a year! Wait a moment 'till I thank the prince! Thank you, prince, for the entertainment you have given us! It was most amusing to hear these young men... It is vile, vile! A chaos, a scandal, worse than a nightmare! Is it possible that there can be many such people on earth? Be quiet, Aglaya! Be quiet, Alexandra! It is none of your business! Don't fuss round me like that, Evgenie Pavlovitch; you exasperate me! So, my dear," she cried, addressing the prince, "you go so far as to beg their pardon! He says, 'Forgive me for offering you a fortune.' And you, you mountebank, what are you laughing at?" she cried, turning suddenly on Lebedeff's nephew. "'We refuse ten thousand roubles; we do not beseech, we demand!' As if he did not know that this idiot will call on them tomorrow to renew his offers of money and friendship. You will, won't you? You will? Come, will you, or won't you?"

"I shall," said the prince, with gentle humility.

"You hear him! You count upon it, too," she continued, turning upon Doktorenko. "You are as sure of him now as if you had the money in your pocket. And there you are playing the swaggerer to throw dust in our eyes! No, my dear sir, you may take other people in! I can see through all your airs and graces, I see your game!"

"Lizabetha Prokofievna!" exclaimed the prince.

"Come, Lizabetha Prokofievna, it is quite time for us to be going, we will take the prince with us," said Prince S. with a smile, in the coolest possible way.

The girls stood apart, almost frightened; their father was positively horrified. Mrs. Epanchin's language astonished everybody. Some who stood a little way off smiled furtively, and talked in whispers. Lebedeff wore an expression of utmost ecstasy.

"Chaos and scandal are to be found everywhere, madame," remarked Doktorenko, who was considerably put out of countenance.

"Not like this! Nothing like the spectacle you have just given us, sir," answered Lizabetha Prokofievna, with a sort of hysterical rage. "Leave me alone, will you?" she cried violently to those around her, who were trying to keep her quiet. "No, Evgenie Pavlovitch, if, as you said yourself just now, a lawyer said in open court that he found it quite natural that a man should murder six people because he was in misery, the world must be coming to an end. I had not heard of it before. Now I understand everything. And this stutterer, won't he turn out a murderer?" she cried, pointing to Burdovsky, who was staring at her with stupefaction. "I bet he will! He will have none of your money, possibly, he will refuse it because his conscience will not allow him to accept it, but he will go murdering you by night and walking off with your cashbox, with a clear conscience! He does not call it a dishonest action but 'the impulse of a noble despair'; 'a negation'; or the devil knows what! Bah! everything is upside down, everyone walks head downwards. A young girl, brought up at home, suddenly jumps into a cab in the middle of the street, saying: 'Good-bye, mother, I married Karlitch, or Ivanitch, the other day!' And you think it quite right? You call such conduct estimable and natural? The 'woman question'? Look here," she continued, pointing to Colia, "the other day that whippersnapper told me that this was the whole meaning of the 'woman question.' But even supposing that your mother is a fool, you are none the less, bound to treat her with humanity. Why did you come here tonight so insolently? 'Give us our rights, but don't dare to speak in our presence. Show us every mark of deepest respect, while we treat you like the scum of the earth.' The miscreants have written a tissue of calumny in their article, and these are the men who seek for truth, and do battle for the right! 'We do not beseech, we demand, you will get no thanks from us, because you will be acting to satisfy your own conscience!' What morality! But, good heavens! if you declare that the prince's generosity will, excite no gratitude in you, he might answer that he is not, bound to be grateful to Pavlicheff, who also was only satisfying his own conscience. But you counted on the prince's, gratitude towards Pavlicheff; you never lent him any money; he owes you nothing; then what were you counting upon if not on his gratitude? And if you appeal to that sentiment in others, why should you expect to be exempted from it? They are mad! They say society is savage and inhuman because it despises a young girl who has been seduced. But if you call society inhuman you imply that the young girl is made to suffer by its censure. How then, can you hold her up to the scorn of society in the newspapers without realizing that you are making her suffering, still greater? Madmen! Vain fools! They don't believe in God, they don't believe in Christ! But you are so eaten up by pride and vanity, that you will end by devouring each other—that is my prophecy! Is not this absurd? Is it not monstrous chaos? And after all this, that shameless creature will go and beg their pardon! Are there many people like you? What are you smiling at? Because I am not ashamed to disgrace myself before you?—Yes, I am disgraced—it can't be helped now! But don't you jeer at me, you scum!" (this was aimed at Hippolyte). "He is almost at his last gasp, yet he corrupts others. You, have got hold of this lad "—(she pointed to Colia); "you, have turned his head, you have taught him to be an atheist, you don't believe in God, and you are not too old to be whipped, sir! A plague upon you! And so, Prince Lef Nicolaievitch, you will call on them tomorrow, will you?" she asked the prince breathlessly, for the second time.

"Yes."

"Then I will never speak to you again." She made a sudden movement to go, and then turned quickly back. "And you will call on that atheist?" she continued, pointing to Hippolyte. "How dare you grin at me like that?" she shouted furiously, rushing at the invalid, whose mocking smile drove her to distraction.

Exclamations arose on all sides.

"Lizabetha Prokofievna! Lizabetha Prokofievna! Lizabetha Prokofievna!"

"Mother, this is disgraceful!" cried Aglaya.

Mrs. Epanchin had approached Hippolyte and seized him firmly by the arm, while her eyes, blazing with fury, were fixed upon his face.

"Do not distress yourself, Aglaya Ivanovitch," he answered calmly; "your mother knows that one cannot strike a dying man. I am ready to explain why I was laughing. I shall be delighted if you will let me—"

A violent fit of coughing, which lasted a full minute, prevented him from finishing his sentence.

"He is dying, yet he will not stop holding forth!" cried Lizabetha Prokofievna. She loosed her hold on his arm, almost terrified, as she saw him wiping the blood from his lips. "Why do you talk? You ought to go home to bed."

"So I will," he whispered hoarsely. "As soon as I get home I will go to bed at once; and I know I shall be dead in a fortnight; Botkine told me so himself last week. That is why I should like to say a few farewell words, if you will let me."

"But you must be mad! It is ridiculous! You should take care of yourself; what is the use of holding a conversation now? Go home to bed, do!" cried Mrs. Epanchin in horror.

"When I do go to bed I shall never get up again," said Hippolyte, with a smile. "I meant to take to my bed yesterday and stay there till I died, but as my legs can still carry me, I put it off for two days, so as to come here with them to-day—but I am very tired."

"Oh, sit down, sit down, why are you standing?"

Lizabetha Prokofievna placed a chair for him with her own hands.

"Thank you," he said gently. "Sit opposite to me, and let us talk. We must have a talk now, Lizabetha Prokofievna; I am very anxious for it." He smiled at her once more. "Remember that today, for the last time, I am out in the air, and in the company of my fellow-men, and that in a fortnight I shall I certainly be no longer in this world. So, in a way, this is my farewell to nature and to men. I am not very sentimental, but do you know, I am quite glad that all this has happened at Pavlofsk, where at least one can see a green tree."

"But why talk now?" replied Lizabetha Prokofievna, more and more alarmed; "are quite feverish. Just now you would not stop shouting, and now you can hardly breathe. You are gasping."

"I shall have time to rest. Why will you not grant my last wish? Do you know, Lizabetha Prokofievna, that I have dreamed of meeting you for a long while? I had often heard of you from Colia; he is almost the only person who still comes to see me. You are an original and eccentric woman; I have seen that for myself—Do you know, I have even been rather fond of you?"

"Good heavens! And I very nearly struck him!"

"You were prevented by Aglaya Ivanovna. I think I am not mistaken? That is your daughter, Aglaya Ivanovna? She is so beautiful that I recognized her directly, although I had never seen her before. Let me, at least, look on beauty for the last time in my life," he said with a wry smile. "You are here with the prince, and your husband, and a large company. Why should you refuse to gratify my last wish?"

"Give me a chair!" cried Lizabetha Prokofievna, but she seized one for herself and sat down opposite to Hippolyte. "Colia, you must go home with him," she commanded, "and tomorrow I will come my self."

"Will you let me ask the prince for a cup of tea?... I am exhausted. Do you know what you might do, Lizabetha Prokofievna? I think you wanted to take the prince home with you for tea. Stay here, and let us spend the evening together. I am sure the prince will give us all some tea. Forgive me for being so free and easy—but I know you are kind, and the prince is kind, too. In fact, we are all good-natured people—it is really quite comical."

The prince bestirred himself to give orders. Lebedeff hurried out, followed by Vera.

"It is quite true," said Mrs. Epanchin decisively. "Talk, but not too loud, and don't excite yourself. You have made me sorry for you. Prince, you don't deserve that I should stay and have tea with you, yet I will, all the same, but I won't apologize. I apologize to nobody! Nobody! It is absurd! However, forgive me, prince, if I blew you up—that is, if you like, of course. But please don't let me keep anyone," she added suddenly to her husband and daughters, in a tone of resentment, as though they had grievously offended her. "I can come home alone quite well."

But they did not let her finish, and gathered round her eagerly. The prince immediately invited everyone to stay for tea, and apologized for not having thought of it before. The general murmured a few polite words, and asked Lizabetha Prokofievna if she did not feel cold on the terrace. He very nearly asked Hippolyte how long he had been at the University, but stopped himself in time. Evgenie Pavlovitch and Prince S. suddenly grew extremely gay and amiable. Adelaida and Alexandra had not recovered from their surprise, but it was now mingled with satisfaction;

in short, everyone seemed very much relieved that Lizabetha Prokofievna had got over her paroxysm. Aglaya alone still frowned, and sat apart in silence. All the other guests stayed on as well; no one wanted to go, not even General Ivolgin, but Lebedeff said something to him in passing which did not seem to please him, for he immediately went and sulked in a corner. The prince took care to offer tea to Burdovsky and his friends as well as the rest. The invitation made them rather uncomfortable. They muttered that they would wait for Hippolyte, and went and sat by themselves in a distant corner of the verandah. Tea was served at once; Lebedeff had no doubt ordered it for himself and his family before the others arrived. It was striking eleven.

X.

After moistening his lips with the tea which Vera Lebedeff brought him, Hippolyte set the cup down on the table, and glanced round. He seemed confused and almost at a loss.

"Just look, Lizabetha Prokofievna," he began, with a kind of feverish haste; "these china cups are supposed to be extremely valuable. Lebedeff always keeps them locked up in his china-cupboard; they were part of his wife's dowry. Yet he has brought them out tonight—in your honour, of course! He is so pleased—" He was about to add something else, but could not find the words.

"There, he is feeling embarrassed; I expected as much," whispered Evgenie Pavlovitch suddenly in the prince's ear. "It is a bad sign; what do you think? Now, out of spite, he will come out with something so outrageous that even Lizabetha Prokofievna will not be able to stand it."

Muishkin looked at him inquiringly.

"You do not care if he does?" added Evgenie Pavlovitch. "Neither do I; in fact, I should be glad, merely as a proper punishment for our dear Lizabetha Prokofievna. I am very anxious that she should get it, without delay, and I shall stay till she does. You seem feverish."

"Never mind; by-and-by; yes, I am not feeling well," said the prince impatiently, hardly listening. He had just heard Hippolyte mention his own name.

"You don't believe it?" said the invalid, with a nervous laugh. "I don't wonder, but the prince will have no difficulty in believing it; he will not be at all surprised."

"Do you hear, prince—do you hear that?" said Lizabetha Prokofievna, turning towards him.

There was laughter in the group around her, and Lebedeff stood before her gesticulating wildly.

"He declares that your humbug of a landlord revised this gentleman's article—the article that was read aloud just now—in which you got such a charming dressing-down."

The prince regarded Lebedeff with astonishment.

"Why don't you say something?" cried Lizabetha Prokofievna, stamping her foot.

"Well," murmured the prince, with his eyes still fixed on Lebedeff, "I can see now that he did."

"Is it true?" she asked eagerly.

"Absolutely, your excellency," said Lebedeff, without the least hesitation.

Mrs. Epanchin almost sprang up in amazement at his answer, and at the assurance of his tone.

"He actually seems to boast of it!" she cried.

"I am base—base!" muttered Lebedeff, beating his breast, and hanging his head.

"What do I care if you are base or not? He thinks he has only to say, 'I am base,' and there is an end of it. As to you, prince, are you not ashamed?—I repeat, are you not ashamed, to mix with such riff-raff? I will never forgive you!"

"The prince will forgive me!" said Lebedeff with emotional conviction.

Keller suddenly left his seat, and approached Lizabetha. Prokofievna.

"It was only out of generosity, madame," he said in a resonant voice, "and because I would not betray a friend in an awkward position, that I did not mention this revision before; though you heard him yourself threatening to kick us down the steps. To clear the matter up, I declare now that I did have recourse to his assistance, and that I paid him six roubles for it. But I did not ask him to correct my style; I simply went to him for information concerning the facts, of which I was ignorant to a great extent, and which he was competent to give. The story of the gaiters, the appetite in the Swiss professor's house, the substitution of fifty roubles for two hundred and fifty—all such details, in fact, were got from him. I paid him six roubles for them; but he did not correct the style."

"I must state that I only revised the first part of the article," interposed Lebedeff with feverish impatience, while laughter rose from all around him; "but we fell out in the middle over one idea, so I never corrected the second part. Therefore I cannot be held responsible for the numerous grammatical blunders in it."

"That is all he thinks of!" cried Lizabetha Prokofievna.

"May I ask when this article was revised?" said Evgenie Pavlovitch to Keller.

"Yesterday morning," he replied, "we had an interview which we all gave our word of honour to keep secret."

"The very time when he was cringing before you and making protestations of devotion! Oh, the mean wretches! I will have nothing to do with your Pushkin, and your daughter shall not set foot in my house!"

Lizabetha Prokofievna was about to rise, when she saw Hippolyte laughing, and turned upon him with irritation.

"Well, sir, I suppose you wanted to make me look ridiculous?"

"Heaven forbid!" he answered, with a forced smile. "But I am more than ever struck by your eccentricity, Lizabetha Prokofievna. I admit that I told you of Lebedeff's duplicity, on purpose. I knew the effect it would have on you,—on you alone, for the prince will forgive him. He has probably forgiven him already, and is racking his brains to find some excuse for him—is not that the truth, prince?"

He gasped as he spoke, and his strange agitation seemed to increase.

"Well?" said Mrs. Epanchin angrily, surprised at his tone; "well, what more?"

"I have heard many things of the kind about you...they delighted me... I have learned to hold you in the highest esteem," continued Hippolyte.

His words seemed tinged with a kind of sarcastic mockery, yet he was extremely agitated, casting suspicious glances around him, growing confused, and constantly losing the thread of his ideas. All this, together with his consumptive appearance, and the frenzied expression of his blazing eyes, naturally attracted the attention of everyone present.

"I might have been surprised (though I admit I know nothing of the world), not only that you should have stayed on just now in the company of such people as myself and my friends, who are not of your class, but that you should let these... young ladies listen to such a scandalous affair, though no doubt novel-reading has taught them all there is to know. I may be mistaken; I hardly know what I am saying; but surely no one but you would have stayed to please a whippersnapper (yes, a whippersnapper; I admit it) to spend the evening and take part in everything—only to be ashamed of it tomorrow. (I know I express myself badly.) I admire and appreciate it all extremely, though the expression on the face of his excellency, your husband, shows that he thinks it very improper. He-he!" He burst out laughing, and was seized with a fit of coughing which lasted for two minutes and prevented him from speaking.

"He has lost his breath now!" said Lizabetha Prokofievna coldly, looking at him with more curiosity than pity: "Come, my dear boy, that is quite enough—let us make an end of this."

Ivan Fedorovitch, now quite out of patience, interrupted suddenly. "Let me remark in my turn, sir," he said in tones of deep annoyance, "that my wife is here as the guest of Prince Lef Nicolaievitch, our friend and neighbour, and that in any case, young man, it is not for you to pass judgment on the conduct of Lizabetha Prokofievna, or to make remarks aloud in my presence concerning what feelings you think may be read in my face. Yes, my wife stayed here," continued the general, with increasing irritation, "more out of amazement than anything else. Everyone can understand that a collection of such strange young men would attract the attention of a person interested in contemporary life. I stayed myself, just as I sometimes stop to look on in the street when I see something that may be regarded as-as-as-"

"As a curiosity," suggested Evgenie Pavlovitch, seeing his excellency involved in a comparison which he could not complete.

"That is exactly the word I wanted," said the general with satisfaction—"a curiosity. However, the most astonishing and, if I may so express myself, the most painful, thing in this matter, is that you cannot even understand, young man, that Lizabetha Prokofievna, only stayed with you because you are ill,—if you really are dying—moved by the pity awakened by your plaintive appeal, and that her name, character, and social position place her above all risk of contamination. Lizabetha Prokofievna!" he continued, now crimson with rage, "if you are coming, we will say goodnight to the prince, and—"

"Thank you for the lesson, general," said Hippolyte, with unexpected gravity, regarding him thoughtfully.

"Two minutes more, if you please, dear Ivan Fedorovitch," said Lizabetha Prokofievna to her husband; "it seems to me that he is in a fever and delirious; you can see by his eyes what a state he is in; it is impossible to let him go back to Petersburg tonight. Can you put him up, Lef Nicolaievitch? I hope you are not bored, dear prince," she added suddenly to Prince S. "Alexandra, my dear, come here! Your hair is coming down."

She arranged her daughter's hair, which was not in the least disordered, and gave her a kiss. This was all that she had called her for.

"I thought you were capable of development," said Hippolyte, coming out of his fit of abstraction. "Yes, that is what I meant to say," he added, with the satisfaction of one who suddenly remembers something he had forgotten. "Here is Burdovsky, sincerely anxious to protect his mother; is not that so? And he himself is the cause of her disgrace. The prince is anxious to help Burdovsky and offers him friendship and a large sum of money, in the sincerity of his heart. And here they stand like two sworn enemies—ha, ha, ha! You all hate Burdovsky because his behaviour with regard to his mother is shocking and repugnant to you; do you not? Is not that true? Is it not true? You all have a passion for beauty and distinction in outward forms; that is all you care for, isn't it? I have suspected for a long time that you cared for nothing else! Well, let me tell you that perhaps there is not one of you who loved your mother as Burdovsky loved his. As to you, prince, I know that you have sent money secretly to Burdovsky's mother through Gania. Well, I bet now," he continued with an hysterical laugh, "that Burdovsky will accuse you of indelicacy, and reproach you with a want of respect for his mother! Yes, that is quite certain! Ha, ha, ha!"

He caught his breath, and began to cough once more.

"Come, that is enough! That is all now; you have no more to say? Now go to bed; you are burning with fever," said Lizabetha Prokofievna impatiently. Her anxious eyes had never left the invalid. "Good heavens, he is going to begin again!"

"You are laughing, I think? Why do you keep laughing at me?" said Hippolyte irritably to Evgenie Pavlovitch, who certainly was laughing.

"I only want to know, Mr. Hippolyte—excuse me, I forget your surname."

"Mr. Terentieff," said the prince.

"Oh yes, Mr. Terentieff. Thank you prince. I heard it just now, but had forgotten it. I want to know, Mr. Terentieff, if what I have heard about you is true. It seems you are convinced that if you could speak to the people from a window for a quarter of an hour, you could make them all adopt your views and follow you?"

"I may have said so," answered Hippolyte, as if trying to remember. "Yes, I certainly said so," he continued with sudden animation, fixing an unflinching glance on his questioner. "What of it?"

"Nothing. I was only seeking further information, to put the finishing touch."

Evgenie Pavlovitch was silent, but Hippolyte kept his eyes fixed upon him, waiting impatiently for more.

"Well, have you finished?" said Lizabetha Prokofievna to Evgenie. "Make haste, sir; it is time he went to bed. Have you more to say?" She was very angry.

"Yes, I have a little more," said Evgenie Pavlovitch, with a smile. "It seems to me that all you and your friends have said, Mr. Terentieff, and all you have just put forward with such undeniable talent, may be summed up in the triumph of right above all, independent of everything else, to the exclusion of everything else; perhaps even before having discovered what constitutes the right. I may be mistaken?"

"You are certainly mistaken; I do not even understand you. What else?"

Murmurs arose in the neighbourhood of Burdovsky and his companions; Lebedeff's nephew protested under his breath.

"I have nearly finished," replied Evgenie Pavlovitch.

"I will only remark that from these premises one could conclude that might is right—I mean the right of the clenched fist, and of personal inclination. Indeed, the world has often come to that conclusion. Prudhon upheld that might is right. In the American War some of the most advanced Liberals took sides with the planters on the score that the blacks were an inferior race to the whites, and that might was the right of the white race."

"Well?"

"You mean, no doubt, that you do not deny that might is right?"

"What then?"

"You are at least logical. I would only point out that from the right of might, to the right of tigers and crocodiles, or even Daniloff and Gorsky, is but a step."

"I know nothing about that; what else?"

Hippolyte was scarcely listening. He kept saying "well?" and "what else?" mechanically, without the least curiosity, and by mere force of habit.

"Why, nothing else; that is all."

"However, I bear you no grudge," said Hippolyte suddenly, and, hardly conscious of what he was doing, he held out his hand with a smile. The gesture took Evgenie Pavlovitch by surprise, but with the utmost gravity he touched the hand that was offered him in token of forgiveness.

"I can but thank you," he said, in a tone too respectful to be sincere, "for your kindness in letting me speak, for I have often noticed that our Liberals never allow other people to have an opinion of their own, and immediately answer their opponents with abuse, if they do not have recourse to arguments of a still more unpleasant nature."

"What you say is quite true," observed General Epanchin; then, clasping his hands behind his back, he returned to his place on the terrace steps, where he yawned with an air of boredom.

"Come, sir, that will do; you weary me," said Lizabetha Prokofievna suddenly to Evgenie Pavlovitch.

Hippolyte rose all at once, looking troubled and almost frightened.

"It is time for me to go," he said, glancing round in perplexity. "I have detained you... I wanted to tell you everything... I thought you all... for the last time... it was a whim..."

He evidently had sudden fits of returning animation, when he awoke from his semi-delirium; then, recovering full self-possession for a few moments, he would speak, in disconnected phrases which had perhaps haunted him for a long while on his bed of suffering, during weary, sleepless nights.

"Well, good-bye," he said abruptly. "You think it is easy for me to say good-bye to you? Ha, ha!"

Feeling that his question was somewhat gauche, he smiled angrily. Then as if vexed that he could not ever express what he really meant, he said irritably, in a loud voice:

"Excellency, I have the honour of inviting you to my funeral; that is, if you will deign to honour it with your presence. I invite you all, gentlemen, as well as the general."

He burst out laughing again, but it was the laughter of a madman. Lizabetha Prokofievna approached him anxiously and seized his arm. He stared at her for a moment, still laughing, but soon his face grew serious.

"Do you know that I came here to see those trees?" pointing to the trees in the park. "It is not ridiculous, is it? Say that it is not ridiculous!" he demanded urgently of Lizabetha Prokofievna. Then he seemed to be plunged in thought. A moment later he raised his head, and his eyes sought for someone. He was looking for Evgenie Pavlovitch, who was close by on his right as before, but he had forgotten this, and his eyes ranged over the assembled company. "Ah! you have not gone!" he said, when he caught sight of him at last. "You kept on laughing just now, because I thought of speaking to the people from the window for a quarter of an hour. But I am not eighteen, you know; lying on that bed, and looking out of that window, I have thought of all sorts of things for such a long time that... a dead man has no age, you know. I was saying that to myself only last week, when I was awake in the night. Do you know what you fear most? You fear our sincerity more than anything, although you despise us! The idea crossed my mind that night... You thought I was making fun of you just now, Lizabetha Prokofievna? No, the idea of mockery was far from me; I only meant to praise you. Colia told me the prince called you a child—very well—but let me see, I had something else to say..." He covered his face with his hands and tried to collect his thoughts.

"Ah, yes—you were going away just now, and I thought to myself: 'I shall never see these people again-never again! This is the last time I shall see the trees, too. I shall see nothing after this but the red brick wall of Meyer's house opposite my window. Tell them about it—try to tell them,' I thought. 'Here is a beautiful young girl—you are a dead man; make them understand that. Tell them that a dead man may say anything—and Mrs. Grundy will not be angry—ha-ha! You are not laughing?" He looked anxiously around. "But you know I get so many queer ideas, lying there in bed. I have grown convinced that nature is full of mockery—you called me an atheist just now, but you know this nature... why are you laughing again? You are very cruel!" he added suddenly, regarding them all with mournful reproach. "I have not corrupted Colia," he concluded in a different and very serious tone, as if remembering something again.

"Nobody here is laughing at you. Calm yourself," said Lizabetha Prokofievna, much moved. "You shall see a new doctor tomorrow; the other was mistaken; but sit down, do not stand like that! You are delirious—" Oh, what shall we do with him she cried in anguish, as she made him sit down again in the arm-chair.

A tear glistened on her cheek. At the sight of it Hippolyte seemed amazed. He lifted his hand timidly and, touched the tear with his finger, smiling like a child.

"I... you," he began joyfully. "You cannot tell how I... he always spoke so enthusiastically of you, Colia here; I liked his enthusiasm. I was not corrupting him! But I must leave him, too—I wanted to leave them all—there was not one of them—not one! I wanted to be a man of action—I had a right to be. Oh! what a lot of things I wanted! Now I want nothing; I renounce all my wants; I swore to myself that I would want nothing; let them seek the truth without me! Yes, nature is full of mockery! Why"—he continued with sudden warmth—"does she create the choicest beings only to mock at them? The only human being who is recognized as perfect, when nature showed him to mankind, was given the mission to say things which have caused the shedding of so much blood that it would have drowned mankind if it had all been shed at once! Oh! it is better for me to die! I should tell some dreadful lie too; nature would so contrive it! I have corrupted nobody. I wanted to live for the happiness of all men, to find and spread the truth. I used to look out of my window at the wall of Meyer's house, and say to myself that if I could speak for a quarter of an hour I would convince the whole world, and now for once in my life I have come into contact with... you—if not with the others! And what is the result? Nothing! The sole result is that you despise me! Therefore I must be a fool, I am useless, it is time I disappeared! And I shall leave not even a memory! Not a sound, not a trace, not a single deed! I have not spread a single truth!... Do not laugh at the fool! Forget him! Forget him forever! I beseech you, do not be so cruel as to remember! Do you know that if I were not consumptive, I would kill myself?"

Though he seemed to wish to say much more, he became silent. He fell back into his chair, and, covering his face with his hands, began to sob like a little child.

"Oh! what on earth are we to do with him?" cried Lizabetha Prokofievna. She hastened to him and pressed his head against her bosom, while he sobbed convulsively.

"Come, come, come! There, you must not cry, that will do. You are a good child! God will forgive you, because you knew no better. Come now, be a man! You know presently you will be ashamed."

Hippolyte raised his head with an effort, saying:

"I have little brothers and sisters, over there, poor avid innocent. She will corrupt them! You are a saint! You are a child yourself—save them! Snatch them from that... she is... it is shameful! Oh! help them! God will repay you a hundredfold. For the love of God, for the love of Christ!"

"Speak, Ivan Fedorovitch! What are we to do?" cried Lizabetha Prokofievna, irritably. "Please break your majestic silence! I tell you, if you cannot come to some decision, I will stay here all night myself. You have tyrannized over me enough, you autocrat!"

She spoke angrily, and in great excitement, and expected an immediate reply. But in such a case, no matter how many are present, all prefer to keep silence: no one will take the initiative, but all reserve their comments till afterwards. There were some present—Varvara Ardalionovna, for instance—who would have willingly sat there till morning without saying a word. Varvara had sat apart all the evening without opening her lips, but she listened to everything with the closest attention; perhaps she had her reasons for so doing.

"My dear," said the general, "it seems to me that a sick-nurse would be of more use here than an excitable person like you. Perhaps it would be as well to get some sober, reliable man for the night. In any case we must consult the prince, and leave the patient to rest at once. Tomorrow we can see what can be done for him."

"It is nearly midnight; we are going. Will he come with us, or is he to stay here?" Doktorenko asked crossly of the prince.

"You can stay with him if you like," said Muishkin.

"There is plenty of room here."

Suddenly, to the astonishment of all, Keller went quickly up to the general.

"Excellency," he said, impulsively, "if you want a reliable man for the night, I am ready to sacrifice myself for my friend—such a soul as he has! I have long thought him a great man, excellency! My article showed my lack of education, but when he criticizes he scatters pearls!"

Ivan Fedorovitch turned from the boxer with a gesture of despair.

"I shall be delighted if he will stay; it would certainly be difficult for him to get back to Petersburg," said the prince, in answer to the eager questions of Lizabetha Prokofievna.

"But you are half asleep, are you not? If you don't want him, I will take him back to my house! Why, good gracious! He can hardly stand up himself! What is it? Are you ill?"

Not finding the prince on his death-bed, Lizabetha Prokofievna had been misled by his appearance to think him much better than he was. But his recent illness, the painful memories attached to it, the fatigue of this evening, the incident with "Pavlicheff's son," and now this scene with Hippolyte, had all so worked on his oversensitive nature that he was now almost in a fever. Moreover, anew trouble, almost a fear, showed itself in his eyes; he watched Hippolyte anxiously as if expecting something further.

Suddenly Hippolyte arose. His face, shockingly pale, was that of a man overwhelmed with shame and despair. This was shown chiefly in the look of fear and hatred which he cast upon the assembled company, and in the wild smile upon his trembling lips. Then he cast down his eyes, and with the same smile, staggered towards Burdovsky and Doktorenko, who stood at the entrance to the verandah. He had decided to go with them.

"There! that is what I feared!" cried the prince. "It was inevitable!"

Hippolyte turned upon him, a prey to maniacal rage, which set all the muscles of his face quivering.

"Ah! that is what you feared! It was inevitable, you say! Well, let me tell you that if I hate anyone here—I hate you all," he cried, in a hoarse, strained voice—"but you, you, with your jesuitical soul, your soul of sickly sweetness, idiot, beneficent millionaire—I hate you worse than anything or anyone on earth! I saw through you and hated you long ago; from the day I first heard of you. I hated you with my whole heart. You have contrived all this! You have driven me into this state! You have made a dying man disgrace himself. You, you, you are the cause of my abject cowardice! I would kill you if I remained alive! I do not want your benefits; I will accept none from anyone; do you hear? Not from any one! I want nothing! I was delirious, do not dare to triumph! I curse every one of you, once for all!"

Breath failed him here, and he was obliged to stop.

"He is ashamed of his tears!" whispered Lebedeff to Lizabetha Prokofievna. "It was inevitable. Ah! what a wonderful man the prince is! He read his very soul."

But Mrs. Epanchin would not deign to look at Lebedeff. Drawn up haughtily, with her head held high, she gazed at the "riff-raff," with scornful curiosity. When Hippolyte had finished, Ivan Fedorovitch shrugged his shoulders, and his wife looked him angrily up and down, as if to demand the meaning of his movement. Then she turned to the prince.

"Thanks, prince, many thanks, eccentric friend of the family, for the pleasant evening you have provided for us. I am sure you are quite pleased that you have managed to mix us up with your extraordinary affairs. It is quite enough, dear family friend; thank you for giving us an opportunity of getting to know you so well."

She arranged her cloak with hands that trembled with anger as she waited for the "riff-raff" to go. The cab which Lebedeff's son had gone to fetch a quarter of an hour ago, by Doktorenko's order, arrived at that moment. The general thought fit to put in a word after his wife.

"Really, prince, I hardly expected after—after all our friendly intercourse—and you see, Lizabetha Prokofievna—"

"Papa, how can you?" cried Adelaida, walking quickly up to the prince and holding out her hand.

He smiled absently at her; then suddenly he felt a burning sensation in his ear as an angry voice whispered:

"If you do not turn those dreadful people out of the house this very instant, I shall hate you all my life—all my life!" It was Aglaya. She seemed almost in a frenzy, but she turned away before the prince could look at her. However, there was no one left to turn out of the house, for they had managed meanwhile to get Hippolyte into the cab, and it had driven off.

"Well, how much longer is this going to last, Ivan Fedorovitch? What do you think? Shall I soon be delivered from these odious youths?"

"My dear, I am quite ready; naturally... the prince."

Ivan Fedorovitch held out his hand to Muishkin, but ran after his wife, who was leaving with every sign of violent indignation, before he had time to shake it. Adelaida, her fiance, and Alexandra, said good-bye to their host with sincere friendliness. Evgenie Pavlovitch did the same, and he alone seemed in good spirits.

"What I expected has happened! But I am sorry, you poor fellow, that you should have had to suffer for it," he murmured, with a most charming smile.

Aglaya left without saying good-bye. But the evening was not to end without a last adventure. An unexpected meeting was yet in store for Lizabetha Prokofievna.

She had scarcely descended the terrace steps leading to the high road that skirts the park at Pavlofsk, when suddenly there dashed by a smart open carriage, drawn by a pair of beautiful white horses. Having passed some ten yards beyond the house, the carriage suddenly drew up, and one of the two ladies seated in it turned sharp round as though she had just caught sight of some acquaintance whom she particularly wished to see.

"Evgenie Pavlovitch! Is that you?" cried a clear, sweet voice, which caused the prince, and perhaps someone else, to tremble. "Well, I *am* glad I've found you at last! I've sent to town for you twice today myself! My messengers have been searching for you everywhere!"

Evgenie Pavlovitch stood on the steps like one struck by lightning. Mrs. Epanchin stood still too, but not with the petrified expression of Evgenie. She gazed haughtily at the audacious person who had addressed her companion, and then turned a look of astonishment upon Evgenie himself.

"There's news!" continued the clear voice. "You need not be anxious about Kupferof's IOU's—Rogojin has bought them up. I persuaded him to!—I dare say we shall settle Biscup too, so it's all right, you see! *Au revoir*, tomorrow! And don't worry!" The carriage moved on, and disappeared.

"The woman's mad!" cried Evgenie, at last, crimson with anger, and looking confusedly around. "I don't know what she's talking about! What IOU's? Who is she?" Mrs. Epanchin continued to watch his face for a couple of seconds; then she marched briskly and haughtily away towards her own house, the rest following her.

A minute afterwards, Evgenie Pavlovitch reappeared on the terrace, in great agitation.

"Prince," he said, "tell me the truth; do you know what all this means?"

"I know nothing whatever about it!" replied the latter, who was, himself, in a state of nervous excitement.

"No?"

"No?

"Well, nor do I!" said Evgenie Pavlovitch, laughing suddenly. "I haven't the slightest knowledge of any such IOU's as she mentioned, I swear I haven't—What's the matter, are you fainting?"

"Oh, no—no—I'm all right, I assure you!"

XI.

The anger of the Epanchin family was unappeased for three days. As usual the prince reproached himself, and had expected punishment, but he was inwardly convinced that Lizabetha Prokofievna could not be seriously angry with him, and that she probably was more angry with herself. He was painfully surprised, therefore, when three days passed with no word from her. Other things also troubled and perplexed him, and one of these grew more important in his eyes as the days went by. He had begun to blame himself for two opposite tendencies—on the one hand to extreme, almost "senseless," confidence in his fellows, on the other to a "vile, gloomy suspiciousness."

By the end of the third day the incident of the eccentric lady and Evgenie Pavlovitch had attained enormous and mysterious proportions in his mind. He sorrowfully asked himself whether he had been the cause of this new "monstrosity," or was it... but he refrained from saying who else might be in fault. As for the letters N.P.B., he looked on that as a harmless joke, a mere childish piece of mischief—so childish that he felt it would be shameful, almost dishonourable, to attach any importance to it.

The day after these scandalous events, however, the prince had the honour of receiving a visit from Adelaida and her fiance, Prince S. They came, ostensibly, to inquire after his health. They had wandered out for a walk, and called in "by accident," and talked for almost the whole of the time they were with him about a certain most lovely tree in the park, which Adelaida had set her heart upon for a picture. This, and a little amiable conversation on Prince S.'s part, occupied the time, and not a word was said about last evening's episodes. At length Adelaida burst out laughing, apologized, and explained that they had come incognito; from which, and from the circumstance that they said nothing about the prince's either walking back with them or coming to see them later on, the latter inferred that he was in Mrs. Epanchin's black books. Adelaida mentioned a watercolour that she would much like to show him, and explained that she would either send it by Colia, or bring it herself the next day—which to the prince seemed very suggestive.

At length, however, just as the visitors were on the point of departing, Prince S. seemed suddenly to recollect himself. "Oh yes, by-the-by," he said, "do you happen to know, my dear Lef Nicolaievitch, who that lady was who called out to Evgenie Pavlovitch last night, from the carriage?"

"It was Nastasia Philipovna," said the prince; "didn't you know that? I cannot tell you who her companion was."

"But what on earth did she mean? I assure you it is a real riddle to me—to me, and to others, too!" Prince S. seemed to be under the influence of sincere astonishment.

"She spoke of some bills of Evgenie Pavlovitch's," said the prince, simply, "which Rogojin had bought up from someone; and implied that Rogojin would not press him."

"Oh, I heard that much, my dear fellow! But the thing is so impossibly absurd! A man of property like Evgenie to give IOU's to a money-lender, and to be worried about them! It is ridiculous. Besides, he cannot possibly be on such intimate terms with Nastasia Philipovna as she gave us to understand; that's the principal part of the mystery! He has given me his word that he knows nothing whatever about the matter, and of course I believe him. Well, the question is, my dear prince, do you know anything about it? Has any sort of suspicion of the meaning of it come across you?"

"No, I know nothing whatever about it. I assure you I had nothing at all to do with it."

"Oh, prince, how strange you have become! I assure you, I hardly know you for your old self. How can you suppose that I ever suggested you could have had a finger in such a business? But you are not quite yourself today, I can see." He embraced the prince, and kissed him.

"What do you mean, though," asked Muishkin, "'by such a business'? I don't see any particular 'business' about it at all!"

"Oh, undoubtedly, this person wished somehow, and for some reason, to do Evgenie Pavlovitch a bad turn, by attributing to him—before witnesses—qualities which he neither has nor can have," replied Prince S. drily enough.

Muiskhin looked disturbed, but continued to gaze intently and questioningly into Prince S.'s face. The latter, however, remained silent.

"Then it was not simply a matter of bills?" Muishkin said at last, with some impatience. "It was not as she said?"

"But I ask you, my dear sir, how can there be anything in common between Evgenie Pavlovitch, and—her, and again Rogojin? I tell you he is a man of immense wealth—as I know for a fact; and he has further expectations from his uncle. Simply Nastasia Philipovna—"

Prince S. paused, as though unwilling to continue talking about Nastasia Philipovna.

"Then at all events he knows her!" remarked the prince, after a moment's silence.

"Oh, that may be. He may have known her some time ago—two or three years, at least. He used to know Totski. But it is impossible that there should be any intimacy between them. She has not even been in the place—many people don't even know that she has returned from Moscow! I have only observed her carriage about for the last three days or so."

"It's a lovely carriage," said Adelaida.

"Yes, it was a beautiful turn-out, certainly!"

The visitors left the house, however, on no less friendly terms than before. But the visit was of the greatest importance to the prince, from his own point of view. Admitting that he had his suspicions, from the moment of the occurrence of last night, perhaps even before, that Nastasia had some mysterious end in view, yet this visit confirmed his suspicions and justified his fears. It was all clear to him; Prince S. was wrong, perhaps, in his view of the matter, but he was somewhere near the truth, and was right in so far as that he understood there to be an intrigue of some sort going on. Perhaps Prince S. saw it all more clearly than he had allowed his hearers to understand. At all events, nothing could be plainer than that he and Adelaida had come for the express purpose of obtaining explanations, and that they suspected him of being concerned in the affair. And if all this were so, then *she* must have some terrible object in view! What was it? There was no stopping *her*, as Muishkin knew from experience, in the performance of anything she had set her mind on! "Oh, she is mad, mad!" thought the poor prince.

But there were many other puzzling occurrences that day, which required immediate explanation, and the prince felt very sad. A visit from Vera Lebedeff distracted him a little. She brought the infant Lubotchka with her as usual, and talked cheerfully for some time. Then came her younger sister, and later the brother, who attended a school close by. He informed Muishkin that his father had lately found a new interpretation of the star called "wormwood," which fell upon the water-springs, as described in the Apocalypse. He had decided that it meant the network of railroads spread over the face of Europe at the present time. The prince refused to believe that Lebedeff could have given such an interpretation, and they decided to ask him about it at the earliest opportunity. Vera related how Keller had taken up his abode with them on the previous evening. She thought he would remain for some time, as he was greatly pleased with the society of General Ivolgin and of the whole family. But he declared that he had only come to them in order to complete his education! The prince always enjoyed the company of Lebedeff's children, and today it was especially welcome, for Colia did not appear all day. Early that morning he had started for Petersburg. Lebedeff also was away on business. But Gavrila Ardalionovitch had promised to visit Muishkin, who eagerly awaited his coming.

About seven in the evening, soon after dinner, he arrived. At the first glance it struck the prince that he, at any rate, must know all the details of last night's affair. Indeed, it would have been impossible for him to remain in ignorance considering the intimate relationship between him, Varvara Ardalionovna, and Ptitsin. But although he and the prince were intimate, in a sense, and although the latter had placed the Burdovsky affair in his hands—and this was not the only mark of confidence he had received—it seemed curious how many matters there were that were tacitly avoided in their conversations. Muishkin thought that Gania at times appeared to desire more cordiality and frankness. It was apparent now, when he entered, that he, was convinced that the moment for breaking the ice between them had come at last.

But all the same Gania was in haste, for his sister was waiting at Lebedeff's to consult him on an urgent matter of business. If he had anticipated impatient questions, or impulsive confidences, he was soon undeceived. The prince was thoughtful, reserved, even a little absent-minded, and asked none of the questions—one in particular—that Gania had expected. So he imitated the prince's demeanour, and talked fast and brilliantly upon all subjects but the one on which their thoughts were engaged. Among other things Gania told his host that Nastasia Philipovna had been only four days in Pavlofsk, and that everyone was talking about her already. She was staying with Daria Alexeyevna, in an ugly little house in Mattrossky Street, but drove about in the smartest carriage in the place. A crowd of followers had pursued her from the first, young and old. Some escorted her on horse-back when she took the air in her carriage.

She was as capricious as ever in the choice of her acquaintances, and admitted few into her narrow circle. Yet she already had a numerous following and many champions on whom she could depend in time of need. One gentleman on his holiday had broken off his engagement on her account, and an old general had quarrelled with his only son for the same reason.

She was accompanied sometimes in her carriage by a girl of sixteen, a distant relative of her hostess. This young lady sang very well; in fact, her music had given a kind of notoriety to their little house. Nastasia, however, was behaving with great discretion on the whole. She dressed quietly, though with such taste as to drive all the ladies in Pavlofsk mad with envy, of that, as well as of her beauty and her carriage and horses.

"As for yesterday's episode," continued Gania, "of course it was pre-arranged." Here he paused, as though expecting to be asked how he knew that. But the prince did not inquire. Concerning Evgenie Pavlovitch, Gania stated, without being asked, that he believed the former had not known Nastasia Philipovna in past years, but that he had probably been introduced to her by somebody in the park during these four days. As to the question of the IOU's she had spoken of, there might easily be something in that; for though Evgenie was undoubtedly a man of wealth, yet certain of his affairs were equally undoubtedly in disorder. Arrived at this interesting point, Gania suddenly broke off, and said no more about Nastasia's prank of the previous evening.

At last Varvara Ardalionovna came in search of her brother, and remained for a few minutes. Without Muishkin's asking her, she informed him that Evgenie Pavlovitch was spending the day in Petersburg, and perhaps would remain there over tomorrow; and that her husband had also gone to town, probably in connection with Evgenie Pavlovitch's affairs.

"Lizabetha Prokofievna is in a really fiendish temper today," she added, as she went out, "but the most curious thing is that Aglaya has quarrelled with her whole family; not only with her father and mother, but with her sisters also. It is not a good sign." She said all this quite casually, though it was extremely important in the eyes of the prince, and went off with her brother. Regarding the episode of "Pavlicheff's son," Gania had been absolutely silent, partly from a kind of false modesty, partly, perhaps, to "spare the prince's feelings." The latter, however, thanked him again for the trouble he had taken in the affair.

Muishkin was glad enough to be left alone. He went out of the garden, crossed the road, and entered the park. He wished to reflect, and to make up his mind as to a certain "step." This step was one of those things, however, which are not thought out, as a rule, but decided for or against hastily, and without much reflection. The fact is, he felt a longing to leave all this and go away—go anywhere, if only it were far enough, and at once, without bidding farewell to anyone. He felt a presentiment that if he remained but a few days more in this place, and among these people, he would be fixed there irrevocably and permanently. However, in a very few minutes he decided that to run away was impossible; that it would be cowardly; that great problems lay before him, and that he had no right to leave them unsolved, or at least to refuse to give all his energy and strength to the attempt to solve them. Having come to this determination, he turned and went home, his walk having lasted less than a quarter of an hour. At that moment he was thoroughly unhappy.

Lebedeff had not returned, so towards evening Keller managed to penetrate into the prince's apartments. He was not drunk, but in a confidential and talkative mood. He announced that he had come to tell the story of his life to Muishkin, and had only remained at Pavlofsk for that purpose. There was no means of turning him out; nothing short of an earthquake would have removed him.

In the manner of one with long hours before him, he began his history; but after a few incoherent words he jumped to the conclusion, which was that "having ceased to believe in God Almighty, he had lost every vestige of morality, and had gone so far as to commit a theft." "Could you imagine such a thing?" said he.

"Listen to me, Keller," returned the prince. "If I were in your place, I should not acknowledge that unless it were absolutely necessary for some reason. But perhaps you are making yourself out to be worse than you are, purposely?"

"I should tell it to no one but yourself, prince, and I only name it now as a help to my soul's evolution. When I die, that secret will die with me! But, excellency, if you knew, if you only had the least idea, how difficult it is to get money nowadays! Where to find it is the question. Ask for a loan, the answer is always the same: 'Give us gold, jewels, or diamonds, and it will be quite easy.' Exactly what one has not got! Can you picture that to yourself? I got angry at last, and said, 'I suppose you would accept emeralds?' 'Certainly, we accept emeralds with pleasure. Yes!' 'Well, that's all right,' said I. 'Go to the devil, you den of thieves!' And with that I seized my hat, and walked out."

"Had you any emeralds?" asked the prince.

"What? I have emeralds? Oh, prince! with what simplicity, with what almost pastoral simplicity, you look upon life!"

Could not something be made of this man under good influences? asked the prince of himself, for he began to feel a kind of pity for his visitor. He thought little of the value of his own personal influence, not from a sense of humility, but from his peculiar way of looking at things in general. Imperceptibly the conversation grew more animated and more interesting, so that neither of the two felt anxious to bring it to a close. Keller confessed, with apparent sincerity, to having been guilty of many acts of such a nature that it astonished the prince that he could mention them, even to him. At every fresh avowal he professed the deepest repentance, and described himself as being "bathed in tears"; but this did not prevent him from putting on a boastful air at times, and some of his stories were so absurdly comical that both he and the prince laughed like madmen.

"One point in your favour is that you seem to have a child-like mind, and extreme truthfulness," said the prince at last. "Do you know that that atones for much?"

"I am assuredly noble-minded, and chivalrous to a degree!" said Keller, much softened. "But, do you know, this nobility of mind exists in a dream, if one may put it so? It never appears in practice or deed. Now, why is that? I can never understand."

"Do not despair. I think we may say without fear of deceiving ourselves, that you have now given a fairly exact account of your life. I, at least, think it would be impossible to add much to what you have just told me."

"Impossible?" cried Keller, almost pityingly. "Oh prince, how little you really seem to understand human nature!"

"Is there really much more to be added?" asked the prince, with mild surprise. "Well, what is it you really want of me? Speak out; tell me why you came to make your confession to me?"

"What did I want? Well, to begin with, it is good to meet a man like you. It is a pleasure to talk over my faults with you. I know you for one of the best of men... and then... then..."

He hesitated, and appeared so much embarrassed that the prince helped him out.

"Then you wanted me to lend you money?"

The words were spoken in a grave tone, and even somewhat shyly.

Keller started, gave an astonished look at the speaker, and thumped the table with his fist.

"Well, prince, that's enough to knock me down! It astounds me! Here you are, as simple and innocent as a knight of the golden age, and yet... yet... you read a man's soul like a psychologist! Now, do explain it to me, prince, because I... I really do not understand!... Of course, my aim was to borrow money all along, and you... you asked the question as if there was nothing blameable in it—as if you thought it quite natural."

"Yes... from you it is quite natural."

"And you are not offended?"

"Why should I be offended?"

"Well, just listen, prince. I remained here last evening, partly because I have a great admiration for the French archbishop Bourdaloue. I enjoyed a discussion over him till three o'clock in the morning, with Lebedeff; and then... then—I swear by all I hold sacred that I am telling you the truth—then I wished to develop my soul in this frank and heartfelt confession to you. This was my thought as I was sobbing myself to sleep at dawn. Just as I was losing consciousness, tears in my soul, tears on my face (I remember how I lay there sobbing), an idea from hell struck me. 'Why not, after confessing, borrow money from him?' You see, this confession was a kind of masterstroke; I intended to use it as a means to your good grace and favour—and then—then I meant to walk off with a hundred and fifty roubles. Now, do you not call that base?"

"It is hardly an exact statement of the case," said the prince in reply. "You have confused your motives and ideas, as I need scarcely say too often happens to myself. I can assure you, Keller, I reproach myself bitterly for it sometimes. When you were talking just now I seemed to be listening to something about myself. At times I have imagined that all men were the same," he continued earnestly, for he appeared to be much interested in the conversation, "and that consoled me in a certain degree, for a *double* motive is a thing most difficult to fight against. I have tried, and I know. God knows whence they arise, these ideas that you speak of as base. I fear these double motives more than ever just now, but I am not your judge, and in my opinion it is going too far to give the name of baseness to it—what do you think? You were going to employ your tears as a ruse in order to borrow money, but you also say—in fact, you have sworn to the fact—that independently of this your confession was made with an honourable motive. As for the money, you want it for drink, do you not? After your confession, that is weakness, of course; but, after all, how can anyone give up a bad habit at a moment's notice? It is impossible. What can we do? It is best, I think, to leave the matter to your own conscience. How does it seem to you?" As he concluded the prince looked curiously at Keller; evidently this problem of double motives had often been considered by him before.

"Well, how anybody can call you an idiot after that, is more than I can understand!" cried the boxer.

The prince reddened slightly.

"Bourdaloue, the archbishop, would not have spared a man like me," Keller continued, "but you, you have judged me with humanity. To show how grateful I am, and as a punishment, I will not accept a hundred and fifty roubles. Give me twenty-five—that will be enough; it is all I really need, for a fortnight at least. I will not ask you for more for a fortnight. I should like to have given Agatha a present, but she does not really deserve it. Oh, my dear prince, God bless you!"

At this moment Lebedeff appeared, having just arrived from Petersburg. He frowned when he saw the twenty-five rouble note in Keller's hand, but the latter, having got the money, went away at once. Lebedeff began to abuse him.

"You are unjust; I found him sincerely repentant," observed the prince, after listening for a time.

"What is the good of repentance like that? It is the same exactly as mine yesterday, when I said, 'I am base, I am base,'—words, and nothing more!"

"Then they were only words on your part? I thought, on the contrary..."

"Well, I don't mind telling you the truth—you only! Because you see through a man somehow. Words and actions, truth and falsehood, are all jumbled up together in me, and yet I am perfectly sincere. I feel the deepest repentance, believe it or not, as you choose; but words and lies come out in the infernal craving to get the better of other people. It is always there—the notion of cheating people, and of using my repentant tears to my own advantage! I assure you this is the truth, prince! I would not tell any other man for the world! He would laugh and jeer at me—but you, you judge a man humanely."

"Why, Keller said the same thing to me nearly word for word a few minutes ago!" cried Muishkin. "And you both seem inclined to boast about it! You astonish me, but I think he is more sincere than you, for you make a regular trade of it. Oh, don't put on that pathetic expression, and don't put your hand on your heart! Have you anything to say to me? You have not come for nothing..."

Lebedeff grinned and wriggled.

"I have been waiting all day for you, because I want to ask you a question; and, for once in your life, please tell me the truth at once. Had you anything to do with that affair of the carriage yesterday?"

Lebedeff began to grin again, rubbed his hands, sneezed, but spoke not a word in reply.

"I see you had something to do with it."

"Indirectly, quite indirectly! I am speaking the truth—I am indeed! I merely told a certain person that I had people in my house, and that such and such personages might be found among them."

"I am aware that you sent your son to that house—he told me so himself just now, but what is this intrigue?" said the prince, impatiently.

"It is not my intrigue!" cried Lebedeff, waving his hand.

"It was engineered by other people, and is, properly speaking, rather a fantasy than an intrigue!"

"But what is it all about? Tell me, for Heaven's sake! Cannot you understand how nearly it touches me? Why are they blackening Evgenie Pavlovitch's reputation?"

Lebedeff grimaced and wriggled again.

"Prince!" said he. "Excellency! You won't let me tell you the whole truth; I have tried to explain; more than once I have begun, but you have not allowed me to go on..."

The prince gave no answer, and sat deep in thought. Evidently he was struggling to decide.

"Very well! Tell me the truth," he said, dejectedly.

"Aglaya Ivanovna..." began Lebedeff, promptly.

"Be silent! At once!" interrupted the prince, red with indignation, and perhaps with shame, too. "It is impossible and absurd! All that has been invented by you, or fools like you! Let me never hear you say a word again on that subject!"

Late in the evening Colia came in with a whole budget of Petersburg and Pavlofsk news. He did not dwell much on the Petersburg part of it, which consisted chiefly of intelligence about his friend Hippolyte, but passed quickly to the Pavlofsk tidings. He had gone straight to the Epanchins' from the station.

"There's the deuce and all going on there!" he said. "First of all about the row last night, and I think there must be something new as well, though I didn't like to ask. Not a word about *you*, prince, the whole time! The most interesting fact was that Aglaya had been quarrelling with her people about Gania. Colia did not know any details, except that it had been a terrible quarrel! Also Evgenie Pavlovitch had called, and met with an excellent reception all round. And another curious thing: Mrs. Epanchin was so angry that she called Varia to her—Varia was talking to the girls—and turned her out of the house 'once for all' she said. I heard it from Varia herself—Mrs. Epanchin was quite polite, but firm; and when Varia said good-bye to the girls, she told them nothing about it, and they didn't know they were saying goodbye for the last time. I'm sorry for Varia, and for Gania too; he isn't half a bad fellow, in spite of his faults, and I shall never forgive myself for not liking him before! I don't know whether I ought to continue to go to the Epanchins' now," concluded Colia—"I like to be quite independent of others, and of other people's quarrels if I can; but I must think over it."

"I don't think you need break your heart over Gania," said the prince; "for if what you say is true, he must be considered dangerous in the Epanchin household, and if so, certain hopes of his must have been encouraged."

"What? What hopes?" cried Colia; "you surely don't mean Aglaya?—oh, no!—"

"You're a dreadful sceptic, prince," he continued, after a moment's silence. "I have observed of late that you have grown sceptical about everything. You don't seem to believe in people as you did, and are always attributing motives and so on—am I using the word 'sceptic' in its proper sense?"

"I believe so; but I'm not sure."

"Well, I'll change it, right or wrong; I'll say that you are not sceptical, but *jealous*. There! you are deadly jealous of Gania, over a certain proud damsel! Come!" Colia jumped up, with these words, and burst out laughing. He laughed as he had perhaps never laughed before, and still more when he saw the prince flushing up to his temples. He was delighted that the prince should be jealous about Aglaya. However, he stopped immediately on seeing that the other was really hurt, and the conversation continued, very earnestly, for an hour or more.

Next day the prince had to go to town, on business. Returning in the afternoon, he happened upon General Epanchin at the station. The latter seized his hand, glancing around nervously, as if he were afraid of being caught in wrong-doing, and dragged him into a first-class compartment. He was burning to speak about something of importance.

"In the first place, my dear prince, don't be angry with me. I would have come to see you yesterday, but I didn't know how Lizabetha Prokofievna would take it. My dear fellow, my house is simply a hell just now, a sort of sphinx has taken up its abode there. We live in an atmosphere of riddles; I can't make head or tail of anything. As for you, I feel sure you are the least to blame of any of us, though you certainly have been the cause of a good deal of trouble. You see, it's all very pleasant to be a philanthropist; but it can be carried too far. Of course I admire kind-heartedness, and I esteem my wife, but—"

The general wandered on in this disconnected way for a long time; it was clear that he was much disturbed by some circumstance which he could make nothing of.

"It is plain to me, that *you* are not in it at all," he continued, at last, a little less vaguely, "but perhaps you had better not come to our house for a little while. I ask you in the friendliest manner, mind; just till the wind changes again. As for Evgenie Pavlovitch," he continued with some excitement, "the whole thing is a calumny, a dirty calumny. It is simply a plot, an intrigue, to upset our plans and to stir up a quarrel. You see, prince, I'll tell you privately, Evgenie and ourselves have not said a word yet, we have no formal understanding, we are in no way bound on either side, but the word may be said very soon, don't you see, *very* soon, and all this is most injurious, and is meant to be so. Why? I'm sure I can't tell you. She's an extraordinary woman, you see, an eccentric woman; I tell you I am so frightened of that woman that I can't sleep. What a carriage that was, and where did it come from, eh? I declare, I was base enough to suspect Evgenie at first; but it seems certain that that cannot be the case, and if so, why is she interfering here? That's the riddle, what does she want? Is it to keep Evgenie to herself? But, my dear fellow, I swear to you, I swear he doesn't even *know* her, and as for those bills, why, the whole thing is an invention! And the familiarity of the woman! It's quite clear we must treat the impudent creature's attempt with disdain, and redouble our courtesy towards Evgenie. I told my wife so.

"Now I'll tell you my secret conviction. I'm certain that she's doing this to revenge herself on me, on account of the past, though I assure you that all the time I was blameless. I blush at the very idea. And now she turns up again like this, when I thought she had finally disappeared! Where's Rogojin all this time? I thought she was Mrs. Rogojin, long ago."

The old man was in a state of great mental perturbation. The whole of the journey, which occupied nearly an hour, he continued in this strain, putting questions and answering them himself, shrugging his shoulders, pressing the prince's hand, and assuring the latter that, at all events, he had no suspicion whatever of *him*. This last assurance was satisfactory, at all events. The general finished by informing him that Evgenie's uncle was head of one of the civil service departments, and rich, very rich, and a gourmand. "And, well, Heaven preserve him, of course—but Evgenie gets his money, don't you see? But, for all this, I'm uncomfortable, I don't know why. There's something in the air, I feel there's something nasty in the air, like a bat, and I'm by no means comfortable."

And it was not until the third day that the formal reconciliation between the prince and the Epanchins took place, as said before.

XII.

It was seven in the evening, and the prince was just preparing to go out for a walk in the park, when suddenly Mrs. Epanchin appeared on the terrace.

"In the first place, don't dare to suppose," she began, "that I am going to apologize. Nonsense! You were entirely to blame."

The prince remained silent.

"Were you to blame, or not?"

"No, certainly not, no more than yourself, though at first I thought I was."

"Oh, very well, let's sit down, at all events, for I don't intend to stand up all day. And remember, if you say, one word about 'mischievous urchins,' I shall go away and break with you altogether. Now then, did you, or did you not, send a letter to Aglaya, a couple of months or so ago, about Easter-tide?"

"Yes!"

"What for? What was your object? Show me the letter." Mrs. Epanchin's eyes flashed; she was almost trembling with impatience.

"I have not got the letter," said the prince, timidly, extremely surprised at the turn the conversation had taken. "If anyone has it, if it still exists, Aglaya Ivanovna must have it."

"No finessing, please. What did you write about?"

"I am not finessing, and I am not in the least afraid of telling you; but I don't see the slightest reason why I should not have written."

"Be quiet, you can talk afterwards! What was the letter about? Why are you blushing?"

The prince was silent. At last he spoke.

"I don't understand your thoughts, Lizabetha Prokofievna; but I can see that the fact of my having written is for some reason repugnant to you. You must admit that I have a perfect right to refuse to answer your questions; but, in order to show you that I am neither ashamed of the letter, nor sorry that I wrote it, and that I am not in the least inclined to blush about it" (here the prince's blushes redoubled), "I will repeat the substance of my letter, for I think I know it almost by heart."

So saying, the prince repeated the letter almost word for word, as he had written it.

"My goodness, what utter twaddle, and what may all this nonsense have signified, pray? If it had any meaning at all!" said Mrs. Epanchin, cuttingly, after having listened with great attention.

"I really don't absolutely know myself; I know my feeling was very sincere. I had moments at that time full of life and hope."

"What sort of hope?"

"It is difficult to explain, but certainly not the hopes you have in your mind. Hopes—well, in a word, hopes for the future, and a feeling of joy that *there*, at all events, I was not entirely a stranger and a foreigner. I felt an ecstasy in being in my native land once more; and one sunny morning I took up a pen and wrote her that letter, but why to *her*, I don't quite know. Sometimes one longs to have a friend near, and I evidently felt the need of one then," added the prince, and paused.

"Are you in love with her?"

"N-no! I wrote to her as to a sister; I signed myself her brother."

"Oh yes, of course, on purpose! I quite understand."

"It is very painful to me to answer these questions, Lizabetha Prokofievna."

"I dare say it is; but that's no affair of mine. Now then, assure me truly as before Heaven, are you lying to me or not?"

"No, I am not lying."

"Are you telling the truth when you say you are not in love?"

"I believe it is the absolute truth."

"'I believe,' indeed! Did that mischievous urchin give it to her?"

"I asked Nicolai Ardalionovitch..."

"The urchin! the urchin!" interrupted Lizabetha Prokofievna in an angry voice. "I do not want to know if it were Nicolai Ardalionovitch! The urchin!"

"Nicolai Ardalionovitch..."

"The urchin, I tell you!"

"No, it was not the urchin: it was Nicolai Ardalionovitch," said the prince very firmly, but without raising his voice.

"Well, all right! All right, my dear! I shall put that down to your account."

She was silent a moment to get breath, and to recover her composure.

"Well!—and what's the meaning of the 'poor knight,' eh?"

"I don't know in the least; I wasn't present when the joke was made. It *is* a joke. I suppose, and that's all."

"Well, that's a comfort, at all events. You don't suppose she could take any interest in you, do you? Why, she called you an 'idiot' herself."

"I think you might have spared me that," murmured the prince reproachfully, almost in a whisper.

"Don't be angry; she is a wilful, mad, spoilt girl. If she likes a person she will pitch into him, and chaff him. I used to be just such another. But for all that you needn't flatter yourself, my boy; she is not for you. I don't believe it, and it is not to be. I tell you so at once, so that you may take proper precautions. Now, I want to hear you swear that you are not married to that woman?"

"Lizabetha Prokofievna, what are you thinking of?" cried the prince, almost leaping to his feet in amazement.

"Why? You very nearly were, anyhow."

"Yes—I nearly was," whispered the prince, hanging his head.

"Well then, have you come here for *her?* Are you in love with *her?* With *that* creature?"

"I did not come to marry at all," replied the prince.

"Is there anything you hold sacred?"

"There is."

"Then swear by it that you did not come here to marry *her!*"

"I'll swear it by whatever you please."

"I believe you. You may kiss me; I breathe freely at last. But you must know, my dear friend, Aglaya does not love you, and she shall never be your wife while I am out of my grave. So be warned in time. Do you hear me?"

"Yes, I hear."

The prince flushed up so much that he could not look her in the face.

"I have waited for you with the greatest impatience (not that you were worth it). Every night I have drenched my pillow with tears, not for you, my friend, not for you, don't flatter yourself! I have my own grief, always the same, always the same. But I'll tell you why I have been awaiting you so impatiently, because I believe that Providence itself sent you to be a friend and a brother to me. I haven't a friend in the world except Princess Bielokonski, and she is growing as stupid as a sheep from old age. Now then, tell me, yes or no? Do you know why she called out from her carriage the other night?"

"I give you my word of honour that I had nothing to do with the matter and know nothing about it."

"Very well, I believe you. I have my own ideas about it. Up to yesterday morning I thought it was really Evgenie Pavlovitch who was to blame; now I cannot help agreeing with the others. But why he was made such a fool of I cannot understand. However, he is not going to marry Aglaya, I can tell you that. He may be a very excellent fellow, but—so it shall be. I was not at all sure of accepting him before, but now I have quite made up my mind that I won't have him. 'Put me in my coffin first and then into my grave, and then you may marry my daughter to whomsoever you please,' so I said to the general this very morning. You see how I trust you, my boy."

"Yes, I see and understand."

Mrs. Epanchin gazed keenly into the prince's eyes. She was anxious to see what impression the news as to Evgenie Pavlovitch had made upon him.

"Do you know anything about Gavrila Ardalionovitch?" she asked at last.

"Oh yes, I know a good deal."

"Did you know he had communications with Aglaya?"

"No, I didn't," said the prince, trembling a little, and in great agitation. "You say Gavrila Ardalionovitch has private communications with Aglaya?—Impossible!"

"Only quite lately. His sister has been working like a rat to clear the way for him all the winter."

"I don't believe it!" said the prince abruptly, after a short pause. "Had it been so I should have known long ago."

"Oh, of course, yes; he would have come and wept out his secret on your bosom. Oh, you simpleton—you simpleton! Anyone can deceive you and take you in like a—like a,—aren't you ashamed to trust him? Can't you see that he humbugs you just as much as ever he pleases?"

"I know very well that he does deceive me occasionally, and he knows that I know it, but—" The prince did not finish his sentence.

"And that's why you trust him, eh? So I should have supposed. Good Lord, was there ever such a man as you? Tfu! and are you aware, sir, that this Gania, or his sister Varia, have brought her into correspondence with Nastasia Philipovna?"

"Brought whom?" cried Muishkin.

"Aglaya."

"I don't believe it! It's impossible! What object could they have?" He jumped up from his chair in his excitement.

"Nor do I believe it, in spite of the proofs. The girl is self-willed and fantastic, and insane! She's wicked, wicked! I'll repeat it for a thousand years that she's wicked; they *all* are, just now, all my daughters, even that 'wet hen' Alexandra. And yet I don't believe it. Because I don't choose to believe it, perhaps; but I don't. Why haven't you been?" she turned on the prince suddenly. "Why didn't you come near us all these three days, eh?"

The prince began to give his reasons, but she interrupted him again.

"Everybody takes you in and deceives you; you went to town yesterday. I dare swear you went down on your knees to that rogue, and begged him to accept your ten thousand roubles!"

"I never thought of doing any such thing. I have not seen him, and he is not a rogue, in my opinion. I have had a letter from him."

"Show it me!"

The prince took a paper from his pocket-book, and handed it to Lizabetha Prokofievna. It ran as follows:

"Sir,

"In the eyes of the world I am sure that I have no cause for pride or self-esteem. I am much too insignificant for that. But what may be so to other men's eyes is not so to yours. I am convinced that you are better than other people. Doktorenko disagrees with me, but I am content to differ from him on this point. I will never accept one single copeck from you, but you have helped my mother, and I am bound to be grateful to you for that, however weak it may seem. At any rate, I have changed my opinion about you, and I think right to inform you of the fact; but I also suppose that there can be no further inter course between us.

"Antip Burdovsky.

"P.S.—The two hundred roubles I owe you shall certainly be repaid in time."

"How extremely stupid!" cried Mrs. Epanchin, giving back the letter abruptly. "It was not worth the trouble of reading. Why are you smiling?"

"Confess that you are pleased to have read it."

"What! Pleased with all that nonsense! Why, cannot you see that they are all infatuated with pride and vanity?"

"He has acknowledged himself to be in the wrong. Don't you see that the greater his vanity, the more difficult this admission must have been on his part? Oh, what a little child you are, Lizabetha Prokofievna!"

"Are you tempting me to box your ears for you, or what?"

"Not at all. I am only proving that you are glad about the letter. Why conceal your real feelings? You always like to do it."

"Never come near my house again!" cried Mrs. Epanchin, pale with rage. "Don't let me see as much as a *shadow* of you about the place! Do you hear?"

"Oh yes, and in three days you'll come and invite me yourself. Aren't you ashamed now? These are your best feelings; you are only tormenting yourself."

"I'll die before I invite you! I shall forget your very name! I've forgotten it already!"

She marched towards the door.

"But I'm forbidden your house as it is, without your added threats!" cried the prince after her.

"What? Who forbade you?"

She turned round so suddenly that one might have supposed a needle had been stuck into her.

The prince hesitated. He perceived that he had said too much now.

"*Who* forbade you?" cried Mrs. Epanchin once more.

"Aglaya Ivanovna told me—"

"When? Speak—quick!"

"She sent to say, yesterday morning, that I was never to dare to come near the house again."

Lizabetha Prokofievna stood like a stone.

"What did she send? Whom? Was it that boy? Was it a message?-quick!"

"I had a note," said the prince.

"Where is it? Give it here, at once."

The prince thought a moment. Then he pulled out of his waistcoat pocket an untidy slip of paper, on which was scrawled:

"*Prince Lef Nicolaievitch,—If you think fit, after all that has passed, to honour our house with a visit, I can assure you you will not find me among the number of those who are in any way delighted to see you.*

"*Aglaya Epanchin.*"

Mrs. Epanchin reflected a moment. The next minute she flew at the prince, seized his hand, and dragged him after her to the door.

"Quick—come along!" she cried, breathless with agitation and impatience. "Come along with me this moment!"

"But you declared I wasn't—"

"Don't be a simpleton. You behave just as though you weren't a man at all. Come on! I shall see, now, with my own eyes. I shall see all."

"Well, let me get my hat, at least."

"Here's your miserable hat. He couldn't even choose a respectable shape for his hat! Come on! She did that because I took your part and said you ought to have come—little vixen!—else she would never have sent you that silly note. It's a most improper note, I call it; most improper for such an intelligent, well-brought-up girl to write. H'm! I dare say she was annoyed that you didn't come; but she ought to have known that one can't write like that to an idiot like you, for you'd be sure to take it literally." Mrs. Epanchin was dragging the prince along with her all the time, and never let go of his hand for an instant. "What are you listening for?" she added, seeing that she had committed herself a little. "She wants a clown like you—she hasn't seen one for some time—to play with. That's why she is anxious for you to come to the house. And right glad I am that she'll make a thorough good fool of you. You deserve it; and she can do it—oh! she can, indeed!—as well as most people."

PART III

I.

The Epanchin family, or at least the more serious members of it, were sometimes grieved because they seemed so unlike the rest of the world. They were not quite certain, but had at times a strong suspicion that things did not happen to them as they did to other people. Others led a quiet, uneventful life, while they were subject to continual upheavals. Others kept on the rails without difficulty; they ran off at the slightest obstacle. Other houses were governed by a timid routine; theirs was somehow different. Perhaps Lizabetha Prokofievna was alone in making these fretful observations; the girls, though not wanting in intelligence, were still young; the general was intelligent, too, but narrow, and in any difficulty he was content to say, "H'm!" and leave the matter to his wife. Consequently, on her fell the responsibility. It was not that they distinguished themselves as a family by any particular originality, or that their excursions off the track led to any breach of the proprieties. Oh no.

There was nothing premeditated, there was not even any conscious purpose in it all, and yet, in spite of everything, the family, although highly respected, was not quite what every highly respected family ought to be. For a long time now Lizabetha Prokofievna had had it in her mind that all the trouble was owing to her "unfortunate character," and this added to her distress. She blamed her own stupid unconventional "eccentricity." Always restless, always on the go, she constantly seemed to lose her way, and to get into trouble over the simplest and more ordinary affairs of life.

We said at the beginning of our story, that the Epanchins were liked and esteemed by their neighbours. In spite of his humble origin, Ivan Fedorovitch himself was received everywhere with respect. He deserved this, partly on account of his wealth and position, partly because, though limited, he was really a very good fellow. But a certain limitation of mind seems to be an indispensable asset, if not to all public personages, at least to all serious financiers. Added to this, his manner was modest and unassuming; he knew when to be silent, yet never allowed himself to be trampled upon. Also—and this was more important than all—he had the advantage of being under exalted patronage.

As to Lizabetha Prokofievna, she, as the reader knows, belonged to an aristocratic family. True, Russians think more of influential friends than of birth, but she had both. She was esteemed and even loved by people of consequence in society, whose example in receiving her was therefore followed by others. It seems hardly necessary to remark that her family worries and anxieties had little or no foundation, or that her imagination increased them to an absurd degree; but if you have a wart on your forehead or nose, you imagine that all the world is looking at it, and that people would make fun of you because of it, even if you had discovered America! Doubtless Lizabetha Prokofievna was considered "eccentric" in society, but she was none the less esteemed: the pity was that she was ceasing to believe in that esteem. When she thought of her daughters, she said to herself sorrowfully that she was a hindrance rather than a help to their future, that her character and temper were absurd, ridiculous, insupportable. Naturally, she put the blame on her surroundings, and from morning to night was quarrelling with her husband and children, whom she really loved to the point of self-sacrifice, even, one might say, of passion.

She was, above all distressed by the idea that her daughters might grow up "eccentric," like herself; she believed that no other society girls were like them. "They are growing into Nihilists!" she repeated over and over again. For years she had tormented herself with this idea, and with the question: "Why don't they get married?"

"It is to annoy their mother; that is their one aim in life; it can be nothing else. The fact is it is all of a piece with these modern ideas, that wretched woman's question! Six months ago Aglaya took a fancy to cut off her magnificent hair. Why, even I, when I was young, had nothing like it! The scissors were in her hand, and I had to go down on my knees and implore her... She did it, I know, from sheer mischief, to spite her mother, for she is a naughty, capricious girl, a real spoiled child spiteful and mischievous to a degree! And then Alexandra wanted to shave her head, not from caprice or mischief, but, like a little fool, simply because Aglaya persuaded her she would sleep better without her hair, and not suffer from headache! And how many suitors have they not had during the last five years! Excellent offers, too! What more do they want? Why don't they get married? For no other reason than to vex their mother—none—none!"

But Lizabetha Prokofievna felt somewhat consoled when she could say that one of her girls, Adelaida, was settled at last. "It will be one off our hands!" she declared aloud, though in private she expressed herself with greater tenderness. The engagement was both happy and suitable, and was therefore approved in society. Prince S. was a distinguished man, he had money, and his future wife was devoted to him; what more could be desired? Lizabetha Prokofievna had felt less anxious about this daughter, however, although she considered her artistic tastes suspicious. But to make up for them she was, as her mother expressed it, "merry," and had plenty of "common-sense." It was Aglaya's future which disturbed her most. With regard to her eldest daughter, Alexandra, the mother never quite knew whether there was cause for anxiety or not. Sometimes she felt as if there was nothing to be expected from her. She was twenty-five now, and must be fated to be an old maid, and "with such beauty, too!" The mother spent whole nights in weeping and lamenting, while all the time the cause of her grief slumbered peacefully. "What is the matter with her? Is she a Nihilist, or simply a fool?"

But Lizabetha Prokofievna knew perfectly well how unnecessary was the last question. She set a high value on Alexandra Ivanovna's judgment, and often consulted her in difficulties; but that she was a 'wet hen' she never for a moment doubted. "She is so calm; nothing rouses her—though wet hens are not always calm! Oh! I can't understand it!" Her eldest daughter inspired Lizabetha with a kind of puzzled compassion. She did not feel this in Aglaya's case, though the latter was her idol. It may be said that these outbursts and epithets, such as "wet hen" (in which the maternal solicitude usually showed itself), only made Alexandra laugh. Sometimes the most trivial thing annoyed Mrs. Epanchin, and drove her into a frenzy. For instance, Alexandra Ivanovna liked to sleep late, and was always dreaming, though her dreams had the peculiarity of being as innocent and naive as those of a child of seven; and the very innocence of her dreams annoyed her mother. Once she dreamt of nine hens, and this was the cause of quite a serious quarrel—no one knew why. Another time she had—it was most unusual—a dream with a spark of originality in it. She dreamt of a monk in a dark room, into which she was too frightened to go. Adelaida and Aglaya rushed off with shrieks of laughter to relate this to their mother, but she was quite angry, and said her daughters were all fools.

"H'm! she is as stupid as a fool! A veritable 'wet hen'! Nothing excites her; and yet she is not happy; some days it makes one miserable only to look at her! Why is she unhappy, I wonder?" At times Lizabetha Prokofievna put this question to her husband, and as usual she spoke in the threatening tone of one who demands an immediate answer. Ivan Fedorovitch would frown, shrug his shoulders, and at last give his opinion: "She needs a husband!"

"God forbid that he should share your ideas, Ivan Fedorovitch!" his wife flashed back. "Or that he should be as gross and churlish as you!"

The general promptly made his escape, and Lizabetha Prokofievna after a while grew calm again. That evening, of course, she would be unusually attentive, gentle, and respectful to her "gross and churlish" husband, her "dear, kind Ivan Fedorovitch," for she had never left off loving him. She was even still "in love" with him. He knew it well, and for his part held her in the greatest esteem.

But the mother's great and continual anxiety was Aglaya. "She is exactly like me—my image in everything," said Mrs. Epanchin to herself. "A tyrant! A real little demon! A Nihilist! Eccentric, senseless and mischievous! Good Lord, how unhappy she will be!"

But as we said before, the fact of Adelaida's approaching marriage was balm to the mother. For a whole month she forgot her fears and worries.

Adelaida's fate was settled; and with her name that of Aglaya's was linked, in society gossip. People whispered that Aglaya, too, was "as good as engaged;" and Aglaya always looked so sweet and behaved so well (during this period), that the mother's heart was full of joy. Of course, Evgenie Pavlovitch must be thoroughly studied first, before the final step should be taken; but, really, how lovely dear Aglaya had become—she actually grew more beautiful every day! And then—Yes, and then—this abominable prince showed his face again, and everything went topsy-turvy at once, and everyone seemed as mad as March hares.

What had really happened?

If it had been any other family than the Epanchins', nothing particular would have happened. But, thanks to Mrs. Epanchin's invariable fussiness and anxiety, there could not be the slightest hitch in the simplest matters of everyday life, but she immediately foresaw the most dreadful and alarming consequences, and suffered accordingly.

What then must have been her condition, when, among all the imaginary anxieties and calamities which so constantly beset her, she now saw looming ahead a serious cause for annoyance—something really likely to arouse doubts and suspicions!

"How dared they, how *dared* they write that hateful anonymous letter informing me that Aglaya is in communication with Nastasia Philipovna?" she thought, as she dragged the prince along towards her own house, and again when she sat him down at the round table where the family was already assembled. "How dared they so much as *think* of such a thing? I should *die* with shame if I thought there was a particle of truth in it, or if I were to show the letter to Aglaya herself! Who dares play these jokes upon *us*, the Epanchins? *Why* didn't we go to the Yelagin instead of coming down here? I *told* you we had better go to the Yelagin this summer, Ivan Fedorovitch. It's all your fault. I dare say it was that Varia who sent the letter. It's all Ivan Fedorovitch. *That* woman is doing it all for him, I know she is, to show she can make a fool of him now just as she did when he used to give her pearls.

"But after all is said, we are mixed up in it. Your daughters are mixed up in it, Ivan Fedorovitch; young ladies in society, young ladies at an age to be married; they were present, they heard everything there was to hear. They were mixed up with that other scene, too, with those dreadful youths. You must be pleased to remember they heard it all. I cannot forgive that wretched prince. I never shall forgive him! And why, if you please, has Aglaya had an attack of nerves for these last three days? Why has she all but quarrelled with her sisters, even with Alexandra— whom she respects so much that she always kisses her hands as though she were her mother? What are all these riddles of hers that we have to guess? What has Gavrila Ardalionovitch to do with it? Why did she take upon herself to champion him this morning, and burst into tears over it? Why is there an allusion to that cursed 'poor knight' in the anonymous letter? And why did I rush off to him just now like a lunatic, and drag him back here? I do believe I've gone mad at last. What on earth have I done now? To talk to a young man about my daughter's secrets—and secrets having to do with himself, too! Thank goodness, he's an idiot, and a friend of the house! Surely Aglaya hasn't fallen in love with such a gaby! What an idea! Pfu! we ought all to be put under glass cases— myself first of all—and be shown off as curiosities, at ten copecks a peep!"

"I shall never forgive you for all this, Ivan Fedorovitch—never! Look at her now. Why doesn't she make fun of him? She said she would, and she doesn't. Look there! She stares at him with all her eyes, and doesn't move; and yet she told him not to come. He looks pale enough; and that abominable chatterbox, Evgenie Pavlovitch, monopolizes the whole of the conversation. Nobody else can get a word in. I could soon find out all about everything if I could only change the subject."

The prince certainly was very pale. He sat at the table and seemed to be feeling, by turns, sensations of alarm and rapture.

Oh, how frightened he was of looking to one side—one particular corner—whence he knew very well that a pair of dark eyes were watching him intently, and how happy he was to think that he was once more among them, and occasionally hearing that well-known voice, although she had written and forbidden him to come again!

"What on earth will she say to me, I wonder?" he thought to himself.

He had not said a word yet; he sat silent and listened to Evgenie Pavlovitch's eloquence. The latter had never appeared so happy and excited as on this evening. The prince listened to him, but for a long time did not take in a word he said.

Excepting Ivan Fedorovitch, who had not as yet returned from town, the whole family was present. Prince S. was there; and they all intended to go out to hear the band very soon.

Colia arrived presently and joined the circle. "So he is received as usual, after all," thought the prince.

The Epanchins' country-house was a charming building, built after the model of a Swiss chalet, and covered with creepers. It was surrounded on all sides by a flower garden, and the family sat, as a rule, on the open verandah as at the prince's house.

The subject under discussion did not appear to be very popular with the assembly, and some would have been delighted to change it; but Evgenie would not stop holding forth, and the prince's arrival seemed to spur him on to still further oratorical efforts.

Lizabetha Prokofievna frowned, but had not as yet grasped the subject, which seemed to have arisen out of a heated argument. Aglaya sat apart, almost in the corner, listening in stubborn silence.

"Excuse me," continued Evgenie Pavlovitch hotly, "I don't say a word against liberalism. Liberalism is not a sin, it is a necessary part of a great whole, which whole would collapse and fall to pieces without it. Liberalism has just as much right to exist as has the most moral conservatism; but I am attacking *Russian* liberalism; and I attack it for the simple reason that a Russian liberal is not a Russian liberal, he is a non-Russian liberal. Show me a real Russian liberal, and I'll kiss him before you all, with pleasure."

"If he cared to kiss you, that is," said Alexandra, whose cheeks were red with irritation and excitement.

"Look at that, now," thought the mother to herself, "she does nothing but sleep and eat for a year at a time, and then suddenly flies out in the most incomprehensible way!"

The prince observed that Alexandra appeared to be angry with Evgenie, because he spoke on a serious subject in a frivolous manner, pretending to be in earnest, but with an under-current of irony.

"I was saying just now, before you came in, prince, that there has been nothing national up to now, about our liberalism, and nothing the liberals do, or have done, is in the least degree national. They are drawn from two classes only, the old landowning class, and clerical families—"

"How, nothing that they have done is Russian?" asked Prince S.

"It may be Russian, but it is not national. Our liberals are not Russian, nor are our conservatives, and you may be sure that the nation does not recognize anything that has been done by the landed gentry, or by the seminarists, or what is to be done either."

"Come, that's good! How can you maintain such a paradox? If you are serious, that is. I cannot allow such a statement about the landed proprietors to pass unchallenged. Why, you are a landed proprietor yourself!" cried Prince S. hotly.

"I suppose you'll say there is nothing national about our literature either?" said Alexandra.

"Well, I am not a great authority on literary questions, but I certainly do hold that Russian literature is not Russian, except perhaps Lomonosoff, Pouschkin and Gogol."

"In the first place, that is a considerable admission, and in the second place, one of the above was a peasant, and the other two were both landed proprietors!"

"Quite so, but don't be in such a hurry! For since it has been the part of these three men, and only these three, to say something absolutely their own, not borrowed, so by this very fact these three men become really national. If any Russian shall have done or said anything really and absolutely original, he is to be called national from that moment, though he may not be able to talk the Russian language; still he is a national Russian. I consider that an axiom. But we were not speaking of literature; we began by discussing the socialists. Very well then, I insist that there does not exist one single Russian socialist. There does not, and there has never existed such a one, because all socialists are derived from the two classes—the landed proprietors, and the seminarists. All our eminent socialists are merely old liberals of the class of landed proprietors, men who were liberals in the days of serfdom. Why do you laugh? Give me their books, give me their studies, their memoirs, and though I am not a literary critic, yet I will prove as clear as day that every chapter and every word of their writings has been the work of a former landed proprietor of the old school. You'll find that all their raptures, all their generous transports are proprietary, all their woes and their tears, proprietary; all proprietary or seminarist! You are laughing again, and you, prince, are smiling too. Don't you agree with me?"

It was true enough that everybody was laughing, the prince among them.

"I cannot tell you on the instant whether I agree with you or not," said the latter, suddenly stopping his laughter, and starting like a schoolboy caught at mischief. "But, I assure you, I am listening to you with extreme gratification."

So saying, he almost panted with agitation, and a cold sweat stood upon his forehead. These were his first words since he had entered the house; he tried to lift his eyes, and look around, but dared not; Evgenie Pavlovitch noticed his confusion, and smiled.

"I'll just tell you one fact, ladies and gentlemen," continued the latter, with apparent seriousness and even exaltation of manner, but with a suggestion of "chaff" behind every word, as though he were laughing in his sleeve at his own nonsense—"a fact, the discovery of which, I believe, I may claim to have made by myself alone. At all events, no other has ever said or written a word about it; and in this fact is expressed the whole essence of Russian liberalism of the sort which I am now considering.

"In the first place, what is liberalism, speaking generally, but an attack (whether mistaken or reasonable, is quite another question) upon the existing order of things? Is this so? Yes. Very well. Then my 'fact' consists in this, that *Russian* liberalism is not an attack upon the existing order of things, but an attack upon the very essence of things themselves—indeed, on the things themselves; not an attack on the Russian order of things, but on Russia itself. My Russian liberal goes so far as to reject Russia; that is, he hates and strikes his own mother. Every misfortune and mishap of the mother-country fills him with mirth, and even with ecstasy. He hates the national customs, Russian history, and everything. If he has a justification, it is that he does not know what he is doing, and believes that his hatred of Russia is the grandest and most profitable kind of liberalism. (You will often find a liberal who is applauded and esteemed by his fellows, but who is in reality the dreariest, blindest, dullest of conservatives, and is not aware of the fact.) This hatred for Russia has been mistaken by some of our 'Russian liberals' for sincere love of their country, and they boast that they see better than their neighbours what real love of one's country should consist in. But of late they have grown, more candid and are ashamed of the expression 'love of country,' and have annihilated the very spirit of the words as something injurious and petty and undignified. This is the truth, and I hold by it; but at the same time it is a phenomenon which has not been repeated at any other time or place; and therefore, though I hold to it as a fact, yet I recognize that it is an accidental phenomenon, and may likely enough pass away. There can be no such thing anywhere else as a liberal who really hates his country; and how is this fact to be explained among *us?* By my original statement that a Russian liberal is *not* a *Russian* liberal—that's the only explanation that I can see."

"I take all that you have said as a joke," said Prince S. seriously.

"I have not seen all kinds of liberals, and cannot, therefore, set myself up as a judge," said Alexandra, "but I have heard all you have said with indignation. You have taken some accidental case and twisted it into a universal law, which is unjust."

"Accidental case!" said Evgenie Pavlovitch. "Do you consider it an accidental case, prince?"

"I must also admit," said the prince, "that I have not seen much, or been very far into the question; but I cannot help thinking that you are more or less right, and that Russian liberalism—that phase of it which you are considering, at least—really is sometimes inclined to hate Russia itself, and not only its existing order of things in general. Of course this is only*partially* the truth; you cannot lay down the law for all..."

The prince blushed and broke off, without finishing what he meant to say.

In spite of his shyness and agitation, he could not help being greatly interested in the conversation. A special characteristic of his was the naive candour with which he always listened to arguments which interested him, and with which he answered any questions put to him on the subject at issue. In the very expression of his face this naivete was unmistakably evident, this disbelief in the insincerity of others, and unsuspecting disregard of irony or humour in their words.

But though Evgenie Pavlovitch had put his questions to the prince with no other purpose but to enjoy the joke of his simple-minded seriousness, yet now, at his answer, he was surprised into some seriousness himself, and looked gravely at Muishkin as though he had not expected that sort of answer at all.

"Why, how strange!" he ejaculated. "You didn't answer me seriously, surely, did you?"

"Did not you ask me the question seriously" inquired the prince, in amazement.

Everybody laughed.

"Oh, trust *him* for that!" said Adelaida. "Evgenie Pavlovitch turns everything and everybody he can lay hold of to ridicule. You should hear the things he says sometimes, apparently in perfect seriousness."

"In my opinion the conversation has been a painful one throughout, and we ought never to have begun it," said Alexandra. "We were all going for a walk—"

"Come along then," said Evgenie; "it's a glorious evening. But, to prove that this time I was speaking absolutely seriously, and especially to prove this to the prince (for you, prince, have interested me exceedingly, and I swear to you that I am not quite such an ass as I like to appear sometimes, although I am rather an ass, I admit), and—well, ladies and gentlemen, will you allow me to put just one more question to the prince, out of pure curiosity? It shall be the last. This question came into my mind a couple of hours since (you see, prince, I do think seriously at times), and I made my own decision upon it; now I wish to hear what the prince will say to it."

"We have just used the expression 'accidental case.' This is a significant phrase; we often hear it. Well, not long since everyone was talking and reading about that terrible murder of six people on the part of a—young fellow, and of the extraordinary speech of the counsel for the defence, who observed that in the poverty-stricken condition of the criminal it must have come *naturally* into his head to kill these six people. I do not quote his words, but that is the sense of them, or something very like it. Now, in my opinion, the barrister who put forward this extraordinary plea was probably absolutely convinced that he was stating the most liberal, the most humane, the most enlightened

374

view of the case that could possibly be brought forward in these days. Now, was this distortion, this capacity for a perverted way of viewing things, a special or accidental case, or is such a general rule?"

Everyone laughed at this.

"A special case—accidental, of course!" cried Alexandra and Adelaida.

"Let me remind you once more, Evgenie," said Prince S., "that your joke is getting a little threadbare."

"What do you think about it, prince?" asked Evgenie, taking no notice of the last remark, and observing Muishkin's serious eyes fixed upon his face. "What do you think—was it a special or a usual case—the rule, or an exception? I confess I put the question especially for you."

"No, I don't think it was a special case," said the prince, quietly, but firmly.

"My dear fellow!" cried Prince S., with some annoyance, "don't you see that he is chaffing you? He is simply laughing at you, and wants to make game of you."

"I thought Evgenie Pavlovitch was talking seriously," said the prince, blushing and dropping his eyes.

"My dear prince," continued Prince S. "remember what you and I were saying two or three months ago. We spoke of the fact that in our newly opened Law Courts one could already lay one's finger upon so many talented and remarkable young barristers. How pleased you were with the state of things as we found it, and how glad I was to observe your delight! We both said it was a matter to be proud of; but this clumsy defence that Evgenie mentions, this strange argument *can*, of course, only be an accidental case—one in a thousand!"

The prince reflected a little, but very soon he replied, with absolute conviction in his tone, though he still spoke somewhat shyly and timidly:

"I only wished to say that this 'distortion,' as Evgenie Pavlovitch expressed it, is met with very often, and is far more the general rule than the exception, unfortunately for Russia. So much so, that if this distortion were not the general rule, perhaps these dreadful crimes would be less frequent."

"Dreadful crimes? But I can assure you that crimes just as dreadful, and probably more horrible, have occurred before our times, and at all times, and not only here in Russia, but everywhere else as well. And in my opinion it is not at all likely that such murders will cease to occur for a very long time to come. The only difference is that in former times there was less publicity, while now everyone talks and writes freely about such things—which fact gives the impression that such crimes have only now sprung into existence. That is where your mistake lies—an extremely natural mistake, I assure you, my dear fellow!" said Prince S.

"I know that there were just as many, and just as terrible, crimes before our times. Not long since I visited a convict prison and made acquaintance with some of the criminals. There were some even more dreadful criminals than this one we have been speaking of—men who have murdered a dozen of their fellow-creatures, and feel no remorse whatever. But what I especially noticed was this, that the very most hopeless and remorseless murderer—however hardened a criminal he may be—still *knows that he is a criminal*; that is, he is conscious that he has acted wickedly, though he may feel no remorse whatever. And they were all like this. Those of whom Evgenie Pavlovitch has spoken, do not admit that they are criminals at all; they think they had a right to do what they did, and that they were even doing a good deed, perhaps. I consider there is the greatest difference between the two cases. And recollect—it was a *youth*, at the particular age which is most helplessly susceptible to the distortion of ideas!"

Prince S. was now no longer smiling; he gazed at the prince in bewilderment.

Alexandra, who had seemed to wish to put in her word when the prince began, now sat silent, as though some sudden thought had caused her to change her mind about speaking.

Evgenie Pavlovitch gazed at him in real surprise, and this time his expression of face had no mockery in it whatever.

"What are you looking so surprised about, my friend?" asked Mrs. Epanchin, suddenly. "Did you suppose he was stupider than yourself, and was incapable of forming his own opinions, or what?"

"No! Oh no! Not at all!" said Evgenie. "But—how is it, prince, that you—(excuse the question, will you?)—if you are capable of observing and seeing things as you evidently do, how is it that you saw nothing distorted or perverted in that claim upon your property, which you acknowledged a day or two since; and which was full of arguments founded upon the most distorted views of right and wrong?"

"I'll tell you what, my friend," cried Mrs. Epanchin, of a sudden, "here are we all sitting here and imagining we are very clever, and perhaps laughing at the prince, some of us, and meanwhile he has received a letter this very day in which that same claimant renounces his claim, and begs the prince's pardon. There I we don't often get that sort of letter; and yet we are not ashamed to walk with our noses in the air before him."

"And Hippolyte has come down here to stay," said Colia, suddenly.

"What! has he arrived?" said the prince, starting up.

"Yes, I brought him down from town just after you had left the house."

"There now! It's just like him," cried Lizabetha Prokofievna, boiling over once more, and entirely oblivious of the fact that she had just taken the prince's part. "I dare swear that you went up to town yesterday on purpose to get the little wretch to do you the great honour of coming to stay at your house. You did go up to town, you know you did—you said so yourself! Now then, did you, or did you not, go down on your knees and beg him to come, confess!"

"No, he didn't, for I saw it all myself," said Colia. "On the contrary, Hippolyte kissed his hand twice and thanked him; and all the prince said was that he thought Hippolyte might feel better here in the country!"

"Don't, Colia,—what is the use of saying all that?" cried the prince, rising and taking his hat.

"Where are you going to now?" cried Mrs. Epanchin.

"Never mind about him now, prince," said Colia. "He is all right and taking a nap after the journey. He is very happy to be here; but I think perhaps it would be better if you let him alone for today,—he is very sensitive now that he is so ill—and he might be embarrassed if you show him too much attention at first. He is decidedly better today, and says he has not felt so well for the last six months, and has coughed much less, too."

The prince observed that Aglaya came out of her corner and approached the table at this point.

He did not dare look at her, but he was conscious, to the very tips of his fingers, that she was gazing at him, perhaps angrily; and that she had probably flushed up with a look of fiery indignation in her black eyes.

"It seems to me, Mr. Colia, that you were very foolish to bring your young friend down—if he is the same consumptive boy who wept so profusely, and invited us all to his own funeral," remarked Evgenie Pavlovitch. "He talked so eloquently about the blank wall outside his bedroom window, that I'm sure he will never support life here without it."

"I think so too," said Mrs. Epanchin; "he will quarrel with you, and be off," and she drew her workbox towards her with an air of dignity, quite oblivious of the fact that the family was about to start for a walk in the park.

"Yes, I remember he boasted about the blank wall in an extraordinary way," continued Evgenie, "and I feel that without that blank wall he will never be able to die eloquently; and he does so long to die eloquently!"

"Oh, you must forgive him the blank wall," said the prince, quietly. "He has come down to see a few trees now, poor fellow."

"Oh, I forgive him with all my heart; you may tell him so if you like," laughed Evgenie.

"I don't think you should take it quite like that," said the prince, quietly, and without removing his eyes from the carpet. "I think it is more a case of his forgiving you."

"Forgiving me! why so? What have I done to need his forgiveness?"

"If you don't understand, then—but of course, you do understand. He wished—he wished to bless you all round and to have your blessing—before he died—that's all."

"My dear prince," began Prince S., hurriedly, exchanging glances with some of those present, "you will not easily find heaven on earth, and yet you seem to expect to. Heaven is a difficult thing to find anywhere, prince; far more difficult than appears to that good heart of yours. Better stop this conversation, or we shall all be growing quite disturbed in our minds, and—"

"Let's go and hear the band, then," said Lizabetha Prokofievna, angrily rising from her place.

The rest of the company followed her example.

II.

The prince suddenly approached Evgenie Pavlovitch.

"Evgenie Pavlovitch," he said, with strange excitement and seizing the latter's hand in his own, "be assured that I esteem you as a generous and honourable man, in spite of everything. Be assured of that."

Evgenie Pavlovitch fell back a step in astonishment. For one moment it was all he could do to restrain himself from bursting out laughing; but, looking closer, he observed that the prince did not seem to be quite himself; at all events, he was in a very curious state.

"I wouldn't mind betting, prince," he cried, "that you did not in the least mean to say that, and very likely you meant to address someone else altogether. What is it? Are you feeling unwell or anything?"

"Very likely, extremely likely, and you must be a very close observer to detect the fact that perhaps I did not intend to come up to *you* at all."

So saying he smiled strangely; but suddenly and excitedly he began again:

"Don't remind me of what I have done or said. Don't! I am very much ashamed of myself, I—"

"Why, what have you done? I don't understand you."

"I see you are ashamed of me, Evgenie Pavlovitch; you are blushing for me; that's a sign of a good heart. Don't be afraid; I shall go away directly."

"What's the matter with him? Do his fits begin like that?" said Lizabetha Prokofievna, in a high state of alarm, addressing Colia.

"No, no, Lizabetha Prokofievna, take no notice of me. I am not going to have a fit. I will go away directly; but I know I am afflicted. I was twenty-four years an invalid, you see—the first twenty-four years of my life—so take all I do and say as the sayings and actions of an invalid. I'm going away directly, I really am—don't be afraid. I am not blushing, for I don't think I need blush about it, need I? But I see that I am out of place in society—society is better without me. It's not vanity, I assure you. I have thought over it all these last three days, and I have made up my mind that I ought to unbosom myself candidly before you at the first opportunity. There are certain things, certain great ideas, which I must not so much as approach, as Prince S. has just reminded me, or I shall make you all laugh. I have no sense of proportion, I know; my words and gestures do not express my ideas—they are a humiliation and abasement of the ideas, and therefore, I have no right—and I am too sensitive. Still, I believe I am beloved in this household, and esteemed far more than I deserve. But I can't help knowing that after twenty-four years of illness there must be some trace left, so that it is impossible for people to refrain from laughing at me sometimes; don't you think so?"

He seemed to pause for a reply, for some verdict, as it were, and looked humbly around him.

All present stood rooted to the earth with amazement at this unexpected and apparently uncalled-for outbreak; but the poor prince's painful and rambling speech gave rise to a strange episode.

"Why do you say all this here?" cried Aglaya, suddenly. "Why do you talk like this to *them?*"

She appeared to be in the last stages of wrath and irritation; her eyes flashed. The prince stood dumbly and blindly before her, and suddenly grew pale.

"There is not one of them all who is worthy of these words of yours," continued Aglaya. "Not one of them is worth your little finger, not one of them has heart or head to compare with yours! You are more honest than all, and better, nobler, kinder, wiser than all. There are some here who are unworthy to bend and pick up the handkerchief you have just dropped. Why do you humiliate yourself like this, and place yourself lower than these people? Why do you debase yourself before them? Why have you no pride?"

"My God! Who would ever have believed this?" cried Mrs. Epanchin, wringing her hands.

"Hurrah for the 'poor knight'!" cried Colia.

"Be quiet! How dare they laugh at me in your house?" said Aglaya, turning sharply on her mother in that hysterical frame of mind that rides recklessly over every obstacle and plunges blindly through proprieties. "Why does everyone, everyone worry and torment me? Why have they all been bullying me these three days about you, prince? I will not marry you—never, and under no circumstances! Know that once and for all; as if anyone could marry an absurd creature like you! Just look in the glass and see what you look like, this very moment! Why, *why* do they torment me and say I am going to marry you? You must know it; you are in the plot with them!"

"No one ever tormented you on the subject," murmured Adelaida, aghast.

"No one ever thought of such a thing! There has never been a word said about it!" cried Alexandra.

"Who has been annoying her? Who has been tormenting the child? Who could have said such a thing to her? Is she raving?" cried Lizabetha Prokofievna, trembling with rage, to the company in general.

"Every one of them has been saying it—every one of them—all these three days! And I will never, never marry him!"

So saying, Aglaya burst into bitter tears, and, hiding her face in her handkerchief, sank back into a chair.

"But he has never even—"

"I have never asked you to marry me, Aglaya Ivanovna!" said the prince, of a sudden.

"*What?*" cried Mrs. Epanchin, raising her hands in horror. "*What's* that?"

She could not believe her ears.

"I meant to say—I only meant to say," said the prince, faltering, "I merely meant to explain to Aglaya Ivanovna—to have the honour to explain, as it were—that I had no intention—never had—to ask the honour of her hand. I assure you I am not guilty, Aglaya Ivanovna, I am not, indeed. I never did wish to—I never thought of it at all—and never shall—you'll see it yourself—you may be quite assured of it. Some wicked person has been maligning me to you; but it's all right. Don't worry about it."

So saying, the prince approached Aglaya.

She took the handkerchief from her face, glanced keenly at him, took in what he had said, and burst out laughing—such a merry, unrestrained laugh, so hearty and gay, that. Adelaida could not contain herself. She, too, glanced at the prince's panic-stricken countenance, then rushed at her sister, threw her arms round her neck, and burst into as merry a fit of laughter as Aglaya's own. They laughed together like a couple of school-girls. Hearing and seeing this, the prince smiled happily, and in accents of relief and joy, he exclaimed "Well, thank God—thank God!"

Alexandra now joined in, and it looked as though the three sisters were going to laugh on for ever.

"They are insane," muttered Lizabetha Prokofievna. "Either they frighten one out of one's wits, or else—"

But Prince S. was laughing now, too, so was Evgenie Pavlovitch, so was Colia, and so was the prince himself, who caught the infection as he looked round radiantly upon the others.

"Come along, let's go out for a walk!" cried Adelaida. "We'll all go together, and the prince must absolutely go with us. You needn't go away, you dear good fellow! *Isn't* he a dear, Aglaya? Isn't he, mother? I must really give him a kiss for—for his explanation to Aglaya just now. Mother, dear, I may kiss him, mayn't I? Aglaya, may I kiss *your* prince?" cried the young rogue, and sure enough she skipped up to the prince and kissed his forehead.

He seized her hands, and pressed them so hard that Adelaida nearly cried out; he then gazed with delight into her eyes, and raising her right hand to his lips with enthusiasm, kissed it three times.

"Come along," said Aglaya. "Prince, you must walk with me. May he, mother? This young cavalier, who won't have me? You said you would *never* have me, didn't you, prince? No—no, not like that; *that's* not the way to give your arm. Don't you know how to give your arm to a lady yet? There—so. Now, come along, you and I will lead the way. Would you like to lead the way with me alone, tête-à-tête?"

She went on talking and chatting without a pause, with occasional little bursts of laughter between.

"Thank God—thank God!" said Lizabetha Prokofievna to herself, without quite knowing why she felt so relieved.

"What extraordinary people they are!" thought Prince S., for perhaps the hundredth time since he had entered into intimate relations with the family; but—he liked these "extraordinary people," all the same. As for Prince Lef Nicolaievitch himself, Prince S. did not seem quite to like him, somehow. He was decidedly preoccupied and a little disturbed as they all started off.

Evgenie Pavlovitch seemed to be in a lively humour. He made Adelaida and Alexandra laugh all the way to the Vauxhall; but they both laughed so very really and promptly that the worthy Evgenie began at last to suspect that they were not listening to him at all.

At this idea, he burst out laughing all at once, in quite unaffected mirth, and without giving any explanation.

The sisters, who also appeared to be in high spirits, never tired of glancing at Aglaya and the prince, who were walking in front. It was evident that their younger sister was a thorough puzzle to them both.

Prince S. tried hard to get up a conversation with Mrs. Epanchin upon outside subjects, probably with the good intention of distracting and amusing her; but he bored her dreadfully. She was absent-minded to a degree, and answered at cross purposes, and sometimes not at all.

But the puzzle and mystery of Aglaya was not yet over for the evening. The last exhibition fell to the lot of the prince alone. When they had proceeded some hundred paces or so from the house, Aglaya said to her obstinately silent cavalier in a quick half-whisper:

"Look to the right!"

The prince glanced in the direction indicated.

"Look closer. Do you see that bench, in the park there, just by those three big trees—that green bench?"

The prince replied that he saw it.

"Do you like the position of it? Sometimes of a morning early, at seven o'clock, when all the rest are still asleep, I come out and sit there alone."

The prince muttered that the spot was a lovely one.

"Now, go away, I don't wish to have your arm any longer; or perhaps, better, continue to give me your arm, and walk along beside me, but don't speak a word to me. I wish to think by myself."

The warning was certainly unnecessary; for the prince would not have said a word all the rest of the time whether forbidden to speak or not. His heart beat loud and painfully when Aglaya spoke of the bench; could she—but no! he banished the thought, after an instant's deliberation.

At Pavlofsk, on weekdays, the public is more select than it is on Sundays and Saturdays, when the townsfolk come down to walk about and enjoy the park.

The ladies dress elegantly, on these days, and it is the fashion to gather round the band, which is probably the best of our pleasure-garden bands, and plays the newest pieces. The behaviour of the public is most correct and proper, and there is an appearance of friendly intimacy among the usual frequenters. Many come for nothing but to look at their acquaintances, but there are others who come for the sake of the music. It is very seldom that anything happens to break the harmony of the proceedings, though, of course, accidents will happen everywhere.

On this particular evening the weather was lovely, and there were a large number of people present. All the places anywhere near the orchestra were occupied.

Our friends took chairs near the side exit. The crowd and the music cheered Mrs. Epanchin a little, and amused the girls; they bowed and shook hands with some of their friends and nodded at a distance to others; they examined the ladies' dresses, noticed comicalities and eccentricities among the people, and laughed and talked among themselves. Evgenie Pavlovitch, too, found plenty of friends to bow to. Several people noticed Aglaya and the prince, who were still together.

Before very long two or three young men had come up, and one or two remained to talk; all of these young men appeared to be on intimate terms with Evgenie Pavlovitch. Among them was a young officer, a remarkably handsome fellow—very good-natured and a great chatterbox. He tried to get up a conversation with Aglaya, and did his best to secure her attention. Aglaya behaved very graciously to him, and chatted and laughed merrily. Evgenie Pavlovitch begged the prince's leave to introduce their friend to him. The prince hardly realized what was wanted of him, but the introduction came off; the two men bowed and shook hands.

Evgenie Pavlovitch's friend asked the prince some question, but the latter did not reply, or if he did, he muttered something so strangely indistinct that there was nothing to be made of it. The officer stared intently at him, then glanced at Evgenie, divined why the latter had introduced him, and gave his undivided attention to Aglaya again. Only Evgenie Pavlovitch observed that Aglaya flushed up for a moment at this.

The prince did not notice that others were talking and making themselves agreeable to Aglaya; in fact, at moments, he almost forgot that he was sitting by her himself. At other moments he felt a longing to go away somewhere and be alone with his thoughts, and to feel that no one knew where he was.

Or if that were impossible he would like to be alone at home, on the terrace-without either Lebedeff or his children, or anyone else about him, and to lie there and think—a day and night and another day again! He thought of the mountains—and especially of a certain spot which he used to frequent, whence he would look down upon the distant valleys and fields, and see the waterfall, far off, like a little silver thread, and the old ruined castle in the distance. Oh! how he longed to be there now—alone with his thoughts—to think of one thing all his life—one thing! A thousand years would not be too much time! And let everyone here forget him—forget him utterly! How much better it would have been if they had never known him—if all this could but prove to be a dream. Perhaps it was a dream!

Now and then he looked at Aglaya for five minutes at a time, without taking his eyes off her face; but his expression was very strange; he would gaze at her as though she were an object a couple of miles distant, or as though he were looking at her portrait and not at herself at all.

"Why do you look at me like that, prince?" she asked suddenly, breaking off her merry conversation and laughter with those about her. "I'm afraid of you! You look as though you were just going to put out your hand and touch my face to see if it's real! Doesn't he, Evgenie Pavlovitch—doesn't he look like that?"

The prince seemed surprised that he should have been addressed at all; he reflected a moment, but did not seem to take in what had been said to him; at all events, he did not answer. But observing that she and the others had begun to laugh, he too opened his mouth and laughed with them.

The laughter became general, and the young officer, who seemed a particularly lively sort of person, simply shook with mirth.

Aglaya suddenly whispered angrily to herself the word—

"Idiot!"

"My goodness—surely she is not in love with such a—surely she isn't mad!" groaned Mrs. Epanchin, under her breath.

"It's all a joke, mamma; it's just a joke like the 'poor knight'—nothing more whatever, I assure you!" Alexandra whispered in her ear. "She is chaffing him—making a fool of him, after her own private fashion, that's all! But she carries it just a little too far—she is a regular little actress. How she frightened us just now—didn't she?—and all for a lark!"

"Well, it's lucky she has happened upon an idiot, then, that's all I can say!" whispered Lizabetha Prokofievna, who was somewhat comforted, however, by her daughter's remark.

The prince had heard himself referred to as "idiot," and had shuddered at the moment; but his shudder, it so happened, was not caused by the word applied to him. The fact was that in the crowd, not far from where lie was sitting, a pale familiar face, with curly black hair, and a well-known smile and expression, had flashed across his vision for a moment, and disappeared again. Very likely he had imagined it! There only remained to him the impression of a strange smile, two eyes, and a bright green tie. Whether the man had disappeared among the crowd, or whether he had turned towards the Vauxhall, the prince could not say.

But a moment or two afterwards he began to glance keenly about him. That first vision might only too likely be the forerunner of a second; it was almost certain to be so. Surely he had not forgotten the possibility of such a meeting when he came to the Vauxhall? True enough, he had not remarked where he was coming to when he set out with Aglaya; he had not been in a condition to remark anything at all.

Had he been more careful to observe his companion, he would have seen that for the last quarter of an hour Aglaya had also been glancing around in apparent anxiety, as though she expected to see someone, or something particular, among the crowd of people. Now, at the moment when his own anxiety became so marked, her excitement also increased visibly, and when he looked about him, she did the same.

The reason for their anxiety soon became apparent. From that very side entrance to the Vauxhall, near which the prince and all the Epanchin party were seated, there suddenly appeared quite a large knot of persons, at least a dozen.

Heading this little band walked three ladies, two of whom were remarkably lovely; and there was nothing surprising in the fact that they should have had a large troop of admirers following in their wake.

But there was something in the appearance of both the ladies and their admirers which was peculiar, quite different for that of the rest of the public assembled around the orchestra.

Nearly everyone observed the little band advancing, and all pretended not to see or notice them, except a few young fellows who exchanged glances and smiled, saying something to one another in whispers.

It was impossible to avoid noticing them, however, in reality, for they made their presence only too conspicuous by laughing and talking loudly. It was to be supposed that some of them were more than half drunk, although they were well enough dressed, some even particularly well. There were one or two, however, who were very strange-looking creatures, with flushed faces and extraordinary clothes; some were military men; not all were quite young; one or two were middle-aged gentlemen of decidedly disagreeable appearance, men who are avoided in society like the plague, decked out in large gold studs and rings, and magnificently "got up," generally.

Among our suburban resorts there are some which enjoy a specially high reputation for respectability and fashion; but the most careful individual is not absolutely exempt from the danger of a tile falling suddenly upon his head from his neighbour's roof.

Such a tile was about to descend upon the elegant and decorous public now assembled to hear the music.

In order to pass from the Vauxhall to the band-stand, the visitor has to descend two or three steps. Just at these steps the group paused, as though it feared to proceed further; but very quickly one of the three ladies, who formed its apex, stepped forward into the charmed circle, followed by two members of her suite.

One of these was a middle-aged man of very respectable appearance, but with the stamp of parvenu upon him, a man whom nobody knew, and who evidently knew nobody. The other follower was younger and far less respectable-looking.

No one else followed the eccentric lady; but as she descended the steps she did not even look behind her, as though it were absolutely the same to her whether anyone were following or not. She laughed and talked loudly, however, just as before. She was dressed with great taste, but with rather more magnificence than was needed for the occasion, perhaps.

She walked past the orchestra, to where an open carriage was waiting, near the road.

The prince had not seen *her* for more than three months. All these days since his arrival from Petersburg he had intended to pay her a visit, but some mysterious presentiment had restrained him. He could not picture to himself what impression this meeting with her would make upon him, though he had often tried to imagine it, with fear and trembling. One fact was quite certain, and that was that the meeting would be painful.

Several times during the last six months he had recalled the effect which the first sight of this face had had upon him, when he only saw its portrait. He recollected well that even the portrait face had left but too painful an impression.

That month in the provinces, when he had seen this woman nearly every day, had affected him so deeply that he could not now look back upon it calmly. In the very look of this woman there was something which tortured him. In conversation with Rogojin he had attributed this sensation to pity—immeasurable pity, and this was the truth. The sight of the portrait face alone had filled his heart full of the agony of real sympathy; and this feeling of sympathy, nay, of actual *suffering*, for her, had never left his heart since that hour, and was still in full force. Oh yes, and more powerful than ever!

But the prince was not satisfied with what he had said to Rogojin. Only at this moment, when she suddenly made her appearance before him, did he realize to the full the exact emotion which she called up in him, and which he had not described correctly to Rogojin.

And, indeed, there were no words in which he could have expressed his horror, yes, *horror*, for he was now fully convinced from his own private knowledge of her, that the woman was mad.

If, loving a woman above everything in the world, or at least having a foretaste of the possibility of such love for her, one were suddenly to behold her on a chain, behind bars and under the lash of a keeper, one would feel something like what the poor prince now felt.

"What's the matter?" asked Aglaya, in a whisper, giving his sleeve a little tug.

He turned his head towards her and glanced at her black and (for some reason) flashing eyes, tried to smile, and then, apparently forgetting her in an instant, turned to the right once more, and continued to watch the startling apparition before him.

Nastasia Philipovna was at this moment passing the young ladies' chairs.

Evgenie Pavlovitch continued some apparently extremely funny and interesting anecdote to Alexandra, speaking quickly and with much animation. The prince remembered that at this moment Aglaya remarked in a half-whisper:

"*What* a—"

She did not finish her indefinite sentence; she restrained herself in a moment; but it was enough.

Nastasia Philipovna, who up to now had been walking along as though she had not noticed the Epanchin party, suddenly turned her head in their direction, as though she had just observed Evgenie Pavlovitch sitting there for the first time.

"Why, I declare, here he is!" she cried, stopping suddenly. "The man one can't find with all one's messengers sent about the place, sitting just under one's nose, exactly where one never thought of looking! I thought you were sure to be at your uncle's by this time."

Evgenie Pavlovitch flushed up and looked angrily at Nastasia Philipovna, then turned his back on her.

"What I don't you know about it yet? He doesn't know—imagine that! Why, he's shot himself. Your uncle shot himself this very morning. I was told at two this afternoon. Half the town must know it by now. They say there are three hundred and fifty thousand roubles, government money, missing; some say five hundred thousand. And I was under the impression that he would leave you a fortune! He's whistled it all away. A most depraved old gentleman, really! Well, ta, ta!—bonne chance! Surely you intend to be off there, don't you? Ha, ha! You've retired from the army in good time, I see! Plain clothes! Well done, sly rogue! Nonsense! I see—you knew it all before—I dare say you knew all about it yesterday-"

Although the impudence of this attack, this public proclamation of intimacy, as it were, was doubtless premeditated, and had its special object, yet Evgenie Pavlovitch at first seemed to intend to make no show of observing either his tormentor or her words. But Nastasia's communication struck him with the force of a thunderclap. On hearing of his uncle's death he suddenly grew as white as a sheet, and turned towards his informant.

At this moment, Lizabetha Prokofievna rose swiftly from her seat, beckoned her companions, and left the place almost at a run.

Only the prince stopped behind for a moment, as though in indecision; and Evgenie Pavlovitch lingered too, for he had not collected his scattered wits. But the Epanchins had not had time to get more than twenty paces away when a scandalous episode occurred. The young officer, Evgenie Pavlovitch's friend who had been conversing with Aglaya, said aloud in a great state of indignation:

"She ought to be whipped—that's the only way to deal with creatures like that—she ought to be whipped!"

This gentleman was a confidant of Evgenie's, and had doubtless heard of the carriage episode.

Nastasia turned to him. Her eyes flashed; she rushed up to a young man standing near, whom she did not know in the least, but who happened to have in his hand a thin cane. Seizing this from him, she brought it with all her force across the face of her insulter.

All this occurred, of course, in one instant of time.

The young officer, forgetting himself, sprang towards her. Nastasia's followers were not by her at the moment (the elderly gentleman having disappeared altogether, and the younger man simply standing aside and roaring with laughter).

In another moment, of course, the police would have been on the spot, and it would have gone hard with Nastasia Philipovna had not unexpected aid appeared.

Muishkin, who was but a couple of steps away, had time to spring forward and seize the officer's arms from behind.

The officer, tearing himself from the prince's grasp, pushed him so violently backwards that he staggered a few steps and then subsided into a chair.

But there were other defenders for Nastasia on the spot by this time. The gentleman known as the "boxer" now confronted the enraged officer.

"Keller is my name, sir; ex-lieutenant," he said, very loud. "If you will accept me as champion of the fair sex, I am at your disposal. English boxing has no secrets from me. I sympathize with you for the insult you have received, but I can't permit you to raise your hand against a woman in public. If you prefer to meet me—as would be more fitting to your rank—in some other manner, of course you understand me, captain."

But the young officer had recovered himself, and was no longer listening. At this moment Rogojin appeared, elbowing through the crowd; he took Nastasia's hand, drew it through his arm, and quickly led her away. He appeared to be terribly excited; he was trembling all over, and was as pale as a corpse. As he carried Nastasia off, he turned and grinned horribly in the officer's face, and with low malice observed:

"Tfu! look what the fellow got! Look at the blood on his cheek! Ha, ha!"

Recollecting himself, however, and seeing at a glance the sort of people he had to deal with, the officer turned his back on both his opponents, and courteously, but concealing his face with his handkerchief, approached the prince, who was now rising from the chair into which he had fallen.

"Prince Muishkin, I believe? The gentleman to whom I had the honour of being introduced?"

"She is mad, insane—I assure you, she is mad," replied the prince in trembling tones, holding out both his hands mechanically towards the officer.

"I cannot boast of any such knowledge, of course, but I wished to know your name."

He bowed and retired without waiting for an answer.

Five seconds after the disappearance of the last actor in this scene, the police arrived. The whole episode had not lasted more than a couple of minutes. Some of the spectators had risen from their places, and departed altogether; some merely exchanged their seats for others a little further off; some were delighted with the occurrence, and talked and laughed over it for a long time.

In a word, the incident closed as such incidents do, and the band began to play again. The prince walked away after the Epanchin party. Had he thought of looking round to the left after he had been pushed so unceremoniously into the chair, he would have observed Aglaya standing some twenty yards away. She had stayed to watch the scandalous scene in spite of her mother's and sisters' anxious cries to her to come away.

Prince S. ran up to her and persuaded her, at last, to come home with them.

Lizabetha Prokofievna saw that she returned in such a state of agitation that it was doubtful whether she had even heard their calls. But only a couple of minutes later, when they had reached the park, Aglaya suddenly remarked, in her usual calm, indifferent voice:

"I wanted to see how the farce would end."

III.

The occurrence at the Vauxhall had filled both mother and daughters with something like horror. In their excitement Lizabetha Prokofievna and the girls were nearly running all the way home.

In her opinion there was so much disclosed and laid bare by the episode, that, in spite of the chaotic condition of her mind, she was able to feel more or less decided on certain points which, up to now, had been in a cloudy condition.

However, one and all of the party realized that something important had happened, and that, perhaps fortunately enough, something which had hitherto been enveloped in the obscurity of guess-work had now begun to come forth a little from the mists. In spite of Prince S.'s assurances and explanations, Evgenie Pavlovitch's real character and position were at last coming to light. He was publicly convicted of intimacy with "that creature." So thought Lizabetha Prokofievna and her two elder daughters.

But the real upshot of the business was that the number of riddles to be solved was augmented. The two girls, though rather irritated at their mother's exaggerated alarm and haste to depart from the scene, had been unwilling to worry her at first with questions.

Besides, they could not help thinking that their sister Aglaya probably knew more about the whole matter than both they and their mother put together.

Prince S. looked as black as night, and was silent and moody. Mrs. Epanchin did not say a word to him all the way home, and he did not seem to observe the fact. Adelaida tried to pump him a little by asking, "who was the uncle they were talking about, and what was it that had happened in Petersburg?" But he had merely muttered something disconnected about "making inquiries," and that "of course it was all nonsense." "Oh, of course," replied Adelaida, and asked no more questions. Aglaya, too, was very quiet; and the only remark she made on the way home was that they were "walking much too fast to be pleasant."

Once she turned and observed the prince hurrying after them. Noticing his anxiety to catch them up, she smiled ironically, and then looked back no more. At length, just as they neared the house, General Epanchin came out and met them; he had only just arrived from town.

His first word was to inquire after Evgenie Pavlovitch. But Lizabetha stalked past him, and neither looked at him nor answered his question.

He immediately judged from the faces of his daughters and Prince S. that there was a thunderstorm brewing, and he himself already bore evidences of unusual perturbation of mind.

He immediately button-holed Prince S., and standing at the front door, engaged in a whispered conversation with him. By the troubled aspect of both of them, when they entered the house, and approached Mrs. Epanchin, it was evident that they had been discussing very disturbing news.

Little by little the family gathered together upstairs in Lizabetha Prokofievna's apartments, and Prince Muishkin found himself alone on the verandah when he arrived. He settled himself in a corner and sat waiting, though he knew not what he expected. It never struck him that he had better go away, with all this disturbance in the house.

He seemed to have forgotten all the world, and to be ready to sit on where he was for years on end. From upstairs he caught sounds of excited conversation every now and then.

He could not say how long he sat there. It grew late and became quite dark.

Suddenly Aglaya entered the verandah. She seemed to be quite calm, though a little pale.

Observing the prince, whom she evidently did not expect to see there, alone in the corner, she smiled, and approached him:

"What are you doing there?" she asked.

The prince muttered something, blushed, and jumped up; but Aglaya immediately sat down beside him; so he reseated himself.

She looked suddenly, but attentively into his face, then at the window, as though thinking of something else, and then again at him.

"Perhaps she wants to laugh at me," thought the prince, "but no; for if she did she certainly would do so."

"Would you like some tea? I'll order some," she said, after a minute or two of silence.

"N-no thanks, I don't know—"

"Don't know! How can you not know? By-the-by, look here—if someone were to challenge you to a duel, what should you do? I wished to ask you this—some time ago—"

"Why? Nobody would ever challenge me to a duel!"

"But if they were to, would you be dreadfully frightened?"

"I dare say I should be—much alarmed!"

"Seriously? Then are you a coward?"

"N-no!—I don't think so. A coward is a man who is afraid and runs away; the man who is frightened but does not run away, is not quite a coward," said the prince with a smile, after a moment's thought.

"And you wouldn't run away?"

"No—I don't think I should run away," replied the prince, laughing outright at last at Aglaya's questions.

"Though I am a woman, I should certainly not run away for anything," said Aglaya, in a slightly pained voice. "However, I see you are laughing at me and twisting your face up as usual in order to make yourself look more interesting. Now tell me, they generally shoot at twenty paces, don't they? At ten, sometimes? I suppose if at ten they must be either wounded or killed, mustn't they?"

"I don't think they often kill each other at duels."

"They killed Pushkin that way."

"That may have been an accident."

"Not a bit of it; it was a duel to the death, and he was killed."

"The bullet struck so low down that probably his antagonist would never have aimed at that part of him—people never do; he would have aimed at his chest or head; so that probably the bullet hit him accidentally. I have been told this by competent authorities."

"Well, a soldier once told me that they were always ordered to aim at the middle of the body. So you see they don't aim at the chest or head; they aim lower on purpose. I asked some officer about this afterwards, and he said it was perfectly true."

"That is probably when they fire from a long distance."

"Can you shoot at all?"

"No, I have never shot in my life."

"Can't you even load a pistol?"

"No! That is, I understand how it's done, of course, but I have never done it."

"Then, you don't know how, for it is a matter that needs practice. Now listen and learn; in the first place buy good powder, not damp (they say it mustn't be at all damp, but very dry), some fine kind it is—you must ask for *pistol* powder, not the stuff they load cannons with. They say one makes the bullets oneself, somehow or other. Have you got a pistol?"

"No—and I don't want one," said the prince, laughing.

"Oh, what *nonsense!* You must buy one. French or English are the best, they say. Then take a little powder, about a thimbleful, or perhaps two, and pour it into the barrel. Better put plenty. Then push in a bit of felt (it *must* be felt, for some reason or other); you can easily get a bit off some old mattress, or off a door; it's used to keep the cold out. Well, when you have pushed the felt down, put the bullet in; do you hear now? The bullet last and the powder first, not the other way, or the pistol won't shoot. What are you laughing at? I wish you to buy a pistol and practise every day, and you must learn to hit a mark for *certain*; will you?"

The prince only laughed. Aglaya stamped her foot with annoyance.

Her serious air, however, during this conversation had surprised him considerably. He had a feeling that he ought to be asking her something, that there was something he wanted to find out far more important than how to load a pistol; but his thoughts had all scattered, and he was only aware that she was sitting by, him, and talking to him, and that he was looking at her; as to what she happened to be saying to him, that did not matter in the least.

The general now appeared on the verandah, coming from upstairs. He was on his way out, with an expression of determination on his face, and of preoccupation and worry also.

"Ah! Lef Nicolaievitch, it's you, is it? Where are you off to now?" he asked, oblivious of the fact that the prince had not showed the least sign of moving. "Come along with me; I want to say a word or two to you."

"*Au revoir*, then!" said Aglaya, holding out her hand to the prince.

It was quite dark now, and Muishkin could not see her face clearly, but a minute or two later, when he and the general had left the villa, he suddenly flushed up, and squeezed his right hand tightly.

It appeared that he and the general were going in the same direction. In spite of the lateness of the hour, the general was hurrying away to talk to someone upon some important subject. Meanwhile he talked incessantly but disconnectedly to the prince, and continually brought in the name of Lizabetha Prokofievna.

If the prince had been in a condition to pay more attention to what the general was saying, he would have discovered that the latter was desirous of drawing some information out of him, or indeed of asking him some question outright; but that he could not make up his mind to come to the point.

Muishkin was so absent, that from the very first he could not attend to a word the other was saying; and when the general suddenly stopped before him with some excited question, he was obliged to confess, ignominiously, that he did not know in the least what he had been talking about.

The general shrugged his shoulders.

"How strange everyone, yourself included, has become of late," said he. "I was telling you that I cannot in the least understand Lizabetha Prokofievna's ideas and agitations. She is in hysterics up there, and moans and says that we have been 'shamed and disgraced.' How? Why? When? By whom? I confess that I am very much to blame myself; I do not conceal the fact; but the conduct, the outrageous behaviour of this woman, must really be kept within limits, by the police if necessary, and I am just on my way now to talk the question over and make some arrangements. It can all be managed quietly and gently, even kindly, and without the slightest fuss or scandal. I foresee that the future is pregnant with events, and that there is much that needs explanation. There is intrigue in the wind; but if on one side nothing is known, on the other side nothing will be explained. If I have heard nothing about it, nor have *you*, nor *he*, nor *she*—who *has* heard about it, I should like to know? How *can* all this be explained except by the fact that half of it is mirage or moonshine, or some hallucination of that sort?"

"*She* is insane," muttered the prince, suddenly recollecting all that had passed, with a spasm of pain at his heart.

"I too had that idea, and I slept in peace. But now I see that their opinion is more correct. I do not believe in the theory of madness! The woman has no common sense; but she is not only not insane, she is artful to a degree. Her outburst of this evening about Evgenie's uncle proves that conclusively. It was *villainous*, simply jesuitical, and it was all for some special purpose."

"What about Evgenie's uncle?"

"My goodness, Lef Nicolaievitch, why, you can't have heard a single word I said! Look at me, I'm still trembling all over with the dreadful shock! It is that that kept me in town so late. Evgenie Pavlovitch's uncle—"

"Well?" cried the prince.

"Shot himself this morning, at seven o'clock. A respected, eminent old man of seventy; and exactly point for point as she described it; a sum of money, a considerable sum of government money, missing!"

"Why, how could she—"

"What, know of it? Ha, ha, ha! Why, there was a whole crowd round her the moment she appeared on the scenes here. You know what sort of people surround her nowadays, and solicit the honour of her 'acquaintance.' Of course she might easily have heard the news from someone coming from town. All Petersburg, if not all Pavlofsk, knows it by now. Look at the slyness of her observation about Evgenie's uniform! I mean, her remark that he had retired just in time! There's a venomous hint for you, if you like! No, no! there's no insanity there! Of course I refuse to believe that Evgenie Pavlovitch could have known beforehand of the catastrophe; that is, that at such and such a day at seven o'clock, and all that; but he might well have had a presentiment of the truth. And I—all of us—Prince S. and everybody, believed that he was to inherit a large fortune from this uncle. It's dreadful, horrible! Mind, I don't suspect Evgenie of anything, be quite clear on that point; but the thing is a little suspicious, nevertheless. Prince S. can't get over it. Altogether it is a very extraordinary combination of circumstances."

"What suspicion attaches to Evgenie Pavlovitch?"

"Oh, none at all! He has behaved very well indeed. I didn't mean to drop any sort of hint. His own fortune is intact, I believe. Lizabetha Prokofievna, of course, refuses to listen to anything. That's the worst of it all, these family catastrophes or quarrels, or whatever you like to call them. You know, prince, you are a friend of the family, so I don't mind telling you; it now appears that Evgenie Pavlovitch proposed to Aglaya a month ago, and was refused."

"Impossible!" cried the prince.

"Why? Do you know anything about it? Look here," continued the general, more agitated than ever, and trembling with excitement, "maybe I have been letting the cat out of the bag too freely with you, if so, it is because you are—that sort of man, you know! Perhaps you have some special information?"

"I know nothing about Evgenie Pavlovitch!" said the prince.

"Nor do I! They always try to bury me underground when there's anything going on; they don't seem to reflect that it is unpleasant to a man to be treated so! I won't stand it! We have just had a terrible scene!—mind, I speak to you as I would to my own son! Aglaya laughs at her mother. Her sisters guessed about Evgenie having proposed and been rejected, and told Lizabetha.

"I tell you, my dear fellow, Aglaya is such an extraordinary, such a self-willed, fantastical little creature, you wouldn't believe it! Every high quality, every brilliant trait of heart and mind, are to be found in her, and, with it all, so much caprice and mockery, such wild fancies—indeed, a little devil! She has just been laughing at her mother to her very face, and at her sisters, and at Prince S., and everybody—and of course she always laughs at me! You know I love the child—I love her even when she laughs at me, and I believe the wild little creature has a special fondness for me for that very reason. She is fonder of me than any of the others. I dare swear she has had a good laugh at *you* before now! You were having a quiet talk just now, I observed, after all the thunder and lightning upstairs. She was sitting with you just as though there had been no row at all."

The prince blushed painfully in the darkness, and closed his right hand tightly, but he said nothing.

"My dear good Prince Lef Nicolaievitch," began the general again, suddenly, "both I and Lizabetha Prokofievna—(who has begun to respect you once more, and me through you, goodness knows why!)—we both love you very sincerely, and esteem you, in spite of any appearances to the contrary. But you'll admit what a riddle it must have been for us when that calm, cold, little spitfire, Aglaya—(for she stood up to her mother and answered her questions with inexpressible contempt, and mine still more so, because, like a fool, I thought it my duty to assert myself as head of the family)—when Aglaya stood up of a sudden and informed us that 'that madwoman' (strangely enough, she used exactly the same expression as you did) 'has taken it into her head to marry me to Prince Lef Nicolaievitch, and therefore is doing her best to choke Evgenie Pavlovitch off, and rid the house of him.' That's what she said. She would not give the slightest explanation; she burst out laughing, banged the door, and went away. We all stood there with our mouths open. Well, I was told afterwards of your little passage with Aglaya this afternoon, and—and—dear prince—you are a good, sensible fellow, don't be angry if I speak out—she is laughing at you, my boy! She is enjoying herself like a child, at your expense, and therefore, since she is a child, don't be angry with her, and don't think anything of it. I assure you, she is simply making a fool of you, just as she does with one and all of us out of pure lack of something better to do. Well—good-bye! You know our feelings, don't you—our sincere feelings for yourself? They are unalterable, you know, dear boy, under all circumstances, but—Well, here we part; I must go down to the right. Rarely have I sat so uncomfortably in my saddle, as they say, as I now sit. And people talk of the charms of a country holiday!"

Left to himself at the cross-roads, the prince glanced around him, quickly crossed the road towards the lighted window of a neighbouring house, and unfolded a tiny scrap of paper which he had held clasped in his right hand during the whole of his conversation with the general.

He read the note in the uncertain rays that fell from the window. It was as follows:

"Tomorrow morning, I shall be at the green bench in the park at seven, and shall wait there for you. I have made up my mind to speak to you about a most important matter which closely concerns yourself.

"P.S.—I trust that you will not show this note to anyone. Though I am ashamed of giving you such instructions, I feel that I must do so, considering what you are. I therefore write the words, and blush for your simple character.

"P.P.S.—It is the same green bench that I showed you before. There! aren't you ashamed of yourself? I felt that it was necessary to repeat even that information."

The note was written and folded anyhow, evidently in a great hurry, and probably just before Aglaya had come down to the verandah.

In inexpressible agitation, amounting almost to fear, the prince slipped quickly away from the window, away from the light, like a frightened thief, but as he did so he collided violently with some gentleman who seemed to spring from the earth at his feet.

"I was watching for you, prince," said the individual.

"Is that you, Keller?" said the prince, in surprise.

"Yes, I've been looking for you. I waited for you at the Epanchins' house, but of course I could not come in. I dogged you from behind as you walked along with the general. Well, prince, here is Keller, absolutely at your service—command him!—ready to sacrifice himself—even to die in case of need."

"But-why?"

"Oh, why?—Of course you'll be challenged! That was young Lieutenant Moloftsoff. I know him, or rather of him; he won't pass an insult. He will take no notice of Rogojin and myself, and, therefore, you are the only one left to account for. You'll have to pay the piper, prince. He has been asking about you, and undoubtedly his friend will call on you tomorrow—perhaps he is at your house already. If you would do me the honour to have me for a second, prince, I should be happy. That's why I have been looking for you now."

"Duel! You've come to talk about a duel, too!" The prince burst out laughing, to the great astonishment of Keller. He laughed unrestrainedly, and Keller, who had been on pins and needles, and in a fever of excitement to offer himself as "second," was very near being offended.

"You caught him by the arms, you know, prince. No man of proper pride can stand that sort of treatment in public."

"Yes, and he gave me a fearful dig in the chest," cried the prince, still laughing. "What are we to fight about? I shall beg his pardon, that's all. But if we must fight—we'll fight! Let him have a shot at me, by all means; I should rather like it. Ha, ha, ha! I know how to load a pistol now; do you know how to load a pistol, Keller? First, you have to buy the powder, you know; it mustn't be wet, and it mustn't be that coarse stuff that they load cannons with—it must be pistol powder. Then you pour the powder in, and get hold of a bit of felt from some door, and then shove the bullet in. But don't shove the bullet in before the powder, because the thing wouldn't go off—do you hear, Keller, the thing wouldn't go off! Ha, ha, ha! Isn't that a grand reason, Keller, my friend, eh? Do you know, my dear fellow, I really must kiss you, and embrace you, this very moment. Ha, ha! How was it you so suddenly popped up in front of me as you did? Come to my house as soon as you can, and we'll have some champagne. We'll all get drunk! Do you know I have a dozen of champagne in Lebedeff's cellar? Lebedeff sold them to me the day after I arrived. I took the lot. We'll invite everybody! Are you going to do any sleeping tonight?"

"As much as usual, prince—why?"

"Pleasant dreams then—ha, ha!"

The prince crossed the road, and disappeared into the park, leaving the astonished Keller in a state of ludicrous wonder. He had never before seen the prince in such a strange condition of mind, and could not have imagined the possibility of it.

"Fever, probably," he said to himself, "for the man is all nerves, and this business has been a little too much for him. He is not *afraid*, that's clear; that sort never funks! H'm! champagne! That was an interesting item of news, at all events!—Twelve bottles! Dear me, that's a very respectable little stock indeed! I bet anything Lebedeff lent somebody money on deposit of this dozen of champagne. Hum! he's a nice fellow, is this prince! I like this sort of man. Well, I needn't be wasting time here, and if it's a case of champagne, why—there's no time like the present!"

That the prince was almost in a fever was no more than the truth. He wandered about the park for a long while, and at last came to himself in a lonely avenue. He was vaguely conscious that he had already paced this particular walk—from that large, dark tree to the bench at the other end—about a hundred yards altogether—at least thirty times backwards and forwards.

As to recollecting what he had been thinking of all that time, he could not. He caught himself, however, indulging in one thought which made him roar with laughter, though there was nothing really to laugh at in it; but he felt that he must laugh, and go on laughing.

It struck him that the idea of the duel might not have occurred to Keller alone, but that his lesson in the art of pistol-loading might have been not altogether accidental! "Pooh! nonsense!" he said to himself, struck by another thought, of a sudden. "Why, she was immensely surprised to find me there on the verandah, and laughed and talked about *tea*! And yet she had this little note in her hand, therefore she must have known that I was sitting there. So why was she surprised? Ha, ha, ha!"

He pulled the note out and kissed it; then paused and reflected. "How strange it all is! how strange!" he muttered, melancholy enough now. In moments of great joy, he invariably felt a sensation of melancholy come over him—he could not tell why.

He looked intently around him, and wondered why he had come here; he was very tired, so he approached the bench and sat down on it. Around him was profound silence; the music in the Vauxhall was over. The park seemed quite empty, though it was not, in reality, later than half-past eleven. It was a quiet, warm, clear night—a real Petersburg night of early June; but in the dense avenue, where he was sitting, it was almost pitch dark.

If anyone had come up at this moment and told him that he was in love, passionately in love, he would have rejected the idea with astonishment, and, perhaps, with irritation. And if anyone had added that Aglaya's note was a love-letter, and that it contained an appointment to a lover's rendezvous, he would have blushed with shame for the speaker, and, probably, have challenged him to a duel.

All this would have been perfectly sincere on his part. He had never for a moment entertained the idea of the possibility of this girl loving him, or even of such a thing as himself falling in love with her. The possibility of being loved himself, "a man like me," as he put it, he ranked among ridiculous suppositions. It appeared to him that it was simply a joke on Aglaya's part, if there really were anything in it at all; but that seemed to him quite natural. His preoccupation was caused by something different.

As to the few words which the general had let slip about Aglaya laughing at everybody, and at himself most of all—he entirely believed them. He did not feel the slightest sensation of offence; on the contrary, he was quite certain that it was as it should be.

His whole thoughts were now as to next morning early; he would see her; he would sit by her on that little green bench, and listen to how pistols were loaded, and look at her. He wanted nothing more.

The question as to what she might have to say of special interest to himself occurred to him once or twice. He did not doubt, for a moment, that she really had some such subject of conversation in store, but so very little interested in the matter was he that it did not strike him to wonder what it could be. The crunch of gravel on the path suddenly caused him to raise his head.

A man, whose face it was difficult to see in the gloom, approached the bench, and sat down beside him. The prince peered into his face, and recognized the livid features of Rogojin.

"I knew you'd be wandering about somewhere here. I didn't have to look for you very long," muttered the latter between his teeth.

It was the first time they had met since the encounter on the staircase at the hotel.

Painfully surprised as he was at this sudden apparition of Rogojin, the prince, for some little while, was unable to collect his thoughts. Rogojin, evidently, saw and understood the impression he had made; and though he seemed more or less confused at first, yet he began talking with what looked like assumed ease and freedom. However, the prince soon changed his mind on this score, and thought that there was not only no affectation of indifference, but that Rogojin was not even particularly agitated. If there were a little apparent awkwardness, it was only in his words and gestures. The man could not change his heart.

"How did you—find me here?" asked the prince for the sake of saying something.

"Keller told me (I found him at your place) that you were in the park. 'Of course he is!' I thought."

"Why so?" asked the prince uneasily.

Rogojin smiled, but did not explain.

"I received your letter, Lef Nicolaievitch—what's the good of all that?—It's no use, you know. I've come to you from *her*,—she bade me tell you that she must see you, she has something to say to you. She told me to find you today."

"I'll come tomorrow. Now I'm going home—are you coming to my house?"

"Why should I? I've given you the message.—Goodbye!"

"Won't you come?" asked the prince in a gentle voice.

"What an extraordinary man you are! I wonder at you!" Rogojin laughed sarcastically.

"Why do you hate me so?" asked the prince, sadly. "You know yourself that all you suspected is quite unfounded. I felt you were still angry with me, though. Do you know why? Because you tried to kill me—that's why you can't shake off your wrath against me. I tell you that I only remember the Parfen Rogojin with whom I exchanged crosses, and vowed brotherhood. I wrote you this in yesterday's letter, in order that you might forget all that madness on your part, and that you might not feel called to talk about it when we met. Why do you avoid me? Why do you hold your hand back from me? I tell you again, I consider all that has passed a delirium, an insane dream. I can understand all you did, and all you felt that day, as if it were myself. What you were then imagining was not the case, and could never be the case. Why, then, should there be anger between us?"

"You don't know what anger is!" laughed Rogojin, in reply to the prince's heated words.

He had moved a pace or two away, and was hiding his hands behind him.

"No, it is impossible for me to come to your house again," he added slowly.

"Why? Do you hate me so much as all that?"

"I don't love you, Lef Nicolaievitch, and, therefore, what would be the use of my coming to see you? You are just like a child—you want a plaything, and it must be taken out and given you—and then you don't know how to work it. You are simply repeating all you said in your letter, and what's the use? Of course I believe every word you say, and I know perfectly well that you neither did or ever can deceive me in any way, and yet, I don't love you. You write that you've forgotten everything, and only remember your brother Parfen, with whom you exchanged crosses, and that you don't remember anything about the Rogojin who aimed a knife at your throat. What do you know about my feelings, eh?" (Rogojin laughed disagreeably.) "Here you are holding out your brotherly forgiveness to me for a thing that I have perhaps never repented of in the slightest degree. I did not think of it again all that evening; all my thoughts were centred on something else—"

"Not think of it again? Of course you didn't!" cried the prince. "And I dare swear that you came straight away down here to Pavlofsk to listen to the music and dog her about in the crowd, and stare at her, just as you did today. There's nothing surprising in that! If you hadn't been in that condition of mind that you could think of nothing but one subject, you would, probably, never have raised your knife against me. I had a presentiment of what you would do, that day, ever since I saw you first in the morning. Do you know yourself what you looked like? I knew you would try to murder me even at the very moment when we exchanged crosses. What did you take me to your mother for? Did you think to stay your hand by doing so? Perhaps you did not put your thoughts into words, but you and I were thinking the same thing, or feeling the same thing looming over us, at the same moment. What should you think of me now if you had not raised your knife to me—the knife which God averted from my throat? I would have been guilty of suspecting you all the same—and you would have intended the murder all the same; therefore we should have been mutually guilty in any case. Come, don't frown; you needn't laugh at me, either. You say you haven't 'repented.' Repented! You probably couldn't, if you were to try; you dislike me too much for that. Why, if I were an angel of light, and as innocent before you as a babe, you would still loathe me if you believed that *she* loved me, instead of loving yourself. That's jealousy—that is the real jealousy.

"But do you know what I have been thinking out during this last week, Parfen? I'll tell you. What if she loves you now better than anyone? And what if she torments you *because* she loves you, and in proportion to her love for you, so she torments you the more? She won't tell you this, of course; you must have eyes to see. Why do you suppose she consents to marry you? She must have a reason, and that reason she will tell you some day. Some women desire the kind of love you give her, and she is probably one of these. Your love and your wild nature impress her. Do you know that a woman is capable of driving a man crazy almost, with her cruelties and mockeries, and feels not one single pang of regret, because she looks at him and says to herself, 'There! I'll torment this man nearly into his grave, and then, oh! how I'll compensate him for it all with my love!'"

Rogojin listened to the end, and then burst out laughing:

"Why, prince, I declare you must have had a taste of this sort of thing yourself—haven't you? I have heard tell of something of the kind, you know; is it true?"

"What? What can you have heard?" said the prince, stammering.

Rogojin continued to laugh loudly. He had listened to the prince's speech with curiosity and some satisfaction. The speaker's impulsive warmth had surprised and even comforted him.

"Why, I've not only heard of it; I see it for myself," he said. "When have you ever spoken like that before? It wasn't like yourself, prince. Why, if I hadn't heard this report about you, I should never have come all this way into the park—at midnight, too!"

"I don't understand you in the least, Parfen."

"Oh, *she* told me all about it long ago, and tonight I saw for myself. I saw you at the music, you know, and whom you were sitting with. She swore to me yesterday, and again today, that you are madly in love with Aglaya Ivanovna. But that's all the same to me, prince, and it's not my affair at all; for if you have ceased to love *her*, *she* has not ceased to love *you*. You know, of course, that she wants to marry you to that girl? She's sworn to it! Ha, ha! She says to me, 'Until then I won't marry you. When they go to church, we'll go too—and not before.' What on earth does she mean by it? I don't know, and I never did. Either she loves you without limits or—yet, if she loves you, why does she wish to marry you to another girl? She says, 'I want to see him happy,' which is to say—she loves you."

"I wrote, and I say to you once more, that she is not in her right mind," said the prince, who had listened with anguish to what Rogojin said.

"Goodness knows—you may be wrong there! At all events, she named the day this evening, as we left the gardens. 'In three weeks,' says she, 'and perhaps sooner, we shall be married.' She swore to it, took off her cross and kissed it. So it all depends upon you now, prince, You see! Ha, ha!"

"That's all madness. What you say about me, Parfen, never can and never will be. Tomorrow, I shall come and see you—"

"How can she be mad," Rogojin interrupted, "when she is sane enough for other people and only mad for you? How can she write letters to *her*, if she's mad? If she were insane they would observe it in her letters."

"What letters?" said the prince, alarmed.

"She writes to *her*—and the girl reads the letters. Haven't you heard?—You are sure to hear; she's sure to show you the letters herself."

"I won't believe this!" cried the prince.

"Why, prince, you've only gone a few steps along this road, I perceive. You are evidently a mere beginner. Wait a bit! Before long, you'll have your own detectives, you'll watch day and night, and you'll know every little thing that goes on there—that is, if—"

"Drop that subject, Rogojin, and never mention it again. And listen: as I have sat here, and talked, and listened, it has suddenly struck me that tomorrow is my birthday. It must be about twelve o'clock, now; come home with me—do, and we'll see the day in! We'll have some wine, and you shall wish me—I don't know what—but you, especially you, must wish me a good wish, and I shall wish you full happiness in return. Otherwise, hand me my cross back again. You didn't return it to me next day. Haven't you got it on now?"

"Yes, I have," said Rogojin.

"Come along, then. I don't wish to meet my new year without you—my new life, I should say, for a new life is beginning for me. Did you know, Parfen, that a new life had begun for me?"

"I see for myself that it is so—and I shall tell *her*. But you are not quite yourself, Lef Nicolaievitch."

IV.

The prince observed with great surprise, as he approached his villa, accompanied by Rogojin, that a large number of people were assembled on his verandah, which was brilliantly lighted up. The company seemed merry and were noisily laughing and talking—even quarrelling, to judge from the sounds. At all events they were clearly enjoying themselves, and the prince observed further on closer investigation—that all had been drinking champagne. To judge from the lively condition of some of the party, it was to be supposed that a considerable quantity of champagne had been consumed already.

All the guests were known to the prince; but the curious part of the matter was that they had all arrived on the same evening, as though with one accord, although he had only himself recollected the fact that it was his birthday a few moments since.

"You must have told somebody you were going to trot out the champagne, and that's why they are all come!" muttered Rogojin, as the two entered the verandah. "We know all about that! You've only to whistle and they come up in shoals!" he continued, almost angrily. He was doubtless thinking of his own late experiences with his boon companions.

All surrounded the prince with exclamations of welcome, and, on hearing that it was his birthday, with cries of congratulation and delight; many of them were very noisy.

The presence of certain of those in the room surprised the prince vastly, but the guest whose advent filled him with the greatest wonder—almost amounting to alarm—was Evgenie Pavlovitch. The prince could not believe his eyes when he beheld the latter, and could not help thinking that something was wrong.

Lebedeff ran up promptly to explain the arrival of all these gentlemen. He was himself somewhat intoxicated, but the prince gathered from his long-winded periods that the party had assembled quite naturally, and accidentally.

First of all Hippolyte had arrived, early in the evening, and feeling decidedly better, had determined to await the prince on the verandah. There Lebedeff had joined him, and his household had followed—that is, his daughters and General Ivolgin. Burdovsky had brought Hippolyte, and stayed on with him. Gania and Ptitsin had dropped in accidentally later on; then came Keller, and he and Colia insisted on having champagne. Evgenie Pavlovitch had only dropped in half an hour or so ago. Lebedeff had served the champagne readily.

"My own though, prince, my own, mind," he said, "and there'll be some supper later on; my daughter is getting it ready now. Come and sit down, prince, we are all waiting for you, we want you with us. Fancy what we have been discussing! You know the question, 'to be or not to be,'—out of Hamlet! A contemporary theme! Quite up-to-date! Mr. Hippolyte has been eloquent to a degree. He won't go to bed, but he has only drunk a little champagne, and that can't do him any harm. Come along, prince, and settle the question. Everyone is waiting for you, sighing for the light of your luminous intelligence..."

The prince noticed the sweet, welcoming look on Vera Lebedeff's face, as she made her way towards him through the crowd. He held out his hand to her. She took it, blushing with delight, and wished him "a happy life from that day forward." Then she ran off to the kitchen, where her presence was necessary to help in the preparations for supper. Before the prince's arrival she had spent some time on the terrace, listening eagerly to the conversation, though the visitors, mostly under the influence of wine, were discussing abstract subjects far beyond her comprehension. In the next room her younger sister lay on a wooden chest, sound asleep, with her mouth wide open; but the boy, Lebedeff's son, had taken up his position close beside Colia and Hippolyte, his face lit up with interest in the conversation of his father and the rest, to which he would willingly have listened for ten hours at a stretch.

"I have waited for you on purpose, and am very glad to see you arrive so happy," said Hippolyte, when the prince came forward to press his hand, immediately after greeting Vera.

"And how do you know that I am 'so happy'?

"I can see it by your face! Say 'how do you do' to the others, and come and sit down here, quick—I've been waiting for you!" he added, accentuating the fact that he had waited. On the prince's asking, "Will it not be injurious to you to sit out so late?" he replied that he could not believe that he had thought himself dying three days or so ago, for he never had felt better than this evening.

Burdovsky next jumped up and explained that he had come in by accident, having escorted Hippolyte from town. He murmured that he was glad he had "written nonsense" in his letter, and then pressed the prince's hand warmly and sat down again.

The prince approached Evgenie Pavlovitch last of all. The latter immediately took his arm.

"I have a couple of words to say to you," he began, "and those on a very important matter; let's go aside for a minute or two."

"Just a couple of words!" whispered another voice in the prince's other ear, and another hand took his other arm. Muishkin turned, and to his great surprise observed a red, flushed face and a droll-looking figure which he recognized at once as that of Ferdishenko. Goodness knows where he had turned up from!

"Do you remember Ferdishenko?" he asked.

"Where have you dropped from?" cried the prince.

"He is sorry for his sins now, prince," cried Keller. "He did not want to let you know he was here; he was hidden over there in the corner,—but he repents now, he feels his guilt."

"Why, what has he done?"

"I met him outside and brought him in—he's a gentleman who doesn't often allow his friends to see him, of late—but he's sorry now."

"Delighted, I'm sure!—I'll come back directly, gentlemen,—sit down there with the others, please,—excuse me one moment," said the host, getting away with difficulty in order to follow Evgenie.

"You are very gay here," began the latter, "and I have had quite a pleasant half-hour while I waited for you. Now then, my dear Lef Nicolaievitch, this is what's the matter. I've arranged it all with Moloftsoff, and have just come in to relieve your mind on that score. You need be under no apprehensions. He was very sensible, as he should be, of course, for I think he was entirely to blame himself."

"What Moloftsoff?"

"The young fellow whose arms you held, don't you know? He was so wild with you that he was going to send a friend to you tomorrow morning."

"What nonsense!"

"Of course it is nonsense, and in nonsense it would have ended, doubtless; but you know these fellows, they—"

"Excuse me, but I think you must have something else that you wished to speak about, Evgenie Pavlovitch?"

"Of course, I have!" said the other, laughing. "You see, my dear fellow, tomorrow, very early in the morning, I must be off to town about this unfortunate business (my uncle, you know!). Just imagine, my dear sir, it is all true—word for word—and, of course, everybody knew it excepting myself. All this has been such a blow to me that I have not managed to call in at the Epanchins'. Tomorrow I shall not see them either, because I shall be in town. I may not be here for three days or more; in a word, my affairs are a little out of gear. But though my town business is, of course, most pressing, still I determined not to go away until I had seen you, and had a clear understanding with you upon certain points; and that without loss of time. I will wait now, if you will allow me, until the company departs; I may just as well, for I have nowhere else to go to, and I shall certainly not do any sleeping tonight; I'm far too excited. And finally, I must confess that, though I know it is bad form to pursue a man in this way, I have come to beg your friendship, my dear prince. You are an unusual sort of a person; you don't lie at every step, as some men do; in fact, you don't lie at all, and there is a matter in which I need a true and sincere friend, for I really may claim to be among the number of bona fide unfortunates just now."

He laughed again.

"But the trouble is," said the prince, after a slight pause for reflection, "that goodness only knows when this party will break up. Hadn't we better stroll into the park? I'll excuse myself, there's no danger of their going away."

"No, no! I have my reasons for wishing them not to suspect us of being engaged in any specially important conversation. There are gentry present who are a little too much interested in us. You are not aware of that perhaps, prince? It will be a great deal better if they see that we are friendly just in an ordinary way. They'll all go in a couple of hours, and then I'll ask you to give me twenty minutes-half an hour at most."

"By all means! I assure you I am delighted—you need not have entered into all these explanations. As for your remarks about friendship with me—thanks, very much indeed. You must excuse my being a little absent this evening. Do you know, I cannot somehow be attentive to anything just now?"

"I see, I see," said Evgenie, smiling gently. His mirth seemed very near the surface this evening.

"What do you see?" said the prince, startled.

"I don't want you to suspect that I have simply come here to deceive you and pump information out of you!" said Evgenie, still smiling, and without making any direct reply to the question.

"Oh, but I haven't the slightest doubt that you did come to pump me," said the prince, laughing himself, at last; "and I dare say you are quite prepared to deceive me too, so far as that goes. But what of that? I'm not afraid of you; besides, you'll hardly believe it, I feel as though I really didn't care a scrap one way or the other, just now!—And—and—and as you are a capital fellow, I am convinced of that, I dare say we really shall end by being good friends. I like you very much Evgenie Pavlovitch; I consider you a very good fellow indeed."

"Well, in any case, you are a most delightful man to have to deal with, be the business what it may," concluded Evgenie. "Come along now, I'll drink a glass to your health. I'm charmed to have entered into alliance with you. By-the-by," he added suddenly, "has this young Hippolyte come down to stay with you?"

"Yes."

"He's not going to die at once, I should think, is he?"

"Why?"

"Oh, I don't know. I've been half an hour here with him, and he—"

Hippolyte had been waiting for the prince all this time, and had never ceased looking at him and Evgenie Pavlovitch as they conversed in the corner. He became much excited when they approached the table once more. He was disturbed in his mind, it seemed; perspiration stood in large drops on his forehead; in his gleaming eyes it was easy to read impatience and agitation; his gaze wandered from face to face of those present, and from object to object in the room, apparently without aim. He had taken a part, and an animated one, in the noisy conversation of the company; but his animation was clearly the outcome of fever. His talk was almost incoherent; he would break off in the middle of a sentence which he had begun with great interest, and forget what he had been saying. The prince discovered to his dismay that Hippolyte had been allowed to drink two large glasses of champagne; the one now standing by him being the third. All this he found out afterwards; at the moment he did not notice anything, very particularly.

"Do you know I am specially glad that today is your birthday!" cried Hippolyte.

"Why?"

"You'll soon see. D'you know I had a feeling that there would be a lot of people here tonight? It's not the first time that my presentiments have been fulfilled. I wish I had known it was your birthday, I'd have brought you a present—perhaps I have got a present for you! Who knows? Ha, ha! How long is it now before daylight?"

"Not a couple of hours," said Ptitsin, looking at his watch. "What's the good of daylight now? One can read all night in the open air without it," said someone.

"The good of it! Well, I want just to see a ray of the sun," said Hippolyte. "Can one drink to the sun's health, do you think, prince?"

"Oh, I dare say one can; but you had better be calm and lie down, Hippolyte—that's much more important."

"You are always preaching about resting; you are a regular nurse to me, prince. As soon as the sun begins to 'resound' in the sky—what poet said that? 'The sun resounded in the sky.' It is beautiful, though there's no sense in it!—then we will go to bed. Lebedeff, tell me, is the sun the source of life? What does the source, or 'spring,' of life really mean in the Apocalypse? You have heard of the 'Star that is called Wormwood,' prince?"

"I have heard that Lebedeff explains it as the railroads that cover Europe like a net."

Everybody laughed, and Lebedeff got up abruptly.

"No! Allow me, that is not what we are discussing!" he cried, waving his hand to impose silence. "Allow me! With these gentlemen... all these gentlemen," he added, suddenly addressing the prince, "on certain points... that is..." He thumped the table repeatedly, and the laughter increased. Lebedeff was in his usual evening condition, and had just ended a long and scientific argument, which had left him excited and irritable. On such occasions he was apt to evince a supreme contempt for his opponents.

"It is not right! Half an hour ago, prince, it was agreed among us that no one should interrupt, no one should laugh, that each person was to express his thoughts freely; and then at the end, when everyone had spoken, objections might be made, even by the atheists. We chose the general as president. Now without some such rule and order, anyone might be shouted down, even in the loftiest and most profound thought...."

"Go on! Go on! Nobody is going to interrupt you!" cried several voices.

"Speak, but keep to the point!"

"What is this 'star'?" asked another.

"I have no idea," replied General Ivolgin, who presided with much gravity.

"I love these arguments, prince," said Keller, also more than half intoxicated, moving restlessly in his chair. "Scientific and political." Then, turning suddenly towards Evgenie Pavlovitch, who was seated near him: "Do you know, I simply adore reading the accounts of the debates in the English parliament. Not that the discussions themselves interest me; I am not a politician, you know; but it delights me to see how they address each other 'the noble lord who agrees with me,' 'my honourable opponent who astonished Europe with his proposal,' 'the noble viscount sitting opposite'—all these expressions, all this parliamentarism of a free people, has an enormous attraction for me. It fascinates me, prince. I have always been an artist in the depths of my soul, I assure you, Evgenie Pavlovitch."

"Do you mean to say," cried Gania, from the other corner, "do you mean to say that railways are accursed inventions, that they are a source of ruin to humanity, a poison poured upon the earth to corrupt the springs of life?"

Gavrila Ardalionovitch was in high spirits that evening, and it seemed to the prince that his gaiety was mingled with triumph. Of course he was only joking with Lebedeff, meaning to egg him on, but he grew excited himself at the same time.

"Not the railways, oh dear, no!" replied Lebedeff, with a mixture of violent anger and extreme enjoyment. "Considered alone, the railways will not pollute the springs of life, but as a whole they are accursed. The whole tendency of our latest centuries, in its scientific and materialistic aspect, is most probably accursed."

"Is it certainly accursed?... or do you only mean it might be? That is an important point," said Evgenie Pavlovitch.

"It is accursed, certainly accursed!" replied the clerk, vehemently.

"Don't go so fast, Lebedeff; you are much milder in the morning," said Ptitsin, smiling.

"But, on the other hand, more frank in the evening! In the evening sincere and frank," repeated Lebedeff, earnestly. "More candid, more exact, more honest, more honourable, and... although I may show you my weak side, I challenge you all; you atheists, for instance! How are you going to save the world? How find a straight road of progress, you men of science, of industry, of cooperation, of trades unions, and all the rest? How are you going to save it, I say? By what? By credit? What is credit? To what will credit lead you?"

"You are too inquisitive," remarked Evgenie Pavlovitch.

"Well, anyone who does not interest himself in questions such as this is, in my opinion, a mere fashionable dummy."

"But it will lead at least to solidarity, and balance of interests," said Ptitsin.

"You will reach that with nothing to help you but credit? Without recourse to any moral principle, having for your foundation only individual selfishness, and the satisfaction of material desires? Universal peace, and the happiness of mankind as a whole, being the result! Is it really so that I may understand you, sir?"

"But the universal necessity of living, of drinking, of eating—in short, the whole scientific conviction that this necessity can only be satisfied by universal co-operation and the solidarity of interests—is, it seems to me, a strong enough idea to serve as a basis, so to speak, and a 'spring of life,' for humanity in future centuries," said Gavrila Ardalionovitch, now thoroughly roused.

"The necessity of eating and drinking, that is to say, solely the instinct of self-preservation..."

"Is not that enough? The instinct of self-preservation is the normal law of humanity..."

"Who told you that?" broke in Evgenie Pavlovitch.

"It is a law, doubtless, but a law neither more nor less normal than that of destruction, even self-destruction. Is it possible that the whole normal law of humanity is contained in this sentiment of self-preservation?"

"Ah!" cried Hippolyte, turning towards Evgenie Pavlovitch, and looking at him with a queer sort of curiosity.

Then seeing that Radomski was laughing, he began to laugh himself, nudged Colia, who was sitting beside him, with his elbow, and again asked what time it was. He even pulled Colia's silver watch out of his hand, and looked at it eagerly. Then, as if he had forgotten everything, he stretched himself out on the sofa, put his hands behind his head, and looked up at the sky. After a minute or two he got up and came back to the table to listen to Lebedeff's outpourings, as the latter passionately commentated on Evgenie Pavlovitch's paradox.

"That is an artful and traitorous idea. A smart notion," vociferated the clerk, "thrown out as an apple of discord. But it is just. You are a scoffer, a man of the world, a cavalry officer, and, though not without brains, you do not realize how profound is your thought, nor how true. Yes, the laws of self-preservation and of self-destruction are equally powerful in this world. The devil will hold his empire over humanity until a limit of time which is still unknown. You laugh? You do not believe in the devil? Scepticism as to the devil is a French idea, and it is also a frivolous idea. Do you know who the devil is? Do you know his name? Although you don't know his name you make a mockery of his form, following the example of Voltaire. You sneer at his hoofs, at his tail, at his horns—all of them the produce of your imagination! In reality the devil is a great and terrible spirit, with neither hoofs, nor tail, nor horns; it is you who have endowed him with these attributes! But... he is not the question just now!"

"How do you know he is not the question now?" cried Hippolyte, laughing hysterically.

"Another excellent idea, and worth considering!" replied Lebedeff. "But, again, that is not the question. The question at this moment is whether we have not weakened 'the springs of life' by the extension..."

"Of railways?" put in Colia eagerly.

"Not railways, properly speaking, presumptuous youth, but the general tendency of which railways may be considered as the outward expression and symbol. We hurry and push and hustle, for the good of humanity! 'The world is becoming too noisy, too commercial!' groans some solitary thinker. 'Undoubtedly it is, but the noise of waggons bearing bread to starving humanity is of more value than tranquillity of soul,' replies another triumphantly, and passes on with an air of pride. As for me, I don't believe in these waggons bringing bread to humanity. For, founded on no moral principle, these may well, even in the act of carrying bread to humanity, coldly exclude a considerable portion of humanity from enjoying it; that has been seen more than once.

"What, these waggons may coldly exclude?" repeated someone.

"That has been seen already," continued Lebedeff, not deigning to notice the interruption. "Malthus was a friend of humanity, but, with ill-founded moral principles, the friend of humanity is the devourer of humanity, without mentioning his pride; for, touch the vanity of one of these numberless philanthropists, and to avenge his self-esteem, he will be ready at once to set fire to the whole globe; and to tell the truth, we are all more or less like that. I, perhaps, might be the first to set a light to the fuel, and then run away. But, again, I must repeat, that is not the question."

"What is it then, for goodness' sake?"

"He is boring us!"

"The question is connected with the following anecdote of past times; for I am obliged to relate a story. In our times, and in our country, which I hope you love as much as I do, for as far as I am concerned, I am ready to shed the last drop of my blood..."

"Go on! Go on!"

"In our dear country, as indeed in the whole of Europe, a famine visits humanity about four times a century, as far as I can remember; once in every twenty-five years. I won't swear to this being the exact figure, but anyhow they have become comparatively rare."

"Comparatively to what?"

"To the twelfth century, and those immediately preceding and following it. We are told by historians that widespread famines occurred in those days every two or three years, and such was the condition of things that men actually had recourse to cannibalism, in secret, of course. One of these cannibals, who had reached a good age, declared of his own free will that during the course of his long and miserable life he had personally killed and eaten, in the most profound secrecy, sixty monks, not to mention several children; the number of the latter he thought was about six, an insignificant total when compared with the enormous mass of ecclesiastics consumed by him. As to adults, laymen that is to say, he had never touched them."

The president joined in the general outcry.

"That's impossible!" said he in an aggrieved tone. "I am often discussing subjects of this nature with him, gentlemen, but for the most part he talks nonsense enough to make one deaf: this story has no pretence of being true."

"General, remember the siege of Kars! And you, gentlemen, I assure you my anecdote is the naked truth. I may remark that reality, although it is governed by invariable law, has at times a resemblance to falsehood. In fact, the truer a thing is the less true it sounds."

"But could anyone possibly eat sixty monks?" objected the scoffing listeners.

"It is quite clear that he did not eat them all at once, but in a space of fifteen or twenty years: from that point of view the thing is comprehensible and natural..."

"Natural?"

"And natural," repeated Lebedeff with pedantic obstinacy. "Besides, a Catholic monk is by nature excessively curious; it would be quite easy therefore to entice him into a wood, or some secret place, on false pretences, and there to deal with him as said. But I do not dispute in the least that the number of persons consumed appears to denote a spice of greediness."

"It is perhaps true, gentlemen," said the prince, quietly. He had been listening in silence up to that moment without taking part in the conversation, but laughing heartily with the others from time to time. Evidently he was delighted to see that everybody was amused, that everybody was talking at once, and even that everybody was drinking. It seemed as if he were not intending to speak at all, when suddenly he intervened in such a serious voice that everyone looked at him with interest.

"It is true that there were frequent famines at that time, gentlemen. I have often heard of them, though I do not know much history. But it seems to me that it must have been so. When I was in Switzerland I used to look with astonishment at the many ruins of feudal castles perched on the top of steep and rocky heights, half a mile at least above sea-level, so that to reach them one had to climb many miles of stony tracks. A castle, as you know, is, a kind of mountain of stones—a dreadful, almost an impossible, labour! Doubtless the builders were all poor men, vassals, and had to pay heavy taxes, and to keep up the priesthood. How, then, could they provide for themselves, and when had they time to plough and sow their fields? The greater number must, literally, have died of starvation. I have sometimes asked myself how it was that these communities were not utterly swept off the face of the earth, and how they could possibly survive. Lebedeff is not mistaken, in my opinion, when he says that there were cannibals in those days, perhaps in considerable numbers; but I do not understand why he should have dragged in the monks, nor what he means by that."

"It is undoubtedly because, in the twelfth century, monks were the only people one could eat; they were the fat, among many lean," said Gavrila Ardalionovitch.

"A brilliant idea, and most true!" cried Lebedeff, "for he never even touched the laity. Sixty monks, and not a single layman! It is a terrible idea, but it is historic, it is statistic; it is indeed one of those facts which enables an intelligent historian to reconstruct the physiognomy of a special epoch, for it brings out this further point with mathematical accuracy, that the clergy were in those days sixty times richer and more flourishing than the rest of humanity and perhaps sixty times fatter also..."

"You are exaggerating, you are exaggerating, Lebedeff!" cried his hearers, amid laughter.

"I admit that it is an historic thought, but what is your conclusion?" asked the prince.

He spoke so seriously in addressing Lebedeff, that his tone contrasted quite comically with that of the others. They were very nearly laughing at him, too, but he did not notice it.

"Don't you see he is a lunatic, prince?" whispered Evgenie Pavlovitch in his ear. "Someone told me just now that he is a bit touched on the subject of lawyers, that he has a mania for making speeches and intends to pass the examinations. I am expecting a splendid burlesque now."

"My conclusion is vast," replied Lebedeff, in a voice like thunder. "Let us examine first the psychological and legal position of the criminal. We see that in spite of the difficulty of finding other food, the accused, or, as we may say, my client, has often during his peculiar life exhibited signs of repentance, and of wishing to give up this clerical diet. Incontrovertible facts prove this assertion. He has eaten five or six children, a relatively insignificant number, no doubt, but remarkable enough from another point of view. It is manifest that, pricked by remorse—for my client is religious, in his way, and has a conscience, as I shall prove later—and desiring to extenuate his sin as far as possible, he has tried six times at least to substitute lay nourishment for clerical. That this was merely an experiment we can hardly doubt: for if it had been only a question of gastronomic variety, six would have been too few; why only six? Why not thirty? But if we regard it as an experiment, inspired by the fear of committing new sacrilege, then this number six becomes intelligible. Six attempts to calm his remorse, and the pricking of his conscience, would amply suffice, for these attempts could scarcely have been happy ones. In my humble opinion, a child is too small; I should say, not sufficient; which would result in four or five times more lay children than monks being required in a given time. The sin, lessened on the one hand, would therefore be increased on the other, in quantity, not in quality. Please understand, gentlemen, that in reasoning thus, I am taking the point of view which might have been taken by a criminal of the middle ages. As for myself, a man of the late nineteenth century, I, of course, should reason differently; I say so plainly, and therefore you need not jeer at me nor mock me, gentlemen. As for you, general, it is still more unbecoming on your part. In the second place, and giving my own personal opinion, a child's flesh is not a satisfying diet; it is too insipid, too sweet; and the criminal, in making these experiments, could have satisfied neither his conscience nor his appetite. I am about to conclude, gentlemen; and my conclusion contains a reply to one of the most important questions of that day and of our own! This criminal ended at last by denouncing himself to the clergy, and giving himself up to justice. We cannot but ask, remembering the penal system of that day, and the tortures that awaited him—the wheel, the stake, the fire!—we cannot but ask, I repeat, what induced him to accuse himself of this crime? Why did he not simply stop short at the number sixty, and keep his secret until his last breath? Why could he not simply leave the monks alone, and go into the desert to repent? Or why not become a monk himself? That is where the puzzle comes in! There must have been something stronger than the stake or the fire, or even than the habits of twenty years! There must have been an idea more powerful than all the calamities and sorrows of this world, famine or torture, leprosy or plague—an idea which entered into the heart, directed and enlarged the springs of life, and made even that hell supportable to humanity! Show me a force, a power like that, in this our century of vices and railways! I might say, perhaps, in our century of steamboats and railways, but I repeat in our century of vices and railways, because I am drunk but truthful! Show me a single idea which unites men nowadays with half the strength that it had in those centuries, and dare to maintain that the 'springs of life' have not been polluted and weakened beneath this 'star,' beneath this network in which men are entangled! Don't talk to me about your prosperity, your riches, the rarity of famine, the rapidity of the means of transport! There is more of riches, but less of force. The idea uniting heart and soul to heart and soul exists no more. All is loose, soft, limp—we are all of us limp.... Enough, gentlemen! I have done. That is not the question. No, the question is now, excellency, I believe, to sit down to the banquet you are about to provide for us!"

Lebedeff had roused great indignation in some of his auditors (it should be remarked that the bottles were constantly uncorked during his speech); but this unexpected conclusion calmed even the most turbulent spirits. "That's how a clever barrister makes a good point!" said he, when speaking of his peroration later on. The visitors began to laugh and chatter once again; the committee left their seats, and stretched their legs on the terrace. Keller alone was still disgusted with Lebedeff and his speech; he turned from one to another, saying in a loud voice:

"He attacks education, he boasts of the fanaticism of the twelfth century, he makes absurd grimaces, and added to that he is by no means the innocent he makes himself out to be. How did he get the money to buy this house, allow me to ask?"

In another corner was the general, holding forth to a group of hearers, among them Ptitsin, whom he had buttonholed. "I have known," said he, "a real interpreter of the Apocalypse, the late Gregory Semeonovitch Burmistroff, and he—he pierced the heart like a fiery flash! He began by putting on his spectacles, then he opened a large black book; his white beard, and his two medals on his breast, recalling acts of charity, all added to his impressiveness. He began in a stern voice, and before him generals, hard men of the world, bowed down, and ladies fell to the ground fainting. But this one here—he ends by announcing a banquet! That is not the real thing!"

Ptitsin listened and smiled, then turned as if to get his hat; but if he had intended to leave, he changed his mind. Before the others had risen from the table, Gania had suddenly left off drinking, and pushed away his glass, a dark shadow seemed to come over his face. When they all rose, he went and sat down by Rogojin. It might have been believed that quite friendly relations existed between them. Rogojin, who had also seemed on the point of going away now sat motionless, his head bent, seeming to have forgotten his intention. He had drunk no wine, and appeared absorbed in reflection. From time to time he raised his eyes, and examined everyone present; one might have imagined that he was expecting something very important to himself, and that he had decided to wait for it. The prince had taken two or three glasses of champagne, and seemed cheerful. As he rose he noticed Evgenie Pavlovitch, and, remembering the appointment he had made with him, smiled pleasantly. Evgenie Pavlovitch made a sign with his head towards Hippolyte, whom he was attentively watching. The invalid was fast asleep, stretched out on the sofa.

"Tell me, prince, why on earth did this boy intrude himself upon you?" he asked, with such annoyance and irritation in his voice that the prince was quite surprised. "I wouldn't mind laying odds that he is up to some mischief."

"I have observed," said the prince, "that he seems to be an object of very singular interest to you, Evgenie Pavlovitch. Why is it?"

"You may add that I have surely enough to think of, on my own account, without him; and therefore it is all the more surprising that I cannot tear my eyes and thoughts away from his detestable physiognomy."

"Oh, come! He has a handsome face."

"Why, look at him—look at him now!"

The prince glanced again at Evgenie Pavlovitch with considerable surprise.

V.

Hippolyte, who had fallen asleep during Lebedeff's discourse, now suddenly woke up, just as though someone had jogged him in the side. He shuddered, raised himself on his arm, gazed around, and grew very pale. A look almost of terror crossed his face as he recollected.

"What! are they all off? Is it all over? Is the sun up?" He trembled, and caught at the prince's hand. "What time is it? Tell me, quick, for goodness' sake! How long have I slept?" he added, almost in despair, just as though he had overslept something upon which his whole fate depended.

"You have slept seven or perhaps eight minutes," said Evgenie Pavlovitch.

Hippolyte gazed eagerly at the latter, and mused for a few moments.

"Oh, is that all?" he said at last. "Then I—"

He drew a long, deep breath of relief, as it seemed. He realized that all was not over as yet, that the sun had not risen, and that the guests had merely gone to supper. He smiled, and two hectic spots appeared on his cheeks.

"So you counted the minutes while I slept, did you, Evgenie Pavlovitch?" he said, ironically. "You have not taken your eyes off me all the evening—I have noticed that much, you see! Ah, Rogojin! I've just been dreaming about him, prince," he added, frowning. "Yes, by the by," starting up, "where's the orator? Where's Lebedeff? Has he finished? What did he talk about? Is it true, prince, that you once declared that 'beauty would save the world'? Great Heaven! The prince says that beauty saves the world! And I declare that he only has such playful ideas because he's in love! Gentlemen, the prince is in love. I guessed it the moment he came in. Don't blush, prince; you make me sorry for you. What beauty saves the world? Colia told me that you are a zealous Christian; is it so? Colia says you call yourself a Christian."

The prince regarded him attentively, but said nothing.

"You don't answer me; perhaps you think I am very fond of you?" added Hippolyte, as though the words had been drawn from him.

"No, I don't think that. I know you don't love me."

"What, after yesterday? Wasn't I honest with you?"

"I knew yesterday that you didn't love me."

"Why so? why so? Because I envy you, eh? You always think that, I know. But do you know why I am saying all this? Look here! I must have some more champagne—pour me out some, Keller, will you?"

"No, you're not to drink any more, Hippolyte. I won't let you." The prince moved the glass away.

"Well perhaps you're right," said Hippolyte, musing. "They might say—yet, devil take them! what does it matter?—prince, what can it matter what people will say of us *then*, eh? I believe I'm half asleep. I've had such a dreadful dream—I've only just remembered it. Prince, I don't wish you such dreams as that, though sure enough, perhaps, I *don't* love you. Why wish a man evil, though you do not love him, eh? Give me your hand—let me press it sincerely. There—you've given me your hand—you must feel that I *do* press it sincerely, don't you? I don't think I shall drink any more. What time is it? Never mind, I know the time. The time has come, at all events. What! they are laying supper over there, are they? Then this table is free? Capital, gentlemen! I—hem! these gentlemen are not listening. Prince, I will just read over an article I have here. Supper is more interesting, of course, but—"

Here Hippolyte suddenly, and most unexpectedly, pulled out of his breast-pocket a large sealed paper. This imposing-looking document he placed upon the table before him.

The effect of this sudden action upon the company was instantaneous. Evgenie Pavlovitch almost bounded off his chair in excitement. Rogojin drew nearer to the table with a look on his face as if he knew what was coming. Gania came nearer too; so did Lebedeff and the others—the paper seemed to be an object of great interest to the company in general.

"What have you got there?" asked the prince, with some anxiety.

"At the first glimpse of the rising sun, prince, I will go to bed. I told you I would, word of honour! You shall see!" cried Hippolyte. "You think I'm not capable of opening this packet, do you?" He glared defiantly round at the audience in general.

The prince observed that he was trembling all over.

"None of us ever thought such a thing!" Muishkin replied for all. "Why should you suppose it of us? And what are you going to read, Hippolyte? What is it?"

"Yes, what is it?" asked others. The packet sealed with red wax seemed to attract everyone, as though it were a magnet.

"I wrote this yesterday, myself, just after I saw you, prince, and told you I would come down here. I wrote all day and all night, and finished it this morning early. Afterwards I had a dream."

"Hadn't we better hear it tomorrow?" asked the prince timidly.

"Tomorrow 'there will be no more time!'" laughed Hippolyte, hysterically. "You needn't be afraid; I shall get through the whole thing in forty minutes, at most an hour! Look how interested everybody is! Everybody has drawn near. Look! look at them all staring at my sealed packet! If I hadn't sealed it up it wouldn't have been half so effective! Ha, ha! that's mystery, that is! Now then, gentlemen, shall I break the seal or not? Say the word; it's a mystery, I tell you—a secret! Prince, you know who said there would be 'no more time'? It was the great and powerful angel in the Apocalypse."

"Better not read it now," said the prince, putting his hand on the packet.

"No, don't read it!" cried Evgenie suddenly. He appeared so strangely disturbed that many of those present could not help wondering.

"Reading? None of your reading now!" said somebody; "it's supper-time." "What sort of an article is it? For a paper? Probably it's very dull," said another. But the prince's timid gesture had impressed even Hippolyte.

"Then I'm not to read it?" he whispered, nervously. "Am I not to read it?" he repeated, gazing around at each face in turn. "What are you afraid of, prince?" he turned and asked the latter suddenly.

"What should I be afraid of?"

"Has anyone a coin about them? Give me a twenty-copeck piece, somebody!" And Hippolyte leapt from his chair.

"Here you are," said Lebedeff, handing him one; he thought the boy had gone mad.

"Vera Lukianovna," said Hippolyte, "toss it, will you? Heads, I read, tails, I don't."

Vera Lebedeff tossed the coin into the air and let it fall on the table.

It was "heads."

"Then I read it," said Hippolyte, in the tone of one bowing to the fiat of destiny. He could not have grown paler if a verdict of death had suddenly been presented to him.

"But after all, what is it? Is it possible that I should have just risked my fate by tossing up?" he went on, shuddering; and looked round him again. His eyes had a curious expression of sincerity. "That is an astonishing psychological fact," he cried, suddenly addressing the prince, in a tone of the most intense surprise. "It is... it is something quite inconceivable, prince," he repeated with growing animation, like a man regaining consciousness. "Take note of it, prince, remember it; you collect, I am told, facts concerning capital punishment... They told me so. Ha, ha! My God, how absurd!" He sat down on the sofa, put his elbows on the table, and laid his head on his hands. "It is shameful—though what does it matter to me if it is shameful?

"Gentlemen, gentlemen! I am about to break the seal," he continued, with determination. "I—I—of course I don't insist upon anyone listening if they do not wish to."

With trembling fingers he broke the seal and drew out several sheets of paper, smoothed them out before him, and began sorting them.

"What on earth does all this mean? What's he going to read?" muttered several voices. Others said nothing; but one and all sat down and watched with curiosity. They began to think something strange might really be about to happen. Vera stood and trembled behind her father's chair, almost in tears with fright; Colia was nearly as much alarmed as she was. Lebedeff jumped up and put a couple of candles nearer to Hippolyte, so that he might see better.

"Gentlemen, this—you'll soon see what this is," began Hippolyte, and suddenly commenced his reading.

"It's headed, 'A Necessary Explanation,' with the motto, '*Après moi le déluge!*' Oh, deuce take it all! Surely I can never have seriously written such a silly motto as that? Look here, gentlemen, I beg to give notice that all this is very likely terrible nonsense. It is only a few ideas of mine. If you think that there is anything mysterious coming—or in a word—"

"Better read on without any more beating about the bush," said Gania.

"Affectation!" remarked someone else.

"Too much talk," said Rogojin, breaking the silence for the first time.

Hippolyte glanced at him suddenly, and when their eye, met Rogojin showed his teeth in a disagreeable smile, and said the following strange words: "That's not the way to settle this business, my friend; that's not the way at all."

Of course nobody knew what Rogojin meant by this; but his words made a deep impression upon all. Everyone seemed to see in a flash the same idea.

As for Hippolyte, their effect upon him was astounding. He trembled so that the prince was obliged to support him, and would certainly have cried out, but that his voice seemed to have entirely left him for the moment. For a minute or two he could not speak at all, but panted and stared at Rogojin. At last he managed to ejaculate:

"Then it was *you* who came—*you—you?*"

"Came where? What do you mean?" asked Rogojin, amazed. But Hippolyte, panting and choking with excitement, interrupted him violently.

"*You* came to me last week, in the night, at two o'clock, the day I was with you in the morning! Confess it was you!"

"Last week? In the night? Have you gone cracked, my good friend?"

Hippolyte paused and considered a moment. Then a smile of cunning—almost triumph—crossed his lips.

"It was you," he murmured, almost in a whisper, but with absolute conviction. "Yes, it was you who came to my room and sat silently on a chair at my window for a whole hour—more! It was between one and two at night; you rose and went out at about three. It was you, you! Why you should have frightened me so, why you should have wished to torment me like that, I cannot tell—but you it was."

There was absolute hatred in his eyes as he said this, but his look of fear and his trembling had not left him.

"You shall hear all this directly, gentlemen. I—I—listen!"

He seized his paper in a desperate hurry; he fidgeted with it, and tried to sort it, but for a long while his trembling hands could not collect the sheets together. "He's either mad or delirious," murmured Rogojin. At last he began.

For the first five minutes the reader's voice continued to tremble, and he read disconnectedly and unevenly; but gradually his voice strengthened. Occasionally a violent fit of coughing stopped him, but his animation grew with the progress of the reading—as did also the disagreeable impression which it made upon his audience,—until it reached the highest pitch of excitement.

Here is the article.

MY NECESSARY EXPLANATION.

"*Après moi le déluge.*

"Yesterday morning the prince came to see me. Among other things he asked me to come down to his villa. I knew he would come and persuade me to this step, and that he would adduce the argument that it would be easier for me to die' among people and green trees,'—as he expressed it. But today he did not say 'die,' he said 'live.' It is pretty much the same to me, in my position, which he says. When I asked him why he made such a point of his 'green trees,' he told me, to my astonishment, that he had heard that last time I was in Pavlofsk I had said that I had come 'to have a last look at the trees.'

"When I observed that it was all the same whether one died among trees or in front of a blank brick wall, as here, and that it was not worth making any fuss over a fortnight, he agreed at once. But he insisted that the good air at Pavlofsk and the greenness would certainly cause a physical change for the better, and that my excitement, and my *dreams*, would be perhaps relieved. I remarked to him, with a smile, that he spoke like a materialist, and he answered that he had always been one. As he never tells a lie, there must be something in his words. His smile is a pleasant one. I have had a good look at him. I don't know whether I like him or not; and I have no time to waste

397

over the question. The hatred which I felt for him for five months has become considerably modified, I may say, during the last month. Who knows, perhaps I am going to Pavlofsk on purpose to see him! But why do I leave my chamber? Those who are sentenced to death should not leave their cells. If I had not formed a final resolve, but had decided to wait until the last minute, I should not leave my room, or accept his invitation to come and die at Pavlofsk. I must be quick and finish this explanation before tomorrow. I shall have no time to read it over and correct it, for I must read it tomorrow to the prince and two or three witnesses whom I shall probably find there.

"As it will be absolutely true, without a touch of falsehood, I am curious to see what impression it will make upon me myself at the moment when I read it out. This is my 'last and solemn'—but why need I call it that? There is no question about the truth of it, for it is not worthwhile lying for a fortnight; a fortnight of life is not itself worth having, which is a proof that I write nothing here but pure truth.

("N.B.—Let me remember to consider; am I mad at this moment, or not? or rather at these moments? I have been told that consumptives sometimes do go out of their minds for a while in the last stages of the malady. I can prove this tomorrow when I read it out, by the impression it makes upon the audience. I must settle this question once and for all, otherwise I can't go on with anything.)

"I believe I have just written dreadful nonsense; but there's no time for correcting, as I said before. Besides that, I have made myself a promise not to alter a single word of what I write in this paper, even though I find that I am contradicting myself every five lines. I wish to verify the working of the natural logic of my ideas tomorrow during the reading—whether I am capable of detecting logical errors, and whether all that I have meditated over during the last six months be true, or nothing but delirium.

"If two months since I had been called upon to leave my room and the view of Meyer's wall opposite, I verily believe I should have been sorry. But now I have no such feeling, and yet I am leaving this room and Meyer's brick wall *for ever*. So that my conclusion, that it is not worth while indulging in grief, or any other emotion, for a fortnight, has proved stronger than my very nature, and has taken over the direction of my feelings. But is it so? Is it the case that my nature is conquered entirely? If I were to be put on the rack now, I should certainly cry out. I should not say that it is not worth while to yell and feel pain because I have but a fortnight to live.

"But is it true that I have but a fortnight of life left to me? I know I told some of my friends that Doctor B. had informed me that this was the case; but I now confess that I lied; B. has not even seen me. However, a week ago, I called in a medical student, Kislorodoff, who is a Nationalist, an Atheist, and a Nihilist, by conviction, and that is why I had him. I needed a man who would tell me the bare truth without any humbug or ceremony—and so he did—indeed, almost with pleasure (which I thought was going a little too far).

"Well, he plumped out that I had about a month left me; it might be a little more, he said, under favourable circumstances, but it might also be considerably less. According to his opinion I might die quite suddenly—tomorrow, for instance—there had been such cases. Only a day or two since a young lady at Colomna who suffered from consumption, and was about on a par with myself in the march of the disease, was going out to market to buy provisions, when she suddenly felt faint, lay down on the sofa, gasped once, and died.

"Kislorodoff told me all this with a sort of exaggerated devil-may-care negligence, and as though he did me great honour by talking to me so, because it showed that he considered me the same sort of exalted Nihilistic being as himself, to whom death was a matter of no consequence whatever, either way.

"At all events, the fact remained—a month of life and no more! That he is right in his estimation I am absolutely persuaded.

"It puzzles me much to think how on earth the prince guessed yesterday that I have had bad dreams. He said to me, 'Your excitement and dreams will find relief at Pavlofsk.' Why did he say 'dreams'? Either he is a doctor, or else he is a man of exceptional intelligence and wonderful powers of observation. (But that he is an 'idiot,' at bottom there can be no doubt whatever.) It so happened that just before he arrived I had a delightful little dream; one of a kind that I have hundreds of just now. I had fallen asleep about an hour before he came in, and dreamed that I was in some room, not my own. It was a large room, well furnished, with a cupboard, chest of drawers, sofa, and my bed, a fine wide bed covered with a silken counterpane. But I observed in the room a dreadful-looking creature, a sort of monster. It was a little like a scorpion, but was not a scorpion, but far more horrible, and especially so, because there are no creatures anything like it in nature, and because it had appeared to me for a purpose, and bore some mysterious signification. I looked at the beast well; it was brown in colour and had a shell; it was a crawling kind of reptile, about eight inches long, and narrowed down from the head, which was about a couple of fingers in width, to the end of the tail, which came to a fine point. Out of its trunk, about a couple of inches below its head, came two legs at an angle of forty-five degrees, each about three inches long, so that the beast looked like a trident from above. It had eight hard needle-like whiskers coming out from different parts of its body; it went along like a snake, bending its body about in spite of the shell it wore, and its motion was very quick and very horrible to look at. I was dreadfully afraid it would sting me; somebody had told me, I thought, that it was venomous; but what tormented me most of all was the wondering and wondering as to who had sent it into my room, and what was the mystery which I felt it contained.

"It hid itself under the cupboard and under the chest of drawers, and crawled into the corners. I sat on a chair and kept my legs tucked under me. Then the beast crawled quietly across the room and disappeared somewhere near my chair. I looked about for it in terror, but I still hoped that as my feet were safely tucked away it would not be able to touch me.

"Suddenly I heard behind me, and about on a level with my head, a sort of rattling sound. I turned sharp round and saw that the brute had crawled up the wall as high as the level of my face, and that its horrible tail, which was moving incredibly fast from side to side, was actually touching my hair! I jumped up—and it disappeared. I did not dare lie down on my bed for fear it should creep under my pillow. My mother came into the room, and some friends of hers. They began to hunt for the reptile and were more composed than I was; they did not seem to be afraid of it. But they did not understand as I did.

"Suddenly the monster reappeared; it crawled slowly across the room and made for the door, as though with some fixed intention, and with a slow movement that was more horrible than ever.

"Then my mother opened the door and called my dog, Norma. Norma was a great Newfoundland, and died five years ago.

"She sprang forward and stood still in front of the reptile as if she had been turned to stone. The beast stopped too, but its tail and claws still moved about. I believe animals are incapable of feeling supernatural fright—if I have been rightly informed,—but at this moment there appeared to me to be something more than ordinary about Norma's terror, as though it must be supernatural; and as though she felt, just as I did myself, that this reptile was connected with some mysterious secret, some fatal omen.

"Norma backed slowly and carefully away from the brute, which followed her, creeping deliberately after her as though it intended to make a sudden dart and sting her.

"In spite of Norma's terror she looked furious, though she trembled in all her limbs. At length she slowly bared her terrible teeth, opened her great red jaws, hesitated—took courage, and seized the beast in her mouth. It seemed to try to dart out of her jaws twice, but Norma caught at it and half swallowed it as it was escaping. The shell cracked in her teeth; and the tail and legs stuck out of her mouth and shook about in a horrible manner. Suddenly Norma gave a piteous whine; the reptile had bitten her tongue. She opened her mouth wide with the pain, and I saw the beast lying across her tongue, and out of its body, which was almost bitten in two, came a hideous white-looking substance, oozing out into Norma's mouth; it was of the consistency of a crushed black-beetle just then I awoke and the prince entered the room."

"Gentlemen!" said Hippolyte, breaking off here, "I have not done yet, but it seems to me that I have written down a great deal here that is unnecessary,—this dream—"

"You have indeed!" said Gania.

"There is too much about myself, I know, but—" As Hippolyte said this his face wore a tired, pained look, and he wiped the sweat off his brow.

"Yes," said Lebedeff, "you certainly think a great deal too much about yourself."

"Well—gentlemen—I do not force anyone to listen! If any of you are unwilling to sit it out, please go away, by all means!"

"He turns people out of a house that isn't his own," muttered Rogojin.

"Suppose we all go away?" said Ferdishenko suddenly.

Hippolyte clutched his manuscript, and gazing at the last speaker with glittering eyes, said: "You don't like me at all!" A few laughed at this, but not all.

"Hippolyte," said the prince, "give me the papers, and go to bed like a sensible fellow. We'll have a good talk tomorrow, but you really mustn't go on with this reading; it is not good for you!"

"How can I? How can I?" cried Hippolyte, looking at him in amazement. "Gentlemen! I was a fool! I won't break off again. Listen, everyone who wants to!"

He gulped down some water out of a glass standing near, bent over the table, in order to hide his face from the audience, and recommenced.

"The idea that it is not worth while living for a few weeks took possession of me a month ago, when I was told that I had four weeks to live, but only partially so at that time. The idea quite overmastered me three days since, that evening at Pavlofsk. The first time that I felt really impressed with this thought was on the terrace at the prince's, at the very moment when I had taken it into my head to make a last trial of life. I wanted to see people and trees (I believe I said so myself), I got excited, I maintained Burdovsky's rights, 'my neighbour!'—I dreamt that one and all would open their arms, and embrace me, that there would be an indescribable exchange of forgiveness between us all! In a word, I behaved like a fool, and then, at that very same instant, I felt my 'last conviction.' I ask myself now how I could have waited six months for that conviction! I knew that I had a disease that spares no one, and I really had no illusions; but the more I realized my condition, the more I clung to life; I wanted to live at any price. I confess I might well have resented that blind, deaf fate, which, with no apparent reason, seemed to have decided to crush me like a fly; but why did I not stop at resentment? Why did I begin to live, knowing that it was not worthwhile to begin? Why did I attempt to do what I knew to be an impossibility? And yet I could not even read a book to the end; I had given up reading. What is the good of reading, what is the good of learning anything, for just six months? That thought has made me throw aside a book more than once.

"Yes, that wall of Meyer's could tell a tale if it liked. There was no spot on its dirty surface that I did not know by heart. Accursed wall! and yet it is dearer to me than all the Pavlofsk trees!—That is—it *would* be dearer if it were not all the same to me, now!

"I remember now with what hungry interest I began to watch the lives of other people—interest that I had never felt before! I used to wait for Colia's arrival impatiently, for I was so ill myself, then, that I could not leave the house. I so threw myself into every little detail of news, and took so much interest in every report and rumour, that I believe I became a regular gossip! I could not understand, among other things, how all these people—with so much life in and before them—do not become *rich*—and I don't understand it now. I remember being told of a poor wretch I once knew, who had died of hunger. I was almost beside myself with rage! I believe if I could have resuscitated him I would have done so for the sole purpose of murdering him!

"Occasionally I was so much better that I could go out; but the streets used to put me in such a rage that I would lock myself up for days rather than go out, even if I were well enough to do so! I could not bear to see all those preoccupied, anxious-looking creatures continuously surging along the streets past me! Why are they always anxious? What is the meaning of their eternal care and worry? It is their wickedness, their perpetual detestable malice—that's what it is—they are all full of malice, malice!

"Whose fault is it that they are all miserable, that they don't know how to live, though they have fifty or sixty years of life before them? Why did that fool allow himself to die of hunger with sixty years of unlived life before him?

"And everyone of them shows his rags, his toil-worn hands, and yells in his wrath: 'Here are we, working like cattle all our lives, and always as hungry as dogs, and there are others who do not work, and are fat and rich!' The eternal refrain! And side by side with them trots along some wretched fellow who has known better days, doing light porter's work from morn to night for a living, always blubbering and saying that 'his wife died because he had no money to buy medicine with,' and his children dying of cold and hunger, and his eldest daughter gone to the bad, and so on. Oh! I have no pity and no patience for these fools of people. Why can't they be Rothschilds? Whose fault is it that a man has not got millions of money like Rothschild? If he has life, all this must be in his power! Whose fault is it that he does not know how to live his life?

"Oh! it's all the same to me now—*now!* But at that time I would soak my pillow at night with tears of mortification, and tear at my blanket in my rage and fury. Oh, how I longed at that time to be turned out—*me*, eighteen years old, poor, half-clothed, turned out into the street, quite alone, without lodging, without work, without a crust of bread, without relations, without a single acquaintance, in some large town—hungry, beaten (if you like), but in good health—and *then* I would show them—

"What would I show them?

"Oh, don't think that I have no sense of my own humiliation! I have suffered already in reading so far. Which of you all does not think me a fool at this moment—a young fool who knows nothing of life—forgetting that to live as I have lived these last six months is to live longer than grey-haired old men. Well, let them laugh, and say it is all nonsense, if they please. They may say it is all fairy-tales, if they like; and I have spent whole nights telling myself fairy-tales. I remember them all. But how can I tell fairy-tales now? The time for them is over. They amused me when I found that there was not even time for me to learn the Greek grammar, as I wanted to do. 'I shall die before I get to the syntax,' I thought at the first page—and threw the book under the table. It is there still, for I forbade anyone to pick it up.

"If this 'Explanation' gets into anybody's hands, and they have patience to read it through, they may consider me a madman, or a schoolboy, or, more likely, a man condemned to die, who thought it only natural to conclude that all men, excepting himself, esteem life far too lightly, live it far too carelessly and lazily, and are, therefore, one and all, unworthy of it. Well, I affirm that my reader is wrong again, for my convictions have nothing to do with my sentence of death. Ask them, ask any one of them, or all of them, what they mean by happiness! Oh, you may be perfectly sure that if Columbus was happy, it was not after he had discovered America, but when he was discovering it! You may be quite sure that he reached the culminating point of his happiness three days before he saw the New World with his actual eyes, when his mutinous sailors wanted to tack about, and return to Europe! What did the New World matter after all? Columbus had hardly seen it when he died, and in reality he was entirely ignorant of what he had discovered. The important thing is life—life and nothing else! What is any 'discovery' whatever compared with the incessant, eternal discovery of life?

"But what is the use of talking? I'm afraid all this is so commonplace that my confession will be taken for a schoolboy exercise—the work of some ambitious lad writing in the hope of his work 'seeing the light'; or perhaps my readers will say that 'I had perhaps something to say, but did not know how to express it.'

"Let me add to this that in every idea emanating from genius, or even in every serious human idea—born in the human brain—there always remains something—some sediment—which cannot be expressed to others, though one wrote volumes and lectured upon it for five-and-thirty years. There is always a something, a remnant, which will never come out from your brain, but will remain there with you, and you alone, for ever and ever, and you will die, perhaps, without having imparted what may be the very essence of your idea to a single living soul.

"So that if I cannot now impart all that has tormented me for the last six months, at all events you will understand that, having reached my 'last convictions,' I must have paid a very dear price for them. That is what I wished, for reasons of my own, to make a point of in this my 'Explanation.'

"But let me resume."

VI.

"I will not deceive you. 'Reality' got me so entrapped in its meshes now and again during the past six months, that I forgot my 'sentence' (or perhaps I did not wish to think of it), and actually busied myself with affairs.

"A word as to my circumstances. When, eight months since, I became very ill, I threw up all my old connections and dropped all my old companions. As I was always a gloomy, morose sort of individual, my friends easily forgot me; of course, they would have forgotten me all the same, without that excuse. My position at home was solitary enough. Five months ago I separated myself entirely from the family, and no one dared enter my room except at stated times, to clean and tidy it, and so on, and to bring me my meals. My mother dared not disobey me; she kept the children quiet, for my sake, and beat them if they dared to make any noise and disturb me. I so often complained of them that I should think they must be very fond, indeed, of me by this time. I think I must have tormented 'my faithful Colia' (as I called him) a good deal too. He tormented me of late; I could see that he always bore my tempers as though he had determined to 'spare the poor invalid.' This annoyed me, naturally. He seemed to have taken it into his head to imitate the prince in Christian meekness! Surikoff, who lived above us, annoyed me, too. He was so miserably poor, and I used to prove to him that he had no one to blame but himself for his poverty. I used to be so angry that I think I frightened him eventually, for he stopped coming to see me. He was a most meek and humble fellow, was Surikoff. (N.B.—They say that meekness is a great power. I must ask the prince about this, for the expression is his.) But I remember one day in March, when I went up to his lodgings to see whether it was true that one of his children had been starved and frozen to death, I began to hold forth to him about his poverty being his own fault, and, in the course of my remarks, I accidentally smiled at the corpse of his child. Well, the poor wretch's lips began to tremble, and he caught me by the shoulder, and pushed me to the door. 'Go out,' he said, in a whisper. I went out, of course, and I declare I *liked* it. I liked it at the very moment when I was turned out. But his words filled me with a strange sort of feeling of disdainful pity for him whenever I thought of them—a feeling which I did not in the least desire to entertain. At the very moment of the insult (for I admit that I did insult him, though I did not mean to), this man could not lose his temper. His lips had trembled, but I swear it was not with rage. He had taken me by the arm, and said, 'Go out,' without the least anger. There was dignity, a great deal of dignity, about him, and it was so inconsistent with the look of him that, I assure you, it was quite comical. But there was no anger. Perhaps he merely began to despise me at that moment.

"Since that time he has always taken off his hat to me on the stairs, whenever I met him, which is a thing he never did before; but he always gets away from me as quickly as he can, as though he felt confused. If he did despise me, he despised me 'meekly,' after his own fashion.

"I dare say he only took his hat off out of fear, as it were, to the son of his creditor; for he always owed my mother money. I thought of having an explanation with him, but I knew that if I did, he would begin to apologize in a minute or two, so I decided to let him alone.

"Just about that time, that is, the middle of March, I suddenly felt very much better; this continued for a couple of weeks. I used to go out at dusk. I like the dusk, especially in March, when the night frost begins to harden the day's puddles, and the gas is burning.

"Well, one night in the Shestilavochnaya, a man passed me with a paper parcel under his arm. I did not take stock of him very carefully, but he seemed to be dressed in some shabby summer dust-coat, much too light for the season. When he was opposite the lamp-post, some ten yards away, I observed something fall out of his pocket. I hurried forward to pick it up, just in time, for an old wretch in a long kaftan rushed up too. He did not dispute the matter, but glanced at what was in my hand and disappeared.

"It was a large old-fashioned pocket-book, stuffed full; but I guessed, at a glance, that it had anything in the world inside it, except money.

"The owner was now some forty yards ahead of me, and was very soon lost in the crowd. I ran after him, and began calling out; but as I knew nothing to say excepting 'hey!' he did not turn round. Suddenly he turned into the gate of a house to the left; and when I darted in after him, the gateway was so dark that I could see nothing whatever. It was one of those large houses built in small tenements, of which there must have been at least a hundred.

"When I entered the yard I thought I saw a man going along on the far side of it; but it was so dark I could not make out his figure.

"I crossed to that corner and found a dirty dark staircase. I heard a man mounting up above me, some way higher than I was, and thinking I should catch him before his door would be opened to him, I rushed after him. I heard a door open and shut on the fifth storey, as I panted along; the stairs were narrow, and the steps innumerable, but at last I reached the door I thought the right one. Some moments passed before I found the bell and got it to ring.

"An old peasant woman opened the door; she was busy lighting the 'samovar' in a tiny kitchen. She listened silently to my questions, did not understand a word, of course, and opened another door leading into a little bit of a room, low and scarcely furnished at all, but with a large, wide bed in it, hung with curtains. On this bed lay one Terentich, as the woman called him, drunk, it appeared to me. On the table was an end of candle in an iron candlestick, and a half-bottle of vodka, nearly finished. Terentich muttered something to me, and signed towards the next room. The old woman had disappeared, so there was nothing for me to do but to open the door indicated. I did so, and entered the next room.

"This was still smaller than the other, so cramped that I could scarcely turn round; a narrow single bed at one side took up nearly all the room. Besides the bed there were only three common chairs, and a wretched old kitchen-table standing before a small sofa. One could hardly squeeze through between the table and the bed.

"On the table, as in the other room, burned a tallow candle-end in an iron candlestick; and on the bed there whined a baby of scarcely three weeks old. A pale-looking woman was dressing the child, probably the mother; she looked as though she had not as yet got over the trouble of childbirth, she seemed so weak and was so carelessly dressed. Another child, a little girl of about three years old, lay on the sofa, covered over with what looked like a man's old dress-coat.

"At the table stood a man in his shirt sleeves; he had thrown off his coat; it lay upon the bed; and he was unfolding a blue paper parcel in which were a couple of pounds of bread, and some little sausages.

"On the table along with these things were a few old bits of black bread, and some tea in a pot. From under the bed there protruded an open portmanteau full of bundles of rags. In a word, the confusion and untidiness of the room were indescribable.

"It appeared to me, at the first glance, that both the man and the woman were respectable people, but brought to that pitch of poverty where untidiness seems to get the better of every effort to cope with it, till at last they take a sort of bitter satisfaction in it. When I entered the room, the man, who had entered but a moment before me, and was still unpacking his parcels, was saying something to his wife in an excited manner. The news was apparently bad, as usual, for the woman began whimpering. The man's face seemed tome to be refined and even pleasant. He was dark-complexioned, and about twenty-eight years of age; he wore black whiskers, and his lip and chin were shaved. He looked morose, but with a sort of pride of expression. A curious scene followed.

"There are people who find satisfaction in their own touchy feelings, especially when they have just taken the deepest offence; at such moments they feel that they would rather be offended than not. These easily-ignited natures, if they are wise, are always full of remorse afterwards, when they reflect that they have been ten times as angry as they need have been.

"The gentleman before me gazed at me for some seconds in amazement, and his wife in terror; as though there was something alarmingly extraordinary in the fact that anyone could come to see them. But suddenly he fell upon me almost with fury; I had had no time to mutter more than a couple of words; but he had doubtless observed that I was decently dressed and, therefore, took deep offence because I had dared enter his den so unceremoniously, and spy out the squalor and untidiness of it.

"Of course he was delighted to get hold of someone upon whom to vent his rage against things in general.

"For a moment I thought he would assault me; he grew so pale that he looked like a woman about to have hysterics; his wife was dreadfully alarmed.

"'How dare you come in so? Be off!' he shouted, trembling all over with rage and scarcely able to articulate the words. Suddenly, however, he observed his pocketbook in my hand.

"'I think you dropped this,' I remarked, as quietly and drily as I could. (I thought it best to treat him so.) For some while he stood before me in downright terror, and seemed unable to understand. He then suddenly grabbed at his side-pocket, opened his mouth in alarm, and beat his forehead with his hand.

"'My God!' he cried, 'where did you find it? How?' I explained in as few words as I could, and as drily as possible, how I had seen it and picked it up; how I had run after him, and called out to him, and how I had followed him upstairs and groped my way to his door.

"'Gracious Heaven!' he cried, 'all our papers are in it! My dear sir, you little know what you have done for us. I should have been lost—lost!'

"I had taken hold of the door-handle meanwhile, intending to leave the room without reply; but I was panting with my run upstairs, and my exhaustion came to a climax in a violent fit of coughing, so bad that I could hardly stand.

"I saw how the man dashed about the room to find me an empty chair, how he kicked the rags off a chair which was covered up by them, brought it to me, and helped me to sit down; but my cough went on for another three minutes or so. When I came to myself he was sitting by me on another chair, which he had also cleared of the rubbish by throwing it all over the floor, and was watching me intently.

"'I'm afraid you are ill?' he remarked, in the tone which doctors use when they address a patient. 'I am myself a medical man' (he did not say 'doctor'), with which words he waved his hands towards the room and its contents as though in protest at his present condition. 'I see that you—'

"'I'm in consumption,' I said laconically, rising from my seat.

"He jumped up, too.

"'Perhaps you are exaggerating—if you were to take proper measures perhaps—'

"He was terribly confused and did not seem able to collect his scattered senses; the pocket-book was still in his left hand.

"'Oh, don't mind me,' I said. 'Dr. B—— saw me last week' (I lugged him in again), 'and my hash is quite settled; pardon me-' I took hold of the door-handle again. I was on the point of opening the door and leaving my grateful but confused medical friend to himself and his shame, when my damnable cough got hold of me again.

"My doctor insisted on my sitting down again to get my breath. He now said something to his wife who, without leaving her place, addressed a few words of gratitude and courtesy to me. She seemed very shy over it, and her sickly face flushed up with confusion. I remained, but with the air of a man who knows he is intruding and is anxious to get away. The doctor's remorse at last seemed to need a vent, I could see.

"'If I—' he began, breaking off abruptly every other moment, and starting another sentence. 'I—I am so very grateful to you, and I am so much to blame in your eyes, I feel sure, I—you see—' (he pointed to the room again) 'at this moment I am in such a position-'

"'Oh!' I said, 'there's nothing to see; it's quite a clear case—you've lost your post and have come up to make explanations and get another, if you can!'

"'How do you know that?' he asked in amazement.

"'Oh, it was evident at the first glance,' I said ironically, but not intentionally so. 'There are lots of people who come up from the provinces full of hope, and run about town, and have to live as best they can.'

"He began to talk at once excitedly and with trembling lips; he began complaining and telling me his story. He interested me, I confess; I sat there nearly an hour. His story was a very ordinary one. He had been a provincial doctor; he had a civil appointment, and had no sooner taken it up than intrigues began. Even his wife was dragged into these. He was proud, and flew into a passion; there was a change of local government which acted in favour of his opponents; his position was undermined, complaints were made against him; he lost his post and came up to Petersburg with his last remaining money, in order to appeal to higher authorities. Of course nobody would listen to him for a long time; he would come and tell his story one day and be refused promptly; another day he would be fed on false promises; again he would be treated harshly; then he would be told to sign some documents; then he would sign the paper and hand it in, and they would refuse to receive it, and tell him to file a formal petition. In a word he had been driven about from office to office for five months and had spent every farthing he had; his wife's last rags had just been pawned; and meanwhile a child had been born to them and—and today I have a final refusal to my petition, and I have hardly a crumb of bread left—I have nothing left; my wife has had a baby lately—and I—I—'

"He sprang up from his chair and turned away. His wife was crying in the corner; the child had begun to moan again. I pulled out my note-book and began writing in it. When I had finished and rose from my chair he was standing before me with an expression of alarmed curiosity.

"'I have jotted down your name,' I told him, 'and all the rest of it—the place you served at, the district, the date, and all. I have a friend, Bachmatoff, whose uncle is a councillor of state and has to do with these matters, one Peter Matveyevitch Bachmatoff.'

"'Peter Matveyevitch Bachmatoff!' he cried, trembling all over with excitement. 'Why, nearly everything depends on that very man!'

"It is very curious, this story of the medical man, and my visit, and the happy termination to which I contributed by accident! Everything fitted in, as in a novel. I told the poor people not to put much hope in me, because I was but a poor schoolboy myself—(I am not really, but I humiliated myself as much as possible in order to make them less hopeful)—but that I would go at once to the Vassili Ostroff and see my friend; and that as I knew for certain that his uncle adored him, and was absolutely devoted to him as the last hope and branch of the family, perhaps the old man might do something to oblige his nephew.

"'If only they would allow me to explain all to his excellency! If I could but be permitted to tell my tale to him!" he cried, trembling with feverish agitation, and his eyes flashing with excitement. I repeated once more that I could not hold out much hope—that it would probably end in smoke, and if I did not turn up next morning they must make up their minds that there was no more to be done in the matter.

"They showed me out with bows and every kind of respect; they seemed quite beside themselves. I shall never forget the expression of their faces!

"I took a droshky and drove over to the Vassili Ostroff at once. For some years I had been at enmity with this young Bachmatoff, at school. We considered him an aristocrat; at all events I called him one. He used to dress smartly, and always drove to school in a private trap. He was a good companion, and was always merry and jolly, sometimes even witty, though he was not very intellectual, in spite of the fact that he was always top of the class; I myself was never top in anything! All his companions were very fond of him, excepting myself. He had several times during those years come up to me and tried to make friends; but I had always turned sulkily away and refused to have anything to do with him. I had not seen him for a whole year now; he was at the university. When, at nine o'clock, or so, this evening, I arrived and was shown up to him with great ceremony, he first received me with astonishment, and not too affably, but he soon cheered up, and suddenly gazed intently at me and burst out laughing.

"'Why, what on earth can have possessed you to come and see *me*, Terentieff?' he cried, with his usual pleasant, sometimes audacious, but never offensive familiarity, which I liked in reality, but for which I also detested him. 'Why what's the matter?' he cried in alarm. 'Are you ill?'

"That confounded cough of mine had come on again; I fell into a chair, and with difficulty recovered my breath. 'It's all right, it's only consumption' I said. 'I have come to you with a petition!'

"He sat down in amazement, and I lost no time in telling him the medical man's history; and explained that he, with the influence which he possessed over his uncle, might do some good to the poor fellow.

"'I'll do it—I'll do it, of course!' he said. 'I shall attack my uncle about it tomorrow morning, and I'm very glad you told me the story. But how was it that you thought of coming to me about it, Terentieff?'

"'So much depends upon your uncle,' I said. 'And besides we have always been enemies, Bachmatoff; and as you are a generous sort of fellow, I thought you would not refuse my request because I was your enemy!' I added with irony.

"'Like Napoleon going to England, eh?' cried he, laughing. 'I'll do it though—of course, and at once, if I can!' he added, seeing that I rose seriously from my chair at this point.

"And sure enough the matter ended as satisfactorily as possible. A month or so later my medical friend was appointed to another post. He got his travelling expenses paid, and something to help him to start life with once more. I think Bachmatoff must have persuaded the doctor to accept a loan from himself. I saw Bachmatoff two or three times, about this period, the third time being when he gave a farewell dinner to the doctor and his wife before their departure, a champagne dinner.

"Bachmatoff saw me home after the dinner and we crossed the Nicolai bridge. We were both a little drunk. He told me of his joy, the joyful feeling of having done a good action; he said that it was all thanks to myself that he could feel this satisfaction; and held forth about the foolishness of the theory that individual charity is useless.

"I, too, was burning to have my say!

"'In Moscow,' I said, 'there was an old state counsellor, a civil general, who, all his life, had been in the habit of visiting the prisons and speaking to criminals. Every party of convicts on its way to Siberia knew beforehand that on the Vorobeef Hills the "old general" would pay them a visit. He did all he undertook seriously and devotedly. He would walk down the rows of the unfortunate prisoners, stop before each individual and ask after his needs—he never sermonized them; he spoke kindly to them—he gave them money; he brought them all sorts of necessaries for the journey, and gave them devotional books, choosing those who could read, under the firm conviction that they would read to those who could not, as they went along.

"'He scarcely ever talked about the particular crimes of any of them, but listened if any volunteered information on that point. All the convicts were equal for him, and he made no distinction. He spoke to all as to brothers, and every one of them looked upon him as a father. When he observed among the exiles some poor woman with a child, he would always come forward and fondle the little one, and make it laugh. He continued these acts of mercy up to his very death; and by that time all the criminals, all over Russia and Siberia, knew him!

"'A man I knew who had been to Siberia and returned, told me that he himself had been a witness of how the very most hardened criminals remembered the old general, though, in point of fact, he could never, of course, have distributed more than a few pence to each member of a party. Their recollection of him was not sentimental or particularly devoted. Some wretch, for instance, who had been a murderer—cutting the throat of a dozen fellow-creatures, for instance; or stabbing six little children for his own amusement (there have been such men!)—would perhaps, without rhyme or reason, suddenly give a sigh and say, "I wonder whether that old general is alive still!" Although perhaps he had not thought of mentioning him for a dozen years before! How can one say what seed of good may have been dropped into his soul, never to die?'

"I continued in that strain for a long while, pointing out to Bachmatoff how impossible it is to follow up the effects of any isolated good deed one may do, in all its influences and subtle workings upon the heart and after-actions of others.

"'And to think that you are to be cut off from life!' remarked Bachmatoff, in a tone of reproach, as though he would like to find someone to pitch into on my account.

"We were leaning over the balustrade of the bridge, looking into the Neva at this moment.

"'Do you know what has suddenly come into my head?' said I, suddenly—leaning further and further over the rail.

"'Surely not to throw yourself into the river?' cried Bachmatoff in alarm. Perhaps he read my thought in my face.

"'No, not yet. At present nothing but the following consideration. You see I have some two or three months left me to live—perhaps four; well, supposing that when I have but a month or two more, I take a fancy for some "good deed" that needs both trouble and time, like this business of our doctor friend, for instance: why, I shall have to give up the idea of it and take to something else—some *little* good deed, *more within my means*, eh? Isn't that an amusing idea!'

"Poor Bachmatoff was much impressed—painfully so. He took me all the way home; not attempting to console me, but behaving with the greatest delicacy. On taking leave he pressed my hand warmly and asked permission to come and see me. I replied that if he came to me as a 'comforter,' so to speak (for he would be in that capacity whether he spoke to me in a soothing manner or only kept silence, as I pointed out to him), he would but remind me each time of my approaching death! He shrugged his shoulders, but quite agreed with me; and we parted better friends than I had expected.

"But that evening and that night were sown the first seeds of my 'last conviction.' I seized greedily on my new idea; I thirstily drank in all its different aspects (I did not sleep a wink that night!), and the deeper I went into it the more my being seemed to merge itself in it, and the more alarmed I became. A dreadful terror came over me at last, and did not leave me all next day.

"Sometimes, thinking over this, I became quite numb with the terror of it; and I might well have deduced from this fact, that my 'last conviction' was eating into my being too fast and too seriously, and would undoubtedly come to its climax before long. And for the climax I needed greater determination than I yet possessed.

"However, within three weeks my determination was taken, owing to a very strange circumstance.

"Here on my paper, I make a note of all the figures and dates that come into my explanation. Of course, it is all the same to me, but just now—and perhaps only at this moment—I desire that all those who are to judge of my action should see clearly out of how logical a sequence of deductions has at length proceeded my 'last conviction.'

"I have said above that the determination needed by me for the accomplishment of my final resolve, came to hand not through any sequence of causes, but thanks to a certain strange circumstance which had perhaps no connection whatever with the matter at issue. Ten days ago Rogojin called upon me about certain business of his own with which I have nothing to do at present. I had never seen Rogojin before, but had often heard about him.

"I gave him all the information he needed, and he very soon took his departure; so that, since he only came for the purpose of gaining the information, the matter might have been expected to end there.

"But he interested me too much, and all that day I was under the influence of strange thoughts connected with him, and I determined to return his visit the next day.

"Rogojin was evidently by no means pleased to see me, and hinted, delicately, that he saw no reason why our acquaintance should continue. For all that, however, I spent a very interesting hour, and so, I dare say, did he. There was so great a contrast between us that I am sure we must both have felt it; anyhow, I felt it acutely. Here was I, with my days numbered, and he, a man in the full vigour of life, living in the present, without the slightest thought for 'final convictions,' or numbers, or days, or, in fact, for anything but that which-which—well, which he was mad about, if he will excuse me the expression—as a feeble author who cannot express his ideas properly.

"In spite of his lack of amiability, I could not help seeing, in Rogojin a man of intellect and sense; and although, perhaps, there was little in the outside world which was of interest to him, still he was clearly a man with eyes to see.

"I hinted nothing to him about my 'final conviction,' but it appeared to me that he had guessed it from my words. He remained silent—he is a terribly silent man. I remarked to him, as I rose to depart, that, in spite of the contrast and the wide differences between us two, les extremites se touchent ('extremes meet,' as I explained to him in Russian); so that maybe he was not so far from my final conviction as appeared.

"His only reply to this was a sour grimace. He rose and looked for my cap, and placed it in my hand, and led me out of the house—that dreadful gloomy house of his—to all appearances, of course, as though I were leaving of my own accord, and he were simply seeing me to the door out of politeness. His house impressed me much; it is like a burial-ground, he seems to like it, which is, however, quite natural. Such a full life as he leads is so overflowing with absorbing interests that he has little need of assistance from his surroundings.

"The visit to Rogojin exhausted me terribly. Besides, I had felt ill since the morning; and by evening I was so weak that I took to my bed, and was in high fever at intervals, and even delirious. Colia sat with me until eleven o'clock.

"Yet I remember all he talked about, and every word we said, though whenever my eyes closed for a moment I could picture nothing but the image of Surikoff just in the act of finding a million roubles. He could not make up his mind what to do with the money, and tore his hair over it. He trembled with fear that somebody would rob him, and at last he decided to bury it in the ground. I persuaded him that, instead of putting it all away uselessly underground, he had better melt it down and make a golden coffin out of it for his starved child, and then dig up the little one and put her into the golden coffin. Surikoff accepted this suggestion, I thought, with tears of gratitude, and immediately commenced to carry out my design.

"I thought I spat on the ground and left him in disgust. Colia told me, when I quite recovered my senses, that I had not been asleep for a moment, but that I had spoken to him about Surikoff the whole while.

"At moments I was in a state of dreadful weakness and misery, so that Colia was greatly disturbed when he left me.

"When I arose to lock the door after him, I suddenly called to mind a picture I had noticed at Rogojin's in one of his gloomiest rooms, over the door. He had pointed it out to me himself as we walked past it, and I believe I must have stood a good five minutes in front of it. There was nothing artistic about it, but the picture made me feel strangely uncomfortable. It represented Christ just taken down from the cross. It seems to me that painters as a rule represent the Saviour, both on the cross and taken down from it, with great beauty still upon His face. This marvellous beauty they strive to preserve even in His moments of deepest agony and passion. But there was no such beauty in Rogojin's picture. This was the presentment of a poor mangled body which had evidently suffered unbearable anguish even before its crucifixion, full of wounds and bruises, marks of the violence of soldiers and people, and of the bitterness of the moment when He had fallen with the cross—all this combined with the anguish of the actual crucifixion.

"The face was depicted as though still suffering; as though the body, only just dead, was still almost quivering with agony. The picture was one of pure nature, for the face was not beautified by the artist, but was left as it would naturally be, whosoever the sufferer, after such anguish.

"I know that the earliest Christian faith taught that the Saviour suffered actually and not figuratively, and that nature was allowed her own way even while His body was on the cross.

"It is strange to look on this dreadful picture of the mangled corpse of the Saviour, and to put this question to oneself: 'Supposing that the disciples, the future apostles, the women who had followed Him and stood by the cross, all of whom believed in and worshipped Him—supposing that they saw this tortured body, this face so mangled and bleeding and bruised (and they *must* have so seen it)—how could they have gazed upon the dreadful sight and yet have believed that He would rise again?'

"The thought steps in, whether one likes it or no, that death is so terrible and so powerful, that even He who conquered it in His miracles during life was unable to triumph over it at the last. He who called to Lazarus, 'Lazarus, come forth!' and the dead man lived—He was now Himself a prey to nature and death. Nature appears to one, looking at this picture, as some huge, implacable, dumb monster; or still better—a stranger simile—some enormous mechanical engine of modern days which has seized and crushed and swallowed up a great and invaluable Being, a Being worth nature and all her laws, worth the whole earth, which was perhaps created merely for the sake of the advent of that Being.

"This blind, dumb, implacable, eternal, unreasoning force is well shown in the picture, and the absolute subordination of all men and things to it is so well expressed that the idea unconsciously arises in the mind of anyone who looks at it. All those faithful people who were gazing at the cross and its mutilated occupant must have suffered agony of mind that evening; for they must have felt that all their hopes and almost all their faith had been shattered at a blow. They must have separated in terror and dread that night, though each perhaps carried away with him one great thought which was never eradicated from his mind for ever afterwards. If this great Teacher of theirs could have seen Himself after the Crucifixion, how could He have consented to mount the Cross and to die as He did? This thought also comes into the mind of the man who gazes at this picture. I thought of all this by snatches probably between my attacks of delirium—for an hour and a half or so before Colia's departure.

"Can there be an appearance of that which has no form? And yet it seemed to me, at certain moments, that I beheld in some strange and impossible form, that dark, dumb, irresistibly powerful, eternal force.

"I thought someone led me by the hand and showed me, by the light of a candle, a huge, loathsome insect, which he assured me was that very force, that very almighty, dumb, irresistible Power, and laughed at the indignation with which I received this information. In my room they always light the little lamp before my icon for the night; it gives a feeble flicker of light, but it is strong enough to see by dimly, and if you sit just under it you can even read by it. I think it was about twelve or a little past that night. I had not slept a wink, and was lying with my eyes wide open, when suddenly the door opened, and in came Rogojin.

"He entered, and shut the door behind him. Then he silently gazed at me and went quickly to the corner of the room where the lamp was burning and sat down underneath it.

"I was much surprised, and looked at him expectantly.

"Rogojin only leaned his elbow on the table and silently stared at me. So passed two or three minutes, and I recollect that his silence hurt and offended me very much. Why did he not speak?

"That his arrival at this time of night struck me as more or less strange may possibly be the case; but I remember I was by no means amazed at it. On the contrary, though I had not actually told him my thought in the morning, yet I know he understood it; and this thought was of such a character that it would not be anything very remarkable, if one were to come for further talk about it at any hour of night, however late.

"I thought he must have come for this purpose.

"In the morning we had parted not the best of friends; I remember he looked at me with disagreeable sarcasm once or twice; and this same look I observed in his eyes now—which was the cause of the annoyance I felt.

"I did not for a moment suspect that I was delirious and that this Rogojin was but the result of fever and excitement. I had not the slightest idea of such a theory at first.

"Meanwhile he continued to sit and stare jeeringly at me.

"I angrily turned round in bed and made up my mind that I would not say a word unless he did; so I rested silently on my pillow determined to remain dumb, if it were to last till morning. I felt resolved that he should speak first. Probably twenty minutes or so passed in this way. Suddenly the idea struck me—what if this is an apparition and not Rogojin himself?

"Neither during my illness nor at any previous time had I ever seen an apparition;—but I had always thought, both when I was a little boy, and even now, that if I were to see one I should die on the spot—though I don't believe in ghosts. And yet *now*, when the idea struck me that this was a ghost and not Rogojin at all, I was not in the least alarmed. Nay—the thought actually irritated me. Strangely enough, the decision of the question as to whether this were a ghost or Rogojin did not, for some reason or other, interest me nearly so much as it ought to have done;—I think I began to muse about something altogether different. For instance, I began to wonder why Rogojin, who had been in dressing—gown and slippers when I saw him at home, had now put on a dress-coat and white waistcoat and tie? I also thought to myself, I remember—'if this is a ghost, and I am not afraid of it, why don't I approach it and verify my suspicions? Perhaps I am afraid—' And no sooner did this last idea enter my head than an icy blast blew over me; I felt a chill down my backbone and my knees shook.

"At this very moment, as though divining my thoughts, Rogojin raised his head from his arm and began to part his lips as though he were going to laugh—but he continued to stare at me as persistently as before.

"I felt so furious with him at this moment that I longed to rush at him; but as I had sworn that he should speak first, I continued to lie still—and the more willingly, as I was still by no means satisfied as to whether it really was Rogojin or not.

"I cannot remember how long this lasted; I cannot recollect, either, whether consciousness forsook me at intervals, or not. But at last Rogojin rose, staring at me as intently as ever, but not smiling any longer,—and walking very softly, almost on tip-toes, to the door, he opened it, went out, and shut it behind him.

"I did not rise from my bed, and I don't know how long I lay with my eyes open, thinking. I don't know what I thought about, nor how I fell asleep or became insensible; but I awoke next morning after nine o'clock when they knocked at my door. My general orders are that if I don't open the door and call, by nine o'clock, Matreona is to come and bring my tea. When I now opened the door to her, the thought suddenly struck me—how could he have come in, since the door was locked? I made inquiries and found that Rogojin himself could not possibly have come in, because all our doors were locked for the night.

"Well, this strange circumstance—which I have described with so much detail—was the ultimate cause which led me to taking my final determination. So that no logic, or logical deductions, had anything to do with my resolve;—it was simply a matter of disgust.

"It was impossible for me to go on living when life was full of such detestable, strange, tormenting forms. This ghost had humiliated me;—nor could I bear to be subordinate to that dark, horrible force which was embodied in the form of the loathsome insect. It was only towards evening, when I had quite made up my mind on this point, that I began to feel easier."

VII.

"I had a small pocket pistol. I had procured it while still a boy, at that droll age when the stories of duels and highwaymen begin to delight one, and when one imagines oneself nobly standing fire at some future day, in a duel.

"There were a couple of old bullets in the bag which contained the pistol, and powder enough in an old flask for two or three charges.

"The pistol was a wretched thing, very crooked and wouldn't carry farther than fifteen paces at the most. However, it would send your skull flying well enough if you pressed the muzzle of it against your temple.

"I determined to die at Pavlofsk at sunrise, in the park—so as to make no commotion in the house.

"This 'explanation' will make the matter clear enough to the police. Students of psychology, and anyone else who likes, may make what they please of it. I should not like this paper, however, to be made public. I request the prince to keep a copy himself, and to give a copy to Aglaya Ivanovna Epanchin. This is my last will and testament. As for my skeleton, I bequeath it to the Medical Academy for the benefit of science.

"I recognize no jurisdiction over myself, and I know that I am now beyond the power of laws and judges.

"A little while ago a very amusing idea struck me. What if I were now to commit some terrible crime—murder ten fellow-creatures, for instance, or anything else that is thought most shocking and dreadful in this world—what a dilemma my judges would be in, with a criminal who only has a fortnight to live in any case, now that the rack and other forms of torture are abolished! Why, I should die comfortably in their own hospital—in a warm, clean room, with an attentive doctor—probably much more comfortably than I should at home.

"I don't understand why people in my position do not oftener indulge in such ideas—if only for a joke! Perhaps they do! Who knows! There are plenty of merry souls among us!

"But though I do not recognize any jurisdiction over myself, still I know that I shall be judged, when I am nothing but a voiceless lump of clay; therefore I do not wish to go before I have left a word of reply—the reply of a free man—not one forced to justify himself—oh no! I have no need to ask forgiveness of anyone. I wish to say a word merely because I happen to desire it of my own free will.

"Here, in the first place, comes a strange thought!

"Who, in the name of what Law, would think of disputing my full personal right over the fortnight of life left to me? What jurisdiction can be brought to bear upon the case? Who would wish me, not only to be sentenced, but to endure the sentence to the end? Surely there exists no man who would wish such a thing—why should anyone desire it? For the sake of morality? Well, I can understand that if I were to make an attempt upon my own life while in the enjoyment of full health and vigour—my life which might have been 'useful,' etc., etc.—morality might reproach me, according to the old routine, for disposing of my life without permission—or whatever its tenet may be. But now, *now*, when my sentence is out and my days numbered! How can morality have need of my last breaths, and why should I die listening to the consolations offered by the prince, who, without doubt, would not omit to demonstrate that death is actually a benefactor to me? (Christians like him always end up with that—it is their pet theory.) And what do they want with their ridiculous 'Pavlofsk trees'? To sweeten my last hours? Cannot they understand that the more I forget myself, the more I let myself become attached to these last illusions of life and love, by means of which they try to hide from me Meyer's wall, and all that is so plainly written on it—the more unhappy they make me? What is the use of all your nature to me—all your parks and trees, your sunsets and sunrises, your blue skies and your self-satisfied faces—when all this wealth of beauty and happiness begins with the fact that it accounts me—only me—one too many! What is the good of all this beauty and glory to me, when every second, every moment, I cannot but be aware that this little fly which buzzes around my head in the sun's rays—even this little fly is a sharer and participator in all the glory of the universe, and knows its place and is happy in it;—while I—only I, am an outcast, and have been blind to the fact hitherto, thanks to my simplicity! Oh! I know well how the prince and others would like me, instead of indulging in all these wicked words of my own, to sing, to the glory and triumph of morality, that well-known verse of Gilbert's:

"'O, puissent voir longtemps votre beauté sacrée
Tant d'amis, sourds à mes adieux!
Qu'ils meurent pleins de jours, que leur mort soit pleurée,
Qu'un ami leur ferme les yeux!'

"But believe me, believe me, my simple-hearted friends, that in this highly moral verse, in this academical blessing to the world in general in the French language, is hidden the intensest gall and bitterness; but so well concealed is the venom, that I dare say the poet actually persuaded himself that his words were full of the tears of pardon and peace, instead of the bitterness of disappointment and malice, and so died in the delusion.

"Do you know there is a limit of ignominy, beyond which man's consciousness of shame cannot go, and after which begins satisfaction in shame? Well, of course humility is a great force in that sense, I admit that—though not in the sense in which religion accounts humility to be strength!

"Religion!—I admit eternal life—and perhaps I always did admit it.

"Admitted that consciousness is called into existence by the will of a Higher Power; admitted that this consciousness looks out upon the world and says 'I am;' and admitted that the Higher Power wills that the consciousness so called into existence, be suddenly extinguished (for so—for some unexplained reason—it is and must be)—still there comes the eternal question—why must I be humble through all this? Is it not enough that I am devoured, without my being expected to bless the power that devours me? Surely—surely I need not suppose that Somebody—there—will be offended because I do not wish to live out the fortnight allowed me? I don't believe it.

"It is much simpler, and far more likely, to believe that my death is needed—the death of an insignificant atom—in order to fulfil the general harmony of the universe—in order to make even some plus or minus in the sum of existence. Just as every day the death of numbers of beings is necessary because without their annihilation the rest cannot live on—(although we must admit that the idea is not a particularly grand one in itself!)

"However—admit the fact! Admit that without such perpetual devouring of one another the world cannot continue to exist, or could never have been organized—I am ever ready to confess that I cannot understand why this is so—but I'll tell you what I *do* know, for certain. If I have once been given to understand and realize that I *am*—what does it matter to me that the world is organized on a system full of errors and that otherwise it cannot be organized at all? Who will or can judge me after this? Say what you like—the thing is impossible and unjust!

"And meanwhile I have never been able, in spite of my great desire to do so, to persuade myself that there is no future existence, and no Providence.

"The fact of the matter is that all this *does* exist, but that we know absolutely nothing about the future life and its laws!

"But it is so difficult, and even impossible to understand, that surely I am not to be blamed because I could not fathom the incomprehensible?

"Of course I know they say that one must be obedient, and of course, too, the prince is one of those who say so: that one must be obedient without questions, out of pure goodness of heart, and that for my worthy conduct in this matter I shall meet with reward in another world. We degrade God when we attribute our own ideas to Him, out of annoyance that we cannot fathom His ways.

"Again, I repeat, I cannot be blamed because I am unable to understand that which it is not given to mankind to fathom. Why am I to be judged because I could not comprehend the Will and Laws of Providence? No, we had better drop religion.

"And enough of this. By the time I have got so far in the reading of my document the sun will be up and the huge force of his rays will be acting upon the living world. So be it. I shall die gazing straight at the great Fountain of life and power; I do not want this life!

"If I had had the power to prevent my own birth I should certainly never have consented to accept existence under such ridiculous conditions. However, I have the power to end my existence, although I do but give back days that are already numbered. It is an insignificant gift, and my revolt is equally insignificant.

"Final explanation: I die, not in the least because I am unable to support these next three weeks. Oh no, I should find strength enough, and if I wished it I could obtain consolation from the thought of the injury that is done me. But I am not a French poet, and I do not desire such consolation. And finally, nature has so limited my capacity for work or activity of any kind, in allotting me but three weeks of time, that suicide is about the only thing left that I can begin and end in the time of my own free will.

"Perhaps then I am anxious to take advantage of my last chance of doing something for myself. A protest is sometimes no small thing."

The explanation was finished; Hippolyte paused at last.

There is, in extreme cases, a final stage of cynical candour when a nervous man, excited, and beside himself with emotion, will be afraid of nothing and ready for any sort of scandal, nay, glad of it. The extraordinary, almost unnatural, tension of the nerves which upheld Hippolyte up to this point, had now arrived at this final stage. This poor feeble boy of eighteen—exhausted by disease—looked for all the world as weak and frail as a leaflet torn from its parent tree and trembling in the breeze; but no sooner had his eye swept over his audience, for the first time during the whole of the last hour, than the most contemptuous, the most haughty expression of repugnance lighted up his face. He defied them all, as it were. But his hearers were indignant, too; they rose to their feet with annoyance. Fatigue, the wine consumed, the strain of listening so long, all added to the disagreeable impression which the reading had made upon them.

Suddenly Hippolyte jumped up as though he had been shot.

"The sun is rising," he cried, seeing the gilded tops of the trees, and pointing to them as to a miracle. "See, it is rising now!"

"Well, what then? Did you suppose it wasn't going to rise?" asked Ferdishenko.

"It's going to be atrociously hot again all day," said Gania, with an air of annoyance, taking his hat. "A month of this... Are you coming home, Ptitsin?" Hippolyte listened to this in amazement, almost amounting to stupefaction. Suddenly he became deadly pale and shuddered.

"You manage your composure too awkwardly. I see you wish to insult me," he cried to Gania. "You—you are a cur!" He looked at Gania with an expression of malice.

"What on earth is the matter with the boy? What phenomenal feeble-mindedness!" exclaimed Ferdishenko.

"Oh, he's simply a fool," said Gania.

Hippolyte braced himself up a little.

"I understand, gentlemen," he began, trembling as before, and stumbling over every word, "that I have deserved your resentment, and—and am sorry that I should have troubled you with this raving nonsense" (pointing to his article), "or rather, I am sorry that I have not troubled you enough." He smiled feebly. "Have I troubled you, Evgenie Pavlovitch?" He suddenly turned on Evgenie with this question. "Tell me now, have I troubled you or not?"

"Well, it was a little drawn out, perhaps; but—"

"Come, speak out! Don't lie, for once in your life—speak out!" continued Hippolyte, quivering with agitation.

"Oh, my good sir, I assure you it's entirely the same to me. Please leave me in peace," said Evgenie, angrily, turning his back on him.

"Good-night, prince," said Ptitsin, approaching his host.

"What are you thinking of? Don't go, he'll blow his brains out in a minute!" cried Vera Lebedeff, rushing up to Hippolyte and catching hold of his hands in a torment of alarm. "What are you thinking of? He said he would blow his brains out at sunrise."

"Oh, he won't shoot himself!" cried several voices, sarcastically.

"Gentlemen, you'd better look out," cried Colia, also seizing Hippolyte by the hand. "Just look at him! Prince, what are you thinking of?" Vera and Colia, and Keller, and Burdovsky were all crowding round Hippolyte now and holding him down.

"He has the right—the right—" murmured Burdovsky. "Excuse me, prince, but what are your arrangements?" asked Lebedeff, tipsy and exasperated, going up to Muishkin.

"What do you mean by 'arrangements'?"

"No, no, excuse me! I'm master of this house, though I do not wish to lack respect towards you. You are master of the house too, in a way; but I can't allow this sort of thing—"

"He won't shoot himself; the boy is only playing the fool," said General Ivolgin, suddenly and unexpectedly, with indignation.

"I know he won't, I know he won't, general; but I—I'm master here!"

"Listen, Mr. Terentieff," said Ptitsin, who had bidden the prince good-night, and was now holding out his hand to Hippolyte; "I think you remark in that manuscript of yours, that you bequeath your skeleton to the Academy. Are you referring to your own skeleton—I mean, your very bones?"

"Yes, my bones, I—"

"Quite so, I see; because, you know, little mistakes have occurred now and then. There was a case—"

"Why do you tease him?" cried the prince, suddenly.

"You've moved him to tears," added Ferdishenko. But Hippolyte was by no means weeping. He was about to move from his place, when his four guards rushed at him and seized him once more. There was a laugh at this.

"He led up to this on purpose. He took the trouble of writing all that so that people should come and grab him by the arm," observed Rogojin. "Good-night, prince. What a time we've sat here, my very bones ache!"

"If you really intended to shoot yourself, Terentieff," said Evgenie Pavlovitch, laughing, "if I were you, after all these compliments, I should just not shoot myself in order to vex them all."

"They are very anxious to see me blow my brains out," said Hippolyte, bitterly.

"Yes, they'll be awfully annoyed if they don't see it."

"Then you think they won't see it?"

"I am not trying to egg you on. On the contrary, I think it very likely that you may shoot yourself; but the principal thing is to keep cool," said Evgenie with a drawl, and with great condescension.

"I only now perceive what a terrible mistake I made in reading this article to them," said Hippolyte, suddenly, addressing Evgenie, and looking at him with an expression of trust and confidence, as though he were applying to a friend for counsel.

"Yes, it's a droll situation; I really don't know what advice to give you," replied Evgenie, laughing. Hippolyte gazed steadfastly at him, but said nothing. To look at him one might have supposed that he was unconscious at intervals.

"Excuse me," said Lebedeff, "but did you observe the young gentleman's style? 'I'll go and blow my brains out in the park,' says he,' so as not to disturb anyone.' He thinks he won't disturb anybody if he goes three yards away, into the park, and blows his brains out there."

"Gentlemen—" began the prince.

"No, no, excuse me, most revered prince," Lebedeff interrupted, excitedly. "Since you must have observed yourself that this is no joke, and since at least half your guests must also have concluded that after all that has been said this youth *must* blow his brains out for honour's sake—I—as master of this house, and before these witnesses, now call upon you to take steps."

"Yes, but what am I to do, Lebedeff? What steps am I to take? I am ready."

"I'll tell you. In the first place he must immediately deliver up the pistol which he boasted of, with all its appurtenances. If he does this I shall consent to his being allowed to spend the night in this house—considering his feeble state of health, and of course conditionally upon his being under proper supervision. But tomorrow he must go elsewhere. Excuse me, prince! Should he refuse to deliver up his weapon, then I shall instantly seize one of his arms and General Ivolgin the other, and we shall hold him until the police arrive and take the matter into their own hands. Mr. Ferdishenko will kindly fetch them."

At this there was a dreadful noise; Lebedeff danced about in his excitement; Ferdishenko prepared to go for the police; Gania frantically insisted that it was all nonsense, "for nobody was going to shoot themselves." Evgenie Pavlovitch said nothing.

"Prince," whispered Hippolyte, suddenly, his eyes all ablaze, "you don't suppose that I did not foresee all this hatred?" He looked at the prince as though he expected him to reply, for a moment. "Enough!" he added at length, and addressing the whole company, he cried: "It's all my fault, gentlemen! Lebedeff, here's the key," (he took out a small bunch of keys); "this one, the last but one—Colia will show you—Colia, where's Colia?" he cried, looking straight at Colia and not seeing him. "Yes, he'll show you; he packed the bag with me this morning. Take him up, Colia; my bag is upstairs in the prince's study, under the table. Here's the key, and in the little case you'll find my pistol and the powder, and all. Colia packed it himself, Mr. Lebedeff; he'll show you; but it's on condition that tomorrow morning, when I leave for Petersburg, you will give me back my pistol, do you hear? I do this for the prince's sake, not yours."

"Capital, that's much better!" cried Lebedeff, and seizing the key he made off in haste.

Colia stopped a moment as though he wished to say something; but Lebedeff dragged him away.

Hippolyte looked around at the laughing guests. The prince observed that his teeth were chattering as though in a violent attack of ague.

"What brutes they all are!" he whispered to the prince. Whenever he addressed him he lowered his voice.

"Let them alone, you're too weak now—"

"Yes, directly; I'll go away directly. I'll—"

Suddenly he embraced Muishkin.

"Perhaps you think I am mad, eh?" he asked him, laughing very strangely.

"No, but you—"

"Directly, directly! Stand still a moment, I wish to look in your eyes; don't speak—stand so—let me look at you! I am bidding farewell to mankind."

He stood so for ten seconds, gazing at the prince, motionless, deadly pale, his temples wet with perspiration; he held the prince's hand in a strange grip, as though afraid to let him go.

"Hippolyte, Hippolyte, what is the matter with you?" cried Muishkin.

"Directly! There, that's enough. I'll lie down directly. I must drink to the sun's health. I wish to—I insist upon it! Let go!"

He seized a glass from the table, broke away from the prince, and in a moment had reached the terrace steps.

The prince made after him, but it so happened that at this moment Evgenie Pavlovitch stretched out his hand to say good-night. The next instant there was a general outcry, and then followed a few moments of indescribable excitement.

Reaching the steps, Hippolyte had paused, holding the glass in his left hand while he put his right hand into his coat pocket.

Keller insisted afterwards that he had held his right hand in his pocket all the while, when he was speaking to the prince, and that he had held the latter's shoulder with his left hand only. This circumstance, Keller affirmed, had led him to feel some suspicion from the first. However this may be, Keller ran after Hippolyte, but he was too late.

He caught sight of something flashing in Hippolyte's right hand, and saw that it was a pistol. He rushed at him, but at that very instant Hippolyte raised the pistol to his temple and pulled the trigger. There followed a sharp metallic click, but no report.

When Keller seized the would-be suicide, the latter fell forward into his arms, probably actually believing that he was shot. Keller had hold of the pistol now. Hippolyte was immediately placed in a chair, while the whole company thronged around excitedly, talking and asking each other questions. Every one of them had heard the snap of the trigger, and yet they saw a live and apparently unharmed man before them.

Hippolyte himself sat quite unconscious of what was going on, and gazed around with a senseless expression.

Lebedeff and Colia came rushing up at this moment.

"What is it?" someone asked, breathlessly—"A misfire?"

"Perhaps it wasn't loaded," said several voices.

"It's loaded all right," said Keller, examining the pistol, "but—"

"What! did it miss fire?"

"There was no cap in it," Keller announced.

It would be difficult to describe the pitiable scene that now followed. The first sensation of alarm soon gave place to amusement; some burst out laughing loud and heartily, and seemed to find a malicious satisfaction in the joke. Poor Hippolyte sobbed hysterically; he wrung his hands; he approached everyone in turn—even Ferdishenko—and took them by both hands, and swore solemnly that he had forgotten—absolutely forgotten—"accidentally, and not on purpose,"—to put a cap in—that he "had ten of them, at least, in his pocket." He pulled them out and showed them to everyone; he protested that he had not liked to put one in beforehand for fear of an accidental explosion in his pocket. That he had thought he would have lots of time to put it in afterwards—when required—and, that, in the heat of the moment, he had forgotten all about it. He threw himself upon the prince, then on Evgenie Pavlovitch. He entreated Keller to give him back the pistol, and he'd soon show them all that "his honour—his honour,"—but he was "dishonoured, now, for ever!"

He fell senseless at last—and was carried into the prince's study.

Lebedeff, now quite sobered down, sent for a doctor; and he and his daughter, with Burdovsky and General Ivolgin, remained by the sick man's couch.

When he was carried away unconscious, Keller stood in the middle of the room, and made the following declaration to the company in general, in a loud tone of voice, with emphasis upon each word.

"Gentlemen, if any one of you casts any doubt again, before me, upon Hippolyte's good faith, or hints that the cap was forgotten intentionally, or suggests that this unhappy boy was acting a part before us, I beg to announce that the person so speaking shall account to me for his words."

No one replied.

The company departed very quickly, in a mass. Ptitsin, Gania, and Rogojin went away together.

The prince was much astonished that Evgenie Pavlovitch changed his mind, and took his departure without the conversation he had requested.

"Why, you wished to have a talk with me when the others left?" he said.

"Quite so," said Evgenie, sitting down suddenly beside him, "but I have changed my mind for the time being. I confess, I am too disturbed, and so, I think, are you; and the matter as to which I wished to consult you is too serious to tackle with one's mind even a little disturbed; too serious both for myself and for you. You see, prince, for once in my life I wish to perform an absolutely honest action, that is, an action with no ulterior motive; and I think I am hardly in a condition to talk of it just at this moment, and—and—well, we'll discuss it another time. Perhaps the matter may gain in clearness if we wait for two or three days—just the two or three days which I must spend in Petersburg."

Here he rose again from his chair, so that it seemed strange that he should have thought it worth while to sit down at all.

The prince thought, too, that he looked vexed and annoyed, and not nearly so friendly towards himself as he had been earlier in the night.

"I suppose you will go to the sufferer's bedside now?" he added.

"Yes, I am afraid..." began the prince.

"Oh, you needn't fear! He'll live another six weeks all right. Very likely he will recover altogether; but I strongly advise you to pack him off tomorrow."

"I think I may have offended him by saying nothing just now. I am afraid he may suspect that I doubted his good faith,—about shooting himself, you know. What do you think, Evgenie Pavlovitch?"

"Not a bit of it! You are much too good to him; you shouldn't care a hang about what he thinks. I have heard of such things before, but never came across, till tonight, a man who would actually shoot himself in order to gain a vulgar notoriety, or blow out his brains for spite, if he finds that people don't care to pat him on the back for his

412

sanguinary intentions. But what astonishes me more than anything is the fellow's candid confession of weakness. You'd better get rid of him tomorrow, in any case.

"Do you think he will make another attempt?"

"Oh no, not he, not now! But you have to be very careful with this sort of gentleman. Crime is too often the last resource of these petty nonentities. This young fellow is quite capable of cutting the throats of ten people, simply for a lark, as he told us in his 'explanation.' I assure you those confounded words of his will not let me sleep."

"I think you disturb yourself too much."

"What an extraordinary person you are, prince! Do you mean to say that you doubt the fact that he is capable of murdering ten men?"

"I daren't say, one way or the other; all this is very strange—but—"

"Well, as you like, just as you like," said Evgenie Pavlovitch, irritably. "Only you are such a plucky fellow, take care you don't get included among the ten victims!"

"Oh, he is much more likely not to kill anyone at all," said the prince, gazing thoughtfully at Evgenie. The latter laughed disagreeably.

"Well, *au revoir!* Did you observe that he 'willed' a copy of his confession to Aglaya Ivanovna?"

"Yes, I did; I am thinking of it."

"In connection with 'the ten,' eh?" laughed Evgenie, as he left the room.

An hour later, towards four o'clock, the prince went into the park. He had endeavoured to fall asleep, but could not, owing to the painful beating of his heart.

He had left things quiet and peaceful; the invalid was fast asleep, and the doctor, who had been called in, had stated that there was no special danger. Lebedeff, Colia, and Burdovsky were lying down in the sick-room, ready to take it in turns to watch. There was nothing to fear, therefore, at home.

But the prince's mental perturbation increased every moment. He wandered about the park, looking absently around him, and paused in astonishment when he suddenly found himself in the empty space with the rows of chairs round it, near the Vauxhall. The look of the place struck him as dreadful now: so he turned round and went by the path which he had followed with the Epanchins on the way to the band, until he reached the green bench which Aglaya had pointed out for their rendezvous. He sat down on it and suddenly burst into a loud fit of laughter, immediately followed by a feeling of irritation. His disturbance of mind continued; he felt that he must go away somewhere, anywhere.

Above his head some little bird sang out, of a sudden; he began to peer about for it among the leaves. Suddenly the bird darted out of the tree and away, and instantly he thought of the "fly buzzing about in the sun's rays" that Hippolyte had talked of; how that it knew its place and was a participator in the universal life, while he alone was an "outcast." This picture had impressed him at the time, and he meditated upon it now. An old, forgotten memory awoke in his brain, and suddenly burst into clearness and light. It was a recollection of Switzerland, during the first year of his cure, the very first months. At that time he had been pretty nearly an idiot still; he could not speak properly, and had difficulty in understanding when others spoke to him. He climbed the mountain-side, one sunny morning, and wandered long and aimlessly with a certain thought in his brain, which would not become clear. Above him was the blazing sky, below, the lake; all around was the horizon, clear and infinite. He looked out upon this, long and anxiously. He remembered how he had stretched out his arms towards the beautiful, boundless blue of the horizon, and wept, and wept. What had so tormented him was the idea that he was a stranger to all this, that he was outside this glorious festival.

What was this universe? What was this grand, eternal pageant to which he had yearned from his childhood up, and in which he could never take part? Every morning the same magnificent sun; every morning the same rainbow in the waterfall; every evening the same glow on the snow-mountains.

Every little fly that buzzed in the sun's rays was a singer in the universal chorus, "knew its place, and was happy in it." Every blade of grass grew and was happy. Everything knew its path and loved it, went forth with a song and returned with a song; only he knew nothing, understood nothing, neither men nor words, nor any of nature's voices; he was a stranger and an outcast.

Oh, he could not then speak these words, or express all he felt! He had been tormented dumbly; but now it appeared to him that he must have said these very words—even then—and that Hippolyte must have taken his picture of the little fly from his tears and words of that time.

He was sure of it, and his heart beat excitedly at the thought, he knew not why.

He fell asleep on the bench; but his mental disquiet continued through his slumbers.

Just before he dozed off, the idea of Hippolyte murdering ten men flitted through his brain, and he smiled at the absurdity of such a thought.

Around him all was quiet; only the flutter and whisper of the leaves broke the silence, but broke it only to cause it to appear yet more deep and still.

He dreamed many dreams as he sat there, and all were full of disquiet, so that he shuddered every moment.

At length a woman seemed to approach him. He knew her, oh! he knew her only too well. He could always name her and recognize her anywhere; but, strange, she seemed to have quite a different face from hers, as he had known it, and he felt a tormenting desire to be able to say she was not the same woman. In the face before him there was such dreadful remorse and horror that he thought she must be a criminal, that she must have just committed some awful crime.

Tears were trembling on her white cheek. She beckoned him, but placed her finger on her lip as though to warn him that he must follow her very quietly. His heart froze within him. He wouldn't, he *couldn't* confess her to be a criminal, and yet he felt that something dreadful would happen the next moment, something which would blast his whole life.

She seemed to wish to show him something, not far off, in the park.

He rose from his seat in order to follow her, when a bright, clear peal of laughter rang out by his side. He felt somebody's hand suddenly in his own, seized it, pressed it hard, and awoke. Before him stood Aglaya, laughing aloud.

VIII.

She laughed, but she was rather angry too.

"He's asleep! You were asleep," she said, with contemptuous surprise.

"Is it really you?" muttered the prince, not quite himself as yet, and recognizing her with a start of amazement. "Oh yes, of course," he added, "this is our rendezvous. I fell asleep here."

"So I saw."

"Did no one awake me besides yourself? Was there no one else here? I thought there was another woman."

"There was another woman here?"

At last he was wide awake.

"It was a dream, of course," he said, musingly. "Strange that I should have a dream like that at such a moment. Sit down—"

He took her hand and seated her on the bench; then sat down beside her and reflected.

Aglaya did not begin the conversation, but contented herself with watching her companion intently.

He looked back at her, but at times it was clear that he did not see her and was not thinking of her.

Aglaya began to flush up.

"Oh yes!" cried the prince, starting. "Hippolyte's suicide—"

"What? At your house?" she asked, but without much surprise. "He was alive yesterday evening, wasn't he? How could you sleep here after that?" she cried, growing suddenly animated.

"Oh, but he didn't kill himself; the pistol didn't go off." Aglaya insisted on hearing the whole story. She hurried the prince along, but interrupted him with all sorts of questions, nearly all of which were irrelevant. Among other things, she seemed greatly interested in every word that Evgenie Pavlovitch had said, and made the prince repeat that part of the story over and over again.

"Well, that'll do; we must be quick," she concluded, after hearing all. "We have only an hour here, till eight; I must be home by then without fail, so that they may not find out that I came and sat here with you; but I've come on business. I have a great deal to say to you. But you have bowled me over considerably with your news. As to Hippolyte, I think his pistol was bound not to go off; it was more consistent with the whole affair. Are you sure he really wished to blow his brains out, and that there was no humbug about the matter?"

"No humbug at all."

"Very likely. So he wrote that you were to bring me a copy of his confession, did he? Why didn't you bring it?"

"Why, he didn't die! I'll ask him for it, if you like."

"Bring it by all means; you needn't ask him. He will be delighted, you may be sure; for, in all probability, he shot at himself simply in order that I might read his confession. Don't laugh at what I say, please, Lef Nicolaievitch, because it may very well be the case."

"I'm not laughing. I am convinced, myself, that that may have been partly the reason."

"You are convinced? You don't really mean to say you think that honestly?" asked Aglaya, extremely surprised.

She put her questions very quickly and talked fast, every now and then forgetting what she had begun to say, and not finishing her sentence. She seemed to be impatient to warn the prince about something or other. She was in a state of unusual excitement, and though she put on a brave and even defiant air, she seemed to be rather alarmed. She was dressed very simply, but this suited her well. She continually trembled and blushed, and she sat on the very edge of the seat.

The fact that the prince confirmed her idea, about Hippolyte shooting himself that she might read his confession, surprised her greatly.

"Of course," added the prince, "he wished us all to applaud his conduct—besides yourself."

"How do you mean—applaud?"

"Well—how am I to explain? He was very anxious that we should all come around him, and say we were so sorry for him, and that we loved him very much, and all that; and that we hoped he wouldn't kill himself, but remain alive. Very likely he thought more of you than the rest of us, because he mentioned you at such a moment, though perhaps he did not know himself that he had you in his mind's eye."

"I don't understand you. How could he have me in view, and not be aware of it himself? And yet, I don't know—perhaps I do. Do you know I have intended to poison myself at least thirty times—ever since I was thirteen or so—and to write to my parents before I did it? I used to think how nice it would be to lie in my coffin, and have them all weeping over me and saying it was all their fault for being so cruel, and all that—what are you smiling at?" she added, knitting her brow. "What do *you* think of when you go mooning about alone? I suppose you imagine yourself a field-marshal, and think you have conquered Napoleon?"

"Well, I really have thought something of the sort now and then, especially when just dozing off," laughed the prince. "Only it is the Austrians whom I conquer—not Napoleon."

"I don't wish to joke with you, Lef Nicolaievitch. I shall see Hippolyte myself. Tell him so. As for you, I think you are behaving very badly, because it is not right to judge a man's soul as you are judging Hippolyte's. You have no gentleness, but only justice—so you are unjust."

The prince reflected.

"I think you are unfair towards me," he said. "There is nothing wrong in the thoughts I ascribe to Hippolyte; they are only natural. But of course I don't know for certain what he thought. Perhaps he thought nothing, but simply longed to see human faces once more, and to hear human praise and feel human affection. Who knows? Only it all came out wrong, somehow. Some people have luck, and everything comes out right with them; others have none, and never a thing turns out fortunately."

"I suppose you have felt that in your own case," said Aglaya.

"Yes, I have," replied the prince, quite unsuspicious of any irony in the remark.

"H'm—well, at all events, I shouldn't have fallen asleep here, in your place. It wasn't nice of you, that. I suppose you fall asleep wherever you sit down?"

"But I didn't sleep a wink all night. I walked and walked about, and went to where the music was—"

"What music?"

"Where they played last night. Then I found this bench and sat down, and thought and thought—and at last I fell fast asleep."

"Oh, is that it? That makes a difference, perhaps. What did you go to the bandstand for?"

"I don't know; I—-"

"Very well—afterwards. You are always interrupting me. What woman was it you were dreaming about?"

"It was—about—you saw her—"

"Quite so; I understand. I understand quite well. You are very—Well, how did she appear to you? What did she look like? No, I don't want to know anything about her," said Aglaya, angrily; "don't interrupt me—"

She paused a moment as though getting breath, or trying to master her feeling of annoyance.

"Look here; this is what I called you here for. I wish to make you a—to ask you to be my friend. What do you stare at me like that for?" she added, almost angrily.

The prince certainly had darted a rather piercing look at her, and now observed that she had begun to blush violently. At such moments, the more Aglaya blushed, the angrier she grew with herself; and this was clearly expressed in her eyes, which flashed like fire. As a rule, she vented her wrath on her unfortunate companion, be it who it might. She was very conscious of her own shyness, and was not nearly so talkative as her sisters for this reason—in fact, at times she was much too quiet. When, therefore, she was bound to talk, especially at such delicate moments as this, she invariably did so with an air of haughty defiance. She always knew beforehand when she was going to blush, long before the blush came.

"Perhaps you do not wish to accept my proposition?" she asked, gazing haughtily at the prince.

"Oh yes, I do; but it is so unnecessary. I mean, I did not think you need make such a proposition," said the prince, looking confused.

"What did you suppose, then? Why did you think I invited you out here? I suppose you think me a 'little fool,' as they all call me at home?"

"I didn't know they called you a fool. I certainly don't think you one."

"You don't think me one! Oh, dear me!—that's very clever of you; you put it so neatly, too."

"In my opinion, you are far from a fool sometimes—in fact, you are very intelligent. You said a very clever thing just now about my being unjust because I had *only* justice. I shall remember that, and think about it."

Aglaya blushed with pleasure. All these changes in her expression came about so naturally and so rapidly—they delighted the prince; he watched her, and laughed.

"Listen," she began again; "I have long waited to tell you all this, ever since the time when you sent me that letter—even before that. Half of what I have to say you heard yesterday. I consider you the most honest and upright of men—more honest and upright than any other man; and if anybody says that your mind is—is sometimes affected, you know—it is unfair. I always say so and uphold it, because even if your surface mind be a little affected (of course you will not feel angry with me for talking so—I am speaking from a higher point of view) yet your real mind is far better than all theirs put together. Such a mind as they have never even *dreamed* of; because really, there are *two* minds—the kind that matters, and the kind that doesn't matter. Isn't it so?"

"May be! may be so!" said the prince, faintly; his heart was beating painfully.

"I knew you would not misunderstand me," she said, triumphantly. "Prince S. and Evgenie Pavlovitch and Alexandra don't understand anything about these two kinds of mind, but, just fancy, mamma does!"

"You are very like Lizabetha Prokofievna."

"What! surely not?" said Aglaya.

"Yes, you are, indeed."

"Thank you; I am glad to be like mamma," she said, thoughtfully. "You respect her very much, don't you?" she added, quite unconscious of the naiveness of the question.

"*Very* much; and I am so glad that you have realized the fact."

"I am very glad, too, because she is often laughed at by people. But listen to the chief point. I have long thought over the matter, and at last I have chosen you. I don't wish people to laugh at me; I don't wish people to think me a 'little fool.' I don't want to be chaffed. I felt all this of a sudden, and I refused Evgenie Pavlovitch flatly, because I am not going to be forever thrown at people's heads to be married. I want—I want—well, I'll tell you, I wish to run away from home, and I have chosen you to help me."

"Run away from home?" cried the prince.

"Yes—yes—yes! Run away from home!" she repeated, in a transport of rage. "I won't, I won't be made to blush every minute by them all! I don't want to blush before Prince S. or Evgenie Pavlovitch, or anyone, and therefore I have chosen you. I shall tell you everything, *everything*, even the most important things of all, whenever I like, and you are to hide nothing from me on your side. I want to speak to at least one person, as I would to myself. They have suddenly begun to say that I am waiting for you, and in love with you. They began this before you arrived here, and so I didn't show them the letter, and now they all say it, every one of them. I want to be brave, and be afraid of nobody. I don't want to go to their balls and things—I want to do good. I have long desired to run away, for I have been kept shut up for twenty years, and they are always trying to marry me off. I wanted to run away when I was fourteen years old—I was a little fool then, I know—but now I have worked it all out, and I have waited for you to tell me about foreign countries. I have never seen a single Gothic cathedral. I must go to Rome; I must see all the museums; I must study in Paris. All this last year I have been preparing and reading forbidden books. Alexandra and Adelaida are allowed to read anything they like, but I mayn't. I don't want to quarrel with my sisters, but I told my parents long ago that I wish to change my social position. I have decided to take up teaching, and I count on you because you said you loved children. Can we go in for education together—if not at once, then afterwards? We could do good together. I won't be a general's daughter any more! Tell me, are you a very learned man?"

"Oh no; not at all."

"Oh-h-h! I'm sorry for that. I thought you were. I wonder why I always thought so—but at all events you'll help me, won't you? Because I've chosen you, you know."

"Aglaya Ivanovna, it's absurd."

"But I will, I *will* run away!" she cried—and her eyes flashed again with anger—"and if you don't agree I shall go and marry Gavrila Ardalionovitch! I won't be considered a horrible girl, and accused of goodness knows what."

"Are you out of your mind?" cried the prince, almost starting from his seat. "What do they accuse you of? Who accuses you?"

"At home, everybody, mother, my sisters, Prince S., even that detestable Colia! If they don't say it, they think it. I told them all so to their faces. I told mother and father and everybody. Mamma was ill all the day after it, and next day father and Alexandra told me that I didn't understand what nonsense I was talking. I informed them that they little knew me—I was not a small child—I understood every word in the language—that I had read a couple of Paul de Kok's novels two years since on purpose, so as to know all about everything. No sooner did mamma hear me say this than she nearly fainted!"

A strange thought passed through the prince's brain; he gazed intently at Aglaya and smiled.

He could not believe that this was the same haughty young girl who had once so proudly shown him Gania's letter. He could not understand how that proud and austere beauty could show herself to be such an utter child—a child who probably did not even now understand some words.

"Have you always lived at home, Aglaya Ivanovna?" he asked. "I mean, have you never been to school, or college, or anything?"

"No—never—nowhere! I've been at home all my life, corked up in a bottle; and they expect me to be married straight out of it. What are you laughing at again? I observe that you, too, have taken to laughing at me, and range yourself on their side against me," she added, frowning angrily. "Don't irritate me—I'm bad enough without that—I don't know what I am doing sometimes. I am persuaded that you came here today in the full belief that I am in love with you, and that I arranged this meeting because of that," she cried, with annoyance.

"I admit I was afraid that that was the case, yesterday," blundered the prince (he was rather confused), "but today I am quite convinced that—"

"How?" cried Aglaya—and her lower lip trembled violently. "You were *afraid* that I—you dared to think that I—good gracious! you suspected, perhaps, that I sent for you to come here in order to catch you in a trap, so that they should find us here together, and make you marry me—"

"Aglaya Ivanovna, aren't you ashamed of saying such a thing? How could such a horrible idea enter your sweet, innocent heart? I am certain you don't believe a word of what you say, and probably you don't even know what you are talking about."

Aglaya sat with her eyes on the ground; she seemed to have alarmed even herself by what she had said.

"No, I'm not; I'm not a bit ashamed!" she murmured. "And how do you know my heart is innocent? And how dared you send me a love-letter that time?"

"*Love-letter?* My letter a love-letter? That letter was the most respectful of letters; it went straight from my heart, at what was perhaps the most painful moment of my life! I thought of you at the time as a kind of light. I—"

"Well, very well, very well!" she said, but quite in a different tone. She was remorseful now, and bent forward to touch his shoulder, though still trying not to look him in the face, as if the more persuasively to beg him not to be angry with her. "Very well," she continued, looking thoroughly ashamed of herself, "I feel that I said a very foolish thing. I only did it just to try you. Take it as unsaid, and if I offended you, forgive me. Don't look straight at me like that, please; turn your head away. You called it a 'horrible idea'; I only said it to shock you. Very often I am myself afraid of saying what I intend to say, and out it comes all the same. You have just told me that you wrote that letter at the most painful moment of your life. I know what moment that was!" she added softly, looking at the ground again.

"Oh, if you could know all!"

"I *do* know all!" she cried, with another burst of indignation. "You were living in the same house as that horrible woman with whom you ran away." She did not blush as she said this; on the contrary, she grew pale, and started from her seat, apparently oblivious of what she did, and immediately sat down again. Her lip continued to tremble for a long time.

There was silence for a moment. The prince was taken aback by the suddenness of this last reply, and did not know to what he should attribute it.

"I don't love you a bit!" she said suddenly, just as though the words had exploded from her mouth.

The prince did not answer, and there was silence again. "I love Gavrila Ardalionovitch," she said, quickly; but hardly audibly, and with her head bent lower than ever.

"That is *not* true," said the prince, in an equally low voice.

"What! I tell stories, do I? It is true! I gave him my promise a couple of days ago on this very seat."

The prince was startled, and reflected for a moment.

"It is not true," he repeated, decidedly; "you have just invented it!"

"You are wonderfully polite. You know he is greatly improved. He loves me better than his life. He let his hand burn before my very eyes in order to prove to me that he loved me better than his life!"

"He burned his hand!"

"Yes, believe it or not! It's all the same to me!"

The prince sat silent once more. Aglaya did not seem to be joking; she was too angry for that.

"What! he brought a candle with him to this place? That is, if the episode happened here; otherwise I can't."

"Yes, a candle! What's there improbable about that?"

"A whole one, and in a candlestick?"

"Yes—no—half a candle—an end, you know—no, it was a whole candle; it's all the same. Be quiet, can't you! He brought a box of matches too, if you like, and then lighted the candle and held his finger in it for half an hour and more!—There! Can't that be?"

"I saw him yesterday, and his fingers were all right!"

Aglaya suddenly burst out laughing, as simply as a child.

"Do you know why I have just told you these lies?" She appealed to the prince, of a sudden, with the most childlike candour, and with the laugh still trembling on her lips. "Because when one tells a lie, if one insists on

417

something unusual and eccentric—something too 'out of the way" for anything, you know—the more impossible the thing is, the more plausible does the lie sound. I've noticed this. But I managed it badly; I didn't know how to work it." She suddenly frowned again at this point as though at some sudden unpleasant recollection.

"If"—she began, looking seriously and even sadly at him—"if when I read you all that about the 'poor knight,' I wished to-to praise you for one thing—I also wished to show you that I knew all—and did not approve of your conduct."

"You are very unfair to me, and to that unfortunate woman of whom you spoke just now in such dreadful terms, Aglaya."

"Because I know all, all—and that is why I speak so. I know very well how you—half a year since—offered her your hand before everybody. Don't interrupt me. You see, I am merely stating facts without any comment upon them. After that she ran away with Rogojin. Then you lived with her at some village or town, and she ran away from you." (Aglaya blushed dreadfully.) "Then she returned to Rogojin again, who loves her like a madman. Then you—like a wise man as you are—came back here after her as soon as ever you heard that she had returned to Petersburg. Yesterday evening you sprang forward to protect her, and just now you dreamed about her. You see, I know all. You did come back here for her, for her—now didn't you?"

"Yes—for her!" said the prince softly and sadly, and bending his head down, quite unconscious of the fact that Aglaya was gazing at him with eyes which burned like live coals. "I came to find out something—I don't believe in her future happiness as Rogojin's wife, although—in a word, I did not know how to help her or what to do for her—but I came, on the chance."

He glanced at Aglaya, who was listening with a look of hatred on her face.

"If you came without knowing why, I suppose you love her very much indeed!" she said at last.

"No," said the prince, "no, I do not love her. Oh! if you only knew with what horror I recall the time I spent with her!"

A shudder seemed to sweep over his whole body at the recollection.

"Tell me about it," said Aglaya.

"There is nothing which you might not hear. Why I should wish to tell you, and only you, this experience of mine, I really cannot say; perhaps it really is because I love you very much. This unhappy woman is persuaded that she is the most hopeless, fallen creature in the world. Oh, do not condemn her! Do not cast stones at her! She has suffered too much already in the consciousness of her own undeserved shame.

"And she is not guilty—oh God!—Every moment she bemoans and bewails herself, and cries out that she does not admit any guilt, that she is the victim of circumstances—the victim of a wicked libertine.

"But whatever she may say, remember that she does not believe it herself,—remember that she will believe nothing but that she is a guilty creature.

"When I tried to rid her soul of this gloomy fallacy, she suffered so terribly that my heart will never be quite at peace so long as I can remember that dreadful time!—Do you know why she left me? Simply to prove to me what is not true—that she is base. But the worst of it is, she did not realize herself that that was all she wanted to prove by her departure! She went away in response to some inner prompting to do something disgraceful, in order that she might say to herself—'There—you've done a new act of shame—you degraded creature!'

"Oh, Aglaya—perhaps you cannot understand all this. Try to realize that in the perpetual admission of guilt she probably finds some dreadful unnatural satisfaction—as though she were revenging herself upon someone.

"Now and then I was able to persuade her almost to see light around her again; but she would soon fall, once more, into her old tormenting delusions, and would go so far as to reproach me for placing myself on a pedestal above her (I never had an idea of such a thing!), and informed me, in reply to my proposal of marriage, that she 'did not want condescending sympathy or help from anybody.' You saw her last night. You don't suppose she can be happy among such people as those—you cannot suppose that such society is fit for her? You have no idea how well-educated she is, and what an intellect she has! She astonished me sometimes."

"And you preached her sermons there, did you?"

"Oh no," continued the prince thoughtfully, not noticing Aglaya's mocking tone, "I was almost always silent there. I often wished to speak, but I really did not know what to say. In some cases it is best to say nothing, I think. I loved her, yes, I loved her very much indeed; but afterwards—afterwards she guessed all."

"What did she guess?"

"That I only *pitied* her—and—and loved her no longer!"

"How do you know that? How do you know that she is not really in love with that—that rich cad—the man she eloped with?"

"Oh no! I know she only laughs at him; she has made a fool of him all along."

"Has she never laughed at you?"

"No—in anger, perhaps. Oh yes! she reproached me dreadfully in anger; and suffered herself, too! But afterwards—oh! don't remind me—don't remind me of that!"

He hid his face in his hands.

"Are you aware that she writes to me almost every day?"

"So that is true, is it?" cried the prince, greatly agitated. "I had heard a report of it, but would not believe it."

"Whom did you hear it from?" asked Aglaya, alarmed. "Rogojin said something about it yesterday, but nothing definite."

"Yesterday! Morning or evening? Before the music or after?"

"After—it was about twelve o'clock."

"Ah! Well, if it was Rogojin—but do you know what she writes to me about?"

"I should not be surprised by anything. She is mad!"

"There are the letters." (Aglaya took three letters out of her pocket and threw them down before the prince.) "For a whole week she has been entreating and worrying and persuading me to marry you. She—well, she is clever, though she may be mad—much cleverer than I am, as you say. Well, she writes that she is in love with me herself, and tries to see me every day, if only from a distance. She writes that you love me, and that she has long known it and seen it, and that you and she talked about me—there. She wishes to see you happy, and she says that she is certain only I can ensure you the happiness you deserve. She writes such strange, wild letters—I haven't shown them to anyone. Now, do you know what all this means? Can you guess anything?"

"It is madness—it is merely another proof of her insanity!" said the prince, and his lips trembled.

"You are crying, aren't you?"

"No, Aglaya. No, I'm not crying." The prince looked at her.

"Well, what am I to do? What do you advise me? I cannot go on receiving these letters, you know."

"Oh, let her alone, I entreat you!" cried the prince. "What can you do in this dark, gloomy mystery? Let her alone, and I'll use all my power to prevent her writing you any more letters."

"If so, you are a heartless man!" cried Aglaya. "As if you can't see that it is not myself she loves, but you, you, and only you! Surely you have not remarked everything else in her, and only not *this?* Do you know what these letters mean? They mean jealousy, sir—nothing but pure jealousy! She—do you think she will ever really marry this Rogojin, as she says here she will? She would take her own life the day after you and I were married."

The prince shuddered; his heart seemed to freeze within him. He gazed at Aglaya in wonderment; it was difficult for him to realize that this child was also a woman.

"God knows, Aglaya, that to restore her peace of mind and make her happy I would willingly give up my life. But I cannot love her, and she knows that."

"Oh, make a sacrifice of yourself! That sort of thing becomes you well, you know. Why not do it? And don't call me 'Aglaya'; you have done it several times lately. You are bound, it is your *duty* to 'raise' her; you must go off somewhere again to soothe and pacify her. Why, you love her, you know!"

"I cannot sacrifice myself so, though I admit I did wish to do so once. Who knows, perhaps I still wish to! But I know for*certain*, that if she married me it would be her ruin; I know this and therefore I leave her alone. I ought to go to see her today; now I shall probably not go. She is proud, she would never forgive me the nature of the love I bear her, and we should both be ruined. This may be unnatural, I don't know; but everything seems unnatural. You say she loves me, as if this were *love!*As if she could love *me*, after what I have been through! No, no, it is not love."

"How pale you have grown!" cried Aglaya in alarm.

"Oh, it's nothing. I haven't slept, that's all, and I'm rather tired. I—we certainly did talk about you, Aglaya."

"Oh, indeed, it is true then! *You could actually talk about me with her*; and—and how could you have been fond of me when you had only seen me once?"

"I don't know. Perhaps it was that I seemed to come upon light in the midst of my gloom. I told you the truth when I said I did not know why I thought of you before all others. Of course it was all a sort of dream, a dream amidst the horrors of reality. Afterwards I began to work. I did not intend to come back here for two or three years—"

"Then you came for her sake?" Aglaya's voice trembled.

"Yes, I came for her sake."

There was a moment or two of gloomy silence. Aglaya rose from her seat.

"If you say," she began in shaky tones, "if you say that this woman of yours is mad—at all events I have nothing to do with her insane fancies. Kindly take these three letters, Lef Nicolaievitch, and throw them back to her, from me. And if she dares," cried Aglaya suddenly, much louder than before, "if she dares so much as write me one word again, tell her I shall tell my father, and that she shall be taken to a lunatic asylum."

The prince jumped up in alarm at Aglaya's sudden wrath, and a mist seemed to come before his eyes.

"You cannot really feel like that! You don't mean what you say. It is not true," he murmured.

"It *is* true, it *is* true," cried Aglaya, almost beside herself with rage.

"What's true? What's all this? What's true?" said an alarmed voice just beside them.

Before them stood Lizabetha Prokofievna.

"Why, it's true that I am going to marry Gavrila Ardalionovitch, that I love him and intend to elope with him tomorrow," cried Aglaya, turning upon her mother. "Do you hear? Is your curiosity satisfied? Are you pleased with what you have heard?"

Aglaya rushed away homewards with these words.

"H'm! well, *you* are not going away just yet, my friend, at all events," said Lizabetha, stopping the prince. "Kindly step home with me, and let me have a little explanation of the mystery. Nice goings on, these! I haven't slept a wink all night as it is."

The prince followed her.

IX.

Arrived at her house, Lizabetha Prokofievna paused in the first room. She could go no farther, and subsided on to a couch quite exhausted; too feeble to remember so much as to ask the prince to take a seat. This was a large reception-room, full of flowers, and with a glass door leading into the garden.

Alexandra and Adelaida came in almost immediately, and looked inquiringly at the prince and their mother.

The girls generally rose at about nine in the morning in the country; Aglaya, of late, had been in the habit of getting up rather earlier and having a walk in the garden, but not at seven o'clock; about eight or a little later was her usual time.

Lizabetha Prokofievna, who really had not slept all night, rose at about eight on purpose to meet Aglaya in the garden and walk with her; but she could not find her either in the garden or in her own room.

This agitated the old lady considerably; and she awoke her other daughters. Next, she learned from the maid that Aglaya had gone into the park before seven o'clock. The sisters made a joke of Aglaya's last freak, and told their mother that if she went into the park to look for her, Aglaya would probably be very angry with her, and that she was pretty sure to be sitting reading on the green bench that she had talked of two or three days since, and about which she had nearly quarrelled with Prince S., who did not see anything particularly lovely in it.

Arrived at the rendezvous of the prince and her daughter, and hearing the strange words of the latter, Lizabetha Prokofievna had been dreadfully alarmed, for many reasons. However, now that she had dragged the prince home with her, she began to feel a little frightened at what she had undertaken. Why should not Aglaya meet the prince in the park and have a talk with him, even if such a meeting should be by appointment?

"Don't suppose, prince," she began, bracing herself up for the effort, "don't suppose that I have brought you here to ask questions. After last night, I assure you, I am not so exceedingly anxious to see you at all; I could have postponed the pleasure for a long while." She paused.

"But at the same time you would be very glad to know how I happened to meet Aglaya Ivanovna this morning?" The prince finished her speech for her with the utmost composure.

"Well, what then? Supposing I should like to know?" cried Lizabetha Prokofievna, blushing. "I'm sure I am not afraid of plain speaking. I'm not offending anyone, and I never wish to, and—"

"Pardon me, it is no offence to wish to know this; you are her mother. We met at the green bench this morning, punctually at seven o'clock,—according to an agreement made by Aglaya Ivanovna with myself yesterday. She said that she wished to see me and speak to me about something important. We met and conversed for an hour about matters concerning Aglaya Ivanovna herself, and that's all."

"Of course it is all, my friend. I don't doubt you for a moment," said Lizabetha Prokofievna with dignity.

"Well done, prince, capital!" cried Aglaya, who entered the room at this moment. "Thank you for assuming that I would not demean myself with lies. Come, is that enough, mamma, or do you intend to put any more questions?"

"You know I have never needed to blush before you, up to this day, though perhaps you would have been glad enough to make me," said Lizabetha Prokofievna,—with majesty. "Good-bye, prince; forgive me for bothering you. I trust you will rest assured of my unalterable esteem for you."

The prince made his bows and retired at once. Alexandra and Adelaida smiled and whispered to each other, while Lizabetha Prokofievna glared severely at them. "We are only laughing at the prince's beautiful bows, mamma," said Adelaida. "Sometimes he bows just like a meal-sack, but to-day he was like—like Evgenie Pavlovitch!"

"It is the *heart* which is the best teacher of refinement and dignity, not the dancing-master," said her mother, sententiously, and departed upstairs to her own room, not so much as glancing at Aglaya.

When the prince reached home, about nine o'clock, he found Vera Lebedeff and the maid on the verandah. They were both busy trying to tidy up the place after last night's disorderly party.

"Thank goodness, we've just managed to finish it before you came in!" said Vera, joyfully.

"Good-morning! My head whirls so; I didn't sleep all night. I should like to have a nap now."

"Here, on the verandah? Very well, I'll tell them all not to come and wake you. Papa has gone out somewhere."

The servant left the room. Vera was about to follow her, but returned and approached the prince with a preoccupied air.

"Prince!" she said, "have pity on that poor boy; don't turn him out today."

"Not for the world; he shall do just as he likes."

"He won't do any harm now; and—and don't be too severe with him."

"Oh dear no! Why—"

"And—and you won't *laugh* at him? That's the chief thing."

"Oh no! Never."

"How foolish I am to speak of such things to a man like you," said Vera, blushing. "Though you *do* look tired," she added, half turning away, "your eyes are so splendid at this moment—so full of happiness."

"Really?" asked the prince, gleefully, and he laughed in delight.

But Vera, simple-minded little girl that she was (just like a boy, in fact), here became dreadfully confused, of a sudden, and ran hastily out of the room, laughing and blushing.

"What a dear little thing she is," thought the prince, and immediately forgot all about her.

He walked to the far end of the verandah, where the sofa stood, with a table in front of it. Here he sat down and covered his face with his hands, and so remained for ten minutes. Suddenly he put his hand in his coat-pocket and hurriedly produced three letters.

But the door opened again, and out came Colia.

The prince actually felt glad that he had been interrupted,—and might return the letters to his pocket. He was glad of the respite.

"Well," said Colia, plunging in medias res, as he always did, "here's a go! What do you think of Hippolyte now? Don't respect him any longer, eh?"

"Why not? But look here, Colia, I'm tired; besides, the subject is too melancholy to begin upon again. How is he, though?"

"Asleep—he'll sleep for a couple of hours yet. I quite understand—you haven't slept—you walked about the park, I know. Agitation—excitement—all that sort of thing—quite natural, too!"

"How do you know I walked in the park and didn't sleep at home?"

"Vera just told me. She tried to persuade me not to come, but I couldn't help myself, just for one minute. I have been having my turn at the bedside for the last two hours; Kostia Lebedeff is there now. Burdovsky has gone. Now, lie down, prince, make yourself comfortable, and sleep well! I'm awfully impressed, you know."

"Naturally, all this—"

"No, no, I mean with the 'explanation,' especially that part of it where he talks about Providence and a future life. There is a gigantic thought there."

The prince gazed affectionately at Colia, who, of course, had come in solely for the purpose of talking about this "gigantic thought."

"But it is not any one particular thought, only; it is the general circumstances of the case. If Voltaire had written this now, or Rousseau, I should have just read it and thought it remarkable, but should not have been so *impressed* by it. But a man who knows for certain that he has but ten minutes to live and can talk like that— why—it's—it's *pride*, that is! It is really a most extraordinary, exalted assertion of personal dignity, it's— it's *defiant!* What a *gigantic* strength of will, eh? And to accuse a fellow like that of not putting in the cap on purpose; it's base and mean! You know he deceived us last night, the cunning rascal. I never packed his bag for him, and I never saw his pistol. He packed it himself. But he put me off my guard like that, you see. Vera says you are going to let him stay on; I swear there's no danger, especially as we are always with him."

"Who was by him at night?"

"I, and Burdovsky, and Kostia Lebedeff. Keller stayed a little while, and then went over to Lebedeff's to sleep. Ferdishenko slept at Lebedeff's, too; but he went away at seven o'clock. My father is always at Lebedeff's; but he has gone out just now. I dare say Lebedeff will be coming in here directly; he has been looking for you; I don't know what he wants. Shall we let him in or not, if you are asleep? I'm going to have a nap, too. By-the-by, such a curious thing happened. Burdovsky woke me at seven, and I met my father just outside the room, so drunk, he didn't even know me. He stood before me like a log, and when he recovered himself, asked hurriedly how Hippolyte was. 'Yes,' he said, when I told him, 'that's all very well, but I *really* came to warn you that you must be very careful what you say before Ferdishenko.' Do you follow me, prince?"

"Yes. Is it really so? However, it's all the same to us, of course."

"Of course it is; we are not a secret society; and that being the case, it is all the more curious that the general should have been on his way to wake me up in order to tell me this."

"Ferdishenko has gone, you say?"

"Yes, he went at seven o'clock. He came into the room on his way out; I was watching just then. He said he was going to spend 'the rest of the night' at Wilkin's; there's a tipsy fellow, a friend of his, of that name. Well, I'm off. Oh, here's Lebedeff himself! The prince wants to go to sleep, Lukian Timofeyovitch, so you may just go away again."

"One moment, my dear prince, just one. I must absolutely speak to you about something which is most grave," said Lebedeff, mysteriously and solemnly, entering the room with a bow and looking extremely important. He had but just returned, and carried his hat in his hand. He looked preoccupied and most unusually dignified.

The prince begged him to take a chair.

"I hear you have called twice; I suppose you are still worried about yesterday's affair."

"What, about that boy, you mean? Oh dear no, yesterday my ideas were a little—well—mixed. Today, I assure you, I shall not oppose in the slightest degree any suggestions it may please you to make."

"What's up with you this morning, Lebedeff? You look so important and dignified, and you choose your words so carefully," said the prince, smiling.

"Nicolai Ardalionovitch!" said Lebedeff, in a most amiable tone of voice, addressing the boy. "As I have a communication to make to the prince which concerns only myself—"

"Of course, of course, not my affair. All right," said Colia, and away he went.

"I love that boy for his perception," said Lebedeff, looking after him. "My dear prince," he continued, "I have had a terrible misfortune, either last night or early this morning. I cannot tell the exact time."

"What is it?"

"I have lost four hundred roubles out of my side pocket! They're gone!" said Lebedeff, with a sour smile.

"You've lost four hundred roubles? Oh! I'm sorry for that."

"Yes, it is serious for a poor man who lives by his toil."

"Of course, of course! How was it?"

"Oh, the wine is to blame, of course. I confess to you, prince, as I would to Providence itself. Yesterday I received four hundred roubles from a debtor at about five in the afternoon, and came down here by train. I had my purse in my pocket. When I changed, I put the money into the pocket of my plain clothes, intending to keep it by me, as I expected to have an applicant for it in the evening."

"It's true then, Lebedeff, that you advertise to lend money on gold or silver articles?"

"Yes, through an agent. My own name doesn't appear. I have a large family, you see, and at a small percentage—"

"Quite so, quite so. I only asked for information—excuse the question. Go on."

"Well, meanwhile that sick boy was brought here, and those guests came in, and we had tea, and—well, we made merry—to my ruin! Hearing of your birthday afterwards, and excited with the circumstances of the evening, I ran upstairs and changed my plain clothes once more for my uniform [Civil Service clerks in Russia wear uniform.]— you must have noticed I had my uniform on all the evening? Well, I forgot the money in the pocket of my old coat—you know when God will ruin a man he first of all bereaves him of his senses—and it was only this morning at half-past seven that I woke up and grabbed at my coat pocket, first thing. The pocket was empty—the purse gone, and not a trace to be found!"

"Dear me! This is very unpleasant!"

"Unpleasant! Indeed it is. You have found a very appropriate expression," said Lebedeff, politely, but with sarcasm.

"But what's to be done? It's a serious matter," said the prince, thoughtfully. "Don't you think you may have dropped it out of your pocket whilst intoxicated?"

"Certainly. Anything is possible when one is intoxicated, as you neatly express it, prince. But consider—if I, intoxicated or not, dropped an object out of my pocket on to the ground, that object ought to remain on the ground. Where is the object, then?"

"Didn't you put it away in some drawer, perhaps?"

"I've looked everywhere, and turned out everything."

"I confess this disturbs me a good deal. Someone must have picked it up, then."

"Or taken it out of my pocket—two alternatives."

"It is very distressing, because *who*—? That's the question!"

"Most undoubtedly, excellent prince, you have hit it—that is the very question. How wonderfully you express the exact situation in a few words!"

"Come, come, Lebedeff, no sarcasm! It's a serious—"

"Sarcasm!" cried Lebedeff, wringing his hands. "All right, all right, I'm not angry. I'm only put out about this. Whom do you suspect?"

"That is a very difficult and complicated question. I cannot suspect the servant, for she was in the kitchen the whole evening, nor do I suspect any of my children."

"I should think not. Go on."

"Then it must be one of the guests."

"Is such a thing possible?"

"Absolutely and utterly impossible—and yet, so it must be. But one thing I am sure of, if it be a theft, it was committed, not in the evening when we were all together, but either at night or early in the morning; therefore, by one of those who slept here. Burdovsky and Colia I except, of course. They did not even come into my room."

"Yes, or even if they had! But who did sleep with you?"

"Four of us, including myself, in two rooms. The general, myself, Keller, and Ferdishenko. One of us four it must have been. I don't suspect myself, though such cases have been known."

"Oh! *do* go on, Lebedeff! Don't drag it out so."

"Well, there are three left, then—Keller firstly. He is a drunkard to begin with, and a liberal (in the sense of other people's pockets), otherwise with more of the ancient knight about him than of the modern liberal. He was with the sick man at first, but came over afterwards because there was no place to lie down in the room and the floor was so hard."

"You suspect him?"

"I *did* suspect him. When I woke up at half-past seven and tore my hair in despair for my loss and carelessness, I awoke the general, who was sleeping the sleep of innocence near me. Taking into consideration the sudden disappearance of Ferdishenko, which was suspicious in itself, we decided to search Keller, who was lying there sleeping like a top. Well, we searched his clothes thoroughly, and not a farthing did we find; in fact, his pockets all had holes in them. We found a dirty handkerchief, and a love-letter from some scullery-maid. The general decided that he was innocent. We awoke him for further inquiries, and had the greatest difficulty in making him understand what was up. He opened his mouth and stared—he looked so stupid and so absurdly innocent. It wasn't Keller."

"Oh, I'm so glad!" said the prince, joyfully. "I was so afraid."

"Afraid! Then you had some grounds for supposing he might be the culprit?" said Lebedeff, frowning.

"Oh no—not a bit! It was foolish of me to say I was afraid! Don't repeat it please, Lebedeff, don't tell anyone I said that!"

"My dear prince! your words lie in the lowest depth of my heart—it is their tomb!" said Lebedeff, solemnly, pressing his hat to the region of his heart.

"Thanks; very well. Then I suppose it's Ferdishenko; that is, I mean, you suspect Ferdishenko?"

"Whom else?" said Lebedeff, softly, gazing intently into the prince s face.

"Of course—quite so, whom else? But what are the proofs?"

"We have evidence. In the first place, his mysterious disappearance at seven o'clock, or even earlier."

"I know, Colia told me that he had said he was off to—I forget the name, some friend of his, to finish the night."

"H'm! then Colia has spoken to you already?"

"Not about the theft."

"He does not know of it; I have kept it a secret. Very well, Ferdishenko went off to Wilkin's. That is not so curious in itself, but here the evidence opens out further. He left his address, you see, when he went. Now prince, consider, why did he leave his address? Why do you suppose he went out of his way to tell Colia that he had gone to Wilkin's? Who cared to know that he was going to Wilkin's? No, no! prince, this is finesse, thieves' finesse! This is as good as saying, 'There, how can I be a thief when I leave my address? I'm not concealing my movements as a thief would.' Do you understand, prince?"

"Oh yes, but that is not enough."

"Second proof. The scent turns out to be false, and the address given is a sham. An hour after—that is at about eight, I went to Wilkin's myself, and there was no trace of Ferdishenko. The maid did tell me, certainly, that an hour or so since someone had been hammering at the door, and had smashed the bell; she said she would not open the door because she didn't want to wake her master; probably she was too lazy to get up herself. Such phenomena are met with occasionally!"

"But is that all your evidence? It is not enough!"

"Well, prince, whom are we to suspect, then? Consider!" said Lebedeff with almost servile amiability, smiling at the prince. There was a look of cunning in his eyes, however.

"You should search your room and all the cupboards again," said the prince, after a moment or two of silent reflection.

"But I have done so, my dear prince!" said Lebedeff, more sweetly than ever.

"H'm! why must you needs go up and change your coat like that?" asked the prince, banging the table with his fist, in annoyance.

"Oh, don't be so worried on my account, prince! I assure you I am not worth it! At least, not I alone. But I see you are suffering on behalf of the criminal too, for wretched Ferdishenko, in fact!"

"Of course you have given me a disagreeable enough thing to think about," said the prince, irritably, "but what are you going to do, since you are so sure it was Ferdishenko?"

"But who else *could* it be, my very dear prince?" repeated Lebedeff, as sweet as sugar again. "If you don't wish me to suspect Mr. Burdovsky?"

"Of course not."

"Nor the general? Ha, ha, ha!"

"Nonsense!" said the prince, angrily, turning round upon him.

"Quite so, nonsense! Ha, ha, ha! dear me! He did amuse me, did the general! We went off on the hot scent to Wilkin's together, you know; but I must first observe that the general was even more thunderstruck than I myself this morning, when I awoke him after discovering the theft; so much so that his very face changed—he grew red and then pale, and at length flew into a paroxysm of such noble wrath that I assure you I was quite surprised! He is a most generous-hearted man! He tells lies by the thousands, I know, but it is merely a weakness; he is a man of the highest feelings; a simple-minded man too, and a man who carries the conviction of innocence in his very appearance. I love that man, sir; I may have told you so before; it is a weakness of mine. Well—he suddenly stopped in the middle of the road, opened out his coat and bared his breast. 'Search me,' he says, 'you searched Keller; why don't you search me too? It is only fair!' says he." And all the while his legs and hands were trembling with anger, and he as white as a sheet all over! So I said to him, "Nonsense, general; if anybody but yourself had said that to me, I'd have taken my head, my own head, and put it on a large dish and carried it round to anyone who suspected you; and I should have said: 'There, you see that head? It's my head, and I'll go bail with that head for him! Yes, and walk through the fire for him, too. There,' says I, 'that's how I'd answer for you, general!' Then he embraced me, in the middle of the street, and hugged me so tight (crying over me all the while) that I coughed fit to choke! 'You are the one friend left to me amid all my misfortunes,' says he. Oh, he's a man of sentiment, that! He went on to tell me a story of how he had been accused, or suspected, of stealing five hundred thousand roubles once, as a young man; and how, the very next day, he had rushed into a burning, blazing house and saved the very count who suspected him, and Nina Alexandrovna (who was then a young girl), from a fiery death. The count embraced him, and that was how he came to marry Nina Alexandrovna, he said. As for the money, it was found among the ruins next day in an English iron box with a secret lock; it had got under the floor somehow, and if it had not been for the fire it would never have been found! The whole thing is, of course, an absolute fabrication, though when he spoke of Nina Alexandrovna he wept! She's a grand woman, is Nina Alexandrovna, though she is very angry with me!"

"Are you acquainted with her?"

"Well, hardly at all. I wish I were, if only for the sake of justifying myself in her eyes. Nina Alexandrovna has a grudge against me for, as she thinks, encouraging her husband in drinking; whereas in reality I not only do not encourage him, but I actually keep him out of harm's way, and out of bad company. Besides, he's my friend, prince, so that I shall not lose sight of him, again. Where he goes, I go. He's quite given up visiting the captain's widow, though sometimes he thinks sadly of her, especially in the morning, when he's putting on his boots. I don't know why it's at that time. But he has no money, and it's no use his going to see her without. Has he borrowed any money from you, prince?"

"No, he has not."

"Ah, he's ashamed to! He *meant* to ask you, I know, for he said so. I suppose he thinks that as you gave him some once (you remember), you would probably refuse if he asked you again."

"Do you ever give him money?"

"Prince! Money! Why I would give that man not only my money, but my very life, if he wanted it. Well, perhaps that's exaggeration; not life, we'll say, but some illness, a boil or a bad cough, or anything of that sort, I would stand with pleasure, for his sake; for I consider him a great man fallen—money, indeed!"

"H'm, then you *do* give him money?"

"N-no, I have never given him money, and he knows well that I will never give him any; because I am anxious to keep him out of intemperate ways. He is going to town with me now; for you must know I am off to Petersburg after Ferdishenko, while the scent is hot; I'm certain he is there. I shall let the general go one way, while I go the other; we have so arranged matters in order to pop out upon Ferdishenko, you see, from different sides. But I am going to follow that naughty old general and catch him, I know where, at a certain widow's house; for I think it will be a good lesson, to put him to shame by catching him with the widow."

"Oh, Lebedeff, don't, don't make any scandal about it!" said the prince, much agitated, and speaking in a low voice.

"Not for the world, not for the world! I merely wish to make him ashamed of himself. Oh, prince, great though this misfortune be to myself, I cannot help thinking of his morals! I have a great favour to ask of you, esteemed prince; I confess that it is the chief object of my visit. You know the Ivolgins, you have even lived in their house; so if you would lend me your help, honoured prince, in the general's own interest and for his good."

Lebedeff clasped his hands in supplication.

"What help do you want from me? You may be certain that I am most anxious to understand you, Lebedeff."

"I felt sure of that, or I should not have come to you. We might manage it with the help of Nina Alexandrovna, so that he might be closely watched in his own house. Unfortunately I am not on terms... otherwise... but Nicolai Ardalionovitch, who adores you with all his youthful soul, might help, too."

"No, no! Heaven forbid that we should bring Nina Alexandrovna into this business! Or Colia, either. But perhaps I have not yet quite understood you, Lebedeff?"

Lebedeff made an impatient movement.

"But there is nothing to understand! Sympathy and tenderness, that is all—that is all our poor invalid requires! You will permit me to consider him an invalid?"

"Yes, it shows delicacy and intelligence on your part."

"I will explain my idea by a practical example, to make it clearer. You know the sort of man he is. At present his only failing is that he is crazy about that captain's widow, and he cannot go to her without money, and I mean to catch him at her house today—for his own good; but supposing it was not only the widow, but that he had committed a real crime, or at least some very dishonourable action (of which he is, of course, incapable), I repeat that even in that case, if he were treated with what I may call generous tenderness, one could get at the whole truth, for he is very soft-hearted! Believe me, he would betray himself before five days were out; he would burst into tears, and make a clean breast of the matter; especially if managed with tact, and if you and his family watched his every step, so to speak. Oh, my dear prince," Lebedeff added most emphatically, "I do not positively assert that he has... I am ready, as the saying is, to shed my last drop of blood for him this instant; but you will admit that debauchery, drunkenness, and the captain's widow, all these together may lead him very far."

"I am, of course, quite ready to add my efforts to yours in such a case," said the prince, rising; "but I confess, Lebedeff, that I am terribly perplexed. Tell me, do you still think... plainly, you say yourself that you suspect Mr. Ferdishenko?"

Lebedeff clasped his hands once more.

"Why, who else could I possibly suspect? Who else, most outspoken prince?" he replied, with an unctuous smile.

Muishkin frowned, and rose from his seat.

"You see, Lebedeff, a mistake here would be a dreadful thing. This Ferdishenko, I would not say a word against him, of course; but, who knows? Perhaps it really was he? I mean he really does seem to be a more likely man than... than any other."

Lebedeff strained his eyes and ears to take in what the prince was saying. The latter was frowning more and more, and walking excitedly up and down, trying not to look at Lebedeff.

"You see," he said, "I was given to understand that Ferdishenko was that sort of man,—that one can't say everything before him. One has to take care not to say too much, you understand? I say this to prove that he really is, so to speak, more likely to have done this than anyone else, eh? You understand? The important thing is, not to make a mistake."

"And who told you this about Ferdishenko?"

"Oh, I was told. Of course I don't altogether believe it. I am very sorry that I should have had to say this, because I assure you I don't believe it myself; it is all nonsense, of course. It was stupid of me to say anything about it."

"You see, it is very important, it is most important to know where you got this report from," said Lebedeff, excitedly. He had risen from his seat, and was trying to keep step with the prince, running after him, up and down. "Because look here, prince, I don't mind telling you now that as we were going along to Wilkin's this morning, after telling me what you know about the fire, and saving the count and all that, the general was pleased to drop certain hints to the same effect about Ferdishenko, but so vaguely and clumsily that I thought better to put a few questions to him on the matter, with the result that I found the whole thing was an invention of his excellency's own mind. Of course, he only lies with the best intentions; still, he lies. But, such being the case, where could you have heard the same report? It was the inspiration of the moment with him, you understand, so who could have told *you?* It is an important question, you see!"

"It was Colia told me, and his father told *him* at about six this morning. They met at the threshold, when Colia was leaving the room for something or other." The prince told Lebedeff all that Colia had made known to himself, in detail.

"There now, that's what we may call *scent!*" said Lebedeff, rubbing his hands and laughing silently. "I thought it must be so, you see. The general interrupted his innocent slumbers, at six o'clock, in order to go and wake his beloved son, and warn him of the dreadful danger of companionship with Ferdishenko. Dear me! what a dreadfully dangerous man Ferdishenko must be, and what touching paternal solicitude, on the part of his excellency, ha! ha! ha!"

"Listen, Lebedeff," began the prince, quite overwhelmed; "*do* act quietly—don't make a scandal, Lebedeff, I ask you—I entreat you! No one must know—*no one*, mind! In that case only, I will help you."

"Be assured, most honourable, most worthy of princes—be assured that the whole matter shall be buried within my heart!" cried Lebedeff, in a paroxysm of exaltation. "I'd give every drop of my blood... Illustrious prince, I am a poor wretch in soul and spirit, but ask the veriest scoundrel whether he would prefer to deal with one like himself, or with a noble-hearted man like you, and there is no doubt as to his choice! He'll answer that he prefers the noble-hearted man—and there you have the triumph of virtue! *Au revoir*, honoured prince! You and I together—softly! softly!"

X.

The prince understood at last why he shivered with dread every time he thought of the three letters in his pocket, and why he had put off reading them until the evening.

When he fell into a heavy sleep on the sofa on the verandah, without having had the courage to open a single one of the three envelopes, he again dreamed a painful dream, and once more that poor, "sinful" woman appeared to him. Again she gazed at him with tears sparkling on her long lashes, and beckoned him after her; and again he awoke, as before, with the picture of her face haunting him.

He longed to get up and go to her at once—but he *could not*. At length, almost in despair, he unfolded the letters, and began to read them.

These letters, too, were like a dream. We sometimes have strange, impossible dreams, contrary to all the laws of nature. When we awake we remember them and wonder at their strangeness. You remember, perhaps, that you were in full possession of your reason during this succession of fantastic images; even that you acted with extraordinary logic and cunning while surrounded by murderers who hid their intentions and made great demonstrations of friendship, while waiting for an opportunity to cut your throat. You remember how you escaped them by some ingenious stratagem; then you doubted if they were really deceived, or whether they were only pretending not to know your hiding-place; then you thought of another plan and hoodwinked them once again. You remember all this quite clearly, but how is it that your reason calmly accepted all the manifest absurdities and impossibilities that crowded into your dream? One of the murderers suddenly changed into a woman before your very eyes; then the woman was transformed into a hideous, cunning little dwarf; and you believed it, and accepted it all almost as a matter of course—while at the same time your intelligence seemed unusually keen, and accomplished miracles of cunning, sagacity, and logic! Why is it that when you awake to the world of realities you nearly always feel, sometimes very vividly, that the vanished dream has carried with it some enigma which you have failed to solve? You smile at the extravagance of your dream, and yet you feel that this tissue of absurdity contained some real idea, something that belongs to your true life,—something that exists, and has always existed, in your heart. You search your dream for some prophecy that you were expecting. It has left a deep impression upon you, joyful or cruel, but what it means, or what has been predicted to you in it, you can neither understand nor remember.

The reading of these letters produced some such effect upon the prince. He felt, before he even opened the envelopes, that the very fact of their existence was like a nightmare. How could she ever have made up her mind to write to her? he asked himself. How could she write about that at all? And how could such a wild idea have entered her head? And yet, the strangest part of the matter was, that while he read the letters, he himself almost believed in the possibility, and even in the justification, of the idea he had thought so wild. Of course it was a mad dream, a nightmare, and yet there was something cruelly real about it. For hours he was haunted by what he had read. Several passages returned again and again to his mind, and as he brooded over them, he felt inclined to say to himself that he had foreseen and known all that was written here; it even seemed to him that he had read the whole of this some time or other, long, long ago; and all that had tormented and grieved him up to now was to be found in these old, long since read, letters.

"When you open this letter" (so the first began), "look first at the signature. The signature will tell you all, so that I need explain nothing, nor attempt to justify myself. Were I in any way on a footing with you, you might be offended at my audacity; but who am I, and who are you? We are at such extremes, and I am so far removed from you, that I could not offend you if I wished to do so."

Farther on, in another place, she wrote: "Do not consider my words as the sickly ecstasies of a diseased mind, but you are, in my opinion—perfection! I have seen you—I see you every day. I do not judge you; I have not weighed you in the scales of Reason and found you Perfection—it is simply an article of faith. But I must confess one sin against you—I love you. One should not love perfection. One should only look on it as perfection—yet I am in love with you. Though love equalizes, do not fear. I have not lowered you to my level, even in my most secret thoughts.

426

I have written 'Do not fear,' as if you could fear. I would kiss your footprints if I could; but, oh! I am not putting myself on a level with you!—Look at the signature—quick, look at the signature!"

"However, observe" (she wrote in another of the letters), "that although I couple you with him, yet I have not once asked you whether you love him. He fell in love with you, though he saw you but once. He spoke of you as of 'the light.' These are his own words—I heard him use them. But I understood without his saying it that you were all that light is to him. I lived near him for a whole month, and I understood then that you, too, must love him. I think of you and him as one."

"What was the matter yesterday?" (she wrote on another sheet). "I passed by you, and you seemed to me to *blush*. Perhaps it was only my fancy. If I were to bring you to the most loathsome den, and show you the revelation of undisguised vice—you should not blush. You can never feel the sense of personal affront. You may hate all who are mean, or base, or unworthy—but not for yourself—only for those whom they wrong. No one can wrong *you*. Do you know, I think you ought to love me—for you are the same in my eyes as in his-you are as light. An angel cannot hate, perhaps cannot love, either. I often ask myself—is it possible to love everybody? Indeed it is not; it is not in nature. Abstract love of humanity is nearly always love of self. But you are different. You cannot help loving all, since you can compare with none, and are above all personal offence or anger. Oh! how bitter it would be to me to know that you felt anger or shame on my account, for that would be your fall—you would become comparable at once with such as me.

"Yesterday, after seeing you, I went home and thought out a picture.

"Artists always draw the Saviour as an actor in one of the Gospel stories. I should do differently. I should represent Christ alone—the disciples did leave Him alone occasionally. I should paint one little child left with Him. This child has been playing about near Him, and had probably just been telling the Saviour something in its pretty baby prattle. Christ had listened to it, but was now musing—one hand reposing on the child's bright head. His eyes have a far-away expression. Thought, great as the Universe, is in them—His face is sad. The little one leans its elbow upon Christ's knee, and with its cheek resting on its hand, gazes up at Him, pondering as children sometimes do ponder. The sun is setting. There you have my picture.

"You are innocent—and in your innocence lies all your perfection—oh, remember that! What is my passion to you?—you are mine now; I shall be near you all my life—I shall not live long!"

At length, in the last letter of all, he found:

"For Heaven's sake, don't misunderstand me! Do not think that I humiliate myself by writing thus to you, or that I belong to that class of people who take a satisfaction in humiliating themselves—from pride. I have my consolation, though it would be difficult to explain it—but I do not humiliate myself.

"Why do I wish to unite you two? For your sakes or my own? For my own sake, naturally. All the problems of my life would thus be solved; I have thought so for a long time. I know that once when your sister Adelaida saw my portrait she said that such beauty could overthrow the world. But I have renounced the world. You think it strange that I should say so, for you saw me decked with lace and diamonds, in the company of drunkards and wastrels. Take no notice of that; I know that I have almost ceased to exist. God knows what it is dwelling within me now—it is not myself. I can see it every day in two dreadful eyes which are always looking at me, even when not present. These eyes are silent now, they say nothing; but I know their secret. His house is gloomy, and there is a secret in it. I am convinced that in some box he has a razor hidden, tied round with silk, just like the one that Moscow murderer had. This man also lived with his mother, and had a razor hidden away, tied round with white silk, and with this razor he intended to cut a throat.

"All the while I was in their house I felt sure that somewhere beneath the floor there was hidden away some dreadful corpse, wrapped in oil-cloth, perhaps buried there by his father, who knows? Just as in the Moscow case. I could have shown you the very spot!

"He is always silent, but I know well that he loves me so much that he must hate me. My wedding and yours are to be on the same day; so I have arranged with him. I have no secrets from him. I would kill him from very fright, but he will kill me first. He has just burst out laughing, and says that I am raving. He knows I am writing to you."

There was much more of this delirious wandering in the letters—one of them was very long.

At last the prince came out of the dark, gloomy park, in which he had wandered about for hours just as yesterday. The bright night seemed to him to be lighter than ever. "It must be quite early," he thought. (He had forgotten his watch.) There was a sound of distant music somewhere. "Ah," he thought, "the Vauxhall! They won't be there today, of course!" At this moment he noticed that he was close to their house; he had felt that he must gravitate to this spot eventually, and, with a beating heart, he mounted the verandah steps.

No one met him; the verandah was empty, and nearly pitch dark. He opened the door into the room, but it, too, was dark and empty. He stood in the middle of the room in perplexity. Suddenly the door opened, and in came Alexandra, candle in hand. Seeing the prince she stopped before him in surprise, looking at him questioningly.

It was clear that she had been merely passing through the room from door to door, and had not had the remotest notion that she would meet anyone.

"How did you come here?" she asked, at last.

"I—I—came in—"

"Mamma is not very well, nor is Aglaya. Adelaida has gone to bed, and I am just going. We were alone the whole evening. Father and Prince S. have gone to town."

"I have come to you—now—to—"

"Do you know what time it is?"

"N—no!"

"Half-past twelve. We are always in bed by one."

"I—I thought it was half-past nine!"

"Never mind!" she laughed, "but why didn't you come earlier? Perhaps you were expected!"

"I thought" he stammered, making for the door.

"*Au revoir!* I shall amuse them all with this story tomorrow!"

He walked along the road towards his own house. His heart was beating, his thoughts were confused, everything around seemed to be part of a dream.

And suddenly, just as twice already he had awaked from sleep with the same vision, that very apparition now seemed to rise up before him. The woman appeared to step out from the park, and stand in the path in front of him, as though she had been waiting for him there.

He shuddered and stopped; she seized his hand and pressed it frenziedly.

No, this was no apparition!

There she stood at last, face to face with him, for the first time since their parting.

She said something, but he looked silently back at her. His heart ached with anguish. Oh! never would he banish the recollection of this meeting with her, and he never remembered it but with the same pain and agony of mind.

She went on her knees before him—there in the open road—like a madwoman. He retreated a step, but she caught his hand and kissed it, and, just as in his dream, the tears were sparkling on her long, beautiful lashes.

"Get up!" he said, in a frightened whisper, raising her. "Get up at once!"

"Are you happy—are you happy?" she asked. "Say this one word. Are you happy now? Today, this moment? Have you just been with her? What did she say?"

She did not rise from her knees; she would not listen to him; she put her questions hurriedly, as though she were pursued.

"I am going away tomorrow, as you bade me—I won't write—so that this is the last time I shall see you, the last time! This is really the *last time!*"

"Oh, be calm—be calm! Get up!" he entreated, in despair.

She gazed thirstily at him and clutched his hands.

"Good-bye!" she said at last, and rose and left him, very quickly.

The prince noticed that Rogojin had suddenly appeared at her side, and had taken her arm and was leading her away.

"Wait a minute, prince," shouted the latter, as he went. "I shall be back in five minutes."

He reappeared in five minutes as he had said. The prince was waiting for him.

"I've put her in the carriage," he said; "it has been waiting round the corner there since ten o'clock. She expected that you would be with *them* all the evening. I told her exactly what you wrote me. She won't write to the girl any more, she promises; and tomorrow she will be off, as you wish. She desired to see you for the last time, although you refused, so we've been sitting and waiting on that bench till you should pass on your way home."

"Did she bring you with her of her own accord?"

"Of course she did!" said Rogojin, showing his teeth; "and I saw for myself what I knew before. You've read her letters, I suppose?"

"Did you read them?" asked the prince, struck by the thought.

"Of course—she showed them to me herself. You are thinking of the razor, eh? Ha, ha, ha!"

"Oh, she is mad!" cried the prince, wringing his hands. "Who knows? Perhaps she is not so mad after all," said Rogojin, softly, as though thinking aloud.

The prince made no reply.

"Well, good-bye," said Rogojin. "I'm off tomorrow too, you know. Remember me kindly! By-the-by," he added, turning round sharply again, "did you answer her question just now? Are you happy, or not?"

"No, no, no!" cried the prince, with unspeakable sadness.

"Ha, ha! I never supposed you would say 'yes,'" cried Rogojin, laughing sardonically.

And he disappeared, without looking round again.

A week had elapsed since the rendezvous of our two friends on the green bench in the park, when, one fine morning at about half-past ten o'clock, Varvara Ardalionovna, otherwise Mrs. Ptitsin, who had been out to visit a friend, returned home in a state of considerable mental depression.

There are certain people of whom it is difficult to say anything which will at once throw them into relief—in other words, describe them graphically in their typical characteristics. These are they who are generally known as "commonplace people," and this class comprises, of course, the immense majority of mankind. Authors, as a rule, attempt to select and portray types rarely met with in their entirety, but these types are nevertheless more real than real life itself.

"Podkoleosin" [A character in Gogol's comedy, The Wedding.] was perhaps an exaggeration, but he was by no means a non-existent character; on the contrary, how many intelligent people, after hearing of this Podkoleosin from Gogol, immediately began to find that scores of their friends were exactly like him! They knew, perhaps, before Gogol told them, that their friends were like Podkoleosin, but they did not know what name to give them. In real life, young fellows seldom jump out of the window just before their weddings, because such a feat, not to speak of its other aspects, must be a decidedly unpleasant mode of escape; and yet there are plenty of bridegrooms, intelligent fellows too, who would be ready to confess themselves Podkoleosins in the depths of their consciousness, just before marriage. Nor does every husband feel bound to repeat at every step, "*Tu l'as voulu, Georges Dandin!*" like another typical personage; and yet how many millions and billions of Georges Dandins there are in real life who feel inclined to utter this soul-drawn cry after their honeymoon, if not the day after the wedding! Therefore, without entering into any more serious examination of the question, I will content myself with remarking that in real life typical characters are "watered down," so to speak; and all these Dandins and Podkoleosins actually exist among us every day, but in a diluted form. I will just add, however, that Georges Dandin might have existed exactly as Molière presented him, and probably does exist now and then, though rarely; and so I will end this scientific examination, which is beginning to look like a newspaper criticism. But for all this, the question remains,—what are the novelists to do with commonplace people, and how are they to be presented to the reader in such a form as to be in the least degree interesting? They cannot be left out altogether, for commonplace people meet one at every turn of life, and to leave them out would be to destroy the whole reality and probability of the story. To fill a novel with typical characters only, or with merely strange and uncommon people, would render the book unreal and improbable, and would very likely destroy the interest. In my opinion, the duty of the novelist is to seek out points of interest and instruction even in the characters of commonplace people.

For instance, when the whole essence of an ordinary person's nature lies in his perpetual and unchangeable commonplaceness; and when in spite of all his endeavours to do something out of the common, this person ends, eventually, by remaining in his unbroken line of routine—. I think such an individual really does become a type of his own—a type of commonplaceness which will not for the world, if it can help it, be contented, but strains and yearns to be something original and independent, without the slightest possibility of being so. To this class of commonplace people belong several characters in this novel;—characters which—I admit—I have not drawn very vividly up to now for my reader's benefit.

Such were, for instance, Varvara Ardalionovna Ptitsin, her husband, and her brother, Gania.

There is nothing so annoying as to be fairly rich, of a fairly good family, pleasing presence, average education, to be "not stupid," kind-hearted, and yet to have no talent at all, no originality, not a single idea of one's own—to be, in fact, "just like everyone else."

Of such people there are countless numbers in this world—far more even than appear. They can be divided into two classes as all men can—that is, those of limited intellect, and those who are much cleverer. The former of these classes is the happier.

To a commonplace man of limited intellect, for instance, nothing is simpler than to imagine himself an original character, and to revel in that belief without the slightest misgiving.

Many of our young women have thought fit to cut their hair short, put on blue spectacles, and call themselves Nihilists. By doing this they have been able to persuade themselves, without further trouble, that they have acquired new convictions of their own. Some men have but felt some little qualm of kindness towards their fellow-men, and the fact has been quite enough to persuade them that they stand alone in the van of enlightenment and that no one has such humanitarian feelings as they. Others have but to read an idea of somebody else's, and they can immediately assimilate it and believe that it was a child of their own brain. The "impudence of ignorance," if I may use the expression, is developed to a wonderful extent in such cases;—unlikely as it appears, it is met with at every turn.

This confidence of a stupid man in his own talents has been wonderfully depicted by Gogol in the amazing character of Pirogoff. Pirogoff has not the slightest doubt of his own genius,—nay, of his *superiority* of genius,—so certain is he of it that he never questions it. How many Pirogoffs have there not been among our writers—scholars, propagandists? I say "have been," but indeed there are plenty of them at this very day.

Our friend, Gania, belonged to the other class—to the "much cleverer" persons, though he was from head to foot permeated and saturated with the longing to be original. This class, as I have said above, is far less happy. For the "clever commonplace" person, though he may possibly imagine himself a man of genius and originality, none the less has within his heart the deathless worm of suspicion and doubt; and this doubt sometimes brings a clever man to despair. (As a rule, however, nothing tragic happens;—his liver becomes a little damaged in the course of time, nothing more serious. Such men do not give up their aspirations after originality without a severe struggle,—and there have been men who, though good fellows in themselves, and even benefactors to humanity, have sunk to the level of base criminals for the sake of originality).

Gania was a beginner, as it were, upon this road. A deep and unchangeable consciousness of his own lack of talent, combined with a vast longing to be able to persuade himself that he was original, had rankled in his heart, even from childhood.

He seemed to have been born with overwrought nerves, and in his passionate desire to excel, he was often led to the brink of some rash step; and yet, having resolved upon such a step, when the moment arrived, he invariably proved too sensible to take it. He was ready, in the same way, to do a base action in order to obtain his wished-for object; and yet, when the moment came to do it, he found that he was too honest for any great baseness. (Not that he objected to acts of petty meanness—he was always ready for *them*.) He looked with hate and loathing on the poverty and downfall of his family, and treated his mother with haughty contempt, although he knew that his whole future depended on her character and reputation.

Aglaya had simply frightened him; yet he did not give up all thoughts of her—though he never seriously hoped that she would condescend to him. At the time of his "adventure" with Nastasia Philipovna he had come to the conclusion that money was his only hope—money should do all for him.

At the moment when he lost Aglaya, and after the scene with Nastasia, he had felt so low in his own eyes that he actually brought the money back to the prince. Of this returning of the money given to him by a madwoman who had received it from a madman, he had often repented since—though he never ceased to be proud of his action. During the short time that Muishkin remained in Petersburg Gania had had time to come to hate him for his sympathy, though the prince told him that it was "not everyone who would have acted so nobly" as to return the money. He had long pondered, too, over his relations with Aglaya, and had persuaded himself that with such a strange, childish, innocent character as hers, things might have ended very differently. Remorse then seized him; he threw up his post, and buried himself in self-torment and reproach.

He lived at Ptitsin's, and openly showed contempt for the latter, though he always listened to his advice, and was sensible enough to ask for it when he wanted it. Gavrila Ardalionovitch was angry with Ptitsin because the latter did not care to become a Rothschild. "If you are to be a Jew," he said, "do it properly—squeeze people right and left, show some character; be the King of the Jews while you are about it."

Ptitsin was quiet and not easily offended—he only laughed. But on one occasion he explained seriously to Gania that he was no Jew, that he did nothing dishonest, that he could not help the market price of money, that, thanks to his accurate habits, he had already a good footing and was respected, and that his business was flourishing.

"I shan't ever be a Rothschild, and there is no reason why I should," he added, smiling; "but I shall have a house in the Liteynaya, perhaps two, and that will be enough for me." "Who knows but what I may have three!" he concluded to himself; but this dream, cherished inwardly, he never confided to a soul.

Nature loves and favours such people. Ptitsin will certainly have his reward, not three houses, but four, precisely because from childhood up he had realized that he would never be a Rothschild. That will be the limit of Ptitsin's fortune, and, come what may, he will never have more than four houses.

Varvara Ardalionovna was not like her brother. She too, had passionate desires, but they were persistent rather than impetuous. Her plans were as wise as her methods of carrying them out. No doubt she also belonged to the category of ordinary people who dream of being original, but she soon discovered that she had not a grain of true originality, and she did not let it trouble her too much. Perhaps a certain kind of pride came to her help. She made her first concession to the demands of practical life with great resolution when she consented to marry Ptitsin. However, when she married she did not say to herself, "Never mind a mean action if it leads to the end in view," as her brother would certainly have said in such a case; it is quite probable that he may have said it when he expressed his elder-brotherly satisfaction at her decision. Far from this; Varvara Ardalionovna did not marry until she felt convinced that her future husband was unassuming, agreeable, almost cultured, and that nothing on earth would tempt him to a really dishonourable deed. As to small meannesses, such trifles did not trouble her. Indeed, who is free from them? It is absurd to expect the ideal! Besides, she knew that her marriage would provide a refuge for all her family. Seeing Gania unhappy, she was anxious to help him, in spite of their former disputes and misunderstandings. Ptitsin, in a friendly way, would press his brother-in-law to enter the army. "You know," he said sometimes, jokingly, "you despise generals and generaldom, but you will see that 'they' will all end by being generals in their turn. You will see it if you live long enough!"

"But why should they suppose that I despise generals?" Gania thought sarcastically to himself.

To serve her brother's interests, Varvara Ardalionovna was constantly at the Epanchins' house, helped by the fact that in childhood she and Gania had played with General Ivan Fedorovitch's daughters. It would have been inconsistent with her character if in these visits she had been pursuing a chimera; her project was not chimerical at all; she was building on a firm basis—on her knowledge of the character of the Epanchin family, especially Aglaya, whom she studied closely. All Varvara's efforts were directed towards bringing Aglaya and Gania together. Perhaps she achieved some result; perhaps, also, she made the mistake of depending too much upon her brother, and expecting more from him than he would ever be capable of giving. However this may be, her manoeuvres were skilful enough. For weeks at a time she would never mention Gania. Her attitude was modest but dignified, and she was always extremely truthful and sincere. Examining the depths of her conscience, she found nothing to reproach herself with, and this still further strengthened her in her designs. But Varvara Ardalionovna sometimes remarked that she felt spiteful; that there was a good deal of vanity in her, perhaps even of wounded vanity. She noticed this at certain times more than at others, and especially after her visits to the Epanchins.

Today, as I have said, she returned from their house with a heavy feeling of dejection. There was a sensation of bitterness, a sort of mocking contempt, mingled with it.

Arrived at her own house, Varia heard a considerable commotion going on in the upper storey, and distinguished the voices of her father and brother. On entering the salon she found Gania pacing up and down at frantic speed, pale with rage and almost tearing his hair. She frowned, and subsided on to the sofa with a tired air, and without taking the trouble to remove her hat. She very well knew that if she kept quiet and asked her brother nothing about his reason for tearing up and down the room, his wrath would fall upon her head. So she hastened to put the question:

"The old story, eh?"

"Old story? No! Heaven knows what's up now—I don't! Father has simply gone mad; mother's in floods of tears. Upon my word, Varia, I must kick him out of the house; or else go myself," he added, probably remembering that he could not well turn people out of a house which was not his own.

"You must make allowances," murmured Varia.

"Make allowances? For whom? Him—the old blackguard? No, no, Varia—that won't do! It won't do, I tell you! And look at the swagger of the man! He's all to blame himself, and yet he puts on so much 'side' that you'd think— my word!—'It's too much trouble to go through the gate, you must break the fence for me!' That's the sort of air he puts on; but what's the matter with you, Varia? What a curious expression you have!"

"I'm all right," said Varia, in a tone that sounded as though she were all wrong.

Gania looked more intently at her.

"You've been *there?*" he asked, suddenly.

"Yes."

"Did you find out anything?"

"Nothing unexpected. I discovered that it's all true. My husband was wiser than either of us. Just as he suspected from the beginning, so it has fallen out. Where is he?"

"Out. Well—what has happened?—go on."

"The prince is formally engaged to her—that's settled. The elder sisters told me about it. Aglaya has agreed. They don't attempt to conceal it any longer; you know how mysterious and secret they have all been up to now. Adelaida's wedding is put off again, so that both can be married on one day. Isn't that delightfully romantic? Somebody ought to write a poem on it. Sit down and write an ode instead of tearing up and down like that. This evening Princess Bielokonski is to arrive; she comes just in time—they have a party tonight. He is to be presented to old Bielokonski, though I believe he knows her already; probably the engagement will be openly announced. They are only afraid that he may knock something down, or trip over something when he comes into the room. It would be just like him."

Gania listened attentively, but to his sister's astonishment he was by no means so impressed by this news (which should, she thought, have been so important to him) as she had expected.

"Well, it was clear enough all along," he said, after a moment's reflection. "So that's the end," he added, with a disagreeable smile, continuing to walk up and down the room, but much slower than before, and glancing slyly into his sister's face.

"It's a good thing that you take it philosophically, at all events," said Varia. "I'm really very glad of it."

"Yes, it's off our hands—off *yours*, I should say."

"I think I have served you faithfully. I never even asked you what happiness you expected to find with Aglaya."

"Did I ever expect to find happiness with Aglaya?"

"Come, come, don't overdo your philosophy. Of course you did. Now it's all over, and a good thing, too; pair of fools that we have been! I confess I have never been able to look at it seriously. I busied myself in it for your sake, thinking that there was no knowing what might happen with a funny girl like that to deal with. There were ninety to one chances against it. To this moment I can't make out why you wished for it."

"H'm! now, I suppose, you and your husband will never weary of egging me on to work again. You'll begin your lectures about perseverance and strength of will, and all that. I know it all by heart," said Gania, laughing.

"He's got some new idea in his head," thought Varia. "Are they pleased over there—the parents?" asked Gania, suddenly.

"N—no, I don't think they are. You can judge for yourself. I think the general is pleased enough; her mother is a little uneasy. She always loathed the idea of the prince as a *husband*; everybody knows that."

"Of course, naturally. The bridegroom is an impossible and ridiculous one. I mean, has *she* given her formal consent?"

"She has not said 'no,' up to now, and that's all. It was sure to be so with her. You know what she is like. You know how absurdly shy she is. You remember how she used to hide in a cupboard as a child, so as to avoid seeing visitors, for hours at a time. She is just the same now; but, do you know, I think there is something serious in the matter, even from her side; I feel it, somehow. She laughs at the prince, they say, from morn to night in order to hide her real feelings; but you may be sure she finds occasion to say something or other to him on the sly, for he himself is in a state of radiant happiness. He walks in the clouds; they say he is extremely funny just now; I heard it from themselves. They seemed to be laughing at me in their sleeves—those elder girls—I don't know why."

Gania had begun to frown, and probably Varia added this last sentence in order to probe his thought. However, at this moment, the noise began again upstairs.

"I'll turn him out!" shouted Gania, glad of the opportunity of venting his vexation. "I shall just turn him out—we can't have this."

"Yes, and then he'll go about the place and disgrace us as he did yesterday."

"How 'as he did yesterday'? What do you mean? What did he do yesterday?" asked Gania, in alarm.

"Why, goodness me, don't you know?" Varia stopped short.

"What? You don't mean to say that he went there yesterday!" cried Gania, flushing red with shame and anger. "Good heavens, Varia! Speak! You have just been there. *Was* he there or not, *quick?*" And Gania rushed for the door. Varia followed and caught him by both hands.

"What are you doing? Where are you going to? You can't let him go now; if you do he'll go and do something worse."

"What did he do there? What did he say?" "They couldn't tell me themselves; they couldn't make head or tail of it; but he frightened them all. He came to see the general, who was not at home; so he asked for Lizabetha Prokofievna. First of all, he begged her for some place, or situation, for work of some kind, and then he began to complain about *us*, about me and my husband, and you, especially *you*; he said a lot of things."

"Oh! couldn't you find out?" muttered Gania, trembling hysterically.

"No—nothing more than that. Why, they couldn't understand him themselves; and very likely didn't tell me all."

Gania seized his head with both hands and tottered to the window; Varia sat down at the other window.

"Funny girl, Aglaya," she observed, after a pause. "When she left me she said, 'Give my special and personal respects to your parents; I shall certainly find an opportunity to see your father one day,' and so serious over it. She's a strange creature."

"Wasn't she joking? She was speaking sarcastically!" "Not a bit of it; that's just the strange part of it."

"Does she know about father, do you think—or not?"

"That they do *not* know about it in the house is quite certain, the rest of them, I mean; but you have given me an idea. Aglaya perhaps knows. She alone, though, if anyone; for the sisters were as astonished as I was to hear her speak so seriously. If she knows, the prince must have told her."

"Oh! it's not a great matter to guess who told her. A thief! A thief in our family, and the head of the family, too!"

"Oh! nonsense!" cried Varia, angrily. "That was nothing but a drunkard's tale. Nonsense! Why, who invented the whole thing—Lebedeff and the prince—a pretty pair! Both were probably drunk."

"Father is a drunkard and a thief; I am a beggar, and the husband of my sister is a usurer," continued Gania, bitterly. "There was a pretty list of advantages with which to enchant the heart of Aglaya."

"That same husband of your sister, the usurer—"

"Feeds me? Go on. Don't stand on ceremony, pray."

"Don't lose your temper. You are just like a schoolboy. You think that all this sort of thing would harm you in Aglaya's eyes, do you? You little know her character. She is capable of refusing the most brilliant party, and running away and starving in a garret with some wretched student; that's the sort of girl she is. You never could or did understand how interesting you would have seen in her eyes if you had come firmly and proudly through our misfortunes. The prince has simply caught her with hook and line; firstly, because he never thought of fishing for her, and secondly, because he is an idiot in the eyes of most people. It's quite enough for her that by accepting him she puts her family out and annoys them all round—that's what she likes. You don't understand these things."

"We shall see whether I understand or no!" said Gania, enigmatically. "But I shouldn't like her to know all about father, all the same. I thought the prince would manage to hold his tongue about this, at least. He prevented Lebedeff spreading the news—he wouldn't even tell me all when I asked him—"

"Then you must see that he is not responsible. What does it matter to you now, in any case? What are you hoping for still? If you *have* a hope left, it is that your suffering air may soften her heart towards you."

"Oh, she would funk a scandal like anyone else. You are all tarred with one brush!"

"What! *Aglaya* would have funked? You are a chicken-hearted fellow, Gania!" said Varia, looking at her brother with contempt. "Not one of us is worth much. Aglaya may be a wild sort of a girl, but she is far nobler than any of us, a thousand times nobler!"

"Well—come! there's nothing to get cross about," said Gania.

"All I'm afraid of is—mother. I'm afraid this scandal about father may come to her ears; perhaps it has already. I am dreadfully afraid."

"It undoubtedly has already!" observed Gania.

Varia had risen from her place and had started to go upstairs to her mother; but at this observation of Gania's she turned and gazed at him attentively.

"Who could have told her?"

"Hippolyte, probably. He would think it the most delightful amusement in the world to tell her of it the instant he moved over here; I haven't a doubt of it."

"But how could he know anything of it? Tell me that. Lebedeff and the prince determined to tell no one—even Colia knows nothing."

"What, Hippolyte? He found it out himself, of course. Why, you have no idea what a cunning little animal he is; dirty little gossip! He has the most extraordinary nose for smelling out other people's secrets, or anything approaching to scandal. Believe it or not, but I'm pretty sure he has got round Aglaya. If he hasn't, he soon will. Rogojin is intimate with him, too. How the prince doesn't notice it, I can't understand. The little wretch considers me his enemy now and does his best to catch me tripping. What on earth does it matter to him, when he's dying? However, you'll see; I shall catch *him* tripping yet, and not he me."

"Why did you get him over here, if you hate him so? And is it really worth your while to try to score off him?"

"Why, it was yourself who advised me to bring him over!"

"I thought he might be useful. You know he is in love with Aglaya himself, now, and has written to her; he has even written to Lizabetha Prokofievna!"

"Oh! he's not dangerous there!" cried Gania, laughing angrily. "However, I believe there is something of that sort in the air; he is very likely to be in love, for he is a mere boy. But he won't write anonymous letters to the old lady; that would be too audacious a thing for him to attempt; but I dare swear the very first thing he did was to show me up to Aglaya as a base deceiver and intriguer. I confess I was fool enough to attempt something through him at first. I thought he would throw himself into my service out of revengeful feelings towards the prince, the sly little beast! But I know him better now. As for the theft, he may have heard of it from the widow in Petersburg, for if the old man committed himself to such an act, he can have done it for no other object but to give the money to her. Hippolyte said to me, without any prelude, that the general had promised the widow four hundred roubles. Of course I understood, and the little wretch looked at me with a nasty sort of satisfaction. I know him; you may depend upon it he went and told mother too, for the pleasure of wounding her. And why doesn't he die, I should like to know? He undertook to die within three weeks, and here he is getting fatter. His cough is better, too. It was only yesterday that he said that was the second day he hadn't coughed blood."

"Well, turn him out!"

"I don't *hate*, I despise him," said Gania, grandly. "Well, I do hate him, if you like!" he added, with a sudden access of rage, "and I'll tell him so to his face, even when he's dying! If you had but read his confession—good Lord! what refinement of impudence! Oh, but I'd have liked to whip him then and there, like a schoolboy, just to see how surprised he would have been! Now he hates everybody because he—Oh, I say, what on earth are they doing there! Listen to that noise! I really can't stand this any longer. Ptitsin!" he cried, as the latter entered the room, "what in the name of goodness are we coming to? Listen to that—"

But the noise came rapidly nearer, the door burst open, and old General Ivolgin, raging, furious, purple-faced, and trembling with anger, rushed in. He was followed by Nina Alexandrovna, Colia, and behind the rest, Hippolyte.

Hippolyte had now been five days at the Ptitsins'. His flitting from the prince's to these new quarters had been brought about quite naturally and without many words. He did not quarrel with the prince—in fact, they seemed to part as friends. Gania, who had been hostile enough on that eventful evening, had himself come to see him a couple of days later, probably in obedience to some sudden impulse. For some reason or other, Rogojin too had begun to visit the sick boy. The prince thought it might be better for him to move away from his (the prince's) house. Hippolyte informed him, as he took his leave, that Ptitsin "had been kind enough to offer him a corner," and did not say a word about Gania, though Gania had procured his invitation, and himself came to fetch him away. Gania noticed this at the time, and put it to Hippolyte's debit on account.

Gania was right when he told his sister that Hippolyte was getting better; that he was better was clear at the first glance. He entered the room now last of all, deliberately, and with a disagreeable smile on his lips.

Nina Alexandrovna came in, looking frightened. She had changed much since we last saw her, half a year ago, and had grown thin and pale. Colia looked worried and perplexed. He could not understand the vagaries of the general, and knew nothing of the last achievement of that worthy, which had caused so much commotion in the house. But he could see that his father had of late changed very much, and that he had begun to behave in so extraordinary a fashion both at home and abroad that he was not like the same man. What perplexed and disturbed him as much as anything was that his father had entirely given up drinking during the last few days. Colia knew that he had quarrelled with both Lebedeff and the prince, and had just bought a small bottle of vodka and brought it home for his father.

"Really, mother," he had assured Nina Alexandrovna upstairs, "really you had better let him drink. He has not had a drop for three days; he must be suffering agonies— The general now entered the room, threw the door wide open, and stood on the threshold trembling with indignation.

"Look here, my dear sir," he began, addressing Ptitsin in a very loud tone of voice; "if you have really made up your mind to sacrifice an old man—your father too or at all events father of your wife—an old man who has served his emperor—to a wretched little atheist like this, all I can say is, sir, my foot shall cease to tread your floors. Make your choice, sir; make your choice quickly, if you please! Me or this—screw! Yes, screw, sir; I said it accidentally, but let the word stand—this screw, for he screws and drills himself into my soul—"

"Hadn't you better say corkscrew?" said Hippolyte.

"No, sir, *not* corkscrew. I am a general, not a bottle, sir. Make your choice, sir—me or him."

Here Colia handed him a chair, and he subsided into it, breathless with rage.

"Hadn't you better—better—take a nap?" murmured the stupefied Ptitsin.

"A nap?" shrieked the general. "I am not drunk, sir; you insult me! I see," he continued, rising, "I see that all are against me here. Enough—I go; but know, sirs—know that—"

He was not allowed to finish his sentence. Somebody pushed him back into his chair, and begged him to be calm. Nina Alexandrovna trembled, and cried quietly. Gania retired to the window in disgust.

"But what have I done? What is his grievance?" asked Hippolyte, grinning.

"What have you done, indeed?" put in Nina Alexandrovna. "You ought to be ashamed of yourself, teasing an old man like that—and in your position, too."

"And pray what *is* my position, madame? I have the greatest respect for you, personally; but—"

"He's a little screw," cried the general; "he drills holes my heart and soul. He wishes me to be a pervert to atheism. Know, you young greenhorn, that I was covered with honours before ever you were born; and you are nothing better than a wretched little worm, torn in two with coughing, and dying slowly of your own malice and unbelief. What did Gavrila bring you over here for? They're all against me, even to my own son—all against me."

"Oh, come—nonsense!" cried Gania; "if you did not go shaming us all over the town, things might be better for all parties."

"What—shame you? I?—what do you mean, you young calf? I shame you? I can only do you honour, sir; I cannot shame you."

He jumped up from his chair in a fit of uncontrollable rage. Gania was very angry too.

"Honour, indeed!" said the latter, with contempt.

"What do you say, sir?" growled the general, taking a step towards him.

"I say that I have but to open my mouth, and you—"

Gania began, but did not finish. The two—father and son—stood before one another, both unspeakably agitated, especially Gania.

"Gania, Gania, reflect!" cried his mother, hurriedly.

"It's all nonsense on both sides," snapped out Varia. "Let them alone, mother."

"It's only for mother's sake that I spare him," said Gania, tragically.

"Speak!" said the general, beside himself with rage and excitement; "speak—under the penalty of a father's curse!"

"Oh, father's curse be hanged—you don't frighten me that way!" said Gania. "Whose fault is it that you have been as mad as a March hare all this week? It is just a week—you see, I count the days. Take care now; don't provoke me too much, or I'll tell all. Why did you go to the Epanchins' yesterday—tell me that? And you call yourself an old man, too, with grey hair, and father of a family! H'm—nice sort of a father."

"Be quiet, Gania," cried Colia. "Shut up, you fool!"

"Yes, but how have I offended him?" repeated Hippolyte, still in the same jeering voice. "Why does he call me a screw? You all heard it. He came to me himself and began telling me about some Captain Eropegoff. I don't wish for your company, general. I always avoided you—you know that. What have I to do with Captain Eropegoff? All I did was to express my opinion that probably Captain Eropegoff never existed at all!"

"Of course he never existed!" Gania interrupted.

But the general only stood stupefied and gazed around in a dazed way. Gania's speech had impressed him, with its terrible candour. For the first moment or two he could find no words to answer him, and it was only when Hippolyte burst out laughing, and said:

"There, you see! Even your own son supports my statement that there never was such a person as Captain Eropegoff!" that the old fellow muttered confusedly:

"Kapiton Eropegoff—not Captain Eropegoff!—Kapiton—major retired—Eropegoff—Kapiton."

"Kapiton didn't exist either!" persisted Gania, maliciously.

"What? Didn't exist?" cried the poor general, and a deep blush suffused his face.

"That'll do, Gania!" cried Varia and Ptitsin.

"Shut up, Gania!" said Colia.

But this intercession seemed to rekindle the general.

"What did you mean, sir, that he didn't exist? Explain yourself," he repeated, angrily.

"Because he *didn't* exist—never could and never did—there! You'd better drop the subject, I warn you!"

"And this is my son—my own son—whom I—oh, gracious Heaven! Eropegoff—Eroshka Eropegoff didn't exist!"

"Ha, ha! it's Eroshka now," laughed Hippolyte.

"No, sir, Kapitoshka—not Eroshka. I mean, Kapiton Alexeyevitch—retired major—married Maria Petrovna Lu—Lu—he was my friend and companion—Lutugoff—from our earliest beginnings. I closed his eyes for him—he was killed. Kapiton Eropegoff never existed! tfu!"

The general shouted in his fury; but it was to be concluded that his wrath was not kindled by the expressed doubt as to Kapiton's existence. This was his scapegoat; but his excitement was caused by something quite different. As a rule he would have merely shouted down the doubt as to Kapiton, told a long yarn about his friend, and eventually retired upstairs to his room. But today, in the strange uncertainty of human nature, it seemed to require but so small an offence as this to make his cup to overflow. The old man grew purple in the face, he raised his hands. "Enough of this!" he yelled. "My curse—away, out of the house I go! Colia, bring my bag away!" He left the room hastily and in a paroxysm of rage.

His wife, Colia, and Ptitsin ran out after him.

"What have you done now?" said Varia to Gania. "He'll probably be making off *there* again! What a disgrace it all is!"

"Well, he shouldn't steal," cried Gania, panting with fury. And just at this moment his eye met Hippolyte's.

"As for you, sir," he cried, "you should at least remember that you are in a strange house and—receiving hospitality; you should not take the opportunity of tormenting an old man, sir, who is too evidently out of his mind."

Hippolyte looked furious, but he restrained himself.

"I don't quite agree with you that your father is out of his mind," he observed, quietly. "On the contrary, I cannot help thinking he has been less demented of late. Don't you think so? He has grown so cunning and careful, and weighs his words so deliberately; he spoke to me about that Kapiton fellow with an object, you know! Just fancy—he wanted me to—"

"Oh, devil take what he wanted you to do! Don't try to be too cunning with me, young man!" shouted Gania. "If you are aware of the real reason for my father's present condition (and you have kept such an excellent spying watch during these last few days that you are sure to be aware of it)—you had no right whatever to torment the—unfortunate man, and to worry my mother by your exaggerations of the affair; because the whole business is nonsense—simply a drunken freak, and nothing more, quite unproved by any evidence, and I don't believe that much of it!" (he snapped his fingers). "But you must needs spy and watch over us all, because you are a—a—"

"Screw!" laughed Hippolyte.

"Because you are a humbug, sir; and thought fit to worry people for half an hour, and tried to frighten them into believing that you would shoot yourself with your little empty pistol, pirouetting about and playing at suicide! I gave you hospitality, you have fattened on it, your cough has left you, and you repay all this—"

"Excuse me—two words! I am Varvara Ardalionovna's guest, not yours; *you* have extended no hospitality to me. On the contrary, if I am not mistaken, I believe you are yourself indebted to Mr. Ptitsin's hospitality. Four days ago I begged my mother to come down here and find lodgings, because I certainly do feel better here, though I am not fat, nor have I ceased to cough. I am today informed that my room is ready for me; therefore, having thanked your sister and mother for their kindness to me, I intend to leave the house this evening. I beg your pardon—I interrupted you—I think you were about to add something?"

"Oh—if that is the state of affairs—" began Gania.

"Excuse me—I will take a seat," interrupted Hippolyte once more, sitting down deliberately; "for I am not strong yet. Now then, I am ready to hear you. Especially as this is the last chance we shall have of a talk, and very likely the last meeting we shall ever have at all."

Gania felt a little guilty.

"I assure you I did not mean to reckon up debits and credits," he began, "and if you—"

"I don't understand your condescension," said Hippolyte. "As for me, I promised myself, on the first day of my arrival in this house, that I would have the satisfaction of settling accounts with you in a very thorough manner before I said good-bye to you. I intend to perform this operation now, if you like; after you, though, of course."

"May I ask you to be so good as to leave this room?"

"You'd better speak out. You'll be sorry afterwards if you don't."

"Hippolyte, stop, please! It's so dreadfully undignified," said Varia.

"Well, only for the sake of a lady," said Hippolyte, laughing. "I am ready to put off the reckoning, but only put it off, Varvara Ardalionovna, because an explanation between your brother and myself has become an absolute necessity, and I could not think of leaving the house without clearing up all misunderstandings first."

"In a word, you are a wretched little scandal-monger," cried Gania, "and you cannot go away without a scandal!"

"You see," said Hippolyte, coolly, "you can't restrain yourself. You'll be dreadfully sorry afterwards if you don't speak out now. Come, you shall have the first say. I'll wait."

Gania was silent and merely looked contemptuously at him.

"You won't? Very well. I shall be as short as possible, for my part. Two or three times to-day I have had the word 'hospitality' pushed down my throat; this is not fair. In inviting me here you yourself entrapped me for your own use; you thought I wished to revenge myself upon the prince. You heard that Aglaya Ivanovna had been kind to me and read my confession. Making sure that I should give myself up to your interests, you hoped that you might get some assistance out of me. I will not go into details. I don't ask either admission or confirmation of this from yourself; I am quite content to leave you to your conscience, and to feel that we understand one another capitally."

"What a history you are weaving out of the most ordinary circumstances!" cried Varia.

"I told you the fellow was nothing but a scandalmonger," said Gania.

"Excuse me, Varia Ardalionovna, I will proceed. I can, of course, neither love nor respect the prince, though he is a good-hearted fellow, if a little queer. But there is no need whatever for me to hate him. I quite understood your brother when he first offered me aid against the prince, though I did not show it; I knew well that your brother was making a ridiculous mistake in me. I am ready to spare him, however, even now; but solely out of respect for yourself, Varvara Ardalionovna.

"Having now shown you that I am not quite such a fool as I look, and that I have to be fished for with a rod and line for a good long while before I am caught, I will proceed to explain why I specially wished to make your brother look a fool. That my motive power is hate, I do not attempt to conceal. I have felt that before dying (and I am dying, however much fatter I may appear to you), I must absolutely make a fool of, at least, one of that class of men which has dogged me all my life, which I hate so cordially, and which is so prominently represented by your much esteemed brother. I should not enjoy paradise nearly so much without having done this first. I hate you, Gavrila Ardalionovitch, solely (this may seem curious to you, but I repeat)—solely because you are the type, and incarnation, and head, and crown of the most impudent, the most self-satisfied, the most vulgar and detestable form of commonplaceness. You are ordinary of the ordinary; you have no chance of ever fathering the pettiest idea of your own. And yet you are as jealous and conceited as you can possibly be; you consider yourself a great genius; of this you are persuaded, although there are dark moments of doubt and rage, when even this fact seems uncertain. There are spots of darkness on your horizon, though they will disappear when you become completely stupid. But a long and chequered path lies before you, and of this I am glad. In the first place you will never gain a certain person."

"Come, come! This is intolerable! You had better stop, you little mischief-making wretch!" cried Varia. Gania had grown very pale; he trembled, but said nothing.

436

Hippolyte paused, and looked at him intently and with great gratification. He then turned his gaze upon Varia, bowed, and went out, without adding another word.

Gania might justly complain of the hardness with which fate treated him. Varia dared not speak to him for a long while, as he strode past her, backwards and forwards. At last he went and stood at the window, looking out, with his back turned towards her. There was a fearful row going on upstairs again.

"Are you off?" said Gania, suddenly, remarking that she had risen and was about to leave the room. "Wait a moment—look at this."

He approached the table and laid a small sheet of paper before her. It looked like a little note.

"Good heavens!" cried Varia, raising her hands.

This was the note:

"Gavrila Ardolionovitch,—persuaded of your kindness of heart, I have determined to ask your advice on a matter of great importance to myself. I should like to meet you tomorrow morning at seven o'clock by the green bench in the park. It is not far from our house. Varvara Ardalionovna, who must accompany you, knows the place well.

"A. E."

"What on earth is one to make of a girl like that?" said Varia.

Gania, little as he felt inclined for swagger at this moment, could not avoid showing his triumph, especially just after such humiliating remarks as those of Hippolyte. A smile of self-satisfaction beamed on his face, and Varia too was brimming over with delight.

"And this is the very day that they were to announce the engagement! What will she do next?"

"What do you suppose she wants to talk about tomorrow?" asked Gania.

"Oh, *that's* all the same! The chief thing is that she wants to see you after six months' absence. Look here, Gania, this is a *serious* business. Don't swagger again and lose the game—play carefully, but don't funk, do you understand? As if she could possibly avoid seeing what I have been working for all this last six months! And just imagine, I was there this morning and not a word of this! I was there, you know, on the sly. The old lady did not know, or she would have kicked me out. I ran some risk for you, you see. I did so want to find out, at all hazards."

Here there was a frantic noise upstairs once more; several people seemed to be rushing downstairs at once.

"Now, Gania," cried Varia, frightened, "we can't let him go out! We can't afford to have a breath of scandal about the town at this moment. Run after him and beg his pardon—quick."

But the father of the family was out in the road already. Colia was carrying his bag for him; Nina Alexandrovna stood and cried on the doorstep; she wanted to run after the general, but Ptitsin kept her back.

"You will only excite him more," he said. "He has nowhere else to go to—he'll be back here in half an hour. I've talked it all over with Colia; let him play the fool a bit, it will do him good."

"What are you up to? Where are you off to? You've nowhere to go to, you know," cried Gania, out of the window.

"Come back, father; the neighbours will hear!" cried Varia.

The general stopped, turned round, raised his hands and remarked: "My curse be upon this house!"

"Which observation should always be made in as theatrical a tone as possible," muttered Gania, shutting the window with a bang.

The neighbours undoubtedly did hear. Varia rushed out of the room.

No sooner had his sister left him alone, than Gania took the note out of his pocket, kissed it, and pirouetted around.

III.

As a general rule, old General Ivolgin's paroxysms ended in smoke. He had before this experienced fits of sudden fury, but not very often, because he was really a man of peaceful and kindly disposition. He had tried hundreds of times to overcome the dissolute habits which he had contracted of late years. He would suddenly remember that he was "a father," would be reconciled with his wife, and shed genuine tears. His feeling for Nina Alexandrovna amounted almost to adoration; she had pardoned so much in silence, and loved him still in spite of the state of degradation into which he had fallen. But the general's struggles with his own weakness never lasted very long. He was, in his way, an impetuous man, and a quiet life of repentance in the bosom of his family soon became insupportable to him. In the end he rebelled, and flew into rages which he regretted, perhaps, even as he gave way to them, but which were beyond his control. He picked quarrels with everyone, began to hold forth eloquently, exacted unlimited respect, and at last disappeared from the house, and sometimes did not return for a long time. He had given up interfering in the affairs of his family for two years now, and knew nothing about them but what he gathered from hearsay.

But on this occasion there was something more serious than usual. Everyone seemed to know something, but to be afraid to talk about it.

The general had turned up in the bosom of his family two or three days before, but not, as usual, with the olive branch of peace in his hand, not in the garb of penitence—in which he was usually clad on such occasions—but, on the contrary, in an uncommonly bad temper. He had arrived in a quarrelsome mood, pitching into everyone he came across, and talking about all sorts and kinds of subjects in the most unexpected manner, so that it was impossible to discover what it was that was really putting him out. At moments he would be apparently quite bright and happy; but as a rule he would sit moody and thoughtful. He would abruptly commence to hold forth about the Epanchins, about Lebedeff, or the prince, and equally abruptly would stop short and refuse to speak another word, answering all further questions with a stupid smile, unconscious that he was smiling, or that he had been asked a question. The whole of the previous night he had spent tossing about and groaning, and poor Nina Alexandrovna had been busy making cold compresses and warm fomentations and so on, without being very clear how to apply them. He had fallen asleep after a while, but not for long, and had awaked in a state of violent hypochondria which had ended in his quarrel with Hippolyte, and the solemn cursing of Ptitsin's establishment generally. It was also observed during those two or three days that he was in a state of morbid self-esteem, and was specially touchy on all points of honour. Colia insisted, in discussing the matter with his mother, that all this was but the outcome of abstinence from drink, or perhaps of pining after Lebedeff, with whom up to this time the general had been upon terms of the greatest friendship; but with whom, for some reason or other, he had quarrelled a few days since, parting from him in great wrath. There had also been a scene with the prince. Colia had asked an explanation of the latter, but had been forced to conclude that he was not told the whole truth.

If Hippolyte and Nina Alexandrovna had, as Gania suspected, had some special conversation about the general's actions, it was strange that the malicious youth, whom Gania had called a scandal-monger to his face, had not allowed himself a similar satisfaction with Colia.

The fact is that probably Hippolyte was not quite so black as Gania painted him; and it was hardly likely that he had informed Nina Alexandrovna of certain events, of which we know, for the mere pleasure of giving her pain. We must never forget that human motives are generally far more complicated than we are apt to suppose, and that we can very rarely accurately describe the motives of another. It is much better for the writer, as a rule, to content himself with the bare statement of events; and we shall take this line with regard to the catastrophe recorded above, and shall state the remaining events connected with the general's trouble shortly, because we feel that we have already given to this secondary character in our story more attention than we originally intended.

The course of events had marched in the following order. When Lebedeff returned, in company with the general, after their expedition to town a few days since, for the purpose of investigation, he brought the prince no information whatever. If the latter had not himself been occupied with other thoughts and impressions at the time, he must have observed that Lebedeff not only was very uncommunicative, but even appeared anxious to avoid him.

When the prince did give the matter a little attention, he recalled the fact that during these days he had always found Lebedeff to be in radiantly good spirits, when they happened to meet; and further, that the general and Lebedeff were always together. The two friends did not seem ever to be parted for a moment.

Occasionally the prince heard loud talking and laughing upstairs, and once he detected the sound of a jolly soldier's song going on above, and recognized the unmistakable bass of the general's voice. But the sudden outbreak of song did not last; and for an hour afterwards the animated sound of apparently drunken conversation continued to be heard from above. At length there was the clearest evidence of a grand mutual embracing, and someone burst into tears. Shortly after this, however, there was a violent but short-lived quarrel, with loud talking on both sides.

All these days Colia had been in a state of great mental preoccupation. Muishkin was usually out all day, and only came home late at night. On his return he was invariably informed that Colia had been looking for him. However, when they did meet, Colia never had anything particular to tell him, excepting that he was highly dissatisfied with the general and his present condition of mind and behaviour.

"They drag each other about the place," he said, "and get drunk together at the pub close by here, and quarrel in the street on the way home, and embrace one another after it, and don't seem to part for a moment."

When the prince pointed out that there was nothing new about that, for that they had always behaved in this manner together, Colia did not know what to say; in fact he could not explain what it was that specially worried him, just now, about his father.

On the morning following the bacchanalian songs and quarrels recorded above, as the prince stepped out of the house at about eleven o'clock, the general suddenly appeared before him, much agitated.

"I have long sought the honour and opportunity of meeting you—much-esteemed Lef Nicolaievitch," he murmured, pressing the prince's hand very hard, almost painfully so; "long—very long."

The prince begged him to step in and sit down.

"No—I will not sit down,—I am keeping you, I see,—another time!—I think I may be permitted to congratulate you upon the realization of your heart's best wishes, is it not so?"

"What best wishes?"

The prince blushed. He thought, as so many in his position do, that nobody had seen, heard, noticed, or understood anything.

"Oh—be easy, sir, be easy! I shall not wound your tenderest feelings. I've been through it all myself, and I know well how unpleasant it is when an outsider sticks his nose in where he is not wanted. I experience this every morning. I came to speak to you about another matter, though, an important matter. A very important matter, prince."

The latter requested him to take a seat once more, and sat down himself.

"Well—just for one second, then. The fact is, I came for advice. Of course I live now without any very practical objects in life; but, being full of self-respect, in which quality the ordinary Russian is so deficient as a rule, and of activity, I am desirous, in a word, prince, of placing myself and my wife and children in a position of—in fact, I want advice."

The prince commended his aspirations with warmth.

"Quite so—quite so! But this is all mere nonsense. I came here to speak of something quite different, something very important, prince. And I have determined to come to you as to a man in whose sincerity and nobility of feeling I can trust like—like—are you surprised at my words, prince?"

The prince was watching his guest, if not with much surprise, at all events with great attention and curiosity.

The old man was very pale; every now and then his lips trembled, and his hands seemed unable to rest quietly, but continually moved from place to place. He had twice already jumped up from his chair and sat down again without being in the least aware of it. He would take up a hook from the table and open it—talking all the while,— look at the heading of a chapter, shut it and put it back again, seizing another immediately, but holding it unopened in his hand, and waving it in the air as he spoke.

"But enough!" he cried, suddenly. "I see I have been boring you with my—"

"Not in the least—not in the least, I assure you. On the contrary, I am listening most attentively, and am anxious to guess-"

"Prince, I wish to place myself in a respectable position—I wish to esteem myself—and to—"

"My dear sir, a man of such noble aspirations is worthy of all esteem by virtue of those aspirations alone."

The prince brought out his "copy-book sentence" in the firm belief that it would produce a good effect. He felt instinctively that some such well-sounding humbug, brought out at the proper moment, would soothe the old man's feelings, and would be specially acceptable to such a man in such a position. At all hazards, his guest must be despatched with heart relieved and spirit comforted; that was the problem before the prince at this moment.

The phrase flattered the general, touched him, and pleased him mightily. He immediately changed his tone, and started off on a long and solemn explanation. But listen as he would, the prince could make neither head nor tail of it.

The general spoke hotly and quickly for ten minutes; he spoke as though his words could not keep pace with his crowding thoughts. Tears stood in his eyes, and yet his speech was nothing but a collection of disconnected sentences, without beginning and without end—a string of unexpected words and unexpected sentiments— colliding with one another, and jumping over one another, as they burst from his lips.

"Enough!" he concluded at last, "you understand me, and that is the great thing. A heart like yours cannot help understanding the sufferings of another. Prince, you are the ideal of generosity; what are other men beside yourself? But you are young—accept my blessing! My principal object is to beg you to fix an hour for a most important conversation—that is my great hope, prince. My heart needs but a little friendship and sympathy, and yet I cannot always find means to satisfy it."

"But why not now? I am ready to listen, and—"

"No, no—prince, not now! Now is a dream! And it is too, too important! It is to be the hour of Fate to me—*my own* hour. Our interview is not to be broken in upon by every chance comer, every impertinent guest—and there are plenty of such stupid, impertinent fellows"—(he bent over and whispered mysteriously, with a funny, frightened look on his face)—"who are unworthy to tie your shoe, prince. I don't say *mine*, mind—you will understand me, prince. Only *you* understand me, prince—no one else. *he* doesn't understand me, he is absolutely— *absolutely* unable to sympathize. The first qualification for understanding another is Heart."

The prince was rather alarmed at all this, and was obliged to end by appointing the same hour of the following day for the interview desired. The general left him much comforted and far less agitated than when he had arrived.

At seven in the evening, the prince sent to request Lebedeff to pay him a visit. Lebedeff came at once, and "esteemed it an honour," as he observed, the instant he entered the room. He acted as though there had never been the slightest suspicion of the fact that he had systematically avoided the prince for the last three days.

He sat down on the edge of his chair, smiling and making faces, and rubbing his hands, and looking as though he were in delighted expectation of hearing some important communication, which had been long guessed by all.

The prince was instantly covered with confusion; for it appeared to be plain that everyone expected something of him—that everyone looked at him as though anxious to congratulate him, and greeted him with hints, and smiles, and knowing looks.

Keller, for instance, had run into the house three times of late, "just for a moment," and each time with the air of desiring to offer his congratulations. Colia, too, in spite of his melancholy, had once or twice begun sentences in much the same strain of suggestion or insinuation.

The prince, however, immediately began, with some show of annoyance, to question Lebedeff categorically, as to the general's present condition, and his opinion thereon. He described the morning's interview in a few words.

"Everyone has his worries, prince, especially in these strange and troublous times of ours," Lebedeff replied, drily, and with the air of a man disappointed of his reasonable expectations.

"Dear me, what a philosopher you are!" laughed the prince.

"Philosophy is necessary, sir—very necessary—in our day. It is too much neglected. As for me, much esteemed prince, I am sensible of having experienced the honour of your confidence in a certain matter up to a certain point, but never beyond that point. I do not for a moment complain—"

"Lebedeff, you seem to be angry for some reason!" said the prince.

"Not the least bit in the world, esteemed and revered prince! Not the least bit in the world!" cried Lebedeff, solemnly, with his hand upon his heart. "On the contrary, I am too painfully aware that neither by my position in the world, nor by my gifts of intellect and heart, nor by my riches, nor by any former conduct of mine, have I in any way deserved your confidence, which is far above my highest aspirations and hopes. Oh no, prince; I may serve you, but only as your humble slave! I am not angry, oh no! Not angry; pained perhaps, but nothing more.

"My dear Lebedeff, I—"

"Oh, nothing more, nothing more! I was saying to myself but now... 'I am quite unworthy of friendly relations with him,' say I; 'but perhaps as landlord of this house I may, at some future date, in his good time, receive information as to certain imminent and much to be desired changes—'"

So saying Lebedeff fixed the prince with his sharp little eyes, still in hope that he would get his curiosity satisfied.

The prince looked back at him in amazement.

"I don't understand what you are driving at!" he cried, almost angrily, "and, and—what an intriguer you are, Lebedeff!" he added, bursting into a fit of genuine laughter.

Lebedeff followed suit at once, and it was clear from his radiant face that he considered his prospects of satisfaction immensely improved.

"And do you know," the prince continued, "I am amazed at your naive ways, Lebedeff! Don't be angry with me—not only yours, everybody else's also! You are waiting to hear something from me at this very moment with such simplicity that I declare I feel quite ashamed of myself for having nothing whatever to tell you. I swear to you solemnly, that there is nothing to tell. There! Can you take that in?" The prince laughed again.

Lebedeff assumed an air of dignity. It was true enough that he was sometimes naive to a degree in his curiosity; but he was also an excessively cunning gentleman, and the prince was almost converting him into an enemy by his repeated rebuffs. The prince did not snub Lebedeff's curiosity, however, because he felt any contempt for him; but simply because the subject was too delicate to talk about. Only a few days before he had looked upon his own dreams almost as crimes. But Lebedeff considered the refusal as caused by personal dislike to himself, and was hurt accordingly. Indeed, there was at this moment a piece of news, most interesting to the prince, which Lebedeff knew and even had wished to tell him, but which he now kept obstinately to himself.

"And what can I do for you, esteemed prince? Since I am told you sent for me just now," he said, after a few moments' silence.

"Oh, it was about the general," began the prince, waking abruptly from the fit of musing which he too had indulged in "and—and about the theft you told me of."

"That is—er—about—what theft?"

"Oh come! just as if you didn't understand, Lukian Timofeyovitch! What are you up to? I can't make you out! The money, the money, sir! The four hundred roubles that you lost that day. You came and told me about it one morning, and then went off to Petersburg. There, *now* do you understand?"

"Oh—h—h! You mean the four hundred roubles!" said Lebedeff, dragging the words out, just as though it had only just dawned upon him what the prince was talking about. "Thanks very much, prince, for your kind interest—you do me too much honour. I found the money, long ago!"

"You found it? Thank God for that!"

"Your exclamation proves the generous sympathy of your nature, prince; for four hundred roubles—to a struggling family man like myself—is no small matter!"

"I didn't mean that; at least, of course, I'm glad for your sake, too," added the prince, correcting himself, "but—how did you find it?"

"Very simply indeed! I found it under the chair upon which my coat had hung; so that it is clear the purse simply fell out of the pocket and on to the floor!"

"Under the chair? Impossible! Why, you told me yourself that you had searched every corner of the room? How could you not have looked in the most likely place of all?"

"Of course I looked there,—of course I did! Very much so! I looked and scrambled about, and felt for it, and wouldn't believe it was not there, and looked again and again. It is always so in such cases. One longs and expects to find a lost article; one sees it is not there, and the place is as bare as one's palm; and yet one returns and looks again and again, fifteen or twenty times, likely enough!"

"Oh, quite so, of course. But how was it in your case?—I don't quite understand," said the bewildered prince. "You say it wasn't there at first, and that you searched the place thoroughly, and yet it turned up on that very spot!"

"Yes, sir—on that very spot." The prince gazed strangely at Lebedeff. "And the general?" he asked, abruptly.

"The—the general? How do you mean, the general?" said Lebedeff, dubiously, as though he had not taken in the drift of the prince's remark.

"Oh, good heavens! I mean, what did the general say when the purse turned up under the chair? You and he had searched for it together there, hadn't you?"

"Quite so—together! But the second time I thought better to say nothing about finding it. I found it alone."

"But—why in the world—and the money? Was it all there?"

"I opened the purse and counted it myself; right to a single rouble."

"I think you might have come and told me," said the prince, thoughtfully.

"Oh—I didn't like to disturb you, prince, in the midst of your private and doubtless most interesting personal reflections. Besides, I wanted to appear, myself, to have found nothing. I took the purse, and opened it, and counted the money, and shut it and put it down again under the chair."

"What in the world for?"

"Oh, just out of curiosity," said Lebedeff, rubbing his hands and sniggering.

"What, it's still there then, is it? Ever since the day before yesterday?"

"Oh no! You see, I was half in hopes the general might find it. Because if I found it, why should not he too observe an object lying before his very eyes? I moved the chair several times so as to expose the purse to view, but the general never saw it. He is very absent just now, evidently. He talks and laughs and tells stories, and suddenly flies into a rage with me, goodness knows why."

"Well, but—have you taken the purse away now?"

"No, it disappeared from under the chair in the night."

"Where is it now, then?"

"Here," laughed Lebedeff, at last, rising to his full height and looking pleasantly at the prince, "here, in the lining of my coat. Look, you can feel it for yourself, if you like!"

Sure enough there was something sticking out of the front of the coat—something large. It certainly felt as though it might well be the purse fallen through a hole in the pocket into the lining.

"I took it out and had a look at it; it's all right. I've let it slip back into the lining now, as you see, and so I have been walking about ever since yesterday morning; it knocks against my legs when I walk along."

"H'm! and you take no notice of it?"

"Quite so, I take no notice of it. Ha, ha! and think of this, prince, my pockets are always strong and whole, and yet, here in one night, is a huge hole. I know the phenomenon is unworthy of your notice; but such is the case. I examined the hole, and I declare it actually looks as though it had been made with a pen-knife, a most improbable contingency."

"And—and—the general?"

"Ah, very angry all day, sir; all yesterday and all today. He shows decided bacchanalian predilections at one time, and at another is tearful and sensitive, but at any moment he is liable to paroxysms of such rage that I assure you, prince, I am quite alarmed. I am not a military man, you know. Yesterday we were sitting together in the tavern, and the lining of my coat was—quite accidentally, of course—sticking out right in front. The general squinted at it, and flew into a rage. He never looks me quite in the face now, unless he is very drunk or maudlin; but yesterday he looked at me in such a way that a shiver went all down my back. I intend to find the purse tomorrow; but till then I am going to have another night of it with him."

"What's the good of tormenting him like this?" cried the prince.

"I don't torment him, prince, I don't indeed!" cried Lebedeff, hotly. "I love him, my dear sir, I esteem him; and believe it or not, I love him all the better for this business, yes—and value him more."

Lebedeff said this so seriously that the prince quite lost his temper with him.

441

"Nonsense! love him and torment him so! Why, by the very fact that he put the purse prominently before you, first under the chair and then in your lining, he shows that he does not wish to deceive you, but is anxious to beg your forgiveness in this artless way. Do you hear? He is asking your pardon. He confides in the delicacy of your feelings, and in your friendship for him. And you can allow yourself to humiliate so thoroughly honest a man!"

"Thoroughly honest, quite so, prince, thoroughly honest!" said Lebedeff, with flashing eyes. "And only you, prince, could have found so very appropriate an expression. I honour you for it, prince. Very well, that's settled; I shall find the purse now and not tomorrow. Here, I find it and take it out before your eyes! And the money is all right. Take it, prince, and keep it till tomorrow, will you? Tomorrow or next day I'll take it back again. I think, prince, that the night after its disappearance it was buried under a bush in the garden. So I believe—what do you think of that?"

"Well, take care you don't tell him to his face that you have found the purse. Simply let him see that it is no longer in the lining of your coat, and form his own conclusions."

"Do you think so? Had I not just better tell him I have found it, and pretend I never guessed where it was?"

"No, I don't think so," said the prince, thoughtfully; "it's too late for that—that would be dangerous now. No, no! Better say nothing about it. Be nice with him, you know, but don't show him—oh, *you* know well enough—"

"I know, prince, of course I know, but I'm afraid I shall not carry it out; for to do so one needs a heart like your own. He is so very irritable just now, and so proud. At one moment he will embrace me, and the next he flies out at me and sneers at me, and then I stick the lining forward on purpose. Well, *au revoir*, prince, I see I am keeping you, and boring you, too, interfering with your most interesting private reflections."

"Now, do be careful! Secrecy, as before!"

"Oh, silence isn't the word! Softly, softly!"

But in spite of this conclusion to the episode, the prince remained as puzzled as ever, if not more so. He awaited next morning's interview with the general most impatiently.

IV.

The time appointed was twelve o'clock, and the prince, returning home unexpectedly late, found the general waiting for him. At the first glance, he saw that the latter was displeased, perhaps because he had been kept waiting. The prince apologized, and quickly took a seat. He seemed strangely timid before the general this morning, for some reason, and felt as though his visitor were some piece of china which he was afraid of breaking.

On scrutinizing him, the prince soon saw that the general was quite a different man from what he had been the day before; he looked like one who had come to some momentous resolve. His calmness, however, was more apparent than real. He was courteous, but there was a suggestion of injured innocence in his manner.

"I've brought your book back," he began, indicating a book lying on the table. "Much obliged to you for lending it to me."

"Ah, yes. Well, did you read it, general? It's curious, isn't it?" said the prince, delighted to be able to open up conversation upon an outside subject.

"Curious enough, yes, but crude, and of course dreadful nonsense; probably the man lies in every other sentence."

The general spoke with considerable confidence, and dragged his words out with a conceited drawl.

"Oh, but it's only the simple tale of an old soldier who saw the French enter Moscow. Some of his remarks were wonderfully interesting. Remarks of an eye-witness are always valuable, whoever he be, don't you think so?"

"Had I been the publisher I should not have printed it. As to the evidence of eye-witnesses, in these days people prefer impudent lies to the stories of men of worth and long service. I know of some notes of the year 1812, which—I have determined, prince, to leave this house, Mr. Lebedeff's house."

The general looked significantly at his host.

"Of course you have your own lodging at Pavlofsk at—at your daughter's house," began the prince, quite at a loss what to say. He suddenly recollected that the general had come for advice on a most important matter, affecting his destiny.

"At my wife's; in other words, at my own place, my daughter's house."

"I beg your pardon, I—"

"I leave Lebedeff's house, my dear prince, because I have quarrelled with this person. I broke with him last night, and am very sorry that I did not do so before. I expect respect, prince, even from those to whom I give my heart, so to speak. Prince, I have often given away my heart, and am nearly always deceived. This person was quite unworthy of the gift."

"There is much that might be improved in him," said the prince, moderately, "but he has some qualities which—though amid them one cannot but discern a cunning nature—reveal what is often a diverting intellect."

The prince's tone was so natural and respectful that the general could not possibly suspect him of any insincerity.

"Oh, that he possesses good traits, I was the first to show, when I very nearly made him a present of my friendship. I am not dependent upon his hospitality, and upon his house; I have my own family. I do not attempt to

442

justify my own weakness. I have drunk with this man, and perhaps I deplore the fact now, but I did not take him up for the sake of drink alone (excuse the crudeness of the expression, prince); I did not make friends with him for that alone. I was attracted by his good qualities; but when the fellow declares that he was a child in 1812, and had his left leg cut off, and buried in the Vagarkoff cemetery, in Moscow, such a cock-and-bull story amounts to disrespect, my dear sir, to—to impudent exaggeration."

"Oh, he was very likely joking; he said it for fun."

"I quite understand you. You mean that an innocent lie for the sake of a good joke is harmless, and does not offend the human heart. Some people lie, if you like to put it so, out of pure friendship, in order to amuse their fellows; but when a man makes use of extravagance in order to show his disrespect and to make clear how the intimacy bores him, it is time for a man of honour to break off the said intimacy., and to teach the offender his place."

The general flushed with indignation as he spoke.

"Oh, but Lebedeff cannot have been in Moscow in 1812. He is much too young; it is all nonsense."

"Very well, but even if we admit that he *was* alive in 1812, can one believe that a French chasseur pointed a cannon at him for a lark, and shot his left leg off? He says he picked his own leg up and took it away and buried it in the cemetery. He swore he had a stone put up over it with the inscription: 'Here lies the leg of Collegiate Secretary Lebedeff,' and on the other side, 'Rest, beloved ashes, till the morn of joy,' and that he has a service read over it every year (which is simply sacrilege), and goes to Moscow once a year on purpose. He invites me to Moscow in order to prove his assertion, and show me his leg's tomb, and the very cannon that shot him; he says it's the eleventh from the gate of the Kremlin, an old-fashioned falconet taken from the French afterwards."

"And, meanwhile both his legs are still on his body," said the prince, laughing. "I assure you, it is only an innocent joke, and you need not be angry about it."

"Excuse me—wait a minute—he says that the leg we see is a wooden one, made by Tchernosvitoff."

"They do say one can dance with those!"

"Quite so, quite so; and he swears that his wife never found out that one of his legs was wooden all the while they were married. When I showed him the ridiculousness of all this, he said, 'Well, if you were one of Napoleon's pages in 1812, you might let me bury my leg in the Moscow cemetery.'

"Why, did you say—" began the prince, and paused in confusion.

The general gazed at his host disdainfully.

"Oh, go on," he said, "finish your sentence, by all means. Say how odd it appears to you that a man fallen to such a depth of humiliation as I, can ever have been the actual eye-witness of great events. Go on, *I* don't mind! Has *he* found time to tell you scandal about me?"

"No, I've heard nothing of this from Lebedeff, if you mean Lebedeff."

"H'm; I thought differently. You see, we were talking over this period of history. I was criticizing a current report of something which then happened, and having been myself an eye-witness of the occurrence—you are smiling, prince—you are looking at my face as if—"

"Oh no! not at all—I—"

"I am rather young-looking, I know; but I am actually older than I appear to be. I was ten or eleven in the year 1812. I don't know my age exactly, but it has always been a weakness of mine to make it out less than it really is.

"I assure you, general, I do not in the least doubt your statement. One of our living autobiographers states that when he was a small baby in Moscow in 1812 the French soldiers fed him with bread."

"Well, there you see!" said the general, condescendingly. "There is nothing whatever unusual about my tale. Truth very often appears to be impossible. I was a page—it sounds strange, I dare say. Had I been fifteen years old I should probably have been terribly frightened when the French arrived, as my mother was (who had been too slow about clearing out of Moscow); but as I was only just ten I was not in the least alarmed, and rushed through the crowd to the very door of the palace when Napoleon alighted from his horse."

"Undoubtedly, at ten years old you would not have felt the sense of fear, as you say," blurted out the prince, horribly uncomfortable in the sensation that he was just about to blush.

"Of course; and it all happened so easily and naturally. And yet, were a novelist to describe the episode, he would put in all kinds of impossible and incredible details."

"Oh," cried the prince, "I have often thought that! Why, I know of a murder, for the sake of a watch. It's in all the papers now. But if some writer had invented it, all the critics would have jumped down his throat and said the thing was too improbable for anything. And yet you read it in the paper, and you can't help thinking that out of these strange disclosures is to be gained the full knowledge of Russian life and character. You said that well, general; it is so true," concluded the prince, warmly, delighted to have found a refuge from the fiery blushes which had covered his face.

"Yes, it's quite true, isn't it?" cried the general, his eyes sparkling with gratification. "A small boy, a child, would naturally realize no danger; he would shove his way through the crowds to see the shine and glitter of the uniforms, and especially the great man of whom everyone was speaking, for at that time all the world had been talking of no one but this man for some years past. The world was full of his name; I—so to speak—drew it in with my mother's milk. Napoleon, passing a couple of paces from me, caught sight of me accidentally. I was very well dressed, and being all alone, in that crowd, as you will easily imagine..."

"Oh, of course! Naturally the sight impressed him, and proved to him that not *all* the aristocracy had left Moscow; that at least some nobles and their children had remained behind."

"Just so! just so! He wanted to win over the aristocracy! When his eagle eye fell on me, mine probably flashed back in response. '*Voilà un garçon bien éveillé! Qui est ton père?*' I immediately replied, almost panting with excitement, 'A general, who died on the battle-fields of his country!' '*Le fils d'un boyard et d'un brave, pardessus le marché. J'aime les boyards. M'aimes-tu, petit?*'

"To this keen question I replied as keenly, 'The Russian heart can recognize a great man even in the bitter enemy of his country.' At least, I don't remember the exact words, you know, but the idea was as I say. Napoleon was struck; he thought a minute and then said to his suite: 'I like that boy's pride; if all Russians think like this child, then—' he didn't finish, but went on and entered the palace. I instantly mixed with his suite, and followed him. I was already in high favour. I remember when he came into the first hall, the emperor stopped before a portrait of the Empress Katherine, and after a thoughtful glance remarked, 'That was a great woman,' and passed on.

"Well, in a couple of days I was known all over the palace and the Kremlin as 'le petit boyard.' I only went home to sleep. They were nearly out of their minds about me at home. A couple of days after this, Napoleon's page, De Bazancour, died; he had not been able to stand the trials of the campaign. Napoleon remembered me; I was taken away without explanation; the dead page's uniform was tried on me, and when I was taken before the emperor, dressed in it, he nodded his head to me, and I was told that I was appointed to the vacant post of page.

"Well, I was glad enough, for I had long felt the greatest sympathy for this man; and then the pretty uniform and all that—only a child, you know—and so on. It was a dark green dress coat with gold buttons—red facings, white trousers, and a white silk waistcoat—silk stockings, shoes with buckles, and top-boots if I were riding out with his majesty or with the suite.

"Though the position of all of us at that time was not particularly brilliant, and the poverty was dreadful all round, yet the etiquette at court was strictly preserved, and the more strictly in proportion to the growth of the forebodings of disaster."

"Quite so, quite so, of course!" murmured the poor prince, who didn't know where to look. "Your memoirs would be most interesting."

The general was, of course, repeating what he had told Lebedeff the night before, and thus brought it out glibly enough, but here he looked suspiciously at the prince out of the corners of his eyes.

"My memoirs!" he began, with redoubled pride and dignity. "Write my memoirs? The idea has not tempted me. And yet, if you please, my memoirs have long been written, but they shall not see the light until dust returns to dust. Then, I doubt not, they will be translated into all languages, not of course on account of their actual literary merit, but because of the great events of which I was the actual witness, though but a child at the time. As a child, I was able to penetrate into the secrecy of the great man's private room. At nights I have heard the groans and wailings of this 'giant in distress.' He could feel no shame in weeping before such a mere child as I was, though I understood even then that the reason for his suffering was the silence of the Emperor Alexander."

"Yes, of course; he had written letters to the latter with proposals of peace, had he not?" put in the prince.

"We did not know the details of his proposals, but he wrote letter after letter, all day and every day. He was dreadfully agitated. Sometimes at night I would throw myself upon his breast with tears (Oh, how I loved that man!). 'Ask forgiveness, Oh, ask forgiveness of the Emperor Alexander!' I would cry. I should have said, of course, 'Make peace with Alexander,' but as a child I expressed my idea in the naive way recorded. 'Oh, my child,' he would say (he loved to talk to me and seemed to forget my tender years), 'Oh, my child, I am ready to kiss Alexander's feet, but I hate and abominate the King of Prussia and the Austrian Emperor, and—and—but you know nothing of politics, my child.' He would pull up, remembering whom he was speaking to, but his eyes would sparkle for a long while after this. Well now, if I were to describe all this, and I have seen greater events than these, all these critical gentlemen of the press and political parties—Oh, no thanks! I'm their very humble servant, but no thanks!"

"Quite so—parties—you are very right," said the prince. "I was reading a book about Napoleon and the Waterloo campaign only the other day, by Charasse, in which the author does not attempt to conceal his joy at Napoleon's discomfiture at every page. Well now, I don't like that; it smells of 'party,' you know. You are quite right. And were you much occupied with your service under Napoleon?"

The general was in ecstasies, for the prince's remarks, made, as they evidently were, in all seriousness and simplicity, quite dissipated the last relics of his suspicion.

"I know Charasse's book! Oh! I was so angry with his work! I wrote to him and said—I forget what, at this moment. You ask whether I was very busy under the Emperor? Oh no! I was called 'page,' but hardly took my duty seriously. Besides, Napoleon very soon lost hope of conciliating the Russians, and he would have forgotten all about me had he not loved me—for personal reasons—I don't mind saying so now. My heart was greatly drawn to him, too. My duties were light. I merely had to be at the palace occasionally to escort the Emperor out riding, and that was about all. I rode very fairly well. He used to have a ride before dinner, and his suite on those occasions were generally Davoust, myself, and Roustan."

"Constant?" said the prince, suddenly, and quite involuntarily.

"No; Constant was away then, taking a letter to the Empress Josephine. Instead of him there were always a couple of orderlies—and that was all, excepting, of course, the generals and marshals whom Napoleon always took with him for the inspection of various localities, and for the sake of consultation generally. I remember there was one—Davoust—nearly always with him—a big man with spectacles. They used to argue and quarrel sometimes. Once they were in the Emperor's study together—just those two and myself—I was unobserved—and they argued, and the Emperor seemed to be agreeing to something under protest. Suddenly his eye fell on me and an idea seemed to flash across him.

"'Child,' he said, abruptly. 'If I were to recognize the Russian orthodox religion and emancipate the serfs, do you think Russia would come over to me?'"

"'Never!' I cried, indignantly."

"The Emperor was much struck."

"'In the flashing eyes of this patriotic child I read and accept the fiat of the Russian people. Enough, Davoust, it is mere phantasy on our part. Come, let's hear your other project.'"

"'Yes, but that was a great idea," said the prince, clearly interested. "You ascribe it to Davoust, do you?"

"Well, at all events, they were consulting together at the time. Of course it was the idea of an eagle, and must have originated with Napoleon; but the other project was good too—it was the 'Conseil du lion!' as Napoleon called it. This project consisted in a proposal to occupy the Kremlin with the whole army; to arm and fortify it scientifically, to kill as many horses as could be got, and salt their flesh, and spend the winter there; and in spring to fight their way out. Napoleon liked the idea—it attracted him. We rode round the Kremlin walls every day, and Napoleon used to give orders where they were to be patched, where built up, where pulled down and so on. All was decided at last. They were alone together—those two and myself.

"Napoleon was walking up and down with folded arms. I could not take my eyes off his face—my heart beat loudly and painfully.

"'I'm off,' said Davoust. 'Where to?' asked Napoleon.

"'To salt horse-flesh,' said Davoust. Napoleon shuddered—his fate was being decided.

"'Child,' he addressed me suddenly, 'what do you think of our plan?' Of course he only applied to me as a sort of toss-up, you know. I turned to Davoust and addressed my reply to him. I said, as though inspired:

"'Escape, general! Go home!—'

"The project was abandoned; Davoust shrugged his shoulders and went out, whispering to himself—'Bah, il devient superstitieux!' Next morning the order to retreat was given."

"All this is most interesting," said the prince, very softly, "if it really was so—that is, I mean—" he hastened to correct himself.

"Oh, my dear prince," cried the general, who was now so intoxicated with his own narrative that he probably could not have pulled up at the most patent indiscretion. "You say, if it really was so!' There was more—much more, I assure you! These are merely a few little political acts. I tell you I was the eye-witness of the nightly sorrow and groanings of the great man, and of that no one can speak but myself. Towards the end he wept no more, though he continued to emit an occasional groan; but his face grew more overcast day by day, as though Eternity were wrapping its gloomy mantle about him. Occasionally we passed whole hours of silence together at night, Roustan snoring in the next room—that fellow slept like a pig. 'But he's loyal to me and my dynasty,' said Napoleon of him.

"Sometimes it was very painful to me, and once he caught me with tears in my eyes. He looked at me kindly. 'You are sorry for me,' he said, 'you, my child, and perhaps one other child—my son, the King of Rome—may grieve for me. All the rest hate me; and my brothers are the first to betray me in misfortune.' I sobbed and threw myself into his arms. He could not resist me—he burst into tears, and our tears mingled as we folded each other in a close embrace.

"'Write, oh, write a letter to the Empress Josephine!' I cried, sobbing. Napoleon started, reflected, and said, 'You remind me of a third heart which loves me. Thank you, my friend;' and then and there he sat down and wrote that letter to Josephine, with which Constant was sent off next day."

"You did a good action," said the prince, "for in the midst of his angry feelings you insinuated a kind thought into his heart."

"Just so, prince, just so. How well you bring out that fact! Because your own heart is good!" cried the ecstatic old gentleman, and, strangely enough, real tears glistened in his eyes. "Yes, prince, it was a wonderful spectacle. And, do you know, I all but went off to Paris, and should assuredly have shared his solitary exile with him; but, alas, our destinies were otherwise ordered! We parted, he to his island, where I am sure he thought of the weeping child who had embraced him so affectionately at parting in Moscow; and I was sent off to the cadet corps, where I found nothing but roughness and harsh discipline. Alas, my happy days were done!"

"'I do not wish to deprive your mother of you, and, therefore, I will not ask you to go with me,' he said, the morning of his departure, 'but I should like to do something for you.' He was mounting his horse as he spoke. 'Write something in my sister's album for me,' I said rather timidly, for he was in a state of great dejection at the moment. He turned, called for a pen, took the album. 'How old is your sister?' he asked, holding the pen in his hand. 'Three years old,' I said. 'Ah, *petite fille alors!*' and he wrote in the album:

"'Ne mentez jamais! Napoléon (votre ami sincère).'

"Such advice, and at such a moment, you must allow, prince, was—"

"Yes, quite so; very remarkable."

"This page of the album, framed in gold, hung on the wall of my sister's drawing-room all her life, in the most conspicuous place, till the day of her death; where it is now, I really don't know. Heavens! it's two o'clock! *How* I have kept you, prince! It is really most unpardonable of me."

The general rose.

"Oh, not in the least," said the prince. "On the contrary, I have been so much interested, I'm really very much obliged to you."

"Prince,", said the general, pressing his hand, and looking at him with flashing eyes, and an expression as though he were under the influence of a sudden thought which had come upon him with stunning force. "Prince, you are so kind, so simple-minded, that sometimes I really feel sorry for you! I gaze at you with a feeling of real affection. Oh, Heaven bless you! May your life blossom and fructify in love. Mine is over. Forgive me, forgive me!"

He left the room quickly, covering his face with his hands.

The prince could not doubt the sincerity of his agitation. He understood, too, that the old man had left the room intoxicated with his own success. The general belonged to that class of liars, who, in spite of their transports of lying, invariably suspect that they are not believed. On this occasion, when he recovered from his exaltation, he would probably suspect Muishkin of pitying him, and feel insulted.

"Have I been acting rightly in allowing him to develop such vast resources of imagination?" the prince asked himself. But his answer was a fit of violent laughter which lasted ten whole minutes. He tried to reproach himself for the laughing fit, but eventually concluded that he needn't do so, since in spite of it he was truly sorry for the old man. The same evening he received a strange letter, short but decided. The general informed him that they must part for ever; that he was grateful, but that even from him he could not accept "signs of sympathy which were humiliating to the dignity of a man already miserable enough."

When the prince heard that the old man had gone to Nina Alexandrovna, though, he felt almost easy on his account.

We have seen, however, that the general paid a visit to Lizabetha Prokofievna and caused trouble there, the final upshot being that he frightened Mrs. Epanchin, and angered her by bitter hints as to his son Gania.

He had been turned out in disgrace, eventually, and this was the cause of his bad night and quarrelsome day, which ended in his sudden departure into the street in a condition approaching insanity, as recorded before.

Colia did not understand the position. He tried severity with his father, as they stood in the street after the latter had cursed the household, hoping to bring him round that way.

"Well, where are we to go to now, father?" he asked. "You don't want to go to the prince's; you have quarrelled with Lebedeff; you have no money; I never have any; and here we are in the middle of the road, in a nice sort of mess."

"Better to be of a mess than in a mess! I remember making a joke something like that at the mess in eighteen hundred and forty—forty—I forget. 'Where is my youth, where is my golden youth?' Who was it said that, Colia?"

"It was Gogol, in Dead Souls, father," cried Colia, glancing at him in some alarm.

"'Dead Souls,' yes, of course, dead. When I die, Colia, you must engrave on my tomb:

"'*Here lies a Dead Soul,*
Shame pursues me.'

446

"Who said that, Colia?"

"I don't know, father."

"There was no Eropegoff? Eroshka Eropegoff?" he cried, suddenly, stopping in the road in a frenzy. "No Eropegoff! And my own son to say it! Eropegoff was in the place of a brother to me for eleven months. I fought a duel for him. He was married afterwards, and then killed on the field of battle. The bullet struck the cross on my breast and glanced off straight into his temple. 'I'll never forget you,' he cried, and expired. I served my country well and honestly, Colia, but shame, shame has pursued me! You and Nina will come to my grave, Colia; poor Nina, I always used to call her Nina in the old days, and how she loved.... Nina, Nina, oh, Nina. What have I ever done to deserve your forgiveness and long-suffering? Oh, Colia, your mother has an angelic spirit, an angelic spirit, Colia!"

"I know that, father. Look here, dear old father, come back home! Let's go back to mother. Look, she ran after us when we came out. What have you stopped her for, just as though you didn't take in what I said? Why are you crying, father?"

Poor Colia cried himself, and kissed the old man's hands

"You kiss my hands, *mine?*"

"Yes, yes, yours, yours! What is there to surprise anyone in that? Come, come, you mustn't go on like this, crying in the middle of the road; and you a general too, a military man! Come, let's go back."

"God bless you, dear boy, for being respectful to a disgraced man. Yes, to a poor disgraced old fellow, your father. You shall have such a son yourself; le roi de Rome. Oh, curses on this house!"

"Come, come, what does all this mean?" cried Colia beside himself at last. "What is it? What has happened to you? Why don't you wish to come back home? Why have you gone out of your mind, like this?"

"I'll explain it, I'll explain all to you. Don't shout! You shall hear. Le roi de Rome. Oh, I am sad, I am melancholy!

"'Nurse, where is your tomb?'"

"Who said that, Colia?"

"I don't know, I don't know who said it. Come home at once; come on! I'll punch Gania's head myself, if you like—only come. Oh, where *are* you off to again?" The general was dragging him away towards the door a house near. He sat down on the step, still holding Colia by the hand.

"Bend down—bend down your ear. I'll tell you all—disgrace—bend down, I'll tell you in your ear."

"What are you dreaming of?" said poor, frightened Colia, stooping down towards the old man, all the same.

"Le roi de Rome," whispered the general, trembling all over.

"What? What *do* you mean? What roi de Rome?"

"I—I," the general continued to whisper, clinging more and more tightly to the boy's shoulder. "I—wish—to tell you—all—Maria—Maria Petrovna—Su—Su—Su......."

Colia broke loose, seized his father by the shoulders, and stared into his eyes with frenzied gaze. The old man had grown livid—his lips were shaking, convulsions were passing over his features. Suddenly he leant over and began to sink slowly into Colia's arms.

"He's got a stroke!" cried Colia, loudly, realizing what was the matter at last.

V.

In point of fact, Varia had rather exaggerated the certainty of her news as to the prince's betrothal to Aglaya. Very likely, with the perspicacity of her sex, she gave out as an accomplished fact what she felt was pretty sure to become a fact in a few days. Perhaps she could not resist the satisfaction of pouring one last drop of bitterness into her brother Gania's cup, in spite of her love for him. At all events, she had been unable to obtain any definite news from the Epanchin girls—the most she could get out of them being hints and surmises, and so on. Perhaps Aglaya's sisters had merely been pumping Varia for news while pretending to impart information; or perhaps, again, they had been unable to resist the feminine gratification of teasing a friend—for, after all this time, they could scarcely have helped divining the aim of her frequent visits.

On the other hand, the prince, although he had told Lebedeff,—as we know, that nothing had happened, and that he had nothing to impart,—the prince may have been in error. Something strange seemed to have happened, without anything definite having actually happened. Varia had guessed that with her true feminine instinct.

How or why it came about that everyone at the Epanchins' became imbued with one conviction—that something very important had happened to Aglaya, and that her fate was in process of settlement—it would be very difficult to explain. But no sooner had this idea taken root, than all at once declared that they had seen and observed it long ago; that they had remarked it at the time of the "poor knight" joke, and even before, though they had been unwilling to believe in such nonsense.

So said the sisters. Of course, Lizabetha Prokofievna had foreseen it long before the rest; her "heart had been sore" for a long while, she declared, and it was now so sore that she appeared to be quite overwhelmed, and the very thought of the prince became distasteful to her.

There was a question to be decided—most important, but most difficult; so much so, that Mrs. Epanchin did not even see how to put it into words. Would the prince do or not? Was all this good or bad? If good (which might be the case, of course),*why* good? If bad (which was hardly doubtful), *wherein*, especially, bad? Even the general, the paterfamilias, though astonished at first, suddenly declared that, "upon his honour, he really believed he had fancied something of the kind, after all. At first, it seemed a new idea, and then, somehow, it looked as familiar as possible." His wife frowned him down there. This was in the morning; but in the evening, alone with his wife, he had given tongue again.

"Well, really, you know"—(silence)—"of course, you know all this is very strange, if true, which I cannot deny; but"—(silence).—"But, on the other hand, if one looks things in the face, you know—upon my honour, the prince is a rare good fellow—and—and—and—well, his name, you know—your family name—all this looks well, and perpetuates the name and title and all that—which at this moment is not standing so high as it might—from one point of view—don't you know? The world, the world is the world, of course—and people will talk—and—and—the prince has property, you know—if it is not very large—and then he—he—" (Continued silence, and collapse of the general.)

Hearing these words from her husband, Lizabetha Prokofievna was driven beside herself.

According to her opinion, the whole thing had been one huge, fantastical, absurd, unpardonable mistake. "First of all, this prince is an idiot, and, secondly, he is a fool—knows nothing of the world, and has no place in it. Whom can he be shown to? Where can you take him to? What will old Bielokonski say? We never thought of such a husband as *that* for our Aglaya!"

Of course, the last argument was the chief one. The maternal heart trembled with indignation to think of such an absurdity, although in that heart there rose another voice, which said: "And *why* is not the prince such a husband as you would have desired for Aglaya?" It was this voice which annoyed Lizabetha Prokofievna more than anything else.

For some reason or other, the sisters liked the idea of the prince. They did not even consider it very strange; in a word, they might be expected at any moment to range themselves strongly on his side. But both of them decided to say nothing either way. It had always been noticed in the family that the stronger Mrs. Epanchin's opposition was to any project, the nearer she was, in reality, to giving in.

Alexandra, however, found it difficult to keep absolute silence on the subject. Long since holding, as she did, the post of "confidential adviser to mamma," she was now perpetually called in council, and asked her opinion, and especially her assistance, in order to recollect "how on earth all this happened?" Why did no one see it? Why did no one say anything about it? What did all that wretched "poor knight" joke mean? Why was she, Lizabetha Prokofievna, driven to think, and foresee, and worry for everybody, while they all sucked their thumbs, and counted the crows in the garden, and did nothing? At first, Alexandra had been very careful, and had merely replied that perhaps her father's remark was not so far out: that, in the eyes of the world, probably the choice of the prince as a husband for one of the Epanchin girls would be considered a very wise one. Warming up, however, she added that the prince was by no means a fool, and never had been; and that as to "place in the world," no one knew what the position of a respectable person in Russia would imply in a few years—whether it would depend on successes in the government service, on the old system, or what.

To all this her mother replied that Alexandra was a freethinker, and that all this was due to that "cursed woman's rights question."

Half an hour after this conversation, she went off to town, and thence to the Kammenny Ostrof, ["Stone Island," a suburb and park of St. Petersburg] to see Princess Bielokonski, who had just arrived from Moscow on a short visit. The princess was Aglaya's godmother.

"Old Bielokonski" listened to all the fevered and despairing lamentations of Lizabetha Prokofievna without the least emotion; the tears of this sorrowful mother did not evoke answering sighs—in fact, she laughed at her. She was a dreadful old despot, this princess; she could not allow equality in anything, not even in friendship of the oldest standing, and she insisted on treating Mrs. Epanchin as her *protégée*, as she had been thirty-five years ago. She could never put up with the independence and energy of Lizabetha's character. She observed that, as usual, the whole family had gone much too far ahead, and had converted a fly into an elephant; that, so far as she had heard their story, she was persuaded that nothing of any seriousness had occurred; that it would surely be better to wait until something *did* happen; that the prince, in her opinion, was a very decent young fellow, though perhaps a little eccentric, through illness, and not quite as weighty in the world as one could wish. The worst feature was, she said, Nastasia Philipovna.

Lizabetha Prokofievna well understood that the old lady was angry at the failure of Evgenie Pavlovitch—her own recommendation. She returned home to Pavlofsk in a worse humour than when she left, and of course everybody in the house suffered. She pitched into everyone, because, she declared, they had 'gone mad.' Why were things always mismanaged in her house? Why had everybody been in such a frantic hurry in this matter? So far as she could see, nothing whatever had happened. Surely they had better wait and see what was to happen, instead of making mountains out of molehills.

And so the conclusion of the matter was that it would be far better to take it quietly, and wait coolly to see what would turn up. But, alas! peace did not reign for more than ten minutes. The first blow dealt to its power was in certain news communicated to Lizabetha Prokofievna as to events which had happened during her trip to see the princess. (This trip had taken place the day after that on which the prince had turned up at the Epanchins at nearly one o'clock at night, thinking it was nine.)

The sisters replied candidly and fully enough to their mother's impatient questions on her return. They said, in the first place, that nothing particular had happened since her departure; that the prince had been, and that Aglaya had kept him waiting a long while before she appeared—half an hour, at least; that she had then come in, and immediately asked the prince to have a game of chess; that the prince did not know the game, and Aglaya had beaten him easily; that she had been in a wonderfully merry mood, and had laughed at the prince, and chaffed him so unmercifully that one was quite sorry to see his wretched expression.

She had then asked him to play cards—the game called "little fools." At this game the tables were turned completely, for the prince had shown himself a master at it. Aglaya had cheated and changed cards, and stolen others, in the most bare-faced way, but, in spite of everything the prince had beaten her hopelessly five times running, and she had been left "little fool" each time.

Aglaya then lost her temper, and began to say such awful things to the prince that he laughed no more, but grew dreadfully pale, especially when she said that she should not remain in the house with him, and that he ought to be ashamed of coming to their house at all, especially at night, "*after all that had happened*."

So saying, she had left the room, banging the door after her, and the prince went off, looking as though he were on his way to a funeral, in spite of all their attempts at consolation.

Suddenly, a quarter of an hour after the prince's departure, Aglaya had rushed out of her room in such a hurry that she had not even wiped her eyes, which were full of tears. She came back because Colia had brought a hedgehog. Everybody came in to see the hedgehog. In answer to their questions Colia explained that the hedgehog was not his, and that he had left another boy, Kostia Lebedeff, waiting for him outside. Kostia was too shy to come in, because he was carrying a hatchet; they had bought the hedgehog and the hatchet from a peasant whom they had met on the road. He had offered to sell them the hedgehog, and they had paid fifty copecks for it; and the hatchet had so taken their fancy that they had made up their minds to buy it of their own accord. On hearing this, Aglaya urged Colia to sell her the hedgehog; she even called him "dear Colia," in trying to coax him. He refused for a long time, but at last he could hold out no more, and went to fetch Kostia Lebedeff. The latter appeared, carrying his hatchet, and covered with confusion. Then it came out that the hedgehog was not theirs, but the property of a schoolmate, one Petroff, who had given them some money to buy Schlosser's History for him, from another schoolfellow who at that moment was driven to raising money by the sale of his books. Colia and Kostia were about to make this purchase for their friend when chance brought the hedgehog to their notice, and they had succumbed to the temptation of buying it. They were now taking Petroff the hedgehog and hatchet which they had bought with his money, instead of Schiosser's History. But Aglaya so entreated them that at last they consented to sell her the hedgehog. As soon as she had got possession of it, she put it in a wicker basket with Colia's help, and covered it with a napkin. Then she said to Colia: "Go and take this hedgehog to the prince from me, and ask him to accept it as a token of my profound respect." Colia joyfully promised to do the errand, but he demanded explanations. "What does the hedgehog mean? What is the meaning of such a present?" Aglaya replied that it was none of his business. "I am sure that there is some allegory about it," Colia persisted. Aglaya grew angry, and called him "a silly boy." "If I did not respect all women in your person," replied Colia, "and if my own principles would permit it, I would soon prove to you, that I know how to answer such an insult!" But, in the end, Colia went off with the hedgehog in great delight, followed by Kostia Lebedeff. Aglaya's annoyance was soon over, and seeing that Colia was swinging the hedgehog's basket violently to and fro, she called out to him from the verandah, as if they had never quarrelled: "Colia, dear, please take care not to drop him!" Colia appeared to have no grudge against her, either, for he stopped, and answered most cordially: "No, I will not drop him! Don't be afraid, Aglaya Ivanovna!" After which he went on his way. Aglaya burst out laughing and ran up to her room, highly delighted. Her good spirits lasted the whole day.

All this filled poor Lizabetha's mind with chaotic confusion. What on earth did it all mean? The most disturbing feature was the hedgehog. What was the symbolic signification of a hedgehog? What did they understand by it? What underlay it? Was it a cryptic message?

Poor General Epanchin "put his foot in it" by answering the above questions in his own way. He said there was no cryptic message at all. As for the hedgehog, it was just a hedgehog, which meant nothing—unless, indeed, it was a pledge of friendship,—the sign of forgetting of offences and so on. At all events, it was a joke, and, of course, a most pardonable and innocent one.

We may as well remark that the general had guessed perfectly accurately.

The prince, returning home from the interview with Aglaya, had sat gloomy and depressed for half an hour. He was almost in despair when Colia arrived with the hedgehog.

Then the sky cleared in a moment. The prince seemed to arise from the dead; he asked Colia all about it, made him repeat the story over and over again, and laughed and shook hands with the boys in his delight.

It seemed clear to the prince that Aglaya forgave him, and that he might go there again this very evening; and in his eyes that was not only the main thing, but everything in the world.

"What children we are still, Colia!" he cried at last, enthusiastically,—"and how delightful it is that we can be children still!"

"Simply—my dear prince,—simply she is in love with you,—that's the whole of the secret!" replied Colia, with authority.

The prince blushed, but this time he said nothing. Colia burst out laughing and clapped his hands. A minute later the prince laughed too, and from this moment until the evening he looked at his watch every other minute to see how much time he had to wait before evening came.

But the situation was becoming rapidly critical.

Mrs. Epanchin could bear her suspense no longer, and in spite of the opposition of husband and daughters, she sent for Aglaya, determined to get a straightforward answer out of her, once for all.

"Otherwise," she observed hysterically, "I shall die before evening."

It was only now that everyone realized to what a ridiculous dead-lock the whole matter had been brought. Excepting feigned surprise, indignation, laughter, and jeering—both at the prince and at everyone who asked her questions,—nothing could be got out of Aglaya.

Lizabetha Prokofievna went to bed and only rose again in time for tea, when the prince might be expected.

She awaited him in trembling agitation; and when he at last arrived she nearly went off into hysterics.

Muishkin himself came in very timidly. He seemed to feel his way, and looked in each person's eyes in a questioning way,—for Aglaya was absent, which fact alarmed him at once.

This evening there were no strangers present—no one but the immediate members of the family. Prince S. was still in town, occupied with the affairs of Evgenie Pavlovitch's uncle.

"I wish at least *he* would come and say something!" complained poor Lizabetha Prokofievna.

The general sat still with a most preoccupied air. The sisters were looking very serious and did not speak a word, and Lizabetha Prokofievna did not know how to commence the conversation.

At length she plunged into an energetic and hostile criticism of railways, and glared at the prince defiantly.

Alas Aglaya still did not come—and the prince was quite lost. He had the greatest difficulty in expressing his opinion that railways were most useful institutions,—and in the middle of his speech Adelaida laughed, which threw him into a still worse state of confusion.

At this moment in marched Aglaya, as calm and collected as could be. She gave the prince a ceremonious bow and solemnly took up a prominent position near the big round table. She looked at the prince questioningly.

All present realized that the moment for the settlement of perplexities had arrived.

"Did you get my hedgehog?" she inquired, firmly and almost angrily.

"Yes, I got it," said the prince, blushing.

"Tell us now, at once, what you made of the present? I must have you answer this question for mother's sake; she needs pacifying, and so do all the rest of the family!"

"Look here, Aglaya—" began the general.

"This—this is going beyond all limits!" said Lizabetha Prokofievna, suddenly alarmed.

"It is not in the least beyond all limits, mamma!" said her daughter, firmly. "I sent the prince a hedgehog this morning, and I wish to hear his opinion of it. Go on, prince."

"What—what sort of opinion, Aglaya Ivanovna?"

"About the hedgehog."

"That is—I suppose you wish to know how I received the hedgehog, Aglaya Ivanovna,—or, I should say, how I regarded your sending him to me? In that case, I may tell you—in a word—that I—in fact—"

He paused, breathless.

"Come—you haven't told us much!" said Aglaya, after waiting some five seconds. "Very well, I am ready to drop the hedgehog, if you like; but I am anxious to be able to clear up this accumulation of misunderstandings. Allow me to ask you, prince,—I wish to hear from you, personally—are you making me an offer, or not?"

"Gracious heavens!" exclaimed Lizabetha Prokofievna. The prince started. The general stiffened in his chair; the sisters frowned.

"Don't deceive me now, prince—tell the truth. All these people persecute me with astounding questions—about you. Is there any ground for all these questions, or not? Come!"

"I have not asked you to marry me yet, Aglaya Ivanovna," said the prince, becoming suddenly animated; "but you know yourself how much I love you and trust you."

"No—I asked you this—answer this! Do you intend to ask for my hand, or not?"

"Yes—I do ask for it!" said the prince, more dead than alive now.

There was a general stir in the room.

"No—no—my dear girl," began the general. "You cannot proceed like this, Aglaya, if that's how the matter stands. It's impossible. Prince, forgive it, my dear fellow, but—Lizabetha Prokofievna!"—he appealed to his spouse for help—"you must really—"

"Not I—not I! I retire from all responsibility," said Lizabetha Prokofievna, with a wave of the hand.

"Allow me to speak, please, mamma," said Aglaya. "I think I ought to have something to say in the matter. An important moment of my destiny is about to be decided"—(this is how Aglaya expressed herself)—"and I wish to find out how the matter stands, for my own sake, though I am glad you are all here. Allow me to ask you, prince, since you cherish those intentions, how you consider that you will provide for my happiness?"

"I—I don't quite know how to answer your question, Aglaya Ivanovna. What is there to say to such a question? And—and must I answer?"

"I think you are rather overwhelmed and out of breath. Have a little rest, and try to recover yourself. Take a glass of water, or—but they'll give you some tea directly."

"I love you, Aglaya Ivanovna,—I love you very much. I love only you—and—please don't jest about it, for I do love you very much."

"Well, this matter is important. We are not children—we must look into it thoroughly. Now then, kindly tell me—what does your fortune consist of?"

"No—Aglaya—come, enough of this, you mustn't behave like this," said her father, in dismay.

"It's disgraceful," said Lizabetha Prokofievna in a loud whisper.

"She's mad—quite!" said Alexandra.

"Fortune—money—do you mean?" asked the prince in some surprise.

"Just so."

"I have now—let's see—I have a hundred and thirty-five thousand roubles," said the prince, blushing violently.

"Is that all, really?" said Aglaya, candidly, without the slightest show of confusion. "However, it's not so bad, especially if managed with economy. Do you intend to serve?"

"I—I intended to try for a certificate as private tutor."

"Very good. That would increase our income nicely. Have you any intention of being a Kammer-junker?"

"A Kammer-junker? I had not thought of it, but—"

But here the two sisters could restrain themselves no longer, and both of them burst into irrepressible laughter.

Adelaida had long since detected in Aglaya's features the gathering signs of an approaching storm of laughter, which she restrained with amazing self-control.

Aglaya looked menacingly at her laughing sisters, but could not contain herself any longer, and the next minute she too had burst into an irrepressible, and almost hysterical, fit of mirth. At length she jumped up, and ran out of the room.

"I knew it was all a joke!" cried Adelaida. "I felt it ever since—since the hedgehog."

"No, no! I cannot allow this,—this is a little too much," cried Lizabetha Prokofievna, exploding with rage, and she rose from her seat and followed Aglaya out of the room as quickly as she could.

The two sisters hurriedly went after her.

The prince and the general were the only two persons left in the room.

"It's—it's really—now could you have imagined anything like it, Lef Nicolaievitch?" cried the general. He was evidently so much agitated that he hardly knew what he wished to say. "Seriously now, seriously I mean—"

"I only see that Aglaya Ivanovna is laughing at me," said the poor prince, sadly.

"Wait a bit, my boy, I'll just go—you stay here, you know. But do just explain, if you can, Lef Nicolaievitch, how in the world has all this come about? And what does it all mean? You must understand, my dear fellow; I am a father, you see, and I ought to be allowed to understand the matter—do explain, I beg you!"

"I love Aglaya Ivanovna—she knows it,—and I think she must have long known it."

The general shrugged his shoulders.

"Strange—it's strange," he said, "and you love her very much?"

"Yes, very much."

"Well—it's all most strange to me. That is—my dear fellow, it is such a surprise—such a blow—that... You see, it is not your financial position (though I should not object if you were a bit richer)—I am thinking of my daughter's happiness, of course, and the thing is—are you able to give her the happiness she deserves? And then—is all this a joke on her part, or is she in earnest? I don't mean on your side, but on hers."

At this moment Alexandra's voice was heard outside the door, calling out "Papa!"

"Wait for me here, my boy—will you? Just wait and think it all over, and I'll come back directly," he said hurriedly, and made off with what looked like the rapidity of alarm in response to Alexandra's call.

He found the mother and daughter locked in one another's arms, mingling their tears.

These were the tears of joy and peace and reconciliation. Aglaya was kissing her mother's lips and cheeks and hands; they were hugging each other in the most ardent way.

"There, look at her now—Ivan Fedorovitch! Here she is—all of her! This is our *real* Aglaya at last!" said Lizabetha Prokofievna.

Aglaya raised her happy, tearful face from her mother's breast, glanced at her father, and burst out laughing. She sprang at him and hugged him too, and kissed him over and over again. She then rushed back to her mother and hid her face in the maternal bosom, and there indulged in more tears. Her mother covered her with a corner of her shawl.

"Oh, you cruel little girl! How will you treat us all next, I wonder?" she said, but she spoke with a ring of joy in her voice, and as though she breathed at last without the oppression which she had felt so long.

"Cruel?" sobbed Aglaya. "Yes, I *am* cruel, and worthless, and spoiled—tell father so,—oh, here he is—I forgot Father, listen!" She laughed through her tears.

"My darling, my little idol," cried the general, kissing and fondling her hands (Aglaya did not draw them away); "so you love this young man, do you?"

"No, no, no, can't *bear* him, I can't *bear* your young man!" cried Aglaya, raising her head. "And if you dare say that *once* more, papa—I'm serious, you know, I'm,—do you hear me—I'm serious!"

She certainly did seem to be serious enough. She had flushed up all over and her eyes were blazing.

The general felt troubled and remained silent, while Lizabetha Prokofievna telegraphed to him from behind Aglaya to ask no questions.

"If that's the case, darling—then, of course, you shall do exactly as you like. He is waiting alone downstairs. Hadn't I better hint to him gently that he can go?" The general telegraphed to Lizabetha Prokofievna in his turn.

"No, no, you needn't do anything of the sort; you mustn't hint gently at all. I'll go down myself directly. I wish to apologize to this young man, because I hurt his feelings."

"Yes, *seriously*," said the general, gravely.

"Well, you'd better stay here, all of you, for a little, and I'll go down to him alone to begin with. I'll just go in and then you can follow me almost at once. That's the best way."

She had almost reached the door when she turned round again.

"I shall laugh—I know I shall; I shall die of laughing," she said, lugubriously.

However, she turned and ran down to the prince as fast as her feet could carry her.

"Well, what does it all mean? What do you make of it?" asked the general of his spouse, hurriedly.

"I hardly dare say," said Lizabetha, as hurriedly, "but I think it's as plain as anything can be."

"I think so too, as clear as day; she loves him."

"Loves him? She is head over ears in love, that's what she is," put in Alexandra.

"Well, God bless her, God bless her, if such is her destiny," said Lizabetha, crossing herself devoutly.

"H'm destiny it is," said the general, "and there's no getting out of destiny."

With these words they all moved off towards the drawing-room, where another surprise awaited them. Aglaya had not only not laughed, as she had feared, but had gone to the prince rather timidly, and said to him:

"Forgive a silly, horrid, spoilt girl"—(she took his hand here)—"and be quite assured that we all of us esteem you beyond all words. And if I dared to turn your beautiful, admirable simplicity to ridicule, forgive me as you would a little child its mischief. Forgive me all my absurdity of just now, which, of course, meant nothing, and could not have the slightest consequence." She spoke these words with great emphasis.

Her father, mother, and sisters came into the room and were much struck with the last words, which they just caught as they entered—"absurdity which of course meant nothing"—and still more so with the emphasis with which Aglaya had spoken.

They exchanged glances questioningly, but the prince did not seem to have understood the meaning of Aglaya's words; he was in the highest heaven of delight.

"Why do you speak so?" he murmured. "Why do you ask my forgiveness?"

He wished to add that he was unworthy of being asked for forgiveness by her, but paused. Perhaps he did understand Aglaya's sentence about "absurdity which meant nothing," and like the strange fellow that he was, rejoiced in the words.

Undoubtedly the fact that he might now come and see Aglaya as much as he pleased again was quite enough to make him perfectly happy; that he might come and speak to her, and see her, and sit by her, and walk with her— who knows, but that all this was quite enough to satisfy him for the whole of his life, and that he would desire no more to the end of time?

(Lizabetha Prokofievna felt that this might be the case, and she didn't like it; though very probably she could not have put the idea into words.)

It would be difficult to describe the animation and high spirits which distinguished the prince for the rest of the evening.

He was so happy that "it made one feel happy to look at him," as Aglaya's sisters expressed it afterwards. He talked, and told stories just as he had done once before, and never since, namely on the very first morning of his acquaintance with the Epanchins, six months ago. Since his return to Petersburg from Moscow, he had been remarkably silent, and had told Prince S. on one occasion, before everyone, that he did not think himself justified in degrading any thought by his unworthy words.

But this evening he did nearly all the talking himself, and told stories by the dozen, while he answered all questions put to him clearly, gladly, and with any amount of detail.

There was nothing, however, of love-making in his talk. His ideas were all of the most serious kind; some were even mystical and profound.

He aired his own views on various matters, some of his most private opinions and observations, many of which would have seemed rather funny, so his hearers agreed afterwards, had they not been so well expressed.

The general liked serious subjects of conversation; but both he and Lizabetha Prokofievna felt that they were having a little too much of a good thing tonight, and as the evening advanced, they both grew more or less melancholy; but towards night, the prince fell to telling funny stories, and was always the first to burst out laughing himself, which he invariably did so joyously and simply that the rest laughed just as much at him as at his stories.

As for Aglaya, she hardly said a word all the evening; but she listened with all her ears to Lef Nicolaievitch's talk, and scarcely took her eyes off him.

"She looked at him, and stared and stared, and hung on every word he said," said Lizabetha afterwards, to her husband, "and yet, tell her that she loves him, and she is furious!"

"What's to be done? It's fate," said the general, shrugging his shoulders, and, for a long while after, he continued to repeat: "It's fate, it's fate!"

We may add that to a business man like General Epanchin the present position of affairs was most unsatisfactory. He hated the uncertainty in which they had been, perforce, left. However, he decided to say no more about it, and merely to look on, and take his time and tune from Lizabetha Prokofievna.

The happy state in which the family had spent the evening, as just recorded, was not of very long duration. Next day Aglaya quarrelled with the prince again, and so she continued to behave for the next few days. For whole hours at a time she ridiculed and chaffed the wretched man, and made him almost a laughing-stock.

It is true that they used to sit in the little summer-house together for an hour or two at a time, very often, but it was observed that on these occasions the prince would read the paper, or some book, aloud to Aglaya.

"Do you know," Aglaya said to him once, interrupting the reading, "I've remarked that you are dreadfully badly educated. You never know anything thoroughly, if one asks you; neither anyone's name, nor dates, nor about treaties and so on. It's a great pity, you know!"

"I told you I had not had much of an education," replied the prince.

"How am I to respect you, if that's the case? Read on now. No—don't! Stop reading!"

And once more, that same evening, Aglaya mystified them all. Prince S. had returned, and Aglaya was particularly amiable to him, and asked a great deal after Evgenie Pavlovitch. (Muishkin had not come in as yet.)

Suddenly Prince S. hinted something about "a new and approaching change in the family." He was led to this remark by a communication inadvertently made to him by Lizabetha Prokofievna, that Adelaida's marriage must be postponed a little longer, in order that the two weddings might come off together.

It is impossible to describe Aglaya's irritation. She flared up, and said some indignant words about "all these silly insinuations." She added that "she had no intentions as yet of replacing anybody's mistress."

These words painfully impressed the whole party; but especially her parents. Lizabetha Prokofievna summoned a secret council of two, and insisted upon the general's demanding from the prince a full explanation of his relations with Nastasia Philipovna. The general argued that it was only a whim of Aglaya's; and that, had not Prince S. unfortunately made that remark, which had confused the child and made her blush, she never would have said what she did; and that he was sure Aglaya knew well that anything she might have heard of the prince and Nastasia

Philipovna was merely the fabrication of malicious tongues, and that the woman was going to marry Rogojin. He insisted that the prince had nothing whatever to do with Nastasia Philipovna, so far as any liaison was concerned; and, if the truth were to be told about it, he added, never had had.

Meanwhile nothing put the prince out, and he continued to be in the seventh heaven of bliss. Of course he could not fail to observe some impatience and ill-temper in Aglaya now and then; but he believed in something else, and nothing could now shake his conviction. Besides, Aglaya's frowns never lasted long; they disappeared of themselves.

Perhaps he was too easy in his mind. So thought Hippolyte, at all events, who met him in the park one day.

"Didn't I tell you the truth now, when I said you were in love?" he said, coming up to Muishkin of his own accord, and stopping him.

The prince gave him his hand and congratulated him upon "looking so well."

Hippolyte himself seemed to be hopeful about his state of health, as is often the case with consumptives.

He had approached the prince with the intention of talking sarcastically about his happy expression of face, but very soon forgot his intention and began to talk about himself. He began complaining about everything, disconnectedly and endlessly, as was his wont.

"You wouldn't believe," he concluded, "how irritating they all are there. They are such wretchedly small, vain, egotistical,*commonplace* people! Would you believe it, they invited me there under the express condition that I should die quickly, and they are all as wild as possible with me for not having died yet, and for being, on the contrary, a good deal better! Isn't it a comedy? I don't mind betting that you don't believe me!"

The prince said nothing.

"I sometimes think of coming over to you again," said Hippolyte, carelessly. "So you *don't* think them capable of inviting a man on the condition that he is to look sharp and die?"

"I certainly thought they invited you with quite other views."

"Ho, ho! you are not nearly so simple as they try to make you out! This is not the time for it, or I would tell you a thing or two about that beauty, Gania, and his hopes. You are being undermined, pitilessly undermined, and—and it is really melancholy to see you so calm about it. But alas! it's your nature—you can't help it!"

"My word! what a thing to be melancholy about! Why, do you think I should be any happier if I were to feel disturbed about the excavations you tell me of?"

"It is better to be unhappy and know the worst, than to be happy in a fool's paradise! I suppose you don't believe that you have a rival in that quarter?"

"Your insinuations as to rivalry are rather cynical, Hippolyte. I'm sorry to say I have no right to answer you! As for Gania, I put it to you, *can* any man have a happy mind after passing through what he has had to suffer? I think that is the best way to look at it. He will change yet, he has lots of time before him, and life is rich; besides—besides..." the prince hesitated. "As to being undermined, I don't know what in the world you are driving at, Hippolyte. I think we had better drop the subject!"

"Very well, we'll drop it for a while. You can't look at anything but in your exalted, generous way. You must put out your finger and touch a thing before you'll believe it, eh? Ha! ha! ha! I suppose you despise me dreadfully, prince, eh? What do you think?"

"Why? Because you have suffered more than we have?"

"No; because I am unworthy of my sufferings, if you like!"

"Whoever *can* suffer is worthy to suffer, I should think. Aglaya Ivanovna wished to see you, after she had read your confession, but—"

"She postponed the pleasure—I see—I quite understand!" said Hippolyte, hurriedly, as though he wished to banish the subject. "I hear—they tell me—that you read her all that nonsense aloud? Stupid bosh it was—written in delirium. And I can't understand how anyone can be so—I won't say *cruel*, because the word would be humiliating to myself, but we'll say childishly vain and revengeful, as to *reproach* me with this confession, and use it as a weapon against me. Don't be afraid, I'm not referring to yourself."

"Oh, but I'm sorry you repudiate the confession, Hippolyte—it is sincere; and, do you know, even the absurd parts of it—and these are many" (here Hippolyte frowned savagely) "are, as it were, redeemed by suffering—for it must have cost you something to admit what you there say—great torture, perhaps, for all I know. Your motive must have been a very noble one all through. Whatever may have appeared to the contrary, I give you my word, I see this more plainly every day. I do not judge you; I merely say this to have it off my mind, and I am only sorry that I did not say it all *then*—"

Hippolyte flushed hotly. He had thought at first that the prince was "humbugging" him; but on looking at his face he saw that he was absolutely serious, and had no thought of any deception. Hippolyte beamed with gratification.

"And yet I must die," he said, and almost added: "a man like me!

"And imagine how that Gania annoys me! He has developed the idea—or pretends to believe—that in all probability three or four others who heard my confession will die before I do. There's an idea for you—and all this by way of *consoling* me! Ha! ha! ha! In the first place they haven't died yet; and in the second, if they *did* die—all of them—what would be the satisfaction to me in that? He judges me by himself. But he goes further, he actually pitches into me because, as he declares, 'any decent fellow' would die quietly, and that 'all this' is mere egotism on my part. He doesn't see what refinement of egotism it is on his own part—and at the same time, what ox-like coarseness! Have you ever read of the death of one Stepan Gleboff, in the eighteenth century? I read of it yesterday by chance."

"Who was he?"

"He was impaled on a stake in the time of Peter."

"I know, I know! He lay there fifteen hours in the hard frost, and died with the most extraordinary fortitude—I know—what of him?"

"Only that God gives that sort of dying to some, and not to others. Perhaps you think, though, that I could not die like Gleboff?"

"Not at all!" said the prince, blushing. "I was only going to say that you—not that you could not be like Gleboff—but that you would have been more like—"

"I guess what you mean—I should be an Osterman, not a Gleboff—eh? Is that what you meant?"

"What Osterman?" asked the prince in some surprise.

"Why, Osterman—the diplomatist. Peter's Osterman," muttered Hippolyte, confused. There was a moment's pause of mutual confusion.

"Oh, no, no!" said the prince at last, "that was not what I was going to say—oh no! I don't think you would ever have been like Osterman."

Hippolyte frowned gloomily.

"I'll tell you why I draw the conclusion," explained the prince, evidently desirous of clearing up the matter a little. "Because, though I often think over the men of those times, I cannot for the life of me imagine them to be like ourselves. It really appears to me that they were of another race altogether than ourselves of today. At that time people seemed to stick so to one idea; now, they are more nervous, more sensitive, more enlightened—people of two or three ideas at once—as it were. The man of today is a broader man, so to speak—and I declare I believe that is what prevents him from being so self-contained and independent a being as his brother of those earlier days. Of course my remark was only made under this impression, and not in the least—"

"I quite understand. You are trying to comfort me for the naiveness with which you disagreed with me—eh? Ha! ha! ha! You are a regular child, prince! However, I cannot help seeing that you always treat me like—like a fragile china cup. Never mind, never mind, I'm not a bit angry! At all events we have had a very funny talk. Do you know, all things considered, I should like to be something better than Osterman! I wouldn't take the trouble to rise from the dead to be an Osterman. However, I see I must make arrangements to die soon, or I myself—. Well—leave me now! *Au revoir.* Look here—before you go, just give me your opinion: how do you think I ought to die, now? I mean—the best, the most virtuous way? Tell me!"

"You should pass us by and forgive us our happiness," said the prince in a low voice.

"Ha! ha! ha! I thought so. I thought I should hear something like that. Well, you are—you really are—oh dear me! Eloquence, eloquence! Good-bye!"

VI.

As to the evening party at the Epanchins' at which Princess Bielokonski was to be present, Varia had reported with accuracy; though she had perhaps expressed herself too strongly.

The thing was decided in a hurry and with a certain amount of quite unnecessary excitement, doubtless because "nothing could be done in this house like anywhere else."

The impatience of Lizabetha Prokofievna "to get things settled" explained a good deal, as well as the anxiety of both parents for the happiness of their beloved daughter. Besides, Princess Bielokonski was going away soon, and they hoped that she would take an interest in the prince. They were anxious that he should enter society under the auspices of this lady, whose patronage was the best of recommendations for any young man.

Even if there seems something strange about the match, the general and his wife said to each other, the "world" will accept Aglaya's fiance without any question if he is under the patronage of the princess. In any case, the prince would have to be "shown" sooner or later; that is, introduced into society, of which he had, so far, not the least idea. Moreover, it was only a question of a small gathering of a few intimate friends. Besides Princess Bielokonski, only one other lady was expected, the wife of a high dignitary. Evgenie Pavlovitch, who was to escort the princess, was the only young man.

Muishkin was told of the princess's visit three days beforehand, but nothing was said to him about the party until the night before it was to take place.

He could not help observing the excited and agitated condition of all members of the family, and from certain hints dropped in conversation he gathered that they were all anxious as to the impression he should make upon the princess. But the Epanchins, one and all, believed that Muishkin, in his simplicity of mind, was quite incapable of realizing that they could be feeling any anxiety on his account, and for this reason they all looked at him with dread and uneasiness.

In point of fact, he did attach marvellously little importance to the approaching event. He was occupied with altogether different thoughts. Aglaya was growing hourly more capricious and gloomy, and this distressed him. When they told him that Evgenie Pavlovitch was expected, he evinced great delight, and said that he had long wished to see him—and somehow these words did not please anyone.

Aglaya left the room in a fit of irritation, and it was not until late in the evening, past eleven, when the prince was taking his departure, that she said a word or two to him, privately, as she accompanied him as far as the front door.

"I should like you," she said, "not to come here tomorrow until evening, when the guests are all assembled. You know there are to be guests, don't you?"

She spoke impatiently and with severity; this was the first allusion she had made to the party of tomorrow.

She hated the idea of it, everyone saw that; and she would probably have liked to quarrel about it with her parents, but pride and modesty prevented her from broaching the subject.

The prince jumped to the conclusion that Aglaya, too, was nervous about him, and the impression he would make, and that she did not like to admit her anxiety; and this thought alarmed him.

"Yes, I am invited," he replied.

She was evidently in difficulties as to how best to go on. "May I speak of something serious to you, for once in my life?" she asked, angrily. She was irritated at she knew not what, and could not restrain her wrath.

"Of course you may; I am very glad to listen," replied Muishkin.

Aglaya was silent a moment and then began again with evident dislike of her subject:

"I do not wish to quarrel with them about this; in some things they won't be reasonable. I always did feel a loathing for the laws which seem to guide mamma's conduct at times. I don't speak of father, for he cannot be expected to be anything but what he is. Mother is a noble-minded woman, I know; you try to suggest anything mean to her, and you'll see! But she is such a slave to these miserable creatures! I don't mean old Bielokonski alone. She is a contemptible old thing, but she is able to twist people round her little finger, and I admire that in her, at all events! How mean it all is, and how foolish! We were always middle-class, thoroughly middle-class, people. Why should we attempt to climb into the giddy heights of the fashionable world? My sisters are all for it. It's Prince S. they have to thank for poisoning their minds. Why are you so glad that Evgenie Pavlovitch is coming?"

"Listen to me, Aglaya," said the prince, "I do believe you are nervous lest I shall make a fool of myself tomorrow at your party?"

"Nervous about you?" Aglaya blushed. "Why should I be nervous about you? What would it matter to me if you were to make ever such a fool of yourself? How can you say such a thing? What do you mean by 'making a fool of yourself'? What a vulgar expression! I suppose you intend to talk in that sort of way tomorrow evening? Look up a few more such expressions in your dictionary; do, you'll make a grand effect! I'm sorry that you seem to be able to come into a room as gracefully as you do; where did you learn the art? Do you think you can drink a cup of tea decently, when you know everybody is looking at you, on purpose to see how you do it?"

"Yes, I think I can."

"Can you? I'm sorry for it then, for I should have had a good laugh at you otherwise. Do break *something* at least, in the drawing-room! Upset the Chinese vase, won't you? It's a valuable one; *do* break it. Mamma values it, and she'll go out of her mind—it was a present. She'll cry before everyone, you'll see! Wave your hand about, you know, as you always do, and just smash it. Sit down near it on purpose."

"On the contrary, I shall sit as far from it as I can. Thanks for the hint."

"Ha, ha! Then you are afraid you *will* wave your arms about! I wouldn't mind betting that you'll talk about some lofty subject, something serious and learned. How delightful, how tactful that will be!"

"I should think it would be very foolish indeed, unless it happened to come in appropriately."

"Look here, once for all," cried Aglaya, boiling over, "if I hear you talking about capital punishment, or the economical condition of Russia, or about Beauty redeeming the world, or anything of that sort, I'll—well, of course I shall laugh and seem very pleased, but I warn you beforehand, don't look me in the face again! I'm serious now, mind, this time I *am really*serious." She certainly did say this very seriously, so much so, that she looked quite different from what she usually was, and the prince could not help noticing the fact. She did not seem to be joking in the slightest degree.

"Well, you've put me into such a fright that I shall certainly make a fool of myself, and very likely break something too. I wasn't a bit alarmed before, but now I'm as nervous as can be."

"Then don't speak at all. Sit still and don't talk."

"Oh, I can't do that, you know! I shall say something foolish out of pure 'funk,' and break something for the same excellent reason; I know I shall. Perhaps I shall slip and fall on the slippery floor; I've done that before now, you know. I shall dream of it all night now. Why did you say anything about it?"

Aglaya looked blackly at him.

"Do you know what, I had better not come at all tomorrow! I'll plead sick-list and stay away," said the prince, with decision.

Aglaya stamped her foot, and grew quite pale with anger.

"Oh, my goodness! Just listen to that! 'Better not come,' when the party is on purpose for him! Good Lord! What a delightful thing it is to have to do with such a—such a stupid as you are!"

"Well, I'll come, I'll come," interrupted the prince, hastily, "and I'll give you my word of honour that I will sit the whole evening and not say a word."

"I believe that's the best thing you can do. You said you'd 'plead sick-list' just now; where in the world do you get hold of such expressions? Why do you talk to me like this? Are you trying to irritate me, or what?"

"Forgive me, it's a schoolboy expression. I won't do it again. I know quite well, I see it, that you are anxious on my account (now, don't be angry), and it makes me very happy to see it. You wouldn't believe how frightened I am of misbehaving somehow, and how glad I am of your instructions. But all this panic is simply nonsense, you know, Aglaya! I give you my word it is; I am so pleased that you are such a child, such a dear good child. How *charming* you can be if you like, Aglaya."

Aglaya wanted to be angry, of course, but suddenly some quite unexpected feeling seized upon her heart, all in a moment.

"And you won't reproach me for all these rude words of mine—some day—afterwards?" she asked, of a sudden.

"What an idea! Of course not. And what are you blushing for again? And there comes that frown once more! You've taken to looking too gloomy sometimes, Aglaya, much more than you used to. I know why it is."

"Be quiet, do be quiet!"

"No, no, I had much better speak out. I have long wished to say it, and *have* said it, but that's not enough, for you didn't believe me. Between us two there stands a being who—"

"Be quiet, be quiet, be quiet, be quiet!" Aglaya struck in, suddenly, seizing his hand in hers, and gazing at him almost in terror.

At this moment she was called by someone. She broke loose from him with an air of relief and ran away.

The prince was in a fever all night. It was strange, but he had suffered from fever for several nights in succession. On this particular night, while in semi-delirium, he had an idea: what if on the morrow he were to have a fit before everybody? The thought seemed to freeze his blood within him. All night he fancied himself in some extraordinary society of strange persons. The worst of it was that he was talking nonsense; he knew that he ought not to speak at all, and yet he talked the whole time; he seemed to be trying to persuade them all to something. Evgenie and Hippolyte were among the guests, and appeared to be great friends.

He awoke towards nine o'clock with a headache, full of confused ideas and strange impressions. For some reason or other he felt most anxious to see Rogojin, to see and talk to him, but what he wished to say he could not tell. Next, he determined to go and see Hippolyte. His mind was in a confused state, so much so that the incidents of the morning seemed to be imperfectly realized, though acutely felt.

One of these incidents was a visit from Lebedeff. Lebedeff came rather early—before ten—but he was tipsy already. Though the prince was not in an observant condition, yet he could not avoid seeing that for at least three days—ever since General Ivolgin had left the house Lebedeff had been behaving very badly. He looked untidy and dirty at all times of the day, and it was said that he had begun to rage about in his own house, and that his temper was very bad. As soon as he arrived this morning, he began to hold forth, beating his breast and apparently blaming himself for something.

"I've—I've had a reward for my meanness—I've had a slap in the face," he concluded, tragically.

"A slap in the face? From whom? And so early in the morning?"

"Early?" said Lebedeff, sarcastically. "Time counts for nothing, even in physical chastisement; but my slap in the face was not physical, it was moral."

He suddenly took a seat, very unceremoniously, and began his story. It was very disconnected; the prince frowned, and wished he could get away; but suddenly a few words struck him. He sat stiff with wonder—Lebedeff said some extraordinary things.

In the first place he began about some letter; the name of Aglaya Ivanovna came in. Then suddenly he broke off and began to accuse the prince of something; he was apparently offended with him. At first he declared that the prince had trusted him with his confidences as to "a certain person" (Nastasia Philipovna), but that of late his friendship had been thrust back into his bosom, and his innocent question as to "approaching family changes" had been curtly put aside, which Lebedeff declared, with tipsy tears, he could not bear; especially as he knew so much already both from Rogojin and Nastasia Philipovna and her friend, and from Varvara Ardalionovna, and even from Aglaya Ivanovna, through his daughter Vera. "And who told Lizabetha Prokofievna something in secret, by letter? Who told her all about the movements of a certain person called Nastasia Philipovna? Who was the anonymous person, eh? Tell me!"

"Surely not you?" cried the prince.

"Just so," said Lebedeff, with dignity; "and only this very morning I have sent up a letter to the noble lady, stating that I have a matter of great importance to communicate. She received the letter; I know she got it; and she received *me*, too."

"Have you just seen Lizabetha Prokofievna?" asked the prince, scarcely believing his ears.

"Yes, I saw her, and got the said slap in the face as mentioned. She chucked the letter back to me unopened, and kicked me out of the house, morally, not physically, although not far off it."

"What letter do you mean she returned unopened?"

"What! didn't I tell you? Ha, ha, ha! I thought I had. Why, I received a letter, you know, to be handed over—"

"From whom? To whom?"

But it was difficult, if not impossible, to extract anything from Lebedeff. All the prince could gather was, that the letter had been received very early, and had a request written on the outside that it might be sent on to the address given.

"Just as before, sir, just as before! To a certain person, and from a certain hand. The individual's name who wrote the letter is to be represented by the letter A.—"

"What? Impossible! To Nastasia Philipovna? Nonsense!" cried the prince.

"It was, I assure you, and if not to her then to Rogojin, which is the same thing. Mr. Hippolyte has had letters, too, and all from the individual whose name begins with an A.," smirked Lebedeff, with a hideous grin.

As he kept jumping from subject to subject, and forgetting what he had begun to talk about, the prince said nothing, but waited, to give him time.

It was all very vague. Who had taken the letters, if letters there were? Probably Vera—and how could Lebedeff have got them? In all probability, he had managed to steal the present letter from Vera, and had himself gone over to Lizabetha Prokofievna with some idea in his head. So the prince concluded at last.

"You are mad!" he cried, indignantly.

"Not quite, esteemed prince," replied Lebedeff, with some acerbity. "I confess I thought of doing you the service of handing the letter over to yourself, but I decided that it would pay me better to deliver it up to the noble lady aforesaid, as I had informed her of everything hitherto by anonymous letters; so when I sent her up a note from myself, with the letter, you know, in order to fix a meeting for eight o'clock this morning, I signed it 'your secret correspondent.' They let me in at once—very quickly—by the back door, and the noble lady received me."

"Well? Go on."

"Oh, well, when I saw her she almost punched my head, as I say; in fact so nearly that one might almost say she did punch my head. She threw the letter in my face; she seemed to reflect first, as if she would have liked to keep it, but thought better of it and threw it in my face instead. 'If anybody can have been such a fool as to trust a man like you to deliver the letter,' says she,' take it and deliver it! 'Hey! she was grandly indignant. A fierce, fiery lady that, sir!"

"Where's the letter now?"

"Oh, I've still got it, here!"

And he handed the prince the very letter from Aglaya to Gania, which the latter showed with so much triumph to his sister at a later hour.

"This letter cannot be allowed to remain in your hands."

"It's for you—for you! I've brought it you on purpose!" cried Lebedeff, excitedly. "Why, I'm yours again now, heart and hand, your slave; there was but a momentary pause in the flow of my love and esteem for you. Mea culpa, mea culpa! as the Pope of Rome says.

"This letter should be sent on at once," said the prince, disturbed. "I'll hand it over myself."

"Wouldn't it be better, esteemed prince, wouldn't it be better—to—don't you know—"

Lebedeff made a strange and very expressive grimace; he twisted about in his chair, and did something, apparently symbolical, with his hands.

"What do you mean?" said the prince.

"Why, open it, for the time being, don't you know?" he said, most confidentially and mysteriously.

The prince jumped up so furiously that Lebedeff ran towards the door; having gained which strategic position, however, he stopped and looked back to see if he might hope for pardon.

"Oh, Lebedeff, Lebedeff! Can a man really sink to such depths of meanness?" said the prince, sadly.

Lebedeff's face brightened.

"Oh, I'm a mean wretch—a mean wretch!" he said, approaching the prince once more, and beating his breast, with tears in his eyes.

"It's abominable dishonesty, you know!"

"Dishonesty—it is, it is! That's the very word!"

"What in the world induces you to act so? You are nothing but a spy. Why did you write anonymously to worry so noble and generous a lady? Why should not Aglaya Ivanovna write a note to whomever she pleases? What did you mean to complain of today? What did you expect to get by it? What made you go at all?"

"Pure amiable curiosity,—I assure you—desire to do a service. That's all. Now I'm entirely yours again, your slave; hang me if you like!"

"Did you go before Lizabetha Prokofievna in your present condition?" inquired the prince.

"No—oh no, fresher—more the correct card. I only became this like after the humiliation I suffered there,

"Well—that'll do; now leave me."

This injunction had to be repeated several times before the man could be persuaded to move. Even then he turned back at the door, came as far as the middle of the room, and there went through his mysterious motions designed to convey the suggestion that the prince should open the letter. He did not dare put his suggestion into words again.

After this performance, he smiled sweetly and left the room on tiptoe.

All this had been very painful to listen to. One fact stood out certain and clear, and that was that poor Aglaya must be in a state of great distress and indecision and mental torment ("from jealousy," the prince whispered to himself). Undoubtedly in this inexperienced, but hot and proud little head, there were all sorts of plans forming, wild and impossible plans, maybe; and the idea of this so frightened the prince that he could not make up his mind what to do. Something must be done, that was clear.

He looked at the address on the letter once more. Oh, he was not in the least degree alarmed about Aglaya writing such a letter; he could trust her. What he did not like about it was that he could not trust Gania.

However, he made up his mind that he would himself take the note and deliver it. Indeed, he went so far as to leave the house and walk up the road, but changed his mind when he had nearly reached Ptitsin's door. However, he there luckily met Colia, and commissioned him to deliver the letter to his brother as if direct from Aglaya. Colia asked no questions but simply delivered it, and Gania consequently had no suspicion that it had passed through so many hands.

Arrived home again, the prince sent for Vera Lebedeff and told her as much as was necessary, in order to relieve her mind, for she had been in a dreadful state of anxiety since she had missed the letter. She heard with horror that her father had taken it. Muishkin learned from her that she had on several occasions performed secret missions both for Aglaya and for Rogojin, without, however, having had the slightest idea that in so doing she might injure the prince in any way.

The latter, with one thing and another, was now so disturbed and confused, that when, a couple of hours or so later, a message came from Colia that the general was ill, he could hardly take the news in.

However, when he did master the fact, it acted upon him as a tonic by completely distracting his attention. He went at once to Nina Alexandrovna's, whither the general had been carried, and stayed there until the evening. He could do no good, but there are people whom to have near one is a blessing at such times. Colia was in an almost hysterical state; he cried continuously, but was running about all day, all the same; fetching doctors, of whom he collected three; going to the chemist's, and so on.

The general was brought round to some extent, but the doctors declared that he could not be said to be out of danger. Varia and Nina Alexandrovna never left the sick man's bedside; Gania was excited and distressed, but would not go upstairs, and seemed afraid to look at the patient. He wrung his hands when the prince spoke to him, and said that "such a misfortune at such a moment" was terrible.

The prince thought he knew what Gania meant by "such a moment."

Hippolyte was not in the house. Lebedeff turned up late in the afternoon; he had been asleep ever since his interview with the prince in the morning. He was quite sober now, and cried with real sincerity over the sick general—mourning for him as though he were his own brother. He blamed himself aloud, but did not explain why. He repeated over and over again to Nina Alexandrovna that he alone was to blame—no one else—but that he had acted out of "pure amiable curiosity," and that "the deceased," as he insisted upon calling the still living general, had been the greatest of geniuses.

He laid much stress on the genius of the sufferer, as if this idea must be one of immense solace in the present crisis.

Nina Alexandrovna—seeing his sincerity of feeling—said at last, and without the faintest suspicion of reproach in her voice: "Come, come—don't cry! God will forgive you!"

Lebedeff was so impressed by these words, and the tone in which they were spoken, that he could not leave Nina Alexandrovna all the evening—in fact, for several days. Till the general's death, indeed, he spent almost all his time at his side.

Twice during the day a messenger came to Nina Alexandrovna from the Epanchins to inquire after the invalid.

When—late in the evening—the prince made his appearance in Lizabetha Prokofievna's drawing-room, he found it full of guests. Mrs. Epanchin questioned him very fully about the general as soon as he appeared; and when old Princess Bielokonski wished to know "who this general was, and who was Nina Alexandrovna," she proceeded to explain in a manner which pleased the prince very much.

He himself, when relating the circumstances of the general's illness to Lizabetha Prokofievna, "spoke beautifully," as Aglaya's sisters declared afterwards—"modestly, quietly, without gestures or too many words, and with great dignity." He had entered the room with propriety and grace, and he was perfectly dressed; he not only did not "fall down on the slippery floor," as he had expressed it, but evidently made a very favourable impression upon the assembled guests.

As for his own impression on entering the room and taking his seat, he instantly remarked that the company was not in the least such as Aglaya's words had led him to fear, and as he had dreamed of—in nightmare form—all night.

This was the first time in his life that he had seen a little corner of what was generally known by the terrible name of "society." He had long thirsted, for reasons of his own, to penetrate the mysteries of the magic circle, and, therefore, this assemblage was of the greatest possible interest to him.

His first impression was one of fascination. Somehow or other he felt that all these people must have been born on purpose to be together! It seemed to him that the Epanchins were not having a party at all; that these people must have been here always, and that he himself was one of them—returned among them after a long absence, but one of them, naturally and indisputably.

It never struck him that all this refined simplicity and nobility and wit and personal dignity might possibly be no more than an exquisite artistic polish. The majority of the guests—who were somewhat empty-headed, after all, in spite of their aristocratic bearing—never guessed, in their self-satisfied composure, that much of their superiority was mere veneer, which indeed they had adopted unconsciously and by inheritance.

The prince would never so much as suspect such a thing in the delight of his first impression.

He saw, for instance, that one important dignitary, old enough to be his grandfather, broke off his own conversation in order to listen to *him*—a young and inexperienced man; and not only listened, but seemed to attach value to his opinion, and was kind and amiable, and yet they were strangers and had never seen each other before. Perhaps what most appealed to the prince's impressionability was the refinement of the old man's courtesy towards him. Perhaps the soil of his susceptible nature was really predisposed to receive a pleasant impression.

Meanwhile all these people-though friends of the family and of each other to a certain extent—were very far from being such intimate friends of the family and of each other as the prince concluded. There were some present who never would think of considering the Epanchins their equals. There were even some who hated one another cordially. For instance, old Princess Bielokonski had all her life despised the wife of the "dignitary," while the latter was very far from loving Lizabetha Prokofievna. The dignitary himself had been General Epanchin's protector from his youth up; and the general considered him so majestic a personage that he would have felt a hearty contempt for himself if he had even for one moment allowed himself to pose as the great man's equal, or to think of him—in his fear and reverence-as anything less than an Olympic God! There were others present who had not met for years, and who had no feeling whatever for each other, unless it were dislike; and yet they met tonight as though they had seen each other but yesterday in some friendly and intimate assembly of kindred spirits.

It was not a large party, however. Besides Princess Bielokonski and the old dignitary (who was really a great man) and his wife, there was an old military general—a count or baron with a German name, a man reputed to possess great knowledge and administrative ability. He was one of those Olympian administrators who know everything except Russia, pronounce a word of extraordinary wisdom, admired by all, about once in five years, and, after being an eternity in the service, generally die full of honour and riches, though they have never done anything great, and have even been hostile to all greatness. This general was Ivan Fedorovitch's immediate superior in the service; and it pleased the latter to look upon him also as a patron. On the other hand, the great man did not at all consider himself Epanchin's patron. He was always very cool to him, while taking advantage of his ready services, and would instantly have put another in his place if there had been the slightest reason for the change.

Another guest was an elderly, important-looking gentleman, a distant relative of Lizabetha Prokofievna's. This gentleman was rich, held a good position, was a great talker, and had the reputation of being "one of the dissatisfied," though not belonging to the dangerous sections of that class. He had the manners, to some extent, of the English aristocracy, and some of their tastes (especially in the matter of under-done roast beef, harness, men-servants, etc.). He was a great friend of the dignitary's, and Lizabetha Prokofievna, for some reason or other, had got hold of the idea that this worthy intended at no distant date to offer the advantages of his hand and heart to Alexandra.

Besides the elevated and more solid individuals enumerated, there were present a few younger though not less elegant guests. Besides Prince S. and Evgenie Pavlovitch, we must name the eminent and fascinating Prince N.— once the vanquisher of female hearts all over Europe. This gentleman was no longer in the first bloom of youth—he was forty-five, but still very handsome. He was well off, and lived, as a rule, abroad, and was noted as a good teller of stories. Then came a few guests belonging to a lower stratum of society—people who, like the Epanchins themselves, moved only occasionally in this exalted sphere. The Epanchins liked to draft among their more elevated guests a few picked representatives of this lower stratum, and Lizabetha Prokofievna received much praise for this practice, which proved, her friends said, that she was a woman of tact. The Epanchins prided themselves upon the good opinion people held of them.

One of the representatives of the middle-class present today was a colonel of engineers, a very serious man and a great friend of Prince S., who had introduced him to the Epanchins. He was extremely silent in society, and displayed on the forefinger of his right hand a large ring, probably bestowed upon him for services of some sort. There was also a poet, German by name, but a Russian poet; very presentable, and even handsome-the sort of man one could bring into society with impunity. This gentleman belonged to a German family of decidedly bourgeois origin, but he had a knack of acquiring the patronage of "big-wigs," and of retaining their favour. He had translated some great German poem into Russian verse, and claimed to have been a friend of a famous Russian poet, since dead. (It is strange how great a multitude of literary people there are who have had the advantages of friendship with some great man of their own profession who is, unfortunately, dead.) The dignitary's wife had introduced this worthy to the Epanchins. This lady posed as the patroness of literary people, and she certainly had succeeded in obtaining pensions for a few of them, thanks to her influence with those in authority on such matters. She was a lady of weight in her own way. Her age was about forty-five, so that she was a very young wife for such an elderly husband as the dignitary. She had been a beauty in her day and still loved, as many ladies of forty-five do love, to dress a little too smartly. Her intellect was nothing to boast of, and her literary knowledge very doubtful. Literary patronage was, however, with her as much a mania as was the love of gorgeous clothes. Many books and translations were dedicated to her by her proteges, and a few of these talented individuals had published some of their own letters to her, upon very weighty subjects.

This, then, was the society that the prince accepted at once as true coin, as pure gold without alloy.

It so happened, however, that on this particular evening all these good people were in excellent humour and highly pleased with themselves. Every one of them felt that they were doing the Epanchins the greatest possible honour by their presence. But alas! the prince never suspected any such subtleties! For instance, he had no suspicion of the fact that the Epanchins, having in their mind so important a step as the marriage of their daughter, would never think of presuming to take it without having previously "shown off" the proposed husband to the dignitary—the recognized patron of the family. The latter, too, though he would probably have received news of a great disaster to the Epanchin family with perfect composure, would nevertheless have considered it a personal offence if they had dared to marry their daughter without his advice, or we might almost say, his leave.

The amiable and undoubtedly witty Prince N. could not but feel that he was as a sun, risen for one night only to shine upon the Epanchin drawing-room. He accounted them immeasurably his inferiors, and it was this feeling which caused his special amiability and delightful ease and grace towards them. He knew very well that he must tell some story this evening for the edification of the company, and led up to it with the inspiration of anticipatory triumph.

The prince, when he heard the story afterwards, felt that he had never yet come across so wonderful a humorist, or such remarkable brilliancy as was shown by this man; and yet if he had only known it, this story was the oldest, stalest, and most worn-out yarn, and every drawing-room in town was sick to death of it. It was only in the innocent Epanchin household that it passed for a new and brilliant tale—as a sudden and striking reminiscence of a splendid and talented man.

Even the German poet, though as amiable as possible, felt that he was doing the house the greatest of honours by his presence in it.

But the prince only looked at the bright side; he did not turn the coat and see the shabby lining.

Aglaya had not foreseen that particular calamity. She herself looked wonderfully beautiful this evening. All three sisters were dressed very tastefully, and their hair was done with special care.

Aglaya sat next to Evgenie Pavlovitch, and laughed and talked to him with an unusual display of friendliness. Evgenie himself behaved rather more sedately than usual, probably out of respect to the dignitary. Evgenie had been known in society for a long while. He had appeared at the Epanchins' today with crape on his hat, and Princess Bielokonski had commended this action on his part. Not every society man would have worn crape for "such an uncle." Lizabetha Prokofievna had liked it also, but was too preoccupied to take much notice. The prince remarked that Aglaya looked attentively at him two or three times, and seemed to be satisfied with his behaviour.

Little by little he became very happy indeed. All his late anxieties and apprehensions (after his conversation with Lebedeff) now appeared like so many bad dreams—impossible, and even laughable.

He did not speak much, only answering such questions as were put to him, and gradually settled down into unbroken silence, listening to what went on, and steeped in perfect satisfaction and contentment.

Little by little a sort of inspiration, however, began to stir within him, ready to spring into life at the right moment. When he did begin to speak, it was accidentally, in response to a question, and apparently without any special object.

VII.

While he feasted his eyes upon Aglaya, as she talked merrily with Evgenie and Prince N., suddenly the old anglomaniac, who was talking to the dignitary in another corner of the room, apparently telling him a story about something or other—suddenly this gentleman pronounced the name of "Nicolai Andreevitch Pavlicheff" aloud. The prince quickly turned towards him, and listened.

The conversation had been on the subject of land, and the present disorders, and there must have been something amusing said, for the old man had begun to laugh at his companion's heated expressions.

The latter was describing in eloquent words how, in consequence of recent legislation, he was obliged to sell a beautiful estate in the N. province, not because he wanted ready money—in fact, he was obliged to sell it at half its value. "To avoid another lawsuit about the Pavlicheff estate, I ran away," he said. "With a few more inheritances of that kind I should soon be ruined!"

At this point General Epanchin, noticing how interested Muishkin had become in the conversation, said to him, in a low tone:

"That gentleman—Ivan Petrovitch—is a relation of your late friend, Mr. Pavlicheff. You wanted to find some of his relations, did you not?"

The general, who had been talking to his chief up to this moment, had observed the prince's solitude and silence, and was anxious to draw him into the conversation, and so introduce him again to the notice of some of the important personages.

"Lef Nicolaievitch was a ward of Nicolai Andreevitch Pavlicheff, after the death of his own parents," he remarked, meeting Ivan Petrovitch's eye.

"Very happy to meet him, I'm sure," remarked the latter. "I remember Lef Nicolaievitch well. When General Epanchin introduced us just now, I recognized you at once, prince. You are very little changed, though I saw you last as a child of some ten or eleven years old. There was something in your features, I suppose, that—"

"You saw me as a child!" exclaimed the prince, with surprise.

"Oh! yes, long ago," continued Ivan Petrovitch, "while you were living with my cousin at Zlatoverhoff. You don't remember me? No, I dare say you don't; you had some malady at the time, I remember. It was so serious that I was surprised—"

"No; I remember nothing!" said the prince. A few more words of explanation followed, words which were spoken without the smallest excitement by his companion, but which evoked the greatest agitation in the prince; and it was discovered that two old ladies to whose care the prince had been left by Pavlicheff, and who lived at Zlatoverhoff, were also relations of Ivan Petrovitch.

The latter had no idea and could give no information as to why Pavlicheff had taken so great an interest in the little prince, his ward.

"In point of fact I don't think I thought much about it," said the old fellow. He seemed to have a wonderfully good memory, however, for he told the prince all about the two old ladies, Pavlicheff's cousins, who had taken care of him, and whom, he declared, he had taken to task for being too severe with the prince as a small sickly boy—the elder sister, at least; the younger had been kind, he recollected. They both now lived in another province, on a small estate left to them by Pavlicheff. The prince listened to all this with eyes sparkling with emotion and delight.

He declared with unusual warmth that he would never forgive himself for having travelled about in the central provinces during these last six months without having hunted up his two old friends.

He declared, further, that he had intended to go every day, but had always been prevented by circumstances; but that now he would promise himself the pleasure—however far it was, he would find them out. And so Ivan Petrovitch *really* knew Natalia Nikitishna!—what a saintly nature was hers!—and Martha Nikitishna! Ivan Petrovitch must excuse him, but really he was not quite fair on dear old Martha. She was severe, perhaps; but then what else could she be with such a little idiot as he was then? (Ha, ha.) He really was an idiot then, Ivan Petrovitch must know, though he might not believe it. (Ha, ha.) So he had really seen him there! Good heavens! And was he really and truly and actually a cousin of Pavlicheff's?

"I assure you of it," laughed Ivan Petrovitch, gazing amusedly at the prince.

"Oh! I didn't say it because I *doubt* the fact, you know. (Ha, ha.) How could I doubt such a thing? (Ha, ha, ha.) I made the remark because—because Nicolai Andreevitch Pavlicheff was such a splendid man, don't you see! Such a high-souled man, he really was, I assure you."

The prince did not exactly pant for breath, but he "seemed almost to *choke* out of pure simplicity and goodness of heart," as Adelaida expressed it, on talking the party over with her fiance, the Prince S., next morning.

"But, my goodness me," laughed Ivan Petrovitch, "why can't I be cousin to even a splendid man?"

"Oh, dear!" cried the prince, confused, trying to hurry his words out, and growing more and more eager every moment: "I've gone and said another stupid thing. I don't know what to say. I—I didn't mean that, you know—I—I—he really was such a splendid man, wasn't he?"

The prince trembled all over. Why was he so agitated? Why had he flown into such transports of delight without any apparent reason? He had far outshot the measure of joy and emotion consistent with the occasion. Why this was it would be difficult to say.

He seemed to feel warmly and deeply grateful to someone for something or other—perhaps to Ivan Petrovitch; but likely enough to all the guests, individually, and collectively. He was much too happy.

Ivan Petrovitch began to stare at him with some surprise; the dignitary, too, looked at him with considerable attention; Princess Bielokonski glared at him angrily, and compressed her lips. Prince N., Evgenie, Prince S., and the girls, all broke off their own conversations and listened. Aglaya seemed a little startled; as for Lizabetha Prokofievna, her heart sank within her.

This was odd of Lizabetha Prokofievna and her daughters. They had themselves decided that it would be better if the prince did not talk all the evening. Yet seeing him sitting silent and alone, but perfectly happy, they had been on the point of exerting themselves to draw him into one of the groups of talkers around the room. Now that he was in the midst of a talk they became more than ever anxious and perturbed.

"That he was a splendid man is perfectly true; you are quite right," repeated Ivan Petrovitch, but seriously this time. "He was a fine and a worthy fellow—worthy, one may say, of the highest respect," he added, more and more seriously at each pause; "and it is agreeable to see, on your part, such—"

"Wasn't it this same Pavlicheff about whom there was a strange story in connection with some abbot? I don't remember who the abbot was, but I remember at one time everybody was talking about it," remarked the old dignitary.

"Yes—Abbot Gurot, a Jesuit," said Ivan Petrovitch. "Yes, that's the sort of thing our best men are apt to do. A man of rank, too, and rich—a man who, if he had continued to serve, might have done anything; and then to throw up the service and everything else in order to go over to Roman Catholicism and turn Jesuit—openly, too—almost triumphantly. By Jove! it was positively a mercy that he died when he did—it was indeed—everyone said so at the time."

The prince was beside himself.

"Pavlicheff?—Pavlicheff turned Roman Catholic? Impossible!" he cried, in horror.

"H'm! impossible is rather a strong word," said Ivan Petrovitch. "You must allow, my dear prince... However, of course you value the memory of the deceased so very highly; and he certainly was the kindest of men; to which fact, by the way, I ascribe, more than to anything else, the success of the abbot in influencing his religious convictions. But you may ask me, if you please, how much trouble and worry I, personally, had over that business, and especially with this same Gurot! Would you believe it," he continued, addressing the dignitary, "they actually tried to put in a claim under the deceased's will, and I had to resort to the very strongest measures in order to bring them to their senses? I assure you they knew their cue, did these gentlemen—wonderful! Thank goodness all this was in Moscow, and I got the Court, you know, to help me, and we soon brought them to their senses."

"You wouldn't believe how you have pained and astonished me," cried the prince.

"Very sorry; but in point of fact, you know, it was all nonsense and would have ended in smoke, as usual—I'm sure of that. Last year,"—he turned to the old man again,—"Countess K. joined some Roman Convent abroad. Our people never seem to be able to offer any resistance so soon as they get into the hands of these—intriguers—especially abroad."

"That is all thanks to our lassitude, I think," replied the old man, with authority. "And then their way of preaching; they have a skilful manner of doing it! And they know how to startle one, too. I got quite a fright myself in '32, in Vienna, I assure you; but I didn't cave in to them, I ran away instead, ha, ha!"

"Come, come, I've always heard that you ran away with the beautiful Countess Levitsky that time—throwing up everything in order to do it—and not from the Jesuits at all," said Princess Bielokonski, suddenly.

"Well, yes—but we call it from the Jesuits, you know; it comes to the same thing," laughed the old fellow, delighted with the pleasant recollection.

"You seem to be very religious," he continued, kindly, addressing the prince, "which is a thing one meets so seldom nowadays among young people."

The prince was listening open-mouthed, and still in a condition of excited agitation. The old man was evidently interested in him, and anxious to study him more closely.

"Pavlicheff was a man of bright intellect and a good Christian, a sincere Christian," said the prince, suddenly. "How could he possibly embrace a faith which is unchristian? Roman Catholicism is, so to speak, simply the same thing as unchristianity," he added with flashing eyes, which seemed to take in everybody in the room.

"Come, that's a little *too* strong, isn't it?" murmured the old man, glancing at General Epanchin in surprise.

"How do you make out that the Roman Catholic religion is *unchristian?* What is it, then?" asked Ivan Petrovitch, turning to the prince.

"It is not a Christian religion, in the first place," said the latter, in extreme agitation, quite out of proportion to the necessity of the moment. "And in the second place, Roman Catholicism is, in my opinion, worse than Atheism itself. Yes—that is my opinion. Atheism only preaches a negation, but Romanism goes further; it preaches a disfigured, distorted Christ—it preaches Anti-Christ—I assure you, I swear it! This is my own personal conviction, and it has long distressed me. The Roman Catholic believes that the Church on earth cannot stand without universal temporal Power. He cries 'non possumus!' In my opinion the Roman Catholic religion is not a faith at all, but simply a continuation of the Roman Empire, and everything is subordinated to this idea—beginning with faith. The Pope has seized territories and an earthly throne, and has held them with the sword. And so the thing has gone on, only that to the sword they have added lying, intrigue, deceit, fanaticism, superstition, swindling;—they have played fast and loose with the most sacred and sincere feelings of men;—they have exchanged everything—everything for money, for base earthly *power!* And is this not the teaching of Anti-Christ? How could the upshot of all this be other than Atheism? Atheism is the child of Roman Catholicism—it proceeded from these Romans themselves, though perhaps they would not believe it. It grew and fattened on hatred of its parents; it is the progeny of their lies and spiritual feebleness. Atheism! In our country it is only among the upper classes that you find unbelievers; men who have lost the root or spirit of their faith; but abroad whole masses of the people are beginning to profess unbelief—at first because of the darkness and lies by which they were surrounded; but now out of fanaticism, out of loathing for the Church and Christianity!"

The prince paused to get breath. He had spoken with extraordinary rapidity, and was very pale.

All present interchanged glances, but at last the old dignitary burst out laughing frankly. Prince N. took out his eye-glass to have a good look at the speaker. The German poet came out of his corner and crept nearer to the table, with a spiteful smile.

"You exaggerate the matter very much," said Ivan Petrovitch, with rather a bored air. "There are, in the foreign Churches, many representatives of their faith who are worthy of respect and esteem."

"Oh, but I did not speak of individual representatives. I was merely talking about Roman Catholicism, and its essence—of Rome itself. A Church can never entirely disappear; I never hinted at that!"

"Agreed that all this may be true; but we need not discuss a subject which belongs to the domain of theology."

"Oh, no; oh, no! Not to theology alone, I assure you! Why, Socialism is the progeny of Romanism and of the Romanistic spirit. It and its brother Atheism proceed from Despair in opposition to Catholicism. It seeks to replace in itself the moral power of religion, in order to appease the spiritual thirst of parched humanity and save it; not by Christ, but by force. 'Don't dare to believe in God, don't dare to possess any individuality, any property! *Fraternité ou la Mort*; two million heads. 'By their works ye shall know them'—we are told. And we must not suppose that all this is harmless and without danger to ourselves. Oh, no; we must resist, and quickly, quickly! We must let out Christ shine forth upon the Western nations, our Christ whom we have preserved intact, and whom they have never known. Not as slaves, allowing ourselves to be caught by the hooks of the Jesuits, but carrying our Russian civilization to *them*, we must stand before them, not letting it be said among us that their preaching is 'skilful,' as someone expressed it just now."

"But excuse me, excuse me;" cried Ivan Petrovitch considerably disturbed, and looking around uneasily. "Your ideas are, of course, most praiseworthy, and in the highest degree patriotic; but you exaggerate the matter terribly. It would be better if we dropped the subject."

"No, sir, I do not exaggerate, I understate the matter, if anything, undoubtedly understate it; simply because I cannot express myself as I should like, but—"

"Allow me!"

The prince was silent. He sat straight up in his chair and gazed fervently at Ivan Petrovitch.

"It seems to me that you have been too painfully impressed by the news of what happened to your good benefactor," said the old dignitary, kindly, and with the utmost calmness of demeanour. "You are excitable, perhaps as the result of your solitary life. If you would make up your mind to live more among your fellows in society, I trust, I am sure, that the world would be glad to welcome you, as a remarkable young man; and you would soon find yourself able to look at things more calmly. You would see that all these things are much simpler than you think; and, besides, these rare cases come about, in my opinion, from ennui and from satiety."

"Exactly, exactly! That is a true thought!" cried the prince. "From ennui, from our ennui but not from satiety! Oh, no, you are wrong there! Say from *thirst* if you like; the thirst of fever! And please do not suppose that this is so small a matter that we may have a laugh at it and dismiss it; we must be able to foresee our disasters and arm against them. We Russians no sooner arrive at the brink of the water, and realize that we are really at the brink, than we are so delighted with the outlook that in we plunge and swim to the farthest point we can see. Why is this? You say you are surprised at Pavlicheff's action; you ascribe it to madness, to kindness of heart, and what not, but it is not so.

"Our Russian intensity not only astonishes ourselves; all Europe wonders at our conduct in such cases! For, if one of us goes over to Roman Catholicism, he is sure to become a Jesuit at once, and a rabid one into the bargain. If one of us becomes an Atheist, he must needs begin to insist on the prohibition of faith in God by force, that is, by the sword. Why is this? Why does he then exceed all bounds at once? Because he has found land at last, the fatherland that he sought in vain before; and, because his soul is rejoiced to find it, he throws himself upon it and kisses it! Oh, it is not from vanity alone, it is not from feelings of vanity that Russians become Atheists and Jesuits! But from spiritual thirst, from anguish of longing for higher things, for dry firm land, for foothold on a fatherland which they never believed in because they never knew it. It is easier for a Russian to become an Atheist, than for any other nationality in the world. And not only does a Russian 'become an Atheist,' but he actually *believes in* Atheism, just as though he had found a new faith, not perceiving that he has pinned his faith to a negation. Such is our anguish of thirst! 'Whoso has no country has no God.' That is not my own expression; it is the expression of a merchant, one of the Old Believers, whom I once met while travelling. He did not say exactly these words. I think his expression was:

"'Whoso forsakes his country forsakes his God.'

"But let these thirsty Russian souls find, like Columbus' discoverers, a new world; let them find the Russian world, let them search and discover all the gold and treasure that lies hid in the bosom of their own land! Show them the restitution of lost humanity, in the future, by Russian thought alone, and by means of the God and of the Christ of our Russian faith, and you will see how mighty and just and wise and good a giant will rise up before the eyes of the astonished and frightened world; astonished because they expect nothing but the sword from us, because they think they will get nothing out of us but barbarism. This has been the case up to now, and the longer matters go on as they are now proceeding, the more clear will be the truth of what I say; and I—"

But at this moment something happened which put a most unexpected end to the orator's speech. All this heated tirade, this outflow of passionate words and ecstatic ideas which seemed to hustle and tumble over each other as they fell from his lips, bore evidence of some unusually disturbed mental condition in the young fellow who had "boiled over" in such a remarkable manner, without any apparent reason.

Of those who were present, such as knew the prince listened to his outburst in a state of alarm, some with a feeling of mortification. It was so unlike his usual timid self-constraint; so inconsistent with his usual taste and tact, and with his instinctive feeling for the higher proprieties. They could not understand the origin of the outburst; it could not be simply the news of Pavlicheff's perversion. By the ladies the prince was regarded as little better than a lunatic, and Princess Bielokonski admitted afterwards that "in another minute she would have bolted."

The two old gentlemen looked quite alarmed. The old general (Epanchin's chief) sat and glared at the prince in severe displeasure. The colonel sat immovable. Even the German poet grew a little pale, though he wore his usual artificial smile as he looked around to see what the others would do.

In point of fact it is quite possible that the matter would have ended in a very commonplace and natural way in a few minutes. The undoubtedly astonished, but now more collected, General Epanchin had several times endeavoured to interrupt the prince, and not having succeeded he was now preparing to take firmer and more vigorous measures to attain his end. In another minute or two he would probably have made up his mind to lead the prince quietly out of the room, on the plea of his being ill (and it was more than likely that the general was right in his belief that the prince *was* actually ill), but it so happened that destiny had something different in store.

At the beginning of the evening, when the prince first came into the room, he had sat down as far as possible from the Chinese vase which Aglaya had spoken of the day before.

Will it be believed that, after Aglaya's alarming words, an ineradicable conviction had taken possession of his mind that, however he might try to avoid this vase next day, he must certainly break it? But so it was.

During the evening other impressions began to awaken in his mind, as we have seen, and he forgot his presentiment. But when Pavlicheff was mentioned and the general introduced him to Ivan Petrovitch, he had changed his place, and went over nearer to the table; when, it so happened, he took the chair nearest to the beautiful vase, which stood on a pedestal behind him, just about on a level with his elbow.

As he spoke his last words he had risen suddenly from his seat with a wave of his arm, and there was a general cry of horror.

The huge vase swayed backwards and forwards; it seemed to be uncertain whether or no to topple over on to the head of one of the old men, but eventually determined to go the other way, and came crashing over towards the German poet, who darted out of the way in terror.

The crash, the cry, the sight of the fragments of valuable china covering the carpet, the alarm of the company—what all this meant to the poor prince it would be difficult to convey to the mind of the reader, or for him to imagine.

But one very curious fact was that all the shame and vexation and mortification which he felt over the accident were less powerful than the deep impression of the almost supernatural truth of his premonition. He stood still in alarm—in almost superstitious alarm, for a moment; then all mists seemed to clear away from his eyes; he was conscious of nothing but light and joy and ecstasy; his breath came and went; but the moment passed. Thank God it was not that! He drew a long breath and looked around.

For some minutes he did not seem to comprehend the excitement around him; that is, he comprehended it and saw everything, but he stood aside, as it were, like someone invisible in a fairy tale, as though he had nothing to do with what was going on, though it pleased him to take an interest in it.

He saw them gather up the broken bits of china; he heard the loud talking of the guests and observed how pale Aglaya looked, and how very strangely she was gazing at him. There was no hatred in her expression, and no anger whatever. It was full of alarm for him, and sympathy and affection, while she looked around at the others with flashing, angry eyes. His heart filled with a sweet pain as he gazed at her.

At length he observed, to his amazement, that all had taken their seats again, and were laughing and talking as though nothing had happened. Another minute and the laughter grew louder—they were laughing at him, at his dumb stupor—laughing kindly and merrily. Several of them spoke to him, and spoke so kindly and cordially, especially Lizabetha Prokofievna—she was saying the kindest possible things to him.

Suddenly he became aware that General Epanchin was tapping him on the shoulder; Ivan Petrovitch was laughing too, but still more kind and sympathizing was the old dignitary. He took the prince by the hand and pressed it warmly; then he patted it, and quietly urged him to recollect himself—speaking to him exactly as he would have spoken to a little frightened child, which pleased the prince wonderfully; and next seated him beside himself.

The prince gazed into his face with pleasure, but still seemed to have no power to speak. His breath failed him. The old man's face pleased him greatly.

"Do you really forgive me?" he said at last. "And—and Lizabetha Prokofievna too?" The laugh increased, tears came into the prince's eyes, he could not believe in all this kindness—he was enchanted.

"The vase certainly was a very beautiful one. I remember it here for fifteen years—yes, quite that!" remarked Ivan Petrovitch.

"Oh, what a dreadful calamity! A wretched vase smashed, and a man half dead with remorse about it," said Lizabetha Prokofievna, loudly. "What made you so dreadfully startled, Lef Nicolaievitch?" she added, a little timidly. "Come, my dear boy! cheer up. You really alarm me, taking the accident so to heart."

"Do you forgive me all—*all*, besides the vase, I mean?" said the prince, rising from his seat once more, but the old gentleman caught his hand and drew him down again—he seemed unwilling to let him go.

"*C'est très-curieux et c'est très-sérieux,*" he whispered across the table to Ivan Petrovitch, rather loudly. Probably the prince heard him.

"So that I have not offended any of you? You will not believe how happy I am to be able to think so. It is as it should be. As if I *could* offend anyone here! I should offend you again by even suggesting such a thing."

"Calm yourself, my dear fellow. You are exaggerating again; you really have no occasion to be so grateful to us. It is a feeling which does you great credit, but an exaggeration, for all that."

"I am not exactly thanking you, I am only feeling a growing admiration for you—it makes me happy to look at you. I dare say I am speaking very foolishly, but I must speak—I must explain, if it be out of nothing better than self-respect."

All he said and did was abrupt, confused, feverish—very likely the words he spoke, as often as not, were not those he wished to say. He seemed to inquire whether he *might* speak. His eyes lighted on Princess Bielokonski.

"All right, my friend, talk away, talk away!" she remarked. "Only don't lose your breath; you were in such a hurry when you began, and look what you've come to now! Don't be afraid of speaking—all these ladies and gentlemen have seen far stranger people than yourself; you don't astonish *them*. You are nothing out-of-the-way remarkable, you know. You've done nothing but break a vase, and give us all a fright."

The prince listened, smiling.

"Wasn't it you," he said, suddenly turning to the old gentleman, "who saved the student Porkunoff and a clerk called Shoabrin from being sent to Siberia, two or three months since?"

The old dignitary blushed a little, and murmured that the prince had better not excite himself further.

"And I have heard of *you*," continued the prince, addressing Ivan Petrovitch, "that when some of your villagers were burned out you gave them wood to build up their houses again, though they were no longer your serfs and had behaved badly towards you."

"Oh, come, come! You are exaggerating," said Ivan Petrovitch, beaming with satisfaction, all the same. He was right, however, in this instance, for the report had reached the prince's ears in an incorrect form.

"And you, princess," he went on, addressing Princess Bielokonski, "was it not you who received me in Moscow, six months since, as kindly as though I had been your own son, in response to a letter from Lizabetha Prokofievna; and gave me one piece of advice, again as to your own son, which I shall never forget? Do you remember?"

"What are you making such a fuss about?" said the old lady, with annoyance. "You are a good fellow, but very silly. One gives you a halfpenny, and you are as grateful as though one had saved your life. You think this is praiseworthy on your part, but it is not—it is not, indeed."

She seemed to be very angry, but suddenly burst out laughing, quite good-humouredly.

Lizabetha Prokofievna's face brightened up, too; so did that of General Epanchin.

"I told you Lef Nicolaievitch was a man—a man—if only he would not be in such a hurry, as the princess remarked," said the latter, with delight.

Aglaya alone seemed sad and depressed; her face was flushed, perhaps with indignation.

"He really is very charming," whispered the old dignitary to Ivan Petrovitch.

"I came into this room with anguish in my heart," continued the prince, with ever-growing agitation, speaking quicker and quicker, and with increasing strangeness. "I—I was afraid of you all, and afraid of myself. I was most afraid of myself. When I returned to Petersburg, I promised myself to make a point of seeing our greatest men, and members of our oldest families—the old families like my own. I am now among princes like myself, am I not? I wished to know you, and it was necessary, very, very necessary. I had always heard so much that was evil said of you all—more evil than good; as to how small and petty were your interests, how absurd your habits, how shallow your education, and so on. There is so much written and said about you! I came here today with anxious curiosity; I wished to see for myself and form my own convictions as to whether it were true that the whole of this upper stratum of Russian society is *worthless*, has outlived its time, has existed too long, and is only fit to die—and yet is dying with petty, spiteful warring against that which is destined to supersede it and take its place—hindering the Coming Men, and knowing not that itself is in a dying condition. I did not fully believe in this view even before, for there never was such a class among us—excepting perhaps at court, by accident—or by uniform; but now there is not even that, is there? It has vanished, has it not?"

"No, not a bit of it," said Ivan Petrovitch, with a sarcastic laugh.

"Good Lord, he's off again!" said Princess Bielokonski, impatiently.

"Laissez-le dire! He is trembling all over," said the old man, in a warning whisper.

The prince certainly was beside himself.

"Well? What have I seen?" he continued. "I have seen men of graceful simplicity of intellect; I have seen an old man who is not above speaking kindly and even *listening* to a boy like myself; I see before me persons who can understand, who can forgive—kind, good Russian hearts—hearts almost as kind and cordial as I met abroad. Imagine how delighted I must have been, and how surprised! Oh, let me express this feeling! I have so often heard, and I have even believed, that in society there was nothing but empty forms, and that reality had vanished; but I now see for myself that this can never be the case *here*, among us—it may be the order elsewhere, but not in Russia. Surely you are not all Jesuits and deceivers! I heard Prince N.'s story just now. Was it not simple-minded, spontaneous humour? Could such words come from the lips of a man who is dead?—a man whose heart and talents are dried up? Could dead men and women have treated me so kindly as you have all been treating me to-day? Is there not material for the future in all this—for hope? Can such people fail to *understand?* Can such men fall away from reality?"

"Once more let us beg you to be calm, my dear boy. We'll talk of all this another time—I shall do so with the greatest pleasure, for one," said the old dignitary, with a smile.

Ivan Petrovitch grunted and twisted round in his chair. General Epanchin moved nervously. The latter's chief had started a conversation with the wife of the dignitary, and took no notice whatever of the prince, but the old lady very often glanced at him, and listened to what he was saying.

"No, I had better speak," continued the prince, with a new outburst of feverish emotion, and turning towards the old man with an air of confidential trustfulness. "Yesterday, Aglaya Ivanovna forbade me to talk, and even specified the particular subjects I must not touch upon—she knows well enough that I am odd when I get upon these matters. I am nearly twenty-seven years old, and yet I know I am little better than a child. I have no right to express my ideas, and said so long ago. Only in Moscow, with Rogojin, did I ever speak absolutely freely! He and I read Pushkin together—all his works. Rogojin knew nothing of Pushkin, had not even heard his name. I am always afraid of spoiling a great Thought or Idea by my absurd manner. I have no eloquence, I know. I always make the wrong gestures—inappropriate gestures—and therefore I degrade the Thought, and raise a laugh instead of doing my subject justice. I have no sense of proportion either, and that is the chief thing. I know it would be much better if I were always to sit still and say nothing. When I do so, I appear to be quite a sensible sort of a person, and what's more, I think about things. But now I must speak; it is better that I should. I began to speak because you looked so kindly at me; you have such a beautiful face. I promised Aglaya Ivanovna yesterday that I would not speak all the evening."

"Really?" said the old man, smiling.

"But, at times, I can't help thinking that I am wrong in feeling so about it, you know. Sincerity is more important than elocution, isn't it?"

"Sometimes."

"I want to explain all to you—everything—everything! I know you think me Utopian, don't you—an idealist? Oh, no! I'm not, indeed—my ideas are all so simple. You don't believe me? You are smiling. Do you know, I am sometimes very wicked—for I lose my faith? This evening as I came here, I thought to myself, 'What shall I talk about? How am I to begin, so that they may be able to understand partially, at all events?' How afraid I was—dreadfully afraid! And yet, how *could* I be afraid—was it not shameful of me? Was I afraid of finding a bottomless abyss of empty selfishness? Ah! that's why I am so happy at this moment, because I find there is no bottomless abyss at all—but good, healthy material, full of life.

"It is not such a very dreadful circumstance that we are odd people, is it? For we really are odd, you know—careless, reckless, easily wearied of anything. We don't look thoroughly into matters—don't care to understand things. We are all like this—you and I, and all of them! Why, here are you, now—you are not a bit angry with me for calling you 'odd,' are you? And, if so, surely there is good material in you? Do you know, I sometimes think it is a good thing to be odd. We can forgive one another more easily, and be more humble. No one can begin by being perfect—there is much one cannot understand in life at first. In order to attain to perfection, one must begin by failing to understand much. And if we take in knowledge too quickly, we very likely are not taking it in at all. I say all this to you—you who by this time understand so much—and doubtless have failed to understand so much, also. I am not afraid of you any longer. You are not angry that a mere boy should say such words to you, are you? Of course not! You know how to forget and to forgive. You are laughing, Ivan Petrovitch? You think I am a champion of other classes of people—that I am *their* advocate, a democrat, and an orator of Equality?" The prince laughed hysterically; he had several times burst into these little, short nervous laughs. "Oh, no—it is for you, for myself, and for all of us together, that I am alarmed. I am a prince of an old family myself, and I am sitting among my peers; and I am talking like this in the hope of saving us all; in the hope that our class will not disappear altogether—into the darkness—unguessing its danger—blaming everything around it, and losing ground every day. Why should we disappear and give place to others, when we may still, if we choose, remain in the front rank and lead the battle? Let us be servants, that we may become lords in due season!"

He tried to get upon his feet again, but the old man still restrained him, gazing at him with increasing perturbation as he went on.

"Listen—I know it is best not to speak! It is best simply to give a good example—simply to begin the work. I have done this—I have begun, and—and—oh! *can* anyone be unhappy, really? Oh! what does grief matter—what does misfortune matter, if one knows how to be happy? Do you know, I cannot understand how anyone can pass by a green tree, and not feel happy only to look at it! How anyone can talk to a man and not feel happy in loving him! Oh, it is my own fault that I cannot express myself well enough! But there are lovely things at every step I take—things which even the most miserable man must recognize as beautiful. Look at a little child—look at God's day-dawn—look at the grass growing—look at the eyes that love you, as they gaze back into your eyes!"

He had risen, and was speaking standing up. The old gentleman was looking at him now in unconcealed alarm. Lizabetha Prokofievna wrung her hands. "Oh, my God!" she cried. She had guessed the state of the case before anyone else.

Aglaya rushed quickly up to him, and was just in time to receive him in her arms, and to hear with dread and horror that awful, wild cry as he fell writhing to the ground.

There he lay on the carpet, and someone quickly placed a cushion under his head.

No one had expected this.

In a quarter of an hour or so Prince N. and Evgenie Pavlovitch and the old dignitary were hard at work endeavouring to restore the harmony of the evening, but it was of no avail, and very soon after the guests separated and went their ways.

A great deal of sympathy was expressed; a considerable amount of advice was volunteered; Ivan Petrovitch expressed his opinion that the young man was "a Slavophile, or something of that sort"; but that it was not a dangerous development. The old dignitary said nothing.

True enough, most of the guests, next day and the day after, were not in very good humour. Ivan Petrovitch was a little offended, but not seriously so. General Epanchin's chief was rather cool towards him for some while after the occurrence. The old dignitary, as patron of the family, took the opportunity of murmuring some kind of admonition to the general, and added, in flattering terms, that he was most interested in Aglaya's future. He was a man who really did possess a kind heart, although his interest in the prince, in the earlier part of the evening, was due, among other reasons, to the latter's connection with Nastasia Philipovna, according to popular report. He had heard a good deal of this story here and there, and was greatly interested in it, so much so that he longed to ask further questions about it.

Princess Bielokonski, as she drove away on this eventful evening, took occasion to say to Lizabetha Prokofievna:

"Well—he's a good match—and a bad one; and if you want my opinion, more bad than good. You can see for yourself the man is an invalid."

Lizabetha therefore decided that the prince was impossible as a husband for Aglaya; and during the ensuing night she made a vow that never while she lived should he marry Aglaya. With this resolve firmly impressed upon her mind, she awoke next day; but during the morning, after her early lunch, she fell into a condition of remarkable inconsistency.

In reply to a very guarded question of her sisters', Aglaya had answered coldly, but exceedingly haughtily:

"I have never given him my word at all, nor have I ever counted him as my future husband—never in my life. He is just as little to me as all the rest."

Lizabetha Prokofievna suddenly flared up.

"I did not expect that of you, Aglaya," she said. "He is an impossible husband for you,—I know it; and thank God that we agree upon that point; but I did not expect to hear such words from you. I thought I should hear a very different tone from you. I would have turned out everyone who was in the room last night and kept him,—that's the sort of man he is, in my opinion!"

Here she suddenly paused, afraid of what she had just said. But she little knew how unfair she was to her daughter at that moment. It was all settled in Aglaya's mind. She was only waiting for the hour that would bring the matter to a final climax; and every hint, every careless probing of her wound, did but further lacerate her heart.

VIII.

This same morning dawned for the prince pregnant with no less painful presentiments,—which fact his physical state was, of course, quite enough to account for; but he was so indefinably melancholy,—his sadness could not attach itself to anything in particular, and this tormented him more than anything else. Of course certain facts stood before him, clear and painful, but his sadness went beyond all that he could remember or imagine; he realized that he was powerless to console himself unaided. Little by little he began to develop the expectation that this day something important, something decisive, was to happen to him.

His attack of yesterday had been a slight one. Excepting some little heaviness in the head and pain in the limbs, he did not feel any particular effects. His brain worked all right, though his soul was heavy within him.

He rose late, and immediately upon waking remembered all about the previous evening; he also remembered, though not quite so clearly, how, half an hour after his fit, he had been carried home.

He soon heard that a messenger from the Epanchins' had already been to inquire after him. At half-past eleven another arrived; and this pleased him.

Vera Lebedeff was one of the first to come to see him and offer her services. No sooner did she catch sight of him than she burst into tears; but when he tried to soothe her she began to laugh. He was quite struck by the girl's deep sympathy for him; he seized her hand and kissed it. Vera flushed crimson.

"Oh, don't, don't!" she exclaimed in alarm, snatching her hand away. She went hastily out of the room in a state of strange confusion.

Lebedeff also came to see the prince, in a great hurry to get away to the "deceased," as he called General Ivolgin, who was alive still, but very ill. Colia also turned up, and begged the prince for pity's sake to tell him all he knew about his father which had been concealed from him till now. He said he had found out nearly everything since yesterday; the poor boy was in a state of deep affliction. With all the sympathy which he could bring into play, the prince told Colia the whole story without reserve, detailing the facts as clearly as he could. The tale struck Colia like a thunderbolt. He could not speak. He listened silently, and cried softly to himself the while. The prince perceived that this was an impression which would last for the whole of the boy's life. He made haste to explain his view of the matter, and pointed out that the old man's approaching death was probably brought on by horror at the thought of his action; and that it was not everyone who was capable of such a feeling.

Colia's eyes flashed as he listened.

"Gania and Varia and Ptitsin are a worthless lot! I shall not quarrel with them; but from this moment our feet shall not travel the same road. Oh, prince, I have felt much that is quite new to me since yesterday! It is a lesson for me. I shall now consider my mother as entirely my responsibility; though she may be safe enough with Varia. Still, meat and drink is not everything."

He jumped up and hurried off, remembering suddenly that he was wanted at his father's bedside; but before he went out of the room he inquired hastily after the prince's health, and receiving the latter's reply, added:

"Isn't there something else, prince? I heard yesterday, but I have no right to talk about this... If you ever want a true friend and servant—neither you nor I are so very happy, are we?—come to me. I won't ask you questions, though."

He ran off and left the prince more dejected than ever.

Everyone seemed to be speaking prophetically, hinting at some misfortune or sorrow to come; they had all looked at him as though they knew something which he did not know. Lebedeff had asked questions, Colia had hinted, and Vera had shed tears. What was it?

At last, with a sigh of annoyance, he said to himself that it was nothing but his own cursed sickly suspicion. His face lighted up with joy when, at about two o'clock, he espied the Epanchins coming along to pay him a short visit, "just for a minute." They really had only come for a minute.

Lizabetha Prokofievna had announced, directly after lunch, that they would all take a walk together. The information was given in the form of a command, without explanation, drily and abruptly. All had issued forth in obedience to the mandate; that is, the girls, mamma, and Prince S. Lizabetha Prokofievna went off in a direction exactly contrary to the usual one, and all understood very well what she was driving at, but held their peace, fearing to irritate the good lady. She, as though anxious to avoid any conversation, walked ahead, silent and alone. At last Adelaida remarked that it was no use racing along at such a pace, and that she could not keep up with her mother.

"Look here," said Lizabetha Prokofievna, turning round suddenly; "we are passing his house. Whatever Aglaya may think, and in spite of anything that may happen, he is not a stranger to us; besides which, he is ill and in misfortune. I, for one, shall call in and see him. Let anyone follow me who cares to."

Of course every one of them followed her.

The prince hastened to apologize, very properly, for yesterday's mishap with the vase, and for the scene generally.

"Oh, that's nothing," replied Lizabetha; "I'm not sorry for the vase, I'm sorry for you. H'm! so you can see that there was a 'scene,' can you? Well, it doesn't matter much, for everyone must realize now that it is impossible to be hard on you. Well, *au revoir*. I advise you to have a walk, and then go to sleep again if you can. Come in as usual, if you feel inclined; and be assured, once for all, whatever happens, and whatever may have happened, you shall always remain the friend of the family—mine, at all events. I can answer for myself."

In response to this challenge all the others chimed in and re-echoed mamma's sentiments.

And so they took their departure; but in this hasty and kindly designed visit there was hidden a fund of cruelty which Lizabetha Prokofievna never dreamed of. In the words "as usual," and again in her added, "mine, at all events," there seemed an ominous knell of some evil to come.

The prince began to think of Aglaya. She had certainly given him a wonderful smile, both at coming and again at leave-taking, but had not said a word, not even when the others all professed their friendship for him. She had looked very intently at him, but that was all. Her face had been paler than usual; she looked as though she had slept badly.

The prince made up his mind that he would make a point of going there "as usual," tonight, and looked feverishly at his watch.

Vera came in three minutes after the Epanchins had left. "Lef Nicolaievitch," she said, "Aglaya Ivanovna has just given me a message for you."

The prince trembled.

"Is it a note?"

"No, a verbal message; she had hardly time even for that. She begs you earnestly not to go out of the house for a single moment all to-day, until seven o'clock in the evening. It may have been nine; I didn't quite hear."

"But—but, why is this? What does it mean?"

"I don't know at all; but she said I was to tell you particularly."

"Did she say that?"

"Not those very words. She only just had time to whisper as she went by; but by the way she looked at me I knew it was important. She looked at me in a way that made my heart stop beating."

The prince asked a few more questions, and though he learned nothing else, he became more and more agitated.

Left alone, he lay down on the sofa, and began to think.

"Perhaps," he thought, "someone is to be with them until nine tonight and she is afraid that I may come and make a fool of myself again, in public." So he spent his time longing for the evening and looking at his watch. But the clearing-up of the mystery came long before the evening, and came in the form of a new and agonizing riddle.

Half an hour after the Epanchins had gone, Hippolyte arrived, so tired that, almost unconscious, he sank into a chair, and broke into such a fit of coughing that he could not stop. He coughed till the blood came. His eyes glittered, and two red spots on his cheeks grew brighter and brighter. The prince murmured something to him, but Hippolyte only signed that he must be left alone for a while, and sat silent. At last he came to himself.

"I am off," he said, hoarsely, and with difficulty.

"Shall I see you home?" asked the prince, rising from his seat, but suddenly stopping short as he remembered Aglaya's prohibition against leaving the house. Hippolyte laughed.

"I don't mean that I am going to leave your house," he continued, still gasping and coughing. "On the contrary, I thought it absolutely necessary to come and see you; otherwise I should not have troubled you. I am off there, you know, and this time I believe, seriously, that I am off! It's all over. I did not come here for sympathy, believe me. I lay down this morning at ten o'clock with the intention of not rising again before that time; but I thought it over and rose just once more in order to come here; from which you may deduce that I had some reason for wishing to come."

"It grieves me to see you so, Hippolyte. Why didn't you send me a message? I would have come up and saved you this trouble."

"Well, well! Enough! You've pitied me, and that's all that good manners exact. I forgot, how are you?"

"I'm all right; yesterday I was a little—"

"I know, I heard; the china vase caught it! I'm sorry I wasn't there. I've come about something important. In the first place I had, the pleasure of seeing Gavrila Ardalionovitch and Aglaya Ivanovna enjoying a rendezvous on the green bench in the park. I was astonished to see what a fool a man can look. I remarked upon the fact to Aglaya Ivanovna when he had gone. I don't think anything ever surprises you, prince!" added Hippolyte, gazing incredulously at the prince's calm demeanour. "To be astonished by nothing is a sign, they say, of a great intellect. In my opinion it would serve equally well as a sign of great foolishness. I am not hinting about you; pardon me! I am very unfortunate today in my expressions.

"I knew yesterday that Gavrila Ardalionovitch—" began the prince, and paused in evident confusion, though Hippolyte had shown annoyance at his betraying no surprise.

"You knew it? Come, that's news! But no—perhaps better not tell me. And were you a witness of the meeting?"

"If you were there yourself you must have known that I was *not* there!"

"Oh! but you may have been sitting behind the bushes somewhere. However, I am very glad, on your account, of course. I was beginning to be afraid that Mr. Gania—might have the preference!"

"May I ask you, Hippolyte, not to talk of this subject? And not to use such expressions?"

"Especially as you know all, eh?"

"You are wrong. I know scarcely anything, and Aglaya Ivanovna is aware that I know nothing. I knew nothing whatever about this meeting. You say there was a meeting. Very well; let's leave it so—"

"Why, what do you mean? You said you knew, and now suddenly you know nothing! You say 'very well; let's leave it so.' But I say, don't be so confiding, especially as you know nothing. You are confiding simply *because* you know nothing. But do you know what these good people have in their minds' eye—Gania and his sister? Perhaps you are suspicious? Well, well, I'll drop the subject!" he added, hastily, observing the prince's impatient gesture. "But I've come to you on my own business; I wish to make you a clear explanation. What a nuisance it is that one cannot die without explanations! I have made such a quantity of them already. Do you wish to hear what I have to say?"

"Speak away, I am listening."

"Very well, but I'll change my mind, and begin about Gania. Just fancy to begin with, if you can, that I, too, was given an appointment at the green bench today! However, I won't deceive you; I asked for the appointment. I said I had a secret to disclose. I don't know whether I came there too early, I think I must have; but scarcely had I sat down beside Aglaya Ivanovna than I saw Gavrila Ardalionovitch and his sister Varia coming along, arm in arm, just as though they were enjoying a morning walk together. Both of them seemed very much astonished, not to say disturbed, at seeing me; they evidently had not expected the pleasure. Aglaya Ivanovna blushed up, and was actually a little confused. I don't know whether it was merely because I was there, or whether Gania's beauty was too much for her! But anyway, she turned crimson, and then finished up the business in a very funny manner. She jumped up from her seat, bowed back to Gania, smiled to Varia, and suddenly observed: 'I only came here to express my gratitude for all your kind wishes on my behalf, and to say that if I find I need your services, believe me—' Here she bowed them away, as it were, and they both marched off again, looking very foolish. Gania evidently could not make head nor tail of the matter, and turned as red as a lobster; but Varia understood at once that they must get away as quickly as they could, so she dragged Gania away; she is a great deal cleverer than he is. As for myself, I went there to arrange a meeting to be held between Aglaya Ivanovna and Nastasia Philipovna."

"Nastasia Philipovna!" cried the prince.

"Aha! I think you are growing less cool, my friend, and are beginning to be a trifle surprised, aren't you? I'm glad that you are not above ordinary human feelings, for once. I'll console you a little now, after your consternation. See what I get for serving a young and high-souled maiden! This morning I received a slap in the face from the lady!"

"A—a moral one?" asked the prince, involuntarily.

"Yes—not a physical one! I don't suppose anyone—even a woman—would raise a hand against me now. Even Gania would hesitate! I did think at one time yesterday, that he would fly at me, though. I bet anything that I know what you are thinking of now! You are thinking: 'Of course one can't strike the little wretch, but one could suffocate him with a pillow, or a wet towel, when he is asleep! One *ought* to get rid of him somehow.' I can see in your face that you are thinking that at this very second."

"I never thought of such a thing for a moment," said the prince, with disgust.

"I don't know—I dreamed last night that I was being suffocated with a wet cloth by—somebody. I'll tell you who it was—Rogojin! What do you think, can a man be suffocated with a wet cloth?"

"I don't know."

"I've heard so. Well, we'll leave that question just now. Why am I a scandal-monger? Why did she call me a scandal-monger? And mind, *after* she had heard every word I had to tell her, and had asked all sorts of questions besides—but such is the way of women. For *her* sake I entered into relations with Rogojin—an interesting man! At *her* request I arranged a personal interview between herself and Nastasia Philipovna. Could she have been angry because I hinted that she was enjoying Nastasia Philipovna's 'leavings'? Why, I have been impressing it upon her all this while for her own good. Two letters have I written her in that strain, and I began straight off today about its being humiliating for her. Besides, the word 'leavings' is not my invention. At all events, they all used it at Gania's, and she used it herself. So why am I a scandal-monger? I see—I see you are tremendously amused, at this moment! Probably you are laughing at me and fitting those silly lines to my case—

"'Maybe sad Love upon his setting smiles, And with vain hopes his farewell hour beguiles.

"Ha, ha, ha!"

Hippolyte suddenly burst into a fit of hysterical laughter, which turned into a choking cough.

"Observe," he gasped, through his coughing, "what a fellow Gania is! He talks about Nastasia's 'leavings,' but what does he want to take himself?"

The prince sat silent for a long while. His mind was filled with dread and horror.

"You spoke of a meeting with Nastasia Philipovna," he said at last, in a low voice.

"Oh—come! Surely you must know that there is to be a meeting today between Nastasia and Aglaya Ivanovna, and that Nastasia has been sent for on purpose, through Rogojin, from St. Petersburg? It has been brought about by invitation of Aglaya Ivanovna and my own efforts, and Nastasia is at this moment with Rogojin, not far from here—at Dana Alexeyevna's—that curious friend of hers; and to this questionable house Aglaya Ivanovna is to proceed for a friendly chat with Nastasia Philipovna, and for the settlement of several problems. They are going to play at arithmetic—didn't you know about it? Word of honour?"

"It's a most improbable story."

"Oh, very well! if it's improbable—it is—that's all! And yet—where should you have heard it? Though I must say, if a fly crosses the room it's known all over the place here. However, I've warned you, and you may be grateful to me. Well—*au revoir*—probably in the next world! One more thing—don't think that I am telling you all this for your sake. Oh, dear, no! Do you know that I dedicated my confession to Aglaya Ivanovna? I did though, and how she took it, ha, ha! Oh, no! I am not acting from any high, exalted motives. But though I may have behaved like a cad to you, I have not done *her* any harm. I don't apologize for my words about 'leavings' and all that. I am atoning for that, you see, by telling you the place and time of the meeting. Goodbye! You had better take your measures, if you are worthy the name of a man! The meeting is fixed for this evening—that's certain."

Hippolyte walked towards the door, but the prince called him back and he stopped.

"Then you think Aglaya Ivanovna herself intends to go to Nastasia Philipovna's tonight?" he asked, and bright hectic spots came out on his cheeks and forehead.

"I don't know absolutely for certain; but in all probability it is so," replied Hippolyte, looking round. "Nastasia would hardly go to her; and they can't meet at Gania's, with a man nearly dead in the house."

"It's impossible, for that very reason," said the prince. "How would she get out if she wished to? You don't know the habits of that house—she *could* not get away alone to Nastasia Philipovna's! It's all nonsense!"

"Look here, my dear prince, no one jumps out of the window if they can help it; but when there's a fire, the dandiest gentleman or the finest lady in the world will skip out! When the moment comes, and there's nothing else to be done—our young lady will go to Nastasia Philipovna's! Don't they let the young ladies out of the house alone, then?"

"I didn't mean that exactly."

"If you didn't mean that, then she has only to go down the steps and walk off, and she need never come back unless she chooses: Ships are burned behind one sometimes, and one doesn't care to return whence one came. Life need not consist only of lunches, and dinners, and Prince S's. It strikes me you take Aglaya Ivanovna for some conventional boarding-school girl. I said so to her, and she quite agreed with me. Wait till seven or eight o'clock. In your place I would send someone there to keep watch, so as to seize the exact moment when she steps out of the house. Send Colia. He'll play the spy with pleasure—for you at least. Ha, ha, ha!"

Hippolyte went out.

There was no reason for the prince to set anyone to watch, even if he had been capable of such a thing. Aglaya's command that he should stay at home all day seemed almost explained now. Perhaps she meant to call for him, herself, or it might be, of course, that she was anxious to make sure of his not coming there, and therefore bade him remain at home. His head whirled; the whole room seemed to be turning round. He lay down on the sofa, and closed his eyes.

One way or the other the question was to be decided at last—finally.

Oh, no, he did not think of Aglaya as a boarding-school miss, or a young lady of the conventional type! He had long since feared that she might take some such step as this. But why did she wish to see Nastasia?

He shivered all over as he lay; he was in high fever again.

No! he did not account her a child. Certain of her looks, certain of her words, of late, had filled him with apprehension. At times it had struck him that she was putting too great a restraint upon herself, and he remembered that he had been alarmed to observe this. He had tried, all these days, to drive away the heavy thoughts that oppressed him; but what was the hidden mystery of that soul? The question had long tormented him, although he implicitly trusted that soul. And now it was all to be cleared up. It was a dreadful thought. And "that woman" again! Why did he always feel as though "that woman" were fated to appear at each critical moment of his life, and tear the thread of his destiny like a bit of rotten string? That he always *had* felt this he was ready to swear, although he was half delirious at the moment. If he had tried to forget her, all this time, it was simply because he was afraid of her. Did he love the woman or hate her? This question he did not once ask himself today; his heart was quite pure. He knew whom he loved. He was not so much afraid of this meeting, nor of its strangeness, nor of any reasons there might be for it, unknown to himself; he was afraid of the woman herself, Nastasia Philipovna. He remembered, some days afterwards, how during all those fevered hours he had seen but *her* eyes, *her* look, had heard *her* voice, strange words of hers; he remembered that this was so, although he could not recollect the details of his thoughts.

He could remember that Vera brought him some dinner, and that he took it; but whether he slept after dinner, or no, he could not recollect.

He only knew that he began to distinguish things clearly from the moment when Aglaya suddenly appeared, and he jumped up from the sofa and went to meet her. It was just a quarter past seven then.

Aglaya was quite alone, and dressed, apparently hastily, in a light mantle. Her face was pale, as it had been in the morning, and her eyes were ablaze with bright but subdued fire. He had never seen that expression in her eyes before.

She gazed attentively at him.

"You are quite ready, I observe," she said, with absolute composure, "dressed, and your hat in your hand. I see somebody has thought fit to warn you, and I know who. Hippolyte?"

"Yes, he told me," said the prince, feeling only half alive.

"Come then. You know, I suppose, that you must escort me there? You are well enough to go out, aren't you?"

"I am well enough; but is it really possible?—"

He broke off abruptly, and could not add another word. This was his one attempt to stop the mad child, and, after he had made it, he followed her as though he had no will of his own. Confused as his thoughts were, he was, nevertheless, capable of realizing the fact that if he did not go with her, she would go alone, and so he must go with her at all hazards. He guessed the strength of her determination; it was beyond him to check it.

They walked silently, and said scarcely a word all the way. He only noticed that she seemed to know the road very well; and once, when he thought it better to go by a certain lane, and remarked to her that it would be quieter and less public, she only said, "it's all the same," and went on.

When they were almost arrived at Daria Alexeyevna's house (it was a large wooden structure of ancient date), a gorgeously-dressed lady and a young girl came out of it. Both these ladies took their seats in a carriage, which was waiting at the door, talking and laughing loudly the while, and drove away without appearing to notice the approaching couple.

No sooner had the carriage driven off than the door opened once more; and Rogojin, who had apparently been awaiting them, let them in and closed it after them.

"There is not another soul in the house now excepting our four selves," he said aloud, looking at the prince in a strange way.

Nastasia Philipovna was waiting for them in the first room they went into. She was dressed very simply, in black.

She rose at their entrance, but did not smile or give her hand, even to the prince. Her anxious eyes were fixed upon Aglaya. Both sat down, at a little distance from one another—Aglaya on the sofa, in the corner of the room, Nastasia by the window. The prince and Rogojin remained standing, and were not invited to sit.

Muishkin glanced at Rogojin in perplexity, but the latter only smiled disagreeably, and said nothing. The silence continued for some few moments.

An ominous expression passed over Nastasia Philipovna's face, of a sudden. It became obstinate-looking, hard, and full of hatred; but she did not take her eyes off her visitors for a moment.

Aglaya was clearly confused, but not frightened. On entering she had merely glanced momentarily at her rival, and then had sat still, with her eyes on the ground, apparently in thought. Once or twice she glanced casually round the room. A shade of disgust was visible in her expression; she looked as though she were afraid of contamination in this place.

She mechanically arranged her dress, and fidgeted uncomfortably, eventually changing her seat to the other end of the sofa. Probably she was unconscious of her own movements; but this very unconsciousness added to the offensiveness of their suggested meaning.

At length she looked straight into Nastasia's eyes, and instantly read all there was to read in her rival's expression. Woman understood woman! Aglaya shuddered.

"You know of course why I requested this meeting?" she said at last, quietly, and pausing twice in the delivery of this very short sentence.

"No—I know nothing about it," said Nastasia, drily and abruptly.

Aglaya blushed. Perhaps it struck her as very strange and impossible that she should really be sitting here and waiting for "that woman's" reply to her question.

At the first sound of Nastasia's voice a shudder ran through her frame. Of course "that woman" observed and took in all this.

"You know quite well, but you are pretending to be ignorant," said Aglaya, very low, with her eyes on the ground.

"Why should I?" asked Nastasia Philipovna, smiling slightly.

"You want to take advantage of my position, now that I am in your house," continued Aglaya, awkwardly.

"For that position *you* are to blame and not I," said Nastasia, flaring up suddenly. "*I* did not invite *you*, but you me; and to this moment I am quite ignorant as to why I am thus honoured."

Aglaya raised her head haughtily.

"Restrain your tongue!" she said. "I did not come here to fight you with your own weapons.

"Oh! then you did come 'to fight,' I may conclude? Dear me!—and I thought you were cleverer—"

They looked at one another with undisguised malice. One of these women had written to the other, so lately, such letters as we have seen; and it all was dispersed at their first meeting. Yet it appeared that not one of the four persons in the room considered this in any degree strange.

The prince who, up to yesterday, would not have believed that he could even dream of such an impossible scene as this, stood and listened and looked on, and felt as though he had long foreseen it all. The most fantastic dream seemed suddenly to have been metamorphosed into the most vivid reality.

One of these women so despised the other, and so longed to express her contempt for her (perhaps she had only come for that very purpose, as Rogojin said next day), that howsoever fantastical was the other woman, howsoever afflicted her spirit and disturbed her understanding, no preconceived idea of hers could possibly stand up against that deadly feminine contempt of her rival. The prince felt sure that Nastasia would say nothing about the letters herself; but he could judge by her flashing eyes and the expression of her face what the thought of those letters must be costing her at this moment. He would have given half his life to prevent Aglaya from speaking of them. But Aglaya suddenly braced herself up, and seemed to master herself fully, all in an instant.

"You have not quite understood," she said. "I did not come to quarrel with you, though I do not like you. I came to speak to you as... as one human being to another. I came with my mind made up as to what I had to say to you, and I shall not change my intention, although you may misunderstand me. So much the worse for you, not for myself! I wished to reply to all you have written to me and to reply personally, because I think that is the more convenient way. Listen to my reply to all your letters. I began to be sorry for Prince Lef Nicolaievitch on the very day I made his acquaintance, and when I heard—afterwards—of all that took place at your house in the evening, I was sorry for him because he was such a simple-minded man, and because he, in the simplicity of his soul, believed that he could be happy with a woman of your character. What I feared actually took place; you could not love him, you tortured him, and threw him over. You could not love him because you are too proud—no, not proud, that is an error; because you are too vain—no, not quite that either; too self-loving; you are self-loving to madness. Your letters to me are a proof of it. You could not love so simple a soul as his, and perhaps in your heart you despised him and laughed at him. All you could love was your shame and the perpetual thought that you were disgraced and insulted. If you were less shameful, or had no cause at all for shame, you would be still more unhappy than you are now."

Aglaya brought out these thronging words with great satisfaction. They came from her lips hurriedly and impetuously, and had been prepared and thought out long ago, even before she had ever dreamed of the present meeting. She watched with eagerness the effect of her speech as shown in Nastasia's face, which was distorted with agitation.

"You remember," she continued, "he wrote me a letter at that time; he says you know all about that letter and that you even read it. I understand all by means of this letter, and understand it correctly. He has since confirmed it all to me—what I now say to you, word for word. After receiving his letter I waited; I guessed that you would soon come back here, because you could never do without Petersburg; you are still too young and lovely for the provinces. However, this is not my own idea," she added, blushing dreadfully; and from this moment the colour never left her cheeks to the end of her speech. "When I next saw the prince I began to feel terribly pained and hurt on his account. Do not laugh; if you laugh you are unworthy of understanding what I say."

"Surely you see that I am not laughing," said Nastasia, sadly and sternly.

"However, it's all the same to me; laugh or not, just as you please. When I asked him about you, he told me that he had long since ceased to love you, that the very recollection of you was a torture to him, but that he was sorry for you; and that when he thought of you his heart was pierced. I ought to tell you that I never in my life met a man anything like him for noble simplicity of mind and for boundless trustfulness. I guessed that anyone who liked could deceive him, and that he would immediately forgive anyone who did deceive him; and it was for this that I grew to love him—"

Aglaya paused for a moment, as though suddenly brought up in astonishment that she could have said these words, but at the same time a great pride shone in her eyes, like a defiant assertion that it would not matter to her if "this woman" laughed in her face for the admission just made.

"I have told you all now, and of course you understand what I wish of you."

"Perhaps I do; but tell me yourself," said Nastasia Philipovna, quietly.

Aglaya flushed up angrily.

"I wished to find out from you," she said, firmly, "by what right you dare to meddle with his feelings for me? By what right you dared send me those letters? By what right do you continually remind both me and him that you love him, after you yourself threw him over and ran away from him in so insulting and shameful a way?"

"I never told either him or you that I loved him!" replied Nastasia Philipovna, with an effort. "And—and I did run away from him—you are right there," she added, scarcely audibly.

"Never told either him or me?" cried Aglaya. "How about your letters? Who asked you to try to persuade me to marry him? Was not that a declaration from you? Why do you force yourself upon us in this way? I confess I thought at first that you were anxious to arouse an aversion for him in my heart by your meddling, in order that I might give him up; and it was only afterwards that I guessed the truth. You imagined that you were doing an heroic action! How could you spare any love for him, when you love your own vanity to such an extent? Why could you not simply go away from here, instead of writing me those absurd letters? Why do you not *now* marry that generous man who loves you, and has done you the honour of offering you his hand? It is plain enough why; if you marry Rogojin you lose your grievance; you will have nothing more to complain of. You will be receiving too much honour. Evgenie Pavlovitch was saying the other day that you had read too many poems and are too well educated for—your position; and that you live in idleness. Add to this your vanity, and, there you have reason enough—"

"And do you not live in idleness?"

Things had come to this unexpected point too quickly. Unexpected because Nastasia Philipovna, on her way to Pavlofsk, had thought and considered a good deal, and had expected something different, though perhaps not altogether good, from this interview; but Aglaya had been carried away by her own outburst, just as a rolling stone gathers impetus as it careers downhill, and could not restrain herself in the satisfaction of revenge.

It was strange, Nastasia Philipovna felt, to see Aglaya like this. She gazed at her, and could hardly believe her eyes and ears for a moment or two.

Whether she were a woman who had read too many poems, as Evgenie Pavlovitch supposed, or whether she were mad, as the prince had assured Aglaya, at all events, this was a woman who, in spite of her occasionally cynical and audacious manner, was far more refined and trustful and sensitive than appeared. There was a certain amount of romantic dreaminess and caprice in her, but with the fantastic was mingled much that was strong and deep.

The prince realized this, and great suffering expressed itself in his face.

Aglaya observed it, and trembled with anger.

"How dare you speak so to me?" she said, with a haughtiness which was quite indescribable, replying to Nastasia's last remark.

"You must have misunderstood what I said," said Nastasia, in some surprise.

"If you wished to preserve your good name, why did you not give up your—your 'guardian,' Totski, without all that theatrical posturing?" said Aglaya, suddenly a propos of nothing.

"What do you know of my position, that you dare to judge me?" cried Nastasia, quivering with rage, and growing terribly white.

"I know this much, that you did not go out to honest work, but went away with a rich man, Rogojin, in order to pose as a fallen angel. I don't wonder that Totski was nearly driven to suicide by such a fallen angel."

"Silence!" cried Nastasia Philipovna. "You are about as fit to understand me as the housemaid here, who bore witness against her lover in court the other day. She would understand me better than you do."

"Probably an honest girl living by her own toil. Why do you speak of a housemaid so contemptuously?"

"I do not despise toil; I despise you when you speak of toil."

"If you had cared to be an honest woman, you would have gone out as a laundress."

Both had risen, and were gazing at one another with pallid faces.

"Aglaya, don't! This is unfair," cried the prince, deeply distressed.

Rogojin was not smiling now; he sat and listened with folded arms, and lips tight compressed.

"There, look at her," cried Nastasia, trembling with passion. "Look at this young lady! And I imagined her an angel! Did you come to me without your governess, Aglaya Ivanovna? Oh, fie, now shall I just tell you why you came here today? Shall I tell you without any embellishments? You came because you were afraid of me!"

"Afraid of *you?*" asked Aglaya, beside herself with naive amazement that the other should dare talk to her like this.

"Yes, me, of course! Of course you were afraid of me, or you would not have decided to come. You cannot despise one you fear. And to think that I have actually esteemed you up to this very moment! Do you know why you are afraid of me, and what is your object now? You wished to satisfy yourself with your own eyes as to which he loves best, myself or you, because you are fearfully jealous."

"He has told me already that he hates you," murmured Aglaya, scarcely audibly.

"Perhaps, perhaps! I am not worthy of him, I know. But I think you are lying, all the same. He cannot hate me, and he cannot have said so. I am ready to forgive you, in consideration of your position; but I confess I thought better of you. I thought you were wiser, and more beautiful, too; I did, indeed! Well, take your treasure! See, he is gazing at you, he can't recollect himself. Take him, but on one condition; go away at once, this instant!"

She fell back into a chair, and burst into tears. But suddenly some new expression blazed in her eyes. She stared fixedly at Aglaya, and rose from her seat.

"Or would you like me to bid him, *bid him*, do you hear, *command him*, now, at once, to throw you up, and remain mine for ever? Shall I? He will stay, and he will marry me too, and you shall trot home all alone. Shall I?—shall I say the word?" she screamed like a madwoman, scarcely believing herself that she could really pronounce such wild words.

Aglaya had made for the door in terror, but she stopped at the threshold, and listened. "Shall I turn Rogojin off? Ha! ha! you thought I would marry him for your benefit, did you? Why, I'll call out *now*, if you like, in your presence, 'Rogojin, get out!' and say to the prince, 'Do you remember what you promised me?' Heavens! what a fool I have been to humiliate myself before them! Why, prince, you yourself gave me your word that you would marry me whatever happened, and would never abandon me. You said you loved me and would forgive me all, and—and resp—yes, you even said that! I only ran away from you in order to set you free, and now I don't care to let you go again. Why does she treat me so—so shamefully? I am not a loose woman—ask Rogojin there! He'll tell you. Will you go again now that she has insulted me, before your eyes, too; turn away from me and lead her away, arm-in-arm? May you be accursed too, for you were the only one I trusted among them all! Go away, Rogojin, I don't want you," she continued, blind with fury, and forcing the words out with dry lips and distorted features, evidently not believing a single word of her own tirade, but, at the same time, doing her utmost to prolong the moment of self-deception.

The outburst was so terribly violent that the prince thought it would have killed her.

"There he is!" she shrieked again, pointing to the prince and addressing Aglaya. "There he is! and if he does not approach me at once and take *me* and throw you over, then have him for your own—I give him up to you! I don't want him!"

Both she and Aglaya stood and waited as though in expectation, and both looked at the prince like madwomen.

But he, perhaps, did not understand the full force of this challenge; in fact, it is certain he did not. All he could see was the poor despairing face which, as he had said to Aglaya, "had pierced his heart for ever."

He could bear it no longer, and with a look of entreaty, mingled with reproach, he addressed Aglaya, pointing to Nastasia the while:

"How can you?" he murmured; "she is so unhappy."

But he had no time to say another word before. Aglaya's terrible look bereft him of speech. In that look was embodied so dreadful a suffering and so deadly a hatred, that he gave a cry and flew to her; but it was too late.

She could not hold out long enough even to witness his movement in her direction. She had hidden her face in her hands, cried once "Oh, my God!" and rushed out of the room. Rogojin followed her to undo the bolts of the door and let her out into the street.

The prince made a rush after her, but he was caught and held back. The distorted, livid face of Nastasia gazed at him reproachfully, and her blue lips whispered:

"What? Would you go to her—to her?"

She fell senseless into his arms.

He raised her, carried her into the room, placed her in an arm-chair, and stood over her, stupefied. On the table stood a tumbler of water. Rogojin, who now returned, took this and sprinkled a little in her face. She opened her eyes, but for a moment she understood nothing.

Suddenly she looked around, shuddered, gave a loud cry, and threw herself in the prince's arms.

"Mine, mine!" she cried. "Has the proud young lady gone? Ha, ha, ha!" she laughed hysterically. "And I had given him up to her! Why—why did I? Mad—mad! Get away, Rogojin! Ha, ha, ha!"

Rogojin stared intently at them; then he took his hat, and without a word, left the room.

A few moments later, the prince was seated by Nastasia on the sofa, gazing into her eyes and stroking her face and hair, as he would a little child's. He laughed when she laughed, and was ready to cry when she cried. He did not speak, but listened to her excited, disconnected chatter, hardly understanding a word of it the while. No sooner did he detect the slightest appearance of complaining, or weeping, or reproaching, than he would smile at her kindly, and begin stroking her hair and her cheeks, soothing and consoling her once more, as if she were a child.

IX.

A fortnight had passed since the events recorded in the last chapter, and the position of the actors in our story had become so changed that it is almost impossible for us to continue the tale without some few explanations. Yet we feel that we ought to limit ourselves to the simple record of facts, without much attempt at explanation, for a very patent reason: because we ourselves have the greatest possible difficulty in accounting for the facts to be recorded. Such a statement on our part may appear strange to the reader. How is anyone to tell a story which he cannot understand himself? In order to keep clear of a false position, we had perhaps better give an example of what we mean; and probably the intelligent reader will soon understand the difficulty. More especially are we inclined to take this course since the example will constitute a distinct march forward of our story, and will not hinder the progress of the events remaining to be recorded.

During the next fortnight—that is, through the early part of July—the history of our hero was circulated in the form of strange, diverting, most unlikely-sounding stories, which passed from mouth to mouth, through the streets and villas adjoining those inhabited by Lebedeff, Ptitsin, Nastasia Philipovna and the Epanchins; in fact, pretty well through the whole town and its environs. All society—both the inhabitants of the place and those who came down of an evening for the music—had got hold of one and the same story, in a thousand varieties of detail—as to how a certain young prince had raised a terrible scandal in a most respectable household, had thrown over a daughter of the family, to whom he was engaged, and had been captured by a woman of shady reputation whom he was determined to marry at once—breaking off all old ties for the satisfaction of his insane idea; and, in spite of the public indignation roused by his action, the marriage was to take place in Pavlofsk openly and publicly, and the prince had announced his intention of going through with it with head erect and looking the whole world in the face. The story was so artfully adorned with scandalous details, and persons of so great eminence and importance were apparently mixed up in it, while, at the same time, the evidence was so circumstantial, that it was no wonder the matter gave food for plenty of curiosity and gossip.

According to the reports of the most talented gossip-mongers—those who, in every class of society, are always in haste to explain every event to their neighbours—the young gentleman concerned was of good family—a prince—fairly rich—weak of intellect, but a democrat and a dabbler in the Nihilism of the period, as exposed by Mr. Turgenieff. He could hardly talk Russian, but had fallen in love with one of the Miss Epanchins, and his suit met with so much encouragement that he had been received in the house as the recognized bridegroom-to-be of the young lady. But like the Frenchman of whom the story is told that he studied for holy orders, took all the oaths, was ordained priest, and next morning wrote to his bishop informing him that, as he did not believe in God and considered it wrong to deceive the people and live upon their pockets, he begged to surrender the orders conferred upon him the day before, and to inform his lordship that he was sending this letter to the public press,—like this Frenchman, the prince played a false game. It was rumoured that he had purposely waited for the solemn occasion of a large evening party at the house of his future bride, at which he was introduced to several eminent persons, in order publicly to make known his ideas and opinions, and thereby insult the "big-wigs," and to throw over his bride as offensively as possible; and that, resisting the servants who were told off to turn him out of the house, he had seized and thrown down a magnificent china vase. As a characteristic addition to the above, it was currently reported that the young prince really loved the lady to whom he was engaged, and had thrown her over out of purely Nihilistic motives, with the intention of giving himself the satisfaction of marrying a fallen woman in the face of all the world, thereby publishing his opinion that there is no distinction between virtuous and disreputable women, but that all women are alike, free; and a "fallen" woman, indeed, somewhat superior to a virtuous one.

It was declared that he believed in no classes or anything else, excepting "the woman question."

All this looked likely enough, and was accepted as fact by most of the inhabitants of the place, especially as it was borne out, more or less, by daily occurrences.

Of course much was said that could not be determined absolutely. For instance, it was reported that the poor girl had so loved her future husband that she had followed him to the house of the other woman, the day after she had been thrown over; others said that he had insisted on her coming, himself, in order to shame and insult her by his taunts and Nihilistic confessions when she reached the house. However all these things might be, the public interest in the matter grew daily, especially as it became clear that the scandalous wedding was undoubtedly to take place.

So that if our readers were to ask an explanation, not of the wild reports about the prince's Nihilistic opinions, but simply as to how such a marriage could possibly satisfy his real aspirations, or as to the spiritual condition of our hero at this time, we confess that we should have great difficulty in giving the required information.

All we know is, that the marriage really was arranged, and that the prince had commissioned Lebedeff and Keller to look after all the necessary business connected with it; that he had requested them to spare no expense; that Nastasia herself was hurrying on the wedding; that Keller was to be the prince's best man, at his own earnest request; and that Burdovsky was to give Nastasia away, to his great delight. The wedding was to take place before the middle of July.

But, besides the above, we are cognizant of certain other undoubted facts, which puzzle us a good deal because they seem flatly to contradict the foregoing.

We suspect, for instance, that having commissioned Lebedeff and the others, as above, the prince immediately forgot all about masters of ceremonies and even the ceremony itself; and we feel quite certain that in making these arrangements he did so in order that he might absolutely escape all thought of the wedding, and even forget its approach if he could, by detailing all business concerning it to others.

What did he think of all this time, then? What did he wish for? There is no doubt that he was a perfectly free agent all through, and that as far as Nastasia was concerned, there was no force of any kind brought to bear on him. Nastasia wished for a speedy marriage, true!—but the prince agreed at once to her proposals; he agreed, in fact, so casually that anyone might suppose he was but acceding to the most simple and ordinary suggestion.

There are many strange circumstances such as this before us; but in our opinion they do but deepen the mystery, and do not in the smallest degree help us to understand the case.

However, let us take one more example. Thus, we know for a fact that during the whole of this fortnight the prince spent all his days and evenings with Nastasia; he walked with her, drove with her; he began to be restless whenever he passed an hour without seeing her—in fact, to all appearances, he sincerely loved her. He would listen to her for hours at a time with a quiet smile on his face, scarcely saying a word himself. And yet we know, equally certainly, that during this period he several times set off, suddenly, to the Epanchins', not concealing the fact from Nastasia Philipovna, and driving the latter to absolute despair. We know also that he was not received at the Epanchins' so long as they remained at Pavlofsk, and that he was not allowed an interview with Aglaya;—but next day he would set off once more on the same errand, apparently quite oblivious of the fact of yesterday's visit having been a failure,—and, of course, meeting with another refusal. We know, too, that exactly an hour after Aglaya had fled from Nastasia Philipovna's house on that fateful evening, the prince was at the Epanchins',—and that his appearance there had been the cause of the greatest consternation and dismay; for Aglaya had not been home, and the family only discovered then, for the first time, that the two of them had been to Nastasia's house together.

It was said that Elizabetha Prokofievna and her daughters had there and then denounced the prince in the strongest terms, and had refused any further acquaintance and friendship with him; their rage and denunciations being redoubled when Varia Ardalionovna suddenly arrived and stated that Aglaya had been at her house in a terrible state of mind for the last hour, and that she refused to come home.

This last item of news, which disturbed Lizabetha Prokofievna more than anything else, was perfectly true. On leaving Nastasia's, Aglaya had felt that she would rather die than face her people, and had therefore gone straight to Nina Alexandrovna's. On receiving the news, Lizabetha and her daughters and the general all rushed off to Aglaya, followed by Prince Lef Nicolaievitch—undeterred by his recent dismissal; but through Varia he was refused a sight of Aglaya here also. The end of the episode was that when Aglaya saw her mother and sisters crying over her and not uttering a word of reproach, she had flung herself into their arms and gone straight home with them.

It was said that Gania managed to make a fool of himself even on this occasion; for, finding himself alone with Aglaya for a minute or two when Varia had gone to the Epanchins', he had thought it a fitting opportunity to make a declaration of his love, and on hearing this Aglaya, in spite of her state of mind at the time, had suddenly burst out laughing, and had put a strange question to him. She asked him whether he would consent to hold his finger to a lighted candle in proof of his devotion! Gania—it was said—looked so comically bewildered that Aglaya had almost laughed herself into hysterics, and had rushed out of the room and upstairs,—where her parents had found her.

Hippolyte told the prince this last story, sending for him on purpose. When Muishkin heard about the candle and Gania's finger he had laughed so that he had quite astonished Hippolyte,—and then shuddered and burst into tears. The prince's condition during those days was strange and perturbed. Hippolyte plainly declared that he thought he was out of his mind;—this, however, was hardly to be relied upon.

Offering all these facts to our readers and refusing to explain them, we do not for a moment desire to justify our hero's conduct. On the contrary, we are quite prepared to feel our share of the indignation which his behaviour aroused in the hearts of his friends. Even Vera Lebedeff was angry with him for a while; so was Colia; so was Keller, until he was selected for best man; so was Lebedeff himself,—who began to intrigue against him out of pure irritation;—but of this anon. In fact we are in full accord with certain forcible words spoken to the prince by Evgenie Pavlovitch, quite unceremoniously, during the course of a friendly conversation, six or seven days after the events at Nastasia Philipovna's house.

We may remark here that not only the Epanchins themselves, but all who had anything to do with them, thought it right to break with the prince in consequence of his conduct. Prince S. even went so far as to turn away and cut him dead in the street. But Evgenie Pavlovitch was not afraid to compromise himself by paying the prince a visit, and did so, in spite of the fact that he had recommenced to visit at the Epanchins', where he was received with redoubled hospitality and kindness after the temporary estrangement.

Evgenie called upon the prince the day after that on which the Epanchins left Pavlofsk. He knew of all the current rumours,—in fact, he had probably contributed to them himself. The prince was delighted to see him, and immediately began to speak of the Epanchins;—which simple and straightforward opening quite took Evgenie's fancy, so that he melted at once, and plunged in medias res without ceremony.

The prince did not know, up to this, that the Epanchins had left the place. He grew very pale on hearing the news; but a moment later he nodded his head, and said thoughtfully:

"I knew it was bound to be so." Then he added quickly:

"Where have they gone to?"

Evgenie meanwhile observed him attentively, and the rapidity of the questions, their simplicity, the prince's candour, and at the same time, his evident perplexity and mental agitation, surprised him considerably. However, he told Muishkin all he could, kindly and in detail. The prince hardly knew anything, for this was the first informant from the household whom he had met since the estrangement.

Evgenie reported that Aglaya had been really ill, and that for two nights she had not slept at all, owing to high fever; that now she was better and out of serious danger, but still in a nervous, hysterical state.

"It's a good thing that there is peace in the house, at all events," he continued. "They never utter a hint about the past, not only in Aglaya's presence, but even among themselves. The old people are talking of a trip abroad in the autumn, immediately after Adelaida's wedding; Aglaya received the news in silence."

Evgenie himself was very likely going abroad also; so were Prince S. and his wife, if affairs allowed of it; the general was to stay at home. They were all at their estate of Colmina now, about twenty miles or so from St. Petersburg. Princess Bielokonski had not returned to Moscow yet, and was apparently staying on for reasons of her own. Lizabetha Prokofievna had insisted that it was quite impossible to remain in Pavlofsk after what had happened. Evgenie had told her of all the rumours current in town about the affair; so that there could be no talk of their going to their house on the Yelagin as yet.

"And in point of fact, prince," added Evgenie Pavlovitch, "you must allow that they could hardly have stayed here, considering that they knew of all that went on at your place, and in the face of your daily visits to their house, visits which you insisted upon making in spite of their refusal to see you."

"Yes—yes, quite so; you are quite right. I wished to see Aglaya Ivanovna, you know!" said the prince, nodding his head.

"Oh, my dear fellow," cried Evgenie, warmly, with real sorrow in his voice, "how could you permit all that to come about as it has? Of course, of course, I know it was all so unexpected. I admit that you, only naturally, lost your head, and—and could not stop the foolish girl; that was not in your power. I quite see so much; but you really should have understood how seriously she cared for you. She could not bear to share you with another; and you could bring yourself to throw away and shatter such a treasure! Oh, prince, prince!"

"Yes, yes, you are quite right again," said the poor prince, in anguish of mind. "I was wrong, I know. But it was only Aglaya who looked on Nastasia Philipovna so; no one else did, you know."

"But that's just the worst of it all, don't you see, that there was absolutely nothing serious about the matter in reality!" cried Evgenie, beside himself: "Excuse me, prince, but I have thought over all this; I have thought a great deal over it; I know all that had happened before; I know all that took place six months since; and I know there was *nothing* serious about the matter, it was but fancy, smoke, fantasy, distorted by agitation, and only the alarmed jealousy of an absolutely inexperienced girl could possibly have mistaken it for serious reality."

Here Evgenie Pavlovitch quite let himself go, and gave the reins to his indignation.

Clearly and reasonably, and with great psychological insight, he drew a picture of the prince's past relations with Nastasia Philipovna. Evgenie Pavlovitch always had a ready tongue, but on this occasion his eloquence, surprised himself. "From the very beginning," he said, "you began with a lie; what began with a lie was bound to end with a lie; such is the law of nature. I do not agree, in fact I am angry, when I hear you called an idiot; you are far too intelligent to deserve such an epithet; but you are so far *strange* as to be unlike others; that you must allow, yourself. Now, I have come to the conclusion that the basis of all that has happened, has been first of all your innate inexperience (remark the expression 'innate,' prince). Then follows your unheard-of simplicity of heart; then comes your absolute want of sense of proportion (to this want you have several times confessed); and lastly, a mass, an accumulation, of intellectual convictions which you, in your unexampled honesty of soul, accept unquestionably as also innate and natural and true. Admit, prince, that in your relations with Nastasia Philipovna there has existed, from the very first, something democratic, and the fascination, so to speak, of the 'woman question'? I know all about that scandalous scene at Nastasia Philipovna's house when Rogojin brought the money, six months ago. I'll show you yourself as in a looking-glass, if you like. I know exactly all that went on, in every detail, and why things have turned out as they have. You thirsted, while in Switzerland, for your home-country, for Russia; you read, doubtless, many books about Russia, excellent books, I dare say, but hurtful to *you*; and you arrived here; as it were, on fire with the longing to be of service. Then, on the very day of your arrival, they tell you a sad story of an ill-used woman; they tell *you*, a knight, pure and without reproach, this tale of a poor woman! The same day you actually *see* her; you are attracted by her beauty, her fantastic, almost demoniacal, beauty—(I admit her beauty, of course).

"Add to all this your nervous nature, your epilepsy, and your sudden arrival in a strange town—the day of meetings and of exciting scenes, the day of unexpected acquaintanceships, the day of sudden actions, the day of meeting with the three lovely Epanchin girls, and among them Aglaya—add your fatigue, your excitement; add Nastasia' s evening party, and the tone of that party, and—what were you to expect of yourself at such a moment as that?"

"Yes, yes, yes!" said the prince, once more, nodding his head, and blushing slightly. "Yes, it was so, or nearly so—I know it. And besides, you see, I had not slept the night before, in the train, or the night before that, either, and I was very tired."

"Of course, of course, quite so; that's what I am driving at!" continued Evgenie, excitedly. "It is as clear as possible, and most comprehensible, that you, in your enthusiasm, should plunge headlong into the first chance that came of publicly airing your great idea that you, a prince, and a pure-living man, did not consider a woman disgraced if the sin were not her own, but that of a disgusting social libertine! Oh, heavens! it's comprehensible enough, my dear prince, but that is not the question, unfortunately! The question is, was there any reality and truth in your feelings? Was it nature, or nothing but intellectual enthusiasm? What do you think yourself? We are told, of course, that a far worse woman was *forgiven*, but we don't find that she was told that she had done well, or that she was worthy of honour and respect! Did not your common-sense show you what was the real state of the case, a few months later? The question is now, not whether she is an innocent woman (I do not insist one way or the other—I do not wish to); but can her whole career justify such intolerable pride, such insolent, rapacious egotism as she has shown? Forgive me, I am too violent, perhaps, but—"

"Yes—I dare say it is all as you say; I dare say you are quite right," muttered the prince once more. "She is very sensitive and easily put out, of course; but still, she..."

"She is worthy of sympathy? Is that what you wished to say, my good fellow? But then, for the mere sake of vindicating her worthiness of sympathy, you should not have insulted and offended a noble and generous girl in her presence! This is a terrible exaggeration of sympathy! How can you love a girl, and yet so humiliate her as to throw her over for the sake of another woman, before the very eyes of that other woman, when you have already made her a formal proposal of marriage? And you *did* propose to her, you know; you did so before her parents and sisters. Can you be an honest man, prince, if you act so? I ask you! And did you not deceive that beautiful girl when you assured her of your love?"

"Yes, you are quite right. Oh! I feel that I am very guilty!" said Muishkin, in deepest distress.

"But as if that is enough!" cried Evgenie, indignantly. "As if it is enough simply to say: 'I know I am very guilty!' You are to blame, and yet you persevere in evil-doing. Where was your heart, I should like to know, your *christian heart*, all that time? Did she look as though she were suffering less, at that moment? You saw her face—was she suffering less than the other woman? How could you see her suffering and allow it to continue? How could you?"

"But I did not allow it," murmured the wretched prince.

"How—what do you mean you didn't allow?"

"Upon my word, I didn't! To this moment I don't know how it all happened. I—I ran after Aglaya Ivanovna, but Nastasia Philipovna fell down in a faint; and since that day they won't let me see Aglaya—that's all I know."

"It's all the same; you ought to have run after Aglaya though the other was fainting."

"Yes, yes, I ought—but I couldn't! She would have died—she would have killed herself. You don't know her; and I should have told Aglaya everything afterwards—but I see, Evgenie Pavlovitch, you don't know all. Tell me now, why am I not allowed to see Aglaya? I should have cleared it all up, you know. Neither of them kept to the real point, you see. I could never explain what I mean to you, but I think I could to Aglaya. Oh! my God, my God! You spoke just now of Aglaya's face at the moment when she ran away. Oh, my God! I remember it! Come along, come along—quick!" He pulled at Evgenie's coat-sleeve nervously and excitedly, and rose from his chair.

"Where to?"

"Come to Aglaya—quick, quick!"

"But I told you she is not at Pavlofsk. And what would be the use if she were?"

"Oh, she'll understand, she'll understand!" cried the prince, clasping his hands. "She would understand that all this is not the point—not a bit the real point—it is quite foreign to the real question."

"How can it be foreign? You *are* going to be married, are you not? Very well, then you are persisting in your course. *Are* you going to marry her or not?"

"Yes, I shall marry her—yes."

"Then why is it 'not the point'?"

"Oh, no, it is not the point, not a bit. It makes no difference, my marrying her—it means nothing."

"How 'means nothing'? You are talking nonsense, my friend. You are marrying the woman you love in order to secure her happiness, and Aglaya sees and knows it. How can you say that it's 'not the point'?"

"Her happiness? Oh, no! I am only marrying her—well, because she wished it. It means nothing—it's all the same. She would certainly have died. I see now that that marriage with Rogojin was an insane idea. I understand all now that I did not understand before; and, do you know, when those two stood opposite to one another, I could not bear Nastasia Philipovna's face! You must know, Evgenie Pavlovitch, I have never told anyone before—not even Aglaya—that I cannot bear Nastasia Philipovna's face." (He lowered his voice mysteriously as he said this.) "You described that evening at Nastasia Philipovna's (six months since) very accurately just now; but there is one thing which you did not mention, and of which you took no account, because you do not know. I mean her *face*—I looked at her face, you see. Even in the morning when I saw her portrait, I felt that I could not *bear* to look at it. Now, there's Vera Lebedeff, for instance, her eyes are quite different, you know. I'm *afraid* of her face!" he added, with real alarm.

"You are *afraid* of it?"

"Yes—she's mad!" he whispered, growing pale.

"Do you know this for certain?" asked Evgenie, with the greatest curiosity.

"Yes, for certain—quite for certain, now! I have discovered it *absolutely* for certain, these last few days."

"What are you doing, then?" cried Evgenie, in horror. "You must be marrying her solely out of *fear*, then! I can't make head or tail of it, prince. Perhaps you don't even love her?"

"Oh, no; I love her with all my soul. Why, she is a child! She's a child now—a real child. Oh! you know nothing about it at all, I see."

"And are you assured, at the same time, that you love Aglaya too?"

"Yes—yes—oh; yes!"

"How so? Do you want to make out that you love them *both?*"

"Yes—yes—both! I do!"

"Excuse me, prince, but think what you are saying! Recollect yourself!"

"Without Aglaya—I—I *must* see Aglaya!—I shall die in my sleep very soon—I thought I was dying in my sleep last night. Oh! if Aglaya only knew all—I mean really, *really* all! Because she must know *all*—that's the first condition towards understanding. Why cannot we ever know all about another, especially when that other has been guilty? But I don't know what I'm talking about—I'm so confused. You pained me so dreadfully. Surely—surely Aglaya has not the same expression now as she had at the moment when she ran away? Oh, yes! I am guilty and I know it—I know it! Probably I am in fault all round—I don't quite know how—but I am in fault, no doubt. There is something else, but I cannot explain it to you, Evgenie Pavlovitch. I have no words; but Aglaya will understand. I have always believed Aglaya will understand—I am assured she will."

"No, prince, she will not. Aglaya loved like a woman, like a human being, not like an abstract spirit. Do you know what, my poor prince? The most probable explanation of the matter is that you never loved either the one or the other in reality."

"I don't know—perhaps you are right in much that you have said, Evgenie Pavlovitch. You are very wise, Evgenie Pavlovitch—oh! how my head is beginning to ache again! Come to her, quick—for God's sake, come!"

"But I tell you she is not in Pavlofsk! She's in Colmina."

"Oh, come to Colmina, then! Come—let us go at once!"

"No—no, impossible!" said Evgenie, rising.

"Look here—I'll write a letter—take a letter for me!"

"No—no, prince; you must forgive me, but I can't undertake any such commissions! I really can't."

And so they parted.

Evgenie Pavlovitch left the house with strange convictions. He, too, felt that the prince must be out of his mind.

"And what did he mean by that *face*—a face which he so fears, and yet so loves? And meanwhile he really may die, as he says, without seeing Aglaya, and she will never know how devotedly he loves her! Ha, ha, ha! How does the fellow manage to love two of them? Two different kinds of love, I suppose! This is very interesting—poor idiot! What on earth will become of him now?"

X.

The prince did not die before his wedding—either by day or night, as he had foretold that he might. Very probably he passed disturbed nights, and was afflicted with bad dreams; but, during the daytime, among his fellow-men, he seemed as kind as ever, and even contented; only a little thoughtful when alone.

The wedding was hurried on. The day was fixed for exactly a week after Evgenie's visit to the prince. In the face of such haste as this, even the prince's best friends (if he had had any) would have felt the hopelessness of any attempt to save "the poor madman." Rumour said that in the visit of Evgenie Pavlovitch was to be discerned the influence of Lizabetha Prokofievna and her husband... But if those good souls, in the boundless kindness of their hearts, were desirous of saving the eccentric young fellow from ruin, they were unable to take any stronger measures to attain that end. Neither their position, nor their private inclination, perhaps (and only naturally), would allow them to use any more pronounced means.

We have observed before that even some of the prince's nearest neighbours had begun to oppose him. Vera Lebedeff's passive disagreement was limited to the shedding of a few solitary tears; to more frequent sitting alone at home, and to a diminished frequency in her visits to the prince's apartments.

Colia was occupied with his father at this time. The old man died during a second stroke, which took place just eight days after the first. The prince showed great sympathy in the grief of the family, and during the first days of their mourning he was at the house a great deal with Nina Alexandrovna. He went to the funeral, and it was observable that the public assembled in church greeted his arrival and departure with whisperings, and watched him closely.

The same thing happened in the park and in the street, wherever he went. He was pointed out when he drove by, and he often overheard the name of Nastasia Philipovna coupled with his own as he passed. People looked out for her at the funeral, too, but she was not there; and another conspicuous absentee was the captain's widow, whom Lebedeff had prevented from coming.

The funeral service produced a great effect on the prince. He whispered to Lebedeff that this was the first time he had ever heard a Russian funeral service since he was a little boy. Observing that he was looking about him uneasily, Lebedeff asked him whom he was seeking.

"Nothing. I only thought I—"

"Is it Rogojin?"

"Why—is he here?"

"Yes, he's in church."

"I thought I caught sight of his eyes!" muttered the prince, in confusion. "But what of it!—Why is he here? Was he asked?"

"Oh, dear, no! Why, they don't even know him! Anyone can come in, you know. Why do you look so amazed? I often meet him; I've seen him at least four times, here at Pavlofsk, within the last week."

"I haven't seen him once—since that day!" the prince murmured.

As Nastasia Philipovna had not said a word about having met Rogojin since "that day," the prince concluded that the latter had his own reasons for wishing to keep out of sight. All the day of the funeral our hero was in a deeply thoughtful state, while Nastasia Philipovna was particularly merry, both in the daytime and in the evening.

Colia had made it up with the prince before his father's death, and it was he who urged him to make use of Keller and Burdovsky, promising to answer himself for the former's behaviour. Nina Alexandrovna and Lebedeff tried to persuade him to have the wedding in St. Petersburg, instead of in the public fashion contemplated, down here at Pavlofsk in the height of the season. But the prince only said that Nastasia Philipovna desired to have it so, though he saw well enough what prompted their arguments.

The next day Keller came to visit the prince. He was in a high state of delight with the post of honour assigned to him at the wedding.

Before entering he stopped on the threshold, raised his hand as if making a solemn vow, and cried:

"I won't drink!"

Then he went up to the prince, seized both his hands, shook them warmly, and declared that he had at first felt hostile towards the project of this marriage, and had openly said so in the billiard-rooms, but that the reason simply was that, with the impatience of a friend, he had hoped to see the prince marry at least a Princess de Rohan or de Chabot; but that now he saw that the prince's way of thinking was ten times more noble than that of "all the rest put together." For he desired neither pomp nor wealth nor honour, but only the truth! The sympathies of exalted personages were well known, and the prince was too highly placed by his education, and so on, not to be in some sense an exalted personage!

"But all the common herd judge differently; in the town, at the meetings, in the villas, at the band, in the inns and the billiard-rooms, the coming event has only to be mentioned and there are shouts and cries from everybody. I have even heard talk of getting up a 'charivari' under the windows on the wedding-night. So if 'you have need of the pistol' of an honest man, prince, I am ready to fire half a dozen shots even before you rise from your nuptial couch!"

Keller also advised, in anticipation of the crowd making a rush after the ceremony, that a fire-hose should be placed at the entrance to the house; but Lebedeff was opposed to this measure, which he said might result in the place being pulled down.

"I assure you, prince, that Lebedeff is intriguing against you. He wants to put you under control. Imagine that! To take 'from you the use of your free-will and your money—that' is to say, the two things that distinguish us from the animals! I have heard it said positively. It is the sober truth."

The prince recollected that somebody had told him something of the kind before, and he had, of course, scoffed at it. He only laughed now, and forgot the hint at once.

Lebedeff really had been busy for some little while; but, as usual, his plans had become too complex to succeed, through sheer excess of ardour. When he came to the prince—the very day before the wedding—to confess (for he always confessed to the persons against whom he intrigued, especially when the plan failed), he informed our hero that he himself was a born Talleyrand, but for some unknown reason had become simple Lebedeff. He then proceeded to explain his whole game to the prince, interesting the latter exceedingly.

According to Lebedeff's account, he had first tried what he could do with General Epanchin. The latter informed him that he wished well to the unfortunate young man, and would gladly do what he could to "save him," but that he did not think it would be seemly for him to interfere in this matter. Lizabetha Prokofievna would neither hear nor see him. Prince S. and Evgenie Pavlovitch only shrugged their shoulders, and implied that it was no business of theirs. However, Lebedeff had not lost heart, and went off to a clever lawyer,—a worthy and respectable man, whom he knew well. This old gentleman informed him that the thing was perfectly feasible if he could get hold of competent witnesses as to Muishkin's mental incapacity. Then, with the assistance of a few influential persons, he would soon see the matter arranged.

Lebedeff immediately procured the services of an old doctor, and carried the latter away to Pavlofsk to see the prince, by way of viewing the ground, as it were, and to give him (Lebedeff) counsel as to whether the thing was to be done or not. The visit was not to be official, but merely friendly.

Muishkin remembered the doctor's visit quite well. He remembered that Lebedeff had said that he looked ill, and had better see a doctor; and although the prince scouted the idea, Lebedeff had turned up almost immediately with his old friend, explaining that they had just met at the bedside of Hippolyte, who was very ill, and that the doctor had something to tell the prince about the sick man.

The prince had, of course, at once received him, and had plunged into a conversation about Hippolyte. He had given the doctor an account of Hippolyte's attempted suicide; and had proceeded thereafter to talk of his own malady,—of Switzerland, of Schneider, and so on; and so deeply was the old man interested by the prince's conversation and his description of Schneider's system, that he sat on for two hours.

Muishkin gave him excellent cigars to smoke, and Lebedeff, for his part, regaled him with liqueurs, brought in by Vera, to whom the doctor—a married man and the father of a family—addressed such compliments that she was filled with indignation. They parted friends, and, after leaving the prince, the doctor said to Lebedeff: "If all such people were put under restraint, there would be no one left for keepers." Lebedeff then, in tragic tones, told of the approaching marriage, whereupon the other nodded his head and replied that, after all, marriages like that were not so rare; that he had heard that the lady was very fascinating and of extraordinary beauty, which was enough to explain the infatuation of a wealthy man; that, further, thanks to the liberality of Totski and of Rogojin, she possessed—so he had heard—not only money, but pearls, diamonds, shawls, and furniture, and consequently she could not be considered a bad match. In brief, it seemed to the doctor that the prince's choice, far from being a sign of foolishness, denoted, on the contrary, a shrewd, calculating, and practical mind. Lebedeff had been much struck by this point of view, and he terminated his confession by assuring the prince that he was ready, if need be, to shed his very life's blood for him.

Hippolyte, too, was a source of some distraction to the prince at this time; he would send for him at any and every hour of the day. They lived,—Hippolyte and his mother and the children,—in a small house not far off, and the little ones were happy, if only because they were able to escape from the invalid into the garden. The prince had enough to do in keeping the peace between the irritable Hippolyte and his mother, and eventually the former became so malicious and sarcastic on the subject of the approaching wedding, that Muishkin took offence at last, and refused to continue his visits.

A couple of days later, however, Hippolyte's mother came with tears in her eyes, and begged the prince to come back, "or*he* would eat her up bodily." She added that Hippolyte had a great secret to disclose. Of course the prince went. There was no secret, however, unless we reckon certain pantings and agitated glances around (probably all put on) as the invalid begged his visitor to "beware of Rogojin."

"He is the sort of man," he continued, "who won't give up his object, you know; he is not like you and me, prince—he belongs to quite a different order of beings. If he sets his heart on a thing he won't be afraid of anything—" and so on.

Hippolyte was very ill, and looked as though he could not long survive. He was tearful at first, but grew more and more sarcastic and malicious as the interview proceeded.

The prince questioned him in detail as to his hints about Rogojin. He was anxious to seize upon some facts which might confirm Hippolyte's vague warnings; but there were none; only Hippolyte's own private impressions and feelings.

However, the invalid—to his immense satisfaction—ended by seriously alarming the prince.

At first Muishkin had not cared to make any reply to his sundry questions, and only smiled in response to Hippolyte's advice to "run for his life—abroad, if necessary. There are Russian priests everywhere, and one can get married all over the world."

But it was Hippolyte's last idea which upset him.

"What I am really alarmed about, though," he said, "is Aglaya Ivanovna. Rogojin knows how you love her. Love for love. You took Nastasia Philipovna from him. He will murder Aglaya Ivanovna; for though she is not yours, of course, now, still such an act would pain you,—wouldn't it?"

He had attained his end. The prince left the house beside himself with terror.

These warnings about Rogojin were expressed on the day before the wedding. That evening the prince saw Nastasia Philipovna for the last time before they were to meet at the altar; but Nastasia was not in a position to give him any comfort or consolation. On the contrary, she only added to his mental perturbation as the evening went on. Up to this time she had invariably done her best to cheer him—she was afraid of his looking melancholy; she would try singing to him, and telling him every sort of funny story or reminiscence that she could recall. The prince nearly always pretended to be amused, whether he were so actually or no; but often enough he laughed sincerely, delighted by the brilliancy of her wit when she was carried away by her narrative, as she very often was. Nastasia would be wild with joy to see the impression she had made, and to hear his laugh of real amusement; and she would remain the whole evening in a state of pride and happiness. But this evening her melancholy and thoughtfulness grew with every hour.

The prince had told Evgenie Pavlovitch with perfect sincerity that he loved Nastasia Philipovna with all his soul. In his love for her there was the sort of tenderness one feels for a sick, unhappy child which cannot be left alone. He never spoke of his feelings for Nastasia to anyone, not even to herself. When they were together they never discussed their "feelings," and there was nothing in their cheerful, animated conversation which an outsider could not have heard. Daria Alexeyevna, with whom Nastasia was staying, told afterwards how she had been filled with joy and delight only to look at them, all this time.

Thanks to the manner in which he regarded Nastasia's mental and moral condition, the prince was to some extent freed from other perplexities. She was now quite different from the woman he had known three months before. He was not astonished, for instance, to see her now so impatient to marry him—she who formerly had wept with rage and hurled curses and reproaches at him if he mentioned marriage! "It shows that she no longer fears, as she did then, that she would make me unhappy by marrying me," he thought. And he felt sure that so sudden a change could not be a natural one. This rapid growth of self-confidence could not be due only to her hatred for Aglaya. To suppose that would be to suspect the depth of her feelings. Nor could it arise from dread of the fate that awaited her if she married Rogojin. These causes, indeed, as well as others, might have played a part in it, but the true reason, Muishkin decided, was the one he had long suspected—that the poor sick soul had come to the end of its forces. Yet this was an exp!anation that did not procure him any peace of mind. At times he seemed to be making violent efforts to think of nothing, and one would have said that he looked on his marriage as an unimportant formality, and on his future happiness as a thing not worth considering. As to conversations such as the one held with Evgenie Pavlovitch, he avoided them as far as possible, feeling that there were certain objections to which he could make no answer.

The prince had observed that Nastasia knew well enough what Aglaya was to him. He never spoke of it, but he had seen her face when she had caught him starting off for the Epanchins' house on several occasions. When the Epanchins left Pavlofsk, she had beamed with radiance and happiness. Unsuspicious and unobservant as he was, he had feared at that time that Nastasia might have some scheme in her mind for a scene or scandal which would drive Aglaya out of Pavlofsk. She had encouraged the rumours and excitement among the inhabitants of the place as to her marriage with the prince, in order to annoy her rival; and, finding it difficult to meet the Epanchins anywhere, she had, on one occasion, taken him for a drive past their house. He did not observe what was happening until they were almost passing the windows, when it was too late to do anything. He said nothing, but for two days afterwards he was ill.

Nastasia did not try that particular experiment again. A few days before that fixed for the wedding, she grew grave and thoughtful. She always ended by getting the better of her melancholy, and becoming merry and cheerful again, but not quite so unaffectedly happy as she had been some days earlier.

The prince redoubled his attentive study of her symptoms. It was a most curious circumstance, in his opinion, that she never spoke of Rogojin. But once, about five days before the wedding, when the prince was at home, a messenger arrived begging him to come at once, as Nastasia Philipovna was very ill.

He had found her in a condition approaching to absolute madness. She screamed, and trembled, and cried out that Rogojin was hiding out there in the garden—that she had seen him herself—and that he would murder her in the night—that he would cut her throat. She was terribly agitated all day. But it so happened that the prince called at Hippolyte's house later on, and heard from his mother that she had been in town all day, and had there received a visit from Rogojin, who had made inquiries about Pavlofsk. On inquiry, it turned out that Rogojin visited the old lady in town at almost the same moment when Nastasia declared that she had seen him in the garden; so that the whole thing turned out to be an illusion on her part. Nastasia immediately went across to Hippolyte's to inquire more accurately, and returned immensely relieved and comforted.

On the day before the wedding, the prince left Nastasia in a state of great animation. Her wedding-dress and all sorts of finery had just arrived from town. Muishkin had not imagined that she would be so excited over it, but he praised everything, and his praise rendered her doubly happy.

But Nastasia could not hide the cause of her intense interest in her wedding splendour. She had heard of the indignation in the town, and knew that some of the populace was getting up a sort of charivari with music, that verses had been composed for the occasion, and that the rest of Pavlofsk society more or less encouraged these preparations. So, since attempts were being made to humiliate her, she wanted to hold her head even higher than usual, and to overwhelm them all with the beauty and taste of her toilette. "Let them shout and whistle, if they dare!" Her eyes flashed at the thought. But, underneath this, she had another motive, of which she did not speak. She thought that possibly Aglaya, or at any rate someone sent by her, would be present incognito at the ceremony, or in the crowd, and she wished to be prepared for this eventuality.

The prince left her at eleven, full of these thoughts, and went home. But it was not twelve o'clock when a messenger came to say that Nastasia was very bad, and he must come at once.

On hurrying back he found his bride locked up in her own room and could hear her hysterical cries and sobs. It was some time before she could be made to hear that the prince had come, and then she opened the door only just sufficiently to let him in, and immediately locked it behind him. She then fell on her knees at his feet. (So at least Dana Alexeyevna reported.)

"What am I doing? What am I doing to you?" she sobbed convulsively, embracing his knees.

The prince was a whole hour soothing and comforting her, and left her, at length, pacified and composed. He sent another messenger during the night to inquire after her, and two more next morning. The last brought back a message that Nastasia was surrounded by a whole army of dressmakers and maids, and was as happy and as busy as such a beauty should be on her wedding morning, and that there was not a vestige of yesterday's agitation remaining. The message concluded with the news that at the moment of the bearer's departure there was a great confabulation in progress as to which diamonds were to be worn, and how.

This message entirely calmed the prince's mind.

The following report of the proceedings on the wedding day may be depended upon, as coming from eye-witnesses.

The wedding was fixed for eight o'clock in the evening. Nastasia Philipovna was ready at seven. From six o'clock groups of people began to gather at Nastasia's house, at the prince's, and at the church door, but more especially at the former place. The church began to fill at seven.

Colia and Vera Lebedeff were very anxious on the prince's account, but they were so busy over the arrangements for receiving the guests after the wedding, that they had not much time for the indulgence of personal feelings.

There were to be very few guests besides the best men and so on; only Dana Alexeyevna, the Ptitsins, Gania, and the doctor. When the prince asked Lebedeff why he had invited the doctor, who was almost a stranger, Lebedeff replied:

"Why, he wears an 'order,' and it looks so well!"

This idea amused the prince.

Keller and Burdovsky looked wonderfully correct in their dress-coats and white kid gloves, although Keller caused the bridegroom some alarm by his undisguisedly hostile glances at the gathering crowd of sight-seers outside.

At about half-past seven the prince started for the church in his carriage.

We may remark here that he seemed anxious not to omit a single one of the recognized customs and traditions observed at weddings. He wished all to be done as openly as possible, and "in due order."

Arrived at the church, Muishkin, under Keller's guidance, passed through the crowd of spectators, amid continuous whispering and excited exclamations. The prince stayed near the altar, while Keller made off once more to fetch the bride.

On reaching the gate of Daria Alexeyevna's house, Keller found a far denser crowd than he had encountered at the prince's. The remarks and exclamations of the spectators here were of so irritating a nature that Keller was very near making them a speech on the impropriety of their conduct, but was luckily caught by Burdovsky, in the act of turning to address them, and hurried indoors.

Nastasia Philipovna was ready. She rose from her seat, looked into the glass and remarked, as Keller told the tale afterwards, that she was "as pale as a corpse." She then bent her head reverently, before the ikon in the corner, and left the room.

A torrent of voices greeted her appearance at the front door. The crowd whistled, clapped its hands, and laughed and shouted; but in a moment or two isolated voices were distinguishable.

"What a beauty!" cried one.

"Well, she isn't the first in the world, nor the last," said another.

"Marriage covers everything," observed a third.

"I defy you to find another beauty like that," said a fourth.

"She's a real princess! I'd sell my soul for such a princess as that!"

Nastasia came out of the house looking as white as any handkerchief; but her large dark eyes shone upon the vulgar crowd like blazing coals. The spectators' cries were redoubled, and became more exultant and triumphant every moment. The door of the carriage was open, and Keller had given his hand to the bride to help her in, when suddenly with a loud cry she rushed from him, straight into the surging crowd. Her friends about her were stupefied with amazement; the crowd parted as she rushed through it, and suddenly, at a distance of five or six yards from the carriage, appeared Rogojin. It was his look that had caught her eyes.

Nastasia rushed to him like a madwoman, and seized both his hands.

"Save me!" she cried. "Take me away, anywhere you like, quick!"

Rogojin seized her in his arms and almost carried her to the carriage. Then, in a flash, he tore a hundred-rouble note out of his pocket and held it to the coachman.

"To the station, quick! If you catch the train you shall have another. Quick!"

He leaped into the carriage after Nastasia and banged the door. The coachman did not hesitate a moment; he whipped up the horses, and they were oft.

"One more second and I should have stopped him," said Keller, afterwards. In fact, he and Burdovsky jumped into another carriage and set off in pursuit; but it struck them as they drove along that it was not much use trying to bring Nastasia back by force.

"Besides," said Burdovsky, "the prince would not like it, would he?" So they gave up the pursuit.

Rogojin and Nastasia Philipovna reached the station just in time for the train. As he jumped out of the carriage and was almost on the point of entering the train, Rogojin accosted a young girl standing on the platform and wearing an old-fashioned, but respectable-looking, black cloak and a silk handkerchief over her head.

"Take fifty roubles for your cloak?" he shouted, holding the money out to the girl. Before the astonished young woman could collect her scattered senses, he pushed the money into her hand, seized the mantle, and threw it and the handkerchief over Nastasia's head and shoulders. The latter's wedding-array would have attracted too much attention, and it was not until some time later that the girl understood why her old cloak and kerchief had been bought at such a price.

The news of what had happened reached the church with extraordinary rapidity. When Keller arrived, a host of people whom he did not know thronged around to ask him questions. There was much excited talking, and shaking of heads, even some laughter; but no one left the church, all being anxious to observe how the now celebrated bridegroom would take the news. He grew very pale upon hearing it, but took it quite quietly.

"I was afraid," he muttered, scarcely audibly, "but I hardly thought it would come to this." Then after a short silence, he added: "However, in her state, it is quite consistent with the natural order of things."

Even Keller admitted afterwards that this was "extraordinarily philosophical" on the prince's part. He left the church quite calm, to all appearances, as many witnesses were found to declare afterwards. He seemed anxious to reach home and be left alone as quickly as possible; but this was not to be. He was accompanied by nearly all the invited guests, and besides this, the house was almost besieged by excited bands of people, who insisted upon being allowed to enter the verandah. The prince heard Keller and Lebedeff remonstrating and quarrelling with these unknown individuals, and soon went out himself. He approached the disturbers of his peace, requested courteously to be told what was desired; then politely putting Lebedeff and Keller aside, he addressed an old gentleman who was standing on the verandah steps at the head of the band of would-be guests, and courteously requested him to honour him with a visit. The old fellow was quite taken aback by this, but entered, followed by a few more, who tried to appear at their ease. The rest remained outside, and presently the whole crowd was censuring those who had accepted the invitation. The prince offered seats to his strange visitors, tea was served, and a general conversation sprang up. Everything was done most decorously, to the considerable surprise of the intruders. A few tentative attempts were made to turn the conversation to the events of the day, and a few indiscreet questions were asked; but Muishkin replied to everybody with such simplicity and good-humour, and at the same time with so much dignity, and showed such confidence in the good breeding of his guests, that the indiscreet talkers were quickly silenced. By degrees the conversation became almost serious. One gentleman suddenly exclaimed, with great vehemence: "Whatever happens, I shall not sell my property; I shall wait. Enterprise is better than money, and there, sir, you have my whole system of economy, if you wish!" He addressed the prince, who warmly commended his sentiments, though Lebedeff whispered in his ear that this gentleman, who talked so much of his "property," had never had either house or home.

Nearly an hour passed thus, and when tea was over the visitors seemed to think that it was time to go. As they went out, the doctor and the old gentleman bade Muishkin a warm farewell, and all the rest took their leave with hearty protestations of good-will, dropping remarks to the effect that "it was no use worrying," and that "perhaps all would turn out for the best," and so on. Some of the younger intruders would have asked for champagne, but they were checked by the older ones. When all had departed, Keller leaned over to Lebedeff, and said:

"With you and me there would have been a scene. We should have shouted and fought, and called in the police. But he has simply made some new friends—and such friends, too! I know them!"

Lebedeff, who was slightly intoxicated, answered with a sigh:

"Things are hidden from the wise and prudent, and revealed unto babes. I have applied those words to him before, but now I add that God has preserved the babe himself from the abyss, He and all His saints."

At last, about half-past ten, the prince was left alone. His head ached. Colia was the last to go, after having helped him to change his wedding clothes. They parted on affectionate terms, and, without speaking of what had happened, Colia promised to come very early the next day. He said later that the prince had given no hint of his intentions when they said good-bye, but had hidden them even from him. Soon there was hardly anyone left in the house. Burdovsky had gone to see Hippolyte; Keller and Lebedeff had wandered off together somewhere.

Only Vera Lebedeff remained hurriedly rearranging the furniture in the rooms. As she left the verandah, she glanced at the prince. He was seated at the table, with both elbows upon it, and his head resting on his hands. She approached him, and touched his shoulder gently. The prince started and looked at her in perplexity; he seemed to be collecting his senses for a minute or so, before he could remember where he was. As recollection dawned upon him, he became violently agitated. All he did, however, was to ask Vera very earnestly to knock at his door and awake him in time for the first train to Petersburg next morning. Vera promised, and the prince entreated her not to tell anyone of his intention. She promised this, too; and at last, when she had half-closed the door, he called her back a third time, took her hands in his, kissed them, then kissed her forehead, and in a rather peculiar manner said to her, "Until tomorrow!"

Such was Vera's story afterwards.

She went away in great anxiety about him, but when she saw him in the morning, he seemed to be quite himself again, greeted her with a smile, and told her that he would very likely be back by the evening. It appears that he did not consider it necessary to inform anyone excepting Vera of his departure for town.

An hour later he was in St. Petersburg, and by ten o'clock he had rung the bell at Rogojin's.

He had gone to the front door, and was kept waiting a long while before anyone came. At last the door of old Mrs. Rogojin's flat was opened, and an aged servant appeared.

"Parfen Semionovitch is not at home," she announced from the doorway. "Whom do you want?"

"Parfen Semionovitch."

"He is not in."

The old woman examined the prince from head to foot with great curiosity.

"At all events tell me whether he slept at home last night, and whether he came alone?"

The old woman continued to stare at him, but said nothing.

"Was not Nastasia Philipovna here with him, yesterday evening?"

"And, pray, who are you yourself?"

"Prince Lef Nicolaievitch Muishkin; he knows me well."

"He is not at home."

The woman lowered her eyes.

"And Nastasia Philipovna?"

"I know nothing about it."

"Stop a minute! When will he come back?"

"I don't know that either."

The door was shut with these words, and the old woman disappeared. The prince decided to come back within an hour. Passing out of the house, he met the porter.

"Is Parfen Semionovitch at home?" he asked.

"Yes."

"Why did they tell me he was not at home, then?" "Where did they tell you so,—at his door?" "No, at his mother's flat; I rang at Parfen Semionovitch's door and nobody came."

"Well, he may have gone out. I can't tell. Sometimes he takes the keys with him, and leaves the rooms empty for two or three days."

"Do you know for certain that he was at home last night?"

"Yes, he was."

"Was Nastasia Philipovna with him?"

"I don't know; she doesn't come often. I think I should have known if she had come."

The prince went out deep in thought, and walked up and down the pavement for some time. The windows of all the rooms occupied by Rogojin were closed, those of his mother's apartments were open. It was a hot, bright day. The prince crossed the road in order to have a good look at the windows again; not only were Rogojin's closed, but the white blinds were all down as well.

He stood there for a minute and then, suddenly and strangely enough, it seemed to him that a little corner of one of the blinds was lifted, and Rogojin's face appeared for an instant and then vanished. He waited another minute, and decided to go and ring the bell once more; however, he thought better of it again and put it off for an hour.

The chief object in his mind at this moment was to get as quickly as he could to Nastasia Philipovna's lodging. He remembered that, not long since, when she had left Pavlofsk at his request, he had begged her to put up in town at the house of a respectable widow, who had well-furnished rooms to let, near the Ismailofsky barracks. Probably Nastasia had kept the rooms when she came down to Pavlofsk this last time; and most likely she would have spent the night in them, Rogojin having taken her straight there from the station.

The prince took a droshky. It struck him as he drove on that he ought to have begun by coming here, since it was most improbable that Rogojin should have taken Nastasia to his own house last night. He remembered that the porter said she very rarely came at all, so that it was still less likely that she would have gone there so late at night.

Vainly trying to comfort himself with these reflections, the prince reached the Ismailofsky barracks more dead than alive.

To his consternation the good people at the lodgings had not only heard nothing of Nastasia, but all came out to look at him as if he were a marvel of some sort. The whole family, of all ages, surrounded him, and he was begged to enter. He guessed at once that they knew perfectly well who he was, and that yesterday ought to have been his wedding-day; and further that they were dying to ask about the wedding, and especially about why he should be here now, inquiring for the woman who in all reasonable human probability might have been expected to be with him in Pavlofsk.

He satisfied their curiosity, in as few words as possible, with regard to the wedding, but their exclamations and sighs were so numerous and sincere that he was obliged to tell the whole story—in a short form, of course. The advice of all these agitated ladies was that the prince should go at once and knock at Rogojin's until he was let in:

and when let in insist upon a substantial explanation of everything. If Rogojin was really not at home, the prince was advised to go to a certain house, the address of which was given, where lived a German lady, a friend of Nastasia Philipovna's. It was possible that she might have spent the night there in her anxiety to conceal herself.

The prince rose from his seat in a condition of mental collapse. The good ladies reported afterwards that "his pallor was terrible to see, and his legs seemed to give way underneath him." With difficulty he was made to understand that his new friends would be glad of his address, in order to act with him if possible. After a moment's thought he gave the address of the small hotel, on the stairs of which he had had a fit some five weeks since. He then set off once more for Rogojin's.

This time they neither opened the door at Rogojin's flat nor at the one opposite. The prince found the porter with difficulty, but when found, the man would hardly look at him or answer his questions, pretending to be busy. Eventually, however, he was persuaded to reply so far as to state that Rogojin had left the house early in the morning and gone to Pavlofsk, and that he would not return today at all.

"I shall wait; he may come back this evening."

"He may not be home for a week."

"Then, at all events, he *did* sleep here, did he?"

"Well—he did sleep here, yes."

All this was suspicious and unsatisfactory. Very likely the porter had received new instructions during the interval of the prince's absence; his manner was so different now. He had been obliging—now he was as obstinate and silent as a mule. However, the prince decided to call again in a couple of hours, and after that to watch the house, in case of need. His hope was that he might yet find Nastasia at the address which he had just received. To that address he now set off at full speed.

But alas! at the German lady's house they did not even appear to understand what he wanted. After a while, by means of certain hints, he was able to gather that Nastasia must have had a quarrel with her friend two or three weeks ago, since which date the latter had neither heard nor seen anything of her. He was given to understand that the subject of Nastasia's present whereabouts was not of the slightest interest to her; and that Nastasia might marry all the princes in the world for all she cared! So Muishkin took his leave hurriedly. It struck him now that she might have gone away to Moscow just as she had done the last time, and that Rogojin had perhaps gone after her, or even *with* her. If only he could find some trace!

However, he must take his room at the hotel; and he started off in that direction. Having engaged his room, he was asked by the waiter whether he would take dinner; replying mechanically in the affirmative, he sat down and waited; but it was not long before it struck him that dining would delay him. Enraged at this idea, he started up, crossed the dark passage (which filled him with horrible impressions and gloomy forebodings), and set out once more for Rogojin's. Rogojin had not returned, and no one came to the door. He rang at the old lady's door opposite, and was informed that Parfen Semionovitch would not return for three days. The curiosity with which the old servant stared at him again impressed the prince disagreeably. He could not find the porter this time at all.

As before, he crossed the street and watched the windows from the other side, walking up and down in anguish of soul for half an hour or so in the stifling heat. Nothing stirred; the blinds were motionless; indeed, the prince began to think that the apparition of Rogojin's face could have been nothing but fancy. Soothed by this thought, he drove off once more to his friends at the Ismailofsky barracks. He was expected there. The mother had already been to three or four places to look for Nastasia, but had not found a trace of any kind.

The prince said nothing, but entered the room, sat down silently, and stared at them, one after the other, with the air of a man who cannot understand what is being said to him. It was strange—one moment he seemed to be so observant, the next so absent; his behaviour struck all the family as most remarkable. At length he rose from his seat, and begged to be shown Nastasia's rooms. The ladies reported afterwards how he had examined everything in the apartments. He observed an open book on the table, Madam Bovary, and requested the leave of the lady of the house to take it with him. He had turned down the leaf at the open page, and pocketed it before they could explain that it was a library book. He had then seated himself by the open window, and seeing a card-table, he asked who played cards.

He was informed that Nastasia used to play with Rogojin every evening, either at "preference" or "little fool," or "whist"; that this had been their practice since her last return from Pavlofsk; that she had taken to this amusement because she did not like to see Rogojin sitting silent and dull for whole evenings at a time; that the day after Nastasia had made a remark to this effect, Rogojin had whipped a pack of cards out of his pocket. Nastasia had laughed, but soon they began playing. The prince asked where were the cards, but was told that Rogojin used to bring a new pack every day, and always carried it away in his pocket.

The good ladies recommended the prince to try knocking at Rogojin's once more—not at once, but in the evening. Meanwhile, the mother would go to Pavlofsk to inquire at Dana Alexeyevna's whether anything had been heard of Nastasia there. The prince was to come back at ten o'clock and meet her, to hear her news and arrange plans for the morrow.

In spite of the kindly-meant consolations of his new friends, the prince walked to his hotel in inexpressible anguish of spirit, through the hot, dusty streets, aimlessly staring at the faces of those who passed him. Arrived at his destination, he determined to rest awhile in his room before he started for Rogojin's once more. He sat down, rested his elbows on the table and his head on his hands, and fell to thinking.

Heaven knows how long and upon what subjects he thought. He thought of many things—of Vera Lebedeff, and of her father; of Hippolyte; of Rogojin himself, first at the funeral, then as he had met him in the park, then, suddenly, as they had met in this very passage, outside, when Rogojin had watched in the darkness and awaited him with uplifted knife. The prince remembered his enemy's eyes as they had glared at him in the darkness. He shuddered, as a sudden idea struck him.

This idea was, that if Rogojin were in Petersburg, though he might hide for a time, yet he was quite sure to come to him—the prince—before long, with either good or evil intentions, but probably with the same intention as on that other occasion. At all events, if Rogojin were to come at all he would be sure to seek the prince here—he had no other town address—perhaps in this same corridor; he might well seek him here if he needed him. And perhaps he did need him. This idea seemed quite natural to the prince, though he could not have explained why he should so suddenly have become necessary to Rogojin. Rogojin would not come if all were well with him, that was part of the thought; he would come if all were not well; and certainly, undoubtedly, all would not be well with him. The prince could not bear this new idea; he took his hat and rushed out towards the street. It was almost dark in the passage.

"What if he were to come out of that corner as I go by and—and stop me?" thought the prince, as he approached the familiar spot. But no one came out.

He passed under the gateway and into the street. The crowds of people walking about—as is always the case at sunset in Petersburg, during the summer—surprised him, but he walked on in the direction of Rogojin's house.

About fifty yards from the hotel, at the first cross-road, as he passed through the crowd of foot-passengers sauntering along, someone touched his shoulder, and said in a whisper into his ear:

"Lef Nicolaievitch, my friend, come along with me." It was Rogojin.

The prince immediately began to tell him, eagerly and joyfully, how he had but the moment before expected to see him in the dark passage of the hotel.

"I was there," said Rogojin, unexpectedly. "Come along." The prince was surprised at this answer; but his astonishment increased a couple of minutes afterwards, when he began to consider it. Having thought it over, he glanced at Rogojin in alarm. The latter was striding along a yard or so ahead, looking straight in front of him, and mechanically making way for anyone he met.

"Why did you not ask for me at my room if you were in the hotel?" asked the prince, suddenly.

Rogojin stopped and looked at him; then reflected, and replied as though he had not heard the question:

"Look here, Lef Nicolaievitch, you go straight on to the house; I shall walk on the other side. See that we keep together."

So saying, Rogojin crossed the road.

Arrived on the opposite pavement, he looked back to see whether the prince were moving, waved his hand in the direction of the Gorohovaya, and strode on, looking across every moment to see whether Muishkin understood his instructions. The prince supposed that Rogojin desired to look out for someone whom he was afraid to miss; but if so, why had he not told *him*whom to look out for? So the two proceeded for half a mile or so. Suddenly the prince began to tremble from some unknown cause. He could not bear it, and signalled to Rogojin across the road.

The latter came at once.

"Is Nastasia Philipovna at your house?"

"Yes."

"And was it you looked out of the window under the blind this morning?"

"Yes."

"Then why did—"

But the prince could not finish his question; he did not know what to say. Besides this, his heart was beating so that he found it difficult to speak at all. Rogojin was silent also and looked at him as before, with an expression of deep thoughtfulness.

"Well, I'm going," he said, at last, preparing to recross the road. "You go along here as before; we will keep to different sides of the road; it's better so, you'll see."

When they reached the Gorohovaya, and came near the house, the prince's legs were trembling so that he could hardly walk. It was about ten o'clock. The old lady's windows were open, as before; Rogojin's were all shut, and in the darkness the white blinds showed whiter than ever. Rogojin and the prince each approached the house on his respective side of the road; Rogojin, who was on the near side, beckoned the prince across. He went over to the doorway.

"Even the porter does not know that I have come home now. I told him, and told them at my mother's too, that I was off to Pavlofsk," said Rogojin, with a cunning and almost satisfied smile. "We'll go in quietly and nobody will hear us."

He had the key in his hand. Mounting the staircase he turned and signalled to the prince to go more softly; he opened the door very quietly, let the prince in, followed him, locked the door behind him, and put the key in his pocket.

"Come along," he whispered.

He had spoken in a whisper all the way. In spite of his apparent outward composure, he was evidently in a state of great mental agitation. Arrived in a large salon, next to the study, he went to the window and cautiously beckoned the prince up to him.

"When you rang the bell this morning I thought it must be you. I went to the door on tip-toe and heard you talking to the servant opposite. I had told her before that if anyone came and rang—especially you, and I gave her your name—she was not to tell about me. Then I thought, what if he goes and stands opposite and looks up, or waits about to watch the house? So I came to this very window, looked out, and there you were staring straight at me. That's how it came about."

"Where is Nastasia Philipovna?" asked the prince, breathlessly.

"She's here," replied Rogojin, slowly, after a slight pause.

"Where?"

Rogojin raised his eyes and gazed intently at the prince.

"Come," he said.

He continued to speak in a whisper, very deliberately as before, and looked strangely thoughtful and dreamy. Even while he told the story of how he had peeped through the blind, he gave the impression of wishing to say something else. They entered the study. In this room some changes had taken place since the prince last saw it. It was now divided into two equal parts by a heavy green silk curtain stretched across it, separating the alcove beyond, where stood Rogojin's bed, from the rest of the room.

The heavy curtain was drawn now, and it was very dark. The bright Petersburg summer nights were already beginning to close in, and but for the full moon, it would have been difficult to distinguish anything in Rogojin's dismal room, with the drawn blinds. They could just see one anothers faces, however, though not in detail. Rogojin's face was white, as usual. His glittering eyes watched the prince with an intent stare.

"Had you not better light a candle?" said Muishkin.

"No, I needn't," replied Rogojin, and taking the other by the hand he drew him down to a chair. He himself took a chair opposite and drew it up so close that he almost pressed against the prince's knees. At their side was a little round table.

"Sit down," said Rogojin; "let's rest a bit." There was silence for a moment.

"I knew you would be at that hotel," he continued, just as men sometimes commence a serious conversation by discussing any outside subject before leading up to the main point. "As I entered the passage it struck me that perhaps you were sitting and waiting for me, just as I was waiting for you. Have you been to the old lady at Ismailofsky barracks?"

"Yes," said the prince, squeezing the word out with difficulty owing to the dreadful beating of his heart.

"I thought you would. 'They'll talk about it,' I thought; so I determined to go and fetch you to spend the night here—'We will be together,' I thought, 'for this one night—'"

"Rogojin, *where* is Nastasia Philipovna?" said the prince, suddenly rising from his seat. He was quaking in all his limbs, and his words came in a scarcely audible whisper. Rogojin rose also.

"There," he whispered, nodding his head towards the curtain.

"Asleep?" whispered the prince.

Rogojin looked intently at him again, as before.

"Let's go in—but you mustn't—well—let's go in."

He lifted the curtain, paused—and turned to the prince. "Go in," he said, motioning him to pass behind the curtain. Muishkin went in.

"It's so dark," he said.

"You can see quite enough," muttered Rogojin.

"I can just see there's a bed—"

"Go nearer," suggested Rogojin, softly.

The prince took a step forward—then another—and paused. He stood and stared for a minute or two.

Neither of the men spoke a word while at the bedside. The prince's heart beat so loud that its knocking seemed to be distinctly audible in the deathly silence.

But now his eyes had become so far accustomed to the darkness that he could distinguish the whole of the bed. Someone was asleep upon it—in an absolutely motionless sleep. Not the slightest movement was perceptible, not the faintest breathing could be heard. The sleeper was covered with a white sheet; the outline of the limbs was hardly distinguishable. He could only just make out that a human being lay outstretched there.

All around, on the bed, on a chair beside it, on the floor, were scattered the different portions of a magnificent white silk dress, bits of lace, ribbons and flowers. On a small table at the bedside glittered a mass of diamonds, torn off and thrown down anyhow. From under a heap of lace at the end of the bed peeped a small white foot, which looked as though it had been chiselled out of marble; it was terribly still.

The prince gazed and gazed, and felt that the more he gazed the more death-like became the silence. Suddenly a fly awoke somewhere, buzzed across the room, and settled on the pillow. The prince shuddered.

"Let's go," said Rogojin, touching his shoulder. They left the alcove and sat down in the two chairs they had occupied before, opposite to one another. The prince trembled more and more violently, and never took his questioning eyes off Rogojin's face.

"I see you are shuddering, Lef Nicolaievitch," said the latter, at length, "almost as you did once in Moscow, before your fit; don't you remember? I don't know what I shall do with you—"

The prince bent forward to listen, putting all the strain he could muster upon his understanding in order to take in what Rogojin said, and continuing to gaze at the latter's face.

"Was it you?" he muttered, at last, motioning with his head towards the curtain.

"Yes, it was I," whispered Rogojin, looking down.

Neither spoke for five minutes.

"Because, you know," Rogojin recommenced, as though continuing a former sentence, "if you were ill now, or had a fit, or screamed, or anything, they might hear it in the yard, or even in the street, and guess that someone was passing the night in the house. They would all come and knock and want to come in, because they know I am not at home. I didn't light a candle for the same reason. When I am not here—for two or three days at a time, now and then—no one comes in to tidy the house or anything; those are my orders. So that I want them to not know we are spending the night here—"

"Wait," interrupted the prince. "I asked both the porter and the woman whether Nastasia Philipovna had spent last night in the house; so they knew—"

"I know you asked. I told them that she had called in for ten minutes, and then gone straight back to Pavlofsk. No one knows she slept here. Last night we came in just as carefully as you and I did today. I thought as I came along with her that she would not like to creep in so secretly, but I was quite wrong. She whispered, and walked on tip-toe; she carried her skirt over her arm, so that it shouldn't rustle, and she held up her finger at me on the stairs, so that I shouldn't make a noise—it was you she was afraid of. She was mad with terror in the train, and she begged me to bring her to this house. I thought of taking her to her rooms at the Ismailofsky barracks first; but she wouldn't hear of it. She said, 'No—not there; he'll find me out at once there. Take me to your own house, where you can hide me, and tomorrow we'll set off for Moscow.' Thence she would go to Orel, she said. When she went to bed, she was still talking about going to Orel."

"Wait! What do you intend to do now, Parfen?"

"Well, I'm afraid of you. You shudder and tremble so. We'll pass the night here together. There are no other beds besides that one; but I've thought how we'll manage. I'll take the cushions off all the sofas, and lay them down on the floor, up against the curtain here—for you and me—so that we shall be together. For if they come in and look about now, you know, they'll find her, and carry her away, and they'll be asking me questions, and I shall say I did it, and then they'll take me away, too, don't you see? So let her lie close to us—close to you and me."

"Yes, yes," agreed the prince, warmly.

"So we will not say anything about it, or let them take her away?"

"Not for anything!" cried the other; "no, no, no!"

"So I had decided, my friend; not to give her up to anyone," continued Rogojin. "We'll be very quiet. I have only been out of the house one hour all day, all the rest of the time I have been with her. I dare say the air is very bad here. It is so hot. Do you find it bad?"

"I don't know—perhaps—by morning it will be."

"I've covered her with oil-cloth—best American oilcloth, and put the sheet over that, and four jars of disinfectant, on account of the smell—as they did at Moscow—you remember? And she's lying so still; you shall see, in the morning, when it's light. What! can't you get up?" asked Rogojin, seeing the other was trembling so that he could not rise from his seat.

"My legs won't move," said the prince; "it's fear, I know. When my fear is over, I'll get up—"

"Wait a bit—I'll make the bed, and you can lie down. I'll lie down, too, and we'll listen and watch, for I don't know yet what I shall do... I tell you beforehand, so that you may be ready in case I—"

Muttering these disconnected words, Rogojin began to make up the beds. It was clear that he had devised these beds long before; last night he slept on the sofa. But there was no room for two on the sofa, and he seemed anxious that he and the prince should be close to one another; therefore, he now dragged cushions of all sizes and shapes from the sofas, and made a sort of bed of them close by the curtain. He then approached the prince, and gently helped him to rise, and led him towards the bed. But the prince could now walk by himself, so that his fear must have passed; for all that, however, he continued to shudder.

"It's hot weather, you see," continued Rogojin, as he lay down on the cushions beside Muishkin, "and, naturally, there will be a smell. I daren't open the window. My mother has some beautiful flowers in pots; they have a delicious scent; I thought of fetching them in, but that old servant will find out, she's very inquisitive.

"Yes, she is inquisitive," assented the prince.

"I thought of buying flowers, and putting them all round her; but I was afraid it would make us sad to see her with flowers round her."

"Look here," said the prince; he was bewildered, and his brain wandered. He seemed to be continually groping for the questions he wished to ask, and then losing them. "Listen—tell me—how did you—with a knife?—That same one?"

"Yes, that same one."

"Wait a minute, I want to ask you something else, Parfen; all sorts of things; but tell me first, did you intend to kill her before my wedding, at the church door, with your knife?"

"I don't know whether I did or not," said Rogojin, drily, seeming to be a little astonished at the question, and not quite taking it in.

"Did you never take your knife to Pavlofsk with you?" "No. As to the knife," he added, "this is all I can tell you about it." He was silent for a moment, and then said, "I took it out of the locked drawer this morning about three, for it was in the early morning all this—happened. It has been inside the book ever since—and—and—this is what is such a marvel to me, the knife only went in a couple of inches at most, just under her left breast, and there wasn't more than half a tablespoonful of blood altogether, not more."

"Yes—yes—yes—" The prince jumped up in extraordinary agitation. "I know, I know, I've read of that sort of thing—it's internal haemorrhage, you know. Sometimes there isn't a drop—if the blow goes straight to the heart—"

"Wait—listen!" cried Rogojin, suddenly, starting up. "Somebody's walking about, do you hear? In the hall." Both sat up to listen.

"I hear," said the prince in a whisper, his eyes fixed on Rogojin.

"Footsteps?"

"Yes."

"Shall we shut the door, and lock it, or not?"

"Yes, lock it."

They locked the door, and both lay down again. There was a long silence.

"Yes, by-the-by," whispered the prince, hurriedly and excitedly as before, as though he had just seized hold of an idea and was afraid of losing it again. "I—I wanted those cards! They say you played cards with her?"

"Yes, I played with her," said Rogojin, after a short silence.

"Where are the cards?"

"Here they are," said Rogojin, after a still longer pause.

He pulled out a pack of cards, wrapped in a bit of paper, from his pocket, and handed them to the prince. The latter took them, with a sort of perplexity. A new, sad, helpless feeling weighed on his heart; he had suddenly realized that not only at this moment, but for a long while, he had not been saying what he wanted to say, had not been acting as he wanted to act; and that these cards which he held in his hand, and which he had been so delighted to have at first, were now of no use—no use... He rose, and wrung his hands. Rogojin lay motionless, and seemed neither to hear nor see his movements; but his eyes blazed in the darkness, and were fixed in a wild stare.

The prince sat down on a chair, and watched him in alarm. Half an hour went by.

Suddenly Rogojin burst into a loud abrupt laugh, as though he had quite forgotten that they must speak in whispers.

"That officer, eh!—that young officer—don't you remember that fellow at the band? Eh? Ha, ha, ha! Didn't she whip him smartly, eh?"

The prince jumped up from his seat in renewed terror. When Rogojin quieted down (which he did at once) the prince bent over him, sat down beside him, and with painfully beating heart and still more painful breath, watched his face intently. Rogojin never turned his head, and seemed to have forgotten all about him. The prince watched and waited. Time went on—it began to grow light.

Rogojin began to wander—muttering disconnectedly; then he took to shouting and laughing. The prince stretched out a trembling hand and gently stroked his hair and his cheeks—he could do nothing more. His legs trembled again and he seemed to have lost the use of them. A new sensation came over him, filling his heart and soul with infinite anguish.

Meanwhile the daylight grew full and strong; and at last the prince lay down, as though overcome by despair, and laid his face against the white, motionless face of Rogojin. His tears flowed on to Rogojin's cheek, though he was perhaps not aware of them himself.

At all events when, after many hours, the door was opened and people thronged in, they found the murderer unconscious and in a raging fever. The prince was sitting by him, motionless, and each time that the sick man gave a laugh, or a shout, he hastened to pass his own trembling hand over his companion's hair and cheeks, as though trying to soothe and quiet him. But alas! he understood nothing of what was said to him, and recognized none of those who surrounded him.

If Schneider himself had arrived then and seen his former pupil and patient, remembering the prince's condition during the first year in Switzerland, he would have flung up his hands, despairingly, and cried, as he did then:

"An idiot!"

XII.

When the widow hurried away to Pavlofsk, she went straight to Daria Alexeyevna's house, and telling all she knew, threw her into a state of great alarm. Both ladies decided to communicate at once with Lebedeff, who, as the friend and landlord of the prince, was also much agitated. Vera Lebedeff told all she knew, and by Lebedeff's advice it was decided that all three should go to Petersburg as quickly as possible, in order to avert "what might so easily happen."

This is how it came about that at eleven o'clock next morning Rogojin's flat was opened by the police in the presence of Lebedeff, the two ladies, and Rogojin's own brother, who lived in the wing.

The evidence of the porter went further than anything else towards the success of Lebedeff in gaining the assistance of the police. He declared that he had seen Rogojin return to the house last night, accompanied by a friend, and that both had gone upstairs very secretly and cautiously. After this there was no hesitation about breaking open the door, since it could not be got open in any other way.

Rogojin suffered from brain fever for two months. When he recovered from the attack he was at once brought up on trial for murder.

He gave full, satisfactory, and direct evidence on every point; and the prince's name was, thanks to this, not brought into the proceedings. Rogojin was very quiet during the progress of the trial. He did not contradict his clever and eloquent counsel, who argued that the brain fever, or inflammation of the brain, was the cause of the crime; clearly proving that this malady had existed long before the murder was perpetrated, and had been brought on by the sufferings of the accused.

But Rogojin added no words of his own in confirmation of this view, and as before, he recounted with marvellous exactness the details of his crime. He was convicted, but with extenuating circumstances, and condemned to hard labour in Siberia for fifteen years. He heard his sentence grimly, silently, and thoughtfully. His colossal fortune, with the exception of the comparatively small portion wasted in the first wanton period of his inheritance, went to his brother, to the great satisfaction of the latter.

The old lady, Rogojin's mother, is still alive, and remembers her favourite son Parfen sometimes, but not clearly. God spared her the knowledge of this dreadful calamity which had overtaken her house.

Lebedeff, Keller, Gania, Ptitsin, and many other friends of ours continue to live as before. There is scarcely any change in them, so that there is no need to tell of their subsequent doings.

Hippolyte died in great agitation, and rather sooner than he expected, about a fortnight after Nastasia Philipovna's death. Colia was much affected by these events, and drew nearer to his mother in heart and sympathy. Nina Alexandrovna is anxious, because he is "thoughtful beyond his years," but he will, we think, make a useful and active man.

The prince's further fate was more or less decided by Colia, who selected, out of all the persons he had met during the last six or seven months, Evgenie Pavlovitch, as friend and confidant. To him he made over all that he knew as to the events above recorded, and as to the present condition of the prince. He was not far wrong in his choice. Evgenie Pavlovitch took the deepest interest in the fate of the unfortunate "idiot," and, thanks to his influence, the prince found himself once more with Dr. Schneider, in Switzerland.

Evgenie Pavlovitch, who went abroad at this time, intending to live a long while on the continent, being, as he often said, quite superfluous in Russia, visits his sick friend at Schneider's every few months.

But Dr. Schneider frowns ever more and more and shakes his head; he hints that the brain is fatally injured; he does not as yet declare that his patient is incurable, but he allows himself to express the gravest fears.

Evgenie takes this much to heart, and he has a heart, as is proved by the fact that he receives and even answers letters from Colia. But besides this, another trait in his character has become apparent, and as it is a good trait we will make haste to reveal it. After each visit to Schneider's establishment, Evgenie Pavlovitch writes another letter, besides that to Colia, giving the most minute particulars concerning the invalid's condition. In these letters is to be detected, and in each one more than the last, a growing feeling of friendship and sympathy.

The individual who corresponds thus with Evgenie Pavlovitch, and who engages so much of his attention and respect, is Vera Lebedeff. We have never been able to discover clearly how such relations sprang up. Of course the root of them was in the events which we have already recorded, and which so filled Vera with grief on the prince's account that she fell seriously ill. But exactly how the acquaintance and friendship came about, we cannot say.

We have spoken of these letters chiefly because in them is often to be found some news of the Epanchin family, and of Aglaya in particular. Evgenie Pavlovitch wrote of her from Paris, that after a short and sudden attachment to a certain Polish count, an exile, she had suddenly married him, quite against the wishes of her parents, though they had eventually given their consent through fear of a terrible scandal. Then, after a six months' silence, Evgenie Pavlovitch informed his correspondent, in a long letter, full of detail, that while paying his last visit to Dr. Schneider's establishment, he had there come across the whole Epanchin family (excepting the general, who had remained in St. Petersburg) and Prince S. The meeting was a strange one. They all received Evgenie Pavlovitch with effusive delight; Adelaida and Alexandra were deeply grateful to him for his "angelic kindness to the unhappy prince."

Lizabetha Prokofievna, when she saw poor Muishkin, in his enfeebled and humiliated condition, had wept bitterly. Apparently all was forgiven him.

Prince S. had made a few just and sensible remarks. It seemed to Evgenie Pavlovitch that there was not yet perfect harmony between Adelaida and her fiance, but he thought that in time the impulsive young girl would let herself be guided by his reason and experience. Besides, the recent events that had befallen her family had given Adelaida much to think about, especially the sad experiences of her younger sister. Within six months, everything that the family had dreaded from the marriage with the Polish count had come to pass. He turned out to be neither count nor exile—at least, in the political sense of the word—but had had to leave his native land owing to some rather dubious affair of the past. It was his noble patriotism, of which he made a great display, that had rendered him so interesting in Aglaya's eyes. She was so fascinated that, even before marrying him, she joined a committee that had been organized abroad to work for the restoration of Poland; and further, she visited the confessional of a celebrated Jesuit priest, who made an absolute fanatic of her. The supposed fortune of the count had dwindled to a mere nothing, although he had given almost irrefutable evidence of its existence to Lizabetha Prokofievna and Prince S.

Besides this, before they had been married half a year, the count and his friend the priest managed to bring about a quarrel between Aglaya and her family, so that it was now several months since they had seen her. In a word, there was a great deal to say; but Mrs. Epanchin, and her daughters, and even Prince S., were still so much distressed by Aglaya's latest infatuations and adventures, that they did hot care to talk of them, though they must have known that Evgenie knew much of the story already.

Poor Lizabetha Prokofievna was most anxious to get home, and, according to Evgenie's account, she criticized everything foreign with much hostility.

"They can't bake bread anywhere, decently; and they all freeze in their houses, during winter, like a lot of mice in a cellar. At all events, I've had a good Russian cry over this poor fellow," she added, pointing to the prince, who had not recognized her in the slightest degree. "So enough of this nonsense; it's time we faced the truth. All this continental life, all this Europe of yours, and all the trash about 'going abroad' is simply foolery, and it is mere foolery on our part to come. Remember what I say, my friend; you'll live to agree with me yourself."

So spoke the good lady, almost angrily, as she took leave of Evgenie Pavlovitch.

Made in United States
North Haven, CT
24 October 2021